RIVALS

Jilly Cooper

CORGI BOOKS

RIVALS
A CORGI BOOK 0 552 13264 0

Originally published in Great Britain by
Bantam Press, a division of Transworld Publishers Ltd

PRINTING HISTORY
Bantam Press edition published 1988
Corgi edition published 1989
Corgi edition reissued 1989 (twice)
Corgi edition reprinted 1989 (twice)

Copyright © Jilly Cooper 1988

This book is set in 10/11pt Linotron 202 Goudy by
Rowland Phototypesetting Ltd, Bury St Edmunds, Suffolk

Corgi Books are published by Transworld Publishers
Ltd., 61–63 Uxbridge Road, Ealing, London W5 5SA, in
Australia by Transworld Publishers (Australia) Pty. Ltd.,
15–23 Helles Avenue, Moorebank, NSW 2170, and in New
Zealand by Transworld Publishers (N.Z.) Ltd., Cnr. Moselle
and Waipareira Avenues, Henderson, Auckland.

Printed and bound in Great Britain by
Cox & Wyman Ltd., Reading, Berks.

DEDICATION

To Annalise Kay
who is as wise as she is
good and beautiful

TO CHELTENHAM

MARTI GLUCKSTEIN'S
COTTAGE

PENSCOMBE

THE FALCONRY
Tony and Monica
Baddingham's House

HAMILTON TERRACE

Professor Graystock's
House

Cameron Cook's
House

Cotchester University

Cotchester
Town Hall

CTV Corinium
Television

Dame Enid
Spink's House

Bishop's Palace

...HYCHEY

Bar Sinister
and Basil
Baddingham's House

Cotchester Cathedral

RIVER FLEET

COTCHESTER HIGH STREET

COTCHESTER

TO LONDON →

ACKNOWLEDGEMENTS

A very large number of people helped me with this book. Most of them work in television and are exceptionally busy. They still found the time to talk to me and – particularly in the case of those from HTV – to entertain me with lavishness and generosity. All of them are experts in their own field. But as I was writing fiction, I only took their advice so far as it fitted my plot. The accuracy of the book in no way reflects their expertise. They were also all so nice to me that it was impossible to base any of the unpleasant characters in the story on any of them.

They include Georgina Abrahams, Rita Angel, William Beloe, Michael Blakstad, Roy Bottomley, James Bredin, Adrian Brenard, Doug Carnegie, Stephen Cole, John Corbett, Jenny Crick, Mike Davey, Geoff Druett, Ron Evans, Su Evans, James Gatward, David Glencross, Stuart Hall, Nick Handel, Tom Hartman, Barbara Hazell, Stan Hazell, Paul Heiney, Bruce Hockin, Alison Holloway, Patricia Houlihan, Bryan Izzard, Philip Jones, Barbara Kelly, Susan Kyle, Maurice Leonard, Barrie MacDonald, Billy Macqueen, George McWatters, Steve Matthews, Lesley Morgan, Malcolm Morris, Jack Patterson, Bob Simmons, Tom Walsh, Ann de Winton, Richard Whitely, Ron Wordley and Richard Wyatt.

Tragically, dear Eamonn Andrews, with whom I was privileged to work for four series on 'What's My Line?', died in November, after the book was finished. His utter integrity, professionalism and gentle humour were a constant source of inspiration while I was writing it.

I should also like to thank the crews, the drivers, the make-up girls and the wardrobe staff with whom I worked over the years, who came up with endless suggestions.

I must thank the people who wrote three books which were invaluable to me in understanding the extraordinarily complicated process by which television franchises are awarded. They are Walter Butler, author of *How to Win the Franchise and Influence People*, Michael Leapman, author of *Treachery? The Power Struggle at TV-am*, and Asa Briggs and Joanna Spicer, joint authors of *The Franchise Affair – Creating fortunes and failures in Independent Television*.

I am also eternally grateful to Peter Cadbury, former Chairman of Westward Television, for giving me access to his autobiography which unaccountably has never been published, to Robin Currie, of the Fire and Rescue Service HQ, Cheltenham, to Toni Westall, secretary to Captain Brian Walpole, General Manager, Concorde, and to Tim and Primrose Unwin for inviting me to some excellent hunt balls.

In addition I need to thank my Bank Manager, Keith Henderson, my publishers, Paul Scherer, Mark Barty-King and Alan Earney and all their staff at Bantam Press and Corgi, and my agent Desmond Elliott, for their faith and continued encouragement.

Three brave ladies, Beryl Hill, Sue Moore and Geraldine Kilgannon, deserve thanks and praise for deciphering my ghastly handwriting and typing several chapters of the manuscript; so does my cleaner, Ann Mills, for mucking out my study once a fortnight.

Finally, once again there are no words adequate to thank Leo, my husband, my children, Felix and Emily, and my secretary, Annalise Kay, whom I regard as one of the family, and who typed ninety per cent of the manuscript. Their collective good cheer, unselfishness and comfort over the past eighteen months knew no bounds.

Bisley, Gloucestershire
1987.

CHARACTERS IN ALPHABETICAL ORDER

JOHNNY ABRAHAMS	Head of News and Current Affairs, BBC.
GEORGIE BAINES	Sales Director, Corinium Television.
LADY BARNSLEY	A member of the Independent Broadcasting Authority (IBA), late of the White Fish Authority.
BIRGITTA	A comely but bolshie nanny working for the Verekers.
HARDY BISSETT	A franchise expert. Late of the IBA.
MR AND MRS BODKIN	Rupert Campbell-Black's couple.
SIR CEDRIC BONNINGTON	Chairman of Mid-West Television.
HUBERT BRENTON	Bishop of Cotchester.
ANTHONY, SECOND BARON BADDINGHAM	Chairman and Managing Director, Corinium Television.
MONICA BADDINGHAM	His wife.
ARCHIE BADDINGHAM	His elder son.
BASIL BADDINGHAM	Tony's illegitimate brother, ace polo player, and owner of the Bar Sinister in Cotchester High Street.
SEBASTIAN BURROWS	A news reporter, Corinium Television.
DAYSEE BUTLER	A very beautiful, stupid PA, Corinium Television.

RUPERT CAMPBELL-BLACK	Minister for Sport. Tory MP for Chalford and Bisley. Ex-member of the British show-jumping team.
MARCUS CAMPBELL-BLACK	His son.
TABITHA CAMPBELL-BLACK	His daughter.
CAMERON COOK	Producer/Director, NBS, New York. Later Head of Drama, Corinium Television.
CHARLES CRAWFORD	Retiring Chairman of the IBA.
JUDGE DAVEY	A member of the IBA.
OWEN DAVIES	Leader of the Opposition.
WESLEY EMERSON	Gloucester and England bowler.
SUZY ERIKSON	An American ex-girlfriend of Rupert Campbell-Black.
LADY EVESHAM	An early feminist, and non-executive Director, Corinium Television.
CHARLES FAIRBURN	Head of Religious Broadcasting, Corinium Television.
JOHNNY FRIEDLANDER	American actor and megastar.
MARTI GLUCKSTEIN	A brilliant East End accountant.
MALISE GORDON	Ex-*chef d'équipe* of the British show-jumping team.
HELEN GORDON	His wife. Ex-wife of Rupert Campbell-Black and mother of Marcus and Tabitha.
LADY GOSLING	Chairman of the IBA.
GRACE	Declan O'Hara's housekeeper.
CRISPIN GRAYSTOCK	Professor of English at Cotchester University and a disgusting lecher.
HENRY HAMPSHIRE	Lord-Lieutenant of Gloucestershire – a much less disgusting lecher.
SIMON HARRIS	Controller of Programmes, Corinium Television.

GEORGINA HARRISON	An undergraduate.
RONNIE HAVEGAL	Head of Co-Productions, NBS, New York.
HAZEL	A BBC make-up girl.
RALPHIE HENRIQUES	An undergraduate at Trinity Dublin.
IVOR HICKS	Corporate Development Controller, Corinium Television.
JILLY	Yet another Vereker nanny, but for once a dependable boot.
BEATTIE JOHNSON	Fleet Street columnist, ghosting Rupert Campbell-Black's memoirs.
GINGER JOHNSON	Financial Director, Corinium Television. No relation to Beattie.
FREDDIE JONES	A multi-millionaire in electronics.
VALERIE JONES	His wife, a nightmare.
SHARON JONES	His overweight daughter.
DEIRDRE KILPATRICK	A researcher at Corinium Television.
LAVINIA	Patrick O'Hara's girlfriend.
BILLY LLOYD-FOXE	Sports Presenter, BBC.
JANEY LLOYD-FOXE	An author and national newspaper columnist.
DERMOT MACBRIDE	A playwright and Angry Not-So-Young man.
JOYCE MADDEN	Lord Baddingham's secretary, Corinium Television.
MRS MAKEPIECE	A 'treasure' who cleans for Valerie Jones and Lizzie Vereker.
KEVIN MAKEPIECE	Her son.
TRACEY MAKEPIECE	Her daughter.
SALLY MAPLES	Head of Children's Programmes, Yorkshire Television.
MIKE MEADOWS	Head of Sport, Corinium Television.
MRS MENZIES-SCOTT	Ex-head of the Women's Institute, a member of the IBA.

GERALD MIDDLETON	Parliamentary Private Secretary to Rupert Campbell-Black.
DECLAN O'HARA	A television megastar.
MAUD O'HARA	His ex-actress wife.
PATRICK O'HARA	His son, an undergraduate at Trinity Dublin.
AGATHA (TAGGIE) O'HARA	His elder daughter.
CAITLIN O'HARA	His younger daughter.
ORTRUD	Yet another of the Verekers' comely nannies.
CYRIL PEACOCK	Lord Baddingham's PA and sometime Press Officer, Corinium Television.
THE VERY REVEREND FERGUS PENNEY	An ex-Prebendary of the Church of England, and a member of the IBA.
PERCY	Lord Baddingham's chauffeur.
PASCOE RAWLINGS	The most powerful theatrical agent in London.
BARTON SINCLAIR	Director of *The Merry Widow*.
SKIP	A beautiful American lawyer.
LORD SMITH	An ex-Secretary of the TGWU.
DAME ENID SPINK	A distinguished composer and Professor of Music at Cotchester University.
PAUL STRATTON	Tory MP for Cotchester. An ex-Cabinet Minister.
SARAH STRATTON	His ravishing second wife and ex-secretary.
SYDNEY	Rupert's driver.
URSULA	Declan O'Hara's secretary.
JAMES VEREKER	Anchorman of 'Cotswold Round-Up', Corinium Television.
LIZZIE VEREKER	His wife, a novelist.
ELEANOR VEREKER	His daughter.
SEBASTIAN VEREKER	His son.
HAROLD WHITE	Director of Programmes, London Weekend Television.
MAURICE WOOTON	A bent Gloucestershire property millionaire.

RIVALS

1

Sitting in the Concorde departure lounge at Heathrow on a perfect blue June morning, Anthony, second Baron Baddingham, Chairman and Managing Director of Corinium Television, should have been perfectly happy. He was blessed with great wealth, a title, a brilliant career, a beautiful flat in Kensington, houses in Gloucestershire and Tuscany, a loyal, much-admired wife, three charming children and a somewhat demanding mistress, to whom he had just bidden a long farewell on the free telephone beside him.

He was about to fly on his favourite aeroplane, Concorde, to his favourite city, New York, to indulge in his favourite pastime – selling Corinium's programmes to American television and raising American money to make more programmes. Tony Baddingham was a great believer in using Other People's Money, or OPM as he called it; then if a project bombed, someone else picked up the bill.

As a final bonus, neatly folded beside him were the morning papers, which he'd already read in the Post House Hotel, and which all contained glowing reports of Corinium's past six months' results, announced yesterday.

Just as he had been checking out of the Post House an hour earlier, however, Tony's perfect pleasure had been ruined by the sight of his near neighbour and long-term rival, Rupert Campbell-Black, checking in. He was scribbling his signature with one hand and holding firmly on to a rather grubby but none-the-less ravishing girl with the other.

The girl, who had chipped nail polish, wildly tangled blonde hair, mascara smudges under her eyes, and a deep suntan, had obviously just been pulled out of some other bed and was giggling hysterically.

'Ru-pert,' she wailed, 'there simply isn't time; you'll miss the plane.'

'It'll wait,' said Rupert, and, gathering up his keys, started to drag her towards the lift. As the doors closed, like curtains coming down on the first act of a play, Tony could see the two of them glued together in a passionate embrace.

A deeply competitive man, Tony had felt dizzy with jealousy. He had seldom, particularly since he had inherited the title and become Chief Executive of Corinium, had any difficulty attracting women, but he'd never attracted anything so wantonly desirable and desiring as that grubby, vaguely familiar blonde.

'More coffee, Lord Baddingham?' One of the beautiful attendants in the Concorde Lounge interrupted Tony's brooding. He shook his head, comforted by the obvious admiration in her voice.

'Shouldn't we be boarding?' he asked.

'We'll be a few minutes late. There was a slight engineering problem. They're just doing a last-minute check.'

Tony glanced round the departure lounge, filled with businessmen and American tourists, and noticed a pale, red-headed young man in a grey pinstripe suit, who had stopped his steady flow of writing notes on a foolscap pad and was looking apprehensively at his watch.

Boarding the plane twenty minutes later, Tony found himself sitting up at the front on an inside seat with a Jap immersed in a portable computer on his right. Across the gangway next to the window sat the young man in the pinstripe suit. He was even paler now and looking distinctly put out.

'Good morning, Lord Baddingham,' said a stewardess, handing Tony that day's newly-flown-in copy of the *Wall Street Journal*.

14

'Engineering fault sorted out?' asked Tony, as the engines started revving up.

Not quite meeting his eyes, the girl nodded brightly; then, looking out of the window, she seemed to relax as a black car raced across the tarmac. Next there was a commotion, as a light, flat, familiar drawl could be heard down the gangway:

'Frightfully sorry to hold you all up; traffic was diabolical.'

All the stewardesses seemed to converge on the new arrival, fighting to carry his newspaper and put his hand luggage up in the locker.

'Won't you be needing your briefcase, Minister?' asked a male steward, shimmying down the gangway.

Rupert Campbell-Black shook his head. 'No thanks, sweetheart.'

'Have a nice zizz then,' said the male steward, going crimson with pleasure at the endearment.

As the doors slammed shut, Rupert collapsed into the seat across the gangway from Tony. Wearing a crumpled cream suit, a blue striped shirt, dark glasses and with an eighth of an inch of stubble on his chin, he looked more like a rock star than one of Her Majesty's ministers.

'Terribly sorry, Gerald,' he murmured to the pale young man in the pinstripe suit. 'There was a terrible pile-up on the M4.'

Smiling thinly, Gerald removed a blonde hair from Rupert's lapel.

'I really must buy you an alarm clock for Christmas, Minister. If you'd missed that lunchtime speech, we'd have been in real stück. Good of them to hold the plane.'

'Thank Christ they did.' Looking round, Rupert saw Tony Baddingham and grinned. 'Why, it's the big Baddingham wolf.'

'Cutting it a bit fine, aren't you?' said Tony disapprovingly.

Both men required each other's goodwill. Rupert, as an MP within Tony's television company's territory, needed the coverage, whereas Tony needed Rupert's recommendation to the Government that he was running a respectable company. But it didn't make either like the other any better.

'Bloody good results you had this morning,' said Rupert, fastening his seat belt. 'I'd better buy some Corinium shares.'

Slightly mollified, Tony congratulated Rupert on his recent appointment as Tory Minister for Sport.

Rupert shrugged. 'The PM's shit-scared about football hooliganism – seems to think I can come up with some magic formula.'

'Setting a Yobbo to catch a Yobbo perhaps,' said Tony nastily, then regretted it.

'I was at Thames Television yesterday,' said Rupert icily, as the plane taxied towards the runway. 'After the programme I had a drink with the Home Secretary and the Chairman of the IBA. They were both saying that you'd better watch out. If you don't spend a bit more of that bloody fortune you're coining from advertising on making some decent programmes, you're going to lose your franchise.'

As Rupert leant forward so Tony could hear him over the engines, Tony caught a whiff of the scent the girl had been wearing in the Post House foyer earlier.

'And you ought to spend some time in the area. How the hell can you run a television company in the Cotswolds, if you spend all your time in London, hawking your ass round the advertising companies?'

'The shareholders wouldn't be very pleased if I didn't,' said Tony, thoroughly nettled. 'Look at our results.'

Rupert shrugged again. 'You're also supposed to make good programmes. As your local MP I'm just passing on what's being said.'

'As one of your more influential constituents,' said Tony, furiously, 'I don't think you should be checking into the Post House with bimbos half your age.'

Rupert laughed. 'That was no bimbo, that was Beattie Johnson.'

Of course! Instantly Tony remembered the girl. Beattie Johnson was one of the most scurrilous and successful women columnists – dubbed by *Private Eye* 'the First not-quite-a-lady of Fleet Street'.

'She's ghosting my memoirs,' added Rupert. 'We were doing research. I always believe in laying one's ghost.'

Below the blank stare of the dark glasses, his curved smiling mouth seemed even more insolent. As the plane revved up, both men turned to look out of the window, and Tony found himself trembling with rage. But not even the splendid, striped-silk-shirted bosom of the air hostess, which rose and fell as she showed passengers how to inflate their life jackets, could keep Rupert's eyes open. By the time they were air-borne, he was asleep.

Tony accepted a glass of champagne and tried to concen-trate on the *Wall Street Journal*. He didn't know which he resented most – Rupert's habitual contempt, his ability to sleep anywhere, his effortless acquisition of women, or the obvious devotion of the palely efficient Gerald, who was now sipping Perrier and polishing the speech Rupert was to deliver to the International Olympic Committee at lunchtime.

There had hardly been a husband in Gloucestershire, indeed in the world, Tony reflected, who hadn't cheered four years ago when Rupert's beautiful wife, Helen, had walked out on him in the middle of the Los Angeles Olympics, running off with another rider and causing Rupert the maximum humiliation.

But, infuriatingly, Rupert had appeared outwardly unaffec-ted and had risen to the occasion by winning a show-jumping gold medal despite a trapped shoulder nerve, and going on two years later to win the World Championship, the only prize hitherto to elude him. Then, giving up show jumping at the pinnacle of his fame, he had moved effortlessly into politics, winning the Tory seat of Chalford and Bisley with ease. Even worse, he had turned out a surprisingly good MP, being very quick on his feet, totally unfazed by the Opposition or the Prime Minister, and prepared to fight very hard for his constituency.

Although scandal had threatened eighteen months ago, when Rupert's then mistress, Amanda Hamilton, wife of the Foreign Secretary, had withdrawn her patronage on finding out that Rupert was also sleeping with her teenage daughter, by this time, in the eyes of a doting Prime Minister, Rupert could do no wrong. Now, as Minister for Sport, with Gerald Middleton as an exceptional private secretary to do all the donkey work, Rupert was free to roam round exuding glamour, raising money for the Olympic team here, defusing a riot against a South African athlete there. Responsibility, however, hadn't cleaned up his private life at all. Divorced from Helen, he could behave as he chose, hence his cavorting with Beattie Johnson in the Post House that morning.

Glancing at Rupert, sprawled out on the pale-grey leather seat, taking up most of Gerald's leg room, beautiful despite the emergent stubble, Tony felt a further stab of jealousy. He couldn't remember a time in his forty-four years when he hadn't envied the Campbell-Blacks. For all their outlandish behaviour, they had always been looked up to in Gloucestershire. They had lived in the same beautiful house in Penscombe for generations, while Tony was brought up behind net curtains in a boring semi in the suburbs of Cheltenham. Tony also had a chip because he only went to a grammar school, where he'd been teased for being fat and short, and because his conventional colourless father (although subsequently ennobled for his work in the war) had been considered far too valuable as a munitions manufacturer to be allowed to go off and fight, unlike Rupert's father, Eddie, who'd had a dazzling war in the Blues.

Even when Tony's father had been given his peerage, Eddie Campbell-Black and his cronies had laughed, always referring to him dismissively as Lord Pop-Pop, as they blasted away slaughtering wild life with one of his products on their large estates.

Growing up near the Campbell-Blacks, Tony had longed to be invited to Penscombe and drawn into that rackety, exciting set. But the privilege had been bestowed on his brother Basil, who was ten years younger and who, because Tony's father had made his pile by then, had been given a pony to ride and sent to Harrow instead of a grammar school, and had there become a friend of Rupert's.

As a result of such imagined early deprivation, Tony had

grown up indelibly competitive – not just at work, but also socially, sexually, and at all games. Spurning the family firm when he left school, he'd gone straight into advertising and specialized in buying television air time. Having learnt the form, from there he moved to the advertising side of television. A brilliant entrepreneur, who felt he was slipping unless he had a dozen calls from Tokyo and New York during Christmas dinner, by changing jobs repeatedly he had gained the plum post of Chief Executive at Corinium Television eight years ago.

Having shot up to five feet ten and lost his puppy fat in his twenties, Tony had in middle age grown very attractive in a brutal sort of way; although with his Roman nose, heavy-lidded charcoal-grey eyes, coarsely modelled mouth and springy close-cropped dark hair, he looked more like a Sicilian wide boy than an English peer. He chose to proclaim the latter, however, by wearing coronets on absolutely everything. And on the little finger on his left hand gleamed a massive gold signet ring, sporting the Baddingham crest of wrestling rams, above the motto chosen by Lord Pop-Pop: Peaceful is the country that is strongly armed.

Considerably adding to Tony's sex appeal was a hunky bull-necked body, kept in shape by self-control and ruthless exercise, and a voice deliberately deep and smooth to eradicate any trace of a Gloucestershire accent. This only slipped when he went into one of his terrifying rages, which flattened the Corinium Television staff against the cream-hessianed walls of his vast office.

In fact, it irritated the hell out of Tony that, despite his success, his fortune and his immense power, Rupert still refused to take him seriously. He would not have been so upset by Rupert's sniping if it had not echoed a warning last night from Charles Crawford, the rotund and retiring Chairman of the Independent Broadcasting Authority (or IBA as they were known). The IBA's job was to grant franchises to the fifteen independent television companies every eight years or so, monitor their programmes and generally beat them with a big stick if they stepped out of line.

After his programme with Rupert and the Home Secretary at Thames Television yesterday, Charles Crawford had gone on to the Garrick to dine with Tony.

'As an old friend,' said Charles, greedily pouring the cream Tony had rejected together with his own supply over his strawberries, 'I don't see what else we can do but give you a stinking mid-term report. You promised us Corinium would provide at least ten hours' drama a year for the network, and all you've produced is one lousy cops-and-robbers two-parter, totally targeted at the American market. Why can't you provide some decent programmes, like Patrick Dromgoole does at HTV?'

For a second Tony gritted his teeth. He was fed up with having Patrick Dromgoole and HTV held up to him as models of perfection. Then pulling himself together he filled up Charles Crawford's glass with priceless Barsac.

'Things are going to change,' he said soothingly. 'I've just poached Simon Harris from the BBC as Programme Controller. He's very hot on drama, and has dreamed up a terrific idea for a thirteen-parter, a cross between James Herriot and "Animal House".'

'Well that's a start,' grumbled Charles, 'but your regional programmes are quite awful too. Your territory – which you conveniently seem to have forgotten – stretches from Oxford to Wales, and from Southampton to Stratford. And you're supposed to cover the whole area. That's why we gave you the franchise.

'We also know you've been spending Corinium advertising profits, which should have been spent improving your programmes, buying up . . .' Charles ticked the list off with his fat fingers, 'a film production company, a publishing firm, a travel agency, a cinema chain, a film library, and a safari park, and what's this I hear about plans to buy an American distribution company? American, for Christ's sake.'

'That's fallen through,' lied Tony. 'It was only an idea.'

'Well, keep it that way. Finally you've got to spend more time in your area. Many of your staff have absolutely no idea what you look like. I could understand if you had to live in the middle of Birmingham or even Manchester, but Cotchester must be the most delightfully civilized town in the country. We awarded you the franchise to reflect the region responsibly, and we've given you a very easy ride up till now.'

And I've given you some bloody good dinners, thought Tony sourly, as Charles sniffed appreciatively at a passing plate of welsh rarebit.

'But when Lady Gosling takes over from me in the autumn,' went on Charles, spooning up the last drop of pink cream, 'you're all going to feel the chill cloud of higher education across the industry. Lady G believes in quality programmes and lots of women at the helm. Go on producing your usual crap, and you'll be out on your ear.'

Having brooded on this conversation and on Rupert Campbell-Black's contumely the entire flight, the only thing that managed to cheer Tony up was when the limousine that met him at Kennedy turned out to be at least three feet longer than Rupert's and twice as plush.

RIVALS

2

Tony's rule, once he got to America, was never to check what time it was in England. To compensate for such an unsatisfactory start to the day, he spent the next few hours in a heady spate of wheeling and dealing, selling the format of two sit-coms and a game show for such a large sum that it wouldn't matter even if they bombed. It was only when he got back to the Waldorf and found three messages to ring his very demanding mistress, Alicia, and, checking the time, realized that he couldn't because it was long after midnight and she'd be tucked up in bed with her husband, that he suddenly felt tired.

He kicked himself for agreeing to dine with Ronnie Havegal, Head of Co-Productions at NBS, particularly as Ronnie had asked if he could bring some producer called Cameron Cook.

'Cameron's a good friend of mine,' Ronnie had said in his Harvard drawl. 'Very bright, just done a documentary on debutantes, up for a Peabody award, real class; they like that sort of thing in England.'

With his royal-blue blazers, butterscotch tan, and streaked hair, Tony had often wondered about Ronnie's sexual preferences. He didn't want to spend an evening avoiding buying some lousy programme from one of Ronnie's fag friends. Yanks always got class wrong anyway.

Christ, he was tired. Unable to master the taps in the

22

shower, he shot boiling lava straight into his eyes. Then, forgetting to put the shower curtain inside the bath, he drenched the floor and his only pair of black shoes.

Tony spent a lot of money on his clothes and ever since he'd seen Marlon Brando in *Guys and Dolls* as a teenager tended to wear dark shirts with light ties. The new dark-blue silk shirt Alicia had given him for his birthday would be wasted on two fags. He would keep it for lunch with Ali MacGraw tomorrow. Dressed, he fortified himself with a large whisky and put the presentation booklet of 'Four Men went to Mow', Simon Harris's new idea for a thirteen-part series, on the glass table, together with a video of possible exteriors and interiors to give the Americans a taste of the ravishing Cotswold countryside.

He was woken by Ronnie ringing up from downstairs. But when Ronnie came through the door, Tony suddenly didn't feel tired any more, for with him was the sexiest, most truculent-looking girl Tony had ever seen. Around twenty-six, she was wearing a straight linen dress, the colour of a New York taxi, and earrings like mini satellite dishes. She had a lean, wonderfully rapacious body, long legs, very short dark hair sleeked back from her thin face, and a clear olive skin. With her straight black brows, angry, slightly protruding amber eyes, beaky nose and predatory mouth, she reminded him of a bird of prey — beautiful, intensely ferocious and tameable only by the few. She gave out an appalling sexual energy.

She was also so rude to Ronnie, who was very much her senior, that at first Tony assumed they must be sleeping together. He soon realized she was rude to everyone.

'This is Cameron Cook,' said Ronnie.

Nodding angrily in Tony's direction, Cameron set off prowling round the huge suite, looking at the large blue urn in the centre of the living-room holding agapanthus as big as footballs, the leather sofas and arm chairs, the vast double bed next door, and the six telephones (with one even in the shower).

'Shit!' Her voice was low and rasping. 'This place is bigger than Buckingham Palace; no wonder you Brits need American co-production money.'

Tony, who was opening a bottle of Dom Perignon, ignored the jibe, and asked Cameron where she came from.

'Cincinnati.'

'City of the seven hills,' said Tony smoothly. 'But you must have bought those legs in New York.'

Cameron didn't smile.

'You don't look like a Lord, more like a Mafia hood. What do I call you: Your Grace, Sir, my Lord, Baron, Lord Ant?'

'You can call me Tony.' He handed her a glass.

Cameron picked up the presentation booklet of 'Four Men went to Mow'. Kicking off her flat black shoes, she curled up, looking very tiny on the huge pockmarked red leather sofa.

'What's this shit?'

'Cameron!' remonstrated Ronnie.

'Corinium's latest thirteen-parter,' explained Tony. 'We aim to start shooting in October.'

'If you get American finance,' said Cameron, sharply.

Tony nodded. 'We'll put it out early in the evening; should appeal to kids and adults.'

'Dumb title. What the shit does it mean?'

'It's the line of an English song,' said Tony evenly.

'Thought it was a series about back yards.'

'It's about four agricultural students living in a house.'

'I can read, thank you,' snapped Cameron, running her eyes down the page. 'And someone finds someone in bed with someone in the first episode. Jesus, and you're expecting this shit to go out as wholesome family entertainment in Middle America, where we haven't seen a nipple on the network for years.'

'Don't listen to Cameron,' said Ronnie. 'She needs a muzzle in the office to stop her savaging her colleagues.'

'Shut up and let me read it.'

Ronnie then proceeded to update Tony on the recent changes at NBS. 'They axed twenty people last week, good people who've been there fifteen years. The new business guys are running the place like a supermarket.'

But Tony wasn't listening. He was watching this incredibly savage girl with her skirt rucked up round her thighs. Christ, he'd like to screw all that smouldering bad temper out of her.

As if aware of his scrutiny, she glanced up.

'There's too much air in this glass,' she said, holding it out for a refill.

'You're too old for TV at twenty-five these days,' Ronnie rattled on obsessively. 'I work with a guy of fifty. He lives in such constant fear of his age getting out, he keeps on having his face lifted.'

Ronnie looked desperately tired. Beneath the butterscotch tan, there were new lines round the eyes. Cameron chucked the presentation booklet back on the glass table.

'Well?' Tony raised his eyebrows.

'Schmaltz, schlock, shit, what d'you want me to say? It's utterly provincial, right, but the dialogue's far too sophisticated. If you're going to appeal to Alabama blacks, Mexican peasants and Russian Jews in the same programme, you can't have a vocab bigger than three hundred words. And I don't know any of the stars.'

'No one had heard of Tim Piggott-Smith, or Charles Dance, or Geraldine James before "Jewel".'

'They'd heard of Peggy Ashcroft. Your characters are so stereotyped. And you've got the wrong hero, Johnny's the guy the Americans will identify with. He's got drive, he comes from a poor home, he's going to make it. The Hon Will's got it already. What's an Hon anyway?'

'A peer's son,' said Tony.

'Well, make him a Lord. Americans understand Lords. And they're all far too wimpish. Americans are pissed off with wimps. We've seen too many guys crying in pinnies. You can't wear your sensitivity on your silk shirtsleeve any more.'

Tony, who'd never done any of these things, warmed to this girl.

'Go on,' he said.

25

'As a nation, we're getting behind the family and the strong patriarch again. There's a large part of the population that want men to reassert themselves, be more aggressive, more accountable, more heterosexual. And you've got a marvellous chance with four guys in a house together to explore friendship between men, I don't mean faggotry; I mean comradeship. It was a great Victorian virtue, but no one associated it with being gay. Today's man shoots first, then gets in touch with his feelings later.'

'Is that how you like your men?' said Tony, getting up to put the video into the machine.

'Shit no, I'm just talking about the viewers. You've got one of the guys ironing the girl's ball gown for her; yuk!'

Tony filled up her glass yet again.

'Have a look at this.'

Up on the screen came a honey-coloured Cotswold village, an ancient church, golden cornfields, then a particularly ravishing Queen Anne house.

'We plan to use this as Will's father's house,' said Tony.

'Bit arty-farty,' snapped Cameron, as the camera roved lasciviously over a lime-tree avenue, waterfalls of old roses, and a lake surrounded by yellow irises.

'Beautiful place,' said Ronnie in awe.

'Mine,' said Tony smugly.

'Don't you have a wife who owns it as well?' said Cameron, feminist hackles rising.

'Of course; she's a very good gardener.'

'Looks like fucking Disneyland,' said Cameron.

Switching off the video machine, Tony emptied the bottle into Cameron's glass and said, 'Corinium did make more than twelve million pounds last year selling programmes to America, so we're not quite amateurs. Some of the points you made are interesting, but we do have to appeal to a slightly more sophisticated audience at home.'

'We ought to eat soon,' said Ronnie. 'You must be exhausted.'

'Not at all,' said Tony, who was looking at Cameron, 'must just have a pee.'

Alone in the bathroom, he whipped out his red fountain pen and in the memo page of his diary listed every criticism Cameron had made. Then he brushed his hair and, smiling at his reflection, hastily removed a honey-roast peanut from between his teeth. Fortunately he hadn't been smiling much at that bitch.

Even in a packed restaurant swarming with celebrities Cameron turned heads. There was something about her combative unsmiling beauty, her refusal to look to left or right, that made even the vainest diners put on their spectacles to have a second glance.

Immediately they'd ordered, Ronnie went off table-hopping. 'Nice guy,' said Tony, fishing.

'Very social register,' said Cameron dismissively. 'Watch him work the room, he makes everyone feel they've had a meaningful intimate conversation in ten seconds flat.'

'Seems a bit flustered about the blood-letting at NBS.'

Cameron took a slug of Dom Perignon. 'He needs a big success. Both the series he set up last year have bombed.'

'Given him an ulcer too.'

Cameron looked at Tony speculatively.

'I guess you've never had an ulcer, Lord Ant.'

'No,' said Tony smoothly. 'I give them to other people. How do the NBS sackings affect you?'

Cameron shrugged. 'I don't mind the sackings or the rows, but now the money men have moved in, I figure I'll have less freedom to make the programmes I want.'

'How d'you get into television?'

'My mother walked out on my father at the height of the feminist revolution, came to New York hell-bent on growth. The only thing that grew was her overdraft. She was too proud to ask for money from my father, so I went to Barnard on a scholarship, and got a reporting job in the Vac to make ends meet. After graduation, I joined the *New York Times*, then moved to the NBS newsroom. Last year I switched over to documentaries, as a writer/producer. At the moment I'm directing drama.'

'Your mother must be proud of you.'

'She thinks I'm too goal-orientated,' said Cameron bitterly. 'She's never forgiven me for voting for Reagan. I don't understand my mother's generation. All that crap about going back to Nature, and open marriages, and communes and peace marches. Jesus.'

Tony laughed. 'I can't see you on a peace march. What are your generation into?'

'Physical beauty, money, power, fame.'

'You've certainly achieved the first.'

'Sure.' Cameron made no attempt to deny it.

'How d'you intend to achieve the rest?'

'I aim to be the first woman to run a Network Company.'

'What about marriage and children?'

Cameron shook her head so violently she nearly blacked her own eyes with her satellite dish earrings.

'Gets in the way of a career. I've seen too many women at NBS poised to close a deal, being interrupted by a phone call, and having to rush home because their kid's got a temperature of 104.'

The waiter arrived with their first course. Escargots for Cameron, gulls' eggs for Tony. Ronnie, who hadn't ordered anything, returned to the table, buttered a roll, but didn't eat it.

'Anyway,' went on Cameron angrily, 'what's the point of getting married? Look at the guys. New York is absolutely crammed with emotionally immature guys quite unable to make a commitment.'

'They're all gay,' said Tony. He peeled a gull's egg, dipped it in celery salt, and handed it to Cameron.

'Bullshit,' she said, accepting it without thanking him. 'There are loads of heterosexuals in New York. I know at least three. And what makes it worse, with the men being so dire, is that New York is absolutely crawling with prosperous, talented, beautiful women in a state of frenzy about getting laid.'

'Give me their telephone numbers,' said Tony lightly.

'Don't be fatuous,' snarled Cameron. 'Guys are turned off by achieving women; they make them feel inferior. What

28

beats me is why women are so dependent on men. You see them everywhere, with their leather briefcases, and their dressed-for-success business suits, rabbiting on about independence, yet clinging onto a thoroughly destructive relationship rather than be without a guy.'

Furiously she gouged the last of the garlic and parsley butter out of her snail shells. The lady, reflected Tony, is protesting too much.

Ronnie was off table-hopping again. The head waiter was now making a great song and dance about cooking Cameron's steak Diane at the table, throwing mushrooms and spring onions into the sizzling butter. The champagne having got to Cameron's tongue, she was also spitting away like the hot fat:

'TV people have no idea what's important. Ask them about their kids, they just tell you what private schools they're enrolled in. That's a very subtle way of telling you how well they're doing. What's the point of having kids? Just as a status symbol.'

'You're a bit of a puritan at heart.' Tony filled her glass yet again. 'Your ancestors didn't come over on the *Mayflower* by any chance?'

'No, but my father was British. I've got a British passport.'

Better and better, thought Tony.

The head waiter was pouring Napoleon brandy over the steak now and setting fire to it. The orange purple flames flared upwards, charring the ceiling, lighting up Cameron's hostile, predatory face. Another waiter served Tony's red snapper, which was surrounded by tiny courgettes, sweetcorn and carrots.

'They employ one guy here to sharpen the turnips,' said Cameron, pinching a courgette from Tony's plate. For a second, she looked at it. 'Tiny,' she added dismissively. 'Like the average New York cock.' And with one bite she devoured it.

Tony laughed, encouraging her in her scorn.

'Enjoy your meal,' said the head waiter, laying the steak in front of Cameron with a flourish.

I wonder if I'm reading her right, thought Tony; anyone that aggressive must either be desperately insecure or impossibly spoilt. Maybe her mother had felt guilty about splitting up from her father, and let Cameron get away with murder.

Ronnie's sole was cold when he returned to the table, shaking his head. 'I hear you had a row with Bella Wakefield this afternoon.'

Cameron raised her eyes to the charred ceiling. 'She's so fucking useless.'

'She *is* the Vice-President's daughter.'

'She pisses me off. Every time she's got a line, which is about once a year, she teeters up on her spike heels, saying, "Cameron, what's my motivation in this scene?" So finally I flip and say: "Pay day on Friday." She went kinda mad.'

'I'm not surprised,' said Ronnie disapprovingly.

The head waiter glided up. 'Everything all right, sir?'

'Perfect,' said Ronnie, who hadn't touched his sole.

'Steak as madam likes it?'

Cameron tipped back her chair. 'If you want the honest truth, it tastes like moderately flavoured socks.'

The smile was wiped off the waiter's face. 'I beg your pardon.'

'Cameron,' hissed Ronnie.

'Like chewing my own laundry. I cannot figure why you waste such expensive ingredients producing something so disgusting. I'd rather drink the brandy straight.'

The head waiter looked as though he was going to cry.

'Would madam like something else?'

'I'll pass,' said Cameron, ostentatiously putting her knife and fork together. 'It's not even worth a doggie bag.'

RIVALS

3

As they came out of the restaurant, limos for Ronnie and Tony glided up. Cameron paused between the two.

'I haven't seen your deb programme yet,' said Tony. 'Why don't we go back to the Waldorf and look at it?'

Ronnie shook his head. 'You guys go. I'm pooped.'

Back in Tony's suite, an almost unbearable tension developed between them. Having poured large brandies, Tony removed his coat. Despite the air conditioning, he could feel damp patches of sweat forming under his arms and trickling down his spine. In silence they watched Cameron's tape. Within five minutes, Tony realized its outstanding quality.

The commentary was cut to a minimum; Cameron had let the debs and their mothers speak for themselves. But you could feel her fierce egalitarian scorn, in the way she had highlighted their silliness and pretension, and the compassion she displayed for the *noveau riche* who tried to break in, and for the wallflower who sat unfêted through ball after ball.

Despite the fact that Cameron had been vile about 'Four Men went to Mow', Tony knew when to be generous.

'They'll adore it in England,' he said at the end. 'I'll ring the Film Purchasing Committee tomorrow and insist they look at it.'

'Thanks.' Cameron got up to rewind the tape. 'I'd better go. I got up at six this morning, and you must be reeling from Concorde lag.'

With that sleek Eton crop, thought Tony, it'd be like making love to a boy. Putting out a hand to halt her he encountered a huge shoulder pad.

'Sit down. I want to talk to you. You got a regular boy-friend?'

'Until three months ago.' She sat down on the far end of the leather sofa.

'What did he do?'

'He was a threat analyst. Spent all day looking at the Soviets, and saying: "They're a threat".'

Tony laughed, edging down the sofa.

'I don't need a man to look after me,' said Cameron defensively. 'Just someone to make the sparks fly. If I'm not having a good time, I quit. Are you happily married?'

'Not overwhelmingly.'

'She a dog?'

'Not at all. It's a marriage of extreme public convenience. We get on very well when we don't see too much of each other.'

This girl is exactly what I need to wake them all up at Corinium, he was thinking. She's superbright, ambitious, aggressive. The IBA would adore the deb programme, it had quality and universal appeal; and being a woman, Cameron would appeal to the incoming chairman, Lady Gosling. Even more important, from the way she had carved up Simon Harris's treatment, she was capable of seeing what was wrong with a programme and subtly gearing it towards the American market without making it too bland. And finally, as she had a British passport, there wouldn't be the usual ghastly hassle about work permits.

'How'd you like to work in England?'

'How much?'

'Thirty grand.'

'You've got to be joking. I'm on a hundred thousand dollars here.'

'It's cheaper living in England, and we could pick up a few bills.'

'I'd have to have somewhere to live,' said Cameron, think-

32

ing longingly of the honey-coloured houses she'd seen on the video.

'We can arrange that.'

'If I'm stuck in the country, I'll need a car.'

'Of course.'

For a minute she glared at him. 'How soon do I get on the Board?'

'Cameron,' said Tony gently, 'I'm the boss of Corinium. I decide that.'

'I'll kick it around,' she said indifferently. 'You'd better sleep with me first.'

Not by a flicker did Tony's swarthy face betray his surprise.

'Why? D'you think afterwards I might not want to offer you the job?'

Cameron smiled for the first time that evening. 'No, I might not want to take it.'

Even in the bedroom she didn't stop fighting, promptly switching on the television.

'God is love,' a lady in a shirtwaister, with very long royal blue eyelashes, was saying, 'not a guy with a stick; He wants us all to enjoy ourselves.'

'And so say all of us,' said Cameron.

Tony turned off the television and, with remarkably steady hands, removed her huge earrings, and massaged the reddened lobes.

'D'you get a good satellite picture from these?'

There wasn't much else to take off. Just the yellow dress and a pair of yellow pants. Tony never dreamed that anyone with such a sinewy, well-muscled body could have such a smooth skin.

'Those Y-fronts went out with the ark,' said Cameron, throwing them in the wastepaper basket. 'I'm going to buy you some boxer shorts.'

Bearing in mind that it was eight o'clock in the morning in England, Tony thought he acquitted himself with honours.

'Mine eyes have seen the glory of the coming of the Lord,' sang Cameron as she finally climbed off him.

'Still fighting the American War of Independence,' murmured Tony into her shoulder.

But just as he was falling asleep, he realized she was rigid and shuddering beside him. Reaching down, he found her hand in her bush.

'I thought you'd come as well,' he said, outraged.

'If you figured that, Buster, you've got a lot to learn.'

'Come here, you bitch.'

Tugging away her hand, he knelt over her, kissing her navel, then very slowly progressing downwards. Lying on the floor, tangled in each other's arms, they were interrupted much later by the telephone.

It was Corinium's sales director, Georgie Baines.

'I thought you'd like the monthly revenue figures, Tony. I didn't wake you?'

'I've been up for hours.'

'You can say that again,' said Cameron, wriggling out from under him.

'They're up four million on last year,' said Georgie jubilantly. For five minutes they discussed business, then Georgie said that Percy, Tony's chauffeur, would like a word.

'Good morning, my Lord,' said Percy. 'We won the Test match by four wickets.'

Tony was almost more delighted by that than by the advertising figures. Hearing water running in the shower, he was about to jump on Cameron once more, when the telephone rang again. After that it kept ringing, ending up with a call from Alicia, Tony's beautiful and demanding mistress.

'Do you spend all your life on the telephone?' she screamed.

There was a knock on the door. Tony hung up and, wrapping a towel round his waist, went to answer it. It was the breakfast he'd ordered before going out last night.

Having signed the bill, he found Cameron in the bathroom, drying her pants with the hair dryer. She was wearing Tony's dark-blue silk birthday shirt, with one of his red paisley ties wound round her waist. Her hair was wet from the shower; she looked sensational.

34

'Come back to bed.'

'Can't. I've got a breakfast meeting. Got to get there early to check the room isn't bugged.'

The telephone rang again.

'You answer it,' said Tony evilly.

Cameron picked it up.

'Someone called Alicia,' she said.

'Say I'm in the shower.'

'She didn't sound very pleased,' said Cameron, putting down the receiver.

Scooping up the mini-bottles of shampoo, conditioner, bath gel, and cologne, she dropped them into her bag. Then, peeling the shoulder pads out of her yellow dress, she fixed them into the shoulders of Tony's dark-blue shirt. As she went into the bedroom, she removed a strawberry as big as a cricket ball from the grapefruit on Tony's breakfast tray.

'What are your plans?' asked Tony.

'I'm in the studios from ten o'clock onwards. I should be through around eight. And you?'

'I've got people to see. I'm lunching with Ali MacGraw – more my age group, sweetie.' He kissed Cameron on the forehead. 'And I want that shirt back.'

'You can wear my yellow dress. If I wear it, Ronnie'll know I haven't been home.' Taking a mirror from her bag, she winced at her reflection in the bright sunlight. 'He'll know it anyway.'

'I'll call you later,' said Tony.

The moment she'd gone, he showered, dressed and, having summoned one of the secretaries from Corinium's American office on 5th Avenue, dictated a completely new treatment for 'Four Men went to Mow'.

In the middle, Alicia rang and demanded who had answered the telephone.

'Your successor,' said Tony, without a trace of compassion, and hung up.

By midday he had a new and beautifully bound presentation booklet for 'Four Men went to Mow', containing a character analysis of the new hero, who was now the working-class boy and not the peer's son (who had become a lord), plus a new list of possible stars, suggested locations, story lines, and a couple of pages of simplified dialogue, all based entirely on Cameron's recommendations.

Ronnie called up as Tony was reading it through.

'How d'you like Cameron?'

'Like wasn't the operative word. What's bugging her?'

'More enfant than terrible,' said Ronnie, who wanted to do business with Tony very badly, 'but she's too ambitious for her own good, and too upfront. There's a streak of idealism which makes her scream and shout till she gets what she wants; and if you're as sexy as she is you antagonize not only women but also the men who don't get to pull you.

'Don't tell anyone I told you, but the programme controller's going to axe her last documentary, and she's been so rude to Bella Wakefield she's being taken off the series. But she's bright,' Ronnie sighed. 'Sadly they don't give a shit about talent here any more. But that's off the record.'

'We haven't spoken,' said Tony.

'As a quid pro quo, can we be the first people to see "Four Men went to Mow?"' asked Ronnie. 'I know Cameron carved it up, but it looked great to me.'

'Of course,' said Tony smoothly.

After an exceptionally affable lunch with Ali MacGraw, who was an old friend, to discuss a long-term project, Tony strolled down to see USBC, the deadly rivals of NBS.

At the plaza of the Seagram building tourists and office workers sat on the walls, eating sandwiches and pizza, trying to woo the blazing sun down between the office blocks on to their bare arms and legs. The flowers in the centre strip of Park Avenue wilted in the heat as Tony sauntered past General Motors and the Pan Am building with their thousand glittering windows, admiring the coloured awnings outside the houses and the beautiful, loping New York girls with their briefcases, who looked back at him with flattering interest. Maybe Cameron was right about the paucity of real New York men.

The Head of Co-Production at USBC and the Daytime

Programme Controller were enchanted by the video of the honey-coloured houses and the Cotswold countryside.

'This series,' Tony told them, his deep, beautiful voice flowing on like vintage port glugging out of a priceless decanter, 'will be a cross between James Herriot and "Animal House", but in a way it's much, much more. We intend to explore real friendship between real men; not homosexuality, but that Victorian virtue, comradeship. The hero, a poor boy from a deprived background, doesn't inherit the earth or the girl, but he finds his integrity. The story, despite its depths, is simple enough to appeal to a Mexican peasant or to an Alabama black.'

Out of the corner of his eye he noticed that the extremely influential VPICDT Prog. (which stood for Vice-President In Charge of Daytime Programming) had just entered the room. Tony warmed to his subject.

'In England,' he went on, 'we are sick of wimps who wear their sensitivity on their silk shirtsleeves. The guys in our story are kind to animals and women, but they shoot from the hip first and get in touch with their feelings later. Nor would they be seen dead in an apron. Let us have men as men again, and bring back dignity and chivalry to our sex.'

Thinking he'd gone slightly over the top, Tony switched briskly to finance. 'We can do it for three-quarters of a million an hour,' he said. 'It'll be thirty per cent cheaper if we make it in England; we'll put up twenty per cent of the cost against Europe and the UK.'

Admiring the discreet blue coronet on Tony's dark-green shirt, the VPICDT Prog., who'd just been bawled out on the phone by his wife for forgetting to collect the suit she'd had altered at Ralph Lauren, reflected that Lord B had real class. And he was right — it was high time men were men again.

'Very interesting, Tony,' he said. 'We'd like to kick the idea around. You in New York for a few days?'

'Yes,' said Tony.

'Showing it to other people?'

'Of course.'

'We'll get back to you as soon as possible.'

Outside it had rained. The trees had taken on a deeper greenness. The city had the warm wet smell of a conservatory. Park Avenue was a solid yellow mass of honking taxis. Quivering with the excitement of wheeler-dealing, Tony knew he ought to ring Ronnie and show him the treatment. Let him sweat, he thought, let Cameron sweat. He went back to the Waldorf, checked out and, without leaving a forwarding address, flew to Los Angeles.

Cameron lived in an eleventh-floor apartment on Riverside Drive with a glorious view of the Hudson River. She got home at about nine after a hellish day, punctuated with screaming matches which had finally culminated in Bella Wakefield turning up on the set wearing two-inch false eyelashes and half a ton of purple eyeshadow to play a Victorian governess. When Cameron had ordered her to take her make-up down, Bella had stormed out, presumably to sob on the Vice-President's already sodden shoulder.

The moment she got in, Cameron played back her recording machine, but there was no message from Tony, not even a click to show he'd rung and hung up because she wasn't there. He hadn't left any messages at NBS either.

Cameron, however, had done her homework. As Tony had learnt from Ronnie that she was brilliant but unbalanced, she in turn had discovered that Tony was an unprincipled shit, much more interested in making money than good programmes, masterly at board-room intrigue, and so smooth he could slide up a hill. Convinced she could handle him, Cameron wasn't at all put out by this information, and decided to accept the job.

She'd always wanted to work in England and track down her English relations. She admired British television, and she'd bitterly envied all those rich girls at Barnard who'd travelled to Europe so effortlessly on Daddy's income. It would also give her a chance to get away from her mother and her mother's appalling lover, Mike. Cameron gave a shudder; she had recurrent nightmares about Mike.

She turned on the light. She would be sad to leave her

apartment, which was painted white throughout, with yellow curtains and rush matting on the polished floors. Furniture in the living-room included a grand piano, a dentist's chair upholstered in red paisley like Tony's tie, a dartboard, and a gold toe, one foot high, which had been surreptitiously chipped from the foot of a cherub in the Metropolitan Museum. Books lined most of one wall, but half a shelf was taken up with videos of the programmes she'd made. These were her identity. Cameron only felt she truly existed when she saw her credits coming up on the screen.

And now this English lord had come along and thrown her into complete turmoil because he hadn't called. Denied a father in her teens, Cameron was always drawn to older men. She was attracted by Tony's utter ruthlessness, and, despite her sniping, sexually it had ended up a great night.

Then why didn't the bastard call? Lord of the Never Rings. Collapsing on the sofa, she gazed out of the window. On the opposite bank, lights from the factories and power stations sent glittering yellow snakes across the black water. Watching the coloured Dinky cars whizzing up and down the freeway, she fell asleep.

When she woke next morning, very cold and stiff, the Hudson had turned to a sheet of white metal, with the power stations smoking dreamily in the morning mist. Perhaps Tony had only offered her a job as a ruse to get her into bed, but she didn't think he was like that. If he'd just wanted to screw her, he'd have said so. Yet when she rang the Waldorf to accept, she was outraged to be told that Tony had checked out, leaving no forwarding address.

'This guy's mighty popular,' said the operator. 'Everyone's been ringing him.'

Nor would Corinium's New York office tell her where Tony had gone, and, even worse, the morning paper had a charming picture of him coming out of the Four Seasons with Ali MacGraw.

In Los Angeles, when he wasn't spreading the word about 'Four Men went to Mow', or finalizing the deal to buy the

American distributors, which he'd had to acquire through a holding company so as not to upset the IBA, Tony thought about Cameron.

Back in New York, two days later, ignoring the increasingly desperate messages from NBS, he went to USBC and after screwing another quarter million dollars a programme out of them on the grounds that Disney were madly interested, he closed the deal.

He returned to the Waldorf, sweating like a pig, had a shower, poured himself an enormous whisky and rang Cameron. He had to hold the telephone at arm's length.

'Where the fuck have you been, you bastard?' she screamed.

'Busy,' said Tony and, when she started to give him an earful, very sharply told her to shut up and calm down.

'I've raised the cash for "Four Men went to Mow".'

'Who put it up?' demanded Cameron.

'USBC. The lawyers are thrashing out the nuts and bolts at the moment.'

'Poor Ronnie. NBS aren't going to be very happy – we didn't even get to see it.'

'Well, there you go.'

'He probably will, right out of the front door, and never come back after this. Ronnie's right – you are a shit.'

'That's no way to address your new boss.'

Cameron's heart was hammering so hard, her palms were suddenly so damp, that the receiver nearly slid out of her hand.

'Hullo, hullo,' said Tony. 'Have you thought about that job I offered you?'

'You just fuck off like that. How do I know I can trust you?'

'Give me the address. I'll be over in half an hour and we'll talk terms.'

Yet when he arrived at Cameron's flat, armed with a bottle of champagne, he was outraged to find an impossibly handsome young man lounging in the dentist's chair, holding a glass that definitely didn't contain mouthwash.

'Who the hell's he?' snarled Tony.

'This is Skip, my lawyer. He dropped by to draw up my contract of employment,' said Cameron.

'Why the hell's he wearing my shirt and tie?'

Cameron laughed. 'Since I'm moving to England, I figured he deserved a leaving present.'

RIVALS
4

On a cold Friday in February, exactly twenty months after he'd signed up Cameron Cook in New York, Tony Baddingham made an infinitely more dramatic and controversial addition to his staff. Having exchanged contracts in the utmost secrecy in the morning, he popped into the IBA headquarters in Brompton Road for a midday glass of sherry with the new chairman, Lady Gosling, to dazzle her with the secret news of his latest acquisition before setting out on the two-hour drive down to Cotchester.

Even on a raw blustery February afternoon, Cotchester's wide streets and ancient pale gold houses gave off an air of serenity and prosperity. To the north of the town, in the market square, a statue of Charles I on his horse indicated that Cotchester had once been a Royalist stronghold. Round the plinth, pigeons pecked among the straw left by the sheep and cattle sold in the market earlier in the day. To the south soared the cathedral, its great bell only muted during rush hour, the shadow of its spire on bright days lying like a benediction over the town.

Dominating the High Street was a fine Queen Anne building, once the Corn Exchange, now the headquarters of Corinium Television. Although, over the last twenty years, the building had been considerably extended at the back to include studios, dressing-rooms, an imposing new board room, and a suite of splendid offices for the directors, nothing except pale-yellow rambler roses had been allowed to alter its imposing façade. On the roof the vast dark red letters CTV could be seen for miles around, letters topped by a splendid ram standing four-square, with a Roman nose and curly horns. Originally chosen as a symbol of the wool trade which once characterized the area, according to some of Corinium's more uncharitable employees the ram could now be used to symbolize Tony Baddingham's sexual excesses.

At the back of the building an entire wall of the board room consisted of a huge window looking out on to the cathedral close, water meadows and willows trailing their yellow branches in the River Fleet, a peaceful scene totally at variance with the tensions and feuds within Corinium Television itself.

These tensions had been exacerbated that particular Friday by Tony returning unexpectedly from London and calling a programme-planning meeting at three o'clock, when he knew most of his staff would be hoping to slope off early.

Tony had actually returned in an excellent mood. His meeting with Lady Gosling had been decidedly satisfactory. Simon Harris, the ex-BBC Golden Boy, and Cameron Cook had so improved Corinium programmes over the last twenty months that he was no longer seriously worried that his franchise would be taken away in mid-term. But, in case there were rival groups who might pitch for the Corinium franchise when it came up for renewal next year, he had made the decision on the way down to clean up Corinium's act well in advance.

Until that time therefore, until Corinium were officially re-selected, he was determined not only to trail some of the most glittering names in television and the arts in front of the IBA, but also to put on some really worthy regional programmes.

It was to map out ideas for these programmes that he'd called the impromptu meeting. Unfortunately half the staff were away. The Head of News was in Munich on a freebie, the Head of Documentaries was in Rome getting a prize, the

43

male Head of Light Entertainment and the comely female Head of Kids' Programmes were both away with gastric flu, which caused a few raised eyebrows, as they had been seen looking perfectly healthy the day before.

Tony took the chair, but was instantly summoned to take an urgent call from Los Angeles. The only people in the room who didn't appear terrified or at least extremely wary of him were Charles Fairburn, Head of Religious Programmes, who'd got pissed at lunchtime, and Cameron Cook, now Head of Drama.

The Head of Sport, Mike Meadows, a once-famous footballer with ginger sideboards, whose muscle-bound shoulders had grown too big for his shiny blue blazer, smoked one cigarette after another.

Simon Harris, the Controller of Programmes, who was principled and intelligent and always saw both sides of every problem, and was therefore labelled indecisive, trembled on Tony's right. He kept his hands under the table to hide a nerve rash he had scratched raw. His thin face twitched. In an attempt to gain some kind of authority he had recently grown a straggly beard. When he took off his coat – Tony always kept the central heating tropical – you could hear the rattle of the Valium bottle, and see the great damp patches under his arms.

Beyond Simon was Tony's PA, Cyril Peacock, DFC, Corinium's ex-Sales Manager, once a stocky, jolly, assertive fellow, sensational at his job. The point of a PA, however, is that he should be utterly loyal. Some Chief Executives in television buy this loyalty with money, which is dangerous, because someone else can buy it with more money. Tony bought it with fear. After making Cyril his PA, and sometime publicity officer, Tony had encouraged him to invest his savings in a company that promptly went broke. Now the terror of the Luftwaffe was someone Tony hung his coat on – a poor old dodderer in his early sixties, with loss of job and pension hanging over his head like a sword of Damocles. Tony took great pleasure in making Cyril do his dirty work – he had four people for him to fire on Monday.

On Tony's left was Miss Madden, his secretary, also in her sixties, plain, and utterly dedicated, whose chilblains were itching because of the central heating, and who never let anyone into Tony's office without an appointment except Cameron Cook, on whom she had a love—hate crush.

Finally, down the table, opposite Cameron sat James Vereker, the impossibly good-looking, beautifully coiffeured Anchorman of the six o'clock regional news programme, 'Cotswold Round-Up'.

James should have been in the newsroom getting ready for the evening's programme, but, hating to miss anything, he had muscled in on the meeting and was now using Tony's absence to rewrite the links he would have to say later on air to fit his own speech patterns.

Glancing across at Cameron, James wondered if she and Tony had rehearsed the whole meeting in bed earlier this week, turning each other on by seeing who could be the most gratuitously bloody to everyone else. He looked at Cameron's dark-brown cashmere jersey, snugly fitting the lean body, the pale-brown suede skirt, the Charles Jourdan boots and the lascivious unmade-up face, and felt a wave of loathing. Today her short hair had been coaxed upwards in gelled spikes, like a hedgehog who'd rolled in chicken fat.

James pointedly moved the arrangement of Spring flowers left over from Wednesday's board meeting up a couple of inches to obscure his view of her and, getting out a packet of Polos, handed one to Miss Madden, who went slightly pink as she accepted it.

James offered Polos to no one else. He knew who to suck up to. Properly courted, Miss Madden would sing his praises to Tony and admit him to the inner sanctum when necessary.

As Tony walked back into the room, everyone rose from their chairs except Cameron, who pointedly ignored him. Perhaps they've had a bust-up, thought James Vereker hopefully.

The good thing about Tony, reflected Charles Fairburn, Head of Religious Programmes, was that he did cut out the

45

waffle. There was a good chance that Charles, who was going to the ballet at Covent Garden that evening, would be out of the building by five.

'I'd like to start,' said Tony briskly, 'by congratulating Cameron on being nominated for a BAFTA award. As you all know, "Four Men went to Mow" has not only been a huge network success, and sold everywhere overseas, but also because of the exceptional camera work, attracted scores of tourists to the area, and last month toppled "Howard's Way" in the ratings. We're looking for more programmes like this that project the area into the network.'

'Hear, hear,' said Cyril Peacock, his false teeth rattling with nerves.

Tony's conveniently forgotten that 'Four Men went to Mow' was my idea in the first place, thought Simon Harris bitterly. Cameron, still ignoring Tony, gazed sourly at the framed photograph on the wall of him smilingly assisting Princess Margaret to plant a cherry tree on the Corinium front lawn.

Christ, they *have* had a row, thought James.

'I'd like to give the go-ahead for a second series,' Tony went on. 'We've got the co-production money again from USBC, but I think it would be a good idea, Cameron, if you introduced perhaps a black unmarried mother into the cottage of the agricultural students to appeal to the IBA.'

Charles Fairburn suppressed a grin. The IBA were crazy about minority groups. Cameron looked outraged.

'Black unmarried mothers don't become agricultural students,' she snarled.

'There's always a first time,' said Tony smoothly. 'She could be the girlfriend of one of the four boys.'

'For Chrissake, why not have a gay shepherdess with one leg?' said Cameron.

'Why not a deaf, unemployed merry peasant?' suggested Charles Fairburn with a hiccup. 'Or a handicapped harvester?'

'That's enough,' snapped Tony.

He then went on to OK plans for an obscure Michael Tippett opera, which Cameron also scowled at, detecting

46

Lady Baddingham's influence (Tony's wife was crazy about opera) and a production of *Midsummer Night's Dream* as a sop to Stratford-on-Avon which was just within the Corinium boundary.

Now it was the turn of James Vereker, who, having finished re-writing his links, helped himself to a glass of Perrier and then suggested Corinium ought to show its 'caring face, Tony' and do a series on poverty and the aged.

'Jesus, how turgid,' said Cameron, glaring at him through the screen of fading daffodils. 'Of all the boring . . .'

Tony raised his hand for silence, his huge signet ring catching the light.

'Not a bad idea. We could do a very cheap pilot to impress the IBA. We don't have to make the series. Perhaps Cyril,' he smiled malevolently at his PA, 'could front it. He's been looking rather old and poverty-stricken lately.'

Cyril Peacock cracked his twitching face, trying to smile back. Thus encouraged, James suggested they should do something 'very strong, Tony' on rioting and drug abuse at Cotchester University. Swiftly Cameron swooped, the falcon Tony had trained, tearing into James:

'What a crappy awful idea,' she screamed. 'D'you want to antagonize the entire Tourist Board because everyone's scared to visit Cotchester any more? No one will want to invest money here. We're trying to boost the area for Chrissake.'

'What about a programme on the role of women in Cotchester town hall?' stammered Simon Harris, tugging at his straggling yellow beard.

'And have the town halls at Bath, Southampton, Oxford, Winchester, Stratford, et cetera et cetera in an uproar because we haven't done programmes on them,' said Cameron crushingly.

'I thought your idea, Tony, of interviewing the wives of celebrities living in the area looked a winner,' said Cyril Peacock, desperate to get back into favour.

' "Behind Every Famous Man"?' Cameron turned on Cyril furiously. 'That was my idea.'

'We could start with one of our director's wives, or perhaps,' Cyril lumbered on, 'even Lady Baddingham.'

Tony looked not unpleased. 'I think that would be a bit close to home.'

'Why not do a series on the very very rich?' said Charles Fairburn, who had not quite sobered up, 'They're far more of a minority group than anyone else. We could start with you, Tony.'

He was quelled by an icy glance from Tony, who, aware that the meeting was slightly lacking in carnage, suddenly realized that his Head of Operations, whose role was to tell creative people what they could not do, was missing.

'Where's Victor Page?' he said ominously.

'Gone to his grandmother's funeral,' said Miss Madden, her lips tightening.

'But he killed off two grandmothers during Wimbledon last year.'

'This was his step-granny,' said Miss Madden. 'His mother married twice.'

'No doubt his other step-grandmother will pop off during next Wimbledon,' said Tony, making a note on his memo pad. That would be five people for Cyril to fire on Monday.

Tony then turned to the points made during his talk with Lady Gosling that morning. There was no need to let his production staff get complacent.

'Several viewers,' he said, 'have complained about field mice copulating too long on our "Nature at Night" programme.'

Charles Fairburn, who had a round red face like a Dutch cheese, suppressed another smile. He'd better do his expenses. He hadn't been anywhere this week, but he needed some cash to buy drinks for his airline-steward friend at the ballet tonight.

'Cloakroom and gratuities £5,' wrote Charles Fairburn. 'Drinks with the Archdeacon £15.' That was pushing it; the Archdeacon was teetotal, but the Accounts Department didn't know it. They'd be shut if Tony didn't wrap up this meeting soon.

'On the kids' programmes front,' went on Tony, 'we've also had complaints about too much violence in "Dorothy Dove".'

'What kind of violence?' asked Simon Harris.

'Pecking Priscilla Pigeon and pulling out all her feathers.'

James was tempted to say his children had absolutely adored that particular episode, but decided not to. The Head of Kids' Programmes had rejected his advances at the Christmas party; he didn't owe her any favours.

'Dorothy Dove is supposed to be a symbol of peace,' said Tony.

'Peaceful is the dove that is strongly armed – or beaked in Dorothy's case,' murmured Charles Fairburn and regretted it.

'There have been complaints,' went on Tony nastily, 'about insufficient religious content in our religious programmes. I'll talk to you after the meeting, Charles, and the IBA are very unhappy about "Rags to Riches".'

Simon Harris turned dark red. It was he who had bought the format for 'Rags to Riches' from America and adapted it for the British network.

'But the ratings are sensational,' he protested.

'I know, but the IBA have pointed out that the contestants are far too glamorous and upmarket. We do need a few unemployed frumps to add a touch of reality, and please remember our ethnic minorities.'

'You can borrow my black unmarried mother,' said Cameron, shooting Tony a venomous look.

'The IBA,' went on Tony, squinting down the polished table, like a daily looking for smears, 'also feel we should have more women on the Corinium Board. After all, Lady Evesham's nearly sixty-five, so we must all wrack our brains for some powerful ladies.'

The men in the room exchanged glances of horror. Would Tony use this as an excuse to put the appalling Cameron Cook on the Board?

'And,' went on Tony swiftly, 'they feel we still haven't enough directors who live in the area.'

That, thought James savagely, also includes Cameron, and her exquisite Regency house on the outskirts of Cotchester.

Now Tony was saying, not without complacency, that Freddie Jones, the electronics multi-millionaire, and Rupert Campbell-Black, the Minister for Sport, who both lived in the area, would be coming in his party to the West Cotchester Hunt Ball that evening, and he would be sounding them out as possible directors.

For a second, outrage overcame the Head of Sport's terror of Tony: 'But Rupert Campbell-Black's been consistently vile about our coverage,' he spluttered. 'You'd think it was our fault Cotchester was bottom of the Third Division.'

'Good name on the writing paper. We've got to keep our local MPs sweet, with the franchise coming up,' said Tony. 'Anyway he's far too tied up with football hooligans to come to more than a couple of meetings a year, so he won't get a chance to make a nuisance of himself.'

'Don't you be too sure of it,' spat Cameron. 'Macho pig.'

Smug in the knowledge that he was the only member of the staff who'd been asked to join Tony's party at the hunt ball that evening, James Vereker couldn't resist saying, as the meeting broke up, how much he and Lizzie, his wife, were looking foward to it, and what time would Tony like them for drinks.

'About eight,' said Tony, gathering up his papers.

James could feel the laser beams of loathing and jealousy directed at him from all around the table, particularly from Cameron. That should rattle the stuck-up bitch, he thought. Since she'd been nominated for a BAFTA, she'd been getting much too big for her Charles Jourdan boots.

As Tony went out of the room, straightening the photograph of himself and Princess Margaret as he passed, James glanced at his watch. Four-thirty. He was on the air in an hour and a half and they would wrap up the programme by seven. If he had to drive the eleven miles home, bath and change, he'd be pushed for time. He'd better have a quick shower and blow dry his hair beforehand; then he could legitimately keep his make-up on — just bronzing gel, a bit of creme puff and dark brown mascara — for the ball. One got so pale in February.

He considered whether to wear his turquoise evening shirt, which brought out the blue-green in his eyes, or a white one with a turquoise bow-tie, then decided on the former. The gel might show up on the white shirt.

Wandering into the newsroom, he selected the secretary who was most in love with him and handed her twenty pages of longhand, entitled 'Poverty and the Aged: A Treatment', by James Vereker.

'I think you'll have rather fun with this one,' he told her. 'Could you centre the title in caps? I don't need it till first thing Monday morning.'

Entirely sobered up now, Charles Fairburn followed Tony into his office. He'd never get to Covent Garden and his airline steward now. But, to his amazement, Tony greeted him warmly: 'Ratings aren't bad, Charles. Wheel in the Bishop of Cotchester, a few Sikhs and a woman priest next week to talk about the meaning of self-denial and Lent; that should keep Lady Gosling happy. Look, I'm reading the lesson in church on Sunday. Rather tricky phrasing, I want to get the sense right. Could you just run through it with me?'

RIVALS
5

James Vereker drove home in his Porsche, warmly aware that
'my programme', as he always referred to it, had gone well.
James Vereker's outstanding qualities, apart from his dazzling
good looks, were his total egotism and chronic insecurity. In
order not to miss himself on television, he had even been
known to take a portable television into a restaurant. A huge
local celebrity, much of whose time was spent opening fêtes
and PAs' legs, he disliked going to London, or even worse
abroad, because no one recognized him. When he'd worked
in radio, he used to dread some crisis blowing up in Southern
Europe or the Middle East in case he couldn't pronounce it.

Aware that he was dismissed as a popinjay by the editors,
journalists and researchers who got 'Cotswold Round-Up' on
air, and who were jealous of his inflated salary and his celebrity
status, he was given to little tantrums, yet couldn't resist
seeking constant reassurance. Cameron Cook had even
suggested the parrot used in Corinium's Christmas production
of *Treasure Island* should be given a permanent squawk-on
part, telling James he was wonderful after every programme.
He kept his job because he was quite good at it and because
he always won the fight for viewers from the BBC.

Back at James's house, Birgitta, the children's curvaceous
nanny, had just lovingly finished ironing both James's white
and turquoise evening shirts, and was scenting herself and
putting on make-up for James's return.

I wish Birgitta would spend slightly more time putting the children to bed, thought James's wife, Lizzie, as they swarmed into her study demanding attention. Lizzie had had two novels published and well reviewed. A third was on the way, but it was causing a great deal of morning sickness.

She and James had been married eight years, and Lizzie had supported James on her publishing salary in the early days when he was trying to break into television. Once very pretty (she had the bright eyes and long questing nose of a vole, and the shaggy light brown hair of a clematis montana clambering over an old apple tree in winter), she had recently put on too much weight.

The Verekers lived in a large messy house with a large messy garden two miles down the valley from Rupert Campbell-Black, where the Frogsmore stream hurtled into a large reed-fringed lake. They had bought Lake House, as it was called, five years ago, just after James had got the job at Corinium, when it had seemed ridiculously cheap. Viewing it in high summer, they had only seen its romantic aspect, not realizing that for at least five months of the year it was so low in the valley that it never saw the sun and would be quite inaccessible when the snows came in winter.

This mattered little to James because he spent so much time at Corinium. When the house got snowed up, he simply didn't come home for several days. But it was not good for Lizzie, who wrote there all day, eating too many biscuits to keep out the cold, or for the children who caught one cold after another, or for the nannies who found it dank and depressing, except when James was at home.

For Lizzie life turned on the children not getting ill, and nannies not leaving so that she had time to write. Unfortunately James couldn't resist pulling the prettier nannies, who invariably walked out, when he moved on to someone else. Lizzie always found out the score by reading the nannies' diaries when they were shopping in Cotchester or nearby Stroud. Birgitta, the current nanny, wrote her diary in Swedish, which Lizzie couldn't understand. But with the aid of a Swedish dictionary she was beginning to crack the code, and the word 'James' appeared rather too often. In fact you only had to see the way Birgitta perked up when James came through the door. Lizzie was used to his infidelity. She realized he needed little adventures to boost his ego, but they still upset her. She would have liked an admirer herself, but felt she was too fat to attract anyone.

Lizzie nearly had a fit when she heard James banging the front door. She'd stopped writing far too late, wrestling to get at least a draft of the first chapter down on paper. Still struggling mentally with her plot, she'd spent too long washing her hair and in the bath. Then she discovered that the long low-cut black silk ball dress which she'd decided to wear was far too tight. Not even shoe horns or the disdainful tugging of Birgitta could get her into it, so she had to wear another dress, dark red velvet to match her distraught face, and calf-length so it wouldn't conceal her ankles which had swelled up in the bath.

Finally, because she couldn't see out, she'd cut her fringe with the kitchen scissors, not realizing that Birgitta had just used them to cut rind off the children's bacon, so now her fringe stuck together and reeked of bacon. She was about to wash it again when James arrived. He hadn't been home so early in months; usually he hung around the Corinium bar mopping up adulation.

'Have a bath, darling,' shouted Lizzie, desperately trying to tone down her face with green foundation.

'I had a shower at the studios,' said James, 'so I've only got to change. We ought to leave in five minutes. How did you think my programme went?'

'Wonderful,' lied Lizzie, who hadn't watched it, starting to panic. As it was dark outside, she couldn't even make up in the car.

'I'll read you an extra story tomorrow, darlings,' she told the children as they clung whining to her on the landing. 'Or perhaps, Birgitta,' she raised her voice hopefully, 'will read you one before you go to bed.'

But Birgitta was watching James, who had decided on the white shirt after all, putting a pink carnation in his buttonhole. Poor Mr Vereker, she thought, looking so handsome in his dinner jacket, going out with such a frump. How much better would she, Birgitta, be in Lizzie's place. James, however, hardly noticed his wife's appearance. His was the one that mattered.

'You look absolutely lovely, James,' said Lizzie dutifully.

Low sepia clouds obscured the moon. As the headlamps lit up grey stone walls, acid green tree trunks and long blonde grasses, Lizzie tried abortively to apply eye liner as James described every little triumph of the planning meeting and his programme afterwards.

'Anyone interesting in our party tonight?' asked Lizzie as he paused for breath.

'Rupert Campbell-Black, Beattie Johnson his mistress, Freddie Jones.'

'Who's he?'

'Don't you ever read the papers?' said James, appalled. 'Mr Electronics.'

Oh God, sighed Lizzie to herself. I daren't ask what electronics are, and I bet I'm sitting next to him at dinner.

'And Paul Stratton and his new wife.'

'Oooh,' squeaked Lizzie. 'That's exciting.'

Three years ago, just after the Conservatives won the last election, Paul Stratton, the Tory MP for Cotchester and the very upright Minister for Home Affairs, with a special brief to investigate sex education in schools, had rocked his constituency and the entire nation by walking out on Winifred, his solid dependable boot of a wife, and running off with his secretary half his age.

Not that his constituents were prudish (having Rupert Campbell-Black in the next door constituency, they were used to the erotic junketing of MPs), but as Paul Stratton had not only used his political career to feather his nest financially, but also set himself up as a pillar of respectability and uxoriousness, constantly inveighing against pornography, homosexuality, easier divorce and the general laxity of the nation's morals, they had found it hard to stomach his hypocrisy.

'Evidently, they've bought a place in Chalford,' said James, 'and Paul and Sarah, I think she's called, are planning to spend weekends down here, re-establishing themselves with the local community.'

'I suppose Tony inviting them this evening heralds the official return of the prodigal son,' said Lizzie. 'I wonder if she's as beautiful as her photographs. I bet Rupert makes a pass at her. He's always enjoyed bugging Paul.'

'Don't be fatuous, they're only just back from their honeymoon,' snapped James, steering round a sharp bend and bringing the conversation neatly back to himself.

'I've got a gut feeling tonight is going to mark a turning-point in my career,' he said importantly. 'Tony's been exceptionally nice to me recently. And when I popped into Madden's office later this evening to find out exactly who was in the party, there was a confidential memo on Tony's desk about the Autumn schedules, which I managed to read upside-down. It appears Corinium are committed to a series of prime time interviews for the Network. I didn't dare read any more, in case Madden got suspicious, but I suspect Tony's got me in mind, and that's why he's asked us this evening.'

Tony Baddingham soaked in a boiling Floris-scented bath, admiring his flat stomach. For once the cordless telephone was mute, giving him the chance to savour the prospect of the evening ahead. One of the joys of becoming hugely successful was that it gave you the opportunity to patronize those who, in the past, had patronized you. Paul Stratton, for example. It was going to be so amusing tonight extending the hand of friendship to Paul and his bimbo wife. How grateful and subservient they'd be.

Then there was Rupert. Tony was not given to fantasy, but more than anything else in the world he longed to be in a position when an abject, penitent, penniless Rupert, who'd somehow lost all his looks, was seeking Tony's favour and friendship. The only reason Tony really wanted Rupert on his Board was in order to dazzle him with his brilliant business acumen.

In wilder fantasy, Tony dreamt of flaunting an undeniably sexy mistress, who would be impervious to Rupert's charms.

'Can't you bloody understand,' he imagined Cameron screaming at Rupert, 'that Tony's the only man there'll ever be in my life?'

Tony added more boiling water to his bath to steel himself against the arctic climate of the rest of the house. There was a running battle between Tony who liked the heat, and whose office, according to Charles Fairburn, provided an excellent dress rehearsal, both physically and mentally, for hell fires, and Monica, his wife, who regarded central heating as a wanton extravagance which ate into one's capital.

'I still feel dreadfully guilty not telling Winifred about Paul and Sarah coming tonight,' said Monica, when later, fully dressed, Tony went into his wife's bedroom and found her sitting at her dressing table vigorously brushing her short fair hair. She was wearing the same emerald-green taffeta she'd worn for the last four hunt balls, which went beautifully with Tony's diamonds, but did nothing to play down the red veins that mapped her cheeks, as a result of gardening and striding large labradors across the Gloucestershire valleys in all weathers. Yet, in a way, her rather masculine beauty, splendid on the prow of a ship or as a model for a Victorian bust of Duty, needed no enhancement.

Monica had once been head girl of her boarding school and had remained so all her life. Winifred Stratton, Paul's ex-wife, had been her senior prefect. Together they had run the school firmly and wisely, diverting the headmistress's attention away from a plume of cigarette smoke rising from the shrubbery, but gently reproaching the errant smoker afterwards. All the lower fourths had had crushes on Monica. Sometimes, even today, unheard by Tony who slept in a separate room, she cried, 'Don't talk in the passage,' in her sleep.

Known locally as Monica of the Glen because of her noble appearance and total lack of humour, she was the only woman to whom Tony was always polite, and also a little afraid. In the icy, high-ceilinged bedroom, opera and gardening books crowded the tables on either side of the ancient crimson-curtained four-poster which Tony visited perhaps once a week. But even after eighteen years of marriage, these visits gave him an incredible sexual frisson.

On the chest of drawers, which contained no new clothes, were silver-framed photographs of their three children. With her sense of fairness, Monica would never let the other two know that she loved her elder son Archie, sixteen last week, the best. Nor that she loved her two yellow labradors, and her great passions, opera and gardening, often a great deal more than her husband.

Running Tony's life with effortful efficiency, she never had enough time for these two passions, but if she was disappointed by the hand life had dealt her, she never showed it. She was not looking forward to this evening, which would involve talking until three o'clock in the morning to all those people Tony considered so important, but she would treat them with the same impersonal kindness whether they were Lords-Lieutenant or electronics millionaires. Always anxious to help humanity collectively (she did a huge amount for charity), Monica was not interested in people individually, or what made them tick or leap into bed with one another, but she was worried about Winifred. Even after she'd married Tony, and Winifred had married the much more brilliant, handsome and ambitious Paul Stratton, they had remained friends and gone to the opera and old school reunions together.

When Paul had run off with his secretary, in a scandal that rocked Gloucestershire almost as much as Helen Campbell-Black walking out on Rupert, Winifred had been utterly devastated, but like a building sapped by dry rot, one couldn't initially see the damage from outside. After Winifred had moved to Spain with her two daughters in a desperate attempt to rebuild her life, Monica missed her friendship desperately, and now, to crown it, Tony had asked Paul and Sarah to join the party tonight, and she, Monica, was expected to smooth over Sarah's first public outing in Gloucestershire.

'I just feel it's revoltingly disloyal to Winifred,' repeated Monica.

She had applied Pond's vanishing cream and face powder, and a dash of bright-red lipstick, which was the extent of her daytime make-up, and was now adding her night make-up: brown block mascara put on with a little brush.

'I swore to Winifred I'd never have that little tramp' – Monica spat on her mascara – 'over the threshold.'

Tony's brows drew together like two black caterpillars.

'Paul is still our local MP, even if he has been booted out of the Cabinet,' he said patiently. 'With the franchise coming up next year, I have to entertain whatever wife he chooses. At least I waited until after they were married.'

As Tony moved forward to do up the clasp of her diamond necklace, Monica caught sight of her husband's reflection. The red tailcoat with dove-grey facings made him look taller and thinner, and gave a distinction to his somewhat heavy good looks, but Monica hardly noticed.

'I still ought to telephone Winifred and tell her.'

'She's in Spain. Let it rest. I'd better go down; they'll be here in a minute.'

Monica glanced at her diamond watch. *Lohengrin* was about to start on Radio 3. If only she could stay at home and listen to it, she thought wistfully. As she slotted a three-hour blank tape into her radio cassette and pressed the record button, she called after Tony, 'Can you tell Victor to up the proportion of orange juice in the Buck's Fizz. We don't want everyone arriving at the town hall plastered like last year.'

RIVALS
6

An hour later, downstairs in the huge dark panelled drawing-room hung with tapestries, members of the party were beginning to unthaw and retreat from the fierce red glow of the beech logs smouldering and crackling in the vast fireplace. Lizzie Vereker, sustained by at least six glasses of Buck's Fizz, had perked up and forgotten her extra pounds and her straining red dress.

Neither Rupert nor Beattie Johnson had arrived yet, but there was plenty to gaze at. Paul Stratton's new wife, for example, was absolutely gorgeous. She had entered the room looking little girlish and apprehensive, eyes cast down, clinging to Paul's arm and hardly speaking. She was wearing a yellow silk dress which matched her thick piled-up gold hair, and a beautiful tobacco-brown fringed silk shawl covering her shoulders and wound high round her neck.

After replying in shy monosyllables to Tony and Monica's questions, she had allowed herself to be introduced to James and also to Tony's youngest brother, Bas, who was a terrific rake with black patent-leather hair, a smooth olive complexion, and a very overdeveloped little finger from twisting women round it. Now a small smile was beginning to play around Sarah's full coral lips at Bas's extravagant compliments, and the shawl was beginning to slip to reveal the most voluptuous golden shoulders and bosom. She and Paul must have been somewhere hot for their honeymoon, decided Lizzie.

Paul didn't seem to have reaped the same benefit. His dark hair, which he'd once brushed straight back, had gone silver grey and been coaxed forward, almost to his eyebrows, and in little commas over his very pink ears. Sarah, being young, had obviously encouraged him into a Paisley bow-tie and a wing collar, the points of which kept being bent over by a new double chin. His once hard angular face seemed to have softened and weakened. He still, however, had the same all-embracing smile that passed over you like a lighthouse beam, and still liked the sound of his own voice. He was now talking to Freddie Jones, the electronics multi-millionaire.

'Three million unemployed,' he boomed, 'is a Mickey Mouse figure. Didn't you see that article about that factory manager who was offering people two hundred and twenty pounds a week merely to stuff mattresses, and simply couldn't get staff? The working classes just don't want to work. They're shored up by moonlighting and the great feather bed of the welfare state.'

Paul made the mistake of thinking that someone with such capitalist instincts would automatically vote Tory. Freddie Jones listened to him carefully but didn't say anything. He was plump and jolly, with rumpled red-gold curls, round, merry grey-blue eyes, a snub nose and an air that life was a tremendous adventure. Lizzie thought he looked much more fun than anyone else.

Across the room, she noticed, James had broken swiftly away from Sarah Stratton, and was now talking to a very slim woman with dimples and short brown curls tied up by a blue bow. She was wearing a pale-blue midi dress with a full skirt and a top, of which the satin lining was the strapless bodice, and the gauze over it covered her arms down to her wrists and her shoulders and tied in a pussy-cat bow at the neck. It was the most ghastly dress Lizzie had ever seen. But the woman, who Lizzie deduced must be Freddie Jones's wife, seemed frightfully pleased with herself, and was laughing away, rolling her eyes and gazing up at James's beautiful bronzed face with excessive admiration.

Apart from Sarah Stratton, Lizzie decided hazily, the men looked much more glamorous than the women this evening, gaudy peacocks in their different tail coats, red with grey-blue facings for the West Cotchester Hunt, red with crimson for the neighbouring Gatherham Hunt, dark blue with buff for the Beaufort. If he hadn't been so good-looking, James in a dinner jacket would have been outclassed.

Helping herself to another Buck's Fizz, Lizzie wandered somewhat unsteadily over to the seating plan for dinner at the Town Hall. She was sitting next to Freddie Jones. James was on Monica Baddingham's right. Maybe his predictions about his brilliant future were about to come true.

Laughing uproariously, two handsome young bloods in red coats now rushed up and started marking the seating plan with red asterisks.

'What *are* you doing?' asked Lizzie.

'Singling out the worst gropers,' said one. 'We're starting with Bas Baddingham and Rupert Campbell-Black.'

'Better put one beside my husband,' said Lizzie.

'Who's he?'

'James Vereker.'

'We were just about to.' They all collapsed with laughter.

'Have some more fizz,' yelled Monica Baddingham in her raucous voice, arriving with a jug which contained almost straight orange juice now. 'I can't think what's happened to Rupert. We'll have to leave in a sec, or we'll be late for dinner.' She drifted off.

'Do we dare put an asterisk by Tony's name?' said one of the young bloods.

'Of course,' said the other, seizing the Pentel.

Giggling, Lizzie glanced across the room to see James beckoning imperiously.

He's had enough of Mrs Jones, so he wants to palm her off on me and press the flesh, thought Lizzie.

Ignoring James, she turned back to the seating plan. Next minute James had crossed the room and seized her wrist.

'May I borrow her?' he asked coldly.

'Of course,' said the young bloods, 'as long as you bring her straight back.'

James dragged Lizzie away. 'Do pay attention when I signal.'

'I was having a nice time.'

'This is work,' hissed James. 'I want you to meet Valerie Jones. She's opening a boutique in Cotchester next month. You must go and buy something.'

Never, never, thought Lizzie sulkily, if she sells dresses like that blue thing she's wearing.

'Lizzie writes novels,' James told Valerie Jones, as if to explain his wife's scruffy appearance.

'I'd laike to wraite novels if I had the taime,' said Valerie Jones, in an incredibly elocuted voice, 'but Ay'm so busy with the boutique and the kids and moving in and we do have to entertain a lot. People are always saying, You should wraite a book, Mrs Jones, you've had such a fascinating laife.'

She screwed her face up in what she obviously thought was a fascinating smile.

Close up, Lizzie noticed that Valerie Jones had very clean nails, perfectly shaved armpits and the very white eyeballs of the non-reader and non-drinker. She was tiny and very pretty in a doll-like way, but Lizzie suddenly understood the expression: blue with cold. Valerie's china-blue eyes were the coldest she'd ever seen. The pink and white skin also concealed the rhinoceros hide of the relentless social climber.

'I'll leave you girls to get acquainted,' said James. 'Better have a word with Paul Stratton, or he'll think I'm avoiding him. We must have a dance later,' he added admiringly to Valerie. 'I bet you're as light as thistledown.'

'Seven stone on the scales this morning,' simpered Valerie.

And six-and-a-half of that's ego, thought Lizzie. 'Where d'you live?' she asked.

'At Whychey,' said Valerie.

'Quite near us,' said Lizzie. 'We're at Penscombe.'

But Valerie wasn't remotely interested in where Lizzie lived.

'And only quarter of an hour from the boutique, so Ay can

rush down there, if there's any craysis, or a special client comes in. They always ask for me.' Valerie put her head on one side. 'Ay don't know why. Ay think Ay tell people the truth. Ay mean, what is the point of selling somebody a gown that doesn't suit them? It's such a bad advertisement for the boutique.'

'Which house in Whychey?' asked Lizzie.

'Oh it's lovely; Elizabethan,' said Valerie. 'We had to do an awful lot though, ripping out all that horrid dark panelling.' Lizzie winced. 'And of course we've completely re-landscaped the garden, but it'll be a year or two before Green Lawns is the paradise we want.'

Lizzie looked puzzled. 'The only Elizabethan house I know in Whychey is Bottom Hollow Court.'

'We changed the name,' said Valerie. 'We thought Green Lawns sounded prettier.'

'Where did you live before?'

'Cheam,' said Valerie, with the flourish of one saying Windsor Castle. 'We never thought we'd find anywhere as perfect as Cheam. All our help broke down and crayed when we left. But Gloucestershire has so much to offer.'

At that moment Monica came up.

'I was just saying, Monica, that Gloucestershire has so much to offer, particularly,' Valerie raised her untouched glass, 'on a gracious evening like tonight.'

'Not if we don't get any grub,' said Monica briskly. 'We've decided not to wait for Rupert. Do either of you need a loo?'

Outside it had turned bitterly cold. Valerie came out of the house smothered in an almost floor-length mink. I hope hounds get her, thought Lizzie savagely, as she watched Freddie open the door and settle Valerie in, before going round to the driving seat.

'Isn't she a poppet?' said James. 'Knew so much about my programme.'

'Sarah Stratton?' asked Lizzie.

'No, Valerie Jones. I do hope Freddie joins the Board. We could do with a few caring wives like Valerie at Corinium.'

Lizzie was dumbfounded. Was James such a dreadful judge of character?

'What did you think of Sarah Stratton?' she asked.

'Not a lot. Didn't even know who I was. You'd have thought Paul would have briefed her.'

Off they set in convoy, cars with silver foxes on the bonnet skidding all over the road, rattling the cattle grids, lighting up the last grey curls of the traveller's joy and the last red beech leaves. Flakes of snow were drifting down as they arrived at Cotchester Town Hall.

'It's already fetlock-deep in Stow,' bellowed a woman who'd just driven up with a white windscreen. 'But of course you're a coat warmer down here.'

Cotchester Town Hall, a splendid baroque edifice, two hundred yards down on the other side of the High Street from Corinium Television, had been built in 1902 to replace the old Assembly Rooms. The huge dining-rooms on either side of the ballroom were filled with tables, packed with laughing, chattering people. But in a noisy, glamorous gathering easily the most glamorous, scrutinized table belonged to Corinium Television. The Krug was circulating (Tony was always generous when the evening was deductible) and dinner was now well underway, but Rupert and Beattie Johnson still hadn't turned up and Sarah Stratton, who should have been on Rupert's right, and Tony, who should have had Beattie on his left, were trying to hide their irritation and disappointment.

Lizzie Vereker, however, was having a lovely time sitting next to Freddie Jones. Totally unpompous, instinctively courteous, noisily sucking up his bortsch, rattling off remarks in a broad Cockney accent at a speed which must tax the most accomplished shorthand typist, he was also, despite a scarlet cummerbund strained double by his wide girth, curiously attractive.

'I don't know anything about electronics,' confessed Lizzie, taking a belt of Krug, 'but I know you're very good at them. James says you're one of the most powerful men in England.'

'My wife doesn't fink so,' said Freddie. 'It's a fallacy women are attracted to power. No one's fallen in love wiv me for years. I'd like to be tall like your 'usband. But I got my height from my muvver and my shoulders from my Dad, and the rest 'ad to go somewhere.' He roared with laughter.

At the head of the table Monica listened politely to James Vereker talking about his programme and his ideas for other programmes, and surreptitiously gazed at Sarah Stratton. Her tobacco-brown shawl had slid right off her golden shoulders now. Her piled-up blonde hair emphasized her long slender neck. The seat beside her, which should have been Rupert's, had now been taken by Bas, Tony's wicked brother, who was chatting her up like mad.

She's so beautiful, thought Monica. What chance could poor Winifred have stood?

She felt jolted and uneasy. She wished she were at home reading gardening books and listening to *Lohengrin*.

Valerie Jones had one aim in life – to rise socially. She had therefore done her homework. Knowing James was coming this evening, she had watched his programme all week so she could comment on every item. She was now sitting next to Paul Stratton, whose recent speech in the House on the proposed Cotchester by-pass she had learnt almost by heart. But Paul was less flattered by her obvious homework than James. He, like Monica, was surreptitiously watching his wife flirting with Bas, and experiencing a tightness round his heart, a jealousy never felt when he was married to Winifred.

Lizzie's and Freddie's conversation had noisily progressed to hunting.

'It was Rupert who got me going,' said Freddie. 'Put me up on a really quiet 'orse last March. I was cubbing by August, and huntin' by November.'

'Weren't you terrified?' asked Lizzie in awe.

'I needed three ports and lemons to get me on to the 'orse for the opening meet, I can tell you. But I reckoned if I fell orf I'd bounce anyway.' He roared with laughter again. 'I'm going to take up shootin' next.'

Huge oval silver plates of roast beef were now coming round.

'How's Rupert getting on with Beattie Johnson?' asked Lizzie, helping herself.

Freddie shrugged. 'Not very well. She keeps 'earing wedding bells, and we all know Rupe's tone-deaf. He said the other day he fort the relationship would last till Cheltenham.'

Lizzie giggled. 'What a typically Rupert remark. Has she finished ghosting his memoirs yet?'

'Probably providing material for the last chapter at the moment,' said Freddie. Digging a serving spoon into a creamy mass of potato dauphinoise, he gave a big helping to Lizzie, and was just helping himself when Valerie called sharply down the table, 'No tatties, Fred-Fred.'

'It's Friday,' said Freddie, the Cockney accent wheedling, as the spoon edged towards his plate.

'No tatties, I said.' Valerie's voice was pure steel.

Freddie put back the potatoes.

Looking across at Lizzie, Sarah Stratton gave her a ghost of a wink.

'You can have my roll, Fred-Fred,' she said, lobbing it across the table to him.

Valerie opened her rosebud mouth and shut it again. She knew one must behave like a lady at all times, and not brawl with one's hubby in public. Then she suddenly noticed that James, who'd ground to a halt with Monica, was looking very put out.

'What's your programme about on Monday?' Valerie asked him across the table.

Paul Stratton, on Monica's left, seized his opportunity. Turning to her, he said in a low voice, 'It's awfully good of you to take Sarah under your wing this evening. I know how close you were to Winifred.'

Monica almost choked on her roast beef. She didn't want to talk about Winifred.

'It meant so much to Sarah,' went on Paul. 'She was so worried about coming tonight.'

She doesn't look worried now, thought Monica, watching Sarah laughing up at Bas.

'I felt guilty at the time,' said Paul rather heartily. 'But we are all sinners, are we not? What happened to Sarah and me was part of a loving relationship. All sides behaved with dignity. I feel I can now walk down Cotchester High Street with my head held high.'

Do you indeed, thought Monica furiously.

'But one can't destroy something that's lasted twenty-five years over-night,' said Paul, spearing a piece of Yorkshire pudding. 'I still miss Win and the girls, particularly when I see old friends like you and Tony.'

He wants my sympathy, thought Monica incredulously. He's utterly destroyed my best friend, and he wants me to feel sorry for *him*.

'Do you correspond with Win?' asked Paul.

Fortunately deliverance appeared in the form of one of the hall porters, who whispered a message in Monica's ear.

'Thank you so much,' she said, and banging the table with her spoon, yelled down to Tony at the other end, 'That was a message from Rupert. He can't make it after all. Something urgent has come up.'

'Probably Rupert's cock,' said Lizzie idly, earning herself a thunderous look of disapproval from James.

'Pity,' said Sarah lightly. 'I was *so* looking forward to meeting him.'

'There'll be other occasions,' said Bas, leaning back as a waitress removed his plate.

Tony, for a minute, was unable to disguise his rage.

'Of all the fucking bad manners,' he exploded.

Rupert's defection put a considerable dampener on the evening. It was not until the syllabub had been handed round in tall glasses that Bas Baddingham, who was among other things a partner in a local estate agents, made an attempt to lighten the atmosphere.

'Has anyone else heard a rumour that Declan O'Hara's bought Penscombe Priory?' he asked.

For a second there was a stunned silence. Then all the women acted with the frantic excitement of dogs when their leads are rattled.

'I'm going on a crash diet tomorrow,' squeaked Lizzie, dropping her spoon with a clatter.

'Oh why didn't we buy a house in Penscombe rather than Chalford?' wailed Sarah Stratton.

'How much did he pay for it?' asked Valerie Jones.

'Half a million' said Bas.

There was a long pause as everyone did frantic sums to work out how much that now made their houses worth.

'That's an awful lot,' grumbled Valerie.

'But it's such a romantic house,' sighed Lizzie, 'and that lovely wild garden.'

'Hellishly cold,' shuddered James.

'And faces North,' said Valerie.

'So does Declan O'Hara,' said Sarah dreamily, earning herself a sharp look from Paul.

'Rather a lot to pay for a weekend retreat,' said James, looking put out.

To hell with impressing Rupert with the secret he'd been hugging to himself all day, thought Tony. He had a good enough audience as it was, and it was too late for any of them to leak the story to the press tonight.

'Declan's going to live here,' said Tony, looking slowly down the table. 'He's joining Corinium in September.'

There was a gasp of excitement, followed by another stunned silence.

Troublesome, tetchy, but monumentally talented, Declan O'Hara was simply the BBC's hottest property. His weekly interviews with the great and very famous went out at prime time and were avidly watched and discussed by the entire nation. Nothing like the normal chat show host, he indulged in no back slapping, nor drinking in the green room, nor bandying round of Christian names before a programme. Nor did he bounce around on long pastel sofas, cosily exchanging confidences.

His victims sat facing him, and, once on air, like a Jesuit

priest, he really listened to them, relentlessly probing with the most devastating questions and waiting so unbearably long for an answer that they invariably stumbled into a confession. To the intense disappointment of his armies of female fans, the camera was constantly trained on the person he was interviewing rather than on Declan himself.

Poor James, thought Lizzie, oh poor, poor James. That must be the series of networked interviews scheduled for the Autumn.

'How the hell did you persuade Declan?' asked Bas.

'He's fed up with the Beeb,' said Tony. 'The last straw was axing his interview with Paisley. People who saw the video said it was absolute carnage. They didn't think Paisley would go the fifteen rounds. Then they hacked great contentious chunks out of his interview with Reagan. He wants to go out live, so this kind of thing can't happen. He will when he joins us.'

'You'll never get people like Reagan coming down to Cotchester,' said Paul Stratton.

'You will for Declan,' said Freddie. 'The BBC must be as sick as a parrot.'

'They're not pleased,' Tony was purring like a great leopard now, 'but it's not exactly our job to please the Beeb.'

Clicking their tongues, the waitresses removed the untouched syllabubs.

'Declan's a bit of a pinko,' said Paul, disapprovingly.

'That's putting it mildly,' said Tony, 'but as it looks as though the socialists will be in power next year unless you lot get your act together, we can't afford to be too right wing any more.'

Trying, for James's sake, to curb her excitement, Lizzie turned to Monica. 'Have you met him?'

'They came to lunch,' said Monica. 'Declan seems a super chap.'

Sarah and Lizzie caught each other's eyes again and giggled at such a totally inadequate description.

'A bit remote,' Monica went on, 'probably shy. His wife is charming.'

'Beautiful?' asked Lizzie.

'Oh yes, exceptional.'

'Pity,' sighed Sarah, earning another scowl from Paul.

'And three utterly ravishing children,' said Monica. 'A boy of twenty at Trinity, Dublin, and two teenage girls about seventeen and fourteen.'

'With Rupert living just across the valley,' said Lizzie, shaking her shaggy head, 'Declan must be barking. He'll have to lock his wife and both daughters up in chastity belts.'

'The youngest kiddy will make a friend for Sharon, although Sharon made a lot of friends at Pony Club camp. I must get them together when the O'Haras move in,' said Valerie.

Catching Sarah's eye yet again, Lizzie decided Sarah was definitely going to be a mate.

A group of young waitresses from other tables were now hovering, wondering if it were the right moment to ask James Vereker for his autograph. Tony was also looking at James and experiencing a glow of pure pleasure. Corinium's most popular presenter was feeling all the pique and disquiet of a big fish who's been basking for years in a rock pool, then suddenly sees the fin of a shark coming over the horizon. James's exquisitely straight nose would be frightfully put out of joint by Declan's arrival. James, Tony decided, had been getting a shade above himself recently. There was nothing Tony loved more than cutting people down to size.

As liqueurs and cigars came round, Tony moved down the table beside Freddie Jones. Now Rupert had stood him up so summarily, he was even keener to get Freddie on to the Board. With satellite television in the offing, Freddie's millions and electronic expertise would be invaluable.

'When Declan arrives, we'll get him to interview you,' said Tony.

Valerie also changed places and sat next to Monica.

'What a lovely meal, Lady Anthony,' she said.

'Oh, please call me Monica.'

'Well, thank you, Monica,' said Valerie gratified. 'You may, if you like, call me Mousie. That's Fred-Fred's pet name for me. I only allow very special friends to become members of the Mousie club.'

Oblivious of Monica's look of amazement and Sarah's and Lizzie's complete hysterics, Valerie ploughed on. 'I wanted to pick your brains, Monica, about public schools. Wayne is eleven but he's extra bright, so we're thinking of Winchester or even Eton, but I just wondered if you and Tony had been satisfied with Rugborough.'

'Well, Archie's very happy there,' said Monica, her raucous voice softening. 'The only problem, if one's got a flat in London, is that Rugborough's on the Central Line and, whenever he gets bored, Archie keeps nipping home on the tube. It drives Tony demented. Archie's supposed to be doing his O-levels.'

'Our problem,' said Valerie smugly, 'is to *stop* Wayne working. Not that he's a sissy, Monica – he's really plucky at sport – but you know how important qualifications are.'

The band was playing 'Red Red Wine'. The brilliantly lit ballroom beckoned. The vast springy floor was now filling up with couples. Like a shaken kaleidoscope, the red coats of the men with their flying tails clashed gloriously with the stinging fuchsia pinks and electric blues of the women's dresses.

'I wouldn't mind if Tony'd given me an inkling beforehand,' said James Vereker furiously, as, oblivious for once of the admiring glances of most of the young girls in the room, he lugged Lizzie round the floor, 'but I looked such a pratt, knowing nothing about it, and Monica actually admitted never watching my programme. Says she prefers BBC 2. What kind of a Chairman's wife is that?'

Lizzie let him rabbit on. She felt terribly sorry for him, but it was such exciting news that Declan was moving to Corinium, and she was fascinated by what was happening on the floor.

Monica was dancing with the Lord-Lieutenant now. For

someone so mad about opera, she had no sense of rhythm. Gyrating three feet apart, they looked like two ostriches on hot bricks.

'*Red red wine,*' sang the Lord-Lieutenant over and over again, which were the only words he knew.

As the tempo speeded up, Valerie took the floor with Freddie, showing off her 'Come Dancing' skills, fishtailing, telemarquing, reversing, correcting Freddie sharply whenever he made a mistake. Freddie, his little black shoes twinkling, laughed and took it in good part.

'What on earth did you find to say to James Vereker's wife?' asked Valerie, as the band paused for a moment. 'What a mess, can't have combed her hair for weeks, and that fraightful gown.'

'Nice lady,' said Freddie firmly. 'I liked her a lot.'

Valerie gazed at Freddie as uncomprehendingly as Lizzie had gazed at James when, earlier, he'd called Valerie 'a poppet'.

'And that new wife of Paul Stratton's looks a handful,' she went on.

Freddie refrained from saying he'd love to have his hands full of Sarah Stratton.

Paul and Sarah were dancing together now. He was holding her close, his hands moving over her flawless gold back, as if testing she were real. Perhaps she'd made a special effort to look particularly stunning tonight, thought Lizzie, knowing Winifred was such a chum of Monica's.

Tony devoted the rest of the evening to wooing Freddie, but he allowed himself the treat of a dance with Sarah. She was really gorgeous, he decided. One could understand exactly why Paul let his heart rule his very swollen head and ditched Winifred, but would he ever hold Sarah? She had obviously fallen in love with Paul because he was powerful and unobtainable. Now his career had taken a nose dive in the party and he'd been sacked from the Cabinet, he was neither of these things. Nervous of losing his seat at the next election, he kept angling for Tony to offer him an executive directorship on the Corinium Board.

73

But Paul shouldn't have patronized Tony in the past. How much more amusing, thought Tony, to employ Paul's new wife instead. Holding her dazzlingly full and exciting body, breathing in the scent of her thickly piled-up blonde hair, trying not to gaze too openly at the beautiful gold breasts, Tony felt the stirrings of lust. If she was any good, she'd be perfect to present the new late night show. That would really put Paul in a tizz.

'It's terribly exciting about Declan,' said Sarah. 'I'm such a fan. Those programmes are like Rembrandts. Did you see the one on Placido Domingo?'

'You must come and meet him as soon as they move in,' said Tony. 'You're going to be a distinct asset to Gloucestershire.'

Suddenly Sarah looked terribly young. Even in the dim light Tony could see she was blushing.

'It was angelic of you to ask us tonight, knowing what friends you were, particularly your wife, of Winifred's. Paul's friends haven't been exactly friendly. They think I've screwed up Paul's career.'

Tony gave a piratical smile. All he needs between his teeth is a cutlass, thought Sarah.

'You've given Paul a cast-iron excuse not to be Prime Minister,' he said. 'He'd never have made it. He has neither the bottle nor the conviction.'

'You're speaking of the man I love,' said Sarah.

'I'm sorry.' Tony didn't sound it. 'I'm going to tell James Vereker to interview you for our new "Behind Every Famous Man" series.'

Sarah smiled, showing very small, white, even teeth.

'You'd do better to interview Valerie. She drives poor Fred-Fred on with a pitchfork.'

'Probably spent half the day reading etiquette books on the correct way to hold your pitchfork,' said Tony.

Back at the table, the waiter poured more Krug, but Tony put a hand over his glass.

'I'm driving to London after this,' he said. 'We're announcing Declan's appointment tomorrow, so all hell's going to break loose.'

'The Gloucestershire poacher strikes again,' said Lizzie, receiving a sharp kick on the ankle from James.

As everyone swarmed out into the High Street after the 'Post Horn Gallop' and 'Auld Lang Syne', they found a thick layer of snow on the pavements. Down the road, high above them, the Corinium red ram was already wearing a white barrister's wig of snow on his curly poll.

'Drive carefully, Tony,' called Monica, as Percy the chauffeur held open the door of the Rolls for her. 'See you tomorrow evening.' Happily she settled back in the grey seat. Soon she'd be home to at least an hour of *Lohengrin* before she fell asleep.

'Bet the old ram's making a Cook's detour via Hamilton Terrace,' said James Vereker savagely, as Tony set off for London in the BMW, waving goodbye to the last of his guests.

Tony drove towards the motorway, but, sure enough, as soon as he'd shaken everyone else off, he did a U-turn and, just as the snow started to fall again, belted back to Cotchester.

RIVALS
7

It was three o'clock in the morning but Cameron Cook was still working on the first story outline for the new series of 'Four Men went to Mow'. On Monday she'd start commissioning writers. Ones that were talented and bullyable were not easy to find.

Beyond having a shower and brushing her teeth, she'd made no preparations for Tony, no satin sheets, no black silk negligées, no Fracas – the sharp, dry scent he so adored and which he brought her by the bucket – sprayed round the room. She was wearing the same brown cashmere jersey she'd worn to the office earlier, tight black trousers and no make-up. After twenty months, the one thing that held Tony was her indifference, her refusal to jump to his ringmaster's whip.

Perhaps he wouldn't turn up at all to punish her for being so bloody at the meeting. But she was so pissed off with him going to the Hunt Ball without her, and even worse inviting that jerk James Vereker, that she'd refused to speak to him after the meeting and stormed off home. She mustn't drop her guard like that. Once Tony detected weakness, he stuck the knife in.

All the same her stint in England had been terrifically exciting. She remembered so well the July day she had arrived. Tony had met her at Heathrow and driven her straight down to Cotchester to the quiet Regency terrace to the honey-gold house he had bought her. It was the only time she'd ever known him nervous.

Inside, as they'd gone from room to room, as finely proportioned and delicately coloured as the eggs of a bird, primrose and Wedgwood blue, lemon-yellow and cream, pale green and white, with large sash windows, and pretty alcoves with shelves for china scooped out of the walls, Cameron hadn't said a word. Apart from a fully equipped kitchen and a television set in the living-room, there was no furniture except a huge brass four-poster in the upstairs attic, which spread across the whole top floor.

Cameron had opened the window and gazed out at her new back yard with its pale-pink roses, and three ancient apple trees at the end. Someone had just mowed the lawn, and, as she breathed in the smell of grass cuttings, and admired the grey-gold spire of Cotchester Cathedral rising from its bright-green water meadows, she burst into tears.

Tony, who hadn't touched her until then, thinking she hated the house, or was feeling homesick, moved forward like lightning and took her in his arms.

'Darling, what's the matter? We'll find something else if you don't like it.'

Then Cameron sobbed into his Prussian-blue silk shirt that it was the loveliest house she'd ever seen, and why didn't they christen the bed – and their love-making turned out to be even more rapturous than it had been in New York.

But that was the last time she'd displayed weakness in his presence. From the moment she'd arrived she'd had no time to consider whether she was homesick or not. When she wasn't producing and master- minding every detail of the thirteen episodes of 'Four Men went to Mow', battling with directors, designers, actors and technicians, who weren't at all pleased to have a twenty-seven-year-old American upstart ordering them around, she was furnishing the house, driving from Southampton to Stratford, from Bath to Oxford, picking up antiques, thoroughly acquainting herself with the Cotswold area and seeking new ideas for programmes.

Otherwise her life revolved around Tony. He managed to

spend several evenings a week with her; people noticed he'd started leaving official dinners and cocktail parties abnormally early. He also took her to all the big events in the television calendar: Edinburgh, Monte Carlo, Cannes, New York, New Orleans, where she'd justified her existence a hundred times over selling Corinium programmes and acquiring new ones.

But there was still the married side of Tony's life, from which she was so ruthlessly excluded. She had only been once to his beautiful house, The Falconry, when Monica and the children were away, and that, she was sure, was because he wanted to show the place off.

Going into the drawing-room, she had exclaimed with pleasure at the Renoir over the mantelpiece.

'Don't touch it,' screamed Tony, 'or you'll have the entire Gloucestershire constabulary on the doorstep.'

Cameron had only met Monica once or twice at office parties, or at the odd business reception. And occasionally Monica sailed into Corinium to collect Tony. The galling thing was she never recognized Cameron. In one way, Monica's lack of interest in Tony's job made it much easier for him to deceive her. In another, brooded Cameron, if you had a rival, you wanted her at least to be aware of your existence.

'Lady Baddingham is a real lady,' Miss Madden was fond of saying when she wanted to get under Cameron's skin.

Cameron liked to think Tony only stayed with Monica because the silly old bag gave him respectability, and he didn't want any scandal before the franchise was renewed.

Getting up from her desk, Cameron wandered round the living-room. It was the only room in the house she'd redecorated, papering the walls in scarlet with a tiny blue-grey flower pattern and adding scarlet curtains, and a blue-grey carpet, sofas and chairs. She had acquired a new piano in England, lacquered in red, but had brought with her from America the dentist's chair upholstered in scarlet Paisley, the dartboard, the gold toe from the Metropolitan Museum, and all the videos of her NBS programmes. Beside them on the shelf were now stacked the thirteen prize-winning episodes of 'Four

Men went to Mow' and the two documentaries Cameron had also made on All Souls' College, Oxford, and on Anthony Trollope, who'd based Barchester on Salisbury, which was, after all, within the Corinium boundary.

On the mantelpiece was a signed photograph of the four young actors who'd starred in 'Four Men went to Mow', and a huge phallic cactus, given to her as an end-of-shoot present by the entire cast. '*Darling Cameron,*' said the card, which was still propped against it, '*You're spikey, but you're great.*'

After all the screaming matches, it had been a great accolade.

Tony obviously wasn't coming, Cameron decided; she'd blown it once and for all. The weekend stretched ahead, nothing but work until more work on Monday.

For consolation, she picked up that week's copy of *Broadcast*, which fell open at a photograph of her cuddling a dopey looking Jersey cow. '*Producer Cameron Cook on location during filming of her BAFTA-nominated series: "Four Men went to Mow",*' said the caption. '*The lucky cow is on the left.*'

Going over to the window, Cameron realized it was snowing. There were already three inches on top of her car, and soft white dustsheets had been laid over the houses opposite. Snow had also filled up the cups of the winter jasmine that jostled with the Virginia creeper climbing up the front of her house. If you wanted to get to the top you had to jostle, reflected Cameron. Tony had hinted he might put her on the Board, but she knew James Vereker, Simon Harris, and all the Heads of Departments would block her appointment to the last ditch. She had interfered at all levels, criticizing every programme, and every script she could lay her hands on. She knew she was unpopular with everyone in the building. But she didn't want popularity, she wanted power and the freedom to make the programmes she wanted without running to Tony for protection.

She was so deep in thought, she didn't notice the BMW drawing up, nor that Tony was outside until he lobbed a snowball against the window. She wished he didn't look so revoltingly handsome in that red coat. Cameron detested hunting, not because she felt sorry for the fox, but because of the bloody-minded arrogance of people like Tony and Rupert Campbell-Black who hunted.

'How was it?' she asked, getting a bottle of champagne from the fridge.

'Great.'

Immediately her antagonism came flooding back.

'How was Rupert?' She knew her interest would bug Tony.

'Bastard didn't turn up. But Bas had heard a rumour that Declan had bought The Priory, so I told everyone he was joining Corinium. It was OK,' he added, seeing Cameron's look of horror. 'It was too late for any of them to ring the papers. You should have seen James's face.'

Cameron grinned.

'That's an improvement,' said Tony. 'Why were you so bloody bootfaced at the meeting?'

'I had a migraine.'

They both knew she was lying. But, excited by dancing with Sarah and upsetting James, and even more by the prospect of bringing Cameron to shuddering gasping submission, Tony didn't want a row. He soon had her undressed and into the huge brass bed, now curtained with pale-grey silk, which he or rather Corinium had paid for, just as they had paid for the whole house. The excuse was that putting up visiting VIPs in Cameron's spare room would be cheaper than the Cotchester Arms, which served awful food and had no air conditioning.

'Do you do this to keep your mind off your work?' asked Tony later, as a naked Cameron straddled him in all her angry, voracious beauty.

Cameron leaned over and took a gulp of champagne.

'Who says it takes my mind off my work? I've got an idea.'

'What?' Feeling those muscles gripping his cock, Tony wondered how he ever refused her anything.

'I want to produce Declan when he arrives in September.'

Leaving Cameron at six o'clock, Tony drove up to London. He'd put on a jersey over his evening shirt, and planned to bath, shave and breakfast at his flat in Rutland Gate. As he was going up a deserted Kensington High Street, his car was splashed by another – some celebrity being raced the opposite way to Breakfast Television at Lime Grove, lights on in the back as he mugged up his notes.

Red coat over his arm, Tony let himself into his flat. For a second he thought he'd been burgled. Clothes littered the hall; bottles, glasses and unwashed plates covered the kitchen table. Then, going into Monica's bedroom, Tony discovered the naked figure of his son Archie, come home once again from Rugborough on the tube, fast asleep in the arms of an extremely pretty, very young girl.

Tony's bellow of rage nearly sent them through the double glazing. The girl dived under the flowered sheets. Archie mumbled that he was terribly sorry, but he'd thought his parents were at the Hunt Ball.

'We were,' snapped Tony. 'Now I'm going to have a bath, and I want her out of here by the time I've finished.'

At least Archie had the manners to take the girl home, reflected Tony, as he soaked for the second time in twelve hours in a boiling bath. Pretty little thing too. He'd always been nervous Archie might turn out a bit AC/DC. Having a very dominant but adoring mother didn't help, but he was pleased to see Archie following in his father's footsteps. Tony was extremely fond of his elder son. He was frying eggs and bacon when Archie returned very sheepishly.

Having bawled him out for his disgraceful behaviour, Tony said, 'Where the hell does your housemaster think you are?'

'In bed, I suppose.'

'But not whose. How old is she?'

'Sixteen.'

'Over age, thank Christ. If you ever use Mummy's bed again, I'll disinherit you. I hope you took precautions.'

'We did,' mumbled Archie. 'I'm really sorry. We were going to change the sheets.'

'Think how upset Mummy would have been.'

'We don't have to tell her, do we?' Archie's round face turned pale.

Thinking he would also have some very fast explaining to do if Monica discovered he hadn't reached the flat until eight o'clock, Tony agreed that they didn't.

'But don't let it happen again. You've bloody well got to pass your O-levels. You know how important qualifications are. Now I suppose you expect me to give you breakfast?'

RIVALS

8

Six months later, on the wettest August day for fifty years, Declan O'Hara moved into Penscombe Priory to the feverish excitement of the entire county. It rained so hard that on 'Cotswold Round-Up' James Vereker caringly warned his viewers about flooding on the Cotchester-Penscombe road. But perhaps, being Irish, reflected Lizzie Vereker the next morning, the rain made Declan and his family feel more at home.

Lizzie's children had gone out to friends for the day; her daily Mrs Makepiece was due later; Ortrud, the nanny who had replaced Birgitta in April, was upstairs no doubt writing about James in her diary. Lizzie had a rare clear day to work. But she was halfway through and very bored with her novel. Outside the downpour had given way to brilliant sunshine and delphinium-blue skies. From her study Lizzie could see the keys on the sycamore already turning coral and yellow leaves flecking the huge weeping willow which blocked her view of the lake. There wouldn't be many more beautiful days this year, reflected Lizzie. Overcome by restlessness and curiosity, she decided to walk up the valley and drop in on the O'Haras. As a moving-in present she would take them some bantams' eggs and the bottle of champagne an adoring fan had given James yesterday.

The trees in the wood that marked the beginning of Rupert's land were so blackly bowed down with rain that it was like walking through a dripping tunnel. Emerging, Lizzie wandered up the meadows closely cropped by Rupert's horses. In the opposite direction thundered the Frogsmore stream, which ran along the bottom of the valley, hurtling over mossy stones, twisting round fallen logs, shrugging off the caress of hanging forget-me-nots and pink campion, and occasionally disappearing altogether into a cavern of bramble and briar.

Coming in the other direction was Mrs Makepiece, who worked mornings for the unspeakable Valerie Jones and who was bursting with gossip. The four Pickfords' vans bearing the O'Haras' belongings had nearly got stuck on Chalford Hill, she told Lizzie, and Declan's son – well, the image of Declan, anyway – had been sighted in the village shop, asking for whisky, chocolate biscuits, toilet paper and lightbulbs, and was quite the handsomest young man anyone had seen in Penscombe since Rupert Campbell-Black was a lad.

'Will they be bringing their own staff from London?' asked Mrs Makepiece wistfully, thinking it would be much more fun working for Mrs O'Hara, who probably paid London prices and wouldn't slave-drive like Valerie Jones. Lizzie said she didn't know. Mrs Makepiece was an ace cleaner, a 'treasure'. Even the exacting Valerie Jones admitted it. Annexing 'treasures' was a far worse sin in Gloucestershire than stealing somebody's husband.

Lizzie wandered on. Having had no lunch because she was on a diet, she kept stopping to eat blackberries, which didn't count. Up on the left, dominating the valley, Rupert's beautiful tawny house dozed in the sunshine. The garden wasn't as good as it had been when Rupert's ex-wife Helen had lived there. The beeches she'd planted round the tennis court were nearly eight feet tall now. Rupert should fly a flag when he was in residence, thought Lizzie. One couldn't help feeling excited when he was at home.

Half a mile upstream, the village of Penscombe, with its church spire and ancient ash-blond houses, lay in a cleavage of green hills like a retirement poster promising a happy future. Lizzie, however, turned right, clambering over a mossy gate into a beech wood, whose smooth grey trunks soared like the pipes of some vast organ. Following a zig-zagging path upwards, which three times crossed a waterfall hurtling down to join the Frogsmore, Lizzie finally stumbled and panted her way to the top.

Across a hundred-yard sweep of lawn, which was now almost a hayfield, rose the confusion of mediaeval chimneys, pointed gables, gothic turrets and crenellated battlements that made up Penscombe Priory. On either side with the sun behind them like a funeral cortège towered great black yew trees, cedars and wellingtonias. To the left of the lawn, where once, before the dissolution of the monasteries, the nuns must have strolled and prayed, grew a tangled rose walk.

Poor O'Haras, thought Lizzie, as she hurried along it. After divorce and death, moving house is supposed to be the most traumatic experience. But, as she skirted a large pond overgrown with water lilies, round to the front of the house which faced into the hillside for shelter, she was suddenly deafened by pop music booming out of two of the upstairs turrets, and opera, she thought it was *Rheingold*, pouring out of the other two.

The old oak front door, studded with nails, was open. On the sweep of gravel outside a van was still being unloaded. Peering inside, Lizzie noticed some very smeary furniture (the O'Haras *would* be needing a 'treasure' after all), a grand piano whose yellow keys seemed to be leering at her, and several tea chests full of books.

Sprawling over the front porch was an ancient clematis which acted as a curtain for the bathroom window above and covered the doorbell, which didn't work anyway. Inside Lizzie called 'Hullo-oo, hullo-oo,' in a high voice.

Next minute a very plain, self-important black and white mongrel appeared, barking furiously and wagging a tightly curled tail.

Turning right down the hall into the kitchen, which was situated in the oldest, thirteenth-century part of the house, Lizzie found a woman, whom she assumed must be Declan's wife Maud. Ravishing, but inappropriately dressed in a pink sequinned T-shirt, lime-green tracksuit bottoms, with a jewelled comb in her long red hair, she was very slowly unpacking china from a tea chest, stopping to smooth out and read each bit of paper it was wrapped in, and drinking whisky out of a tea cup.

On the window seat, training a pair of binoculars on Rupert Campbell-Black's house, knelt a teenage girl with spiky short pink hair, a brace on her teeth and a pale, clever charming face. In her black clumpy shoes, wrinkled socks and black woolly cardigan, she looked like a tramp who'd just changed into his old clothes. Neither of them took any notice when Lizzie came in. But a very tall girl in jeans and a dark-green jersey, with a cloud of thick black hair, strange silver-grey eyes, and a smudge on her cheek, who was quickly unloading china, looked up and smiled.

'I live down the valley,' announced Lizzie. 'I've brought you some eggs and a bottle. Don't open it now. It's a bit shaken up. Put it in the fridge.'

'Oh, how really kind of you,' said the dark girl. She had a soft deep slightly gruff voice, like a teddy bear's growl. She looked very tired.

Maud, having finished reading her piece of newspaper, glanced up and gave Lizzie the benefit of her amazing eyes which were almond-shaped, sleepy, fringed with very thick dark red lashes, and as brilliantly green as Bristol glass. Deciding Lizzie was worthy of interest, she introduced her daughters Taggie, short for Agatha, the tall dark one, and Caitlin, the little redhead.

The sink was crammed with flowers still in cellophane. Sidling over, Lizzie noticed one lot was from Tony and Monica Baddingham, wishing the O'Haras good luck in their new house and a long and happy association with Corinium.

'All the nation's press tramped through here yesterday in the mud trying to interview Declan,' grumbled Maud. 'TV Times has been here all morning photographing us moving in. Two local papers are due this afternoon, and a man from the Electricity Board has been rabbiting on like Mr Darcy about the inferiority of our connections and says the whole place will have to be rewired. Have a drink.'

She extracted a mug wrapped in a page of *New Statesman*, splashed some whisky into it for Lizzie and filled up her own tea cup.

'It's a glorious house,' said Lizzie, raising her mug to them. 'Welcome. We're all wildly excited you've come to live here.'

'After yesterday's deluge, we've discovered it leaks in half a dozen places,' said Maud, 'so we shall probably have to have a new roof as well.'

'We're thinking of letting our grounds to some cows,' said Caitlin, putting down her binoculars and helping herself to a chocolate biscuit, which she proceeded to share with the black and white mongrel who was drooling on the window seat beside her.

'Moving's very disorientating,' she went on. 'Daddy's trying to work upstairs, and he's frantic because he's lost his telephone book. Taggie's lost her bra.'

'Caitlin!' The tall girl blushed.

'And I've lost my heart,' continued Caitlin, training her binoculars back on Rupert Campbell-Black's house. 'Will you introduce me?'

'He's not here that much,' said Lizzie. 'But when he is, I'm sure he'll introduce himself.'

'It's not fair,' moaned Caitlin. 'I'm going to bloody boarding school next week, and I won't get first crack at him. He's bound to fall for Taggie – or even Mummy,' she said dismissively.

There was a knock on the door and a removal man came in with a yellowing dress in a polythene bag: where did Mrs O'Hara want this put?

'My wedding dress,' said Maud theatrically, rising to her feet and holding it against her. 'Just to think, twenty-one years ago.'

'Ugh,' said Caitlin. 'It's gross. How did you get Daddy in that? But I suppose he didn't see you till he came up the aisle, and then it was too late.'

'Caitlin, hush,' chided Taggie, as Maud's face tightened with anger. 'Mummy looked beautiful; you've seen the photos.'

87

'Oh, put it in my bedroom,' snapped Maud, going back to the *New Statesman*.

'I'm not sure I'm going to like living in the country,' said Caitlin, fiddling with the wireless. 'No Capital Radio, no *Standard*, no second post.'

'No second post!' Taggie's gasp of dismay was interrupted by a knock on the door. Another removal man wanted to know where the piano was to go.

'On the right of the front door,' said Maud.

'Not there,' shrieked Caitlin. 'Wandering Aengus is shut in there, and that stupid bugger Daddy's let him out twice already.'

And there's Daddy, the nation's biggest megastar, thought Lizzie.

'Aengus is our cat. He's a bit unsettled,' said Taggie, smiling apologetically at Lizzie.

'Oh look,' sighed Maud, unwrapping a baby's bottle. 'That was Patrick's when he was a baby.'

Caitlin tapped the fast-emptying whisky bottle with a finger. 'And this was Daddy's when he was forty-two,' she said accusingly.

'Oh, go away,' said Maud, shooting her another dirty look.

Peering at a pile of books in the corner, Lizzie was highly gratified to see a copy of her first novel.

'I wrote that,' she blurted out.

'Did you?' said Maud in amazement, picking up the book and examining the photograph on the inside flap.

'When I was thinner,' said Lizzie humbly.

'It was really good,' said Maud. 'I thoroughly enjoyed it.'

At that moment a punk Lord Byron wandered into the room. He had flawless cheek bones, short dark glossy vertical hair, and an inch of violet shadow under his eyes, which were like Maud's only darker and much more direct; obviously the son Patrick who had so dazzled the village shop.

'Darling,' said Maud in excitement, 'this is Lizzie Vereker. She wrote this marvellous novel, and she lives down the valley, so perhaps Penscombe won't be such a cultural desert after all.'

Patrick said, 'Hullo, Lizzie,' and announced that he'd liked the book too, and where did his mother want the piano?

'In the big drawing-room.'

'Too cold; you'll never play it in there,' said Caitlin.

'Put it in the small sitting-room, then,' said Maud.

'There won't be room for anything else in there, not even a piano stool,' protested Patrick.

'Oh well, you sort it out, darling, you're so good at that sort of thing,' said Maud.

'And don't let Aengus out,' screamed Caitlin.

Patrick's reply was drowned by a bellow of rage from outside and Declan stormed in holding a piece of paper in one hand and the cordless telephone in the other. Lizzie caught her breath. She'd never expected him to be so tall and broad in the shoulders, or quite so heroic looking. He had very thick dark hair streaked with grey, and worry and hard work had dug deep lines on either sides of his mouth and round his eyes, which were as sombre and dark as the rain-soaked yew trees outside. But even with half-moon spectacles fallen down over his broken nose, a quarter of an inch of stubble and odd socks, one had to admit his force.

'This is Lizzie Vereker,' announced Maud. 'She's brought us some eggs and a bottle of champagne, and she writes lovely books.'

Declan glared at Lizzie as though she didn't exist.

'I can't find the focking A-D directory.' His Irish accent was much more pronounced than the rest of the family. 'I can't find my focking telephone book. I can't get through to Claridge's. I can't get any answer from directory enquiries in London. I've been trying for the last half-hour.'

He dialled the number again, then held out the receiver, so they could all hear the parrot screech of the unobtainable.

'Shall I try?' said Lizzie. 'You have to dial 192 for London directories in the country, and then 01 before the number.'

Two minutes later she got through to Claridge's and handed the telephone to an amazed and grateful Declan, who asked to be put through to Johnny Friedlander.

Lizzie almost fainted. Johnny Friedlander was a brilliant,

madly desirable American actor, with a well-known cocaine habit, and a penchant for under-age school girls.

'*The* Johnny Friedlander,' she mouthed at Taggie.

Taggie nodded and smiled.

Declan was put straight through, and invited Johnny on to his first programme for Corinium next month.

'I'd ask you to stay with us,' Declan went on in his world-famous husky infinitely sexy smoker's voice, 'but we're in shit order this end, and you'd do better in a hotel. We can have dinner after the programme. I'll get our contract people to talk to your people. Thanks, Johnny, I can't think of a better person to kick off the series.'

'But he's never given an interview ever,' said Lizzie in wonder, as Declan came off the telephone.

'I know. Isn't it great?' Declan suddenly smiled, a wide, slightly gap-toothed grin, which made him look much more like Taggie, and made Lizzie feel utterly weak at the knees. 'And all because you know how to use a telephone,' he went on. 'If I'd left it any later, he'd have been looped or refused point blank. I'll certainly read your book.'

He turned to Maud. 'D'you hear that, darling? Johnny's coming on the programme.'

'That's nice,' said Maud, without interest. 'Hell,' she went on, reaching the end of another torn bit of paper, 'this piece on Princess Michael is continued on page eight. Do see if you can find it, Taggie.'

She started frantically burrowing in the tea chest, throwing discarded bits of newspaper all over the floor. Taggie raised her eyes to heaven.

Lizzie turned to Declan: 'What are you writing at the moment?'

'Cheques mostly,' said Declan.

Gazing out of the window, towards the pond, he suddenly started, and grabbed the binoculars from Caitlin, nearly garrotting her with the straps.

'Grasshopper warbler,' he said a second later. 'Pretty rare for this part of the world. There are some marvellous birds round here.'

'There could be some marvellous blokes too,' said Caitlin, rubbing her neck and snatching back the binoculars to train them once more on Rupert's house, 'if they were ever at home.'

'I'm off to the public library, darling,' said Declan, attempting to kiss a still scrabbling Maud on the cheek.

'But you haven't had any breakfast or lunch,' said Taggie in distress.

'Trust you to push off leaving us to do all the work,' grumbled Maud.

'Leaving Taggie to do all the work,' said Declan with a slight edge to his voice.

After he'd gone, and Maud and Lizzie had had some more whisky, the doorbell rang.

'Probably the local paper, and your father's not here,' said Maud, who was now reading about Boy George.

But it was another bouquet of flowers, brought in by Caitlin.

'Who are they for?' asked Taggie, hope flaring then dying in her eyes, when Caitlin opened the envelope and read: *To Declan and Maura*. 'That's a new one, Mum.'

Seeing the flash of irritation on Maud's face, Lizzie wondered quite how much fun it must be to be married to such a famous man. Lizzie had experienced the same thing in a smaller way being married to James, but she wasn't stunningly beautiful like Maud. It must be awful looking like that, and having people getting your name wrong, and wanting to gawp all the time at your husband.

'Where's Grace?' said Maud fretfully.

'Not up yet,' said Caitlin. 'Said she couldn't sleep because of the quiet. I suggested the removal men should drive their vans round and round hooting under her window to remind her of the juggernauts in Fulham. Grace is our so-called housekeeper,' she explained to Lizzie. 'Patrick says she ought to join the RSPCA, she's so kind to spiders.'

'I must go,' said Lizzie regretfully.

'Have another drink,' said Maud, not looking up.

'Have some lunch,' said Taggie. 'I was just going to make some omelettes.'

'I must work,' said Lizzie. 'Thanks awfully. The children'll be home soon; it must be nearly four.'

'I'll walk some of the way with you,' said Caitlin. 'Gertrude needs a walk. Do you want to come with us, Mummy?' Her voice was suddenly conciliatory, as though she regretted cheeking her mother.

'No thanks,' said Maud vaguely. 'I must measure up some windows for curtains.'

'Curtains, indeed,' muttered Caitlin as she and Lizzie left the room. 'The only thing my mother measures with any efficiency is her length after parties.' Then, noticing Lizzie's raised eyebrows, 'I'm afraid I'm at the age when one tends to criticize one's parents a lot. Sadly one can't sever the umbilical cord gently. It has to be done with a razor blade and without an anaesthetic.'

Along a winding passage Caitlin opened a door into a large octagonal room, the base of one of the mediaeval turrets. Tall, narrow ecclesiastical windows with stained glass in the top panes provided the only interruption to shelves and shelves of books.

'Daddy's library,' said Caitlin. 'I thought, being a writer, you'd like it.'

'How lovely,' gasped Lizzie.

'I think Daddy bought the house because it already had shelves in.'

They went out of the West door on the other side of the house, past stables and a clock tower with a roof covered in ferns and dark moss, through a vegetable garden which had been taken over by nettles, and an orchard whose stunted lichened trees grew no higher than seven feet, because of the constant blasting of the winds.

'Patrick says it's going to take a fleet of gardeners to keep this place in order,' said Caitlin. 'And what with my school fees, and the re-wiring, and the new roof, and Mummy's *House and Garden* fantasies, Daddy's bloody well going to need his new salary.'

Out in the sunshine Lizzie noticed how pale and thin Caitlin was and thought a few terms playing games and eating stodge

92

at a vigorous girls' boarding school would do her no harm. Gertrude bounced ahead, plunging into the beech wood after rabbits. Certainly, slithering down the wood was easier than climbing up.

'Is Rupert Campbell-Black as attractive as everyone says?' asked Caitlin.

'Yes,' sighed Lizzie. 'He seems to get more so.'

'They say he was very wild in his youth.'

'Well, he's had a rather extended youth.'

'And brainy.'

'Well, street bright, and very sharp with money.'

'My brother Patrick is like that. I have brains. Taggie has beauty. Patrick has both.'

'Oh you're going to be very beautiful,' said Lizzie truthfully.

'I may blossom,' said Caitlin beadily. 'But at present I am undernourished, and my teeth leave a lot to be desired. I had to make the dentist put this beastly brace on. My mother only believes in going to the dentist when one's teeth hurt.'

'And Taggie seems very efficient in the kitchen,' said Lizzie. 'Isn't *she* bright?'

'Not at all. She's dyslexic, poor darling, hardly stumbles through Mills and Boon, and she has fearful trouble with recipe books, which is a pity, as she wants to be a cook. Patrick said it was ghastly when she was small, everyone thought she was retarded because she couldn't read. Mummy shouted at her all the time, never thought of taking her to an educational psychologist.'

The wall at the bottom of the beech wood marked the end of Declan's land. Caitlin scrambled over it and held out a hand to help Lizzie.

'How beautiful,' she said, gazing at the flat water meadows and the bustling little stream. 'I can imagine mediaeval knights jousting here in the old days.'

She whistled to Gertrude who'd belted the other way, and who now rushed back, splashing and drinking in the stream.

'The ghastly thing about having brilliant famous parents,' Caitlin went on, 'is you never feel the centre of the universe, because they're so obsessed with their own lives. And if you do brilliantly at school, everyone nods sagely and says Declan's daughter, it's in the genes; and if you do badly like poor Tag, they just assume you're lazy or bloody-minded. Tag's self-confidence was in tatters when she left school.'

'But she's so beautiful,' protested Lizzie.

'I know, but she doesn't realize it. She's madly in love with Ralphie Henriques, one of Patrick's even more brilliant friends. After months of pestering, he seduced Tag at a May Ball at Trinity this year. God, look at those blackberries!' Caitlin started tearing them off the bushes with both hands and cramming them into her mouth.

'I hoped Tag would tell me *exactly* what it was like. One can't obtain one's entire sexual education from the pages of Jackie Collins, but she just clammed up, and he never rang her again. Just one postcard from Cork, and nothing since. Can you imagine doing that to Tag? That's why she waits for every post and jumps on every telephone. Patrick says Ralphie's got someone else, some pert little blonde who reads Sophocles in the original. Poor Tag can't even read English in the original.'

'What about Patrick?' asked Lizzie. 'Does he like Trinity?'

'He feels right there. He thinks my father has betrayed his roots working in England, and he also rather despises Daddy for being in television. God, these blackberries are good. Perhaps Rupert smiled at them.'

'But your father's a genius,' said Lizzie, shocked. 'Those interviews are works of art.'

'I know, but Patrick thinks Daddy ought to write books. He's been working on a biography of Yeats for years, and he used to write wonderful plays.'

'What's Patrick going to do when he leaves Trinity?'

'He'll write. He's much more together than Daddy. I know Daddy makes pots of money, but it all gets spent, and he's always having frightful rows at work. Patrick's calmer. He's a prose version of Daddy, really. And for someone with such high principles, he thinks nothing of running up the most enormous debts, which of course Mummy settles out of Daddy's despised television earnings.'

'Jolly easy to have principles when someone else picks up the bill,' said Lizzie.

'Right,' said Caitlin. 'Patrick's also a bit smug because he attracts the opposite sex so effortlessly. Do you think Gertrude will get lonely in the country? Should we get her a dog friend?'

They had crossed the stream now, to the same side as Rupert's house. Despite the lack of wind, thistledown was drifting everywhere as though a pillow had just burst. Panting up the slope, and turning in their tracks, they could just see the creepered battlements and turrets of The Priory above its ruff of beech trees, now warmed by the late afternoon sun. Climbing had also given Caitlin's pale freckled face a tinge of colour.

'Think of all those nuns living there in the middle ages,' she sighed ecstatically, 'gazing across the valley, yearning for Rupert Campbell-Black's ancestors.'

Lizzie decided not to spoil such a romantic concept by pointing out that Rupert's house hadn't been built until the seventeenth century.

'It *is* a romantic house, isn't it?' said Caitlin, still gazing at The Priory. 'Exciting things must happen to us all — even Tag — in a place like that.'

'I'm sure they will,' said Lizzie.

'I'd better go home now,' said Caitlin. 'Can I come and see you next time I'm back for the weekend?'

Lizzie floated home. What richness, what a fascinating afternoon. The prospect of new friends excited her these days almost as much as new boyfriends had when she was young. She was still bubbling over when James got home later than usual.

'What did you think of my programme?' he asked.

Lizzie had to confess she'd forgotten to watch it, because she'd dropped in and had a drink with the O'Haras.

'Did Declan say anything about me or the programme?' demanded James.

'No,' said Lizzie.

'Didn't you tell them you were married to me?' said James, utterly scandalized.

'I forgot,' said Lizzie. 'I'm awfully sorry, but there was so much going on, and the O'Haras are just *so* glamorous.'

RIVALS
9

Declan O'Hara had two obsessions in life: his work, and, rare in a profession that tends to regard a broken marriage as the only essential qualification, his wife.

He was born in a thatched cottage on a green hillside in the Wicklow mountains, where his father scratched a living from the land. When Declan was ten, his father broke his back falling from a tractor when drunk, and was thus rendered useless for heavy work, so the family moved back to Cork, his Protestant mother's home town. Here his mother proceeded to bring up Declan and his three brothers by taking endless cleaning and secretarial jobs, aided by occasional handouts from her parents. Her one joy in an exhausting life was Declan, who fulfilled his promise at school by winning a history scholarship to Trinity, Dublin. Soon he was writing poetry and plays, working freelance for the *Irish Times* and sending money home.

One evening in his second year at Trinity, he dropped into the theatre to see *The Playboy of the Western World*. Maud, with her red hair and her amazing green eyes, was the toast of Dublin as Pegeen Mike. Declan went round in a daze for three days afterwards, then sat down, wrote a play for her in a month, and posted it off. Impressed by the play, Maud asked him backstage and was even more impressed by this roaring black-eyed boy with his volcanic moods and his gift for words. The theatre put on the play for a three-month run.

It was an instant success, with Maud's extra radiance being noted by all the critics. By the sixth week she was pregnant and married Declan as soon as the play came off. Although stunned with amazement and joy that this glorious creature was his, Declan soon realized there was no way he could support her and a baby by writing plays, so he junked his academic career and got a full-time job, doing profiles on the *Irish Times*.

There was talk of Maud returning to the stage when Patrick grew older, but then Taggie came along, and then Caitlin. Habitually strapped for cash, Declan moved to television, where, although his family in Cork thought he was joining the circus, he soon became a star. Snapped up by the BBC in London, that milker of Irish talent, in a year he was writing and fronting his own programmes, culminating in a series of interviews which had promptly climbed to the top of the ratings and remained there for two years.

For not only was Declan the most natural thing ever seen on television, but, unlike other presenters and chat show hosts, he never showed off or talked about himself, and he always did his homework. To get public figures, as a result of this quiet, sympathetic, utterly relentless probing, to reveal facets of their character never seen before made for spellbinding television.

These revelations, however, did not always please the BBC who got rattled if a Sinn Fein leader appeared too attractive or a politician too unpleasant. Known as the terror of Lime Grove because of his black glooms and his sporadic bouts of heavy drinking, Declan bitterly resented interference from above. He finally walked out because the Governors, heavily leant on by the Home Secretary, pulled his interview with Ian Paisley, and because Tony Baddingham offered to triple his salary and Declan couldn't see any other way of paying his tax bill or ever clearing his overdraft.

After his early childhood in Wicklow, too, Declan had always yearned to live in the country. He truly believed it would be cheaper than London, that he would have more time to spend with his family, particularly Maud, and to finish his biography of Yeats.

Maud herself was lazy, egotistical and selfish. She idled her time away reading novels, and token scripts, spending money and talking. Playing second fiddle, on the other hand, is not an easy part. When she married Declan, she had been the star, pursued by half the men in Dublin, and the mistress of the Director. Then she had to watch Declan rise to international fame, while her career dwindled away through lethargy and terror of failure, on the excuse that she was always too busy with the children. Underneath, she was desperately jealous of Declan's success, and one reason he had never become spoilt was because Maud showed no interest in his career and was constantly mobbing him up.

There was a tremendously strong erotic pull between them, but, even after twenty-one years, Declan still felt he hadn't really won her. He was also in a Catch-22 situation. In order to support Maud's wanton extravagance he was forced to work all hours, which meant she got bored and spent more, and, to goad him, toyed with other men. Another reason Declan had moved to the country was that last year one of her toyings had got out of hand.

A week after the O'Haras moved into The Priory, Declan started work at Corinium. He didn't sleep at all the night before. It was a long time since February, when he'd accepted the job, but Maud had immediately started spending in the expectation of riches, culminating in a vast Farewell to Fulham party. Christ knew how he was to pay for that, or for all Maud's re-decorating schemes.

Nor had his friends at the BBC been backward in telling him that Tony Baddingham was a shit, or that ITV, notoriously more reactionary and restrictive than the Beeb, would be far harder to work for. In the end, too, as he had been desolate to leave Ireland, he was sad to leave the BBC, particularly as so many of the staff had come out on strike when his programme on Paisley had been axed. They had then held a succession of riotous and tearful leaving parties,

99

finally clubbing together to give him the *Complete Oxford Dictionary of National Biography*. But all his life Declan had walked away from the safe thing – that was his instinct.

As he lay in the huge double bed, smoking one cigarette after another, watching dawn creep through the curtainless windows, Maud slept peacefully beside him. Her red hair spilled over the rose-pink pillow case, the whole of the dark-blue duvet was wrapped round her hips, and her breasts fell sideways on to a pale-green bottom sheet. Nothing ever matched in their house, reflected Declan.

He longed to make love to her to ease the panic and tension, but there was no way she'd wake before ten o'clock. She was as obsessive about sleep as he was about work. Tony had told him to roll up at eleven, but knowing work was the only way out of his black panic, Declan decided to go in early. He was expecting a pile of Johnny Friedlander's cuttings from America.

Thank God for Taggie, he thought, as he put on a beautifully ironed black and green checked shirt. Grace the housekeeper, who also never rose before ten, had an ability to singe or iron buttons off everything she touched.

As he went into the kitchen to pick up his car keys, Taggie came barefoot and hollow-eyed down the back stairs in her nightgown.

'Daddy, you shouldn't be up yet.'

'Couldn't sleep. Thought I might as well go in.'

'You must have some breakfast, or at least a cup of coffee.' When he shook his head, she put her arms round him.

'It'll be OK, I know it will. Remember you're the best in the world.'

Declan reached the Corinium Television building at a quarter to eight, just as the night security man on the car park was about to go off. Seeing a pair of vaguely familiar eyes looking over the half-open window of the absolutely filthy Mini, he raised the horizontal pole, and, having waved Declan through, went back to enjoying Page Three of the *Sun*.

Walking through the revolving front door, absolutely sick

100

with nerves, Declan found the place deserted except for a cleaner down the passage morosely pushing a mop, and a young man in pink trousers arranging roses on the marble-topped reception desk.

Aware that every other girl who worked in the building was at home washing her hair, putting on her prettiest clothes, and emptying scent bottles over herself in anticipation of Declan's arrival, the receptionist had just nipped down to Make-up to re-do her eyes before the hordes started arriving at nine.

Declan therefore waited a few minutes, admired the framed awards on the wall, which seemed all to have been won by Cameron Cook, then, still finding no one at Reception, took a lift to the fifth floor, where he eventually discovered a coffee machine and an office with his name on it at the end of the passage.

It was a splendid office with a thick blue carpet, a huge bare desk with empty drawers, two empty filing cabinets, a radio cassette, two television sets, a video machine and a large bunch of red roses, which had obviously been arranged by the pink-trousered youth. Out of the window was a marvellous view of the close, and the water meadows still white with dew. But even more marvellous on the virgin sheet of pink blotting paper lay a pile of mail including two fat airmail envelopes. Lighting a cigarette, sitting down at his desk, Declan was soon totally immersed in Johnny Friedlander's cuttings – most of them highly speculative and fictitious because Johnny never gave interviews.

The great bell of Cotchester Cathedral had tolled the hour three times when suddenly a red-faced middle-aged lady, reeking of Devon Violets, and with tightly permed hair, barged into his office, gave a squawk of amazed relief and shot out again, shrieking down the passage, 'He's here, Lord B, he's here.'

Next minute Tony Baddingham erupted into the room, absolutely purple with rage. 'Where the fuck have you been?'

Declan sat back in his chair. 'Sitting here, since about eight o'clock.'

'Why the hell didn't you tell anyone?'

'There was no one here to tell.'

With a colossal effort Tony gained control of himself and shook Declan's hand. 'Well, welcome anyway. Look, I've got most of the national press outside waiting to witness your arrival. We nearly had the police out.'

'They said you'd left home at seven-thirty,' said the lady reeking of Devon Violets, who was Tony's secretary, Miss Madden. 'We thought you might have had a car crash.'

'Or second thoughts,' said Charles Fairburn, Head of Religious Programmes, shimmying in and giving Declan a great kiss on both cheeks. 'You're not to be bloody to him on his first day, Tony. First days in an office are like birthdays. No one's allowed to be bloody to you.'

'Fuck off, Charles,' snarled Tony.

'See you later, darling,' said Charles, whisking out again, nearly colliding with an ashen Cyril Peacock.

'They're getting awfully fed up, Tony. Where the hell can the stupid fucker have got to?'

'He's been here all the time,' said Tony nastily. 'You just didn't look, Cyril. Another classical Peacock-up.'

'Oh, hello Declan. Welcome to Corinium,' said Cyril, his false teeth rattling even more violently with nerves. 'Marvellous to see you. They're all waiting for you in the car park, getting very hot.'

'Uh-uh,' Declan shook his head, looking mutinous. 'I've got nothing to say to them.'

'Well for a start you might like to refute that piece in the *Guardian* claiming you joined Corinium merely to clear your overdraft and not as a vocational choice,' said Tony with a cold smile.

'I interview people, I don't give interviews,' said Declan, not budging. 'The press made enough fuss when we arrived at Penscombe, staking us out all bloody night.'

Tony tried a different tack. 'It'll be such a thrill for all the staff,' he said suavely. 'All we want is pictures of you driving into the car park for the first time and having a glass of champagne in the board room afterwards, and then we can all get down to work.'

Declan suddenly decided he needed a drink.

'All right, I'll go and get my car.'

'You can't do that. They'll see you,' said Tony.

'Give Cyril your keys. He'll drive it round to the front, then you can drive in again.'

'It's a Mini, parked in the far corner,' said Declan.

As Declan drove his absolutely filthy Mini into the parking slot with his name on, which was between Tony's maroon Rolls Royce with the silver Corinium ram on the bonnet, and Cameron's green Lotus, there was absolutely no reaction from the crowd of reporters and cameramen. The next minute, however, there was a furious banging on the roof. Declan wound down the window half an inch. He could see a beaky nose, and a predatory mouth.

'Yes?' he said.

'You can't park here, asshole,' said an enraged female voice.

'Why not?'

'Can't you read, you fucking dumbass? This slot's reserved for Declan O'Hara.'

'Is it indeed?' said Declan softly. 'Then I've come to the right place.'

Winding up the window, he got out, towering over Cameron Cook, who gasped and stepped back as she instantly recognized the tousled black curls, the brooding dark eyes and the familiar face as battered as the Irish coastline. Shock made her even more hostile.

'Where the fuck have you been? You should have been here at eleven. It's nearly twenty past.'

'So I was, crosspatch, in my office. Nobody thought to look.'

There was a shout as the press recognized Declan and surged forward, their cameras clicking away like weaving looms, hugely enjoying the contrast between Declan's rusty banger and Tony's gleaming Rolls. From every window female staff, their clean hair flopping, screamed and cheered with excitement. Declan grinned up at them and waved.

In the Gent's, James lowered the Venetian blind a quarter of an inch and was delighted to see how old Declan was looking and that he was not even wearing a suit or a tie. Tony would not like that at all.

Outside there was almost a punch-up, as the Corinium camera crew battled to get the press out of the way, so they could get their own cameras in and film Declan's arrival for the lunchtime news bulletin.

Inside the building everyone surged forward to say hullo to Declan. The corridor was swarming with *Midsummer Night's Dream* fairies coming back from their mid-morning coffee-break. As Declan fought his way through them, shaking hands, Bottom took off his ass's head to have a better look. Next minute, Titania struggled to Declan's side, her crown askew, and kissed him on both cheeks.

'Darling, marvellous you've arrived. We must lunch later in the week. Love to Maud.'

'Wish we'd never started this fucking production,' said Tony, punching more fairies out of the way.

Mercifully he kept the press conference short: 'We are all absolutely delighted Declan's joined Corinium,' he said, when everyone had been given a glass of champagne. 'We feel he has a tremendous contribution to make, and has just the right kind of incandescent talent to revitalize our current affairs schedule.'

Declan suppressed a yawn.

'Why d'you move, Declan?' asked the very young girl reporter from the *Cotchester Times*.

'Well, to misquote Dr Johnson,' said Declan, 'we weren't tired of life, but we were a bit tired of London.'

'This Dr Johnson,' persisted the reporter earnestly, 'is he a private doctor?'

He'll crucify her, thought Cameron, waiting for the kill.

But Declan merely laughed. 'No, definitely National Health,' he said.

The press conference, in fact, was affability itself, compared with the meeting that followed in Tony's office.

As Tony, Declan and Cameron trooped past the tiny outer office where Cyril Peacock waited, grey and sweating, for Tony's reprisals after the disaster of Declan's arrival, they found Simon Harris, Controller of Programmes, lurking apprehensively in Miss Madden's office.

'I'm terribly sorry I wasn't here when Declan arrived,' said Simon, following Tony into his office. 'Fiona's had to go into hospital, so I had to take the kids to school.'

'Couldn't the nanny have done it?' snapped Tony.

'She's had to take the baby to the clinic.' Simon scratched at his eczema mindlessly.

'I'm so sorry,' Declan turned to Simon. 'Is your wife OK?'

'Multiple sclerosis,' said Simon helplessly. 'She's in for new tests.'

'I'm so sorry,' said Declan again. 'We met briefly at the Beeb.' He held out his hand.

The hand that limply gripped his was wet and trembling. Christ, he's aged, thought Declan, appalled. Simon looked awful. His eyes were unbecomingly frightened, the shoulders of his grey suit were coated in scurf.

'Well, sit down,' said Tony irritably, deliberately waving Cameron and Declan towards the squashy dark-green leather sofa which lined two walls of his vast office. Simon Harris had to make do with a hard straight-backed chair right in front of Tony. Despite the room's size, the plethora of television sets, video machines, and huge shiny-green tropical plants, plus Tony's massive empty desk and vast carved chair, made it seem unpleasantly overcrowded. A bowl of flesh-coloured orchids on Tony's desk and, despite the warmth of the day, central heating turned up like the tropical house at the zoo, increased the jungle atmosphere. Any moment Declan expected a leopard to pad out from behind the filing cabinet. As he'd already downed a couple of glasses of champagne, he wanted to go on drinking. But it was at least half an hour until lunchtime.

'After lunch, Declan,' said Tony, 'I'll hand you over to Cameron, but I thought I'd like to be in at the kick-off.'

Declan looked at Cameron in her sleeveless orange T-shirt

and her short black leather skirt. Her hair was greased back, her eyes fierce. She looks like a vulture who's spent the morning at Vidal Sassoon, thought Declan. He loathed meetings; he wanted to get back to his Johnny Friedlander cuttings.

Furious at having made an idiot of herself in the car park, Cameron was determined to regain the whip hand and weighed straight in: 'My goal is to give your programme more pizazz,' she said. 'We've chosen several possible signature tunes. Once we've decided on the right one, we can go ahead and cut a disc, which should go straight to the top of the charts with a nice profit for Corinium. But we ought to get it recorded at once. Could you listen to them this afternoon?'

Declan's eyes, which never left the face of the person he was listening to, seemed to darken.

'I know what tune I'm having,' he said flatly. 'The opening of the first movement of Schubert's Fifth Symphony.'

'Too up-market.'

'The programme's up-market. It's a great tune, and it's in the public domain, so we won't have to pay copyright. All we have to do is to record a jazzed-up version and pay the arranger.'

'Am I hearing you right?' exploded Cameron. 'This isn't fucking Radio 3.'

'No,' agreed Declan. 'But it's what I want, so we're having it.'

Cameron was spitting, but she particularly didn't want to lose face in front of Tony and Simon, so she tried another tack which would certainly have worked with James Vereker.

'I keep hearing the same complaint about your programmes.'

'What?' said Declan softly.

'The viewers don't see enough of you. We want to feature you much more in the interview, that's why we've designed a terrific set with book shelves and some really good abstracts, and this jade-green sofa.'

'No,' interrupted Declan sharply. 'I only interview people face to face.'

106

'Confrontational TV's kinda dated,' taunted Cameron.

Simon Harris opened his mouth to protest and shut it again.

'I'm not using a sofa,' said Declan firmly.

'Well, we'll argue about that later,' said Cameron.

'We will not. We'll decide now. I want two Charles Rennie Mackintosh chairs, facing each other six feet apart on pale steely-blue circular rostra.'

'Steely blue?' screeched Cameron.

'Steely blue,' said Declan firmly, 'so they rise like islands from a floor of dark-blue gloss. Then carrying on the dark blue up the bottom of the cyclorama into a limitless white horizon.'

'This is insane!' Outraged, Cameron swung round to Tony for help. 'Well?'

But Tony was calmly doing his expenses.

'It's Declan's programme,' he said smoothly. 'He knows by now how to get the best out of people.'

'How does he know until he's tried a sofa?'

'Sofa's make it look like any other chat show,' mumbled Simon.

'No one's asking you, dumbass,' hissed Cameron.

She's like a hawk not a vulture, decided Declan. She prefers her victims alive. He imagined her cruising the hillside, scanning the ground for prey, or darting down a woodland ride, scattering terrified small birds.

Squaring her shoulders, Cameron turned back to Declan. 'And we're scrapping the introductory package,' she said. 'We want you talking to camera for two or three minutes about the guest, to replace all those dreary stills and clips with a voice over.'

'The point of those dreary stills and clips with a VO,' said Declan, dangerously quietly, 'is that they concentrate the viewers' minds on the guest and set the tone of the interview. I get uptight enough as it is without having to ponce about making a long spiel on autocue. This way I can concentrate on the first questions.'

'I *must* disagree on this one,' said Tony, putting down his red fountain pen. 'The point is, Declan, that you have immense presence. It's you the viewers turn on for. You should open the programme talking to camera in a really decent suit,' he added, raising a disapproving eyebrow at Declan's scuffed leather jacket, check shirt and ancient jeans. 'It'll be up to Cameron to make you relax and be less uptight.'

Through half-closed eyes Declan looked at Cameron who was now pacing up and down through the rubber plants burning up the calories. No wonder she was so thin.

'She?' said Declan incredulously, '*She* make *me* relax?'

'We've got to be different from the Beeb,' snarled Cameron, 'or they'll just say we're serving up the same old garbage.'

'Anyway we've got three weeks to kick the idea around,' said Tony, 'and to cheer you up, Declan. I know Cameron's had a great time dreaming up people for you to interview.'

'We've checked out on all their availability,' said Cameron.

'Well, you can just uncheck them again,' said Declan harshly. 'I decide who I'm going to interview.'

Cameron stopped in her tracks, glaring at him. 'They may not be hot enough.'

Declan then stunned the three of them. He was kicking off with Johnny Friedlander on September 21, he announced, followed by Jackie Kennedy the week after.

Frantic now to keep her end up, Cameron snarled that Jackie Kennedy would just rabbit on about her boring publishing job.

'She may indeed,' said Declan, 'but she's also going to talk about her marriages, and her life as a single woman in New York.'

'You and she should have much in common, Cameron,' said Tony bitchily.

Cameron ignored him, but a muscle pounded in her cheek. 'Isn't it going to overextend your budget, flying her over?' she demanded.

Declan suddenly relaxed and gave Cameron the benefit of the wicked gap-toothed schoolboy grin: 'She's coming over on a private visit, and she'll probably stay with us,' he said.

Fifteen love to Declan, thought Simon Harris joyfully. Then it was game and first set when Declan announced that in subsequent weeks he'd be doing the French Foreign Secretary who was in the middle of a gloriously seamy sex scandal, followed by Mick Jagger, and the most controversial of the royal Princesses.

Desperately fighting a rear-guard action, Cameron said she had lined up a couple of ace researchers, who'd better get started on Johnny Friedlander and Jackie Kennedy at once.

There was a long pause. Very slowly Declan got out a cigarette, lit it, inhaled deeply, and only just avoided blowing smoke in Cameron's face.

'I do my own research,' he said softly.

'For Chrissake,' screamed Cameron, 'you can't cover subjects like this singled-handed!'

'I have done for the past ten years. For better or worse, what you've bought is not my face, but my vision – what I can get out of people.'

'It's a team effort,' hissed Cameron.

'Good,' said Declan amiably. 'Then I suggest we put your researchers on to finding some decent footage and stills.'

'We've got an excellent library,' said Simon, tugging his beard.

'Shut up!' howled Cameron.

Tony was lasciviously fingering one of the flesh-coloured orchids. Glancing round, Declan tried to analyse the expression on his face. He's enjoying it, he thought with a shudder, he's excited by seeing her rip people apart.

Noticing the disapproval on Declan's face, Tony looked at his watch.

'That was a very stimulating exchange of views,' he said, getting to his feet, 'but I, for one, need some lunch.' Then, deliberately excluding Simon, he added, 'Cameron and I've booked a table at a little French restaurant a couple of miles outside Cotchester. We hope you'll join us, Declan, and we can carry on the – er – discussion.' He smiled expansively.

Declan didn't smile back. 'Thanks, but I'm lunching with

Charles Fairburn. We worked together at the Beeb,' he added, by way of slight mitigation.

Tony was about to order Declan to cancel, then decided there would be oodles of time later to get heavy. Besides, the clash of wills had turned him on so much he had a sudden craving to take Cameron back to Hamilton Terrace for a quickie.

'What are your plans for the afternoon?' Cameron asked Declan sulkily.

'I'm going home,' said Declan. 'I've got Johnny's cuttings and all my reference books are there.'

'I trust you'll do most of your research in the building and report regularly to me and Tony,' she said. 'This is a group effort. OK? We want to be fully briefed at all times. Cock-ups occur at Corinium when no one knows what anyone else is doing.'

As she flopped down again on the green leather sofa, Declan immediately got up, as if he couldn't bear to share the same seating. From the depths of the sofa, he seemed to Cameron almost to touch the ceiling, his massive rugger player's shoulders blocking out the light, his face bleak and uncompromising. She never dreamed he'd be so dauntingly self-confident.

'I have to be left alone,' he said, speaking only to her. 'It's the only way I can operate.'

'I'm producing this programme,' she said furiously.

'Yes, but it's *my* programme you're producing.'

For a second they glared at each other, then a knock on the door made them start. Round it, like the rising sun, came Charles Fairburn's red beaming face.

'Are you through, sweeties?' he said blithely. 'Because I've come to take Declan to din-dins.'

They lunched at a very pretty pink and white restaurant off the High Street. Pretty waiters in pink jerseys and pink-and-white striped bow-ties converged on Charles.

'We've got your usual table,' they said, sweeping him and Declan off into a dark corner.

110

'Good boys,' said Charles. 'You know how I detest windows, they show up my red veins. Now get your little asses into gear and bring me a colossal dry Martini, and my friend here would like? Whisky is it still, Declan?'

'Bad as that, is it?' asked Declan three minutes later, as Charles drained his dry Martini and asked the waiter for another one.

'Well, I don't want to slag off the company on your first day, dear boy, but things are a shade tense.'

'Cameron Cook,' said Declan, tearing his roll savagely apart.

'Got it in one.'

'What's her position in the company?'

'Usually prostrate. She's Tony's bit of crumpet. Officially she's Head of Drama – particularly appropriate in the circs as she's always making scenes, but she's also got a finger up to the elbow in every other pie. That's how she talked Tony into letting her produce your programme.'

'Simon Harris has aged twenty years. He used to be such a whizz-kid.'

'Well, he's a was-kid now, and totally castrated. He's been threatening to have a nervous breakdown since Cameron arrived. Unfortunately he can't walk out, because he's got a second mortgage on his house, an invalid wife, three young children, and two to support from his first marriage.'

'Quite a burden.'

'Makes one feel like Midas by comparison, doesn't it?'

'Not quite,' said Declan, thinking of his tax bill.

'Well, Cameron, as you no doubt observed, jackboots all over Simon and every time he or anyone else queries her behaviour she bolts straight to Tony. The food is utterly wonderful here,' Charles went on, smiling at the prettiest waiter. 'I'll have liver and marmalade and radicchio salad. Ta, duckie.'

Declan, who liked his food plain, ordered steak, chips and some french beans.

'And we'd like a bottle of No. 32, and bring us another

111

whisky and a dry Martini while you're about it,' said Charles. 'Hasn't he got a sweet little face?' he added, lowering his voice.

As soon as the waiter had disappeared to the bar, however, Charles returned to the subject of Corinium: 'The entire staff are in a state of revolt. They've all been denied rises, and they're forced to make utterly tedious programmes in order to retain the franchise. James Vereker's ghastly "Round-Up" is just a wank for local councillors and Tony's business chums; and the reason why *Midsummer Night's Dream* is taking so long is that you can't get a carpenter to build a set – they're all up at The Falconry building an indoor swimming pool and a conservatory for Tony, when they're not installing a multi-gym and jacuzzi for Cameron.'

Declan grinned. Charles, he remembered from the BBC, had always had the ability to make things seem less awful.

'Nor,' added Charles, draining his third dry Martini and beckoning to the pretty waiter to pour out the claret, 'are the staff overjoyed that you've been brought in at a vast salary – yes they all read the *Guardian* yesterday – to wow the IBA. Gorgeous Georgie Baines, the Sales Director, who's stunning at his job incidentally, and whose expenses are even larger than mine, went straight in and asked Tony for a rise this morning. Tony refused, of course. Said they were paying you the market price. Depends what market you shop in, shouted Georgie, and stormed out.

'Thank you, duck,' he added as the waiter placed a plate of liver reverently before him.

Declan stubbed out his cigarette. Suddenly he didn't feel remotely hungry any more.

'Anyway,' said Charles, cheering up as the Martinis began to take effect, 'the staff like the idea of you, Declan. Christ, this liver is ambrosial. I've told them you're a good egg.'

'Thanks,' said Declan dryly.

'They all admire your work, and they can't wait to see the fireworks when you tangle with Ms Cook.'

'I already have,' said Declan, watching the blood run out

as he plunged the knife into his steak. 'Tell me about Tony.'

'Complete shit, but extremely complex. One never knows which way he's going to jump. Believes in deride and rule, plants his spies at all levels, so really we're all spying on each other. But he does have alarming charm, when it suits him. Because he's so irredeemably bloody most of the time, when he's nice it's like a dentist stopping drilling on a raw nerve.'

'What's the best way to handle him?'

'Well, he claims to like people who shout back at him like Cameron does; but, unfortunately, after a row, you and I can't make it up with him in bed, which I bet is where he and Cameron are now. Things were so much more peaceful when he spent all his time in London, but the IBA's warning him to spend more time in the area neatly coincided with his falling in love (though that's hardly the word) with Ms Cook, so he's down here making a nuisance of himself most of the time now.'

Charles suddenly looked contrite.

'You're not eating a thing, dear boy. Have I upset you?'

'Yes, but I'd rather know the score.'

'My budget has been so slashed,' said Charles, pinching one of Declan's chips, 'that I intend to interview two rubber dummies in dog collars on the epilogue tonight. Not that anyone would notice.'

'Will Tony leave Monica?'

'I doubt it. Any scandal, even a piece in *Private Eye*, is the last thing he wants with the franchise coming up. The pity of it, Iago, is that Ms Cook is very good at her job, once you dispense with all the crip-crap about checking out on your availability. I've acted as her walker at the odd dinner, when she had to take a man and didn't want to rouse Tony's ire. And she can be quite fun when she forgets to be insecure. If she had someone really strong to slap her down, there'd be no stopping her.'

'There doesn't seem much stopping her at the moment,' said Declan gloomily.

'If she gets on the Board, we're all in trouble,' said Charles, pinching another chip. 'But we have great hopes you're going

113

to rout her, Declan; now let's have another bottle and you can tell me all about poor bored Maud, and that ravishing son of yours.'

Back at Corinium, James Vereker fingered the prettiest secretary from the Newsroom with one hand as he re-read today's fan mail for comfort with the other.

'I do really think,' he said petulantly, 'Tony might have had the manners to introduce me to Declan.'

RIVALS
10

A fortnight after Declan started at Corinium his younger daughter, Caitlin, went back to her new boarding school in Oxfordshire, and his elder daughter, Taggie, disgraced herself by being the only member of the family to cry.

Caitlin's last week at home coincided with her mother Maud discovering the novels of P. D. James. As a result Maud spent her days curled up on the sitting-room sofa, holding P. D. James on top of a pile of games shirts, shorts and navy-blue knickers. When anyone came into the room, she would hastily whip the clothes over her book and pretend assiduously to be sewing on name tapes. The same week Grace, the housekeeper, discovered the local pub.

As well as getting the house straight, therefore, and feeding everyone, and coping with Grace grumbling about the incessant quiet and imagined ghosts and having to drag dustbins to the end of a long drive, the task of getting Caitlin ready for school fell on Taggie.

It was not just the gathering of tuck, the buying of lacrosse sticks, laundry bags, and the New English Bible (which Declan hurled out of the window, because it was a literary abomination, and which had to be retrieved from a rose bush) and the packing of trunks which got Taggie down. Worst of all was scurrying from shop to shop in Gloucester, Cheltenham, Cotchester, Stroud and finally Bath, trying to find casual shoes and a wool dress for chapel which Caitlin didn't think gross and the school quite unsuitable.

Caitlin spent the morning of her departure peeling glow stars off her bedroom ceiling, and sticking large photographs of Gertrude the mongrel, Wandering Aengus the cat, Rupert Campbell-Black and smaller ones of her family into a photograph album, and dressing for school. On the first day back, girls were allowed to wear home clothes. By two o'clock she was ready.

'Are you auditioning for *Waiting for Godot?*' asked Declan, as she walked in wearing slashed jeans and an old dark-blue knitted jersey she'd extracted from Gertrude's basket.

By two-thirty the car was loaded. Only then did Maud decide to wash her hair and glam herself up to impress the other parents. They finally left at four by which time Caitlin was in a frenzy they were going to be late.

'Goodbye, my demon lover,' she cried, blowing a kiss to Rupert Campbell-Black's house as the rusty Mini staggered down the drive. 'Keep yourself on ice until I come home again.'

No one spoke on the journey. Declan, with his first interview in a week's time, could think of nothing but Johnny Friedlander. Maud was deep in P. D. James. Taggie and Caitlin sat on the back under a pile of lacrosse sticks, radios, records, teddy bears, with the trunk like a coffin behind them.

After three-quarters of an hour they reached the undulating leafy tunnels of Oxfordshire, and there, high on the hill surrounded by regiments of pine trees, rose the red-brick walls of Upland House, Caitlin's new school.

'My head ought to be filled with noble Enid Blyton thoughts about comradeship,' grumbled Caitlin to herself, as they were overtaken by gleaming BMWs and Volvos bearing other girls and their belongings, but all she could think was how embarrassing it was to turn up with such famous parents in such a tatty car.

As they arrived so late, all the beds near the window in Caitlin's dormitory had been bagged, and Caitlin had to be content with the one by the door, which meant she'd be the first to be caught reading with the huge torch that her mother had given her as a going-back present.

While Taggie, her fingers still sore from sewing on name-tapes, unpacked the trunk, Maud drifted about wafting scent and being admired by passing fathers. Declan sat on Caitlin's bed gazing gloomily at all those glass cubes full of photographs of black labradors, ponies and double-barrelled mothers looking twenty years younger than those in the dormitory. He wondered if he'd been mad to let Maud persuade him to send Caitlin away.

He also thought how incredibly glamorous the other fourteen-year-olds looked, drifting about with their suntans and their shaggy blonde hair, and how excited they would have made Johnny Friedlander with his penchant for underage girls.

As they left, with all the girls surreptitiously gazing out of the window to catch a glimpse of Declan, Maud did nothing to endear herself to Caitlin's housemistress by calling out, 'Don't worry, Caitlin darling, you can always leave if you don't like it.'

''Bye Tag,' said Caitlin cheerfully. 'Don't cry, Duckie. I'll be OK. Keep your eyes skinned for Rupert. I won't look while you drive away. It's unlucky.'

'She'll be all right, sweetheart,' said Declan, reaching back and patting Taggie's heaving shoulders, until he had to put both hands on the wheel to negotiate the leafy tunnels once more and was soon deep in thought again.

'Don't be silly, Taggie,' snapped Maud irritably. 'I'm Caitlin's mother. I'm the one who minds most about losing my darling baby, but I'm able to control myself,' and she went back to P. D. James.

Going to bed that night, Taggie felt even worse. In Caitlin's bedroom, she found a moth bashing against a window pane and the needle stuck in the middle of a *Wham* record, and she realized there was no one to leave the light on in the passage for any more, to ward off the ghosts and hobgoblins.

Up in her turret bedroom, which was like sleeping in a

tree top, and which creaked and leaked and yielded in the high winds like an old ship, she looked across the valley and saw at long last a light on in Rupert's house. Caitlin would have been so excited.

'Oh please God,' she prayed, 'look after her, and don't let boarding school curb her lovely merry nature.'

The O'Hara children, having been dragged up by a lot of housekeepers, and frequently neglected by their parents, were as a result absolutely devoted to one another.

Taggie, in particular, had never enjoyed an easy relationship with her mother, whom she adored but who intimidated her. Ten days late when she was born, Taggie had been a very large baby. Labour had been so long and agonizing, Maud had nearly died. Declan, insane with worry, thanked God he was a Protestant, and not faced with the painful Catholic preference for saving the baby rather than the mother. Both survived, but the doctors thought later that Taggie's dyslexia might be due to slight brain damage sustained at birth.

Maud, shattered and weakened, never took to Taggie the same way as she had to Patrick who'd been born with such ease. As a child Taggie developed normally except that she walked and spoke very late, and even when she was four was only able to manage single syllables and might have been talking Japanese.

At school in Dublin, the staff, eagerly awaiting another dazzlingly bright pupil like Patrick, were disappointed to find that Taggie couldn't read or write. She was also very clumsy and hopeless at dressing herself, putting shoes on the wrong foot, clothes back to front, doing up the wrong buttons and quite unable to tie her laces. Because she couldn't tell the time, and had no sense of direction, she always ended in the wrong classroom, bringing the wrong books, and because she was so tall, people automatically assumed she was older than her age, and dismissed her as even more lazy and stupid.

Patrick, two and a half years older, was constantly fighting her battles, but he couldn't help her in class, when the other children teased her and the teachers shouted at her, nor during those agonizing sessions at home when Maud lost her temper and screamed, but in the end got so bored that she sometimes ended up doing Taggie's homework for her.

Patrick never forgot those pieces of homework, smudged with tears of frustration, sweaty from effort, and later peppered with red writing and crossings-out from the teachers.

Early detection of dyslexia and special teaching can quickly put a child within reach or even on a level with the rest of the class. Taggie was left to flounder, constantly losing confidence, until at eleven she came to England with the family and was about to be put in a school for backward children.

In the end it was Patrick, who got a scholarship to Westminster with ease and who, acquiring a friend there with a dyslexic older sister, persuaded his parents to have Taggie tested by an educational psychologist. He pronounced Taggie severely dyslexic and said she should be sent immediately to a special school.

Maud now felt even more ambiguous about Taggie. She never told anyone what the psychologist had said to her in that brief bitter exchange after he'd seen Taggie, nor would she ever admit that she felt desperately guilty for not seeking help for the child's problems earlier.

Nor was there any way, once the condition was diagnosed, that Maud would ever have the patience and routine to spend each evening helping Taggie with her reading and learning of the alphabet. Declan was always too busy. So it was Patrick, and later Caitlin, who came to her rescue.

Five years of specialist teaching produced dramatic improvements. At sixteen Taggie wrote her first essay. She still wasn't confident in the order of the alphabet, she still read slowly and hesitantly, following the text with her finger. She had never really mastered joined up writing, and punctuation was a closed book. Her spelling was atrocious and she still didn't automatically know her left from her right, and had to think back to the kitchen in Fulham and Patrick saying: 'Window on the right, Tag, Aga on the left.'

It still took her ages to write letters or recipes, and when

119

they moved to The Priory it took her much longer than the others to find her way round all the rooms. She also always double-checked telephone numbers, asking people to repeat them, ever since the nightmarish day when one of Maud's lovers had rung from America and asked if Maud could ring him back. Taggie had taken the number down wrong, and he'd never rung again. Occasionally, when she was drunk, Maud would bring this incident up: how Taggie had lost her the one great love of her life.

But at the end of her school career, although Taggie only managed O-levels in cooking and needlework, she left with an excellent final report: '*Taggie is a dear girl*,' wrote her headmaster. '*Kind, hardworking, responsible; she deserves to do very well in life.*'

Offered a place at a catering college, she preferred to learn the hard way, and worked in a restaurant belonging to a friend of her father's. After two years, coinciding with the family's move to Penscombe, he regretfully told Taggie that although he would do anything to keep her, there was nothing else he could teach her.

She cooked, he said, by instinct, by pinches, a pinch of this here, a pinch of that there. Given a barrel of self-confidence, he told Declan, Taggie could be another Escoffier.

Inspired, Taggie was longing to start her own cooking business. There must be hundreds of people in Gloucestershire who needed someone to do dinner parties, or fill up their deep freezes at Christmas or at the beginning of the school holidays. But so much of her time lately had been spent looking after the family, or crying herself to sleep at night over Ralphie Henriques. Maybe now Caitlin had gone back and Patrick was on his way to Trinity, via three weeks in France, she could get started.

The following morning did little to raise Taggie's spirits. She missed Caitlin and her acid asides dreadfully; the morning post brought no letter from Ralphie, and when Patrick rang from France, where he was staying with Ralphie's family, to report he had arrived safely, he made no mention of him. When Taggie finally steeled herself to ask how he was, Patrick had replied that he was fine.

'Doing a lot of water-skiing and drinking. But honestly, duck, I think you'd do better to cut your losses and find yourself a nice rosy-cheeked Gloucestershire farmer.'

Taggie was protesting that she didn't want a Gloucestershire farmer when Maud swanned in, enraged that Taggie hadn't told her that it was her beloved Patrick on the line, and seized the telephone.

As the alternatives that afternoon included picking apples, making green tomato chutney, or getting on Maud's nerves, Taggie decided to take Gertrude for a walk and explore the village. In an attempt to beat her dyslexia she tried to learn a new word every day and use it. Today's word was 'abhorrent'. There was certainly nothing abhorrent about Penscombe that afternoon: the wind that shook her turret bedroom last night had dropped, while the little Beatrix Potter cottages, covered in velvety purple clematis, were white in the afternoon light. A lot of Bovver boys on their motorbikes by the war memorial eyed Taggie with great interest. A nice farmer who lived down the valley asked her how they were all getting on and said they must come and have supper when the long nights began. At the village shop Mrs Banks gave her a mutton bone for Gertrude and the new *TV Times* with Declan's picture on the front, and an old lady with a blue greyhound stopped outside and exhorted her to look after the badgers who lived in the sets at the top of the Priory wood.

Cheered up by their friendliness, Taggie set out for home. She could feel the heat of the road through her espadrilles, thistledown drifted idly, and the sky was brilliant blue except for a few little violet clouds on the horizon. If only Ralphie were here with his hand in hers. Turning down the drive of yews, hollies, laurels, which almost hid The Priory from the top road, she remembered her promise to keep her eyes skinned for Rupert. She glanced across the valley, then gasped with horror as she saw a huge mushroom of brown smoke rising into the sky and realized that two of Rupert's fields on the far side of the house were on fire.

She ran down the drive to The Priory, dashed into the kitchen and unearthed the Gloucestershire telephone directory. Oh God, she must keep calm. When she panicked, her reading went to pieces, and she had even more difficulty with the alphabet.

Callan, Calvay, Cam Auto Repairs, Camamile – with agonizing slowness her finger moved down the column. There were two Campbells, one in Gloucester, another in Nailsworth, then the list moved on to Cambridge and Campden. No Campbell-Blacks. Rupert must be ex-directory, like her father.

Out of the window great clouds of smoke were belching from Rupert's red-hot flickering fields, the flames spreading ever nearer to the house. Taggie dialled 999. All the fire engines were out, explained the man at the other end, but they'd ring Cotchester. 'Don't worry, my love, we'll get one over as soon as possible.'

All the same, thought Taggie, she'd better rush over and warn Rupert. He might not be able to see the fire from the house, although he'd probably be able to smell it. It would be so awful if any of the horses got trapped in their stables. . . .

She raced across the lawn with Gertrude, slithered down the beech wood, bumping on her bottom most of the way, and ran across the water meadows; then she leapt the bustling Frogsmore, before starting the steep climb up the other side. Ripping her clothes on barbed wire, oblivious of stinging nettles and brambles tearing at her bare arms and legs, losing an espadrille on the way, she panted on, past surprised horses knee deep in lush grass, past ancient oaks and beeches, skirting the lake, tearing across Rupert's lawn, in through the french windows into a beautiful pale-yellow drawing-room, by which time she was so puffed she couldn't even shout 'Fire'.

Although the front door was open, no one was about. Returning to the garden through the french windows, her breath coming in great painful gasps, Taggie was about to run towards the stables when she heard shrieks of laughter coming from the tennis court on the left of the house, which was completely hidden by a thick beech hedge. As she raced down a gravel walk putting up red admirals, gorging themselves on the white buddleia on either side, she heard another shriek of laughter.

'I can't hit a bloody thing. I should never have had so much to drink at lunch,' said a girl's voice.

'Tit-fault. Your tits were at least six inches over the line,' said a man's voice, a clipped light flat, very distinctive drawl.

'Cock fault then,' said the girl, giggling hysterically. 'You must be at least ten inches over the line.'

'You flatter me,' said the man. 'I wouldn't be if you didn't excite me so much.'

'Fire,' gasped Taggie to the beech hedge, but no sound came out.

The man was laughing now. 'We'll finish this set, and then I'll finish you off upstairs.'

Taggie raced round the beech hedge until she came to a gap.

'Fire,' she croaked.

Then, very slowly, she realized to her utter horror that a tall, blond, lean, very suntanned man, and a beautiful girl with catkin blonde hair tied up in a pink ribbon, and a golden body like distilled sunflowers, were playing tennis with no clothes on at all.

The man was serving. His body rippled with muscle as the ball scorched across the net. Dropping her racket, the girl gave a shriek and rushed to the side of the court, breasts flopping everywhere, and covered herself with a pale-pink shirt. The man proceeded to serve the second ball very hard into the far netting, then sauntered almost insolently towards the net near Taggie, over which was hanging a darkblue towel.

'Fire,' mumbled Taggie, clapping her hands over her eyes.

'What did you say?' shouted the man. 'It's OK. You can look now.'

Very gingerly, Taggie lowered her hands. He had wrapped

123

the dark-blue towel round his loins now. With his sleek blond hair, broad brown shoulders, and long, wickedly mocking eyes, as cornflower blue as the great expanse of sky behind him, he was quite unmistakable, from Caitlin's photographs, as Rupert Campbell-Black.

Acutely aware of her heaving breasts and sweating red face, Taggie muttered, 'Your fields are on fire.'

'They're meant to be,' said Rupert.

'Whatever for?'

'Quickest way to get rid of the stubble after the harvest.'

'But it's the most a-a-abhorrent thing I've ever heard,' whispered Taggie, utterly appalled. 'What about the r-rabbits and voles and field mice and moles and all the poor birds?'

Rupert shrugged. 'They've got legs; they can run away.'

'Not that quickly,' said Taggie furiously. 'You're a murderer.'

'I suppose,' snapped Rupert, thoroughly nettled, 'that you want me to stop ploughing my fields because it's cruel to worms, earwigs, beetles, woodlice and all the poor bugs.' He was mimicking Taggie now. 'Do you want me to give them a state funeral?'

The blonde girl giggled. She was very young, only a few years older than Taggie.

'Oh shut up!' screamed Taggie, losing her temper. 'How would you like someone to set fire to you when you were in bed?'

Rupert nodded at the blonde. 'She frequently does.'

'Don't be disgusting. You're utterly abhorrent, the sort of person who always has to be killing something; hunting, fishing, shooting.'

At that moment, a lot of dogs, back from their walk with one of Rupert's grooms, swarmed barking on to the court. There were Jack Russells, spaniels, a black labrador, and a beautiful shaggy blue lurcher, which bounded joyfully up to Gertrude, who bridled and curled her tail up even tighter.

Taggie pointed to the lurcher. 'I bet you use that for coursing,' she said furiously.

'Why don't you take that ugly brute back to its pigsty,' said

Rupert, picking up a green tennis ball and hurling it at Gertrude, 'and stop interrupting other people's innocent afternoon pleasures.'

'Don't you d-dare be beastly to Gertrude.'

Reaching for his racket, Rupert let his towel drop: 'Forty love wasn't it, darling?'

The blonde girl giggled again. But next moment the pussy-cat smile was wiped off her face as, with a manic jangling of bells, three fire engines roared up the drive.

'Fucking hell!' screamed Rupert.

Taggie gave a sob and fled back across the valley, her face flaming as much as her poor torn stung legs. Beastly, horrible, abhorrent man. Looking up in front of her she could see The Priory. Except for Declan's twelve acres, all the land in the valley belonged to Rupert. Now, thought Taggie with a shudder, it seemed to curl round The Priory like a man trapping a woman at a party, putting his hands on the wall on either side of her, so she couldn't escape.

Back home she found Maud sitting outside, wearing a big black hat to protect her white skin from the early evening sun, which had just crept round the side of the valley to admire her. She was drinking vodka and tonic and immersed in P. D. James.

'I've just met Rupert Campbell-Black,' said Taggie.

Maud glanced up and saw Taggie was puce in the face, with her black cloudy hair standing up on end in a tangled mess, her red dress ripped and her long legs and arms scratched and bleeding and covered with white nettle stings.

'My God,' said Maud, roused out of her usual languor, 'I know he's got a fearful reputation, but surely you didn't let him get that far?'

RIVALS
11

The following Sunday Monica Baddingham gave a lunch party at The Falconry to welcome Maud and Declan to Gloucestershire and launch the new conservatory built by Corinium's studio carpenters. Accustomed to going out to lunch in London where people seldom ate before two o'clock or even two-thirty, Maud and Declan didn't leave home until half past one. Declan tried to persuade Taggie to come too, but she blushingly refused when she heard Rupert might be there.

'I'm sure Monica said left at The Dog and Trumpet,' said Maud, applying a second layer of coral gloss to a pouting bottom lip.

Declan was in a vile temper. Not only had Maud made him late yet again by washing her hair at the last moment, but he had spent all morning trying to cut their hayfield of a lawn with a mower that kept choking on Gertrude's shredded mutton bones. Now they seemed to be driving half way round Gloucestershire.

'Why the hell can't you take directions down properly?' he snarled.

'He's your boss. You should have taken down the directions. Anyway it was you who wanted to move to the bloody country. Let's go home.'

'They're giving the focking party for us. Why the hell don't they put names on their houses in the country?'

'You don't.'

'That's because I don't want anyone to come and see me.'

Declan was also aware that, although his wife was looking a billion dollars in a very low-cut black silk dress, a green shawl which matched her eyes, black stockings and black high heels, with her shiny red hair piled under the big black hat, she was quite unsuitably dressed for Sunday lunch.

'There it is,' said Declan at last, as he drove through two lichened gate posts topped with rather newer stone rams. 'Christ, people are leaving already.'

As a dark-green BMW passed them coming the other way, the woman who was driving wound down the window:

'Love your progamme. Frightfully sorry, we've *got* to go to a christening. Welcome to Gloucestershire; you must come to dinner. Better hurry or there won't be any drink left.'

'Jesus,' muttered Declan.

The Baddinghams' splendid Queen Anne house lay in a hollow surrounded by lush parkland. The stable clock was always kept twenty minutes fast so that people might worry they were late, and be encouraged to leave early.

In huge gold letters against a black background above the second door of the porch was written: *Peaceful is the Country that is strongly armed.* In the hall, stuffed heads of deer, tiger, stag and buffalo gazed down glassily.

'My head'll be up there next,' muttered Declan as Tony came out of the drawing-room, plainly in a bait.

'Can't you ever get the time right, Declan? We've been trying to have lunch for three-quarters of an hour.'

'I'm terribly sorry,' said Maud in her most caressing tones. 'Declan and I are used to London hours.'

'Well, you'd better acquire a few rural habits. The Pimm's has run out; what d'you want to drink?'

'Oh, there you are.' Monica swept in wearing a blue cotton shirtwaister and open-toed sandals on her big bare feet. 'Taggie said you were on your way; pity you didn't bring her, I've got so many spare men. Have a quick drink, and then we'll have lunch. It's probably the last time we'll be able to eat outside this year,' she added wistfully, thinking how much she'd prefer to be dividing the regale lilies.

Having given Maud a drink, she led her through the vast tapestried drawing-room out to the new conservatory, which stretched the entire back of the house at ground floor level and was crammed with statues of goddesses, iron seats painted white, lilies, palms, aspidistras and plants still wrapped, which people had brought as conservatory-warming presents.

'Beautiful,' murmured Maud, taking a huge slug of whisky.

Everyone, gathered on the lawn, turned round and stared.

'Come into the garden, Maud,' bellowed Charles Fairburn, who was already tight. Mistiming his kiss, his round red shiny face cannoned off Maud's like a billiard ball.

'Looking beautiful as usual,' he said, drawing her aside.

'You're not to monopolize her, Charles,' said Monica bossily.

'I promise I'll introduce her to everyone,' said Charles. 'Your husband's certainly been stirring things up at Corinium,' he added, lowering his voice.

'Really,' said Maud, only mildly interested.

She'd never been wild about Charles. He knew too much about her, and with such fantastic men around she didn't want to waste her first party on one who was both drunk and gay.

'Is that very good-looking man over there Rupert Campbell-Black?' she asked.

'Unfair to Rupert,' said Charles. 'That's James Vereker, Corinium's most popular presenter, drinking Perrier and working the room. He's fearfully put out by your husband joining Corinium.'

James was, in fact, absolutely furious. He'd arrived as late as he dared in order to make an entrance, then Declan had swanned in even later. Now he was trapped by three of Monica's friends who 'did an enormous amount for charity', silly old bags who all wanted him to open their Autumn bazaars and Christmas fayres for nothing. To look at Monica's toe nails, thought James in disgust, you'd have reckoned she weeded the garden with her feet; and Paul Stratton, who'd put on a hell of a lot of weight, looked ludicrous in those tight new jeans, and a denim shirt undone to the waist to reveal scanty grey chest hair. James, who'd nearly worn jeans and an unbuttoned blue shirt, was so glad he'd put on instead a new grey jersey with a pink elephant on the front, knitted by one of his adoring fans.

'Come and meet Maud O'Hara, James,' yelled Charles Fairburn.

James extracted himself from the old bags and wandered over. Maud O'Hara was certainly extraordinarily beautiful.

'Is that pink elephant on your bosom meant to reproach the rest of us for not drinking Perrier?' said Charles.

'If the cap fits, Charles,' smirked James. 'Don't you think it's a nice sweater, Maud? Sent me by a fan.' He smiled engagingly.

Charles peered at the sweater: 'Not sure about the collar.'

'It might look better if you wore a brooch,' said Maud.

James suddenly decided he didn't think Maud was beautiful at all.

'Hullo,' said Lizzie Vereker, coming over and hugging Maud, 'lovely to see you, I'm so pleased you've met James. Thank you for all that lovely whisky the other day. Are you straight yet?'

'Don't ever ask *me* that question,' said Charles with a shudder. 'What's all this about five fire engines rolling up at Rupert's house and catching him playing nude tennis with a blonde. Talk about Wobble-don.'

Lizzie giggled: 'Rupert's convinced some animal rights freak called the fire brigade because she thought he was cruel to burn his stubble.'

'Who was the blonde?' asked Charles. 'Beattie Johnson?'

'No, that finished months ago. Rupert won't say. The *on dit* is that she's the girl playing Mustard Seed in *Midsummer Night's Dream*.'

'Have you heard that Titania's so petrified of getting AIDS, she's refusing to kiss Bottom until he's had a blood test?' said Charles.

'Is Rupert here?' asked Maud, who was not interested in Corinium gossip.

'Somewhere. Probably wandered off down one of those garden glades in which everyone except Monica behaves badly,' said Lizzie.

'Speak for yourself,' said James disapprovingly.

It was certainly a beautiful garden. Rising out of a sea of lavender, roses coming up for a second pale-pink innings rampaged up the walls of the house. Pastel drifts of delphiniums, Japanese anemones, and Michaelmas daisies were sheltered from the bitter winds by yew hedges nine feet high. Two plump labradors panted on lawns as smooth as an Oxford quad. Beyond was a fish pond and a water garden, fed by the same winding River Fleet that flowed through Cotchester.

'What are you going to do about the Priory garden?' asked Lizzie.

'Get a donkey to keep down the lawn,' said Maud.

'I hope to God we eat soon,' said a harassed-looking man with a moth-eaten yellow beard, and a sleeping baby hanging from a baby sling. He was also hanging on to two frantically struggling children by the scruffs of their necks.

'There is a limited amount of time one can entertain one's kids feeding Tony's fish,' he added helplessly.

Lizzie introduced Simon Harris. All his skin seemed to be flaking in the open air, thought Maud.

'How's Fiona?' asked Lizzie.

'Still in hospital for another three weeks. It's the nanny's day off, or I'd never have brought this lot,' said Simon, as the two hyperactive horrors strained at their collars like bull terriers after a cat. 'If they get at Monica's Meissen I'm finished. I just couldn't resist a square meal,' he added pathetically.

Lizzie opened her mouth to ask him to supper, then closed it again. Simon was so boring at the moment, and she knew James, who was convinced Simon was about to get the bullet, would think it a waste of time.

The panting labradors struggled to their feet, waving their tails as Monica appeared at the conservatory door.

'Lunch,' she said. 'You stay outside with the children,' she added firmly to Simon. 'I'll get someone to bring you something out. I like children normally, but Simon's two will keep pulling the dogs' ears, and they keep knocking over my new plants,' she added in an undertone to Maud.

As Maud walked into the dining-room, Declan came towards her looking really happy for the first time that week: 'Darling, you must meet Rupert. He knows Johnny very well. He's given me some great stuff about him. It's added a totally new dimension to his character.'

Maud caught her breath. How could I ever have mistaken James Vereker for *that*, she wondered.

Rupert and Declan were both tall and broad in the shoulder, but there the resemblance ended. Declan, with his heavily lined, broken-nosed, shaggy-haired splendour, was like a battle-scarred charger returning from the wars. Rupert was like a sleek capricious thoroughbred, rippling with muscle and breeding, about to win the Derby at a canter. Yet in their great fame and their intrinsic belief (despite Declan's current self-doubts) that they were still the greatest in the world at what they did, they were the same, and therefore separate from the rest of the party. At that moment both James and Maud felt a bitter stab of envy, that Declan had been admitted so effortlessly to the same club to which Johnny Friedlander and Rupert belonged.

'Welcome to Penscombe.' Rupert kissed Maud on the cheek. 'I'm sorry I wasn't at home when you moved in, but I've been frantically busy.'

'So we hear, Rupert,' said Charles archly. 'What's this about fire engines and a burning bush?'

'Fuck off, Fairburn,' said Rupert, grinning.

'Come on, don't hold up the queue,' said Monica, beckoning from behind a long white table. 'You're getting Coronation chicken again, I'm afraid.'

Maud stood in front of Declan and Rupert, gulping down her third glass of wine and feeling totally unnerved.

'I know your house very well,' Rupert told her. 'I remember pursuing something that wasn't a fox across your haha at one party. Ended up ripping the front of my trousers off on the barbed wire. How's the garden?'

'A groundsel estate, and the nettles are on the warpath,' said Declan.

'Better get those tackled professionally,' said Rupert, 'or you'll never get rid of them. I've got a man who'll do it for you.'

'What about the wood?' asked Declan.

'Forestry commission'll give you a grant for that. They'll whip out all the dead stuff and plant you new young trees as a quid pro quo for the firewood.'

'How wonderfully positive you are,' murmured Maud. 'Perhaps you can give me advice on re-decorating our bedroom?'

'Re-decorating's never been a priority of mine. Not in bedrooms,' said Rupert.

'Tuck in, Maud,' said Monica impatiently. 'And you haven't met my brother-in-law, Bas. He's dying to meet you.'

Bas was about five inches taller than Tony and decidedly attractive in a sleek, wicked, Latin way. He kissed Maud's hand, then turned it over and buried his lips in her wrist.

'Calèche,' he murmured. 'I adore it. Do you wear it all over?'

Maud laughed. 'Are you local?'

'Near enough as the helicopter flies. I can land on the palm of your hand. I've got wine bar in Cotchester High Street,' he went on. 'Most of my evil brother's staff gather there to plot against him. No doubt your famous husband will shortly join them. You must get him to bring you in one day.'

'Don't be silly, Bas,' said Monica briskly. 'You haven't met Paul Stratton, Maud, our MP for Cotchester, nor his wife Sarah.'

She looks more like his daughter, thought Maud. With his anxious, lined, somewhat petulant face, and his brushed-forward blue-grey hair, Paul looked like one of those once-famous television personalities who eke out a middle-aged existence advising housewives to buy soap powder in television commercials.

Even Maud, who had a dismissive attitude to the charms of her own sex, had to admit that the wife was ravishing.

'Ah, the newly-weds,' said Bas, kissing Sarah on the mouth. 'When are you going to start being unfaithful to Paul? We're in Beaufort country here, you know, high fences and low morals.'

'*Basil*,' snapped Monica. 'Do stop holding up the queue. And you haven't met Freddie Jones, our electronic whizz kid have you, Maud?'

'Oh my goodness, you are smashing,' said Freddie in wonder. 'I 'ear Rupert's going to provide your 'usband with an 'orse.'

Maud felt marvellous. It was such a long time since she'd been admired by so many attractive men, so much more macho than all those wimps in London, and for once people were paying more attention to her than Declan. This dress always worked.

'Come along, Mrs O'Hara,' said Rupert, who, while Maud was busy fascinating, had loaded up two plates, acquired a bottle of white and two glasses, and put them on a tray. 'D'you want to be indoors or out?'

'Indoors,' said Maud joyfully. 'I freckle so easily.'

Rupert found them a window seat in the conservatory.

'Monica's done this rather well,' he said, looking round. 'I gather it's cost Corinium even more than your husband's first week's salary. You want to avoid this house in winter; it's the sort of place eskimos send their children as punishment.'

On cue, Simon Harris's two hyperactive monsters roared past, sending an aspidistra flying. Ten seconds later they were followed by Simon Harris, with Coronation chicken all over his beard. The baby in the sling was bawling its head off.

'Did they go this way?' asked Simon frantically.

There was a crash from the drawing-room.

'I'm afraid so,' said Rupert.

Maud wrinkled her nose as he rushed out.

'That baby needs changing.'

Rupert laughed. 'All his children do. I'd take the lot back to Harrods if I was him.'

Rushing almost as fast in the opposite direction came Paul Stratton searching for Sarah, who was sitting on a wall giggling with Bas.

'Paul's jeans appear to be castrating him even more than his new wife,' said Rupert, forking up chicken at great speed. 'If he bends over, his eyes will pop out.'

Maud admired the length of Rupert's pale-brown cord-uroyed thighs. After four large glasses of wine, she suddenly had an irresistible urge to touch one of them.

'She's beautiful, his wife,' said Maud.

'She's a tramp,' said Rupert, 'and Paul's living in Cloud Cuckold Land.'

'What's Bas like?' asked Maud, putting her chicken down on the floor untouched.

'Divine,' said Rupert. 'One of my best mates. Runs a phenomenally successful wine bar, dabbles in property, hunts four days a week in winter, plays polo all summer, and screws all the prettiest girls in four counties. Can't be bad.'

'He doesn't look like Tony,' said Maud.

'They had different fathers. After twenty-three years of utter fidelity to Lord Pop-Pop, Tony's mother fell for an Argentinian polo player. The result to everyone's amazement was Bas. Hence the name of the wine bar – the Bar Sinister.'

Maud laughed. Many men had told her that her laugh was beautiful – low, musical, joyous.

'Tell me about your children,' said Rupert, who'd finished his chicken.

'I've got a son, Patrick.'

'I'm not interested in him.'

'And a daughter of just eighteen.' Seeing Rupert's eyes gleam, Maud added hastily, 'But she's shy and retiring; doesn't go out much. And one of fourteen, who's madly in love with you; she's kept her binoculars trained on your house ever since we arrived.'

'That's nice. They're adorable at that age.'

'She's got a brace on her teeth, and going through a very plain stage,' said Maud even more hastily. 'Tell me about Freddie Jones.'

'He's a saint.'

'Because he buys your horses?'

'Not entirely. I've offered Declan a horse if ever he wants a day's hunting.'

'Declan rides very well,' said Maud. 'He grew up on a farm. Who's that little woman who's bending his ear at the moment, who keeps making silly faces? He looks as though he needs rescuing.'

Rupert glanced round. 'Not by me, he doesn't. That's Freddie's wife, Valerie, the Lady of the Mannerism; won't rest till she's Queen of England. Freddie unfortunately thinks she is already. Keeping down with the Joneses is an eternal problem round here.'

'You're very black and white, aren't you?' said Maud, noticing his long fingers and wishing they were unbuttoning her silk dress.

'I like people or I don't.'

Looking up, Maud gave Rupert the benefit of her most bewitching smile. The great expanse of white eyeball and the beautiful teeth (unfairly even and white after so few visits to the dentist) really did light up her face. At the same time her hair escaped from its jewelled comb and cascaded down her back.

'I hope you like me,' she murmured.

'I don't know yet,' said Rupert slowly, looking at her mouth and then her breasts. 'I like your husband very much, but you're certainly too disturbing to be living across the valley.'

Glancing through the conservatory window at Maud's pale, rapt face, Declan thought she looked far more exotic than any of Monica's orchids and felt a sick churning jealousy. Rupert had his back turned. Maud was weaving her spells again.

'*You need but lift a pearl-pale hand,*' Declan quoted to himself despairingly, '*And bind up your long hair and sigh, And all men's hearts must burn and beat.*'

Oh Christ, if only he could get away from this party, and spend a few hours on his Yeats book. And in three days he'd got to interview Johnny. He'd done his duty at this party.

He'd talked to the appallingly pompous Paul Stratton, and asked Simon Harris about his wife, and answered questions from fearful bone-headed locals about the famous people he'd interviewed, and listened to at least three women who had daughters reading English at University, who wanted to go into television, and now he was trapped by this monstrous dwarf.

'It's so wonderful to be able to stand at the bottom of one's drive,' said Valerie Jones, 'and not be able to see one's house.'

She was wearing a cricket sweater and white flannels, and rabbited relentlessly on like an obnoxious player who wouldn't stop bowling when the umpire said Over.

'We couldn't be happier with Green Lawns,' she went on smugly. 'We looked at The Priory, you know. It was on the market for ages, but it's awfully cold, and I really couldn't live in a property that didn't get sun until the evening. I must have sunshine.'

She held her silly face up to the sun. Declan longed to clout a six into it. He could see Maud was running her hand through her hair now, shaking it out. Her body was arched towards Rupert. Unnoticed by either of them, the fatter of Monica's labradors was busy gobbling up Maud's chicken.

'Even Freddie was nervous about meetin' you,' Valerie was saying. 'Ay said, don't be silly, Fred-Fred. Famous folk are just like everyone else. Most of them are on drugs, and very lonely, because all their friends have deserted them.'

'I wish some of ours would desert us,' said Declan grimly. 'That's why we moved to the country.'

In the hall Tony was throwing out Simon Harris. The elder monster had just smashed a Ming bowl.

'Was it very old?' stammered Simon, white-lipped.

'Only just over six hundred years,' hissed Tony. 'Out, OUT.'

'I'll pay for it.'

'It would take you two years' salary, which I don't think you'd like from the way you're always whining about money.

136

Now, bugger off, before those little bastards break the whole place up.'

'I must go,' said Rupert.

'Oh,' said Maud, put out. She wanted the afternoon to go on for ever. It was as though the sun had gone in.

'I've got to pick up my children from my ex.'

'How old are they?'

'Eight and ten.'

'You must bring them over to see us. Taggie, my daughter, dotes on children. She'd keep them out of our hair. Has your ex-wife married again?'

'Yes,' said Rupert getting to his feet, 'to my old *chef d'équipe*, Malise Gordon. He used to manage the British team when I was show jumping. Bit of a tartar, so I feel their twin rays of disapproval if I roll up late.'

At that moment Freddie Jones rolled up with two over-loaded plates of Pavlova.

''ullo my darlings; brought you some sweet.'

'Not for me, I'm off,' said Rupert.

'How's my horse getting on?' said Freddie.

'Bloody well. I think we'll run him in a two-mile chase at Cheltenham. He's ready for it.'

They were interrupted by frantic tapping on the window pane. Valerie Jones was glaring in: No dessert, Fred-Fred, she mouthed.

Lizzie Vereker took Valerie's place beside Declan: 'D'you need rescuing?'

'I did,' said Declan. 'I don't any more. She nails your feet to the floor, but I'm trained to cut across wafflers.' He shook his head. 'How's the book going?'

'Backwards,' said Lizzie. 'Are you nervous about your first programme?'

'Yes. I shouldn't be allowed out before a series starts. I get so wound up, I can't talk to anyone.'

'Good luck with Johnny,' said Rupert, pausing on his way out.

'Come and have dinner with us after the programme,' said Declan.

'Can't. I'm off to Ireland. I know we're both hellishly pushed, but let's get together soon. I'll come and look at your wood. 'Bye, darling.' He gave Lizzie a kiss.

As he crossed the deserted hall Sarah Stratton came out of the downstairs loo, reeking of Anaïs Anaïs. Glancing back towards the garden, Rupert saw that James was nose to nose with Paul Stratton, each mistakenly assuming he was furthering his own career.

'Come and feed the fish,' said Rupert, taking Sarah's hand.

He led her down a grassy ride, flanked on either side by yew hedges, to the fish pond. Stuffed to bursting by Simon Harris's monsters, the carp didn't even bother to ruffle the surface of the water lilies.

'Any repercussions?' asked Rupert.

Sarah shook her head. 'It seems funny, belting away from your tennis court with a pink dress over my head. The entire Gloucestershire fire brigade will recognize my bush, but not my face.'

Rupert grinned, and pulled her inside the thick curtain of a weeping ash. After he'd kissed her, he said: 'When are we going to finish the set?'

'Very soon, please.'

Her smooth golden face was green in the gloom; she looked like a water nymph.

'How was Maud O'Hara?' she asked.

'Seemed pretty unmoored to me,' said Rupert.

'Looks as though she'd like to tie herself to you.'

'Were you jealous?'

Sarah nodded.

'Pity your husband's summer recess coincides with mine.'

'He's never away,' moaned Sarah, as Rupert's fingers moved between her legs. 'Why don't we nip into the gazebo?'

'Got to pick up the children. I'm late already.'

'When am I going to see you?' gasped Sarah, as Rupert's other hand slid down underneath her pants at the back.

'Come to Ireland with me. I'm leaving on Wednesday afternoon.'

'I can't. My ghastly step-children are coming for a couple

of weeks on a trial visit. I know who it's going to be a trial
to as well. Paul's going to Gatwick on Tuesday to meet
them.'

'That'll give us at least five hours. Ring me at home the
minute he leaves.'

'Hulloo,' called a male voice.

Frantically straightening her dress, Sarah shot out through
the ash tree curtain and bent once more over the fish pond
to hide her flaming face.

Wiping off her pale-pink lipstick, Rupert followed in a
more leisurely fashion.

'Sarah and I were talking about horses,' he told an apoplectic Paul. 'If you're going to fork out for a groom, feed and
grazing for two hunters, you're talking about at least fifteen
thousand a year. Better if Sarah kept something at my yard.'

'We'll discuss it in our own time, thank you,' spluttered
Paul. 'We must go, Sarah.'

Back in the conservatory, Maud was being heavily chatted
up by Bas.

'Shove off, Bas,' Monica told him. 'Declan wants to go
and I want two minutes with Maud.'

'I'll come and see you,' said Bas, blowing Maud a kiss.

He's very attractive, thought Maud dreamily, but not in
Rupert's class.

'I'm sure you're a joiner,' said Monica, who was now busily
dead-heading a pale-blue plumbago growing up a white-
washed trellis.

'No,' said Maud, 'I'm an actress.'

Very firmly, but charmingly, she managed to resist all
Monica's urging that she should get herself involved in any
kind of charity work.

'The children come first,' said Maud simply.

'But two of them are away,' protested Monica, 'and Taggie's
eighteen.'

'But still dyslexic,' sighed Maud. 'She needs her mother,
and of course Declan needs his wife.'

'But you must do something for charity,' persisted Monica.

'It's such a good way of meeting new people, and it's awfully easy to get bored in the country.'

'I never get bored,' lied Maud. 'There's so much to do to the house. I can't pass a traffic light at the moment without wondering whether yellow would go with red in one of the children's bedrooms.'

Driving home, Maud put a hand on Declan's thigh, edging it upwards. Pixillated by Rupert's interest, and Bas's extravagant compliments, hazy with drink, she felt wildly desirable and alive again.

'Let's go straight to bed.'

'What about Taggie?' said Declan.

'Say we're both tired.'

Declan curled a hand into the front of her black dress.

'They all wanted you.'

'Did you like that?' whispered Maud.

'I know how hard I've got to fight to keep you,' he said harshly and felt her nipples hardening.

Back in their bedroom at The Priory, he undressed her slowly down to her suspender belt and stockings, so black against the soft white skin.

'When did you get those bruises?' she said sharply, as he took off his shirt.

'This morning. The focking mowing machine kept stopping and I didn't.'

12

Gertrude, the mongrel, was walked off her feet in the next three days. When Maud wasn't drifting up and down the valley in a new lilac T-shirt and matching flowing skirt, hoping to bump into Rupert, Declan was striding through the woods, trying to work out what questions he would ask Johnny Friedlander and driving Cameron Cook crackers because he was never in when she wanted to talk to him.

Cameron's patience was further taxed by her PA getting chicken-pox, and having to be replaced by Daysee Butler, easily the prettiest girl working at Corinium but also the stupidest.

'Why d'you spell Daisy that ludicrous way?' snarled Cameron.

'Because it shows up more on credits,' said Daysee simply.

Like all PAs that autumn, Daysee wandered round clutching a clipboard and a stopwatch, wearing loose trousers tucked into sawn-off suede boots, and jerseys with pictures knitted on the front.

'It's just like the Tit Gallery with all these pictures floating past,' grumbled Charles Fairburn.

Programme day dawned at The Priory with Declan roaring round the house.

'Whatever's the matter?' asked Taggie in alarm.

'I have absolutely no socks. No, don't tell me. I've looked

behind the tank in the hot cupboard, and in all my drawers, and in the dirty clothes basket. Utterly bloody Patrick and utterly bloody Caitlin swiped all my socks when they went back, so I have none to wear.'

'I'll drive into Cotchester and get you some,' said Taggie soothingly.

'Indeed you will not,' said Declan. 'I'm driving into Cotchester, and I'm buying thirty pairs of socks in such a disgossting colour that none of you will ever wish to pinch them again.'

He was very tired. He hadn't slept, panicking Johnny might roll up stoned or not at all. And yesterday he and Cameron had been closeted together for twelve hours in the edit suite, putting together the introductory package, rowing constantly over what clips and stills they should use. Daysee Butler's inanities hadn't helped either. Nor had Declan's dismissing as pretentious crap an alternative script Cameron pretended one of the researchers had written, but which she in fact had toiled over all weekend. She couldn't run to Tony, who was in an all-day meeting in London, but got her revenge while Declan was recording his own beautifully lyrical script, by making him do bits over and over again because of imagined mispronunciations or technical faults or bangings outside. They parted at the end of the day not friends.

Having bought his socks, Declan arrived at the studios around five. A game show was underway in Studio 2; the Floor Manager was flapping his hands above his head like a demented seal as a sign to the audience to applaud. *Midsummer Night's Dream* had ground to a halt in Studio 1, because Cameron, dissatisfied with the rushes, had tried to impose an 'out-of-house lighting cameraperson' on the crew, who had promptly downed tools. The Rude Mechanicals, with no prospect of a line all day, were getting pissed in the bar.

Deferential, glad-to-be-of-use, Deirdre Kilpatrick, the researcher on 'Cotswold Round-Up', as dingy as Daysee Butler was radiant, was taking a famous romantic novelist to tea before being interviewed by James Vereker.

'James will ask you your idea of the perfect romantic hero, Ashley,' Deirdre was saying earnestly. 'And it'd be very nice if you could say: "You are, James", which would bring James in.'

'I only go on TV because my agent says it sells books,' said the romantic novelist. 'Oooh, isn't that Declan O'Hara? Now, he *is* the perfect romantic hero.'

Declan slid into his dressing-room and locked the door. A pile of good luck cards and telexes awaited him. He was particularly touched by one from his old department at the BBC saying, 'Sock it to them.'

'Da-glo yellow sock it to them,' said Declan, chucking thirty pairs of socks in luminous cat-sick yellow on the bed.

There was a knock on the door. It was Wardrobe.

'D'you want anything ironed?'

Declan peered gloomily in the mirror: 'Only my face.'

He gave her his suit, light grey and very lightweight, as he was going to be under the hot lights for an hour. She hung up his shirt and tie, then squealed with horror at the yellow socks.

'You can't wear those.'

'They won't show,' said Declan.

In Studio 3 two technicians were sitting in Declan's and Johnny's chairs, while the crew sorted out lighting and camera angles. Crispin, the set designer, whisked about in a lavender flying-suit. The set was exactly as Declan had wanted, except the Charles Rennie Mackintosh chairs had been replaced by wooden Celtic ones, with the conic back of Declan's rising a foot above his head like a wizard's chair: a symbol of authority and magic.

As a gesture of defiance, on the steel-blue tables which rose like mushrooms at the side of each rostrum, Crispin, the designer, had placed blue-and-red-striped glasses and carafes.

'I want plain glasses,' snapped Declan.

'Oh, they're so dreary.' Crispin pouted.

'I want them – and get rid of those focking flowers.'

'Cameron ordered them specially.'

Declan picked up the bouquet threateningly.

'Are you trying to bury me?'

'All right, no flowers,' said Crispin sulkily.

At six-thirty there was a very scratchy run-through.

'Can't you *ad lib* us through your line of questioning?' asked Cameron.

'No.'

'You must know your first question.'

'Depends on his mood.'

'May be looped, you mean. Your bloody fault, asking a junkie on the first programme.'

Declan went off and shook in the men's lavatory for half an hour. When he returned to the studio the crew were lining up their four cameras before the meal break.

'Have you heard the latest Irish joke?' the Senior Cameraman was saying. 'There was this Paddy who went into a chemist for his heroin fix.'

The crew gathered round, grinning at the prospect of more Hibernian idiocy. Halfway though the story the Senior Cameraman realized he'd lost his audience. Next moment, he was grabbed by the scruff of the neck.

'You may be the best focking cameraman in ITV,' roared Declan, 'but you'll not work on my programme if you're going to tell Irish jokes. You don't dare tell jokes about Jews and blacks or cripples any more; why pick on the poor bloody Irish?'

With a final shake, which threw the Senior Cameraman half-way across the studio, he stalked out.

'I'll report you to my shop steward,' screamed the Senior Cameraman rubbing his neck.

In the bar they were gathering to catch a glimpse of Johnny Friedlander and to support Declan by watching his programme. There was still a latent *esprit de corps* at Corinium. Someone had deliberately changed the colour on the bar television, so James Vereker's face looked like a Jaffa orange.

'What's your idea of a romantic hero, Ashley?' he was saying.

'You are, James.'

'That's very sweet of you, Ashley.' James smoothed his streaks. 'What's romantic about me?'

'Well, you're so caring, James, and you've got an inner strength like Leslie Howard.'

'Turn the sound down,' screamed a Rude Mechanical, hurling a handful of peanuts at the screen.

'Anyone seen Declan?' asked Daysee Butler, putting her top half, which had Goofy appropriately knitted on the bosom, round the door to a chorus of wolf-whistles. It was getting perilously close to transmission time.

'In the bog,' said Charles Fairburn. 'I'm surprised he doesn't move his dressing-room in there. Can't even keep down a brandy.'

'Declan,' shouted the Senior Cameraman. 'You can stop worrying. Daysee's too embarrassed to come in 'ere, but Johnny Friedlander's people have just phoned to say they've come off the M4 and they'll be wiv us in twenty minutes.'

'Thank Christ for that,' groaned Declan.

'And 'ere's a letter for you.' A piece of writing paper appeared under the door.

'*Dear Declan*, it said. '*We're sorry we was telling Paddy jokes. We won't any more, you was quite right.*'

All the crew had signed it.

'*PS. Have you heard the one about the Englishman, the Welshman and the Scotsman?*'

Declan grinned, then he glanced at his watch, and nearly threw up again. He'd be on air in less than an hour.

Johnny Friedlander arrived in a black limo which seemed to stretch the length of Cotchester High Street. He was accompanied by a publicity girl and four security men. In a second limo were four lawyers. Looking at the bulges in the security men's suits, the press allowed Johnny to be smuggled into the building without too much hassle.

From the start Johnny's visit to Corinium went off with a bang. Taking one look at the ravishing Daysee, he pulled her into his dressing-room and locked the door. The four security men stood outside with folded arms.

145

'Who's she?' asked Johnny's publicity girl in horror.

'A piece of ass,' said one of the security men.

'Are you quite sure she's not a reporter?'

'Couldn't report a burglary,' said Charles Fairburn, whisking past, thoroughly overexcited by so much security muscle.

In his dressing-room a pretty make-up girl with sheep in a field knitted on her bosom fussed around Declan. He wished he could lie down in her field and go to sleep.

'At least let me paint out the dark rings and give you a bit of base; you're so pale,' she murmured. 'And we'll have to do something about the beard area. You really ought to shave.'

'I'm shaking so much I'll cut myself.'

'I'll shave you.'

Next moment Cameron stormed in.

'Johnny Friedlander's barricaded himself into his dressing-room with Daysee.'

'Best place for him,' said Declan. 'At least if he's having a bang, he's not snorting coke.'

In his fifth-floor office, Tony Baddingham, even more nervous than Declan, was dispensing Krug to his special guests, who included several big advertising clients, the Mayor and Mayoress of Cotchester and Freddie and Valerie Jones. By a ghastly mischance, they had also been joined by the Reverend Fergus Penney, a former Prebendary of the Church of England. A fearful old prude constantly inveighing against sex on television, he had recently become a member of the IBA board, and was currently on a tour of the Independent television companies. Now, primly sipping Perrier, he kept peering across the corridor to the board room, where the press, assembled to watch Declan's first programme on a big screen pulled down against the far wall, were getting drunk and stuffing their faces with quiche and chicken drumsticks.

In a corner of the board room, as disapproving as the ex-Prebendary, sat Johnny's four lawyers, also sipping Perrier and fingering calculators at the prospect of litigation.

'Why the fuck d'you ask so many press?' Tony hissed to

146

Cyril Peacock, who knew he'd have been equally roasted if only a handful had turned up.

Nor did the fact that Tony had been entirely responsible for hiring Declan stop him now blaming everything on Simon Harris. 'You ought to be able to control Declan, Simon. That's what you're here for. He hasn't even given Cameron a running order.'

'All she needs now is a prayer sheet,' said Charles.

'Declan's my favourite telly star,' the Lady Mayoress was saying excitedly to Valerie. 'I can't wait to meet him later.'

'Oh, we know him quaite well,' said Valerie Jones, on the strength of last Sunday's lunch party. 'He always singles me out – because Ay tell him the truth. Ay think famous folk get so bored with flattery.'

A curious tension was building up through the building.

'Declan's just cut me dead,' complained James Vereker, going into the bar. 'Awfully uncool to get so uptight.'

Daysee came out of Johnny's dressing-room, looking as though she'd found the Holy Grail.

'He's having a quick shower,' she said. 'Then he wants Make-up.'

'Well, send in a boot,' said Cameron. 'We don't want him banging her as well.'

It was five minutes to blast off. The four security men had taken up their positions in the studio. In the control room the production team sat at a desk like a vast dashboard, gazing at two rows of monitor screens. On four of the monitors which came direct from the studio, Cameron could see Johnny Friedlander's carved, beautiful, degenerate face with its hollow cheek bones and Californian suntan. His fair hair was the red-gold of willows in winter, the irises of the deep-set Oxford-blue eyes were almost as dark as the pupils. Thin almost to the point of emaciation, he lounged easily in his three-thousand-dollar suit, with the sleeves rolled up to the elbow. But the air of relaxation was false.

'Why the hell did I agree to do this shit?' he drawled.

'I'm sorry,' said Declan, meaning it.

147

'Aw that's OK. I just don't feel I've got proper lines when they're my own. Rupert called, by the way. He said: "You can trust this guy, he's one of us."'

In his earpiece Declan could hear Daysee saying: 'The pink strapless is more dressy, but my holiday tan's nearly gone.'

'Can we have some level?' asked the Floor Manager. 'What did you have for breakfast, Johnny?'

Johnny laughed. 'You want to get me arrested?'

On Cameron's left, Daysee was checking different stop-watches. The moment they were on air she would forget pink strapless dresses and become as cool as a computer, timing the programme to the second.

On the right sat the vision-mixer in a red T-shirt, hands at the ready over regiments of square buttons, lit up like spangles, ready to punch up the correct picture when Cameron demanded it.

'Good luck, everyone,' said Cameron, crossing her fingers. 'Stand by Studio, stand by Opening Titles, stand by Music.'

'One minute to air,' said Daysee, clenching her stop-watch and glaring at the leaping red number of the clock. 'Twenty seconds, ten, five, four, three, two, one and in.'

Schubert's Fifth Symphony started on its jolly jazzed-up course. On the screen a rocket exploded in coloured stars above a night-lit Cotchester, and then cascaded down to form the word Declan. A great cheer went up in the bar. Tony puffed on his cigar.

'I want another gin and tonic,' said an already drunk reporter from the *Mail on Sunday*.

'Shut up,' said Johnny's four lawyers in unison, who were listening to the opening package like hawks, in the hope of finding something defamatory.

As Daysee cued Declan in, as a concession to Cameron, he swung round to talk directly to camera. For a moment his throat went dry. He's forgotten his first question, thought Cameron in anguish. Then he said: 'I welcome my first guest in this new series with the greatest humility. He is simply the best actor to come out of America in the last fifteen years.

But this is the first interview you've ever given.' He turned to Johnny, 'Why?'

'I hate publicity,' drawled Johnny. 'If all journalists were exterminated life would be just fine.'

Up in the board room a howl of protest went up from the press, who stopped filling up their drinks and started listening.

'The press detest success,' went on Johnny, 'and they screw up your sex life. However much you try not to get fed up, it pisses you off when you read lies that your latest girlfriend's been two-timing you with some Greek masseur. Every day, my exes are offered millions to tell all.'

'How d'you cope?' said Declan.

'I don't read press cuttings any more. I just weigh them; if they're light I start worrying.'

'By deliberately avoiding publicity, aren't you actually courting it?'

'Don't give me that crap,' said Johnny lightly.

And they were off, sparring, laughing, fooling about almost like two old friends discussing someone they knew and liked, but frequently disapproved of. Johnny was being absolutely outrageous now about his exploits with his leading ladies, but he drawled out his answers so honestly and engagingly that the press quickly forgave him for his earlier sniping. The lawyers were clutching their heads, but they were laughing and even the ex-Prebendary was looking moderately benign.

It's going to be all right, thought Cameron. 'Ten minutes to the commercial break, Declan,' she said into his earpiece. Following a tip-off from Rupert, Declan then said, 'And you're about to face your greatest acting challenge . . .'

Johnny raised an eyebrow.

' . . . playing Hamlet at Stratford next year,' said Declan. Johnny looked startled. Upstairs the board room was in an uproar.

'No one knows that,' screamed the lawyers. 'The god-dammed contracts haven't been fucking exchanged yet.'

'I figured I ought to have a crack at it,' said Johnny. 'Women don't get taken seriously as actresses these days until they allow themselves to look ugly and sweaty and get raped on screen. Guys still have to play Hamlet. And I like the guy. I mean he had a stepfather problem. I don't figure Claudius bumped off Hamlet's father at all. That was Hamlet's fantasy; he hated his stepfather. I hated mine.'

'Why?'

'He married my mother. I was jealous. He was a bass-tard.'

'Why?'

Tony drew on his cigar; the lawyers fingered their calculators; even the press were still.

Declan paused, waiting unbearably long. On his pale-blue island in a sea of dark blue, Johnny suddenly seemed terribly vulnerable.

'He groped my baby sister the whole time,' he said. 'So I quit. My stepfather called to say my mother was dying of cancer. I didn't believe him, so I didn't go home.' Johnny put his head in his hands. 'But she did die the next day. She topped herself. I ain't never told no one that.'

'Why did she commit suicide?' asked Declan quietly.

Johnny looked up, his eyes cavernous. 'She was jealous because my stepfather preferred my sister. Christ, what a mess.'

'Out of order,' screamed the lawyers apoplectically. The Prebendary was looking equally outraged.

'Are you worried, being American, you won't be taken seriously as Hamlet?' asked Declan.

Relieved at a change of subject, Johnny fast recovered his poise. 'He was a Dane, for Christ's sake. He didn't speak like Leslie Howard.'

In the bar James and the lady novelist exchanged caring smiles.

'It's the acting that matters,' went on Johnny. 'I could play him like JR.'

He launched into 'To be or not to be' in broad Texan; it was so funny, the cameramen could hardly keep their cameras still. Halfway through Johnny slid into Prince Charles's accent, which was even funnier; then for the last ten lines, he played it straight and was so good that Declan felt

150

his hair standing on end. At the end, Johnny said, 'That'll be five hundred pounds, please,' in a camp Cockney accent.

'You'll be taken seriously,' said Declan.

'I can switch moods, that's why I'm a good movie actor,' said Johnny. 'But to be on stage four hours, that's something else. But then I've always lived dangerously. . . .'

Declan took a deep breath. 'Is that why you went back to America to face trial?'

'That is definitely out of order,' screamed the lawyers, positively orgasmic now at the prospect of lucrative litigation. 'We agreed he wouldn't talk about that.'

'I went back because I missed the States,' said Johnny. He still appeared relaxed, but his knuckles were white points as he gripped the arms of his chair.

'Have you always fancied very young girls?'

'Sure, if they're pretty. Most men do. This one was very pretty.'

'Did you know she was only fourteen?'

The Prebendary was about to have a seizure.

'I think you ought to have a word with the control room,' he spluttered to Tony.

'Sure, I guess it was wrong, but she was so sweet, I really cared for her. I know I screwed her, but I don't figure I screwed her up. She's very happily married with a baby now.'

'How d'you get on in prison?'

Johnny's eyes were cavernous again. 'It's not a very nice place to be. But if you're a famous movie star you're trapped anyway; going to gaol is just exchanging one kind of captivity for another. And I learnt a lot. I could burglarize your place tonight, while you were in it. And I'm shit-hot at insider trading.'

Declan stretched out his legs.

'Extraordinary coloured socks,' said the girl from the *Mail on Sunday*, pouring herself another gin.

'Did they give you a hard time inside?' Declan asked Johnny.

151

'Not really. One guy who couldn't count – he thought the girl was four not fourteen – worked me over a bit, but I made some good friends.'

'Have you never fancied older women?'

Johnny thought for a minute, then he smiled wickedly.

'No, they have droopy asses. Droopy asses are so cold in bed.'

The telephone rang in the control room.

'For Christ's sake, get him off sex,' yelled Tony. 'The lawyers are going to take us to the cleaners, and Fergus Penney's having a coronary. We'll lose the franchise if you don't shut him up.'

'It's a fucking good programme,' said Cameron, and hung up.

Then she took the telephone off the hook.

'Five seconds to the cue dot,' intoned Daysee. 'Five, four, three, two, one.' She flicked the cue switch to warn people all over the network to get ready in sixty seconds to roll in the commercials, which were, after all, the life-blood of the station.

As the End-of-Part-One caption came up, Johnny shot out of the studio, saying he must have a leak.

'You stay here,' Cameron screamed at Daysee. 'Well done, Declan.'

Johnny may not have been able to have Daysee in the break, but he had certainly taken something. In the second half he was even more outrageous, but utterly relaxed. Declan, in his wizard's chair, had only to prompt him here, jog his memory there, and curb his amazing honesty when he looked like going over the top.

The floor manager thrust the back of his hand with splayed-out fingers towards Declan to indicate five minutes more.

'I was on location in Texas,' Johnny was saying as he waved his cigarette around. 'Staying in my hotel was this glorious German girl. She gave me her room number, told me to come up in half an hour. I must have been looped. When I hotfooted upstairs later and banged on her door, someone let me in, but the room was in darkness.'

'Oh Christ,' thought Cameron. 'What's he going to say?'

'Well, I undressed and got into bed, and I reached out, and I felt a boob, like a wrinkled fig. I figured this was odd. Then moving down I found I could play Grieg's Piano Concerto on her ribs, so I groped for the light, and there were her teeth grinning at me from a glass beside the bed. I don't know which of us screamed the louder. I mean, she must have been ninety, if she was a day. I mean, under-age girls are one thing, gerontophilia's quite another.' Johnny smiled helplessly.

'Disgusting,' spluttered the Prebendary and Valerie Jones in unison.

'Anyway I shot down the bed as the security men broke in, and the old sweetie didn't give me away. I sent her a whole roomful of flowers the next morning, and,' Johnny paused wickedly – Oh Christ, thought Tony, as the Prebendary turned even more purple – 'she still sends me Christmas cards.'

The floor manager was waving a couple of fingers at Declan for two minutes more.

'Now you're going to play Hamlet, have you got any ambitions left?'

'I guess I'd like to make a happy marriage,' said Johnny seriously. 'I went to see my grandma the other day, she's been married sixty years. Now that is achievement – like building a cathedral brick by brick, a real life's work. I guess I won't achieve it, but that's what I'd like.'

'Aaaaah,' said Daysee Butler, so moved that she flicked the cue switch too early.

Now Declan was smiling and thanking Johnny for coming on the programme.

On came Schubert, jauntier than ever, up rolled the credits, but alas because of Daysee's early cue, just as Cameron Cook's name was about to come up at the end, the screen went royal blue and the Corinium television logo appeared, with the little red ram seeming to hold his horned head

153

even higher than usual. A second later they were into the commercials.

Another great roar went up in the bar and the board room. Even the crew broke into rare spontaneous applause and crowded round Declan and Johnny. Upstairs, the press raced for the telephones.

'I must talk to Declan about those yellow socks. I'm definitely going to do a fashion piece,' said the girl from the *Mail on Sunday*, pouring herself another gin.

'Great,' said Freddie Jones, 'really great. Congratulations.'

The lawyers came up and pumped Tony's hand. 'We were shitting bricks at the end, but Johnny came across great, a really nice guy, an attractive guy.'

Valerie Jones was nose to nose with the Prebendary.

'Disgraceful,' she was saying. 'My daughter Sharon is only fourteen and when one thinks . . .'

'Screw the Prebendary,' said Tony five minutes later, as he came off the telephone in his office. 'Lady Gosling thought it was terrific.'

'It was,' said Miss Madden. 'Declan wants a word.'

'That was a terrific programme. Well done,' said Tony, picking up another telephone.

'Thanks,' said Declan. 'D'you mind if we don't come up? Johnny doesn't want to see anyone. He's reached a stage when he might go right over the top. I'm taking him home for a quiet dinner.'

Through the door Tony could see the press and even the lawyers getting drunk. The Prebendary was still nose to nose with Valerie. Corinium had walked a tightrope that evening and got away with it.

'Understood,' said Tony. 'I'll talk to you tomorrow, but congratulations anyway.'

As Cameron went into the board room, everyone cheered. Tony even forgot himself sufficiently to march over and hug her. His eyes were blazing with triumph.

'Lady Gosling rang to say how much she liked it. She sent special congratulations to you.'

But Cameron felt utterly drained and despairing. Not just

because of her lost credit, but because she had produced and directed a programme in which she'd had no part. It had lived and fortunately not died with Declan.

RIVALS
13

Declan's first programmes for Corinium were a colossal success. The press agreed that Johnny Friedlander was the best interview he'd ever done, that the ones with Jackie Kennedy and the Princess were even better, and the ones with Mick Jagger and Harold Pinter even better than that. The programmes sold everywhere abroad, and there was even talk at the Network meetings of moving the series to seven-thirty on Thursday in an attempt to knock out 'EastEnders'. Declan sweat shirts, mugs and posters were selling faster than bikinis in June and Schubert must have looked down from heaven and been surprised but delighted to see his Fifth Symphony galloping up the charts.

Once the first programme was over Declan was much less aggressive and uptight and even drank in the bar with the crew, but he was no less intransigent about wanting his own way. Cameron smouldered and bided her time. Tony was besotted with Declan at the moment, but, knowing the nature of the two men, Cameron realized it wouldn't last.

Meanwhile, although the flood of resignations at Corinium had been arrested by Declan's arrival, Simon Harris was getting nearer his nervous breakdown and the staff were muttering even more mutinously into their glasses of Sancerre at the Bar Sinister that Cameron was about to be put on the Board.

But, to stop Cameron getting smug, Tony, ever the bubblepricker, finally invited the ravishing Sarah Stratton to lunch and arranged for James Vereker to interview her in the 'Behind Every Famous Man' series early in November. Cameron was livid and vented her rage on the rest of the staff.

The same week Sarah was due to be interviewed, Tony summoned Declan to his office.

'How's your cold?' Declan asked Miss Madden as he walked through the outer office.

'Much better,' said Miss Madden, flushing. 'How amazing of you to remember. Better hurry. Cameron's in there already.'

Cameron was lounging menacingly by the window, wearing a black polo neck, black leather trousers and spiky high heels. Declan wondered if she walked all over Tony in bed in them. The room was full of cigar smoke. Tony was drinking a brandy, but didn't offer Declan one.

'Sit down. Congratulations to both of you,' he said briskly. 'I've just heard off the record that we got our highest local rating ever for your interview with the Princess.'

Declan sank into one of the low squashy sofas, which, with his long legs, were desperately uncomfortable unless one was lying down.

Tony leant back in his chair: 'Cameron and I have decided it's time you spread your wings, Declan.'

Declan looked wary.

'We'd like you to interview Maurice Wooton this week.'

'He's not big enough,' said Declan flatly. Lord Wooton was a high-profile Cotchester property developer but of little interest nationally. 'And I'm already doing Graham Greene this week.'

'That's OK,' said Cameron. 'Do Lord Wooton as a special after the ten o'clock news on Friday night.'

'Why can't James do him?'

'James is already doing Sarah Stratton in the Famous Man slot on "Cotswold Round-Up". Besides, we want you.'

'I'm only contracted to do one interview a week.'

'Don't worry,' said Tony. 'We'll pay you extra. We just want you to get really involved in the station.'

'I don't have the time.' It was so hot in Tony's office that Declan could feel his shirt drenched in sweat.

'That's what researchers are for,' said Cameron, as though she was explaining to a two-year-old. 'Deirdre Kilpatrick's been working on Maurice Wooton all week. She's come up with some terrific stuff. After all,' she added tauntingly, 'a guy as great as Henry Moore wasn't too proud to employ studio assistants.'

Like a dog struggling out of a weed-clogged pond, Declan heaved himself up from the squashy sofa. 'I do my own research,' he said coldly, and walked out.

Hooray, thought Cameron, it's begun to work.

On Thursday morning Cameron rang Declan at home. It was his official day off. He'd stayed up until four in the morning reading Graham Greene. Inspired, he was determined to spend the next two days on his Yeats biography, and here was Cameron's horrible rasp ordering him to come into a meeting tomorrow at eleven o'clock.

'So we can kick some ideas around about the line you might take with Maurice Wooton.'

Declan hung up on her. When he hadn't shown up by eleven-thirty the following morning, Cameron rang The Priory in a fury. She got Maud, who said she was sorry but Declan was in bed.

'At this hour? Is he ill?'

'Not at all,' said Maud. 'He's reading.'

'Put him on.'

Declan told Cameron to go and jump in the River Fleet and that he'd no intention of coming in for any meeting. Tony then rang Declan and ordered him to come in that evening and interview Maurice Wooton. Declan, having just received an eighty-thousand-pound tax bill, which he had no way of ever paying unless he went on working at Corinium, said he'd be in later, but wouldn't submit questions beforehand.

He slid into Corinium around two o'clock, when he knew Cameron and Tony would still be at lunch, and went down to the newsroom to talk to Sebastian Burrows, the youngest, brightest and therefore most frustrated of the reporters.

'Deirdre Kilpatrick's been working like mad on your Maurice Wooton interview,' said Seb.

'Deirdre Kill-Programme,' said Declan.

Seb grinned: 'You can say that again. Maurice is emerging as a total sweetie.'

'You got any dirt on him?' asked Declan.

'He's one of Tony's best friends, isn't that enough?'

'Not quite – anything concrete?'

Sebastian's thin face lit up. 'I've got enough to send him down for ten years, but I daren't use it.'

'Give it to me,' said Declan. 'I'm going out.'

On the same Friday, Rupert Campbell-Black, having spent all week in meetings with the FA and the Club Managers trying to thrash out some suitable compromise on football hooliganism, decided he felt like a pit pony who needed a day off, and went hunting with Basil Baddingham.

Scent was very bad, however. It rained all day and the foxes sensibly decided to stay in their earths. Having re-boxed their horses, Rupert and Bas got back to Rupert's dark-blue Aston-Martin to find the windscreen covered with leaves like parking tickets. Removing their drenched red coats and hunting ties, and putting on jerseys, they drove home through the yellow gloom.

'Who shall we do this evening?' said Bas, who was feeling randy.

'No one,' sighed Rupert. 'I've got my red box to go through, and I've got to look in at some fund-raising drinks party.'

'Pity,' said Bas slyly, 'I was going to show you the most amazing girl.'

'That's different,' said Rupert. 'Where does she live?'

'Penscombe Priory.'

Thinking Bas meant Maud, Rupert said, 'Isn't she a bit long in the tooth for you?'

'No, I'm talking about the daughter,' said Bas. 'She's absolutely stunning.'

.

Back at The Priory, Grace, the housekeeper, who was making ridiculously slow progress sorting out the attic, stumbled on a trunk of Maud's old clothes. Maud, who had just finished her last P. D. James and was suffering from withdrawal symptoms, wandered upstairs and started trying them on. Now she was parading round in a black-and-red-striped mini which fell just below her groin and showed off her still beautiful legs.

'I remember walking down Grafton Street in 1968 in this,' she said, 'and an American clapping his hands over his eyes, and screaming: "Oh my Gard, can they go any higher?" My hair was down like this.' Maud pulled out the combs so it cascaded down her back. 'I was only twenty-four.'

'You don't look a day more than that now. Amizing,' said Grace.

'Oh, I adored this dress too.' Maud tugged a sapphire-blue mini with a pie-frill collar out of the trunk. 'I wore it to Patrick's christening. I wonder if I can still get into it.'

'Fits you like a glove,' said Grace, who was trying on a maxicoat. 'Amizing.'

As Maud admired herself in an ancient full-length mirror propped against the rafters, she heard Gertrude barking. Not displeased with her appearance, she went downstairs, then paused halfway. Below her in the hall, she could see two heads: one very dark, the other gleaming blond. Her heart missed a beat.

'Maud,' yelled Bas, 'are you in?'

'I'm up here,' said Maud with the light behind her.

Bas looked up. 'Caitlin,' he said. 'I thought you'd gone back.'

'It's me.' Maud came slowly down the stairs. 'Grice and I were being silly trying on my old clothes.'

'How old were you when you first wore that?'

'About twenty-one.'

'You look about sixteen today,' said Bas, kissing her.

'Flattery will get you an enormous drink. I assume that's what you've come for. Grice,' Maud yelled up the stairs, 'can you come down and fix some drinks? I'll go and change.'

'Don't,' said Rupert. 'I bet Declan fell in love with you in that dress. I'm quite safe,' he went on, also kissing Maud. 'Some bloody hunt saboteur sprayed me with Anti-Mate this afternoon.'

'Where's Declan?' asked Bas, as they went into the kitchen.

'Ordered in to do an extra programme,' said Maud, getting a bottle of whisky out of the larder.

'My evil brother got the screws on him already?' asked Bas. 'Have you got anything to eat? I'm absolutely starving.'

'There's some chocolate cake and a quiche in the larder,' said Maud, splashing whisky into three glasses. 'Have a look and see what you can find.'

Rupert prowled round the room. There was a huge scrubbed table in the centre of the room, with chairs down either side. Poetry and cookery books crammed the shelves in equal proportions. A rocking-horse towered over Gertrude's basket in the corner. Aengus the cat snored on some newly ironed shirts by the Aga. On the walls were drawings of Maud in *Juno and the Paycock*, and a corkboard covered with recipes and photographs of animals, cut by Taggie out of newspapers. Apart from a television set on a chest of drawers, every other available surface seemed to be littered with letters, bills, colour swatches, photographs waiting to be stuck in, dog and cat worming tablets, biros that didn't work, newspapers and magazines.

'Nice kitchen,' said Rupert.

'It's like the room described by Somerville and Ross when they were packing up before moving,' said Maud. 'Under everything, there's something.'

Valerie Jones, who dropped in half an hour later, didn't think it was a nice kitchen at all. She was shocked to find Maud showing at least six inches of bare thigh, and Rupert and Basil with their long-booted legs up on the table, all getting tanked up on Declan's whisky. Rupert was eating bread and bramble jelly and reading the problem page in *Jackie*. Bas was finishing up the remains of a mackerel mousse with a spoon. Gertrude, eyeing the remains of the quiche and the large chocolate cake, was now sitting drooling on the table on a pile of unironed sheets, which would no doubt go straight back on the beds, thought Valerie with a shudder.

Valerie herself, natty in a ginger tweed suit and a deer-stalker, said she had just been to a Distressed Gentlefolk's Committee Meeting with Lady Baddingham, and, deciding to 'straike while the iron was hot', had looked in to see if Maud had any jumble for the Xmas Bazaar next month.

'Having just moved, you must have lots of old junk to throw out.'

'Only her husband,' said Bas, starting on the quiche.

'Hush,' reproved Maud softly. 'Funnily enough, I've just been trying on all my old clothes. This was the dress I wore at Patrick's christening. The priest gathered up my skirt with the christening robes by mistake and all the congregation were treated to the sight of my red pants.'

Valerie didn't want to hear about Maud's pants. 'Then you must have lots of jumble,' she said.

'I never throw clothes away,' said Maud.

'Well, I've brought you a brochure of our Autumn range,' said Valerie, determined to turn the visit to some advantage.

'Kind,' said Maud, chucking the brochure into the débris on the Welsh dresser. 'Have a drink.'

'Ay'm driving. Have you got anything soft?' said Valerie.

'Not round here, with Maud wearing that dress,' said Rupert, cutting himself a piece of chocolate cake.

'I'll have a tea then,' said Valerie, 'and I'd love a piece of that gâteau, and those bramble preserves look quite delicious.'

'Taggie picked the blackberries down your valley; we ought to give you a pot,' Maud said to Rupert, as she put the kettle on. She felt wildly happy.

At that moment Grace walked in, wearing Maud's red and black mini.

'This is Amizing Grice,' said Maud.

'Amizing,' said Grace, gazing at Rupert in wonder. 'I'm just off to that lecture on glass-blowing at the Women's Institute, Maud,' she went on. 'See you later.'

'I didn't know there was a WI meeting tonight,' said Valerie, perplexed.

'Straight up to the pub,' explained Maud, as the front door banged.

'It's not a very good idea to be on Christian name terms with one's help,' said Valerie reprovingly. 'We don't really do it in Gloucestershire, you know.'

''Bye, Grace! Have a good evening,' yelled Rupert.

Valerie's small mouth tightened. Watching Maud pouring boiling water over a teabag, she hoped the mug was clean.

'This quiche is seriously good,' said Bas. 'And for Christ's sake leave some of that chocolate cake, Rupert.'

'Did Grace make it?' enquired Valerie. Maybe Grace was more of a treasure than she had at first appeared.

'Grace can't cook a thing,' said Maud. 'Taggie made all this. She wants to break into catering and do people's dinner parties.'

'She'd better come and work at the Bar Sinister,' said Bas. 'Darling, I wondered where you'd got to.' He swung his feet off the table and stood up as Taggie came in.

She was very pale, with her hair in a thick black plait down her back, and wearing one of Declan's red shirts above long, long bare legs.

'Hullo,' she said in delight to Bas. Then, embarrassed that he aimed straight at her mouth, turned her head slightly so he ended up kissing her hair. At that moment, over his shoulder, she saw Rupert. She gave a gasp of horror and turned as red as her shirt.

To Valerie's equal horror, Maud removed the teabag from Valerie's tea with her fingers. Then she introduced Taggie to everyone.

Smiling at Valerie, but totally ignoring Rupert, Taggie took a tin of baked beans out of the fridge and started to eat them with a spoon.

'I'm sure we've met before,' said Rupert, puzzled. 'You're not a Young Conservative, are you?' Then, suddenly he twigged and started to laugh. 'I remember now. It was at a tennis party.'

Taggie blushed even deeper.

'Brilliant quiche, stunning mousse, marvellous chocolate cake,' said Bas with his mouth full.

'Oh, it was for Daddy's supper,' began Taggie, distressed, then stopped herself. Sometimes she could murder her mother. She was about to go upstairs when Bas grabbed her hand and, sitting her down beside him, tried to persuade her to work for him at the Bar Sinister.

'It's really kind of you,' mumbled Taggie, 'but I worked in a restaurant for two years. I want to branch out on my own.'

'You can come and cook my breakfast any day of the week,' said Rupert. She looked so different from the angry child who'd screamed at him about his stubble. 'You were quite right,' he added to Basil.

Again Taggie ignored him.

'It's very good of Bas,' said Maud with a slight edge to her voice. 'Most girls would leap at a job like that. I always had to de-emphasize my career for Declan,' she added fretfully.

Taggie, however, was totally thrown. She couldn't take in what Bas was saying. She was only conscious of this horrible monster, who'd haunted her nightmares for weeks, whom she'd last seen oiled, brown-skinned, erect in every sense of the word and as totally unselfconscious of his nakedness as a Zulu chief, and who was now drinking her father's whisky and laughing at her across the table. Out of sheer nervousness, she leapt up and turned on the television.

'Pratt,' yelled Rupert, as James Vereker appeared on the screen.

Over at Corinium Television Sarah Stratton sat in Hospitality going greener (perhaps that was why it was called a green room), and wishing she'd never agreed to go on James's programme.

The appalling Deirdre Kill-Programme (as everyone called her now) had visited her at home earlier in the week and worked out lots of questions that James could ask Sarah to promote discussion and bring in James's caring nature.

Paul, furious that Sarah had been asked on, and not him, went on and on about how her high profile wouldn't help his career at the moment. He was also furious that she'd spent a fortune for the occasion on a new black mohair dress with daisies embroidered on the front and huge padded shoulders, which she was not sure suited her. Thank God Rupert was at some Tory fund-raising bash at the moment, and wouldn't watch the programme. Earlier, James had paid a fleeting visit to Hospitality to say hullo, rather like a famous surgeon in an expensive hospital, popping in before he removes half your intestine.

Ushered into the studio during the commercial break, Sarah was now sitting on the famous pale-pink sofa beside him. Catching sight of herself on the monitor, she wished she hadn't worn the mohair; it was much too hot and the padded shoulders made her look like an American footballer. On rushed the make-up girl to tone down her flushed face.

'Collar up, James,' said Wardrobe.

'I did it deliberately, Tessa,' said James. 'Thought it looked more casual. Remember to look at me, not the camera, Sarah.' She was desperately nervous, which didn't help. Glancing round at the idiot board to find out what question he was supposed to ask her first, he saw chalked in large letters: 'James Vereker can't do his programme without having a bonk first'.

'Turn it over,' hissed James, as a burst of 'Cotswold Round-Up' theme music signified the end of the commercial break.

Sarah, who had also seen the idiot board, screamed with laughter, and it was thus that the viewers had their first glimpse of her.

'Sarah Stratton,' said James, reading from the turned-over board, 'you've been married to Paul Stratton, our member for Cotchester for nearly nine months now. How do you see your role as the wife of an MP, Sarah?'

Sarah straightened her face: 'To support my husband in every possible way,' she said, gazing straight at the camera.

In the O'Haras' kitchen, Rupert turned up the sound.

'Isn't that Lizzie Vereker's husband?' said Maud. 'I like Lizzie.'

165

'She's lovely,' said Rupert. 'If she lost three stone, I'd marry her.'

'James is hell,' said Basil. 'Put him in front of a camera, you can't get him down with a gun.'

'Some viewers may find the following scenes disturbing,' said Rupert. 'Sarah's nervous. Look at the way her eyes are darting and she's licking her lips. Looks bloody good, though.'

Whatever she thought to the contrary, Sarah looked stunning on camera. She was now saying how hard it was falling in love with a married man.

'I put no pressure on Paul to leave his first wife,' she said demurely.

'Bollocks,' howled Bas. 'She carried a chisel round in her bag for years, trying to chip Paul off like a barnacle.'

'But because he did eventually leave her for me,' went on Sarah, 'and *he* made the decision, I'm branded a scarlet woman.'

'With some justification,' said Rupert. 'And her husband is as mean as the grave. It's so hard to get a drink in his house, the PM ought to make him the Minister for Drought. Which is not something anyone could accuse *you* of, Maud darling,' he added, as Maud splashed the last of the whisky into his glass.

Taggie, who was ironing sheets, was as perplexed as Rupert had been earlier. 'I'm sure I've seen her somewhere before,' she muttered, then once again went absolutely scarlet as she realized that Sarah was the beautiful blonde who'd been playing nude tennis with Rupert.

'She's quite excellent at ball play,' said Rupert, reading Taggie's thoughts. 'And *you're* going to burn that sheet.'

Furiously, Taggie went on ironing. Fortunately a diversion was created with Valerie asking how Caitlin was getting on at Upland House.

'It seems more like St Trinian's than Enid Blyton,' said Maud. 'Caitlin says they all smoke like chimneys and have bottles of Malibu under the floorboards. But I had a nice half-term report from her house mistress, saying Caitlin was a dear girl who'd settled in well, but was too easily satisfied.'

166

'Not something her future husband is going to grumble about,' said Rupert, who was watching Taggie. He liked making her blush.

'Caitlin's like Taggie,' said Maud. 'Watches too much television.'

'Sharon's only allowed to watch occasionally at weekends,' said Valerie smugly. 'When I was young, my sister and I made our own amusements.'

'So did I,' agreed Rupert, 'until Nanny told me it would make me go blind.'

Ignoring him, Valerie thought how much more attractive was James, with his charming boyish smile, than Rupert, who was always leading Freddie astray and making *risqué* remarks.

James, winding up Sarah's interview, asked her if she had any plans for a career.

'You must know – as a very famous man yourself,' Sarah answered admiringly, 'that wives of famous men have to take second place.'

'It is possible to be famous and caring, Sarah,' said James huskily.

'Of course,' said Sarah. 'I'm just saying if you marry someone who's been married before, you're just that little bit more anxious to make the marriage work, to *not* put your own career first – to prove everyone wrong who said it wouldn't last. So you just try harder.'

Taggie was shocked. How *could* Sarah say that, when she was busy having an affair with Rupert? It was only after a few minutes Taggie realized that Valerie was telling her all about the boutique.

'You must pop in some time,' said Valerie. 'I know it's difficult, dressing when you're so tall, but I'm sure I could find something lovely for you.'

'That's really kind,' said Taggie gratefully.

Rupert, watching Taggie, decided she really was very beautiful. It was as though someone had taken a fine black pen and drawn lines along her lashes and round the irises of those amazing silver-grey eyes. Her nose was too large, but

167

the curve of the soft pink mouth emphasized by the very short upper lip was adorable, and he'd like to see all that lustrous black hair spilling over a pillow. She must be nearly five foot ten, he reckoned, and most of it legs, and she had the gentle, apologetic clumsiness of an Irish wolfhound, who can't help knocking off teacups with its tail.

Noticing Rupert observing Taggie with such lazy, almost lustful affection, Maud felt a stab of jealousy.

'Go and get another bottle of whisky from the larder, Tag,' she said sharply, 'and clear away all these plates.'

'But it's Daddy's last bottle,' protested Taggie.

Furious, Maud turned on her. 'As if your father would deny a guest a drink in his own house.'

Trembling, Taggie switched off the iron, fetched the bottle from the larder and dumped it on the table with a crash. Gertrude was whining by the back door.

'I'll take you out, darling,' said Taggie, pulling on a pair of black gumboots.

'Do wrap up warm,' said Valerie. 'And if you want to get on in the country, you should wear green wellies,' she added kindly.

'If you really want to get on in the country,' drawled Rupert, 'you should get that dog's tail straightened.'

It was the final straw. Giving him a filthy look, Taggie went out, slamming the back door behind her.

'What's up with her?' asked Bas.

'In love,' said Maud, unscrewing the bottle of whisky. 'Some friend of Patrick's who hardly knows she exists. You know how moody teenagers are.'

Outside it was deliciously mild. The wind was shepherding parties of orange leaves across the lawn and sighing in the wood. The stream after the recent rain was hurtling down the garden. Above, russet clouds like stretched cotton wool didn't quite cover the sky. Every so often through a chink glittered a brilliant star. Still shaking, Taggie tramped down the rose walk that so often in the past must have been paced by nuns, like her, praying for deliverance.

'Oh, please God, get that horrible horrible man out of the house.'

She couldn't stop thinking of Rupert's lean oiled body, under the dark-blue jersey and mud-spattered white breeches. It was obvious her mother was wildly attracted to him; she'd seen the rapt expression, the flushed cheeks, the wild drinking so often before. And Rupert was leading her mother on, making those beastly salacious (there, at last she'd used her word for the day) remarks, and drinking all her father's drink, and eating all his supper.

Despite the mildness of the night, she shivered as she contemplated the rows ahead if Maud started one of her things. She, Taggie, would get dragged in to provide alibis. Well, she wouldn't cover up for her mother this time, she wouldn't, she wouldn't.

Her father didn't want hassle at the moment; he needed keeping calm. Turning towards the house, its great battlements and turrets confronting the shadowy garden with a timeless strength, she felt slightly comforted. Surely the house would look after them.

After 'Cotswold Round-Up', James and Sarah, both feeling rather elated, were soon cut down to size.

'What did you think of the interview, Cameron?' asked James.

'I'd rather watch slugs copulate,' snapped Cameron.

Sarah in turn rang Paul. 'Was I OK?' she asked eagerly.

'You were very clear,' said Paul. 'Have you seen Tony?'

'Yes,' said Sarah sulkily.

'Did he say anything about putting me on the Board?'

'No,' said Sarah.

'Come and have a drink,' said James, as she slammed down the receiver.

'Yes please,' said Sarah.

Soon after Taggie took Gertrude out, Valerie went home. Maud, Basil and Rupert carried on carousing. Going into the kitchen much later, Taggie was relieved to find only Bas and Maud.

'Daddy's interviewing Lord Wooton in a few minutes,' she said.

'My husband,' Maud told Basil, 'always becomes the person he's interviewing. When he did Margaret Thatcher he spent the week wearing power suits, talking about "circumstarnces", and calling me Denis in bed.'

Noticing Taggie's look of disapproval, Basil patted the chair beside him and said the interview should be interesting as Tony was pulling out every stop to get Maurice Wooton to join the Corinium Board.

Rupert returned from the downstairs loo, waving the *New Statesman*. 'Don't tell me Declan reads this,' he said in outrage.

Maud nodded. 'And actually believes it.'

'But he can't be a socialist when he earns such a vast salary.'

'I know,' sighed Maud. 'He's utterly inconsistent.'

'I expect he'd like to give some of it away,' protested Taggie angrily, 'if everyone didn't spend it all.'

'If you can't keep a civil tongue in your head,' snapped Maud, 'you'd better go to bed.' She'd never known Taggie answer back like this.

Over in Studio 3 Declan always went into himself before a programme, but he nodded when Tony came on to the floor, reeking of brandy and waving a huge cigar. Tony was in an excellent mood; two of Corinium's news stories had been used with a by-line by ITN; he'd just had an excellent dinner with Maurice Wooton, and now he'd got his way about Declan doing this interview, it was the thin end of the wedge. Declan couldn't refuse to do other specials now – Freddie Jones next week, perhaps.

'Maurice is just having a pee. He's been made-up,' he said to Declan. 'Give him a nice easy ride. He may have a reputation as a hatchet man, but he runs a huge empire, he's devoted to his grandchildren and does an enormous amount for charity. He's also delightful if you get him on to opera or his cats.'

'Just show his caring face, Declan,' said Cameron from the control room. 'And Camera 2, can you try to avoid Lord Wooton's bald patch?'

Tonight's vision mixer, sitting in front of her row of lit-up buttons, massaged her neck and opened a Kit Kat. It had been a long day. Daysee Butler fingered her stop-watch. In his earpiece Declan could hear her talking about her boyfriend: 'He's cooking supper for me tonight, cod in cheese sauce out of a packet. He's got such charisma.'

Lord Wooton was now being ushered in by the floor manager. He had plainly had too much to drink with Tony, but Make-up had toned him down with green foundation, and blacked out his greying sideboards. His revoltingly sensual face with the big red pouting lower lip was just like one of Tony's orchids, thought Declan, as he rose to his feet to welcome him.

'Very warm night,' said Lord Wooton.

'Very,' said Declan.

The introductory package, which Cameron had written, was full of nice stills and clips of Lord Wooton romping with cats, visiting children in hospital, playing cricket with grandsons, watching the first bricks of various buildings being laid, and collecting an OBE at the Palace. He was plainly delighted.

'Don't know where they dug up all those old photographs,' he said untruthfully.

'Ten seconds to end of opening package, Declan,' said Daysee from the control room.

Surreptitiously Declan removed his earpiece and put it in his pocket. His first question was sycophancy itself.

'As the leading property developer in Gloucestershire, probably the whole of the West Country, you must be proud of your achievement.'

Maurice Wooton put his hands together happily.

'One is only as good as the people who work for one, Declan,' he said smoothly. 'You must know that. I have first-rate people, hand-picked of course.'

171

'Pity you don't take better care of them,' said Declan amiably.

He then proceeded to carve Maurice Wooton up, starting with one of his managers who'd been sacked while he was in hospital recovering from open-heart surgery, then proceeding to another who'd been given no compensation when he broke his back falling off some scaffolding.

Tony rang Cameron in the control box.

'What the fuck's going on?' he roared. 'Tell him to ask Maurice about his fucking grandchildren.'

'I can't get through to him,' yelled Cameron. 'He's taken out his earpiece.'

'Well, tell the floor manager to tell him to put it fucking back in again.'

Ignoring all Maurice Wooton's spluttering denials, Declan moved on to illegal takeovers, shady deals, and then produced a just-published secret Town Hall report, which claimed that, despite a huge grant from the Council, his firm had built a block of flats cheap to faulty specifications.

Temporarily speechless now, Maurice Wooton was mouthing like a great purple bull frog.

'Another even more unattractive aspect of your business career,' went on Declan relentlessly, 'was the way you bribed three Labour councillors in the housing department at Cotchester Town Hall to give you the contract for the tower block development on Bankside.'

'This is preposterous,' exploded Maurice Wooton.

'You deny it?'

'Of course I do.'

Out of the corner of his eye, Declan could see the floor manager making frantic signals for him to replace his earpiece.

Ignoring them, he said: 'Why, then, do Councillor Bridie, Councillor Yallop, and Councillor Rogers have five thousand pounds entered on their bank statements, paid in by you from a Swiss bank account? Here are the photostats of the bank statements, the cheques, and your letters to them.' Declan brandished them under Maurice Wooton's hairy expanding crimson nostrils, then threw them down on the table. 'Thank

God there are some Town Hall officials left with integrity.'

Cameron was so insane with rage, she stubbed her cigarette out by mistake on the hand of the vision mixer, who, screaming, pressed the wrong button, which ran in telecine of a lot of very fat schoolgirls doing an eightsome reel.

'Go back to one, take fucking one,' screamed Cameron.

The schoolgirls disappeared in mid-dance to be replaced by Maurice Wooton, standing up and shouting at Declan that the whole thing was a trumped-up pack of lies, and he was going home to ring his lawyers. Next moment he'd stormed out, leaving the studio in uproar. Declan sat turned to stone in his chair.

To their great disappointment, Corinium's viewers were then treated to soothing music and a film showing close-ups of Cotchester's wild flowers, so they missed Tony roaring into the studio, so angry he could hardly get the words out.

'I've spent five years courting that man,' he spluttered. 'He was just about to join the Board and put fifteen million into our satellite project.'

Declan rose to his feet, towering over Tony.

'You should have given me time to research him properly,' he said coldly. 'I might have found something nice to ask him, but I doubt it.' And with that, he walked out of the studio.

Back at The Priory, Rupert, wiping his eyes, turned to Maud: 'That was the best television programme I've seen for years and free schoolgirls thrown in, too. After Tony Baddingham, Maurice Wooton is without doubt the biggest shit in England, and your husband is the first socialist I've ever really admired. The Corinium switchboard must be absolutely jammed, or "preserved", as dear Valerie would say, with congratulatory calls.'

At that moment the telephone rang. Rupert picked it up.

'Brilliant programme,' said a voice. 'It's the Western Daily Press. Is Declan in?'

'What did I tell you?' said Rupert, handing the receiver to

Maud. 'Don't look so cross,' he added to Taggie. 'I'll nip home in a minute and get your father another bottle.'

After Rupert had returned with the whisky, and he and Bas had left, Taggie watched her mother go to the hall mirror, fluff up her hair on top and smooth the dress over her hips, before sitting down at the drawing-room piano. She must be very drunk, thought Taggie, judging by the number of wrong notes.

What on earth could she give her father for supper, she wondered wearily, as she started to load the washing-up machine. Perhaps she ought to accept Bas's offer of a job, and get out and meet people. She couldn't eat her heart out for Ralphie for ever. She heard the front door bang. Going into the hall, she saw Declan gazing into the drawing-room at Maud playing Schumann in the dress she'd worn when they were first married, living blissfully on no money in Ireland. Her hair almost touched the piano stool.

Putting his hands on her shoulder, he said, 'Why did you put that on?'

'Grice and I were tidying away some of my old clothes.'

'You look beautiful.'

Schumann halted abruptly, as Declan's hands slid under the pie-frill collar. 'Let's go to bed.'

As Maud walked upstairs in front of him, his hands slid up between her bare thighs:

'Christ, you're wet.'

Maud smiled sleepily. 'I've been thinking all evening about your coming home.'

RIVALS
14

Tony would have sacked any other member of his staff for savaging Maurice Wooton like that. As it was he spent the weekend poring over Declan's contract with the lawyers. Unfortunately there was no clause about not presenting his victims with unpalatable truths. So in the end Tony merely wrote Declan a sharp note accusing him of misconduct and warning him that if he stepped out of line a second and third time he'd be out on his ear.

Tony's guns were further spiked by the Government immediately ordering an investigation into Cotchester Town Hall's Housing policy, and by the very favourable press coverage of the programme and Corinium in particular.

'*Corinium show their teeth at last*,' wrote the *Western Daily Press*.

'*Corinium prove they're no longer a Tory poodle*,' wrote the *Guardian*.

Hardest for Tony to take was an enthusiastic telephone call from the IBA: 'Splendid stuff, Tony. No one can accuse you of political bias now.'

The following Wednesday there was a Corinium Board meeting. Tony's temper was not improved when one of the non-executive directors, old Lady Evesham, Vice Chancellor of the local university, arrived on her bicycle in the pouring rain, just as Tony rolled up in the Rolls. Why did the stupid old bag always arrive an hour early and go nosing round the office, talking to staff and stirring up trouble? Hoping she'd go away, Tony cringed behind the *Financial Times*. Next minute she was tapping on the window. Grudgingly, Tony lowered it a few inches.

'Congratulations,' said Lady Evesham, thrusting her wrinkled, whiskery muzzle towards him. 'That interview with Maurice Wooton's the sort of thing we should be doing all the time. Routing out injustice. Man's a rogue. I shall seek out Declan and tell him so in person.'

Tony, however, had other things on his mind. In the same telephone call praising Declan's interview, the IBA had complained that Corinium still wasn't giving sufficient attention to the Southampton end of the area.

'Charles Fairburn has just finished a programme on Isaac Watts,' Tony had countered swiftly.

'Who's he?' asked the IBA's Head of Television.

'Famous philosopher, poet, teacher.' Tony hastily consulted the advance programme notes. 'Watts Square in Southampton is named after him. Wrote "Oh God, our help in ages past".'

'That's not much help in ages present,' said the IBA. 'People in Southampton will hardly regard one hour on the Sunday Godslot as good enough. We're talking about news coverage. There was nothing for example about HMS *Princess Michael of Kent* catching fire at the docks on Friday. The BBC devoted seven minutes to the story.'

'I'll look into it,' said Tony.

As a result of this conversation, Tony summoned his two most valuable executive directors, who usually worked in London but who had come down for the board meeting, into his office beforehand. Known as 'Beauty and the Beast', Georgie Baines and Ginger Johnson looked after sales and finance respectively.

Gorgeous Georgie, who had big brown eyes and even bigger expenses, was up to every single fiddle and lived in the big advertising agencies' pockets, which he lined as effectively as his own. He also made vast sums of money for Corinium. Ginger Johnson, the Beast, was a thug, with carroty hair and a beetroot face, like a particularly unappetizing winter salad. As Financial Director, he saw that the vast sums netted by Georgie were administered as remuneratively as possible. All the most important business on the agenda was always done by the three men before the board meeting.

Going into Tony's office that Wednesday, Georgie and Ginger found him looking at a map of the area.

'If we're going to hang on to the franchise,' said Tony, 'we've got to be properly represented.'

'So?' said Georgie, who'd heard this all before.

'We're going to build a studio here.' Tony jabbed the red dot of Southampton with his finger.

'Cost a fortune,' said Ginger, aghast. 'Even a small studio'll set us back five million. We don't need a studio there.'

'Nor do we want to make any more programmes,' said Georgie. 'Programmes cost too much money.'

'The IBA will love the idea,' said Tony happily. 'More programmes, more employment, better coverage. We don't have to actually build the fucking thing. But if we wave Board sanction and some provisional architect's plans under the IBA's nose, it'll keep them quiet until the franchise is in the bag.'

'I'm sure the Board won't wear it, when we're slashing budgets everywhere else,' said Ginger.

'Leave it to me,' said Tony.

Tony was at his best and his most urbane at board meetings. On his right and left sat Georgie looking beautiful, and Ginger looking ugly. Beyond them sat Simon Harris, who never spoke, and Miss Madden taking the minutes. Beyond these two, down the long elm table, sat members of the Great and the Good, including an MP for Stroud, a winner at Badminton, a famous composer who lived in Oxford, an educationalist from Stratford, a bishop, a famous footballer, and several industrialists who lived in the area, and, of course, Lady Evesham.

As the meeting got under way, everyone expressed great satisfaction at the kudos Declan's programmes had given

Corinium. Resolutions were then passed, budget cuts agreed. Lady Evesham then held up the meeting for at least twenty minutes. First she handed round marmite sandwiches. Having risen at six to write her biography of Emily Pankhurst, she was very hungry. Then she raised a complaint from 'an unnamed young woman researcher' – actually Deirdre Kilpatrick – who'd been denied the right to breastfeed in the newsroom.

'Oh Christ,' thought Tony, glaring at Simon Harris.

Typically, it was Simon who had given Deirdre the go-ahead to bring her baby in, because he thought bonding was all important. Deirdre had then proceeded to whip out great grey tits all over the building. As the *coup de grâce*, Baby Kilpatrick had regurgitated milk into one of the newsroom word processors just as Charles Fairburn was showing the Bishop of Salisbury round the building. Charles had promptly fainted and Tony had banished the baby.

Now Tony cleared his throat: '*I* told the girl not to bring her baby in any more,' he said to Lady Evesham. 'It was quite old enough to go on the bottle, and she's got a perfectly good nanny at home. It distracted my reporters in the newsroom.'

'Surely they should be above that kind of distraction?' said Lady Evesham frostily. 'This is the twentieth century.'

'If one girl is allowed to bring her baby in, they all will.'

The famous footballer, who was given to ribaldry, then said it was always the ugly old feminist boots who wanted to breastfeed in public. If the pretty ones wanted to do it, none of the blokes would mind. He received a stony glare from Lady Evesham.

Tony, who thoroughly agreed with the famous footballer, but had to pretend to look disapproving, thought it was high time Lady Evesham resigned, and Cameron, who wouldn't stand any truck with breastfeeders, took her place on the Board.

Saying he'd look into it, Tony moved briskly on to the subject of cutting costs. He then proceeded to bore the meeting rigid with details of expenditure on stationery and calculators, and whether it was really necessary to supply the sales' staff with portable computers. Everyone glazed as he compared the merits of endless different models.

It was two minutes to one. Hearing the chink of bottles in the director's dining-room next door, everyone perked up. A delicious smell of boeuf Wellington drifted under the door.

'Well, that's all for the day,' said Tony. Then, as everyone dived for their bags and briefcases, he added, 'Except for one item that may not be on everyone's agenda: the proposed new studio in Southampton. The question of our not giving sufficient attention to the Southampton end of the territory has been raised before.'

'Hear, hear,' said the footballer, who'd once played for the Saints.

'You've all agreed the idea of a new studio in principle,' went on Tony.

The directors scratched their heads. . . . Had they? They were instantly distracted by another waft of boeuf Wellington.

'The building of the studios will create a lot of employment in the area,' said Tony briskly. 'We've got a costing which can be easily accommodated within the budget. Ginger?' He cocked an eyebrow at Ginger Johnson.

'Easily,' said Ginger.

'And you're for it, Georgie?'

'Very much so,' said Georgie, who was lost in admiration. 'Simon?'

Simon Harris had been so unnerved by the breastfeeding incident that he nodded even before Tony got his name out.

'Oh look, it's snowing,' said the footballer, distracting people even further.

'Everyone else in favour?' Tony smiled down the table.

Lady Evesham's was the only dissenting hand.

'Good,' said Tony, gathering up his papers. 'Come and have a drink everyone and meet Declan O'Hara.'

Any further thoughts about studios evaporated as they surged next door.

There was great excitement at Corinium the following Wednesday, when Dame Nellie Finegold, a friend of Lady

Evesham, and one of the last surviving suffragettes, who'd agreed to come on Declan's programme that evening, dropped dead from a heart attack.

Even greater excitement was caused when the Prime Minister, who was in Gloucestershire opening a new hospital and later dining with the Cotchester Regiment, graciously agreed to step into Dame Nellie's shoes to balance Declan's extremely favourable interview with the Leader of the Opposition the previous week. The Prime Minister, appreciating the value of preaching to eighteen million viewers, thought she could handle Declan. Her one condition, which Tony leapt at, was that Declan should submit questions first, and make an undertaking not to depart from them.

'This is our chance to nail him,' Tony told Cameron gleefully. 'If he submits questions today, we can insist he does the same for all future interviews. Then we can manipulate him to our own advantage. You've seen how lethal he can be with Maurice; just think what havoc he could cause in an election year.'

Declan looked tired and tense as he walked into Tony's office waving a sheaf of the Prime Minister's cuttings. Tipping back his chair, Tony stretched his legs and gazed consideringly at him for a moment.

'This is a big day for you, Declan.'

Declan grunted. 'I'm very much looking foward to shaking her by – ' he paused – 'the neck.'

'Now, now,' said Tony, 'let's keep it all sweetness and light.'

'The PM's only coming on the programme if she knows exactly what you're going to ask her, and no funny business,' said Cameron.

'Don't be ridiculous,' snapped Declan. 'Why should she be treated differently to anyone else?'

'Because she's the PM, dumbass, and the IBA is ultimately answerable to her, so she's got to be kept sweet.'

'Not by me she hasn't.'

'Don't be so fucking pigheaded,' screeched Cameron.

180

An almighty row followed, ending in Declan flatly refusing to do the interview and walking out.

Cameron and Tony exchanged glances of joy and horror – what the hell were they going to do? The Prime Minister was already in the area. She was due at the studios at seven-forty to go on air at eight. The network had been trailing Declan's dramatic change of guest since lunchtime.

'James will have to do it,' said Tony. 'But we won't announce the change of plan until just before transmission, or we'll lose the audience.'

In his office, having just re-written his links for 'Cotswold Round-Up', James switched off the wireless because he was fed up with hearing Declan's signature tune. Turning to his fan mail, he found a letter from Sarah Stratton thanking him for his standard letter thanking her for coming on the programme. Nice bold handwriting, thought James; he was sure those huge loops to the Ls meant something. During their drink at the bar, he'd decided she was very attractive, and wondered by what ruse he could see her again. But a second later, as Cameron burst into his office, his thoughts were only for one woman: the Prime Minister.

'Deirdre's working on your questions at the moment,' said Cameron. 'We've got to rush them over to the PM at Gloucester so she can look at them while she's changing. We should be able to let you have them about five. If you've got any questions to add, let Deirdre know. Here's a brief of what the PM's been up to in the last two months, but you're pretty well briefed anyway, aren't you?'

James blushed. It was the first compliment Cameron had ever paid him.

'I thought Declan was doing this interview.'

'Declan's sick,' said Cameron.

'Seriously?' said James, trying to look suitably caring.

'Not nearly seriously enough,' said Cameron viciously.

As soon as she'd gone, thanking God he'd had his hair streaked last week, James rang Lizzie: 'I'll be late. I've got to interview the PM.'

'My God! Ask her when she last got laid.'

'Don't be silly, this is for real. I'm sending a driver over for my blue suit, and could you put in my jade-green silk shirt, and the sapphire-blue tie. And could you phone the Strattons and ask them to record the programme.' He wanted Sarah to witness his hour of glory. 'I don't trust our machine one hundred per cent.'

You mean you don't trust me to remember, thought Lizzie.

Cameron, popping in to the studio later on her way to the control room, was nearly knocked sideways by Aramis.

'She's arrived. Tony'll bring her through in a minute. Are you nervous?'

'Not yet,' said James, re-plumping cushions on the pastel-pink sofa.

'Nice change from Declan,' said Cameron. 'Good luck.'

Perhaps he'd maligned Cameron, thought James, as he combed his hair for the hundredth time and removed the shine on his nose with Nouveau Beige creme puff. He used to use Gay Whisper, but had decided the name had rather unfortunate connotations.

The Prime Minister, like most women, had a weakness for charming, handsome men. Seeing her appearing through the black curtain, radiant in dark-blue taffeta, being guided over the cables and uneven surfaces by Tony, James leapt to his feet. For a second Diorella fought with Aramis. Aramis won easily.

'Welcome to Cotchester, Prime Minister. I can't tell you how privileged I feel to meet you,' said James, giving her the benefit of his beautiful aquamarine eyes, now subtly enhanced by the jade-green shirt and the sapphire-blue tie. Then, when she offered him her hand, he bowed his streaked head and kissed it reverently.

'Silly cunt,' muttered the Senior Cameraman.

'Come and sit down,' said James.

Down came the famous bottom on the pastel-pink sofa.

'I'll leave you in good hands, Prime Minister,' said Tony.

'Indeed, Lord Baddingham,' said the PM in her low voice. The interview was pure Barbara Cartland. Aware no difficult questions would be forthcoming, the PM was at her most relaxed and charming, and unbent to James as she'd never done before on television.

'Prepared only to see the steely side of your character, Prime Minister, some people make the ridiculous mistake of thinking you don't care about the unemployed or the old and poverty-stricken.'

'Mr Vereker – ' the Prime Minister's voice dropped an octave – 'if only you could realize the sleepless nights we spend worrying about hypothermia, particularly with another winter coming on.'

'How many more times is the stupid asshole going to use the word "caring",' snarled Cameron to Tony, who'd stayed with her in the Control Room.

'Hush, she's really unbuttoning,' purred Tony.

During the commercial break, the PM became positively skittish.

'They'll be into heavy petting in a minute,' said Cameron as James leant forward in sycophantic ecstasy.

At the end of the second half the Prime Minister even shed tears as she talked of her worries as a mother.

'But you are a mother to all of us,' said James, handing her his Aramis-scented handkerchief.

'Pass me the motion discomfort bag,' groaned Cameron.

'It's good,' said Tony. 'Should win her a lot of votes.'

'Ten seconds to out, James,' said Cameron, flicking on the key switch. 'Close the programme.'

'Thank you, Prime Minister, for showing us your caring face,' said James, 'and please come back to Cotchester again soon.'

As the credits went up, they could be seen laughing and joking together.

'I'm going to frow up,' said the Senior Cameraman.

'Come back, Declan,' muttered the Floor Manager, 'nothing needed to be forgiven.'

'I would love a tape of that programme, Mr Vereker,' said the Prime Minister.

Outside, a second Corinium camera crew filmed her

183

departure, lethargically cheered by a hand-picked crowd of Corinium staff.

'I hope we get overtime for this,' said Charles Fairburn, waving a Union Jack, as a jubilant James, Cameron and Tony accompanied the PM down the steps. Settled in her car, ready to depart to a late dinner with the Cotchester Regiment, the PM wound down her window.

'I hope Mr O'Hara feels better soon,' she said earnestly. 'This flu virus can be very pulling down.'

'About time the mighty Mr O'Hara was pulled down from his seat,' said Cameron, as soon as she had driven off.

'What a caring lady,' sighed James.

He woke next morning to find himself temporarily famous. Both the BBC and ITN picked up the interview, which was fulsomely praised the next day by the Tory press. Only the *Mirror* and the *Guardian* grumbled that James had let the PM get away with murder.

By Friday the story had got out that Declan hadn't been ill at all, but had simply refused to do the interview with the Prime Minister.

'*The Rows Begin Again*,' said a huge headline in the *Sun*.

At the BBC and around the network, people smirked knowingly. They'd known the honeymoon wouldn't last.

15

Declan was having a row about money with Maud in the kitchen when the telephone rang.

'Yes,' he snapped.

'This is Valerie Jones,' said an ultra-refined, vaguely familiar voice.

'Yes,' said Declan, who was no wiser.

'We met at Lady Monica's buffet luncheon. I was wearing a cricket jumper.'

'Oh yes,' Declan twigged – the extremely silly mid-on.

'Fred-Fred and I were wondering if you could come and dayne on December 7th, that's tomorrow week, just a few close friends. Tony and Monica Baddingham. . . .'

Declan had heard enough. He was sorry, he said, but they had a previous engagement.

Maud was absolutely furious. 'We never go out,' she stormed. 'How dare you refuse for me? I might have wanted to go.'

'It was that horrendous dwarf we met at the Baddinghams; bound to have been hell.'

'There might have been other amusing people there. How can we ever meet anyone, if you turn down everything?'

Maud's sulk lasted all day. Declan was trying to get to grips with the volatile, volcanic personality of John McEnroe, who was coming on the programme on Wednesday. Maud's black mood permeated the whole house and totally sabotaged his concentration. At dusk, unable to bear it any longer, he went downstairs and apologized.

'I'm sorry; it was selfish of me. I must work, but you go on your own. I hate it, but I've got to get used to it. Are you lonely?' he went on as Maud clung to him. 'D'you want to go back to London?'

She shook her head violently. 'I just miss my friends. I was wondering if we could give a tiny party for Patrick's birthday on New Year's Eve.'

Declan's heart sank. 'Not really, not this Christmas. We simply can't afford it.'

'It's his twenty-first,' pleaded Maud. 'He's always had such lousy birthdays, having them so near Christmas. Just the tiniest party, half a dozen couples. Taggie can do the food; it'll be good training for her. She's not getting any response from those cards.'

Declan was about to say they still hadn't paid for the Fulham Farewell when the telephone rang again. Taggie picked it up in the kitchen. Five minutes later she rushed, pink-faced with excitement, into the drawing-room.

'The most p-p-prodigious – ' her word for the day – 'thing has happened. Valerie Jones got one of my cards and she's asked me to do her dinner party next Friday. Isn't it prodigious?'

'It is, indeed,' said Declan, disentangling himself from Maud and hugging her.

'She asked us,' said Maud fretfully. 'What are you going to cook for her that we won't get?'

'I've got to go over tomorrow and discuss menus,' said Taggie.

Maud seized her chance. 'Daddy's agreed we can have a little party for Patrick on New Year's Eve,' said Maud, ignoring Declan's look of horror, 'so you can start thinking up some nice food for that.'

Taggie's already euphoric face lit up even further: 'What a prodigious idea.'

Upstairs in her turret bedroom, she clutched herself, pressing her boiling face against one of the thin, cool ecclesiastical windows. If Patrick was having a party, how could Patrick's best friend not be there? She was going to see Ralphie again.

Cooking for Valerie's dinner party was Taggie's first big job, but her nerves were nothing to Valerie's. Valerie was livid with Freddie for asking Rupert, who was coming down to Gloucestershire for a constituency meeting and to present the cup at the Cotchester–Bristol football Derby. Originally he was supposed to be bringing some French actress, but she'd got stuck on location in Scotland. So Valerie'd had to find a spare woman at the last moment. She settled for Cameron Cook who had just won an American award for a documentary about arranged marriages which she'd produced last Spring. Having talked to her briefly at Declan's first programme, Valerie had no idea she was Tony's mistress.

And now Valerie wouldn't stop flapping round the kitchen tasting and criticizing everything Taggie was making – 'A soupçon more cayenne in the cucumber sauce, Agatha – ' or fretting whether they should have cheese before pudding, or who should sit next to whom.

'It says,' she announced, poring over the etiquette book, 'that the most important man should sit on my right.'

'That's me,' said Freddie, roaring with laughter.

'Don't be silly, Fred-Fred,' snapped Valerie, 'and don't pick.'

'That fish pâté's champion,' said Freddie, who'd only been allowed a small salad at lunch.

'Are you going to be all day with that dessert, Agatha?' said Valerie, beadily looking at the huge ice cream and meringue castle, around which Taggie was curling whipped cream to simulate pounding waves. 'The place is a frightful mess.'

'I promise I'll clear up in time. Everything's done but this.'

People were due at eight to eight-thirty to dine at nine. The pheasants, simmered with cranberries and ginger, had to go in at six forty-five.

'You've still got the menus to write out, one for each end

of the table,' said Valerie. 'It would be naice to have them in French.'

Taggie went pale. She couldn't even spell them properly in English; she'd always had trouble with pheasant. She started to shake.

'I'm going to check the rest of the house,' said Valerie.

The lounge looked beautiful. She'd got florists in to provide two beautiful pink arrangements. The dining-room was also a symphony in pink, with a centrepiece of roses. Valerie adored pink; it was so feminine and went so well with her mauve velvet evening gown with the flowing skirt and the trumpet sleeves. She was glad they weren't having soup – Freddie drank it so noisily. She'd worked out where everyone was going to sit. Now, standing at the end of the table, Valerie practised her commands:

'Bring in the appetizer, please, Agatha. Take away the entrée, Agatha. Bring in the dessert.'

Then there was the tricky bit, catching all the women's eyes. She glanced at alternate chairs. 'Shall we go upstairs?'

What happened if that awful Rupert read the message wrong and followed her upstairs too? He was quite capable. For safety, she'd better say: 'Shall we *ladies* go upstairs?'

'We've got a right one 'ere,' said Reg, the hired butler, who'd already well stuck into the Mouton Cadet. 'Yakking away to herself in the dining-room.'

'What am I to do about this menu?' said Taggie helplessly.

'I'll help you. I'm doing French for O-levels,' said Sharon, the daughter of the house, who'd inherited her father's bulk and his sweet nature. 'I'm sure the French for pheasant is *payson.*'

Mrs Makepiece, Valerie's daily, who'd come to help with the washing up, was just raking the shagpile in the lounge, flicking away non-existent dust when Valerie rushed in and realigned the *Tatlers* and *Harpers*, leaving the *Gloucester and Avon Life* specially open at a picture of herself at the NSPCC fashion show in Cheltenham. It was seven o'clock. She'd better take a bath and change.

.

In the kitchen, Taggie finished the pudding and put the pheasants into the oven. She must remember to add chopped dill to the prawn sauce. She wished Valerie hadn't wanted things quite so elaborate. Everything was going swimmingly until Valerie came down dressed, and insisted Taggie put on a maid's black dress and a white apron which came miles above her black-stockinged knees, and then made her put her hair up. Even Taggie baulked at the white maid's cap.

'I expect you to answer the door,' said Valerie, 'supervise everything in the kitchen and wait at table.'

'You're in the army now,' sung Reg, the hired butler, now on his third bottle.

'Will you come and watch "Dynasty" with me?' Sharon asked Taggie.

'You're not watching rubbish like that, Sharon. You're to hand round nibbles and make yourself pleasant,' snapped Valerie, nearly jumping out of her skin, as music blared out from the speakers all over the house.

'It's Daddy's signature tune,' said Taggie in delight.

'Turn that horrible din down, Fred-Fred,' screamed Valerie.

'Monica loves classical music,' said Freddie.

'Oh well, leave it on, then.'

The doorbell rang. 'Go and answer it, Agatha. Put the men's coats in the downstairs toilet, and the ladies' coats upstairs in the master bedroom, and then direct them towards the lounge, where Mr Jones and I will receive them.'

It was Paul and Sarah Stratton. For a second Taggie and Sarah stared at each other, remembering their previous encounter on Rupert's tennis court. Then, with a wicked little smile, Sarah took off her red velvet cloak. Her tan had gone, but a black taffeta dress, off-the-shoulders and with a bustle, showed off her beautiful, opulent figure. Never having seen Paul before, Taggie thought he looked dreadfully old and careworn to be married to such a glowing over-excited young girl.

The next arrival was Cameron Cook, who Taggie recognized from Declan's description and tried not to hate. Declan had omitted to say she was so beautiful, and wonderfully dressed this evening in a dark-red smoking jacket and black tie with a wing collar, her hair sleeked back to show off her smooth white forehead and thick black brows. She looked straight through Taggie, and, having no coat to take, stalked past her into the drawing-room.

She was shortly followed by Tony and Monica. Tony'd been away at a conference, and for once, because he was cleaning up Corinium's act, hadn't taken Cameron with him. Now he was unflatteringly unpleased to see her. The big smile he switched on like a light bulb switched off as though there'd been a mega powercut. He always felt twitchy when Cameron and Monica were in the same room, and, even worse, Cameron, it seemed, had been invited for Rupert, his old rival. And there was Declan's bloody signature tune blaring out. He was still extremely off Declan, but his hopes of having a good bitch about him this evening had been foiled by the presence of Declan's stupid daughter.

'This music is wonderful,' exclaimed Monica.

'Come and see it in action,' said Freddie, bearing her off to witness the electronic wizardry in his study.

'Have you got any Wagner?' said Monica.

Next moment, to Valerie's horror. Siegfried's funeral march pounded deafeningly through the house.

'What the hell are you doing here?' hissed Tony to Cameron.

'I was asked,' said Cameron coldly.

'We must be very careful.'

'Of course,' said Cameron, holding her glass out to Reg for an instant refill. 'We mustn't jeopardize the franchise.'

Valerie was telling Paul about the house: 'We replaced those dreary old mullioned windows with picture windows.'

'How on earth did you get planning permission?' said Paul in horror. 'I thought this was a listed building.'

'Grade 1,' said Valerie smugly. 'Fred-Fred has friends in high places.'

'Please God, don't let the sauce curdle,' prayed Taggie in the kitchen as she added egg yolks and vinegar.

'Door, love,' said Reg, giving her a pinch on the bottom. 'You look much the sexiest of the lot.'

It was Lizzie and James, who'd plainly had a row because of Lizzie's catastrophic navigation. James loved making an entrance, but not arriving half an hour after his boss, who was looking bootfaced and standing as far away from Cameron as possible talking to Paul Stratton. James immediately gravitated towards Sarah and thought how nice it was to see Cameron out of her depth socially, and for once rather insecure.

Lizzie, who looked awful (she'd worked too late on her novel again and had not had time to wash her hair), had brought some bantams' eggs for Freddie and Valerie, and was thrilled to see Taggie: 'I know it'll all be delicious; don't worry.'

Valerie looked at her watch yet again: quarter past nine and no Rupert.

'Doesn't matter,' said Freddie, filling up everyone's glasses. 'Nice to relax on a Friday.'

'Freddie's equipment is quite staggering,' said Monica returning from the study.

Sarah caught Lizzie's eye and giggled.

Mashing the potatoes in the kitchen, Taggie was going frantic. Everything would be ruined unless they ate soon.

'Off you go,' said Reg, as the doorbell rang.

Crimson with rage and embarrassment, bending her legs to make her maid's dress look longer, Taggie answered the door. Grinning, Rupert walked into the hall. 'Called any good fire engines lately?'

'Would you like to take off your coat?' said Taggie stiffly.

'I'd much rather take off your dress,' said Rupert. 'You look like the object of all red-blooded men's fantasies. I'm late. I'd better go and make my peace.'

Valerie hid her rage less well than Taggie: 'Rupert, where *have* you been?'

Cameron choked on her champagne. Having never actually met Rupert and having been poisoned by Tony's almost pathological jealousy, she'd expected him to just be another loud-mouthed, upper-class English shit. In the flesh he was glorious, and much more American-looking than English.

Having apologized to Valerie, Rupert turned to kiss Monica.

'You haven't met Cavendish Cook, have you, Rupert?' said Monica.

'How do you do, sir,' said Rupert, admiring Cameron's smoking jacket.

'Cavendish works for Tony,' went on Monica. 'I gather you won another prize last week, Cavendish; jolly good show. I meant to watch the programme last summer, but unfortunately they were doing *Meistersinger* on BBC 2 the same night, and I was videoing that as well as watching it.'

James was in ecstasy – Cavendish Cook! There were some advantages in Monica's addiction to BBC 2 after all.

Seeing Sharon sneaking through the hall towards the kitchen, Valerie gave an eldritch screech.

'Sharon, Sharon, come in here and give Auntie Monica some nibbles. She keeps sloping off to watch "Dynasty",' she added to Monica. 'I won't have my kids watching soaps.'

'Oh I love "Dynasty",' said Monica, smiling at Sharon. 'Do tell me whether Blake and Crystal have made it up.'

Rupert walked over to James, who was still talking to Sarah.

'That was a bloody good interview you did with the PM,' he said. 'And she thought you were marvellous. Asked me for your address so she could write to you.'

James, who'd always hated Rupert, melted faster than a snowball in the microwave. Then Rupert turned to Sarah, kissing her white shoulder.

'Evening, my darling, that's an incredibly sexy dress, I don't know why you bother to wear any clothes at all. Bloody cold outside. I think it's going to snow.'

'I can never get home if it snows,' grumbled James. 'I'm thinking of installing a put-you-up in my office.'

Seeing Tony was still talking to Paul, Rupert said: 'Tony Baddingham's got a put-you-down in *his* office.'

Cameron laughed.

James, who was not going to be egged on to bitching about Tony in front of Cameron, said, 'I always feel Tony is much maligned.'

'I entirely agree,' said Rupert, draining his whisky, 'but not nearly enough.'

Sitting next to Rupert at dinner, Sarah found herself talking gibberish. The awful thing about adultery, she thought, was that one had to remember in public that one hadn't heard things that one's lover had told one in private.

'I saw your "Behind Every Famous Man" interview with James,' said Rupert, as he unfolded his napkin. 'Very good. Were you nervous?'

'Desperately,' said Sarah, blushing.

As they had discussed the whole thing and how ghastly James had been at length in bed yesterday afternoon, and because, under the table, Rupert's hand was already creeping up between the slit in her skirt, Sarah found it impossible not to giggle.

'I think I've found you a horse,' went on Rupert, giving her his blank, blue-eyed stare. Then he solemnly proceeded to describe it down to its last fetlock. As he'd also given her the same details yesterday, she found it even more difficult to keep a straight face, particularly as Paul, pretending to listen to Valerie, had ears on elastic trying to hear what they were saying.

Fortunately, distraction was provided by Taggie bringing round the fish mousse. Not remembering her left from her right, having served Monica, she moved backwards to serve James.

'Clockwise,' screeched Valerie.

There was another awful moment for Taggie when she saw Rupert and Lizzie having hysterics over the menu.

'Gingered French peasant, cravat sauce and desert château,' translated Rupert.

'Our hostess's French is slightly Stratford atte Bowe,' whispered Lizzie.

'What's that?' said Valerie sharply from the other end of the table.

For a second Lizzie caught Taggie's anguished eye, and instantly identified the author of the menu: 'Just saying how good your French is,' she said to Valerie.

Valerie nodded smugly: 'Crusty bread anyone?' she cried waving the basket. 'I will not have white bread in this house.'

'I love it,' said Freddie wistfully.

'So do I,' said Rupert. 'I'll send you a loaf for Christmas.'

Sitting opposite Tony, trying desperately not to catch his eye, Cameron longed to be able to sparkle and scintillate, but how could she with Paul Stratton on one side, watching his wife like a warder and James on the other talking about himself?

'How's your series on "Caring for the Elderly" getting on?' she asked.

James brightened. 'We think we've found a presenter at last – a Mrs Didbody. She's a seventy-five-year-old coloured lady, a widow with a daughter of fifty. Which makes her a single parent,' added James triumphantly.

'A real franchise grabber,' said Cameron, who was watching Rupert. He was easily the most attractive man she'd seen since she came to England, probably ever. It was a combination of elegance, deadpan arrogance, and a total inability to resist stirring things up. He was plainly having it off with Sarah Stratton.

'What exactly are electronics?' Monica was saying to Freddie in her piercing voice. 'What exactly d'you do?'

Cameron saw a look of fury on Tony's face, but Freddie seemed delighted by her interest.

'I make everythink really: videos, televisions, synthesizers, compact disks, floppy disks, silicon chips.'

'I always muddle up silicon with cellulite,' said Monica.

'With my computers,' went on Freddie proudly, 'scientists on the ground can place satellites in orbit. All satellites now carry my computers on board.'

'Good heavens,' said Monica. She could see now how useful Freddie'd be to Tony.

Tony was not enjoying himself. It was one of life's ironies, he thought, that at dinners like this Monica always sat next to all the brilliant achieving men, who usually didn't interest her at all (although she did seem to be having fun with Freddie), and he got stuck with their unachieving wives. Lizzie Vereker on his left looked a complete mess.

'That was delicious,' she said taking another piece of bread to wipe up the last vestiges of prawn sauce. 'Did you make it?' she asked Valerie slyly.

'Yes,' said Valerie, as Taggie was out of the room.

'How's Archie?' Lizzie asked Tony.

'Doing Business Studies for A-levels,' said Tony with a grin, 'which he thinks allows him to tell me exactly where I'm going wrong in running Corinium.'

The only time he's nice, thought Lizzie, is when he talks about his children.

'Sharon is doing *The Dream* for her O-levels,' said Valerie, ringing a bell.

Taggie, who was chopping parsley for the courgettes, threw down the knife and ran into the dining-room, tugging down her horribly short dress.

'Can you clear away the appetizer, Agatha,' said Valerie.

Returning to the kitchen with the plates, Taggie found Reg the butler, very drunk now, carving the pheasants. She wished he wouldn't cut quite such huge slices, there might not be enough to go round.

'Tender as a woman's kiss,' said Reg, helping himself to a slice. 'You're another Mrs Beeton, Agatha.'

'Oh, it does look yummy. Can I have a bit?' said fat Sharon.

'Have some later,' said Taggie, as she poured the sauce over, and scattered parsley over the courgettes. 'I must take it in.'

'I'll take round the courgettes,' said Sharon, who wanted to gaze at Rupert.

Taggie took the pheasant round the right way this time.

195

She noticed Rupert still had his hand inside Sarah's slit skirt, the revolting man, but had to remove it to help himself to pheasant. Was she imagining it or was he deliberately rubbing his black elbow against her breast as he did so? When she took round the potatoes, she stood as far away as possible, arching over him like a street light. As she moved down the other side of the table, his wicked dissipated blue eyes seemed to follow her, making her even more hot and bothered. Reg was taking round the Mouton Cadet now, and had reached Valerie.

'We had Sharon in 1972,' she was telling Paul, 'and we were married in, er . . .'

'Watch it,' said Reg, giving her a great nudge.

Rupert grinned broadly. Sarah and Lizzie giggled.

Valerie, knowing one must behave with dignity at all times, ignored the innuendo. 'That will be all, Reginald and Agatha. I'll ring if anyone wants second helpings.'

'We're televising Midnight Mass at Cotchester Cathedral this year,' said Tony as he put his knife and fork together. 'I'm reading the first lesson. Are you reading the second?' he asked Paul, knowing he wasn't.

'No,' said Paul, looking very put out. 'We'll be away.'

'I wonder who is reading it then,' said Tony.

'I am,' said Rupert.

'You said you were going skiing,' said an unguarded Sarah. 'I mean,' she added, looking thoroughly flustered, 'you said you'd be away at Christmas.'

There was an awkward pause.

'This pheasant is wonderful,' said Lizzie.

'I'll give you the recipe if you like,' said Valerie. 'Don't pick your bones, Fred-Fred,' she snapped, then stopped hastily as she saw that Rupert was picking his.

All the same, it was going wonderfully well, reflected Valerie later, as Taggie cleared away the cheese board. Everyone was talking like mad and seemed to enjoy the novelty of the men moving two places on. It was a good thing Rupert was sitting next to Cameron now, who'd seemed rather out of it earlier. In five minutes, Taggie would bring on the moated castle.

Turning to Cameron, Rupert thought how different she was to Sarah, as lean and hungry as Sarah was replete and voluptuous.

'I'm dying to have a pee,' he murmured, 'just for an excuse to prowl round and see what a ghastly cock-up our hostess has made of a once-ravishing house. I used to come to children's parties here.'

'I can't imagine you as a kid.'

'I always cheated at doctors and nurses.'

Across the table, he noticed Sarah deliberately flirting with James, to make him jealous perhaps or to put Paul off the scent.

To Valerie's disapproval Cameron got out a cigarette. Picking up a pink candle, Rupert lit it for her.

'You hunt with the same pack as Tony?' she asked.

'Sometimes,' said Rupert softly. 'Sometimes after the same quarry.'

Looking round at his suddenly predatory, unsmiling face, she felt a quivering between her legs. Christ, she wanted him.

'D'you want a lift home?' he said.

'No.' She could have wept. 'I brought my own car.'

'The Lotus?' said Rupert.

She nodded.

'Nice Corinium perk,' said Rupert, instantly returning to his former flippant mood. 'I see James has finally got himself a Porsche. I'll have to get rid of mine.'

'I don't know much about horses,' murmured Cameron, frantic to hold his attention, 'except my boss's wife looks like one.'

'You won't oust her by bitching,' said Rupert. Then, aware that Tony had suddenly stopped talking to Sarah and they were both listening, he said, 'There are three things you need in a horse: balance, quality and courage. Same as a woman, really.'

'I'd add intelligence,' said Cameron.

197

'I wouldn't.'

'Don't you like achieving women?'

'I don't like ballbreakers.'

There was a chorus of oohs and aahs as Taggie came in with the moated ice cream castle. It was the last lap. Once she'd served this, and cleared away, she could relax.

'What d'you do at Corinium?' Rupert asked Cameron, as he idly watched Taggie moving round the table. She was bright pink in the face, her tongue clenched between her teeth in her efforts to hold the pudding steady. Any make-up had sweated off. Her dark hair was fighting the pins that held it up. But nothing could disguise the length of leg, or the long dark eyelashes, or the voluptuous swell of her breasts. She was going anti-clockwise again, but most people were too plastered to notice.

'I produce Declan,' said Cameron. 'Why don't you come on the programme?'

'What?' said Rupert, dragging his thoughts back from Taggie.

'Come on the programme. I'm sure you and Declan would strike sparks off each other.'

'I don't want to,' said Rupert flatly. 'I don't need that kind of wank, and you'd never hear any chat above the rattle of skeletons tumbling out of cupboards.'

Having just served Valerie, Taggie was moving slowly round towards him.

'How d'you get on with Declan?' he asked Cameron wickedly.

'Utterly obnoxious,' said Cameron. 'He really pisses me off.'

Rupert watched Taggie to see if she'd rise.

'Very pretty,' he said, examining the pudding. 'Feel I ought to get planning permission before I dig into this. Thanks, angel,' he added, helping himself to a piece of battlement and a dollop of cream.

Ignoring him, Taggie moved round to his other side to serve Cameron.

'How on earth does Declan's wife put up with him?' asked Cameron.

'You'd better ask Taggie,' said Rupert. 'Maud's her mother.'

Cameron paled visibly. Noticing Taggie for the first time, she tried to remember what ghastly things she'd said about Declan.

'I'm sorry. I didn't realize.'

In embarrassment she helped herself to too much pudding. The whole thing swayed. Rupert could smell Taggie's body, could feel how hot, and nervous and trembling she was. Her skirt was so short. Almost without thinking, he put a leisurely hand between her thighs.

The next moment Taggie gave a shriek and dropped the very considerable remains of the pudding all over Cameron's seven-hundred-pound smoking jacket and black satin trousers.

'You stupid bitch,' screamed Cameron, forgetting herself. 'What the fuck d'you think you're doing?'

In tears Taggie fled to the kitchen.

Remembering one must behave with dignity at all times, Valerie swept an almost hysterical Cameron upstairs.

Lizzie turned on Rupert: 'You bastard,' she yelled. 'Don't you realize this was her first job? She's been trying to break into catering for months. She cooked like an angel and you had to fuck it up.'

'With looks like that,' said Rupert, retrieving pieces of broken plate from the floor, 'I wouldn't have thought a career was that important.'

'Don't be so fucking insensitive. Didn't you know poor darling Taggie's dyslexic? Can't you imagine how ghastly it is being the only unbright one in such a brilliant family?'

'Oh Christ,' said Rupert, truly appalled. 'I simply didn't know. It was entirely my fault, Freddie. I couldn't resist goosing your cook, but really you shouldn't have dressed her in such sexy clothes. I'd better go and apologize.'

'Leave her bloody alone,' said Lizzie, rushing out to the kitchen to comfort a sobbing Taggie, who was being ineffectually patted by a swaying Reg.

199

'Go and get a cloth and a dustpan and brush, and clear up the mess,' Lizzie told him, 'and give everyone another drink.'

'There there, duck.' She hugged Taggie.

'I'm so sorry. I wanted everything to be perfect for Mrs Jones,' sobbed Taggie.

'You mustn't worry. It was the most marvellous food anyone's had in years.' Lizzie pulled off a piece of kitchen roll to dry Taggie's eyes. 'Rupert's a bastard. He just can't resist a beautiful girl.'

'Cameron is changing into one of my ge-owns,' said Valerie, sweeping in.

'I'm so sorry, Mrs Jones,' said Taggie in a choked voice.

'I was just telling her how brilliantly she cooked,' said Lizzie.

Valerie was livid. She'd been shown up as not doing the cooking at all.

'Pull yourself together, Agatha,' she said sharply. 'Go and collect the rest of the plates, and see if Lord Baddingham and Miss Cook would like some fresh fruit, as they didn't get any dessert.'

'Cameron got her just dessert,' giggled Lizzie.

'I can't go back in there,' said Taggie aghast.

'You will,' said Valerie, 'if you want to work for me again.'

In the dining-room James was furious with Lizzie for making such a fuss over Declan's idiot daughter, and Sarah was furious with Rupert for so openly groping Taggie. She'd tried to be laid back about her affair with him, but now all she could feel was a red-hot lava of jealousy pouring over her.

Tony, on the other hand, was delighted by the turn of events. 'Child's clearly over-emotional and unbalanced like her father,' he kept saying.

'Bloody good cook,' said Freddie.

And when Taggie, very tear-stained and head hanging, brought in a bowl of peaches and grapes, Monica leaned out and squeezed her hand.

'Delicious dinner, my dear. I've got a girl's lunch next

week. Perhaps you'd like to help me out with that? Nothing elaborate, very cosy. I'll ring you tomorrow.'

Gulping gratefully, Taggie said she'd love to.

Attention was then taken off her by the return of Cameron, wearing one of Valerie's black ge-owns. It was perfectly frightful with a bow on the bum, and much too tight.

'I prefer you as a bloke,' said Rupert, wiping a blob of cream off her chair.

'I'm desperately sorry,' mumbled Taggie, as she passed Cameron, 'I'll pay for it.'

'You couldn't begin to,' hissed Cameron.

'Don't be a bitch,' said Rupert sharply. Putting a hand on Taggie's arm, he said, 'I'm really sorry, angel, it was all my fault.'

Taggie didn't say anything, but seemed to shrink away.

James sidled up to Valerie.

'One of my programmes is on in a minute. Would anyone mind if I slipped upstairs and watched it?'

'Of course,' said Valerie. 'In fact I think, ladies, we'll all go upstairs.'

Cameron got her own back by flatly refusing to go and staying to drink port with the men. Little good it did her. Tony got Freddie in a corner and persuaded him to have lunch immediately after Christmas to discuss his joining the Corinium Board, and, leaving Cameron with the frightful Paul, Rupert went off to the kitchen. Here he found Taggie loading the washing-up machine and making coffee.

'Go away!' she sobbed. 'You're the most m-m-m-malefic man I've ever met.'

''ere, 'ere,' groaned Reg from underneath the kitchen table.

RIVALS
16

The following Monday Declan stormed into Cameron's office without knocking. 'You were at Valerie Jones's dinner party.'

'Right,' said Cameron coolly. Inside she quailed, wondering if Taggie had told Declan how she'd screamed and sworn at her, and how earlier she'd bitched about Declan to Rupert.

'I gather Taggie tipped the pudding over you. I'm sorry,' said Declan. 'If you can't get the marks out, I'll be happy to refund you.'

'It was no big deal,' said Cameron, absolutely weak with relief. 'I took them along to the cleaners on Saturday, they'll be just fine.'

'Then we'll pick up your cleaning bill.'

'Rupert can bloody well do that.'

Declan's face hardened. 'The bastard – poor little Tag. She was distraught.'

'She did really well,' protested Cameron, feeling she could afford to be generous. 'The food was terrific, and Monica asked her to do a lunch for her.'

'I know. Monica rang on Saturday. That cheered Taggie up.'

'It was all Rupert's fault,' said Cameron, deciding to put the boot in.

'Wait till I get my hands on the bastard.'

'Why don't I ask him on to your programme?' said Cameron idly. 'That'd be a much more subtle way of burying him.'

Declan paused in his prowling and thought for a minute. It was violently against all his principles to ask someone deliberately on to the programme in order to do a hatchet job.

'He really screwed her up,' insisted Cameron, who wanted an excuse to ring Rupert.

'All right,' said Declan.

Even Tony was temporarily roused out of his anti-Declan mood. 'Bloody good idea. If Declan does a Maurice Wooton on Rupert, I'll double his salary.'

Cameron rang Rupert. 'I'm just checking out on your availability over the next few months.'

'You should have come home with me on Friday,' said Rupert.

Because he was horrendously busy and not given to intro-spection and would much rather spend any spare second in Gloucestershire on constituency work, or with his children or his horses, or in bed with Sarah Stratton, Rupert then told Cameron he had no intention of going on Declan's programme.

Cameron played her trump card. 'I'll tell Declan you're too chicken.'

That nettled Rupert: 'Don't be silly. All right, I'll think about it.'

And with that Cameron had to be content.

As Christmas approached Declan grew more depressed. He was totally disillusioned with Tony. He felt like a damsel in distress, who, having been rescued from the BBC by St George, had promptly been put on the game. Not a day passed without some loaded request to open Monica's Christmas Bazaar for the Distressed Gentlefolk, or draw the raffle at the NSPCC Ball (tickets seventy-five pounds each), or take part in Corinium's Pantomime to Help the Aged, or turn on the lights in Cotchester. Declan refused them all, which increased Tony's animosity and enabled James Vereker to step caringly into his shoes. The implication was the same: if you bothered to make use of our excellent research team, you could pull your weight as a member of the Corinium team.

Sapped by endless rows. Declan was aware his programme was losing its edge. He was still very high in the ratings, but he knew people were beginning to turn on in the hope he'd be better this week.

Desperate for some kind of intellectual satisfaction, he was getting up at five every day to spend three or four hours on his Yeats biography, but was too drained to make any real progress. He was also grimly aware that he wasn't paying enough attention to Maud. After a long bout of lethargy, excited about Caitlin and Patrick coming home for Christmas, she was having one of her spates of frantic energy, which invariably involved spending money. She came to the office Christmas party and charmed absolutely everyone.

Patrick arrived the next day, walking through the door slightly drunk, with four suitcases of washing.

'Is this the Priory laundry?'

'Why did you come by taxi?' asked Maud, flinging her arms round his neck.

'Because I wrote off the Golf yesterday.'

At that moment Caitlin rang from school.

'Patrick's home,' said Maud in ecstasy.

'Well he can come and collect me in the Golf, the Mini's too shaming.'

Christmas Eve saw scenes of frantic revelry at Corinium. The whole building thrummed with lust. Seb Burrows from the newsroom scaled the front of the building when drunk, and placed Charles Fairburn's Russian hat on one of the red horns of the Corinium ram. Another joker put rainbow condoms on the horns and tail of the bronze Corinium ram in the board room, just before Tony ushered in the local representative from the IBA for a Christmas drink. Secretaries with tinsel in their hair ran shrieking down the passage blowing squeakers. Just as James Vereker passed the board room door, carrying a pile of Christmas presents from caring fans out to his car, four shrieking secretaries converged on him and unzipped his flies. His trousers dropped, to reveal seasonal boxer shorts covered with Santas, just as Tony was ushering the IBA man out. Tony was absolutely livid, but not so livid as Cameron, who'd opted to work over Christmas for want of anything better to do, when she discovered Tony had dispatched Miss Madden to choose Christmas presents both for her and Monica.

'I bought two diamond bracelets,' whispered Miss Madden conspiratorially. 'I thought you might like to choose first.'

'I'll take the bigger one,' said Cameron grimly.

James was even more annoyed to find that Declan had ten times more Christmas cards than he had, and that the Christmas tree in Reception completely obscured James's framed photograph. Declan's photograph had been deliberately left unhidden for all to admire.

Despite being horribly broke, Declan sold a first edition of Trollope and gave everyone who worked on his programme, including Cameron, a Christmas pudding and a pep pill for Christmas. He also took them out to a splendid lunch at The Dog and Trumpet outside Cotchester, whose manager subsequently barred anyone from Corinium Television from ever crossing the threshold again.

As the Senior Cameraman pointed out, 'You don't need directions to go to one of Corinium's Christmas parties – just follow the blue flashing lights.'

Afterwards they all conga-ed down Cotchester High Street back to the office, where Declan found Charles Fairburn, who was meant to be organizing the live transmission of Midnight Mass from Cotchester Cathedral that evening, drinking Cointreau and doing his expenses.

Russian hat £100, wrote Charles, dinner with Dean and Chapter £80. Dinner with Chapter £100. 'The trouble with you, Declan,' he said, shaking his head, 'is that you're not creative enough in your expenses.'

In the newsroom the Corinium weather man leant out of the window at sunset, just to check that the forecast he was about to give on air of a very fine evening was correct. Next moment he received a bucket of cold water over his newly washed hair.

'It's raining, you berk,' shouted a voice from above.

Declan took a box of chocolates up to Miss Madden, who'd always been nice to him. After she'd thanked him profusely, she confided that her nephew, who was a chorister, had been chosen to sing a solo at Midnight Mass.

'My heart felt like bursting with pride, and I wanted to cry at the same time,' she said.

Cotchester by midnight, with the golden houses and the great cathedral floodlit, was at its most beautiful. The huge blue spruce just inside the cathedral gates, which was normally a glorious sight festooned with fairy lights at Christmas, was sadly bare this year, because the conservationists, headed by Simon Harris, had claimed the lights were harmful to it.

The church which was lit by candles, white fairy lights on the Christmas tree and television lights, was absolutely packed, with people hoping both to appear on television and to catch a glimpse of Declan O'Hara.

Tony read the first lesson and stumbled twice, to his entire staff's delight. Rupert read the second in his flat drawl, and hardly a girl in the congregation, except Taggie, didn't long to have him in her stocking the following morning.

'Please God, if you think it's right, give me Ralphie,' prayed Taggie.

Caitlin, taking communion, couldn't stop thinking about AIDS. But she knew one had to swallow three pints of saliva before one caught it. As she clumped down the aisle in her new black suede brothel-creepers and her wildly fashionable da-glo cat-sick yellow socks, she could have sworn Rupert was looking at her. In the long wait while everyone else took communion, Patrick, also wearing wildly fashionable da-glo cat-sick yellow socks, held out a cracker and Caitlin pulled it with a loud bang.

'I wonder if Aengus and Gertrude knelt down at midnight to honour the birth of Christ,' said Patrick, as they drove home. Far from honouring anyone's birth, sulking at being left behind, Aengus had knocked off and smashed several balls from the Christmas tree and Gertrude had opened three presents from underneath and also chewed the label off a small parcel for Taggie. Inside was the most beautiful silver pendant inlaid with amethysts on a silver chain. She gasped as she slowly read the note:

'Darling Taggie, I'm sorry I've been such a sod. Have a lovely Christmas. See you on New Year's Eve. All Love R.'

'Oh it's beautiful,' she said with a sob, and fled upstairs, clutching herself in ecstasy.

Outside, the stars and the new moon seemed to be shining just for her. Ralphie had remembered after all, and in seven days she'd see him again.

17

By New Year's Eve the Christmas decorations at The Priory were sagging, the evergreens had brewer's droop, and Wandering Aengus, having smashed every coloured ball on the Christmas tree, had taken up crash-landing in the Christmas cards.

Outside, a force five gale, Hurricane Fiona, as Patrick had called her, was rampaging up the valley, rattling the windows, and howling down the chimneys. On the lawn a huge pink-and-white-striped marquee, heated by gas burners, wrestled with its moorings.

'Perhaps we could enter it for the Americas Cup,' said Caitlin.

'We can line all the drunks round the bottom to hold it down,' said Patrick, taking another slug of Moët.

'You'll be one of them if you don't stop knocking back that stuff,' said Caitlin reprovingly.

'It's my birthday. Everyone is entitled to behave appallingly on their birthday. *Oh, I've got the key-hee-hee of the door, never been twenty-one before.*' He was extremely happy because, unknown to his father, his mother had given him a new Golf for his birthday.

As Maud had gone off to the hairdressers and to pick up a new dress that was being altered, Patrick and Caitlin carried on doing the seating plan she had started. Taggie had tried to write names on some of the cards, but was in such a state

of excitement about Ralphie's arrival that her spelling had
gone totally to pot. Worried about the marquee coming
down, she had gone off to ring the firm who'd put it up. Her
arms ached from mashing the potato for a dozen enormous
shepherds' pies. She seemed to have put crosses in a million
sprouts and peeled a billion grapes for the fruit salad. The
garlic bread lay like a pile of silver slugs in its aluminium foil.
The turkey soup only needed heating up. The kedgeree for
breakfast was in four huge dishes on top of the deep freeze,
with cucumber, prawns and hard-boiled eggs, ready chopped
to add at the last moment. Patrick's birthday cake, in the
shape of a shamrock, rested in the fridge.

An extension lead still had to be found for the disco, a
bulb was needed for the outside light, and Caitlin still hadn't
written out large cards to show people where the loos were
and where to hang their coats.

But things were gradually getting under control. Taggie
had never felt so tired in her life. She had cooked herself
into the ground, but she kept telling herself that if she got
through everything and didn't grumble, God would reward
her with Ralphie.

Back in the marquee, Caitlin was hastily rewriting new
name cards for people Taggie had seriously misspelt.

'Monknicker Baddingham,' she giggled. 'Do let's leave that
one. Put Monknicker on Daddy's right.'

'I'll put Joanna Lumley on his left. He needs some fun,'
said Patrick, 'although, as it's my birthday, I ought to have
her next to me.'

'Look,' screeched Caitlin. 'Utterly bloody Mummy's put
Rupert Campbell-Black next to her. I'm bloody sitting next
to him.'

Removing the card from Maud's right, she bore it off and
placed it reverently beside hers, three tables away and behind
a huge flower arrangement, so her mother couldn't spy.

'In fact – ' she scribbled Rupert's name on to a second card
– 'I'm going to put him on both sides of me so there's no slip
up.'

Looking at his place, Patrick noted that he was sitting next to Lavinia, his current girlfriend, and someone called Sarah Stratton.

'Oh, I'll swap her,' said Caitlin, seizing Sarah's card. 'She's ancient — at least twenty-six.'

'I was rather excited by the sound of her,' said Patrick. 'Mum said she was very beautiful and voluptuous, with a rich crumbling husband. My only answer is to marry a rich wife. I wish Pa would cut me out of his will. If I inherit all his debts, I'm finished.'

'Oh well, I'll swap Sarah back again,' said Caitlin. 'I've put Tag next to Ralphie.'

Patrick shook his head: 'I wouldn't. He and Georgina Harrison have been inseparable all term. He's bringing her tonight.'

'Well, why did he send Tag that amethyst pendant then, and apologize for being such a sod?'

'Sounds *most* unlikely. Last week he couldn't afford to buy his mother a box of handkerchiefs for Christmas, and he still owes me fifty pounds. Are you sure it was Ralphie?'

'Quite sure, the two-timing shit.'

'Shut up, she's coming.'

'I got through to the tent man; he's coming over. He says they're going all round Gloucester double-checking their erections,' said Taggie with a giggle, then turned pale as the doorbell rang.

But it was only two young pink and white Old Etonians who were doing the disco, and Maud back from the hair-dressers, with her hair set in a mass of snaky curls.

'It looks lovely, Mummy,' said Taggie.

'It looks gross,' muttered Caitlin.

The telephone rang. It was Bas Baddingham.

'Darling Maud, may I bring my new new lady?'

'Of course,' said Maud. 'More the merrier. Damn,' she added as she put down the telephone, 'another really attractive spare man paired up. Who the hell's going to dance with Cameron Cook?'

'You haven't asked *her*?' said Taggie in horror, thinking of the wrecked smoking jacket. 'Daddy can't stand her.'

'How many d'you reckon are coming?' said Patrick, giving a glass of Moët to each of the pink and white Etonians, who were both staring at Taggie.

'About two to three hundred,' said Maud airily.

'But we haven't hired nearly enough plates or knives or forks or anything,' said Taggie aghast, 'or got anywhere to seat them.'

Maud turned to Patrick. 'Pop across the valley to Rupert's and borrow some,' she said.

'I didn't know he was coming too,' whispered Taggie, even more horrified. 'I thought he was away skiing.'

'He's come back specially for the party,' said Maud dreamily. 'It was too windy for him to land the helicopter but I've just seen him driving through Penscombe. Well, if there's nothing else for me to do, I'm going upstairs to paint my nails.' As she went out, running her eyes over the table seating, she caught sight of Rupert's cards on both sides of Caitlin.

Tearing one up in a rage, she put the other back on her right. 'You will not sit next to Rupert, Caitlin, you're going to sit next to Archie Baddingham and like it.' She turned back to Taggie.

'Has Grace made up the beds for all Patrick's friends?'

'Someone insulted her in the pub at lunchtime,' said Taggie. 'Introduced her as Declan O'Hara's scrubber, so she's gone to bed in a huff.'

'Well, get her up,' snapped Maud. 'At least you've got Valerie Jones's char and her two children and that butler Reg and his friends coming to help, but you better make up some more beds.'

'They can all sleep in armchairs,' said Patrick soothingly as he gathered up his new car keys. 'I'll go and borrow those plates from Rupert.'

'I've made up a bed for Ralphie in the spare room,' said Taggie, blushing.

At six-thirty Declan returned home having recorded an interview with the Bishop of Cotchester, which he was aware was totally lacking in sparkle. He had been wracked with increasing foreboding during the day, as one person after another – Charles Fairburn, James Vereker, Simon Harris, Daysee Butler and then, horrors, Cameron Cook and Tony Baddingham – said they'd see him this evening. Maud had obviously got tighter than he'd realized at the Corinium Christmas party. But he never expected the frantically billowing pink and white tent on the lawn or the tables laid for two hundred people, or the disco boys checking acoustics, or the three hundred bottles of Moët on ice in various baths round the house.

Roaring upstairs, he found Maud lying on the bed naked except for a face pack and an Optrex eyepad.

'What the fuck is going on? Do you want to ruin me?' He slammed the door behind him.

In the drawing-room below, a group of Patrick's glamorous friends, who'd just arrived and were having a drink, could see the mistletoe hanging from the chandelier trembling beneath Declan's demented pacing. Then they heard Maud screaming.

'Oh dear,' sighed Caitlin, 'Daddy doesn't seem in a party mood.'

Upstairs, Taggie was frantically making up beds for Patrick's friends. Perfectly happy to sleep together in the narrowest of beds all term at Trinity Dublin, now they were sleeping in the house of one of their friend's parents, all the girls, overcome by a fit of morality, said they wanted separate rooms.

The din was increasing in her parents' room.

Maud was careful not to be too provocative. She didn't want her eye blacked. Eye-shadow and mascara were more becoming.

'*Peace on earth, and mercy mild, God and sinners reconciled,*' sang Caitlin outside the door. 'Shut up you two, you're upsetting Gertrude.'

Taggie could hear another lot of Patrick's friends arriving downstairs, crying: '*Happy Birthday.*' Running to the banisters, she could see Patrick's exquisite girlfriend, Lavinia, giving him a present. She was followed by a beautiful dark girl and behind her – Taggie caught her breath – just under the mistletoe in the hall, stood Ralphie. He seemed to have got even more beautiful with his big blue eyes and blond curls.

In a panic she rushed back into the spare room, put another log on the fire, and re-arranged the Christmas roses in the blue jug beside the bed. At least they had curtains in this room, and a really comfortable bed for Ralphie – and perhaps her. Taggie clutched herself; she must not be presumptuous. There was a knock on the door.

'Come in,' croaked Taggie, hanging on to the mantelpiece for support.

The beautiful dark girl she'd seen in the hall came through the door. She was very slim and tiny, not more than five foot one.

'Oh what a lovely room,' she said, dumping a squashy bag and a black ruched dress on the bed, 'and a fire too. You are kind. Will I be able to have a bath?'

'Of course,' stammered Taggie, 'but it may not be a hot one.'

'You must be Taggie,' said the girl. 'You look just like Patrick. Oh, look at the lovely Christmas roses! You shouldn't have bothered.'

Taggie, blushing so hard she felt she could fry an egg on her face, said, 'Actually this is Ralphie's room.'

'And mine,' said the girl happily. 'I'm Georgina Harrison, Ralphie's girlfriend.'

Patrick had never seen such grief. Taggie seemed almost deranged, her whole body shuddering and shuddering with sobs.

'I can't bear it, I can't bear it, I love him so much.'

'Angel, I know you do. But really it's not on. He's frightfully shallow, and you're simply not his type. It's not anything you've done, you're just too large for him. It's like expecting a chihuahua to mate with a wolfhound. Well, not quite, but, being small, he feels daunted by tall girls. He said to me last summer, "Your sister'd be absolutely heartbreaking, if only she were tiny." '

'I can't shrink.'

'Go off and nibble a mushroom.'

'Don't make jokes,' sobbed Taggie.

'Sweetheart, you've got to pull yourself together and get dressed. Mum and Dad have stopped rowing, but there's no way they can organize the grub. Mrs Makepiece has arrived with two frightful teenage children, and Grace and Reg the butler and his friends are all getting stuck into the Moët. You must go down and supervise them. Now be a good girl and dry your eyes. I'm not twenty-one every day.'

Maud had the ability to make houses look beautiful. There were no curtains on the windows, but huge fires crackled in all the downstairs rooms, which were lit by hundreds of red candles and decorated by huge banks of holly, yew and laurel. She was also totally unfazed by being a hostess, or by the frightful row she'd just had with Declan. She had certainly never looked more beautiful. The Medusa curls had dropped a little after her bath, and framed her pale face to which the heat from the fires had given a touch of colour. She was wearing a very low-cut ivy-green taffeta dress with a bustle, which brought out the witchy green of her eyes and clung to her figure. She'd lost seven pounds, hardly eating a thing over Christmas. Pearls gleamed at her wrists, her ears and her throat. If she couldn't ensnare Rupert tonight, she never would.

'New dress,' snarled Declan, tying his black tie in the drawing-room mirror.

'Oh, this old thing,' said Maud mockingly.

'The old thing's in the dress,' said Caitlin sourly.

Pinching some of her mother's scent, she had seen the bill for the dress, and really thought her mother had overdone it this time. Why did she need to spend that much money on clothes when she'd already got a man? Caitlin was worried that her father was deliberately setting out to get drunk, and even more worried about poor old Taggie. But at least at a ball with hundreds of people, Taggie might meet someone new.

'Pretend it's a job, pretend it's a job,' Taggie told herself through gritted teeth, as she stirred the great vats of turkey soup.

'Could you possibly ask Caitlin to make sure Aengus is locked in one of the bedrooms? I'm afraid he might get under a car,' she said to Mrs Makepiece's daughter, Tracey, who, dressed in the tightest of black skirts and a white tricel shirt and pearls, was upwardly mobilizing her spiky hair in the kitchen mirror. Tracey was plainly avid to have a crack at one of Patrick's friends.

Outside, Mrs Makepiece's punk son Kevin was directing cars into a nearby field, and coming in frequently to fortify himself against the cold with slugs of wine. Reg and his two friends were doing sterling work drinking and circulating drink. Grace was already pissed. 'Goodness you look tired,' she said to Taggie. 'What 'ave you been up to?'

Gertrude grew hoarse with barking as more and more people poured in. The party was plainly a success. Maud had produced a splendid mix: lots of London friends, who were knocked out by the beauty of the house and how good Maud was looking. Many of them had brought teenage children who were borne off upstairs for Malibu and coke in Caitlin's bedroom. Then there were Patrick's glamorous friends from Trinity, a large contingent from Corinium Television, and all Maud and Declan's new friends from Gloucestershire, who were thoroughly over-excited to see so many London celebs. With two hours' hard drinking before dinner, most people were soon absolutely plastered.

Bas Baddingham stunned everyone by turning up with a most beautiful wife – somebody else's.

'She left Alistair on December 12th, and was out hunting the very next day,' said Valerie Jones in a shocked voice.

Valerie could also be heard saying repeatedly that she was simply exhausted after so many parties. 'Fred-Fred and Ay simply longed for a poached egg in front of TV tonight, but we felt we couldn't let the O'Haras down,' she said to Lizzie Vereker. 'What a crush, I hope we daine soon.'

'Did you have a good Christmas?' Lizzie asked Freddie.

'Amizing,' said Freddie. 'Got some triffic presents. The staff gave me a fireman's helmet, cos I'm always rushin' about, and Rupert sent me a loaf of Mother's Pride.'

Lizzie giggled.

'Typical,' said Valerie, her lips tightening.

'And those bantams' eggs you gave us were triffic, too. You can taste the difference. I 'ad one for my breakfast this morning.' Freddie beamed at Lizzie.

'Nonsense, Fred-Fred,' said Valerie with a little laugh, 'that egg came from Tesco's.'

James, who'd skipped lunch because he was having his roots touched up, was drinking more than usual and thinking what a lot of amazingly beautiful women there were around: Joanna Lumley over there, and Patricia Hodge, and Pamela Armstrong, and Selina Scott and Ann Diamond.

Maud was looking sensational too, and there was Sarah Stratton, *not* looking as good as usual. There were black rings under her eyes, but she still exuded wantonness.

Sarah was, in fact, in a foul mood. She hadn't had any lunch either, because she'd been hunting for a dress to wear this evening. She had missed Rupert horribly over Christmas. He obviously couldn't ring her, as Paul had been home all the time, but she hadn't even had a postcard, and then in Nigel Dempster's column that morning there'd been a picture of Rupert skiing, with his arm round an incredibly glamorous French actress called Nathalie Perrault. She'd kill him when she saw him.

Where the hell was he, anyway? Who could she flirt with to irritate him? The most attractive men in the room, Sarah decided, were Declan, who was already drunk, and Declan's son, a raving beauty, who was going to be very formidable in a few years' time when he filled out. Sarah shimmied out to the marquee and, finding Rupert's place card, moved it next to hers. How dare the bastard dally with Nathalie Perrault?

Bloody Paul had read Dempster too, and made sly little digs about it all day.

Tony, to his amazement, was thoroughly enjoying the party. Shrewd enough to appreciate his vanity, Maud was treating him as the guest of honour, keeping him constantly plied with celebrities, mostly beautiful women, and introducing him to them as: 'Declan's gorgeous boss. You must get him to ask you down to Corinium, darling.' Tony was soon purring like a great leopard let loose in a goat farm.

Archie, Tony's beloved son, was getting plastered upstairs with Caitlin's friends. Poor fat Sharon Jones was desperately shy. Caitlin had introduced her to boy after boy, ordering them to look after her, but within seconds Sharon had waddled back to her increasingly irritated mother.

'I told you, go and make some friends of your own age,' hissed Valerie furiously.

Mrs Makepiece sidled up to Maud. 'Miss Taggie says we ought to eat; everything's ready.'

'We can't till Rupert arrives,' said Maud firmly. 'Tell her to wait ten minutes.'

The doorbell rang. Perhaps this was him. She went into the hall, but Declan got there first, and it was only Simon Harris barging in with the two hyperactive monsters, and the baby in a carrycot.

'Hullo, Declan,' panted Simon. 'Sorry we're late. Nice of you to invite the whole brood.' Then, seeing Declan's look of horror, he explained, 'I talked to someone called Grace, who said it'd be quite all right.'

Looking around, deciding that this was the sort of nice messy house that wouldn't mind children, Simon let go of the two little monsters. 'Where shall I put the baby?'

At that moment, Rupert sauntered through the open door with snow on his dinner jacket and in his hair, the dingy grey pallor of Simon Harris throwing his Gstaad suntan into even greater relief.

'Rupert,' said Maud joyfully, 'you made it.'

She looked so beautiful, glowing under the hall mistletoe,

that Rupert kissed her on the mouth. 'You look sensational,' he said.

'Not nearly as sensational as you,' whispered Maud. 'You must have had wonderful weather.'

'I can feel the temperature dropping here,' said Rupert, as Declan turned on his heel and stalked off towards the kitchen. 'What's up with him?'

'Oh he's just in a bait.' Maud turned to the passing Reg. 'Bring Mr Campbell-Black a bucket of whisky.'

Going back to the kitchen via the marquee, Caitlin put her place card back on Rupert's right and removed Wandering Aengus who was sitting on Valerie's plate.

'Wonderful party,' she said to Taggie who was grimly pouring turkey soup into bowls on trays. 'Rupert's arrived looking like a red Indian, so Mummy says we can eat now, and Daddy's terribly drunk.'

'Daddy's not the only one,' said Taggie. 'You should see Reg and his friends. Both Tracey and Kev have already buggered off upstairs, and good old Grace is singing "This Joyful Eastertide".'

18

Tony Baddingham was even happier at dinner sitting between Joanna Lumley and Sarah Stratton.

'I know by rights you should be on *my* right,' Maud had whispered in his ear, 'but I thought you deserved a treat.'

'Freddie and Ay'll be leaving early,' said Valerie as she went into dinner. 'The West Cotchester are meeting at Green Lawns tomorrow.'

'They're not meeting anywhere,' said Rupert. 'It's frozen solid outside, so we can all get frightfully drunk.'

He wondered what had happened to Taggie. He couldn't find her name on the seating plan.

'You're over here, next to me,' Maud called to Rupert, patting the seat beside her.

'And next to me,' beamed Caitlin, bolting up to the table and whipping away Cameron Cook's place card which was on his other side.

Maud could have murdered Caitlin, but she didn't want a scene in public.

'You better say Grace,' giggled Caitlin, who'd been at the Malibu, 'and she'll come running in singing "This Joyful Eastertide".'

It was obvious, reflected Tony with satisfaction, that Maud and Declan had had the most frightful row – probably about money. Earlier in the day Declan had very forcibly stressed that it was a tiny party, just a few friends, but there must be at least three hundred people here and by the way the Moët was being splashed about, nothing had been stinted, which was good, because the broker Declan got, the more dependent he'd be on Corinium, and the more Tony could torment and manipulate him.

Then, looking across the room at Maud's enraptured face turned towards Rupert, her elbows pressed together to deepen her cleavage, her turkey soup untouched, he decided it was more likely that Declan was upset because his wife had a thumping great crush on Rupert. This suited Tony even better, because it meant Declan would crucify Rupert even more when he interviewed him in the New Year.

Sarah Stratton, who'd stopped to say hullo to Rupert on the way in, was looking rather bleak as she sat down beside Tony.

'I'm glad we're next to each other,' he said. 'I wanted to talk to you.'

'Have you made any New Year's resolutions?' said Sarah, picking up her soup spoon.

'Yes,' said Tony, his swarthy pirate's face suddenly looking as though he was going to fight off a flotilla of rival clipper ships, 'to keep the franchise.'

'I'll drink to that,' said Sarah.

'I wouldn't mind,' said Simon Harris across the room, helping himself to a seventh piece of garlic bread, 'but Tony came roaring in today saying I'm not having fucking language like that on any fucking programme going out from my fucking station.'

'Sorry to bother you, Mr Harris,' said Mrs Makepiece, 'but your baby's crying.'

It was not surprising the baby was upset, surrounded as it was upstairs by scenes of Petronian debauchery, as teenagers smoked, drank, necked, and screamed with laughter as they opened another packet of Tampax and shot the cotton wool out like cannons.

Archie was sharing a bottle of Moët with Caitlin, who had briefly abandoned Rupert at dinner to smoke an illicit cigarette.

'What has an Upland House girl in common with a Tampax?' Archie asked her.

'Dunno,' said Caitlin.

'They're both stuck-up cunts.'

Caitlin screamed with laughter. 'Have you got a girlfriend?'

'I did,' said Archie, 'but she went off me because of my zits.'

'You mustn't worry about zits,' said Caitlin kindly. 'It means you're producing lots of Testosterone and will make a wonderfully vigorous lover later. Piss off, you snotty little buggers,' she screamed, as Simon Harris's monsters raced up and down giggling at the necking teenagers and threatening each other with one of Rupert's borrowed knives.

'My father said all your family were weirdos,' said Archie, 'but I think you're cool.'

Declan, whom Maud had put deliberately between Monica and Valerie, so he couldn't make a scene, was so drunk he was in danger of seriously jeopardizing his career. He didn't even realize Monica was talking about *Otello* until she got onto Iago.

'He's an even more evil character than Scarpia,' she was saying.

'Much more,' agreed Declan. 'Very like your husband in fact.'

'Garlic bread, either of you?' said Valerie, unable to believe her ears.

'Your husband is an absolute shit,' said Declan.

'I know,' said Monica calmly, as she tore off a piece of garlic bread. 'However, I have three children and I don't believe in divorce.'

'Nor do I,' said Declan, filling up both their glasses.

Valerie was absolutely livid when the farmer on her left said, 'You live at Long Bottom Court, don't you?' She didn't want to talk to him at all. She wanted to listen to what Monica was saying to Declan.

'You won't try and wind Tony up too much at work, will

221

you?' went on Monica. 'You're very good for Corinium. They need people with integrity. I'd like you to stay.'

'I'm not sure your husband would.'

'I think we'd both better stop discussing Tony,' said Monica gently, 'or we might become very indiscreet. This is a very good party. Maud's looking so beautiful.'

'Has anyone ever told you you're a beautiful woman?' said Declan.

Monica went pink. 'That's jolly well overdoing it. You really ought to eat some of this shepherd's pie. It's frightfully good.'

But Declan was looking at Maud who was gazing at Rupert. '*O heart! O heart!*' he murmured, '*if she'd but turn her head.*'

'*You'd know the folly of being comforted,*' said Monica, finishing the quotation for him. 'Don't worry about Rupert,' she went on briskly. 'Bertie Berkshire once described him as a "particularly nasty virus, that one's wife caught sooner or later", but we all get over it.'

Declan looked back at her, startled. 'Even you?'

Monica sighed. 'Even me, although Rupert had no idea. Don Giovanni must have been very like him. He can't resist the conquest, and I think, although he won't admit it, he still misses show-jumping desperately, and it's a question of constantly filling the aching void.'

'He's usually filling other people's wives' aching voids,' said Declan bitterly.

At last Maud had to stop monopolizing Rupert and turn to Declan's old boss at the BBC, Johnny Abrahams, who was sitting on her left.

'Lovely party, darling,' he said. 'Hope you can pay for it. What's up with Declan? Not working out with Tony Baddingham? I did warn him.'

'Don't be silly,' said Maud. 'You know Declan always has rows wherever he is. But look at him now, getting on like a house on fire with Tony's wife.'

'You can talk to me now,' said Caitlin to Rupert.

'How d'you do? I saw you at Midnight Mass,' said Rupert. He liked her merry face and her bright beady eyes.

222

'Tell me,' he went on lowering his voice, 'is your sister ever going to forgive me?'

'Ah,' said Caitlin, 'well, you haven't been very nice to her. I heard about the groping at the dinner party, which was pretty crass, and the row over the stubble burning. Taggie probably over-reacted there; she's so soppy about animals, she spends her time prising frozen worms off the paths in this weather. What really pissed her off was that you were so unkind about Gertrude.'

'Gertrude?' said Rupert, bewildered.

'Our dog. You may think Gertrude is very plain, but we're all devoted to her. Taggie's led such a sheltered life, she's never left home like Patrick and me, and she and Gertrude have never been parted.'

Rupert grinned. 'Perhaps I should have sent Gertrude a pendant instead.'

'Oh my God,' said Caitlin in horror, 'it was *you*! Because you signed it R, we all assumed it was from Ralphie. Taggie's mad about him, you see.'

'Glad I gave her a happy Christmas,' said Rupert acidly.

'But she's not happy now, because Ralphie's turned up with another woman.'

'Which is he?'

'That blond over there. Taggie likes blonds, so if you give her time . . .'

'Caitlin,' said Maud very sharply, 'go and tell Taggie to clear away the fruit salad plates. We must have Patrick's cake, or we'll be still sitting here at midnight.' She turned to Rupert. 'We've managed to get tickets for *Starlight Express* the week after next. D'you want to come?'

'Don't talk about things that happen after I go back,' grumbled Caitlin, getting up.

'Taggie, Taggie,' she squealed, racing into the kitchen, 'Mummy wants the plates cleared, then we can have Patrick's cake.'

'There isn't anyone to clear them,' said Taggie in despair. 'Both the Makepiece children have vanished, and I can't find Mrs Makepiece or Grace, or Reg, or either of Reg's friends.'

'Never mind that now,' said Caitlin. 'This is *far* more exciting. It was Rupert who sent you that pendant, because he was sorry about goosing you at Valerie Jones's.'

'There's no way we're going to get 300 slices out of this.' Taggie nearly dropped Patrick's cake. 'What did you say?'

'Rupert sent you the pendant.'

'He couldn't have,' whispered Taggie. 'I hate him.'

'No, you don't. He's really nice. Go and sit next to him. I'll try and find Reg and his mates to carry the cake in and people can eat it on their fruit salad plates. Go on, Tag.'

'Never, never,' gasped Taggie. She was deathly pale now. 'I'm going to send it back.'

Maud's plans had gone seriously awry. She had wanted them all to be dancing and she and Rupert to be standing under one of Caitlin's hundred bunches of mistletoe at midnight, but they were still sitting at the tables waiting for Patrick to cut his cake. Why on earth couldn't Taggie be more efficient?

At five minutes to midnight Declan got somewhat unsteadily to his feet, and tapped the table with his knife. 'I'm very pleased to see you all here tonight,' he said, 'and I'd just like to drink my son Patrick's health. He's a good boy and he's given us a lot of pleasure over the years.'

'And me too,' piped up Patrick's girlfriend, Lavinia, and everyone laughed and sang 'Happy Birthday' and said 'Speech! Speech!' As Reg and his mates staggered in very perilously carrying the cake, Patrick stood up. Speaking in public didn't rattle him in the least. He had all Declan's assurance:

'I'd like to thank my father and mother for having me,' he said, 'and giving me such a wonderful party, and for my sister Taggie for doing all the work, and making this wonderful cake.' For a second Maud looked furious at the loudness of the cheers. 'Thank you all for coming, and for all your presents, which I'll open later when I get a moment.'

There were more loud cheers. Then, just as Caitlin finished lighting the candles, like the dark stranger coming over the

224

threshold, Cameron Cook walked in. She was wearing an extremely tight-fitting, strapless, black suede dress, which came eight inches above her knees. Three-inch cross-laced gaps on either side from armpit to hem made it quite plain she was wearing nothing but Fracas and Mantan underneath. There was a heavy metal chain round her neck, and among the heavy silver bangles worn over her long black suede gloves gleamed Tony's diamond bracelet.

Anyone else would have looked tarty in that dress, but Cameron, with her marvellously lean, sinuous, rapacious beauty, succeeded in looking both menacing and absolutely staggering.

'Holy shit,' said Patrick into the microphone.

Everyone screamed with laughter.

'Blow out your candles,' said Caitlin.

Still gazing at Cameron, Patrick blew them out with one puff, then turned to Declan. 'Who the hell's that?'

'The biggest bitch in television,' said Declan bleakly.

'She may well be your future daughter-in-law,' said Patrick.

'Christ, I can just see her with a whip,' muttered Bas to Rupert.

'Perhaps that's what gets your brother going.'

Basil turned to Daysee Butler: 'Did you know your boss was heavily into SM?'

'Who's she?' said Daysee.

'Sorry I'm late,' said Cameron, fighting her way through the crowd to Maud's side. 'We've had a lot of hassle at work.'

'Lovely to see you at any time,' said Maud. 'Caitlin,' she added pointedly, terrified that Caitlin might start monopolizing Rupert again, 'will get you something to eat.'

'She needs a drink,' said Patrick.

Goodness, he's pretty, thought Cameron. Like Declan, but purer-looking, somehow.

'Aren't you going to cut your cake?' she said to him.

'I've got to wish,' said Patrick. Never taking his eyes off her, he slowly plunged the knife into the cake, right up to the hilt.

'I didn't have time to buy you a present,' said Cameron.

225

'You brought yourself,' said Patrick, slightly mockingly. 'Just what I wanted.'

Filling up his glass with champagne, he handed it to her.

'Thanks.' Taking it, Cameron drained the glass.

Just at that moment, from speakers all round the tent, Big Ben boomed out the twelve strokes of midnight. As everyone started kissing everyone else and cheering, Patrick drew Cameron into his arms and kissed her on and on and on.

At last they broke away.

'The *coup de foudre*,' said Patrick softly. 'I've waited twenty-one years for this to happen.'

'Look at Tony's face,' whispered Lizzie Vereker to Charles Fairburn with a shiver.

As the last notes of 'Auld Lang Syne' rang out, Declan could be heard saying, 'Bloody January again.'

Plates were being cleared away, tables pushed back and the marquee cleared for dancing, as the women drifted upstairs to do their faces. Telling Cameron he wouldn't be a second, Patrick went off to the kitchen to thank Taggie. Oblivious that Monica might be watching, Tony fought his way over to Cameron and seized her arm: 'What the hell are you playing at?'

Cameron winced. 'Celebrating Christmas. It hasn't been great so far.'

'I couldn't get away.'

'I guess not.'

'That dress is deliberately provocative,' snarled Tony.

'Well, if it deliberately provokes you, it's doing a great job.'

'Why are you so fucking late?'

'Titania's four months gone.'

'Shit. How d'you know?'

'Wardrobe told me,' said Cameron.

'And she's admitted it?'

'Sure.'

'Who's the father?'

'She's not sure. It could be Bottom, or Theseus or even Peter Quince.'

'Jesus – we'll just have to shoot round her.'

Patrick never made it to the kitchen. Declan dragged him into the library.

'For Christ's sake, Cameron's out of bounds.'

'Why?'

'She's Tony Baddingham's mistress.'

'So. Are you frightened of losing your job?'

For a second Patrick thought Declan was going to hit him.

'It's not that. You've no idea of the evil of both of them.'

'He may be, she's not. She just needs someone of her own age to play with for a change.'

'He's taught her some very unpleasant habits,' said Declan heavily.

'Like arguing with you, I suppose,' said Patrick.

'She's out of your league.'

'I don't give a fuck,' said Patrick, walking out.

'You don't have to take your clothes off to have a good time, oh no,' sang Jermaine Stewart from the disco. *'You can dance and party all night.'*

Still arguing with Tony, seeing both Monica and Patrick bearing purposefully down on her, Cameron escaped to check her face. After Patrick's kiss, she certainly couldn't have any lipstick left. Upstairs, in the only bedroom that didn't seem to be inhabited by necking teenagers, she found Sarah Stratton brushing her hair.

'Good party,' said Sarah.

'It seems so.'

'I'm glad I bumped into you,' said Sarah. 'Tony's offered me a job at Corinium. Ought I to take it?'

'Sure,' said Cameron coolly.

'You don't think he's just after my body?'

'No way,' said Cameron, who was having difficulty applying lipstick, her hands were trembling so much.

'I just wondered.' Sarah dropped her head, brushing all her hair downwards. 'Tony and Monica are an awfully weird couple, you know. Paul's ex-wife, Winifred, used to be Monica's best chum. I've often wondered if they weren't a bit dykey.' Sarah tossed her head back, so her hair rose, then cascaded wildly onto her shoulders.

'Monica evidently told Winifred,' she went on, 'that Tony made such incredible sexual demands on her that she had to move into a separate bedroom. He wanted it two or three times every night. Now she restricts him to once a week, like church. Perhaps that's why he's so lecherous.'

As if in a dream, Cameron watched Sarah spray Anaïs Anaïs between her breasts, then behind her kneecaps and finally, pulling out her pants, on her blonde bush.

'Did Tony make a pass at you?' Cameron said in a frozen voice.

'Not exactly – but he was terrifically complimentary,' said Sarah. 'And I must say for an older man he's not unattractive.'

As they came downstairs James Vereker was hovering. Deliberately ignoring Cameron, he asked Sarah to dance. Oh well, thought Sarah, anything to make Rupert jealous.

'How did you get on with Tony's mistress?' asked James.

'Oh my Christ, is she?' gasped Sarah, appalled, and she told James what had happened. 'I'd better not take that job at Corinium after all,' she said finally.

'She'd certainly have it in for you,' said James. 'She has it in for any beautiful woman.' (And man for that matter, he nearly added.) 'If you came to Corinium – ' his arm tightened round her – 'I'd look after you and show you the ropes.'

'Isn't television frightfully difficult?'

'Not if you've got a teacher who really cares,' said James.

I'll kill Tony, I'll absolutely kill him, thought Cameron as, seething with rage, she went into the marquee. Both Tony and Patrick were waiting. Patrick was quicker.

'Come and dance,' he said, taking her hand. 'I'm not going to let you go for the rest of the evening, probably not for the rest of my life.'

'D'you always move in so fast?' said Cameron, laughing.

'No, I wished for you when I cut my cake.'

'You mustn't tell wishes; they might not come true.'

'Mine always do,' said Patrick calmly.

Taggie was mindlessly washing up in the kitchen when Simon Harris's little monsters returned and, saying they were hungry, broke through the clingfilm over the kedgeree and started eating it with their hands. Something finally snapped inside Taggie.

'Bugger off, you little horrors,' she screamed.

'Talking to me?' said a voice.

Rupert was standing in the doorway. He was as brown as he'd been last summer when he'd had no clothes on. Taggie went scarlet.

Rupert grinned. 'Your mother was only telling me the other day, how much you adore children.' Then, turning on the monsters, 'Go on, fuck off, you little sods. Out, OUT!'

Muttering venomously, the monsters sidled out, cramming birthday cake into their mouths as they went.

'It was the most lovely dinner,' said Rupert gently, noticing Taggie's reddened eyes. 'Will you please stop playing Cinderella and come and dance.'

'I've got too much to do, thank you, and thank you for the pendant. I didn't realize.' She stumbled on the words.

At that moment Simon Harris came in with spewed-up rusk all over his dinner jacket, carrying a bawling baby.

'Could you possibly hold her for me while I heat up a bottle?' he asked Taggie.

Of two evils, Taggie chose the prettier. 'There's a saucepan over there,' she said and, feeling Rupert's hand close over hers, she followed him into the marquee.

'I'm a very, very bad dancer,' she muttered.

'Doesn't matter,' said Rupert. 'We can sway in a dark corner.'

'*Never seen you look so lovely as you do tonight,*' sang Chris de Burgh, '*Never seen you shine so bright.*'

Taggie's hair smelt of shepherd's pie. As he drew her to him, Rupert could feel the substantial softness of her breasts, compared with the incredible slenderness of her waist. Her body was rigid with tension and embarrassment. She had absolutely no sense of rhythm at all. It was like a very slim elephant dancing at the circus.

'Did you have a nice Christmas?' asked Rupert.

'Yes.'

'Did you get nice presents?'

'Yes.'

'Come on my angel, relax.' His hands moved over her back, gentling her as though she was one of his young horses. 'Look! Gertrude's followed us. She knows I'm a rotter and she won't let you out of her sight.'

Catching Gertrude's disapproving eye, Taggie gave a half laugh, half sob.

Rupert reached down and stroked Gertrude. 'Good Gertrude, beautiful Gertrude. See, I am trying.'

'*Lady in red, Lady in red,*' sang everyone as they swayed round the floor, which were the only words they knew.

Rupert took Taggie's face in his hands. She was so tall her eyes were only just below his.

'Don't be so sad,' he murmured. 'You'll get over him.'

Taggie started. 'How d'you know?'

'Caitlin told me. You thought the pendant was from him. I'm sorry.'

'It was very kind,' said Taggie stiffly. 'I just don't accept presents from men.'

'I see. Only from boys.'

As Chris de Burgh finished and Wham started, he gripped her waist, knowing she was about to bolt.

'*Last Christmas, I gave you my heart,*' sang George Michael, '*But the very next day you gave it away.*'

Across the room Taggie could see Ralphie and Georgina dancing together. He was stroking her cheek with his hand. With a low moan, Taggie tugged herself away from Rupert. Cannoning off startled couples, she fled from the marquee upstairs to the loo to cry her eyes out once again.

Patrick danced on and on with Cameron. They didn't talk much because they were easily the best dancers in the room. Tony, grinding his teeth down to the gums, didn't dare move in with Monica looking on.

'That's the best thing I've seen in years,' said James Vereker, who was dancing on and on with Sarah.

'What?' said Sarah.

'Cameron getting off with Declan's son. At best it'll screw up Tony and Cameron. At worst it'll put Tony even more off Declan.'

Although Paul was hovering, looking thunderous, Sarah carried on dancing with James until she saw Rupert going past. Breaking away, she screamed out to him.

To keep her quiet Rupert bore her off to dance. Paul could see them rowing all the way round the floor, in that rigid-jawed way as though they'd had too many injections at the dentist.

'Why have you been deliberately ignoring me?'

'I haven't. It's just that Paul has been watching us like a Wimbledon linesman.'

'Never put you off in the past.'

'Did you have a good Christmas?'

'Of course I didn't. You obviously did, if the *Daily Mail*'s anything to go by. I don't require fidelity from my husband,' said Sarah hysterically, 'but I do from my lover.'

'Then you've picked the wrong guy, sweetheart. We've had a good time.'

Sarah looked up, aghast. 'Is it over then?'

'No, not necessarily. I'm just not prepared to offer you an exclusive.'

'Bastard,' hissed Sarah. 'I thought you were serious.'

'You were wrong, and frankly, angel, I don't think you make a very good MP's wife. Paul looks a shambles.'

In the kitchen, surrounded by undergraduates and dirty plates and glasses, Declan was declaiming Yeats:

> *And the flame of the blue star of twilight, hung low*
>   *on the rim of the sky,*
> *Has awaked in our hearts, my beloved, a sadness that*
>   *may not die.*

Cameron stood listening to him, her hand in Patrick's.

'He recites best when he's drunk,' whispered Patrick. 'Loses all self-consciousness.'

'He should do a programme on Yeats,' marvelled Cameron.

'Hardly of local interest.'

'We could do it for Channel Four.'

Upstairs, Maud was arranging her breasts in the green dress, and putting scent on her hair, and applying coral blusher to her pale cheeks. Her freckles were like a sprinkling of nutmeg tonight.

'I'm not middle-aged,' she whispered to herself. 'I'm still young and beautiful.'

'*I get no kick from champagne*,' sang the disco. '*Pure alcohol doesn't thrill me at all.*'

The message was all in the music, thought Maud. Go forth and multiply and seek love.

Going downstairs, she could hear Declan declaiming in the kitchen. She was safe for half an hour or so. Screams and shouts were coming from the direction of Caitlin's room.

The berries of the mistletoe gleamed brighter than her pearls under the hall light. It was three in the morning; soon Taggie would be serving kedgeree. As if in answer to her prayer, Maud heard Rupert's voice, 'Darling, I was looking for you.'

Taking her hand, he led her into the study where Caitlin, taking no chances, had hung more mistletoe. Rupert's hand felt so warm and dry, and the ball of his thumb was so pudgy, noticed Maud. That was the fortune-teller's clue to a passionate highly-sexed nature. It was certainly the only spare flesh on his body. Maud's heart was pounding. She must try and be distant, a little mysterious. As he turned towards her, her eyes were on a level with his black tie. She longed to caress the lovely line of his jaw. It's going to happen, she thought in ecstasy, as Rupert shut the door to blot out the screams and raucous laughter, and coming towards her, gazed deeply into her eyes.

232

'Angel, I've been wanting to ask you something from the moment we met, certainly from the moment I came over here with Bas after hunting. You won't be cross with me?'

'No, no,' whispered Maud. She was having difficulty breathing.

'You probably think I'm the biggest shit in the world.'

'I don't. I don't. I just think people misunderstand you.'

She could smell the faint lemon tang of his aftershave as he moved nearer.

'I'm absolutely mad,' began Rupert.

'Go on,' stammered Maud.

'About little Taggie, and she can't stand me. Could you possibly put in a good word for me?'

'Taggie,' said Maud in outrage, 'TAGGIE!'

She might have been Lady Bracknell referring to the famous handbag.

'For Christ's sake,' she screamed, 'Taggie's eighteen, you're thirty-seven. She's dyslexic, which makes her seem even younger. How dare you, you revolting letch, how dare you, how DARE you?' And, bursting into tears, she fled upstairs and locked herself in her bedroom.

She couldn't bear it, she, who'd always got anyone she wanted, being spurned under the mistletoe by the biggest rake in Gloucestershire. And for Taggie, of all people, which made it far, far worse. Almost pathologically jealous of Taggie, there was no one in the world Maud would less like to lose a man to. Was that to be her fate, growing older and less attractive, until no one wanted her?

An hour later in the kitchen Declan was still declaiming to an enraptured group.

'Christ, I wish I wasn't too tight to make notes,' said Ralphie.

'You see why he can't go on doing crappy interviews with the Bishop of Cotchester,' said Patrick to Cameron.

Cameron nodded.

•

A woman of so shining loveliness, [Declan was saying]
That men threshed corn at midnight by a tress,
A little stolen tress.

He looked up and saw Maud. 'A *little stolen tress*,' he repeated slowly.

For a minute they gazed at each other.

There is grey in your hair, [he began very softly]
Young men no longer catch their breath,
When you are passing.

Maud turned away, her face stricken.

Declan dropped his cigarette into the sink and, stepping over the enraptured seated undergraduates, caught up with Maud on the stairs. Not having had anything to drink for a couple of hours, he was sobering up.

'What's the matter? Did he turn you down?'

Maud nodded, tears spilling out between her eyelashes.

'I've seen it coming since September. I wanted to warn you.'

'Why didn't you then?'

Declan sighed: 'Has there ever been any point? He's no good for you. He's a traveller. It might have lasted a week, a month, then he'd have dumped you.'

He put his huge hands round her neck above the pearl choker.

'I'm sorry,' she mumbled. 'He's just so attractive.'

'I know. Hush, hush.' He raised his thumbs to still her quivering mouth. 'Let's go to bed.'

'We can't in the middle of a party.'

'What better time?'

'I've spent so much money.'

'Doesn't matter,' said Declan as they went up the remaining stairs.

'I love you,' he said softly, 'and I'm the only one of the lot of them who understands you.'

'I know,' whispered Maud.

234

Declan shut the bedroom door behind them.

Caitlin, going past, heard the key turn. Removing the sign outside the loo on which she had earlier written *Ladies*, Caitlin turned it over, wrote *Do Not Disturb, Sex in Progress*, and hung it on her parents' door.

Downstairs, the party showed no signs of winding down.

'I love yew,' said Lizzie, looking at a dark clump of greenery in the corner, as she danced round with Freddie.

'I love you,' said Freddie, giving her a squeeze. 'Honestly, on my life and at least a bottle-and-a-half of Moët.'

It was obvious that Tony wasn't going to be able to prise Cameron away from Patrick for even a second.

'We must go,' he said bleakly to Monica.

'All right,' said Monica reluctantly. 'I haven't seen Archie for hours. Where is he?'

'Upstairs, I think,' said Caitlin.

Monica swayed up the stairs, hanging onto the banisters. She hadn't drunk so much since she was a deb; it was really rather fun.

Finding several rooms heavily occupied by couples, she finally tracked down her elder and beloved son on a *chaise-longue* on the top floor, absolutely superglued to Tracey Makepiece, his hand burrowing like a ferret inside her white tricel shirt.

'Archie,' thundered Monica. 'Drop!'

Archie dropped.

'We're leaving,' said Monica, 'at *once*.'

Downstairs, she told Tony what Archie had been up to.

'Christ,' exploded Tony, 'he might put her in the club. Get him out of this bloody house as fast as possible.'

'I don't know where Declan and Maud are. We ought to thank them,' said Monica, as Archie shuffled sheepishly down the stairs.

Having witnessed the incident, Valerie gave her little laugh: 'One must learn to be democratic, Ay'm afraid these days, Monica. Sharon, of course, gets on with all classes.'

'Evidently,' said Caitlin, sliding down the banisters and

beaming at Valerie. 'She's been wrapped round Kevin Make-piece for the last two hours.'

Giving a screech close to death, Valerie bolted upstairs.

Caitlin turned to Monica, Tony and Archie with a beatific smile on her face. 'I bet Kev a pound he wouldn't neck with Sharon. I suppose I'll have to pay him now.'

'Are your parents around?' said Monica.

'I'm afraid they've gone to bed,' said Caitlin.

'Well, if you'd just tell them how very much we all enjoyed it,' said Monica.

'You may have enjoyed it,' hissed Tony, slipping on the icy drive in his haste to get to the Rolls and the frozen chauffeur, 'but frankly it was the most bloody party I've ever been to, and that child Caitlin is a minx.'

'She's sweet,' protested Archie with a hiccup.

'If you have anything more to do with any of the O'Hara children I'll disinherit you.'

About five in the morning, having behaved just as badly as everyone else, Rupert came back into the drawing-room looking for the whisky decanter, and saw a black and white tail sticking out from under the piano.

'Gertrude,' he said.

The tail quivered. Crouching down, Rupert found both Gertrude and Taggie.

'What on earth are you doing?'

'A drunk's passed out in my bed,' said Taggie with a sob. 'Every other bedroom in the house is occupied; a bloody great party, including Ralphie and his blonde are in the kitchen, so I can't wash up, the disco people haven't been paid, Mummy and Daddy have gone to bed, and I don't want to be a wallflower and cramp everyone's style.'

'You won't cramp mine. Come on.' Rupert dragged her out.

An empty champagne bottle rolled out at the same time.

'You drink all that?'

'Nearly.'

Rupert threw a couple of logs on the dying fire and then

236

sat Taggie down on the sofa beside him. Gertrude took up her position between them.

'It's been a wonderful party,' he said.

'It hasn't,' said Taggie despairingly. 'It's been a disaster. Patrick's got off with Lord Baddingham's m-mistress, which'll make Lord Baddingham go even more off Daddy. And Mummy's got a terrific crush on someone.' She blushed, remembering it was Rupert, and added hastily, 'I'm not sure who, and poor Daddy's got to pay for it all. I tried and tried to keep the cost down, but then Mummy went off and ordered all that champagne, and invited hundreds and hundreds of people.'

'Your father must earn a good screw from Corinium,' said Rupert reasonably.

'He does —' Taggie cuddled Gertrude like a terrified child clutching a teddy bear — 'but it's not nearly enough. He's got a massive overdraft and we still haven't paid for our leaving party in London, and he got another huge tax bill yesterday, and he hasn't paid the last one yet, and Mummy and Caitlin and Patrick won't take it seriously. They think Daddy's a bottomless pit who'll always provide.

'To produce his best work,' she went on, 'he's got to be kept calm. That's why we moved to the country for some peace and for him to finish his book. And he loathes Lord Baddingham, he thinks he's dreadfully cor — cor . . .' She blocked on the word.

'Corrupt,' said Rupert.

'That's right, and shouldn't be running Corinium at all. Daddy's so headstrong, I'm sure he'll walk out if there are any more rows, and he says the BBC won't have him back.'

Despite being drunk, Rupert appreciated it wasn't at all an ideal set-up.

'Of course the BBC would,' he said. 'Your father's a genius. He's got everything going for him.'

'Except us,' said Taggie with a sob. 'We're all a drain on him.'

'You're not,' said Rupert.

'I am. Ralphie doesn't love me. No one will ever love me.'

Rupert let her cry for a few minutes, then made her laugh by putting his black tie on Gertrude.

'I'm so sorry,' stammered Taggie, wiping her eyes on someone's discarded silk shawl. 'I'm being horribly s-s-self-indulgent.'

'You're not.' Suddenly Rupert felt very avuncular and protective as he did when one of his dogs cut its paw. He wished a visit to the vet and a few stitches could cure Taggie's problems.

'I'm going to get that drunk out of your bed and then you can go to sleep.'

'I must pay the disco – but no one seems to want them to stop – and the Makepieces. I've got the money.' She got a large wad of tenners out of the George V Coronation tin on the desk.

'I'll pay them,' said Rupert, taking the money. 'You're going to bed.'

Up in Taggie's turret bedroom, with some effort, Rupert lifted Charles Fairburn out of the bed and, lugging him down the winding stairs, put him on the *chaise-longue* recently vacated by Archie and Tracey Makepiece. As Taggie's room was like the North Pole, he returned with a duvet he'd whipped off a fornicating couple in the spare room. Taggie had got into a red flannel nightgown and cleaned her teeth. Lady in Red, thought Rupert. She had huge black circles under her eyes. She looked about twelve.

'Everything'll work out all right,' he said, tucking her in.

'You've been so kind,' stammered Taggie. 'I'm sorry I was so rude to you before, and thank you for the pendant.'

But as Rupert put out a hand to touch her cheek, Gertrude, still in her black tie, growled fiercely.

'You may have forgiven me,' said Rupert, 'but Gertrude hasn't.'

RIVALS
19

At seven-thirty the disco was still pounding. All over the house Patrick's friends, with ultra-fashionable cat-sick yellow socks over their eyes like aeroplane eye masks, had crashed out on arm chairs and sofas. Charles snored happily on his *chaise-longue*. In the small sitting-room, watched balefully by Gertrude still in Rupert's black tie, Cameron and Patrick opened Patrick's presents, throwing the wrapping paper into the fire to ignite the dying embers. Cameron had never seen such loot: gold cufflinks, Rolex watches, diamond studs, a Leica camera, a Picasso drawing, a Matthew Smith, a red-and-silver-striped silk Turnbull and Asser dressing-gown.

Patrick was like the prince in the fairy story, thought Cameron, whom each of the neighbouring kings was trying to win over with more and more extravagant presents. She thought bitterly back to her own twenty-first birthday. Neither of her parents had even bothered to send her a card.

'You'll never remember who gave you what. That's neat,' she added, as Patrick drew out a copy of *The Shropshire Lad* from some shiny red paper.

'Very,' said Patrick. 'First edition. What have you got there?'

'Silver hip flask, from someone called All my Love Lavinia. She's had it engraved. Who's she?'

'My Ex,' said Patrick, collapsing onto the sofa to read *The Shropshire Lad*.

'How Ex?'

'About two minutes before midnight last night. Listen: *When I was one-and-twenty, I heard a wise man say, Give crowns and pounds and guineas, but not your heart away.* Hope that's not prophetic. I wish Housman hadn't used the word "Lad" so often; so appallingly hearty. Who's that from?'

Cameron pulled a long, dark-brown cashmere scarf from a gold envelope. 'Georgie and Ralphie.'

'I bet Georgie paid for it – kind of them, though.'

He got up and wound the scarf round Cameron's neck, holding on to the two ends and slowly drawing her towards him.

'It's yours. Everything I have is yours,' he said, kissing her, only breaking away from her because the telephone rang.

He grinned as he put down the receiver. It was the vicar of Penscombe asking if they could turn the disco down for an hour so he could take early service.

'I must go,' said Cameron.

'You must not. I'll tell those disco boys to go and have some breakfast and then you and I are going to watch the sun rise.'

Wearing three of Patrick's sweaters, a pair of Taggie's jeans, rolled over four times at the ankle, Caitlin's gumboots, and a very smart dark-blue coat with a velvet collar left over the banisters by Bas Baddingham, Cameron set out with Patrick.

'I've shaved so I won't cut your face to ribbons,' he said.

'The wind'll do that,' grumbled Cameron.

The wind, in fact, had dropped, but a vicious frost had ermined all the fences, roughened the surface of the snow and turned the waterfall in the wood to two foot-long icicles. Gertrude charged ahead leaping into drifts, tunnelling the snow with her snout.

'Wow, it's beautiful,' said Cameron, as the valley stretched out below them. 'How much of it's yours?'

'To the bottom of the wood. The rest of the valley belongs to Rupert Campbell-Black.'

Christ, it's a kingdom, thought Cameron, looking across at the white fields, the blanketed tennis court, Rupert's golden house with its snowy roof and the bare beech wood rearing up behind like a huge spiky white hedgehog.

'We're trying to get him on your father's programme.'

'Why bother? Pa could interview him by morse code across the valley. He's the most awful stud. Evidently resentful husbands all over Gloucestershire bear scars on their knuckles from trying to bash down bedroom doors.'

'He was there last night,' said Cameron.

'Was he?' said Patrick. 'I only had eyes for you.'

They had reached the water meadows at the bottom of the wood. Here the snow had settled in roots of trees, in the crevices of walls, and in six-foot drifts anywhere it could find shelter from yesterday's blizzard. The blizzard had also laid thick white tablecloths of snow fringed with icicles on either side of the stream which ran with chattering teeth down the valley. It was deathly quiet except for Rupert's horses occasionally neighing to one another. But it was getting lighter.

'Nice scent,' said Patrick, burrowing his face in her neck. 'What is it?'

'Fracas.'

'Very appropriate. Who gave it to you?'

'Tony.'

'Why hasn't he got a neck?' Patrick hurled a snowball into the woods. Gertrude hurtled after it. 'You'd have thought with that much money he could have bought himself a neck.'

'Shut up,' said Cameron. 'Tell me, do your mother and father always slope off to bed in the middle of their own parties?'

'It's a very odd marriage,' said Patrick, pointing his new Leica at her. 'Look towards the stream, darling. My father has always seen my mother as Maud Gonne.'

'The woman Yeats was fixated on?'

'Right. Yeats fell in love with her at exactly the same age my father fell in love with my mother. Look, badger tracks.' Patrick bent down to examine them. 'Maud Gonne was a rabid revolutionary. Yeats knew he wouldn't impress her with poetry, so he got caught up in a political movement to unite Ireland. Then she married John MacBride, another revolutionary. Broke Yeats's heart, but it made him write his best poetry. He claimed Maud Gonne was beyond blame, like Helen of Troy.'

'But your mother isn't a revolutionary, for Christ's sake, and she hasn't married someone else.'

'No, but she has Maud Gonne's tremendous beauty, and my father has an almost fatalistic acceptance that she's above blame and will have affairs with other men.'

'Doesn't your mother care for him?'

'In her way. I once asked her why she messed him about so much. She said that, with every woman in the world after him, she could only hold him by uncertainty.'

Cameron digested this.

'But if he only loves her, and doesn't want all these women, why can't she stop playing games and love him back?'

'That's far too easy. She's convinced that, once he's sure of her, his obsession would evaporate. So the games go on.'

'I wish they wouldn't,' said Cameron. 'It sure makes him cranky to work with.'

She sat on a log and watched Patrick write 'Patrick loves Cameron' in huge letters in the snow. Then he got out his hip flask, now filled with brandy, and handed it to her.

'You warm enough?'

Cameron nodded, taking a sip.

'Do you have a drinking problem?' she asked, as Patrick took a huge slug.

Patrick laughed. 'Only if I can't afford it. Whisky's twelve pounds a bottle in Dublin. Will you come and stay with me at Trinity next term?'

It's crazy, thought Cameron. He's utterly unsuitable and eight years younger than me, but the snow had given her such a feeling of irresponsibility, she hadn't felt so happy for years. The only unsettling thing was that he reminded her so much of Declan. They had the same arrogance, the same assumption that everyone would dance to their tune. Patrick seemed to read her thoughts.

'Don't worry, I'm not at all like my father. Being Capricorn,

242

I have a very shrewd business head. I may be overexacting, but I'm also cool, calculating and calm, whereas my father is very highly strung and overemotional. Capricorns also have excellent senses of humour and make protective and loving husbands.' He grinned at her. The violet shadows beneath the brilliant dark eyes were even more pronounced this morning, but nothing could diminish the beauty of the bone structure, the full slightly sulky curve of the mouth, or the thickness of the long dark eyelashes.

'Not a very artistic sign, Capricorn,' Cameron said crushingly.

'What about Mallarmé?' said Patrick. 'One of the bravest, most dedicated of poets. He was Capricorn. He knew what slog and self-negation is needed to produce poetry. He understood the loneliness of the writer. Look, here's the sun.'

Hand in hand they watched the huge red sun climbing up behind the black bars of the beech copse on the top road, blushing at its inability to warm the day.

'Looks like Charles Fairburn spending a night inside for soliciting,' said Patrick.

'God, I wish I had a crew,' said Cameron. 'D'you realize you can only afford to film sunrises in winter in this country? In summer it rises at four o'clock in the morning. That's in golden time, when you have to pay a crew miles over the rate for working through the night. Christ, I hate the British unions.'

Patrick turned towards her. 'I only like American-Irish unions. Let me look at you.'

Her dark hair, no longer sleeked back with water, was blown forward in black tendrils over her cheek bones, and in a thick fringe which softened the slanting yellow eyes, and the beaky nose. Her skin and her full pale lips were amber in the sunshine.

Patrick sighed and took another photograph. 'Even the sun's upstaged. You're so dazzling, he'll have to wear dark glasses to look at you.'

Cameron laughed. He'd be terribly easy to fall in love with, she was shocked to find herself thinking.

'How many more terms have you got?' she asked as they wandered back.

'Two.'

'What are your future goals?'

'To take you to bed when we get home.'

'Don't be an asshole! Apart from that?'

'Get a first, then write plays.'

'Just like that?'

'Just like that. I've started one already.'

'What's it about?'

'Intimidation – by British soldiers in Ulster.'

'You're crazy – neither the BBC nor ITV would touch it, particularly in an election year. Nor will the West End.'

'Broadway would, and a success there would come here.'

'Very self-confident, aren't you?'

'Not particularly. I just know what I want from life.'

He moved closer, putting his hands inside the three jerseys warming them on her small breasts.

'I want you most.'

Back at The Priory, people were beginning to surface. Bas, having put so many Alka Seltzers in a glass of water they'd fizzed over the top, was trying to find his overcoat. Caitlin was eating Alpen and reading *Lady Chatterley's Lover*. Taggie was serving breakfast to Simon Harris's monsters, trying to give the baby its bottle and comfort Simon Harris who was sobbing at the kitchen table with his face in his hands.

'Oh Patrick, thank goodness you're back,' she said. 'Could you possibly ring the doctor about . . .' She nodded in Simon Harris's direction.

'No,' said Patrick, backing out of the kitchen. 'Sorry, darling, I'm busy.'

'I'm going home to call the office and get some sleep,' said Cameron.

'No,' said Patrick, suddenly frantic. 'If we go to sleep it won't be my birthday any more and we'll break the spell.'

He took her up the winding stairs to his bedroom in the east turret, which was painted dazzlingly white, as though the snow had fallen inside. There were no carpets or curtains, and the only furniture was a desk, a chair, a green and white sofa piled high with books, and a vast red-curtained oriental four-poster with bells hanging from the tops of the posts. The view, however, was magnificent, straight across the valley and up to Penscombe. You could see the weathercock on top of the church spire glittering in the sunlight.

A volume of Keats lay open on the bed: the pages were covered with pencilled notes. Picking it up, Cameron crawled under the duvet and tried to decipher Patrick's writing. Looking up, she saw the ceiling was painted dove grey with little stars picked out in white.

If only she'd had a room like this when she was young, she thought bitterly. Patrick went off to get them some breakfast. He took longer than anticipated. Taggie was on the telephone ringing up some doctor about Simon Harris, but she ran after him and buttonholed him as he was going back upstairs with a tray, dragging him into the sitting-room, distraught that he had Cameron in his room.

'She's Tony Baddingham's c-c-concubine.'

'Is that your word for the day?' said Patrick coldly.

'No, that's what Daddy calls her. Do you want to ruin his career?'

'Tony B couldn't be that petty, firing a megastar like Pa, just because I took his mistress off him.'

'He could! He's really evil!'

'Well if he's that evil, Pa shouldn't be working for him. Now, get out of my way, sweetheart. The coffee's getting cold.'

'And I've had enough of entertaining your friends,' Taggie screamed after him.

'Bicker, bicker,' said Caitlin, looking up from *Lady Chatterley's Lover*. 'Pity it isn't Spring, then Cameron could festoon your willy with forget-me-nots. Oh my God,' she screamed, as an ashen Daysee Butler shuffled downstairs in a white towelling dressing-gown. 'It's The Priory ghost.'

Upstairs, Patrick found Cameron wearing her new red and silver dressing-gown and reading Keats. The sun shining through the stained glass of one of the windows had turned her face emerald, ruby and violet like a nymph of the rainbow. Patrick felt his heart fail.

He had brought up croissants, Taggie's bramble jelly, a bunch of green grapes, a jug of Buck's Fizz and some very strong black coffee. Cameron, who'd had no dinner the night before, was starving and ate most of it. It was astonishing, thought Patrick, that she looked desirable even with croissant crumbs on her lips. But even the black coffee couldn't keep her awake for long. Patrick didn't sleep. He sat making notes on Keats, which was one of his set books, but spending more time gazing at her. In sleep her face lost all its aggression.

It was almost dark when she woke up. For a second she looked bewildered and utterly terrified.

'It's all right,' said Patrick gently. 'You're safe now.'

She got up and looked out of the window. Orion, the swaggering voyeur, was looking in at her. The great yews and cedars were black against the snow. She could hear an unearthly strangulated croaking.

'What's that?'

'Foxes barking. It's a love call. Come here.'

'Not till I've cleaned my teeth.'

Grabbing her bag she went down the landing, terrified of bumping into Declan. Instead, coming out of the bathroom she found Caitlin and Maud having a row.

'I'm nothing like Lady Chatterley,' Maud was screaming. 'Good evening, Cameron. Nothing at all.'

'You're so lucky to have a family,' said Cameron as she slid back under the duvet beside Patrick. He was still wearing a jersey and trousers.

'How many times have you been home, since you came over here?' he asked.

'I haven't.'

'Why not? One must see one's family occasionally if only to fight with them.'

The argument outside was growing more clamorous.

'My parents are divorced. My father's married again. My

mother lives with someone. I don't want to talk about it,' said Cameron shrilly. Suddenly she was trembling, her teeth chattering, her eyes darting and frightened.

'You must,' said Patrick. 'How can I love you properly if I don't know everything about you?'

'No!' It was almost a scream.

'Come on. It'll help, I promise.'

They argued for some minutes before she gave in.

Suddenly he reminded her again of Declan. He had the same gentle but relentlessly probing voice, the same way of never taking his eyes off her face, and almost hypnotizing her into telling him everything.

'My mother walked out on my father when I was fourteen,' said Cameron tonelessly. 'Decided she wanted to be her own person. She dabbled in a lot of things, peace marches, consciousness raising, but she wasn't sufficiently focused and when the money ran out she moved to a female commune. Took me with her, but left my dog behind, because it was male.' Cameron gave a bitter, choked laugh, 'I never forgave her for that. My father got married again, and got all tied up with his new wife. Then Mom shacked up with Mike.'

'Your step-father?'

There was a long pause.

'You could call it that. Mike was a dyke. My mother wrote a piece about coming out in the *Village Voice*. All her friends thought she was real brave. My classmates just sniggered and nudged each other.'

'You poor little baby.' Patrick took her trembling hands.

'Then Mike and Mom moved to Cincinnati and Mike got the job of City Editor on the local paper. I could have put up with her being gay, but she was a real bull dyke, more macho than a guy really, with a skin like the surface of the moon, and hip measurements in treble figures, and a beer-gut spilling over her leather belts.' Cameron shuddered. 'She had a huge motorbike and she used to take Mom on the pillion. They joined a crazy organization called "Dykes on Bikes" and roared round the country in black leather going to gay parades.'

247

Patrick drew her to him. He could feel the pouring sweat, the terrible fits of shivering sweeping over her.

'Go on, darling,' he whispered.

'I prayed Mike would crash and kill herself. Then, as a last straw, Mom decided their union should be blessed and went off and got pregnant by AID. Mike was mad about the idea at first, strutted round as though she was the real father. Then when the baby arrived, it was a boy, poor little sod, and she got jealous. Mom was over forty. She had a terrible labour. She was in hospital for ten days. I was alone in the house with Mike. Every night she came home plastered. Then one evening I remember she spent about ten minutes getting her key into the lock. I was trying to work in my room. I can't tell you. I've never told anyone this.' She was suddenly frantic like a cat struggling and clawing to escape. Patrick held onto her. 'It's OK. You've got to trust me. Come on, sweetheart, come on.'

'Mike yelled for me to come downstairs and fix her some supper.' Cameron's voice was toneless again, and so quiet Patrick could hardly hear her.

'I was frying her eggs and bacon when suddenly she came up behind me and started to grope me, ripping my clothes off, trying to kiss me. Ugh. She was terribly strong. I swung the pan round and hit her with it. Then I ran out into the night.'

Cameron put her fingers in her hair, rubbing the ball of her hand over and over again against her forehead, as if to blot out the memory. Patrick waited.

'I went to some neighbours. I lied that Mike had tried to beat me up. They said they'd expected it for months. They called Dad in Washington. He came the next day and took me to live with him. He'd been dying to get something on Mom and Mike and the court ruled I should stay with him.'

'What happened then?'

'It didn't work,' said Cameron wearily. 'The honeymoon wore off. My stepmother's a lawyer, my father's a diplomat; they had a young baby. They're Very Civilized People and Very Busy; they couldn't handle a savage like me. I disrupted

248

their lives, I made awful scenes, stayed out all night. They couldn't see I was crying out for someone to care. I ran away from them too in the end. I got a scholarship to Barnard, worked in the Vac to support myself, got a job on the *New York Times*, and finally moved to television. The rest is hysterics.' She gave her bitter mirthless laugh again.

'You poor darling.' Patrick pulled her back into his arms again, kissing her forehead. No wonder she was screwed up and aggressive and desperately insecure after that. He'd never felt so sorry for anyone in his life.

'Didn't you have a boyfriend to look after you?'

'Oh I screwed around like crazy, just to prove I was heterosexual. Then the AIDS scare started in the States. Then Tony came along.'

'Hardly the ideal father figure,' said Patrick.

'I'm not dependent on him,' snarled Cameron too quickly. 'I'm not dependent on anyone. The only time I feel I belong is when my credits come up on the screen.'

She was shuddering violently now, furious with herself for dropping her guard and revealing so much.

'I guess you'll run to Declan now and tell him the whole thing, so you can have a good laugh.'

'Don't be childish,' snapped Patrick. 'I'm going to look after you. I'll blot out all the bad memories, even if it takes a lifetime.'

Never taking his eyes off her face, he started to unbutton his shirt.

'It's too soon,' she whispered.

'I'm not going to fuck you,' said Patrick. 'I'm just going to hold you close. You've got to learn that someone loves you for other things besides your heavenly body, and your skills as a career bitch.'

Patrick was as good as his word. Gradually the shuddering stopped and he soothed all the tension out of her. Exhausted by so much revelation, she even slept again. At midnight she insisted on going back to her house. He was very loath to let her go.

'Let me get dressed. I'll run you home.'

'I've got my car.'

'I want to see your house.'

'That's Tony's patch.'

'Not any more. Tony's past history.'

Cameron sighed. 'I guess it's a bit more problematical than that.'

'I feel like Demeter letting Persephone go back to the underworld,' said Patrick as he fastened her seat belt. 'For Christ's sake, drive carefully. The roads are like glass. I'll ring you tomorrow. I love you.'

Hell, thought Cameron, as she drove up to the house, I must have left the living-room light on. She glanced in the hall mirror. Not a scrap of make-up. Despite the sleep, the circles under her eyes were darker than her eyebrows. Patrick had really seen her in the raw, yet she felt strangely cleansed and at peace at having told him everything. Tomorrow they'd make love. She knew it would be wonderful. The slow lazy smile of anticipation was wiped off her face when she went into the living-room and found Tony.

The videos of her programmes lay scattered over the floor. The ashtray was filled with cigar butts. The whisky bottle, which had been half-full, was empty now. Tony was a slow drinker; he must have been there hours. Cameron shut the door and leant against it, her heart crashing. With a particularly unpleasant smile on his face, Tony picked up some papers lying on the table.

'I've been looking at your contract,' he said amiably. 'D'you want to leave now or work out your notice?'

It was as though the last twenty-four hours had never existed. Here was reality. Her whole career, her only security, was crashing round her ears in ruins.

'I haven't done anything. You can't fire me,' she whispered in terror.

'I don't have to. Your contract runs out in six weeks. Such a pity you blew it.' He examined his square, beautifully manicured fingernails. 'I came round to tell you that Simon Harris gave in to his nervous breakdown and was carted off to a loony bin this afternoon on extended leave. But you know what I feel about unpunctuality and twenty-four hours is a little late to come home from the ball.'

'But I never normally see you on a Sunday,' said Cameron illogically. She seemed too stunned to take anything in.

'That doesn't mean I don't expect you to be here.'

Smiling, he picked up his glass of whisky.

'You bloody little whore,' he said softly. The next moment he'd hurled it in her face.

For a second she was speechless, as the liquid dripped down on to the suede dress.

'How odd,' she said in a strained, high voice. 'Every time I buy something new and expensive some jerk spills something all over it.' Then she lost her temper.

'You bastard,' she screamed. 'I haven't taken a weekend off in three years. I'm always at your fucking beck and call.'

'That's what I pay you for,' said Tony. His eyes were sparkling with pleasure now.

'You bloody don't. If you paid me golden time for the hours I put in for you, I'd be Howard Hughes by now. You frig around doing exactly what you like, expecting me to behave like a fucking nun, except when you require my services. Well, it's not bloody good enough.'

She sprang at him, trying to claw his face, but he grabbed her wrists. He was not bull-necked and thick-armed for nothing. As his grip tightened, Cameron gasped with pain.

'I'd put up with it,' she said through clenched teeth, 'if the relationship was remotely even. You raise hell if I date anyone else, but you're quite free to take darling Sarah Stratton out to lunch and make passes at her and offer her a job.'

Tony's eyes gleamed. 'So that's it. Who told you that?'

'She did,' yelled Cameron, desperately struggling to get away. 'And she said you still sleep with Monica.'

Tony grinned. 'She must have an excellent spy system.'

'The Old Bag system. Monica told Winifred, who told Paul, who told Sarah that, as you were always pestering her, Monica restricts you to once a week. And you told me you hadn't laid a finger on her for years. You bloody liar.'

'It's rather exciting sleeping with Monica,' mused Tony. 'There's a rarity element about it.'

'So that's why you sent Madden tripping out to James Garrett on Christmas Eve to buy us both diamond bracelets. Jesus Christ!'

Starting to laugh, Tony let go of her wrists. 'You discovered that too, did you? Poor little Cameron, you must have been festering over Christmas. Jealousy is the most destructive of emotions, you know. It hurts only oneself.'

'I hate you,' screamed Cameron, wrenching off the bracelet and hurling it at him. Missing him, it hit the window, slithering scratchily down the glass like a fingernail on a blackboard.

'Get out! I'll move out tomorrow, but leave me alone now.' She collapsed, sobbing, on the sofa. Regurgitating her past with Patrick earlier had only underlined how terrifying it was to have no security. She was a panic-stricken sixteen-year-old again, racing through the night away from Mike with nowhere to go.

Tony poured two fingers of brandy into a glass, then moved towards her, until she could feel the solidness of his thigh against hers. She resisted the temptation to cling on to it, as a child might fling its arms around a tree for comfort.

'You were jealous, really jealous,' purred Tony. 'Was that why you led that boy on?'

'Sure.'

He caught her hair, yanking her head back. 'Did you sleep with him?'

'Yes,' she muttered. Then, terrified he was going to hit her or throw the brandy into her face, 'But not the way you think, I was so goddam tired. I hadn't slept for nights worrying about everything. I crashed out on his bed.'

'And nothing happened?'

'Nothing, nothing! He's just a kid.' Oh please make him believe her.

'Did Declan know you spent the night there?'

'No, I never saw him. He never came out of the bedroom.' With the franchise coming up this year, Tony decided, he didn't really want to lose her, but he was going to enjoy torturing her a bit more.

'And you promise never to see the boy again?'

'I promise,' said Cameron wearily. 'But he may try to see me.'

'We'll have to put pressure on Declan to stop him then, won't we?' said Tony silkily, as he took off Cameron's jacket.

'That is a very disturbing dress. I'd rather you didn't wear it in public again.'

Putting his hand under the skirt, he jabbed two fingers up inside her.

Cameron winced. 'I can't, Tony, not tonight. I'm really pooped.'

'You can,' said Tony softly, 'if you want to be Controller of Programmes.'

Three days after Patrick's party Taggie was gingerly testing her heart and finding that the ache for Ralphie was much less acute than she'd expected it to be when the doorbell rang.

In the doorway stood Rupert. His suntan was already beginning to fade.

'Hullo,' he said, soulfully gazing into her eyes. 'Since your wonderful party, I haven't been able to eat a thing.'

'Oh my goodness,' stammered Taggie, her heart beginning to thump.

Rupert grinned. 'Could I possibly have my knives and forks and plates back?'

Taggie was used to unrequited love. Patrick, however, was not. Hopelessly spoilt by his mother, accustomed to attracting girls effortlessly, he couldn't believe Cameron didn't want to see him any more.

Despite Declan's tirades and Taggie's pleading, he continued to pester her with letters and telephone calls. Then, when these were not answered, he hung round the Corinium studios and outside her house.

Cameron, in fact, had hardly had time to think. As well as producing Declan's programme and coping with her new job as Acting Controller of Programmes, she had to face a virtual palace revolution from a staff outraged by her appointment.

The afternoon before he was due to go back to Trinity, Patrick rang Cameron at the office. Expecting a call from Rupert about coming on Declan's programme, Cameron unthinkingly picked up the telephone instead of leaving it to her secretary.

'Can I speak to Cameron?' said Patrick.

Cameron froze. Putting on a cockney accent, she said, 'I'm afraid she's not at her desk at the moment.'

'Where is she?' snapped Patrick. 'Lying with the Managing Director under *his* desk.'

Cameron hung up.

The telephone was ringing again as she got home that evening. Running into the hall, she snatched up the receiver. It was Rupert answering her call.

'We were talking about a date for you to come on Declan's programme,' she said with a confidence she didn't feel. 'I was just hoping to firm you up.'

Rupert laughed. 'Extraordinary terminology you use in television.'

His diary was ridiculously full, but to her amazement he said he could make a Wednesday in February, which turned out to be St Valentine's Day. He'd been so adamant he wouldn't do the programme.

'And in case I don't bump into Declan beforehand, can you ask him if he's free for dinner afterwards?'

Cameron didn't say that after Declan had taken Rupert to the cleaners she thought it most unlikely.

'That was a good party on New Year's Eve,' said Rupert. 'I saw you bopping in your suede dress. I hoped you'd jump out of your skin.'

The next moment Cameron nearly did jump out of her skin, as she felt a kiss on the back of her neck. Patrick had walked in through the unlocked door.

254

'Get out,' hissed Cameron, clapping her hand over the receiver.

Shaking his head, Patrick sauntered into the living-room. She caught a blast of whisky as he passed.

Talking gibberish, furious at having to wind up her conversation with Rupert so abruptly, she said goodbye and went into the living-room, where she found Patrick hurling darts at the dart board.

'Nice place you've got here. I can see why you wouldn't want to give it up in a hurry.'

'Get out,' screamed Cameron.

'Not until you tell me why you didn't ring back.'

He went up to the board, and pulled out the darts. His hands were shaking, his eyes were black hollows in a deathly pale face. He must have lost pounds; he looked terrible.

'There was no reason to call back. We had a fun day.'

'A fun day?' he asked incredulously. 'Was that all it meant to you, after the sunrise, and all you told me about your mother and Mike and you falling asleep in my arms?'

'Shut up,' hissed Cameron, looking round in terror, expecting Tony to pop up from under the piano.

Patrick picked up a huge bunch of anemones which he'd left on the dentist's chair.

'I bought you these. For Christ's sake, I love you. Can't you understand that?'

In answer Cameron snatched the flowers from him and hurled them into the fireplace. Patrick winced and turned back to the dart board. The first dart missed, crashing into the wall, the second hit the glass in the frame of one of Cameron's awards, the third hit a plate.

'Pack it in,' said Cameron more calmly. 'If Tony turns up, he'll kill us both.'

'He's a fiend. I've been checking up on him,' said Patrick, sitting down at the piano. 'He's so avaricious,' he went on between crashing chords, 'even the bags under his eyes have got gold in them, and he's corrupting you too, turning you into his pet Rottweiler to savage any of his staff he wants to reduce to jelly. You'll never get out of the Underworld if you stay with him.'

'Tony suits me,' said Cameron over the din. 'We've been together for three years, OK? My career's the only thing that matters.'

'So you agreed to drop me if he made you Controller of Programmes?'

'You flatter yourself. What can you offer me?'

Patrick's hands came down in a jumble of discords. '*I, being poor*,' he said bitterly, '*can only offer you my dreams.*'

'Stop talking like a prime-time soap.'

'You should know, you make enough of them. Can I have a drink?'

'You've had enough,' snarled Cameron. 'Tony'll be here in a minute.'

'And he'll settle you in that dentist's chair,' said Patrick scornfully, 'and say "open wide", and then it's Wham, bam, thank you, Mammon. My Christ.'

He slammed the piano lid down and got to his feet.

'Don't be obnoxious,' hissed Cameron.

On New Year's Day, when she'd sobbed in his arms, he'd seemed so strong. Suddenly now he looked terribly young and frightened. Cameron was too insecure herself to be drawn to frailty.

'I'm truly sorry,' he muttered. 'It hurts loving you, that's all. Look, I'll do anything. I'll chuck Trinity, get a job. It'll be easy with Pa's connections.'

'Always fall back on Daddy, don't you?' taunted Cameron. 'You bitch about his philistine programme, but you'll bleed him white when it suits you. Well I'm not having you bleeding *me* white. Can't you get it into your Neanderthal skull that I don't want you around?'

Guilt at the way she'd treated him made her even more brutal.

'I can't help myself,' said Patrick, going towards the door. 'La Belle Dame sans merci has me totally in thrall.'

He went to the nearest pub and drank until long after closing time. The landlady felt sorry for the beautiful, obviously desolate young man sitting there quietly gazing into space.

At midnight Patrick parked his car four houses down from Cameron's and got out. It was a punishingly cold night. Cotchester slumbered beneath her eiderdown of snow. In a sky russet from the streetlamps huge stars flickered. Icicles glittered from Cameron's gutters. In front of the house beside Cameron's green Lotus was parked Tony's bloody great dark-red Rolls Royce with the Corinium ram on the bonnet. There was a light on in the top of the house – Cameron's bedroom, guessed Patrick. He imagined Tony brutally clambering over her lovely body. The Sunday before last she'd lain in his arms, pliant as a child. He wanted to plunge one of the icicles into Tony's heart.

Wearing only a jersey and an old pair of cords, he was shivering violently now. Then he noticed that Tony's car keys were still in the dashboard. Trying the car door he found it open. The lecherous bugger had obviously been in such a hurry to get at Cameron he'd forgotten to lock it.

Easing open the door, pulling out the keys, Patrick chucked them into a nearby flower bed. They landed deep in a lavender bush, hardly scattering the snow.

At four o'clock in the morning Tony looked at his watch. 'I must go.'

Cameron didn't dissuade him. She was utterly shattered. To eradicate any memory of Patrick, Tony had recently insisted on indulging in sexual marathons. Four times that night, he thought smugly; no one could accuse him of losing his touch. Cameron daren't complain. She was also twitchy that Patrick might do something insane to rock the boat.

Hearing Tony let himself out, she was just falling asleep when she heard a key turn in the door. It was a sound that always unnerved her, reminding her of Mike. For a wild moment of dread and longing she thought it might be Patrick.

'Did I leave my keys here?' shouted Tony.

By the time they'd upended the entire house, the car and

the drive, screamed at each other and nearly frozen to death, the lights had come on in the houses opposite and curtains were twitching in the houses on either side. There was no way Tony could start the Rolls, or get someone to help push it out of the way. If he rang Percy, his chauffeur, it would be round the entire network in a flash, so he spent the next three hours frantically and abortively ringing round the country, trying to find another set of keys.

In the end he had to order a taxi from the station. His temper was not improved by the driver recognizing him and slyly my Lording him all the way home.

Arriving at The Falconry, he had to provide Monica with a ridiculously convoluted explanation that he'd decided to come home that night, but that his car had gone into a skid on the motorway and he'd had to abandon it. He then had to keep her in bed in the morning, so she wouldn't drive into Cotchester and see his car parked outside Cameron's house.

As it was, poor, loyal Cyril Peacock tracked down a key and removed the Rolls by midday, but by then almost the entire Corinium staff had seen the car on their way in to work and had had a good laugh. That afternoon, Cameron passed the staff noticeboard. Beneath the card announcing her appointment as Acting Controller of Programmes, some-one had added the words: 'and Mistress of the Rolls'.

Later that day, Patrick rang Cameron from Birmingham Airport to say goodbye.

'Did you steal Tony's keys?' she shouted.

'Tell him to look under the lavender on the left of the front door.'

Cameron let Patrick have it. 'You stupid asshole. If Monica had come by and seen the car, you'd have landed Tony in a divorce court.'

'I thought that's what you wanted.'

'Don't be so fucking infantile.'

'I couldn't help it.' Patrick's voice faltered. 'I can't bear to think of that great toad in bed with you.'

'Get out of my life,' screamed Cameron. 'You don't know the rules.'

'I love you.' Patrick was almost crying.

'Well, I don't love you. You're a fucking nuisance. Piss off and try and do something worthwhile with your life.'

She was dead scared of telling Tony about the keys, but was amazed to find that he was grimly pleased.

'What a very silly little boy to put such a very large nail in his father's coffin.'

20

At the end of January the IBA formally asked for applications for the new franchises. These applications, which had to be provided not only by the fifteen incumbent independent companies, but also by any rival consortium who sought to oust them, often ran to hundreds of beautifully bound pages, giving details of finance, staffing policies, plans for future programmes and proposed boards of management.

After the applications were handed in in early May, the IBA would study them and then conduct a series of public meetings around the country, attempting to find out whether the public felt well-served by their particular local television company. After private meetings between the IBA and all the individual contenders in October and November, the franchises would be finally awarded in December.

Anticipating a long year full of lobbying and hustling, Tony Baddingham's immediate task in the New Year was to strengthen the Corinium Board. Knowing the IBA and particularly Lady Gosling's penchant for women, he intended to make Cameron a director. But he wanted to punish her as long as possible for stepping out of line with Patrick, and, as the staff were still in a state of mutiny over her appointment, he didn't want a strike on his hands in franchise year. The staff, however, had short memories. Cameron had found Simon Harris's affairs in such a shambles that Tony had quite enough excuses to dispense with his services when he came out of hospital, but that would have to be done discreetly too. Then he could appoint Cameron to the Board just before the applications went in.

Tony also had his lunch with Freddie Jones, who, heavily pressured by Valerie, was poised to join the Corinium Board. His only reservation was whether, with his electronics empire and his race horses and his hunting, he would have sufficient time. If he were a director, he wanted to do some directing.

As an added incentive to Valerie, however, Tony invited Freddie shooting the last Saturday in January, and asked some extremely grand people to shoot as well. Never having shot with Freddie before, Tony issued a warning to the other guns beforehand.

'Freddie Jones is a bit of a rough diamond, but exceptionally able. He's going to be very useful on our board, if you know what I mean. But I'm not sure how good a shot he is, so bring your tin hat.'

In the master bedroom at Green Lawns Freddie Jones lay beside his wife in the vast suede oval bed, covered with dials for quadraphonic stereo, radio, dimmer switches, razors and vibrators which Valerie used to massage her neck. They had to leave for Tony's about nine. It was now only six forty-five, which left plenty of time for sex, thought Freddie hopefully. They had already drunk two cups of tea from the Teasmade. Reaching across, Freddie put his hand on Valerie's bush, fingering her clitoris from time to time as a door-to-door salesman, not very hopeful of entrance, might press a doorbell.

Valerie sighed. She knew no wife should deny her husband his conjugal rights, but one of the joys of Freddie getting up early to go hunting every Saturday meant that she could pretend to be asleep as she did every weekday when he left for work at six-thirty.

Valerie did everything to avoid sex. She had already taken back to Jolly's of Bath the absurdly sexy black lingerie an ever-hopeful Freddie had bought her for Christmas and replaced it with some peach satin sheets for the guest bedroom. She always wore woollen nightgowns buttoned up to the neck. If only she could sew up the bottom as well! The pressing finger was getting more insistent.

'D'you want to come, Fred-Fred?'

'Do you?'

'Not really. I want to be fresh for Tony and Monica.'

'Will you help me then?'

Valerie sighed again. Kneeling, she raised the red woollen nightgown, so Freddie could admire her candy pink nipples and her neatly clipped bush. She loathed watching him, but at least it stopped her getting messy.

'You're so beautiful,' sighed Freddie. 'You've got the body of a little girl.'

'Here's some tissues. Don't waste a clean towel, Fred-Fred.'

He had barely finished his lonely act before Valerie had reached up to press another switch on the bedhead which instantly sent boiling water gushing out of the 22-carat-gold mixer taps into the vast onyx and sepia marble double bath next door. Then, remembering she didn't want a flushed face, Valerie twiddled another knob to lower the temperature.

Snowdrops spread in a milk-white blur on either side of Tony Baddingham's drive. The guns, in their dung-coloured clothes, gathered outside The Falconry, pulling on gumboots and bellowing at excited dogs that whisked about lifting their legs on Monica's aconites.

At nine-thirty, just as it stopped raining, Freddie's freshly cleaned red Jaguar roared up the drive.

'Oh dear,' said Freddie, leaning out of the window and roaring with laughter at the other guns' filthy Landrovers, 'I forgot to chuck a bucket of mud over my car before I came out. Amizing, those snowdrops,' he said, clambering out. 'Just like a big fall of snow.'

He was wearing a red jersey, a Barbour and no cap on his red-gold curls. Next minute Valerie emerged from her side in a ginger knickerbocker suit, with a matching ginger cloak flung round her shoulders, and a ginger deerstalker.

'Christ,' muttered Tony to Sarah Stratton.

'It's Sherlock Lovely Homes,' said Sarah, making no attempt not to laugh. 'All she needs is a curved pipe and a spy glass.'

'What's that?' asked Valerie gaily.

'We were admiring your – er – outfit,' said Sarah quickly.

'All from my Spring range,' said Valerie, looking smug. 'Better hurry, it's selling like hot cakes.'

Tony oozed forward, exuding charm.

'You both know Sarah and Paul Stratton of course, and my brother Bas,' he said smoothly, and when he went on to introduce Valerie to the Lord-Lieutenant Henry Hampshire, two peers and a Duke from the next county, Valerie nearly had the orgasm Freddie had so longed to give her earlier. Fred-Fred must definitely join the Corinium Board, thought Valerie. It might be a Prince, or even a King, next time.

'Hullo, Valerie,' said Monica, who was wearing a green sou'wester over a headscarf. 'Would you like a cup of coffee?'

'Naughty,' chided Valerie, waving a tan suede finger. 'I said you must call me Mousie, No, I won't have a coffee, thank you.'

She didn't want to have to go to the toilet behind a hawthorn bush mid-morning in front of all the gentry.

They were about to set off when the phone rang loudly in Freddie's car.

''Ullo, Mr Ho Chin, how are fings?' said Freddie in delight. 'Grite, grite. Fifty million, did you say? Yeah, that seems about right. Look, 'ave a word with Alfredo and see if 'e wants to come in too, and phone me back. Yes, I'll be on this number all day.'

The guns exchanged looks of absolute horror, as Freddie extracted the telephone from the car, all set to bring it with him.

Tony sidled up. 'D'you mind awfully leaving that thing behind? Might put off the pheasants.'

''Course not,' said Freddie, putting it back in the car. 'If Chin can't get me 'ere, he'll ring my office.'

'D'you take your telephone hunting too?' asked an appalled Paul.

'Always,' said Freddie.

They started off up an incredibly steep hill behind the house. It was one of those mild January days that give the illusion winter is over. A few dirty suds of traveller's joy still hung from the trees. No wind ruffled the catkins. It was hellishly hard going. Valerie, wishing she hadn't worn her long johns, tried not to pant.

As it started to rain, she put up her ginger umbrella which kept catching in the branches. On the brow of the hill the guns took up their position, which they'd drawn out of a hat earlier. Except for Freddie's distracting red-gold curls, the flat caps along the row were absolutely parallel with the gun barrels. Shooting in the middle of the line between Tony and the Duke, Freddie jumped from foot to foot swinging his gun through the line like Ian Botham hooking.

The Duke, who had three daughters and was hoping for a son so the title wouldn't pass to a younger brother, was not the only gun looking at Freddie with extreme trepidation.

'I'm 'ot,' said Freddie, shedding his Barbour. Seeing the Duke's and Tony's looks of horror at Freddie's red jersey and Bas laughing like a jackass, Valerie, who'd been yakking non-stop to Sarah Stratton about puff-ball skirts, sharply told Freddie to put it back on. For once Freddie ignored her.

Suddenly the patter of rain on the flat caps was joined by the relentless swish of the beaters' flags.

'Come on, little birdies,' cooed Paul, caressing the trigger.

I hate him for being him and not Rupert, thought Sarah despairingly.

A lone pheasant came into view, high over Freddie's head.

'Bet he misses,' said Paul.

The Duke and Tony raised their guns in case he did.

But a shot rang out and the pheasant somersaulted like a gaudy catherine wheel and thudded to the ground.

Next moment a great swarm appeared, some steeply rising, some whirring close to the ground. There was a deafening fusillade and the air was full of feathers as birds cartwheeled and crashed into the grass.

The whistle blew; the first drive was over. Dogs shot off to retrieve the plunder. It was plain from the number of brace being amassed by Freddie's loader that he'd shot the plus twos off everyone else.

'Freddie Jones seems a bloody good shot,' said Bas.

'Beginner's luck,' snapped Paul, who had easily shot the least.

For the next drive the guns formed a ring round a little yellow stone farmhouse with a turquoise door and a moulting Christmas tree in the back yard.

Once more the shots rang out, once more the sky rained pheasants. To left and right, Freddie, the Duke and the Lord-Lieutenant were bringing down everything that came over. Tony fared less well. Valerie was standing behind him with Monica and her endless chatter put him off.

At the end of the drive Tony's loader, knowing the competitive nature of his boss, pinched a brace from Bas on one side and another from the Lord-Lieutenant who was gazing admiringly at Sarah.

'Those are mine!' said the Lord-Lieutenant sharply.

'Sorry,' said Tony smoothly. 'My loader's very jealous of my reputation.'

'Jealous loader, indeed,' muttered the Lord-Lieutenant.

The next drive was a long one, with the guns dotted like waistcoat buttons down the valley. Valerie was bored. Only the birds and the chuckling of a little stream interrupted the quiet. Monica, who found shooting as boring as Corinium Television, was plugged into the Sony Walkman Archie had given her for Christmas. Now she was transfixed by the love duet from *Tristan und Isolde*, eyes shut, dreamily waving her hands in time to the music and tripping over bramble cables.

Sarah was equally uncommunicative. Weekends were the worst, she reflected, because, knowing Paul was at home, Rupert would never ring. She'd only come out today for something to do. Spring returns, she murmured, looking at the ruby and amethyst haze of the thickening buds, but not my Rupert. He had been so keen, but suddenly after Valerie's dinner party he had lost interest. Was it Nathalie Perrault, or Cameron Cook, or even Maud O'Hara he was running after now? Perhaps he was just busy and would come back.

A diversion was provided by the arrival of Hermione Hampshire, the Lord-Lieutenant's wife, who looked like a sheep, had a ringing voice and appeared to be on so many of the same committees as Monica that she even merited having the Walkman turned off.

'Freddie's been shooting wonderfully,' said Monica kindly, and then started rabbiting on to Hermione Hampshire about shooting lunches.

Valerie listened to them. One could pick up lots of tips about pronunciation from the gentry. But it was confusing that Monica said 'Eyether' and Hermione said 'Eether'.

In the next field she was somewhat unnerved by some black and white cows who cavorted skittishly around, startled by the gunfire. She edged closer to Monica and Hermione.

'D'you know,' Monica was saying, 'I never spend less than forty minutes on a cock.'

Valerie was shocked to the core. She'd always imagined Monica was somehow above sex.

'I agree,' said Hermione Hampshire in her ringing voice. 'I never spend less than thirty minutes on a hen.'

'They're talking about plucking,' whispered Sarah with a giggle, 'and I don't think either of them have heard of rhyming slang.'

It was the last drive before lunch. Freddie, like a one-man Bofors, was bringing down pheasants with relentless accuracy.

'Got my eye in now,' he said, grinning at the Lord-Lieutenant.

He raised his gun as another pheasant flew towards him, then swore as it crashed prematurely to the ground.

'Sorry,' said Tony, who couldn't bear being upstaged a moment longer. 'Thought you were unloaded.'

266

This time it was carnage. The air was raining feathers. Dogs circled, loaders went round breaking the necks of the wounded.

Lucky things, thought Sarah. I wish someone would put me out of my misery.

'I love your dog,' she said to Henry Hampshire. 'I saw a beautiful springer the other day with a long tail.'

'Good God,' said Henry Hampshire, appalled, and strode off leaving her in mid-sentence.

'I thought you said you hadn't shot before,' said Tony as they walked back to the house.

'Not pheasant,' said Freddie, 'but I was the top marksman at Bisley for two years.'

Entering the garden, they passed two yews cut in the shape of pheasants.

'You couldn't even hit those today, could you, Paul?' said Tony nastily.

After so much open air and exercise, everyone fell on lunch. There was Spanish omelette cut up in small pieces on cocktail sticks, and a huge stew, with baked potatoes, and a winter salad, and plum cake steeped in brandy and Stilton, with masses of claret and sloe gin.

Freddie was in terrific form. His curls had tightened in the rain. Looking more like a naughty cherub than ever, he kept his end of the table in a roar with stories of his army career and his first catastrophic experiences out hunting.

Henry Hampshire, who had a lean face and turned-down eyes, shed his gentle paternalistic smile on everyone, even Sarah.

'D'yer really think Springers look better with long tails?' he asked her.

Sarah had a lot to drink at lunch. She looks like a Renoir, thought Tony, all blonde curls, huge blue eyes and languor.

'Have you made up your mind about joining Corinium?' he asked her.

'Yes, I'd love to. I'll come in and sign the contract tomorrow.'

267

'Only a three months' trial,' said Tony, who never took chances, 'but I think you'll love it. This will be a very exciting year.'

Christ, I'd like to take her to bed, he thought. Cameron was being very uptight at the moment.

'Not too worried about me getting you on the telecasting couch?' he added, lowering his voice.

Sarah went crimson. 'Cameron must have told you about that. I picked her brains, I didn't realize you and she . . . I'm sorry.'

'Don't give it a thought,' said Tony, pouring her some more sloe gin.

'No more Stilton, Fred-Fred,' chided Valerie. 'What a lovely meal, Monica.'

'Taggie O'Hara did the whole thing,' said Monica. 'I can't thank you enough for putting me on to her. She's going to fill up the deep freeze before the children come home at half-term.'

Valerie, who was feeling a little out of things because everyone was laughing at Freddie's jokes, turned to the Duke. After two glasses of claret she'd be calling him your grouse in a minute.

'We have a lovely home,' she said complacently. 'Green Lawns. I hope we shall receive you there one day. The Hunt was supposed to gather there on New Year's Day. Do you ride to hounds?'

'Well, a bit,' said the Duke, who had his own pack.

'Freddie's been asked to hunt with the Belvoir. That's the smartest pack in the country,' boasted Valerie.

Everyone except Valerie knew that Belvoir was not pronounced as it was spelt. Everyone except Tony was well-bred enough to keep their traps shut. Buy Tony was fed up with her stupid chatter.

'If you were really smart, Valerie, you wouldn't call it Belvoir. It's pronounced Beaver.'

There was an embarrassed pause.

'How long have you lived in Gloucestershire?' asked the Duke, who was a kind man.

The women went off to various loos. Freddie went off to take a telephone call from Tokyo.

'What a very amusing fellow Freddie Jones is,' said the Lord-Lieutenant.

'And very very bright,' said Tony. 'That's why I need him on my Board. Cable and Satellite isn't just about technology or delivery systems, you know; it's about marketing programmes. Freddie's a genius at marketing. Shame we couldn't include his jumped-up bitch of a wife as part of the bag.'

'Not on a cocks-only day,' said Bas.

Everyone laughed.

The guns were waiting to start off for the last two drives of the day. Freddie was still on the telephone to Tokyo. Valerie was admiring the azaleas in Monica's conservatory.

It was unfortunate that when Freddie came into the hall he found Sarah Stratton in Valerie's deerstalker giggling frantically and brandishing Valerie's tan mackintosh cape, at which Basil was pretending to charge like a bull.

'Olé,' said Tony, who was grinning in the doorway.

'It's selling laike hot gâteaux,' squealed Sarah. Then, seeing Freddie, she went very pink and asked him if he thought the deerstalker suited her.

At that moment Valerie came into the hall.

'You look delaightful,' she said excitedly. 'I've got identical ones in stock. I'll set one asaide for you.'

'I really feel I've made a breakthrough with Sarah Stratton,' Valerie kept telling Freddie as they drove home.

Having done her stuff in the morning and during lunch, Monica felt justified in staying behind in the afternoon and doing some gardening. Before she got stuck into pruning, she popped into the kitchen to thank Taggie, but found her looking absolutely miserable standing on one leg.

'What on earth's the matter?' said Monica, alarmed. 'Everything was wonderful.'

269

Taggie hung her head. 'I'm desperately sorry, Lady Baddingham, but I didn't realize it was a shooting lunch. I know it sounds p-p-priggish, but I don't app-p-prove of shooting. I think it's very cruel; all those poor pheasants, and I'd rather not cook for those kind of lunches any more. You probably won't want me to do any more cooking now. I'm so sorry, as I like working for you so much.'

Monica's face softened. 'Don't give it a thought. It was very brave of you to stick up for your principles. The shooting season's virtually over now, anyway. I quite understand, as long as you go on doing other lunches and dinner parties for me and filling up the freezer.'

When Tony came out of a meeting on Monday morning, Miss Madden greeted him with the news that Freddie had rung.

'Get him for me, would you?' said Tony.

He smiled expansively as he was put through.

'Freddie, hullo. You shot bloody well. Everyone was most impressed.'

'Thank you very much for asking us,' said Freddie.

'We must make it a regular thing next season.' Tony made a thumbs-up sign to Cameron.

'I don't fink so,' said Freddie coldly. 'I'm not joining your board.'

'Why ever not?' said Tony, astounded.

'I don't like people patronizing Valerie. I know you was all laughing at her.'

'It was a joke,' protested Tony. 'We're all devoted to Mousie.'

'I don't mind anyone laughing at me, but no one puts 'er down.' And Freddie put down the receiver.

The tragedy was that Valerie was absolutely livid with Freddie, who was not prepared to hurt her by telling her why he'd backed off. Valerie – over whose head the cracks about the Belvoir and the boutique had gone completely – ranted on and on about how Monica had become such a good friend and Tony had promised to film the boutique and put her on

270

'Behind Every Famous Man', and what amusing people the Duke, the Lord-Lieutenant, the Strattons, Bas and even the O'Haras were, and now she supposed all they'd do was mix with boring businessmen.

Even when Tony dispatched Sarah to the boutique to buy the cloak, the knickerbocker suit and the deer stalker, Freddie didn't relent.

RIVALS
21

Tony couldn't directly blame Declan for Freddie Jones's defection, but he blamed him for everything else: for inciting rebellion in the newsroom with his subversive lefty attitudes, for egging Charles Fairburn on to put in larger and larger expenses, for Cameron's bad temper which was no doubt caused by Declan's handsome son Patrick, for Declan's trouncing of Maurice Wooton, which had made Tony so anxious to get Freddie on the Board and waste so much time and money wooing him, only to be rejected.

It was generally agreed at Corinium that Tony had never sustained a mood of utter bloody-mindedness for quite so long, and the only way Declan could redeem himself would be to crucify Rupert Campbell-Black when he interviewed him on St Valentine's Day – a massacre Declan looked forward to with grim relish.

As he researched the programme, Declan found himself increasingly fascinated by the complexities of Rupert's character. He was obviously very good at his job. The Ministry for Sport, when Rupert was offered it, had been merely a PR post, answerable to the Ministry of the Environment, with the Home Office dealing with any major disasters like football riots.

Rupert, however, had refused to take on the job unless he was given sole responsibility for all sport in the country and any trouble that ensued. The gamble paid off. He had had spectacular success in curbing football hooliganism, he had raised a vast amount of money for sport, particularly the next Olympics. He had had rows with the Teachers' Unions over the decline of competitive sport in schools, with the Football Association, rows with fellow ministers, even rows with the PM. But he got things done and he cut through waffle. Utterly sure of his own judgement, he was sometimes too arrogant, and, having been a great athlete himself, he tended to side with the players rather than the management, but when he went against officials it was always because he'd discovered a weakness in their argument. He was extremely lucky in Gerald Middleton, his private secretary.

Declan also noted Rupert's appallingly deprived childhood, not of material things, but of love and stability. His beautiful mother was on her fifth marriage. His father's fourth marriage had just come unstuck. Then there was his taking over of the family home at Penscombe, with its four hundred acres, when he was only twenty-one and just making the big time in show-jumping, and soon having it running at a thumping profit. There were the frequent rumblings in the press about his cruelty to his horses, or at least ruthlessly overjumping them. There was the compulsive womanizing that hardly stopped with marriage or divorce. Even today, when he should be setting a good example, far too many women appeared only too anxious to say 'Yes Minister'.

Declan had spoken to Rupert's best friend, Billy Lloyd-Foxe, now Head of Sport at the BBC, who had nothing but praise for the way Rupert had helped him in the past, curing him of alcoholism and virtually saving his marriage. He also talked to Malise Gordon, Rupert's old *chef d'équipe*, now married to Rupert's ex-wife Helen, who said Rupert's urge to win was the strongest motivating force in his character. 'Whatever he does, he'll get to the top.' He talked to numerous exes, who all described Rupert as impossible but irresistible, not least because he made them laugh, and to several cabinet ministers, who spoke of him with respect rather than affection.

Everyone cited Rupert's phenomenal energy. After the

punishing hours of show-jumping he took the gruelling work load of Sports Minister in his stride. Accustomed to adulation and easy conquest on the show-jumping circuit, he had been unaffected both by the reverence and sycophancy which surrounds MPs and the brickbats thrown at them by the press and in the House. Because he was fearless and not short of money, he made a surprisingly good MP, happy to kick up a fuss on behalf of his constituency whenever necessary. Chalford and Bisley were proud. Once again Rupert had put them on the map.

This, therefore, was the man that Declan read every word written about and became obsessed with as he strode through the frozen Gloucestershire valleys, or tossed and turned in his bed at night. This was the man, he thought, as he worked out his questions, with a black, churning, sickening hatred, who could at any moment take Maud or Taggie or even Caitlin off him. On the surface Maud seemed to have got over her passion for Rupert. She had discovered Anthony Powell's novels, and was steadily reading her way through the twelve volumes of *A Dance to the Music of Time*, aided by rather too much whisky of an evening. She was very listless, but this could be attributed to the length and severity of the winter. She showed no interest in his interview with Rupert.

St Valentine's Day dawned, causing the usual flutter of excitement at Corinium Television, and giving hernias to the postmen staggering up Cotchester High Street under sackfuls of coloured envelopes.

None of these envelopes, however, were addressed to Cameron. Not that she really noticed. Since she'd taken over Simon Harris's job, she was working herself into the ground.

Not only was she still producing Declan and overseeing the production of a new series of 'Four Men went to Mow', but she was now in sole charge of Corinium Programmes, and seemed to spend her time scheduling, commissioning, arguing about budgets, or going to meetings with other Programme Controllers in London.

Patrick bombarded her with increasingly anguished letters

to which she didn't reply. Only that morning he'd sent her a huge Valentine bunch of lilies of the valley at home.

Darling Cameron [said the accompanying letter],
I am going into a decline. Decline O'Hara. I've lost so much weight my friends are convinced I've got AIDS. Having been told by you to make something of my life, you will be pleased that I have given up drink (almost) and am writing my play and working hard. The play is no longer about British intimidation in Ireland, but about a young boy in love with an older woman, who can't tear herself away from an absolute bastard. Don't worry about libel, I've given Lord Bad Hat red hair. I suppose I ought to thank you for making me experience unhappiness in love. Did you know James Joyce actually encouraged his wife to have affairs, so he could find out what it was like to be a cuckold?
'Jim' (isn't that a ghastly let down), wrote Mrs Joyce, 'wants me to go with other men, so he can write about it.' Stupid pratt, he couldn't have loved her.
My mother says my father is incredibly ratty. Are things going very badly at Corinium? Before you tear this letter up, remember it will be worth something one day, and might well keep you in lonely old age, when your ancient lover, Baddingham, has croaked. I love you and remain in darkness, Patrick.

As she left for the office, Cameron put the lilies of the valley outside the back door in case Tony came home with her after Declan's programme. Not that that was likely. Their relationship had deteriorated. They fought less, but formerly their rows had been the snapping of foreplay. Now when Tony made love to her there was a brutality and coldness never there before.

To make matters worse, Sarah Stratton, in all her radiant beauty, had joined Corinium as a prospective presenter, and her pussy-cat smile, her blonde halo of hair, her soft angora bosom and her wafts of Anaïs Anaïs, had affected the men in the building like Zuleika Dobson. James Vereker, wearing a different pastel pullover every day and behaving like a lovesick schoolboy, had been nicknamed Hanker-man by the newsroom. The Head of News was taking the task of initiating Sarah very seriously indeed. Even Tony chose every opportunity to see if she was all right, summoning her to drinks in his office after work, or to join board-room lunches to impress visiting bigwigs. Cameron consequently got more histrionic and ratty with the staff.

'If Simon and Cameron are anything to go by,' observed Charles Fairburn, 'control is the one ingredient unnecessary for the job of Controller of Programmes.'

James had so many Valentines he decided to do a little item on 'Cotswold Round-Up' to thank his fans and conduct a studio discussion as to whether men were more romantic and caring than they used to be. Sarah received one Valentine card postmarked Penscombe with no writing inside. Having never had a letter from Rupert, she couldn't be sure the flashy blue scrawl on the envelope was his, but she was almost certain. Declan's Valentines arrived by the sackful, but he was too preoccupied with Rupert to open them.

Taggie had a trying day. No one sent her any Valentines. She was doing dinner for the Lord-Lieutenant that evening and had made a huge ratatouille and left it to cool overnight in the larder, only to find that Declan had put the whole lot out on the lawn for the badgers, who'd refused to touch it. Declan's only distraction these days, apart from bird-watching, was putting food out at night and crouching in a dimly-lit kitchen waiting for the foxes and badgers to turn up.

Now he was roaring round the house in bare feet, complaining once again that his utterly bloody children had swiped every single one of the da-glo cat-sick yellow socks that he had made so fashionable. Looking for a pair under Caitlin's bed, he found a vodka bottle, empty except for a cockroach, and said once again that they really must sack Grace.

'Absolutely not,' said Maud firmly. 'I need my Greek chorus.'

Declan was just leaving for the studios, weighed down with

poisoned rapiers to stick into Rupert, when Taggie came rushing into the kitchen, speechless with excitement and brandishing a vast Valentine covered in hearts, which had just arrived by special delivery, and which played 'The White Cliffs of Dover' on the xylophone every time you opened it.

'What the hell's that?'

'It's from Rupert. He's sent Gertrude a Valentine.'

'Whatever for?' snapped Maud.

'He once said she was ugly. He must have changed his mind. How gratuitously' – Taggie brought out her word for the day in triumph – 'kind of him.'

'Bloody hell,' thought Declan as he went out into the dank February drizzle. 'Not content with groping Taggie and ensnaring Maud, he's now trying to seduce my dog.'

Taggie ran after him. 'You won't give Rupert too hard a time, will you?'

Throughout the network Declan's interview with Rupert had been trailed every hour on the hour during the day. Make-up had drawn lots as to who was to attend to him. Declan tried to snatch a quiet couple of hours in his office sharpening his poisoned rapiers, but was interrupted by one member of staff after another trooping in to grumble about Tony.

'He bollocked me for not giving the reps extra bonuses in January,' said Georgie Barnes, the Sales Director. 'If I had, he'd have bollocked me for squandering Corinium's resources.'

'Last week he shouted at me because my desk was a mess,' moaned Cyril Peacock. 'So I had a big tidy out. Then, when he came in this afternoon and found me with an empty desk, he bawled me out for doing nothing.'

Charles Fairburn was furious because, for the seventh week running, his request for a hundred pounds to replace the fur hat Seb Burrows had put on the Corinium Ram at Christmas had been crossed off his expenses.

Sarah Stratton, wearing a clinging pale-grey angora dress,

sat in the newsroom with the Head of News who was showing off his muscle by demanding why the BBC had had a story at lunchtime which his reporters had missed.

'Of course "Cotswold Round-Up" is the company's flagship,' he told Sarah. 'We lose or retain the franchise according to whether or not the programme truly represents local news and views. We have to be consistent, questioning, responsible and entertaining. It's the one area where interference from Cameron or Tony isn't tolerated. The autonomy of the newsroom is undisputed.'

Beside him the internal telephone rang. Taking his hand off Sarah's knee, the Head of News picked up the receiver and turned pale.

'Of course, Lord B. I quite understand. I'll put someone on the story right away.'

Sarah smiled into her paper cup and said nothing.

On the air now, James Vereker, having thanked all his fans ver' ver' much for their caring Valentines, was interviewing a local witch who'd just made a record. She was wearing a black mini and crinkled black boots, and had huge bare mottled thighs which she kept crossing and re-crossing so James could see everything.

'I'm sure you're a very caring person, Tamzin,' said James, averting his eyes, 'but don't you think the general public has a rather more sinister idea of witches?'

'Turn him into a toad,' screamed Seb Burrows in the newsroom, throwing a paper dart at the screen.

'Wish she'd make an effigy of Tony and stick pins into it,' said Charles Fairburn.

'We could market a Baddingham pin cushion,' said Seb. 'It'd sell even better than Declan T-shirts.'

Sarah wasn't listening. Rupert will be here soon, she thought. She'd warned Paul she might be late, because Tony wanted her to help at some PR party. Tony, in fact, had asked her up to the board room to watch Rupert's interview and impress a couple of big advertisers. Rupert was bound to pop in after the programme.

278

I know he sent me the Valentine, thought Sarah, wriggling in ecstasy. He must want to come back.

Rupert, in fact, had had a very tough day. He had had an acrimonious meeting with the UEFA Committee, who were still refusing to let English soccer teams play in Europe next season. He'd had to smooth over the scandal of a Chinese ping-pong player caught shoplifting in an Ann Summers sex shop. He'd tried to persuade the Advertising Institute that there was no very good reason why a large condom manufacturer shouldn't sponsor the Rugby League Cup Final next year, and coped with the Health Authority up in arms because a famous racing driver had gone on 'Wogan' in a Marlboro T-shirt. Because all these meetings ran late, he had only had half an hour to harangue a group of headmasters on the decline of competitive sport in schools, which had been exacerbated by the teachers' strike.

Finally, just as he was leaving for Cotchester, the PM had summoned him, wanting him to lean on the British Lions to cancel their tour of South Africa to encourage the athletes to boycott the European Games next month.

Rupert lost his temper. 'Politics shouldn't be brought into sport,' he snapped. 'I'm not going to pressure anyone to boycott anything. You've absolutely no idea what it's like to be an athlete. How would you have liked it if the day you became Prime Minister, someone had ordered you to refuse the job, and you'd been almost certain you'd never get another chance? You can't force people to abide by principles you wouldn't dream of sticking to yourself.'

And the Prime Minister had dismissed Rupert very frostily, saying she hoped he'd have second thoughts on the matter.

'I feel like a football at the end of the Cup Final,' said Rupert as he collapsed into the black Government car beside Sydney, his official driver. 'Everyone's having a go at me today. Who won the three-thirty?'

They discussed racing until the Heathrow exit, then Rupert fell asleep. Sydney liked working for Rupert. He enjoyed the glamour and Rupert's erratic hours brought him spectacular overtime.

Gerald Middleton, Rupert's private secretary, sat in the back with the light on, going through Rupert's red box, streamlining as much as possible, pencilling in little notes on what action to take. Glancing at the sprawled elegant figure in front, with the head fallen sideways, Gerald fought the temptation to stroke the sleek blond hair. Rupert would never know the self-control Gerald had to exert day after day, never to betray his feelings. It must be some death wish that made him pour all his energies into Rupert's career, ensuring Rupert's rapid escalation up the political scale to the head of a far grander ministry, away from Gerald – that is, unless Rupert did something silly, like going on Declan's programme tonight.

Gerald looked at his watch. They were cutting it very fine. Just as well – Rupert wouldn't have time for too many whiskys in Hospitality beforehand.

Cameron went to the control room early. She liked to have half an hour before the programme to take a deep breath and think about what she had to do. As she closed the door, the *Jaws* theme belted out from the sound room next door. This joke had been going on ever since she was made Controller of Programmes. She found it very unfunny, but, looking though the glass windows and the vertical blinds at the guffawing sound men on one side and the vision controllers on the other, it obviously creased up everyone else.

Rupert's cool unsmiling face stared out at her from every single monitor screen, except those that would feed in stills, telecine and video tape to illustrate aspects of Rupert's life during the programme. On the studio floor they were checking the order of the stills. Up on the monitor came pictures of Rupert winning the World Cup and standing on the Olympic rostrum with his arm in a sling, of his beautiful ex-wife Helen, of Beattie Johnson and Nathalie Perrault and Amanda Hamilton, wife of the Foreign Secretary. There was Jake Lovell, Rupert's arch-rival on the circuit, and his *chef d'équipe*, Malise Gordon, who'd ended up with Helen. They looked like characters in some glamorous Hollywood mini-series. Declan was clearly hell bent on carnage.

The rest of the crew drifted into the studio after their dinner break. Daysee Butler, weighed down with stop watches and blue mascara and wearing a new pale-pink jersey with a large grey cat knitted on the front, took up her position on Cameron's left.

'Rupert'll be here in five minutes. Go and meet him, Daysee, and take him straight to Make-up,' said Cameron.

On the monitor she could already see Declan slumped in his wizard's chair. Flicking the key switch, she warned him of Rupert's arrival.

'Are you going to have a drink with him beforehand?'

'I am not.'

He looks shattered, thought Cameron. He'd lost so much weight recently. His black hair was even more threaded with grey. The violet shadows under his eyes reminded her of Patrick. But she mustn't think of Patrick.

'Just do a Maurice Wooton on him, Dec, and Tony'll die happy.'

'As long as he dies,' growled Declan, 'I don't care if he's happy or not.'

Rupert, Sydney and Gerald waited in Reception, looking at photographs of Declan, Charles Fairburn and James Vereker, who was no longer obscured by the Christmas tree.

'Fuckin' 'ell, it's Farah Fawcett Major,' said Sydney, as Daysee swayed down the royal-blue steel staircase, giving them the benefit of her bouncing strawberry-blonde hair and undulating figure.

'Can I take you straight to Make-up, Minister?' said Daysee.

'Can't you and I go to the Cotchester Arms instead?' said Rupert.

Daysee looked at her watch. 'I don't think there's time,' she said seriously. 'You're on in fifteen minutes.'

'I don't want any make-up. All I need is a vast whisky,' said Rupert.

Gerald handed Daysee some photographs.

281

'Here are the pix of the '76 Olympic Games.'

'Oh thanks,' said Daysee. 'I'll get Graphics to soft-mount them.'

'Sounds like a contradiction in terms,' said Rupert.

'Soft-mounting means sticking a photograph on a background from which it can easily be peeled off,' explained Daysee patiently.

'Definitely Farah Fawcett NCO,' muttered Rupert to Gerald as they follow Daysee upstairs.

'You're lovely and brown,' said the make-up girl, applying a touch of Nouveau Beige to the shine on Rupert's nose and forehead.

'Skiing last weekend,' said Rupert.

He wondered for the millionth time why the hell he'd agreed to do this interview. Partly, he knew, it was Cameron taunting him about being afraid of Declan. But, in between frantic hard work and cavorting in bed and on the ski slopes with Nathalie Perrault, he had kept remembering Taggie in floods at Patrick's party over her father's catastrophic finances.

Daysee brought Rupert a dark mahogany whisky, which Gerald immediately took to the make-up department wash basin and diluted with water.

'You haven't eaten all day, Minister.'

'Yes, Nanny,' said Rupert.

'I'd better take you down,' said Daysee.

Gerald straightened Rupert's blue spotted tie.

'For Christ's sake be careful. If he asks you anything you don't like, just say you didn't come on the programme to discuss personal matters. Don't bitch up other ministers. Try not to lose your temper.'

Rupert grinned. 'Anyone would think I was off to my first term at prep school.'

Gerald didn't smile. 'You behave like it sometimes.'

22

Large orange letters outside the studio said: No Entry When Flashing.

'I should think not,' said Rupert, draining his whisky and giving the glass to Daysee. 'Do they want me to expose myself on air?'

'Christ, he's photogenic,' said Cameron in the gallery, as she watched Rupert sit down opposite a tense, unsmiling Declan. 'Look at that jawline, and the way his eyes lengthen when he smiles.'

'Declan's nervous,' said the Vision Mixer, as the sound man tested both men for level. 'Listen to the quiver in his voice.'

In his earpiece, Declan could now hear Daysee discussing a boyfriend who was coming to dinner tomorrow.

'The recipe says lots of garlic, but I think I'll leave it out. That Rupert's dead attractive, isn't he?'

Declan looked at Rupert, lounging, so relaxed, radiating élitism and privilege with his Red Indian suntan, his beautifully cut suit and his blue silk shirt matching his insolent blue eyes. He thought of Taggie sobbing with humiliation after Valerie Jones's party, and of Maud sobbing in his arms the night of Patrick's twenty-first, and his resolve hardened.

'Either of you need a touch-up?' asked the make-up girl, whisking on with her steel basket.

'I'd love to give you one,' said Rupert.

The make-up girl blushed. Rupert leaned forward and looked at the name-tape on one of Declan's odd socks. It said Charlotte Webster-Lee.

'She's a friend of Caitlin's,' snapped Declan.

'I think I used to know her mother very well,' said Rupert. 'Is Charlotte blonde with blue eyes?'

Can't he let up for a second? thought Declan savagely.

Trouble ahead, decided Rupert, as he chatted idly with the crew about Cotchester's chances against Wandsworth United on Saturday. This man's out to bury me.

'One minute to air, Declan,' said the Floor Manager.

'Good luck,' said Cameron.

'Stand by tape,' said Daysee.

The floor manager raised his hand to cue Declan, the red light flashed on, and he was off.

'My guest tonight needs no introduction. He has been described as the greatest show jumper in the world, the handsomest man in England, the icing on the cake of the Tory party. He is, of course, the Minister for Sport, and the MP for Chalford and Bisley, Rupert Campbell-Black.'

Dispensing with the introductory package, Declan weighed straight in: 'Do you mind being described as the handsomest man in England?'

'Why should I?'

'You're not frightened of being dismissed just as a pretty face?'

'No.'

'Of being dragged into the Tory party just to add an element of much-needed glamour?'

'No, because it's not true.'

'For what other reason could you possibly have been brought in?' said Declan dismissively.

'I know more about sport than anyone else in the party,' said Rupert simply. 'Having lasted in show jumping for sixteen years on what must be the most gruelling circuits in the world, I can cope with the pressures. One day you're king of the castle in show jumping, next day you're bottom of the

284

heap. It's helped me to be resilient about the ups and downs of politics.'

'Do you find politics as satisfying as show-jumping?'

'Of course not, but it has its compensations.'

'What are they?'

'The Olympic Fund has just passed four million and we've still got eighteen months to go. Soccer violence is down by seventy per cent. Comprehensive schools are gradually upping competitive sport and' – Rupert grinned nastily – 'England trounced Ireland at rugger last Saturday.'

Gerald, sipping Perrier in the board room, winced. That was a cheap point. Rupert shouldn't have made it.

'The Government makes two hundred million pounds a year from tax on football pools,' accused Declan, 'and yet you're asking the clubs to spend two million this year tightening up their security to reduce football violence. Why don't you give them some help?'

'With footballers earning one hundred thousand pounds a year and stars like Garry Lineker changing hands for over a million I think the football clubs can put their own houses in order.'

'Some people feel you're taking a strong line on soccer violence because it's electorally attractive.'

'Do they?' said Rupert politely.

Shit, thought Declan, I walked right into that one.

Rupert relented: 'Just because something is electorally attractive, doesn't make it wrong. I want to clean up the terraces and make them safe places for fathers to take their families again – or the game'll be drained of its support and future talent.'

Declan changed tack: 'I see from the evening paper that you're backing the British Lions tour of South Africa, thereby giving your blessing to a corrupt and evil regime.'

'Rubbish,' said Rupert, wondering if the PM was listening. 'Sport's outside politics. Athletes are so briefly at their peak, they should be allowed to compete where and against whom they like. It's bloody easy to have principles when you're not making the sacrifices.'

And so the programme went on, with nice bitchy repartee flashing back and forth, but on the whole Rupert deflected Declan's needling easily.

Then Declan said: 'You've been described as the Prime Minister's blue-eyed boy.'

'Boy's pushing it. I'm thirty-seven,' said Rupert, 'but as I've got blue eyes, I don't see how I could be anything else.'

'She seems to prefer good-looking men.'

'She'd need her head examined if she didn't,' said Rupert coldly. 'Do you prefer dogs yourself?'

'You've always got on well with women,' said Declan. 'Wasn't it Amanda Hamilton –' a large glamorous picture of the Foreign Secretary's wife appeared on the screen – 'who drew you into politics?'

'And her husband Rollo,' said Rupert quickly. 'They both encouraged me.'

Despite repeated probing from Declan, Rupert refused to give an inch on the subject of Amanda Hamilton.

'It was Mrs Hamilton,' said Declan pointedly, 'who drove you down to your first meeting with your constituency. Do you find a conflict between your ministerial and constituency duties?'

'Of course,' snapped Rupert. 'I don't have enough time to devote to my constituency. They come first; they're the people who voted me in. I've lived in the area all my life, and I don't want a bloody great motorway half a mile from Penscombe any more than they do.'

Gerald put his head in his hands.

Tony, purring with pleasure, was pacing up and down the board-room carpet. 'Rupert is beginning to lose his temper,' he said softly.

I can't help it, thought Sarah, I still love him.

'Was it merely lust for power that drove you into politics?' asked Declan dismissively.

'It certainly wasn't the money, or the free time,' snapped Rupert. 'Most ministers are hopelessly overworked. The civil service want control and pile work on to keep us quiet. Sometimes you get home at three in the morning after a session in the House, then still have to go through your box. That's when the trouble starts. You're so zonked you OK a nuclear power station in your constituency and six months later you realize to your horror what you've done. I'm very lucky. I have an exceptional private secretary in Gerald Middleton. He does all my donkey work, and wraps my knuckles if I go too far. I'm also lucky,' went on Rupert, yawning ostentatiously, 'because on the circuit I learnt to grab sleep at any time.'

'With anyone?' said Declan. He was taunting Rupert now.

'No,' drawled Rupert. 'I've always been selective.'

'That's not what your press cuttings say.'

A still of Samantha Freebody, the starlet who'd told all about sleeping with Rupert while he was married, appeared on the screen, followed by a succession of beauties including Amanda Hamilton's daughter, Georgina, Beattie Johnson and Nathalie Perrault.

'Coming to 2. We must catch Rupert's reaction after this lot,' said Cameron. 'Take 2.'

But Rupert's face was expressionless.

Declan picked up a cutting from the table: 'One Gloucestershire peer has described you as "rather a nasty virus, that everyone's wife caught sooner or later".'

'If you'd seen his wife, it's definitely later,' said Rupert lightly, but there was a muscle going in his cheek.

'With the advent of AIDS, don't you feel you should mend your ways?'

'Sure,' said Rupert. 'I'm giving up casual sex for Lent.'

Tony was getting restless, and, picking up a telephone, dialled the control room:

'Tell Declan to stop farting around and put the boot in.'

'Tony says put the boot in, Declan,' Cameron told Declan. 'Get him on to cruelty.'

Declan squared his shoulders. 'Over the past two years you've expressed sympathy for the football hooligans.'

Rupert stared at his shoes. 'Most of them probably lead appallingly dull lives during the week. Many are out of work, or just turning lathes in a factory. The terraces are their stage, their chance to vent the frustrations of the week. They generally riot because they're losing, or there's been a bad penalty at half-time.'

'You were a bad loser, weren't you?' said Declan gently.

It was the voice of Torquemada, the pale intent face of the Grand Inquisitor.

Rupert looked wary: 'What's the point of competing — except to win?'

'Even to the extent of beating up your horses?'

Rupert's eyes narrowed, but he just stared back at Declan, saying nothing.

'Look at this picture,' said Declan, showing a still of a horse so thin it was almost a skeleton.

'This was one of your horses, Macaulay. You beat him up so badly he wouldn't jump for you, so you sold him to the Middle East, where he ended up in the stone quarries.'

'That was bad luck,' said Rupert. 'I sold half-a-dozen horses to the same Sheik. One of them's at stud in America now. Two of them are still with him. The horse didn't click with him so he sold it on.'

'And your deadly enemy Jake Lovell nursed the horse back to health, and then entered it in the World Championship, and in the finals, when you all had to ride each other's horses, Macaulay wasn't very keen on having you on his back. Remember this?'

On the screen came a clip of Rupert being finally bucked off, then being chased round the ring by the maddened horse, before taking refuge in the centre of a vast jump.

'Coming to 2, take 2,' screamed Cameron, frantic once again to get the reaction on Rupert's face. But once again it was completely blank. Only his long fingers clenched round the glass of water on the table betrayed any emotion.

'He's going to walk out,' said Tony happily.

'You'd beaten up that horse so badly,' said Declan, almost in a whisper, 'that it remembered and went for you. What d'you feel seeing that clip today?'

There was another long pause.

288

'That I was in the wrong sport,' said Rupert slowly. 'With me running that fast, neither Seb Coe nor Ovett would have had a chance against me in the 1500 metres.'

For a second the two men glared at each other. Then Rupert grinned and Declan started to laugh.

'Have you got any regrets you treated your horses so badly?'

'I didn't treat them all badly or they wouldn't have jumped so well. Of course I regret it, but it helped me understand the football hooligans; poor sods out of work, their fathers out of work, often their grandfathers too. Out of sheer frustration at not winning, they resort to violence.'

'You were in work.'

'I know. There was really no excuse.'

'You treated women very badly in the past.'

Rupert shrugged helplessly. 'I liked winning there too.'

'Jake Lovell,' went on Declan remorselessly, 'was your arch rival because you bullied him at school.'

'Are we having oranges at half-time?' protested Rupert, shaking his head.

Declan smiled slightly. 'Jake Lovell finally got his revenge by running off with your wife, Helen, in the middle of the 1980 Olympics. How did you feel at the time?'

Rupert'll kill Declan in a minute, thought Gerald in panic. No one's ever dared ask him these questions.

'I was principally outraged that she should distract me and Jake, when we should have been concentrating on a team gold,' said Rupert.

'But you still got your medal, despite dislocating your shoulder, and riding with one arm.'

'That was just to show them that, even riding one man short and one man injured, we could beat the whole world.'

Prompted by Declan, Rupert went on to talk about the Olympics and Rocky, the horse he'd won a gold medal on, who still lived at Penscombe.

'I'm so cruel to Rocky,' drawled Rupert, 'that he has the entire run of my garden, and spends his time trampling over the flower beds and peering in at the drawing-room window.'

I like this man. Why I am trying to crucify him? thought Declan.

I like this man, even though he's trying to crucify me, thought Rupert.

Tony went into the next-door office to ring Cameron, so the advertisers wouldn't hear him.

'Declan's gone soft, for Christ's sake. Tell him to fucking nail him.'

'What did you feel,' Declan was asking now, 'when Helen split up with Jake and married your old team manager?'

'Well, I didn't let off fireworks. It was like one's childhood sweetheart marrying one's headmaster.'

'Do you mind her being happy now?'

'Not at all,' said Rupert in surprise. 'It's better for the children. Anyway she deserved it; she had a rough time with me.'

'In what way?'

'Show-jumping and marriage don't mix. I was never there when she needed me. When she was having Marcus I was stuck on an alpine pass. She was an intellectual and I hardly know Oscar Wilde from Kim Wilde. Then the dogs were always getting in the bed.'

'Yes,' said Declan. 'People say you were fonder of your black labrador, Badger, than of Helen.'

'I had him first,' said Rupert flatly. 'He lived with me six years after she left me. *He* never criticized or tried to improve me.'

'Is that what you want from women, uncritical adulation?'

Rupert grinned. 'Probably.'

The questions were still barbed, but the animosity had gone.

'Your name's been linked since your divorce with some dazzling women. Have you ever thought of marrying again?'

'Just because I enjoy flying on Concorde doesn't mean I want to buy the plane. These questions are giving me earache,' grumbled Rupert.

Out of the corner of his eye, Declan could see the Floor Manager holding up his hand for three minutes.

'When you get any free time, what's the thing you like doing best?'

Rupert put his head on one side: 'I thought this was supposed to be a family programme.'

'You must have some hobbies,' said Declan hastily.

'Hunting, shooting, fishing,' said Rupert.

'All the blood sports.' Declan's lip was curling.

'Not all. I didn't include being interviewed by you on television.'

'*Touché*,' said Declan, laughing. 'Who are your heroes? If you could choose, who would you like to meet in an afterlife?'

For a second Rupert seemed to have difficulty in speaking: 'I'd like to see Badger again,' he muttered.

'Oh, how sweet,' said Daysee, who was now revving up for her most important moment: pressing the cue switch. The Floor Manager was making wind-up signals to Declan.

'Looking back on your sixteen years in show-jumping, can you remember the hardest thing you had to do? Was it getting the first bronze, winning the King's Cup three years running, clinching the team gold in 1980, or finally winning the World Championship?'

There was another long pause.

'What was the hardest thing?' Declan urged him.

Just for a second the despair showed through on Rupert's face.

'The thing that nearly killed me,' he said bleakly, 'was giving it up.'

As Schubert's Fifth Symphony pounded out and the credits came up, Declan most uncharacteristically could be seen getting out of his chair and shaking Rupert by the hand. As soon as they were off air, Cameron came down onto the studio floor. Maybe it was because she was blinking in the unaccustomed light after the darkness of the control room, but for once her yellow eyes seemed to have lost all their aggression.

'Great programme, Declan. Best you've done for us – and

you were marvellous.' Flushing slightly she turned to Rupert. 'Declan threw you some really tough questions and you handled them so well.'

'I hope my boss thinks so,' said Rupert. 'Coming on your programme's rather like being interrogated by the IRA. I was expecting electrodes any minute.'

Cameron had amazing legs, he noticed, as she walked upstairs in front of them.

Up in Hospitality, Tony Baddingham was feeling far from hospitable, but had to restrain himself in front of his two big advertisers, who were terrific fans both of Declan and Rupert, and who felt they had just witnessed a great gladiatorial contest. With a shaking hand, the normally teetotal Gerald helped himself to a triple whisky.

'Wasn't it wonderful?' said Sarah, busily powdering her nose and undoing another pearl button of her little grey dress. 'Declan brought out a really vulnerable side of Rupert. I'm sure he just needs the love of a good woman.'

And the attention of a whole harem of mistresses as well, thought Gerald. He had disapproved very strongly of Rupert's affair with Sarah, regarding it as political dynamite. He hoped it wasn't going to start again.

But, as Rupert walked in with Declan and Cameron, Sarah rushed up and flung her arms round his neck, giving him the benefit of unsupported breasts and half a bucket of Anaïs Anaïs. 'Darling, you were wonderful, so honest.'

'Not much else I could do without walking off the set.'

'When am I going to see you?' murmured Sarah. 'Thank you so much for your Valentine.'

But before Rupert had time to answer her, Gerald muscled in.

'I'm sorry, Minister, I never dreamed Declan'd go that far.'

Rupert raised an eyebrow at Gerald's glass of whisky.

'Are we in trouble?'

'I don't know,' said Gerald. 'The press are going berserk already. I told the switchboard to say you'd left. We'll have to smuggle you out by a side door.'

292

Tony, having introduced the big advertisers to Rupert, went and vented his fury on Declan.

'I thought I told you to fucking well crucify him.'

'I tried to,' said Declan coldly, 'but he was too good for me,' and, turning on his heel, he headed towards the drinks.

Seeing Tony coming to give her an earful, Cameron grabbed a plate of quiche and took it over to Rupert, who, to Sarah's fury, turned away from the group to talk to her. After the tension of the interview, he was gripped by the lust that always used to overwhelm him after a big show-jumping class. In the old days he would have screwed a groom or a show-jumping groupie in the back of his lorry. Tonight he was sure he could choose between Daysee, Sarah or Cameron. Daysee was too thick, Sarah too possessive, Cameron on the other hand had a reckless, scrawny nymphomania and pulling her would have the added charm of irritating the hell out of Tony.

'Well,' he said icily, 'I had to box bloody clever to get out of that one. I suppose Tony put Declan up to it.'

'I'm sorry,' said Cameron.

Glancing up, she found she couldn't tear her eyes away.

'Being sorry isn't enough,' said Rupert softly. 'I'm going to get my own back.'

Cameron gasped. She could see Tony bearing down on them.

'I was wondering if you'd like to come on another programme? It's the third Thursday in March,' she stammered.

'And have open-heart surgery all over again without an anaesthetic? No, thanks. Besides it's Cheltenham.'

'It's not until the evening,' said Cameron quickly. 'All we'd want you to do is to judge "Miss Corinium Television" with Declan. There are some beautiful girls entered.'

'I might just be able to drag myself away,' said Rupert, 'as long as you promise me a night in the Cotchester Arms with the winner as second prize.'

'What's the first prize?' said Cameron, knowing the answer.

'A night in the Cotchester Arms with you,' said Rupert, 'and my God, I'd make you walk differently in the morning.'

It was several seconds before they both realized that a tense-looking Gerald was tapping Rupert on the arm.

'Telephone. It's the PM.'

'Oh Christ,' said Rupert. 'Back benches here I come.'

'Well done,' said the Prime Minister in her rich deep voice that always sounded like Carnation Milk pouring out of a tin. 'We were very proud of you.'

'You were?' said Rupert in amazement.

'Well, what else could you have done, faced with that spiteful little pinko? You handled him very well. That interview will do us a lot of good in the opinion polls.'

'Good God,' said Rupert putting down the telephone, 'she actually liked it.'

'Was that really the PM?' said one of the big advertisers in awe.

'Did she mention me?' said James, who'd rolled up from a Save-the-Aged fund-raising party.

'I've booked a table for us at the Horn of Plenty at nine-thirty,' said Cameron casually to Rupert. 'The cars are waiting downstairs.'

Despite her off-hand manner, Rupert noticed she was quivering with expectancy, like a greyhound ordered to sit when the woolly rabbit sets off round the track. Then he caught a glimpse of Declan, looking grey and utterly shattered. Once again he remembered Taggie's tears on New Year's Eve.

'Sweet of you,' he said to Cameron, 'but Declan and I are going back to Penscombe. We've got things to discuss.'

Aware of Tony watching her, Cameron hid her bitter disappointment. Being very young, Sarah had no such reserve. 'You can't go,' she wailed. 'We'll be far too many girls.'

'James can come instead,' said Tony smoothly. 'That's if he hasn't got to rush home to Lizzie.'

'Of course not,' said James.

'That's rather uncaring of you,' said Sarah sulkily.

'Work comes first,' said James sanctimoniously. 'And you haven't told me what you thought of my Valentine, Sarah.

294

I thought it was rather nice that it was sold to raise money for the Cat's Protection League.'

Back at Penscombe, two Jack Russells, a young black labrador, two springer spaniels and a blue lurcher threw themselves on Rupert in ecstasy. Once inside, Rupert whisked Gerald and Declan past tapestried hunting scenes and portraits of ancestors, only pausing to point out a huge oil painting of Badger, into the kitchen, which was low-beamed with a flagstone floor, and a window looking over the valley. As Gerald found a bottle of whisky and three glasses and Rupert investigated the fridge and the larder, Declan looked at the pictures on the wall. They were mostly paintings of dogs and horses and framed photographs of two incredibly beautiful children.

'That's Tabitha,' said Rupert, pointing to a little girl on a pony festooned with rosettes.

'She's magic,' said Declan.

'She's doing bloody well in junior classes already.'

'Does the boy ride?' said Declan, looking at the sensitive, nervous face and the huge eyes.

'No. He gets asthma, but he skis well, and he's extremely clever.' There was a slight edge to Rupert's voice.

'Can I have a look round?' asked Declan.

'Go ahead,' said Rupert.

As he wandered through beautiful pastel room after pastel room admiring the incredible pictures: a Romney, a Gainsborough, a Lely, a Thomas Lawrence, and two Stubbs for starters, and the lovingly polished furniture, he thought the whole house was like a museum, beautiful but crying out for someone to live in it, or like a horse, constantly bridled, saddled and groomed to perfection, but with no one to ride it.

Finding the library, Declan was lost in admiration. He'd never seen such books in a private house – first editions of Scott, Dickens, Trollope, Wordsworth, Keats and Shelley, and a whole set of Oscar Wilde, and other books so rare there couldn't be more than half-a-dozen copies in the country.

Half an hour later Rupert found him, oblivious of time, immersed in a first edition of *Middlemarch*.

'Supper. Christ, you can't read in this light!'

'Can I come and live here?' said Declan, shaking his head in bewildered reverence.

'Borrow anything you like whenever you want to. No one else reads them. Helen pretended to, but never seemed to get beyond the first chapter.'

Laid out on the kitchen table was smoked salmon, brown bread, gulls' eggs and half a heated-up chicken pie. Gerald had also made a tomato salad and fried some potatoes.

'It's very good of you,' mumbled Declan. 'I couldn't have faced dinner with Tony.'

'Not up to Taggie's standard, I'm afraid,' said Rupert, adding casually, 'How is she?'

'Very pleased with Gertrude's Valentine.'

'Oh, she got it?' said Rupert. 'Ironic that the first Valentine I ever sent in my life should be to a dog.'

They talked about politics, horses and sport, and then Rupert filled Declan in on local gossip, and some of the early history of Penscombe.

'I hope Penscombe waits for me,' sighed Declan. 'I've been so busy since we've lived here, I've never had a chance to explore it. I haven't even been into the local pub yet.'

It was not until they'd both got pretty drunk, and Gerald had gone to bed, that Rupert asked how things were at Corinium.

'Bloody awful,' said Declan.

'Tony?'

Declan nodded wearily. 'I seem to go from Baddingham to worse.'

'He didn't look very happy after the programme.'

'He wasn't. He wanted me to carve you up.'

Rupert grinned. 'You had a bloody good try. I know why Tony was out for my blood, but why you? Just because I'm a Tory?'

'No, for screwing up Tag at Valerie Jones's dinner party.'

'Ah.'

'And I thought you were after her at Patrick's birthday party.'

Suddenly Declan didn't want to mention Maud.

Rupert inhaled deeply on his cigar. 'Would that have been so bad?'

'She's eighteen and desperately insecure,' said Declan roughly. 'She's simply not equipped to cope. You'd break her like a moth caught in the typewriter keys.'

'Ouch,' said Rupert wincing.

'I saw them all slavering this evening,' went on Declan, 'Sarah, Cameron, that imbecile Daysee. You could have had any of them. Just spare Taggie.'

Rupert, however, was reluctant to drop the subject.

'But she seems incredibly competent. She cooked brilliantly for Valerie and she coped with your party on New Year's Eve virtually single-handed.'

'Oh, she's competent enough,' said Declan. 'You mustn't assume people with dyslexia are thick, just because they have difficulty reading and writing. Albert Einstein, Leonardo da Vinci and Thomas Edison were all dyslexic. So was General Patton. He could never learn the alphabet or his tables by heart.'

'Good God,' said Rupert in alarm. 'So we can expect to see Taggie commanding the Third Army at any minute.'

Declan grinned.

Rupert filled up their glasses with brandy.

'Is Tony really giving you a hard time?'

'Septic tankwise, I'm up to here.' Declan drew a finger across his throat.

He got up and wandered slightly unsteadily towards the window.

'Beautiful house this. Where's The Priory from here?'

Rupert pointed to the left, where, through a spiky fuzz of trees, a light was burning. 'Taggie's still awake, that's her bedroom,' he added without thinking. Then, when Declan instantly looked bootfaced, 'It's all right. I had to bodily remove some drunk from her room the night of your party because Taggie wanted to go to bed – alone.'

As Rupert joined Declan beside the window, dogs, sprawled all over the floor, sleepily thumped their tails.

'D'you know what I've always wanted to do?' said Rupert idly. 'Buy that wood below your house.'

'Pretty useless piece of land,' said Declan.

'Fifty yards to the right of the stream you could make the most perfect dry ski slope. You wouldn't see it from the road. It'd be hidden by trees on both sides.'

'How much d'you reckon it's worth?'

'About thirty-five grand,' lied Rupert.

'Seems a helluva lot,' said Declan, stroking Jack Russells with both hands.

'You could still walk through the rest of the wood if you wanted to,' said Rupert.

But Declan wasn't listening. Thirty-five grand would get me off the hook for the moment with the tax man, he thought, and pay the electricity bill and Caitlin's school fees.

'Think about it, anyway,' said Rupert. 'You also need a day off. Come out hunting on Saturday week. I'll lend you a horse.'

When Declan finally got back to The Priory, he left all the car lights on, flattened several purple crocuses on the edge of the lawn and drove slap through a flower bed.

Waiting for him on the stairs, both looking equally disapproving, were Taggie and Gertrude.

'Why,' said Taggie, 'were you so g-g-gratuitously beastly to Rupert?'

23

On the third Monday in March Cameron Cook had the sadistic idea of summoning the entire Corinium staff to a power breakfast in Studio 1 at eight o'clock in the morning. While they blearily consumed croissants and muesli, and orange juice (scrambled egg was considered to contain too much cholesterol), Tony gave them a rousing pep talk on how each one of them could personally help retain the franchise.

'This is a very exciting time,' said Tony heartily. '"Dorothy Dove" and "Four Men went to Mow" have yet again been nominated for BAFTA Awards. Our new series on the elderly, "Young as You Feel", starts next week. And we're delighted to announce that our new presenter is going to be Naomi Hargreaves, who, as you know, climbed Everest last year at the age of sixty-five.

'Our new networked quiz, "Master Dog", to find the canine brain of Britain, starts recording on Wednesday. The new series of "Four Men went to Mow" starts at the end of April and a performance of Michael Tippett's *Midsummer Marriage* will be recorded in Cotchester Park in early June. James Vereker's and Sarah Stratton's new afternoon programme starts on Monday week.' Tony smiled warmly at Sarah, and received a black look from Cameron. 'And we all wish them the best of luck.

'Finally, *Midsummer Night's Dream*,' Tony added with a

sigh of relief, 'is virtually in the can. We anticipate two days re-shooting, tomorrow and Wednesday, leaving Studio 1 free for "Miss Corinium Television" on Thursday.'

To put Declan down, Tony had deliberately not mentioned his programme, but now, looking round the packed studio, he discovered to his fury that Declan didn't appear to be present.

Declan, in fact, was at home, having got up at five to wrestle with his Yeats biography. Looking at the pile of scribbled notes and typed pages on his desk, he felt like Vidal Sassoon confronted by the wild woman of the West with fifty years of burrs and tangles in her hair. He wished he had Vidal Sassoon's skills. He was so tired, he hadn't had an original thought for weeks. Matters had not been helped by Grace finally walking out at the weekend because Declan had bawled her out for drinking all his whisky. Maud, furious at losing her ally and sparring partner, blamed Declan for the whole thing and was refusing to talk to him.

His black gloom was interrupted by Ursula ringing up to say she had flu.

'Poor thing. Stay in bed,' said Declan. 'Can I bring you anything?'

'No, but I'm terribly sorry, I forgot to remind you about Cameron's power breakfast,' said Ursula.

At Corinium Tony was winding up his peroration: 'I have no doubt that Corinium will retain the franchise, but I cannot remind you too strongly that this year we are on show. The IBA will not only be monitoring our programmes more closely, and examining our finances and our staff relations, but they will be looking to see how we conduct ourselves both as individuals and as a company. Any complaints from a local body, pressure group or a restaurateur will count as the blackest mark. Seb Burrows' twenty-first birthday party last week, for example, completely broke up the Beaufort room at the Cotchester Arms. If you ever have another twenty-first birthday, Seb –' Tony's big smile flashed on – 'you'll be fired.'

Realizing some sort of joke had been made, the staff tittered feebly.

'Finally I must warn you that that scourge of violence and, particularly, sex, the Reverend Fergus Penney, ex-Prebendary of the Church of England, will be visiting the station tomorrow, so for Christ's sake behave yourselves and make him feel welcome. And remember above all, appearance does matter.'

Exactly on cue, Declan walked in, deathly pale, hair unbrushed, stubble blacking his jaw, and his jersey inside out.

'I'm sorry, Tony,' he said, 'I forgot.'

'We've just finished,' said Tony coolly. 'I'm afraid you've missed the boat, but that's nothing unusual.'

'Where are you going?' shouted Cameron, as Declan turned towards the exit.

'Home,' snapped Declan, 'I've got a lot of lying down to do.'

The next day, 21st March, was the first day of Spring. The Head of News sent a crew off to photograph lambs playing in a field. James wore a new primrose yellow tracksuit to urge viewers to join his new sponsored Slim-for-Spring campaign to raise money for heart research, and Declan came in to interview Guilini. The programme, for once, was being recorded as Guilini was flying to New York for a concert straight afterwards.

The fair Daysee Butler, keen to do her bit for the franchise, accepted an invitation to lunch from someone almost as grand as Guilini. As it was programme day, she only sipped Perrier and ate one course of chef's salad. Her very distinguished companion, however, departed from his usual Perrier and put away a large whisky before lunch, a whole bottle of claret during, and a large brandy afterwards. He hardly touched his monkfish, but was charmed that Daysee should peel his Mediterranean prawns for him as she told him, admittedly rather monotonously, how she got every programme out on time.

On the drive back from the restaurant, which was several miles outside Cotchester, Daysee's very distinguished companion, mindful that it was the first day of Spring, pulled into a side road to admire some leaping lambs and leapt on poor Daysee. By the time he had torn half the buttons off her yellow angora jersey with the picture of Donald Duck on the front, and grabbed goatily at her thighs, laddering her stockings, Daysee was so frightened she dashed out of the car and, taking off her high heels, ran sobbing across Cotchester water meadows, across the tarmac of the car park and in through the back door of Corinium Television. Here she collided with Tony, who had lunched not wisely but too well. The sight of poor Daysee with her blonde hair awry, her mascara streaked with tears, her stockings muddy and laddered, and her yellow jersey half torn off her beautiful body, melted even Tony's stony heart.

'My dear child, what *is* the matter?'

'Someone's just tried to rape me,' wailed Daysee.

Next minute she was whisked up in the fast lift to Tony's office and ensconced on the squashy leather sofa, sobbing her heart out while Tony poured her a vast brandy.

'There, drink this.'

'I mustn't,' sobbed Daysee. 'I'll never be able to count Declan's programme out on time.'

'Nonsense! One glass of brandy won't hurt you. Anyway, it's only some tinpot conductor.'

Getting out his red silk handkerchief smelling of Paco Rabanne, Tony dried Daysee's eyes. She was really very, very pretty.

'Now, tell me who it was.'

'I c-c-can't.'

'Come on, you can trust me.' He sat down on the sofa beside her.

'It was such a shock,' whispered Daysee. 'I thought he was just interested in our programmes. I wanted to help Corinium win the franchise.'

'I know you did,' said Tony warmly. 'That's what makes it so reprehensible. Just give me his name.'

302

'I'd truly rather not.'

'Someone connected with work?'

Daysee gulped and nodded.

Better and better, thought Tony, mentally rubbing his hands. How wonderful if it were Declan or even James.

'If we don't get him for rape, we'll clobber him for sexual harassment,' he said, trying not to sound too eager.

Daysee shook her head in bewilderment. 'I was convinced he was just interested in my mind.'

Noticing the ten inches of thigh and the glorious depth of cleavage revealed by the torn jersey, Tony sidled down the dark-green squashy sofa and said, 'Of course he was.'

Daysee looked up, her huge eyes spilling over once more with tears. Tony put an arm round her shoulders.

'Come on, my dear, we can't allow animals like him to roam at large. He may strike again and succeed next time. Think of your female colleagues. Don't worry, I'll see your name's kept out of the papers. Now tell me who it was.' Gently he stroked her silky hair.

'It was the Prebendary,' murmured Daysee.

'What!' exploded Tony.

'The Reverend Fergus Penney from the IBA,' whispered Daysee miserably.

Instantly the solicitous smile was wiped off Tony's face. His arm jumped off her shoulders as though they were red hot.

'I don't want to hear any more about this business,' he said chillingly. 'If you value your job, don't blab about it to anyone. And I hope you've learnt your lesson, not to wear such short skirts or tight sweaters to the office in future.' With that he slammed his door in poor Daysee's face.

Still trying to be a loyal Corinium employee, Daysee tried to keep her trap shut. But Declan, noticing her reddened eyes and lack of bounce during the afternoon and being infinitely more skilled at getting confidences out of people than Tony, soon had the whole story from her with the help of a few whiskys from his office bottle.

'Lord Baddingham said the Prebendary was so against sex and violence,' sobbed Daysee.

'Only on television,' said Declan grimly. 'It's fine in real life.'

As he was intending to take Thursday off to go to the Gold Cup with Rupert, Declan went into the office on Wednesday to wade through a mountain of post. After the row with Maud about the telephone and drink bills which she'd hidden behind the recipe books in the kitchen, Corinium, with all its ructions, seemed the quieter place. The tax man had also called the day before to collect twenty thousand pounds, and, being told Declan was out, said he would call again next day, which was another reason for not hanging around at home. He was beginning to think there was no alternative except to sell Rupert the wood. The only thought that sustained him was that he was due for a two-month break at the end of April, but, as things were going, he'd have to spend the time off doing programmes in America to raise some cash.

He was also aware that his programmes had been very lacklustre recently. The one on Rupert had attracted huge ratings and newspaper coverage, but Declan in retrospect was bitterly ashamed of it, knowing that initially he'd let personal animosity overwhelm his detachment. Since then, the programmes had had the bite of a rubber duck.

God, he was tired. He looked at the mountain of post, a lot of it probably bills. Ursula was still away. He could smell today's special, boeuf bourguignon, flavoured from a packet no doubt, drifting down from the canteen, as could the contestants of 'Master Dog' who were barking hungrily in Studio 2.

He picked up the first memo. *'The Gay and Lesbian Sub-Committee of the ACTT has been re-named the Sexuality Sub-Committee.'*

On cue, Charles Fairburn drifted in, having just collected his expenses.

'Come and have a drink at the Bar Sinister.'

Declan shook his head. 'Got to deal with all this.'

'Never grumble about fan mail,' chided Charles. 'Think of poor me going off to Southampton first thing tomorrow to supervise Holy Communion for the Deaf. Have you been asked to Tony's bash for Badminton? He's put the little red ram logo on the corner of all the invites so he can offload the whole thing on expenses.'

'He won't ask me,' said Declan grimly.

'No, you are a bit out of favour, poor dear,' said Charles sympathetically, 'and you work harder than any of us. I'm expecting to get the Old Queen's Award for Lack of Industry any minute. That's better; at least you're smiling. And I'll tell you something else to cheer you up even more. In Studio 2 you'll find a lot of lovable mongrels rummaging for choc drops which have all melted under the lights, on caring James's pastel sofa. James is going to be livid when he gets back from another three-hour lunch with Mrs Stratton.'

The telephone rang. 'Corinium Waifs and Strays,' said Charles, picking it up. 'Oh, hi, Madden dear. All right, I'll send him along. Tony's leaving for London in twenty minutes, thank God,' he told Declan, 'but he wants a word with you first. I'd take the slow lift. He's in a vile mood.'

Tony, in fact, seemed in an excellent mood, purring away like a great cat about to enjoy an extended game of mouse-taunting.

'Ah, Declan. Shut the door behind you and sit down.'

As usual the central heating was turned up so high Declan felt he was having a hot flush.

'I wonder if you'd explain this.'

Tony threw Declan a picture postcard of a huge crocodile with gaping jaws. On the other side was scrawled in huge black writing: 'Here's a picture of your boss. Bloody hot here. If I don't talk to you before, I'll pick you up at The Priory at eleven o'clock. Rupert.'

There was no address or stamp.

'Who the fock opened this?' asked Declan.

'We open all mail during franchise year,' said Tony

smoothly. 'Just to check whether any of our staff are being propositioned by other franchise contenders.'

'This place gets more like the KGB every minute.' Declan made no attempt to hide his rage.

'I also see you've taken up élitist sports,' went on Tony, happily handing Declan the *Daily Express*, which was folded back at a picture of Rupert and Declan out hunting.

'Burying the hatchet after their recent encounter on "Declan",' read the caption.

Tony shook his head. 'You're not keeping very good company, Declan.'

'Then why has Rupert been asked to judge Miss Corinium tomorrow?'

'That's a slip-up of Cameron's. It won't happen again. There's also a piece in yesterday's *Standard* quoting you as saying you've given up hope for Lent. Not a very positive attitude. Be a bit more careful when you talk to the press in future.'

Tony got up and wandered towards the drinks cupboard.

'Like a drink?'

Declan shook his head.

'Just as well,' said Tony, pouring himself one. 'I gather you were plastered when you interviewed Guilini yesterday.' Then, as Declan opened his mouth to protest, he went on, 'I saw your old boss, Johnny Abrahams, from the BBC last night. He said they'd let you go at just the right time, that you were burnt out.'

'The bastard,' said Declan furiously. 'He's got a bloody nerve.'

'I hoped you'd take it like that,' said Tony softly, 'because I am very worried about your ratings. Only ten million for the week ending 2nd March. Cameron was at a network meeting yesterday and they're now considering what was unthinkable a few months ago, shifting your programme from peak time to shallower waters, perhaps a ten-thirty or even an eleven o'clock slot.'

'That's insane,' said Declan. 'We only got ten million because the BBC have moved "Dallas" against us. We'll get it back.'

'I doubt it,' said Tony brutally. 'Quite honestly you've lost your authority, Declan. There was a time when every interview made the front page of every newspaper. Now even the critics ignore them. You didn't make a single national last week.'

'I will next week. Bob Geldof's coming on.'

'Bit old hat – all that Aid stuff.'

Tony tipped back his chair, stretched his legs, and gazed at Declan considerately. 'I'm so sorry,' he said. 'I know how depressing it is for stars when they drop down from Number One. I do hope you're not overdoing things. Why are your hands shaking?' He looked complacently down at his own beautifully manicured hands. 'Mine don't shake.'

Declan stood up. 'That's because you don't have to work with people like you,' he snarled.

Out of the window he could see a posse of lovable mongrels scampering across the water meadows after an aniseed trail, being pursued by a panting camera crew.

Tony also rose to his feet: 'I'm trying to be sympathetic,' he said in a voice that froze even Declan's blood, 'and all I get is abuse.'

He pressed a button. Miss Madden appeared so quickly she must have been listening at the door.

'Declan's leaving,' said Tony imperiously.

Back in his office, trembling from head to foot, Declan got a bottle of whisky from the cupboard and, pouring two inches into a paper cup, drained it. The first thing that really registered in his post was a typescript and a letter from Patrick. He had finished his play and sent it to Declan to read:

Dearest Pa,
I've been poisonous enough about your stuff in the past, now I'm going to get a taste of my own medication (as Cameron would say). Please read it and tell me the truth. Give my love to Cameron, if you're still speaking. See you next week.
Love Patrick.

Patrick, Declan reflected, was a bloody sight better at getting down to things than he was. He was about to start reading when there was a knock on the door. It was Miss Madden, puce as a beetroot, bringing him a cup of coffee and two rounds of roast beef sandwiches.

'You don't eat enough.'

'You mean I'm drinking too much. That's terribly sweet of you, darling. How much do I owe you?'

'It's a present,' said Miss Madden, blushing even more deeply. 'As Lord B's gone to town and Ursula's sick, I thought you might like some help with your mail. I can polish off that lot in no time. I expect it's mostly from fans.'

'I doubt it.'

'Don't take Lord B's remarks too much to heart. He's only trying to goad you. Please don't walk out. We need you here.'

Declan was touched, and dutifully sat down and went through his post. When Miss Madden had taken it away, he felt unable to settle down to Bob Geldof's cuttings. Wandering down the corridor, he found James and Sarah recording their first afternoon programme in front of a small geriatric audience.

James was interviewing a large woman in a pin-striped suit and a monocle, who looked not unlike Thomas the Tank Engine. Insufficiently briefed, having spent far too long lunching with Sarah, he was frantically leafing through his notes to find out something about her. At last he turned up Deirdre's list of questions. Christ, she was a fucking composer. James was tone-deaf.

'A very good afternoon and welcome to Dame Edith Spink,' he said.

The audience clapped lethargically.

'May I call you Edith?'

'You may, but my name's actually Enid,' said the lady composer.

Flustered, James consulted his notes. He'd kill Deirdre after the programme.

'I'd like to say, Enid, how much I personally have enjoyed all your symphonies.'

'I've only written one,' snapped Dame Enid.

From the darkness by the door, Declan was beginning to enjoy himself. Dame Enid Spink was an extremely distinguished musician who lived on the borders of Wiltshire and Gloucestershire, and was probably only second to Michael Tippett as a composer in Britain. A notorious lesbian and a feminist, she was already furious that Corinium were doing Michael Tippett's opera this year rather than one of hers.

'You've just visited the States, Enid,' ploughed on James, 'to conduct your newest opera. Er, what do the Americans think of your work?'

'Bloody stupid question,' said Dame Enid. 'I didn't ask them all. There are about two-hundred million, you know.'

Bitch, thought James furiously, I'll fix her.

'Many critics,' he read from Deirdre's notes, 'say this latest opera of yours isn't up to standard.'

Crash came Dame Enid's hands down on her wide-apart pinstriped thighs. 'Name four,' she thundered.

'Pardon?' stammered James.

'Name four of those critics,' persisted Dame Enid.

James couldn't. Dame Enid stalked off the set.

James mopped his brow, thanking Christ the programme wasn't live. He was lucky that it was not until ten minutes later that Cameron put in an appearance and therefore entirely missed the encounter.

Now it was Sarah's turn. Her task was to interview some female rugger players and a group of lady buyers in suits with pussy-cat bows on whether it was still a man's world, followed by a studio discussion in which James would whizz round the audience with a roving mike.

Although there was already an extremely competent director, Cameron, in her role as Programme Controller, couldn't resist sticking her oar in, making an already nervous Sarah fluff her introductory patter over and over again. Now Cameron had come down on the studio floor.

'Thank you so much for spending March with us,' she told the tittering audience after the tenth take.

Sarah fluffed her patter again.

'This is really an elaborate way of handing in your notice, Sarah,' taunted Cameron to more titters. Sarah looked imploringly at James, who, sitting on the yellow sofa, suddenly seemed very interested in his cuticles. Sarah fluffed the patter again.

'If you don't pull your finger out,' Cameron told her, 'we'll be going out live.'

Declan had seen enough. 'Stop being a fucking bitch,' he yelled, marching up to Cameron.

The crew, grinning broadly, gave him a round of applause. The audience, wildly excited to see such a megastar and thinking it was part of the show, started to clap and cheer too.

'How dare you lay that number on me?' screamed Cameron over the din. 'I'm going home.'

'Put the kettle on,' the Floor Manager shouted after her. 'We'll all be round for tea in half an hour.'

Down the steps swarmed the audience, crowding round Declan, clamouring for his autograph.

'You're very like yourself,' said one lady.

'Thank you so much, Declan,' said Sarah tearfully.

'Now you can get on with the programme,' said Declan, beating a hasty retreat.

Utterly dispirited after his outburst, Declan returned to his office and, getting out the whisky bottle, settled down to read Patrick's play. As he finished it, he was equally consumed with pleasure and despair, because the play was quite simply marvellous: incredibly original, funny, very moving, slightly over the top, but possessing all the vigour and fearlessness of youth. Reading it made Declan realize once again what an utter cock-up he'd made of his own career.

Emptying the bottle, very drunk now, he wandered into the corridor, ending up in the big studio where they were shooting the last re-take of *Midsummer Night's Dream*.

Even the cardboard trees seemed to pulsate with mid-summer heat and enchantment. Declan stood in the shadows, tears pouring down his face, impossibly moved by the poetry. Would *he* ever write anything good again?

Feeling a tap on his shoulder, he jumped violently. It was Cameron. Rubbing his eyes frantically, he followed her out into the corridor.

'I'm sorry I came on strong this afternoon,' she said. ' "Four Men went to Mow" starts again next month. I guess I'm uptight.'

'I guess you are,' said Declan ungraciously. 'Pick someone your own weight next time. Sarah could be very good if you don't frighten her off too soon.'

He stalked into his office, rather laboriously gathered up the pages of Patrick's play, and chucked the whisky bottle into the wastepaper basket with a clang.

'As Tony's opening people's post, I suppose he's frisking wastepaper baskets as well,' he snarled at Cameron. 'That should really convince him I'm drinking too much. I imagine it was you who told him I was drunk on the programme yesterday.'

Cameron blushed. 'No way.'

'Well, I wasn't.' He went on gathering papers together.

'What's that?' said Cameron, anxious to change the subject.

'Patrick's play.'

'Any good?'

'Exceptional. You'll be sorry one day you passed him up.'

'I'm sure you won't be,' snapped Cameron.

'No.' Declan's brooding eyes looked at her contemptuously. 'I can't imagine anything that would have filled me with more horror. He sent his love by the way.'

Cameron tried again: 'Look, I know it's screwing you up working here.'

'I'm surprised you talk in the present tense,' growled Declan, going towards the door.

311

'Don't forget you're judging "Miss Corinium Television" tomorrow. We want you and Rupert here by seven,' said Cameron.

'About all I'm fit for,' said Declan wearily, and walked out.

Declan was not a vain man, but if anything could have boosted his self-confidence it was that day at Cheltenham. Whenever he put his nose out of Freddie's tent to have a bet, he was mobbed, and the combination of him and Rupert together among that horse-loving, strongly Irish crowd, caused almost as much excitement as the returning winner of the Gold Cup. To add to everyone's high spirits, Freddie's horse danced home an effortless winner in the second race. Nor was it anyone's fault that, as a result of a freak snowstorm, the Gold Cup was postponed for an hour, or that Rupert had a monkey each way on the winner. Consequently Rupert and Declan got unbelievably drunk and didn't reach Cotchester until seven forty-five.

'Is this the Forest of Hard-On?' said Rupert, as he tripped over a lot of stacked-up cardboard trees outside Studio 1.

'Wrong play,' said Declan. 'They were supposed to represent Greece.'

Cameron, Tony and James, who was compèring the programme in a midnight-blue dinner jacket with a dinky rose-pink bow-tie, were all absolutely livid they were so late.

'It's a bloody disgrace,' stormed Cameron. 'There's no time to brief you. Go into my office and you'll have a chance to meet the other judges and the fifteen finalists before transmission.'

The other judges were a male pop star called Big Lil, the Mayor of Cotchester, the head of the local tourist board and a naval officer called Ron, who'd just returned from sailing round the world single-handed.

'After a girl-less ten months,' whispered Rupert, 'he'll have to be lashed to his chair.'

'We're now selecting the last seven,' Cameron told the judges. 'You should look for the kind of girl you can take anywhere.'

'In the broom cupboard, under the mulberry tree,' said Rupert.

As each girl sidled in, Tony and Cameron fired questions at them. Miss Bisley came from Cotchester. Miss Painswick from Bisley. Miss Chipping Sodbury was so well stacked she could have won a National Front award.

When Miss Wotton-under-Edge said her ambition was to run a home for homeless pussies, Rupert and Declan got serious giggles. Fortunately the room was ill-lit.

'They all talk like Valerie Jones,' said Rupert.

Having selected the last seven, they all adjourned to Studio 1, which was now organized with tables, at which sat the so-called invited audience, and the contest was on air.

The fifteen contestants then teetered on in bathing dresses and four-inch heels. Although the judges had already pre-selected their last seven, as far as the audience, the contestants and the viewers were concerned they were picking them now. Seeing the girls in bathing dresses for the first time, however, Declan and Rupert realized some of the ones they *hadn't* chosen had much better figures and legs and noisily tried to change their minds.

'You're supposed to be picking the first three now,' hissed Cameron. 'And stop making that bloody awful row.'

As Declan and Rupert rushed out to have a pee in the commercial break, Rupert grabbed a bottle of champagne from one of the tables, shoving it under his coat. Cameron, waiting in the corridor as they came out of the lavatory, shoved them into an empty dressing-room. 'Big Lil's going to sing his new single while the last seven change and you two can bloody well stay in here and behave yourselves.'

Rupert put on Bottom's head, which was hanging on a hook, and read out a notice on the wall: 'We apologize to all artistes for any inconvenience caused by accommodating them in a temporary dressing-room.'

'I am a Pees Arteeste,' said Declan, taking a swig from Rupert's bottle. Totally forgetting they were miked up, they starting discussing the contest.

'Why's James Vereker wearing red shoes?' asked Rupert.

'Must be the blood running down from all the people sticking knives in his back,' said Declan.

'What d'you think of Miss Bisley's bottom?' said Rupert from the furry depths of his ass's head.

'Terrific,' said Declan. 'What d'you think of Miss Chipping Sodbury's tits?'

'Wonderful, but not as good as Miss Wotton-under-Edge's crotch.'

'Which one d'you think Tony Baddingham's fucking?' said Declan.

'The whole lot,' said Rupert, collapsing on the bed with laughter.

Declan leant against the wall, shaking. 'And Daysee Butler will get it out to the second.'

Next minute a chalk-white sound man erupted through the door to tell them they were being overheard by everyone in the control room, including Cameron and Tony. After that Declan found events became slightly hazy. Miss Bisley was crowned Miss Corinium Television and even wept a few tears, but not enough to streak her waterproof mascara.

'I'll see you in my office in half an hour,' hissed Tony to Declan, as he ushered the Mayor and a lot of visiting VIPs upstairs.

'I won't be long,' Declan told Rupert. 'Wait in the car.'

He got his contract out of the filing cabinet in his office and took the lift to the fifth floor. He felt curiously elated.

As he stood in the doorway of the board room he heard Miss Bisley saying to Miss Painswick that Miss Cotchester's trouble was that she had an unphotogenic crotch.

Tony was talking to his VIPs, who included the Prebendary and who were all ogling the girls. Declan went up and tapped Tony on the shoulder.

'I'd like a word now.'

'Piss off.'

'Now – in your office,' said Declan, 'unless you want me to tell these creeps exactly what I think of you.'

'Do be careful,' said Miss Madden, who was sitting at her typewriter in a mauve satin dress.

Sauntering after Tony, Declan blew her a kiss.

'You look beautiful,' he told her.

'How dare you?' thundered Tony, as Declan slammed the door behind them.

'Because you're rotten,' said Declan. 'So rotten, even maggots throw you up.'

Tony went purple. 'You've flouted my authority at every opportunity,' he spluttered.

Slowly Declan walked towards him, huge, cavernous-eyed and menacing. 'Violence isn't the answer,' he said softly, 'but it's a bloody good start.'

Tony backed up against the wall, licking his lips, eyes darting, hand edging towards the intercom button.

'Don't touch me,' he croaked. 'I'll get you for GBH.'

'The H would be so fucking G,' said Declan, 'that you'd never open your big mouth again, you bastard.'

As he raised his hand, Tony cringed away until his head crashed against the framed photograph of himself and the Queen. Then he realized that Declan was holding a folded-up piece of paper.

'This is my contract,' said Declan grimly. Slowly and with great relish he tore it into tiny pieces and sprinkled it over Tony's head. Then he turned towards the door.

For a second Tony was struck dumb, but, as Declan's hand touched the door handle, he said, 'Can I take it you've resigned?'

'Indeed you can,' said Declan. 'I've prostituted myself for – ' he counted up on his fingers – 'seven months too long, and tonight I'm going to have the first night's sleep since I started working for you.'

'Has it occurred to you that you're breaking your contract?'

'I don't give a fuck,' said Declan, opening the door. 'I'm not staying here till you break me, like you broke Cyril, and Simon and half the poor mentally crippled sods in this building.'

The moment he'd gone Tony pressed the re-wind button on the tape recorder and poured himself a huge glass of brandy.

'Miss Madden,' he shouted, extracting the tape from the cassette, 'can you transcribe this at once? Make a dozen copies. Then sweep up these bits of paper and put them in an envelope marked Declan O'Hara's contract. What the fuck are you crying for?'

'He was a nice man,' sobbed Miss Madden. 'He always asked me about my life as though it mattered to him.'

Outside in the car park the wind had dropped and the moon was shining dimly through the clouds like a ten-watt bulb.

Rupert, still wearing Bottom's head, had finished the bottle of champagne.

'Sorry to keep you,' said Declan, getting into the car.

'How did it go?'

'I'm out.'

'Christ!' Rupert pulled off the ass's head. 'I thought you had a water-tight contract?'

'Unfortunately it wasn't whisky-tight,' said Declan. 'Let's go and get seriously drunk.'

RIVALS
24

Taggie slept fitfully, worried about her father, disturbed by a restless Gertrude, who imagined every creak and rattle of creeper blown against the turret windows was Declan returning. Waking at five, Taggie glanced out across the valley, as she always seemed to be doing these days, and saw that Rupert's lights were on. She tried not to envy her father spending a whole day with him; he'd had such a ghastly time at work lately, he deserved a break. Going downstairs to check if the car was back she froze with horror to see it once more parked across a flowerbed with all the lights on. Rushing outside, she found it empty and stealthily started to search the house. Declan was not in the bedroom – her mother sprawled diagonally across the bed as though denying him access – nor in the spare room. He wasn't in Patrick's room, or the kitchen, or either of the drawing-rooms or the dining-room.

She was beginning to panic that he'd gone for a walk in the wood and fallen down the ravine when she heard an excited squeak from the library. Gertrude had found him, still dressed, passed out cold over his desk. In his hand he still held the pen with which he had been writing his Yeats biography. He had knocked over a glass of whisky which had spilt over the open page of the notebook, blurring the drunken scrawl.

Taggie wrapped a couple of blankets round him, and put a cushion under his head, but he didn't stir.

He woke six hours later with a debilitating hangover and an even worse sense of foreboding. Staggering groaning into the kitchen, he found Maud reading Anthony Powell upside-down and looking bootfaced. Without being asked, Taggie tore four Alka-Seltzers from their blue and silver metal wrapping and dropped them into a glass. Declan took a gulp, retched and fled from the room.

'Well,' said Maud, when he came back, even more white and shaking, 'what kept you?'

'I don't remember,' growled Declan.

The telephone rang and he clutched his head, groaning. It was the *Scorpion*, the most seamy of the tabloids. Could they speak to Declan?

'He's not here,' said Taggie quickly.

'I gather he's resigned from Corinium. D'you know where I can get hold of him?'

Taggie went pale. 'Are you sure?'

'Quite. The press office confirmed it.'

'No. He's definitely not here.' Taggie slammed down the telephone.

Declan glared at her with bloodshot eyes, sensing trouble. 'What am I supposed to have done?'

Taggie looked nervously at her mother.

'Come on,' said Declan.

'G-given in your notice.'

'Kerist! Did I really?'

'You bloody idiot,' hissed Maud. 'Ring up Tony at once and apologize. Say you were drunk.'

At that moment Ursula arrived, looking pale from her flu, but very overexcited by events. Joyce Madden had rung her in tears in the middle of the night and told her what had happened.

'I was just telling Declan to ring Tony and say he's sorry,' said Maud. 'They're bound to take him back. He's such a big star.' The contempt was undeniable.

'I'm not sure they will,' sighed Ursula.

'Sit down,' said Taggie, pulling out a chair. 'I'll make you a cup of tea.'

'Declan's got a contract,' said Maud, 'and he was far too plastered to put anything in writing last night.'

Ursula turned to Declan who was sitting with his head in his hands.

'Don't you remember anything?'

'I remember a lot of girls in bathing dresses, who were rather ugly, and Rupert dressed up as a horse, and I think I remember having a row with Tony,' he muttered.

'You did,' said Ursula. 'You gave him an earful. Then you tore up your contract and scattered it all over him and resigned.'

'Oh Jesus!' Declan opened a bloodshot eye. 'Did I really?'

'And Tony taped the entire conversation, and Joyce Madden transcribed it at once, and no doubt copies are winging their way to the IBA and the ITCA and God knows who else at this moment.'

'You stupid idiot,' whispered Maud.

Fear is the parent of cruelty. Having found Declan impossible to live with for the past few months, she had considerable sympathy with Tony. Declan's career, albeit meteoric, had always been peppered with rows. She was totally unable to appreciate the pressures he'd been under. She proceeded to be blisteringly unsympathetic.

'Well, I'm not going back,' said Declan at the end of her tirade.

'You have no choice. The BBC wouldn't touch you with a barge pole. You'll have to crawl for once.'

'Oh Mummy,' protested Taggie, putting heavily sweetened, very strong cups of tea in front of Declan and Ursula.

Declan warmed his shaking hands round the mug which had a picture of a girl whose bikini disappeared when the mug was filled with boiling liquid. Like my career, thought Declan.

'It's all your fault,' went on Maud, 'taking days off to go hunting, going on the bat with Rupert before a programme. You're like a couple of schoolboys.'

All the animosity she harboured after Rupert had rejected her and embraced Declan seemed to pour forth like scalding lava.

'I rang up Personnel and resigned too,' said Ursula importantly. 'I'm not working for a police state any more.'

Oh Christ, thought Declan, that means I'll have to pay her salary myself until she gets another job. But he put a hand on her arm.

'Thanks, darling. That was very loyal of you.'

Everyone jumped as the telephone rang. Maud picked it up. It was the *Star*. Maud could never resist journalists.

'We're a bit hazy this end,' she said. 'Declan hasn't told us anything. What happened?'

The reporter, enchanted by Maud's soft, caressing tones, told her.

'I see,' said Maud grimly. 'Where's Rupert?'

'Well, he arrived in London ten minutes late to chair a seminar on "Alcoholism in the ex-Athlete". Looked like a prime target, but he refused to comment.'

'Thanks,' said Maud. 'We'll ring you back when he comes in. How could you?' She rounded on Declan. 'Slagging off Tony when you were miked up. I thought you were supposed to be a professional.'

Declan hardly heard her. 'We'll have to sell the house,' he said bleakly.

The telephone rang again. Declan got up and seized the receiver. 'Will you fucking go away?' he screamed.

'Charming,' said a shrill voice. 'This is Caitlin, your daughter, if you hadn't forgotten, and why hasn't someone come to pick me up?'

'Oh God,' said Taggie in anguish, catching the gist. 'I thought she broke up this afternoon.'

'Well, you'd better go and get her,' snapped Maud, who had forgotten to pass on the message.

'I'm going out,' said Declan.

'Whatever for?' screamed Maud.

'To do some thinking.'

'Well, you'd better come up with something pretty quickly. I have no intention of selling this house.'

With four Anadin Extra, four Alka-Seltzers, a cup of strong tea and the remains of last night's whisky churning uneasily inside him, Declan set out. A mild and sunny day with a gentle breeze had followed yesterday's torrential rain, freak snow storms and razor-sharp winds. Everything sparkled. For the first time in months the birds ignored Declan's bird-table and were busy singing and courting in the trees.

Down the Frogsmore, in one day, Spring seemed to have arrived. Primroses nestled on the bank. Coltsfoot exploded sulphur yellow beneath his feet, celandines arched back their shiny yellow petals in the sunshine; even the most uncompromising spiked red blackberry cable was putting out tiny pale-green leaves.

In the fields above, he could see Rupert's horses pounding round in their New Zealand rugs, tails held high, like children let out of school. In the woods, he found the first anemones and blue and white violets. Far above him the woodpecker was rattling away at a tree trunk. He could almost hear the buds bursting open.

Why the hell had he blown it all in his fucking intellectual arrogance? All he'd had to do was to endure working at Corinium until the end of April, then in the break look around for another job. Now that he'd left in a blaze of drunken publicity with plummeting ratings, no one would want him.

He crushed a wild garlic leaf between his fingers. The smell reminded him of lunches in Soho and endlessly plotting with his cronies to make a better world at the BBC. He'd loved London, but he didn't want to go back.   It was so hot that, on the way home, he took off his coat and sat down on the bank of the stream for a long time, watching the water as it glittered and squirmed with pleasure beneath the sunshine. Gertrude splashed about, and, picking up a stick, bounced up to Declan hoping he'd pull the other end; then, when he wouldn't, dropped it and licked his face.

An old man, walking his ancient Jack Russell back from Penscombe, stopped for a chat. His grandfather used to be the gamekeeper at The Priory, he said, a hundred years ago, when the land stretched for three hundred acres across the north side of the Penscombe–Chalford Road. He'd kept the place like a new pin. It was sad to see the state it had fallen into, the rotting trees and collapsing walls everywhere. Declan felt ashamed.

'You can tell Spring's come at last,' said the old man, 'because all the blackbirds are singing.'

But not for me any more, thought Declan in despair.

Then the old man peered closer. 'Didn't you used to be Declan O'Hara?' he said.

By late afternoon Taggie was shattered. Ursula, having parried the press all day, had gone home. After another terrible row with Maud, Declan had barricaded himself into the library, refusing to talk to anyone. Caitlin sat on the kitchen table with her arm round Gertrude, both watching Taggie stuffing a chicken with a mixture of apricots, sausage meat, breadcrumbs and garlic. Used to the central heating and constant chatter of Upland House, Caitlin was shivering like a whippet and gabbling away nonstop.

'There are going to be no more balls against boys' schools,' she announced. 'Last Friday we danced against Rugborough and one lot of boys took some fifth formers up on the garage roof and they were all smoking and drinking and telling the teachers to fuck off, and Miss Lovett-Standing – think of being saddled with a name like that – the gym mistress, found three condoms in the rhododendrons next morning.

'I came top in the exam on *The Mayor of Casterbridge*,' went on Caitlin. Then, seeing Taggie struggling to understand a recipe for potatoes Lyonnaise, her lips moving slowly as she read, she added kindly, 'but a sixth former who did the same paper last year told me all the answers beforehand. And two girls in the upper sixth are having abortions this holidays.'

'That's nice,' said Taggie absent-mindedly.

'Taggie, you're not listening.'

322

'I'm sorry. I'm so worried about Daddy.'

'He'll be OK. Someone will snap him up.'

'I don't know. He's lost all his confidence. I've never known him so down.'

'That's hangover,' said Caitlin.

Her ability to spread mess everywhere was even greater than Maud's. Her open trunk lay in the hall and lacrosse sticks, tapes, posters, rolled-up art work, wet towels, coloured files, a teddy bear and a squashy bag, overflowing with underwear, were scattered in a trail all the way to the kitchen. She was wearing a very expensive pink T-shirt, pinched from Maud at half-term, over which all her friends had written messages in biro, a puffball skirt, laddered tights and black clumpy stompers, and was now eating muesli out of a cup with a teaspoon.

'Christ, this house is cold.'

The telephone rang again for the hundredth time. The line was awful.

'Can I speak to Declan?' said a male voice.

'He can't talk to anyone,' said Taggie hysterically.

'Is that Taggie?'

'Yes,'

'It's Rupert. How's your father?'

'Not great.' Taggie felt herself going very red, and turned her back on Caitlin. 'He walked out, you know.'

'It was partly my fault. He was in an exocet mood. I should have stopped him storming in to see Tony, but he's better out of it; it was killing him. Are you all right, sweetheart?'

The sudden gentleness in his voice made her want to burst into tears.

'I'm fine,' she mumbled.

'Well, tell him I'll be over later.'

Upstairs, Declan turned on the five forty-five news and found Tony Baddingham, with a red carnation in his buttonhole, giving a press conference.

'The truth of the matter,' he was saying, 'is that Declan O'Hara tendered his resignation last night, and we accepted it.'

Stupid word 'tendered', thought Declan. There was nothing tender about it at all.

'Naturally, we're very sad to lose Declan,' said Tony, looking absolutely delighted, 'but, quite frankly, there have been a series of disagreements and there's a general feeling at Corinium that when people get too big for their boots, we'd prefer them to go off and wear out other people's carpets.'

Declan switched off and looked down at the floorboards. He hadn't got any carpets to wear out, and probably now he never would have. The telephone rang again. It was one of the Corinium shop stewards.

'Fuckin' idiot,' he chided Declan, 'you should've hung in and let him fire you.'

'I know,' said Declan almost apologetically. 'I felt I had to retain some shred of integrity.'

'Wish you'd come to us. Look, the lads want to come out. You've only got to ask. We'll black out the 'ole network for you, Declan, and get you reinstated.'

Declan was so moved he couldn't say anything for a minute. Then he said gruffly that there wouldn't be any point.

'I can't work for Tony any more, but thanks very much all the same, and say goodbye and thanks to all the boys for me.'

It was dark outside now, but a robin was singing on the bare honeysuckle outside his window. It had turned up at exactly six-thirty for the last week now, as if to cheer him on.

'*Art thou the bird whom man loves best,*' he murmured to himself, '*The pious bird with the scarlet breast, Our little English robin?*'

Tears filled his eyes. Oh God, what was he going to do?

Taggie knocked on the door and, getting no answer, walked in. She found him looking so haggard and despairing that she ran across the room, stumbling over the piles of papers and books all over the floor, and put her arms round him.

'Please don't be so sad. It doesn't matter if we go back to London. We were all happy there. You've just got to get your confidence back. Rupert rang, by the way. He's coming round.'

Going upstairs to her bedroom, she was horrified by how awful she looked. She'd been so busy she hadn't had a moment to wash or even clean her teeth all day. She knew she had no chance with Rupert, that it was appallingly presumptuous, but for once she wanted to look her best when she saw him. Caitlin's welcome-home supper could wait, she decided. She was going to have a bath and wash her hair.

Caitlin wolf-whistled when Taggie came into the kitchen an hour later. She was wearing a red-and-black-striped polo-necked jersey which Patrick had given her for Christmas, tucked into black jeans which were in turn tucked into black boots. As her hair was still damp she'd tied it back with a black ribbon. She wore no make-up except smudged black eyeliner, which made her silver-grey eyes look huge and almost luminous. A hot bath and the hairdryer had given her pale cheeks quite enough colour.

'Because you so seldom bother,' said Caitlin critically, 'one forgets how beautiful you are: much more so than anyone else I know.'

'Oh, don't be silly,' muttered Taggie in embarrassment, putting the chicken into the top-right oven of the Aga.

'How soon will it be ready?'

'About nine.'

'Good, I can watch "Dynasty". Who are you going out with?'

'No one.' Taggie busied herself with draining the parsnips. 'You like parsnip purée, don't you?'

'Adore it. You haven't answered my question.'

'No one.'

'Then why are you done up like Gertrude's dinner?'

'I just felt awful,' muttered Taggie apologetically, as she threw the parsnips into the blender. 'I didn't have time to wash all day.'

'Hum,' said Caitlin beadily, as she watched Taggie add curry powder, then butter, then cream to the parsnips.

'As I just got up into yesterday's clothes, I felt I must change,' went on Taggie, even more embarrassed.

'Fee, fi, fo fumble,' said Caitlin, 'I smell the blood of Rupert Campbell.'

'Oh shut up,' said Taggie, turning on the blender.

Caitlin waited until she had turned it off.

'I am Campbell-Black but comely,' said Caitlin giggling. *'Rise up, my love, my fair one, and come away, For lo, the winter is past, the rain is over and gone. The flowers appear on the earth; the time of the singing of birds is come, and the turtle-necked sweater is worn in our land.'*

'Oh shut up,' screamed Taggie. Picking up Gertrude's rubber ring, she hurled it at Caitlin, missed and nearly hit Rupert, who, finding the door open, had let himself in, followed by Freddie Jones. Taggie stood rooted to the spot with horror. Gertrude went into a frenzy of outraged barking that someone had entered the house without her knowing.

'Hello, Gertrude,' said Rupert. 'How extraordinarily good you look today. Nice dog, Gertrude, well done, hurrah, what a beautiful curly tail you've got.' Bending down, he stroked the bemused Gertrude over and over again.

Taggie giggled.

'That's better,' said Rupert. He looked a bit pale after yesterday's excesses, but seemed in excellent spirits.

'Hullo,' he said to Caitlin. 'How are you?'

'Fine.' Caitlin beamed. 'I was just quoting the Bible to my sister to keep her on the straight and narrow.'

'Cait*lin*,' pleaded Taggie in despair, frantically concentrating on spooning the purée out of the blender to hide her blushes.

Rupert went over to Taggie and, putting a hand on the back of her neck, drew her towards him. With most women, he would have dropped a kiss on the tops of their heads, but Taggie was so tall, he was able to rest his lips for a second against her temple.

'There, angel, you mustn't worry about your papa. Frederico, the whizz kid, and I will sort him out.'

'I'll get you a drink,' stammered Taggie. 'What would you like? Daddy's in the library.'

'I'd like a Bacardi and Coke, love,' said Freddie, 'and if

Rupe 'ere can keep it down, he'd like a whisky and soda.'

'If there isn't any Malibu, I'll have a Vod and Ton, Tag,' added Caitlin.

Fleeing into the larder, Taggie paused before she got down the bottles. Unbelievingly she touched her left temple where Rupert had kissed it, then, moving her fingers to her lips, kissed them in ecstasy. What was happening to her? She wondered if Caitlin's welcome-home chicken would stretch to six.

''Ullo, Declan,' said Freddie, as they went into the library and found him slumped at his desk. 'I've just seen that fucker Tony on the news. You're well shot of the smarmy bastard.'

Sitting down on the window seat, Rupert waited until Taggie had brought in the drinks. Then he shut the door behind her and said, 'Look, Frederico and I have been talking about you for some time. To put it bluntly, both being hard-nosed businessmen, we hate to see a hot property like you being wasted.'

'We've decided to form our own independent production company,' said Freddie, 'an' employ you to make programmes for the network, Channel 4 and the overseas market.'

It took a lot of tough talking to persuade Declan they weren't just being kind. He looked at his untouched glass for a second; then a real gleam of excitement came into his eyes. 'I've got a better idea. Why don't we pitch for the Corinium franchise, and boot out Tony.'

Freddie and Rupert looked at each other. 'Aren't we too late?'

'Not at all,' said Declan. 'If we step on it. The applications don't have to be in until the beginning of May.'

'We know all the right people,' said Rupert. 'So there won't be any problems getting our Board together.'

'And we won't have any trouble getting the backing,' said Freddie, jumping up and down with excitement. 'An' I can provide you wiv all the technical know-how.'

'And I know the Corinium Programmes backwards,' said Declan, 'so we can submit better programme plans standing on our heads.'

Taggie popped her head round the door: 'Anyone want more drinks?'

Too excited to be deflected, Declan shook his head. So did Freddie, who'd hardly touched his glass. Only Rupert handed out his. 'Please, angel,' he said with a grin, 'and could I have soda this time?'

'Oh goodness, did I give you Coke? I'm really sorry, and poor Mr Jones must have had Bacardi and soda.'

'I don't think he's noticed,' said Rupert.

As Freddie and Declan got more and more excited over their plans, Rupert thought about Taggie, how she'd trembled when he kissed her, and how adorable she'd looked with her long legs in those black boots, and her hair tied back like a boy soldier. But he mustn't think about her, he told himself grimly. She was Declan's kid daughter, totally out of bounds. Wrenching his mind back, he heard Declan saying: 'In fact Tony's only trump card with the IBA is Cameron Cook, and the staff are in a state of uproar about her as it is.'

'How would it be if I seduced her on to our side?' said Rupert idly.

'We don't want *her*!' Declan exploded. 'She's a treacherous evil bitch.'

'Not once I've sorted her out,' said Rupert. 'I was always good with difficult horses. I guarantee to have her eating out of my hand in a few weeks.'

25

Overwhelmed by the day's vicissitudes, Declan went to bed and didn't emerge for thirty-six hours, waking on Saturday morning to thank God he wouldn't ever have to work for Tony again, before falling back to sleep. On Sunday he woke to a glorious day and apologized to his darling Maud for being such a bear. She apologized for being such a bitch and, after he had explained about bidding for the franchise and selling the wood to Rupert to raise some cash, they vowed that things would be better between them and made passionate, ecstatic love. Replete, tranquillized, Maud wondered why she had ever wanted to look at anyone else. Taggie, as she cooked lunch later, listened to her mother singing and playing Schubert *lieder*. She found these staggering *volte-faces* bewildering, but felt only relief that the row was over.

Rupert, having spent Saturday hunting and on constituency business, rose early on Sunday and tried out each of a new intake of horses that had arrived from Ireland earlier in the week. One dark bay mare was really exceptional, incredibly quick off the mark with a huge wild jump. In a couple of years he could have made a world-class horse out of her. He felt, as always, that reluctance to sell her on, that temptation to have one more crack at show-jumping, then put the thought sternly behind him. An election was in the offing this summer and there was the franchise to be won. He was seeing Declan and Freddie that afternoon to work out a plan of campaign. They had arranged to meet at Freddie's house because they wanted to keep their bid secret until the applications went in, and because the press were still hanging around Penscombe Court and The Priory hoping to get some juicy story about Declan's exit from Corinium.

Handing the mare back to one of the grooms, Rupert mounted his old Olympic gold medal horse, Rocky, for a ride round the estate, as he always did if he was at home on a Sunday. The pack of dogs raced ahead putting up pheasants, chasing rabbits, snuffling down badger sets and foxes' earths. Rocky loved these outings, and to prove they were both still great, Rupert put the old horse over the occasional wall and any streams or fallen logs in their path. Rupert's eagle eye missed nothing, a loose wire here, a tree blown across a fence there, which would have to be repaired before sheep were moved in, how poor or good the grass was in each field, and how the winter barley was spreading in an emerald-green haze over the rich brown earth.

In the distance he could hear Penscombe church bells ringing, and the rattle of a clay shoot. Across the valley The Priory was in shadow with the sun behind it. The beech trees in front were a crimson blur as the buds thickened. Soon the leaves would be out and he wouldn't be able to see the house any more. Taking the muddy track that wound high above the Frogsmore, he noticed the first primroses blooming happily and safely under wild rose and bramble bushes, the spiky branches keeping the predatory grazing horses and cattle away.

In their sweet pale trusting innocence, the primroses reminded him of Taggie, who, he felt, could only blossom in life if she were fiercely protected. He suddenly wished he could be those spiky powerful branches keeping away anyone who threatened her. He imagined putting her on his gentlest horse, showing her all over his land, pointing out his favourite places, then making love to her among the wild flowers, as he had done to so many other women before – but with Taggie it would be different. Christ, he must get a grip on himself and get stuck into someone else very quickly. Thank goodness Nathalie Perrault was arriving this evening for a few days, and there was still the conquest of Cameron Cook to be orchestrated.

Back at Penscombe, stripped for a bath, Rupert got on to the scales and winced. Twelve and a half stone: at six feet two, no one could call him fat, but it was a far cry from the honed muscular leanness, the eleven stone, produced by eight hours in the saddle, which he'd trained down to before the Olympic Games and the World Championship. Too many dinners, too much booze, not enough exercise, he was hopelessly unfit. If he was going to seduce Cameron, he'd have to knock off a stone first – that meant no alcohol, and just meat, fish and vegetables for the next month.

When he rolled up at Freddie's house, Declan, looking ten years younger, had already arrived, and he and Freddie were poring over a book called *How to Win The Franchise*.

'The first thing we gotta do is appoint a chairman,' said Freddie.

'Better be you,' said Rupert.

'OK,' said Freddie, 'but we'll need someone respectable like a lord or a bishop or somefing as deputy chairman.'

'We must also remember,' said Declan, 'that the IBA, despite all their pronouncements about quality, are looking for applicants who won't go broke in the first eighteen months, and who'll be able to produce programmes that'll keep the company in the black over the next eight years. That's why we need a very experienced MD and a very strong Programme Controller.'

'You'd better be MD, then,' said Rupert.

'But I'm terrible with money.'

'You know about television. I'll be Financial Director, and I'll get hold of a shit-hot accountant to keep an eye on you. Sandwiched between him and me and Freddie, you can't go far wrong.'

'I've got just the man for Programme Controller,' said Declan: 'Harold White, ex-ITN and BBC. Currently Director of Programmes at London Weekend. He's bloody good.'

331

'I've been doing some sums,' said Freddie. 'We'll need at least fifteen million to keep the station going for the first two years, but before that we'll need at least two hundred grand up front as burn money to pay for brokers, bankers, running costs and to launch the publicity campaign.'

'Which we'll forfeit if the bid fails,' said Declan.

'Right,' said Freddie. 'Why don't we put that up ourselves? Give us some control.'

Rupert was about to agree. Then, catching sign of Declan's twitching face, said, 'Let's argue about that later. Now which do we find first, board or backing?'

'Backing's easy,' said Freddie. 'Let's get the right people first. Apart from the directors, who are actually going to run the station, we need some local millionaires, and a liberal sprinkling of the great and the good as non-executive directors.'

'Before we approach anyone, we'd better come up with a name,' said Rupert.

'I've been thinking. What about Venturer?' said Declan.

'Sounds all right,' said Freddie. 'What's it say it means in the dictionary?'

'Someone who's daring and willing to take risks, someone who's prepared to brave dangers, or embark on a possibly hazardous journey.'

In Declan's deep husky voice it sounded wonderfully romantic.

'Perfick. What we going to use as a logo?'

'I've been thinking about that too,' said Declan. 'You know that bronze I admired in your sitting-room, Rupert?' He turned back to Freddie. 'It's of a boy in an open-necked shirt and knickerbockers with bare legs. He's shading his forehead with his hand as he gazes into the distance. It's ravishing and it's got the right mix of strength and grace and vision.'

'I've seen it, it's grite,' said Freddie in excitement. 'We'll get someone to draw it; then we can put it on all our stationery and on the front of the application.'

'We'd better get T-shirts and ties and car stickers printed,' said Rupert, 'and posters too. Just imagine a poster of Taggie in a Victory for Venturer T-shirt!'

'What about a studio?' said Declan.

'Well if Tony Baddingham's prepared to sell the Corinium building, it would be much cheaper to take over that,' said Rupert. 'But, in case he turns really nasty, we'd better make contingency plans.'

Valerie Jones was absolutely livid. She never admitted reading the *Scorpion*, but the weekend fish had arrived in Saturday's edition, and Valerie couldn't miss the huge headline announcing that Declan had resigned from Corinium while getting disgustingly drunk with Rupert, and now they were both closeted together in Fred-Fred's den, and the air was thick with cigar smoke, and she was sure they were up to no good. She'd grumbled so much in the past about Freddie blasting her out with his music that he'd had the room thoroughly sound-proofed. Now she couldn't hear a word that was going on inside, even when she went outside and pretended to pull non-existent weeds out of the flowerbed under the window. How could they keep the windows closed on such a lovely day?

'Shall I take them in afternoon tea?' said poor fat Sharon, who still cherished a long-range crush on Rupert.

'No,' snapped Valerie. 'You haven't done your religious study yet. Miss Fidduck said at least an hour a day; nor have you groomed Merrylegs. What is the point of your father buying you an event horse?'

As Sharon waddled upstairs, Valerie could bear it no longer.

'Afternoon tea,' she announced ten minutes later, barging into Freddie's den with a tray.

Declan was striding up and down the room scattering cigarette ash. Freddie was whizzing round excitedly in his revolving chair. Rupert lounged on the sofa, playing with one of Freddie's executive games, which involved clashing huge ball-bearings against each other. All three of them looked up with ill-concealed irritation.

'What a fug,' said Valerie, dumping down the tray and throwing open the window, so all Freddie's papers blew around.

'I don't know how you can stay inside. I hope you won't be long, Fred-Fred. We're due at Sir Arthur's for cocktails at six-thirty and you promised to walk round the grounds with me beforehand.'

She turned to Rupert and Declan: 'We're opening Green Lawns to the public in July. All proceeds to the NSPCC. I'm surprised you're not opening Penscombe Court this year, Rupert,' she added, raising her voice to cover the increasing clash of ball-bearings.

'You can hardly expect the public to look at a lot of weeds,' said Rupert.

'But you've got buckets of time to get it shipshape. It seems so selfish not to raise the money if you can.' Valerie gave her little laugh.

'I'm sure the NSPCC would prefer a cheque,' said Rupert evenly.

'I don't expect Maud'll be interested in opening *your* garden,' went on Valerie, turning to Declan. 'I've just read all about your exploits in the *Sunday Express*. Tony Baddingham is quoted as saying one of the reasons you left Corinium was because you couldn't face being knocked out by "Dallas".'

As Freddie gently shooed her out, Rupert and Declan both reflected that not throttling Valerie before December would be infinitely harder than winning the franchise.

The next five weeks were frantic. Many of the bidders for franchises in other territories had spent several years perfecting their applications, raising the cash, and getting their boards together. To speed up the operation, Freddie, Declan and Rupert divided the role of recruiting officer between them.

'There's no point enlisting people who won't contribute anything,' said Declan. 'We mustn't confuse celebrity with

334

attainment, and they *must* live in the area. Once we land a really big fish, the rest will follow.'

Hubert Brenton, Bishop of Cotchester, whom luckily Declan hadn't bitched up during his New Year's Eve interview and who was currently furious with Tony for deciding to televise Easter Communion at Gloucester Cathedral rather then Cotchester, was the first to be signed up. Declan invited him to lunch at The Priory the following week, and, as it was Lent and a Friday, Taggie cooked the most succulent Coquille St Jacques, followed by sole Veronique. Maud, with a cross round her neck and her titian hair drawn back in a bun, gravely asked the Bishop to say Grace, and pointed out the beautiful spring flowers in the centre of the table, which her children had sent her for Mothering Sunday.

Rupert, who, as part of his getting-fit-for-Cameron-Cook campaign, was off the booze, provided the most exquisite white wine. Caitlin, who, unlike poor Sharon Jones, had passed her religious studies O-level, was able to converse with the Bishop at length about St Luke, and particularly the Prodigal Son.

There was a dicey moment when she dropped her bread, butter-side down, and said 'Shit', but by then the Bishop was fortunately talking to Maud about his recent trip to the Holy Land. Fortunately, too, he'd been wandering round the Sea of Galilee last weekend and missed the newspaper reports of Declan's exit from Corinium. Over the lemon sorbet, Declan and the Bishop discussed how thrilling it would be to dramatize Lytton Strachey's brilliant essay about Cardinal Newman and Cardinal Manning, who had both lived in Oxford, which was, after all, within the franchise area.

After lunch Maud, Taggie and Caitlin discreetly withdrew, and Declan produced Rupert's venerable port.

'Not drinking?' asked the Bishop, as Rupert passed the decanter on.

'No, My Lord,' said Rupert gravely. 'I've given it up for Lent.'

The Bishop, who was very hot on sex and violence, had always thoroughly disapproved of Rupert, but perhaps at long last, after such a turbulent past, he was trying to shed his jetset playboy image and forge a more satisfying way of life.

Declan and Freddie steered the conversation round to Corinium Television and the appalling poverty of their religious programmes, and then raised the subject of their rival bid. They very much hoped the Bishop would join Venturer and become their Deputy Chairman.

'Television today,' said the Bishop warmly, 'is a key factor for the quality of life and for establishing values.'

For the past ten years, he went on, he had had special responsibilities for communication in the diocese and he saw joining Venturer as a way of extending a work that interested him greatly.

'We know busy people don't do fings for nuffink,' said Freddie, cosily. 'If we win the franchise, there'll be a very small director's fee, say ten thousand a year, which could always go to your favourite charity.'

Signing up Henry Hampshire, the Lord-Lieutenant, was even easier. Freddie and Rupert wooed him over a very expensive lunch in London. Henry, as it turned out, was absolutely furious with Tony for flogging a field ten miles from The Falconry, but only a quarter of a mile from and in full view of Henry's house, to some property developers. He was also a very old friend of Rupert's, having a wife too plain for even Rupert to have had a crack at, and had liked Freddie when they'd met shooting at Tony's.

'Any money in it?' he asked, having flogged two stone lions last week to pay a tax bill.

'Fucking fortune,' said Rupert. 'We'd need a bit up front.'

'Don't mind that,' said Henry. 'As long as you arrange for me to meet Joanna Lumley. Suppose I could always sell a Stubbs.'

'You needn't go that far,' said Rupert, shocked. 'We only want about ten grand. What about that minor Pre-Raphaelite, the one over the chimney-piece in the sitting-room?'

'Good idea,' said Henry. 'Never liked it. Silly girl lying in the water, covered in flowers. Someone should have taught her the backstroke.'

At the end of lunch, Henry tried to pay.

'No, no,' said Freddie. 'Honest, it's on Venturer.'

'Oh well, if you can get it on corsts,' said Henry.

Strong on his homework, Declan investigated the likes and dislikes of Lady Gosling, Chairman of the IBA. He also discovered that her best friend, Dame Enid Spink, was the composer interviewed so disastrously by James Vereker. Declan called on Dame Enid in her rooms at Cotchester University, where she was director of music, and found her ferociously conducting to a gramophone record of her latest opera, *The Persuaders*.

'Worst programme I've ever been on,' boomed Dame Enid, as she and Declan dipped pieces of stale seed cake into tea the colour of mahogany. 'In fact Corinium's whole attitude to music is utterly philistine. Last time the franchises came up for grabs, that treacherous little fart, Tony Baddingham, promised to finance a Cotchester Youth Orchestra. Not a penny have we seen.'

Declan said truthfully that Venturer wouldn't be prepared to finance anything except television programmes until they broke even, but he hoped Dame Enid would advise them on their music programmes.

'If you get the franchise,' asked Dame Enid, 'would you get rid of that little squirt James Vereker?'

'Indeed we would,' said Declan.

Once Dame Enid agreed, it was a piece of cake to recruit Professor Crispin Graystock, a rich left-wing English Literature don who had dry, unmanageable hair like Worzel Gummidge's dipped in soot, wild eyes and a wet formless face, and who longed to be a television star because he thought it would help sell his slim and unutterably dreary volumes of poetry.

Although he was still smarting over not being included in the new *Oxford Companion to English Literature*, Crispin

Graystock was regarded as a considerable heavyweight in the academic world.

Freddie Jones took Lord Smith, the even more left-wing ex-secretary of the Transport and General Workers Union, out to yet another very expensive lunch, where, with his mouth crammed simultaneously with lobster and Pouilly Fuissé, Lord Smith agreed to join Venturer, and provide a substantial cash investment from Union funds.

'Doesn't he feel guilty about getting involved with such a capitalist organ as Venturer?' said Rupert disapprovingly.

'Not at all. Once I told him the money to be made,' said Freddie. 'He feels television is for the people.'

Rupert, seeking a shit-hot money man, rang up Marti Gluckstein, arguably the most brilliant accountant just this side of the law.

'How'd you like to join our bid for the Corinium franchise?'

'I've already turned down four other groups,' said Marti in his nasal Cockney twang. 'I loathe television.'

'You'd have to buy a house in the area,' said Rupert. He could feel Marti shudder all the way down the telephone wires.

'I loathe the country,' said Marti.

'Don't have to live here,' said Rupert. 'Just buy a place and sell it the moment we clinch the franchise. Prices are going up so fast in the Royal triangle, you'll double your money by the time you sell it. I'll find you one.'

The prospect of making such a fast buck clinched it.

'Marti Gluckstein's a crook,' said Declan in outrage, when Freddie and Rupert jubilantly told him the good news.

'Don't be anti-semitic,' said Rupert primly.

'And he doesn't live in the area.'

'He's just bought a cottage in Penscombe,' said Rupert blithely. He was quickly learning he had to box very carefully round Declan's integrity.

Bearing in mind the IBA's obsession with minority groups, particularly ethnic ones, Declan, who knew nothing about cricket, recruited Wesley Emerson, a six-foot-five West

Indian bowler and the hero of Cotchester Cricket Club, whom he'd met at a Sports Aid drinks party.

Rupert was as outraged as Declan had been about Marti Gluckstein. 'You're crazy,' he yelled. 'It was only me and the Government stepping in with some very fast talking that stopped Wesley getting busted in New Zealand this winter. He was snorting coke on the pitch, and he's the biggest letch since Casanova.'

'I thought that was your prerogative,' said Declan coldly. 'Talk about the kettle calling the pot Campbell-Black.'

'I didn't realize we were talking about minority gropes,' snarled back Rupert.

It took all of Freddie's diplomacy to calm them down.

Basil Baddingham was the easiest of all to recruit. Rupert signed him up as they checked on the edge of a beech covert during the last meet of the season.

'D'you really want to infuriate Tony?' asked Rupert.

'How much?' said Bas, after Rupert had explained.

'Ten grand.'

'Cheap at the price. You're on,' said Bas.

Having assembled their Board of the great and the good, Venturer now needed some heavyweight production people. This had to be handled with great delicacy. Anyone worth their salt had already been approached by other consortiums. Two department heads at Yorkshire had just been sacked when it was discovered they'd joined a consortium in the Midlands. Most ITV companies, and the BBC as well, had threatened to boot out anyone found having dealings with any new franchise applicants, even in another area. As Declan was only too aware, Tony was already going through all incoming mail, monitoring telephone calls and checking through desk drawers and wastepaper baskets after dark.

Declan therefore proceeded with extreme caution, winkling out home telephone numbers and promising total anonymity. Early in April he rang Harold White, programme controller at LWT, arguably the most brilliant and innovative brain in television.

'Harold, it's Declan.'

'How extraordinary,' said Harold. 'I've been trying to get your home telephone number all day. We're bidding for Granada. You interested in joining our consortium?'

'Not really, but thanks all the same,' said Declan. 'We've just moved here, and I couldn't face another move. How about joining ours?'

One of the pledges that Venturer planned to make to the IBA was that, if they won the franchise, they would take over most of the Corinium staff below board level. But there were three people Declan was anxious to secure for Venturer in advance, in case they were lured away by another consortium.

'I want Charles Fairburn,' he told Rupert.

'He'd fight with the Bishop of Cotchester, the lazy fat poof,' said Rupert.

'Charles knows the area like the back of his handbag,' said Declan, 'and he's very bright. He's just bored out of his skull. I'd move him away from Religious Programming and put him in charge of Documentaries.'

Declan didn't recognize Charles when he rolled up at The Priory. He was wearing a false nose, a ginger moustache, a ginger felt hat with a Tyrolean feather and dark glasses.

'Can't be too careful, dear,' he said, whisking into the house. 'James Vereker spent three hours at lunchtime getting his hair streaked yet again, and Tony's absolutely refusing to believe he didn't go to an interview.'

Declan was glad he was alone with Charles when he asked him to join Venturer as Head of Documentaries, because Charles promptly burst into tears. For an awful moment Declan thought he'd insulted him.

'I'm sorry,' he muttered. 'I had a feeling you were bored with religion.'

'I am, I am,' sobbed Charles. 'You don't understand! The absolute bliss of the thought of getting away from Corinium! You've no idea how we all miss you.'

It was only then that Declan realized, despite the quips and the jokey exterior, the strain Charles must have been under for years.

'Tony demoralizes one so much, one feels one will never be good enough to work for anyone else again. I can't thank you enough, Declan. Do you think there's any chance of us getting it?'

Declan was touched by the 'us'.

'Well, a tenant whose record is good,' he said, 'stands a better chance than a new applicant of unknown potential. But Tony's record isn't exactly good, and we're getting together an incredibly strong team. Now if I tell you who they are, will you promise to keep your trap shut, because if one word of this gets out before the applications go in, Tony'll start tarting up Corinium's bid and exoceting ours.'

'Mum's the word,' said Charles wiping his eyes. 'Mummy's always been the word in fact. I wish you'd met Mummy, Declan. Now, is there anyone else at Corinium you want me to sound out?'

Declan said he was interested in gorgeous Georgie Baines, the Sales Director, and Seb Burrows from the newsroom.

'Very good choice,' said Charles approvingly. 'Both stunningly able. Seb's in dead trouble. He dug up a terrific story about a bent vet in league with one of Tony's millionaire farmer friends. Unfortunately he used hidden mikes and secret cameras without getting clearance and, when Tony pulled the programme, Seb handed it over to the BBC. If Seb wasn't Cameron's protégé, he'd be out on his ear by now. You're not interested in her are you? She's tipped for a BAFTA this week.'

Declan shook his head violently. He hoped that Rupert had forgotten about Cameron.

Rupert rang Declan that evening from London.

'We need a really good Head of Sport. How about Billy Lloyd-Foxe?'

'Excellent. I've heard nothing but good about Billy,' said Declan. 'Will you talk to him?'

The following day Rupert had a drink with his best friend

and old show-jumping partner. Billy, who was working for the BBC and very strapped for cash, looked tired and pale. Janey, his journalist wife, had just had another baby; they weren't getting much sleep at night. He absolutely jumped at Rupert's proposition, particularly when Rupert offered to treble his salary.

'You'd have to come back and live in Gloucestershire.'

'Try and stop me. You know I hate London. Might there be something in it for Janey?'

''Course there would,' said Rupert. 'How extraordinary we didn't think of her before. The IBA are dotty about women. She could have her own programme. Those chat shows she did for Yorkshire were terrific. Tell her not to write anything too outrageous in her column before Christmas. We won't know whether we've got the franchise until December.'

'What happens in the meantime?' said Billy, who felt guilty that Rupert was buying him large whiskies, and only drinking Perrier himself. 'I'd adore to join Venturer, but until you can pay me a salary, and the franchise is safely in the bag, I can't really afford to burn my boats with the Beeb.'

'It's all right,' said Rupert. 'Georgie Baines, Seb Burrows, Harold White and Charles Fairburn are all in exactly the same boat. All that happens is we attach a strictly confidential memo to our application saying we've signed up a Head of Sport, a Sales Director, a Programme Controller, etc., who are all wildly experienced, but for security reasons we can't reveal their names until we go up to the IBA for the interview in November.'

'How very cloak and dagger,' said Billy. 'I must say it'll be fun working together again.'

'We need some more women,' said Declan. 'Janey Lloyd-Foxe is gorgeous and talented, but a bit lightweight, and Dame Enid's almost a man anyway.'

'I'm going to have a crack at Cameron Cook. I'm working on it,' said Rupert, who'd already lost twelve pounds in weight.

'Not safe,' growled Declan. 'She'd shop us to Tony.'

Together Freddie and Rupert raised the money.

Rupert, in between his punishing work load as Sports Minister, had several meetings with Henriques Bros, the London Merchant Bank. He found it very difficult not drinking and sticking to his diet over those interminably long lunches, but at least it left him with a clear head. By the second week in April he'd organized a potential seven-million-pound loan.

Freddie's methods were more direct. He invited half a dozen rich cronies to lunch in his board room and got Taggie up to London to do the cooking. With the boeuf en croute he produced a claret of such vintage and venerability that a one-minute silence was preserved as the first glass was drunk.

'Christ, that's good,' said the Chief Executive of Oxford Motors.

Freddie tipped back his chair, his red-gold curls on end, his merry grey eyes sparkling: 'I can only afford to drink wine like this once a year,' he said, 'but I'd like to be able to drink it every day, and that's where all you gentlemen come in.'

By the end of lunch, having bandied the names of Marti Gluckstein, Rupert and Declan around the table, Freddie was well on the way to raising the eight million.

Jubilant, he travelled back to Gloucestershire by train and, seeing a plump lady walking down the platform, recognized Lizzie Vereker and whisked her into a first-class carriage. His mood of euphoria, he soon discovered, was matched by Lizzie's. Thanks to a wonderful new nanny, who seemed impervious to James's advances, she'd finished and delivered her new novel and the publishers loved it. It was an excuse for her to buy him an enormous drink, she said, but she didn't know if British Railways stocked Bacardi and Coke.

'Leave it to me,' said Freddie, and came back with two half-bottles of Moët.

'How's James?' he asked, as the train whizzed through Slough.

343

'Frightfully cross,' said Lizzie. 'People keep ringing him up asking for Declan's home number because they want him to join their consortiums. Have you seen Declan?'

'No,' lied Freddie, and wished he didn't have to. Looking at Lizzie's round, smiling face and capacious cashmere bosom, Freddie couldn't help thinking how nice it would be if Lizzie joined Venturer. She had just the right emollient quality to keep everyone happy. She had three novels under her belt and lived in the area. He gave her a lift home. Although the trees were still leafless, the wild garlic and the dog mercury were sweeping like a great emerald-green tide over the floor of the woods.

'Oh I love Spring,' sighed Lizzie. 'The bluebells will be out soon. I've only been away two days and it's like missing "EastEnders"; you suddenly discover nature's moved on another instalment without you.'

'I know I shouldn't ask,' said Freddie as the red Jaguar pulled up outside her house, 'but will you have lunch with me one day?'

'I know I shouldn't accept,' said Lizzie, 'but yes, please.'

Dropping in at The Priory on the way home, Freddie found Declan and Rupert in the library surrounded by tapes. Declan was busy writing the section of the application which would tear Corinium's programmes to shreds.

He and Rupert were now watching a tape of 'Cotswold Round-Up'. Sarah was interviewing some old lady who couldn't pay her gas bill and James was sitting on the pink sofa looking caring.

'Christ, she's pretty,' said Declan. 'She'd be dazzling if she were properly produced. We do need some more women.'

'No, no, no, no,' said Rupert. 'She really *is* lightweight.'

'What would you feel about Lizzie Vereker?' said Freddie, his voice thickening.

'Good idea,' said Declan. 'She writes very well.'

'And she's so sweet,' said Rupert, 'and it would infuriate James.'

'And she lives in the area,' they all chorused.

'Let's recruit her later in the year,' said Declan. 'She's too near to Tony and I really don't want him to know what we're up to before the applications go in.'

RIVALS
26

On the second Monday in April, Ursula, who was still working for Declan, although he could ill afford her salary, was due to lunch with her old friend Joyce Madden.

'See if you can find out Tony's whereabouts next weekend,' Rupert had asked her on the telephone beforehand.

Ursula, who loved conspiracy, came back from lunch and half a bottle of Sauternes bustling with excitement, and rang Rupert.

'Joyce told me in the strictest confidence that Tony and Cameron are off on a naughty to Madrid this weekend. Cameron's flying out on Friday afternoon. Evidently she wants some peace to polish Corinium's application before it goes off to the IBA. Tony's giving a party at The Falconry on Friday night because it's Badminton weekend and a nice excuse to ask all his posh friends paid for by Corinium. Then he's flying to Madrid on Saturday lunchtime. They're staying in the same hotel and on Sunday night Cameron's picking up some award for "Four Men went to Mow". They're both flying home on separate planes on Monday.'

'Well done, thou good and faithful servant,' said Rupert. 'Could you bear at this stage not to mention this to Declan?'

Later in the day Rupert went to a reception to welcome some visiting Russian gymnasts, during which they gave a demonstration of their skills. Watching them go into incredibly graceful contortions on parallel bar and rug, Rupert wondered whether Cameron Cook was as supple and agile as that in bed. How the hell was he to get her on her own to launch his attack? Then inspiration struck. The moment the party was over he beetled out to his Government car and rang his friend the handsome Duke, who lived at Badminton.

'Could you do me a great favour?'

'Depends how great,' said the Duke.

'You've got the Princess staying next weekend, haven't you?'

'Yes.'

'Could you possibly ask Tony and Monica Baddingham to dinner on Saturday night?'

'Do I have to? I don't mind Monica, but he's such a ghastly snob.'

'I'll knock half a grand off that Irish mare.'

'Oh, all right then.'

'I'm going away this weekend,' Rupert told Gerald Middleton next morning as they went through the diary. 'I bumped into the Secretary of State for Scotland last night, who reminded me that Hearts are playing Madrid on Saturday, and it seemed wrong that no one from our department was going.'

Gerald raised his eyebrow.

'They're the only British team in the semi-final,' said Rupert blandly.

'You're meant to be chairing a meeting opposing the Swindon/Gloucester motorway in Gloucester on Friday night,' said Gerald, who didn't approve of dates being broken.

'I know. Ring them and say I'm terribly sorry. They have my full support, but they'll have to get someone else. And can you get me a couple of presents for the wives of the British Ambassador and the Spanish Minister for Sport?'

'I hope you're not overdoing things,' said Gerald reprovingly. 'You've lost an awful lot of weight recently. Don't forget you've got a second appointment with Doctor Benson tomorrow.'

Gerald was very worried. Rupert had been edgy for the last

month, which could at first be put down to his not drinking, but this weekend he'd been really bad-tempered and two trips to the doctor in three days seemed ominous, particularly when you had screwed around as much as Rupert.

Rupert, however, rolled up at The Priory in the highest spirits the following evening to find Declan still surrounded by tapes and Basil Baddingham sitting on the edge of his desk drinking a Bloody Mary and discussing tactics.

'I was just telling Declan that I've found you a possible building in case Tony won't let us buy the existing Corinium studios,' said Bas. 'Cotchester Hall's coming on to the market in November. Why are you looking so bloody pleased with yourself?'

Rupert waved a piece of paper in front of them.

'I had an AIDS test this week and I'm clear.'

'Christ,' said Bas, examining it. 'Is there no justice in the world?'

'How long did it take you to get the results?' asked Declan.

'Forty-eight hours,' said Rupert, 'but I had to bung them.'

'I'd be far too frightened to go,' said Bas.

'I came to tell you,' said Rupert, retrieving his piece of paper, 'that I'm going away for the weekend.'

'But we've got our first Venturer meeting on Sunday,' protested Declan. 'Everyone's coming – even Harold White and Marti Gluckstein.'

'Christ, he's never been to the country in his life,' said Rupert. Then, hurriedly remembering the cottage he was supposed to be buying for Marti, asked, 'Where are you having it, at the Bar Sinister?'

'Too close to Tone,' said Bas. 'Freddie's earmarked a fantastic little pub in the middle of Salisbury Plain which no one knows and which has amazing food. The landlord just runs it for fun.'

Declan was still looking disapproving. 'You ought to be there. Meetings are essential at this stage to establish some kind of *esprit de corps*. And we'll all be tossing ideas around.'

'You know I never have any,' said Rupert.

'I thought you were chairing the motorway meeting,' said Bas.

'Had to cancel it,' said Rupert. 'If I don't spend more time in my constituency other than on Venturer business, they're going to drop me.'

'Burke only visited his constituency once in six years,' said Declan.

Rupert laughed. 'He wasn't such a berk then.'

'Where *are* you going?' asked Bas.

'To Madrid to watch some soccer.'

'Balls,' said Bas. 'You're up to something.'

'I need a break,' said Rupert. 'Man cannot live by bread alone; he needs crumpet.'

There is a moment every Spring when even the most dedicated workaholic is overwhelmed by restlessness and longs to cast clouts and wander hand in hand with a new love through the burgeoning countryside. Cameron Cook was no exception. The weather had suddenly turned so warm as she packed for Madrid on Friday morning that she was able to wander naked round her bedroom with the smell of newly mown grass drifting in through the wide-open windows. The apple trees at the bottom of her backyard were still bare, but the long grass round their gnarled grey trunks was filled with bright blue cillas, polyanthus and narcissi. Beyond the fence two mallard had nested in the rushes on the edge of the water meadows, and in the distance the willows, bowed over the river, were fringed with palest green.

Although Cameron had read that there was a heatwave in Madrid, it wouldn't catch her on the hop. She had spent several hours a week over the last month on the sun bed, baking her body to that dark smooth gold that Tony loved. She was in great shape too; her coach at the gym last night had told her that, apart from a few professional athletes, her body was the most perfect and finely tuned he had ever handled. She admired it every time she passed the long mirror. Yet only yesterday Tony had shattered her confidence once again.

349

In order to discuss some change in the running order, she had barged into Sarah Stratton's dressing-room yesterday afternoon and found her sharing a bottle of champagne with Tony. Sarah's gold hair was prosaically in rollers and she was sitting in a dove-grey silk petticoat which showed off her cleavage and had got rucked up to show a strip of flesh between the top of her dove-grey silk French knickers and her pale grey stockings. She was actually perfectly decently dressed and Tony was leaning against the wall six feet away from her, but there was something about the way they stopped talking when Cameron came in. Normally Cameron would have bawled Sarah out for drinking before a programme, but she couldn't with Tony countenancing it. Instead she had a row with Tony after work.

Tony was quite unrepentant.

'Poor darling Sarah, she was a bit nervous about interviewing the head of the Chamber of Commerce, in case it influenced the franchise. After all they are an important pressure group. She was asking my advice on her best line of questioning. Her great strength,' he went on, with a nasty smile, 'is that she's not afraid to show a man she's vulnerable, and she is *so* deliciously feminine.'

'And I'm not, I suppose?'

Tony shrugged and ruffled her spiky hair.

'No one could call you feminine, darling.'

So this morning, in a rage, Cameron, who had never worn baby-doll nighties or anything underneath her clothes other than the briefest bikini pants, rushed out and spent a fortune on matching underwear and nightgowns and negligées.

In other more subtle ways her self-confidence had been eroded recently. Ironically, since Tony had made her Programme Controller, a role she'd coveted for so long, she'd become less secure, because she spent so much time in meetings and was doing less and less of the thing she was really good at – making programmes. All the prizes she was now winning were for work done last year. The new series of 'Four Men went to Mow', starting next week, would largely be produced, directed and re-written by other people. Having clawed her way to the top, she realized, as many men had realized before her, that the view from there wasn't that great; in fact it was bloody scary. Finally, she was aware that by flexing her muscles in the office, in bed and in the gym, she was frightening guys off. In the last three years Patrick and Tony were the only ones who'd fallen in love with her, and Tony was showing every sign of getting bored.

Out on the water meadows and the cathedral close she could see office workers in shirt sleeves and cotton dresses, many of them probably from Corinium, sneaking out to early lunches, wandering arm in arm, carrying bottles to drink under the willows.

She glanced at the status symbols littered in ludicrously expensive confusion over her bed – the Charles Jourdan shoes, the Hermés scarves, the Filofax, the Rayban shades, the huge Rolex watch, the backless kingfisher-blue Jasper Conran for Sunday night's presentation – what was the point of all these spiralist trappings if there was no one to share them with? Her mood of despair lasted all the way to Madrid.

There, however, the black limo that met her at the airport and the splendour of her magnificent suite in a hotel paid for by the Spanish television authorities, gradually cheered her up.

There were two bedrooms in the suite, each with two beds, a huge living-room stuffed with antiques and lit by huge chandeliers, and an enormous bathroom with soft and hard loo paper, a hair dryer and two beautiful white towelling dressing-gowns. There was a bottle of champagne in a bucket of ice and a huge basket of fruit with pomegranates, persimmons and apples as big as grapefruit. Pink carnations floated in the finger bowls; there were flowers in every room to match the pale pink walls, and silver trays of chocolates. And this was just her suite. Tony's suite next door was identical.

'Hey diddly dee, a plutocrat's life for me,' sang Cameron, demolishing a tray of chocolates. Then she started worrying about spots. She'd better stop.

There were also telephones everywhere, even in the shower. Tony would be circulating at his drinks party now.

351

It brought her up with a nasty jolt that no one else in the world would like to be called by her, except Patrick and she didn't know where he was.

She strolled out on to the balcony and saw that there was a little garden restaurant below, with a summer house and floodlit lemon trees and a lawn with a fountain. The tables were filled with handsome, hawklike men with sleek black hair, and beautiful women in suits with very padded shoulders, who were all talking their heads off and having a wonderful time.

Going back into the living-room to attack a pomegranate, she noticed an etching of the Judgement of Paris on the wall. Juno and Athene, both fully dressed, were looking furious, as Venus, who was flashing an ankle and a bare boob, was awarded the apple. Venus looked just like Sarah Stratton. Cameron turned the picture to the wall. It must be tiredness that suddenly made her feel so unbelievably down again. She couldn't be bothered with supper; taking two Mogadon, she crashed out.

She got up early, spent two hours working out camera angles for the first part of 'Four Men went to Mow', then spent the rest of the morning working on Corinium's application. God it was turgid, longer than *Gone with the Wind* and infinitely less readable: all those Brownie points being notched up with promises to employ independent production companies and set up audio-visual workshops, or subsidize roving repertory companies and youth orchestras. There was also a lot of guff about grass-roots involvement and worker participation schemes. A few figures had been provided, but there was very little talk of profits.

Unable to face tinkering with it any more, Cameron lunched at the hotel, wandered round Madrid, which seemed to be packed with Scottish football supporters, then spent two hours restoring her sanity looking at the Goyas and El Grecos in the Prado. The telephone was ringing as she let herself into her suite. It was Joyce Madden.

'Lord B's terribly sorry.' Cameron could tell Madden wasn't. 'He's been trying to get you all afternoon. He's sorry but he won't be able to fly out for the awards. Something's cropped up. The Duke's asked him to dine at Badminton tonight. He says he can't refuse, particularly in franchise year. Hullo, hullo . . .' but Cameron had hung up.

She was so angry she ate all the chocolates on the silver tray. How dare he, the bastard! Standing her up for a bloody dinner party. Bloody star-fucker.

Absolutely on cue there was a knock on the door and in came a valet bringing a huge bunch of roses.

'*Sorry I can't make it, Darling,*' said the card. '*Good luck tomorrow, All love, Tony.*'

Cameron was so furious she went out and hurled the roses over the balcony, watching them whizz round and round until they landed on a mob of cheering fans.

'Bastard, fucker, asshole,' screamed Cameron at the top of her voice, then let out an enormous fart, which seemed the only way she could demonstrate her utter contempt for Tony.

'Hush,' drawled a voice, 'you'll frighten the pigeons.'

Cameron swung round and gave a gasp of appalled embarrassment.

For there, laughing his handsome head off on the next-door balcony, his face as brown as the glass of whisky in his hand, lounged Rupert.

'What are you doing here?' muttered Cameron.

'Watching Hearts win a football match. Never thought I'd get in here, but they had a last-minute cancellation, a Mr Smith.' He grinned wickedly. 'What an extraordinary coincidence to find you here. Why are you looking so bad-tempered?'

'I am bad-tempered. The TV doesn't speak English.'

'You expecting guests?'

'Not any more.'

'So that bouquet you were bombing the masses with was a peace offering from the Oily Baron?'

'You're *so* fucking perceptive,' said Cameron sulkily. Then rage overcame pride. 'Madden just called to say he can't make it. He's been summoned to dine at Badminton.'

'Probably has,' said Rupert. 'I know there's a dinner party

there tonight and the Princess is going. Let's have a drink.
Your place or mine?'

'Mine,' said Cameron. 'Give me half an hour while I take
a bath and dress.'

'I wouldn't bother.' said Rupert. 'You're overdressed as it
is.'

It was all going too fast for her. What the hell was Rupert
doing here? It could hardly be coincidence. He was the
biggest rake in the world. No one emerged unscathed. So
why was she feeling so wildly elated, washing her ears when
she'd washed them that morning, and trimming her bush,
and rubbing Fracas into her belly and inner thighs? As she
slid into her new peach satin underwear it seemed to be
caressing her in anticipation. For once she didn't need
blusher, the glow came from within. Finally, she put on a
pale apricot tunic, very demure and clinging with all the
buttons done up, but with the hemline six inches above the
knee, making her legs seem endless.

All powerful men are attractive. Men who are powerful
and kind are irresistible. For once Rupert seemed to have
abandoned his flip cracks and his sexual innuendoes. He
appeared to be really, really interested in her career, in
Corinium's programme plans and how they were approaching
their application for the franchise. He was also incredibly
well informed. She'd always thought he was only interested
in sport and screwing.

Cameron was enjoying herself so much she didn't notice
she'd drunk almost an entire bottle of champagne and Rupert
had hardly touched his glass of whisky. As the boat race is
usually won in the first two minutes by one crew surging ahead
and taking advantage of smoother water, so the conquest of
Cameron was really achieved in that first hour when she was
off-guard and feeling bruised and vulnerable because Tony
had stood her up. As Rupert got up to fill her glass yet again,
he pointed to the mound of paper on her desk.

'What are you doing?'

'Working on the final application.'

'Anyone bidding against you?' asked Rupert, idly.

'Tony's discovered a group of Bristol businessmen calling themselves Mid-West are having a go. They claim we're too Cotchester-orientated. But I don't figure they're much cop.'

That's three of us pitching, thought Rupert, reflecting that, as Cameron Cook had such wonderful legs, spying on her was no hardship at all.

'Is Tony worried?' he asked.

'No way, but we can't afford to be complacent. Southern lost their franchises in 1980, and they didn't appear to have done anything wrong. The IBA have to make some changes to be seen to be doing their job properly.'

'What about Declan? Tony lost a network slot there. How's he going to replace him?'

'I'm not sure. Declan cost Tony so much dough, and he really zapped him out. Tony can't stand not being able to bully people. He's much less uptight since Declan walked out, but he needs a replacement. I guess he'll poach some top front-of-camera person in the next few weeks, just to distract people from Declan's departure. The media are still sniffing round.'

'Any idea who it might be?' said Rupert.

'No. Tony loves to surround himself in mystery.'

'How are you enjoying being Programme Controller?'

Cameron shrugged. 'Not as much as I expected. There's so much hassle. Admin bores me rigid. Thinking up brilliant ideas, which other people promptly screw up. I had to sack four people last week. You ever done that?'

'Frequently,' said Rupert. Christ, he thought, as Cameron rabbited on, her mouth's like a dumper. I could use her to unblock my drains.

'You should get out,' he said when she finally paused for breath. 'Any of the network companies would snap you up.'

Cameron looked at the bulky application on the desk. 'I'd like to see Corinium retain the franchise. I'll probably look around in the Autumn. Although why I hang in with that bastard, I can't think. Is it usual to be asked to dine with royalty at the last moment?'

'No,' said Rupert.

'So Tony must have known about the dinner party for ages, and didn't have the guts to tell me he wouldn't be coming out.'

'Probably didn't want you to make other arrangements,' said Rupert, emptying the bottle into her glass.

He was shrewd enough to realize that, having existed on a diet of Tony for three years, and having been flaunted at work and on the occasional jolly abroad but ruthlessly excluded from anything else, what Cameron was missing was a legitimate social life. He got to his feet.

'Well, thanks for the drink. I'm going out to dinner.'

Cameron's happiness drained away. 'Goodbye,' she said coldly, gazing at the plane trees in the square which were turning pink in the setting sun. 'Well, go on then,' she snapped a few seconds later.

'Stop sulking,' said Rupert. 'You're invited as well.'

'To a restaurant?'

'No, a private house.'

'They won't want me.'

'Yes they will. Nicky and Mary. You'll adore them. I'm just going to put on a tie.'

Next door he extracted a tape recorder the width and size of half a pencil from his top pocket, removed the tape, and put it in a secret drawer at the back of his brief case. There'd be too much noise at dinner to isolate anything interesting.

Nicky and Mary turned out to be the British Ambassador and his beautiful wife, who'd been a mad success in Madrid. They lived in a ravishing house a few miles from the centre of the town and the dinner party was just as grand as the one Tony and Monica were enjoying in England, but everyone was so friendly and easy-going and knew all about Cameron coming to Madrid to accept an award, that she instantly felt at home.

Mary, who had known Rupert at the height of his show-jumping career, was a good enough friend not to mind his totally upsetting the rigid protocol usually observed in diplomatic circles by bringing an extra guest, though it did mean a last-minute arrangement of the *placement*. At dinner Cameron sat between the Italian Ambassador and a Spanish duke, who both spoke perfect English. The gossip about royalty, politics and the jet set was sensational, but it was generally accepted that nothing would be passed on.

As Cameron ate the most delicious ravioli filled with scallop and lobster she had ever tasted, the Spanish Duke, who had slicked-back ebony hair, and hooded eyes, talked to her about the national character. 'As a people we are obsessed with death, but indifferent to it as long as the right attitude is struck. Note the matador's lack of concern for his own life. Life should be enjoyed now, not devoted to working for some distant fulfilment.'

Cameron looked at Rupert, who was seated on the other side of the table, laughing with his beautiful hostess.

Reading her thoughts, the Duke went on, 'Rupert in some ways is very Spanish, very brave, very macho, very sad underneath.'

'Sad?' said Cameron, amazed. 'Rupert?'

The Duke nodded. 'You never saw him in the show ring? It was magnificent. All the grace and courage, and apparent effortlessness of the matador. It must have been terrible for him to give it up. I thought he would drink or womanize himself to death.'

'He's made a great success of Minister for Sport,' said Cameron.

'It would hurt his pride not to make a success of anything, but he is still not fulfilled, and if the Tories lose the election, as everyone thinks they will, he'll be out of a job. He needs a great love in his life. I 'ope you are she.' He raised his glass to her.

'What was his wife like?'

The Duke kissed his bunched-up fingers. 'So beautiful, but quite wrong, nervy and not really interested in him, only what she thought he could become. You can't change Rupert, only make him more secure.'

With the Cochinillo everyone turned to talk to the person on their left.

'Rupert is very lucky,' said the Italian Ambassador. 'He has always had beautiful women, but seldom so clever. I believe you come to Rome next month for another prize?'

I'm having fun, thought Cameron in amazement. Tony's virtually kept me in prison for three years. For the first time since New Year's Eve with Patrick, I'm really having fun.

Rupert took her home just after midnight. They sat on opposite sides of the back of the embassy car and he made no attempt to touch her. In the darkness, she could see his profile, Spanish too with its thick slicked-back hair and forehead which ran down in a dead straight line to his nose. The only luxuriance in such a finely planed face were the wicked long blue eyes which she couldn't see in the dark, and the fullness of the lower lip. I want him she thought, helplessly; I want to be the woman who brings him fulfilment.

To their left a lot of drunken Scottish football fans were splashing about in a fountain. Above them soared the statue of Christopher Columbus.

'Can we get out and look at him?' said Cameron. 'After all, he did discover America.'

As they got out, Rupert's hair gleamed in the moonlight.

'Rupert,' screamed one of the Scottish fans. 'Look, it's Rupert.'

'No, thank you very much,' said Rupert, pulling Cameron back into the car.

Furious with herself for wanting him so badly, Cameron spoke only in monosyllables all the way back to the hotel. Totally ignoring the two smiling footmen who leapt forward to turn the revolving door for her, she shot into the elevator. In such a small space, you wouldn't have thought it possible to be so far apart, but Cameron felt her belly button touching her spine. Falling out of the elevator, she set out at a run across the patterned carpet, then, realizing she'd turned the wrong way, had to retrace her steps. What the hell was the matter with her, Controller of Programmes, mega-prize-winner, woman of substance, flapping around like a blackbird trapped in a fruit cage?

'I must be pooped,' she said in an over-bright voice. 'Thank you so much,' she mumbled outside her door, and, the moment Rupert had opened it for her, she shot inside.

Rupert made no attempt to retain her. 'Good night,' he said yawning. 'Sleep well.'

Alone in her mammoth suite, Cameron nearly went into orbit with frustration. In the mirror she could see her eyes glittering feverishly, her breath coming in great gasps, her nipples sticking through the apricot dress like thimbles. She half expected to see a pulse jumping between her legs.

She was nearly thirty. Perhaps she was losing her touch and Rupert really didn't want to sleep with her. She couldn't stand it. Ripping off the dress and the temptress's satin underwear he hadn't even seen, she went into the bathroom and turned on the cold shower, letting the icy jet blast away all the Fracas and the body lotion and the gel, and, hopefully, the desire. She turned it on so hard that it was a few seconds before she realized the telephone was ringing. No doubt it was Tony, establishing his ascendancy, so she let it ring just to worry him. After two minutes she picked it up.

'I don't see why Christopher Columbus should have a monopoly,' said a light clipped drawl. 'I want to discover America too.'

Cameron leant against the wall, feeling giddy with relief.

'Cameron.'

'Yes?'

'Who are we fooling?'

'I don't want to get hurt. Or get AIDS.'

'You won't,' said Rupert triumphantly. 'I had a test last week. I'm as clear as one of Valerie Jones's picture windows. I've got a certificate to prove it.'

'I'm amazed you haven't run off millions of copies on Ministry for Sports' stationery,' said Cameron, 'and circulated them to all interested parties.'

'Don't be bitchy. What about you?'

'I had a medical for insurance last month.'

'Tony must have bonked you since then. One could catch

something far nastier than AIDS from him. Now am I going to have to swing across the balcony like Tarzan or are you going to let me in?'

Rupert had cleaned his teeth and was still wearing his blue striped shirt and suit trousers. Without the camouflage of his jacket, Cameron could see how divinely proportioned he was, hunky on the shoulders, and lean and streamlined everywhere else. The golden meanie, she thought. As he came towards her, she clutched the towel round her, looking very young and vulnerable with her hair flat and wet from the shower, like a guard dog who's been uncharacteristically caught with its hackles down.

'Everyone's into prolonged courtship these days,' she gabbled. 'I don't want you to think I'm easy.'

'I don't.' Very gently Rupert took off the huge Rolex watch she'd forgotten to remove in the shower. 'I just want to see if you've got a designer cunt.'

He stopped her reply by kissing her; the towel slid to the floor.

It was a very good thing, he reflected later, that he'd lost all that weight and been jogging for an hour every morning, or he'd never have coped with the pace. Cameron was like an electric eel, knew every sexual permutation in the book, could twist herself into any position, and ordered him around like a sergeant-major.

'You are incredible,' he murmured into the back of her head, 'you'd make a matchstick feel like a cigar.'

'I need a bit more stimulation on my clitoris,' demanded Cameron.

Rupert obliged. 'In England, we pronounce it clitter-is.'

'It's *cly*-toris, and please be gentle.'

After two hours' fairly sustained screwing in both bedrooms, on the sofa in the drawing-room, under the shower, and admiring themselves in every mirror, they collapsed onto the carpet and Rupert came for the fourth and, from his point of view, final time.

'I haven't come yet,' said Cameron in his ear.

Rupert was astounded. 'What was wrong, for Christ's sake?'

'Nothing. It was the best first fuck I've ever had, I'm too uptight and too pissed, I guess.'

'Well, I'm not jumping ship till you do, so you may as well relax and stop fighting.'

Wriggling downwards, he parted her sodden bush. 'I am, after all, a member of the Cly-Tory Party,' he said in muffled tones.

RIVALS
27

Waking first, Cameron reached out and immediately realized she wasn't with Tony. Rupert had the most enormous erection, so like a Cruise missile that Cameron half expected to see lots of Greenham women camped round the bed looking disapproving and waving CND banners. Getting up, she drew back the curtain an inch. Rupert was certainly the best-looking man she'd ever been to bed with, and, despite her sniping, the best lay. Once she'd let him take over last night, everything had been perfect. She knew too that, in the space of fourteen hours, she was a different person. She'd been dependent on Tony for security but never happiness. For the first time in her life, she was in love and it terrified her.

The ring of the telephone woke Rupert up. It was Tony, all smarm, calling from his car, so the line wasn't very good. This was a good thing as Rupert started kissing Cameron all over in the middle, and so distracted her she couldn't remember anything practical, like what time the awards were or when she flew in tomorrow, or concentrate on the witty remarks Tony had made to the Princess.

'It's Tony,' she wrote frantically on the telephone message pad.

'So?' wrote Rupert.

'I'm so sorry,' gasped Cameron. 'I was working very late on the application.'

'How's it shaping?'

'Very well,' shrieked Cameron, as Rupert, grinning broadly, lunged Cruise into her. 'Look, I've got to go, I'm off to Toledo. I'll ring you before I leave tomorrow morning. You're insupportable,' she howled at Rupert, as she slammed down the telephone.

'How was the dinner party?'

Cameron grimaced. 'Said he only accepted because he felt the Duke needed his support and it was always a bit nerve-racking entertaining royalty.'

Rupert had to bury his face in her neck to stop himself laughing.

Afterwards he wanted to go back to sleep, but Cameron, who felt one shouldn't waste a minute in a foreign country, made the mistake of dragging him off to Toledo.

'You are now entering the Imperial capital,' read a large sign as they drove through the ancient city gates.

'I can think of things I'd much rather enter,' said Rupert broodily.

'Hardly Cyril Smith country,' he went on, as the official car rumbled cautiously up incredibly narrow streets, where the flowers in the window boxes on either side seemed to bend over to kiss each other beneath a thin blue strip of sky.

Cameron's hopes that Rupert might like the cathedral were soon dashed. He whizzed past the ravishing stained-glass windows, the carved pillars and the breathtaking pictures as though he was riding against the clock. A Velasquez Borgia reminded him of Tony. After gazing at a Rubens Madonna and Child for three seconds, he said they both should be dispatched to Weightwatchers. The El Grecos finished him off altogether because they all reminded him of his ex-wife's husband, Malise Gordon.

Just inside the entrance to the cathedral was a gift shop selling not only religious relics and postcards, but also flick knives, swords, guns, thumbscrews and racks. Was this symbolic of the torture Rupert was going to put her through? wondered Cameron. To cheer him up, she insisted they stop for Margueritas at a nearby bar. Rupert pronounced them absolutely disgusting: neat salt water with added salt water. They'll all be at the first Venturer lunch on Salisbury Plain, he thought sourly, getting drunk and enjoying themselves. He wished he were there too.

As they were leaving Toledo, Cameron suddenly thought wistfully of Patrick and how much he would have enjoyed wandering round the city and the cathedral.

'Can we just drive up to the top and look back?' she asked the chauffeur.

The view took her breath away. The whole of Toledo sprawled out on the hillside, little houses, palaces, churches, bleached and baked over the centuries by the burning sun to the palest terracottas, roans, corals and ochres, with the occasional black-green cypress as an exclamation mark. On the right flowed the Tagus, like dark-green glass, going into a flurry of foaming water as it dropped down a level, then becoming absolutely still again, as though someone had added gelatine.

'Christ, I'd like to bring a film crew here,' said Cameron. Then she looked at Rupert's face, which was as still and cold as the dark-green water.

I've lost him, she thought despairingly. I should have let him sleep.

But, as they were driving back to Madrid, his hand along the back of the seat suddenly touched her hair. It was as though he'd sawn through the ropes and dragged her off the railroad track as the express thundered towards her.

She melted towards him. 'What's the matter?'

'I'm sorry.'

'Don't you like culture?'

'Not a lot. It's already happened, and I hate being trapped. The first time Helen and I stayed in Madrid, she went to Toledo by herself and raved on and on and on about it. I even remember her making Malise blush when she told him he was pure El Greco. She was crazy about sightseeing. I'm afraid the things I disliked in her I don't like any better in other people.'

'But you can't expect people always to do what you want.'

'I don't, but if they want to do something, I'd rather they went off and did it alone, and then not gas about it afterwards.'

'What were you doing all the time she was sightseeing?'

'I was show-jumping,' said Rupert.

When they got back to the room, they made love again, with less energy but more tenderness.

'Can I get down?' said Cameron finally as she straddled him.

'You are *able* to get down,' said Rupert, quoting his old nanny, 'but whether you *may* is another matter.'

Cameron caressed his cheek. 'Are you coming with me tonight?'

Rupert shook his head. 'Not safe. There'll be too many press.'

Despite no sleep, Cameron looked so seductive in her new kingfisher-blue backless that Rupert nearly dragged her back to bed again.

'Uh, uh.' Cameron skipped out of the way. 'I'll stagger onto the podium like John Wayne as it is. I hope I don't fall asleep in the speeches.'

As soon as she walked into the Reception she realized that it was a very good thing she'd come by herself. There was Ivor Hicks, Corinium's corporate development controller, chatting up a tough-looking Spanish woman. She also recognized people from Granada and TVS, and one of Robert Maxwell's henchmen.

'What the hell are you doing here?' she whispered to Ivor.

'Tony's after a stake in Spanish television,' said Ivor. 'The Government here's creating three new channels. Tony wants twenty-five per cent of one of them. Maxwell, Granada and TVS are after the same thing.'

Cameron sighed. 'That means less money for programmes.'

'But more security for Tony, in case he loses the franchise,' said Ivor. 'Diversification is the name of the game.'

Rupert gave Cameron half an hour. Then, seeing her going into dinner on television, he went systematically through her Filofax, dictating her future appointments into his tape recorder – and a lot of Tony's that she'd listed. Then he opened her briefcase, and removed the Corinium application. It was very bulky, like smuggling in *Lady Chatterley's Lover* when he was at Prep School.

At first the pretty girl on the reception desk told Rupert the office was closed and there was no way the application could be photostated. But Spanish guests at the hotel seldom had such blond hair, or such blue eyes, or such good teeth, or waved so many thousands and thousands of pesetas in front of her. She would see what she could do, she said. She'd have to secrete the application into the office, it might take a little time, as the manager was about. She'd ring Rupert's room as soon as it was done. Sweating, he went back upstairs and paced up and down drinking whisky. On television the awards were well underway. Stars were tottering up on to the platform wiping their eyes and thanking every member of the crew, and every madre and padre for the help they had given. What if Cameron had been on already and, overcome with lust, was belting back to him?

Going downstairs again, he met the receptionist, very flustered, but with the completed copy. It was only when he got back to his room that he realized the silly cow had put it back out of order; the sections on 'Master Dog' and 'Dorothy Dove' didn't follow on and James Vereker's afternoon programme was in the middle of Engineering specifications. It was a long and laborious task to get them in the right order, and even then Rupert wasn't sure he'd done it right. For the third time he rushed down to get the various chapters stapled together.

He was just getting back into the lift when he saw Cameron coming through the revolving door. Pressing the button, he creaked up to the seventh floor, rushed along to her room, which he'd rashly left open because he didn't have a key and double-locked it on the inside.

With trembling hands he shoved the original back in her briefcase, hoping it was the right way up, snapped the clasp

366

and shoved the copied pages inside his jacket under his arm.
The next minute there was a tantivy on the door.

'Rupert, open up,' said Cameron.

Pretending to rub the sleep out of his eyes, he opened the
door. 'Sorry, sweetheart, I didn't want to be disturbed by
maids replacing chocolates and turning down beds. How was
it?'

'Scary,' said Cameron. 'I'll never, never be mean to any
front-of-camera people again. Wasn't it awful when I dried?'

'You were sweet,' lied Rupert, 'and they were all so touched
you tried to speak Spanish.'

Fortunately Cameron was a bit pissed. 'Have you eaten?'
she asked.

'I wasn't hungry,' said Rupert, edging towards the door.
'In fact I've got a bloody awful headache.'

'I've got some Panadol,' said Cameron, going to her briefcase.

'I've got something even stronger next door,' said Rupert
hastily. 'I'll be back in a minute.'

Back in his suite, he nearly died. He'd never had nerves
like this in the old days when he was show jumping, and
screwing everyone else's wives. With shaking, sweating
hands, he stuffed the photostated application in the secret
compartment of his briefcase.

Cameron had kicked off her shoes and was lying on the
bed drinking white wine when he got back.

'Good thing you didn't come,' she said. 'There were so
many people who'd have recognized you. I picked up a *Sunday
Times*.'

'Thanks.'

Rupert turned immediately to the sports page, she noticed,
then the smile was wiped off his face.

'Fucking hell!' He turned to the front page.

'What's the matter?'

'Riots after both semi-finals of the FA Cup,' he howled.
'Petrol bombs thrown at the police, two policemen stabbed,
cars overturned and burnt, shop windows smashed, twenty
people taken to hospital, forty-five arrests. Fucking, fucking

367

hell! I play hookey for one weekend and this happens.'

In a second he was on to Gerald in London.

'I've been trying to get you since yesterday, Minister.'

There were obviously other people in the room or Gerald would never have been so formal.

'Is it very serious?'

'Yes – four people are still in intensive care.'

'I'll fly back tonight.'

'I'm sorry, Minister. After all your hard work, it's a most tragic setback.'

By one o'clock, Rupert managed to get on to a private jet, arranged by the British Ambassador. He seemed to have forgotten Cameron's existence until he was leaving.

'I'm sorry to walk out on you, angel. I'm just so pissed off. I was so certain I'd pegged the violence.' He took her face in his hands. 'Look, it's been great. I won't ring you in case I get Tony, but promise to ring me. Here's Gerald's number; he'll know where to find me.'

And he was gone.

It's a beginning, thought Cameron, hanging over the balcony to see if she could catch a glimpse of him getting into his car. It was still warm. Breathing in the scent of the lemon trees rising from the little garden, she had a sudden vision of Rupert's beautiful house in Gloucestershire and all that wonderful sweep of land, and decided the only status symbol she really wanted was a Cartier wedding-ring with R C-B and CC engraved inside.

RIVALS
28

Rupert went back to England slap into a political storm. The dramatic drop in football hooliganism had been a high spot of the Tory administration. Now, after a sickening day of violence, their claims were looking very dubious. With an election in the offing, the opposition were roaring for blood and, in an emergency debate on Monday night, tabled a motion of no confidence in the Minister for Sport and howled for Rupert's resignation. Although Rupert was certain left-wing militants were behind the riots and hinted as much in the House, he couldn't prove it yet and the Government won the debate by the narrowest majority. Some of his own side were not displeased by events; Rupert had been the PM's darling for too long. The Cup Final was not until 11th May, but all Rupert's energies were now channelled into seeing the violence wasn't repeated.

He spent most of the next week trying not to lose his temper with the pack of reporters snarling at his heels as he visited the two devastated football clubs, and comforted those who'd been hurt in the riots. As a result, he didn't get down to Penscombe until late Wednesday afternoon, landing the helicopter on the lawn.

He had only been away a week, but already bluebells were flaming like Bunsen burners in his woods, and the crimson glow of the beeches had turned to a rusty terracotta as green leaves burst out of their narrow brown buds. Although brilliant sunshine and blue skies welcomed him, across the valley he could see an April shower tumbling darkly out of a huge purple cloud on to The Priory.

However angry he was, returning to Penscombe always soothed him. He was greeted by messages from Gerald that the two stabbed policemen were now off the danger list and that Cameron Cook had rung three times, leaving a number. Instead of calling her, he had a quick shower and drove over to The Priory where the rain had almost stopped, leaving a heady smell of wet earth and nettles. As he walked through the door, he was greeted by an even headier smell of frying garlic and onions. Taggie must be home, which unconsciously soothed him even more. He'd go and see her when he'd reported in. In the library he found Freddie, Bas and Charles giving a slightly unreceptive Declan tips on how to write the application.

'What a focking awful week you're having,' said Declan. 'You poor bastard. You must feel like Sisyphus.'

'I don't know who he is,' said Rupert, 'but I'm sure I do.'

'Get him a drink, Bas,' said Declan.

'Only Perrier,' said Rupert. 'I've got to fly back and vote after this. How did the first Venturer meeting go?'

The others looked at each other. Was the sun shining through the stained glass window or was Freddie blushing?

'It was somewhat hazardous,' said Declan.

'Did you all fall out?' asked Rupert, taking the Perrier from Bas, and trying to find an inch on one of the window seats that wasn't covered with books and tapes to sit on.

'Charles and Dame Enid did,' said Bas with a grin.

'Shut up,' giggled Charles.

'You tell him, Freddie,' said Declan.

'Well, we all went down to this pub on Salisbury Plain,' said Freddie sheepishly, 'which I could've sworn was always deserted, and we'd just settled into pre-lunch drinks and managed to stop Wesley Emerson offering the Bishop a joint, and got over the fact that Charles, here, turned up dressed as a woman . . .'

'Knowing the IBA's obsession with the fair sex, I thought it fitting,' interrupted Charles demurely.

'. . . when the entire nation's press arrived in three coaches to 'ave a beano before witnessing the launching of a new tank at some army base down the road.'

'Christ,' Rupert started to laugh. 'Did any of them see you?'

'Billy the Kid couldn't have emptied a saloon bar faster,' said Freddie, 'and Charles and Dame Enid got stuck trying to climb out of the Ladies'.'

'It was seriously funny,' said Bas. 'We all hotfooted it back to The Priory for a Chinese takeaway, and the whole thing seemed to bring us closer together. I must say I'd forgotten how stunningly attractive Janey Lloyd-Foxe is.'

'And belongs to Billy,' said Rupert firmly.

Through the window he could see Taggie, who'd gone out into the garden to pick some thyme from the herb garden, gazing in rapture at a rainbow. She had the most adorable bottom, he decided, which became even more adorable when she bent over the flower bed in her jeans.

'Rupert,' said Bas, 'are you still with us?'

'Looking at the rainbow,' said Rupert, hastily opening his briefcase.

'Never knew rainbows were female and five foot ten,' said Bas slyly.

'Fuck off,' said Rupert. 'Anyway, I've got a stunning bit of news to cheer you all up. I've brought you an Easter present, Declan.'

Triumphantly he chucked the two tapes and the photostat of the Corinium application down on Declan's desk.

'What's this?' said Declan, putting on his spectacles.

'Two extraordinarily informative conversations with Cameron Cook, and a photostat of the corrected final draft of Corinium's application.'

Freddie, Bas and Charles were so excited, none of them noticed Declan's look of thunderous disapproval, or that he'd dropped the application as though it was a wasp-infested pear.

'Where did you get that?' asked Freddie in awe.

'I spent the weekend in Madrid and in bed with Cameron.'

Basil's jaw clanged. 'Does my brother know?'

'Tony was due out there,' said Rupert, 'but I arranged for a chum to offer Tony an invite for Saturday night he couldn't refuse.'

Basil started to laugh. 'To meet HRH at Badminton?'

'My God, was that your doing?' said Charles in amazement. 'Tony was boasting about it to everyone.'

'So he stood up Ms Cook,' said Rupert, wandering over to the drinks table and splashing more Perrier into his glass, 'who was not overly delighted until I suddenly appeared on the adjacent balcony like *Private Lives* and took Tony's place.'

'What was she like?' asked Bas, fascinated.

'Fucks like a stoat,' said Rupert. 'In fact the end-away definitely justified the means. Although I had to endure some hellish sightseeing on Sunday before she went off to collect her prize. That was when I got the application photostated.'

'Bloody good,' said Freddie.

'You ought to join the CIA,' said Bas.

'She'll be after your blood, your untainted AIDS-free blood, when she finds out,' said Charles delightedly.

'She won't,' said Rupert. 'She hadn't a clue. Well?' He turned to Declan for approval.

But Declan was looking infinitely more thunderous than the cloud that had drenched The Priory earlier.

'You can't focking do that,' he exploded.

'Why ever not?'

'Because it's bloody dishonest.'

'I must be dreaming,' said Rupert incredulously. 'Declan dear, we're pitching for a business with a hundred-and-twenty-five-million-pound turnover, not playing fucking tiddlywinks. Have a read. You can find out exactly what Tony's up to and pre-empt it. It's the most turgid stuff, much more effective than Mogadon. Tony seems to be promising an unchecked flow of good causes and Elizabethan drama for the next ten years!'

'I'm not going to read it,' said Declan roughly. 'We're playing this thing straight.'

'Now come on, Declan,' protested Freddie. 'Think of the clout it'll give us.'

'Never cast a clout till May is out,' giggled Charles.

'Shut up, Charles,' snapped Declan. Then, turning to Rupert, who was now absolutely shaking with rage, 'I repeat, we're playing it straight.'

'Tony is evil,' hissed Rupert. 'Don't you think he'd do the same thing to you, given the chance? I thought you were out to get him.'

'Not by sinking to his methods,' said Declan coldly.

'Then what are you doing asking the Bishop to lunch, dressing Maud up like a nun and asking him to say Grace?'

'That's different.'

'It is NOT!' Rupert was furiously pacing up and down the floorboards now. 'And what are you doing poaching half Tony's staff? I'm amazed you didn't ring Tony first and ask his permission.'

'That's entirely different,' yelled Declan. 'What you've done is stolen Corinium's property. It's a criminal offence.'

'Isn't Charles Corinium's property?' yelled back Rupert.

'Ooo,' said Charles, looking excited. 'They're fighting over me.'

'Shut up,' screamed Rupert and Declan, both turning on him.

'Charles came of his own volition,' said Declan, 'but Cameron had no idea what you were up to.'

'She certainly enjoyed it,' snarled Rupert. 'Don't you go feeling sorry for her, and Jesus, the hassle I went to, getting that thing photostated. I practically had to bang the receptionist.'

'Never been a hardship for you,' said Declan icily, and, picking up the application and the two tapes, he chucked them into the wastepaper basket. Bas, Freddie and Charles winced. Rupert went very still.

'And if any of you try and retrieve them, I'll put them in the boiler,' added Declan.

'All my life I've been accused of lacking application,' drawled Rupert, 'then when I actually get hold of one . . .'

'It's not a joke,' roared Declan.

'I'm not laughing,' said Rupert bleakly. 'Fuck you, Declan, and screw your bloody franchise.'

'Now, wite a minute,' said Freddie, leaping to his feet.

But Rupert had walked out. In the hall he nearly sent Taggie flying. She was carrying a pile of Aertex shirts and green skirts upstairs. Caitlin was going back to school next week.

'What on earth's the matter?' she said in alarm.

'Your fucking father.'

'What's he done? Come into the kitchen.'

'It's what he won't do.' For a second Rupert debated whether to walk out, but he was so angry with Declan he had to tell someone, so he followed her into the kitchen.

'I'll get you a drink.'

'I'm not drinking. And I'll never touch a drop of your father's liquor again.'

'What's happened?' said Taggie, bewildered. Then, realizing the steak and kidney she was frying on the Aga was catching, ran across the kitchen to give it a stir.

'I've just spent all last weekend in Madrid screwing Cameron Cook,' said Rupert furiously, 'to get her on our side, and to get information about Corinium's application, and by Sunday night I not only had her eating out of my hand, but had secretly photostated the entire application.'

He was so angry, he didn't notice that Taggie's wooden spoon had stopped moving.

'What's Daddy objecting to?' said Taggie in a strangely high voice.

'He won't read it. He thinks it's taking unfair advantage. Jesus, no wonder he's broke.'

At that moment Freddie appeared in the doorway. But, seeing Rupert was talking to Taggie, he decided she'd be better at calming him down than any of them and tiptoed back to the library.

'Let me make you a cup of tea,' said Taggie.

By the time the kettle had boiled and the tea had brewed for three minutes, and Rupert had told her the whole story, she'd recovered her composure. After all, Rupert was entitled to go to bed with whom he chose, and perhaps he just did it with Cameron because he wanted to get hold of the application document, she thought hopefully, although Cameron was terribly beautiful and Patrick would be absolutely heart-broken if he found out. Oh God, what a terrible muddle.

Rupert leant against the Aga, looking moodily at a huge vase of bluebells.

'From our wood,' said Taggie, trying to lift the conversation. 'Aren't they lovely?'

Rupert was about to snap that they were from his wood now.

'Don't try to placate me,' he said coldly.

Taggie handed him a cup of tea. Then she took a deep breath. 'I think Daddy's right,' she stammered.

Rupert looked up. 'You what?' he said, unbelievingly. 'Not you, too?'

'He wouldn't feel right with himself. It's like cheating in exams. To most people it wouldn't matter, but he's got such utter integ . . . ' Taggie stumbled over the word.

'Integrity, and I haven't, I suppose.'

'Of course you have, but of a different kind. If you won the franchise because he'd spied on Tony Baddingham, he wouldn't be able to live with himself.'

'Well, he's not living with me any longer. D'you think Tony won't wheel out every trick in the book, once he finds out we're bidding against him? Your father's trying to fight a nuclear war with a pop gun.'

'It's because he disapproves of Lord Baddingham so much. He couldn't descend to his level. That's why he's bidding against him.'

'Not with me, he ain't,' said Rupert, putting down his mug. 'I'm out.'

'Oh please not,' pleaded Taggie. 'It's so lovely for them having you as part of the consortium. You've got such c-c-charisma.'

'Is that your word for the day?' snapped Rupert.

'No, it's my word for always about you,' said Taggie,

blushing crimson. 'Honestly, they think you're marvellous.'

'Funny way of showing it,' said Rupert, walking towards the door.

Taggie ran after him, her eyes filling with tears.

'Oh, please. Daddy really needs you. You and Freddie were so wonderful when he was down, I know he seems terribly clever but he's not street bright like you.'

Gazing at her, Rupert noticed how her tears and the old grey denim shirt of Declan's she was wearing emphasized the strange silver-grey of her eyes.

'Darling Taggie,' he said, his face softening, 'how can anyone refuse you anything?'

'Then you'll stay?'

Rupert shrugged. 'I suppose so . . . but I'm extremely pissed off.' He reached into his pocket and rooted out a crimson leather box. 'I got you an Easter egg in Madrid. I hope you'll like it better than the present I brought your father.'

Inside the box Taggie found a little gold egg, speckled with rubies and diamonds. She gave a gasp.

'Look further,' said Rupert.

Opening the egg, she found a tiny gold bird with ruby eyes.

'Poor thing's got conjuctivitis,' said Rupert.

'I can't believe it,' breathed Taggie. 'No one brings me presents like that. Oh thank you so so much. I love it.'

Blushing furiously again, she leant forward and kissed him on the cheek. She's the little sister I never had, Rupert told himself firmly.

'Your steak and kidney's burning,' he said.

'Are you staying for supper?'

'No, I've got to go back and vote.'

'What on?'

'Capital punishment for terrorists.'

Taggie looked horrified.

'They're not going to bring it back, are they? Daddy'd leave the country.'

In the library Freddie was tearing a strip off Declan. 'This is the big league, if you'll excuse me saying so. Rupert's a very clever operator, and we can't afford to lose 'im. You've got to learn to argue wivout rancour, Declan. You can't stick your chest out all the time.'

'What do you know about it?' growled Declan.

'I've never 'ad a strike at work,' said Freddie, 'because I don't judge everyone the same. I cultivate their individual skills. You're always bangin' on about giving creative people the right atmosphere to work in. Then, when Rupert does somefink really creative, you shit on 'im.'

Watched in awed amazement by Bas and Charles, Freddie calmly retrieved the application from the wastepaper basket.

Declan gazed at him appalled: 'But, it's dishonest, for fock's sake. You wouldn't have nicked that document, would you?'

'Wouldn't 'ave 'ad the nerve,' said Freddie. 'But now we've got it, I'm certainly goin' to 'ave a little look. This is war, as Rupert said, not tiddlywinks. You don't want to be too 'igh-minded, Declan.'

By the time Sydney his driver had dropped Rupert off at Westminster, the yellow stone of the House was softened by floodlighting and Big Ben shone like a great sugar sifter against an inky blue sky.

'Only one vote,' Rupert told Sydney. 'I'm paired after that, but I've got a hell of a lot of work still to do. Can you come back about twelve-thirty?'

Nodding good evening to the policeman on the gate, Rupert went through the Member's entrance, an expression that usually made him laugh. Glancing at the monitor he saw that Owen Davies, the Labour leader, was winding up for the abolitionists. Time for a large drink . . . he was bloody tired, and he'd never had any doubts that stringing up was the answer for terrorists. But as he headed for the bar he thought fleetingly of Taggie's horror of capital punishment, and Declan's passionate disapproval, and decided to listen to the debate instead.

As he entered the chamber the Ministers of Employment and of Health moved slightly apart to make room for him on the green leather front bench.

'Owen's in barnstorming form,' whispered the Minister of Health.

Hearing a din behind him, Rupert glanced round to see Paul Stratton, who was violently pro-hanging for everything, particularly wife-pinching, looking excited for the first time in months.

'Rubbish,' Paul yelled. 'Resign, check your figures. What's the point of having British soldiers out there if we don't support them?'

Owen Davies, a brilliant orator on the dullest subject, was on magnificent form tonight. What about all those people who'd been imprisoned for terrorism, he demanded, who'd later been found innocent? How much more terrible if they'd been hanged. What evidence was there in any country that the death penalty curbed terrorism, and, conversely, didn't hanging make sainted martyrs out of the most vicious thugs?

It was great emotional stuff. But, putting aside the soft cadences, the eloquence, the Welsh voice, Rupert suddenly knew Owen was right. Every moment you could feel the spirits of the Anti-Hanging lobby rising. The Bring-Back brigade looked turned to stone. The Prime Minister, who was almost more pro-hanging than Paul Stratton, looked most bootfaced of all. Owen Davies sat down to a storm of applause.

Scenting blood, the abolitionists roared for the PM to get up. 'On your feet. Don't be bashful.'

But the PM wasn't budging. Instead, she let the Home Secretary, who was decidedly ambivalent about the merits of hanging anyway, wind up. Every time he opened his mouth, he was howled down, but he ploughed on bravely with his prepared speech, careful not to emphasize that terrorism was on the increase, but droning on about deterrents and the need to support the forces of law and order. As ten o'clock approached, the abolitionists worked themselves into the kind of frenzy only seen at Cardiff Arms Park when there's two minutes to go and the Welsh are just in the lead. Then, as Big Ben tolled ten o'clock, the noise subsided and the house divided.

The Ayes, looking tight-lipped and apprehensive, shuffled to the right. The Noes, looking elated, sauntered to the left. Without a moment's deliberation, ignoring the outraged looks of the PM, the Chief Whip and most of the Front Bench, Rupert joined the Noes. Owen Davies, turning in delighted amazement, tapped Rupert on the shoulder. 'I didn't know you were one of us.'

'I wasn't until I heard you,' said Rupert.

The Minister of Health, a pacific and gentle soul, also joined the Noes.

'We'll be on the carpet tomorrow,' he said.

'She'll have to call an election any minute,' said Rupert.

'An even tenner on 10th June,' said the Minister of Health.

'Done,' said Rupert.

Feeling suddenly shattered and not wanting a bollocking from the PM, Rupert beat a quick retreat to his office, a small room on the lower Minister's floor. Inside, the walls were covered with signed photographs of famous athletes: Pat Eddery, Ian Botham, Maradona, John McEnroe, Pat Cash, Gary Lineker, Dino and Fenella Ferranti, to name only a few. Above the filing cabinet was a picture of Wesley Emerson, the local cricketing hero who had joined the Venturer consortium, and who Rupert had saved from getting busted.

'Thanks, Rupe, Wesley Emerson,' he had scrawled in black pentel across the blue sky behind him.

I should think so too, reflected Rupert whenever he looked at the photo.

Having taken off his tie, and undone his top button, he poured himself a large whisky and soda. Christ, he was tired. He'd been on the go since five that morning and hadn't had any real sleep for a week. Making him feel even more tired was the red box full of work, the buff envelope on the blotter full of constituency letters to be signed, and the even bigger pile of mail to be read, which was probably mostly abusive letters about the football riots.

The admirable Gerald had scribbled a note: 'Gone to Madam Butterfly. Back about one-thirty. Ring if you need me.'

In the corner of the room was a hard olive-green sofa, where Rupert was supposed to snatch some sleep during late-night sittings. It had never looked more seductive. If he had an hour's kip, he might work better. He had another six o'clock start in the morning. The telephone ringing made him jump.

'Rupert, it's Cameron.'

Christ, he'd completely forgotten to ring her back.

'Angel! You got home safely?'

'Well, I'm not lying in a pile of wreckage at the bottom of the Bay of Biscay.' All the insecurity and truculence had returned to her voice. It must have cost her a lot to ring.

'I'm sorry I didn't ring back. It's been frantic, and I didn't want to tread on Tony's bunions. When am I going to see you?' He suppressed a yawn.

'Christ knows,' snapped Cameron. 'Tony's taking me away for the weekend.'

'To Buckingham Palace?'

Cameron didn't laugh. 'To LA, to close a couple of deals over Easter. Then we fly straight to Cannes to meet with our various co-production partners and firm up existing relation-ships. I won't be back till Monday week.'

Rupert glanced at the calendar. Monday week was 22nd April. He'd be away until the 26th and the franchises had to be in on the 29th. That would give him hardly any time after she got back to persuade her to join Venturer. He ought to establish interim ascendancy over Tony by seeing her this evening.

'Where are you?' he asked.

'At home.'

'Alone?'

'Yes.'

'I'll drive down.'

'Are you crazy? D'you know what time it is?' But it was impossible for her to keep the elation out of her voice.

'I've got at least an hour's work,' said Rupert. 'The drive at this time of night should take an hour and a half. I can't afford to get done for speeding. I'll be with you about two.'

Thank God, he'd had a shower and changed at Penscombe earlier in the evening; it seemed a thousand years ago. He trusted Sydney, but not entirely, so he dismissed him and took the Ferrari, which was parked outside his Westminster flat. Torrential rain on the motorway gave way to moonlight as he reached the outskirts of Cotchester. The cathedral clock was tolling the hour; the shadow of the spire lay thick and black across the watermeadows. He was so tired he'd never be able to get it up.

Cameron, however, opened the front door with nothing on.

'I might have been the milkman,' said Rupert reprovingly.

'You're not that late,' she whispered.

As her warm, oiled and scented body twined round him, she was obviously so delighted to see him that miraculously Rupert woke up.

Bounding upstairs after her, he decided this was one relationship he would have absolutely no difficulty firming up.

29

Although Cameron was kept ludicrously busy selling herself and Corinium's programmes, she was shattered by how much she missed Rupert. LA was bad enough, but Cannes seemed so tantalizingly near. Every minute on the Corinium stand or on the front, or at the numerous parties, or in her hotel bedroom, conveniently next to Tony's, she expected Rupert to appear grinning like a Cheshire cat.

On her second Thursday away from him, however, her black mood was caused by rage rather than longing. One of Tony's myriad subsidiary companies, Falconry Films Inc., had made a lousy mini-series called 'Stowaway', about an aristocratic orphan who disguised herself as a cabin boy on a clipper ship and got off with the pirate captain. And now Tony had actually sailed a real clipper ship, at vast expense, into Cannes Harbour as a publicity stunt and was holding a huge bash on board. Sourly watching all the fatcat international buyers and their bikinied bimbos stuffing their faces with champagne and caviare, Cameron felt they were guzzling all the profits she'd made Corinium from 'Four Men went to Mow'.

The Mediterranean suited Tony; his olive skin had already turned mahogany. As he purred round the clipper ship in his dark glasses and discreetly coroneted black shirt, clinching deals and pinching bottoms, he looked more like a pirate king than ever.

Cameron had had plenty of time to compare Tony with Rupert while she was away. Both were reputed to be absolute shits. But, while Tony was coldly sensual, utterly venal, eaten up with envy and sadistically dedicated to putting people down, Rupert, Cameron felt, was only sharp-tongued because he was arrogant and easily bored. Apart from the day they went to Toledo, when he'd been reminded too much of Helen (which showed he was capable of deep feeling), he had been angelic and really interested not only in her as a woman, but in her career, and her programmes. She had been so touched that he'd driven all the way down to Cotchester on that last night, and that after he'd made love to her he hadn't fallen asleep as most men would, but stayed awake pestering her with questions about what she and Tony would be doing and selling in LA and Cannes.

It was a relief too that he couldn't call her, so she didn't go through the roof with expectation every time the telephone rang. Instead, at grave risk, she'd rung him twice from LA and every day from Cannes.

There was no doubt, too, that she was the flavour of the month at the festival. The third series of 'Four Men went to Mow' had already been pre-sold world wide. The Corinium publicity department had taken a full page advertisement in *Broadcast* that week, with a stunning photograph of Cameron holding a baby lamb, with the caption: '*Cameron Cook works for Corinium, meet her on stand 329*', then listing all the prizes she'd won in the last year. Everyone wanted to congratulate her and offer her work.

Back at The Priory, Declan was still working on the Venturer application, only pausing occasionally to pick up the binoculars on the window seat to check on some newly-arrived migrant bird; swallows, housemartins, whitethroats were all winging in now. Last night he had even heard the first nightingale in the wood.

'*Our duty,*' wrote Declan, '*is to tell the truth, to be relevant, entertaining and interesting, to monitor power and expose its abuse, to be nobody's mouthpiece.*'

Christ, it was difficult not to use clichés, to be concise: *To bring the balloon of the mind that bellies and drags in the wind,* as Yeats had so perfectly put it, *into its narrow shed.*

'*We will give the area a nationally recognized television identity,*' he wrote. '*This we feel Corinium has failed to do. In their last application they promised to provide a new studio, a new youth orchestra, a trust fund for the arts and sciences, adequate training schemes and worker participation at board level. This they have failed to do.*

'*They also promised that fifty per cent of their profits after tax would go to shareholders, and the rest would be ploughed back into making programmes. This they have also failed to do.*'

He was about to tackle Venturer's programme plans, when Gertrude leapt barking off the sofa, scattering papers, as Rupert and Freddie walked in.

'Christ, you're a slut, Declan,' said Rupert, looking round at the files, tapes, coffee cups and overflowing ashtrays that covered every available inch of space. 'Why don't you let Taggie tidy up a bit?'

'I'm superstitious,' grumbled Declan. 'I never tidy up between books in case I throw pages away.'

Rupert threw a copy of *Broadcast*, open at Cameron's advertisement, down on Declan's desk. 'We must have her for Venturer.'

'She's riding far too high to be interested in us,' said Declan quickly.

'She's not. She's really pissed off,' said Rupert. 'She was on to me from Cannes only half an hour ago grumbling that Tony'd blued forty-five grand hiring a boat to promote some crappy mini series not even made by Corinium.'

'We need some 'eavy-weight ladies,' said Freddie, moving the binoculars and sitting on the window seat.

'Think how useful Cameron would be for the rest of the year as a mole in the Corinium camp,' said Rupert.

'We've got Georgie and Seb and Charles,' protested Declan.

'None of them sleep with Tony,' persisted Rupert. 'We can use her to manipulate him.'

'More likely Tony'll use her to manipulate you.'

'No one manipulates me,' said Rupert haughtily. 'I don't mean to sound conceited, but I do know when a woman's absolutely mad about me.'

'You do sound conceited,' snapped Declan. 'She may be mad about you at the moment, but it's a long, long time from May to December, and if you get bored or start playing her up she'll bolt straight back to Tony with all our secrets.'

'Look,' said Rupert patiently, 'she's Tony's only trump card. If the IBA know from the start she's with us, it'll totally discredit him.'

'It's a risk wurf taking,' said Freddie. 'We needn't tell her too much.'

'I've got to tell her anyway,' said Rupert flatly. 'If she reads that we're pitching for the franchise in the press on Tuesday morning, she'll never forgive me and there'll be no hope of ever getting her.'

Declan shook his head. 'I want it to go on record,' he said grimly, 'that I utterly deplore the idea of using her as a mole. It's unethical and dangerous. Nor is Cameron going to be very pleased when you tell her what you've been up to already.'

Freddie scratched his curls. 'I 'aven't told Valerie yet,' he confessed. 'Been putting it off. Don't fink she'll be very pleased either.'

Valerie, in fact, was absolutely livid. Having studied her very good friend Monica Baddingham's behaviour, Valerie had decided it was upper class to be keen on gardening and she must therefore channel more of her energy into transforming Green Lawns into an absolute paradise. Wearing new gardening gloves and a tan scarf tied at the back of her very clean neck to keep her curls neat, and kneeling on a new green rubber mat, Valerie was now tackling her favourite spot, the mauve and pink garden. Fat mauve clumps of aubretia fell over the walls, candy-pink double cherries danced in the breeze above serried ranks of mauve and pink tulips. Such a pity, sighed Valerie, that none of them would be out for her

Opening in July. And then Freddie had to drop this disgusting bombshell about the franchise.

'We can't do that to Monica and Tony,' she shrieked. 'It's so unsupportive. Ay'll never hold my head up high on the Distressed Gentlefolk's Committee. Who else is behind it?'

Freddie took a deep breath: 'Declan O'Hara.'

Valerie was so cross she weeded up a purple tulip. 'That drunk – he's practically IRA, and Sharon nearly got raped at their New Year's Eve party.'

'And Rupert,' said Freddie, quailing.

'Rupert,' screamed Valerie, as purple now as the tulip she was trying to force back into the earth. 'He's a bounder. No female is safe. The evil way I saw him looking at Sharon's legs when she was wearing her tennis shorts the other day. Even worse, I found a snap-shot of him in her brassière drawer yesterday. And both Declan and Rupert are enemies of poor Tony,' said Valerie. 'Monica will be outraged.'

Like a small boy plunging into icy water, Freddie battled on: 'And Marti Gluckstein and Bas.'

'Both crooks.'

'And Arfur Smiff.'

'Common little man and a leftie,' sniffed Valerie.

'Professor Graystock and Wesley Emerson.'

'A black man,' said Valerie, incensed. 'His wife's black too. She might start poppin' into the boutique.'

'And Dame Enid.'

Valerie stamped her foot. 'That disgusting old lezzie, with Sharon in her teens. Frederick Jones, have you taken leave of your senses! You must have been plottin' this for weeks. Ay insist you drop out.'

'And Henry Hampshire and Hubert Brenton,' said Freddie.

'And what's more . . .' screamed Valerie, then stopped in her tracks as the names registered.

'Who did you say?'

Freddie repeated the last two names.

'Not the Lord-Lieutenant, and the Bishop of Cotchester?'

'Yup,' said Freddie grinning.

Dropping her trowel, Valerie leapt to her feet.

'Well, that does put a different laight on things. If anyone can keep Rupert in order, they can. I haven't met the Bishop's waife, but Hermione Hampshire is charming. When can I tell everyone?'

'Any time after Monday lunchtime.'

Back from Cannes, Cameron plunged into the first five days of shooting 'Four Men went to Mow'. Rupert was abroad, smoothing the path for the next World Cup in South America and playing in a Pro-Am tennis tournament to raise money for the Olympic fund, so he and Cameron didn't meet up until late on Friday.

Cameron always drove too fast. Fortunately there was little traffic on the road that Friday night as she scorched round corners and shot crossroads in her frenzy to reach Rupert. Hardly a light was on in Penscombe village, but huge, quivering stars and a full moon lit her path. The chestnuts lining Rupert's drive had reached a perfect pitch of pale greenness to welcome her. And as she screeched to a halt in front of the house, her headlights flood-lit a big white magnolia in full flower on the edge of the lawn – a thing of such unearthly incandescent beauty Cameron just gazed and gazed. I want to marry Rupert, she thought, and be as beautiful a bride as that tree.

The next moment the front door opened and the pack of dogs swarmed round the car, wagging and barking. She didn't even mind their paws scrabbling the paintwork. Rupert followed them, blond hair silver in the moonlight. Wearing a clean pink-and-white-striped shirt, reeking of expensive cologne, he had obviously just bathed and cleaned his teeth. Holding his arms out he swept her off the ground above the tidal wave of dogs.

'But they're lovely,' she cried as he put her down in the hall, and, kneeling, she hugged the dogs as they surged forward, shoving, nudging and licking her bare arms and legs in welcome.

'How strange and how nice,' said Rupert, leading her into the drawing-room. 'I never imagined you'd like dogs.'

There was a bottle of Dom Perignon on ice, which Rupert immediately opened, and a huge plate of smoked salmon and some buttered wholemeal rolls on the table.

'After a long hard day, I don't believe in screwing on an empty stomach,' said Rupert, 'and I'm certainly going to give you a long hard night.'

Cameron moved up behind him, fingering the powerful shoulders, feeling the thrust of the muscular buttocks against her belly, melting against him with lust.

'How are things at Fort Knocks-off?' asked Rupert.

Cameron shook her head. 'I feel like a mole.'

Rupert nearly spilled the champagne he was pouring. 'How d'you mean?'

'If you'd been stuck in a studio for twelve hours, you'd worry you'd never see the light again.'

'Oh, I see,' said Rupert, relieved. 'And you've got over Cannes?'

'Almost.' Cameron took a great slug of champagne. 'That's better. D'you know, I was approached by five different groups to join their consortiums?'

'Very flattering,' said Rupert, piling smoked salmon onto a roll and handing it to her. 'Anyone interesting?'

'Not bad. Unfortunately they're all pitching against companies like Granada and Yorkshire, who are virtually impregnable, and if Tony got a sniff of it, I'd be out on my ear.'

'How is he?' Rupert filled up her glass.

'Appallingly twitchy. Someone leaked the story of the clipper ship to Dempster, doubling the cost of the party.'

'Press always get things wrong,' said Rupert blandly. It was he who had fed the story. He examined his glass of whisky. 'Has the Corinium application gone in?' he asked idly.

'Yes, thank God,' said Cameron, who was shaking hands with one of the Springer spaniels. 'Tony's handing it in to the IBA tomorrow morning.'

Rupert heaved a sigh of relief. If Cameron flipped when he told her about Venturer later tomorrow, at least it would be too late for her to alter Corinium's application.

Slowly Cameron was taking in the beauty of the room, registering the Romney, the Gainsborough, the Stubbs and the Lely on the pale-yellow walls. Determined not to be impressed, she asked almost too aggressively, 'How can you possibly live on your own in this great barn?'

'I don't,' said Rupert. 'I've got Mr and Mrs Bodkin who look after me, and the children are often here at weekends, and there's – er – usually a house guest.'

I asked for that, thought Cameron, biting her lip.

'Don't worry.' Rupert read her thoughts. 'In order not to besmirch the memory of our last blessed encounter, I've been holding my own ever since. I suppose you've been sating yourself on Lord B?'

'Much less than before,' said Cameron quickly.

The grandfather clock struck midnight.

'D'you know what day it is now?' asked Rupert.

'1st May,' said Cameron, glancing at her Rolex.

'D'you know our local poem?' said Rupert, grinning and putting on a Gloucestershire accent:

> *First of May, first of May,*
> *Outdoor fucking starts today.*
> *But as usual it do rain.*
> *So we fucks off indoors again.*

As he moved towards her he stopped, smiling. 'Will it be too cold for you outside?'

'Not if you keep me warm,' whispered Cameron.

Outside under the moonlit magnolia he took off her clothes, slowly kissing her all over where each garment had been, until she was squirming and helpless with desire. She could feel the dew-drenched lawn under her back. Rupert's cock was really incredible. As he slid inside her, she felt all the amazed joy of a canal lock suddenly finding it can accommodate the QE2.

When she made love to Tony, she always shut her eyes. She didn't want to see the uncharacteristically untidy hair, the bulging eyes, the clenched teeth, the veins knotting on his forehead as he came. She liked him sleek and in control. With Rupert she kept her eyes open all the time because he was the stuff of fantasy, and because she didn't want to miss a second.

Deciding the ground was too hard for her, he later insisted she went on top.

'You're so beautiful,' he said, watching her transported maenad face, ghostly in the moonlight.

Lousy at accepting compliments, Cameron had to joke. 'Didn't your mother tell you off for lying on the grass?'

'I'm not lying,' said Rupert, arching his back up into her. 'I'm telling the truth.'

As Cameron opened, so did the heavens.

'But as usual it do rain,' murmured Rupert, moving in and out of her. 'D'you want to fuck off inside again?'

'Not for ages,' gasped Cameron. 'At least it'll wash off the sweat.'

She woke in Rupert's huge Jacobean four-poster to find him gone and a note beside the bed saying he was doing a morning surgery at his constituency and would be back around lunchtime.

Looking round the beautiful room with its peachy walls, corn-coloured carpet, yellow-and-pink-striped silk curtains on the four-poster and at the windows, and rose-pink silk *chaise-longue*, Cameron felt she was waking in the middle of a sunrise. It was an incredibly feminine room for a man. Then she remembered the pale-blue hall and the pale-yellow drawing-room, and decided it must all be Helen's taste. On the dressing table, amid Rupert's clutter of betting slips, silver-backed brushes, cigar packets and loose change, were photographs of his children. The girl, exactly like Rupert, had the same arrogant blue-eyed stare; the boy had very dark red hair and large dark wary eyes. Having met Rupert's pack last night, Cameron felt seven step-dogs might be an easier proposition to take on than two step-children. Helen must have been spectacular to produce kids like that. Mad on sight-seeing, she was plainly a sight herself.

Outside, through a frame of rampant, budding clematis, lay the valley, pale green except for the occasional wild cherry tree in flower, or the blackthorn breaking in white waves over the hedgerows. From an ash grove by the lake she could hear the haunting, sweet cry of the cuckoo. How could Helen have walked out on such a view and such a man?

Having showered and dressed, Cameron went downstairs. The dogs lying in the hall thumped their tails and followed her into the kitchen. There the housekeeper, Mrs Bodkin, was friendly but unfazed by her presence. Perhaps, like people in trains, she could afford to be friendly, knowing Cameron wouldn't be in situ for long. She mustn't get jealous and paranoid. Tony was turned on by rows. Rupert, she suspected, would be bored, and walk away from them.

She took some orange juice and coffee out onto the terrace. That must be Declan's house across the valley, still just visible through the thickening beech wood.

She wondered what he'd been up to since his fall from grace. How strange that on 1st January with Patrick she'd looked across at Rupert's house and thought, What a kingdom, and now, four months later, here she was.

She stopped only briefly to glance at the library and the first editions, which could be examined at length on a less lovely morning, then set out with the dogs to explore. There was a wonderful untamed beauty, rather like Maud O'Hara, about the garden. Green leaves were uncurling on the tangled old roses, the peacocks and crowing cocks once clipped out of the yew hedges were looking distinctly shaggy. The swimming-pool was full of leaves, the beech hedge round the tennis court was in need of a cut, the lawns dotted with daisies were still lit along the edges by pools of dying daffodils. Rupert and this place need a woman, thought Cameron, to cherish and sort them out.

The stables, on the other hand, were immaculate, and filled with beautiful, well-muscled horses. More horses were out in the fields. The girl grooms treated Cameron with the same we've-seen-them-all-come-and-go politeness displayed by Mrs Bodkin.

I'll show them, thought Cameron, as she set out through the beech woods. I'm the one who's going to hang in.

The ground was still carpeted with bluebells. Only when she pressed her face close could she distinguish their faint sweet hyacinth scent from the rank sexy stench of the wild garlic. The dogs charged ahead, but the shaggy lurcher called Blue kept bounding back solicitously to check she was all right, shoving his wet nose in her hand, giving her a token lick. It was all so beautiful; she had never felt so happy or so right anywhere.

She had wandered for a mile or two when suddenly she breathed in a sticky, sweet familiar scent that made her tremble. Ahead, a copse of poplars, rising like flaming amber swords, was wafting balsam down the woodland ride towards her, evoking the times she used to inhale Friar's Balsam under a towel as a child, reminding her all too violently of her mother and Mike. Instantly her euphoria evaporated. She glanced at her watch. It was half past twelve. She must get back. Grey clouds were creeping over the sun; it had become much cooler. She even felt a spot of rain. As she dropped down the wood towards the house an owl hooted. Surely it shouldn't hoot at midday? Through the trees she could see the lake grey and blank now as a smudged mirror, and as she reached the big lawn she gave a moan of horror. Last night's deluge had stripped all the petals from the magnolia, scattering them over the grass. Last night's bride was naked now.

The dogs converged, barking, as a car drew up at the front door. Cameron hoped it was Rupert, but it turned out to be a youth delivering some boxes of T-shirts, who gazed at Cameron in admiration.

'This is the first lot. Mr C-B wanted them in a hurry,' he said. 'Tell him the stickers, the posters and the badges'll be ready by Monday.'

Cameron couldn't resist having a look. The T-shirts were a beautiful cerulean blue, with a dark bronze drawing of a boy shading his forehead on the front and the words *Support Venturer* on the front and the back. They must be for some

392

sporting event. Taking one upstairs, Cameron stripped off and put it on. It fell just below her bush. Suddenly feeling incredibly randy, she hoped Rupert hadn't got anything planned for the afternoon. As it was much colder, she shut the window, trapping a tendril of clematis which was already wilting and bruised from being trapped on previous occasions. Trying to insinuate its way into Rupert's bedroom, like her and every other woman, thought Cameron wryly.

Next minute the front door banged. Very slowly she walked downstairs. Rupert was looking at the boxes in the hall.

'They're great,' she said. 'Can I keep one?'

Rupert glanced up and froze for a second.

'Hullo, angel. Did you sleep well?'

'So well,' murmured Cameron seductively, 'that I'm ready to be exhausted again.' She lifted the T-shirt to show him her bush. Then, when he didn't react as she'd expected and come bounding up the stairs, she said, 'What is Venturer, anyway?'

Rupert's eyes seemed to have gone a darker, more opaque shade of blue and lost all their sparkle. 'Come and have a drink,' he said.

Disappointed, Cameron followed him into the drawing-room. Suddenly he seemed incredibly tense and, when she refused a drink, poured himself two fingers of neat whisky and drank it in one gulp. Then he pulled her down on to the sofa beside him.

'Look, sweetheart, this is a bit difficult, but there's something I've got to tell you.'

Cameron went white. Suddenly in that baggy T-shirt, she looked as fragile, pale and defenceless as one of the anemones that strewed the paths of Rupert's woods.

'You want to pack me in?' she whispered.

'No, no, quite the reverse.' Very gently he smoothed a tendril of dark hair behind her ear and stroked her rigid, quivering cheek.

'But you may want to pack me in. Freddie Jones, Declan and I are pitching for the Corinium franchise. We've called ourselves Venturer.'

At first she was so relieved that he wasn't trying to end the relationship she couldn't think straight.

'You and Declan? How long has this been going on?'

'Since the day after Declan walked out.'

'So turning up in Madrid wasn't only to see a football match?'

'No.'

'Or showing such interest in my career and the goings on at Corinium?'

'No.'

'Did you read the application in my briefcase?'

'I photostated it.'

She was trembling violently now and her lips were quite white.

'Don't worry,' he reassured her. 'Declan was so appalled by my skulduggery he refused to read it; so we haven't pinched anything.'

'And I suppose you arranged those riots as an excuse to fly straight home once you'd got what you wanted?'

'Uh-uh,' protested Rupert. 'Two stabbed cops, twenty-five people injured and a burnt-down stand is going too far even for me.'

'But driving down to see me before I flew out to LA and all those questions you asked me? Did you give that "Stowaway" story to Dempster?'

Rupert nodded. Truth, however devastating, was the only answer now.

'And, Christ, how much have I already told you this weekend?' whispered Cameron, looking at her watch. 'And our application's already gone in.'

Rupert had expected rage, tantrums, having his face clawed, but not this numb state of shock.

'I trusted you,' she said slowly. 'You're the first person I've trusted since I was fourteen. I thought you were so caring, you bloody Judas. This is the worst thing that's ever happened to me.'

'It isn't as awful as it seems,' said Rupert soothingly. 'I thought you were the sexiest thing on two legs the moment

I saw you. Didn't I offer you a lift home after Valerie's dinner party? I would have moved in both at Declan's party, if young Patrick hadn't been making the running, and at Corinium, if Tony hadn't been hanging about. If I hadn't fancied you to death, I'd never have bothered coming out to Madrid. I wanted to level with you but I didn't know how you'd react. We couldn't afford to let you rush back to Tony and tell him everything, in case he exoceted our bid before it got off the ground.'

Cameron leapt to her feet, tugging down the T-shirt. 'And I figured you were really interested in me. What a joke. I know how Declan detests me. He must have cracked up, and I suppose Patrick and that dumbass Taggie were in on it too. Christ, you must have been all laughing yourselves sick.'

She was crying now – angry, agonized rasping tears, and Rupert suddenly appreciated her terrible insecurity, her paranoia, her vulnerability and her terror; for the first time his heart was truly touched by her. Getting up, he tried to take her in his arms and comfort her.

'Angel, you've got it wrong. No one's laughing at you. I want you, I absolutely adore you. We all want you to join Venturer. We were just picking our moment. We've got an absolutely alpha line-up, but you'd be the jewel in our crown, and you'd be totally free to make the programmes you wanted.'

'Get out of my way!' screamed Cameron. 'I hate you! I never want to see you again!' And, diving under his outstretched arms, she bolted out of the door.

Rupert had never felt such a shit in his life. She'll have to get her clothes and her suitcase from upstairs, he thought; I can cut her off on her way downstairs. But Cameron shot straight out of the front door, and next moment he heard the wheels of the Lotus crunching on the gravel. Tony was probably still on his way down from London and Cameron couldn't rage round to The Falconry in nothing but that T-shirt, but she'd be on to him on the telephone in a flash. The early-warning system had gone off. It was just a matter of time before the H-bomb landed.

30

All over the country on Sunday, 2nd May, the independent companies and those consortiums who sought to oust them were assembling, colour-coding and ring-binding forty copies of their application document on A4 paper – complete with attached confidential material – to be delivered to the IBA headquarters in Brompton Road by noon the following day.

Corinium, to be on the safe side, had submitted their application the day before. Venturer, who were pushed for time, spent a wildly exciting Sunday at Freddie's house in Holland Park knocking their final draft into shape.

Everyone agreed that Declan had done a masterly job. But Freddie and Marti Gluckstein, who arrived looking like a costive lizard, felt Declan's bald and somewhat arrogant claim that 'We can find £15 million; just ring Henriques Bros' was inadequate, and were therefore considerably extending the financial section. Freddie and Lord Smith were going through the technical specifications with a toothcomb, while Harold White, Janey Lloyd-Foxe, Charles Fairburn, Dame Enid and Professor Graystock were having fun jazzing up the programme content.

Bas, having provided architects' plans for the conversion of Cotchester House into studios and offices should Tony turn nasty, was now playing chemmy with Henry Hampshire, the Lord-Lieutenant, who hadn't spent a Sunday in London for twenty-five years, and with Wesley Emerson, who had nothing really to add to the bid except his illustrious presence. The Bishop was driving up to London immediately after Evensong. Maud, who'd come for the ride, was playing the piano. Upstairs, Ursula and Freddie's secretary were frantically typing and re-typing drafts and then running okayed pages off on the word processor.

Taggie was in the kitchen. She had given everyone pâté and cheese for lunch, and was now making chicken Estragon for the celebration dinner. Four plump boiling chickens, carrots and onions were already simmering in a huge pan on the Aga. There was an extremely complicated and hazardous sauce to be made later, involving egg yolks, cream and lemon juice which might easily curdle. But at least having tramped the length of Notting Hill Gate that morning, she'd found some fresh tarragon.

From the next-door room she could hear screams of laughter.

'We must do a series on local studs called "Dongs of Praise",' Janey Lloyd-Foxe was saying. 'We can start off with Rupert; then we won't have to pay him a fee.'

'Rupert'd screw a fee out of us anyway,' said Charles.

'Well, the programme's about screwing,' said Janey.

Janey was absolutely gorgeous, thought Taggie. Rupert had said she was nearly forty, but, except for the fine pencilling of lines round her wicked dark brown eyes, you'd never have known it. Poor Billy, her husband, was abroad covering the Paris Tennis Tournament for the BBC, and Janey had turned up with the most adorable baby, who was so fat, smiling and gurgling that even the men wanted to hold her. And Janey was so blonde and beautiful, and had such wonderful brown breasts after a week in Portugal, that no one minded her breast-feeding at all.

'I've got a terrific idea for a game show,' Janey was now saying. 'You have a panel and they have to guess who the celebrity is by interviewing the cleaners who work for them. We call it "Daily Daily". Mrs Makepiece can give us some wonderful stories about James Vereker, and Mrs Bodkin would be riveting about Rupert's goings on. Mrs Bodkin used to work for us,' continued Janey, shifting the baby to her right breast. 'The first time we got a cordless telephone she found it in our bed and, assuming it was some auto-erotic device, discreetly hid it in my pants' drawer. Then, when it started ringing, Billy, who was expecting some summons to jump for Britain, went frantic trying to find it.'

Everyone screamed with laughter.

'Don't you think it's a brilliant idea, Declan?'

'No,' said Declan, who already adored Janey. 'The IBA would think it otterly ondemocratic.'

'Well, what about an English "Dallas", wife-swapping in the Royal triangle?' said Janey.

'Later,' said Declan, 'when we've got the franchise.'

They were all so bright and clever, thought Taggie wistfully. She had contributed nothing. 'An army marches on its stomach,' Declan was fond of telling her, but she was sure that everyone would have been just as happy with an Indian takeaway this evening and that her father had only suggested she did the food in order to involve her.

In the house opposite, a lot of young people were sprawled on the drawing-room carpet drinking red wine and reading the Sunday papers. It all came back to reading, thought Taggie despairingly. If she didn't keep at it, she'd lose the ability more and more, like not talking French. She *must* try harder.

She pored over the Estragon recipe in the book, but half the words were in French. Embarrassed at having to resort to a tape recorder she shut the door, so no one could hear.

She was worried about Rupert too. He'd been edgy and refused to eat anything when he'd popped in earlier, then furious because he'd forgotten to bring up the T-shirts. He'd also taken an instant dislike to Professor Graystock, whom he hadn't met before, and who had black straggly hair, like a jumble-sale crone, a wet, sensual mouth and a pale, waxy, formless face.

'Who's he in mourning for?' Rupert asked Taggie in horror.

'No one, I don't think.'

'Must be. Look at his fingernails and the inside of his collar.'

Then Rupert had pushed off, promising he and the T-shirts would be back later. Taggie was sure he didn't look after himself properly. If she made the chicken particularly nice, he might eat something this evening.

At eight o'clock the first bottle of Bollinger was cracked as they waited for the final draft to be ready. Declan had just re-written the last page to give the whole thing a uniformity of style. Ursula and Freddie's secretary were busy collating everything and Freddie and Declan were now folding up the confidential memos listing Harold White, Georgie Baines, Charles, Seb and Billy as Heads of various departments and putting these memos into envelopes.

'Pity we can't add Cameron Cook,' sighed Freddie.

'Rupert would have rung by now if he had anything to report,' said Declan, who preferred it that way.

Dame Enid and Maud, both well away, were now playing duets. The Lord-Lieutenant had lost so much money to Bas he'd probably have to sell another Pre-Raphaelite, but he couldn't have enjoyed himself more. There were so many pretty women to gaze at, and they were all such splendid chaps, and Rupert had promised he should meet Joanna Lumley very soon.

Janey, who was well stuck into the Bollinger, was breast-feeding again.

'Mother and child – a lovely sight,' said the Bishop who'd just arrived.

'So much prettier than Deirdre Kill-Programme and her disgusting brat,' said Georgie Baines to Seb Burrows.

'Please,' said Charles Fairburn faintly.

'That baby's drinking neat Bollinger,' said Bas. 'That's why it's so cheerful.'

'I hope all our burn money isn't being squandered on bubbly,' said Professor Graystock, who was on his fourth glass.

'It isn't,' said Taggie quickly. 'Rupert's paid for all of it.'

Helped by Seb, she was now putting out big plates of

chicken Estragon and rice salad. She'd worried herself sick that the sauce had gone wrong, but mercifully it had thickened as it cooled.

'That looks marvellous, Taggie. I wish you'd marry me when I grow up,' said Bas, who was now comfortably ensconced on the sofa with Janey and a full bottle.

'This tomato salad is out of this world,' said Seb, carrying the bowl in.

Taggie liked Seb. He had a good body, hunky without being fat, thick light-brown hair, short at the back and long at the front, very direct slate grey eyes and he was very nearly as tall as she was.

Then, as Big Ben struck nine, the applications were ready: forty copies of beautifully typed, ring-bound pages. On the front, beneath the clear plastic cover, was a drawing of a beautiful boy with his hand to his forehead, standing on the capitals T and U of the word Venturer against a clear cerulean background. On the back, also protected by a plastic cover, was an exquisite water-colour map of the area, painted by Caitlin, including the towns and villages, with little drawings of the relevant houses, where all the prospective Venturer directors lived, and with pale blue arrows from each of them converging on Cotchester. It had cost a lot to print, but they'd all thought it was worth it.

Everyone went mad with excitement as they sat round reading, and at last holding in their hands tangible proof that it was all really happening.

'Don't spill drink over them, for Christ's sake,' said Declan.

'It's very good, Declan,' said Harold White. 'I'd forgotten how well you write. I love the bit about "carpets being so thick and offices so sound-proofed on the Corinium directors' floor, that all one can hear is the faint rustle of nests being feathered".'

'I liked that bit too,' said Declan, blushing.

'And I love this bit about Corinium's local news programmes being presented by "pretentious pastel-clad narcissists",' boomed Dame Enid. 'That boring little fart Vereker won't like that one bit.'

'I hope that's not actionable,' said Professor Graystock primly. 'And are you quite sure there was a Roman camp at Whychey?'

'Quite,' said Declan.

'I like my cottage,' said Marti Gluckstein, examining the map at the back. 'I must come and look at it some time. Ouch!' he yelled, as Freddie kicked him sharply on the ankle.

'Sorry, but Declan thinks you spend every weekend there,' whispered Freddie.

'I do like your ideas for religious programmes,' said Janey, smiling up at the Bishop, who went very pink.

Declan saw that everyone's glasses were full, then got to his feet. 'I'd just like to thank you all for having the courage to join Venturer, and for all the hard work you've put in already. But I must warn you, this has been the easy bit. Once it's out in the open that we're pitching for Corinium, Tony Baddingham is going to do everything to discredit us and rake up dirt about all of us. Our only hope is to stick together and trosst each other.' He smiled round at everyone. 'This is a very very proud day for me. Let's all raise our glasses.'

'Victory to Venturer,' said Henry Hampshire, and amazingly, unselfconsciously, everyone followed suit.

'I shall compose a battle song for Venturer and we'll make a record,' said Dame Enid.

'I hope it's better than the song cycle she's just written,' muttered Seb to Taggie. 'It sounded more like a lot of tom cats being garrotted by knicker elastic. This chicken is just as much a work of art as your father's application,' he went on. 'Can I have some more?'

Everyone jumped as the doorbell went.

'I can't help thinking it's Tony with a pitchfork,' said Georgie Baines nervously.

But it was only the man with the T-shirts and once again everyone went wild and put them on, including the baby and Gertrude. They were baggy enough, having been ordered to Caitlin's specification, to fit Dame Enid and Charles Fairburn, and even the Bishop wore one over his dog collar. Janey wore hers just over pants to show off her long brown legs, and, after a lot of persuading, Taggie did the same.

'They're much better than Corinium's T-shirts,' said Seb in delight. 'They're custard yellow with Caring Corinium written across the front. Tony eschewed the symbol of the Corinium ram as being too libidinous.'

More champagne was drunk and food eaten. Then the photographer arrived.

'Where the hell's Rupert?' said Declan irritably.

'I think we ought to get on and get this pickie taken without him,' said Freddie in an undertone. 'Lord Smiff's shipped enough to float the *QE2* an' Wesley's on somefink else, and he's supposed to drive back to Leeds tonight for an eleven o'clock start.'

'He better go first thing tomorrow,' said Declan. 'We don't want him busted the day the applications go in.'

Bas and Janey were still nose to nose on the sofa; the baby had fallen asleep in Bas's arms.

'Line up for the photograph everyone,' shouted Freddie.

Seb dragged Taggie in from the kitchen. She loathed group photographs. She was always taller than half the men.

'You're as much a part of Venturer as anyone else,' said Seb.

Taggie sat on the sofa, Gertrude on her knee, bristling in a child's T-shirt, with Maud on one side and Janey and the baby on the other. Bas stood behind Janey. Taggie suddenly noticed his suntanned fingers caressing the back of Janey's neck and hastily looked away.

'Straighten your T-shirt, so I can see all the Venturers,' said the photographer. 'Look nice and happy please. Can you get the little dog to prick up his ears? Lovely! Smile please.'

He was still snapping away two minutes later when Taggie gave a shriek of pain as Gertrude leapt off her bare legs, barking furiously, as Rupert came through the door.

He had that same look of blazing triumph on his face, reflected Janey, that he used to have in the old days when one of his horses won a big class and he used to ride it out of the ring, giving its neck great slaps of joy. He hadn't looked like that for years.

Rupert paused in the doorway.

'Ladies and Gentlemen,' he drawled, 'may I introduce Venturer's Head of Drama.'

Taggie gave a gasp of horror; Harold White went white. Seb, Georgie and Charles nearly jumped out of the window in terror, as Rupert turned round and, putting his arm around Cameron's shoulders very much in a gesture of possession, drew her into the room.

She looked very pale and very shy, but incredibly beautiful, with her face strangely softened by love.

Maud broke the stunned silence. For months, despite Declan's denials, she had suspected Rupert of having a growing preference for Taggie. It was the one thing she couldn't have stood. Joyfully, she welcomed such a public transferring of his affections to Cameron. Rushing forward, she hugged them both.

'Congratulations, darlings. Now I'm convinced Venturer's going to get the franchise.'

'Don't look so worried,' said Rupert mockingly to the cringing Corinium contingent. 'Cameron's on the level. Her name's going to be put forward on the confidential memo like the rest of you, and she's going to stay working for Corinium until December.'

Charles decided to make the best of a bad job. 'Welcome to Venturer, sweetie,' he said, kissing Cameron.

'Fucking hell,' muttered Seb to Georgie.

'Look at the way she's looking at Rupert,' said Georgie. 'He's got her exactly where he wants her.'

'As long as he stays wanting her,' said Seb, shaking his head.

Janey's baby woke up suddenly and started bawling its head off.

'Probably got a hangover,' said Bas.

Soon the champagne was circulating again. Cameron was sitting on the sofa now, flipping through the application document with one hand, clinging onto Rupert's hand with the other.

'Why's Taggie crying in the kitchen?' Dame Enid asked Maud.

'I expect she'd like to be able to read her father's application like everyone else,' said Maud airily. 'She's dyslexic, you see.'

'Poor darling,' said Dame Enid. 'She's a bloody good cook. I'm going to have thirds.'

Seb put his arm round Taggie in the kitchen. 'You OK, babes?'

'Fine,' she muttered blowing her nose on a drying-up cloth. 'I'm just tired, I guess.'

'Your application's dazzling,' said Cameron, following Declan over to the drinks table where he was opening another bottle. 'Miles, miles better than ours. Any slight doubts I might have had about joining Venturer have been dispelled by reading it. I do hope Rupert hasn't railroaded you all into accepting me?'

'I don't want any bullying,' said Declan, glaring at her. 'One's only as good as one's work force and don't you ever forget it.'

I'm going to have to put in a lot of spade work to win him over, thought Cameron, but all that really mattered was that Rupert loved her.

Freddie clapped his hands. 'Let's get this pickie finished.'

'Come on, Cameron,' said Charles, brandishing a T-shirt.

'I'm not sure I ought to appear in it,' stammered Cameron, suddenly realizing what compromising evidence it would be.

'Put it on,' snapped Declan.

Charles slid the T-shirt over her head and once again they all lined up, George and Seb taking up their position on either side of her, with Charles standing behind.

'Straighten your T-shirts, look happy everyone,' said the photographer.

'Let's get one thing straight beside T-shirts, Miss Cook,' said Georgie out of the corner of his handsome mouth, as he beamed into the camera.

'If you shop us to Tony, we'll shop you,' said Seb as he also beamed into the camera.

'And don't forget, there are well over two hundred shopping days to 15th December,' said Charles.

As Venturer had called a press conference for the following afternoon, Declan stayed the night at Freddie's house and Taggie drove her mother and Gertrude back to Penscombe just after midnight.

Maud was plastered and went on and on about how nice Janey was, and wasn't it a turn-up for the books Rupert rolling up with Cameron, and did Taggie think Rupert had offered her marriage or to move into Penscombe or what. Taggie answered in monosyllables and fortunately, as they passed the Reading exit, Maud fell into a drunken sleep.

Taggie then proceeded to give herself a very good talking to. What the hell was she feeling so miserable about? Rupert was as far beyond her as the huge stars daisying the black lawn of sky above, and plainly as impervious to her love. It was the stupid sort of crush teenagers had on pop stars or actors, someone to dream about when you were tucked up in bed, or wandering through the woods.

Rupert had probably been kind to her because he missed his own children. The silver necklace, Gertrude's Valentine, the little Easter Egg, were all presents you might give a child, she told herself firmly. And saying that no one could resist her (Taggie wished she could memorize recipes and how to spell words as easily as she remembered every conversation she'd had with Rupert) was just the sort of thing he'd say to any girl. Cameron was beautiful, brilliant, sophisticated and tough. Taggie was sure she only disliked her because she'd upset Declan and hurt Patrick so much, but Rupert wouldn't stand any nonsense, so maybe they were well suited.

Next minute she felt a cold nose nudging her elbow and put out her hand to stroke Gertrude, who slid forward along the hand brake until she could climb onto Taggie's knee and settle down with a martyred sigh.

Taggie knew she shouldn't allow Gertrude to lie there. On

405

a motorway it was particularly dangerous. But she needed the comfort. She was not someone who regarded happiness as a right, but the ghastly shock of seeing Cameron and Rupert so obviously in love tonight made her realize how happy, without being conscious of it, she'd been since Valentine's Day, when Rupert began dropping in at The Priory whenever he was at home. Despite the talking to, she didn't think she'd ever felt so unhappy in her life.

RIVALS
31

At noon the lists closed. The information office at the IBA then had a frantic three and a half hours going through the applications and extracting the names and addresses of those involved for a press release at three-thirty.

Down at Cotchester three of the four Corinium moles made themselves scarce. Charles Fairburn drove to the Forest of Dean to spend two days in an enclosed order, ostensibly interviewing monks. Georgie flew to Manchester to see a big pet-food client. Cameron disappeared to Stow-on-the-Wold on location, leaving strict instructions that she wasn't to be interrupted. Seb Burrows, being a true journalist and hating to miss the fireworks, hung around the newsroom.

Corinium staff not involved with the Venturer bid were also kept busy. James Vereker slipped home with Sarah Stratton for an extended lunch hour. Daysee Butler, who'd been out in the evenings so much recently she hadn't watched any television, was reading the soap updates in the *Mail*, as she soaked up the sun in her bikini in the Cathedral close. Tony Baddingham and Ginger Johnson were having a celebrity board-room lunch with the French co-producers of 'Stowaway', having just sold it both to NBS and BBC. What a relief, they all agreed, they hadn't killed off the handsome pirate villain, as a sequel was already planned.

How nice it was too, thought Tony, to lunch with Europeans who still appreciated a good blow-out and decent claret, compared with the Yanks who seemed totally addicted to rabbit food and Perrier.

By three forty-five Tony was back in his office. In half an hour he would have sobered up and be wondering who to bully. Now he merely felt lecherous. All those pale-green trees and pale half-naked girls stretched out among the buttercups. The first flush and flesh of Spring always got him going. Having spent a weekend without Cameron, he decided to drop in and see her after the Chamber of Commerce dinner that night, an event which had to be endured in a franchise year.

Still feeling randy, he was about to summon Sarah Stratton to discuss her posing with a lamb for a Caring Corinium poster when Miss Madden buzzed. 'Barney Williams from the *Telegraph*, Lord B. He wants to talk about the franchise.'

'Put him on.' Tony extracted a cigar from the box on his desk and relaxed in his leather chair, preparing to be generous about Mid-West's pathetic bid.

Barney Williams came straight to the point. 'Did you know Declan O'Hara put in a rival bid?'

Tony laughed heartily. 'Is this some kind of joke?'

'I'm afraid it isn't.'

'Who else is involved?'

'Rupert Campbell-Black, Freddie Jones.'

'Whaaaat!'

It sounded like a great oak tree crashing to the ground. Even through sound-proofed doors, Miss Madden jumped in the next-door office. Then Tony was leaning on the buzzer.

'Miss Madden!' he yelled. 'Take these names down. Who else?' he asked Barney.

'Henry Hampshire, the Bishop of Cotchester, Marti Gluckstein.'

'He's never been to Gloucestershire.'

'Evidently he has a weekend cottage there. Janey Lloyd-Foxe, Dame Enid Spink, Lord Smith.'

'He can't join. He's a union member.'

'Ex-member – just. Crispin Graystock. Wesley Emerson – he's the only bit of name-plate engineering. They're all pretty heavyweight, in fact, and, oh yes, there's your brother Bas. Bit Jacob and Esau isn't it?'

Tony gave a low hiss that was almost a sigh.

'And you had absolutely no idea?' asked Barney.

'None.'

'And they're all friends of yours?'

'They were.'

'They're calling a press conference in London at four-thirty. Will you be doing the same, or can I have a quote now?'

'I've nothing to say until I've talked to my Board!'

Tony slammed down the telephone. Bastards! Traitors! Every single one of them. They'd all eaten his salt, and he'd absolutely no inkling. What kind of fucking newsroom did he have? The maddened bull's roar could be heard all down the passage.

'Ginger, Cyril, Georgie, Cameron, Charles! Come in here.'

'Georgie's in Manchester,' said Miss Madden, 'and Cameron's on location.'

'Get them back.'

Ginger Johnson thought Tony was going to have a coronary. He was magenta in the face, veins bulged like huge snakes on his forehead. He seemed to be popping out of his dark-green collar. Ginger wanted Tony's job, but not until the franchise was safely in the bag.

'What on earth's up?'

Tony was so angry as he paced up and down, fists clenched, froth flecking his mouth, he could hardly get the words out to tell him. Once he lit a cigar from the wrong end, then hurled it out of the window. Without taking the top off, he tried to pour himself a stiff whisky, then banged the bottle down.

'What have they called themselves?' asked Cyril Peacock, who was taking down the inevitable notes.

'Venturer – adventurers more likely – every bloody one of them! God, I'll crucify them! I'll take them to the cleaners!'

Ginger went to the drinks cupboard and poured Tony a large brandy. He was equally shocked at the possible loss of a £125 million turnover, but, having no personal vendettas with any of the Venturer team, he didn't feel Tony's paranoia or passionate sense of being deliberately ganged up on.

Miss Madden buzzed: 'It's the *Sun*, Lord B, and just hang on a minute . . . Beryl says the *Mirror* are on the other line.'

'Tell them Lord B's in conference and to ring back in half an hour,' said Ginger, taking the initiative. 'Don't talk to them now,' he added to Tony. 'Get your breath back. The most important thing at this stage is not to show we're rattled. Leave the mud-slinging to Venturer. We've got seven months to put the boot in. The only possible approach now is Olympian. These boring little pygmies are yapping at my heels, but I can't feel it.'

'Should we call a press conference?'

'Certainly not. They're not worth it. Why show them we're panicking?'

Downstairs in the newsroom Seb Burrows picked up his telephone. It was ITN: 'Hello, Seb. Christ, what a story!'

'What story?' said Seb innocently.

ITN told him. 'Did you know anything about it?'

'None of us did. Christ!'

'Can you interview Tony for us for the five forty-five news?'

'I'll try. I don't imagine he'll be in carnival mood.'

But, to Seb's amazement, Tony agreed. By the time the crew got up to Tony's office, every award Corinium had ever won, including the EMMYs and the BAFTAs nicked from Cameron's office, had been put on the bookshelf or hung on the wall behind Tony's head.

The earlier storm had subsided; Tony's rage was ice cold now. He had even extracted a salmon-pink carnation from the vase on the desk to put in his buttonhole.

'What's your reaction to Venturer's bid?' asked Seb.

Tony gave a big, but slightly dismissive smile: 'Well, they're good chaps, all jolly good friends of mine. I'm sure there's a lot of merit in their application, but frankly I'm more interested in the things Corinium are doing – like announcing plans for a ten-million-pound studio near Southampton, which'll mean about four hundred extra jobs, and spending two million on new equipment at Cotchester, to enable us to make even better programmes, and meet with every confidence the challenge of cable and satellite. We've won a lot of awards over the last few years.' He waved airily at the trophies glittering behind him. 'We provide an excellent local news service and make jolly good programmes, and there we rest our case.'

I'm not getting anywhere, thought Seb.

'People are saying that Declan O'Hara and your brother Basil have been deliberately plotting to oust you since Declan walked out of here last March in a blaze of publicity.'

Tony examined his nails. 'Are they?' he said with another big smile.

Ask a silly question, thought Seb, kicking himself.

'Had you any idea they were engaged in a rival bid?'

'None. I wish them luck. It would be a dull race if there were no other contenders, but it doesn't dent my confidence.'

'Which consortium, Mid-West or Venturer, worries you the most?'

'Neither. I congratulate Venturer on putting an application together at such short notice and with such secrecy. I'll be interested to see what's in it in due course.'

'And you feel no bitterness towards Freddie Jones and Rupert Campbell-Black and Henry Hampshire, who have all enjoyed your hospitality?'

'None at all,' laughed Tony, as though the idea had never occurred to him. 'Nor do Corinium have any desire to get involved in mudslinging. Let "Dorothy Dove", who recently won us a BAFTA award, be a symbol of our company, non-combative but victorious.'

The moment the camera stopped rolling the smile was wiped from Tony's face. 'Now bugger off, all of you, but come back the moment "Cotswold Round-Up" is over, Seb, and bring James Vereker with you.'

Cameron ignored Tony's summons to return at once and insisted on carrying on shooting until the four-thirty tea break. It was vital to be as bolshie as usual, or Tony would

411

suspect something. As she drove through the angelic spring greenness with the roof down, she heard a flash on the five-thirty news that Declan O'Hara, after a mega-bust-up with Corinium in March, was now getting his revenge on Tony by heading a rival bid for Corinium. Rupert, Freddie, Dame Enid, the Bishop, Wesley, Lord Smith and Janey were also mentioned. Cameron waited in terror for her name to be tagged on at the end.

She was still in a state of shock after the weekend. When she'd run out on Rupert on Saturday, she'd gone straight home and rung Tony at home — something he'd told her never to do — and promptly got Monica. Remembering that Tony had the French co-production people over for the weekend, who were probably *Mon Dieu*-ing over Monica's fading stretch of daffodils at that moment, she'd hung up. For the next twenty-four hours she crouched shuddering in her bedroom, telephone off the hook, all doors locked, not answering the bell, going through every kind of torture at the prospect of life without Rupert. The craving had got so bad that when, on Sunday afternoon, he'd smashed the pane of her french windows at the back, let himself in, pounded up the stairs, and taken her in his arms, telling her he couldn't go on without her, the sheer relief of having him back made her agree to anything. She would join Venturer; she would stay at Corinium and spy on Tony.

'A Ms is not nearly as good as a Mole,' Rupert had told her as he'd dropped her off at Hamilton Terrace at four o'clock that morning. God knows when either of them would get any sleep.

But at last the crunch had come. All day she'd been snapping at the cast for acting badly. Now she had to give a BAFTA performance herself. At least she'd heard the news bulletin, so she didn't have to simulate complete surprise when she saw Tony.

But as she drove into her slot in the Corinium car park and read the words 'Cameron Cook, Controller of Pro-grammes' she felt she should cross out the last three and put Traitor.

She reached Tony's office just before the main BBC news. The commercials, with the sound turned down, were airing on ITV. Tony, Ginger and Cyril were all watching. Cameron went straight up to Tony and put her arms round him.

'I'm so sorry, I heard it on the radio. They're all traitors, but Freddie and Bas are the worst of all.'

'Was Bas mentioned on the radio?' said Cyril, pencil poised. 'What station?'

'I don't remember,' said Cameron hastily. 'Some local bulletin, but I was switching about to see what I could find out.'

Christ, that was a near one, she thought, going to the drinks cupboard and pouring herself a stiff vodka and tonic. She'd have to be careful with the liquor too; she was so tired, other indiscretions might slip out. How the hell had Guy Burgess kept his communist affiliations a secret for so long if he was always pissed?

The BBC led on the story. Beautiful weather apart, there wasn't much news. After some introductory waffle about the contenders now circling in the paddock, they went straight over to the Venturer press conference. Not wanting him to see her face, Cameron took up her position behind Tony, leaning against the wall with her hand on his shoulder. He seemed calm enough, but she could feel the knotted tension of his muscles. A tic was leaping in his jaw and the carnation in his buttonhole had already wilted, as though poisoned by his venom.

The Venturer team looked splendid. Declan had been so hostile last night that she hadn't noticed how well he was looking, already tanned from gardening and sitting outside writing the application. Half the heavy lines seemed to have been ironed out of his face. And there was Rupert laughing with Janey, who looked amazing, bearing in mind the amount she'd drunk yesterday. Rupert had said she was the one person Cameron need never be jealous of, but she removed her hand from Tony's shoulder, in case she clutched it convulsively. Rupert looked marvellous, too. Christ, he was beautiful. Any minute, she thought, taking such a large slug of vodka that

413

it spilled down the tall glass all over her face, she'd wake up.

There was also a massive contingent of press there. People were standing on tables, fighting for space.

'Why have you pitched for the Corinium franchise, Declan?' asked the BBC.

'We want to create a company that is genuinely local,' said Declan. 'And we want to make some bloody good programmes.'

'And a fortune into the bargain?' said the *Mirror*.

Everyone laughed. Declan grinned. 'That too. Then we can afford to make even better programmes.'

Soon, however, the vitriol was flowing freely.

'Corinium have lost touch with the public and their region. They need a good shake-up,' said Rupert.

'After eight years in business,' said Freddie, 'it seems amazing that Tony B has only just decided to build a studio near Southampton.'

'I appeared on "Cotswold Round-Up" recently,' boomed Dame Enid. 'I was interviewed by some pastel-clad pansy –' she winked at Declan – 'who didn't know what the hell he was talking about. It was the worst programme I've ever been on.'

'What drew you in, Bishop?' asked the *Catholic Herald*.

'Television today is a key factor in the quality of life, in the community, in the establishment of Christian values,' said the Bishop heartily. 'I hope to play a part through Venturer in making television more uplifting and more enjoyable.' He wagged a finger. 'One doesn't exclude the other, y'know.'

Realizing the Bishop was all set to deliver a sermon, Rupert cut in, 'The Bishop feels as I do, that there's far too much sex and violence on Corinium's programmes.'

'Fucking hypocrite,' thundered Tony.

'Very much so,' agreed the Bishop. 'On "Four Men went to Mow" young people are continually going to bed with other young people and shown not to be taking precautions.'

'Corinium's drama record as a whole,' added Janey, 'is abysmal.'

'Bitch,' hissed Cameron in genuine outrage. 'How dare she!'

'There are, of course, good people working at Corinium,' said Declan, 'but they're hamstrung by a greedy and incompetent management.'

Tony puffed on his cigar, the knuckles of his left hand whitening as he made a dagger of the silver paper knife on his desk. Cyril's doodles became more extravagant.

'Having worked at Corinium for seven months,' went on Declan, 'I know just how bad things are.'

'Isn't that actionable?' said Ginger furiously.

But Tony held up his hand for silence as the *Star* asked Declan who Venturer were poaching from other companies.

Declan smiled again. 'We have a string of incredibly talented people who will take over as Heads of the various departments the moment we win the franchise,' he said, 'but as they're all working for ITV or the BBC, we can't tell you who they are.'

'What d'you feel about your other rival, Mid-West?' said the *Sun*.

Rupert laughed. 'Well, they were advertising for ideas for programmes in the local paper last week,' he said, 'so they must be a bit short on imagination, and as their regional trump card is a geography master who's never been to London I can't say we feel very threatened.'

The BBC, obviously feeling they'd given Venturer enough coverage, turned to the wonderful weather.

Tony immediately switched over to 'Cotswold Round-Up' who put out an outwardly impartial report about there being two contenders for the Corinium franchise, then ran Tony's interview with Seb in full. This was immediately followed by a link from James Vereker saying that Declan must have got to know Rupert when he interviewed him for Corinium.

Next the clip was run in from the programme in which Declan quoted the Gloucestershire peer describing Rupert as 'a nasty virus everyone's wife caught sooner or later'. And Rupert replying: 'If you could see his wife, it'd definitely be later.'

415

Finally came Declan's questions as to whether Rupert was going to mend his ways because of AIDS, and Rupert cracking back that he was giving up casual sex for Lent. Without any qualifying comment, the programme then switched to a story about playing-fields.

'That was offensive,' said Cameron furiously. 'That clip should *never* have been taken out of context.'

'The IBA won't like it one bit,' said Ginger, shaking his head.

'I didn't authorize it,' lied Tony quickly. 'I can't help it if my newsroom get a little protective and leap to my defence.'

Cameron felt sick. It was going to be much dirtier and more difficult than she'd thought. Things became worse when Seb and James rolled up after 'Cotswold Round-Up'. Tony, utterly businesslike now, said their chief object should be to dig up as much dirt on Venturer as possible and then get other people to leak the stories.

'We've got to appear whiter than white and above it all. Here's the list of their consortium.' Tony handed copies to James and Seb. 'Declan was desperately pushed for cash when he left Corinium. How's he managed to be in funds again? Investigate any IRA sympathies. His wife's a tart. See if there's any rift there.'

'Rupert's a government minister,' said Ginger. 'That's out of order for a start. He could influence the PM to lean on the IBA to give Venturer the franchise.'

'Excellent,' said Tony. 'Ring up Paul Stratton, Ginger. He detests Rupert. Get him to ask a question in the House about it. And find out who Rupert's sleeping with, Seb. It's bound to be different from yesterday. If anything moves, or rather stays still, he'll fuck it. Sarah Stratton used to sleep with him; she may still be. Talk to her.'

Seb didn't dare look at Cameron. Suddenly, he felt desperately sorry for her.

'Lord Smith likes the fleshpots far too much for a socialist,' went on Tony. 'He's got his own house with five bedrooms and a very nice car. See if he's been using union funds. Graystock's a pinko, too. Investigate any communist sympathies. He's also divorced, got a second house, and definitely sent his second child to a private school. Hang round the University, Seb, and see if he's ever fiddled with one of his students, or put one in the club.'

'Ditto Dame Enid,' said Ginger with his dry mirthless laugh. 'She's probably miffed we're doing a Michael Tippett opera this year and not one of hers.'

'That's possible,' said Tony. 'Good story to leak to the gossip columns. And the Bishop of Cotchester must have had a choirboy in his time.'

He ran his finger down the list. 'Henry Hampshire's a terrible letch; keep an eye on him. Janey Lloyd-Foxe is a whore. She left Billy for a bit and went off with one of his sponsors, and they're always broke. There's bound to be some dirt there. And Wesley Emerson's a cinch. He's always stoned or dipping his wick. We've just got to pick our moment to leak a really juicy story.'

Ginger shook his head. 'Got to be careful, there. Wesley's such a local hero, the public'll forgive him anything. He took five wickets today, only person who did.'

'Send Sarah Stratton to interview him,' said Tony. 'That should do the trick.'

James's stomach gave a terrific rumble; his extended lunch with Sarah today had not included food. 'I think we should be careful about smirching Corinium's caring face,' he said palely.

'I agree,' said Cameron, who'd also gone very white. 'Can't we just, as you said, stand on our record? We're better than them. It seems so tacky to sink to their level.'

'Don't be fucking stupid,' snapped Tony. 'This is war. I don't believe Marti Gluckstein lives in Penscombe either. Find out his alleged address and go and bung the neighbours.'

'I'll do that story,' said Seb quickly.

'Charles is a friend of both Rupert's and Declan's,' said Tony. 'He can find out what they're up to. Where the hell is he, anyway?' He turned furiously on Cyril.

'Gone to an enclosed order for two days,' stammered Cyril. 'They're not on the telephone.'

'Well, drive over and fetch him back, sunshine,' said Tony with exaggerated patience. 'If you both value your jobs, see that he rings me at home tonight after eleven o'clock.'

He opened his briefcase and took out a clean shirt and a tie. 'I've got to go to the Chamber of Commerce dinner. So bugger off, all of you. I want to talk to Cameron.'

After they'd gone Cameron couldn't stop shaking. 'It's so awful,' she kept saying.

'I think it might be rather fun,' said Tony softly. 'When the right moment comes, I'll press the destruct button on the lot of them. They've no idea what they've taken on.'

As he came towards her, his breath was foul, as though all the hatred had churned and rotted inside him. His body stank of stale sweat. Trying not to flinch when he grabbed her, Cameron said, 'I thought you were dropping by this evening?'

'I'd like to, but it's not safe. Press'll be hanging round. Venturer might even put a private dick on to me.'

He was so mad to get inside her, he broke the elastic of her panties. It was all over in a minute.

'The bastards,' he groaned. 'They've all betrayed me.'

Then he took her throat between his hands. 'If you ever betray me, I'll kill you.'

Down the High Street at Radio Cotchester the Controller of Programmes received an irate telephone call from the Managing Director who'd never been near the station since Princess Michael opened it five years ago.

'I've just heard a very favourable interview with Bas Baddingham,' he roared. 'I don't want any more crap like that on Radio Cotchester. Tell all our presenters and DJs we're backing Corinium a hundred per cent throughout this campaign. After all, Tony Baddingham owns twenty per cent of us.'

Up the High Street at the *Cotchester News* the Editor was reading tomorrow's leader: '*Tony Baddingham's words to Declan O'Hara that people who get too big for their boots should go and wear out other people's carpets must ring hollow in his ears today when the mega-star Irishman and Penscombe resident headed a bid to oust Tony Baddingham and walk on Corinium's carpets himself after 15th December. Venturer, as he's called his consortium, appears to be soundly based financially, rich in talent and determined to grasp the infinite . . .'*

The Editor had read enough and buzzed for his leader writer. 'You can't publish this! We own twenty per cent of Corinium, and Tony Baddingham owns twenty-five per cent of us. Go back and rewrite it.'

'Corinium may not be perfect,' the leader writer retyped defiantly. *'What company is? But it has now reached a level of performance far beyond that which any newcomer could achieve in a few years. Corinium has a massive expansion programme, it has won countless awards, it has all the expertise it needs, and it has Cameron Cook.'*

Then he went out and got drunk.

Cameron finally tracked down Rupert at the House after he'd voted.

'Sweetheart, are you OK?' he said. 'How's Sledge-Hammer House of Horror? Has Tony had a seizure?'

'I hate you and I hate myself,' stormed Cameron. 'How dare Janey Lloyd-Foxe say Corinium's drama was abysmal, and that bloody Bishop attacking the morals of "Four Men went to Mow"!'

'That was tactless. I'm sorry, but if we don't knock you, Tony'll suspect something. How did he take it?'

'Fine,' said Cameron. 'Very together, very positive.'

'That's not what Barney Williams told me. He said it really pulled the Krug from under Tony's feet, and that he was quite hysterical. All this expansive crip-crap about welcoming competition came much later in the day.'

Cameron wasn't interested. 'Look, Rupert, I'm not sure I'm going to be any good as a double agent.'

'What's happened?'

'Seb's got to trail you to find out who you're sleeping with.'

Rupert laughed. 'He's going to have a very boring time

then. The only person I'm sleeping or likely to stay awake with is you.'

'Are you sure?' Cameron's voice broke. 'I'm so confused. It all happened so fast. I need to see you, just to talk.'

'I need to fuck,' said Rupert. 'I want you so badly at this moment, but it'd be madness. The press are still baying round. We've got to be careful.'

'I don't think I can handle it.'

'Yes, you can. You're very brave and strong, that's what I adore about you. You're very tired too. Take a couple of Mogadon and sleep in. And sustain yourself with the thought that one day in December we'll be awarded tickets on the one surviving gravy train.'

'I thought we were only interested in making good programmes,' said Cameron disapprovingly.

'Oh well, that, too,' said Rupert.

32

Within a week the IBA had provided the press with précis of all the applications and placed a copy of each application in their library so that the public could come and look at them.

Immediately, Tony dispatched Miss Madden to the IBA to transcribe Venturer's application in her neat shorthand. Going through the revolving doors, she met Ursula, Declan's secretary, on a similar mission.

'I'm not supposed to talk to you,' said Joyce.

'Nor I you,' said Ursula.

Both agreed, however, that much time could be saved if Ursula posted Joyce a copy of Venturer's application and Joyce sent Ursula a copy of Corinium's. Then they could pretend they had transcribed and typed them themselves, and pop over to Harrods instead for a lunch of breaded plaice, fruit salad and several glasses of sweet sherry before going to the cinema.

'We mustn't discuss the franchise or I'll get sacked,' said Joyce, 'but you've no idea how demented Lord B. was when he heard Declan was bidding against him. He's really out to get him now. It's a shame we're on different sides. I always liked Declan. He was such a nice man.'

Having read Venturer's application, Tony launched his counter-offensive.

'It would be foolish to denigrate the competition,' he told the press expansively, and then proceeded to do so.

He also spent a lot of time playing his staff off against each other, having them in individually, offering them large drinks and cigars in his most urbane and disarming manner, then telling each one they were the one person he really relied on to spy on the rest. Pinned on the board was a new notice reiterating instant dismissal for any member of staff found having dealings with any of the Venturer or Mid-Week consortiums.

The Bishop of Cotchester was therefore rather bewildered when, every time he walked down the High Street or round the Cathedral close and tried to pass the time of day with any of the eight hundred Corinium staff, they bolted like squirrels up the nearest tree.

The following Sunday Declan called a Venturer meeting at The Priory. Janey and Billy couldn't make it, nor could Wesley Emerson. But Wesley had vindicated himself by already taking twenty-five wickets and wearing the Venturer T-shirt on every possible occasion.

Georgie, Seb and Charles (who was wearing a tin hat and brandishing a riot shield borrowed from Wardrobe) all turned up giggling hysterically in James Vereker's very distinctive pale-blue Porsche.

'The silly bugger left it in the Corinium car park and a second set of keys in his office,' said Georgie. 'We're going to abandon it outside your house later this afternoon, Enid, then ring up Tony and tip him off.'

'How's it going?' said Freddie.

'Tony's in a vilely twitchy mood,' said Charles, 'bugging everyone's telephones. You'd better watch out, Declan. If our chief engineer rolls up in a yellow van heavily disguised as a British Telecom mechanic, don't let him in.'

It was such a mild day they all sat outside. Apple blossom and lilac were both out and wafting their sweet fragrance. Cow parsley frothed up to meet the trailing young green leaves and white candles of the horse chestnuts round the lawn. The rushing stream was clogged with forget-me-nots and marsh marigolds, and, although the bluebells were fading, the wood was now lit up by the white flowers of the wild garlic. It was definitely a day to be in love. Rupert turned up with Cameron, who was safe because Tony had gone to Rugborough to watch Archie play cricket. She and Rupert had obviously just got out of bed. Their hair was still wet from the shower. She sat on the lawn propped against him, her hand on his thigh. They looked lean, glamorous and intensely separate.

Great excitement was caused by the arrival of the rest of the Venturer publicity material: badges, car stickers, bookmarks, peaked caps with adjustable straps at the back, which had to be taken in to fit Henry Hampshire's narrow stoat's head but let out for Dame Enid and Declan. The *pièce de résistance* was the poster. It was a blow-up from the group photograph of Taggie with Gertrude on her knee, both wearing Venturer T-shirts.

'It's fuckin' gorgeous,' said Freddie. 'Every garage mechanic will put it up in the service bay.'

'I'll have some for the bar,' said Bas.

'And I for the Close,' said the Bishop.

Both Dame Enid and Professor Graystock wanted several for the common room.

'Dirty old letch,' muttered Rupert, glaring at the Professor.

'I'll keep mine under my pillow,' said Seb, 'in case Tony drops in for coffee one evening.'

Only Cameron had been scornful when Rupert had showed the poster to her earlier.

'It's too fucking kitsch for words,' she snapped.

'I thought you might like to have a look at Corinium's rival offering,' said Georgie, unrolling a poster of Sarah Stratton cuddling a baby calf with a caption 'Corinium Cares' underneath. Her T-shirt had rather too many buttons undone.

'"Corinium Bares", more likely,' said Rupert dismissively. 'Venturer have definitely won the battle of the Crumpet. Here, let me carry that, angel,' he went on, leaping to his feet as Taggie came out with a huge chocolate cake and a plate of cucumber sandwiches on a tray.

Taggie couldn't meet his eyes, nor did she say anything when she saw the poster. It reminded her too poignantly of when she'd still been happy, when Rupert had not yet rolled up with Cameron.

After tea Declan came to the serious bit.

'For the next two months,' he told them, 'while the IBA are sifting through the applications before the public meetings begin in July, our job is to get Venturer across to the area. We got off to an excellent start. With such a dazzlingly flamboyant panel –' he grinned round at them – 'publicity has been no problem. Now we've got to get out and meet the people who matter – in the Town Halls, the Chambers of Commerce, the Rotary Clubs all round the area – and show them we're not just a bunch of dilettantes.

'We've also got to cast our net wide to cover schools, colleges, churches, young farmers, job centres, the police, sports clubs, political groups, race relations officers, etc., etc. We must let them know what we intend to do, find out how we can help them, and then sign them up as friends of Venturer. We'll collect a huge petition of names and organizations to send the IBA. But it'll have far more effect if they can also be persuaded to write a private letter to Lady Gosling giving their support.

'We must try to cover the entire area,' he went on. 'I know you're all busy and it's going to be a long hard slog, and obviously none of the Corinium moles or Billy or Harold can be seen to be doing anything.'

'I'll help,' pleaded Taggie. 'Please let me. I can drive round the area delivering handouts and telling people how good you are.'

'How can she possibly explain to anyone why they should support Venturer,' said Cameron too loudly to Rupert, 'if she can't read the fucking application?'

Seeing Taggie go crimson with mortification, Seb leapt to her defence. 'Put it on tape,' he said. 'I'll do it for you, Taggie. If I can't go round the area canvassing, it's the least I can do.'

Seb was as good as his word. Over the next two days he

not only put the most important points of the application on tape for her, but also the answers she should give to any questions.

'If they're a Leftie organization,' he explained, 'say we've got Professor Graystock, Lord Smith and your Dad in the consortium. If they're Tory, plug Freddie, Henry, Rupert and Marti Gluckstein. If they're SDP, bandy Dame Enid's name around.

'If anyone starts grumbling about sex and violence,' he went on, 'say we've got the Bishop of Cotchester and he's going to oversee all our programmes. On the other hand, if anyone says we haven't got enough sex and violence, say we've got Rupert, Bas and Wesley Emerson in the consortium.'

He coached her over and over again until her spiel was word-perfect. Taggie found him incredibly kind and patient.

'I wish I'd been taught by people like you at school,' she said wistfully.

And so the hard grind started. But as Rupert was chronically busy, and Freddie was tied up with his electronics empire, and Declan was locked into his biography of Yeats, and both professors were frantically coaching their students for finals, in the end most of the work fell to Taggie. With a car full of stickers, badges and posters, she drove round the vast area visiting everyone from trade unionists to youth leaders, from mothers' unions to arts councils, taking in every imaginable pressure group, begging them to sign her petition, to write to the IBA and best of all to come along and cheer Venturer at the public meeting in July. Because of her beauty, sweetness and passionate belief in her father's and Venturer's cause, she had surprising success.

Sometimes she was joined by the Bishop, sometimes by Dame Enid, which was great fun. Dame Enid had a convertible and they drove through the glorious Spring together with the roof down, getting brown, sucking lemon sherbets and calling an awful lot of people 'boring little farts' after they'd safely got them signed up. Driving round with Professor Graystock was less fun. He had a horrible habit of squeezing

Taggie's bare legs when he made a point, so she took to wearing trousers.

The third Saturday in May, however, was a very bad day for Taggie. She was tired because she'd been up very late doing a dinner party for Valerie Jones the night before. As she was scheduled to tour the Winchester area, which she didn't know, she'd put directions to all the places she had to visit on tape, but even so she got terribly lost and flustered.

On one of her calls she'd got the SDP muddled up with the Labour Party and started plugging Dame Enid when she should have been pushing Lord Smith and Professor Graystock. Then she'd called on a vile headmaster who'd made her tremble because he reminded her of school. 'How can Venturer help your school personally?' she asked.

'Well, get a pencil, write it down,' he said bossily.

'I'll remember it,' stammered Taggie.

'Write it down,' snapped the headmaster.

'I can't.' Taggie hung her head. 'I'm dyslexic.'

He was incredibly nice after that, giving her a glass of sherry. His eldest son who'd been killed in Northern Ireland had been dyslexic and he got out a lot of photographs to show her.

It was half past nine and getting dark when Taggie left and after ten before she managed to find her way to the gates of the local cricket club.

Perhaps they'd all gone home. But she could hear great whoops and catcalls coming from the pavilion, and, as she drew up outside, moths were bashing against the lighted windows.

Cricket – Taggie took a deep breath – that meant she had to plug Wesley Emerson's involvement and Venturer's entirely fresh approach to cricket coverage. Going through the door, she quailed. They were obviously having some all-male dinner. She couldn't see the white table-cloth for glasses. Scores of huge-shouldered men with brick-red faces and beer guts seemed to be grinning at her with unfocused lechery. A tawny giant up at the top table, fiddling with the microphone, looked vaguely familiar.

426

'I'm so sorry,' she stammered, clutching her stickers, posters and her petition, 'I'll come back some other time.'

'No, come in, sweetheart,' they all yelled.

A chunky dark youth rose to his feet and swayed unsteadily towards her.

'If you're from the Shalvation Army, I'm beyond shaving,' he said.

'Come back, darling,' roared the rest, as Taggie backed out through the door.

A slightly older man, who came up to Taggie's shoulders, and who seemed less inebriated than the rest, said he was the club secretary and asked if he could help.

'I just wanted to tell you about Venturer,' mumbled Taggie, 'and hoped you might sign our petition and put our stickers in your cars.'

'I'd much rather put you in my car,' said the chunky dark youth to roars of applause.

The club secretary then led her to the microphone and introduced her to the Captain, who had hard, rather unpleasant blue eyes. 'Lady wants to tell us about television,' he said.

'Well, go on then,' said the Captain nastily.

The tawny giant smiled at Taggie and sat down.

'I just wanted to tell you about Venturer television,' Taggie began in her soft growling teddy-bear voice. 'You probably know we're p-pitching for the Corinium franchise. We need your help in our campaign. We want to know how we can help you.'

'Give us a blow job, Lofty,' said a wag down the table to howls of laughter.

A bread roll sailed through the air, just missing her. Taggie blushed even deeper but ploughed on.

'Strip, strip, strip, strip,' intoned the Captain, banging on the table.

Soon the entire room took up the cry.

'Shut up, you meatheads,' yelled the tawny giant. 'Let her finish.'

Amazingly, after that they did shut up and, except for

427

the occasional Tarzan howl, heard her out in silence.

'I want you to know finally,' said Taggie, 'that Venturer will be providing an entirely new approach to cricket coverage. We're very interested in cricket at all levels, and er –' she froze for a second trying to remember – 'and Wesley Emerson –' she brought out the name in triumph – 'is a key member of our consortium and is specially interested in promoting cricket in schools, so you'll have some really good colts coming on in the future. Please support Venturer. Thank you very much.'

'I suppose we can now get on with the speeches,' said the Captain over the thunder of applause.

'I'm so sorry.' Taggie picked up the petition. 'Could you possibly sign this?' she asked the tawny giant who'd been so kind to her.

'Of course.' He took the petition from her. 'D'you want it signed to anyone?'

'No, no, just your name and the name of the cricket club.'

'That's a bit difficult, Lofty,' said the Captain bitchily. 'We don't play cricket, you see.'

'But this is a cricket club,' said Taggie, aghast.

'Maybe it is, darling, but this is the Winchley Rugby Club dinner and Bill Beaumont here –' he indicated the tawny giant – 'is our guest of honour and is waiting to speak to us, if you'd be so kind as to bugger off.'

Grabbing the petition, leaving the posters and the car stickers, Taggie fled sobbing into the night. How could she have been so stupid? She was absolutely no help to Venturer at all.

Her dyslexia always got worse when she was upset. As a result she got desperately lost on the way home. She couldn't read any of the unfamiliar names on the signposts, and once it got really dark she was frightened to stop the car and ask strangers the way. There were no stars, or moonlight or street lamps to guide her along the country lanes. She seemed to have been going round for hours and hours, until at last she saw a sign she could recognize: *Penscombe 2m.*

428

Gertrude was noisily delighted to see her, but the trail of clothes in the hall and up the stairs told her that her parents had gone up somewhat precipitately to bed. The débris of their dinner was still on the kitchen table, one of the lids of the Aga was up and Aengus had knocked over a half-full bottle of whisky which was still dripping on to the flagstones.

'Oh God,' sighed Taggie. 'Can't they ever do anything for themselves?'

The cow parsley she'd picked that morning was already shedding petals like scurf all over the Welsh dresser.

Nothing lasts, she thought in despair.

Across the valley, Rupert's house was almost blotted out by the trees. There were no lights on. He was probably tucked up in bed with Cameron. It was always when she was really tired that the longing became unbearable.

Rupert, in fact, had spent the day at the Cup Final, making the main speech at the official dinner afterwards. Despite horrific setbacks, he was the first Minister for Sport who'd tackled hooliganism head on, and when he sat down they cheered him to the rooftops.

After the dinner was over, however, he beat a discreet retreat, taking a bottle of brandy over to that other Wembley stadium, home of the Horse of the Year Show, where he persuaded an obliging groundsman with a couple of tenners to put on the lights.

Sitting in the competitors' stand, drinking out of his bottle, he proceeded hazily to relive his past glories as a show jumper. And suddenly the huge arena seemed to be filled with coloured jumps and with the ghosts of all his great horses: Revenge, Rocky, Belgravia, Mayfair, Arcturus, Snakepit and even the cussed Macaulay. He could hear the sound of the bell, the screams of the Pony Club, the roar of applause, even the voice of the commentator, Dudley Diplock, who always got the names wrong. Oh Christ, what was he to do?

Putting his head in his hands, he was overwhelmed with despair as he realized, despite his political triumphs and the buzz of pitching for the franchise and stealing Cameron from

Tony, how hopelessly empty his life was now. He hadn't got fat when he'd given up show jumping, or taken to drink, except tonight, or to boring other people with endless anecdotes about his sporting glories as so many other great athletes had. But something had died inside him.

It was nearly midnight. The government car was still waiting outside. The groundsman wanted to lock up.

'Probably fallen asleep,' said Sydney, Rupert's driver. 'He's a devil for dropping off anywhere. I'll go and wake him.'

But when Sydney tapped him on the shoulder, the face Rupert raised was so stricken and haggard, that Sydney was prompted to ask if there'd been a death in the family.

'Only myself,' muttered Rupert, chucking away the empty bottle and stumbling to his feet. 'Only myself.'

Taggie had just finished clearing up and feeding Gertrude the corned beef hash which Declan normally loved but had left half-eaten this evening, when the doorbell rang. Gertrude ran out barking as loudly as she could with her mouth full. Taggie followed, hastily kicking her mother's rather grubby bra and French knickers under the radiator. For a second she thought she must be dreaming, for there, swaying in a dinner jacket, clutching a red box, was Rupert.

'Hullo, angel. Thought I'd catch up on the gossip. Is your father in?'

'Yes, but he and Mummy have gone to bed.'

'I'm sorry. I saw a light on. Thought he might be working late.'

'Do you want a drink?'

Oh God! Suddenly she remembered. Aengus had knocked over the whisky.

'I've had enough,' said Rupert. 'I'd love a cup of coffee.'

His normally sleeked-back blond hair had flopped over his forehead, his black tie was crooked, his blue eyes crossing. Taggie realized he was absolutely plastered.

'You didn't drive down?' she said in horror.

'No, no, Syd dropped me off, Now, whatever I do I mushn't

430

lose this.' Carefully he put his red box down on the kitchen table. 'My red box, my unread box. I sometimes wonder if anyone would notice if I threw the whole lot in the Thames.'

'Where have you been?' said Taggie, putting the kettle on, wondering if by some miracle he might have had a bust-up with Cameron.

'To the Cup Final.'

'Of course. You were making a speech. How did it go?'

'All right, I suppose. The speech that the department had written was so ghastly I tore it up and told a lot of blue stories instead. I hope no one was there from Corinium with a tape recorder.'

'And they liked it?'

'They seemed to. They could afford to be kind. It's probably the last one I'll make.'

'What d'you mean?' Taggie put three spoonfuls of sugar into the blackest cup of coffee and put it down on the table in front of him.

'Thanks, darling. The PM's announcing the election date as Thursday 24th June. At least I won a bet on it.'

'But you'll win,' said Taggie, sitting down at the table beside him.

Rupert shrugged. 'I'm not sure we will. The awful thing is, I don't give a bugger. I'm fed up with politics.'

'You'll feel differently tomorrow,' said Taggie.

At that moment Gertrude strolled in, looked beadily at Rupert, then, to Taggie's amazement, jumped on to his knee and gave his face a quick lick, before settling down, leaving white hairs all over his dinner jacket. Rupert stroked her and laughed.

'There are some small victories left to me,' he said.

'Was C-C-Cameron with you?'

Taggie felt it would be better if they could talk about her openly.

'No, it was much too public. Every photographer would have picked us up. Anyway, Tony's *in situ* this weekend.'

'It must be awfully difficult for you both.'

'Worse for her. At least I don't have to sleep with Tony. I wish she wasn't so fucking insecure. She's like a Jack Russell. One spends one's time removing her from the target of her aggression – usually oneself.'

'Patrick said she had a terrible childhood,' said Taggie. 'He didn't give any details,' she added quickly. 'Just said she'd really been through it.'

What on earth am I doing defending her, she wondered.

'I don't believe all that junk about terrible childhoods,' said Rupert. 'I've had four stepmothers and five stepfathers. You had Declan and Maud, which is even worse.'

Taggie giggled.

'We're not screwed up,' said Rupert.

That was debatable, thought Taggie.

Rupert picked up the petition. 'Look at all these names!' His eyes ran down page after page. 'Christ, you've been working hard.'

'It wasn't so good today,' said Taggie. Then she told him about the rugger club.

Rupert was absolutely furious. 'The bastards,' he howled. 'Give me their names and I'll get their ground ploughed up. But what can you expect from a lot of rugger yobbos? Poor darling, I'm so sorry. It must have been awful.'

He yawned without even putting his hand over his mouth, showing a long pink tongue, and teeth without a single stopping. Then he said, 'Why have you written L and R on the back of your hands?'

Blushing, Taggie shoved her hands under the table.

'I'll drive you home,' she said quickly.

As she started up the car, the tape came on. Frantic with embarrassment, she tried to tug it out of the machine, but Rupert's hand closed over hers like a vice.

'Leave it.'

'Turn left at the A412,' said Taggie's deep breathy voice, 'then keep going for two miles, then turn left just before the Old Mill pub, then keep going till you come to a big barn, turn right, then left up a winding road. Winchley Women's Institute is at the top on the right.'

432

Pulling out the tape, Rupert looked up at the windscreen, on which a large capital L and R were stuck on opposite sides.

'You poor little duck,' he said softly.

The chestnut candles were shedding their white petals along his drive, a couple of horses blinked in the gloom. As Taggie drew up in front of the house, he said again, 'You poor little duck.'

Taggie hung her head. 'I can't map-read very well. It takes me so long and signposts are difficult too, because I don't know the words. If I put it on tape it speeds everything up, and we've got so much ground to cover before July.'

Rupert couldn't bear it. What was it about Taggie that so often brought a lump to his throat?

'Angel, you can't go round on your own. Particularly not at night.'

'I don't always. Dame Enid's come with me, and the Bishop, and Professor Graystock once or twice.'

Rupert shuddered. 'That's worse than being alone.'

Enforced celibacy was not natural to Rupert. It was like asking a man who smoked sixty cigarettes a day only to smoke ten cigarettes one day a week. Denied Cameron, he was certainly not used to sleeping alone. Still very drunk, he only just stopped himself taking Taggie in his arms to comfort her, and Christ knows where that would have led to. Declan would take him apart and Cameron would bolt straight back to Tony.

Getting out of the car, however, a brilliant idea struck him. 'I'll be travelling all round the area canvassing over the next month. You can come with me and hand out Venturer posters and stickers, and paddle the Venturer canoe at the same time. We can even use the Tory loudspeaker to plug Venturer when no one from the Party's listening.'

'Is that allowed?' said Taggie in awe.

'Politics is a dirty business,' said Rupert blandly. 'The Socialists paid a lot of actors twenty-five pounds to dress up in shit order and pretend to be a dole queue for their election poster last time.'

33

Next morning Caitlin rang up The Priory, wild with excitement.

'Gertrude's in the *Daily Mail*! She looks so sweet.'

'What's she doing?' asked Taggie.

'Wearing a Venturer T-shirt and an expression of absolute outrage. She's sitting on your knee. You look nice, much better than that old tart Sarah Stratton.'

'Oh goodness,' said Taggie. 'What's the piece about?'

'The headline says: "*Rival Beauties weigh in for the Battle of the Box*",' read Caitlin. 'They've used the two posters of you and Sarah. "*Will the blonde or the brunette pack the greater punch?*" it starts. Then there's a lot of guff about Sarah being Paul Stratton's second wife, and Corinium's latest star presenter, who pulls in three hundred fan letters a week.'

'Then it goes on: "*The dark horse (or rather beauty) in the race is Agatha O'Hara, 18-year-old daughter of TV megastar Declan O'Hara, who's bidding to oust his ex-boss Lord Baddingham in the Corinium franchise fight. Agatha runs her own business*" . . . get you . . . "*cooking for the great and famous, but sadly she can no longer undertake dinner parties for her favourite client, Tony Baddingham's wife, Monica, in case state secrets slip out over the soufflé.*"'

'Gosh,' said Taggie in amazement. 'Where did they get all that from? I hope Lady B isn't cross. How are you anyway?'

'All right. Fed up with revising. Can you send me some

money? And tell bloody Mummy and Daddy to write.'

'They've been really busy with the franchise and things,' said Taggie.

'Mummy's never busy with anything,' said Caitlin bitterly.

The long, hard grind of getting Venturer's message across to the people who mattered continued throughout the long, hot summer. But things were much easier now for Taggie. Several other papers reproduced the poster and, as she toured the area, people began to know all about Venturer, recognize her, welcome her and even ask her to autograph the poster.

More important, she spent much of May and June driving around with Rupert on his campaign trail. Leaving him to canvass or to rally support for other South-West Tory MPs. Taggie nipped off to visit vicars, youth clubs and Chambers of Commerce.

Rather too often for Tony Baddingham or Central Office's liking, the two campaigns merged. Rupert was not above urging people to support Venturer on the Tory loudspeaker, or sticking Venturer posters up on the van alongside those urging the public to vote Conservative. Everywhere he and Taggie went, they handed out Venturer publicity material and had great fun after dark, driving round plastering the gateposts of Corinium directors, and even the Corinium building itself, with 'Support Venturer' stickers.

To add to Tony's apoplexy, Rupert conducted the entire campaign in a blue Venturer T-shirt and twice appeared similarly clad on 'Cotswold Round-Up', and, even worse, with huge 'Support Venturer' posters on the Tory party van behind him.

Tony was quoted as saying the Venturer T-shirts had been chosen entirely by Rupert to match his blue eyes, and that no doubt the boy shading his forehead on the front symbolized all those Gloucestershire husbands trying to see where Rupert had hidden their wives. Rupert cracked back that everyone knew who the Corinium Ram was supposed to symbolize.

And so the mudslinging went on, with the local press and radio stations uniformly backing Corinium, but the National and Trade press, having scrutinized the applications and the candidates, universally agreeing that Venturer had the more exciting programme plans. Dame Enid wrote a battle song, sung by Maud, called 'Everything Venture', which to Venturer's relief didn't get into the charts.

On 24th June Labour won the election by twenty seats, with the SDP holding the balance of power. Paul Stratton lost his seat. Rupert kept his. He had, in fact, fought a brilliant campaign. Taggie's presence seemed to soothe him, so he was far less acerbic with bores and hecklers, and, as he was one of the only Tories returned with a much increased majority, Central Office had to stop grumbling about him using Tory funds and equipment to promote Venturer.

In an unprecedented move, Owen Davies, the new Labour Prime Minister, asked Rupert whether he would like to stay on as Minister for Sport if the post was made non-political. Rupert was deeply touched, but refused. He was fed up with swimming galas and ping-pong matches, and there was a big row brewing about players taking drugs at Wimbledon, which he was only too happy to hand on to his successor. He was also immediately offered a job by the International Olympics Committee, but refused that too for the moment, knowing it would mean more buzzing round the world.

He wanted a breathing space, to spend the rest of the summer at home concentrating on the yard, seeing something of his children and putting in a lot of spade work with Cameron, who was getting increasingly uptight. Falling more and more in love with Rupert, she found it almost impossible to pander to Tony's sexual needs and cope with the demanding job of Programme Controller at Corinium. While Rupert was fighting the election, he'd been constantly hounded by the press, baying for franchise gossip and trying to catch him out in some new affair, so he and Cameron had had to be doubly careful.

'All this secrecy's just like adultery, darling,' said Rupert on one of their few meetings. 'Very good training for when you're married.'

'That is the most cynical remark I've ever heard,' stormed Cameron.

'Not at all. The secret of a happy marriage is not getting found out.'

'How d'you know? You didn't have a happy marriage.'

'That's because I was always getting found out.'

As the election was over, and Tony was tied up all day in meetings in London, she and Rupert had arranged to meet at a hotel outside Henley. As they settled down to Bloody Marys and a splendid view of the Thames, a barge came chugging up stream. Two young girls in bikinis were sunbathing on deck. Cameron watched Rupert run an expert eye over them. Now he had free time on his hands, would she find it increasingly difficult to hold him? All the same, she was still not prepared to burn her boats with Corinium until Venturer had safely won the franchise, and, she had to confess, all the secret meetings with Rupert did give the affair a certain edge.

'Come on,' he said, draining his Bloody Mary and picking up the keys of their hotel bedroom. 'I want to indulge in some mole-molesting.'

But she who lives more lives than one, more deaths than one, must die. Next day, in the Corinium canteen, Daysee Butler and Deirdre Kilpatrick took their cottage cheese and kiwi-fruit salads to a corner table and didn't notice Cameron sitting next door.

At first there were the usual grumbles about bosses and crews, but just as Cameron had abandoned her shepherd's pie half-eaten and started on her yoghurt, Deirdre said, 'I don't usually read the *Scorpion* but did you see that story that Rupert Campbell-Black's having an affair with a cook?'

'Cameron Cook?' said Daysee in amazement. 'Lord B won't like that.'

'Not Cameron Cook – a cook. Declan O'Hara's daughter. She does directors' lunches and things. She's seriously pretty. Well, according to the *Scorpion*, she's been canvassing with Rupert and now they're absolutely inseparable.'

Looking down, Cameron saw she had squeezed her yoghurt so hard that it had spurted all over the table. Without

437

attempting to clear up the mess, she walked out of the canteen into Cotchester High Street and the nearest telephone box.

Rupert was trying out one of his new, very young horses over a row of fences in the field beyond the stables. When the telephone suddenly rang in his pocket, the horse nearly took off back to Ireland. Even when he'd pressed the answer button to silence the ringing, it took all his strength to pull up the terrified animal. All Cameron could hear was a muffled thunder of hooves and expletives.

'Hullo,' Rupert said finally.

'Have you seen the *Scorpion*?'

'Yes. So what?'

'All about you and Ms O'Hara.'

'That was yesterday's *Scorpion*. They've linked me with Mary Whitehouse this morning.'

'Can't you be fucking serious?' screamed Cameron. 'Everyone's talking about it.'

'Good,' said Rupert. 'At least it keeps the heat off us.' Then, as Cameron showed no signs of calming down, he added, 'Darling, there's nothing in it, I promise you. As Taggie said in today's *Star*, "Rupert's old enough to be my father. In fact he's a friend of my father's".'

'Doesn't mean a thing – Augustus John was old enough to be a lot of girls' great-grandfather – that didn't stop him. Oh Christ . . .' she screamed as her money ran out. 'I'll call you back in a minute.'

'Please don't until you've cooled down,' said Rupert. 'I don't want both you and the horse having hysterics at the same time.'

Next time they met, it took a great deal of sweet-talking to win her round.

The next big event in the franchise battle was the public meeting held in Cotchester Town Hall at the beginning of July. Chaired by members of the IBA board, it was supposed to give the general public the chance to air their grievances about existing programme content and quiz the rival applicants about their plans. It also gave the IBA the opportunity

438

to observe the applicants in action and gauge the degree of local support.

In fact, the audience consisted mostly of Corinium, Venturer and Mid-West staff and their local supporters, members of consortiums from other franchise areas who would soon go through the same ordeal, picking up tips, local councillors whose sole object was to persuade Venturer or Mid-West that their borough was the perfect site for the new studios, members of Gay Lib, the Women's Movement and other pressure groups, and a handful of the public, only interested in gazing at Declan, Rupert and Wesley Emerson.

Much-needed rain had been bucketing down all day, but it stopped just before the meeting was due to start. Venturer arrived first. As Rupert had given them all a pep talk about being properly dressed, Declan had sulkily put on a suit and a tie.

'And you can get out of jeans,' he had snapped in turn at Taggie. 'I've hardly seen your legs since you were born.'

Taggie, having rifled through her wardrobe in despair, had rushed into Cheltenham and bought a beautiful violet dress with a scooped neckline, a nipped-in waist and flounced gypsy skirt. Newly washed, her dark hair fluffed down to her shoulder blades as though she'd beaten it with an egg whisk.

Declan, in somewhat unflattering amazement, told her she looked absolutely gorgeous. She was glad she did, when she later found that Sarah Stratton, Cameron, Daysee and Janey had all pulled out the stops. To Taggie's delight she also found the audience packed with people whose support she had sought in her drives round the area. Local councillors, race relations officers, social workers, ladies from the WI, from as far afield as Southampton, Oxford and Stratford, had turned up and now surged forward to shake her hand.

'We've still got your lovely poster up; we've written to the IBA; we've been following Venturer's programme with such interest,' they all said. 'We thought we'd come and cheer you on.'

'Remember me?' said a gaunt-looking man in a crumpled

lightweight suit, which had obviously just been unearthed from a trunk in the attic.

'Of course,' said Taggie, quite overwhelmed. 'How wonderful of you to turn up.'

It was the headmaster with the dyslexic son.

A diversion was caused when Marti Gluckstein, who'd never been to the country before, tried to enter the hall wearing gumboots, a waterproof deerstalker, a riding mac and holding an umbrella over his head.

'Don't bring that thing in here. It's unlucky!' boomed Dame Edith.

'Come on, Marti, I'll buy you a stiff drink before we kick off,' said Bas, guiding Marti back through the puddles over the road to the Cotchester Arms for a quick de-robing.

Sprinting after them, Rupert handed Bas his hip flask. 'Can you fill this up with weak rum for Wes? His attention span will never last the course unlaced.'

Wesley, having taken another five wickets that afternoon, and having just been picked for the third test, had been celebrating and was now busy signing autographs.

The next arrivals were three shiny red-faced stocky young men, who'd obviously been in the Cotchester Arms since opening time, who strode up to Taggie waving their tickets. The shortest one, who had hard blue eyes and crinkly hair, thrust a melting box of chocolates into Taggie's hand.

'Hullo, Agatha,' he said. 'Bet you didn't expect us.'

'Sorry we were a bit rowdy when you dropped in,' said the second.

'Thought we'd come and give you a bit of support,' said the third.

It was the Captain and two props from Winchley Rugger Club. Tears filled Taggie's eyes as she hugged them all. 'How sweet of you. Come and meet my father. He adores rugger.'

Declan shook them all by the hand several times. 'Treat Corinium like the Welsh at Twickenham,' he said. 'And here they come.'

A great theatrical hiss went up from the Venturer camp as

440

the Corinium mafia trooped in. They were led by Tony, very brown from Ascot. Wearing a new dark-pink and blue silk shirt, a pink tie, and a pink carnation in his buttonhole, he managed to flash his teeth at everyone in the room except Venturer. He was followed by Ginger Johnson, Georgie Baines, who'd obviously had a few to steady his nerves, Mike Meadows, Head of Sport, Charles Fairburn, Seb Burrows, Simon Harris, who'd been allowed back in a consultancy capacity to impress the IBA, and whose straggly beard had turned quite white, Cyril Peacock, false teeth rattling, sweating through his suit, and Cameron, truculent in an elongated black T-shirt which came five inches above her knees. Sarah Stratton, wearing a dress in Virgin Mary-blue, with a white Puritan collar also to impress the IBA, brought up the rear with James Vereker, whose head was held high so more people could recognize him.

'I fear the Greeks when they come bearing Presenters,' muttered Declan.

'Who's chair?' James asked Charles Fairburn as the Corinium contingent sat down in the front row.

'Dunno. Belongs to the Town Hall, I should think,' said Charles.

'No,' said James impatiently, 'who's Chair?'

'I've just told you.'

'I'm asking you, who is chairing the meeting?'

'Oh.' Comprehension dawned on Charles's round red face. 'Might be Old Mother Goose –' which was everyone's nickname for Lady Gosling – 'but I wouldn't have thought she'd have bothered to come this far.'

Cameron grabbed a seat at the end of the row by the window, as far away from Tony as possible. All she could see was one of his beautifully polished black shoes, rotating as if he were doing an ankle-slimming exercise – a sign that he was nervous. The company *in situ* always got more flak at public meetings than those seeking to oust it. Tony, frightened of ridicule, knew he was in for a bumpy evening. The entire Corinium contingent studiously ignored Venturer – the committed from distaste, the moles from embarrassment.

441

Henry Hampshire, however, who'd been to a drinks party, had no such reservations.

'Hello everyone,' he beamed as he came through the door. 'Hullo, Taggie darling, you're looking beautiful. Hullo, Rupert.' Then, turning to the cringing Corinium contingent, boomed, 'Oh look, there's Charles, Georgie and Cameron. Must go and say hello.'

'Hen-ree,' hissed Rupert, grabbing his arm and whispering in his ear. 'You're not supposed to know they're on our side.'

'What?' said Henry loudly. 'What's that? How d'yer mean, not on our side? 'Course they are.'

Fortunately Tony was talking to the Archdeacon and didn't hear. As Rupert tried to explain, Henry looked as deflated as an English setter who's been told he's not going on a walk, then cheered up when he saw Daysee Butler.

'Who's she? She on our side?'

'No, she's with Corinium.'

'Damn shame, pretty girl like that, and that's Sarah Stratton next to her, isn't it? She's a damn pretty girl too. Why isn't *she* on our side? Met her shooting at Tony's.'

And next moment Henry had broken away from Rupert's restraining hand and marched across the room to talk to Sarah, who introduced him to Daysee.

'Just saying to Rupert, pretty girls like you should be on our side.'

Sarah giggled: 'I don't think Tony'd like that very much. How's your Springer spaniel?'

'How incredible you remembering that,' said Henry, now beaming down on the two girls like an English setter waving his plumy tail at two bitches. 'What are you both doing afterwards?'

'Bugger off, Henry,' snarled Tony.

'Hen-ree,' Rupert dragged him off.

Fortunately at that moment a diversion was provided by Basil returning with Marti, quite soberly dressed now, and Janey Lloyd-Foxe in a pink flying-suit.

'Hullo, Rupert darling.' Janey kissed him full on the mouth. 'Sorry I'm late.'

Rupert tugged up her zip to the bounds of decency, saying, 'For Christ's sake go and distract Henry.'

Basil took Rupert aside. 'I've filled up the hip flask for Wesley.' Then, dropping his voice, he whispered, 'Those lovely lips just puckered up to meet yours were round my dick at eight o'clock this morning.'

'What?' exploded Rupert. 'What did you say?'

'You heard,' said Basil, grinning.

'How dare you,' thundered Rupert. 'She's married to my best friend.'

''Course she is, and very happily. I'm just making sure she doesn't suffer from post-natal depression when Billy's away.'

Rupert might well have hit Bas across the room if the IBA – three members of the Board and various members of their staff – hadn't trooped in and taken up their places on the platform.

'We *are* honoured,' Charles whispered to James. 'Old Mother Goose *is* in the chair. The IBA must regard the outcome as by no means certain then, if she's come all this way to have a look.'

'I can't think why you're looking so cheerful,' said James fretfully. 'Venturer's bound to offer me a job if they get the franchise. I mean I am "Cotswold Round-Up", but, as they've got the Bishop to handle religious programmes, I can't see them wanting you.'

'Who are those deadbeats over there?' Janey asked Bas.

'The Mid-West consortium,' said Bas. 'Can't think they'll bother us much.'

Rupert, having at last persuaded Henry to stop chatting up Daysee and sit down, collapsed into a seat between Taggie and Declan.

'How the hell am I going to keep this lot under control until December?' he said.

Taggie giggled: 'Henry's certainly fallen for Daysee.'

'Let me not to the marriage of true mindlessness admit impediments,' said Declan.

.

443

The audience were now occupying every seat in the body of the hall, with Corinium spread out along the front row and Cameron at the far end by the window. Next to her, at right-angles, on a single row of chairs, sat the Mid-West consortium, who looked a pretty moth-eaten bunch. Facing them, also on a single row of chairs, forming a square with the platform, sat Venturer.

Lady Gosling, decided Cameron, looked more like a hedge-hog than a goose, a Mrs Tiggywinkle, with small twinkling intelligent eyes, a long thin nose, a pointed chin and rather wild grey hair, held down on either side by tortoise-shell slides. She wore no make-up and, despite the warmth of the evening, was smothered in several shawls over her olive-green wool dress. The cosy exterior, however, was deceptive and hid a rapier mind. As Head of an Oxford college, Gwendolyn Gosling had taught Russian. Her fellow dons were not altogether joking when they nicknamed her 'Khruschev'. There was shrewdness beneath the amiability, and the twink-ling eyes, like the stars, gave off little warmth.

For a hideous moment at the beginning of the meeting it looked as though no one was going to ask any questions. Then a man in spectacles got up and grumbled about the reception in Gloucester. Corinium's Chief Engineer got up to answer him, and the stupor produced by engineers at public meetings allowed everyone time to collect their thoughts.

More straightforward complaints then followed from local councillors who had not yet been interviewed by James on 'Cotswold Round-Up' that coverage in their area was pitiful.

Mrs Makepiece, James's daily, then rose to her feet, and, disclaiming any connection with Corinium, said 'Cotswold Round-Up' was the best programme on telly, and why couldn't it be on seven days a week. This was greeted by bellows of 'Rubbish' and 'Offside' from Taggie's rugger players.

One of the Corinium shop stewards, who'd just screwed a two-thousand-pound rise out of Tony for all his members, as well as a fat bribe for himself, shouted from the back that he wouldn't trust Declan O'Hara's mob further than he could throw them. His claim that industrial relations at Corinium

444

were second to none, however, were greeted by cries of 'si-down' from all over the hall.

'As Corinium fork out immediately whatever the unions demand and most of the technicians earn more than the Prime Minister, I should think industrial relations are second to none,' yelled Bas, to loud cheers from the Venturer supporters.

The Chairman of Chipping Sodbury's WI then rose to her feet and said in a ringing voice that her institute was sick to the teeth of news about Cotchester and nothing about Chipping Sodbury.

Remembering 'Miss Corinium Television', Rupert caught Declan's eye. 'She's forgotten Miss Chipping Sodbury's tits,' he whispered across Taggie.

Both men started to shake with laughter, until quelled by a cold look from Lady Gosling.

Tony rose to reply. 'I can assure you, madam,' he said smoothly, 'that, by an extraordinary coincidence, "Cotswold Round-Up" is due to visit Chipping Sodbury later this week.'

'Are we?' said James to Sarah, looking startled.

'In fact,' Tony went on warmly, 'we have super plans for the entire Cotswold area.'

'You've been here eight years. Why haven't we seen any of them?' bellowed Taggie's headmaster.

More cheers all round were counterpointed by snores from Mrs Makepiece.

'I've studied both Venturer's and Corinium's applications at the public library,' went on Taggie's headmaster, 'and Venturer's programme plans seem infinitely more imaginative. What I would like to ask Lord Baddingham is how much have his grandiose new plans for a multi-million-pound studio, for slots for every possible minority group, for cultural improvement and for spectacular entertainment been spawned by editorial inspiration or desire to hang on to his very lucrative franchise?'

Tony was about to rise and shout back over the deafening cheers, but James was too quick for him. 'James Vereker, "Cotswold Round-Up",' he announced, getting to his feet and turning sideways so he could be recognized both by the platform and the floor.

'Who's a pretty boy then?' catcalled Taggie's rugger captain.

'As anchorman of "Cotswold Round-Up,"' said James, 'I know I speak for each and everyone of us at Corinium from Tony Baddingham downward when I say that Corinium's ethos can be summed up in two words.'

'Bloody terrible,' said Taggie's rugger captain, to screams of laughter.

'Two little words –' James ploughed on – 'Corinium cares.'

'The only fing Tony Baddingham cares abart is making a fast buck,' shouted Freddie, to more deafening cheers.

Mrs Makepiece snored so loudly that she woke herself up. 'Let's get up a partition,' she said loudly.

Cameron knew she ought to stand up and defend Corinium, but she didn't relish getting ripped apart by Declan. She was saved by the Women-in-Broadcasting lobby, who all had moustaches and who complained that there weren't enough women in any of the consortiums. Lady Gosling nodded in agreement, and made notes.

The meeting droned on. Wesley Emerson had had a hard day in the field. No one but Rupert and Bas realized that each time his noble head nodded onto his right buttonhole he was taking a long suck of rum from a straw to Rupert's hip flask in his breast pocket.

Outside in Cotchester Park, the lime trees were in flower; their sweet delicate scent, stronger after the downpour, drifted in through the open window. Cameron watched the house martins swooping after insects, flashing their white bellies. The tennis courts were packed with people playing vigorous Wimbledon-inspired tennis. In a week or so they'd revert to their usual patball. She glanced surreptitiously across at Rupert, who was sitting next to that drip Taggie, who (whatever Rupert said to the contrary) had a thumping crush on him.

Nothing except for the occasional yawn, not even a glance

in her direction, betrayed the fact that Rupert had left her bed at six o'clock that morning. Cameron wondered sometimes if she'd imagined the whole thing. She was so deep in thought, she had to be nudged in the ribs by Seb to answer a question from a pale girl from Gay Lib as to whether the lesbian shepherdess who'd appeared briefly in the last series of 'Four Men went to Mow' would appear in the next one.

As Cameron sat down, the Chairman from Chipping Sodbury's WI returned to the attack. 'Nothing that comes from Corinium TV,' she said, 'is truly regional. Even Dorothy Dove speaks with a London accent.'

Another rabble-rouser, again heavily bunged by Tony, then rose to his feet.

'While we're on the subject of accents,' he sneered, 'in the first week of July four people were brutally butchered by the IRA. Do we really want an Irishman, namely one Declan O'Hara, bearing in mind his left-wing attitudes and the subversive nature of many of his programmes, to be the Chief Executive of an English television company?'

'Out of order,' screamed the Venturer contingent.

'Offside, put it in straight,' roared the rugger players.

Declan, who'd gone white, was just about to answer.

'Careful,' whispered Rupert.

'I'd like the speaker to withdraw that remark,' said Lady Gosling frostily. 'Next question, please.'

The Clean-Up Television Campaign, headed by the Archdeacon, then started slamming sex and violence, followed by the Bishop of Cotchester who said how concerned he was about his flock, and that he would be working with Venturer to reduce not only sex and violence, but the very widespread blasphemy on television. He was just getting into his stride when Henry Hampshire's ancient gardener staggered to his feet.

'I like to go to bed very early,' he grumbled. 'I do wish Corinium wouldn't put all those sexy fil-lums on so late at night, because I and the missus can never stay awake to watch them.'

Everyone roared with laughter, including Lady Gosling, who then clapped her hands and said it was with great regret that she had to bring this very stimulating meeting to a close as they were running out of time. They would end, she added, with a seven-minute sales pitch from each of the three contenders.

Tony rose first, deliberately turning his back on Venturer and talking half to the platform and half to the audience.

'Good evening,' he began suavely. 'I am the Chief Executive of – er –' he glanced down at his notes and everyone laughed – 'Corinium Television. We have noted,' he went on, 'the very perceptive and instructive points raised tonight, and, although we don't agree with all of them, anyone who would like a further answer to his – or indeed, her –' he smiled broadly – 'question, please write to me personally.'

'Wanker,' muttered Rupert under his breath. He folded his arms belligerently and, with the hand that was hidden, fought a violent urge to caress the side of Taggie's left breast which swelled so seductively beneath her violet dress. She looked so ravishing this evening, and she'd done so well to get all those strange but incredibly influential people to the meeting.

Firmly clenching his hand away from Taggie, he looked across at Cameron, who was gazing moodily into space with a kind of deadpan, terrorist truculence. She reminded him of the girl grooms he used to pull in the old days. He desperately wanted a fuck, but he wouldn't get Cameron tonight. Tony, overexcited by the meeting, would no doubt take advantage of that release. Rupert was finding the enforced celibacy more and more trying, and, bloody hell, what was Bas doing pulling Janey? It seemed as though he was the only person in the world behaving himself.

Having finished a rousing spiel about Corinium's long and honourable record, Tony was now paying tribute to 'the thriving, creative community' he had the privilege to lead. 'We are aware, Ladies and Gentlemen, that there is life west of Harrods, our hearts are not in "Dallas", nor is our HQ in London. Our company is run by people from the region, who have a special place in the Cotswolds and, indeed, in West

Country life. Corinium is its own man here. We will be biased, we will fight for the West, we are pledged to serve the whole community. Above all we care.'

He sat down to moderate cheers. Then it was Mid-West's turn.

A fat man with straggly white hair staggered to his feet and then took ages to find his notes. 'That's obviously the geography master who never found his way to London,' whispered Rupert to Taggie.

'I am deeply honoured,' began the fat man.

'Name, name,' yelled the audience.

'My name is Cedric Bonnington,' he mumbled. 'I hope to be Chairman of Mid-West Television.'

'Well, don't be bashful, speak up,' shouted Tony's rabble-rouser.

Sadly, Cedric didn't. In a low mumble he laboriously read out that he was very interested in all the fascinating points that had been made by the floor.

'I cannot reveal who our backers are,' he droned on, 'but very substantial funds will be available should the very talented group, whose names I also cannot divulge at this stage, win the franchise.'

'He'll probably get it,' said Georgie Baines to Seb Burrows.

'What about women?' yelled the Women-in-Broadcasting lobby.

Cedric consulted his notes. The company's Programme Controller, whose name he also couldn't divulge, he said, would be a woman of the widest experience.

'Madame Cyn,' yelled Rupert.

'Mary Whitehouse,' said Tony's shop steward.

The audience waited for more exciting revelations, and, when none materialized, egged on by the Corinium consortium, who'd all got to their feet, started to drift away. It was almost dark outside; the pubs beckoned.

'No one's going to stay and listen to Daddy,' said Taggie in anguish, and, as Declan got up to speak, people were swarming out into the High Street.

'I'd like first to answer the speaker who questioned the

449

right of an Irishman to run an English television company,' he began softly. 'As much right perhaps as that great Irishman, the Duke of Wellington, to command a British army.'

He spoke without notes. As people poured back into the hall again, the deep soft husky voice carried easily round the hall.

'I am proud to be Irish,' he went on, 'and, to echo the words of another great Irish patriot, Irwin Cobb, I too had an ancestor who was out with the pikes in '98. He was captured by the English and tried for treason. They hanged him by the neck until he was dead, but his soul goes marching on, transmitting to his descendants, of whom I am proud to be one, the desire to fight against tyranny whenever I come across it. I also love and honour British television. It is the best in the world. That's why I and so many of my countrymen – Eamonn Andrews, Terry Wogan, Robert Kee, Frank Delaney, Dave Allen, Henry Kelly, Patrick Dromgoole, Gloria Hunniford – are over here, learning from it and, I hope, contributing to it.

'But we still go on fighting tyranny and oppression whenever we find it. I found it in the few months I worked for Corinium. That's why I walked out, and why, with my English friends –' he turned and smiled briefly at the Venturer consortium – 'I have put in a bid to oust Lord Baddingham.'

He then proceeded to carve up Tony and tear Corinium's boring sycophantic programmes to shreds. Only at the end did be briefly outline how Venturer would be different, how they would truly both represent the area and foster local talent. 'I would like all great artists of the future to be able to say they had their first chance at Venturer.'

The audience stood up and cheered him for nearly three minutes. Stony-faced, Tony strode out of the hall. Cameron tried to follow him, but, trapped by the crowd, she watched Rupert, Declan, Taggie and the rest of Venturer, plus their supporters, jubilantly swanning off to the Bar Sinister for drinks on the house. Rupert never gave her a backward glance. Sick with desire, she wondered how much longer she could go on playing a double game.

Although the *Cotchester News* reported the meeting a rousing success for Corinium and published numerous rigged readers' letters of support, it was generally agreed that Venturer had won that round.

34

After his humiliation at the public meeting, Tony stepped up his campaign to discredit Venturer. Flipping through a list of their names the following morning, he decided his newsroom had been singularly inept in uncovering any dirt. The Bishop of Cotchester, it seemed, had neither fiddled with the collection nor with any of his more cherubic choir boys; Dame Enid had never straddled anything more exciting than her cello; Professor Graystock was recognized as an old goat, but no more so than the average don. On the other hand, Henry Hampshire was plainly capable of being led astray by Daysee Butler. Perhaps she ought to be sent off to interview him.

Nothing as yet on Rupert, except an alleged walk-out with Taggie O'Hara, which Tony didn't believe. She was far too gormless. All the same it might be a good idea to allow her to cook for Monica again. Primed with a few late-night brandies, she might become indiscreet about the moles who were joining Venturer from other companies. In addition Monica had been so outraged because Tony'd banished Taggie from the house that she'd refused to give any more dinner parties, and Tony did need to entertain some of those boring but influential local dignitaries who might otherwise drift towards Venturer.

He added Taggie's name to the list, but that didn't bring him any nearer Rupert. He made a note to track down Beattie

Johnson, who'd been writing Rupert's memoirs when Rupert booted her out last year. There must be some grievances to fan there.

Freddie Jones, Tony decided blackly, was Venturer's greatest asset. He was so solid, so dependable, so popular, so hugely successful after such a lowly start, which appealed to a crusading streak in the IBA. Ha! thought Tony, *cherchez la femme*. He buzzed Miss Madden. 'Will you tell James Vereker to come up.'

James was not happy. Even through his layers of egotism he realized he'd made a fool of himself at the public meeting. He was still miffed because no one had asked him to join their consortium, and, opening a new edition of *Who's Who in Television* that morning, he'd discovered two columns devoted to Declan and not even a reference to himself.

James brushed his hair and put on a tie. He hoped Tony wasn't still miffed about the public meeting.

Tony, however, was at his most amiable, steering James towards the squashy green sofa, when usually he made male staff perch on hard-backed chairs, telling Madden they didn't want to be disturbed, offering James a large drink.

James normally only drank Perrier at lunchtime, both for his figure and to keep his wits about him for his programme, but now he felt it fitting to accept a large Bell's, just to show that he and Tony were both males capable of holding their liquor.

'I've got a very special mission for you, James,' said Tony.

Half an hour later James returned to his office in a state of euphoria to find Sarah exuding Anaïs Anaïs and expectancy.

'Are we lunching, darling?'

'Probably,' said James. 'I've got to make a call.'

When he rang Valerie Jones, she was absolutely 'delaighted' to hear from him. 'Oh, don't mention that silly franchise. If one can't talk to one's friends,' she said. 'I was going to phone you and your – er – lovely wife –' she always forgot Lizzie's name – 'to remind you that we're opening Green Lawns to the public on Saturday, and we hoped you'd both pop in. It is looking really rather lovely at the moment.'

453

'What an extraordinary coincidence,' said James. 'I was phoning to say of course we've got your opening in our diary and we were hoping we might come and film it for "Cotswold Round-Up". We're only covering the best gardens. Tony and Monica's, of course, and the Duchess's at Badminton. Hullo, hullo, are you still there?'

'She's fainted,' said Sarah.

'Of course I am,' shrieked Valerie.

'Could I come for a recce this afternoon? Will Freddie be there?'

'He's away.'

'Good,' said James wolfishly. 'Give me a chance to get you on my own.'

Valerie's tinkle of laughter showed she was not displeased.

'What *are* you playing at?' asked Sarah as James hung up.

'Tony wants a spy in the Venturer camp. He's chosen me because he thinks I'm the one guy who can charm secrets out of Valerie.'

'The spy who came in from the cold frame,' giggled Sarah. 'Are you going to stick poison umbrellas into Valerie's garden gnomes?'

It was a muggy, still afternoon, French-grey sky on the horizon deepening to forget-me-not blue overhead. The tall seeding grasses in the hayfields were turning gold against the deep summer greens of the trees. At the bottom of the Jones's drive was a large sign saying: 'Garden Open on 13th July, to be televised on "Cotswold Round-Up". Come and meet James Vereker in person – proceeds to the Red Cross.'

Smirking, James drove up a black tarmac drive as wide as the M1. Long before he reached the house he was almost blinded by a blaze of colour. Every flowerbed was packed with serried clashing ranks of French marigolds, yellow calceolaria, royal-blue cineraria, flaming-red geraniums, billiard-ball pink zinnias and mauve asters. As he drew up in front of the house a lorry was unloading plants. Having denuded every garden centre for miles around, Valerie was now hiring four hundred scarlet salvias and three hundred yellow begonias from Rent-a-Garden.

Round the corner came a sweating youth pushing a wheel-barrow crammed with scarlet and mauve petunias. Next moment Valerie came screaming after him, brandishing a small fork.

'What are you doing, Spicer?'

'Putting them on the rubbish heap, ma'am.'

'They're meant to be planted in the wheelbarrow, you idiot. Can't you recognize creative gardening when you see it? Take it straight back to the patio.'

Then she saw handsome James getting out of his pale-blue Porsche and her face softened.

'James,' she said, holding out both her hands, 'it's been too long.'

'You're looking lovely, Mousie,' said James, taking her hands and holding them, also a little too long. 'And so's your garden.'

'It's a miracle if it is,' said Valerie. 'Our darling old gardener dropped dead last week – wasn't it maddening? – and we're having to make do with jobbing gardeners, like that idiot. No, not that way,' she screamed as another jobbing gardener was carted across the lawn slap into a bed of mauve dahlias by an out-of-control computerized mower.

When she'd finished berating that gardener, Valerie swept James round to the patio and asked him if he'd rather have iced coffee first or wander round.

James said he'd rather have iced coffee, and sat down very quickly on the hammock seat, for fear of being concussed by half-a-dozen hanging baskets weighed down by every colour of petunia. But although he coyly patted the seat beside him, once Valerie had poured the iced coffee she insisted on prowling the patio, dead-heading petunias and showing off her slim figure in the floral pink shirt-waister.

'What's happened to your poor legs?' asked James, noticing several marks on the back of her calves.

'Bites,' sighed Valerie. 'I seem fatally attractive to midges.'

'And to men, Mousie.'

Valerie smiled. She wasn't going to tell James that Henry Hampshire had promised to take Freddie and her fly-fishing, and that she'd spent all day practising on the lawn and catching the backs of her legs with the hooks.

'Tony sent his special love, so did Monica,' lied James.

'Oh, we miss them both,' sighed Valerie. 'I do wish Freddie'd never got caught up in this stupid franchise. It's all so pointless.'

'D'you get roped into meetings?' asked James, sipping his coffee and wincing because the orange marigolds and magenta petunias in a nearby tub reminded him rather too forcibly of Ginger Johnson's face.

'No, no,' said Valerie, 'but the socializing side of it's quite fun. Henry took us to As-Cot; we had cocktails with him on the way home. I was shocked by the number of weeds in his seat. But they have made rather lovely use of white buddleia in the walled garden.'

'With such interesting programme plans, Venturer must have roped in some pretty considerable production people,' said James idly.

'I hope you like our border of massed glads over there,' said Valerie. 'Bring your coffee and let's have a wander.'

Having admired every petal, every gnome, every plastic Venus de Milo, James still hadn't learned anything more about Venturer.

'Freddie used to pop into Corinium a lot,' he said as they passed a dolphin regurgitating Blue Loo into a pond. 'Does he still see any of his old friends there? I bet they're knocked-out by this lovely garden.'

'It is lovely, isn't it?' said Valerie smugly, 'but I wish we could grow rhodos in Gloucestershire.'

'Are Venturer recruiting their staff locally?' asked James. 'Who else have they signed up?'

But Valerie was off leaping across a stream to tug up some mare's tail.

'I know Tony's keeping an eye out for moles at Corinium,' fished James as Valerie joined him again.

'So are we,' said Valerie. 'Moles are Freddie's biggest worry.'

456

'Perhaps we should compare notes, Mousie,' said James.

As they were now hidden from the house by a row of yellow conifers, he slid his hand around her waist. It was nice and trim.

'Well, Freddie's been putting down Mole-Ban everywhere,' said Valerie, 'but I'm still terrified I'm going to wake up tomorrow and find mole hills all over the lawn.'

James gave up. Mousie was far too preoccupied with her plot to think about plotting at the moment. He arranged that he and the crew would arrive at about three-thirty, and asked if she could keep any Venturer T-shirts and posters to a minimum.

'Tony feels you're so special and that a lovely garden is above personalities. But we really can't use the footage on "Round-Up" if it's full of plugs for Venturer.'

As James was filming gardens all Saturday afternoon, Lizzie had planned to work on her book. Then, feeling rather old and dried-up, she rubbed a lot of skin-food into her face, only to realize she'd forgotten her neck, which is supposed to betray your age most, so she rubbed the excess skin-food down into it. Then she remembered you were supposed never to rub skin-food downwards as it made your face droop. Would her life have been different, she wondered, if she'd always remembered to rub skin-food upwards? Would James have stayed faithful to her? Unwisely, knowing it would hurt her, she snooped around in James's drawers and found a ravishing photograph of Sarah Stratton under his boxer shorts. Feeling utterly miserable, she thought how nice it would be to see Freddie Jones again. Abandoning any thought of work, she decided to go along to Valerie's opening.

As she drove through Green Lawns's electric gates, she noticed a large 'Support Venturer' sticker on the huge sign announcing that James and Corinium Television would be present that afternoon. Lizzie felt so off James that she couldn't even be bothered to peel the sticker off. In the car park she found Rupert unashamedly sticking more Venturer stickers on everyone's windscreens.

'Darling.' He kissed her. 'Divided as we are by our rival consortiums, we shouldn't consort, but do let's go round together. I need a good laugh. Mrs Jones's new rockery is like the polar bear pit at the zoo; she's been training blow lamps on her roses all night and twenty-four-hour fluorescent lighting in the greenhouse is forcing out the Christmas roses.'

Lizzie laughed. 'You can't bring that dog,' she said as Rupert let Beaver out of his car. 'Particularly if he's not on a lead. Mrs Jones will have a coronary.'

'Good,' said Rupert, locking the car. 'Look how well he's trained,' he went on as Beaver lifted his leg on a cohort of salmon-pink petunias. 'Do you think Valerie drills her flowers every morning?'

'It's just like a park,' said Lizzie as they walked towards the house.

'Unfair to parks,' said Rupert.

On the edge of the lawn a stall was selling clothes from Valerie's boutique, with the mark-up going to the Red Cross. Models, sweating in Valerie's Autumn Range, wandered aimlessly round, fanning themselves with price tags. There was not a Venturer plug in sight.

'What a lot of people,' said Rupert. 'Judging by the mob on the lawn, your husband's holding court. Let's go the other way. Isn't that hell!' He pointed to a crescent-shaped flower bed crammed with fuchsias and French marigolds that looked as if it had been dug out by a pastry cutter. 'Lady Valerie of Vulgaria's gift for self-publicity is only equalled by her appalling taste.'

As they proceeded giggling down the crazy pavement, they could hear Valerie graciously dispensing advice on the other side of the yellow conifer hedge.

'How d'you manage to grow such whopping glads?' asked a neighbour admiringly.

'I feed them with Grow-More,' said Valerie.

'She's obviously been feeding her children the same thing,' muttered Rupert as poor fat Sharon, blushing at the sight of Rupert, waddled past them.

'Hullo, Bishop,' they could now hear Valerie screaming.

'How good of you to look in. I'm about to be interviewed on TV, but you'll find Fred-Fred in the grounds.'

'It'd be grounds for divorce if I was married to her; the only person not allowed into Valerie's opening is Fred-Fred. The frigid bitch,' said Rupert, grabbing Lizzie's arm. 'Come on, buck up, let's look at the pond. I don't want to get trapped with the Bishop.'

'I thought the Bishop was on your side,' said Lizzie, panting after him.

'He is, and a god-awful bore too. He's mad about Taggie, so he keeps dropping in at The Priory unannounced, and finding Maud and Declan having a bonk, or hurling plates at one another, which, bearing in mind the Bishop's views on sex and violence, doesn't go down very well.'

'I thought it was you having a walk-out with Taggie,' said Lizzie slyly as they passed Hybrid Teas, massed in clashing colours above totally weedless beds.

Rupert raised his eyes to heaven. 'Would that I were! She's *so* sweet.'

'Why aren't you then?'

'Declan would do his nut, and she's too young.'

'Never deterred you in the past.'

'Ah, but it's franchise year.' Rupert bent down to press a Venturer sticker on the bare belly of a plastic Venus de Milo. 'And we're all having to behave ourselves, as I'm sure your husband knows. Why have you got that rash on your hands?' he asked more gently as Lizzie whipped off the same sticker.

'The doctor says it's stress-related,' said Lizzie bitterly. 'Mistress-related, more likely.' Suddenly she could bear it no longer. 'James is having an affair with Sarah Stratton. I shouldn't have told you that. You'll leak it to *Private Eye* and discredit Corinium even further.'

'Why don't you leave him? He's such a cunt,' said Rupert, putting another sticker as a figleaf over a cherub, and dragging Lizzie on before she could remove it.

'Helen didn't leave you.' Lizzie paused to examine the pond which was a mass of scarlet and yellow water lilies. 'God, isn't this hell?'

'She did in the end,' said Rupert. 'Besides, I'm not a cunt.'

They had reached the end of the garden now; cornfields the colour of French mustard and bluey-green woods stretched to the horizon. On the right, a red tractor chugged back and forth, anxious to get the hay baled and away before tonight's promised rain.

'Heaven to see some decent country,' said Rupert. 'Do you think "cunt-ricide" means murdering one's mistress?'

Lizzie laughed. 'You do cheer me up. I wish someone would murder Sarah.'

Leaving the pond, they wandered back to the house and walking under a weeping willow went slap into Freddie.

He looked very tired, and only nodded at them politely until he realized who they were. Then he jumped up and down with pleasure, giving Lizzie a big hug.

''Ullo, Rupe, 'ullo Lizzie. 'Ow are you, love? You look grite. Better not let Valerie see Beaver, Rupe, she's a bit uptight. Been dead-'eading petunias in her sleep all night; fink she's abart to dead-'ead me. I've had this bleedin' lot up to 'ere. Let's go inside and 'ave a drink. Val's doing her TV interview. Finks the sun shines out of James Vereker's arse. Oh, sorry, love –' he squeezed Lizzie's arm – 'I quite forgot he was your 'usband!'

'James thinks the same,' said Rupert, spiking another sticker on a garden gnome's fishing rod. 'I'm sure he's only here because he wants to worm secrets out of your wife, Freddie.'

Although, watching the way Freddie and Lizzie were looking at each other, Rupert reflected that Lizzie, with all her warmth and sympathy, would be far more skilled at getting Venturer's secrets out of Freddie.

Cameron had expected to spend Friday night with Tony, but he'd decided to fly to France a day early, leaving her with an unexpected free evening. Unable to get in touch with Rupert, she'd taken two Mogadon, slept alone and very well for the first time in months and woke feeling rested and happy. As she wasn't due to meet Rupert until the evening, she decided to wander along and see how James was getting on filming gardens. She didn't stay long at The Falconry. The garden was too wonderful, and she didn't like such tangible proof of Monica's skills. She was surprised Tony hadn't stayed at home to crow.

By comparison Valerie's garden was utterly dreadful, but had certainly attracted large crowds, particularly round the television crew. Fighting her way through until she was blocked by a large bed of purple and salmon-pink gladioli, Cameron saw James up the other end interviewing Valerie and quickly stifled a scream of laughter. Valerie was dressed for Ascot in a yellow and white shirt-waister and a huge buttercup-yellow hat trimmed with yellow roses, but was totally unaware that someone had stuck a 'Support Venturer' sticker on her bottom.

Looking across the sea of mauve and salmon-pink, Cameron caught her breath in joy, because there, beside Freddie and Lizzie Vereker, also trying very hard not to laugh, was Rupert. As if drawn by her longing, he looked up and gave a brief grin of surprise before instantly resuming his normal deadpan expression.

'Cotswold Round-Up/Green Lawns/Take Four,' said the second assistant, snapping the clapper board.

'One only has to look at your flower beds, Valerie,' said James as the camera panned slowly in on the sea of mauve and salmon-pink, 'to appreciate what a truly caring gardener you are. Tell us your secret.'

'Well, James,' began Valerie; then her little laugh turned to a squawk of rage as the normally well-trained Beaver, suddenly seeing Cameron, who'd spent a great deal of time sharing his master's bed recently, crashed across the bed of gladioli, snapping and flattening most of them, and throwing himself on her in total ecstasy.

Just for a few seconds, to a crescendo of Valerie's squawks, Cameron and Rupert were caught on camera, absolutely collapsing with laughter, before Rupert sharply called Beaver off.

461

As she drove home rather tight later in the evening with James, Lizzie said, 'Cameron's the one you and Tony should be watching. I'm certain she's having an affair with Rupert.'

'Don't be ridiculous,' snapped James. 'Cameron only cares about Corinium.'

On Sunday night on his way back from France, where he'd made great strides in acquiring a stake in French television, Tony dropped in at the office to see how The Falconry garden looked on video. The cameraman had left the tape on his desk. Loosening his tie, pouring himself a large drink, Tony put the tape in the machine and lay back on his squashy sofa to watch. He was enchanted with the results. Monica had really come up trumps this year. How right he'd been not to leave her for Cameron – when one considered the ghastly shambles Paul Stratton had made of his career after he'd left Winifred. Having played back The Falconry footage twice more, he decided to have a good laugh, and ran the tape on to have a look at Valerie's garden. Having located it, he played the tape back five times, particularly freezing the frame on the last ten seconds.

Then he walked out of the building not even bothering to lock the drinks cupboard or his office door, and drove straight over to Hamilton Terrace. Cameron was not there. Letting himself in, he searched systematically through the house. In the bedroom wastepaper basket he found what he was looking for. A pile of tiny torn-up scraps of paper. No one tore paper up that small unless they wanted to hide something. And it was an added precaution, as Cameron wasn't expecting to see him until tomorrow night and by that time the daily would have emptied the basket. It took him a long time to put the pieces together because his hands were trembling so much, but finally he was able to read the words: *Venturer meeting, Henry's house, 12.30 Sunday.*

Cameron got home about midnight. Sated and reeling from Rupert, she hadn't even bothered to shower afterwards as she wanted to keep the sweat and smell of him on and

462

inside her body as long as possible. Dropping her briefcase in the hall, she wandered into the drawing-room. The bulb that turned on by the door had blown, so in the faint light from the street lamps she groped her way across the room to turn on the light by her desk. The next minute she leapt in terror as a hand shot out, grabbing her leg just above the knee. Burglars, was her first panic-stricken thought; then, as a light flashed on, she saw Tony crouched on the sofa like a venomous toad.

'What are you doing skulking in the dark?' she stammered.

'What are *you* doing,' said Tony in a voice that utterly froze her blood, 'going to a Venturer meeting at Henry Hampshire's house today?'

Cameron's gasp of horror gave it all away: 'I-I-I had a tip-off. I went along to spy. I just hung around outside the gates, trying to see who was going in.'

'Who gave you the tip-off?'

Cameron's mind raced. 'I overheard people talking in the Bar Sinister – in the next booth.'

'You bloody liar,' hissed Tony. 'And how long has Rupert been stuffing you?'

'He isn't,' gibbered Cameron, wincing as his hand tightened on her leg. 'He's a bastard. The last person I'd shack up with.'

Tony tugged her towards him, burying his nose briefly in her groin.

'You reek of him, you fucking whore. And how come his dog knows you so well? It's all on tape, sweetheart.'

And the next moment he'd hit her across the room. She fell with a crash, catching her head on the bookshelf. Then he was on her again, picking her up by her shirt and smashing his left fist into her face. This time she crashed back into a small table, knocking over a vase of buddleia.

He's going to kill me, she thought, as he lunged at her again, kicking her in the ribs until she groaned for mercy. Yet, at the same time, another part of her terror-crazed mind was thinking that she had to get out of there before he got his hands on her briefcase which contained all her notes on the meeting, and, even worse, the names of the Corinium moles.

As he dragged her to her feet and hit her again, she managed to grab a chair and, swinging it round, caught him on the side of the head, narrowly missing his eye with one of the legs. It gave her a breathing space. Grabbing the vase of buddleia that was now leaking onto the floor, she hurled it at him and stumbled out of the room, banging the door behind her. Gathering up her briefcase, she just managed to put up the double catch on the front door, locking him in as she slammed it. By the time he'd managed to clamber out of the drawing-room window, she'd started up the Lotus and was on her way to Rupert's.

Putting her hand up to her head where she'd hit the bookcase, she could feel her hair sticky with blood. Looking in the driving mirror she saw more blood pouring out of her right eye and nearly blacked out. She had got to make it to Rupert's with the briefcase, or Tony would catch up and kill her. Somehow, in a daze of pain and sickness, constantly wiping the blood out of her eyes, she managed to reach Penscombe.

Rupert's front door was unlocked. The hall was dimly lit. Tripping over the dogs she screamed for him.

'Angel, how nice. Have you forgotten something?' he said, coming down the stairs wearing only a pair of jeans and reading *Horse and Hound*.

Then she found and switched on the main hall light and he saw her properly. Her right eye had closed up now and her upper lip was cut and terribly swollen. Her face, hair and shirt were drenched in blood.

'My Christ,' he said, appalled. 'What the fuck happened?'

'Tony found out.'

'My poor little baby.' He raced down the stairs, drawing her into his arms, feeling the stickiness of her blood-soaked hair and the frantic racing of her heart. 'The bastard, where is he? Let's get you a doctor, then I'm going round to kill him.'

'I'm OK,' mumbled Cameron. 'He had provocation. You'd

probably have done the same thing under the circs.' The next moment she passed out.

When she regained consciousness she was in Rupert's double bed, dressed in one of his shirts, with most of the blood washed off. A Doctor Benson, who was rather smooth and glamorous, had rolled up in his dinner jacket, reeking of brandy and Gold Spot, and, after examining her, assured her that her face wouldn't be marked. Having patched her up, saying she might have to have stitches in her head in the morning, he gave her a shot to sedate her.

'I don't want my head shaved,' she muttered when Rupert came back.

'Your hair's so short it's practically shaved already,' said Rupert, sitting down on the bed and taking her hands. 'I'm so desperately sorry, angel. I got you into it.'

It took all Cameron's pleading to stop him going straight round to Hamilton Terrace or even to The Falconry to beat Tony to a pulp.

'Think of the adverse publicity. It'll only trivialize Venturer's bid.'

'Nothing trivial about those bruises,' said Rupert, touching her swollen lip with his finger. 'How did he rumble us?'

'Saw the video of Valerie's opening and Beaver's crash-landing in the gladioli. And somehow he found out I was at the Venturer meeting yesterday.'

Very, very gently Rupert was stroking her cheek. Despite the pain in almost every part of her body, she had never felt safer or closer to him.

'Hell knows no fury like a womanizer scorned,' he said lightly. 'Well, he had to know some time. You'd better move in here.'

Cameron utterly despised women who cried in front of men. It was taking an unfair advantage and outraged her feminist principles. But once the tears started spilling out of her bruised eyes, she found she couldn't stop them.

'Is it such a ghastly thought?' said Rupert, taking her in his arms.

'No, no it's the nicest thought in the world. I guess I don't want to railroad you.'

'You're not. You've no idea how I hated letting you go back every time, particularly to Tony. I'm sick of never seeing you. Don't worry about your brilliant career. I'll look after you. And tomorrow, as a symbol of your new dependence, I'm going to chuck that beastly briefcase into the lake.'

Cameron managed a weak smile. 'You had better take the papers out first, or Tony'll be dropping by, using the truth drug on your duck.'

She was drowsy with dope now, so he laid her back on the pillow.

'I'll try not to get under your feet,' she muttered. 'I d-do love you – so so much.'

'I know you do.' Rupert got to his feet. 'Now go to sleep.'

'Please don't go.' She was suddenly frantic. 'You will sleep here, won't you?'

''Course I will. I'll be back in a minute. I'm just going to take the dogs out.'

Wandering mindlessly through the garden, Rupert found himself on the edge of the lake, breathing in the soapy smell of the meadowsweet, listening to the frogs croaking. There were no stars, and, glancing across the valley, he saw Taggie's turret was in darkness.

Valerie Jones was absolutely furious when nothing about her Opening appeared on 'Cotswold Round-Up', but not nearly as angry as Declan when Rupert told him what had happened.

'What the fock were you doing taking a dog you can't control to Valerie's opening?'

'I control my dogs a bloody sight better than you.'

'We're not talking about me. Think of the adverse publicity.'

'There won't be any. I refrained from beating Tony to a pulp.'

Declan sighed. 'And how the hell is Tony going to explain the overnight loss of his mistress and Programme Controller to his staff? Someone's going to leak the story. Pirated tapes of Beaver's flatfoot through the gladioli are no doubt circulating the network already, and it won't be long before they reach the press and the IBA.'

'It was terribly funny. I wish you'd seen Valerie's face.'

'It's not funny,' thundered Declan. 'I suppose you're used to having your character blackened but it won't do Venturer any good. The IBA don't like this kind of thing.'

He couldn't understand how Rupert could be so unrattled by such a catastrophe. He supposed he'd always lived in the eye of the storm.

'I don't know who comes out worse,' Declan went on, 'you setting out coldly and deliberately to seduce Cameron so we

467

had a mole on our side, or Tony who beat her up. A lot of people will feel Tony was justified. He was only acting in the heat of the moment.'

'Oh, come off it,' snapped Rupert. 'Talk about making mountains out of moles. The story we leak is that Cameron and I were attracted to each other when we met, when you interviewed me in February. We resisted it because we were on opposing sides for as long as we could, but now she's moved in with me and Venturer has the best Head of Drama in the country. Christ, we're both free agents. It's Tony who's the adulterer and the mistress-basher. He won't want to make a big thing of it because of Monica and the IBA.'

A story was duly leaked and appeared in the *Mail* the next day that Cameron Cook had changed sides, moved in with Rupert and that Tony was devastated to lose his star producer. No reference was made to Cameron being Tony's mistress, or of her being beaten up by him.

Rumour, however, was rife and by Wednesday Corinium had leaked a counter-story accusing Venturer of poaching and cold-blooded enticement, and putting the blame firmly on Rupert.

'A lonely, single woman nearing thirty, worried about missing the marital boat, is in a particularly vulnerable position,' Tony was quoted as saying.

Rupert was furious. 'All we have to do is give a photograph of Cameron's bruises to the press.'

'Don't be so bloody stupid,' said Declan crushingly. 'You've no proof Tony did it and not you. It isn't as though you've exactly got a blameless reputation when it comes to beating up.'

Tony, once he had cooled down, was absolutely shattered by Cameron's defection. He'd had no idea how much both he and Corinium had come to depend on her, both as an inspiration and a sparring partner.

Discovering through his spies that Rupert would be in London opening a new sports stadium on Thursday, Tony drove over to Penscombe to see her. Surrounded by Rupert's pack of dogs, with Mrs Bodkin in the kitchen and Mr Bodkin strimming the long grass round the lake, Cameron felt safe to let him in. Dressed in an orange bikini, she still looked as though she'd just done fifteen rounds with Barry McGuigan.

Tony followed her out to the pool, which sparkled brilliant turquoise in the sunshine and was no longer filled with leaves. It killed him to see her in this beautiful opulent setting, stretched out oiled on one of Rupert's reclining chairs, guarded by Rupert's lurcher Blue, who lay by her feet panting, but growling every time Tony approached.

Immediately Tony begged her to come back, telling her for the first time how much he loved her and, when that had no effect, offering to leave Monica and marry her. He didn't even lose his temper when she told him to bugger off.

'Your job's open for you to come back whenever you want it, and here are the keys to Hamilton Terrace.' He threw them on to the table. 'The house may belong to Corinium, but it's still yours when you need it. Come and get your clothes whenever you want to. I shouldn't have beaten you up, but I love you and I just saw red.'

'Just like you did the last time I came home late after spending the day with Patrick,' said Cameron. 'Get out.'

Tony, predictably, couldn't remain nice for long. 'You know it's only a matter of time until Rupert ditches you,' was his parting shot. 'Five days, five weeks; he may even keep you five months until Venturer finally don't get the franchise; then he'll kick you out like all the rest and you'll come running back to me.'

Cameron didn't believe Tony would leave Monica, particularly during the franchise year, but at least it now meant she could pick up her clothes, her books, and, much more important, her tapes and prizes from Hamilton Terrace. She also felt privately that it was nice to have Tony as a bolthole in case Rupert started playing her up.

Rupert, in fact, couldn't have been more angelic those first few days, fussing over her, seeing she didn't get too tired, ensuring Mrs Bodkin made her delicious food (which Cameron privately thought contained far too much seasoning and fats), making love to her with surprising gentleness and subtlety, so he didn't crush her bruised ribs or her battered face.

The weather was beautiful too – long hot days, followed by short sweet nights. Cameron was happy to sleep and read and sunbathe and explore Rupert's woods and fields with the dogs. Gradually, as the black eye and the swelling on her lips disappeared, she felt she was healing inside and out.

The only drawback was Mr and Mrs Bodkin, shadowy, polite, running Rupert's life like clockwork, but always there in the background. Cameron wanted Rupert on her own, she was not used to servants. She wanted to wander round the house naked and make love in the kitchen if she felt like it. She was also inclined to treat Mr and Mrs Bodkin like Corinium minions, rapping out orders, snapping at slowness and even more at ignorance.

Even Rupert, famous for his caprice and short fuse with staff, had to pull her up repeatedly: 'Taggie O'Hara increases her vocabulary by learning a new word every day. You could start off with: please and thank you.'

Any reference to Taggie sent Cameron through the roof, so, the second week after she moved in, determined to prove to Rupert that she could cook and run a house much better than Taggie, she persuaded Rupert to give Mr and Mrs Bodkin a few days off.

'I'm better,' she insisted. 'I want to look after you. I'm going to cook you some decent food. You're getting far too much cholesterol.'

'Do I look as though it's harming me?' said Rupert, who was eating white bread and dripping sprinkled with salt as he sat immersed in the *Scorpion*.

'No, but it's futile to abuse a magnificent constitution. It'll catch up with you. And why don't you try to read the *Guardian* occasionally instead of that trash?'

'Because it uses much too long words and makes snide remarks about my party,' said Rupert.

'But objective criticism's valuable, for Chrissake.'

'Not to me. I only like people who think I'm perfect. I'd better get Mr and Mrs Bodkin back for the weekend. The children are coming on Saturday. They make a hell of a lot of work.'

'Oh, don't,' said Cameron, suddenly excited. 'Let's look after them ourselves. We'll have picnics and barbecues and all muck in. It'll be so much fun.'

Like many insecure people, Cameron was much easier to live with when she was down. After she'd been beaten up, it was her intense vulnerability that had appealed to Rupert. Wanting to protect her, he'd asked her to move in. But as she got better, her natural aggression and stridency started to reassert itself.

The day before the children were due, Cameron decided to make a big paella for dinner; the rest could be heated up for them the following day. Discovering in the middle she'd forgotten to get any saffron or squid, she dispatched Rupert to the village shop.

'I'm sure they won't stock them,' grumbled Rupert, who wanted to read *Horse and Hound*.

The kitchen wireless was blaring out Dame Enid's latest tone poem; the *New Statesman* and the *Times Literary Supplement* lay on the kitchen table all giving Rupert an unpleasant feeling of *déjà vu*. It was too much like Helen all over again.

'Well, drive into Stroud then,' snapped Cameron.

She'd forgotten what a rat race paella was to make, but she was determined to cook better than Taggie.

'And get some Parmesan as well,' she shouted after him.

The village shop had recently been converted into a tiny supermarket with shelves all round the walls, and a partition, also with shelves on both sides, running parallel to the counter. If the ubiquitous Mrs Makepiece, who did for Lizzie and Valerie and one morning a week for Maud now, hadn't been holding forth so noisily and indignantly at the head of the queue, Rupert would never have slid into the shop unobserved. Picking up a red wire basket, he chucked in some Jaffa cakes because the children liked them, and a tin of corned beef because he liked it; he couldn't find any squid, but he supposed a tin of pilchards in tomato sauce would do as well – a squid pro quo.

As he moved round to the spice shelf, Mrs Makepiece, encouraged by a chorus of clicking tongues, raised her voice. 'Declan and 'er ladyship have pushed off on some second honeymoon in the Lake District, leaving her all on her own.'

Rupert stiffened, gazing unseeingly at rows of paprika, dill and cayenne.

'All alone in that 'uge 'ouse,' went on Mrs Makepiece, 'and we all know it's 'aunted. Well, 'alf the lights fused, so Taggie went to the fuse box and read the instructions all wrong – she's disconnected, you know, the poor lamb, and she blew all the fuses, and had to shiver all night in the dark, with only Gertrude, that's her little dog, for company.'

Despite the baking heat of the day, Rupert had gone absolutely cold. Taggie might have killed herself fiddling about with that fuse box.

'She was crying her heart out this morning when I come in,' said Mrs Makepiece, egged on by the row of shocked faces. 'At first she wouldn't tell me what was the matter. Then I made us a nice cup of tea and it came out – they'd all forgotten her birthday.'

Rupert was so enraged he dropped the basket and walked straight out of the shop with the pilchards, which he had forgotten to chalk up.

The moment he got home he rang Ursula. 'Where the fuck are Maud and Declan?'

'Windermere.'

'Give me their number.'

'I promised not to; they don't want to be disturbed. This is a patch-up operation. Declan's been devoting too much time to his biography.'

'They forgot Taggie's birthday.'

'Oh, my God!'

'And you should have bloody well reminded them. Give me the number.'

Declan and Maud were out when he rang. He left a message

472

for Declan to ring him, saying it was about the franchise and very urgent.

Then he rang Taggie. 'Happy birthday, darling. Cameron and I are going to take you out to dinner. No, I don't want any "buts". We'll pick you up about eight.'

He was still sweating with horror at the thought of the poor little duck all alone in that big house in the dark with all those winding stairs and long passages.

'Bloody Maud and Declan,' he howled as he went into the kitchen.

'What on earth have they done now? Don't turn it off, it's Vivaldi,' protested Cameron. 'Did you get the squid?' Then, as Rupert handed her the pilchards, 'These won't do, dumbass. And where's the Parmesan and the saffron?'

'They forgot Taggie's birthday,' said Rupert bleakly.

'Well, that's not such a big thing.' Then, seeing the rage on Rupert's face, 'Haven't you forgotten your kids' birthdays?'

'No – yes, I suppose so, but Helen always remembers.'

When he told Cameron what had happened, and that they were taking Taggie out to dinner, she hit the roof. 'But it was our last night on our own. This was to be a celebration I was cooking specially for us.'

'There'll be plenty of time for that in the future.'

The telephone rang. It was Declan. Fuelled by indignation, and also because Declan had been so censorious about him and Cameron, Rupert let him have it. 'You fucking hypocrite, always banging on about tyranny and exploitation. The worst case I've seen is going on under your roof.'

'What the fock are you talking about?'

'Taggie. She works like a slave for the bloody lot of you, and all you can do is leave her alone in a huge house, with the fuses blown, and then forget her birthday.'

'Oh, my Christ,' said Declan, appalled. 'Have we really?'

'You get on the telephone the moment I ring off and say how sorry you are.'

'We ought to come back.'

'No. Cameron and I'll look after her tonight. You come home first thing tomorrow and bring her a decent present, 'not a crappy book of Wordsworth's poems she can't read.'

'God, I feel terrible,' said Declan. 'Now, what was this urgent thing about the franchise?'

'That was it,' said Rupert furiously. 'If she hadn't worked her ass off trailing around the area, rounding up names for your bloody franchise, we wouldn't be ahead in the race now.'

Crashing down the telephone, he poured himself a huge whisky. He was absolutely shaking with rage.

'Well, well, well,' said Cameron, chucking the wooden spoon on to the drying rice and switching off the hot plate. 'What gives with Taggie O'Hara?'

'She doesn't deserve parents like that. She's only a baby.'

'Nineteen today, to be exact. Well beyond the age of consent.'

She knew it was madness to bitch, but she couldn't help herself. 'You've got a very soft spot – or is it a hard spot – for her, haven't you? Are you nurturing some secret passion? What I want to know is where does that put me?'

Rupert looked her up and down. There wasn't a trace of tenderness in his face now.

'You're living here, aren't you?'

'At the moment.'

'Let's get one thing straight,' he said softly. 'If you want to go on living here, stop being such a fucking bitch.'

Draining his whisky, he picked up his car keys. 'I'm going to get her a present. You can ring up the White Elephant in Painswick and book a table for three at nine o'clock.'

Henry Hampshire's Springer spaniel had recently had six puppies. They'd all gone to new homes except the runt whose paw, broken when someone stepped on it, was still in plaster. The puppy had a freckled face, a bright pink mouth, crossed eyes that looked as though he'd been on the booze all night, and a stumpy tail which agitated his whole body.

'He's a great character,' said Henry. 'You can have him for a hundred pounds.'

'With a broken paw? Don't be ridiculous.'

'Plaster comes off next week. Then he'll be as right as rain. Won't stop him going all day in the field.'

'Fifty,' said Rupert.

'You've got to be joking. The others went for two hundred and fifty each. Mother was best of breed at Crufts, father won every field trial in the country.'

'Fifty,' said Rupert. 'He'll always be slightly lame.'

'Oh, all right,' said Henry. 'I had lunch with Daysee Butler today.'

'Well, you shouldn't,' snapped Rupert. 'You're bound to give away trade secrets.'

'Well, you still haven't laid on Joanna Lumley,' grumbled Henry. 'Daysee said Tony's flown to LA to search for a new Programme Controller.'

When Rupert got back to Penscombe, Cameron had washed her hair, and changed into the clinging kingfisher-blue dress she'd worn to get her award in Madrid; it had slits to sunburnt mid-thigh on both sides. She looked apprehensive, very beautiful, and came straight up and put her arms round Rupert's neck.

'I was jealous. I'm sorry.'

He breathed in Fracas, the dry bitter sexy scent she always wore; it made his senses reel.

'I'm sorry too,' he said. 'I over-reacted, but I feel so sorry for her.'

Under the blue dress he could feel Cameron's nipples stiffening. Glancing at the kitchen clock he saw that it was a quarter to eight.

'We haven't got time. It'd muss you up.'

'*You* have,' said Cameron.

Dropping to her knees, she unzipped his flies. This was one skill she knew she was better at than Taggie O'Hara.

A battered dark-green GTI was parked outside The Priory as they drove up. The front door was open; the hall was filled with clothes, books and suitcases.

'Perhaps she won't want to come out to dinner,' murmured Cameron hopefully.

''Course she will,' said Rupert.

It was debatable who got the worse shock, Cameron or Rupert, when they went into the kitchen and found Taggie sobbing in the arms of a tall black-haired, incredibly beautiful young man. The only difference was that Cameron instantly recognized Patrick, whereas Rupert did not. Patrick looked round, still with his arms round Taggie.

'Well?' he said icily.

Taggie glanced up, gave a gasp, then tugging herself away from Patrick, blindly snatched at some kitchen roll, frantically wiping her eyes and blowing her nose.

'I'm sorry,' she mumbled. 'Hullo, Rupert, hullo, Cameron. How are you?'

She was amazed to see Rupert glaring at Patrick with such hostility. Perhaps he resented him as Cameron's ex.

'I don't think you've met my brother Patrick, have you?' she said quickly.

'Your brother!' Instantly the hostility was gone. 'I didn't twig. It was your party on New Year's Eve, wasn't it? How did your finals go?'

'Perfectly all right,' said Patrick shortly.

Turning back to Taggie, Rupert dumped two bottles of Dom Perignon on the table beside Patrick's white carrier bag of duty free.

'Happy birthday, angel. They're just out of the fridge. Open them,' he added to Patrick, totally unaware of the look of utter loathing that Patrick was shooting in his direction.

Oh hell, thought Cameron, poor Patrick. Taggie must have told him about me moving in with Rupert.

Cutting short Taggie's stammering thanks for the champagne, Rupert seized her hand and led her out to the car. 'Come and see your proper present.'

'You d-don't have to bother,' stammered Taggie in the hall. 'I'm having a lovely birthday. Mummy and Daddy have just rung. They're bringing my present back tomorrow afternoon. They couldn't pick it up until today, and Patrick brought me back the most gorgeous Arran sweater. He's just

got back. He had so much stuff to bring after three years.'
She was rattling now, on the verge of tears again.

'Sweetheart, what's the matter?'

'I'm absolutely fine,' she said. How could she possibly
explain to him that the blown fuses, the night in the dark,
and the forgotten birthday, were mere irrelevancies, that it
was Cameron finally moving in with him that had brought
the world down round her ears.

She knew he couldn't ever be serious about someone as
stupid and unsophisticated as she, but, as they'd gone round
the country together, they'd become friends, and now she'd
never see him again without Cameron.

'You were all on your own last night in the dark,' he
said.

'Who told you?'

'Mrs Makepiece told the whole village shop.'

'It was my fault. I read the directions on the fuse box
wrong.' She tried to smile. 'I seemed to spend the whole
night pushing poor Gertrude round the house in front of me.
Things seem to creak so much if you're in the dark.'

Rupert took her hands. 'Look, next time something awful
happens, will you promise to ring me? That's what I'm across
the valley for. It crucifies me to think of you all by yourself
and frightened like that.'

She wouldn't look at him – all he could see was her
reddened, swollen eyelids. Reluctantly he let her go.

Outside, the puppy, with its speckled paws on the car
ledge, was grinning out through the open window.

'Oh, how adorable,' breathed Taggie. 'What's he done to
his paw?'

'It's nearly better. He's your birthday present. I was going
to buy you a guard dog, but I got sidetracked.'

Taggie was in ecstasy. No one had ever given her anything
so lovely.

'Gertrude will be very jealous to begin with,' warned
Rupert, as the puppy rushed off on to the lawn, quartering
frantically, pursuing various cat and dog smells. 'You'll have
to make a lot of fuss of her.

He noticed Taggie was still wearing jeans and an old torn red-and-white-striped shirt of Declan's.

'Aren't you going to change? We've booked a table for nine. Patrick can come too. I've never met him properly.'

Taggie blushed. 'It's terribly kind of you but we're fine on our own.'

'Don't be silly, I'm not having you cooking on your birthday.'

'Patrick and I haven't seen each other for ages.'

'You've got the rest of the summer.'

'He's going abroad tomorrow. He – er – he—'

'Yes,' said Rupert, pulling her down beside him on to the old bench on the side of the lawn.

Taggie blushed even more deeply. 'He adores Cameron, you see, and he's absolutely d-d-devastated about her moving in with you.'

'Ah,' said Rupert.

Taggie was frantically peeling paint off the bench. As the puppy bounded back to them, she gathered him up, cuddling him for comfort.

'Patrick could accept her having an affair with Tony because he thought she was doing it for her career, b-but you're different.'

'Why?' said Rupert, suddenly anxious to know the answer.

Taggie buried her crimson face in the puppy's ginger ears.

'Because one wouldn't need any incentive . . .'

'Is that your word for the day?'

'No.' She shook her head frantically. '. . . any incentive to move in with you.'

Inside, Cameron was gazing at Patrick. He's grown up, she thought. He's much tougher and more detached and less vulnerable.

'How did you really get on in your finals?'

'Got a first.'

'Have they told you?'

478

'No, but I know.'

He got a packet of Marlboro's out of the duty-free bag and lit himself a cigarette without offering her one. As the match flared she could see the bitterness in his face.

'I gather you've just become our next-door neighbour,' he said.

'Aren't you going to wish me joy?'

'What joy? He'll only make you miserable. Christ, you've got awful taste in men,' he added irritably. 'Tony was a disgusting thug. This man –' he couldn't bring himself to say Rupert's name – 'is like a foxhound. Can't you understand? You can't domesticate him. He'll always be hunting for something new. It's in his blood. He'll get bored with you in a few weeks, and if he doesn't, you'll get bored with him; he's the most ghastly philistine, never read a book in his life.'

'He's street-wise.'

'That expression always seems to me a euphemism for someone with extremely shady morals, which means he'll dump you sooner or later – and he'll smash your career. Tony at least encouraged that.'

'You're just jealous.'

'Not any more,' said Patrick wearily. 'I am ashes where once I was fire.'

'He's very funny. You'll like him when you get to know him.'

'I'm not going to give myself the chance. I'm going abroad tomorrow.'

Cameron was put out. She liked talking to Patrick. Now they weren't hamstrung by Tony's jealousy, she'd hoped he might grow into a friend, and that his admiration, like Tony's, would act as a spur to Rupert.

'Where are you going?'

'Australia – to work on a sheep farm. I'm not hanging round for the rest of the year seeing you all scrapping over the franchise and watching your relationship with that bastard self-destruct.'

'He isn't all bastard. Look how kind he's been to Taggie.' Cameron was fishing now.

479

'He's totally fucked her up.'

Cameron's throat went dry. 'Has he tried anything?'

'Nothing according to Tag. Just swans in in his bloody *droit de seigneur*, Lord Bountiful fashion, bombarding her with presents – silver necklaces, Fabergé eggs.'

'Fabergé eggs?' said Cameron, appalled.

'Oh, Taggie didn't know that it was. He brought her that back from Madrid. I don't know what's on offer today. A Monet perhaps, or a Henry Moore!'

'A puppy,' said Cameron in a frozen voice. 'This is it.'

The next moment Aengus shot into the kitchen, tail fluffed out like a lavatory brush, growling ferociously, and took refuge under the kitchen dresser. The puppy frolicked after him, trying to join him under the dresser, then let out a piercing shriek as Aengus caught him with a punishing right hook on his pink nose. Instantly Gertrude bustled in, the personification of outrage. The puppy bounced up to her, then let out another shriek as Gertrude bit him sharply on the ear.

'Oh Christ,' said Patrick. 'Not content with disrupting humans, Rupert has to disrupt animals as well.'

'For Christ's sake open one of those bottles,' said Cameron.

'I don't want a drink,' said Patrick sulkily.

'You'll need it. We've come to take you out to dinner.'

'Well, we're not coming. We don't want any of your fucking charity. Poor little O'Hara kids, eating their hearts out. Let's throw them a few crumbs of comfort.'

A black lock of hair had fallen over his forehead, a muscle was going in the beautiful pale right cheek. His eyes were as dark and forbidding as the depths of the huge cedar outside the window.

'Please don't hate me so much,' Cameron was amazed to find herself pleading. 'I really need a friend to talk to.'

They both jumped as the telephone rang. It was Caitlin who was staying with a friend in Newbury, ringing to wish Taggie many happy returns. By the time they had finished talking, Rupert and Cameron had left.

'How did you get rid of them?' asked Taggie.

'I told them both to fuck off and that we didn't need their charity,' said Patrick, opening one of Rupert's bottles. 'At least we can now get drunk at their expense!'

36

Cameron and Rupert had a disastrous dinner at the White Elephant after that. Rupert was outraged at being thrown out by Patrick. 'Arrogant little fucker, just like his father.'

'I thought you adored his father.'

'Not when he's playing God, or neglecting his children.'

'You certainly aren't neglecting one of them – silver necklaces, Fabergé eggs, handicapped puppies – singularly appropriate in a franchise year.'

'Oh, shut up.'

The row continued until they got to bed, when Rupert maddened Cameron most of all by falling asleep when she was in mid-harangue. She woke next morning, feeling suicidal, to find Rupert gone. Wondering if he were already collecting his children, she went downstairs, found the paella gathering flies on the oven and chucked it out. There was a chicken in the fridge. She supposed she'd better roast it for lunch. Dispiritedly, she peeled some potatoes, put them on to parboil, then started to make a french dressing. There wasn't any dill. If she sent Rupert off to the village shop he'd come back with nutmeg.

Outside, the sun was shining through the mist like a dog's identity disk. Cameron longed to go out to the pool and swim off her hangover. Until last night, with the Bodkins away, she had at last been able to enjoy a marvellously sybaritic few days with Rupert, swimming and sunbathing naked, brazenly tantalizing him away from whatever he was doing. She had even galloped bareback down the valley at twilight one night with no clothes on, until Rupert had caught up with her, pulled her off the horse and pulled her in the meadowsweet. Cameron had half-hoped that Taggie, on a late-night walk with Gertrude, might have caught them at it and realized that at last Rupert had found someone with a sex drive equal to his own.

But last night's row had ruined all that, and now, with the kids around, there'd be no more nude frollicking this week-end. She jumped as the dogs barked and the front door banged.

'Cameron,' yelled Rupert.

As he sauntered into the kitchen, blithe as a skylark, as though there'd been no row at all, Cameron frantically stirred the french dressing.

'We're out of dill,' she said.

'Dildos! Hardly need one of those with me around! I'm sorry I don't give you presents,' he went on, kissing the back of her neck. 'Vainly, I thought my presence was enough. Which hand will you have?'

'Both,' said Cameron sulkily.

'Telepathic,' said Rupert, uncurling his fingers.

Glittering on each palm was a diamond ear-ring, a two-inch-long chandelier, lit by little diamonds instead of crystals. Cameron was speechless. Incredulously, she ripped out the gold hoops she normally wore and hooked on the diamonds, running to the kitchen mirror, rubbing away the steam with her sleeve to have a look.

The ear-rings hung halfway down her slender neck, throwing rainbows of light on the lean, tense jawline, illuminating and softening the truculent hostile little face. Next minute Rupert's reflection appeared beside hers.

'Like them?'

In answer, she turned, kissing him with a fury and passion he'd never known in her. Cupping her face with his hands, he felt the tears sliding into his fingers. Very gently he unhooked the ear-rings.

'Shame to take them off so soon, but I must have you before I pick up the children.'

By the time they'd finished, the potatoes were too soft to roast, so Cameron mashed them instead.

Groggy with love, she waited to love Rupert's children. At half past one, trailing barking dogs, Tabitha erupted into the kitchen. Her cheeks were flushed, her eyes bright with excitement. She was clutching a huge box of chocolates.

'Mrs Bodkin! Mrs Bodkin!' She slithered to a halt in front of Cameron. 'Where's Mrs B?'

'Away for the weekend.'

'Daddy never told us. Are you the temp?'

'Well, not too temporary I hope!' said Cameron, smiling. 'You must be Tabitha?'

'Well, I'm not Marcus.' At nine, Tabitha was as blonde and as effortlessly elegant as Rupert. She stared at Cameron with the wary blue eyes of a stray kitten.

She was followed by Marcus, who at eleven was very thin, with very dark red hair, huge surprised yellow eyes, and pale delicate freckled features. He looked like a fawn liable to bolt at any minute. None of the photographs all over the house had captured their beauty, nor the way their totally different looks complimented each other.

'You must be Marcus, then,' said Cameron. 'I hope you're both hungry. There's roast chicken for lunch.'

'Not yet,' said Tabitha, grabbing an apple out of the fruit bowl. 'I'm going down to the stables.'

Marcus smiled shyly and apologetically. 'I've got a letter from my mother for Mrs Bodkin. I'd better give it to you. The chocolates were for her, perhaps you'd like . . .' His voice trailed off.

'No, no,' said Cameron, 'leave them for her.'

Helen's writing was very Vassar: '*Dear Mrs B,*' she had written, '*I hope your arthritis is better and the kids won't make too much work. Marcus's medication is in his suitcase. Please see he takes it, if he gets uptight. I enclose a list of their clothes. Could you tick them off before they come home? They lost so much last time, and can you see Tabitha learns her vocabulary, and that both do half an hour's piano practice, and say their prayers at night? I also enclose stats of their reports. Can you give them to Mr C-B? Yours sincerely, Helen Gordon.'*

Christ, she's formal, and a Born-again too, thought Cameron. Then she smiled at Marcus. 'Is Daddy on the way?'

'He's gone to the yard. Can I do anything?'

'Tell him and Tabitha lunch'll be ready in ten minutes.'

Putting on the cabbage and removing the chicken from the baking dish, Cameron started to make the gravy, and at the same time read the kids' reports. Tab's was perfectly frightful except for sport. Marcus's was brilliant. He returned to the kitchen looking apprehensive.

'They're trying out some new pony for Tab. Daddy said would half past two be OK?' Then, quailing at Cameron's expression of fury, he said quickly, 'If you don't mind I'll go and unpack.'

How, thought Cameron furiously, can I possibly keep up Taggie O'Hara standards when I get fucked about like this? Then she remembered the diamond ear-rings, and the fact that Rupert hadn't seen the kids for a few weeks, and decided not to make a fuss.

In fact they were back in forty minutes.

'I'm starving,' said Tab, heading straight for the larder. 'I thought you said lunch was ready.' She came out tearing open a packet of crisps with her teeth.

'Don't eat that. It'll spoil your lunch,' said Cameron. Ignoring her, Tab sat down at the table with *Pony* magazine.

Rupert came in with a large vodka and tonic for Cameron. 'Hullo, darling –' Cameron noticed how Tabitha looked up, eyes narrowed at the endearment – 'sorry we're late. Geoffrey Gardener brought the pony over specially. I wanted Tab to try him.'

'Any good?'

'We're going to keep him over the weekend.'

'He's called Biscuit,' said Tabitha.

'Here are the kids' reports and a letter from Helen,' said Cameron as Rupert started to carve.

'I only eat breast,' said Tab, when Rupert handed her a leg.

'Well, give it to Marcus, then,' said Rupert, who was reading the reports at the same time.

Cameron opened her mouth and shut it again. She noticed Marcus was very nervous around his father, and that, while Rupert hardly glanced at Marcus's report, he spent ages reading Tabitha's.

'"Tabitha must learn not to be so competitive at netball." What the fuck do they mean by that?' he said furiously. 'You can't be too competitive at games.'

'I should be in the netball team next term,' boasted Tab, 'and I'm easily the youngest. I don't want any,' she added to Cameron, snatching her plate away, so a large dollop of mashed potato fell on the table. Cameron's lips tightened as she scooped it up and put it on Rupert's plate.

'Or any cabbage or salad.'

'You must have veggies. I'm sure you do at home.'

'This is home.' Tabitha's blue-eyed stare was as arrogant as Rupert's. 'Isn't it, Daddy? This is home,' she repeated to Rupert, who was still reading the headmistress's report.

'Of course it is, angel,' he said, kissing her.

'Marcus's report is excellent,' said Cameron warmly.

'Ninety-five per cent for Latin, that's almost indecent,' said Rupert with an edge to his voice. Then he read on: ' "Marcus has made very good progress in Geography as he has only attended half the classes". What were you doing during the other half? Going to strip clubs?'

Marcus flushed. 'The pollen count was very high. I was off sick quite a lot of days.'

'I wish I had asthma and could bunk-off school,' said Tab, feeding the rest of her chicken to a slavering Beaver.

Rupert, having finished the reports, was now immersed in the racing pages of *The Times*.

'There's a horse called Venturer in the three-thirty,' he said to Cameron. 'We must have a bet.'

'Put a pound on each way for me,' said Tab. 'We're doing a project on snakes next term.'

'You could start off by interviewing Tony Baddingham,' said Rupert, picking up the telephone.

Now here's a chance to help Tabitha and win her confidence, thought Cameron.

'You could start off with Adam and Eve,' she said, helping herself to salad.

'The project's about snakes, not sex,' said Tab rudely.

'Eve got tempted by the snake, stupid,' said Marcus. 'That's why they left the Garden of Eden. It's a jolly good idea,' he added, kindly, to Cameron.

'My project's about real snakes,' snapped Tab.

Getting up from the table and rummaging in her squashy bag, she produced a photograph which she handed to Rupert as he came off the telephone.

'This is the pony Malise bought me. She's brilliant at cross-country because she won't stop.'

'D'you mean you've already got a pony?' asked Cameron, shocked.

'Yes, she's called Dollop the Trollop, and she shakes hooves for a polo.'

'Then why is Daddy buying you another one?'

Tabitha looked at Cameron as though she were crackers.

'Because I need at least two if I'm going on the junior circuit next summer. I can, can't I, Daddy?'

'Your mother's not crazy about the idea unless your school work picks up,' said Rupert, who was still frowning at the photograph. 'That pony's too short in front.'

Tabitha had learned to be manipulative, to play off the rivalry between her father and stepfather.

'Malise and Mummy don't want me to enter for the Pony Club Mounted Games at Wembley even if I'm picked,' she announced slyly. 'Because I'll miss a week of school.'

'Don't be bloody silly,' said Rupert angrily. 'I'll have a few sharp words with your mother.'

'Who'd like fruit salad?' said Cameron, as she cleared away the first course.

'Not me,' said Tab. 'Is there any ice cream in the freezer?'

Cameron had spent a long time that morning peeling grapes. 'If you don't like fruit salad, I'm afraid you'll have to go without,' she said sharply.

'Then I'll have another packet of crisps,' said Tab. 'I can come over every weekend this summer, Daddy, except the last week in August which is Pony Club camp.'

'Good,' said Rupert.

Oh, please no, thought Cameron. She was sure it was only out of kindness that Marcus had a second helping of fruit salad.

Fortunately, spirits were raised when Venturer won by three lengths, which meant that Rupert and Tabitha were richer by three hundred pounds and eight pounds respectively.

'Can we go into Stroud and spend it?' Tabitha climbed on to Rupert's knee, the kitten again, but this time tactile and adoring.

'Christ, no, not on a Saturday afternoon.'

'Can we watch *Amityville I* tonight?'

'No way,' said Cameron. 'It doesn't start until ten and it'll give you nightmares for months.'

'When we don't have to get up next morning Mummy always lets us watch late-night films,' lied Tab.

'Balls,' said Rupert. 'If it's that frightening, you're not watching it.'

'Can we go into Stroud and get a James Bond video then?' persisted Tab. 'And I need some pink hair spray for a punk party next week.'

'I'll take you, if you like,' conceded Cameron.

The journey to Stroud was the most successful part of the weekend. The roof of the Lotus was down and, although Marcus went white, Tab thoroughly approved of Cameron's driving.

'This is a nice car, and you go much faster than Mummy. Can I have an ice cream?'

'May I. You may if you promise to eat your supper.'

On the way back, however, Tabitha smiled sweetly at Cameron. 'You haven't got a husband, have you? Why don't you get one?'

'I'd like to,' said Cameron, thinking longingly of Rupert.

'But not my Daddy,' hissed Tabitha.

'It is absolutely ludicrous,' said Cameron to Rupert as, later, they listened to Tabitha sulkily crucifying Beethoven's Minuet in G on the drawing-room baby grand. 'This is a Saturday during the vacation *and* she's got to learn her vocabulary.'

'Helen is petrified the children will inherit my lack of brains.'

'Marcus is clearly superbright,' said Cameron. 'He's such a sweet, sensitive kid.'

'Takes after his mother,' snapped Rupert. 'Tab takes after me. My reports were much worse than hers.'

'She doesn't strike me as being dumb,' said Cameron, 'just unmotivated.'

'She looks OK,' said Rupert coldly. 'And she rides like a dream. What else matters?'

Supper was decidedly scratchy. Tab ostentatiously gave all her shepherd's pie to Beaver. Afterwards Rupert packed both children off upstairs to watch James Bond. Cameron was reading the *Guardian* in the drawing-room and feeling absolutely shattered. How the hell did mothers cope day in and day out, when piercing screams rent the air? The next minute Marcus had run into the room, waving the remote control. He had difficulty breathing.

'I don't think Tab should watch this video. It's called *For Your Eyes Only*, but it's not James Bond.'

'You got it, didn't you?' said Rupert unhelpfully.

A second later Tab came storming in and tried to grab the remote control. When Marcus held it above his head she went for him, kicking his shins and giving him a karate chop in the stomach which doubled him up.

'Stop it,' shouted Rupert, pulling her off.

'It's a lovely film,' screamed Tabitha. 'It's all about ladies licking each other.'

'I'd better come and have a look,' said Rupert.

He returned, grinning. 'Marcus was right. It's a blue film about Lesbians.' He threw the video on the sofa beside Cameron. 'We must have a watch later.'

She was wearing a sleeveless T-shirt, and he slid his hands inside caressing her armpits, then feeling for her breasts. It was ridiculous the way he could turn her to jello.

'I don't fancy your bedroom without a lock on it,' she said. 'The only safe place with this mob around is the john.'

More shrieks issued from upstairs, followed by a crash on the terrace outside. Going out through the french windows, Rupert found the remote control with all its entrails spilling out.

Cameron stormed upstairs. She'd been looking forward to watching *Dido and Aeneas* on Channel Four later, and now they'd be stuck with BBC 1.

'Why did you chuck that out of the window?' she yelled at Tab. 'I know it was you.'

'Marcus won't let me watch *Amityville*,' sobbed Tab. 'I hate him! I hate him!'

Rupert put her to bed screaming. Cameron was relieved at only having to deal with Marcus's asthma attack.

'I'm sorry about Tab,' he murmured as she finally tucked him in.

'Surely she doesn't behave like this at home?'

'Of course she doesn't. Both Malise and Mum are quite strict, so when she comes here she sort of runs wild. And she and Daddy love each other so much,' he added wistfully.

'He loves you too,' said Cameron, giving him a kiss.

Down the passage Cameron found Rupert talking to Tab, who was tucked up in bed with Paddington Bear, gloomily transvestite in the family christening robes.

'You really ought to be asleep, Tab,' she said. 'Marcus says Mummy puts your lights out at nine.'

'Marcus is a bloody sneak,' said Tabitha, yawning.

'Have you said your prayers?'

'OK.' Tab rolled out of bed. 'Dear God,' she prayed loudly, 'please bless Daddy, Mummy, Marcus, Dollop and Beaver. And please give me Biscuit, if you think that's right, God.' Then her fingers opened a fraction. She could see Cameron still hovering on the landing, hopeful of a mention. 'And please God, make Mummy and Daddy get married again, so I can come and live at Penscombe for always; make me a good girl, Amen.'

Cameron walked back to Rupert's bedroom, quivering with rage. Rupert thought it was very funny. 'Isn't she awful? She asked me earlier why I didn't sell my double bed as I didn't need it any more.'

As Marcus predicted, Tab had terrible nightmares and ended up in Rupert's bed. Turned on by the blue movie, Rupert and Cameron waited until she was asleep and then went downstairs and barricaded themselves into the dining-room.

'I've never screwed anyone in here before,' said Rupert. 'Should we put mats down in case we scorch the table?'

In fact, twelve feet of polished mahogany is not the ideal surface on which to make love. Straddling Rupert, her knees aching, Cameron took a long time. She was just capitulating to pleasure when a bright red face, as apoplectic as any Mr Barrett of Wimpole Street, appeared through the hatch.

'What,' thundered Tabitha, 'are you doing to my Daddy?'

'I'm trying to keep him warm,' replied Cameron through gritted teeth.

Things went from bad to worse the next day. Rupert went off to see his constituency secretary. Tab vanished to the stables and, despite Cameron sending repeated messages, didn't return for lunch. Grimly setting out to collect her, Cameron found Tabitha, watched by an idling trio of grooms, jumping the new pony, which ground to a halt each time it came up to a large wall.

'This pony don't jump,' yelled Tabitha.

'Think of something really nasty before take-off, and then give him a good whack,' advised one of the grooms.

Tab rode towards the wall with great determination: 'I'm going to think of CAMERON,' she howled, bringing her whip down on Biscuit's quarters. The grooms screamed with laughter, and then cheered as Biscuit cleared the wall by a foot. Tabitha leapt off the pony, cuddling him and stuffing him with pony nuts. 'Good boy, good boy.'

'Lunch, Tabitha,' said Cameron icily.

Even Tabitha looked faintly sheepish and ran on ahead back to the house.

There are a million children in England living with replacement parents, in fact one in seven is a stepchild, thought Cameron furiously, as she stalked back to the house. They can't all be awful. Just fantasy. You're doing research for a documentary on the in-coming stepmother, she told herself.

'Where's Daddy?' demanded Tab as Cameron went into the kitchen.

'Not coming back till later this afternoon.'

'I don't want any lunch till he gets back.'

'Sit *down*,' ordered Cameron.

'I will if you sit down first,' said Tab with a giggle.

Not looking behind her, Cameron collapsed heavily on to a whoopee cushion which Tab had slipped on to her chair, and which let out a succession of noisy farts. Tab screamed with laughter; even Marcus grinned. For Cameron the noise was too embarrassingly reminiscent of her encounter with their father on the balcony of her Madrid hotel.

'You bloody children, stop winding me up.'

'Don't speak to us like that,' said Tab coldly. 'You're not our mother.'

Cameron walked out of the kitchen and went and swam twenty lengths in the pool to work off her rage. Going upstairs, she discovered Tabitha must have changed at least four times that day and used the carpet of Rupert's bedroom as a dirty clothes' basket.

'Tab,' she bellowed.

'Yes.' Tab appeared from the television room, eating a Mars bar.

'Pick up your clothes, OK?'

'Mrs Bodkin picks them up.'

'Mrs Bodkin is not here. Pick them *up*.'

'Bloody shan't.'

Cameron moved towards her.

'Don't you touch me,' hissed Tab, her little face a mask of spite. 'Because of child molesters like you, I'm learning karate at school,' and, clenching her fist in a black-power salute, she shot under Cameron's arm, downstairs and back to the stables.

A blinding headache nudged Cameron's skull. What was the name of that silent order Charles Fairburn disappeared to the day the franchise applications went in? She took a Valium and went down to the kitchen where she found Marcus trying to clear up lunch.

He had put the roasting pan undrained in the sink so the grease floated thick and yellow on the top of the water.

'I'm sorry about Tab,' he mumbled.

'You make up for it,' Cameron said, hugging him.

'It's not all her fault,' said Marcus, fairly. 'She's used to Daddy's total attention when she's here, and Mrs Bodkin fussing over her. She looked after Tab when she was a baby, you see. When Tab says she wants lunch she's given it, and if she doesn't like it when it arrives that doesn't matter much either. She's just not used to a stranger saying, "Do this, don't do that".'

Cameron gazed at the sea of fat, feeling reproved. 'I'm sorry.'

'It isn't your fault,' said Marcus, busily sloshing water all over the surfaces as he wiped them down with a dripping dishcloth.

'I'm not around kids that much. How d'you relate to Malise?'

'OK. He's strict, but he's fair. He's very old. His grand-children are older than me.'

'Would you like your parents to get married again?'

Marcus went green. 'No, absolutely not.'

'Tab would.'

'Oh, Tab gets on much better with Daddy than I do,' said

493

Marcus bitterly. 'And if she was here she could ride all the time.

As Rupert probably wouldn't have eaten at lunchtime, Cameron decided to make him a nice dinner. Just the two of them; the kids could go to bed early. Marcus chatted to her while she cooked and, when she'd finished, offered to play the piano for her. He was just playing a Chopin impromptu quite magically when Tab charged in with Wham full blast on the wireless.

'Turn it off,' said Cameron sharply.

'Why should I?'

'Turn it *off*,' yelled Marcus, but he stopped playing and shut the piano.

Immediately Tab grinned and turned off the wireless.

'I've never been so bored in my life,' she said moodily.

Cameron's suggestion that she could unload the dishwasher was met once again with the cold blue stare.

'I'm starving. What's for supper?'

'Spaghetti hoops.'

'Yuk. What's that cooking in the oven?'

'Boeuf Provençal.'

'My favourite thing. And there are kiwi fruits in the larder. That's also my favourite thing.'

'As you haven't eaten anything I've cooked for you yet,' said Cameron coolly, 'you're going to have spaghetti hoops cooked by Mr Heinz, and then you're going to bed early. I want to spend some time with your father – alone.'

Rupert came home around half past seven, and amazed Cameron by backing her up. 'Go up to bed both of you. Cameron's looked after you all day and she needs a break. You can watch "Howard's Way".'

'Tab's been insupportable all day,' Cameron was appalled to find herself saying as soon as the children went out of the room.

Later Rupert went upstairs and Cameron toured wearily round the house, picking up kids' clothes. If she put a wash on tonight she could iron them first thing in the morning.

Rupert found Tab curled up in bed in a blue nightie, looking through a photograph album of when Helen and Rupert were married: 'Wasn't I a sweet little baby? Look at me riding on Badger's back.'

Rupert was not to be deflected. 'Why have you been so bloody to Cameron?' he said, sitting down on the bed. 'I told you to be nice to her.'

'I hate her,' said Tab calmly, 'and all the grooms hate her, and they say Mr and Mrs Bodkin hate her because she's so bossy. Even Beaver and Blue hate her.'

'Rubbish! Beaver and Blue adore her.'

'Shows how thick they are, then.'

'I told you to be nice to her,' repeated Rupert sternly.

'It's all God's fault,' said Tab, petulantly pulling the duvet up to her chin. 'I prayed specially hard to him this morning to make me really nice to Cameron, and he did absolutely nothing about it.'

Rupert thought it so funny he had to go straight off and tell Cameron. He found her in the drawing-room, rigid with anger.

'What was this doing on my side of the bed?' She handed Rupert a prayer book bound in ivory. 'Look inside,' she said shrilly.

'*To my own darling Rupert*,' read Rupert slowly. '*All my love, Helen. All other things to their destruction draw, only our love hath no decay.*' He grinned at Cameron. 'Well, Helen certainly goofed on that one, didn't she?'

'Tab must have put it there,' hissed Cameron.

'Don't be fucking stupid. She wouldn't understand words like decay and destruction.'

'Bullshit,' screamed Cameron. 'She's the most destructive kid I've ever met, and she certainly understands "To my own darling Rupert, All my love, Helen".'

'What's wrong with that?' protested Rupert. 'Most children do want their mothers and fathers to love each other. Didn't you?'

'She's insanely spoilt.' Cameron could hear the obsessive rattle in her voice. 'Can't you see how she fawns all over you and freezes out everyone else? Your whole relationship with her is overly symbiotic.'

'I don't know what symbiotic means.' Rupert's voice was suddenly brutally icy. 'But it's fuck all to do with you how I handle my children. I suggest you read this prayer book yourself. It might teach you a little Christianity.'

'Where are you going?' she said as he went towards the door.

'To bed. I don't want any dinner. And you can bloody well sleep in the spare room.'

A minute later she heard the front door open and the dogs barking. Terrified Rupert had stormed out, she ran into the hall to find Mr and Mrs Bodkin blinking in the light, clutching their suitcases and looking sheepish.

'I hope you didn't mind us coming home a day early,' muttered Mrs Bodkin, 'but we wanted to see the children, and I thought you might need a bit of help with their meals and their washing. Mrs Gordon likes everything back in good order.'

Cameron was never so pleased to see anyone. 'Sure, it's OK,' she said. 'I shouldn't have made you have the weekend off. We've all missed you. There's some supper in the oven if you're hungry.'

The next moment she was sent flying by Tabitha tearing downstairs and throwing herself into Mrs Bodkin's arms. 'Oh, Mrs B,' she said in a choked voice, 'I'm so glad you're home. It's so horrid when you're not here.'

The next day passed without incident until the afternoon. Cameron, who knew she should have disarmed Tab by being sweet, or at least outwardly unmoved, spent the day sulking, thawing out, then sulking again. The children were due to go back to Warwickshire after tea. Rupert had bought the pony, Biscuit, for Tab, and would drive pony and two children back in the trailer.

Mrs Bodkin finished the ironing and packed the children's cases, while Rupert and the children watched *High Society* on television. Ecstatic about the new pony, Tabitha sprawled on

496

Rupert's knee, defiantly covering him with kisses. Cameron, determinedly doing the *Guardian* crossword, sat on the sofa as far away from Rupert as possible. They hadn't spoken since last night. The sight of Cameron's long smooth brown thighs in the shortest of khaki shorts, however, was finally too much for Rupert. As the credits came up at the end he stretched out, putting a hand on her leg.

'Don't touch her,' screamed Tab. 'It's disgusting,' and, bursting into tears, she fled upstairs. Rupert followed her to find out what was the matter. He came down shaking his head. 'It's the same old story. She wants me and Helen to get together again like Bing Crosby and Grace Kelly, so she can live here all the time.'

The following morning Rupert got a letter from Taggie: *Dear Roopurt,* she had written, *thank you for the luvly puppy. He is sweet we called him Clawdeeus becos patrick says it goes with gurtrude. they love eech other now. thank you for the shampain. Sorry we did not come out to dinner. I hope you understand. Yours sincearly Taggie O'Hara.*

Rupert wanted to weep.

'Is that from one of the children?' said Cameron, reading over his shoulder. 'They don't teach them much spelling in class. Christ, it's from Taggie. She's completely illiterate. How could Maud and Declan have produced something quite so dumb?'

The weekend left Cameron exhausted and with a numb sense
of failure. What sort of monster was she to detest an innocent
little girl of nine? Desperate for someone to dump on, she
was tempted to ask Seb or even Charles Fairburn out to
lunch, but decided it was too risky. Tony might easily have
bugged their telephones. She longed to talk to Declan. He
was so wise and she craved his approval beyond anything,
but she didn't think this was the way to win it. He'd just
assume she'd been treating Tab like a Corinium employee.
In the end she rang up Janey Lloyd-Foxe who, stuck at home
with a new baby and frantically trying to finish a book, was
only too happy for any distraction. They met for lunch in
London.

Janey rolled up looking stunning and fantastically brown.
'It's typing topless in the garden,' she explained. 'My bum
and legs are as white as blackboard chalk because they're
hidden under the table. I've got to finish this bloody book
because we're desperately broke. Billy's absolutely fed up with
the BBC, too. I do hope Venturer get the franchise. D'you
think we will?'

'Hard to tell,' said Cameron. 'We ought to on form, but
there are so many wild cards in the pack, and Declan and
Rupert really aren't getting on at the moment.'

'They're both so tricky and self-willed,' grumbled Janey.
'Hello.' She beamed up at an Italian waiter who was utterly

mesmerized by her brown breasts which seemed to squirm in her low-cut pink dress like day-old puppies. 'Neither of us wants to work this afternoon, so let's kick off with duo enormo vodkos et tonicos, then we can get wildly drunk and indiscreet. You are lucky not having to worry about schedules and costings any more,' Janey added, as the waiter floated back to the bar. 'It must be bliss being supported by Rupert.'

'He's not very pleased with me,' confessed Cameron, pleating the tablecloth. Then she told Janey about the weekend.

'Darling,' said Janey, taking a hefty belt of vodka, 'get one thing straight. It's not you. I told Helen yonks ago that she never need worry about Rupert marrying again because no one would take on Tab. She's adorable until she suspects anyone might take Rupert away from her, then she's Catherine de Medici crossed with all the Borgias! Mind you,' Janey went on, plunging a cauliflower floret deep into a bowl of mayonnaise, 'Tab hasn't had it easy. Helen tries to be fair, but it's obvious to anyone that Marcus is the Granny Smith of her eye. She's never got on with Tab.'

'Marcus is a really nice kid,' said Cameron. 'Why's Rupert so mean to him?'

'Jealousy. Rupert and Helen were going through one of their many bad patches when Marcus was born. Helen lavished all her affection on Marcus. Rupert started lavishing all his affection on show jumping and other women. It doesn't help that Marcus looks just like Helen, and Rupert doesn't want any reminders of her around him any more.'

'But Marcus just longs for Rupert's approval.'

'I know,' said Janey. 'It's really sad. Just as Rupert used to long for Helen's approval, but she always dismissed him as a handsome hunk and show jumping as a very second-class occupation.'

As the waiter wheeled up the hors d'oeuvres trolley Janey's eyes fell lasciviously on Mediterranean prawns, stuffed aubergine and oeuf à la Russe.

'Go on,' urged Cameron. 'It's my treat.'

'What are you going to have?' asked Janey, as the waiter piled up her plate.

'Just cold salmon and a radicchio salad.'

'Oh, that sounds nice,' said Janey. 'I'll have that next, and lots of white wine.'

'What was Helen like?' said Cameron, trying not to sound too interested as a second besotted waiter helped them to Sancerre.

'Oh, a sweet old thing really, but very earnest and high-minded, not like *us*.' Even grinning with her mouth full of tarragon-flavoured mushrooms, Janey had all the charm in the world, thought Cameron. The 'like us' seemed to unite them in a conspiracy of naughtiness and fun.

'Did she love Rupert?'

'Ish,' said Janey. 'She always disapproved of him. Mind you, he was *disgraceful* in those days. But underneath all that stunning self-assurance and sex appeal, and lack of introspection, he does need the clapping. He wouldn't be so competitive if he didn't. He's so macho, what he really needs is some very gentle, calm, submissive girl who thinks he's absolutely marvellous.'

Like Taggie O'Hara, thought Cameron savagely.

'Goodness, I shouldn't have eaten all that,' said Janey later as she put her knife and fork together. 'But I suppose I can make the excuse that I still haven't got my figure back after the baby.'

'Has Tab truly fought with all Rupert's girlfriends?' asked Cameron.

'Well, he turns them over so fast it's hard to remember,' said Janey. Then, catching sight of Cameron's face, she added quickly, 'But I'm sure it'll be different now he's met you. They liked Beattie Johnson, I think, but she was such a slut, she never imposed any régime on them, and never minded if they were frightened of the dark and wanted to get into Rupert's bed. The more the merrier as far as Beattie was concerned. I'm amazed they got any sleep with her drunken snoring.'

Knowing both Janey and Beattie Johnson had pages on national newspapers, Cameron suspected an element of professional jealousy.

500

'What d'you figure I should do about Tab?' she asked despairingly. 'Rupert's planning to have her over every weekend this summer.'

'He won't,' said Janey soothingly. 'He'll get distracted. But actually I think you ought to go back to work. You're far too bright to hang about all summer brooding about Tab and being Rupert's concubine.'

'It's so hard,' said Cameron. 'I've had plenty of offers, but all from companies in other parts of the country, and I don't want to leave Rupert. I've been offered loads of freelance work too, but nothing that grabs me. I guess you're right, I must do something.'

'You probably miss the bustle at Corinium, and Tony Baddingham too. I've always thought he was very attractive in a dark satanic way.'

'We were together for three years,' admitted Cameron. 'He had his moments, but he was a devil.'

'That forked tongue must have made him very good at oral sex,' said Janey wickedly.

Cameron laughed.

Having hardly touched her lunch, she put her knife and fork together. Leaning over, Janey forked up Cameron's salmon and, wrapping it in a paper napkin, put it in her bag.

'D'you mind if I take it home for my cat, Harold Evans? He's fourteen tomorrow and he loves salmon as much as he hates London.'

While Cameron was in London with Janey, Rupert went over to The Priory in an attempt to melt the dangerous *froideur* that seemed to have developed between him and Declan.

Declan, however, seemed enchanted to see him. Switching off Brahms' Fourth, and making a heavily gin-laced jug of Pimm's – 'Just the kind of focking English upper-class drink you would like!' – he took Rupert out into the garden.

'Is that the new puppy's work?' said Rupert, noticing a shredded bedroom slipper on the lawn and the flattened flower beds.

'I'm afraid so. He's been re-christened High Claudius, as

501

he rolled on onspeakable fox's crap yesterday, and, roshing in, leapt all over Professor Graystock who'd dropped in to drool over Taggie! At least he got rid of the Professor double quick – so he does have his advantages! It's all right,' he added hastily, misreading the sudden bootfaced expression on Rupert's face, 'he's a dear little dog – we all love him. Caitlin's taken him and Gertrude for a walk.'

He poured the Pimm's into two pint mugs, then put the jug in the shade under a nearby chestnut tree. It was another glorious afternoon. Grasshoppers scraped like toy violins in the long grass, a marbled white butterfly basked on a cushion of thyme. Through the silver trunks of the beech trees they could just see Rupert's cornfields turning gold. Even the birds were silent, worn out with feeding their young.

Declan stretched out. 'It's days like this that make that terrible long winter seem worthwhile. D'you know we've been here for nearly a year?'

'Here's to many more,' said Rupert, noticing how tired Declan was looking again. 'How's the book going?'

'All right, except that I'm constantly disturbed by my wife and daughter screaming at each other.'

'Taggie screaming?' said Rupert in surprise.

'Never Taggie. Maud and Caitlin. Maud's menopause appears to be coinciding with Caitlin's adolescence. I'm thinking of calling in the International Peacekeeping Force.'

'I could have done with them this weekend,' said Rupert, swotting an ant. 'My children were staying. Tab and Cameron were like weasels at each other's jugulars. Why can't women get on with each other? Men never fight.'

Declan laughed. 'I'd never have cast Cameron as Mary Poppins.'

Idly they discussed the franchise. Declan had recruited a very good girl from Yorkshire Television as Head of Children's Programmes. Then, heavily prompted by Rupert, he confessed he was desperately pushed again for money.

'Have you spent all that thirty-five thousand already?' said Rupert disapprovingly. 'You shouldn't keep sloping off to grope Maud in the Lakes.'

'I know, but I'd been working flat out and she's so restless. And I've just paid a massive tax bill and Patrick's fare to Australia and Caitlin's school fees for last term. And I've never seen anything like the electricity bill. Talk about electric shock treatment. Poor Tag's the only breadwinner. She's over at Monica's at the moment, filling up her deep freeze.'

'Can't she shove Tony in as well?' said Rupert, fishing a piece of cucumber out of his mug. 'I expect he'll force the poor darling to taste everything first in case she's poisoning them.'

Declan wasn't listening. His Mini, which was a 1976 model welded together by dog hair, rust and mud, which had only passed its MOT for the last few years as a result of prayer and huge sums of money changing hands, had finally given up the ghost, he told Rupert.

'You can borrow one of my cars for the moment,' said Rupert. 'In actual fact, what you need is a massive cash injection. D'you want an advance from the Venturer kitty?'

'We'll need all of that. I've got to earn it. I've spent the last week writing a script for a fifty-minute dramatized documentary on Yeats.'

'Who?'

'The Irish poet. The man I'm writing the book about,' said Declan impatiently.

'Ah,' said Rupert. Then, regaining the ascendancy, 'Doesn't sound like a money-spinner to me.'

'Will be – if it's good enough. I've sold the idea to Channel Four. And the IBA will be in raptures. Lady Gosling's half-Irish.'

Lying on his back, listening to the hum of insects and the idle cooing of the wood pigeons, gazing up at Taggie's bedroom window, Rupert suddenly had a brainwave. 'If Freddie and I put up some more money, you can afford to have Cameron produce and direct it, so we can keep it in the family.'

'Indeed you will not,' said Declan mutinously. 'Cameron and I don't get on.'

Rupert turned towards Declan, eyes squinting against the sun: 'Time you bloody learned. She really thinks you're great. She just has a communication problem. And it'll give her something to do. She's like a sheep dog, she needs work.'

'To stop her getting in your hair?' snapped Declan.

Rupert, who hadn't had any lunch, had now finished all the fruit in his Pimms and was reduced to eating the mint. 'I'm thinking of Venturer, not myself,' he said sanctimoniously, as Declan filled up both their mugs. 'We just don't want her getting restless and running back to Tony.'

'It'd mean several weeks in Ireland,' said Declan. 'We'll have to go on a recce fairly soon, and once we've cast it and fixed up the people to interview, I want to start shooting in early September. Then we'll need another week at the end of November to do the Coole woods in Autumn.'

'Perfect,' said Rupert. 'I'll be popping over to Ireland all the time from now on for the Autumn sales, so Cameron won't suffer too badly from withdrawal symptoms.'

'It's a terrible gamble,' said Declan broodingly. 'She and I never got on at Corinium; why should we get on now?'

'Because Tony won't be there putting the boot in. I promise you, Cameron really, really admires your work.'

Declan blushed slightly. 'Well, she's got to read the script before committing herself. I'm not having her working on something she doesn't like one hundred per cent.'

Cameron rang Declan later that evening, trying to keep the excitement out of her voice. 'I've just got back from London and read your script. I just love it. The characters are terrific and all the ideas for interviews are just great. The text reads so beautifully; it's superb.'

Declan was utterly disarmed by such uncharacteristic enthusiasm. For any writer, waiting for the first reaction is a nail-biting experience. Ursula, who'd typed the script out, had said she'd loved it, but then she was paid to.

'I'd just adore to do it,' went on Cameron, 'if you really figure I'm the right person?'

'Sure you are,' said Declan. 'I've just been talking to Jeremy at Channel Four and told him you might be interested. He's mad about the idea.'

'You look as though you're floating on Eire,' said Rupert as Cameron put down the telephone.

'You won't mind my being away so much?'

'Yes,' said Rupert, taking her in his arms, 'of course I will, but you've got to have your freedom. I did when I was show jumping. It was the one thing that fuelled me.'

Cameron blushed. 'Do you swear it was Declan's idea I should direct it?'

'Would I lie to you?' said Rupert blandly. 'He asked me to ask you. He really admires your work. He just has a communication problem.'

'Oh, wow!' sighed Cameron. 'I feel like the first woman on the moon.'

38

Deliriously happy to be working again, Cameron threw herself into producing Declan's programme. Much of her time was spent in London or over at The Priory and she turned one of Rupert's upstairs bedrooms into a study so she could work there as well. Rupert, who'd been neglecting the yard and his business interests, and still had a full diary as an MP despite the summer recess, was also kept very busy. This suited them both; they continued to argue a lot, but sex at least was miraculous when they met. Even the children's visits seemed less of a hassle. Mrs Bodkin did all the work, and when Tabitha became unbearable, which was most of the time, instead of rowing with her, Cameron retreated upstairs to work.

On the franchise front, the IBA had now sifted through everyone's lengthy applications with a toothcomb and fired off letters to all the consortiums containing supplementary questions about programme plans, management structure, studios and general finance.

'We promised them a cross between Camelot and Utopia,' said Declan, 'and now we've got to justify it.'

The long written answer to this letter was almost as crucial in winning the franchise as the original application. Once again, therefore, the Venturer team had to get together to thrash out policy. Meetings at anyone's house were now considered too risky, as Tony had stepped up his espionage since Cameron had defected.

'I was followed down Cotchester High Street by the most ravishing piece of rough trade this morning,' said Charles Fairburn petulantly, 'but I couldn't work out if it was my lucky day or he was a member of the Baddingham KGB.'

Rupert, being such a practised adulterer, was therefore deputed to find a meeting-place where they wouldn't be found out. He chose a seedy room over a nightclub in a back street in Cheltenham.

'If this is where you bring your mistresses,' grumbled Georgie Baines when he arrived for the first meeting, 'I can see why they get fed up.'

Night after night, therefore, through the end of July and a long hot August, Declan, Freddie, Bas, Rupert, Cameron, Lord Smith, Harold White, and the Corinium Moles – when they could get away – met up to hammer out the answers. Charles Fairburn still turned up every time in a different disguise, which made everyone giggle. They needed to. Declan, deadly serious now, insisted everyone drank only Perrier until the meeting was over. They were nearly half-way through their long ordeal in the franchise fight and nervous tension was mounting.

At least they were spared the Bishop, who was spending a month in the Holy Land, and Professor Graystock, who was in Greece researching a book. But they missed Dame Enid, who'd gone on a walking tour in Wales with a woman friend, and, after 12th August, when he pushed off to Scotland to shoot, they missed the inanities of the Lord-Lieutenant. They'd all grown very fond of Henry. Janey Lloyd-Foxe, hampered by two children and a book to finish, seldom showed up. Billy was in Australia making a film about rugger for the BBC.

For Wesley Emerson, August was a wicket month. He took 8 for 42 against the Australians in the Leeds Test. Venturer basked in his reflected glory.

The letter with the answers to the supplementary questions was dispatched to the IBA at the beginning of September, by which time the franchise wives were getting very fed up. The long summer holidays were slowly grinding to a halt. The smell of moulding leaves and bonfires, the sight of huge red suns and dewy cobwebs hanging on the fences, reminded them with a pang that summer had already had its run.

Sarah Stratton, for example, not only had Paul hanging round at home, out of work and grumpily demoralized, but also his ghastly daughters who never stopped implying that Daddy would be Prime Minister now if he had stayed with Mummy, and that by going out to work Sarah was neglecting him. Sarah and James's afternoon programme was off the air for the summer. Paul and the girls watched the local news and knew that Sarah finished at seven, or even six-thirty on 'Crossroads' days. The studio was only twenty minutes from home. All were waiting bootfaced to start supper if she weren't home by eight.

Valerie Jones was increasingly irritated that Freddie seemed to be spending so much time on the stupid franchise. Completely off gardening since James had failed to immortalize her opening, Valerie had dragged Wayne and Sharon off to a villa in Portugal for a month. She'd all but persuaded Taggie to join them, and to do the cooking, until that fiendish Rupert talked her out of it, so instead they got a local slut called Conceptiona, who got so terribly on Fred-Fred's nerves (he hated foreign food anyway) that he buzzed off back to Gloucestershire saying he had too much on. As he'd been wandering round the villa with *nothing on* at all, in order to get a suntan (no doubt Rupert's fiendish influence again) this seemed very illogical.

Monica Baddingham also had, as Cameron would have said, a somewhat 'stressful' summer. There had been no discussion between her and Tony about Cameron's defection, beyond the fact that Corinium had lost a megastar and an essential weapon in the franchise battle. Privately Monica realized Tony was utterly devastated. Being humane and kindly, she felt very sorry for him, in the same way as she did for her poor distressed gentlefolk, her battered wives, her stray dogs and everyone else who was the recipient of her inexhaustible charity.

It was tragic that Tony couldn't level with her. Comforting him, they might have grown closer. But at least she listened patiently to his diatribes against Declan and Rupert, and stoically accepted that he would want to sleep with her more than once a week until he found a new mistress.

Much more worrying was that Archie, her favourite child, now seventeen and not due to take his A-levels until next year, was still enjoying a most unsuitable fling with the ghastly Tracey Makepiece, whom he'd met at the O'Hara New Year's Eve party. Both Monica and Tony were terrified Archie would make her pregnant and be forced into an early marriage; or, because the Makepieces didn't believe in abortion or adoption, the baby Baddingham would be taken into the bosom of the Makepiece family and be a drain on Archie's quite insufficient pocket money for the rest of his life.

'Why the hell can't you find a girl of your own class?' roared Tony, forbidding Archie to see her any more. Archie had obviously taken no notice. One morning in early August, putting on Archie's Barbour by mistake, Monica found a letter in Tracey's loopy handwriting: '*I will love you dearest, until all the seas run dry.*' Archie had promptly been shunted off to Tuscany for three weeks.

Most despondent of all the wives, however, was Maud. No one had fallen in love with her for ages, and Declan, having been totally obsessed with the franchise, and then his Yeats programme, was now totally obsessed with both. Not wanting to leave Maud when she was so depressed, apprehensive about going to Ireland with Cameron, Declan tried to persuade Maud to make a return to acting and play Yeats's great love, Maud Gonne, in the programme, so she could come with them. Maud, terrified of failure, turned him down flatly and then detested herself for doing so. It was as though she was deliberately pushing him into an affair with Cameron.

Finally, Caitlin had been home most of the summer, full of teenage moodiness, criticizing everything Maud did, particularly her clothes, which Caitlin claimed were so out of date they should be called 'a first world wardrobe'. Maud was not amused; she'd always prided herself on being able to go to a party in a pair of Declan's pyjamas, with a jewelled comb in her hair, and look marvellous.

One morning towards the end of August Maud read a piece in the *Daily Mail* about Princess Michael entering a new golden age of maturity and confidence. She's the same age as me, thought Maud broodily, and I'm ten years younger than Joan Collins, and look how great she looks. Why am I riddled with self-doubt and about as confident as a mongrel at Crufts?

Having borrowed a hundred pounds and her new violet dress off Taggie, she decided to ignore Declan's bank balance as well and go into Cotchester and buy some new clothes. As she got ready, Caitlin wandered into her bedroom.

Even in the space of the holidays she seemed to have shot up several inches, and was as tall as Maud now. Her brace was off her teeth, she'd grown her hair and peroxided it canary yellow. Chronic sulkiness was the only thing that stopped her being incredibly pretty.

Changing her parting slightly, Maud noticed three grey hairs and tugged them out in horror.

'You'd quadruple the men after you if you had short hair or used Sun-In or a bit of gel,' said Caitlin; 'and that's Taggie's dress you're wearing.'

'When I was your age,' countered Maud, 'I had hundreds of boys after me. I can't think why you don't.'

'I'm choosey, that's why. Why don't you have your face lifted?'

Maud gazed at her reflection. Perhaps she ought to, but unable to face a filling at the dentist, she'd never cope with the pain. Anyway she'd rather have her spirits lifted. Her body looked OK still, but crêped when it was squeezed, which didn't seem very often these days. I'm over the hill, she thought with a shiver, as she started to put on her make-up. Declan will go off to Ireland – and with Cameron Cook.

'Eyeliner goes on much better if you pull your eyelids out,' said Caitlin, 'and you're not going to wear those ghastly slingbacks?'

'Better than your revolting clodhoppers,' said Maud furiously. 'It's like sharing a house with a carthorse. And what are you going to do with yourself all day?'

'I'm going to spend the morning dyeing my hair,' said Caitlin.

Cotchester was full of tourists, drifting aimlessly down the High Street, photographing the cathedral and the ancient houses, and the statue of Charles I. By contrast, Monica Baddingham, striding purposefully through the crowds, was like a powerboat chugging through a flotilla of yachts on a windless day. She detested shopping – such a time-consuming activity. But she needed batteries for her Walkman and there was a new recording of *Don Giovanni* on order which, maddeningly, hadn't arrived, and she had to pick up some scores of *The Merry Widow*.

Every year the West Cotchester Hunt put on a play which was performed to large noisy audiences in November. This year they had decided to be slightly more ambitious and join forces with Cotchester Operatic Society to put on *The Merry Widow*.

Monica had already been appropriately cast as Valencienne, a virtuous wife. Charles Fairburn had been inappropriately cast as her randy admirer Camille. Bas Baddingham was still dickering over whether to play the male lead, Count Danilo, but as yet the director, Barton Sinclair – ex-Covent Garden, no less – was still searching for someone to play Hanna, the Merry Widow. He was holding auditions in Cotchester Town Hall that very day, but was deeply pessimistic that anyone would be beautiful or stylish enough, or have a sufficiently good voice. Luck, however, was on Barton Sinclair's side. Outside the Bar Sinister Monica bumped into Maud.

'How jolly nice,' said Monica in her raucous voice as she kissed Maud. 'I've been hoping I'd run into you for ages. I wanted to say how wonderful Taggie's been. Completely saved my life cooking for all the hordes this summer. You must be so proud of her.'

Maud said, yes, she supposed she was.

'But she's getting too thin,' went on Monica. 'She used to be so round, soft and smiling. I hope she's not taking on too much. You, on the other hand, look splendid. How's Declan?'

'Oh, obsessed with the wretched franchise,' said Maud fretfully.

'Isn't it a ghastly bore?' sighed Monica. 'Tony can't think of anything else. But I don't see why, just because our husbands are on different sides, we can't be friends.'

It was very hot in Cotchester High Street. The cool garlic-scented gloom of the Bar Sinister beckoned.

'Nor do I,' said Maud. 'Why don't we go in and have lunch?'

'What a good idea,' said Monica in excitement. 'Ploughman's lunch, and half a pint of cider.'

Maud's aims were slightly more ambitious, and they were soon sitting down with Muscadet and crespolini.

'Oh, look, there's James Vereker and Sarah Stratton,' said Monica. 'What's Declan doing at the moment?'

'He's off to Ireland with Cameron Cook,' said Maud.

'Oh.' Monica's forkful of crespolini stopped on the way to her mouth. 'But I thought . . .'

'. . . she was living with Rupert. Yes, she is, but she's making a film with Declan in Ireland.'

Her tongue loosened by a third glass, Maud told Monica about Declan's trying to persuade her to play Maud Gonne, and how her nerve had failed. 'I couldn't face Cameron screaming at me when I didn't come up to scratch,' she confessed. 'Her sarcasm could strip furniture, and I've always found it difficult to act in front of Declan.'

Monica, at this point, became very thoughtful. 'But you would like to go back?'

'Oh yes, but at the moment I've got about as much self-confidence as a leveret at a coursing meeting.'

Monica fished in her shopping bag and brought out one of the scores of *The Merry Widow*. On the cover was a painting of a beautiful woman, with hair swept up under a big pink hat and a waist, in its swirling cyclamen-pink dress, as slender as her neck. She was raising a glass of champagne in one long purple-gloved hand. Four handsome men with black twirling moustaches were raising their glasses to her in admiring salute.

It was Maud's perfect fantasy. What did gel and Sun-In matter to that woman?

'Why don't you start with something less ambitious than Maud Gonne?' said Monica. 'We're desperate for someone to play the Merry Widow.'

'I couldn't,' faltered Maud. 'It's a very demanding part.'

'Nonsense,' said Monica briskly. 'You'd waltz it.'

'What are my two favourite women doing lunching at my restaurant without telling me?' said a voice.

It was Bas, absolutely black from a fortnight's polo in America.

'Bas,' said Monica delightedly. 'I know I'm not supposed to talk to you either, after the dreadful way you've betrayed Tony, but sit down and help me persuade Maud to audition for Hanna.'

Bas needed little persuading. Up to now he'd by-passed Maud in his amorous travels, partly because he had long-range aims for Taggie and partly because he'd realized how dotty Maud had been about Rupert at Christmas. Certainly, in the soft lighting of the Bar Sinister, she looked stunning today, and that violet dress was very becoming. It emphasized her white skin and just missed clashing with the gorgeous red hair, and all those undone buttons showed off a Cheddar Gorge of cleavage. Another bottle of Muscadet was ordered.

'Bas is toying with the idea of playing your leading man,' said Monica.

'Hopefully it'll lead to other things,' said Basil, rubbing one of his long muscular, polo-playing thighs against Maud's as he re-filled her glass.

Later, not even allowing her a cup of black coffee to sober her up, Basil and Monica frogmarched Maud down the High Street to the Town Hall where the director, Barton Sinclair, had reached screaming point, having heard ten amateur hopefuls murdering the score.

Up on stage now, the eleventh, a very made-up blonde,

who'd never see fifty again, was crucifying the Vilja song. The pianist was desperately trying to keep in time with her. A huge bluebottle buzzing against a window pane was having more success.

'She'd be too fat even if you looked through the wrong end of your binoculars,' whispered Bas to Maud. 'At least you can do better than that.'

'I can't,' muttered Maud in terror. 'That's Top G she's missing.'

As she tried to bolt, Bas's arm closed round her waist. 'Yes, you can,' he murmured. 'Just think of the fun we can have rehearsing together night after night, and it won't be all singing I can tell you.'

'Thank you very much,' said Barton Sinclair in his chorus-boy drawl.

'I sang the part in 1979,' said the blonde, teetering down the steps in her four-inch heels. 'It brought the house down.'

'Pity you weren't buried under the rubble,' muttered Barton. 'We'll be in touch. I'll be making a decision at the end of the week,' he told her. Then, waiting until she was safely out of the door, he turned to Monica. 'That's the lot, thank God. Talk about scraping the barrel organ.'

'I'm going home,' said Maud.

'Could you hear just one more?' said Monica.

Barton Sinclair looked at his watch and sighed: 'Do I have to? I was hoping to get the three forty-five back to Paddington.'

'It'll be worth getting the next train, I promise you,' said Monica. 'This is Maud O'Hara. She used to act and sing professionally.'

Barton Sinclair straightened his flowered tie, and smoothed his straggly mouse-brown hair.

'You certainly look the part,' he said.

'I haven't practised,' bleated Maud, the crespolini and the Sancerre churning like a tumble-dryer inside her.

'Try the same song,' said Barton, handing her the score. 'Take it slowly, Mike,' he added to the pianist.

'You come in on the last quaver of the fourth bar,' the pianist told Maud kindly.

Below her, Maud could see their faces: Monica's eager, flushed and unpainted, Basil's sleek and mahogany, and Barton Sinclair's London night owl and deathly pale. They seemed infinitely more terrifying than a first night audience at Covent Garden.

'I can't,' she whispered, wringing her sweating hands.

'Go on, darling,' said Bas. 'We're all on your side.'

Off went the pianist. Maud fluffed the opening.

'I'm sorry. Could we start again?'

'Of course,' said Barton.

Off went the pianist again, and Maud opened her mouth.

> *There once lived a Vilja, a fair mountain sprite,*
> *She danced on a hill in the still of the night.*

Her voice was sweet, true and hesitant, but suddenly, as she launched into the main theme, it seemed to soar out glorious and joyful, stilling the bluebottle and taking the dust off the rafters, and the four other people in the room felt the hair rising on the backs of their necks.

'A star is re-born,' whispered Monica, wiping her eyes.

'I *am* going to have a nice Autumn,' reflected Basil. 'Over forty, they're always so grateful!'

'*Vilja, Oh, Vilja, be tender and true,*' sang Maud, triple pianissimo, '*Love me and I'll die for you.*'

For a second there was silence, then her audience burst out clapping and cheering.

'*Come into Covent Garden, Maud,*' sang Basil.

'You've got the part,' said Barton Sinclair. 'The only problem is how much you're going to show up the others.'

'Thank you, Barton,' said Monica and Basil in unison.

After that they all went back to the Bar Sinister for several more bottles of Muscadet and Barton Sinclair only just made the six forty-five.

•

Tony and Declan were very apprehensive when they heard the news of such close fraternization between the rival franchise sides. On reflection, however, Tony decided he'd definitely got the better bargain. While Maud was a rattle who drank far too much, Monica drank very little and was incredibly discreet.

'Keep your trap shut and your ears open,' Tony told her. 'You may learn some interesting things.'

'I'm not pumping anyone,' said Monica firmly. 'It's simply not on. Only if anyone lets anything drop.'

'It'll be knickers if Bas has anything to do with it,' said Tony.

Declan, however, who was going to have to spend the second half of September and much of October in Ireland with Cameron, was principally relieved that Maud was so much happier. The sound of her carolling away upstairs practising her songs reminded him of the carefree days in Dublin when they were first married. Perhaps, if *The Merry Widow* were a success, she'd have enough confidence to take up acting professionally again.

Caitlin, who had now dyed her custard-yellow hair so black it almost looked blue, found her mother's euphoria even more irritating than her previous picky depression, and decided to push off to London for a few days to stay with some schoolfriends. She was going back the week after next and might as well have some fun before the prison doors clanged round her again.

She found Taggie in the kitchen fainting over a final reminder from the Electricity Board. 'I can't think why it's so high.'

'Mummy's vibrator's battery-operated, so it can't be that,' said Caitlin. 'Hullo, darling,' she added, hugging Claudius.

'He's in disgrace,' sighed Taggie. 'He's just eaten one of Mummy's new slingbacks.'

'Good thing; they were gross,' said Caitlin. 'Every Claud has a silver lining! Can you lend me fifty pounds to go to London?'

'I haven't got it,' protested Taggie. 'I've just lent Daddy a hundred pounds for a new pair of cords for Ireland.'

'At least I'll be gone for nearly a week, so you won't have to feed me,' cajoled Caitlin. 'So that's worth fifty.'

'And we haven't done your trunk yet,' wailed Taggie. 'You've grown out of everything, you need new Aertex shirts, and both your games' skirts are split.'

'Oh, sew them up,' said Caitlin airily. 'We can't possibly afford new ones if we're so poor.'

39

After a riotous five days in London, Caitlin rolled up at Paddington Station with just enough money for her half-fare home. Her blue-black hair was coaxed upward at the front into a corkscrew quiff. She was wearing peacock feather earrings, a black and white sleeveless T-shirt, a black Lycra mini which just covered her bottom, laddered black tights, huge black clumpy shoes, all of which belonged to various friends of hers, a great deal of black eye make-up, and messages in Biro all over her arms.

It was hardly surprising, therefore, that the man at the ticket desk refused to believe she was under sixteen. A most unseemly screaming match ensued, which first amused then irritated the growing queue of passengers behind Caitlin, who began to worry they might miss their trains home.

'My father is a very very famous man,' screamed Caitlin as a last resort, 'and he'll get you.'

'Don't threaten me, young lady,' said the booking clerk.

'It's people like you who turn liberals like me into racists,' screamed Caitlin even louder. 'You're just discriminating against me because I'm white. I'll report you to the Race Relations Board.'

At that moment Archie Baddingham, on his way home from his three weeks' banishment in Tuscany, reached the top of the neighbouring first-class queue. Hearing the din, and recognizing Caitlin's shrill Irish accent from New Year's Eve, he bought her a ticket.

'Remember me?' he said, tapping her on the shoulder.

'No, yes,' said Caitlin. 'You're Archie, aren't you? Can you lend me my fare, this stupid asshole won't believe I'm under sixteen.'

'I've got you a ticket,' said Archie.

'I can't accept a ticket from you,' stormed Caitlin irrationally. 'Your father's been absolutely shitty to my father.'

'My father's shitty to everyone,' said Archie, calmly taking her arm. 'Come on, we'd better move it.'

They only just caught the train on time, but managed to find two single seats opposite each other.

'I've never travelled first class,' said Caitlin, stretching out on the orange seat and squirming her neck luxuriously against the headrest.

Archie looked wonderful, she thought. Like her, he'd shot up and lost weight. He was wearing black 501s, rolled up above black socks and black brogues with a black polo-neck tucked into a western belt with a silver buckle, black crosses in his ears, and a brown suede jacket. His blond hair, washed with soap to remove any shine, was long at the front and cut short at the back and sides. His still slightly rounded face looked thinner because of a suntan almost as dark as his eyes.

'Why are you so disgustingly brown?' asked Caitlin.

'I've just spent three weeks in Tuscany. My parents booted me out there to get over a girl.'

'Tracey-on-the-Makepiece.'

Archie grinned, making him look even more attractive. 'How d'you know that?'

'You were superglued to her at Patrick's twenty-first.'

'So I was. Actually, I'm over her, but Dad and Mum thought I wasn't, so I thought I might as well take advantage of a free holiday. Have you been away?'

'We never go anywhere. My parents are always broke. No, it's quite OK. Nothing to do with your father. They're just hopeless with money.' There was a pause. Caitlin gazed out of the window, wondering what to say next.

'What would you like to drink?' asked Archie.

'They got any Malibu?'

'I doubt it.'

'Well, vodka and tonic, then. Can I come with you?'

The Inter-City, belting towards Bristol, swayed like a drunk as they walked towards the buffet car.

'Have you had any lunch?' asked Archie, admiring her narrow waist and slim legs which were more ladder than tights.

'No,' said Caitlin.

'I'll buy you some grub then,' said Archie.

'Been to a funeral?' said the gay barman, running a lascivious eye over Archie's black clothes.

'*Passengers are reminded that it is an offence to serve intoxicating liquor to persons under the age of eighteen,*' read Caitlin loudly, as Archie paid for everything.

'Keep your vice down,' hissed Archie.

The journey back to their seat, with each of them carrying white plastic trays of vodkas and tonics, glasses, bacon sandwiches, Mars bars, and packets of crisps, was much more hazardous. They had no hands to steady themselves against the lurching train.

'Terribly sorry,' mumbled Caitlin, going scarlet, as for the third time she cannoned off a commuter back into Archie.

'Who's complaining?' said Archie.

'Thank you so much,' said Caitlin as they sped past slow winding rivers, rolling fields, and clumps of yellowing trees. 'This bacon sandwich is the best thing I've ever tasted.'

'I'm surprised you can say that with Taggie cooking for you,' said Archie. 'Every time my father compliments my mother on the food, it turns out Taggie's made it. How is she?'

'Bit low. She's hopelessly hooked on Rupert Campbell-Black.'

'Won't do her any good,' said Archie, pouring out a second vodka and tonic for Caitlin. 'He strikes women down like lightning bolts. Anyway, he's bonking my father's ex.'

'Cameron Cook,' said Caitlin dismissively. 'She's a

crosspatch, isn't she? I can't see what men see in her. My brother was crazy about her, and now she's gone off to make a film in Ireland with Daddy. I hope they don't end up in bed. People usually do on location, don't they? I'd loathe her as a stepmother.'

'Dad was mad about her. I was shit-scared he'd leave Mum and marry her,' said Archie, breaking a Mars bar and giving half to Caitlin. 'I dread my parents getting a divorce, in case they marry again and leave all their money to their new children.'

Caitlin giggled. 'Mine haven't any to leave.'

'I hear your mother's joined the cast of *The Merry Widow*. Mum told me on the telephone that she's streets ahead of everyone else.'

'At least it's got her off my back,' said Caitlin. 'She drives me crackers: "Where are you going? Who with? Why were you so long on the telephone? Who was that on the telephone? Was it a good party? Did you meet anyone nice?" Christ! Not that she's interested.'

'My mother over-reacts,' said Archie. 'She thinks the world will end if she finds a half-eaten tin of baked beans under the sofa. And she's so embarrassing! Christ, we were at a party earlier these holidays and she suddenly asked me in a loud voice if I needed a Kirby grip.'

He raked his blond locks back from his bronzed forehead.

'It looks great,' said Caitlin, 'particularly now the sun's bleached it.'

A lot of passengers got out at Didcot, so they practically had the carriage to themselves. As the cooling towers of Didcot power station belched out unearthly white steam against a darkening charcoal grey sky, the gay barman came by with a black plastic bag, gathering up rubbish.

'I want to keep my tonic tin,' said Caitlin, grabbing it back.

As she put it in her bag, Archie examined the heart-shaped face, the pointed chin, echoed by the widow's peak, the small, beautifully shaped green eyes, the snub nose, the coral-pink mouth, sweet now it was no longer set in a sulky petulant line, the blue-black mane parted on the left, which she kept lifting with her fingers and tossing over to the right.

Glancing up, she caught him staring at her and smiled.

'That's it,' said Archie wonderingly. 'Your brace has gone.'

'So have your zits,' said Caitlin.

Archie went pink: 'I fancied you the moment I saw you.'

'What about Tracey?'

'She was just a net,' said Archie.

They were nearing Cotchester now, dense woods clinging to steep hills on each side of the line giving way to lighted houses.

Archie removed his ear-rings, putting them in his pocket, because he said his father would only make a fuss. Then blushing again, he forced a tenner into the pocket of Caitlin's clinging Lycra skirt.

'What's this for?' asked Caitlin in amazement. 'I owe *you* money.'

'For a taxi,' said Archie. 'Percy, my father's chauffeur, is meeting me, and if we give you a lift he's bound to sneak to Dad.'

'It's just like the Montagues and the Capulets,' sighed Caitlin. 'I hope we don't end up like Romeo and Juliet.'

'I'll ring you tomorrow,' said Archie, 'and hopefully we can fix an evening when all our parents are away.'

Opening his bank statement next morning, Archie nearly fainted. To make matters worse, it was his mother's birthday on Friday and he'd promised to buy her the latest recording of *The Flying Dutchman*. Normally he'd have tapped his father, who was a far easier touch than Monica, but Tony was still in Edinburgh for the International Television Festival. Besides, if Tony discovered he was financing a date with Caitlin, Archie would be crated straight back to Tuscany.

He'd been stupid to show off and buy them both first-class tickets and all that booze. If only he'd been back at school, he could have raised the cash smuggling in some booze and fags, or even porn mags, and selling them to other boys on the black market.

Nor was Caitlin the kind of girl who could be fobbed off with hamburgers and a video; she needed something special.

Grimly aware that he hadn't touched any of the ridiculous amount of holiday work he'd been set, Archie gazed gloomily at the same page of Aristophanes for twenty minutes, then threw the book across the room. If he hurried he might reach the Bar Sinister before lunch and catch his Uncle Basil before he rushed off to polo or some amorous jaunt.

He found Bas humming the Vilja song from *The Merry Widow* and taking fifty pounds out of his own till.

'Can I have a quiet word?' said Archie.

'You can have several noisy ones if you like,' said Bas. 'I thought your father had forbidden you to talk to me. Where is Rambo, anyway?'

'In Edinburgh,' said Archie. 'And please don't pump me.'

He admired his uncle, who always had the loudest tweed jackets and the prettiest girls of anyone he knew.

'Have a drink?' said Bas, taking down a bottle of Chambery and two glasses.

'Yes, please. If I work really hard in the kitchens for three days, will you let me sign the bill for dinner for two on Saturday night?'

'Are you bringing Tracey Makepiece?'

'No.'

'Good. There *are* limits. I really was on Tony's side for once on that score. Yes, you can, then.'

On Saturday night Taggie's violet dress paid its second visit to the Bar Sinister in ten days – this time with Caitlin inside it. But, with the waist jacked into nothing by a black corset belt, and the skirt turned up from mid-calf to mid-thigh by Taggie, it was almost unrecognizable. Archie, having scrubbed mussels for three days in the kitchen, and suffered agonies of doubt, like Mr Toad, that his hands would ever be unwrinkled again, felt he had really earned his date. Basil was out that evening, but all the waiters were in on the secret and gave Archie and Caitlin a table in an alcove where no one else would see them. Determined to get his wages' worth,

Archie ordered a bottle of Dom Perignon and they started off with a wine race, seeing who could drink a half-pint of champagne fastest to get things warmed up. But after that they found that they were so excited by each other's company they weren't very hungry.

'This is the most delicious thing I've ever eaten,' said Caitlin as she toyed with foie gras on radicchio. 'I can't think why I can't eat more of it.'

Archie slowly undressed a giant prawn and dipped it in dill sauce. 'Try this.'

'Gosh, it's yummy. I wish school food was like this. Nellie Newstead found a used Band-Aid in her shepherd's pie last term. Aren't you dreading going back?'

'Not if you promise to write to me.'

Caitlin looked up. God, she's sweet when she smiles, thought Archie.

'Every day, if you like,' said Caitlin.

'I've looked up the distance between Rugborough and Upland House,' said Archie. 'It's only about forty miles. A mate of mine's passed his test, so we'll drive over and take you out one Sunday; and it'll be half-term soon.'

Archie was wearing a dinner jacket over black baggy trousers and a grey and white shirt over a Sisters of Mercy T-shirt. He looks incredibly cool, thought Caitlin lovingly.

As if in a dream, she watched his sunburnt hand closing over her white one; his palm felt so warm and dry that suddenly she longed for him to touch her all over.

Archie ordered another bottle of champagne.

'You really shouldn't,' protested Caitlin. 'It's frightfully expensive in restaurants, and I already owe you for my ticket and my taxi.'

'You can pay me in kind,' said Archie, gently stroking the inside of her wrist. 'A pound a kiss. No, I won't be able to afford it, a penny a kiss.'

'*Da mi basia mille*,' sighed Caitlin.

'What's that?'

'Catullus. Give me a thousand kisses.'

'Are you frightfully clever?'

'Of course, that's why I chose you.'

They screamed with laughter; suddenly the stupidest things seemed funny. Archie thought he should try and be poetic too.

'Your eyes are the same colour as beech leaves in spring,' he said, gazing into them. 'You're like a little wood nymph.'

'A dry-ad,' said Caitlin, taking a swig of her champagne. 'Nothing very dry about me.'

'What are we going to do after this?' said Archie, getting out a packet of Sobranie. 'Did you say your parents are both away?'

'Daddy's in Edinburgh, probably killing your father, but Mummy might be back from her rehearsal, although she seems to be getting later and later.'

'There's no one at home,' said Archie. 'I'll get them to get us a taxi.'

It was only when she got up to walk out of the restaurant that Caitlin realized how drunk she was. It's like InterCity all over again, she told Archie. Only by grabbing her arm did he prevent her cannoning off every table.

He kissed her all the way back to The Falconry. Caitlin, who'd spent three days practising kissing the palm of her hand, found Archie's mouth a great deal more exciting.

And when they were ensconced on Monica's huge flowered chintz sofa, having both carefully removed each other's ear-rings, Archie discovered that Caitlin's small, incredibly springy white breasts were far more thrilling than Tracey Makepiece's. It was just a question of preferring nectarines to melons. And her waist was so tiny, once he'd removed the black corset belt, that he was terrified he might snap her in two. But nothing could exceed her enthusiasm.

'I do hope I'm not too pissed to remember every minute of this tomorrow,' she said.

'Have you ever been to bed with anyone before?' Archie mumbled into the gel-stiffened straw of her hair.

'Never. Have you?'

'Yes.'

'Lots?'

'About two and three-quarters.'

525

'A man of experience,' sighed Caitlin in ecstasy.

Undoing a few more buttons, Archie, who was down to his Sisters of Mercy T-shirt now, kissed his way down her shoulder until he was sucking her right nipple. He was also wrestling with his conscience as to whether he ought to take her to bed. He wanted to like mad, but he was pissed enough to botch it, and she was certainly so pissed she might easily regret it in the morning. He had a condom in the breast pocket of his dinner jacket, which was hanging over the chair. But if he got up to get it, it might destroy the mood. But again it was unlikely they'd have an empty house to themselves for months.

As her little hands slid inside his T-shirt, he found his hand, as if magnetized, creeping up her legs.

'I'm climbing your ladders to paradise,' he whispered.

The next minute he jumped out of his skin as a great white light shone in at the window.

'Holy shit,' said Archie.

'Ooh,' squeaked Caitlin in excitement, 'it's a close encounter.'

'Bloody sight too close!' said Archie. 'It's my father flying in from Edinburgh.'

It was too late to make a bolt for it. With lightning presence of mind, Archie turned on a side light, plugged a tape in the video, pressed twelve on the remote control and did up Caitlin's buttons.

'I'll ring for a taxi as soon as I can and take you home. We'll just have to try and bluff it out.'

The next minute James Vereker's new pilot on 'Keeping Fit for the Elderly' burst on to the screen.

Tony, fortunately, had been hosting a very successful dinner for the IBA and, after several belts of brandy on the way home, was in a mellow mood. It soon became even mellower when he found his favourite son in the drawing-room with an enchantingly pretty little brunette. She looked vaguely familiar, but Tony was too vain to put on his spectacles, and by no stretch of the imagination could she be called Tracey Makepiece.

'This is Caitie,' said Archie heartily. 'I was just going to ring for a taxi to take her home.'

'Where does she live?' said Tony.

'Chalford,' lied Archie.

'I'll take her,' said Tony expansively. 'No distance at all. Let's all have a drink.'

'Caitie's tired,' said Archie desperately.

'She doesn't look it,' said Tony, admiring Caitlin's flushed cheeks and glittering green eyes. 'There's a bottle of Moët in the fridge.'

Shoving Caitlin's corset belt under a pink-and-white-striped cushion, Archie reluctantly left the room.

'Why are you watching this tape?' asked Tony as a lot of geriatrics with purple faces started doing press-ups.

'I love Corinium's programmes,' said Caitlin dreamily. 'I adore "Master Dog". We've got two dogs, one's very thick, one's brilliant. I'm sure she'd win.'

'You'd better give me a ring in the office next week,' said Tony. 'We're always looking for bright dogs.'

'I'm going back to school.'

'Where d'you go?'

'Upland House.'

Better and better, thought Tony in delight; the girl was a lady.

'D'you know my niece, Tonia Martin?'

'Frightful slag,' said Caitlin. 'She nearly got sacked last term for having boys in her room. She's got a terrible reputation at Stowe, too.'

Tony was enchanted. His sister's daughter was always being held up as a paragon of virtue.

'And d'you by any chance know Caro McKay? Teaches Biology, I think.'

'Of course. She teaches me.' Caitlin beamed. 'Ghastly old dyke. She and Miss Reading live in a two-bedroom house with a spare room.' She screamed with laughter. Tony joined in.

Once Caitlin got an audience, there was no stopping her. Archie was torn between hysterical laughter and total panic

527

as she regaled Tony with one scurrilous story after another about the daughters of his friends and colleagues.

After the bottle was finished, Tony insisted on driving her home. The only way Tracey would have got out of the house, reflected Archie, would have been in a hearse. Bitterly ashamed of himself, he funked going with them; he couldn't face the return journey.

It was a lovely night. A butter-coloured moon was gliding in and out of threatening blue-black clouds, gilding their edges. Mist was rising. There was a smell of dying bonfires and wet leaves.

'What a heavenly car,' said Caitlin, playing with the electric windows.

'How long have you known Archie?' asked Tony.

'About nine months. I don't mean to suck up, but I do think you've brought him up well. He's so considerate.'

Tony purred. 'He is a nice boy. Wish he'd work a bit harder. Have you taken your O-levels yet?'

'Last term.'

'Get a few?'

'Eleven,' said Caitlin simply. 'You seem more pleased than my mother,' she added bitterly a minute later.

Archie's father, she decided, was really, really nice. Extraordinary how her father and Tag got everything wrong. He was soon saying she might like to come to the Hunt Ball if she could get off school, and even suggested skiing in the Christmas holidays.

'Oh, I'd love to,' said Caitlin.

As they neared Penscombe, she noticed the car telephone. 'Oh, how lovely, you are lucky. Can I use it?'

'Of course,' said Tony.

The length of Caitlin's slender white thighs on the black leather seat reminded him almost unbearably of Cameron. He'd been hoping he'd bump into her at Edinburgh, but she hadn't shown up. Without thinking, Caitlin rang The Priory. It was two o'clock in the morning and no one answered for ages.

'Hullo,' murmured a sleepy voice.

'Taggie, darling,' said Caitlin, 'did I wake you?'

Tony nearly ran into a wild rose bush. Suddenly the temperature in the car dropped below zero.

'What did you say your surname was?' said Tony as Caitlin put back the receiver.

'O'Hara,' said Caitlin in a small voice.

'Declan's daughter?'

'Yes.'

'What the fuck are you playing at? Did your father put you up to this?'

'Oh, please don't tell him,' gasped Caitlin. 'He'd be furious.'

'Not any more furious than I bloody am,' roared Tony. 'The little snake! I'll murder Archie when I get home.'

'Oh, please don't!' Caitlin, who'd had a great deal too much to drink, burst into tears.

'For Christ's sake,' exploded Tony.

'I like you so much,' sobbed Caitlin, 'and I thought you liked me.'

'I do,' said Tony in exasperation, handing her his blue spotted handkerchief, reeking of the inevitable Paco Rabanne. 'I just can't stand your father.'

'*The fathers have eaten sour grapes,*' sniffed Caitlin dolefully, '*and the children's teeth are set on edge.*'

'And you're not going to tell Declan that you're going out with Archie?'

'Christ, no,' said Caitlin. 'I don't want to get butchered in my prime.'

Tony did a lot of thinking as he drove home. When he turned on the light in Archie's room, he found him huddled under the duvet, with his pyjamas buttoned up to the neck, desperately pretending to be asleep. Not for the first time, however, Tony astounded his son.

'You can go on seeing that girl as long as you try and find out as much as you can about Venturer.'

'That's immoral,' said Archie, shocked.

'Don't be bloody wet,' said Tony brutally. 'D'you want Corinium to lose the franchise?'

'No.'

'Or for me to forfeit four hundred thousand minimum a year?'

'No,' said Archie.

If he was rich, he reflected, he wouldn't have to scrub mussels for three days every time he wanted to take Caitlin out to dinner. One day she would live in The Falconry with him. His father was right, he decided, blood was thicker than water. If Declan didn't get the franchise, he, Archie, would look after Caitlin.

Taggie had a very wearing September. Getting a besotted and reelingly untogether Caitlin packed up and back to Upland House was bad enough, but dispatching Declan to Ireland was even worse.

As the departure date drew nearer, he grew increasingly reluctant to leave Maud or his precious franchise, which was just coming up to the boil.

Maud was plainly revelling in *The Merry Widow*. Declan was glad, but was her euphoria slightly over the top? And was it really necessary for her to have a bath, wash her hair and pinch yet more of Taggie's clothes before every rehearsal? And when she carolled the words '*All the world's in love with love, and I love you,*' over and over again from the Southern Turret, who were they really aimed at? As the yellow woods turned gold and the swallows seemed to postpone their departure, and even the huge red suns sunk more slowly into Rupert's woods in order to hear Maud's exquisite notes floating down the valley, Declan prayed she wasn't leading her leading man on too much.

Maud herself was much happier after Caitlin had gone back to school. No one was quicker on the draw than a teenager in love, which ruled out any illicit incoming telephone calls for Maud. But now it seemed Cameron Cook was always in the house, monopolizing the telephone and Declan, and not being deferential enough to Maud, the arrogant bitch. Anyone would think they were going off on a six months' polar expedition rather than three silly weeks on location.

Maud also bitterly resented Cameron treating Taggie like a slave. Only this morning, on the eve of departure, Perry O'Donovan, who'd been cast as Yeats, wanted Cameron to call him back, and Taggie had taken the number down wrong.

'Don't keep apologizing,' screamed Cameron, running out of breath after five minutes of invective. 'Just get it right in future.'

The only person allowed to exploit and scream at Taggie, reflected Maud, should be Maud herself.

The eve of departure, in fact, was full of spats, and now at dusk Declan was in the library firing off last-minute instructions to Freddie, who was just back from Portugal again, and Rupert, who was just off to Virginia for a few days. Between them they would probably run things far more smoothly than Declan. The appalling Professor Graystock had also dropped in, returned from his working holiday in Greece to get ready for the new university year, and was, as usual, swilling Declan's whisky. Dame Enid had just come down from upstairs, after going through Maud's *Merry Widow* score with her and making some extremely helpful suggestions.

'She'll be totally irresistible,' Dame Enid told Declan as she accepted a large pink gin. 'Wish I were playing her leading man.'

Cameron sat in the corner going through her lists for tomorrow with half an ear on the meeting. She'd checked that everyone – actors, wardrobe, make-up, and crew – knew where to meet her and Declan at Birmingham Airport; she'd double-checked that the air-conditioned coach would be waiting to take them to Sligo by early evening, and that the hotel overlooking the bay would be expecting them for dinner.

Glancing across the room at Rupert, who was gazing moodily out of the window at Claudius chewing a library book, she knew that he was bored. There was nothing he loathed more than other people's waffle. He'd been affectionate enough recently, but slightly detached; perhaps he always distanced himself before a separation. She hated the thought of him going to Virginia on his own. She couldn't imagine American women leaving anything as beautiful or as explosively macho alone. She'd lived with him for sixty-eight days and – she glanced at her watch – eighteen hours, and she still wanted him continually.

'Now, you all know that I'm on the end of the telephone,' Declan was saying. 'By the time I get back we should have the date for our IBA interview. Then we can start having dry-runs. I've booked Hardy Bisset to coach us. He's ex-IBA so he's witnessed the interviewing process from the other side. 'There's also a permanent exhibition on the history of television at the IBA,' he went on. 'Parties of school-children and tourists visit it every day. I think you should all try and have a look at it before the interview so you at least know something about the business you're intending to run. Go in, in ones or twos, or it'll look too obvious. We must get Wesley, Marti, Bas and particularly Henry along there, or they'll make complete pratts of themselves at the interview. I think that's all.'

He ran his hands through his hair and leaned back in his chair surveying the chaos on his desk in despair.

Rupert turned away from the window. 'When d'you reckon Yeats'll be finally in the can?' he said.

'For Chrissake, dumbass,' screamed Cameron, 'I've told you a hundred times, it's pronounced "Yates".'

Declan raised a disapproving eyebrow. Dame Enid was much more up front. 'You haven't learned to pronounce the word "hostile" yet, young lady,' she snapped, 'but you certainly manage to be it most of the time.'

'Thank you, Enid. The age of chivalry is not entirely dead,' said Rupert lightly, but his face had lost all expression.

Oh, God, thought Cameron, I shouldn't have said that.

'The answer to your question,' said Declan to Rupert, 'is sometime in December. We'll have to edit and do all the VOs when we get back.'

'I hope you've got in the story about Yeats cutting his precious fur coat in half because he didn't want to disturb a cat who was sitting on it,' said Dame Enid. 'Must have been a good bloke to do that.'

'Or the time that he signed a lot of cheques "Yours sincerely, W. B. Yeats",' said Professor Graystock, determined not to be upstaged. 'Or even the story . . .' he began.

Rupert had had enough – fucking intellectuals. He walked out of the library, out of the front door, and down the garden. Migrating arrows of birds were flapping down the valley. There had been a storm at lunchtime; roses were pulping and disintegrating; tobacco plants prostrated themselves like palms before his feet. Beyond the garden, in one of his fields, the grass had been flattened by the deluge, as though a herd of elephants had been having a gang bang.

Half a dozen young steers grazing there had recently been joined by a Guernsey cow and a little chocolate-brown calf, which a grateful neighbouring farmer had sent Rupert as an early birthday present. Now he could see the steers pushing the baby calf away and drinking her mother's milk. With her long-legged gawkiness, her big eyes and long fringed eyelashes, the calf reminded him of Taggie. He looked at the mother's pink udder with its four teats. Perhaps Cameron would pronounce them 'tates'. Fucking intellectual. He'd get the mother and calf moved to a field of their own tomorrow.

Instead of returning to the library, he went round to the kitchen and found Taggie listening to pop music and trying to iron a great pile of Declan's shirts and read a recipe at the same time.

'*Dashing away with a smoothing iron, she stole my heart away,*' said Rupert.

Taggie gave a start. 'I don't see how anyone could steal anybody's heart away when they're ironing,' she mumbled. 'One gets so red in the face.'

'And you're about to singe that shirt,' said Rupert.

Hastily Taggie upended the iron. 'You're just the person I wanted to see. Sarah Stratton wants me to do a dinner party for her the week after next, and she's given me this recipe all in French, and I can't make head nor tail of it.'

Rupert, who'd had plenty of experience of Sarah's writing, took the piece of paper and reeled off the recipe.

'Oh marvellous! Could you read it out to me?' said Taggie, grabbing a pencil.

Rupert was about to take the pencil, saying it'd be much quicker if he scribbled it down himself. Then he remembered something he'd read recently about encouraging dyslexics. Very slowly, making sure he didn't get too far ahead, resisting the urge to touch Taggie's white neck, revealed in all its vulnerability as her black ponytail fell sideways, he read it out.

'You are brilliant,' sighed Taggie as she finished. 'No one else could translate it. Daddy doesn't read French, nor Mummy, nor even Cameron.'

Suddenly Rupert felt ten feet tall again. What a bugger he had to fly to Virginia tomorrow, but he desperately needed a new stallion and he hoped to get in a few days' hunting. He was about to make a firm date for dinner the moment he got back when the repulsive Professor Graystock wandered in.

'Ah, Taggie,' the Professor's formless mouth widened, showing crooked yellow teeth. 'I'm frightfully hungry; only had time for a bowl of soup at lunchtime. Could I have something to eat? Nothing fancy, simple repast, bread and cheese will be quite sufficient.'

Disgusting old goat, thought Rupert with a shudder, typical leftie with his second house, and no school fees to pay, bumming off anyone he regarded as capitalist. Taggie tried to smile. The Professor gave her the creeps, too. He still never missed an opportunity to squeeze her, or gaze at her breasts, or make *risqué* remarks.

'Cameron's looking for you, Rupert,' said the Professor pointedly. 'She wants to go home.'

Rupert took no notice and went on stroking Aengus, who was stretched out by the Aga.

Mouth watering, the Professor watched Taggie put out a

loaf of wholemeal bread, some Brie and Cheddar, and half a pound of butter.

'Any celery?' he asked. 'I'm partial to celery. With Father in Ireland and Mother rehearsing all the time, you're going to be rather lonely, Taggie. Perhaps you'll come over one evening to the campus and cook supper for a lonely old man?'

'She's working every night,' snapped Rupert. 'Someone's got to keep this doss house in whisky.'

'No need to over-react, dear boy,' said the Professor, cutting a doorstep of bread and spreading it thickly with butter. 'I've got an intellectual poser for you both. What would you have done –' he leered at Taggie – 'if you'd discovered, as I did last term, your most brilliant first-year student – guaranteed to get a first – in bed in college with a naked girl? Would you have sent him down?'

'If she'd been pretty,' said Rupert coldly, 'I'd have confiscated her.'

Cameron felt twitchy as she packed. She was still kicking herself for showing Rupert up in front of the others, but she got so uptight before she went on location. It was a million times worse than before a period. At the bottom of her bags she'd packed a book on coping with stepmotherhood. When she came back from Ireland, she was determined to get it together with Marcus and Tab. Wandering into Rupert's dressing-room, she found him also packing. He was catching Concorde in the morning.

'I love you,' she said, putting her arms round him. 'You will fly out to Ireland when you get back from the States, won't you?'

'Of course,' said Rupert, as he hastily flipped a book called *Overcoming Dyslexia* under a pile of shirts.

For a man so confident in business matters, Freddie Jones was surprisingly timid in matters of the heart. For months he had longed to ring up Lizzie Vereker, but only screwed up the courage the day Declan and Cameron left for Ireland.

'How about lunch today?' he said, wading straight in.

'Where's Valerie?' asked Lizzie.

'In Portugal.'

Because she had the curse, two large spots, dirty hair, hairy legs, unpainted toe nails, needed a hundred years to go on a crash diet and had been caught on the hop, Lizzie said no, she was frantically busy. Then felt absolutely miserable. 'What about next week?' she asked hopefully.

'Valerie'll be home,' said Freddie despondently.

'Well, ring me anyway,' said Lizzie.

All week Lizzie was very absent-minded. She spilt red wine over a review copy which she hadn't reviewed, and which James intended to give to his mother for a birthday present. On Thursday morning she kept filling up cups of coffee with cold water and even swallowed a conditioning pill herself which she'd intended to give to the dog. Perhaps she'd go barking mad. She knew she ought to be working on her new book, but all she could think about was Freddie. Distracted and miserable, she walked in the pouring rain down to the lake. A moorhen was summoning her chicks into the rushes with a strange fluted call. The beeches trailed their red leaves in the raindrop-pitted water. Suddenly Lizzie heard shouting from the french windows. It was Jilly, her treasure of a nanny, who seemed even more of a treasure when she said Mr Jones was on the telephone.

''Ullo,' said Freddie. 'Fort you might like to go for a picnic?'

'But it's pouring,' said Lizzie joyfully.

'We could 'ave it indoors at Green Lawns.'

'Where's Valerie?'

'At the Nearly New Sale for the Distressed Gentlefolk.'

Anticipating adultery was rather like going to the doctor, mused Lizzie as she painted her nails, washed her hair, bathed and shaved and cleaned her ears. Then she rubbed body lotion into every centimetre of her body – one really had to get oneself up.

The only problem was that she had forgotten that the Corinium Television gardener (one of James's perks) came that morning. He must have been amazed to see so many gallons of soapy water gushing into the bathroom drain, and to see Lizzie emerging so startlingly painted and scented at midday, to announce that she was off to the Nearly New Sale and then going on to do some shopping, so would he weed the main herbaceous border, which she had already thanked him profusely for weeding last week. She'd even rung James to tell him she was going to the sale and to ask if he needed anything in Cotchester.

Lizzie had had no intention of going to bed with Freddie that day. She wouldn't have if she hadn't bought a lovely blue tweed skirt for a pound at the clothes stall and passed Valerie noisily manning the produce stall on the way out.

'Look,' cried Lizzie, waving the skirt, 'look at my lovely bargain.'

'You'll never get into that!' said Valerie crushingly. 'That used to be Sarah Stratton's.'

Valerie was looking very Sloane, Lizzie decided, in a pale-blue cashmere jersey, dark-blue stockings and Gucci shoes, with her hair drawn off her forehead in a velvet bow.

'Do you know what that absolute swine Tony Baddingham is threatening to do?' Valerie went on, lowering her voice. 'Build twenty homes on a field next to our grounds. It'll ruin our view. I mean, we *are* designated an area of outstanding natural beauty.'

'He won't get planning permission,' said Lizzie.

'Probably will, with all those bribes he offers. Tell James to absolutely refuse to interview any of the Planning Committee on "Cotswold Round-Up". So embarrassing when Monica and I are such close friends.'

Valerie's beady eyes fell on Lizzie's purse. 'Now what are you going to buy? I'm sure James likes beetroot slices in vinegar. I'll give you a penny off.'

'I'll buy that coffee cake; it looks delicious. How long are you stuck here for?' asked Lizzie.

'Until four o'clock,' said Valerie crossly. 'Someone has to hold the fort.'

'It's the fort what counts,' murmured Lizzie.

•

'I fort you was never coming,' said Freddie as he opened the
door. In the kitchen was a bottle of Dom Perignon on ice
and a huge plate of smoked salmon. Freddie had picked
Rupert's brains about seducing techniques.

'The ideal picnic,' sighed Lizzie. 'I brought us some coffee
cake for pudding.'

They stayed in the kitchen, in case they messed up the
cushions poised on their points on Valerie's settees. Briefly
they discussed the franchise.

'D'you think you'll get it?'

'I know we will,' said Freddie. 'Now let's talk about us. I
want to see a great deal of you, Mrs Vereker, but it won't be
easy wiv Tony Baddingham, an' Valerie, an' James breaving
down our necks.'

'James won't be,' said Lizzie.

'Where is he at the moment?'

'Inside Sarah Stratton, I should think.'

They both roared with laughter and, for the first time,
Lizzie found she didn't mind. She liked everything about
Freddie, she decided – the way his eyes turned down at the
corners, and his beer gut, and the damp patches under his
arms because he was so nervous, and the way he smoked
with his cigar between finger and thumb to eke it out, and
coiled into the palm of his hand as though he was still
hiding it from the foreman, who was probably now called
Valerie.

As a writer, she told herself firmly as Freddie led her
upstairs, one has to experience life. All the same she didn't
think she would have gone to bed with Freddie on that first
day, and certainly not in Valerie's bedroom, if she hadn't
found four of her favourite books in the spare room bookshelf,
which she'd lent to Valerie when she'd had flu and which
Valerie'd sworn she'd given back to Lizzie.

When they got upstairs Freddie initially seemed far more
interested in showing off his gadgets – the eight-horsepower
jacuzzi and the bath which turned on by remote control and
regulated the water from the bed, which was huge and oval,
with its great dashboard of buttons at the head.

'Shall we sleep in it,' whispered Lizzie, 'or hi-jack it and fly it to paradise?'

'You do say the loveliest fings,' said Freddie, drawing her close. His paunch slotted in below her splendid breasts, so it was very easy for them to kiss.

'What music would you like?' asked Freddie.

'Brahms's Second Piano Concerto,' said Lizzie.

Next moment, incredibly, it flooded through the room. 'I must have a pee first,' said Lizzie, wading through the shagpile to the bathroom.

'I'll get undressed,' said Freddie.

Lizzie washed herself with Valerie's flannel, but not too much, in case she rubbed away all the lubrication. She wanted Freddie to know how excited she was. For a second she examined the lips of her labia, just peering out of her bush, like a wrinkled old tortoise, then shoved them inside. How could men possibly find women beautiful down there? Would her opening be prettier than Valerie's? she wondered.

Coming out, she opened the wrong door and nearly went into the linen cupboard. Goodness it was tidy, as though it had been laid out with a set square. Adultery certainly taught you about other people's houses. She expected Freddie to be completely undressed by the time she got back, but he had so much jewellery to remove that she beat him to it.

'I've dreamed and dreamed of this moment,' said Freddie as he stretched out beside her. 'Ever since we first met at that 'unt ball, eighteen monfs ago. I fort, what a lovely lady.'

'I'm so fat,' sighed Lizzie.

'You're not,' said Freddie. 'It's much more fun climbing Everest than the foothills.'

Lizzie put her hand on his cock. 'And it's so nice to see software becoming hardware.'

'And I'm going to declare this an area of outstanding natural beauty,' said Freddie. Reaching for his glass of champagne on the bedside table, he emptied it into her bush and proceeded to lick it all off. After Mousie's fragility, he reflected as he climbed on top of her, it was like having a wonderfully sturdy cob between your thighs.

540

'I hope you're using a Condom Perignon,' mumbled Lizzie half-laughing and half-crying with pleasure as he entered her.

Brahms's Second Piano Concerto was her favourite piece of music, but from then on she forgot its existence until the last ecstatic bars of the final Allegretto.

'You're absolutely perfick,' whispered Freddie. 'You're the big fing in my life now.'

'I love you,' said Lizzie.

'And I love you,' said Freddie.

Afterwards they had another bottle and ate all the coffee cake, and longed to make love again, but decided it was too risky. To establish an alibi, Lizzie then went shopping in Cotchester, so drunk and happy she could hardly get the clothes back on the hangers. Coming out of the chemist, having bought a huge guilt present of Aramis for James, which she thought she might give to Freddie, she heard a car tooting.

Not being vain, she didn't even turn round when it went on tooting, and only did so when Tony Baddingham lowered his electric window and yelled out to her.

Keeping her mouth tight shut so he wouldn't catch the champagne fumes, wondering if he could see the words 'adulterer and traitor' branded on her forehead, she edged towards him.

'You're looking great,' said Tony smoothly. 'Really great. Must have been a good holiday. What have you been buying?'

'Scent for James,' said Lizzie.

'How very nice,' said Tony. 'And it isn't even his birthday! You're a good wife, Lizzie. Look forward to seeing you on Saturday week.'

'Saturday?' said Lizzie, bewildered.

'Sarah Stratton's dinner party,' said Tony. 'We'll have a good talk then.'

Back at Lake House, Lizzie rushed upstairs, washed off all her make-up and scent, removed the nail polish from her toes and got into her old clothes in case James came home early.

541

Fortunately he was very late, so she was able to watch almost the entire production of *Midsummer Night's Dream* by herself. It was magical, despite Titania's bulge, and must have won Corinium a lot of Brownie points in the franchise battle. Throughout the performance, Lizzie kept thinking of Freddie, and how cuddly and sweet and kind he'd been, and how she wanted him to make love to her over and over again.

'Funny goings on at Venturer,' said James in a pleased voice, pouring himself an uncharacteristic drink the moment he got in. 'Evidently Cameron's pushed off to Ireland with Declan, and I've just seen Bas coming out of the Bar Sinister with Maud.'

Funny goings on everywhere, thought Lizzie dreamily, what with James and Sarah, and her and Freddie, and Rupert probably still hankering after Taggie. It was as though they'd all been affected by Puck's mischievous witchery like the mortals and Titania in *Midsummer Night's Dream*. James fell asleep the moment his head touched the pillow.

'I am the mistress of a very nice man,' wrote Lizzie ecstatically in her diary before she turned out the light.

41

The first Saturday in October Taggie overslept. Working late, she hadn't got to bed until four. She was just making a cup of coffee when Wandering Aengus, mewing horribly, padded in with a live fieldmouse in his mouth.

'Beast,' yelled Taggie, hurling a dishcloth at him. She missed, but Aengus was so startled he dropped the fieldmouse, which took refuge under the dresser.

Having shut the enraged and growling cat in the larder, Taggie managed to rescue the mouse with a dustpan and brush and put it in a cardboard box. Dressed in only the briefest nightie and gumboots, she carried the box across the lawn to set it free at the edge of the fields. Very gently she tipped it out, but the poor little thing didn't move; perhaps it had died of shock. Next moment she nearly died too. Coming towards her out of the blue mist across the dew-drenched field on a big, sweating dark-brown horse, rode Rupert. As he raised his hat, Taggie put her finger to her lips and showed him the mouse which was still motionless.

'Aengus caught it,' she whispered. 'D'you think it'll survive?'

Rupert privately thought a quick shove with his boot would put the mouse out of its misery, but, knowing this would upset Taggie, said it might just be frozen with fear, and why didn't they leave it for a bit. Gazing at Taggie's nightgown and gumboots, he asked her if she was going out. Taggie went crimson and said she'd been doing a late dinner party. There was a long pause. Casting desperately round for something to say, Taggie mumbled that it was a nice day.

'Very. I've been cubbing,' said Rupert.

'Oh, poor little things,' said Taggie in horror. 'Did you kill any?'

'No,' lied Rupert. 'I brought you these,' he went on, producing some huge mushrooms out of his riding-coat pocket.

'Oh, aren't they beautiful?' Distracted, Taggie examined their pleated pink undersides, 'How really kind. Thank you so much.'

Anyone would have thought he'd given her another Fabergé egg, thought Rupert. Stammering furiously, she asked him if he'd like some breakfast.

'I hoped you'd say that. I'll drop off my horse and come back.'

Taggie raced upstairs and was appalled to see that her nightie had a huge tear, her eyes were full of sleep, and her mascara was all smudged. Frantically she washed, put on an old pair of black sawn-off cords and a dark-brown T-shirt which seemed to be the only things Maud hadn't pinched, and started cooking breakfast. She steeled herself to the possibility that Rupert would get caught up in some drama at the yard, or at home, and forget to return; or that Maud, smelling frying bacon, would come down and join them. But he was back in a quarter of an hour with a bottle of champagne for Buck's Fizz, and Maud stayed upstairs, perfecting a song called 'Jogging in a one-horse gig'.

'She really is working at it,' said Rupert, edging the bottle open with his thumbs.

'It's wonderful. She's so much happier,' said Taggie, thinking how black and luscious the white mushrooms had gone, and tipping most of them onto Rupert's plate.

'I hope Tony Baddingham and your father don't bump into each other on the first night,' said Rupert as the cork flew through the window into the long grass outside, 'or either your mother or Monica really will be a merry widow!'

He picked up the *Guardian* which had a grim front-page story about the rocketing AIDS figures. Thank God he'd had that test.

It was such a lovely day, they had breakfast outside on the peeling white bench. Despite the warmth, the cedars, wellingtonias and yews flanking the house were already full of orange leaves from the nearby horse chestnuts, and the ground was littered with conkers. Lavender, roses, and evening primroses still bloomed on, bravely waiting for the first frost.

'I've never felt such hot sun in October,' said Rupert, taking off his jersey. 'With a few more leaves off the trees, I'll be able to see your house again.'

'How was America?' asked Taggie, dividing her bacon rind between a slavering Gertrude and Claudius.

'Good,' said Rupert, deciding not to mention four magnificent days hunting in Virginia. 'I've found a marvellous stallion, and a brood mare for Freddie. Which reminds me, I saw Freddie's red Jaguar parked outside Mrs Vereker's house while "Cotswold Round-Up" was on the air last night. If he's going to err and stray, he ought to find a more discreet car.'

Taggie giggled. 'Lizzie's so nice, isn't she?' she said, breaking a sausage in half for the dogs.

'She certainly deserves some fun. James treats her like an old wheelchair he can fall back into in old age. This breakfast is quite marvellous. Why are you giving all yours to the dogs?'

'I don't usually eat breakfast,' mumbled Taggie, taking a slug of Buck's Fizz.

Rupert ran his eyes over her. 'You're losing weight. I'll have to start adding molasses and carrots to your oats.'

'*Jogging in a one-horse gig, any time of night or day,*' sang Maud from upstairs, '*Careless of the weather, very close together, lovers fall in love that way.*'

Rupert raised his eyebrows and filled up Taggie's glass.

Please God, she prayed, make this moment go on for ever and ever. The next moment Gertrude had joined them on the bench seat on Taggie's side, not giving herself enough room, so Taggie had to move closer to Rupert.

'Well done, Gertrude,' said Rupert, grinning. 'You really are on my side.'

Taggie's heart seemed to be beating completely out of time to Maud's singing. Frantically, she stroked Gertrude.

'Heard from your father?' asked Rupert.

'No,' stammered Taggie. 'Have you heard from Cameron?'

'Not recently.'

There was another long pause. A conker plummeted on to the shaggy lawn. Laughing and watching her, Rupert waited.

'You mustn't worry about Daddy and Cameron being on their own together for so long,' Taggie finally blurted out. 'I know Daddy's wildly attractive, but he is utterly obsessed with Mummy.'

Rupert was about to deny that he was remotely worried about Cameron. Instead he removed a long dark hair from her shoulder and put it in his shirt pocket.

'I dreamed about you last night.'

'You did?' said Taggie in amazement. 'Was it nice?'

'Lovely, and extremely disturbing.' He trailed the back of his fingers down her arm. Taggie quivered and stopped stroking Gertrude.

'It's the last night of the Horse of the Year Show tonight,' went on Rupert. 'Tabitha's in the final of the mounted games. It's a good evening. Why don't you come with me? We could have dinner afterwards.'

Taggie nearly wept. 'Sarah Stratton's giving a dinner party. I've got to work.'

'Pity,' said Rupert lightly.

Gertrude stuck her nose under Taggie's trembling hand, jerking it upwards, urging Taggie to stroke her again. Gertrude and me, thought Rupert.

'The Baddinghams and the Verekers are going, so they'll all talk about the franchise. I'll probably be made to stay in the kitchen,' babbled Taggie.

'Well keep your ears open and put a pint of arsenic in Tony's whisky. They certainly won't get Buck's Fizz like this tonight. Paul's so mean he makes it with Babycham.'

Damn, damn, damn, thought Taggie as she followed him to the door.

'I'm off to the Tory Party Conference next week,' said Rupert, getting into his car. 'I'll ring you when I get back. That was a lovely breakfast, thank you. By the way,' he added ultra-casually as he drove off, 'I hope you noticed I didn't burn my stubble this year.'

In a complete daze Taggie finished off the Buck's Fizz. Rupert had dreamt about her, *and* he'd asked her out, *and* he hadn't burnt his stubble. The whole thing was desperately confusing. She ran upstairs and looked out of her window. It was true. Instead of charred patches all over the valley, his cornfields were still yellowed by stubble, or reddy-brown after being ploughed up. She couldn't possibly be the reason, but it was so nice of him to say so.

There were so many things she ought to do, picking apples, planting the indoor bulbs, getting in the geraniums. There were large bowls of picked mulberries and blackberries reproachfully gathering fluff in the fridge, waiting to be turned into jam. And she must make some tomato chutney, not to mention painting the bench and mowing the lawn.

Suddenly she heard an enraged mewing from the larder. She'd forgotten Aengus. She couldn't even get cross that he'd eaten half the turbot mousse she'd made for the first course this evening. At least when she went out to search for the fieldmouse it had run away.

By the time she'd reached the Strattons' house she'd sobered up. Paul was still out playing golf. Sarah was in a panic because she wanted everything to be perfect for Tony, her boss, and even more so for James.

'Giving a dinner party is far worse than going on television,' she moaned. 'Look, I know it sounds horrendously Valerie Jones, but do you mind pretending I've done the cooking tonight? Especially the main course, which is a particular favourite of a friend of mine,' added Sarah, going pink. 'If anyone rings, pretend you're our daily, Mrs Maggs.'

Then, leaving Taggie with a mile-long list of instructions, she swanned off to Bath to buy a new dress.

At least everything was tidy, the table laid and the house clean. Taggie got out the French recipe that Rupert had translated for her. An hour and a half later, she was getting on well. The beef daube was sizzling in the oven, the pudding was in the fridge and just needed whipped cream and sugared violets, and she'd done the vegetables earlier. All she had to do was to make another fish mousse. Perhaps she'd just better double-check the beef.

'Oh, my God,' she said aghast as she licked the spoon. She tried again from the other side of the dish, and then the centre, where it was even worse. She must have been so distracted by her encounter with Rupert that she'd added a tablespoonful of salt instead of sugar. She tested the sugar in the glass bowl and went green. It was definitely salt.

The beef was quite inedible, absolutely impregnated with salt, and she'd used up all the other ingredients. It was after five and she'd never get to Cotchester in time. She gave a whimper of horror. She'd wrecked Sarah's party and she knew Sarah could be extremely difficult if things didn't go right.

The telephone rang. Oh God, she sobbed, I've got to remember to be the daily. Trembling, she picked up the receiver.

'Hullo,' crackled a voice from a car telephone.

'Mrs Stratton be shopping, thank you very much. Who be you?' mumbled Taggie.

Rupert laughed. 'That is the worst Gloucestershire accent I've ever heard. How's it going?'

Taggie burst into tears. 'It was James's favourite recipe and she's supposed to have made it for him,' she sobbed.

'Cheer up or you'll cry more salt into the beef,' said Rupert calmly. 'Get on with the fish mousse. I'll be over in half an hour.'

He arrived twenty-five minutes later. He screeched the Aston-Martin to a halt in a cloud of dust and nearly tipped Beaver and Blue, who were sitting on the back seat, through the windscreen, then he sauntered into the kitchen with a huge casserole dish containing boeuf Bourguignon for twelve from Luigi's, the local five-star restaurant in Cheltenham.

'Oh, you're lovely,' said Taggie, flinging her arms round his neck.

'Hands off! We've no time for dalliance!' said Rupert briskly, as he emptied the Bourguignon into one of Sarah's big bowls and chucked Taggie's salty remnants into Luigi's casserole dish. 'Don't tell Paul and Sarah what happened,' he added. 'Just pretend this is how the recipe turned out. They'll all be too pissed to notice, anyway. I'd better beat it, or she'll be back from shopping and start accusing me of bugging the room.'

Still stammering her thanks, Taggie followed him out to the car. An owl was hooting. A semi-circle of orange moon was rising out of the sycamores.

'The moon was a mandarin segment, as Valerie Jones would say,' said Rupert.

'I can't ever begin to thank you,' bleated Taggie.

Rupert pulled her towards him, dropping a kiss on her cheekbone.

'Oh yes, you can, angel. Just wait till I get back from Blackpool.'

The patron saint of cooking guided Taggie that evening. The food was positively ambrosial, and Sarah took all the credit, particularly for Luigi's boeuf Bourguignon, which was so tender you could cut it with a spoon.

'D'you remember that daube we had at the White Elephant at Painswick?' whispered Sarah to James as they went in to dinner. 'Well, I wrote to them for the recipe and I've made it for you tonight.'

Putting on his horn-rimmed spectacles to have a closer look across the table, Tony Baddingham decided he hadn't been wrong about Lizzie Vereker. Whether it was the Marbella sun or a stone off, or just some new inner contentment, she looked sensational.

The talk during dinner was mostly of the rocketing AIDS figures. They also drank to 'Master Dog' which was edging up on 'EastEnders' in the ratings; but they waited until Taggie was safely out of the room to discuss the franchise.

'There are some quite fascinating developments,' Tony said tantalizingly, 'but I'm not prepared to leak them until November, when it'll be nearer the IBA meetings and people are properly back from their holidays and reading newspapers again. And then, my God, Venturer will wish they'd never tried to take us on.' He paused as Taggie came in with the salad.

Not that she would have taken anything in that night. In the kitchen she was frantically trying to watch the Horse of the Year Show, hoping to catch a glimpse of Rupert. At least she saw Tabitha in the mounted games – utterly adorable and so like Rupert as she jumped up and down waiting for the baton, then grabbing it and scorching up the arena. The finals were just coming up when Sarah summoned Taggie to clear away the pudding.

By this time Tony was banging on about AIDS again.

'By the year 2000, unless we get our act together in this country, we'll have sixteen million cases. The message from America is loud and clear, affairs are *passé*.' He gazed down the table. 'Monogamy and fidelity in marriage are in fashion again. It's vital that everyone is made aware of the dangers of AIDS. It's up to us at Corinium to set the ball rolling.'

James felt that Sarah had been so very very caring to go to all that trouble with the daube that, in the hall after dinner, he was foolish enough to behave in a thoroughly unmonogamous fashion and be caught by Tony not only kissing her, but putting his hand inside her new silk dress.

On Monday morning Tony summoned James to his office. 'I've been thinking a lot about our conversation about AIDS on Saturday night,' he began briskly. 'I've decided it's time for you to have your own series, which we'll almost certainly sell to the network.'

'That's very good of you, Tony,' said James.

'I want to make a series examining all aspects of marriage,' went on Tony.

'Financial, dual careers, how much housework should the caring husband do,' rattled off James excitedly. 'Sex, rows, decorating the house.'

'That's right,' said Tony. 'We could perhaps even introduce children and the pressures they put on a marriage. But basically the whole series will be aimed at couples who are getting behind marriage again, who want to avoid AIDS by staying with the same person for the rest of their lives. We'll call it "How to Stay Married".'

'With the AIDS panic, it'll be a real franchise-grabber,' said James excitedly.

'Exactly,' said Tony urbanely. 'And I want you and a very charming lady not far from your heart to front it.'

'I don't even have to guess, Tony,' said James warmly, 'but d'you really feel she's experienced enough?'

'More important,' said Tony, who was enjoying himself, 'she's a natural. She's not too obviously glamorous, but she's got just the right kind of lovely warm bubbly personality that'll make couples talk and trigger off a really good audience reaction.'

James bowed his head. 'I know Sarah will appreciate the very great honour you're bestowing on her, Tony, both to combat AIDS and to help Corinium retain the franchise.'

'I'm not talking about Sarah, you berk,' said Tony icily. 'I mean your wife, Lizzie, and if you value your job, the less you see of Mrs Stratton over the next three months the better.'

Taggie spent the next week dreaming of Rupert. She knew he loved and lived with Cameron, who would be back in a week or so, but she couldn't help herself. On Thursday she watched him on television at the Party Conference making a brilliant speech saying that the Tories must get off their fat backsides and start thinking positively about unemployment and the way it directly affected hooliganism and rioting in the inner cities. Taggie, detecting Declan's influence, felt very proud.

On Friday night a slight distraction was provided by Caitlin coming home for a long weekend, with her black hair dyed white at the front, still utterly besotted with Archie.

'He went into the town and brought eighty cans of beer back in a taxi and smuggled them in and sold them to the other boys on the black market in order to buy me this gorgeous jersey. I haven't taken it off since he sent it me, so please can you wash it tonight, and my black jeans so I can wear them tomorrow? Archie's taking me out to lunch. What's Mummy doing for the rest of the day?'

'Rehearsing, I think,' said Taggie.

Exactly on cue, Maud wandered in, looking radiant. 'Hullo, darling, how's school?'

'Ghastly. Anyone with layered hair is being sent home, so I'm going to get mine layered on Monday.'

'I've bought some apples,' said Maud, waving a large paper bag at Taggie. 'They're so cheap in the market.'

And they cost nothing in the orchard, thudding on to the grass every two minutes, Taggie wanted to scream. She wanted to murder her mother sometimes.

'That's a nice jersey,' said Maud, looking at Caitlin. 'Where did you get it?'

'It was a present,' said Caitlin noncommittally. 'You will wash it carefully, won't you, Tag? How's *The Merry Widow?*' she asked her mother.

'Oh, exhausting, but fun,' said Maud, pouring herself a large whisky. 'I – er – thought I might go to the cinema with some of the cast tomorrow night,' she added casually. 'Taggie's cooking. Will you be all right on your own, Caitlin?'

'Brilliant,' beamed Caitlin. 'Stay out as long as you like. I've got masses of work. Have dinner and make a night of it. I've got to read *Antony and Cleopatra* and write an essay on *Streetcar Named Desire*. I think it's extraordinary that they shut us up in single-sex schools and then give us these amazingly erotic set books.'

By the time Taggie had cleared up supper and washed and ironed Caitlin's jersey and jeans and put them in the hot cupboard it was two o'clock in the morning. Admittedly her progress had been slowed up by constantly looking out of the window to watch for Rupert's helicopter landing on the lawn, or his car coming up the drive. But there was nothing. Perhaps he'd gone to Ireland to see Cameron after all.

It seemed she'd hardly fallen asleep when she was roused by an hysterical Caitlin. 'That bugger Mummy used all the water, so I can't wash my hair or have a bath, and even worse she's gone off in my new jersey and jeans. And now I can't wear it for Archie, and he'll never believe I haven't lost it, like Desdemona's handkerchief. I hate, hate, hate her, bloody old cow, and she's bound to split my jeans.'

'I'll run you into Cotchester and buy you something else,' said Taggie. 'I got paid in cash yesterday.'

'It's no good,' screamed Caitlin. 'I wanted Archie to see me in his jersey. I'll kill her, I'll absolutely kill her.'

Nothing Taggie could say would calm her down.

'I'll ring up Rupert and see if you can have a bath there,' said Taggie in the end.

Throat dry, heart thumping, hands drenched in sweat and trembling, Taggie misdialled the number three times in her nervousness. When Rupert didn't answer immediately, she nearly put the telephone down.

'Hullo.' He sounded irritable and very sleepy.

'It's Taggie.'

'My darling.' His voice softened.

'I'm desperately sorry,' she began. Then, stammering worse than ever, she explained what had happened, but didn't mention Archie's name. 'Could I possibly rush Caitlin over to wash her hair and have a bath?'

'Of course,' said Rupert, 'as long as we can all have it together.'

Rupert hadn't shaved when they arrived. He was wandering around in bare feet, having obviously just put on the white shirt and the black dinner-jacket trousers he'd been wearing last night. He looked bugeyed.

'I won't stop,' mumbled Taggie, desperate not to impose on him. 'I'll pick Caitlin up in an hour, OK?'

Rupert pulled her into the house. 'Don't be boring. As I'm

553

such a notorious reprobate, you ought to stay and chaperone Caitlin.'

Caitlin promptly started raging on about Maud. 'Bloody old cow, nicking all the water, and my seducing kit. What does she want with it? I bet she's up to someone, the old tart. It's high time my father came home.'

'Cait-lin,' remonstrated Taggie, going pink. 'Rupert hasn't got all day. I thought you wanted to be ready by twelve. Go and have a bath.'

Grinning, Rupert took Caitlin upstairs and showed her where everything was. Taggie glanced at some photographs of Tabitha at Wembley which were lying on the kitchen table.

'Aren't these gorgeous?' she said, as Rupert came back. 'I saw a bit of it on television at Sarah Stratton's, but I missed the final. Did her team win?'

'No, but they came third, and she did well. *Horse and Hound* described her as a "chip off the old Campbell-Black"; which was nice.'

'Marvellous,' said Taggie. 'Am I in your way?' she asked as Rupert paused on his way to the fridge.

'No, I just like standing behind you. I know you'll spring to her defence, but your mother is an absolute disgrace. Swanning off with all Caitlin's clothes at her age. Maud's trouble is that she wants to have her cake and eat it, and make trifle out of it as well.'

Taggie giggled, but she said, 'I know, but it's such a relief that she's happy and working again. She might even start doing it professionally, and she's so beautiful,' Taggie sighed. 'It's hardly surprising all the cast's in love with her.'

Rupert privately deduced that Maud must be in love with one of the cast to have lost enough weight to get into Caitlin's jeans, but merely said, 'I've got a hangover. Let's have a drink.'

'I mustn't,' said Taggie, 'or I'll make another cock-up of cooking tonight.'

'Don't say you're working again?' said Rupert, appalled. Taggie nodded dolefully.

'Jesus,' said Rupert. 'I'd better make a date with you for *next* October.'

'I'm so sorry,' stammered Taggie, hanging her head, 'It's n-not that I wouldn't love to.'

'I've got an idea,' said Rupert. 'My children are coming over this afternoon. Why don't you come out with us for the day tomorrow, and help me entertain them?'

'I'll make a picnic,' said Taggie, suddenly excited.

'No, you won't. For once you're not going to cook a thing.'

With both Maud and Caitlin plundering her wardrobe, Taggie was at her wit's end as to what to wear. Feeling desperately guilty, with the Electricity Board, the television hire firm, the village shop, and God knows who else baying to be paid, she blued, or rather greyed, Friday lunchtime's cash wages on a pale-grey cashmere polo-neck which brought out the silver-grey in her eyes and clung to her in all the right places. There was no more money, so she'd have to wear her old black cords.

Next morning Maud whizzed off very early to yet another rehearsal. Caitlin, who nobly said she'd dogsit and read *Antony and Cleopatra*, hustled Taggie out of the house.

'You look delectable. Randy Rupe won't be able to keep his hands off you. Don't hurry back. I'm quite OK on my own –' she smirked wickedly – 'or, almost on my own. The Hon Arch will be dropping by *plus tard*. Or Marble Arch, as I call him, now he's lost his suntan.'

Tabitha, amid the swirling pack of dogs, answered the door looking belligerent. She was wearing a pink sweater embroidered with blue flowers and a blue puff-ball skirt.

'Hullo,' said Taggie in delight. 'I recognize *you*; you were on television last Saturday. You were wonderful, and what a beautiful clever pony. He was much the fastest. What's his name?'

'Biscuit,' said Tabitha coldly.

'Can I see him?'

'He's at my other house.'

'Oh, what a shame. I've brought him some carrots.' Taggie

rummaged round in a carrier bag, 'and I've made you some fudge.'

'Thank you,' said Tab, looking slightly mollified. 'Can I have a bit now?'

'I don't see why not. I like your puff-ball skirt. I wanted to get one, but my knees are far too knobbly.'

'Mummy says hers are, too,' said Tab. 'Perhaps they're not suitable for grown-ups.'

Stroking the dogs, Taggie sat down on one of the stone seats inside the porch.

'What's your name again?' said Tabitha.

'Taggie. It's really Agatha, isn't that awful? Tabitha's so much nicer. My parents call me Tag, sometimes, which sounds just like Tab, doesn't it? I expect when Marcus shouts Tab we'll both go charging into the kitchen to see what he wants and bump into each other in the doorway.'

Tabitha stared at her consideringly, and suddenly she smiled.

'And you're nine and a quarter?' said Taggie.

'Yes,' sighed Tab, pushing her blonde hair out of her eyes. 'Can't you see my wrinkles?'

Taggie giggled. 'Still, it's awfully young to be in the Mounted Games. Were you the youngest?'

'Yes,' said Tab. 'If you come back to Warwickshire with us tonight you can see Biscuit. We've got a foal here. Would you like to come and see it?'

'Yes, please,' said Taggie.

The front door opened; it was Marcus. 'Hullo,' he said. 'Daddy wants to know where you've got to.'

'She's talking to me, stupid,' said Tab. 'She's brought you some fudge.'

'Tag,' bellowed Rupert from the kitchen, 'where are you?'

'Here,' said Tab and Tag in unison. Then they both looked at each other and burst out laughing.

Taking Taggie's hand, Tabitha dragged her into the kitchen. 'Can she come back to Warwickshire with us this evening and see Biscuit?' said Tabitha.

Rupert, who was drinking black coffee and reading the racing pages of the *Sunday Times*, looked surprised.

'Of course she can. I thought you'd kidnapped her.'

'She's brought us fudge, and carrots for Biscuit, and a big bottle of cough mixture,' said Tabitha, unpacking the carrier bag.

'It's sloe gin,' said Taggie, blushing. 'I made it yesterday. You mustn't drink it for three months.'

'Thank you, angel,' said Rupert, kissing her on the cheek. 'I hope I don't have to wait that long for you,' he murmured in an undertone.

'Come *on*, Taggie,' said Tabitha impatiently. 'I thought you wanted to see the foal. This fudge is smashing.'

They had lunch in Cheltenham in an up-market hamburger bar. The children, who insisted on sitting on either side of Taggie, had huge milkshakes. Rupert, who complained he had alcohol shakes, ordered a carafe of red.

'That jersey suits you,' he said approvingly to Taggie. 'How d'you manage to keep it out of Maud's clutches?'

Taggie blushed. 'I slept with it under my pillow.'

'We're doing a "Messiah" at the end of term,' announced Tabitha, sucking air noisily from the bottom of her milkshake. 'There are going to be two trumpets and a drum, and real fathers in the chorus. I'm in the altos. They're much naughtier because they're mostly boys, silly twits.'

'D'you like singing?' asked Taggie.

'No. Mrs Brown takes us. She's just got married. She takes us for history too. She was reading a book called *Improving your Home* in class this week.'

'She was reading a book about drains in our class,' said Marcus.

'And that's what I pay your school fees for,' grumbled Rupert. 'I wish they'd organize a sponsored walk to Save the Parents.'

Having ordered, he looked across at Taggie, who was talking to Marcus about conkers.

'We used to roast them slowly in the oven to harden them up.'

'We soak them in vinegar,' said Marcus.

'My sister Caitlin used to put them in the hot cupboard and they always fell down behind the boiler and went mouldy. We've got masses at The Priory if you want any more, but I expect you've got hundreds already.'

Christ, she's sweet, thought Rupert, noticing the way the grey cashmere moulded the full breasts.

'Mary had a little lamb and surprised the midwife,' said Tabitha to her father.

'Really,' said Rupert absent-mindedly.

'Mary had a little lamb and surprised the midwife. It's a joke.'

'Ha, ha,' said Rupert, filling up Taggie's glass.

'Why d'you always say ha ha and not mean it? Can I have a packet of Frazzles?'

'No,' said Rupert. 'Here's your lunch.'

'Can I have punk hair like Cameron?' said Tabitha, picking bits of mushroom out of her salad and putting them round the edge of her plate.

'No.'

'Why not?'

'Because I don't like short hair.'

'You've got very nice hair,' said Marcus to Taggie, blushing scarlet as he bit into his hamburger.

'Yes,' agreed Rupert. 'She has.'

Tabitha gazed dreamily into space. 'Mrs Bodkin must have slept with Mr Bodkin an awful lot of times.'

'What on earth makes you think that?' asked Rupert in amazement.

'She told me she'd had four miscarriages,' said Tab.

Taggie didn't dare look at Rupert. She thought she had never been happier in her life. Suddenly the most ordinary things – a hamburger smothered in tomato ketchup, the mural of the village street round the wall, with its milk cart and postman – were illuminated because she was with Rupert and these adorable children.

'Everything all right, Meester Campbell-Black?' asked the Manager.

'Perfect,' said Rupert. 'Could we have another carafe of red?'

'I would like to congratulate you,' went on the Manager, looking round rapturously at Marcus, Tab and Taggie. 'I never knew you haff three such beautiful children.'

RIVALS
42

After lunch, they went for a walk in Rupert's woods. It was ridiculously mild. Insects moved leisurely in the rays slanting through the thinning beech trees, like specks of dust caught in the light from a projector. Birds sang drowsily, orange leaves drifted down on to already orange paths. The squirrels, stupefied by the sun, were fooling around on the ground instead of gathering nuts.

'What are you singing at school?' asked Taggie.

'"Green grow the rushes-oh,"' said Tab.

'*I'll sing you three-oh,*' sang Marcus.

'*What is your three-oh?*' sang back Tab.

'*Three for the rivals, Two, two the lily-white boys, Clothed all in green-o,*' replied Marcus, his pure treble echoing through the soaring cathedral of beech trunks. Then both children took up the chant:

'*One is one and all alone, And ever more shall be so.*'

'Lovely,' sighed Taggie.

'Three for the rivals sounds like Corinium, Venturer and Mid-West,' said Rupert.

He used up a couple of reels of film, then, exhausted after a strenuous week at Blackpool, fell asleep under a chestnut tree, while Taggie played games with the children.

'D'you know,' she said, drawing them away down the ride so they wouldn't wake Rupert, 'that every time you catch a falling leaf, you get a happy day? Let's see if we can catch thirty, so we can give Daddy a really happy November when he wakes up.'

'Easy peasy,' said Tabitha, leaping forward as a yellow sycamore leaf pirouetted through the air towards her, then, caught by a puff of wind, dummied round her and fluttered to the ground.

'It's harder than it looks,' panted Marcus, reaching out as a twig of ash leaves floated tantalizingly out of his grasp. 'Would those have counted as seven?'

'Not really,' said Taggie.

'Bugger,' screamed Tab, as she just missed a beech leaf.

'Hush,' said Taggie. 'We mustn't wake Daddy.'

Silently they raced round the wood trying to suppress their screams of joy whenever they managed to catch a leaf. After a particularly piercing yell, when Tab tripped over a bramble cable but managed to hang on to a wand of chestnut leaves, Rupert woke up; but he pretended to be asleep. Watching Taggie, gambolling long-legged over the beech leaves, pony-tail flying, looking, as the Manager had thought, not a day over fourteen, he was suddenly kneed in the groin with longing.

'Here you are, Daddy,' said Tabitha, her hands full of leaves, 'a whole happy month for you.'

Rupert, who privately thought that the only thing that could make him happy at the moment was a whole month in bed with Taggie, said thank you very much.

'Can we go and see the new Woody Allen?' asked Tabitha.

Rupert looked at his watch: 'It's nearly four o'clock. You'll be very late back.' The last thing he wanted to do was to go to the cinema.

'We can go on our way home,' pleaded Tabitha.

'We've done our homework,' said Marcus.

Rupert turned to Taggie who said she'd adore to see it; anything to prolong the day with Rupert.

'I'm going to sit next to Taggie,' said Tabitha, seizing her hand.

561

'I'm going to sit next to her too,' said Marcus, taking her other hand.

'If she sits on my knee, you can both sit next to her,' said Rupert.

Severely jolted, he felt it was increasingly necessary to make a joke about the whole thing.

The Woody Allen was extremely funny, but Taggie hardly took any of it in, she was so aware of Rupert slumped in the seat beyond Tabitha gazing totally unmoved at the screen. How awful for Rupert being left by Helen and losing these heavenly children, living alone by himself in that big house.

'*One is one and all alone and ever more shall be so,*' sang Tabitha as they drove home.

Taggie felt Rupert's loss far more acutely when she met Helen, who was simply the most beautiful woman she'd ever seen, with huge serious yellow eyes and long red hair drawn back in two combs from her freckled face, and incredibly slim ankles and wrists. She had the same colouring as Maud, reflected Taggie, but while Maud cavorted untrainably through life like a red setter bestowing her favours indiscriminately, Helen would be far more fastidious and sparing with her affections. Helen was like a red deer. If you tamed and won the confidence of anything so delicate and nervous, you'd feel incredibly proud.

But before she had much time to observe Helen or her husband, Malise, who seemed very old, Taggie was dragged off to the stables by Tabitha to meet Biscuit and Dollop. Then she had to see Marcus's room and then Tabitha's room, both extraordinarily tidy (in fact, the whole house was incredibly tidy for a Sunday evening), by which time it was well past the children's bedtime.

Back in the drawing-room, Taggie found Helen tapping her beautifully shod foot and looking at the clock, and Rupert standing in front of an unlit fire, holding an empty glass and looking absolutely glazed.

'What would you like to drink?' Malise asked Taggie.

Taggie glanced at Rupert, who almost imperceptibly moved his head in the direction of the door.

'Nothing, thank you very much,' she said.

'We must go,' said Rupert. 'I've got to get this child home.'

So the day was to end just like that. Taggie suddenly felt suicidal. Malise, seeming to sense her depression, said, 'Helen and I are tremendous fans of your father's. I do hope he gets the franchise. Corinium's programmes are absolutely ghastly.'

'Oh, *The Dream* was excellent the other night,' protested Helen. 'Marcus said Cameron Cook had something to do with that, Rupert. You must bring her over sometime. I'd love to discuss the production with her. It was a most original interpretation. They set it in Victorian England and had some fascinating parallels between Queen Victoria and John Brown and Titania and Bottom.'

Rupert stifled a huge yawn.

'I think Taggie and Rupert want to go, darling,' said Malise gently, putting his arm round Helen's shoulders.

He has the most charming smile, thought Taggie. I can see why she finds him attractive, but not compared with Rupert, and he is *terribly* old. The children came to see them off.

'Promise, promise, we can see you next time we come over,' said Tabitha, clinging to her like a monkey.

'Thank you so much for the fudge,' said Marcus.

'Rupert is awful,' said Helen, having packed the children upstairs to have baths. 'That girl must still be at school.'

'She's a bit older than that, but not much,' said Malise, straightening the Sunday papers. 'D'you know, she gives me the same ghastly sense of forboding I had when I first met you?'

'I hope you haven't fallen in love with her too,' said Helen, somewhat too archly.

'No. One just knows he's going to break her heart,' said Malise grimly, 'and feels powerless to do anything about it.'

'He may have mellowed,' said Helen. 'She's the first girl he's ever brought here, and the kids obviously adore her.'

Malise shook his head. 'He's like a hound. You can't domesticate him. Hunting'll always be in his blood.'

Rupert was very quiet on the drive back to Penscombe. Taggie, feeling utterly miserable because the day was almost over and the Aston-Martin seemed to be gobbling up the miles, assumed he was merely depressed because his ravishing wife and children didn't live with him any more. Rupert, however, for the first time in his life, was battling seriously with his conscience.

Taggie was Declan's teenage daughter; he was committed to Cameron, who was already paranoid about Taggie, and there were deadly serious things like franchises to be won.

Then, in the light from a street-lamp in Cheltenham, he caught sight of Taggie. Everything seemed to turn upwards, her nose, her long sooty eyelashes, her adorably short upper lip, and those beautifully soft breasts, which he'd dreamed of the other night. His conscience lost.

'Would you like some dinner?'

'Oh yes, please,' said Taggie joyfully. 'If you're sure you're not too tired and I look smart enough?'

'Never, never get smart,' said Rupert. 'I loathe done-up women.'

'They're such adorable children,' said Taggie. 'And so beautiful. Not surprising really with such a beautiful mother.' In the darkness of the car, now they were out of the town, it seemed easier to talk. 'Is it absolutely agony every time you see her again?'

'Agony,' said Rupert soulfully. Then, shooting a sideways glance at Taggie, he explained, 'Because she bores the fucking tits off me.'

Taggie gave a gasp of shocked laughter.

'I can't think how the hell I stayed married to her for seven years. While you were upstairs, she gave me the entire plot of the Italian film they'd seen that afternoon, and, if Malise hadn't shut her up, we'd have had a five-act analysis of *Midsummer Night's Dream*. How he puts up with it!'

'He seems very nice,' said Taggie, 'but he's almost like a grandfather to the children.'

'Thirty years older than Helen,' said Rupert, 'but he's made her very happy.'

'And what happened to you after she walked out?' asked Taggie.

'Oh well, I had one or two fish of my own I was frying at the time,' admitted Rupert. 'But the fat began to spit too much, so I backed off. Then I had a long stint with an engaging tramp called Beattie Johnson, and then a few games of tennis with Sarah Stratton.'

'Oh God,' moaned Taggie.

Rupert laughed. 'I'm half-tempted to stop the car and see how much you're blushing. Were you terribly shocked when you saw us?'

'Yes, no, yes,' mumbled Taggie. 'More for Gertrude, really. She's led such a sheltered life. It must have been awful all those fire engines turning up.'

'We were bloody lucky,' said Rupert. 'Cameron tells me that the Corinium newsroom give the Cotchester Fire Brigade so much booze at Christmas that invariably the firemen tip them off and keep their hoses running until the television crew arrive. Sarah and I in the buff would have been a sensation on "Cotswold Round-Up".'

Taggie giggled. She didn't like to tell him how much in the last few months the memory of his oiled, mahogany-tanned, wonderfully constructed body had haunted her dreams.

The White Elephant at Painswick was packed and taking last orders, but still managed to find a corner for Rupert. Taggie fled to the loo. All she had in her bag was a defunct mascara wand, a comb, some scent and a picture of Claudius. If only she could clean her teeth. She made do with soaking the roller towel, rubbing some soap on it, rubbing her teeth, then rinsing her mouth out with water. Then she de-tangled her hair and put it back in its ponytail.

When she got back to the table, Rupert, realizing she

would be totally floored by the French menu, had ordered a bottle of Pouilly Fumé and smoked salmon and scrambled eggs for both of them.

'And you're going to eat the lot.'

At first they discussed the children.

'I wish they got on better with Cameron,' sighed Rupert, 'but, being totally unused to children, she makes neither extra beds nor allowances.'

It was good that they could talk about Cameron naturally now, thought Taggie, suddenly longing to touch the fan of fine lines at the corner of Rupert's eyes. Perhaps she could become his long-term confidante, and even when he was eighty, he'd come roaring over to The Priory and tell her he'd met some marvellous new fifty-year-old. At least it'd be better than not seeing him.

'Does it still upset you going to the Horse of the Year Show when you're not winning all the cups any more?' she asked tentatively.

'Yes,' he said. 'That's why I wanted you to come along last week –' he took her hand – 'to hold *my* hand. I don't think I realized at the time how desperately I minded giving up. Just stopping overnight after the World Championship, burying myself in politics, refusing to recognize I was suffering from withdrawal symptoms far worse than any junkie. There's so little time to think while you're show jumping. Even on those interminable drives there was always Billy to yak to, or some horse to natter about, always something to look forward to, a prize to be won, someone else's time to be beaten, a horse to be sorted out, a girl to be laid. I suppose I never gave myself time to grow up, and when Helen buggered off I blocked that out too.'

Still holding her hand, he looked into her loving, infinitely understanding and sympathetic eyes. Christ, he'd never admitted things like this to anyone, not even Billy. Then she asked the same question: 'Does it still hurt seeing Helen?'

Rupert shrugged. 'I got bored with hating her, I guess. The only thing that really irks me is that Malise succeeded where

I failed. I can't honestly say I've ever made any woman happy, or not for very long.'

'You make me very happy,' said Taggie gruffly.

For a second they gazed at each other and he watched the colour mounting in her cheeks.

'I'd like to try,' he said softly. 'I'll just pay the bill and we'll go.'

As he drove her slowly back to Penscombe, Chris de Burgh was singing 'Lady in Red' on the car radio. It was such a beautiful night. The moon was hiding behind a vast ebony cloud shaped like a yew tree, tipping its edges with silver; the rest of the pearly grey sky was threaded with stars. A few windows were still lit up in the village like cardboard cut-outs.

Just before he reached the right turn up the long chestnut avenue to Penscombe Court, Rupert slowed the car down almost to a standstill and raised a finger to Taggie's cheek.

'Are you quite sure, angel?'

He could feel her cheekbone rubbing frantically against his finger as she nodded. Totally adrift with love, she had no thought of refusing.

'Fucking hell,' howled Rupert, as they drew up outside the house. Parked outside, beside Taggie's car, was a Lotus. In the moonlight it could have been any dark colour.

Cameron, thought Taggie in horror.

But the girl who came out of the front door had thick lustrous hair, as golden yellow as the sycamore leaves swirling across the gravel. It was Sarah Stratton. Sobbing, she threw herself into Rupert's arms.

'I must talk to you.'

'I must go,' said Taggie.

'No, don't,' said Rupert sharply. Then, realizing what he was saying, added, 'Well, it is a bit late. We'll check through the rest of those names tomorrow, and we'll tackle the southern part of the region later in the week.'

'Oh, the fucking franchise,' screamed Sarah.

Leaving time only to squeeze Taggie's hand and say he'd

ring her tomorrow, Rupert took Sarah into the drawing-room, where she collapsed sobbing on the sofa. The temperature suddenly seemed to have dropped several degrees. The house felt horribly cold and empty without Taggie and the children.

It was a few minutes before he could get any sense out of Sarah. Evidently James Vereker had given her the bullet.

'Tony ordered him to. He said everyone was gossiping about me and James, and it doesn't do Corinium's reputation any good in a franchise year. Jesus, and when you think of the way he was carrying on with Cameron.'

'*Was* is the operative word,' said Rupert, pouring Sarah a glass of brandy. 'There's no prude like a reformed rake.'

'I know James loves me,' sobbed Sarah hysterically, 'but that shit Tony offered him the carrot of his own thirteen-part series on staying married, and ordered him to front it with Lizzie. Tony's convinced the IBA will adore the idea, what with all this panic about AIDS.'

Rupert whistled. 'That's quite shrewd.'

'So James and the podgy frump have to present a lovey-dovey united front until the franchise is in the bag, and James is going to go along with it.'

'Ambition should be made of sterner stuffing,' said Rupert idly. 'And how's Lizzie taking it?'

'Oh, lapping it up, I should think,' said Sarah viciously. 'Must be the first time anyone's slept with her in yonks.'

Hum, thought Rupert. 'Well, you'll just have to be a bit more discreet until after 15th December,' he said.

'That's what I said, but James is refusing even to have a drink with me. If I talk to him in the passage at Corinium, he scuttles off like a daddy longlegs. He won't even gossip during the break in "Round-Up". I know he's vain and ambitious, but I love him. I can't live without him.' Her voice rose to a shriek.

Slumped on the sofa, in a rucked-up amber mini-skirt, and a saffron yellow jersey, with her tousled tawny hair and her tear-streaked face, Sarah should have been the epitome of desirability. But, comparing her hard, petulant, demanding little face to Taggie's, so sweet, so infinitely kind and gentle, Rupert wondered how the hell he'd ever fancied her.

'I can't live without him,' Sarah repeated shrilly. 'I'll never get over it.'

'I hate to point it out,' said Rupert, 'but you said exactly the same thing to me after Christmas, and you've got over me pretty thoroughly, and no doubt when Paul thought he ought to do his duty and stay with Winifred you said the same thing to him.'

'You can't compare the two,' said Sarah furiously. 'I've just spent a whole weekend with Paul,' she added with a shudder.

'Paul's palled, has he?' said Rupert, topping up her glass.

'I can't stand living with him a moment longer. He won't stop pawing me,' wailed Sarah. 'And he's so old. I mean he's nineteen years older than me. It was all right when I started working for him. I was twenty and he was thirty-nine and he seemed so wonderfully forceful and dynamic and experienced. But now I'm twenty-nine and he's forty-eight, and his body's going, and he looks all grey and rumpled when he wakes in the morning, and he wears cornplasters and snows scurf on his suits, and he's always clearing his throat and picking his nose behind the *FT* and peering at me over his spectacles.' Sarah's voice rose to a screech again as she catalogued his crimes. 'I can't stand it.'

Mindlessly, Rupert patted her heaving shoulder, as he bleakly worked out that the age gap between him and Taggie was exactly the same, or would be when he was thirty-eight next month. Gradually Sarah stopped crying.

'The one thing that puts men off is scenes,' said Rupert. 'You'll just have to grin and not bare it until 15th December. Everyone's going to be behaving in a pretty tense way for the next two months. I honestly can't see James and Lizzie's rapprochement lasting very long, and at least if you concentrate on your career at Corinium you'll be able to support yourself. You won't be able to afford two hunters, a Lotus and Jasper Conran dresses if Tony kicks you out, which he will do if you don't leave Vere-karing alone.'

Sarah sat up and rubbed the mascara from under her eyes.

'I suppose I'd better seduce Tony, but he's got one cloven hoof in the grave too. You and Cameron are so lucky – being near in age.'

Then her eyes narrowed. 'And while we're on that subject, what were you doing rolling up with the Galloping Gormless just now?'

Rupert's mind raced. He'd got to kill that rumour stone dead. If Sarah told Tony he'd been out with Taggie, Tony'd make sure it went straight back in a wildly exaggerated form to Cameron.

'I had the children for the weekend,' he said carefully. 'Cameron's away, so Taggie was helping me amuse them. She's nearer their age.'

'Well, that's a relief,' said Sarah. 'I thought for one ghastly moment you were after her as well. I mean, she's simply not up to it. Very sweet and all, but not very bright. A bit loco, James thinks. The last thing she needs is a lascivious old ram like you. You'd crucify her. Anyway you're far too old. It'd be just like Paul and me in a few years' time.'

It was like a dentist hitting a raw nerve with a high-speed drill. Rupert never dreamed remarks could hurt him quite so much. Mercifully he was saved by the telephone. Then the dentist seemed to hit another nerve.

'Christ, I've missed you,' said Cameron's seductive rasp. 'Sorry I haven't called, but we've been up to here. Perry O'Donovan's such an asshole, and he can't stand Esther McDermott. She's an asshole too, and they've both had such rows with Declan, he's walked off the set twice.'

'So it's all going as planned,' said Rupert.

As Cameron rattled on about the cock-ups and frustrations of filming, all he could hear was prison doors clanging shut on him.

'So we've managed to finish a day early,' she said finally.

'God, what a bore,' said Rupert who hadn't been listening.

'Sweetest, this is a terrible line, I said I'll be coming home a day early. Declan and I are flying in tomorrow.'

'Great,' said Rupert, feeling sick. 'I'll come and meet you.'

'No, I've got the car at the airport. I'll see you late

570

afternoon, and darling,' her voice dropped huskily, 'I've been celibate for three weeks. We've got a lot of catching up to do, so cancel any appointments for the rest of the day. I love you.'

'Me too,' said Rupert automatically.

'Good,' said Sarah, as Rupert put down the receiver and went and poured himself a large whisky. 'An absolute bastard like you needs an utter bitch like her to keep you in order.'

After she'd left, Rupert couldn't face going to bed. He took the dogs into the garden. As they weaved about snuffling and barking after badgers and masochistically lifting their legs on rose bushes, he looked across the valley. The moon had set; black clouds covered the sky; a chill wind was shepherding beech leaves irritably across the lawn; The Priory was in darkness, except for one light in Taggie's bedroom. Rupert almost wept. He longed to ring her now to explain why he wouldn't be ringing her tomorrow, or any day after that, but he didn't dare in case he weakened.

Sarah was right. He was too old, too shop-soiled, too reprobate. He'd only bring her unhappiness. Besides, Cameron was coming home tomorrow and he couldn't jeopardize the franchise by risking her running back to Tony. It was his fault; he'd gone into the whole thing with his flies open. Not only had the prison door clanged shut, but he could hear a huge key turning for ever in the lock.

One is one, and all alone, and ever more shall be so, he thought despairingly.

43

Across at The Priory, by some lucky chance, a starry-eyed but slightly sheepish Maud swanned in at five to twelve just in time to take a telephone call from Declan saying he was coming home tomorrow. Cameron would drop him off and, bar fogs or airport strikes, he would be with her by twilight.

All next day Taggie waited for Rupert to ring, and by some vicious twist of fate, as she cleaned the house and cautiously dusted and hoovered round the chaos of precious papers in her father's study and put clean sheets on her parents' bed, the telephone rang incessantly. But it was only Archie ringing once again to say goodbye to Caitlin, or members of the cast ringing for Maud, or every member of Venturer ringing to ask whether Declan was back. Each time, Taggie pounced on the telephone, and each time, like a stray dog dumped bewildered on the motorway hoping each passing car might be her master returning, when it wasn't Rupert she slunk back in utter despair. And as the day ebbed, so did her hopes. Once Cameron was home, he wouldn't ring.

The weather had changed too, and as the grey skies closed in on the October afternoon, the black tracery of ivy fretted against the casement windows and sharp bitter winds swept the leaves from the lime walk and drove them in withered heaps along the dry gravel paths. However many jerseys she put on, however much she raced about the house, Taggie was still cold, while upstairs Maud oiled and scented herself for Declan's return, no doubt leaving a horrible mess both in the bathroom and bedroom, which Taggie had just cleaned.

In the kitchen, having put some green tomato chutney to cook on the Aga, Taggie was trying to find a place on Caitlin's incredibly skimpy pants to sew a name tape. Caitlin, having scattered breadcrumbs all over the dresser, dumped papers and magazines on the table, left the orange juice carton out and her scrambled-egg pan unwashed in the sink, was now peeling an orange.

> Give me to drink mandragora,
> That I might sleep out this great gap of time
> My Archie is away [she moaned].

'One day you'll be sewing the name Caitlin Baddingham and a coronet on my pants. Don't you think I'll make a good Lady Baddingham?' She dropped a deep curtsey. 'I'm going to bunk out of school next weekend so I can see him.'

'I wouldn't,' said Taggie, breaking off a thread with her teeth. 'You'll get expelled and it's bound to get in the papers. Oh, for God's sake,' she snapped, as Caitlin dropped her orange peel on the table, 'can't you ever throw anything in the bin?'

'Don't nag,' said Caitlin. 'When I grow up I'm going to live in a really messy house.'

'What happens when you meet a fantastic man at a party and want to bring him back for a cup of coffee afterwards?'

'I'd go to his house,' said Caitlin. 'How can I live without Archie till next weekend?'

How can I live without Rupert for ever? thought Taggie, getting up to give the tomato chutney a stir. She jumped as Gertrude and Claudius rushed in and leapt on to the window-seat, bristling furiously. They were followed by Maud in a big fluffy pink towel.

'What on earth are you cooking?' she demanded in outraged tones.

'Tomato chutney,' said Taggie, through gritted teeth.

'What a disgusting smell to welcome home your poor

father, and there are cows in the garden doing great splattering cowpats all over the lawn and the paths, which is even worse. They must be Rupert's. Ring him up and tell him to take them away.'

'You ring him,' screamed Taggie. 'I can't do everything.'

'Temper temper,' said Maud, exchanging surprised glances with Caitlin. 'Well, I certainly haven't got time to ring. Someone's got to be ready to welcome him.'

'Scrubbing off other men's fingerprints,' said Caitlin scornfully, as Maud flounced off upstairs.

She put a hand on Taggie's shoulder.

'You OK?'

'N-not really.'

'Is it Rupert? Did you have a lovely day?'

Taggie nodded. 'But Sarah Stratton was waiting for him when we got back, so I came home. He said he'd ring, but . . .' Her voice trailed off. She stared at the great congealing brown mass of onions, brown sugar and tomatoes. Her mother was right. It was a repulsive smell.

'I'll ring him about the cows,' said Caitlin. 'That'll remind him.'

But when she got through, Rupert was on the other line and the secretary said she'd send the farm manager over at once to remove the cows.

'Rupert's probably terribly busy,' said Caitlin consolingly. Then, as the telephone rang, 'There, that'll be him now.'

'You answer it,' gasped Taggie. Please God make it be Rupert, she whispered over and over again into the vat of chutney.

'Hullo, Upland House Bakery. Which tart would you like to fill?' said Caitlin. 'Oh Archie, darling, I won't survive either.'

She was interrupted by frantic barking. Gertrude and Claudius shot off the window-seat, taking the cushions with them, and rushed into the hall as a car crunched on the gravel.

'My father's just got back. He'd lynch me if he knew I was talking to you,' said Caitlin hastily. 'I'll write tonight. Love you madly. *Ciao*.'

Fighting back the tears, Taggie went out to welcome Declan. He looked wonderful, incredibly suntanned from filming outside and much less tired. He was about to hug her when she was sent flying by Maud, a tornado of Arpège and desire, wearing Taggie's new grey cashmere jersey. Throwing herself on Declan, she buried her face in his chest so that he shouldn't see the guilt flickering in her eyes.

'Darling, you're so brown and handsome,' she murmured. 'I've missed you every single minute.'

Caitlin, lounging in the doorway, whistled, then she quoted sardonically:

> When my love swears that she is made of truth,
> I do believe her, though I know she lies.

Declan was too delighted to find Maud in such good spirits to take in what Caitlin was saying. 'Cameron's outside,' he said. 'Come and say hullo while I unload the car.'

Taggie's heart sank as Cameron came through the door. Like Declan, she looked wonderful. Her face seemed even softer, her hair less severe. She was wearing a cream silk shirt tucked into brown suede jodhpurs above tight, shiny brown boots. Either it had been a highly successful shoot or she was obviously over the moon about seeing Rupert again.

Ignoring Taggie and Caitlin, she went straight up to Maud and hugged her. 'Ireland was terrific, but we sure missed you. If you'd been playing Maud Gonne, we'd get an Emmy. Esther McDermott was just awful. But Declan was such an inspiration. His sarcasm can bruise, but, wow, it makes you grow.'

'Really,' said Maud, not altogether enthusiastically.

Taggie, unable to take any more, went out to the car, where she had no difficulty in picking out her father's battered roped-together leather case from Cameron's Louis Vuitton. On the second journey she picked up a couple of carrier bags.

'No,' said Cameron sharply, appearing in the doorway. 'Those are gifts for Rupert and the kids. I must show you what I got Tabitha, Maud.'

She produced a little leather pony, with a girl rider, and bridles and saddles that came off.

'Isn't it neat?'

'Lovely,' said Maud without interest.

Cameron had bought a beautifully illustrated book of Irish legends for Marcus, and a pair of gold cuff links for Rupert, which she insisted on showing to Taggie.

'I'll get his crest put on later,' she said. Taggie stared at her dumbly.

'Very nice, I'm sure,' said Caitlin tartly. Then, looking at Cameron's jodhpurs, 'Are you going for a ride?'

'I sure am,' said Cameron with a sudden lascivious smile. 'After three weeks away I need one, and not on the back of a horse. I'm off, Declan,' she yelled into the house, 'I'll call you as soon as I know when we can see the rushes.'

'Bitch,' screamed Caitlin at the departing Lotus. Taggie shook her head. Cameron was the one who Rupert belonged to.

Taking a bottle of duty-free whisky, Declan and Maud went up to bed. Taggie also went up to her room, and, with trembling hands, tried to hold Caitlin's binoculars still as she looked across the valley to Penscombe Court. Enough leaves had come off the trees now for her to see lights on downstairs in the kitchen and the drawing-room. Then, like a firefly lighting up the almost leafless chestnut avenue, she saw Cameron's Lotus storming up Rupert's drive. In an unbearably short time another light went on, which Taggie knew from Tabitha's guided tour of the house yesterday was Rupert's bedroom. No one bothered to draw the curtains.

Taggie collapsed on the bed. What was that expression her father was always quoting? *The heart transfixed upon the huddled spears.* She knew what it meant now. Two minutes later there was a bang on her door.

'Go away,' she groaned.

Caitlin walked in with the dogs, who leapt on to the bed, frantically trying to lick away Taggie's tears.

'You got over Ralphie; you'll get over Rupert,' said Caitlin.

'Anyway you may not have to. He's got to keep that bitch sweet until after the franchise.'

'Bugger the franchise,' sobbed Taggie. 'What would you do if you saw Archie and some woman in bed?'

'I'd light a cigarette, have a drink and go and stuff my face,' said Caitlin. 'Look, I hate intruding on your grief, but the tomato chutney smells even more disgusting burning, and as those carnal beasts won't emerge from their bedroom before morning, I'm afraid you'll have to take me back to Uplift House.'

'There's a pauper just behind me and he's treading on my tail,' groaned Declan the following morning as, reeling from hangover and too much sex, he went through the pile of final reminders and endless requests from charity organizations for his time, his money or 'one of his very personal things'.

'Why don't you send them all a lock of your hair?' suggested Ursula.

'I'd be bald in a week.'

'It's only because you're a household name that people mistakenly assume you're rolling,' said Ursula soothingly.

'I'll be a poorhouse-hold name at this rate.' Declan winced as he bent down to retrieve an unopened letter that had fallen under the table among the débris of biros and pencils chewed up by Claudius. 'This looks more interesting.'

The letter was from the IBA telling Venturer that their interview would be at ten o'clock on 29th November at the IBA headquarters at 80 Brompton Road.

Declan immediately swung into action and called a Venturer meeting the following week. The room over the night-club in Cheltenham was considered too risky, so a suite was booked in an obscure Bloomsbury Hotel. For security's sake, a large board in the lobby announced in white plastic letters that the O'Hara, Black & Jones Drainage Co. Sales Conference was being held in the Virginia Woolf Suite on the fourth floor. The whole of Venturer turned up except Dame Enid, who had a concert in New York, Janey Lloyd-Foxe, whose baby had gastric flu, and Bas who had ostensibly been caught up in some crisis at the Bar Sinister.

Cameron took special trouble with her appearance, wearing a new very waisted red silk suit with padded shoulders, a very plunging neckline and an extremely short skirt. This was because she was meeting Rupert's best friend, Billy Lloyd-Foxe, for the first time. He'd been away making a film on rugger for the BBC for the past three months and Cameron was determined to make a good impression. She needn't have worried. Billy came up to her straight away with that famous smile which had been described as 'able to beam into millions of homes without the aid of satellite'.

'Hullo, gosh, I've been longing to meet you,' he said, kissing her. 'I'm mad about "Four Men went to Mow". Janey's taped all the episodes for me. It's exactly how Rupe and I used to carry on before we were married. It was just starting in Australia when I left, and being marvellously received.'

He was extremely attractive, Cameron decided. His light-brown hair had gone greyer and he'd thickened out since his show-jumping days, but he had such a young face, and his turned-down eyes were so merry you didn't notice the broken nose or the doubling chin. He also had a sweetness and an air of life being hilarious, but at the same time a little bit too much for him that had endeared him as much to the BBC viewers as to everyone in the sporting world. Janey was mad to mess him around, thought Cameron. She wondered if that was why Bas wasn't here today.

Rupert and he seemed to know each other so well, they slipped into familiarity like a pair of old bedroom slippers, arguing about horses, finishing each other's sentences, howling with laughter at each other's jokes. It was nice to see Rupert happy again, thought Cameron. His fuse had been very short since she got back. She suspected, although he denied it, that he hated being in opposition – a shadow minister of his former self.

'When you come back to Penscombe, we're bloody well going to start a racing stable,' Rupert was saying in an undertone.

'I thought we were going to run a television station,' said Billy.

'We are, but with the revenue coming in, we'll have access to a hundred and twenty-five million a year. Just think what we can do with that.'

'Good God,' said Billy in amazement. 'Christy may be able to go to Harrow after all. I must have a drink.'

At that moment Declan tapped a large mahogany table in the centre of the room and asked everyone to sit down on the row of chairs lined up on the opposite side.

'Where's the bar?' asked Rupert.

'No one's having anything to drink until we've finished,' Declan said firmly.

Wesley's face fell. Billy turned pale. 'What is this, a concentration camp?'

'Concentration –' Declan smiled thinly – 'is what we're after tonight. If you're all swilling booze and getting up to get each other drinks, you won't take in what I'm saying. There's Perrier if anyone wants it.'

'Now I know why it's called a dry run,' said Billy sulkily. 'Come and sit by me,' he said to Cameron, patting a chair. 'At least I can cheer myself up gazing at your legs.'

Cameron looked like a cross between Joan Collins and Donald Duck, Billy decided, frightfully glamorous but somewhat high-powered.

'I'm frightfully hungry. Can we at least ring for some sandwiches?' said Professor Graystock, deliberately pressing against Cameron's breasts and having a good look as he leant over to pinch one of Billy's cigarettes.

'Later,' said Declan.

Billy, Harold White, Seb Burrows, Georgie Baines and Sally Maples, the children's editor Declan had recruited from Yorkshire Television, then jumped out of their skins when an unknown man in spectacles with a crew cut and a purposeful expression walked in.

'It's all right,' said Declan soothingly. 'This is Hardy Bissett. He used to work for the IBA and knows exactly what sort of questions they'll ask us at the interview. He's going to drill us over the next few weeks.'

'Who's that turgid old crone in the portrait over the mantelpiece?' Billy whispered to Cameron.

'Virginia Woolf,' whispered Cameron.

'I'd do anything to keep her from my door!' said Billy. 'What did she do for a living – belly dancing?'

'A fine writer,' said Professor Graystock reprovingly.

Declan found Hardy a chair beside him on the other side of the table. Then he said, 'The IBA meeting, as you all know now, is fixed for 29th November. The good thing is that Corinium's meeting is the afternoon before, so there won't be any problem for those of you who have to go to both meetings.'

Everyone jumped again as a fat man waddled into the room wearing a stocking over his head, waving a blue plastic toy gun, saying, 'This is a shoot-out.'

Then he peeled the stocking off with a broad grin and said, 'Boo!' It was Charles Fairburn.

'Oh, for fock's sake, Charles,' exploded Declan. 'This is serious. I was just explaining that ours and Corinium's meetings are on different days, so you won't bump into Tony and Ginger Johnson coming out of the IBA as you go in. But please think up excuses to be out of the office on the 29th well in advance. We want as many of you there as possible.'

'Are you sure no one will see us?' asked Sally Maples nervously. 'We've all been threatened with the sack again this week.'

'So have we,' said Billy.

Declan shook his head. 'All you have to do is to drive into the underground garage at the back of the IBA – you needn't go near the front at all – nd you'll be whisked up to the eighth floor.

'By now,' he went on, 'the IBA will have digested our applications and answers to the supplementary questions, and noted our performance at the public meeting. They will obviously have some idea as to whom they want to award the franchise. But have no doubt, the interview on the 29th is key. Just as important as a viva to an undergraduate taking finals.'

'I wouldn't know about that,' murmured Billy.

'I'm now going to hand you over to Hardy,' said Declan, sitting down, 'who'll take you through the dry run.'

Hardy Bissett, despite his bristly crew cut, had an air of officialdom which unnerved them all. Getting to his feet, he tapped the table with a biro: 'This is exactly the kind of table you'll sit along during the interview, except the IBA table is oval-shaped. Facing you will be the twelve members of the Authority, with Lady Gosling in the centre. None of them know anything much about television. They are worthy public figures, academics, business people. One of them, Mrs Scott-Menzies, for example, is the ex-Chairman of the WI. Another used to run the Post Office. Another is an ex-Labour Minister of Education. Yet another, whom I think you've come across, Declan, is the Reverend Fergus Penney, a disgusting old goat who was once a Prebendary of the Church of England.

'It is essential for you to memorize all their names. All important people in their own field once, they tend to be vain and enjoy recognition. Behind them during the meeting will sit half a dozen officials who work for the Authority, who know *all* about television. They do not speak during the interview, but they brief before and advise afterwards, and will be watching you all like hawks.'

Billy mopped his brow. 'It sounds most alarming,' he sighed.

'God, that man's disgusting,' thought Rupert, as Professor Graystock pinched yet another of Billy's cigarettes.

As if reading Rupert's thoughts, Hardy Bissett said, 'One of the crucial things at the interview is to appear to like and admire each other and prove you are not merely a star-studded bunch after a quick buck, but actually capable of forming a workable and amicable team. As you will be sitting in an almost straight line and will not be able to catch each other's eyes, it is also crucial to work out in advance who will field what questions. Freddie perhaps should answer any technical questions, the Bishop should deal with religion, Dame Enid with music, Charles the arts, and so on.

'It is also vital that everyone has their say. One excellent consortium lost the breakfast franchise a few years ago because their chairman, a newspaper editor, answered all the questions quite brilliantly, thereby convincing the IBA that they would be too much of a one-man band.

'All right.' He clapped his hands together. 'Enough waffle. To begin with I'll fire questions directly at individuals. Later on in rehearsals we'll get to the stage when I can fire a question in the air, and the appropriate person will leap to answer it. Now remember, the interview will last at least an hour.'

'I won't if I don't get a drink,' grumbled Billy.

'Shut up,' snapped Hardy Bissett. He turned to Henry Hampshire. 'I'm interested to know why as Lord-Lieutenant you decided to join the Venturer consortium?'

For a second, Henry mouthed helplessly like a goldfish. 'Because Rupert told me I'd make a fortune,' he said, 'and that he'd introduce me to Joanna Lumley.'

Everyone screamed with laughter except the Bishop, Declan and Hardy Bissett.

'Which Rupert hasn't done yet, what?' said Henry, delighted at the reaction.

'This is meant to be a dry run,' said Hardy icily. He turned to Wesley. 'How d'you intend to retain the cultural traditions of the ethnic minorities in your area, Mr Emerson?'

Wesley looked blank. 'Don't know, man. Declan promised me a fortune too, but he didn't say anything about Joanna Lumley.'

Billy wiped his eyes. 'This is wonderful,' he whispered to Cameron.

Like a terrier, Hardy Bissett caught Billy off guard. 'As Venturer's head of sport,' he asked sharply, 'how d'you intend to revolutionize Corinium's sporting coverage?'

'Er-hum,' said Billy helplessly. 'Making programmes is a bit like sex. I do it all the time, but I'm afraid I never talk about it. Programmes are living things, particularly sport,' he went on apologetically. 'They seem to materialize as you go along.'

'Very lucid,' said Hardy so sarcastically that Billy went crimson. He then turned to Professor Graystock. 'I wonder, Professor, if you might be able to provide us with a more serious answer to the question I asked Wesley?'

The Professor cleared his throat. 'At Venturer we would naturally give the ethnic minorities the chance to develop their own programmes in their own way,' he said in his fulsome drone. 'This will keep alive the cultures and traditions which would otherwise be neglected as the minorities become fully integrated into the population.'

'Excellent, Professor,' said Hardy. 'That's more like it, although you could have gone on to specify some of the programmes and had a crack at Corinium's abysmal record at the same time.'

He turned to Freddie. 'Have you got a definite policy towards industrial relations?'

Freddie looked somewhat apprehensively at Rupert. 'I and my Managing Director, Declan, and my Financial Director, Rupert, are all firmly committed believers in industrial democracy.'

'Are we?' said Rupert in amazement.

'Shut up,' hissed Cameron. 'Will you and Billy stop taking the piss.'

Sulkily Rupert got out the *Evening Standard* and surreptitiously started reading his Scorpio horoscope, which was all about career opportunities and staying cool in the face of provocation. Then, because he read Taggie's horoscope as automatically as his own these days, his eyes moved up three places to Cancer.

'*As there is a new moon this week,*' wrote Patric Walker, '*you are probably wondering where the next blow will fall and feel everyone is against you.*'

Oh the poor little duck, thought Rupert, suddenly overwhelmed with longing and protectiveness. She'd been so adorable the other day. He never dreamed he'd miss her so much.

'Rupert,' snapped Cameron. 'Hardy wants to know if we've got an employment policy.'

'Yes,' said Rupert coolly. 'We'll employ very good people. We'll pay them extremely well to work, and if they don't we'll tell them to fuck off.'

The Bishop and Professor Graystock exchanged pained glances. Declan's bitten fingernails drummed on the table.

'Slightly too simplistic,' said Hardy Bissett acidly. 'I hope someone else has something a little bit more illuminating to say on the subject.'

At the end of half an hour Hardy called a halt.

'That was absolutely appalling,' he said bluntly. 'Declan, you're fielding too many questions — can't say I blame you with these morons — and getting totally carried away by your own blarney. So are you, Bishop.' The Bishop turned purple. 'You're both far too long-winded. The rest are much too short. You should be answering the questions in a sentence, and then immediately using the subject to dive into another area where you want to make a point. The object is to put across Venturer's message and make your pitch whatever questions you're asked.'

'Christ,' said Billy to Rupert as the Professor nicked yet another of his cigarettes, 'it's like one of those terrible nightmares of being back at school. Who is this fink on my right who talks like a British Telecom technical manual?'

'Professor Graystock,' said Rupert. 'Declan brought him in. He's a disgrace.'

'We'll have another half-hour session,' said Hardy Bissett. 'Then we'll have a drink.' He turned to Freddie. 'Mr Jones, how did the idea for Venturer originate?'

Freddie scratched his curls.

'Well, it was like this, Rupert an' me 'ad both 'ad an up-and-downer wiv Tony Baddingham over different fings. Declan was having a rough time of it. Tony's a fug, make no bones abart it, got a board made up of professional accountants, who use profits for anyfing other than making programmes; won't take risks; that's why their share of the ratings is dropping. Anyway, Declan 'ad a barney wiv him and walked out. Rupe and I both fink Declan's terrific; he's a real man of stature; could become the Lord Reef of ITV, so we decided to pitch for the franchise.

'We all live in the area,' he went on. 'Rupe's lived there all 'is life. Declan, Cameron and I are comparative new-comers, more like Cafflic converts, so we love it wiv a passion, and we just feel it's being shabbily represented by Corinium.'

'Well done,' said Rupert. But once again the Professor and the Bishop exchanged pained glances.

After that Harold White and Cameron were both excellent on programme plans, Georgie was brilliant on advertising, and Seb marvellously bitchy about the newsroom and 'Cotswold Round-Up'. But at the end Hardy Bissett was just as scathing.

'Look at you,' he said mockingly, 'cringing on the back of your seats trying to make yourself invisible to an examiner who might ask you the awkward question. You've got to sit forward, be eager and positive, bursting with enthusiasm.'

'Gimme a drink, then,' murmured Billy.

'But it was better than last time,' went on Hardy. 'You've got just over a month to get your act together, and if we keep going over the same ground night after night –' Billy and Rupert exchanged looks of horror; Freddie glanced at his watch – 'you're bound to improve. It's obvious our moles won't be able to make every evening. But I'm glad to say most of them, not all –' Hardy glared pointedly at Billy – 'acquitted themselves well and are obviously less in need of coaching than the rest of you. I congratulate you, Declan, on your poaching skills. Just don't get rumbled, any of you, between now and December.'

When they'd all got drinks, Declan gave them a brief progress report. 'You needn't be too disheartened by our abysmal showing today. Elsewhere things are looking good. The most dramatic bit of news is that Mid-West have pulled out. They can't raise the cash evidently, so their Geography master will probably never get to London now.' He grinned. 'This means it's a two-horse race – just us and Corinium.'

Everyone was wildly excited by this information, except Rupert. Two two the rivals now, he thought bitterly. Why did everything remind him of Taggie?

'I've also heard off the record that the IBA have had at least three thousand letters from local organizations pledging their support for Venturer,' Declan went on. 'Tony was also supposed to appear on a programme on Radio Cotchester this week, with me and the West of England man from the IBA, but he's backed off because he claims a programme interspersed with pop records is not the right vehicle for serious discussion, i.e., he's got cold feet.

'The story's been leaked to tomorrow's papers. Finally Ladbroke's make us five to four on today, so we're on our way.'

'So am I,' said Freddie, going towards the door.

Rupert followed him. 'Where are you going?'

'To a meetin',' said Freddie, looking shifty.

'With Mrs Vereker?' said Rupert. 'For Christ's sake be careful. Sarah Stratton rolled up at my house in hysterics the other day, saying James had been told to back off and concentrate on Lizzie, as they're going to make this marriage series together.'

'I know,' said Freddie. 'Makes fings very difficult. That's why Lizzie and me's meeting up here.'

'It's a bloody good story,' said Rupert. 'Corinium presenter ordered to give up his presenter mistress and concentrate on his wife in order to win franchise. The *Scorpion* would adore it.'

'No!' said Freddie, appalled. 'It'd hurt Lizzie, and hurt her kids to have their father's name plastered all over the papers.'

'Frederick, dear,' said Rupert patiently, 'it's a good story, I said. It'll discredit Corinium and make a complete mockery of the marriage programme if everyone knows it's a sham. D'you want to win this franchise or not?'

Freddie shook his head stubbornly. 'Not if it 'urts Lizzie. Anyway, you're barking up the wrong tree, mate. Fact that

Tony's told James to drop his mistress and concentrate on making his marriage work will only score Brownie points with the IBA. Besides, if the papers start sniffin' round James, they might easily cotton on to Lizzie and me.'

Rupert sighed. 'If Declan and I can behave ourselves, I can't think why you can't.'

As soon as Freddie had gone, the Bishop and the Professor, who was clutching a huge whisky in one hand and a vast plate of smoked salmon sandwiches in the other, closed in on Rupert.

'Could we have a word?' said the Bishop.

'We're a bit concerned about Freddie Jones,' said the Professor with his mouth full.

'Charming chap, of course,' said the Bishop smoothly. 'Definitely one of nature's gentlemen, but a little bit of a rough diamond.'

'Rough diamonds are a consortium's best friend,' said Rupert lightly, but there was a deterrent steeliness about his eyes.

'Ha, ha,' said the Bishop heartily. 'However, as I was saying, Crispin Graystock knows several members of the IBA who we'll be meeting on the 29th. I myself am not unfamiliar with quite a few of them either. Mrs Menzies-Scott is an old friend, and of course I've exchanged views with the Prebendary. We just feel that Freddie Jones is not quite the right vehicle to put Venturer's message across.'

'What d'you mean, vehicle?' snapped Rupert. 'Freddie's not a van!'

'Well, someone who talks about Lord Reef and Cafflic converts and refers to Tony Baddingham as "a fug" –' delicately the Professor mimicked Freddie's accent – 'and extols the joys of "miking vast sums of money", will hardly go down very well with the IBA.'

'To be frank,' said the Bishop, 'poor Freddie can hardly string a sentence together.'

'Freddie is a star,' said Rupert furiously. 'He's far the most genuine person Venturer's got. He runs one of the most successful companies in the country and he's got the common touch.'

'A very common touch,' said the Professor, stuffing two more sandwiches into his face and gargling them down with a huge slug of whisky.

'All we're suggesting,' said the Bishop soothingly, 'is that Freddie Jones may be very much at home on the shop floor, with businessmen, even with the press, but not with the clergymen, academics, ladies of the Women's Institute and senior statesmen he's going to encounter on the 29th.'

'We feel very strongly that he should stick to technical specifications, take more of a back seat and perhaps take a few elocution lessons,' added the Professor.

'I know an ex-actor who lives in Will-is-den,' said the Bishop, taking Rupert's stunned silence as assent, 'who's worked absolute miracles with somewhat – er – provincial young curates, who have difficulty taking services and giving sermons.'

'I've never heard such a bloody awful idea in my life,' exploded Rupert. 'D'you want to castrate Freddie, to take away all his spontaneity and bounce? And coming from two jumped-up ex-grammar school boys who talk about "Will-is-den", and "substarntial involevement" makes it all the more laughable. Do you want Freddie to talk like a fucking toastmaster?'

'I beg your pardon?' thundered the Bishop, turning puce.

'And for someone who calls himself a Christian and another a practising socialist, you're both a bloody disgrace,' added Rupert.

'I hope you'll withdraw that remark,' spluttered the Professor, showering Rupert with whisky-soaked crumbs.

'Sausage rolls, anyone?' said Cameron, coming over and shoving a plate between them. 'What on earth's the matter?'

'The Bishop and the Professor have just pointed out that Freddie is a social embarrassment to Venturer and should take some elocution lessons,' said Rupert furiously and stalked out of the room.

It took all Cameron's and, later, Declan's tact to calm the

Bishop and the Professor down. Both threatened to resign, demanded Rupert's resignation or at least most humble apologies, and were only placated by a large and very expensive dinner at the Gay Hussar.

It was two-thirty in the morning before Declan got home to Penscombe, but he found Taggie still up laying out apples in an upstairs spare room. With all the bills flooding in, it might be all they had to live on soon.

'How did it go?' she asked.

'Awful, but Hardy Bissett says it's always ghastly to begin with. He'll knock them into shape. Billy Lloyd-Foxe turned up.'

'Is he nice?' said Taggie.

'Enchanting,' said Declan. 'Exactly the right kind of person to calm everyone down. With the last fence in sight, they're all getting incredibly twitchy.'

Then he told Taggie about Rupert's row with the Bishop and the Professor.

'Rupert was right. Poor Freddie,' said Taggie indignantly.

'He was not,' said Declan. 'Winding up other members of the consortium at this stage is insane. Keeping the Bishop sweet is absolutely crucial. Rupert was flip and obstructive the whole way through the meeting. I don't know what's got into him, or how poor Cameron puts up with him.'

It was poor Cameron now, reflected Taggie grimly.

'She was fantastic at the meeting,' Declan went on, with unexpected warmth. 'The more I see of her, the better I think she is. In fact all the moles distinguished themselves, even Sally Maples, once she got over her nerves. And Charles keeps everyone's spirits up. And Billy, as I said, just has an enchanting personality, which is bound to endear us to the IBA. I hate to sound over-confident –' he reached over and touched the skirting board – 'but if we don't do anything bloddy silly between now and December, our chances of getting the franchise must be focking good.'

44

In the first week in November Tony Baddingham called a press conference. He looked on top of the world, the scarlet poppy in his buttonhole adding just the right note of concerned sobriety to offset the hedonistic effect of a splendid Los Angeles suntan.

He had been in LA, he told the waiting army of reporters and cameramen, to sign up a brilliant new woman programme controller who would start in the new year.

'Assuming you win the franchise?' asked ITN.

'There's no doubt about that,' said Tony smugly.

'Is she better than Cameron Cook?'

'I have no doubt about that either,' said Tony even more smugly.

He went on to say that Corinium had set aside sixteen million pounds next year for new programmes and pledged to have 'an even fresher and more responsible approach to covering the region'.

'The old fox is up to something,' muttered the *Mail on Sunday*. 'He didn't get us here just for this crap.'

'What about advertising?' asked the *Observer*.

'Revenue may be down,' Tony replied smoothly, 'but so is the advertising revenue of all the ITV companies.'

It had been a bad summer for advertising, he explained, because the weather had been so good, but this had boosted

Corinium's leisure interests, so shareholders could expect excellent mid-term results in December.

'Why weren't you prepared to face Declan O'Hara on Radio Cotchester?' asked the *Scorpion*.

'Because Corinium prefer to rest on their laurels and not indulge in vulgar abuse and –' Tony lowered his voice, so the journalists had to crane forward to catch what he was saying – 'Declan O'Hara might not have been quite so happy to face me had he been aware that I know everything he's been up to.'

'Here it comes,' said ITN, as Tony very slowly got out a cigar and made a great play of cutting off the end before lighting it.

'Declan O'Hara,' he went on slowly, 'has been poaching my staff. This summer he enticed Cameron Cook away, but as early as May he had signed up my sales director, Georgie Baines, my religious editor, Charles Fairburn, and my finest news reporter, Sebastian Burrows. I'd like also to warn the BBC, London Weekend, and Yorkshire Television, that Billy Lloyd-Foxe, Harold White and Sally Maples –' Tony enunciated the names particularly carefully so all the journalists could get them down – 'are also signed up and poised to move to Venturer in the most unlikely event of them winning the franchise.'

There was a stunned silence.

'How the hell did you find all this out?' asked the *Mail on Sunday*, almost sent flying by the unseemly dash for the telephones.

'I wouldn't be chief executive of Corinium if I didn't know everything that was going on in my own company,' said Tony grimly, 'and I intend to keep it that way for many years to come. Unlike Venturer,' he added dismissively, 'whose security is even worse than MI5.'

For twenty-four hours Tony left the three Corinium moles to sweat, and the whole Corinium building in a turmoil of rumour and speculation. James Vereker, for one, was absolutely furious on initially hearing the news. How dare Declan ignore him and sign up Charles, who was nothing but a fat drunken fag, or Seb, who was infinitely junior to James in the newsroom, or Georgie, of whose longer eyelashes James was inordinately jealous? Then James's fury turned to pleasure, as he realized that all three moles would be for the high jump. He even gave several interviews to the nationals, saying he was utterly disgusted by their disloyal, uncaring behaviour, and that he felt huge sympathy for Tony Baddingham in his hour of desertion.

James was therefore not the only member of Corinium's staff hanging round the newsroom waiting for fireworks the following morning, after word whistled round the building that Tony had sent for Georgie Baines. Seb was demented with worry, thinking of the loan he'd wheedled out of his bank manager for a new Ferrari. Charles could only take another gulp of claret and think greyly of his five-figure overdraft and the mortgage he'd just taken out on a tumble-down cottage near Penscombe.

Half an hour later Georgie Baines staggered into the newsroom making agonized faces and clutching his bottom as though he'd just been given twelve of the best. Then, very slowly, he drew the latest Corinium Company Report out of the seat of his trousers, then roared and roared with laughter.

'Tony gave me an absolute bollocking,' he told his amazed audience, 'said if I have any more dealings with Venturer, he'll sue me for breach of contract, but it's made him realize how much I'm worth to Corinium. So he's doubled my salary, and made me Deputy Managing Director – so you better all behave yourselves, my darlings.'

'Oh, how sweet,' said Daysee Butler, bursting into tears.

'You're not joining Venturer then?' asked Seb.

'Not for the moment,' said Georgie. Then, rubbing his hands, 'And now that I'm deputy MD I'm going to start getting heavy. Off with his head!' he yelled, pointing at a very discomforted James Vereker. 'And don't you go giving any more interviews to the press about me and disloyalty, you little twerp.'

Muttering about being seriously misquoted, James bolted

out of the newsroom, whereupon everyone cheered and started opening bottles to celebrate.

Seb was summoned ten minutes later and received more or less the same treatment.

'Tony's sending me to the New York office for six months to get me out of the way,' he said. 'Then, if I behave myself, I can come back. I suppose it's better than the sack.'

'Much, much,' said Charles Fairburn, draining his bottle of red. Feeling vastly relieved that he wasn't going to be out on his ear, Charles too obeyed a summons from above.

'*Mea culpa*,' he said in mock seriousness, winking at Miss Madden as he sauntered into Tony's office.

Five minutes later he was back in the newsroom, trembling like a great white blancmange. Everyone stopped their revelling.

'Whatever's the matter?' said Georgie, who'd been tangoing in and out of the desks with Daysee Butler.

'I've been sacked,' whispered Charles. 'On the spot, and he's not giving me any redundancy money because I was warned three times.'

Over at the BBC, at London Weekend and Yorkshire Television, Billy Lloyd-Foxe, Harold White and Sally Maples, all ashen and trembling and mindful of their overdrafts and their dependants, denied any involvement with Venturer and were all suspended from programme-making pending further investigation, and warned that the most tenuous contact with Venturer would mean the sack.

The story was front page in every paper for several days. Declan and Rupert, as the best-known members of Venturer, were blamed for enticement, which no one minded about very much, and lousy security, which, however, reflected very badly on their management skills. Worst of all, Venturer was now left without a sales director, a programme controller, a children's editor, a sports editor, and a head of news, until Seb, enraged by the cavalier sacking of Charles Fairburn, told Tony to stuff his New York job and resigned as well. This was all very high-minded of Seb, but now meant that

Venturer's fast diminishing kitty was faced with paying both his and Charles's salaries. Seb would have no difficulty finding another job, but, at fifty-one and a notorious piss artist, Charles was far more of a problem.

Venturer, meanwhile, had been thrown into complete pandemonium. On the afternoon of Tony's putsch, Rupert, Freddie and Declan met up at The Priory.

'There must be a countermole, or how could Tony have found out all these things?' said Declan. Freddie, however, was scrabbling under Declan's desk. Then he took Declan's telephone apart.

'Bugged,' he said bleakly. 'I'll get my men in at once to sweep the room and check all the phones. It's possible the 'ole place is bugged. They'd better do your phones as well, Rupe.'

Declan was appalled. 'Christ knows how much Tony has found out, then.'

'If he smashes Venturer, he finks he'll get Cameron back,' said Freddie. 'I said we was dealing with a villain. He's out to bury us.'

'But how the hell did his men get in here to bug the telephone?' said Rupert. 'The dogs would frighten anyone away, and there's always someone in the house.'

As Taggie was out doing a dinner party in Cheltenham, Declan sent for Maud. 'Has anyone called to check the telephones lately?' he asked.

'Yes,' said Maud, 'someone from British Telecom came last Friday; such a delightful young man. He said his mother's favourite opera was *The Merry Widow*. He heard me rehearsing and made me sing the Vilja song over and over again.'

'What was he doing here?' asked Declan wearily.

'His department had been notified that we'd been overcharged, so he was checking all the telephones to see if they were using up too many units,' said Maud beaming. 'He said they might be able to give us a rebate. I quite forgot to tell you.'

Declan put his head in his hands.

'How long was he here?' he groaned.

'About three hours,' said Maud.

Rupert and Freddie exchanged glances of horror. If it hadn't been so terrible, it would have been funny.

'That was your bugger,' said Rupert.

'D'you mean to say all that time he was bugging our house?' said Maud indignantly. 'And I gave him three cups of tea with sugar and a Penguin.'

'I'm sorry,' sighed Declan after she'd gone, 'I'm not making excuses for her, but I don't think it's quite as simple as that. Tony knew about *all* the moles, but I've never rung Billy on this telephone. Rupert's always been the one to get in touch with him. And because I was ultra-conscious of security, I've always made a point of directly contacting all the moles from a callbox outside Penscombe, so the calls couldn't be traced back. Anyway, if the telephone was only bugged last Friday, I rang everyone about the dry run before that. I've got a horrible feeling someone tipped Tony off.'

'All right,' said Freddie, sitting down heavily on a lot of tapes, 'let's go through the list of possibilities. Taggie was working at Sarah Stratton's a fortnight ago and the Baddinghams and the Verekers were both there.'

'Don't be bloody silly,' snapped Rupert, who was pacing up and down the room. 'Of course it's not Taggie. She's entirely responsible for all those letters being sent to the IBA and what the fucking hell's she got to gain by leaking secrets to Tony?'

Freddie raised his eyebrows. 'No need to overreact. She could have just let somefink slip to Sarah over the dishes.'

'And how d'you know the Verekers and the Baddinghams were at the Strattons the other night?' said Rupert, still furious. 'I suppose Lizzie told you. Lizzie's much more likely to have told Tony.'

'Lizzie's nothing to do with us,' said Declan irritably. 'Do keep to the point, Rupert.'

'Lizzie's something to do with Freddie,' persisted Rupert. 'You could easily have talked in your sleep.'

Freddie turned dark red. 'There's nuffink going on there.'

'Hum,' said Rupert.

Declan looked disapproving. 'Is there?' he said icily.

Freddie shuffled his feet. 'I'm very fond of Lizzie. I haven't told her anyfing.'

Declan then admitted that Maud had told him Caitlin had been out once with Archie Baddingham, but they were just a couple of kids, and he was quite certain Caitlin knew nothing of importance. Anyway she was back at school now.

'Caitlin knows everything,' said Rupert. 'She doesn't miss a trick, and she might easily have seen Sally Maples or Harold.'

'They've never been to the house,' said Declan. 'I suppose one of the moles could have turned countermole.'

'More than their life's wurf,' said Freddie, shaking his head. 'If they shopped us, they automatically shop themselves. Georgie is the only one it might have been, and he was far too upset when Tony broke the news yesterday. I expect Tony's got the thumbscrew on him now, getting the rest of Venturer's secrets out of him.'

'What about Maud?' said Rupert. 'She's always hanging around with Monica.'

'When did my wife ever take the slightest interest in the franchise? She doesn't know a thing,' said Declan bitterly.

'Valerie's got a soft spot for James Vereker,' suggested Rupert.

Freddie sighed. 'Valerie's like Maud, simply not interested.'

'Much as I'd like to suspect the Bishop and Professor Graystock,' said Rupert, 'they're far too motivated by greed and self-interest to shop us, and the same goes for Marti.'

'Not if Tony made it worth their while,' said Declan. 'I wouldn't rule them out.'

'Well, Basil's in the clear,' went on Rupert, 'and I honestly think Wesley and Henry are too thick, or in Wesley's case too spaced out to remember anyone's names anyway. But I suppose they're possibilities.'

'Everyone's a possibility,' said Declan bleakly, 'and finally there's Cameron. She's my choice. I've had my doubts about her all along.'

'Balls,' said Rupert irritably. 'She's far too obsessed with us winning the franchise and, since she came back from Ireland, with making movies with you.'

'And frankly,' said Freddie, 'she's far too smitten by our Rupe.'

When Declan said nothing, Rupert protested: 'Cameron's got a lot of faults, but she's basically honest. That's why she so loathed carrying on with Tony and Corinium while she was sleeping with me.'

'I've always suspected she was treacherous,' said Declan. 'How do we know she hasn't been spying for Tony from the very beginning?'

'Don't let's get Le Carré-ed away,' said Rupert. 'We'll just have to keep an eye on her.'

'We'll have to keep an eye on everyone,' said Declan grimly.

In an atmosphere of sniping and growing suspicion, Venturer carried on preparations for the IBA interview. There were secret communications with Georgie, Billy, Harold and Sally, arranging that they would join Venturer if and when the franchise was won – it no longer seemed a certainty – but there was no way they could be present at the IBA meeting on 29th November. Night after night without them, therefore, Hardy Bissett fired endless questions at the rest of the consortium, until they were word perfect, and answered almost without thinking. Then he accused them of being too glib.

One evening Charles Fairburn, desperately trying to hide his anxiety about being fired, turned up dressed as Lady Gosling in a grey wig, half-moon spectacles, and hundreds of shawls, and proceeded to lay everyone in the aisles by answering questions in a high soprano until Hardy sharply slapped him down.

But the questions rolled on: 'How d'you hope to promote interest in scientific matters in your schedule? What is your attitude to training schemes? How will you ensure equal opportunity for women in your company?'

'By screwing every one of them,' answered Rupert.

'Don't be bloody flip,' yelled Hardy. 'You can be funny, but never flip, and, with a female chairman, never never be funny about women.'

Rupert was bored and fed up. Why the fuck couldn't they tell the truth, that they just wanted to make good programmes and a lot of money, and dispense with all this flannel? He was relieved when Cameron and Declan set off to Ireland for a final week's shooting. He needed some space and time to think. He spent most of the week they were away in London on political work and keeping the rattled Venturer backers happy. Outside his office the last of the plane leaves were drifting down, reminding him unbearably of Taggie. He still had the thirty leaves she and the children had given him. They hadn't brought him much bloody happiness. He steeled himself not to ring her up, or drop round. He was truly terrified how much he wanted to.

When Rupert didn't take advantage of Cameron's week away
to ring her, Taggie wanted only to retreat into her turret
room in utter despair. But, alas, Monica had asked her to do
the food for the first night party for *The Merry Widow* next
Saturday, and when she wasn't cooking and freezing in both
senses of the word (now the cold weather had set in, The
Priory was absolutely arctic) Taggie was calming down or
boosting the morale of an increasingly demanding and nervous Maud. Corinium were showing highlights of the first
night and Maud was counting on Declan getting back from
Ireland in time. She couldn't face such an ordeal alone.

In addition the press were on the prowl for a story. Both
Venturer and Corinium consortiums were turning out in force
and dinner jackets for the first night. The newly sacked
Charles Fairburn was playing Monica's lover, Declan's exquisite wife was making her stage comeback, and her leading man
was the handsome Bas who was on opposing sides to his
loathed brother Tony. With Declan due back from Ireland,
with Rupert Campbell-Black's live-in lover, who was also
Tony's ex, it was clear that there were endless possibilities
for fireworks. '*Cotchester*', wrote Nigel Dempster slyly, '*are
celebrating Guy Fawkes Day ten days late this year*'.

The *Merry Widow* dress rehearsal on Friday afternoon was
disastrous. The presence of the television crew on a dry run
threw the entire cast. Tempers flared, lights dimmed too

early, lines were fluffed or forgotten. The television director decided to put two cameras in the dress circle and in the two boxes on either side of the stage, so they wouldn't have to take out any stall seats. The technicians stood around yawning, one sound man even fell asleep and snored loudly throughout the second act. James Vereker (Cotchester's dusty answer to Humphrey Burton, according to Charles Fairburn) would be presenting the programme.

'Just as well we bombed early,' said Barton Sinclair, *The Merry Widow*'s director, but he seemed far from happy.

Over in County Galway Cameron and Declan were at the end of their last day's filming. Declan, in a dark-blue fisherman's jersey and jeans, his thick black hair lifting in the gentle west wind, was speaking to camera.

'*Hallow this spot,*' he began softly. '*Here once stood the proud white Georgian house which belonged to Lady Gregory. Here for the last thirty years of his life, Yeats spent every summer and most of his winters. That's a long time to put up with not the easiest of house guests –*' Declan smiled briefly – '*even bearing in mind the number of servants large houses employed in those days. Here in this tranquil, ordered household, Yeats's genius was able to blossom on and on like a rose right into the winter of his days. "I doubt," said Yeats, "if I'd have done much with my life, but for Lady Gregory's firmness and care."*'

'Cut!' shouted Cameron. 'That was excellent. We'll now do close-ups of the copper beech on which he carved his initials, and then straight down to the lake for the last shot. We'd better hurry. The sun'll set in three-quarters of an hour.'

Twenty minutes later Declan was standing on the shore of the lake with a huge blood-red sun sinking gradually behind the coloured trees and casting a warm glow on his face.

'*While Yeats stayed at Coole Park,*' said Declan, bending down and picking up a pebble and sending it spinning across the still water, '*he wrote his poetry in a room looking towards this lake, a time lovingly remembered in his poem "The Wild Swans at Coole".*' He began to quote softly:

> *The trees are in their autumn beauty,*
> *The woodland paths are dry,*
> *Under the October twilight the water*
> *Mirrors a still sky . . .*

Oh, that husky, heartbreakingly sexy voice, thought Cameron, feeling the hairs lifting yet again on the back of her neck. She could go to the stake for Declan at times like this. They'd been so lucky with the weather too. Enough leaves still hung from the trees to pretend it was October, but one hard frost would have stripped them in a day.

The crew, going out to get plastered at an end-of-shoot party, tried to persuade Declan and Cameron to join them, but because they were both tired and faced a late night at *The Merry Widow* tomorrow, they opted for a quiet dinner at the hotel. Afterwards they sat alone in the bar. Apple logs cracked merrily in the grate, giving off a sweet cider smell. Occasionally the flames flared, lighting up Declan's face, as he sat immersed in the *Galway Post*, his whisky hardly touched.

Cameron was happy to watch him, memorizing every tiny black bristle of stubble, every deeply trenched line on the battered, craggy Western hero face. Without seeing the rushes, she knew they had made a great programme. Schemes were afoot for other programmes, but this first would always be the most exciting. Exploring and luxuriating in each other's talent, she had learnt so much from him already. Despite the fact that all the crew were at times victims of his almost feudal caprice, he certainly inspired devotion. He allowed no insubordination. Only that morning he'd roared at the sound man for giving the hung-over PA a Bloody Mary for breakfast. He was irascible, with an extremely short fuse, and got so wrapped up in the work that he frequently upset people, but he was so mortified afterwards and so ready to apologize, that they always forgave him, not least because he had more charm than anyone Cameron had ever met.

Tomorrow, she thought, putting another log on the fire,

she'd return to Rupert and reality, or was it unreality, with both of them following their separate careers in that huge house with nothing in common except the franchise, only coming together literally for sex in that huge pink and yellow silk-curtained four-poster.

She wanted to marry Rupert more than anything in the world, to tame and hold such a beautiful man, and have access to all that wealth and privilege. Rupert was her fix, but she was frightened how increasingly she was drawn to Declan. Together they could make an amazing team. He would understand her far better than Rupert, and she would look after him, and sort out his money problems far more efficiently than that parasitic, feckless, hopeless Maud. And what would happen to her and Rupert if they lost the franchise?

Declan looked up and smiled: 'I'm neglecting you. How's your drink?'

The barman had wandered off to talk to Mrs Rafferty about some cows, or it might be cars (Cameron had difficulty with the Irish pronunciation), and had left the whisky bottle and a jug of water on the table for them.

Cameron was even learning to like whisky without ice; she'd be saying dustbin and petrol soon.

As Declan filled her glass she said, 'This time in a month, we'll know if we've won. I was just wondering if there was life after franchise for me and Rupert.'

The dark brooding eyes bored into her. 'I'd like to think there was. I've grown very fond of you both.'

'Honest?' stammered Cameron.

'Honest. Under all that bitching and stridency, you're as soft as thistledown. The only problem is that you may be too good at your job for Rupert. He needs a wife to come home to, not one to come home with.'

'A little stately home maker,' said Cameron bitterly.

'Partly. He must be the dominant Tom. You'd compete with him, and I'm not sure he could handle you becoming a big star.'

Then, suddenly, out of the blue, never having mentioned

it before, he asked: 'Why were you so focking awful to Patrick?'

Cameron gasped. 'I guess I liked him too much. I was scared. He was so attractive, so élitist, so certain, yet so magnificently unprepared for the knocks that life was bound one day to give him. And Tony was pathological about any competition. All I cared about then was getting to the top, so I could have the space and freedom I needed. There was no way a penniless student could be part of my future goals. I didn't figure he had sufficient weight.'

'Patrick has more weight than anyone,' said Declan, 'and he's more together. I wish you'd read that play.'

'And I knew how violently you disapproved of me and Patrick,' said Cameron slyly.

'Indeed I did,' Declan grinned. 'But I know you better now. He'd suit you better than Rupert. And he wouldn't mess you about.'

But it's you I want, thought Cameron, resisting a terrible urge to reach out and touch Declan's hand, and then drag him up the black polished winding stairs to her hard narrow bed.

Wondering if she was crazy to jeopardize what had certainly been their most intimate conversation yet, she said: 'Maud messes *you* about enough.'

'Maud,' said Declan, topping up his glass, 'is a dramaholic. That's why she devours novels, soap operas and newspapers like a junkie. Occasionally her heroine-addiction spreads to real life, and she has to live out one of these romantic plots. It never lasts very long.'

'Has she got something going at the moment?'

Declan looked out of the window at the moon, peering through the bars of an elder tree like a prisoner. Then he drained half his whisky in one gulp.

'Yes,' he said harshly, 'Bas.'

'Doesn't it crucify you?'

Declan shrugged. 'Adultery isn't the only kind of infidelity. I'm unfaithful to her each time I get locked into work. I can't help myself any more than she can. And if you marry someone like Maud you accept the conditions that beautiful people are the blood royal of humanity and not governed by the same rules as ordinary mortals.'

'She's not that beautiful,' protested Cameron, glancing at her own extremely satisfactory reflection in the mirror above the fireplace.

'She is to me,' said Declan simply.

Cameron wanted to shake him. 'How can you be sure one of these men won't come along one day and walk off with her altogether?'

'She doesn't go after other men for sex,' said Declan arrogantly. 'She knows she'll never better what she has with me. She does it for excitement, flattery and the relief from the loneliness anyone who lives with a writer has to endure.'

Cameron got up to examine a horse brass, pulling her big black leather belt forward with her thumbs so he could appreciate the slenderness of her waist.

'Have you ever cheated on her?' she muttered into the flames.

'No.'

'Have you eve wanted to?' she whispered to his reflection in the mirror.

'Yes,' said Declan simply. 'All this week.'

Cameron stayed motionless by the fire until the heat from the flames became too strong. 'Then it wasn't just me?'

'It's going on location,' said Declan flatly. 'When you create something you both know is special, it seems natural to have some kind of consummation.'

'One devoutly to be wished,' said Cameron fiercely.

'And ludicrously prevalent in television,' said Declan. 'It happens on shoots all the time.'

'Not like this,' pleaded Cameron. Turning, she went up to him. Idly he reached out and fingered the huge low-slung silver buckle of her belt.

'It'd complicate things,' he said roughly. 'At a time we don't need complications. Maud would disintegrate; I can't afford to fall out with Rupert. I can't afford anything at the moment.'

'Don't joke. It's too important,' hissed Cameron, moving her legs between his, pressing her groin forward against the palm of his hand. She felt Declan tremble.

'We'd be so good together, let's go upstairs now,' she urged. They both jumped as the barman returned.

'Not much wind tonight,' he said blithely, 'but what there is is blowing terrible hard.'

'You look frozen,' said Declan. 'Sit down and have a drink.'

Fuck fuck fuck, or rather no fuck, Cameron screamed inwardly, as the barman collected a glass and sat down between them.

'You'll be being a bit of a writer, Declan,' he said. 'Did ye know there's another of your kind living not ten minutes from here? Anglo-Irish, name's MacBride.'

Declan froze, like a dog hearing a rabbit in the undergrowth. 'Dermot MacBride, he lives here?'

'Came in the other night. Said he'd just finished a play, but he didn't think anyone'd be interested. Thought they'd all forgotten him.'

'Him!' said Declan incredulously. 'Do you forget Ibsen or Miller? Have you got his address?'

'I've his number,' said the barman. 'He wanted some manure for his garden.'

'Name's familiar,' said Cameron.

'The angriest of all the angry young men,' said Declan, 'and easily the most unpleasant, and the most talented. He made a bomb from his first play, then the second was so venomous and obscene no one would touch it. He took umbrage and vowed never to write another word. Christ, it's like a new novel from Salinger. Give me the number,' he said to the barman, 'I'm going to ring him.'

'But it's half past eleven,' protested Cameron.

Declan was back, ecstatic, ten minutes later. 'He'd gone to Dublin. I rang him there. I'm going to see him at eleven tomorrow morning.'

'Cutting it a bit fine,' said Cameron. 'The flight's at one. Maud,' she added bitterly, 'would totally disintegrate if you missed it.'

'I'll see him alone,' said Declan. 'He's not keen on women. I'll keep a taxi waiting and meet you at the airport.'

He put his hand on her head, briefly stroking her hair: 'We'd better go to bed, we've got an early start in the morning.'

As Saturday wore on, Maud was increasingly in need of Declan. To fill in time, she went to the hairdressers, and even had a manicure, but her hand shook so much the manicurist had trouble getting the polish on. She also bought good luck cards for the rest of the cast, and some champagne in case by some miracle anyone came backstage to see her afterwards.

Arriving at the theatre, she gave a gasp of terror at the huge lights on metal stands trained on the main entrance, ready to film the arriving celebrities, and huge cables running from these and from the cameras inside the theatre to a variety of OB vans. She felt even sicker at the sight of a make-up caravan, a mobile dressing-room for James, and a double-decker catering bus for the technicians.

Even though the town hall was less than 300 yards from the Corinium Television building, union rules required all these facilities.

Going into her dressing-room, Maud gasped again, but this time with delight, because she'd never seen so many flowers – from the family, and Rupert and Cameron, and the Verekers, and the Joneses and the Baddinghams, and so many of her friends in London. There were also scores of good luck cards, and a telex from darling Patrick in Brisbane. But so much good will made her feel even more nervous. What happened if she let them all down?

She looked at her watch: five o'clock. She needed twenty minutes alone with the script to absorb the notes Barton had given her yesterday. Then her make-up would take an hour, by which time Declan would be here, and he could do up her dress and her jewellery and they could have a quiet hour together. But, as she tried to concentrate on the script, she was interrupted by the arrival of more and more flowers, and by Monica popping in to see if she were all right, and by Bas who'd brought her a fluffy stuffed black cat which miaowed good luck when you pressed it. Maud was enchanted.

'And we've got time to rehearse "Love Unspoken" just once more,' she said.

'Let's rehearse it lying down,' said Bas, who'd just come back from hunting and was feeling randy.

'Not before a performance,' said Maud, shocked. 'I couldn't possibly concentrate.'

'Well I'm not risking you going down on me with chattering teeth,' said Bas. 'So I'd better buzz off back to the Bar Sinister and pay the wages. We're doing a roaring pre-theatre trade.'

As Taggie carried great saucepans of chicken Marengo in through the stage door, she could see people gathering in the foyer hoping for returns. The advance publicity and the possibility of the audience appearing on television had made it a total sell-out.

As she fell over cables and bits of scenery, she could hear, behind every dressing-room door, the cast warming up like the record department at Harrods. She felt simply terrified for her mother. Once she'd unloaded the stuff, there wasn't much to do. The puddings were cold. The salads only needed dressing and she had just to put the chicken, the mashed potato and the garlic bread in the oven to heat up.

If the ovens were turned on low during the interval, everything would be ready, in case anyone was frightfully hungry, by the final curtain. Thank goodness Monica had provided plenty of people to help serve and wash up. As she came in with the last chocolate meringue cake, the telephone was ringing by the stage door.

'Maud O'Hara,' shouted the doorman.

'My mother,' said Taggie. 'Shall I take it and see if it's urgent?'

It was.

'Maud,' said the all-too-familiar, seductive rasp.

'No, it's Taggie.'

'Your fucking father's missed the plane.'

'Oh, my God, are you sure?'

''Course I bloody am, I was on it,' snapped Cameron. 'The next one doesn't land until nine forty-five. I've arranged for a car to pick him up and bring him straight to the theatre.'

'But M-Mummy'll die. She's been going through our leaking roof with nerves all week.'

'Tranq' her till we get there,' said Cameron. 'I've got to change, and then Rupert and I'll be over.'

With a sinking heart, Taggie knocked on Maud's door.

'Declan,' said a low excited voice.

Maud, wearing only a sliding emerald-green towel now, sat at the brilliantly lit mirror, different eyeshadows littering the shelf in front of her, as though a paintbox had been upended. She had just spent forty minutes on her eyes. Huge, gold-green, hypnotic, impossibly seductive, like two separate works of art, they seemed almost too dominant for the heart-shaped, delicately flushed face.

'You look beautiful,' said Taggie nervously. 'And what wonderful flowers.'

'Where's Daddy?' demanded Maud. 'He should have been here five minutes ago. Is he parking the car?'

Taggie took a deep breath, and was almost asphyxiated by the heady smell of fuchsias and jasmine. 'I'm sorry, he missed the plane,' she said. Then, as Maud opened her mouth to scream, 'But he'll be here for the end of the last act and the party. He didn't mean to.'

Going into hysterical sobs, Maud put her hands up to her eyes and deliberately smeared the make-up all over her face, neck and shoulders. Taggie winced. It was like seeing the Mona Lisa slashed with a razor.

'I don't believe it,' sobbed Maud. 'He can't do this to me. The one night I need him. He did it on purpose because he was jealous. He doesn't like me having the limelight.' Her voice rose to a screech. 'I can't go on, I can't.'

Hearing the din, Monica rushed in wearing only her petticoat with one eye made up, demanding what was the matter.

'You *must* go on,' she said in a shocked voice. 'Don't be so jolly wet and selfish. They're all coming to see you.'

608

'He did it on purpose,' screamed Maud, rocking backwards and forwards. 'If it had been an act of God like an engine fault or fog I could have forgiven him, or even a crash.'

'Oh don't say that,' said Taggie, turning pale.

'And you can shut up,' yelled Maud. 'You and your father are just the same, never think of anything but your bloody work.'

'That's jolly unfair,' said Monica.

There was something almost obscene about Maud's daubed screaming face and neck, and her bare shoulders and breasts as the towel slipped downwards.

Monica yanked it up round her, tucking it in, as Barton burst in. But neither Monica's rallying exhortations, nor Barton's hair-tearing, nor Charles's jokes could shift Maud. Finally they all lost their tempers and shouted at her like some operatic trio admonishing a wrong-doer, and Cameron, who'd heard a great deal too much in praise of Maud recently, was only too happy to make it a quartet when she arrived.

'For Chrissake, Maud,' she screeched, 'you can't let the cast and the audience down. Don't be so fucking unprofessional.'

'I'm not going on,' Maud screamed back. 'And why did Declan miss that plane?'

'He went to see . . .' began Cameron, then realizing she couldn't mention Dermot MacBride in front of Monica who might tell Tony, 'to see someone very important about the franchise.'

It was like a spark from the fire landing in a box of matches. Maud went berserk.

'All he thinks about is his fucking franchise,' she screamed, her face a shuddering grotesque coloured pulp of rage and misery, and, turning on her flowers, she started to tear them apart, pulling off the heads and then the petals and throwing them on the floor.

'Shouldn't we slap her face?' said Cameron longingly.

'Stop it, Maud,' said Monica angrily. 'That's wanton and destructive.'

'I don't care,' screamed Maud, ripping apart poor Taggie's yellow roses.

In despair, Taggie went out into the passage and ran slap into Rupert, who was no doubt about to add his own particularly vicious brand of invective. Behind him members of the cast and the Corinium television crew were peering curiously out of doors and round corners.

'Where is she?' said Rupert grimly.

'Oh, please. They're all shouting at her. They don't realize how frightened she is.'

Rupert paused, weighing up the options, then, like a wand fleetingly restoring her happiness, he touched Taggie's cheek with his finger: 'Go and get a large brandy, angel. I'll sort her out. Shut up the lot of you,' he yelled, as he went into the dressing-room.

'We'll have to play the understudy,' said Barton despairingly, 'even though she's fifteen stone and about to draw her pension.'

The floor was entirely carpeted with petals now.

'She won't go on,' said Cameron contemptuously.

'I'm not surprised with you lot yelling at her,' said Rupert. 'Get out, everyone.' And he slammed the door on them.

Rupert sat down on the bed and pulling Maud into his arms, gently stroking the silken shoulders, letting her cry, until gradually the sobbing and shuddering ceased.

'There,' said Rupert encouragingly. 'There's a brave girl.'

'He wanted me to go to Ireland with them and play Maud Gonne,' said Maud in a choked voice.

'I know.' Rupert went on stroking her.

'I wanted to do it so badly, but I funked it. I didn't want to fail again, particularly in front of Cameron. I'm sure she's having an affair with Declan. I kept imagining them meeting secretly after a day's shooting, and discussing how terrible I'd been.'

'You're a dick,' said Rupert gently.

'Declan fell in love with me the first time he saw me acting. I wanted him to fall in love with me all over again tonight.'

'Declan adores you. He's never looked at anyone else.'

610

'Then why isn't he here?' Maud's voice grew shrill again. For a second Rupert thought he'd lost her.

'He went to see Dermot MacBride.'

'*The* Dermot MacBride?'

Rupert nodded. 'He's written a new play. Declan felt if Venturer could tell the IBA we'd bought an option, it would really give us the edge.'

Maud quivered with rage. 'I loathe the franchise,' she said tonelessly.

'Declan's only obsessed with it because he sees it as the one way he'll get you out of your financial mess. You don't want to sell The Priory, do you?'

Maud shook her head violently: 'Could it come to that?'

'It almost has,' said Rupert.

There was a knock on the door.

'I don't want to see anyone,' said Maud hysterically.

Rupert wrapped the towel round her again. But it was only Taggie with an enormous brandy for Maud and an equally huge whisky for Rupert.

'Thanks, sweetheart.' He took them from her. 'Now beat it.'

Maud took such a huge gulp that she choked. Rupert didn't tell her he suspected Declan had deliberately missed the plane because his nerve had failed and he couldn't bear seeing Maud humiliated. Nor did he say that the press were howling like jackals outside and that, if she didn't go on, the publicity, with both her and Declan letting everyone down, would be devastating for Venturer.

'I'm disappointed,' he said idly. 'I heard you practising at The Priory so often. I wanted to hear it for real, and see the others make absolute tits of themselves by comparison. Look, you've had a shock, why not get back into your jersey and jeans and finish that brandy.'

There was a long, long pause.

'Better not,' said Maud shakily, putting down her glass, 'or I'll start forgetting my words. I'd do better with a drop of oil to get me through all those skylarking bits.'

Rupert said nothing, but, reaching for the huge blue tin

611

of cleansing cream, he took off the lid, gouged out a white blob and very slowly began to smear it over Maud's face, blurring away the ravages.

'How did you know to use that?'

'I've watched enough actresses take their make-up off in my time.'

'Most of mine's come off on you,' said Maud, suddenly contrite, as she noticed his hopelessly streaked evening shirt.

'Treat it as war paint,' said Rupert. 'Later I'll be doing battle with Tony.'

Docile as a child, Maud let him remove all the smeared make-up: 'You won't leave me?'

'I'll stay with you the entire evening, but I have to admit making up your face is beyond even my skills.'

Outside, Barton looked at his watch for the hundredth time. It was ten past seven. The press were howling for a decision. The understudy was already changed. If only he could make an announcement that the performance was starting late at least it would keep the audience happy.

'If she weren't going on,' said Cameron, 'Rupert would have come and told us.'

'He was always good at boxing difficult horses,' said Bas, who had changed into his stage clothes and was now raring to go in and comfort Maud.

As her door opened, everyone surged forward. Coming out, Rupert put a finger to his lips, then made a thumbs up sign: 'Has anyone got any eyedrops?'

'Mine are by appointment to the Queen Mother,' said Monica, diving into her dressing-room to get them. 'They jolly well make your eyes sparkle.'

Out in the foyer, Tony was now welcoming the Mayor and Mayoress and the Reverend Fergus Penney from the IBA, who was visiting Cotchester for the performance.

'I have to warn you there may be hold-ups,' purred Tony happily. 'Declan O'Hara, who usually misses the boat, has missed the plane this time and failed to turn up on the night of his poor wife's famous comeback. She's gone to pieces and is refusing to go on, so the understudy is waiting in the wings. I'm afraid one really can't rely on Venturer,' he added to Fergus Penney, 'but at least we can all pass the time pleasantly enough having a glass of champagne.'

Steering them through a door marked *Private*, he found his latest acquisition wearing a new black and gold dress to complement her newly streaked hair and getting stuck into the Bollinger.

'Can I introduce Lizzie Vereker,' said Tony warmly. 'I told you she and James are fronting our new series to discourage the spread of AIDS: "How to Stay Married", didn't I, Fergus?' he added to the Prebendary, who was now licking his thin lips at the sight of Lizzie's curves.

'Norman and I could give you a few tips on that,' said the Mayoress. 'We're celebrating our forty-fifth next week.'

'You must come on Lizzie's programme then,' said Tony, raising his glass. 'Cotchester's most distinguished married couple.'

I can't bear it, thought Lizzie, allowing her glass to be filled up. In this dress she felt as though she'd been gift-wrapped at Harrods. She longed to get out into the foyer and see if Freddie had arrived. Because of James's new uxoriousness and a general tightening up of security, she and Freddie had only managed to talk on the telephone this week.

Outside in the auditorium Sarah Stratton was spinning out the signing of autographs. Anything not to be trapped in the middle of the second row with Paul and thus not able to accost James as he came past. James, absolutely livid at being mistaken for the manager by some enraged theatregoer whose seats had been double-booked, was now trying to explain the extremely complicated plot of *The Merry Widow* to the viewers.

The Bishop, mingling with his flock and pressing the flesh, misconstrued Freddie's abstractedness as animosity and wondered darkly whether Rupert had passed on his remarks about Freddie being a rough diamond.

As the five-minute bell went, Tony glanced at his watch. Seven thirty-five. Bugger, they were hardly going to be late at all. At least they could rely on the understudy to be perfectly awful.

'I think we'd better find our seats,' he said.

Charles, wearing pantaloons so tight he felt he was standing inches above the ground, peered through a chink in the thick Prussian-blue velvet curtains, as he and Monica and the chorus, all in evening dress, waited in the wings to go on.

'It's absolutely packed,' he reported in a hollow voice. 'People are standing at the back and in the side aisles. The première of "The Messiah" in Dublin was such a sell-out that the men were told to leave off their swords. Pity that people weren't frisked at the door today. I bet your husband's carrying a long knife, Monica dear. No, it's no use looking reproving, he's given me the bullet, I can say what I like,' and, turning, he stuck a rather green tongue out through the curtains as Tony came in.

Taggie helped Maud pile up her hair with two *diamanté*

614

combs and zipped her into her slinky black ball dress. Then, leaving Rupert and Bas to do up her jewellery, she slipped into her seat. There were only two empty seats between her and Cameron, but they should have been inhabited by Rupert and Declan, so the gap seemed wider than the Atlantic. Judging by Cameron's set profile it was obvious that she was seething because Rupert wasn't beside her, particularly as a smirking Tony had just rolled up with the Mayor and was sitting directly behind them.

Cameron was seething even more that, after not seeing her for three months, Tony should catch her when she'd only had a few minutes to change and hadn't showered or washed her hair. She was wearing the smoking jacket which Taggie'd tipped dessert over last year and which didn't evoke very happy memories either. It definitely needed clean hair and very dramatic make-up to carry it off. She felt horribly butch. Dame Enid, who was conducting the orchestra in a dinner jacket, had been giving her some very hot looks, but at least she didn't look as awful as Taggie, who must have lost a stone and was wearing a dreadful brown dress that was just the wrong length and made her look completely flat-chested.

There was a gap on Taggie's left too. Where the hell was Caitlin? wondered Taggie. She'd arrived by taxi half an hour ago and, despite promising to behave, had promptly disappeared.

All round, Taggie could hear the roar and sizzle of anticipation as the lights went out and the orchestra started. The cameramen, who'd been forced into dinner jackets by Tony, took up their positions behind their cameras, the soundmen made a final check of the microphones, as Caitlin, apologizing profusely, clambered along an irritated row of people and collapsed panting by Taggie's side.

'Do up the buttons of your shirt,' said Taggie furiously. In the row behind, from the other side, having kicked the Mayoress in the varicose veins and trodden on the Prebendary's bunions, the Hon Archie, the bow of his black tie under his left ear, collapsed panting beside a bootfaced Tony.

Next moment Tony's bootfaced expression turned to one

of apoplexy: 'How dare you wear a made-up tie?' he hissed, as the Prussian-blue velvet curtains creaked back on the Pontevedrian Embassy in Paris. The Ambassador was giving a ball, and the guest of honour about to arrive was the Merry Widow.

After a rousing opening number by the chorus, it was Monica's and Charles's turn. Monica, playing the ambassador's beautiful ex-actress wife, couldn't act for toffee. But by tackling the part with the same breezy competence with which she ran charity committees or bathed labradors, she gave the rest of the cast a much-needed confidence. And Charles looked so sweet in his tight pantaloons, swearing eternal and extremely camp devotion, that it was rather like a skittish Billy Bunter getting off with the head girl.

'My marriage is sacred to me,' warbled Monica, to the smirks of the audience, who all knew she was married to Tony.

'If marriage is sacred to you,' sang back Charles, lasciviously stroking her bare arm, 'there's not very much I can do,' to even more smirks from the audience, who nearly all knew Charles was gay. And they liked it even better when his moustache fell off and he nearly split his pantaloons bending over to pick it up.

'What a lot of gold fillings Monica's got,' whispered Caitlin to Taggie, 'and, waving that baton, Dame Enid looks as though she's playing Stickie with Gertrude. When's Mother Courage coming on?'

'Any minute,' said Taggie, who was praying.

Maud, clinging to both Bas's and Rupert's hands, stood shivering like a whippet in the wings. Although her black velvet dress was Turn-of-the-Century in fashion, Basil, for some reason, was dressed as a Regency buck. The longest legs in Gloucestershire were set off by gleaming black boots and pantaloons, the cut of his slate-blue coat would have had Beau Brummel in raptures and his sleek black hair had been coaxed forward into Byronic curls. He looked the perfect Georgette Heyer hero.

'You look gorgeous,' he whispered to Maud.

'So do you,' said Maud, whose teeth were chattering loud enough to provide the castanets in the orchestra.

'You'll be all right,' said Rupert, patting her shoulder.

And suddenly she was. There was no more need of Rupert's presence; she was really keen to get on stage. She must gather the audience into the play and say every line exactly right. She was only nervous because she was a young provincial widow, a little shy but heartbreakingly beautiful, about to be launched on Parisian society.

There was a terrific roll of drums, a tantivy of horns, and she glided into the glittering ballroom, standing deliberately under the huge chandelier so all her jewels sparked and the audience could take in the beauty of her body in the tight black dress, and her pallor which only set off her red lips and her brilliant red hair.

'*Gentlemen no more,*' sang Maud, pianissimo.

'*I've never seen the Spring going to a ball before,*' sang a swooning French aristocrat, played by the bank manager of Lloyds, Cotchester. '*You throw us into ecstasies, lovely lady.*'

And for once the words were believable. Now Maud was singing again, the exquisite voice hitting F sharp as clear as a bell.

'Shit,' murmured Caitlin. 'She's fucking good.'

'Oh, thank God,' breathed Taggie. 'It's going to be all right.'

I can't bear it, thought Cameron. She'd dismissed Maud as a sluttish, middle-aged parasite with unfashionably long hair, who dressed like a tramp, and here she was bringing the entire audience to their feet at the end of her first number.

Bas's entrance stepped up the excitement even more. He had a glorious, slightly husky voice and added just the right touch of rakish Latin glamour.

'Shit,' said Caitlin again. 'Lucky Mummy. He's *dead* attractive.'

The sexual tension between him and Maud was incredible, particularly when offset by Monica and Charles, who, stepping up the camping, got more and more like Dignity and Impudence. Having dispatched all the competition, Bas was

617

left alone on the stage with Maud at the end of the first act.

'*Music so sweet*,' he crooned softly, dancing round and round her, tempting her into his arms, '*speaks to the heart and the feet.*' And finally, triumphantly, he swept her into a waltz.

Elegant, incredibly romantic, they revolved under the chandelier until the curtain came down to a deafening roar of applause and a fusillade of bravoes.

After the first act, even though there was the Vilja song and several big numbers to come, Maud felt nothing but relief. It didn't matter that Declan hadn't turned up. She even sent Rupert back to his seat. She felt totally insulated. She'd been so petrified, and concentrated so hard on getting that first act perfect, that now she felt on automatic pilot. All trace of tears had gone. And although Charles almost stole the show when he bent down to retrieve his moustache yet again and his trousers split to reveal pink boxer shorts covered in pale-blue teddy bears, it was Maud's night. When the final curtain came down she was cheered to the rooftops, taking curtain call after curtain call, as the whole audience, even Tony, were on their feet, yelling and clapping like promenaders.

Rupert turned to Taggie. 'We did it,' he said triumphantly.

'No,' she said. 'You did it.'

'Don't cry,' said Basil, as he and Maud took their final bows.

'You were better than anyone could have dreamed,' said Barton Sinclair, pale beside the made-up actors, as he kissed Maud's hand and, to roars of applause handed her a huge bouquet of flowers that appeared through the curtains.

'I saw *The Merry Widow* in Paris,' said Valerie Jones petulantly to Professor Graystock. 'It was quite a different opera. But then it was performed by professionals.'

'I wouldn't call *Die Lustige Witwe* opera,' said the Professor, showing off that he knew the German title, 'but I did think Maud O'Hara was marvellously in voice.'

'I'd like to meet Maud O'Hara,' said the Prebendary. 'She seems an interesting person.'

'You shall in a minute,' said Tony cosily.

Maud rushed back to her dressing-room to change out of her gold last-act dress into a blue silk suit she'd bought for the occasion. After that it was bedlam, people pouring in and out, hugging, kissing and congratulating her. The champagne went in a flash. The press bombarded her with questions, but she was not to be drawn on the subject of Declan. 'My husband's in Ireland on business,' she said firmly. 'He'll be here later.'

At the party everyone kept coming up and saying how marvellous she'd been, but she still felt curiously detached, as though nothing could dent her now.

'I wonder if you'd like to have lunch one day,' said the Prebendary, his voice thickening. 'Now I'm in the autumn of my life, I enjoy the company of lovely women.' He was furious when the Bishop came up and joined them, with a plate piled high with Taggie's food.

'Evening, Fergus, you look very fit. Good to see Venturer pulling their weight this evening. Maud, my dear, you were absolutely splendid, such good tunes too, nice to see my flock enjoying it so much. Can I get you some refreshment?'

'I'd love another drink,' said Maud.

'Well, go and get her one,' said the Prebendary irritably.

'Here's a waiter coming,' said the Bishop, not budging. 'I must tell you about my recent trip to the Holy Land, Fergus.'

The Prebendary didn't want to hear about the Holy Land one bit, particularly when Maud excused herself. She was just going over to thank Rupert once again when she felt a warm hand on her back.

It was Tony. '*Even the ranks of Tuscany could scarce forbear to cheer*,' he said softly. 'Couldn't you hear me yelling like a schoolboy?'

'Was it really all right?'

'Stupendous. There wasn't a man in the audience who wasn't madly in love with you. I'm sorry your husband didn't make the grade. But then making the grade has never been one of his specialities, has it?'

'Unfortunately he takes the franchise as seriously as you,' said Maud bitterly.

'Ah,' said Tony with an evil smile. 'But the difference is, he's not going to win.'

'Maud, my dear,' said Monica, bringing forward a distinguished-looking man in a leather jacket with greying hair. 'I didn't tell you before, but this is Pascoe Rawlings.'

Maud's jaw dropped. Pascoe Rawlings was simply the most powerful theatrical agent in London.

'Were you in the audience?' said Maud.

'And in total raptures,' said Pascoe, drawing her out of the shadowy corner and under the naked light bulb hanging in the wings and examining her face carefully. 'Yes, close-up you're even better. Look, Jonathan Miller's casting *A Doll's House*. Can you have lunch with me very early next week?'

The party was, in fact, a great success. James spent the evening holding Lizzie in front of him like a riot shield to ward off the advances of Sarah Stratton, and only let her go because he wanted to be introduced to Pascoe Rawlings. The next moment Freddie had whipped Lizzie behind one of the huge cardboard pillars which had stood in the Pontevedrian ballroom.

'This is a pillar of unrespectability,' said Lizzie.

'I love you,' said Freddie desperately.

'And I love you. James is going to London tomorrow night.'

'What time will the children be asleep?'

'By nine,' said Lizzie, 'even if I have to drug them.'

'I'll be there at nine-firty,' said Freddie.

In her mother's dressing-room, on a floor of wilting petals, Caitlin lay in Archie's arms and had no need of words.

Taggie spent the evening removing plates, keeping out of Rupert's way and sticking up for her father. It was not just Tony who thought he'd behaved appallingly.

'So unsupportive,' snapped Cameron.

'He ought to have his knuckles rapped,' said Monica, 'but in a way that storm of grief seemed to enhance her performance.'

'I always said you can never trust the Irish,' said Valerie Jones.

'D'you think Declan's coming back tonight?' whispered Bas in Maud's ear at midnight, 'because if he isn't . . .'

Everyone stopped talking as Tony tapped his glass with a spoon.

'On behalf of Corinium Television,' he said suavely, 'I'd like to thank our Mayor and Mayoress and, of course, you, Prebendary, for being here this evening. I want to congratulate Barton and all the cast of *The Merry Widow* for a truly splendid performance, but most of all I think we should praise Maud O'Hara, who, under the most difficult circumstances –' he smiled at Maud – 'was without doubt the star of the evening.'

Exactly on cue, Declan walked in. He was deathly pale and still wearing yesterday's jeans and dark-blue jersey. But such was his presence that, as usual, he made everyone else seem like pygmies.

Charles Fairburn, who was pissed, gave a very theatrical hiss. 'Hullo, Declan dear, I'm surprised you haven't popped up through a trap door in a great puff of sulphur and brimstone.'

'Good morning, Declan,' drawled Tony, ostentatiously looking at his watch, 'you're late. Four and a half hours late to be exact. What kept you? I do hope you're not as late as this when you go to the IBA on Friday week, or there's even less chance of Venturer winning the franchise.'

Declan ignored him and walked up to Maud.

'I'm desperately sorry, darling,' he said. 'I hear you were sensational. I knew you would be.'

Indignation overcame Monica's normal good manners: 'You knew nothing of the sort, you beastly man, you ought to be hung, drawn and quartered. She was absolutely super, but no thanks to you. You wait till you see the video.'

'There was a good reason,' said Declan, not taking his eyes off Maud, 'but as I don't like some of the company you're keeping this evening, I'll tell you later. Let's go.'

'But she's the guest of honour,' said Monica furiously.

Just for a second everyone expected Maud to slap Declan's face. Instead she reached up and hugged him.

'Poor darling,' she said, 'you *must* be tired. Thank you all –' marvellously theatrically, the big star now, she turned slowly round, smiling at everyone in the room – 'for a lovely, lovely party.'

Then, taking Declan's arm, she dutifully followed him off the stage.

Caitlin, who'd just emerged from Maud's dressing-room with Archie, shook her head. 'I'll never understand that couple,' she said.

On the way out Maud and Declan passed Rupert and Cameron. 'Rupert saved me,' said Maud, ignoring Cameron, whom she had not forgiven for her abuse earlier.

'I know,' said Declan, 'Taggie told me on the way in.'

Briefly he took Rupert aside. 'Look, I'm sorry I focked everything up, but Dermot MacBride insisted I sat down and read the whole play. I didn't realize his mother was from Gloucestershire and the play's all about his childhood just outside Stroud. He's giving it to us, with an option on the next play. I'm going to fix a price with his agent tomorrow. It's a focking good play.'

'It better be,' said Rupert icily. 'You nearly paid for it with a far higher price than money.'

Six days later the Gatherum, which was the neigbouring
hunt to the West Cotchester, held their hunt ball in Henry
Hampshire's beautiful mouldering Elizabethan house. This
was the last time the two consortiums would meet before
their encounters with the IBA next week, and once again
the whole place seemed to divide like the Dreyfus case. At
one table sat Freddie and Valerie, Henry Hampshire, very
much on his best behaviour as host and in the presence
of his wife Hermione, Declan and Maud and Rupert and
Cameron. Bas was turning up later with some ex-mistress,
whose husband was conveniently in America.

Two tables away sat the Baddinghams, Ginger Johnson
and his wife, Georgie Baines, with his long eyelashes cast
down, and his wife, Paul and Sarah Stratton, and James and
Lizzie Vereker. Although some of the women in both parties
exchanged occasional banter and smiles, the men of one side
studiously ignored those of the other side.

Maud appeared to be the only member of the Venturer
party in tearing spirits. The two subsequent performances of
The Merry Widow on Tuesday and Wednesday had been just
as successful. She had had hundreds of letters and telephone
calls of congratulation, and yesterday she had lunched with
Pascoe Rawlings, who was arranging for her to audition as
soon as possible for *A Doll's House*. Tonight she looked
stunning with her red-gold hair piled up, and an old-gold

623

taffeta dress which looked suspiciously new, turning her green eyes a tigerish yellow. No doubt when Bas arrived, after the success of *The Merry Widow*, the band could be prevailed upon to play a quick waltz, and Bas would sweep her on to the floor.

Cameron, who'd been editing the Yeats rushes all week, and working hard with Declan on additional programme plans to present to the IBA next Friday, looked thin and drawn. She was worried Declan seemed suddenly distant. There was none of the intimacy they'd achieved in Ireland. Tonight, obviously hating being so near Tony, he was pale and edgy. As the only member of the party in a dinner jacket rather than a red coat, his black lowering presence seemed to accentuate Venturer's gloom and tension.

Cameron was even more worried about Rupert, who had gone increasingly into his shell since she'd come back from Ireland. He also looked desperately tired. The new Socialist majority was so tiny that the Tories were determined to contest it to the full on every vote, which meant endless late night sittings. The interminable IBA rehearsals, even though both Henry and Wesley were word perfect now, were also taking their toll. Even Freddie didn't seem his usual bouncy self. Only Valerie was appallingly unchanged.

'What are you doing, Fred-Fred?' she screeched, as Freddie started crawling around under the priceless Jacobean table.

'Lookin' for bugs.'

'You're more laikely to find woodworm,' said Valerie disapprovingly. 'I can't think why Henry and Hermione don't junk all this nasty dark stuff and invest in some decent Repro. And have you seen the state of the place?' Valerie had already had a prowl round some of the bedrooms, the long gallery and the grand staircase with its heraldic leopards. 'All the plaster's peeling. There's so much damp, and you should have seen the moths flutter out when I touched the drapes in Hermione's bedroom.'

'Didn't you realize this is a moth sanctuary?' said Rupert gravely. 'You know Henry is Venturer's conservation expert.'

Valerie looked at Rupert sharply. She was never sure if he wasn't mobbing her up.

'Actually I wanted to pick your brains,' she said, lowering her voice, 'about Fred-Fred's birthday. There was an article in *The Times* yesterday saying the latest thing in the hunting field is to have a brass flask of sherry attached to your saddle.'

'Sounds hell,' said Rupert with a yawn. 'The only thing I want attached to my saddle is my bum.'

At that moment Tony paused in front of the Venturer table – surveying them with amusement.

'I see the devil has cast his net,' he said loudly.

'If the holes in his net were as big as your mouth, we'd all escape,' drawled Rupert.

Everyone at the surrounding tables howled with laughter and Tony retreated discomforted.

'And Ladbroke's has us at 2–1 on today,' Rupert yelled after him.

Valerie turned to Cameron. 'You're looking a bit washed out. I don't think black's really your colour – too deadening. Why don't you pop into the boutique and buy something naice for all the Christmas functions coming up?'

'What's the difference between a shop and a boutique?' asked Henry, who'd got bored of welcoming people.

'They sell exactly the same stuff, but a boutique is about five times as expensive,' said Rupert.

Valerie looked very boutique-faced as Rupert turned his back on both of them.

People were sitting down at their tables now and the waitresses were beginning to carry plates of smoked trout down the aisles. Looking round, Rupert noticed the place was absolutely crawling with beautiful, only-too-available women. It was just the sort of evening he once would have revelled in, getting drunk and off with half of them, behaving atrociously, not a cordoned-off four-poster untested. What the hell was the matter with him? He didn't even want to sleep with Cameron any more.

'Where's Taggie?' asked Valerie, picking up her fork. 'No, leave your bread roll, Fred-Fred.'

'Dog-sitting,' said Maud, holding up her glass for more Muscadet. 'I don't know what's got into her at the moment, she's so lethargic. I tried to persuade her to come this evening, but she wouldn't. She hadn't got a partner. When I was her age I had hordes of boys chasing after me.'

'When all this franchise business is sorted out, we must all put our heads together and find her a decent guy,' said Cameron.

'Don't be fucking silly,' snapped Rupert. 'You can't find people for other people. Taggie's perfectly capable of finding someone herself.' He put his fork down, his trout hardly touched, and, refusing wine, asked the waiter to bring him a bottle of whisky.

Across at the Corinium table, Sarah Stratton plonked herself down beside James.

'You shouldn't be here,' he hissed, giving her the sort of look delphinium growers reserve for slugs. 'The High Sheriff's wife is supposed to be sitting there.'

'I shifted the place cards,' hissed back Sarah. 'You don't want to sit next to that old bag.'

'But you've totally ruined Monica's placement,' said James in outrage. 'And that means Tony's got to sit next to the High Sheriff's wife, which he won't like one bit.'

'Serve him right for trying to split us up. I love you.'

'Keep your voice down.' James looked furtively round.

'I'll talk even louder if you don't let me stay. Surely you must have a programme in your marriage series on coping with temptation? Well, you can bloody well research it tonight.'

Home at The Priory, Taggie, having dispatched her parents to the ball, was wondering forlornly what to do for the rest of the evening. The only decent film on television was Italian, and she wouldn't be able to read the subtitles fast enough to get the gist of it. It was a vicious night. The wind was howling round the windows, trying to get in out of the cold. The snow was falling steadily, already lining the window-ledge and bowing down the evergreens. At least there was a nice fire in the little sitting-room. Gertrude, Aengus and Claudius were all stretched out in front of the blaze. The logs came from their wood, or rather it was Rupert's wood now; everything seemed to come back to him.

How will I ever get through my life without him, she thought hopelessly, when I can't even face a much-longed-for free evening?

She jumped at a sudden pounding on the door. The bell was still blocked up with loo paper to discourage creditors. Outside was Hazel, one of the make-up girls from the BBC, who'd once worked on Declan's programme and become a great family friend. Flakes of snow like brilliants in her hair gave her an added glamour. She'd been doing a job in Bristol and was on her way home.

'Everyone's out except me,' apologized Taggie, 'but come in and have a drink.'

'What a lovely house, really Gothic,' said Hazel in awe as they went into the sitting-room.

'Not too large,' she squawked, as Taggie poured her a vodka and tonic. 'I've got to drive back to London.'

'You must stay the night,' urged Taggie. 'You can't drive in this weather and Daddy'll be d-devastated to have missed you.'

'I can't believe Caitlin's taking O-levels. She was such a wee little thing,' said Hazel twenty minutes later. 'And Patrick got a first, and he's as tall as your Dad. I do hope your Dad gets the franchise. We're all rooting for him at the Beeb. Tony Baddingham's such a shit.'

The telephone rang. It was Bas. 'Taggie, babe, you're coming to the ball.'

'I can't,' squeaked Taggie. 'I've got someone here.'

'Well get rid of them. Annabel, my date, has been out all day with the Belvoir, and the snow's too bad for her to drive down, and anyway, she's bushed. So I've got no one to go with and I can't think of anyone more delicious than you.'

'I haven't got anything to wear.'

'Fret not, I'll be over in an hour with some frocks.'

'I've been asked to the Hunt Ball,' said Taggie in awe.

'Wonderful,' said Hazel excitedly. 'I'll dog-sit. Go and wash your hair and have a bath. I'll make you up. You'll come up beautifully.'

Bas, naughty as his word, arrived an hour later with a back seat loaded up with ball dresses.

'Where did you get them?' asked Taggie incredulously.

'Corinium's wardrobe department,' said Bas. 'Their security is atrocious.'

'What a gorgeous man,' murmured Hazel enviously, 'and I've had some heart-throbs through my fingers in my time.'

'This dress is made by B-A-L-Main,' spelt out Taggie slowly. 'What happens if I put my foot through it?'

'Try the crimson one,' said Bas. 'It's much the best colour for you and at least it won't show up the red wine that's bound to get poured over you.'

'It's awfully low-cut,' said Taggie dubiously.

'All the better,' said Hazel, checking the Carmen rollers. 'Hurry up and decide. I want to do your hair.'

Back at the ball, dinner was over and dancing had begun. It was a measure of Monica's niceness that no one else but she knew that Valerie had auditioned and been turned down for both Maud and Monica's parts in *The Merry Widow*. Still smarting from the rejection (she would have been *so* much better than Maud), Valerie was now determined to demonstrate her dancing skills and had dragged a reluctant Freddie on to the floor. She was soon bawling him out.

'Can't you concentrate for one minute, Fred-Fred? I said fish-tail not telemarque.'

Through a swirling herbaceous border of red coats and brilliantly coloured dresses, Freddie could see Lizzie in fuchsia pink being humped round the floor by James, who'd at last managed to shake off Sarah.

As they passed Tony sitting at the Corinium table, James deliberately pressed his cheek and his body against Lizzie's.

I can't stand it, thought Lizzie wretchedly. She'd imagined it would be better seeing Freddie tonight, than not seeing him at all, but it made everything much, much worse.

Watching across the room, Freddie wanted to punch James

on his perfectly straight nose, and then whisk Lizzie upstairs on to a moth-infested four-poster and tear off her fuchsia dress and kiss her all over.

'Fred-Fred,' screeched Valerie in his ear, 'are you tipsy? This is a foxtrot.'

Declan danced with Maud, who was well away. Over his shoulder she glanced at her gold watch. Bas was very late. At the Venturer table it was plain to Cameron, watching Rupert pour another large whisky, that he was deliberately setting out to get drunk. People kept pausing to say hullo, but, seeing the set expression on his face and the sinister glitter in his eyes, they didn't stay long. Cameron, acutely conscious of Tony two tables away talking in lowered tones to Ginger Johnson and watching her every move, tried to talk to Rupert. A slow anger rose in her when he only answered in monosyllables.

Why make it so obvious that you've absolutely no interest in me, she wanted to scream. Was he deliberately goading her to go back to Tony?

'The next dance is definitely mine,' said Henry to Cameron.

'Oh, good. Here's Bas at last,' said Maud, pinning up a tendril of hair at the back.

'Good Lord,' said Henry in wonder, his glass of wine poised halfway to his lips. 'What a stunning girl!'

'Annabel Kemble-Taylor's hardly a girl,' said Rupert, who had his back to the floor. 'Half Leicestershire's been up her.'

'She is pretty. Most dramatical,' said Freddie, putting on his spectacles. 'Blimey, it's Taggie.'

Rupert swung round and caught his breath. There, undulating across the floor, rouged, lipsticked, her eyes vast and black-lined with kohl, black hair a mass of snakey ringlets, her shoulders, far creamier and lusher than Maud's, rising out of a ruched crimson dress with a bustle, was indeed Taggie. Everyone was turning round to gawp at her. Basil, who'd been slowly stalking her for fourteen months, looked beside himself with pride.

'You look like a Christmas cracker,' he whispered in her ear, as he fingered the ruched dress, 'and, my God, I can't wait to pull you.'

Taggie giggled. She was slightly overwhelmed by how different Hazel had made her look and the sensation she seemed to be creating. Her only aim was to please Rupert. She wanted to show him that she had at last grown up. But as he stared at her, his face totally unsmiling, her courage failed and she gave the dress a desperate tug upwards. Then, just as she and Bas reached the Venturer table, the band started again.

'Lady in Red,' said Basil in delight. 'How appropriate.' And, taking Taggie's bag from her and dropping it in front of Rupert in a curiously insolent gesture, he swept her onto the floor.

'I can't dance,' pleaded Taggie, half-laughing. 'I truly, truly can't.'

'You can with me,' said Bas, putting his hand round her waist. 'This is a nice slow one to start with. This song could have been written for you, you are so so beautiful. *'Never seen you looking so lovely as you do tonight,'* he sang, *never seen you shine so bright.'*

'I find all this lipstick a bit strange,' said Taggie.

'Don't worry, I'll kiss it all off later.'

Taggie blushed. He was at least five inches taller than her, and so supple and strong, and with such a Latin sense of rhythm, that Taggie was soon following him perfectly in time.

'You dance beautifully,' he said, laying his cheek against her hair.

'I can do it,' said Taggie excitedly. 'I can really dance.'

'The lady in red is dancing with me, sang Bas gazing deep into her eyes, *'There's nobody here, just you and me.'* What a good thing Annabel had such an exhausting day with the Belvoir.'

'Lady in red, Lady in red,' sang Taggie dreamily and tunelessly, not knowing any of the other words. 'It is a most gorgeous song.'

'And you're the most gorgeous girl,' said Basil, french-kissing her shoulder.

'Very fast man across country, Bas,' said Henry approvingly.

'Very fast man on the dance floor,' said Freddie. 'Don't they go well togevver?'

Maud was looking extremely wintry. Cameron was watching Rupert. His face was like marble, but the tendons on the back of his hand, which was clenched round his glass, were like underground cables. He never took his eyes off Taggie as she and Bas moved round the floor. Then, suddenly, as the music stopped and Bas bent his otter-sleek head and kissed Taggie on her crimson mouth, his hand tightened on the glass so convulsively that it shattered. Amazingly he didn't cut himself, but there was glass everywhere.

'My Auntie was so superstitious,' said Valerie, as a waitress rushed in with a dustpan and brush, 'that if she broke something precious she'd rush down to the bottom of the garden and smash two jam jars to break the run of bad luck.'

'As Rupert's heart's just been broken as well,' said Cameron viciously, 'we only need smash one more thing.'

'Shut up,' snarled Rupert, pouring a slug of whisky into a nearby wine glass.

Declan shot him a warning look. Nor were matters improved by Bas arriving at the table with Taggie.

'Haven't I done well?' he said smugly. 'Annabel dropped out, so the understudy took her place. I knew you'd be pleased, Maud darling,' he added blithely as he bent down to peck Maud's gritted cheek. 'You were just complaining yesterday Taggie never had any fun.'

'You look absolutely perfick,' said Freddie.

'Where did that gown come from?' asked Valerie accusingly.

'Corinium wardrobe department,' said Basil, lobbing Freddie's roll at Georgie Baines at the next table. 'Suits her, doesn't it?'

'She looks great,' said Declan proudly. 'But make sure it isn't bugged.'

'All the bug would pick up is the hammering of her heart because she's with me,' said Bas, squeezing Taggie's hand.

Taggie glanced shyly across at Rupert, who was now looking at her with complete indifference. Suddenly she felt utterly deflated. Even with every stop pulled out, there was no way she could win him. But there was little time to fret. Next minute a thoroughly over-excited Henry had whisked her off to dance. They were just circling decorously when the band broke into 'Rock around the Clock'.

'Ha ha ha,' said Henry, suddenly galvanized like an over-adrenalized tarantula. 'I know this tune. There's life in the old dog yet.' And he flung Taggie across the floor with great energy.

Every time he twirled her round he nearly pulled her out of her cracker dress. He'll discover a paper hat and a motto in a minute, she thought as she frantically tugged it up again. As soon as the band stopped, a young blood swooped and asked her to dance, and then another, and another. Each one took her telephone number and said they'd ring her.

Great excitement, because it was regarded as highly symbolic, was caused at the Corinium table when Tony won a portable television on the Tombola.

'He won't be needing that much longer,' growled Declan, who was getting increasingly worried about Rupert.

Freddie had also vanished, ostensibly to fetch Valerie some lemon squash, but he'd been away for three-quarters of an hour, and James Vereker could be seen hunting everywhere for Lizzie as he tried to escape from Sarah. Bas claimed another dance with Taggie and persuaded the band to play 'Lady in Red' again. As he and Taggie danced past them, all the band stood up in salute to her beauty.

Rupert was three-quarters of the way down his bottle of whisky when he was tapped sharply on the shoulder by one of his more forceful lady constituents.

'I know this isn't the time, but could we have a word about the Swindon–Gloucester motorway?'

She had a face the colour and texture of corned beef and it was now very close to Rupert's.

'Bugger the motorway,' he said.

The corned beef seemed to engorge and darken like the interior of black pudding.

Getting to his feet, leaving her mouthing apoplectically, Rupert reached the dance floor just as Taggie and Bas were coming off. Grabbing Taggie's hand, he dragged her back onto the floor. Alone in the centre, they gazed at each other. Slowly Rupert examined the huge, blackened, almost feverish eyes, the trembling ruby mouth, the quivering white breasts hardly covered by the crimson ruching. Adoring the way she looked normally in old clothes, with hardly any make-up, he detested this new grown-up, glamorous Taggie.

'What's the matter?' she stammered, stepping back as though scorched by the disapproval in his eyes. 'I hoped you'd l-l-like it.'

'You look like a complete tart,' he said viciously, 'and as you're with Bas, you're obviously going to behave like one.'

Taggie gave a gasp of horror as, turning on his heel, Rupert walked straight back to the table.

'What was that about?' taunted Cameron. 'I thought you liked little girls with bust measurements bigger than their IQs.'

'I like them better than fucking American smart asses,' snarled Rupert.

Spitting with fury, passing heraldic shields, suits of armour and antlers of several kinds of deer, Cameron fled to the Ladies. Rupert was a bastard, an utter asshole. But as she looked at her reflection in the ancient, dusty mirror, which should have flattered her, she couldn't blame him for neglecting her. She looked awful, and the black dress she'd thought so sophisticated and understated had understated her so much she was practically invisible. Why the hell hadn't she worn her black suede dress? Savagely she daubed her cheekbones with blusher and emptied the remains of a bottle of Jolie Madame – what a singularly inappropriate name – over her wrists and neck.

Coming out into the long gallery, she saw Tony emerging from behind a suit of armour and went sharply into reverse. He was too quick for her. Grabbing her wrists, he drew her into an alcove behind a huge urn filled with blue hyacinths. She tried to wriggle away, but he was too strong for her. Oh, why did that sweet, heady smell make her almost faint with longing?

'I've missed you,' he said, as he regained his breath. 'I've never stopped missing you. I need you. Corinium needs you. Come back to us.'

'Don't be fucking infantile,' hissed Cameron. 'After the dirty trick you've pulled on us?'

'I'm going to bury Venturer,' he said evilly, 'and you'll go under too. You've just no idea what I've got up my sleeve.'

Cameron tried not to appear fazed: 'You'll never get away with it. The IBA knows you're as bent as hell.'

'By the time I've finished with Venturer I'll look like a shining white angel.'

Drawing her towards him, he slowly fingered her rib cage, then pressed the ball of his hand up against her breast, at the same time running the other hand equally slowly over her bottom. It was an act of assessment – not of lust.

'Dear, dear,' he sighed, 'you used to have such a beautiful body. Now you could do a commercial for famine relief.'

'Don't be disgusting.'

'I'm just sad you've lost your looks.' The hand still rotated on her bottom. She shuddered, unable to stop the squirming, helpless, revolted longing. Tony always did this to her.

'I've been working, for Chrissake.'

'You always thrived on work. You're having Rupert trouble. I watched you tonight and last Friday.'

Suddenly Cameron realized what the scent of the blue hyacinths reminded her of – the much fainter smell of bluebells in Rupert's wood the first weekend she spent at Penscombe.

'He's got the hots for Taggie O'Hara, hasn't he?' gloated Tony. 'Everyone's talking about it.'

In the distance the band was belting out 'Mac the Knife'. It was as though Tony was turning it in her heart.

'Bullshit,' she said with a sob, and fled away from him, hearing his laughter following her all down the long gallery.

Cameron was so distraught, she didn't see Declan standing in the shadows of a high tallboy. Worried about her scrap with Rupert, he'd come looking for her, wanting to comfort and steady her. He was about to call out. The next moment he froze as he saw a man emerging from behind the urn. The glint of his huge signet ring as he smoothed his hair, and the almost orgasmic expression on his face as he passed, made him instantly recognizable.

Declan went straight back to the Venturer table, but found only Maud and Freddie.

'You was so dramatical in *The Merry Widow*,' Freddie was saying.

'Was I really?' said Maud, looking very happy.

'What's hup?' said Freddie in alarm as he saw Declan's face. Sitting down, Declan came straight to the point.

'I've just seen Cameron talking to Tony.'

'Just saying 'ullo.'

'No, it was a long and very intimate conversation. She was in tears when she left him. He looked delighted with himself.'

'Shit,' said Freddie. 'It's Rupert's fault. He's been diabolical to Cameron all evening.'

'What's much, much worse is that she and I have been working on the Dermot MacBride deal and the Royal Shakespeare negotiations all week. If she leaks those to him we're stymied.'

'I still don't fink she's like that,' said Freddie. 'They was probably just reminiscing.'

'We're off,' said a voice.

It was Bas with his arm round a somewhat tearstained Taggie.

'You've only just arrived,' said Maud hysterically.

'I know, but we've got somewhere else to go on to,' said Bas.

Suddenly there was a shriek of excitement as Henry rode a horse into the ballroom and round the floor, followed by hounds. He had snow on his shoulders and his black hat, and all the hounds had snow on their faces and their frantically wagging sterns. Everyone came rushing in to cheer them. There were terrific view holloas, as a hound trotted calmly up to the Corinium table and lifted its leg on the back of Tony's chair.

'Wish that dog was a member of the IBA,' said Freddie.

By the time the hounds had gone, Cameron and Rupert were back at the table. Rupert, Declan noticed, had snow on his hair too and was shivering uncontrollably. Maud, too, seemed suddenly terribly upset, particularly when Valerie pointed out how keen Bas seemed on Taggie.

'Much better for him to find someone nearer his age,' she said smugly. 'Where are they, anyway?'

'Gone,' said Declan.

'Where?' asked Rupert, looking up sharply.

'I don't know.'

'Get your coat,' said Rupert to Cameron.

He was waiting in the hall, glaring at a buffalo whose eyes were as glassy as his own, making no effort to conceal his impatience.

'It's not easy extracting one's coat from underneath a heaving husband and someone else's wife,' snapped Cameron.

Outside, the snow was already four inches deep. As the long dresses of departing guests trailed over the white lawn, flurrying flakes seemed to blur the great house and a party of whooping young bloods, all no doubt with Taggie's telephone number in their breast pockets, engaged in a snowball fight. Cameron felt she had gone back four hundred years.

'I'll drive. You're drunk,' she said to Rupert as they reached the car.

Careful, she told herself, as the Aston-Martin slid all over the road like Thumper on the ice, he's reached that pitch of drunkenness that will erupt into violence at any minute. Having been beaten up by Tony, she was terrified of it happening again. But as they drew up outside the front of Penscombe Court, Rupert waited until she got out of the car, then slid across into the driving seat and set off in a tremendous flurry of snow.

Sobbing uncontrollably, Cameron let herself into the house and, shouting at the dogs to get out of her way, went straight to Rupert's office and started searching. In the bottom drawer of his desk, under the lining paper, she found what she was looking for – that impossibly ill-spelt and ill-punctuated letter Taggie had written Rupert, thanking him for Claudius, and two photographs of her running in the wood. She stiffened when she saw the second. Rupert's kids were there as well as Taggie. They were holding her hands and laughing. The leaves were flame-red on the beech trees, so it must have been autumn, and Tab was wearing her puff-ball skirt, so it must have been this year. Shit – and they all looked so happy. It must have been while she was away in Ireland. That was why Rupert had been so reluctant to have the kids over since, and insisted on taking them out on his own, in case they babbled on about Taggie. That was almost the worst thing, that she had utterly failed with the children, where Taggie had succeeded. Also under the lining paper, which she couldn't interpret, was a pile of faded leaves.

Rupert knew he was far too drunk to drive, but he didn't care. Anyway, he had always jumped horses when he was pissed with that much more dash and brilliance. Unable to stop himself, he drove straight into Cotchester and parked outside the Bar Sinister. The roofs of the honey-coloured houses were completely hidden with snow now. Flakes were landing like huge polar bears on his bonnet, almost obscuring his vision, but not so much that he couldn't see the lights in the flat above. Bas was plainly at home.

Christ – why had he been such a shit to Taggie? She'd looked so fucking gorgeous and he'd detested it because he wanted to keep her as his little teenager. At the back of his mind he'd expected her to be always there. Rationally he knew he must never make a play for her, that one day she'd find some nice dull kind boy of her own age to take care of her. But he hadn't thought the whole thing through, or realized he'd be driven into a maddened frenzy of jealousy because she'd been stolen from under his nose by the second worst rake in the county who was probably expertly initiating her into the pleasures of the flesh at this moment.

He slumped on the steering wheel, groaning. He wanted to break down the door, to kill Bas, to drag Taggie back to The Priory like a father out of a Victorian melodrama. In his misery he didn't even feel the cold. Gradually the snow obscured the entire windscreen and he had to turn on the engine to start up the wipers, when suddenly the balcony doors opened and Bas and Taggie came out. She was wearing Bas's red coat. Winding down the window, Rupert could hear her cries of joy at the beauty of the snow. Next moment Bas had gathered up the snow along the balcony rail to make a snowball and handed it to her, but she only managed to chuck it a few yards down the ghostly whitening street.

'Tell you never played cricket at school,' said Bas fondly.

Then, drawing her close by the lapels of his coat, he slowly kissed her. They were so preoccupied, they didn't even notice Rupert. Totally sobered up, he drove back to Penscombe.

The rest of the weekend was like the Phoney War. Rupert and Cameron were perfectly polite to each other. She worked on the franchise, he was off to Rome on Sunday for a meeting with the International Olympics Committee, but would be home on Wednesday night.

The only time she saw him with his guard down was when she caught a glimpse of him watching a Lassie film in the study. He was clutching Beaver and the tears were running down his cheeks.

48

After lunch next day, having scraped the frozen snow off the bird table and fed the birds for the fourth time, Declan had great difficulty getting out of his drive to visit Freddie. The gritters had been at work on the main roads, but the side lanes were murder. For once the beauty of the black and white landscape held no charms for him. He passed several cars, totally submerged, which must have been abandoned last night, and a farmer frantically trying to dig out some sheep before dusk. The sky was a dull mustard yellow, promising more snow. What would happen if none of the Venturer consortium could get up to London for the IBA meeting? Freddie's drive had already been lavishly gritted.

'I sent the Council a grittings telegram,' he said with a huge laugh. 'In fact I bunged them a few tenners so they made a detour past the 'ouse.'

He poured Declan a large brandy and took him into his study. The house was blissfully warm after The Priory. Outside, Valerie's garden had never looked more beautiful, totally hidden by snow, the gaudy colours wiped out, the vast rockery transformed into a mini-Andes, the garden gnomes and the plastic cherubs fluffed out into creatures of fable. Even the serried ranks of hybrid teas had become a white army hoisting up fistfuls of snow. If Valerie moved to the Arctic, reflected Declan, she might become an arbiter of garden taste, a Vita Sackville-North.

639

Freddie was in terrific spirits, brandishing the *Telegraph* with a piece on the forthcoming franchise struggle.

'It says four incumbent companies are vulnerable and names Corinium as one of them. It also says: *"Venturer, Corinium's rival must be reckoned a considerable creative and management force."* Then it goes on to say: *"Corinium are strongly challenged, and as a result their shares are selling at a substantial discount to assets."*'

'I don't understand what that means,' said Declan.

'Don't matter. It's good, believe me. We're on our way, boy.'

'What are we going to do about Cameron and Tony?'

Freddie chewed on his cigar. 'I can't believe she's turned.'

'I don't want to, but we still haven't discovered who leaked the names of the other moles to Tony.'

'How was she in Ireland?' asked Freddie.

'Wonderful,' said Declan wistfully.

'Well then, my guess is that she's dotty about Rupert, and when he started giving 'er the runaround last night, Tony seized his chance and accosted her on the way back from the Ladies.'

Declan thought it was more complex. To bolster her chronic insecurity, Cameron had to have a man in her life, and after that last night in Galway, when she'd made such a definite play for him, he didn't think she was Rupert's exclusive property any more. He was also furious how much seeing her with Tony had upset him.

'We've fought this fight absolutely straight up to now,' said Freddie.

'Except for Rupert seducing Cameron in the first place.'

'But so much is at stake now,' Freddie went on, 'that we'd better put a private detective on Tony and get Rupert to slip a tiny bug into Cameron's 'andbag.'

The snow was falling again, flakes tumbling down dark against the muddy yellow sky, then getting lost to view as they reached ground level.

'Better not involve Rupert at this stage,' said Declan. 'If he realizes she's been hobnobbing with Tony, he might get really rough and send her scuttling back to Tony for good. Anyway, she's got a dozen bags. Rupert's bound to bug the wrong one, and he's off to Rome for three days tomorrow.'

'OK,' said Freddie, stubbing out his cigar and getting to his feet. 'We'll start wiv a private detective on Tony. I know an ace one. Leave it wiv me.'

Declan sensed that Freddie was anxious to get rid of him. 'Where's Valerie?' he asked.

'Visiting her sister in Cheam.'

'Do you want to come over for supper?'

Freddie shook his head. 'It's not really a night to go out, thanks. I've got an 'ell of a lot of work to do. I keep forgetting I'm the Chief Executive of a public company.'

Committing adultery, Freddie reflected ruefully after Declan had gone, made one tell an 'orrible lot of lies. James Vereker was spending the night in London at another Corinium dry run. Lizzie's nanny was away for the weekend. He must remember to ring Valerie before he left, so she didn't ring and find him not at home.

As he arrived at Lizzie's, he felt glad that the steadily falling snow would cover any wheel tracks by morning. Lizzie was looking out for him, so no doorbells should wake the children.

She welcomed him in a primrose-yellow silk dressing-gown, rosy, warm and Floris-scented from the bath. The lights were low in the bedroom, but a fire burned merrily in the grate. Reflected tongues of flame lasciviously licked the ceiling. Making a mental note to throw away the evidence first thing in the morning, Lizzie said there was a bottle of Moët to be opened. Instead, Freddie opened her silk dressing-gown and felt his heart stop. Lizzie was wearing just black high heels and a black corset which pushed up her breasts, moulded her waist and stopped just above her damp blonde bush, except for four black suspenders holding up black fishnet stockings.

'You are the loveliest fing I've ever seen,' murmured Freddie. 'Come live wiv me, and be my love. Leave it on,' he added as Lizzie started unhooking.

Kneeling down, he removed her high heels and, kissing

her instep, slowly kissed his way up until he could bury his face in the soft marshmallow of her thighs. Lizzie bent down to take off his jersey and shirt, feeling his stomach muscles tauten as she unbuckled his trouser belt. There was a huge mirror on the ceiling. James adored to watch his own reflection when he made love. Beside his lithe and taut bronzed beauty, Lizzie had always felt like a Beryl Cook lady. With Freddie she felt slim and beautiful and wanted to watch the whole thing.

'I never rated swucksont-nurf before,' said Freddie happily.

The snow had grown two inches on the window ledge. Freddie had grown several inches and diminished again. The logs had died in the grate before Lizzie leaned up on her elbow smoothing the red-gold curls on his chest.

'I love you,' she said softly, so as not to wake him.

Freddie opened an eye. 'I meant it when I said come live wiv me and be my love,' he said.

The following Tuesday morning James Vereker had a rare and intimate breakfast with his five-year-old daughter Eleanor. Usually James fled the din of little children in the morning and either had his muesli, prunes and herbal tea in bed or breakfasted at the Corinium canteen after a work-out in the gym. This week he and Lizzie were recording their second programme in the series on the way children enrich and restrict a marriage. James had already written his script which began: 'As a caring parent, I . . .' and was now, in between reading the *Guardian*, doing a little research into fatherhood.

Sebastian, Ellie's brother, who'd already got soaked making a snowman and nearly drowned testing the ice on the lake, was upstairs having his clothes changed by Jilly, the dependable boot of a nanny. Lizzie was working. Ellie was eating a boiled egg, dreamily dipping buttered toast soldiers into the yolk.

'I hope you'll watch "Round-Up" tonight,' James said to her. 'We're visiting the zoo and filming a new polar bear cub, which is called James after me.'

'I saw Freddie bare the other night,' said Ellie dreamily.

'I don't think I know Freddie Bear,' said James. 'Do the BBC make it, or is it one of ours?'

'I saw Freddie bare,' repeated Ellie.

'I heard you,' said James patiently. 'Is it a new cartoon?'

'No – Freddie bare. He was on the bed with Mummy. They were struggling.'

James put down his spoon. 'I beg your pardon?'

'I wanted a drink of water, so I went into Mummy's room. Freddie and Mummy were in bed. Freddie was bare, but Mummy was wearing long socks with her bottom hanging out.'

James went very red in the face.

'Are you trying to tell me that Mummy was in bed with someone – er – someone who wasn't Daddy?'

'Yes,' beamed Ellie. 'Freddie with the big tummy. He's nice, he brings us Smarties.'

'You're not to make up wicked fibs,' said James furiously. 'Jilly!' he yelled for the dependable boot. 'It's time the children went to school.'

Lizzie had the effrontery to giggle when James confronted her.

'It's not funny,' thundered James.

'No, it isn't. Oh dear, I hope the poor darling isn't totally put off sex for life.'

'Is that all you can say? What about me?'

'Nothing would put you off sex for life,' said Lizzie.

'Stop being frivolous. I cannot believe you'd cheat on me with that dreadful, overweight, common little man.'

'Freddie is a very nice man,' said Lizzie.

'He's totally dishonourable and so are you.'

'What about all *your* affairs?'

'They're finished,' said James sanctimoniously. 'And being in the media one is inevitably the target of certain attentions. Anyway, it's different for men.'

'Don't blame Freddie then.'

'Freddie,' said James, working himself up into a fury, 'is a member of the rival consortium. I feel utterly betrayed. It's like fraternizing in the war.'

'Well, I'm not having *my* head shaved,' screamed Lizzie.

'And what's this about wearing long socks and your bottom hanging out?'

Lizzie giggled again. 'It must have been my fishnet stockings and my corset.'

'You dress up like a prostitute! Whatever for?'

'To excite him,' said Lizzie simply.

'You never bothered to do that for me,' said James indignantly.

Lizzie watched James catch sight of himself in the mirror. Smoothing his hair, he composed his features into an expression suitable for a wronged husband. He's just the wrong husband, she thought.

'I suppose you realize,' said James nastily, 'Freddie's only been running after you to worm Corinium secrets out of you. I shall have to tell Tony of course. We have to report anything suspicious. He'll be delighted to have something on Mr Squeaky Clean at last. I shan't blame you. I'll say being somewhat unsophisticated and unused to male attention, you fell for it.'

'I've heard enough,' said Lizzie furiously. 'Freddie is the most honourable man I've ever met. After you junked Sarah, because Tony ordered you to clean up your marital act, she went screaming round to Rupert and told him everything.'

James winced.

'Rupert was all set to give the story straight to the *News of the World*. It would have been a goody: "*Corinium stud ordered to give up mistress by boss in order to present image of idyllic marriage to viewers and IBA.*" There were plenty of Corinium people, including Sarah, who'd have enjoyed shopping you to the press. And the whole thing would have been a lovely black blot on Corinium's escutcheon. But Freddie wouldn't let Rupert do it. Unlike Tony, he feels that sort of thing is below the belt. He didn't want mine, or the children's names, dragged in; said it wasn't fair having them branded as the offspring of an adulterer – and a pratt,' she added as an afterthought.

'You uncaring bitch,' spluttered James.

'And what is more,' continued Lizzie coldly, 'if you breathe a word about me and Freddie to anyone, I'm leaving you, and then your silly marriage programme's going to look even sillier.'

The moment James left the house, Lizzie burst into tears. She was still crying when Jilly the dependable boot got back from the school run. In the end Lizzie told her the whole story.

'I'd no idea poor darling Ellie came into our bedroom that night.'

'She'd have screamed if she'd been frightened,' said Jilly comfortingly. 'She was perfectly happy on the way to school on Monday; only interested in whether the lake would be frozen enough to slide on.'

She picked up a table which James had knocked over as he rushed from the room.

'If it comes to a split, I'd like to stay with you. You're the best boss I've ever had, and I love the kids. I don't mind taking a cut in salary if things get hard. There, there, there's no need to start crying again.'

Freddie was just going into a board meeting when Lizzie rang him.

'I'll come and get you.'

'No, no,' said Lizzie. 'We've got to lie low. I don't want to give Tony any ammunition at this stage. Venturer doesn't need it, and think of Valerie, Sharon and Wayne. We'll just have to play safe and not see each other till after 15th December.'

'That's over a fortnight,' said Freddie aghast.

'Well, we must try, anyway.'

Freddie was utterly distracted at the meeting. When an outside director congratulated him on the new billion-pound deal with the Japs, he looked blank. When another informed him that the ex-Chairman, General Walters, had died of a heart attack, Freddie said, 'Triffic news. Keep up the good work!'

Outside in the beautifully kept company gardens, the sun, like a huge red Christmas bauble, was setting down the side of a large yew tree. Freddie shivered at the thought that the sun might be setting on his relationship with Lizzie. Then one of his secretaries summoned him from the meeting. There was a call, she said, on his very, very, very private line whose number was only known to Lizzie – and now the private detective. It was the latter ringing: he'd seen Tony and Cameron go into the Royal Garden Hotel early that afternoon. They'd spent ninety minutes in the Residents' Lounge. He'd walked through twice and there'd been no one else there.

Freddie's heart sank. He told the detective to keep on tailing Tony and immediately rang Declan, who was utterly shattered. They both decided, however, that if Cameron had spilled any more beans, it was too late to muzzle Tony now. If, as was just possible, she hadn't, she was still too important a trump card with the IBA to be frightened off.

They decided to wait until Rupert returned from Rome tomorrow before tackling her.

Next morning, after a restless night, Declan woke up to more snow, and, not wishing to risk either car, walked down to the village shop to get the papers. Yesterday at The Priory, they'd had a power cut and frozen pipes. Today the washing machine and the tumble dryer were kaput, and it was warmer out than in. Three-foot icicles hung from the faulty gutters. The evergreens lining the drive were bent double by the snow. Every blade of grass edging the road was rimed with frost and burned with a white heat of its own.

The traffic was crawling so slowly that Declan didn't bother to put the dogs on leads. Gertrude, a bit lame from the hard ground, still rushed into every cottage front garden and barked at the snowmen. Claudius, encountering his first snow this year, was wild with excitement, plunging into drifts, leaping to catch the snowballs Declan hurled for him. As Declan passed the white church, he sent up a prayer that Venturer might win. On such a beautiful day, one couldn't fail to be optimistic. But as he walked into the village shop Mr Banks, who was a great newspaper reader, waved *The Times*.

'Lord Baddingham's been blowing his own trumpet again.'

Declan felt his throat go dry, his stomach churned.

'Page five,' went on Mr Banks, handing the paper to Declan.

' *Baddingham Set for Victory*,' said the headline. There was a very nice picture, taken from above and at a slight angle to reduce the heavy jowl. Tony was smiling and showing excellent teeth. The interview had been written by a well-known financial journalist.

As he was so confident of retaining the franchise, Tony had told him, he was only too happy to reveal Corinium's plans for next year. They were very happy to welcome three new directors on to the Board, all production people, including Ailie Bristoe, who'd just spent three years in Hollywood and who would be Director of Programmes. They were also very excited about their new networked thirteen-part series on marriage which, Tony predicted, would turn James and Lizzie Vereker into big stars.

It was safe enough stuff. Declan sat down on the snow-covered window-ledge outside the shop, obscuring the postcard advertisements for lost gerbils, daily women and second-hand carrycots in the window.

Corinium, he read on, had also made arrangements with the Royal Shakespeare to televise special productions of whatever Shakespeare plays children in the area would be taking for O- and A-levels each year. Then they would offer the videos for sale. They'd also be filming Johnny Friedlander's *Hamlet*, which had been postponed until the summer.

Shit, thought Declan in horror, those were both Cameron's ideas. But most exciting of all, he read on, was that Corinium had signed up a new play by Stroud-born playwright, Dermot MacBride, with an option on the second. There followed a lot of guff about MacBride's towering genius, and how happy

647

Tony was to welcome this lost son of Gloucestershire back into the fold.

'We paid a lot for MacBride,' Tony had admitted.

But, as the financial journalist pointed out, the publicity value alone would be worth thousands of pounds to Corinium.

'Please don't obscure my advertisement,' said a shrill voice. 'I'll never get a cleaner that way.'

Looking up, Declan discovered an old lady with a red nose glaring at him. Looking down he saw Gertrude and Claudius sitting at his feet, shivering miserably. Slipping and sliding, falling over twice, moaning with rage, Declan ran home to The Priory.

'Look at fucking that!' He brandished *The Times* under Maud's nose. 'Tony's bought Dermot MacBride's play. Cameron must have leaked it to him.'

'I always thought she was untrustworthy,' said Maud, who was plucking her eyebrows.

Declan's hands were so cold it took him a long time to dial the number of Dermot MacBride's agent.

'We had a deal. What the fuck are you playing at?'

'The contract hadn't been signed,' said the agent defensively. 'My duty is to get the best deal for my authors. Tony offered three times as much as you.'

'You could have come back to me. I'd have matched his offer.'

'He said if I talked to you the deal was off.'

'That's the last deal I'll ever do with you,' roared Declan.

'Never mind. I'm retiring at Christmas.'

Through the window, Declan watched the Priory robin furiously driving a rival robin away from the bird table.

'How did Tony know about our deal?'

'Dunno. He phoned about five yesterday. I spoke to Mac-Bride. We exchanged contracts this morning. It'll buy a few gold watches for me.'

The moment Declan put down the telephone, Freddie rang.

'Have you seen the *Cotchester News*? There's a bloody great picture of you an' me, an' Rupert, an' Basil, an' 'Enry – all

648

in our red coats out huntin' wiv big grins on our faces, wiv a caption: "*Do you want these butchers to run your television station?*"'

'That's libellous,' howled Declan. 'Have you seen *The Times?*'

'Yes,' said Freddie grimly. 'Unfortunately that's not.'

'I'm not waiting for Rupert to get back,' said Declan. 'I'm going round to have it out with Cameron right now.'

But when he got to Penscombe, Mrs Bodkin told him Cameron had gone out and wasn't expected back until evening. Guilt, thought Declan in a fury.

Cameron got home around eight that evening. She knew she shouldn't have played truant, but, having brooded agonizingly about Rupert since the hunt ball, she felt she had to get out of the house. The heavy frost had made the white valley look so beautiful that morning. Why should I give up all this without a fight? she had thought. Rupert was an alpha male, he was exceptionally handsome, funny, very rich, clever in a totally different way to herself, and, now that she'd given him six months' intensive training on pleasing a woman rather than automatically pleasing himself, spectacular in bed.

A great believer in positive action, she drove into Cheltenham to the branch headquarters of 'Mind the Step', a support group for step-parents and step-children, which had just opened. Cameron figured the subject would not only make a good programme, but might help her love Rupert's children and understand her own tortured relationship with her mother and Mike. She had a long talk with the organizer, who then gave her several names and addresses. Driving round Gloucestershire, Cameron was amazed how many people welcomed her in. At their wits' end, hemmed in by snow and coping with step-children at home for several days, they were only too happy to talk to someone.

Listening to the shrill invective, to half-hearted attempts at love, to occasional genuine affection, to grown women blaming their own step-mothers for lack of love, which prevented them in turn loving their own husbands and children, Cameron forgot her own miseries. She decided it would make a marvellous programme and was already pre-selecting the people to interview.

Like Declan on his way to the village shop that morning, she returned to Penscombe with a feeling of optimism. She found messages from Mrs Bodkin that Rupert had rung twice, Freddie three times and Declan four.

Going into the kitchen, she poured herself a large vodka and tonic and decided to scribble down some ideas for the 'Step' programme while it was still in her head. Searching for a biro on the kitchen shelf, she found the yellow sachet that had been included with the flowers that Tony had sent her after he beat her up, which you were supposed to add to the water to make the flowers last longer. Stabbed with sudden misery, she wished she could sprinkle the sachet on Rupert to prolong their relationship.

With a lurch of apprehension, she heard the dogs barking in the hall. Not Rupert, the welcome wasn't clamorous enough, but it was obviously someone they knew. She went into the hall.

'Declan!' Her face lit up. 'Sorry I didn't call back. I've had a great idea for a programme.'

'On treachery?' asked Declan bleakly. 'You're an expert on that subject.'

'What are you talking about? Do you want a drink?'

'No thanks.' He followed her into the drawing-room. 'You seen *The Times*?'

'Haven't seen any papers. I've been playing hookey.'

Declan picked up *The Times* from the table. It took him ages to find the right page.

'Here.' He thrust it at her.

'What a crazy photo of Tony,' she said, settling down on the sofa for a good read. 'They've made him look almost benign. Oh my God,' she whispered a minute later, the laughter vanishing from her face. 'I don't believe it. How the fuck did he find out?'

'You tell me.'

Something chilling in his tone made her look up in alarm. He had moved close and seemed to tower above her, his legs in the grey trousers rising like two trunks of beech trees, the massive shoulders blocking out the light, and, in his deathly pale face, the implacable ever-watchful eyes of the Inquisitor.

Cameron shivered. 'What d'you mean?'

'I saw you plotting with Tony on Friday night.'

'He was waiting for me when I came out of the john, for Chrissake.'

'So Freddie and I had him followed.'

Cameron's eyes flickered.

'You're not going to tell me you and Tony were talking just about cucumber sandwiches for an hour and a half in the Royal Garden yesterday afternoon,' said Declan.

Cameron suddenly looked the picture of guilt.

'Sure I saw him. We had tea. I needed advice on, on –' she flushed scarlet – 'a personal matter.'

'You gave him all our programme plans, just as last month you told him the names of all the moles. No doubt he's got lots of other info about Venturer up his pinstriped sleeve for the meeting tomorrow.'

Cameron looked furious and terrified now – the hawk cornered by her captor about to strike.

'I didn't tell him anything.'

'You bloody liar,' thundered Declan. 'How long have you been spying for him? Ever since the beginning, since Rupert got his legover in Madrid?'

'How could I possibly spy for Tony?' she screamed. 'He beat me up, for Chrissake. This –' she waved *The Times* piece at Declan – 'sabotages everything we've worked for. Someone else leaked it.'

'Why did you bother to go to London on the worst day of the winter?' snarled Declan.

Blue, the lurcher, who'd been hovering nervously, jumped up on the sofa beside Cameron and, glaring at Declan, started to whine querulously at him. The other dogs licked their lips. Beaver slunk out of the room.

'Blue believes me,' pleaded Cameron. 'Why the fuck should

I come to Ireland, and work so hard on the programme plans, if I was spying for Tony? He's given my old job to Ailie Bristoe.'

'That's a front.'

'Bullshit,' said Cameron furiously. 'Is this some kind of a nightmare? Are you back at Corinium? Am I your guest tonight? Where's the fucking thumbscrews and the rack, or do you use electrodes and knee-capping like the fucking IRA?'

Grabbing her arm, Declan yanked her to her feet.

'No one else knew about Dermot MacBride. How much else have you told him?'

Ignoring the low growl from Blue, he started to shake her like a rat.

'You arrogant, pig-headed Irish asshole,' yelled Cameron. 'Why don't you believe me?'

Maddened because she'd let him down, violent because he felt guilty about wanting her so much, Declan slapped her very hard across the face. The next minute Blue leapt at him, burying his teeth in Declan's arm.

'Leave!' screamed Cameron. 'Leave, Blue.' Grabbing the dog's collar she tugged him off, then, almost carrying him back onto the sofa beside her, collapsed sobbing into his shaggy coat.

Pulling himself together, Declan lit two cigarettes, but, as he handed one to Cameron, Blue gave another ominous growl.

'It's OK, boy,' gasped Cameron.

She wiped her eyes frantically on her sleeve, then took the lighted cigarette. Inhaling deeply, she felt she was drawing the fires of hell into her lungs. Blue struggled up on his front paws and licked her face.

'My only friend,' she said tonelessly. 'You'd better have a tetanus jab,' she added to Declan.

Massaging his arm, Declan retreated to a respectable distance in front of the empty fireplace.

'OK, what was the personal problem? And why Tony?'

'I know he's a shit, but sometimes I figure he's the only person in the world who truly cares for me.'

652

'After beating you up?'

Cameron fingered her reddened cheek and shrugged. 'Seems to be catching.'

'I'm sorry.'

Cameron took a deep breath. 'I saw Tony because Rupert doesn't love me any more, and I can't handle it.'

'Just because he was bloody-minded at the ball,' said Declan scornfully. 'We're all uptight at the moment.'

Cameron's lip was trembling again. 'Rupert doesn't give a shit about the franchise. All he cares about is Taggie.'

'Taggie?' said Declan, flabbergasted. 'My Taggie? Are you out of your mind?'

'He saw her when we were in Ireland. In his bottom desk drawer, under the lining paper, he's hidden pictures of her with his kids.' Cameron gave a sob. 'And he's also kept some totally illiterate thank-you letter she sent him.'

Declan was utterly appalled.

'Rupert and Taggie,' he growled so furiously that Blue started rumbling back at him, like rival storms across a valley. 'I'm not having that profligate bastard laying a finger on Taggie.'

'But it's OK for him to finger me,' hissed Cameron, 'I'm only a mole.'

Earlier that afternoon Rupert had flown in from Rome and gone straight to his office in Whitehall. Ignoring a long list of telephone messages, he signed his letters, gathered up the rest of the post, made sure he was paired for the Finance debate that evening and set out for Gloucestershire. Slumped in the corner of a first-class carriage with his hand round a large Bell's, he looked at the snowy landscape turned electric blue in the twilight. Even in London it wasn't thawing. It had been a wasted visit to Rome. He'd made no contribution to the International Olympics Conference. He hadn't been able to sleep, or eat, or think straight, he was so haunted by the image of Taggie and Basil on the Bar Sinister balcony, or of Taggie's gasping with pleasure in Basil's expert embrace.

He tried to concentrate on the *Standard*, but beyond the

fact that Corinium shares had unaccountably rocketed, and Patric Walker forecast a stormy day for him tomorrow, and warned Cancers, which was Taggie's sign, to ignore all outside influences, he couldn't take anything in. Sitting opposite, an enchanting blonde was eyeing him with discreet but definite interest. Glancing at her slim knees above very shiny black boots, Rupert reflected that by now, in the old days, he would have bought her a large vodka and tonic and been investigating the prospect of a quick bang at the Station Hotel, Cotchester – if not at Penscombe. What the hell was happening to him? His secretary in London had given him a carrier bag of Christmas cards to sign for constituents and party workers. Wearily he scribbled *Rupert Campbell-Black* in a few, but not *love*, not for anyone in the world except that feckless Taggie.

Unknown to him, Taggie was slumped, shivering and equally miserable, in a second-class carriage down the train. She'd been doing an early Christmas lunch for some overseas sales reps in Swindon which had seemed to go on for ever. She always found train journeys unnerving, having to read all the strange station names and the platform directions and the train times. Today by mistake she'd got on a train going back to London and had to get off and wait in quite inadequate clothing on Didcot station for half an hour.

As Declan had taken the new Mini, Maud had borrowed Taggie's car to buy a new dress for her audition for *A Doll's House* tomorrow. She'd promised to meet Taggie at Cotchester if Taggie rang and told her what train she was coming on. But when Taggie had tried to ring her at Didcot there was no answer.

Rupert thought he was dreaming when he saw Taggie ahead of him on the platform at Cotchester. The snakey curls had dropped; she was back to her old ponytail. As she walked up the steps of the bridge, he noticed a man behind admiring her long black-stockinged legs. Fucking letch; Rupert wanted to kill him. As she turned to hand in her ticket, under the overhead light bulb he noticed the black shadows under her eyes. Too much sex, he thought savagely.

No one was there to meet her; there were no taxis; the telephone box didn't work. Peering out through the square glass panes, Taggie's legs nearly gave way beneath her as she saw Rupert getting into his car. Rushing out into the street, she waved at him. There was a moment of blind hope as she thought he waved back as he stormed past spraying snow all over her, but he was only adjusting his driving mirror.

The only answer was to walk into Cotchester and find another telephone box, or perhaps ask Bas to run her home. Why the hell hadn't she worn boots? She wasn't thinking straight at the moment. The icicles glittered from the station roof as she went past. Ahead she could see the white spire of Cotchester cathedral glinting in the moonlight with all the coloured windows lit up by a service inside. The next minute a car skidded to a halt beside her.

'What the hell are you doing?'

'Trying to find a telephone box to ring Mummy,' she muttered through furiously chattering teeth. Her lips were a livid green, her nose bluey-brown in the orange street light.

'Get in,' said Rupert. Viciously he punched out the number he knew so well. He let the telephone ring for two minutes. There was no answer.

'Mummy's on the toot as usual,' he said. 'I'll run you home.'

'Oh please don't bother.'

'It's not exactly out of my way,' he said sarcastically.

The frozen snow twinkled like rhinestones in the moonlight. Once they'd got out of Cotchester on to the country lanes there was only room for single-line traffic between the huge polar drifts. They didn't speak for a few miles, then, glancing sideways, Rupert saw the tears pouring down her face.

'What the fuck's the matter now?'

'I thought we were friends.'

'Then why did you go to bed with Bas?'

'I didn't. I meant to, because I was so miserable about you. I thought if I got some really good experience, you might fancy me a bit, but when it came to the crunch, I couldn't do it. I love you too much.'

Rupert stopped the car, pulling it into a gateway.

'I'm desperately sorry,' sobbed Taggie, groping in her bag for a paper handkerchief. 'I know it must be boring having every woman you meet in love with you. I didn't want to be one of them. I've tried so hard to get over you. Work doesn't help at all. It's just that you've been so kind looking after us, sorting Mummy out the other night and getting all that food when I made an up-cock at Sarah Stratton's dinner party, and giving me all those lovely things, and buying the wood for far more than it's worth.'

'Who told you that?' said Rupert, appalled.

'Ursula did. She saw Daddy's bank statement. It was the only good thing in it. I'm sorry for being such a drip.'

Rupert raised clenched fists to his temples in a superhuman effort not to reach out for her. Taggie mistook the gesture for sheer horror at being propositioned by yet another girl.

'I'm sorry.'

'For Christ's sake stop apologizing.' Rupert started speaking very slowly and deliberately as if he was addressing some loopy foreigner. 'Look, it wouldn't work. I'm terribly fond of you, Tag, but I'm far too old. Remember that hamburger bar manager who thought you were my daughter? I've never been faithful to anyone for more than a few weeks, and I'm not going to ruin your life by having a brief fling with you.'

'My life's ruined already,' sobbed Taggie, who'd soaked one paper handkerchief and was desperately searching in her pockets for another.

'You'll get over me,' said Rupert, handing her his.

'Like that five-bar gate in front of us,' said Taggie helplessly.

What made it worse was that the car got stuck and they had to push it out and Taggie slipped over and Rupert picked her up, then almost shoved her away, as though she was white hot, so desperate was his longing to take her in his arms.

The Priory was in darkness when they got back.

'Tell your father I'll ring him later,' said Rupert, cannoning off a low wall in his haste to get away.

Across the valley he could see lights on in his house. He

656

couldn't face Cameron at the moment. If only he could dump on Billy, but it was Wednesday and Billy would be at the television centre presenting the sports programme. Mindlessly he drove back to Cotchester and parked outside Basil's flat.

One look at Rupert's set white face was enough. Bas poured him a large whisky.

'Taggie said there wasn't a leg-over situation.'

'There wasn't,' said Bas. 'Not through lack of trying on my part. She is utterly adorable, but she utterly adores someone else, you lucky sod.'

Rupert drained his whisky.

'I'm not going to do anything about her.'

'Why ever not?' said Bas incredulously. 'It's on a plate.'

'I'm too old, shopsoiled, evil . . .'

'Oh, don't be so fucking self-indulgent. All these histrionics and tantrums are just the last frantic struggles of the lassooed bronco. You've never been in love before. It's really very nice, if you stop fighting it. Everyone's got to hang up their condom sometime. Taggie'd be worth it.'

'I don't want to talk about it.'

'OK,' said Bas, filling up their glasses.

'Am I interrupting you?'

'Not excessively. I was just looking at the books. The Bar's had a staggering year, thanks to all those malcontents from Corinium drowning their sorrows and plotting my big brother's downfall. Won't be so good next year, with you and Freddie and Declan running things. They'll all be working so hard, they won't have time for a lunch hour. D'you really think we'll get it?'

''Course we will,' said Rupert, thinking he really didn't give a fuck any more.

Bas shook his head. 'Tony gave a bloody good interview to *The Times* this morning. Came across as Mr Caring.' He threw the paper in Rupert's direction.

Rupert ignored it. 'Did she really say she loved me?'

'Yes, she did, which I find extraordinary, knowing you as I do.'

Rupert shook his head in bewilderment.

'It's never, never hit me like this before either. I'm still not going to do anything about it.'

49

Up in London that night the fourteen directors and senior
staff of Corinium Television had an extremely successful final
dry run before their meeting at the IBA the next afternoon.
Tony, in a new dark-blue pin-stripe suit paid for by Corinium,
was in coruscating form.

'They can have one drink,' he told Ginger Johnson beforehand, 'and then not one drop until we've been round the
course – and I'm going to grill them.'

No one at the meeting tomorrow, he said, was to speak until
he'd introduced them. There was now, as a result of recent
hiring and firing, a most satisfactory preponderance of ex-pro-
duction people on the Board who would do most of the talking.
The money-men, like Ginger and Georgie Baines, who
brought in the vast advertising revenue, would keep a low
profile. In fact it would be better if the word 'profit' were not
mentioned at all. All the men had had hair cuts.

'No doubt,' muttered Sarah Stratton to James Vereker,
'there will be a nail inspection in the morning.'

Afterwards they all dined wisely but not too well at the
Carlton Tower, where they were staying overnight. No shellfish was allowed, nor liqueurs after dinner. Everyone was very
impressed with Ailie Bristoe, the new Programme Controller,
who'd flown over from Hollywood for the occasion, and
seemed as beautiful as she was bright. James Vereker, in
particular, thought she looked very caring.

'I'm surprised Tony hasn't put the women in separate hotels,' grumbled Sarah, as they were all sent up to bed early.

'Be sure to order a *Scorpion* for tomorrow,' was Tony's parting shot. 'You'll all find it very interesting reading.'

Back in Gloucestershire, Declan finally stormed out of The Priory around ten o'clock, having failed to get a confession out of Cameron. Utterly devastated that he and Freddie could possibly think she was the mole, Cameron was slumped on the sofa, still cuddling Blue when the telephone rang. It was some girl, saying Rupert wouldn't be back until the morning, but he sent his love. There was a terrific din in the background and the girl sounded as though she was ringing from a bar. Bastard, thought Cameron, but she was too proud to ask where he was. As she put the telephone down it rang again.

'Can I speak to Rupert Campbell-Black?'

'He's not here.'

'Is that Cameron Cook?'

'This is she.'

The voice thickened and became oily as though it was asking for extended credit.

'This is the *Messenger* here. Wondered what you feel about Rupert's memoirs in the *Scorpion*.'

'I don't know what you're talking about.'

'Rupert's really done it this time. Bloody bad timing on the day before your IBA meeting.'

Cameron had had a long day and was not connecting well but gradually it sank in that Beattie Johnson had finally got her revenge on Rupert by telling all to the *Scorpion*. Not only, according to the *Messenger* reporter, had she produced every kind of salacious detail about her two years with Rupert and the unbelievably kinky things they'd got up to, but, even worse, revealed intimate details of his sex life with other women, including Helen.

'Oh my God!' whispered Cameron. 'Does he mention me?'

'Not yet, sweetheart,' said the reporter, who'd already seen and admired Cameron's photograph, 'but you may be in Saturday's instalment. They're trailing the spread that's going out on Friday, the morning you go to the IBA. It's all about Rupert's affair with Amanda Hamilton, wife of the shadow Foreign Secretary. Very pretty lady, evidently she liked being spanked.'

Cameron groaned.

'And there's a particularly damaging bit tomorrow,' said the reporter, who was beginning to enjoy himself. 'I'll read it. Beattie writes: "*I always felt Rupert was unnaturally close to fellow show jumper Billy Lloyd-Foxe. Rupert admitted that when they were in Kenya, he, Helen and Billy and his journalist wife Janey (who left Billy for nine months soon after they were married) had a naughty foursome. Did Helen (who started an affair with Jake Lovell shortly after this incident) discover the true nature of Rupert's sexual preference that night?*"'

'I don't want to hear any more,' screamed Cameron, slamming down the receiver. It rang again. It was the *Sun*.

'Go away,' she screamed.

Immediately she'd put down the receiver, she dialled out.

'Fuck off, all of you,' snarled a voice.

'Declan, it's Cameron. Have you heard about Rupert's memoirs?'

'Yes,' said Declan, 'and I don't know where the fuck to get hold of him.'

'Nor do I,' sobbed Cameron.

The juggernauts rumbling along Cotchester High Street woke Rupert next morning to the worst hangover in recorded history. Moaning, he pulled the blankets over his head. There was a knock on the door.

'Bugger off. I feel terrible.'

'You're not going to feel any better when you read this,' said Bas, handing him a Fernet Branca and the *Scorpion*, which Rupert read in silence.

'The dirty bitch,' he said softly. 'She said she'd get me in the end.'

It was as though some terrible monster from his past had put a hand up from a manhole and dragged him down into the mire and slime below. He went straight to the lavatory and threw up.

'Lend me a toothbrush, and then a telephone,' he said to Bas. He was put straight through to Freddie.

'Look, I've only just seen the *Scorpion*. I'm ringing up to resign.'

'Don't be daft,' said Freddie.

'I've got to. There are two more days to go, and it's bound to get worse. Unless I pull out, there's no way you'll get the franchise.'

'Don't be rash, mate. We won't be much good at running a TV station if we can't ride out somefink like this. Got to stick togevver. Come over 'ere and we'll sort out the best plan of action, but you're not resigning.'

'Up to me really,' said Rupert. 'I must see Cameron, and then I'll be over.'

Arriving at Penscombe, he found cars parked all the way up his drive, and the gravel in front of the house completely hidden by journalists, photographers and television crews. Corinium had even had the temerity to send a mobile canteen. Stony-faced, greyer than the trampled snow, Rupert got out of his car.

'Fuck off, the lot of you,' he snarled as they all surged forward. 'I've got to talk to my lawyer.'

'What about the franchise?' asked the *Mail on Sunday*.

'Come on, Rupe,' said the *Star*. 'Give us a quote. We've waited all fucking night.'

'I've got nothing to say. I'll put my dogs on you if you don't beat it.' Fighting his way into the house, he slammed the door behind him.

'Well, well, well,' said Cameron from halfway up the stairs.

She wore no make-up, and her hair was sleeked back from her face which was deathly white.

'I'm sorry,' began Rupert.

'Fuck off,' screamed Cameron, as a photographer appeared at a side window. Racing downstairs, she drew the curtains.

'Come upstairs,' said Rupert.

They went into his bedroom, the set for so much of the

662

action in the first instalment of the memoirs. Almost as though the great four-poster would contaminate her, Cameron gave it a wide berth and went over to the fireplace.

'How could you?' she whispered. 'Have you told people those sort of things about me?'

'Never, never,' said Rupert. Suddenly dizzy, he slumped on the flowered chintz-covered chair in front of Helen's old dressing table. 'Beattie was a special case. The thing that turned her on was stories of my screwing other women. She must have had a tape recorder running under the bed the whole time.'

'Then you did say those things. They're disgusting, insupportable.' She shuddered. 'You realize your career's finished? You'll be kicked out of the party. I hope you've already resigned from Venturer. And I suppose Saturday's instalment will be all about your touching designs on Taggie O'Hara. How the great rake was reformed and approached his waiting bride with a tenderness which was all the more careful, the more considerate because he knew the depths of her apprehension – Ker-rist!' Her voice rose to a screech.

Rupert looked at her incredulously. Expecting the exocet from the front, he was suddenly being torpedoed from underneath.

'You're in love with her, aren't you?' said Cameron.

Rupert looked across the valley at his white fields. He'd always seen them as arms protecting Taggie. Now they seemed like a great predatory polar bear, crushing The Priory to death.

He turned back to Cameron.

'OK,' he said flatly, 'I do love her. If I'm honest, I've loved her ever since New Year's Eve, probably long before that. I'm desperately sorry, I know I've dealt you a marked card. I'm much too fond of you to kid you along any longer, just for the sake of the franchise, that you and I are going to end up together.'

Cameron opened her mouth to yell at him, but Rupert raised his hand for a second's more silence.

'I didn't know a thing about these memoirs coming out – not that you'd want me anyway after reading them – but I want you to know that I was intending to level with you today about Taggie.'

For a second Cameron seemed to sway with frenzy, like a viper about to strike, then she screamed: 'You won't get her. Declan knows about it too, and there's no way he'll let you ever get your filthy depraved hands on his darling daughter.'

'I know there isn't,' said Rupert. 'This –' he picked up the *Scorpion* and wearily dropped it in the wastepaper basket – 'has finally done for us.'

'Serve you fucking right,' yelled Cameron. 'I'm getting out of here, and I never want to see you again.'

She rushed downstairs out of the front door, then kicked and punched her way through the waiting journalists, sending several of them leaping for safety as the Lotus stormed down the drive.

'Nice quiet girl,' said the *Mail on Sunday*, picking himself out of the snow.

Arriving at Green Lawns, Rupert found Freddie and Declan desperately trying to salvage the IBA meeting. As a result of Rupert's memoirs, two of the major financial backers had pulled out and Professor Graystock had resigned. As Rupert went into Freddie's study, the Bishop rang up:

'I'm afraid in the light of Rupert Campbell-Black's quite appalling revelations, I shall have to withdraw my support for the Venturer bid.'

'You can't,' said Freddie, aghast. 'The meeting's tomorrow morning. Your not being there will really tip the scales. I fort the Church of England were supposed to forgive sinners.'

'I have to set a good example to my flock,' said the Bishop and rang off.

'Lily-livered bastard,' said Freddie furiously. 'We're well shot of 'im.'

'He'd have impressed the IBA,' said Declan bleakly, who couldn't look Rupert in the eye. Was it because of Taggie or the memoirs?

'Then I must resign,' said Rupert. 'It's the only honourable thing to do.'

'No, you won't,' said Freddie. 'It don't add up. Beattie Johnson was a slut, but she 'ad a good 'eart. I don't fink she'd 'ave written those fings wivout considerable financial inducement. Seb Burrows has got nuffink to do at the moment. I'm going to put him on to the story and see what he can dig up. And can't we slap an injunction on the *Scorpion?*'

Rupert shook his head wearily. 'I wish we could, but I'm afraid it's all true. Although, it's appallingly slanted. The only wrong thing is that Billy and I aren't gay. Seven-eighths of it was never, never meant for publication, but she was such a fucking good listener, and you know I can never resist making people laugh. We were together for two years, for Christ's sake.'

'How's Cameron taken it?' asked Declan harshly. 'She was in a terrible state last night. Thinks you and she are kaput.'

Rupert slumped on the sofa, putting his head in his hands.

'We are. I've just told her.'

Declan lost his temper. It was like an earthquake and a volcano erupting at the same time.

'Can't you ever keep your fucking trap shut? First you tell everything to Beattie Johnson, then you have to give Cameron the boot. Don't you realize this'll screw up any final chance we have of getting the franchise? No Bishop, no professor, no financial backing, no Cameron – she'll bolt straight back to Tony and tell him everything she hasn't told him already.'

'What d'you mean?' Rupert looked up, the bloodshot eyes suddenly alert.

'Haven't you read *The Times* yet?'

'Bas muttered something about it last night, but I forgot to read it.'

'Cameron leaked all our plans to Tony on Tuesday.'

'Don't be ridiculous.'

'We put a private detective on to Tony. They spent an hour and a half together in the Royal Garden.'

'So?' said Rupert. 'They were having a bunk-up. Cameron's straight, I swear it.'

'So do I,' said Freddie.

'Well, it's purely academic now, since Rupert has seen fit to kick her out.'

'I'm sorry, Declan.'

'It's not bloody good enough.'

Unshaven, putty-coloured, his shirt on its second day, his suit crumpled, Rupert looked so desolate and so ill, slumped on the sofa, that Freddie went over and put a hand on his shoulder.

'Could 'appen to anyone. You'll come out of it.'

'Venturer won't. I've done for the lot of you.'

At that moment Valerie marched in.

'I've read every word of your disgusting memoirs,' she screeched. 'I don't want you in the house. You might give Wayne or even Fred-Fred some horrid disease.'

'Shut up,' snapped Freddie. 'He's 'ad enough punishment. Now just bugger off and bring us some black coffee.'

Feeling he was such an irritant to Declan, Rupert left soon after that. Holing up in Bas's flat, he spent the rest of a nightmare day on the telephone, trying to resign from the party, from his constituency and from the International Olympics Committee. To his frustration no one would accept. The Leader of the Opposition, for example, was amazingly sanguine:

'Wait until the franchises have been awarded,' she said. 'That tramp Beattie Johnson took me to the cleaners just before I became leader – slanted the whole interview. Jolly nearly cost me the job. The Amanda Hamilton business is unfortunate, I grant you, but Rollo's only Shadow Foreign Secretary at the moment, and you haven't done anything illegal. There's been absolutely no security leak, and it isn't as though you were married when you were in office. Just hang on a bit.'

Amanda Hamilton, on the other hand, was absolutely

gibbering with anger when Rupert rang her. Rollo was intending to sue, she said.

Malise Gordon, by contrast, was icy cold with rage that Helen's name had been dragged into it.

'I'm not excusing what's happened,' said Rupert, 'but I was very raw when Helen left me. Beattie lived with me for two years. Naturally I confided in her about my marriage, it never entered my head she'd shop me. None of the stuff that's been printed was intended for the memoirs. Will you tell Helen how desperately sorry I am? I did tell Beattie hundreds of good things about her, which she conveniently forgot to put in.'

'I'm sure that'll be a great comfort to Helen,' said Malise acidly.

'Look, I'm going abroad immediately after the IBA meeting tomorrow,' said Rupert. 'I won't be back for Christmas. I must see the children before I go.'

'I don't think that's at all a good idea,' said Malise crushingly, 'and I know Helen won't either. Tab's far too young to understand, and I doubt if Marcus will ever speak to you again after the things you said about his mother. The press are howling round the place; your presence would only exacerbate things. Just bugger off and leave us all alone.'

'I must explain –' just for a second Rupert's voice faltered – 'that whatever's happened, I still love them. For Christ's sake, Malise.'

'You can always write,' said Malise, and hung up.

Rupert sat slumped for a long time. Then he borrowed two hundred pounds in cash from Basil's till, a piece of writing paper and an envelope.

'*Darling Taggie,*' he wrote, '*I'm sorry I was bloody the last two times we met. Of course we're still friends. One day you'll find some nice boy who's worthy of you, and he'll be the luckiest sod in the world. In the meantime could you spend the enclosed on Christmas presents for Marcus and Tab. You'll know instinctively what they'd like. Thank you for everything. God bless you . . . Rupert.*'

Shoving the cash and the letter in an envelope, he gave it to Bas to deliver to The Priory.

Towards nightfall, over at Green Lawns, Freddie and Declan were just trying to prevent another backer pulling out when the private detective rang on another line. He had something too important to tell them over the telephone. He'd be straight round. He turned out, to Declan's surprise, not to be some seedy unfrocked cop in a dirty mac, but a delightfully understated, mouse-haired young Wykehamist with an innocent pink and white face. Nor did he beat about anyone's bush.

'Tony Baddingham spent yesterday afternoon in a Stow-in-the-Wold motel with a woman. I've got pictures of them arriving separately and then leaving together, and exchanging kisses in the car park.'

He threw the pictures down on the table. Fascinated, Freddie and Declan got up to have a look. In the first photograph the woman had her black coat collar turned up and was wearing a black beret, dark glasses and her hair tied back. In the second, coming out of the motel, her coat was unbuttoned, she was laughing, holding the dark glasses and the beret in one hand, with her glorious red hair trailing down her back. In the third, she was kissing Tony in front of Taggie's car.

'Is this some kind of a joke?' hissed Declan.

'I'm afraid not,' said the private detective. 'I'm awfully sorry, Mr O'Hara. After they'd gone I talked to the receptionist. After I'd bunged her, she admitted they'd been there several times before. She showed me the register – they'd signed in as Mr and Mrs Jones. The girl remembered Mrs O'Hara because she was so beautiful.'

Declan started to shake. It was like seeing the first stroke of the woodcutter's axe going into a great oak tree, thought Freddie.

'But it was Bas, not Tony,' muttered Declan.

'Bas must have been a front,' said Freddie.

'Look how upset she was the other night when Taggie

turned up with Bas,' said Declan, frantically trying to convince himself.

'That's because she's jealous of Taggie,' said Freddie wisely. 'It was only later she got really upset, which was when you told us you'd just seen Cameron with Tony – and she did know all about Dermot MacBride and the Shakespeare plays.'

'I don't believe it,' muttered Declan. 'She wouldn't. I must find her.' He stumbled towards the door.

'For Christ's sake, drive slowly,' warned Freddie.

As Declan walked into The Priory Maud came out of the drawing-room with a glass of champagne in her hand. She was wearing a black polo-neck jersey, a black coat, black stockings, black flat shoes and a black beret on the back of her head. She was very pale, she wore no lipstick, but her skin had a glowing luminosity and her eyes were huge and dreamy. Declan thought she had never looked more beautiful, and suddenly knew she was as guilty as hell.

'Darling – I got it!' she said ecstatically.

'What?'

'The part – Nora – in A Doll's House. We start rehearsing immediately after Christmas and they're paying me four hundred a week, so our money worries are all over.'

How little she knows about anything, thought Declan – how can a child have done such terrible things?

'Where's Taggie?' he asked.

'Cooking supper, I think. You don't seem very pleased for me, darling.'

As if in a dream he led her into the drawing-room, shutting the door and then opening it again to let in Claudius and Gertrude. Gertrude had a Bonio sticking out of the side of her mouth like a pipe. She could sit there for hours, saliva hanging in festoons. Declan leant against the door for support, watching Maud put a log on the fire. Despite all Maud's grandiose plans for The Priory, there were still no curtains at the windows which were as black as her clothes.

'How long have you been having an affair with Tony?' he asked almost conversationally.

Maud's face went as blank as a digital clock in a power cut.

'I don't know what you're talking about.'

'Don't prevaricate. I've got evidence.' Declan threw the photographs down on the sofa. Slowly Maud examined them.

'Rather good, that one.' She took a leisurely sip of her champagne. 'I might use it as a publicity photograph.'

'How long's it been going on?'

'Since September.'

'So you told him everything?'

Maud shrugged: 'I really don't remember. We found so much to talk about.'

This can't be happening to me, thought Declan. I don't feel anything. It's as though we're discussing two characters in a play.

'But why Tony? Bas I can understand, but not –' for the first time he betrayed any emotion – 'not that filthy venomous toad.'

Maud looked at him for a moment, her hand gently stroking Claudius's ears.

'Because he was kind, because he listened to me, because he was interested in me as a person – not just as a hole between two legs.'

Her sudden uncharacteristic coarseness shocked Declan almost more than her betrayal.

'Tony!' he said in amazement, 'kind?'

Suddenly Maud flipped. 'You're so obsessed with your fucking franchise,' she yelled, 'you don't know anyone else exists, except when you want to fuck them. You couldn't even forget it for one moment to get back for my first night, when I really needed you. Christ – I needed you! And then swanning in and ordering me away from my own first-night party.

'I was only fooling around with Tony until then. It was only after that that it got serious. He arranged for me to meet Pascoe Rawlings. He saw that a car delivered me to Pascoe's office last week and brought me back. He fixed for me to be driven to the audition today, and even though he'd got his

IBA meeting this afternoon, he still rang me this evening to see how I'd got on. You'd even forgotten I was going.' She laughed; it was a horrible sound without any merriment. 'The great interviewer, so praised for his judgement of character and his consideration to the staff, who doesn't know a thing about his own wife.'

'Can't you understand that he's using you?' said Declan slowly. 'The only thing that turns Tony on is acquisition. You've just lost us the franchise, and you were going to stand by and let me blame Cameron.'

'Serve her right – arrogant little bitch,' cried Maud hysterically.

Outside in the hall Taggie could hear her mother's screams getting louder and louder. Oh God, her father didn't need upsetting any more when he had the IBA meeting in the morning. Next moment the drawing-room door burst open.

'I'm leaving you,' screamed Maud.

'Come back,' roared Declan.

'Never, and don't send Ursula looking for me at the Lost Property Office, because I won't be there.' She shot past Taggie and out of the front door, banging it so hard the whole hall rattled.

Taggie ran to open it. Outside it was snowing again. She watched Maud drive off in her car, hell for leather, down the drive.

'What on earth's the matter?' she said, turning to Declan, who was standing as if blasted white by lightning.

'She was the mole.'

Taggie gave a gasp. 'She couldn't be. She can't have meant to.'

'She did,' said Declan in a voice of utter despair, 'because I neglected her. It's all my fault. I blamed Cameron last night and Rupert today, and just now I blamed her. But through my focking obsession and hubris I've brought us all down.'

50

For Rupert next morning the press was crucifixion – ranging from highly moralistic pieces about the chronic Tory failure to keep their noses clean to double-page spreads with pictures charting the rise and fall of the Tory party golden boy. The tabloids had dug up several of Rupert's more bitter exes, who, having done a great deal more than kiss, were now only too happy to tell. The seamiest tabloid of all had a huge frontpage headline: 'Campbell-Blackguard,' above an enchanting picture of Tabitha.

'In the playground of exclusive Bluebell's school (fees £1,500 a term),' ran the copy, 'a little child sobs alone. In a voice hardly above a whisper, Tabitha Campbell-Black told the Scorpion:

'"I don't mind my friends not playing with me any more, but I don't want Daddy to die of AIDS."'

'This is the final fucking limit,' howled Billy Lloyd-Foxe, hurling the Scorpion across the room. 'I'm coming with you to the IBA.'

'The Beeb will sack you if they find out,' said Janey, who was painting her nails because it was less hassle than cleaning them. 'And as I turned down a hundred grand yesterday to tell all about our life with Rupert, and this suit cost nearly as much, I don't think you can afford to.'

'I don't care,' said Billy mutinously. 'Rupert's my best friend, and anyway since Beattie implied I was gay yesterday, I shall certainly be snapped up by Radio 3.'

At Freddie's house, the remnants of the Venturer consortium gathered before the meeting. With no Bishop, no Professor, no Cameron and none of the moles, their numbers were utterly depleted and their bid in tatters. The second day of Rupert's memoirs was even worse, with intimations of underage school girls. Freddie had spent half the night trying to persuade a demented Declan that they'd got to shop Tony, not just for seducing Maud and bugging their houses, but because Seb was working on excellent evidence that Tony had bribed Beattie Johnson to sing to the rooftops, just at a time when it would be most damaging to Venturer.

But like Wellington at Waterloo refusing to turn the guns on the enemy commandant, Declan refused to let anyone condemn Tony. He didn't want Maud's name dragged into it. He was clearly still suffering from shock. He looked terrible.

'A black ram is tupping my white ewe,' he kept saying over and over again, 'and it was all my fault.'

Rupert, who arrived with Bas, didn't look much better, but at least he'd got a grip on himself. The meeting had to be got through. There were people not to be let down, there would be the rest of his life to mourn for Taggie and probably his children as well. Helen had rung this morning, saying she was applying for a court order to deny him access.

Even Henry Hampshire arrived walking wounded, wearing a dark suit with uncharacteristically flared trousers, and with his leg in plaster.

'Horse put its foot down a rabbit hole,' was all he would say about it.

''Morning.' He went up to Rupert, who was huddled on the sofa trying to keep down a cup of coffee. 'Enjoying your memoirs; great stuff.' He lowered his voice. 'I had a crack at Mandy Hamilton myself twenty years ago. God, she was pretty. Might have made more progress if I'd known she liked having her bottom smacked.'

Rupert managed a pale smile. 'At least it kept you out of the papers.' Then, also lowering his voice, he added, 'Look,

I don't think there's any chance now of us getting the franchise. Tony's now odds on and we've gone way out.'

'Better have a bet then,' said Henry, limping towards the telephone. 'Anyway, I've had more fun in the last six months than I can ever remember. We'll have to bid for another area next time.'

Dame Enid arrived next, resplendent in a pinstriped trouser suit with an even wider white stripe than Tony's, a bright blue tie, and an Al Capone hat.

'Stick 'em up, it's a shoot out,' said Marti Gluckstein, who came with her. He was dressed in a lurid green Norfolk jacket and knickerbockers, and sucking on a pipe.

'Did you get that at Valerie's boutique?' said Bas, then hastily shut up in case Freddie overheard.

'Thought I ought to appear as the country squire,' said Marti. 'Where's the Bishop?'

'Pulled out, I'm afraid,' said Freddie, handing him and Dame Enid cups of coffee.

'Good riddance, pompous old fart,' said Dame Enid, helping herself to sugar. 'Can't you pull a rabbi out of a hat to replace him?' she added to Marti.

Marti smirked. 'For you, my dear, anything.'

'Crispin Graystock's pulled out too,' said Freddie.

'Well, thank God we've got rid of the two worst wafflers,' said Dame Enid philosophically. 'Graystock's got complete verbal diarrhoea.'

'Which reminds me,' said Henry, hobbling off at great speed towards the lavatory, 'had the most ghastly trots all night. Sure I'm going to botch my answers.'

The moment he arrived, Lord Smith went straight up to Rupert. 'Really feel for you, lad,' he said. 'But everyone regards the *Scorpion* as fiction. That Beastly Johnson did me over once. Took down what I said, but twisted it like barley sugar. I've got a message from Alf Smithers. Chairman of the FA,' he added, by way of illumination, when Rupert didn't react.

'I know,' said Rupert flatly. 'He was my cross.'

'He's not cross now. Told me to wish you luck today. Said

you were the best Sports Minister they've ever 'ad. They all wish you'd come back. What's up with Declan?'

'Wife trouble,' said Rupert.

'Happens at franchise time,' said Lord Smith. 'When we bid for the Midlands eight years ago, the wives got so fed up, they was all at it – even mine.'

'Only two more to come,' said Freddie, trying to cheer up his own and everyone's spirits. 'And 'ere they are,' he went on, as Seb and Charles came through the door.

'We're going to have a fuller house than you thought,' said Charles. 'I've just seen Billy, Janey, Harold White and Sally Maples getting out of a taxi.'

Freddie had tears in his eyes as he welcomed them. 'You shouldn't have come. It's totally out of order,' he said. 'I know what you're risking, but I won't say I'm not bloody pleased to see you.'

Declan seemed hardly to notice, but Rupert's jaw quilted with muscles when he saw Billy. 'You're fucking insane,' he said roughly.

'I like "lorst" causes, as Henry would say,' said Billy cheerfully. 'Anyway, I brought you luck at the LA Olympics. And you brought me luck, too. If I hadn't done the commentary for the BBC, they'd never have given me a job.'

'Which you're about to lose.'

As the hands of the clock inched past nine-thirty, they decided that there was no point waiting any longer. Cameron wasn't coming.

'Pity,' sighed Hardy Bissett, going round straightening ties. 'Now, don't forget, no sniping – solidarity is all. Sit up straight. Burst with enthusiasm. You're bursting a little too much, Janey darling.' He did up two buttons of her shirt. 'Although, on reflection, if you're sitting anywhere near the Prebendary, undo them again and press your elbows together.'

It was still bitterly cold when they set out for the IBA in their cars. The snow in the park was the colour of dirty seagulls. In High Street, Ken. the shop windows with their jolly snowmen, spangled Christmas trees and muffled bright-eyed tots hurling snowballs were at variance with the sullen sky outside, and the shoppers shuffling blue-lipped and bad-tempered along the slushy pavements.

Janey's scent was making Rupert feel sick. In a greengrocer's shop, he noticed, they were already selling mistletoe, the one thing he wouldn't need this Christmas.

'Oh look, there's Father Christmas,' said Janey, pressing a button to lower the window, as the car swung round The Scotch House into Brompton Road.

'Please Santa,' she called out to him, as he marched alongside the car, 'will you put a franchise in my stocking?'

'Ho, ho, ho,' said Father Christmas, hoisting his sack onto his back and batting his long black eyelashes at Janey. 'For a pretty little girl like you, I just might.'

'My Christ,' said Janey, with a scream of laughter, as he turned right in front of the car and strode purposefully across the road through the revolving doors of the IBA. 'It's Georgie Baines.'

'I wish I'd thought of that,' said Charles petulantly. 'I wanted to come as Gwendolyn Gosling again, but I thought I'd better play it straight.'

To avoid the press, and preserve the utmost security, the convoy of cars turned right down Lancelot Place, entering the IBA from the back by the underground car park. From here their passengers were whisked up to the eighth floor and, although the moles nervously looked for reporters in every dark corner, they were all safely led along the corridor and installed in an empty office.

'I feel like a courtier waiting for an audience with Louis XIV: "Please don't banish me to my estate in the Loire, Sire",' said Charles, as he peered out of the window on to another IBA block of offices, where every secretary seemed to be clutching paper cups of coffee and reading Rupert's memoirs.

'God, I'm nervous,' said Henry, mouthing the answers to possible questions. 'D'you think I should say brilliant wild life "photographer" or "cameraman"?'

'Cameraman,' said Billy. 'Photographer is press, and we don't like them very much at the moment.'

'I wish I could take in a calculator,' said Marti in a hollow voice.

'D'you think they'll shine lights in our faces?' asked Janey.

'They didn't yesterday, but then Corinium has a better track record,' said a voice. It was Georgie Baines, who'd shed his Father Christmas disguise and was now wearing a dark suit and fluffing up his dark curls.

Everyone crowded round him in delight.

'Of course! You went in yesterday afternoon with Corinium,' said Freddie.

'Wearing a different tie,' said Georgie.

'How long were you in there?' asked Seb.

'Exactly an hour,' said Georgie.

'What was it like?'

'Falling off a log. Not one difficult question. Tony's star is definitely in the ascendant, that's why *I'm* here. I've always believed rats should desert a rising shit.'

'How did you manage to get away?' asked Janey, removing a last bit of white beard from Georgie's chin.

'Tony thinks I'm at Saatchi's.'

A female IBA official was going spare trying to organize everyone's entrance into the board room in a pre-ordained order, so the Authority would know who they were.

'I expected eleven people,' she said in bewilderment. 'There seem a great many more. I know who you are,' she said to Janey, 'and you,' she said to Rupert, keeping her distance, 'and you,' she turned to Declan, looking perplexed as though she hardly recognized him.

'Are you the Bishop of Cotchester?' she asked Marti as she consulted her notes. Everyone giggled. 'And I wasn't expecting you, Mr White, or you, Billy, or you, Miss Maples, and certainly not you *again*, Mr Baines.'

'Well we're all here,' said Harold White. 'We belong to Venturer.'

'Have you all got your two photographs?'

Everyone duly produced them.

'Had to go into Woolworths to get it taken,' announced Henry. 'Never been there before. Rather a lark.'

The female official scratched her head in despair: 'And where's Cameron Cook?'

'Not coming, nor the Bishop, nor Professor Graystock. They've dropped out,' said Freddie helpfully. 'Nor Wesley Emerson. He's still wiv us, but he's playing in a test match abroad.'

'No, I'm not,' said a voice deeper than the Caribbean Sea.

It was Wesley in a Support Venturer T-shirt and an England blazer. He was greeted with screams of delight. Dame Enid thumped him on the back till he pleaded for mercy.

'How did you manage to get away?'

'Pulled a muscle, man,' said Wesley, grinning from ear to ear. 'But I haven't slept all night, so I hope there's no tricky questions about ethnic minorities.'

Rupert took him aside. 'You really are fantastic,' he said.

Wesley grinned. 'I read all that shit about you, man. Same thing happened to me; thought we ought to show a united front.'

'I really think I've got you all sorted out,' said the IBA lady. 'I'll just check that Lady Gosling's ready.'

After that there was a dreadful quarter of an hour wait.

'It's just like standing outside the headmaster's study,' said Seb. 'Are we going to have to run round the pitch fifty times or get six of the best?'

'Amanda Hamilton'd like that,' said Charles. Then, seeing the bleak expression on Rupert's face, 'Oh come on, Rupert, one's got to laugh.'

Rupert, who'd been thinking of Taggie, didn't really think one did have to.

'Must go to the lavatory,' said Henry.

'Will you all come in, please?' said the IBA lady.

'Good luck, everyone,' said Freddie.

'Remember the old bat who isn't Lady Gosling is Mrs Menzies-Scott, ex-chairman of the WI,' hissed Georgie.

The twelve members of the authority, flanked by six senior staff from the IBA, were already seated along one side of the beautifully polished oval table, as Venturer filed in and took up their places opposite them.

In the centre sat Lady Gosling in a thick brown tweed suit and a bottle-green cardigan. Despite the warmth of the room, a thermal vest could be seen peeping above her brown check shirt. Mrs Scott-Menzies of the WI, who'd been foolish enough to wear a rust angora jersey, had already turned puce in the heat. Other members of the panel included such worthies as the ex-Labour Minister for Education, who gave Lord Smith the ghost of a wink, a Welsh Judge Davey, a Catholic bishop, the Prebendary, who had an expression of extreme distaste on his face, several dons, two ex-chairmen from public companies, and Lady Barnsley, late of the White Fish Authority, who was alleged to have an orgasm every time she saw a celebrity. Handbag rammed protectively against her groin, she was now gazing at Rupert with a mixture of terror and excitement. Three other Authority members, who'd been avidly reading the memoirs, hastily shoved them away as Venturer came in.

'I wish I'd brought my autograph book,' whispered Judge Davey, who was generally regarded as the group wag.

Freddie sat in the middle facing Lady Gosling, flanked by Rupert and Declan. On Rupert's right, as obvious and disfiguring as a lost front tooth, was a space where Cameron should have been. Janey was up the end of the table, with only Henry beyond her, so he could stick out his plaster leg. The Prebendary sat opposite them, gazing at Janey with pursed lips. Surreptitiously, she undid a couple of the buttons of her grey silk shirt. It was like dining at Lady Margaret Hall, she thought as she looked at the worthy unpainted faces of the women opposite. She wished she'd soft-pedalled her eye make-up.

Henry was gazing out of the window at Knightsbridge Barracks. 'Used to work there,' he announced in a loud whisper. 'You'd never believe there was a squash court on top.'

Lady Gosling, who had not winked at her friend Dame Enid, greeted them with the utmost coolness.

'I'm sorry you were kept waiting so long. It was because of the very considerable changes in the numbers attending. I see all the so-called "moles" –' one could feel her fastidiously putting quotes round such a slang word – 'have decided to show up, despite the threat of dismissal, and we certainly weren't expecting you,' she added to Wesley. 'We gathered you were playing in a test match.'

Wesley gave her the benefit of his heavenly banana-split smile.

'I was, Mrs Menzies-Scott.'

'Gosling,' hissed Janey.

'I'm sorry, Mrs Gosling, I got injured. And coming to this meeting seemed more important. After all, we'll be running a television company for a long long time.'

'Hum,' said Lady Gosling. 'Somewhat hubristic of you. And where are the Bishop and Professor Graystock?'

Freddie cleared his throat.

'Er, they've withdrawn because of a conflict of interests.'

'One can understand that,' said Lady Gosling heavily.

'And Cameron Cook?'

Freddie opened his mouth.

'I'm here,' said a voice behind him. 'I'm so sorry, Lady Gosling, my cab ran into another car in the Old Brompton Road.'

It was Cameron in her scarlet silk suit, bringing a wonderful warmth and colour into the room. She was very pale beneath her blusher, and wearing tinted glasses, but totally self-possessed. Sliding into the seat beside Rupert, she very deliberately put a hand over his, then smiling down the row said once again: 'I'm so sorry, everyone.'

'You little beauty,' said Freddie under his breath.

Cameron's arrival seemed to pull Venturer magically together. The first questions were about finance and technical specifications, and initially fielded by Freddie. Then, like a tigerish scrum-half, he passed the ball out to his wings,

Rupert, Bas, Lord Smith, Marti, and Georgie Barnes, who'd arrived with a pile of revenue forecasts.

Freddie in fact was the life and soul of the application. A born showman, puffing on his cigar, giving occasional infectious roars of laughter, he exuded honesty, energy and huge enthusiasm for the task.

The Prebendary, who was still looking beady, didn't throw Wesley on ethnic minorities, but, seeing him yawning, asked him why he personally wished to oust Corinium as the franchise holder.

'I live in the area, man,' drawled Wesley. 'I'm absolutely fed up, like everyone else in this consortium, with having to watch such God-awful programmes.'

Even Lady Gosling suppressed a smile, and nodded to Lady Barnsley, who rather nervously asked if the applicant's programme plans were based on its view of the characteristics and needs of the franchise area. It was a sod. There was a long pause.

'Almost entirely,' said Cameron. 'We all know and love and live in the area, so we want to put something back, and give it a regional identity. We want to make friends with the viewers, to make them feel part of one great Venturer family.

'But our approach would be the same if we were pitching for any area in the British Isles. Great television comes from telling people the truth, from entertaining them so well they don't realize they're being educated. We want to make documentaries and dramas that tackle the problems we all face, coping with unemployment, loneliness, adolescence, being in love. Even –' she smiled, testing the age group of the panel – 'with the traumas of having one's grandchildren to stay over Christmas.' The panel smiled warmly back.

'Cameron can hardly say this for herself,' chipped in Charles, 'but I'd just like to add that with her and Declan, we have the most exciting team to hit the screen since Ivory and Merchant. They've both been in Ireland making a film on Yeats for Channel Four. I saw the uncut version last week. It is utter magic and will bring Yeats's poetry and the beauty of the Irish countryside to millions of new viewers. It would be nice to think they could do the same for the Cotswold area.'

Lady Gosling nodded sagely, noticing, however, that Declan was gazing blankly into space and taking no part in the proceedings.

Everyone drank a great deal of Highland Spring water. Dame Enid and Charles were superb on the arts; Billy charmed all the panel on sport; Janey had some wonderful ideas for women's interests; Seb made them laugh on news coverage, saying that the Corinium Head of News was so idle, he consulted his opposite number at the BBC every morning, so they could both cover the same local events, and there would be absolutely no danger of either of them being bawled out for scooping the other.

Henry started off brilliantly when Judge Davey asked him about his involvement in the consortium. He was just waxing lyrical on capturing the wild life of the area on film, and appearing to scratch his plaster for the third time, when Janey suddenly realized he was pulling up the flare of his trousers and reading the whole thing off his plaster and got the most frightful giggles. Terrified that the Prebendary, who was sitting next to Henry, would take his eyes off her bosom for one second and see what Henry was up to, Janey nudged Henry sharply in the ribs.

'Ouch! — shrews, voles, badgers,' ended Henry lamely, dropping his trouser-leg and thus losing his impromptu autocue.

'I love badgers,' said Lady Barnsley, looking very excited. 'We've got some in our wood.'

'Have you really?' said Henry. 'So have we, and so has Declan actually. I passed two big chaps having a fight in my drive the other night. They were so preoccupied, I managed to get really close up.'

'Did you really?' said Lady Barnsley.

Lady Gosling, however, had had enough about badgers. She looked straight at Declan, who was still slumped in his chair totally unrecognizable from the dazzlingly charismatic, self-confident demagogue who'd laid into Tony Baddingham at the public meeting.

'Who is going to run the company?' she asked him.

'I'm chairman,' said Freddie, when Declan didn't answer. 'I intend to devote at least one day a week to Venturer if not more. 'Enry's non-executive deputy chairman, Rupert'll handle finance and admin with Harold. Declan and Cameron will oversee programmes. Georgie will be in charge of sales. Charles, Janey, Sally, Billy and Seb will all be Heads of various departments. Marti, Bas, Lord Smiff, Dame Enid an' Wesley will be non-executive directors. But they'll all act on a consultancy basis, and add to the smooth running of the company.'

'But who is really going to run the company?' persisted Lady Gosling.

No contribution was clearly forthcoming from Declan, so Rupert looked at Lady Gosling squarely. 'I am,' he said.

'I would have thought,' said Lady Gosling icily, 'that your very limited business experience doesn't include the creation of new companies. It's a tough skill to acquire.'

'When I was twenty-one,' snapped Rupert, 'I started my own show-jumping business, which has now developed into a yard, which turns over ten million a year. I'm also an MP, and on top of all this I ran an extremely successful sports ministry for four years. I shall also have the constant and incredibly able advice of all my directors, particularly Harold, who's been in charge of LWT's programmes for the last few years.'

'The entire Board would support Rupert as Chief Executive,' said Bas.

All of Venturer murmured their assent except Wesley who was sleeping peacefully.

'He did come on an overnight flight,' explained Janey, giving him a nudge.

'Howzat,' said Wesley, waking up.

Lady Gosling looked with infinite disapproval from Wesley to Declan, to Rupert to Billy, then up the table to Janey. 'Don't you feel there are too many celebrities, too many prima donnas in your consortium? Can you honestly convince us that Venturer will be able to stick effectively together as a team?'

'Yes,' said Rupert evenly, once more looking her straight in the eye. 'It hasn't been an easy week with my so-called "memoirs" coming out, but except for the Bishop and the Professor, we're all here, aren't we?'

Lady Gosling dropped her eyes first.

Glancing at the clock on the wall, Cameron could see they'd been in there an hour and a half. Was that a good sign, or did the IBA merely want to prove Venturer's inferiority beyond doubt? Knowing nothing about Maud's affair with Tony, she had also realized there was something seriously wrong with Declan. He hadn't contributed to the discussion at all. By now he ought to be revving up for his final peroration, tearing Corinium limb from limousine, but he was saying nothing.

She looked down the row, at Janey and Billy radiating panache and glamour and high spirits when she knew how desperately broke they were, at Charles who had no future if Venturer went down, at Georgie, Sally and Harold, who'd certainly jeopardized their careers, at Henry dreaming of bosoms and badgers, at Wesley who'd flown thousands of miles to support them and probably jeopardized his test career as well, at Rupert who, despite the devastating blows that had been dealt him that week, had performed so incredibly bravely, and back to Declan, who had taught her humanity. They were her friends, the people she most wanted to work with.

Lady Gosling looked at her watch, and poured herself a glass of Highland Spring. 'Well, we've listened to you all, and studied your bulky application. Has anyone anything else to say?'

There was a long agonizing pause:

'I have,' said Cameron, getting to her feet, as slim and brave in her red suit as the young Portia.

'Ladies and Gentlemen, last week at one of the northern

684

television stations a young Head of News hanged himself.' She glanced along the row of shocked reproving faces. 'Sure, we've all been fed the official story that he had domestic and financial problems. The truth was he couldn't handle all the pressures in the run-up to the franchise awards. He was being so bullied to get so many different lobbies, local worthies, friends of his Managing Director on to his programme to impress you, the IBA, so that his lousy bosses could keep their franchise and go on making a fortune. This is a tragedy and a disgrace,' went on Cameron fiercely, 'and an appalling indictment on the whole IBA and ITV system. We in production should not feel we've got to put on worthy uplifting boring programmes every eight years in order to impress you and retain the franchise. We should make good programmes all the time.'

She turned, pointing to the framed document on the wall, giving the IBA its own coat of arms and motto: 'Your motto is *Servire populo*. But you're not serving the people if you're encouraging the companies to make programmes that please you, which you feel the people ought to watch, rather than what they want to watch. I worked for Tony Baddingham for four years,' she went on bitterly.

'And produced some very good uplifting programmes that weren't boring,' said Lady Gosling dryly.

Cameron grinned. *'Touché.'* Then instantly she became serious again. 'But that was because Tony Baddingham was *inordinately* fond of me and gave me *carte blanche* to ride roughshod over all the staff, and also gave me an unlimited budget, while cutting the budgets of all other programmes to nothing. Morale at Corinium was and is absolutely rock bottom.

'Declan O'Hara —' she looked at Declan, pleading with him to glance up or react in some way — 'is one of the all-time greats of television. But when he was at Corinium, he was very nearly broken by Tony, who forced him to interview people of total insignificance, big businessmen, local dignitaries, people whose influence he believed he needed to win the franchise. Fortunately Declan escaped and formed Venturer.

I've spent the last two months working with him and learnt that you don't need to terrorize people, or reduce them to hanging themselves, to make good programmes. Once you've got the authority, if you'll forgive the pun, you get far more out of people by kindness and interest in their welfare.'

The Welsh judge put on his spectacles for a better look at Cameron. Really she was a most astonishingly attractive girl. She could read for the Bar if ever she got fed up with television.

'ITV audience figures are plummeting,' went on Cameron accusingly, 'because so many of the programmes are so awful, and because most of the companies are run by accountants who aren't prepared to take risks any more. Why spend ten million on a serial which may fail, when for peanuts you can buy a quiz from another company?

'Venturer's going to change all that. We're going to revitalize ITV and not only make really good programmes right across the board, but also change the scheduling of the whole network so it's based on an exact analysis of what the public wants. At the moment it is simply a ragbag of whatever happens to be lying around, or fits in with the resources of the contributing company. We know what difficulties lie ahead. We know we can't produce profitable results if we have to make continually uplifting programmes. We'll need your help, understanding and guidance all along the way. But I promise you, unlike Corinium, we are not April when we woo, and December when we wed. I'm sorry, I've gone on too long.' She collapsed back into her chair, embarrassed.

It was some comfort that Rupert put his hand over hers with real pride.

'Normally your chairman would sum up at this stage, but I think we've all heard quite enough about Venturer's policy from Miss Cook,' said Lady Gosling. 'Thank you all for coming.'

After all the effort it was a very curt dismissal. Feeling utterly despondent, Venturer filed out of the room. Even worse, as they were smuggled out of the underground car park they went slap into the press, who were out in force clamouring to get a quote from Rupert about the memoirs. Fortunately they concentrated on getting pictures of him and didn't notice the rest of the moles cringing inside the convoy of cars.

For want of anything better to do, they all went back to Freddie's for a wake. On the way there, Janey, Billy and Freddie told Cameron about Declan and Maud.

'But the IBA ought to be told,' stormed Cameron. 'Someone's got to wise them up what an absolute bastard Tony is.'

'You made a pretty good job of it just now,' said Freddie. 'And Declan won't hear of it.'

As soon as he got to Freddie's, Rupert took Cameron aside.

'Thank you for turning up, sweetheart. You were absolutely marvellous.'

Cameron shrugged. 'If you can get a gold with a dislocated shoulder, I can talk too much with a broken heart.'

'Christ, I admire you.'

'I'd so much rather you'd loved me,' said Cameron sadly.

For a second Rupert lowered her dark glasses, and winced to see how red and swollen from crying her eyes were.

'I'm so sorry, angel. You know you can stay on at Penscombe as long as you like. I won't be there for the next few weeks.'

'Where are you going?' asked Cameron, suddenly frantic.

'America, this afternoon. The only hope is to get the hell out of England until the dust settles.'

'So you won't be back for Christmas?'

Rupert shook his head wearily. 'What Christmas?'

'Or for the IBA verdict on the 15th?'

'The result's a foregone conclusion. Couldn't you feel the tidal waves of disapproval and distaste emanating from those tweed bosoms throughout the interview? We haven't a hope.'

'Probably not,' said Cameron, glancing at Declan who was now slumped in a chair, shivering uncontrollably with an untouched glass of whisky in his hand. 'But Declan's going to need a lot of support in the next few days.'

'Not from me,' said Rupert bitterly. 'The best thing for all

687

the O'Haras would be to have me out of their hair.' He looked at his watch. 'I'd better be off.'

'Can I ask you just one favour?' said Cameron. 'Could I possibly keep Blue?'

The doorbell rang and they both jumped thinking it might be Taggie. Freddie's secretary answered it and the next moment a man marched into the room. For a second Cameron thought she was hallucinating, for it seemed as if the old Declan, the forceful, confident, aggressive, clear-eyed, sun-tanned Declan, whom she remembered so clearly that first day he arrived at Corinium, had just walked through the door. Then she realized it was Patrick, thickened out, weath-ered and bronzed from five months working on a sheep farm. He'd obviously come straight from the airport, and being Patrick, even in a family crisis, had bothered to buy duty free whisky and cigarettes. He'd need them both over the next few days.

Near to tears, Declan rose to his feet. Ignoring everyone else in the room, Patrick went over and put his arms round him.

'It's all right, Pa,' he said gently, 'I rang home first. Taggie told me about Mum. It was a terrible thing for her to do, but she had reasons. It'll be all right. It's you she loves. She'll come back.'

He was like the father comforting the child.

'She sabotaged the franchise,' groaned Declan, 'and it was all my fault.'

'Rubbish,' said Patrick. 'The responsibility for that lies elsewhere.'

He let go of Declan and turned towards Rupert, his face hardening. 'You deliberately set out to seduce Cameron be-cause you wanted her on Venturer's side, didn't you? Well that's for fucking *her* up.' The next moment he'd smashed his fist into Rupert's right jaw and, as Rupert reeled sideways, caught totally by surprise, Patrick hit him again on the right eye with his other fist. 'And that's for fucking up Taggie,' he added, as Rupert crashed to the ground.

In the press over the weekend there was endless speculation

as to which of the wronged husbands named in Rupert's bonk-statement (as the memoirs were now known), had given Rupert the black eye.

RIVALS
51

The next two weeks were terrible for Venturer. Deeply guilty that his utter failure to pull himself together at the meeting had finally cost them the franchise, Declan went home to Penscombe. Taggie and Patrick made sure he was never alone, as he seemed to sink deeper and deeper into depression, constantly vacillating between loathing Maud for betraying him and longing to have her back. There was no word from her; she seemed to have totally vanished.

Patrick, displaying patience and understanding way beyond his years, spent hours talking to his father: 'Taggie said Mum was absolutely gibbering with terror before *The Merry Widow*. It was such a colossal distance from obscurity back to the limelight. A little amateur production perhaps to you, but to her it wasn't just an extra step to cross the Frogsmore, but a vast leap over a five-hundred-foot-deep ravine. She needed you so desperately to witness her triumph or catch her if she fell.'

'I know,' groaned Declan. 'Because I always had to fight so hard to keep her, I never realized how much she needed me.'

'And you know she lives any part she plays. In her head she's now become poor bullied Nora in *A Doll's House*, marching out with a slammed door on an insensitive tyrannical husband. She wanted to hit back, to slam the door on your figures.

'And finally you mustn't underestimate the influence of Tony Baddingham. I know the effect he had on Cameron. He is pure Iago. He only had to point out how brilliant, beautiful and sexually voracious Cameron was; how you were spending more and more time with her; how could the two of you *not* be having an affair? You know what an imagination Mum has. This was even more immediate than P. D. James. Imagine, too, the appalling things he must have said about you, and finally the escape from poverty he offered her: new dresses, new jewels, furs, no more brown envelopes, or creditors at the gate, even warmth.' Patrick shivered. After the Australian summer The Priory central heating left a great deal to be desired. 'And he was around all the time, and you were away, or preoccupied with the franchise or Yeats, and Mum was probably turned on because the whole thing was so utterly *verboten*. All he had to do was to switch on his electric carving knife, dip it in washing-up machine powder and turn it in the wound.'

Declan winced: 'I can understand all that, but deliberately to hand over all our secrets.'

'She may not have done,' said Patrick. 'Taggie was out a lot cooking. Tony probably came to the house. The plans were on your desk. Your writing isn't *that* indecipherable.'

'D'you think I should go round to The Falconry and kill him?'

Patrick gave a wintry smile. 'I wouldn't. You know how Lady Gosling abhors violence.'

Taggie, who was kept enormously busy cooking for parties and filling up people's deep freezes for Christmas, made heroic attempts to be cheerful, but she worried Patrick far more than Declan. Never one to grumble, she refused to discuss Rupert, but Patrick knew she was bleeding to death inside.

Outside, the weather was frantically warmer, the snow thawed in patches, leaving fantastic shapes, a sea horse there, a camel here. All down the valley the streams that tumbled into the Frogsmore were still frozen into dirty grey glaciers. Wandering numbly through the fields with the dogs, Taggie only noticed the flattened tufts of thick tawny grass sticking up through the snow, like the heads of a thousand Ruperts slain in battle.

'*Too long a sacrifice,*' quoted Patrick bitterly, thinking too of his own situation, '*can make a stone of the heart.*'

Cameron, mercifully, was still very busy editing Yeats (Declan had lost all interest in the project), and setting up the programme on stepmothers which Channel Four had commissioned. She popped over on several occasions to cheer Declan up, but managed to avoid times when Patrick was at home. Patrick didn't know if she'd gone back to Tony, or whether Tony was looking after his mother. He and Taggie decided it would be better to do nothing until after the franchise results were announced.

Sunday, 15th December was D-Day. The form was that from nine o'clock onwards, in an atmosphere of high drama and secrecy, the existing managing directors of all the commercial television companies would roll up at the IBA in their limos at quarter of an hour intervals. Driving past the battalions of reporters, photographers and camera crews, they would be ushered once again into the building from the underground car park and be whizzed up in the lift to yet another empty office. Here, not unlike the suitors in *The Merchant of Venice*, they would be handed a sealed envelope from Lady Gosling and then be left alone to open it and learn if they had held onto their franchise, or whether, as in some instances, they had to merge with their rivals. Allowed a few minutes to digest this information, they would then be summoned to Lady Gosling's office for a brief word of congratulation or commiseration. Afterwards they would leave the building by the back door or by the front, having sworn not to reveal a word of the results to the press. After all the existing contractors had been seen, the contenders, who hoped to depose them, would come in one by one after lunch and endure the same procedure.

At four-thirty Lady Gosling would call a press conference to announce the results, which would simultaneously be rushed to the Stock Exchange and the Home Secretary, who would inform the Prime Minister.

Tony Baddingham was so certain he had retained the Corinium franchise that he'd taken a suite overnight at the Hyde Park Hotel.

Expectation had been boosted by front-page forecasts in most of the Sunday papers of a definite Corinium victory. The Krug was therefore flowing at a reception for the press and for all Tony's Corinium supporters, as he left for his twelve o'clock appointment with the IBA.

Tony was relieved the contenders weren't being seen until the afternoon. He would need police protection if he met Declan in the lift. He preferred to gloat over Venturer's utter humiliation at a distance.

It was a bitterly cold grey day, with an icy wind, which razor-cut the face far more effectively than any East End villain. Rather than walk the two hundred yards from the Hyde Park Hotel to the IBA, Tony made Percy drive round the park and approach 80 Brompton Road from South Kensington. Innumerable cameramen and journalists were mingling on the pavement with the Christmas shoppers as his Rolls drew up.

Never one to resist publicity, Tony decided to go in through the front door and let Percy take the Rolls round to the car park. There was a frenzy of activity and popping of flashbulbs as he got out. Tony had always kept a high profile; most of the press recognized him. Posing for thirty seconds in his Garrick tie and new £900 suit, he told the grey forest of microphones that he didn't believe in jumping the gun, but he was confident, quietly confident, that he'd still be in business that afternoon, before scurrying through the revolving doors of the IBA.

'Arrogant focker,' snarled Declan who was watching ITN at Freddie's house. 'Don't talk about guns in my presence, you bastard.'

'Don't watch it,' said Patrick, switching off the television. 'It'll only upset you. You ought to change soon, and have a shave.'

'What's the point of looking pretty for a firing squad?'

The door bell rang. Declan started. Why did he pray each time it might be Maud?

'I'll answer it,' said Freddie.

Freddie's heart was heavy. He knew there was no hope of Venturer getting the franchise, but he'd tried to keep everyone's spirits up for the last two weeks and tried even harder to be a good husband to Valerie. In return Valerie hadn't even bothered to come up to London today, she so detested failure. But as Freddie peered through the spyhole, he felt his heart expand in joy and gratitude, for there, her face as red and purple with cold as a mandrill's bottom, stood Lizzie. Never was a door opened so fast. As he drew her into the house out of the sight of any lurking press, she fell into his arms.

'You shouldn't be here,' he mumbled incoherently.

'I know I shouldn't,' said Lizzie, 'but James is being so smug, and I couldn't sit around drinking Tony's champagne. I thought it would poison me.'

At Tony's house in Rutland Gate, totally oblivious of the franchise affair, with only thought for one another, Caitlin O'Hara and Archie Baddingham met up on the first day of the school holidays.

'Are you sure it's safe,' asked Caitlin as they went into Monica's bedroom, 'and your father won't descend down the chimney like Father Christmas?'

'No, they'll be whooping it up all day at the Hyde Park,' said Archie. 'And poor Mum will spend her time fending off kisses from ghastly drunken hangers-on like James Vereker. I'm sorry your father hasn't got it.'

'It's a shame,' said Caitlin. 'He worked jolly hard. So did Tag.'

'I'll support you,' said Archie, putting a bottle of Sancerre and two glasses on his mother's bedside table. 'Look, are you sure you want to go through with this, and wouldn't rather wait until after we're married?'

Caitlin, who, despite her habitual air of unconcern, was

trembling like an earthquake, shook her head. 'Most people sleep together first these days, just to find out whether they're sexually compatible. Anyway, I reached the age of consent last week. It's awfully tidy in here.' She looked round in amazement. 'You ought to see my parents' bedroom. D'you think we ought to put a red towel underneath us? It'd be so awful if I bled all over your mother's sheets.'

'What time is it?' whispered Archie.

'One forty-five,' said Caitlin, looking at the flickering red figures of the digital clock. 'Why?'

'I want to remember what time the most important thing in my life took place,' said Archie, as he unbuttoned her black cardigan.

He looks terrible, thought Taggie, as she brushed Declan's dark-blue suit and straightened his tie. The new Harvie and Hudson green-and-blue-striped shirt Cameron had bought him last week in honour of the occasion was already too big. In the last fortnight the thick black hair had become almost entirely silver, and despair and grief had dug even deeper trenches on his forehead and on either side of his mouth.

The clock struck two.

'Car's here, Declan,' called Freddie from the hall.

'Good luck,' said Taggie, hugging him. 'It'll be over in half an hour.'

One by one the members of Venturer shook Declan's hand and wished him well. Billy gave him the faded four-leaf clover he'd worn in his boot when he'd won the show-jumping silver in Colombia. Henry Hampshire gave him a piece of white heather, foisted on him by a gypsy outside Harrods that morning. Rupert had sent a telex from LA. Professor Graystock and the Bishop of Cotchester were no doubt at this moment enjoying their second helpings of roast beef in Gloucestershire. Everyone waved to Declan as he set off.

'Majestic though in ruin,' said Patrick ruefully.

'Not yet,' boomed Dame Enid. 'Don't be so defeatist, boy.'

•

The media went berserk as Declan's car drew up. It had been a long, cold, somewhat boring day. Not admitted inside the IBA for reasons of security, they had spent their time belting the hundred yards between the front of the building and the back, desperate to get a story. Managing Directors of television companies are enormously powerful but not always very well-known men. One camera crew had had the embarrassment of asking their own Chief Executive what television company he worked for. Another crew wasted a lot of film on their own press officer.

But everyone knew Declan. Many of the crews had worked with him, and loved him, and wished he could have won. The Christmas shoppers, battered by the cold and each other, knew him too, and cheered and mobbed him. It took him several minutes to fight his way across Brompton Road and, as he went in through the revolving doors, a fat woman gave him a piece of holly for good luck. Coming the other way was Johnny Abrahams, his old boss at the BBC who'd put in a bid to oust Granada.

'How did you do?' asked Declan.

'They told us to go home,' said Johnny despondently.

Declan was taken up in the grey steel lift to the eighth floor and ushered into a large office which said 'Members' Viewing Room' on the door. Inside, a lot of maroon chairs were lined up in front of a large screen. The grey telephone in the corner was dead. A smell of turkey drifted down the passage, the aftermath of Lady Gosling's festive lunch. Out of the window he could see Knightsbridge and the north-east corner of Harrods, strawberry roan against a sullen grey sky with its coloured flags fretted by the icy wind.

He looked down at the piece of holly which still had two red berries. It was nice that all those people had been pleased to see him. Perhaps one day, when he'd got this mockery of a franchise behind him, he might work again. He wondered what Maud was doing; probably celebrating at the Hyde Park Hotel with Tony by now. Directly below him was Lancelot Place. It was ironic that he was the Arthur who'd promised the IBA Camelot, and Tony was the Lancelot who'd stolen his Guinevere. Oh Christ, he groaned, how could he possibly ever do anything in life without her?

'Mr O'Hara.'

Declan started violently, looking round stupidly. A kind-faced woman in spectacles had walked through the door with a tray full of envelopes and handed a white one and a larger brown one to him.

'Your envelopes. Best of luck.'

'Thank you,' muttered Declan.

He waited politely until she'd gone, then shoved them in his coat pocket. Like bills, he never believed in opening unpleasant things. Out of the window he saw a group of horses and riders jingling back to the stables at Hyde Park, back to oats and a warm straw bed. Christ, how peaceful in life to be a horse. And how beautiful they were. He'd have to put The Priory on the market immediately, but he might get a day or two's hunting before he left.

'Mr O'Hara.'

'I'm sorry. I was just leaving.'

'Would you come upstairs and have a word with Lady Gosling?'

'Not much point really. Nice of her to bother, though.'

'She asked me to collect you,' said the bespectacled woman firmly.

Lady Gosling sat in her office, behind a huge desk. The Director General and his deputy sat on the sofa. The room was full of smoke. They'd obviously all had a good lunch.

'Good afternoon, Mr O'Hara.' Lady Gosling rose slightly, holding out her thin freckled hand.

Declan held out his, realized he was still holding the bit of holly, and blushed.

'Rather premature to celebrate,' said Lady Gosling dryly. 'I should sit down if I were you.'

Declan mumbled he would prefer to stand.

'Well,' she began sternly. 'There were certainly some patchy moments in your bid. Freddie Jones obviously has an exceptional grasp of finance, and Cameron Cook was first class. What a very bright, courageous girl. And, of course, some of your programme plans are extremely interesting.'

What's she going on about? thought Declan wearily. It was like a condemned man being told that he's got a really sympathetic hangman.

'Some of the publicity, on the other hand, has been perfectly frightful,' went on Lady Gosling fiercely. 'And your security left a lot to be desired. However, we were impressed by this.' She handed Declan some sheets of paper.

At the top of the first were three typewritten lines. It was a little time before Declan's tired eyes could make out what they said.

'We, the undersigned, wish to state we would like to support Declan O'Hara's bid for the Corinium franchise. He makes the kind of television we believe in, and in the brief time he was at Corinium we were all impressed by his utter integrity and kindness to staff at all levels. If his consortium were awarded the franchise we would all like to work for him.'

Slowly, slowly, Declan's eyes travelled down the list of names: Georgie Baines, Cyril Peacock, Daysee Butler, Deirdre Kilpatrick, Mike Meadows, then on to PAs, tea girls, secretaries, production buyers, designers, security men, receptionists, best boys, gaffers, producers, sparks, riggers, researchers, make-up girls, engineers, floor managers, directors, commissionaires, canteen ladies, sound men, vision mixers. He turned the page. The list went on in three columns down to the bottom of the next page, and then down to the bottom of the next and swam before his eyes.

Declan turned towards the window. The horses had all gone in. He pressed his hands to his eyes, his great shoulders shaking.

'That's a most impressive document,' said Lady Gosling gently. 'I should frame it and look at it if ever you feel low.'

Declan turned to her, frantically rubbing his eyes.

'I'm sorry to let them down,' he said in a choked voice. 'It was good of you to show it to me.'

'On the contrary,' said Lady Gosling. 'You haven't let them down at all. Why don't you open those envelopes.'

Still clutching his piece of holly, Declan's hands were trembling so much, he tore the white envelope and had to piece the letter together.

'*Dear Mr O'Hara,*' he read incredulously, '*We have great pleasure in telling you that the Venturer Consortium has been awarded the Corinium franchise.*'

Declan read the letter three times in silence. Then he opened the brown envelope, which contained contractual details.

'I wouldn't bother to try and absorb those at the moment,' chipped in the Director General, also in a slightly unsteady voice, 'but it's all good news. Well done.'

In silence Declan shook hands with them, then presented the piece of holly to Lady Gosling and walked out of the room. Totally forgetting Freddie's driver waiting in the underground car park, he took a lift to the ground floor. Outside the building the press surged forward.

'How d'yer do, Declan?'

Then, seeing he was fighting back the tears, they divided and let him through as he walked unsteadily off in the general direction of Holland Park.

Gathered round the radio, because there was no television news till six o'clock, the Venturer consortium pounced on every bit of news. A great cheer went up when the reporter said that Tony Baddingham had been seen driving away from the building looking stony-faced.

'Perhaps we haven't come to another wake, after all,' said Freddie, in amazement. 'Let's have a drink anyway.'

'Maybe the IBA want us to merge in some way with Corinium,' suggested Cameron.

'Count me out then,' said Charles. 'I'd rather stay on the dole.'

They all jumped as the wireless crackled.

'The latest news on the franchise front,' said the commentator, 'is that Declan O'Hara has just come out of the IBA building in tears, so I'm afraid things look bleak for Venturer. He's just walked through the crowds and was last seen heading towards South Kensington tube station like a man in deep shock.'

Cameron looked at Patrick. 'That's that, then.'

'That bugger Baddingham's beaten us after all,' said Dame Enid furiously. 'I'm bloody well going to tell Gwendolyn Gosling how he enticed Maud away and bribed Beattie Johnson. I don't give a damn what Declan says, we must be able to appeal.'

'I don't fink we can,' said Freddie wearily. 'The decision's final.'

'Nothing's final,' said Dame Enid briskly.

Taggie went white. 'You don't think Daddy will do something silly?'

'Of course not,' snapped Cameron, because she had thought the same thing and was frightened too.

Lizzie took Freddie's hand. 'I'm so sorry, darling.'

Freddie shook his head, near to tears too, unable to speak.

Next minute Freddie's chauffeur rang from the car: 'I 'eard the bad news on the radio, Mr J. I've picked up Mr O'Hara at South Ken.'

'Is he OK?' said Freddie.

'Well, he's not making much sense, but I'll bring him back to Holland Park.'

Ten minutes later Declan walked into the drawing-room. For a second he looked like a thundercloud, so they all knew finally there was absolutely no hope. Then for the first time in weeks, he gave his wicked schoolboy grin: 'It's all right, my darlings. We got it.'

There was a stunned silence, followed by an explosion of cheering; everyone was hugging each other. Janey burst into tears, so did Charles. Dame Enid and Billy were wiping their eyes.

'Fuckin' 'ell,' yelled Freddie, jumping up and down.

'Good Lord,' said Henry.

Taggie suddenly found herself hugging Cameron. 'We got it,' they both screamed simultaneously.

'Are you quite, quite sure?' said Bas incredulously. 'Can we see the proof?'

Grinning broadly, Declan got the torn white letter out of his pocket. Everyone crowded round to have a look.

'Bloody hell, it's true,' said Janey, giving a whoop of joy and hugging Billy. 'We can move back to Penscombe.'

'I'm going to be the next Trevor MacDonald,' shouted Wesley.

'I might even keep my cottage after all,' said Marti.

'What decided them finally to give it to us?' Cameron asked Declan over the Tarzan howls and the deafening fusillade of champagne corks.

'Mostly you,' said Declan, putting an arm round her shoulders. 'They thought you were marvellous, and they adored Freddie, but it was everyone,' he went on, raising his hand for silence. 'It was all of you turning up at the IBA that finally swung it. A case of everyone ventured, everything won. In the end, none but the brave deserved the franchise.' He wiped his eyes. 'I'm so proud and happy for us all.'

'So am I,' said Henry, who'd been laboriously doing sums on the back of an envelope, 'I had one thousand pounds on us at 2–1.'

'Christ,' said Bas. 'You can almost buy Joanna Lumley for that.'

Everyone screamed with laughter and started hugging everyone else all over again.

Over at Rutland Gate, Caitlin lay in Archie's arms.

'Are you sure that was all right,' he asked her for the hundredth time, as he stroked her flat white belly.

'Of course it was.'

'I thought guys were supposed to go off girls the moment they'd had them, but I love you more than ever. You're so beautiful. Did it hurt very much?'

Caitlin giggled: 'One has to suffer to be beautiful. And we've got the whole holidays ahead of us. Have you got masses of work to do?'

'Yes,' said Archie.

'So have I. We can do it together.'

701

'Are you hungry? I am. I'll see if there's anything in the larder.' Archie got up. Naked, still slightly plump, but to Caitlin entirely beautiful, he peered through the curtains. At three-thirty, it was getting dark.

'Holy shit,' said Archie. 'My mother's just getting out of a taxi.'

Frantically Caitlin kicked the bottle under the bed, put the two glasses in the bedside cupboard, dragged on her jeans, her black cardigan and her boots, and shoved her shirt, bra, pants and socks into her carrier bag. Archie turned off the bedroom lights.

Going into the drawing-room a minute later, Monica found Archie and Caitlin sitting on either side of an empty fireplace. Caitlin was reading *Country Life* upside-down.

'Hullo, Mummy,' said Archie heartily, getting up and kissing her. 'I thought you'd be at Dad's celebration piss-up. I was about to join you.'

'It's been cancelled,' said Monica numbly. 'We've lost the franchise.'

'What!' exploded Archie. 'We couldn't have. All the papers said it was in the bag.'

'They were wrong. For security, the IBA leave MI5 standing.'

'My God, I'm sorry.'

Caitlin couldn't take it in. 'D'you mean Daddy's got it?' she said slowly.

'I don't know.' Monica looked at Caitlin dazedly. 'I suppose so.'

Still in her fur coat and headscarf, she sat down very suddenly on the sofa, stared at her rough gardening hands, with their huge diamonds, and burst into tears. Archie, who'd only seen his mother cry once years ago when one of her labradors had to be put down, was utterly helpless. It was like watching the *Titanic* sink.

'I just feel so sorry for him,' sobbed Monica. 'I know he's done dreadful, dreadful things, left no stone unturned to try and win the franchise, but he wanted to beat Rupert and Declan so very badly.'

702

Rushing across the room, Caitlin put her arms round Monica.

'I'm so sorry. I'm delighted for Daddy of course, but it's like the Boat Race. Someone's got to win, but it doesn't stop it being horribly, desperately, publicly humiliating for the crew who don't. There, please don't cry. Get her some brandy,' she ordered Archie. 'Will you be terribly poor?'

'No,' gulped Monica, 'I don't think so. Tony's got all his other companies. It's just that he minded so much, and it's such a shock. He was so certain.'

Struggling to her feet, desperately wiping her eyes, saying she must find a handkerchief, she stumbled off to her bedroom.

Thinking of the unmade bed, Archie and Caitlin looked at each other in horror.

'I must be going senile,' gulped Monica when she returned, wiping her eyes and blowing her nose. 'I could have sworn I made my bed this morning.'

'You've been under a terrific strain,' said Caitlin sympathetically. 'My father topped up a whisky and soda with milk the other day.'

'But I never leave it unmade,' whispered Monica. 'I can't afford to go to pieces. Tony's going to need so much support.'

She made a face like a little girl drinking medicine as she took a gulp of the brandy.

'I'll go and make it for you,' said Caitlin. 'That'll make you feel better. Then Archie and I are going to get you some lunch.'

In the middle of Venturer's amazed and joyful celebrations, the telephone rang. Dame Enid picked it up. Not bothering to put her hand over the receiver, she yelled: 'It's the boring old fart for you, Declan.'

'Congratulations, Declan,' said the Bishop of Cotchester heartily. 'Delighted you've finally got the franchise. With the festive season nearly upon us, I've been pondering much on the nature of forgiveness. I think, on balance, my flock will understand if I overlook Rupert Campbell-Black's lamentable behaviour. I would like to reconsider my position *vis-à-vis* Venturer.'

A beatific smile spread over Declan's face: 'Flock off,' he said, and hung up.

Cameron sat on the sofa cuddling Blue.

'A penny for your thoughts,' said Patrick, sitting down beside her. 'Although, now you've won the franchise, I suppose they're much more expensive than that.'

Cameron grinned: 'I was thinking how odd it is to feel so wildly happy when one's heart is breaking.'

'It's relief,' said Patrick, filling up her glass, 'to discover you're going to survive after all.'

He glanced across at Taggie who, with a fixed smile on her face, was gathering up glasses like a zombie.

'I'm not sure my sister is.'

'What's she got to complain about?' said Cameron bitterly. 'Rupert loves her.'

'She hasn't got a clue he does,' said Patrick, 'and he's not going to do anything about it. He's probably out on the tiles at some Hollywood orgy at this moment, busy forgetting her. Freddie and Pa have been trying to get through to him all evening, but there's no answer.'

Cameron looked at her watch.

'It must be breakfast time in LA,' she said.

52

Over in California Rupert was slowly going out of his mind with misery. Leaving England had made everything far, far worse. He couldn't eat or sleep. He must be dying if he didn't even want to drink. All he could do was long for Taggie. He'd never dreamed anything could hurt so much.

'Rupert,' said Suzy Erikson, his beautiful hostess, as they breakfasted by the pool, having just come in after an all-night party, 'I've been talking to you for twenty minutes, and you haven't heard a single word.'

'I know. I'm sorry.'

'I've also trailed all the most glamorous women in Holly-wood in front of you for the past fortnight and you've paid no attention to any of them.'

'I know. I'm sorry about that too.'

'Still brooding about your Irish teenager?' said Suzy, plung-ing a spoon into her melon. 'Go home and screw her. It's the only way you'll get her out of your system.'

Rupert looked at his cooling cup of coffee. 'I can't, I mustn't fuck her up,' he repeated dully. 'Apart from Billy, she's the only genuinely good person I've ever met.'

'That seems rather a good omen,' said Suzy. 'Billy's the only person you've ever been faithful to, and the only one you haven't fucked up either.'

As Rupert got up to prowl up and down the terrace, Suzy thought how much weight he'd lost and how really ill he looked. Having some years ago been desperately in love with him, she'd always longed to see him brought to his knees. But now, so abject was his despair, she could only feel sorry for him.

'I want to look after her,' he was saying. 'She's the only person who's ever made me want to find a dragon and slay it for her sake, although,' he added with a half-smile, 'she wouldn't appreciate it. She doesn't like cruelty to animals at all.'

'Good thing she didn't know you in the old days,' said Suzy. 'Have you got a picture?'

Rupert walked back to his chair and extracted a creased snapshot from the inside pocket of his boating jacket, which was hanging over the back of the chair. It was one he'd taken in the woods. Taggie was pink-faced from catching leaves with the children.

'Not a great beauty, is she?' said Suzy with a certain satisfaction. Rupert snatched back the photograph.

'She is,' he said icily. 'She's the most beautiful girl I've ever seen.'

'Hum,' said Suzy. 'Well, if you think that, you have got her badly.'

An extremely tense silence was broken by the telephone.

'Someone called Declan O'Hara for you,' said Suzy. 'He seems kinda drunk.'

Rupert steeled himself for abuse.

'We've got it, we've focking got it,' yelled Declan.

'You what?'

'Not just us – you as well. We've focking got the franchise.'

Judging from the shrieks and whoops, there was the most terrific party going on in the background. Rupert wished, after the initial passionate relief, he could feel more excited and respond appropriately to Declan's almost incoherent ecstasy. Then he talked to Freddie, who was calmer but equally euphoric, and briefly to Cameron who sounded pretty overexcited as well. Then Declan snatched back the telephone.

'Isn't it focking marvellous? You'd better come back soon,

706

and we can find out if we know how to run a television company – what's that? Oh Taggie says to wish you a Happy Christmas.'

Switching off the telephone, Rupert walked to the edge of the shimmering pale-blue pool and looked up at the snowy peaks of the Santa Monica mountains that rose like one of Taggie's puddings. He wondered if the snow had thawed at Penscombe.

'I'm going home,' he said.

'To propose to your pink-faced Amazon?'

Rupert shook his head violently. 'No, no. I just think if I was in the same country as her, it might hurt less.'

The journey home was hell. All the air hostesses fluttered round him, plying him with champagne and delicious things to eat, which he left untouched. By some ghastly irony, the film was the Woody Allen which he'd seen with the children and Taggie. He took in as little of it as he had the first time. He tried to sleep, but it was as though he was destined to watch eternal television with Taggie's face on all four channels. He dropped off for a few minutes as the plane flew over Ireland, but dreamed of her and woke in utter desolation to find she wasn't there.

Heathrow at seven-thirty on a raw December morning was still dark.

'Good morning, Mr Campbell-Black,' said the passport man, who didn't even get a nod.

As he waited for his luggage, Rupert watched the carousel going round. It was the last circle of hell, he reflected, for people who never got the person they wanted in life. His heart was so heavy, he'd have to pay excess baggage on it. As he went through the green door at Customs, he thought of all the times in the old days when he'd sauntered through carrying dope or illegal currency in the bottom of his boots. Now he had nothing forbidden to declare but his hopeless love for Taggie.

Once through the barrier, he looked wearily round for his driver, but no one came forward. Christ, that was all he needed. He set off towards the telephones, passing a fleet of people brandishing cards with names on. Suddenly a particularly large placard caught his eye. On it was painted in huge letters: Rooput Cambel-Blak. Only one person could spell that badly! He must be going mad. Then, below the placard, he saw a pair of very long, very slim legs in familiar faded jeans. The legs were shaking frantically, so was the placard. Rupert, finding too that his legs would hardly hold him up, walked towards it. Very gently he pushed it down, seeing first the mane of black hair, then two silver-grey eyes, then the deathly white face, and the desperately trembling mouth he'd dreamed of kissing for months now.

'Oh Tag,' he said despairingly.

'I can't help it,' she sobbed. 'I'll do anything. I'll drive you around. I'll look after your children. I'll cook, clean your house, muck out your horses, weed your garden. I just want to be near you. I can't bear it any longer.'

The next moment the placard crashed to the ground and Rupert had taken her face in his hands, feeling the contrast between the softness of her cheeks and the frantic tension of her jaw. And just to prove to himself she was real, he wonderingly kissed her lips, and her wet salty eyes, and then her forehead.

'I'm such a selfish bastard,' he muttered into her hair.

'I'm used to selfish people,' sobbed Taggie. 'I'd be lost without them.'

'And what about the memoirs?' There was so much uncertainty and despair in his voice that Taggie drew slightly away from him. Then she laughed despite her tears. 'I couldn't read them. That's one advantage of being dyslexic.'

Rupert started to laugh too, and then, taking her in his arms, gave her a kiss that, everyone gathered round said afterwards, should for length and passion have gone straight into the *Guinness Book of Records*.

'I love you,' he gasped as he came up for air. 'I've never loved anyone like I love you.' Then, aware that she was still trembling, added, 'It's all right, darling,' and suddenly he knew that it was and he'd never let her go again.

'Mr Minister,' said a voice, 'I mean, Mr Shadow Minister.'

Glancing round, Rupert saw they were surrounded by press. Holding Taggie close, he whispered, 'Where's the car?'

'Outside, just through the door.'

'We'll make a dash for it.'

On the motorway he managed to shake off the reporters, took an exit into some Royal Berkshire countryside and pulled up with a jerk in a lay-by. Then, removing both their seat belts, he turned to face her, taking her hands.

'I want you to know . . .' it was he who was stammering now . . . 'that I only joined the fucking consortium because of you. In fact, I only came back from Gstaad for your rotten brother's twenty-first because I wanted to have a crack at you. I only let myself be interviewed by your father because I thought he'd think me a wimp if I didn't, and I might be able to ingratiate myself with him. I only bought his bloody wood for that ludicrously inflated price because I love you. The only reason I didn't move in months ago was because in the one unselfish gesture of my life (and Christ, it was the most difficult), I thought it was unfair to foist my sodding bloody-minded nature on you. No one could have had a more appalling past.'

Taggie put up a hand to his lips to halt him. 'I don't care about your past,' she said shakily. 'All I want to be is your future.'

It was not long before the car had misted up completely, and Rupert stopped kissing her and wrote, 'I adore you. Will you marry me?' on the windscreen.

And underneath Taggie wrote, 'Yes pleese.'

Back on the motorway it was light now, and Taggie could see how grey and thin Rupert looked, and how blackly shadowed he was under the eyes.

'I just can't wait to feed you up,' she wailed.

Looking ahead, she saw the pallid full moon, which like a sympathetic friend had peered in at different windows of her turret bedroom throughout the night as she paced the floor boards wondering whether or not she should go and meet

Rupert. Now, clearly dying to go to bed, the moon kept on bobbing round clumps of trees or above the frozen white downs, as if just managing to keep awake to see how the story ended. Silently, thankfully, Taggie made a joyful thumbs-up sign as the moon finally disappeared from view.

'How did you screw up the courage to come and meet me?' asked Rupert, putting his hand on her thigh as they turned off the motorway.

'I went to see the children and gave them your presents yesterday afternoon. I was so desperate, it was the nearest I could get to you. They were so sweet, and Malise and Helen were really nice. They asked me to stay to supper, and after the children went to bed, I talked to Malise. He said he and Helen had over-reacted about the memoirs, and he was sorry, and how happy Helen had made him, and he was thirty years older than her, and he told me to go for it.'

'Really?' said Rupert in amazement. 'Good for Malise.'

'Where are we going?' asked Taggie, snuggling up to him.

'To ask your father's permission. If he won't give it, we'll have to elope, but I don't want it hanging over us.'

'You'll have to see Mummy as well.'

'She's back!' said Rupert in outrage. 'When, for Christ's sake?'

'The day before yesterday, the evening we got the franchise.'

'That figures,' said Rupert dismissively. 'Realized she'd backed the wrong horse.'

'No,' said Taggie. 'She saw Daddy crying on television when he came out of the IBA. You know how emotional he is, and she thought it was from unhappiness because he'd lost it, and felt so sorry for him that she rushed back and turned up at Freddie's house in the middle of the celebrations, just after Daddy'd rung you in fact. It was so odd. I'm not boring you?' she added quickly.

'You never, never bore me,' said Rupert, touching her cheek.

'Well, d'you know what Mummy said when she first saw him? Such a strange remark that I remembered it. She said:

710

"My Oberon! what visions have I seen! Me thought I was enamoured of an ass." Patrick says it comes from *Midsummer's Night Dream*. Anyway, they were both crying and fell into each other's arms, and disappeared into Freddie and Valerie's bedroom.'

'Pa and Ma for the course,' said Rupert, shaking his head.

Taggie giggled. 'It was a bit embarrassing. Hordes of press and television people turned up to interview Daddy and photograph him about getting the franchise, and he'd locked himself in with Mummy. So Freddie and Cameron had to field all the questions.

'And then, even worse, Valerie arrived. She'd beetled up from London the moment she'd heard Venturer had won to get in on the act, and she found everyone plastered, and Freddie kissing Lizzie Vereker on the sofa. So she stormed off to bed, and she couldn't get in because Mummy and Daddy were in there already.'

'Christ, we'll never behave like that, will we?' said Rupert putting his hand over hers. 'Still, I'm glad they're back together again.'

All the same Rupert was surprisingly nervous about confronting his future father-in-law. He needn't have bothered. When he went into the library Declan was poring over all sorts of leaflets for electronic equipment, spread out on the table.

'Rupert. Great to see you, good of you to come back so quickly. Come and look at this stuff. We're going to bid for satellite next.'

Rupert took a deep breath. 'I actually came back to ask for your daughter's hand in marriage, Declan.'

'Have you? Declan peered over his spectacles at Taggie. 'I thought you might. Well, she certainly looks happier than she's done for the past nineteen years, so I'd better say yes. We've got a hell of a lot to do here. Can you start work before Christmas?'

'No, I bloody can't. I'm going to be on my honeymoon over Christmas.'

711

'So soon. Can't you wait till the Spring and go to Paris? Maud and I went to Paris. I'd better call her and we'll have a drink. Good thing you didn't turn up yesterday, we were all so hungover, you might not have had such a genial reception. Maud!' he yelled up the stairs.

Maud wandered down, looking pretty wretched after her prolonged disappearance, but with plenty of her old insouciance, and embraced them both.

'She's obviously so glad to be home, she wouldn't have minded you marrying the cat,' Rupert said to Taggie afterwards.

A bottle of champagne had been opened, when Patrick marched in, looking like a thundercloud.

'Oh Christ, here comes Frank Bruno,' said Rupert, ducking behind Taggie.

'I've just heard the news on Radio One,' said Patrick coldly. 'I suppose none of you has had the decency to tell Cameron.'

'Oh dear,' said Declan. 'I'll ring her.'

'It's my responsibility. I'll do it,' said Rupert.

'I'll do it,' said Patrick heavily.

He took the telephone into the drawing-room next door and dialled the number of Cameron's house in Hamilton Terrace. She took a long time to answer.

'I've just heard,' she said in a flat voice.

'It must hurt, I'm very sorry.'

'You needn't be,' snapped Cameron. 'Why should I care if your sister's finally got him, when it's all over between him and me?'

'Still hurts,' said Patrick reasonably. 'Not much fun seeing someone get a clear round on a horse you were bucked off by. I'll be over later.'

'Whatever for?' Cameron's voice was shrill with hostility. 'I'm going out.'

'You stay where you are.'

Cameron collapsed on her bed. She had nowhere to go anyway. She supposed her house belonged to Venturer now. Outside, the shoppers were trailing argumentatively home in the rain, weighed down by Christmas presents. Then, like a

712

frozen pipe that suddenly bursts with a thaw, Cameron, for the first time since Rupert left for America, gave way to tears.

Around five-thirty, when there seemed nothing left to weep out of her system, she tried to pull herself together, took Blue for a quick desolate walk across the water meadows and had a bath. At half-past-six and seven she was interrupted by carol singers. At a quarter-past-seven she was disturbed by two men with a van, who said they had some stuff to deliver.

'What stuff?' snapped Cameron.

'Six tea chests full of books, records and some clothes.'

'Don't be fucking stupid! You've got the wrong house! Take it away!' she screamed.

At that moment Patrick walked purposefully through the door, carrying two squash rackets and a portable typewriter under one arm and a large ginger cat under the other.

'I don't like cats, nor does Blue,' snarled Cameron.

'You will,' said Patrick soothingly. 'Just give me five minutes,' he added to the van driver, as he pushed Cameron into the sitting-room and shut the door behind him.

'What the bloody hell are you playing at, and what's all that shit they're delivering?'

'I'm moving in,' said Patrick, putting the ginger cat down. Immediately Blue bounced up to the cat, dropping gracefully down on his front paws, head on one side. The cat hissed, tail like a Christmas tree, and took a fierce swipe at Blue's nose. Blue gave a yelp and retreated between Cameron's legs.

'They'll get used to each other,' said Patrick, 'just like we will.'

'We bloody won't.'

'Yes, we will. I love you.'

'You can't any more. I've been such a bitch,' said Cameron, going very pale. 'Anyway, I love Rupert.'

'No you don't, or you wouldn't have gone to bed with my father in Ireland.'

'I didn't,' stammered Cameron.

'Yes, you did on the last night, and he felt so guilty about it afterwards, that's why he didn't get back for Mum's play.'

'Don't you mind?' said Cameron, appalled. 'It's practically incest.'

'It is not. It's you I'm interested in, and, anyway,' said Patrick with more than a touch of Declan's arrogance, 'as I'm a much younger, more beautiful, more together, about to be much more successful version of my father, it's perfectly logical that you should fall in love with me.'

'You're a toy boy,' said Cameron as his hands tightened round her waist.

'I'm not. I'm a man of substance. The BBC have just bought my first play and commissioned another. I'm going to write a kid's play called "Noddy in Toyboyland".'

Cameron grinned. 'You'd better cancel the contract, and I'll produce them both.'

'Nope,' said Patrick firmly. 'I never mix business with pleasure, and you, my dear, dear love are only pleasure.'

'I love Rupert,' wailed Cameron.

'Don't be silly,' said Patrick, drawing her close to him.

'Well, perhaps I don't,' said Cameron bewildered, as a few minutes later they were interrupted by a loud knock on the door.

'Can we unload the stuff now, sir?' said the driver.

Patrick looked at Cameron questioningly.

'Oh well, I guess you bloody well can.'

As the men stumped out to the van, Patrick smiled down at her: 'I just want to check out on your availability for the next thousand years.'

'I've never seen such a change in Taggie,' said Caitlin to Archie next morning. 'She keeps giggling all the time, and grinning from ear to ear, and she's suddenly got terribly protective. Rupert's been asleep for twenty-four hours in the spare room, and the most amazingly important people have rung up, and she hasn't let any of them talk to him.'

'That's nice,' said Archie, kissing her. 'They say love hits you with even more of a thunderbolt when you're old.'

Rupert woke to blue skies and birds singing outside, a fire in the grate and total panic inside. He had no idea where he or Taggie was. Then suddenly he became aware of something warm and furry, and realized Gertrude was lying in the small of his back. Slowly the events of yesterday reasserted themselves and he felt so happy he nearly went back to sleep again. Next minute the door opened very cautiously.

'I'm awake,' said Rupert.

'You did sleep well,' said Taggie in delight as she put down the breakfast tray piled with orange juice, coffee, croissants and home-made apple jelly.

'Because I felt safe for the first time in my life. Come here.' Rupert patted the bed, and when he kissed her, she smelt equally of toothpaste and her mother's scent.

Afterwards he stroked her face incredulously. 'I still can't believe I'm going to spend the rest of my life with you.'

'Nor I you,' sighed Taggie.

'I was going to bring you bacon and eggs,' said Taggie, spooning a pip out of the orange juice, 'but I thought if you hadn't been eating, it might be too rich for you.'

Then she giggled. 'A girl from the *Daily Mail* rang up just now.'

'What did she want?' asked Rupert, thinking how wonderfully it suited her to be so happy.

'She said, "How did you first meet your fiancé and what was he doing?" I couldn't say you were playing nude tennis with Sarah Stratton, so I said Basil brought you round for a drink. And the Leader of the Opposition rang twice. Evidently the Government's fallen and there's going to be an election. She wants you to ring her urgently. I said you were asleep.'

Rupert's eyes gleamed. 'I've got a feeling you're going to be far, far more use to me than I ever dreamed. We'd better get married at once. I'm allergic to the word fiancée; even you can't glorify it.'

'I certainly can't spell it,' said Taggie.

Later, downstairs, they discussed marriage plans.

'I suppose it'll have to be Cotchester Registry office,' said Maud, who was thinking about her wardrobe.

'I got married in a registry office the first time round,' said Rupert. 'As it's the real thing this time –' he raised Taggie's hand to his lips and kissed it – 'we thought we might get married in church. I'm sure we can find some trendy parson in London who won't mind my being divorced.'

'I've got a better idea,' said Declan, reaching for his telephone book.

'Tabitha's going to be a bridesmaid,' said Taggie to Caitlin. 'Would you like to be one too?'

'Only if I can wear jeans,' said Caitlin.

Declan, having for once dialled the right number, was put straight through to the Bishop of Cotchester. He immediately apologized for being so shirty on the telephone the other day and wondered whether the Bishop would reconsider coming on to the Venturer Board after all.

After some huffing and puffing about having to take a stand over Rupert Campbell-Black's disgusting memoirs, the Bishop said he would be delighted, and wrote down the date of the first board meeting.

'There's just one other thing,' said Declan. 'My daughter, Taggie, is getting married and her one wish is to be married by you in Cotchester Cathedral.'

Taggie turned crimson. 'It isn't true!' she squeaked, looking at Rupert who had started to laugh.

The Bishop once again told Declan that he'd be delighted. He'd become extremely fond of Taggie in the past year.

'Just the simplest service,' said Declan. 'Only family and very close friends and, of course, all our Venturer supporters.'

'Splendid, splendid,' said the Bishop. 'And who is the very, very lucky young man?'

'Well, I'm just coming to that,' said Declan.

THE END

RIDERS

BY JILLY COOPER

'Sex and horses: who could ask for more?' *Sunday Telegraph*

If you thought you knew what to expect of Jilly Cooper — bursts of restless romance, strings of domestic disasters, flip fun with the class system — RIDERS will come as a pleasurable surprise.

A multi-stranded love story, it tells of the lives of a tight circle of star riders who move from show to show, united by raging ambition, bitter rivalry and the terror of failure. The superheroes are Jake Lovell, a half-gipsy orphan who wears gold earrings, handles a horse — or a woman — with effortless skill, and is consumed with hatred for the promiscuous upper-class cad, Rupert Campbell-Black, who has no intention of being faithful to his wife, Helen, but is outraged when she runs away with another rider.

Set in the tense, heroic world of show-jumping, Jilly Cooper's novel moves from home-country gymkhanas through a riot of horsey events all over the world, culminating in the high drama of the Los Angeles Olympics.

'Blockbusting fiction at its best'
David Hughes, *The Mail On Sunday*

'I defy anyone not to enjoy her book. It is a delight from start to finish' Auberon Waugh, *Daily Mail*

0 552 12486 9

OTHER JILLY COOPER TITLES
AVAILABLE FROM CORGI BOOKS

Jilly Cooper was born in Hornchurch, Essex in 1937 and grew up in Yorkshire. Her writing career began in 1956, when she got a job as a cub reporter on the *Middlesex Independent*. Following several short stories for women's magazines, Jilly Cooper started contributing a regular column to *The Sunday Times* in 1969. She stayed with them until 1982 when she joined *The Mail on Sunday* as a bi-monthly columnist.

Her first book, *How to Stay Married*, was written in 1969. Since then she has written or helped to compile twenty-five others including six romances: *Emily, Bella, Harriet, Octavia, Prudence* and *Imogen,* and the bestselling *Rivals*. Her most recent non-fiction books are *Animals at War* and *The Common Years*. She has also written a television series, *It's Awfully Bad for Your Eyes, Darling,* and has often appeared as a television guest herself.

Jilly Cooper is married to publisher, Leo Cooper, and they live in the Cotswolds. They have two children, Felix and Emily, four cats and two mongrels.

Also by Jilly Cooper

RIVALS
IMOGEN
PRUDENCE
OCTAVIA
HARRIET
BELLA
EMILY
LISA & CO
CLASS

and published by Corgi Books

Riders

Jilly Cooper

CORGI BOOKS

RIDERS
A CORGI BOOK 0 552 12486 9

Originally published in Great Britain by
Arlington Books Ltd.

PRINTING HISTORY
Arlington Books edition published 1985
Arlington Books edition reprinted 1985 (three times)
Corgi edition published 1986
Corgi edition reprinted 1986 (seven times)
Corgi edition reprinted 1987 (twice)
Corgi edition reprinted 1988 (three times)
Corgi edition reprinted 1989 (twice)

This book is set in 10/11 pt Baskerville

Corgi Books are published by Transworld Publishers
Ltd., 61–63 Uxbridge Road, Ealing, London W5 5SA, in
Australia by Transworld Publishers (Australia) Pty. Ltd.,
15–23 Helles Avenue, Moorebank, NSW 2170, and in New
Zealand by Transworld Publishers (N.Z.) Ltd., Cnr. Moselle
and Waipareira Avenues, Henderson, Auckland.

Printed and bound in Great Britain by
Cox & Wyman Ltd., Reading, Berks.

DEDICATION

*To Beryl Hill,
the Artur Rubinstein of the typewriter,
with love and gratitude*

Acknowledgements

Since I started *Riders* fifteen years ago, an enormous number of people have helped me with the book. They are all experts in their fields. But this being a work of fiction, I took their advice only as far as it suited my plot, and the accuracy of the book in no way reflects on their expertise!

They include Ronnie Massarella, Caroline Silver, Alan Smith, Brian Giles, Douglas Bunn, Michael Clayton, Alan Oliver, Bridget Le Good, John Burbidge, Diana Downie, Raymond Brooks-Ward, Harvey Smith, Dr Hubert and Mrs Bessie Crouch, Dr Timothy Evans, Heather Ross, Caroline Akrill, Dick Stilwell, Sue Clarke, Sue Gibson, Andrew Parker-Bowles, John and Tory Oaksey, Marion Ivey, Rosemary Nunelly, Elizabeth Richardson, Elizabeth Hopkins, Julia Longland, Susan Blair, Ann Martin, Kate O'Sullivan, Marcy Drummond, John and Michael Whitaker, David Broome and Malcolm Pyrah.

I owe a special debt of gratitude to dear Sighle Gogan, who spent so many hours talking to me about show jumping, and arranged for me to meet so many of the people who helped me, but who tragically died in January last year.

I should also like to thank my bank manager, James Atkinson, for being so patient and Paul Scherer and Alan Earney of Corgi Books for being so continually encouraging, and Tom Hartman for being one of those rare people who actually makes authors enjoy having their books edited.

An award for gallantry must go to the nine ladies who all worked fantastically long hours over Christmas, deciphering my appalling hand-writing and typing the 340,000 word manuscript. They include Beryl Hill, Anna Gibbs-Kennet, Sue Moore, Margaret McKellican, Corinne Monhaghan, Julie Payne, Nicky Greenshield, Patricia Quatermass and my own wonderful secretary, Diane Peter.

The lion's share of my gratitude must go to Desmond Elliott for masterminding the whole operation so engagingly, and all his staff at Arlington, who worked so hard to produce such a huge book in under five months.

Finally there are really no words adequate to thank my husband Leo and my children Felix and Emily, except to say that without their support, good cheer and continued unselfishness the book would never have been finished.

I

Because he had to get up unusually early on Saturday, Jake
Lovell kept waking up throughout the night, racked by
terrifying dreams about being late. In the first dream he
couldn't find his breeches when the collecting ring steward
called his number; in the second he couldn't catch any of
the riding school ponies to take them to the show; in the
third Africa slipped her head collar and escaped; and in the
fourth, the most terrifying of all, he was back in the
children's home screaming and clawing at locked iron
gates, while Rupert Campbell-Black rode Africa off down
the High Street, until turning with that hateful, sneering
smile, he'd shouted:

'You'll never get out of that place now, Gyppo; it's where
you belong.'

Jake woke sobbing, heart bursting, drenched in sweat,
paralysed with fear. It was half a minute before he could
reach out and switch on the bedside lamp. He lit a cigarette
with a trembling hand. Gradually the familiar objects in
the room reasserted themselves: the Lionel Edwards prints
on the walls, the tattered piles of *Horse and Hound*, the books
on show jumping hopelessly overcrowding the bookshelves,
the wash basin, the faded photographs of his mother and
father. Hanging in the wardrobe was the check riding coat
Mrs Wilton had rather grudgingly given him for his
twenty-first birthday. Beneath it stood the scratched but
gleaming pair of brown-topped boots he'd picked up
second-hand last week.

In the stall below he could hear a horse snorting and a
crash as another horse kicked over its water bucket.

1

Far too slowly his panic subsided. Prep school and Rupert Campbell-Black were things of the past. It was 1970 and he had been out of the children's home for four years now. He mostly forgot them during the day; it was only in dreams they came back to torment him. He shivered; the sheets were still damp with sweat. Four-thirty, said his alarm clock; there were already fingers of light under the thin yellow curtains. He didn't have to get up for half an hour, but he was too scared to go back to sleep. He could hear the rain pattering on the roof outside and dripping from the gutter, muting the chatter of the sparrows.

He tried to concentrate on the day ahead, which didn't make him feel much more cheerful. One of the worst things about working in a riding school was having to take pupils to horseshows. Few of them could control the bored, broken-down ponies. Many were spoilt; others, terrified, were only riding at all because their frightful mothers were using horses to grapple their way up the social scale, giving them an excuse to put a hard hat in the back window of the Jaguar and slap gymkhana stickers on the windscreen.

What made Jake sick with nerves, however, was that, unknown to his boss, Mrs Wilton, he intended to take Africa to the show and enter her for the open jumping. Mrs Wilton didn't allow Jake to compete in shows. He might get too big for his boots. His job was to act as constant nursemaid to the pupils, not to jump valuable horses behind her back.

Usually, Mrs Wilton turned up at shows in the afternoon and strutted about chatting up the mothers. But today, because she was driving down to Brighton to chat up some rich uncle who had no children, she wouldn't be putting in an appearance. If Jake didn't try out Africa today, he wouldn't have another chance for weeks.

Africa was a livery horse, looked after at the riding school, but owned by an actor named Bobby Cotterel, who'd bought her in a fit of enthusiasm after starring in *Dick Turpin*. A few weeks later he had bought a Ferrari and, apart from still paying her livery fees, had forgotten about

2

Africa, which had given Jake the perfect opportunity to teach her to jump on the quiet.

She was only six, but every day Jake became more convinced that she had the makings of a great show jumper. It was not just her larkiness and courage, her fantastic turn of speed and huge jump. She also had an ability to get herself out of trouble which counterbalanced her impetuosity.

Jake adored her – more than any person or animal he had known in his life. If Mrs Wilton discovered he'd taken her to a show, she'd probably sack him. He dreaded losing a job which had brought him his first security in years, but the prospect of losing Africa was infinitely worse.

The alarm made him jump. It was still raining; the horror of the dream gripped him again. What would happen if Africa slipped when she was taking off or landing? He dressed and, lifting up the trap door at the bottom of his bed, climbed down the stairs into the tackroom, inhaling the smell of warm horse leather, saddle soap and dung, which never failed to excite him. Hearing him mixing the feeds, horses' heads came out over the half-doors, calling, whickering, stamping their hooves.

Dandelion, the skewbald, the greediest pony in the yard, his mane and back covered in straw from lying down, yelled shrilly, demanding to be fed first. As he added extra vitamins, nuts and oats to Africa's bowl, Jake thought it was hardly surprising she looked well. Mrs Wilton would have a fit if she knew.

It was seven-thirty before he had mucked out and fed all the horses. Africa, feed finished, blinking her big, dark-blue eyes in the low-angled sun, hung out of her box, catching his sleeve between her lips each time he went past, shaking gently, never nipping the skin. Mrs Wilton had been out to dinner the night before; it was unlikely she'd surface before half past eight; that gave him an hour to groom Africa.

Rolling up his sleeves, chattering nonsense to her all the time, Jake got to work. She was a beautiful horse, very dark brown, her coat looking almost indigo in the shadows. She

3

had two white socks, a spillikin of white down her forehead, a chest like a channel steamer funnel, huge shoulders and quarters above lean strong legs. Her ears twitched and turned all the time, as sensitive as radar.

He jumped when the stable cat, a fat tabby with huge, whiskers, appeared on top of the stable door and, after glancing at a couple of pigeons scratching for corn, dropped down into the straw and curled up in the discarded warmth of Africa's rug.

Suddenly Africa jerked up her head and listened. Jake stepped outside nervously; the curtains were still drawn in Mrs Wilton's house. He'd wanted to plait Africa's mane, but he didn't dare. It would unplait all curly and he might be caught out. He went back to work.

'Surely you're not taking Africa to the show?' said a shrill voice. Jake jumped out of his skin and Africa tossed up her head, banging him on the nose.

Just able to look over the half-door was one of his pupils, Fenella Maxwell, her face as freckled as a robin's egg, her flaxen hair already escaping from its elastic bands.

'What the hell are you doing here?' said Jake furiously, his eyes watering. 'I said no one was allowed here till ten and it can't be eight yet. Push off home.'

'I've come to help,' said Fenella, gazing at him with huge, Cambridge-blue eyes fringed with thick blond lashes. Totally unabashed, she moved a boiled sweet to the other side of her face.

'I know you're by yourself till Alison comes. I'll get Dandelion ready . . . please,' she added. 'I want him to look as beautiful as Africa.'

'Shut up,' hissed Jake. 'Now shove off.'

'Please let me stay. There's nothing to do at home. I couldn't sleep. I will help. Oh, doesn't Smokey look sweet curled up in the rug? Are you really taking Africa?'

'Mind your own business,' said Jake.

Fen took the boiled sweet out of her mouth and gave it to Dandelion, who was slavering over the next half-door, then kissed him on the nose. Her shirt was already escaping from

4

the jeans which she wore over her jodhpurs to keep them clean.

'Does Mrs Wilton know?' she asked.

'No,' said Jake.

'I won't tell her,' said Fen, swinging on Africa's door. 'Pattie Beasley might, though, or Sally-Ann; she's always sneaking about something.'

Jake had already sweated uncomfortably over this possibility.

'They're probably too thick to notice,' she went on. 'Shall I make you a cup of tea? Four spoonfuls of sugar, isn't it?'

Jake relented. She was a good kid, cheerful and full of guts, with an instinct for horses and a knowledge way beyond her nine years.

'You can stay if you keep your trap shut,' he said. 'I don't want Mrs Wilton waking up yet.'

After she had spilt most of the tea in the saucer, Fen tied Dandelion up outside Africa's box and settled down to washing his white patches, managing to get more water over herself than the pony.

Jake half-listened as she chattered on incessantly about her sister Tory, who was doing the season but not enjoying the parties at all, and who often had red eyes from crying in the morning.

'She's coming to the show later.'

'Does your mother know you're here?' asked Jake.

'She wouldn't notice if I wasn't. She's got a new boyfriend named Colonel Carter. Colonel Cart-ah, he calls himself. He laughs all the time when he's talking to Mummy and he's got big yellow teeth like Dandelion, but somehow they look better on a horse.

'They're coming to the show too. Colonel Carter is bringing a lot of soldiers and guns to do a display after the open jumping. He and Mummy and Tory are going to lunch up at the Hall. Mummy bought a new blue dress specially; it's lovely, but Tory said it was jolly expensive, so I don't expect she'll be able to afford to buy me a pony yet; anyway she says Tory being a deb is costing a fortune.'

5

'Shampoo and set, darling,' she said to Dandelion twenty minutes later as she stuck the pony's tail in a bucket of hot, soapy water. 'Oh, look, Africa's making faces; isn't she sweet?' The next moment Dandelion had whisked his tail at a fly, sending soapy water all over Fen, Africa's rug and the stable cat, who retreated in high dudgeon.

'For God's sake, concentrate,' snapped Jake.

'Mummy's picture's in *The Tatler* again this week,' said Fen. 'She gets in much more often than poor Tory. She says Tory's got to go on a diet next week, so she'll be thin for her drinks party next month. Oh *cave*, Mrs Wilton's drawing back the kitchen curtains.'

Hastily Jake replaced Africa's rug and came out of her box.

Inside the kitchen, beneath the ramparts of honeysuckle, he could see Mrs Wilton, her brick red face flushed from the previous night's drinking, dropping Alka Seltzer into a glass of water. Christ, he hoped she'd get a move on to Brighton and wouldn't hang around. Picking up the brush and the curry comb he started on one of the ponies.

Mrs Wilton came out of the house, followed by her arthritic yellow labrador, who lifted his leg stiffly on the mounting block, then as a formality bounded after the stable cat.

Mrs Wilton was never known to have been on a horse in her life. Stocky, with a face squashed in like a bulldog, she had short pepper and salt hair, a blotchy complexion like salami, and a deep bass voice. All the same, she had had more success with the opposite sex than her masculine appearance would suggest.

'Jake!' she bellowed.

He came out, curry comb in one hand, brush in the other.

'Yes, Mrs Wilton,' though she'd repeatedly asked him to call her Joyce.

They gazed at each other with the dislike of the unwillingly but mutually dependant. Mrs Wilton knew that having lost both his parents and spent much of his life in a children's home, Jake clung on to the security of a

6

living-in job. As her husband was away so much on business, Mrs Wilton had often suggested Jake might be more comfortable living in the house with her. But, aware that he would have to share a bathroom and, if Mrs W had her way, a bedroom, Jake had repeatedly refused. Mrs Wilton was old enough to be his mother.

But, despite finding him sullen and withdrawn to the point of insolence, she had to admit that the horses had never been better looked after. As a result of his encyclopaedic knowledge of plants and wild flowers, and his incredible gypsy remedies, she hadn't had a vet's bill since he'd arrived, and because he was frightened of losing this substitute home, she could get away with paying him a pittance. She found herself doing less and less. She didn't want to revert to getting up at six and mucking out a dozen horses, and it was good to be able to go away, like today, and not worry.

On the other hand, if he was a miracle with animals, he was hell with parents, refusing to suck up to them, positively rude to the sillier ones. A lot had defected and gone to Mrs Haley across the valley, who charged twice as much.

'How many ponies are you taking?' she demanded.

'Six,' said Jake, walking towards the tackroom, praying she'd follow him.

'And you'll get Mrs Thomson to bring the head collars and the water buckets in her car. Do try to be polite for once, although I know how hard you find it.'

Jake stared at her, unsmiling. He had a curiously immobile face, everything in the right place, but without animation. The swarthy features were pale today, the full lips set in an uncompromising line. Slanting, secretive, dark eyes looked out from beneath a frowning line of brow, practically concealed by the thick thatch of almost black hair. He was small, not more than five foot seven, and very thin, a good jockey's weight. The only note of frivolity was the gold rings in his ears. There was something watchful and controlled about him that didn't go with youth.

Despite the heat of the day, his shirt collar was turned up as if against some imagined storm.

'I'll be back tomorrow,' she said, looking down the row of loose boxes.

Suddenly her eyes lit on Africa.

'What's she doing inside?'

'I brought her in this morning,' he lied easily. 'She yells her head off if she's separated from Dandelion and I thought you'd like a lie in.'

'Well, put her out again when you go. I'm not having her eating her head off.'

Despite the fat fee paid by Bobby Cotterel, thought Jake.

She peered into the loose box. For an appalling moment he thought she was going to peel back the rug.

'Hullo, Mrs Wilton' shrieked Fen. 'Come and look at Dandelion. Doesn't he look smart?'

Distracted, Mrs Wilton turned away from Africa.

'Hullo, Fen, dear, you're an early bird. He does look nice; you've even oiled his hooves. Perhaps you'll bring home a rosette.'

'Shouldn't think so,' said Fen gloomily. 'Last time he ate all the potatoes in the potato race.'

'Phew, that was a near one,' said Fen, as Mrs Wilton's car, with the labrador's head sticking out of the window, disappeared down the road.

'Come on,' said Jake, 'I'll make you some breakfast.'

Dressing later before he set out for the show, Jake transferred the crushed and faded yellow tansy flower from the bottom of his left gum-boot to his left riding boot. Tansy warded off evil. Jake was full of superstitions. The royal gypsy blood of the Lovells didn't flow through his veins for nothing.

2

By midday, a blazing sun shone relentlessly out of a speedwell blue sky, warming the russet stone of Bilborough Hall as it dreamed above its dark green moat. To the right on the terrace, great yews cut in the shape of peacocks seemed about to strut across the shaven lawns, down into the valley where blue-green wheat fields merged into meadows of pale silver-green hay. In the park the trees in the angelic softness of their new spring growth looked as though the rain had not only washed them but fabric-conditioned them as well. Dark purple copper beeches and cochineal-red may added a touch of colour.

To the left, the show ring was already circled two deep with cars and more cars in a long gleaming crocodile were still inching slowly through the main gate, on either side of which two stone lions reared up clenching red and white bunting between their teeth.

The headscarf brigade were out in full force, caught on the hop by the first hot day of the year, their arms pale in sleeveless dresses, silk-lined bottoms spilling over shooting sticks, shouting to one another as they unpacked picnics from their cars. Hunt terriers yapped, labradors panted. Food in dog bowls, remaining untouched because of the heat, gathered flies.

Beyond the cars, crowds milled round the stalls selling horsiana, moving aside to avoid the occasional competitors riding through with numbers on their backs. Children mindlessly consumed crisps, clamoured for ices, gas balloons and pony rides. Fathers hung with cameras, wearing creased lightweight suits smelling of mothballs, wished they could escape back to the office, and, for consolation, eyed the inevitable hordes of nubile 14-year-old girls, with long wavy hair and very tight breeches, who seem to parade permanently up and down at horse shows.

Bilborough Hall was owned by Sir William Blake, no relation to the poet, but nicknamed 'Tiger' at school. Mingling with the crowds, he gossiped to friends, raised his hat to people he didn't know and told everyone that in twenty years there had only been one wet Bilborough show. His wife, a J.P. in drooping tweeds and a felt hat, whose passion was gardening, sighed inwardly at the ground already grey and pitted with hoof marks. Between each year, like childbirth, nature seemed to obliterate the full horror of the Bilborough show. She had already instructed the under-gardener, to his intense embarrassment, to go around with a spade and gather up all the manure before it was trodden into the ground.

'Oh, there you are, William,' she said to her husband, who was genially trying to guess the weight of a piglet. 'People are already arriving for luncheon; we'd better go and do our stuff.'

Down by the horse lines, Jake Lovell, tying up a weedy grey pony more securely, was slowly reaching screaming point. The family of the unspeakably hopeless Pattie Beasley (none of whom had ever been on a horse) had all turned up in jodhpurs. Sally-Ann Thomson's frightful mother hung around the whole time, talking at the top of her voice, so all the other competitors turned around and laughed at her.

'It doesn't matter about winning, dear,' she was now telling Sally-Ann. 'Competing and having fun is all that matters.'

'Bloody rubbish,' thought Jake. 'They all sulk if they're not placed.'

After Sally-Ann's pony had bolted with her, and Pattie Beasley's cob had had a kicking match with the priceless winner of the under 13.2 showing class, causing loss of temper on all sides, Jake had refused to let any of the

children ride their ponies until the jumping in the afternoon. He had nearly had a mutiny on his hands.

'Why can't I do some practice jumps on Syrup?'

'Why can't I ride Stardust over to get an ice cream?'

'Oh, Snowball's trodden on my toe.'

'How d'you rate Sally-Ann's chances in the junior
jumping?' asked Mrs Thomson, sweating in an emerald
green wool suit.

'Non-existent,' snapped Jake.

'Joyce Wilton said Sally-Ann was the best little horsewoman in Surrey.'

'Can Pattie enter for the potato race?' asked Mrs Beasley.

'If she wants to waste her money, the secretary's tent's
over there.'

Sally-Ann's mother returned to the attack: 'We've paid
for the pony all day.' (Mrs Wilton charged £12 a gymkhana.) 'My little girl should be able to ride as much as she
likes.'

Jake's head throbbed with the effort of filtering out
conversation. The clamour went on, deafening, shrill and
demanding. He might as well get a job as a nanny. No
wonder sheepdogs had nervous breakdowns. No wonder
mothers battered babies and babies battered mothers. He
wanted to turn off the din, like the wireless, and lie down in
the long lush grass by the river and go to sleep.

His eye ran over the row of bored, depressed-looking
ponies standing on three legs, tails swishing ineffectually
against the flies, occasionally flattening their ears at one
another. They're trapped like me, he thought.

His face became less frosty as he came to little Fenella
Maxwell, standing on a bucket, replaiting the long-
suffering Dandelion's mane for the third time. She was a
good kid. Surprisingly she wasn't spoilt by her bitch of a
mother, who would be guzzling champagne up at the big
house with the nobs by now.

His eyes softened even more when they came to rest on
Africa. Not dozing like the ponies, she looked around with
her huge eyes, taking everything in, reassuring herself

constantly that Jake was still there.

The prospect of the open jumping and the risk he was running made him steadily more sick with nerves. He lit another cigarette.

Next time a huge horse box drew up, a groom got out, unfastened the ramp and led out a beautifully plaited-up grey, sweating in a crimson rug with dark blue binding. A girl wearing a white shirt, a black coat, skin-tight breeches and long black boots walked over and looked the horse over critically. She had a haughty pink and white face. Jake thought how attractive some women looked in riding clothes, the austerity and severity of the uniform contrasting with the wild wantonness beneath. He imagined her long thighs threshing in ecstasy, while the hat, tie and haughty pink and white face remained primly in place. He imagined laying her on a bed of straw, as tempting as a newly made bed.

As if aware of Jake's scrutiny, she turned around. Jake looked away quickly, determined not to give her the satisfaction of knowing she was being fancied.

'Lavinia!' A handsome dark boy, white teeth gleaming in his suntanned face, pulled up his huge chestnut horse beside her.

'Christopher. Hullo. I thought you were in Marbella.'

'Just got back.'

'Come and have a dwink.' She couldn't say her Rs. 'Mummy's parked the car by the collecting wing.'

'Love to.' He rode on.

Bloody upper classes, thought Jake, all making so much bloody noise. He was fed up with wearing a cheap riding coat and third-hand boots that were already killing him. He wanted a horse box, and a groom whisking out different horses like a conjurer producing coloured handkerchiefs, and a tackroom wall papered with red rosettes, and a beautiful pink and white girl asking him respectfully how many strides there were between the gate and the rustic poles.

A shrill piping voice brought him back to earth.

12

'I've bought you an ice cream,' said Fenella Maxwell. 'You ought to keep up your strength. Oh, look, they're bringing out the jumps for the junior jumping. I know I'm going to let Dandelion down. Mummy and Tory'll miss it if they don't stop stuffing themselves.'

Inside Bilborough Hall, Tory Maxwell, Fenella's elder sister, looked up at a large Rubens, in which a huge pink fleshy Venus was being pursued by half the satyr population of Ancient Greece, while adoring cherubs arranged her rippling pearl-strewn hair. 'She's much fatter than me,' thought Tory wistfully. 'Why wasn't I born in the 17th century?'

She had huge grey eyes and long, straight, light brown hair, which her mother insisted she wore drawn back off her forehead and temples and tied in a bow on the crown of her head. A style which made her round, pleading, peony red face look bigger than ever. She was tallish and big boned, with a huge bust that bounced up and down as she walked. However she stood on the scales, she weighed eleven stone.

She'd just got the curse, which made her feel even fatter, and, however many layers of *Erace* she put on, a large red spot on her chin glowed through like a lighthouse. She was getting hotter and hotter, but she couldn't take off the jacket of her red suit because the skirt was fastened precariously by a nappy pin. Her ankles had swelled and, having kicked off her tight shoes, she wondered if she'd ever be able to get back into them again. She wondered if she'd ever been more miserable in her life. Then, with a stab of pain, she remembered last night's dance and decided she was comparatively blessed.

During the week-days she was at a finishing school in London, learning to cook, to type, and to arrange flowers by ramming bits of rhubarb into chicken mesh. By night she practised the art of wallflower arrangement, going to drinks parties and dances and trying to appear as though she belonged to one of those chattering, laughing groups of debs and their admirers. Occasionally, hostesses took pity on her and brought up wilting, reluctant young men who talked politely or danced one dance, then drifted away.

The more miserable she got, the more she ate. But never at dances, never in front of her mother. She would wait for everyone to go out or to bed, then wolf three bowls of cornflakes swimming in double cream. Yesterday she'd eaten a whole box of chocolates, which had been given to her mother by an admirer, and then had to rush out to the shops and buy another box to replace it before her mother got back.

Why couldn't she be like Fen, and have something like horses to be passionately interested in and keep her nose out of the trough? Why did she have to stay inside on this lovely day when she wanted to be outside, picnicking with Fen and Jake? At the thought of Jake, dark-faced and unpredictable, whom she had never spoken to, her stomach felt weak, her mouth dry. Oh Jake! At night she wrote him long passionate letters which she always tore up. Small men were supposed to like big girls; look at D. H. Lawrence and Stanley Spencer. Perhaps having no parents, and being brought up in a children's home, he might be looking for a mother figure, but he didn't seem to be showing much sign so far.

Tory's mother, Molly Maxwell, had enjoyed her lunch *enormously*. She was delighted to be asked. Colonel Carter, who had accompanied her, had enjoyed himself too. It had been fun being able to introduce him to Sir William, and they'd got on well talking about the war. She combed her hair surreptitiously; Gerald had done it beautifully this week. Why was Tory hanging round like a wet blanket? Sir William's sons were there. All of them Old Etonians, nice looking and so suitable, and Tory hadn't addressed a word to any of them all through lunch, just sat like a pig, and taking a second helping of pudding when she thought her mother wasn't looking.

'Poor Molly,' she could imagine people saying, 'poor

14

Molly to be saddled with such a lump.'

'No, I won't have any more wine, thank you, Sir William.' She didn't want to get red in the face. Her new, silk-lined dress and jacket in periwinkle blue was most becoming. This afternoon she'd probably take the jacket off; her arms were still slender and already turning brown.

She was really enjoying Tory doing the season. Jennifer's Diary, this week, had described her as the chic and most attractive mother of Tory Maxwell. At least one deb's delight and several fathers had declared themselves madly in love with her. And now Colonel Carter was getting really keen and sending roses twice a week.

To top everything, last night she had heard two young bloods discussing Tory.

'Wonder if it would be worth marrying her for her money,' said the first.

'I'd certainly marry her for her Mummy,' said the second. 'Molly Maxwell is absolutely gorgeous.'

Molly thought that was too amusing for words.

Molly was a bit short of cash at the moment. Her rather stolid husband had paid her a great deal of alimony, but when he inconveniently died, he had left all his money, unaccountably, in trust for Tory. That was another grudge; what did Tory want with an income of £5,000 a year?

Tory looked across at her mother. 'I'm the fruit of her womb, and I hate her, hate her, hate her,' she thought, 'for her ankles slender as a gazelle's, and her flexible high insteps, and thin Knightsbridge legs, and her painted malicious face, and her shrill clipped voice, not unlike Fen's! Look at Sir William bending over her.'

'No, really,' Molly was saying, 'is it by Ferneley? How fascinating. No, do tell me.'

And that dreadful Colonel Carter, Colonel Bogus more likely, handsome as an ageing movie star, matinee-idling about, a cliché of chauvinism, his large yellow teeth gleaming amicably beneath his greying moustache, as he blamed even the weather on the Socialists.

'No, my younger daughter Fen's riding,' Molly was

15

saying to Sir William. 'She's absolutely horse-mad; up first thing mucking out, never get her to wear a dress. Oh, I see you take *The Tatler* too; not for the articles really; but it's such fun to see which of one's chums are in this week.'

'No, not my only child,' Tory could hear her mother going on. 'There's Tory over there; yes, she's more like her father . . . Yes, just eighteen . . . Well, how kind of you to say so. I suppose I was rather young when I got married.'

'Mustn't monopolize you,' said Sir William, getting up from his chair and noticing Colonel Carter hovering. 'Come and sit down, Carter; can't say I blame you.'

Next moment, Sir William was hurrying across the room to welcome the two judges, Malise Gordon and Miss Squires, who, on a tight schedule, had only time for a quick bite. Malise Gordon, having accepted a weak whisky and soda, refused to follow it with any wine. He took a small helping of salmon but no potatoes, not because he was worried about getting fat, but because he liked to practise asceticism. An ex-Cavalry officer, much medalled after a good war, Colonel Gordon not only farmed but also judged at shows all around the country during the summer, and was kept busy in the winter as the local MFH. He was inclined to apply army discipline to the hunting field to great effect and told people exactly what he thought of them if they talked at the covert side, rode over seeds or left gates open. In addition to these activities, he played the flute, restored pictures in his spare time and wrote poetry and books on military history. Just turned fifty, he was tall and lean with a handsome, hawklike face, high cheekbones and dark hair hardly touched with grey.

That is easily the most attractive man in the room, thought Molly Maxwell, eyeing him speculatively as she accepted Colonel Carter's heavy pleasantries, and let her laugh tinkle again and again round the room. Malise Gordon was now talking to Sir William's wife, Lady Dorothy. What an old frump, thought Molly Maxwell. That dreadful fawn cardigan with marks on it and lace-up shoes and the sort of baggy tweed skirt you'd feed the chickens in.

16

As an excuse to be introduced to Malise, Molly got up and, wandering over to Lady Dorothy, thanked her for a delicious lunch.

'Absolutely first rate,' agreed Colonel Carter, who'd followed her.

'Would you like to see around the garden?' said Lady Dorothy.

Malise Gordon looked at his watch.

'We better go and supervise the junior jumping,' he said to Miss Squires.

'Oh, my daughter's in that,' said Molly Maxwell, giving Malise Gordon a dazzling smile. 'I hope you'll turn a blind eye if she knocks anything down. It would be such a thrill if she got a rosette.'

Malise Gordon didn't smile back. He had heard Molly's laugh once too often and thought her very silly.

'Fortunately, jumping is the one event in which one can't possibly display any favouritism.'

Colonel Carter, aware that his beloved had been snubbed, decided Malise Gordon needed taking down a peg.

'What's the order for this afternoon?' he asked.

'Junior jumping, open jumping, then gymkhana events in ring three, then your show in ring two, Carter.'

A keen territorial, Colonel Carter was organizing a recruiting display which included firing twenty-five pounders.

'We're scheduled for 1700 hours,' snapped Colonel Carter. 'Hope you'll have wound your jumping up by then, Gordon. My chaps like to kick off on time.'

'I hope you won't do anything silly like firing off blanks while there are horses in the ring,' said Malise brusquely. 'It could be extremely dangerous.

'Thanks, Dorothy, for a splendid lunch,' he added, kissing Lady Dorothy on the cheek. 'The garden's looking marvellous.'

Colonel Carter turned purple. What an arrogant bastard, he thought, glaring after Malise's broad, very straight

17

back as he followed Miss Squires briskly out of the drawing room. But then the cavalry always gave themselves airs. Earlier, at the briefing, Malise had had the ill manners to point out that he thought a horse show was hardly the place to introduce a lot of people who had nothing better to do with their afternoons than play soldiers. 'I'll show him,' fumed Colonel Carter.

Outside, hackney carriages were bouncing around the ring, drawn by high-stepping horses, rosettes streaming from their striped browbands, while junior riders crashed their ponies over the practice fence. By some monumental inefficiency, the organizers of the show had also ended up with three celebrities, who'd all arrived to present the prizes and needed looking after.

Bobby Cotterel, Africa's owner, had originally been allotted the task, but at the last moment he'd pushed off to France, and such was the panic of finding a replacement that three other celebrities had been booked and accepted. The first was the Lady Mayoress, who'd opened the show and toured the exhibits and who had now been borne off to inspect the guides. The second was Miss Bilborough 1970, whose all-day-long make-up had not stood up to the heat. The third was a radio celebrity, with uniformly grey hair and a black treacle voice named Dudley Diplock. Having played a doctor in a long-running serial, he talked at the top of his voice all the time in the hope that the public might recognize him. He had now commandeered the microphone for the junior jumping.

Fen felt her stomach getting hollower and hollower. The jumps looked huge. The first fence was as big as Epping Forest.

'Please, God, let me not have three refusals, let me not let Dandelion down.'

'Oh, here comes Tory,' she said as Jake helped her saddle up Dandelion. 'She went to a dance last night but I don't think she enjoyed it; her eyes were awfully red this morning.'

Jake watched the plump, anxious-faced Tory wincing

18

over the churned-up ground in her tight shoes. She didn't look like a girl who enjoyed anything very much.

'Did you have a nice lunch? I bet you had strawberries,' shrieked Fen, climbing onto Dandelion and gathering up the reins. 'I'm just going to put Dandelion over a practice fence.

'This is my sister, Tory,' she added.

Jake looked at Tory with that measure of disapproval he always bestowed on strangers.

'It's very hot,' stammered Tory.

'Very,' said Jake.

There didn't seem much else to say.

Fortunately, Tory was saved by the microphone calling the competitors into the collecting ring.

'Mr Lovell, I can't get Stardust's girths to meet, she's blown herself out,' wailed Pattie Beasley.

Jake went over and gave Stardust a hefty knee-up in the belly.

Fen came back from jumping the practice fence. Immediately Dandelion's head went down, snatching at the grass.

'You pig,' squealed Fen, jumping off and pulling bits out of his mouth. 'I just cleaned that bit. Where's Mummy?' she added to Tory.

'Going over the garden with Lady Dorothy,' said Tory.

'She must be bored,' said Fen. 'No, there she is over on the other side of the ring.'

Looking across, they could see Mrs Maxwell standing beside Sally-Ann Thomson's mother, while Colonel Carter adjusted her deck chair.

'Colonel Carter stayed last night,' said Fen in disgust. 'I couldn't sleep and I looked out of the window at about five o'clock and saw him go. He looked up at Mummy's bedroom and blew her a great soppy kiss. Think of kissing a man with an awful, droopy moustache like that. I suppose there's no accounting for tastes.'

'Fen,' said Tory, blushing scarlet. She looked at Jake out of the corner of her eye to see if he was registering shock or amusement, but his face was quite expressionless.

'No. 58,' called out the collecting ring steward.

A girl in a dark blue riding coat on a very shiny bay mare went in and jumped clear. Some nearby drunks in a Bentley, whose boot groaned with booze, hooted loudly on their horn.

'How was her ladyship's garden?' asked Colonel Carter.

'I think I was given a tour of every petal,' said Molly Maxwell.

'You must have been the fairest flower,' said the Colonel, putting his deck chair as close to hers as possible. 'My people used to have a lovely garden in Hampshar.'

The radio personality, Dudley Diplock, having mastered the microphone, was now thoroughly enjoying himself.

'Here comes the junior champion for Surrey,' he said. 'Miss Cock, Miss Sarah Cock on Topsy.'

A girl with buck teeth rode in. Despite her frenziedly flailing legs the pony ground to a halt three times in front of the first fence.

'Jolly bad luck, Topsy,' said the radio personality. 'Oh, I beg your pardon, here comes Miss Sarah Cock, I mean Cook, on Topsy.'

A girl on a heavily bandaged dappled grey came in and jumped a brisk clear round.

Next came Sally-Ann Thomson.

'Here's my little girl,' said Mrs Thomson, pausing for a moment in her discussion of hats with Mrs Maxwell. 'I wonder if Stardust will go better in a running martingale.'

Stardust decided not and refused three times at the first fence.

'We really ought to buy her a pony of her own,' said Mrs Thomson. 'Even the best riders can't do much on riding-school hacks.'

Mrs Maxwell winked at Colonel Carter.

Round followed round; everyone agreed the standard was frightful.

'And here we have yet another competitor from Brook Farm Riding School; Miss Pattie Beasley on Swindle.'

Swindle trotted dejectedly into the ring, rolling-eyed and

thin-legged, like a horse in a medieval tapestry. Then, like a car running out of petrol, she ground to a halt in front of the first fence.

Jake raised his eyes to heaven.

'Jesus Christ,' he muttered.

Swindle's third refusal was too much for Patty's father, who'd bought breeches specially to attend the show. Rushing across the grass he brandished a shooting stick shouting 'Geron'. Terrified, Swindle rose like a stag from the hard ground and took a great leap over the brush fence, whereupon Patty fell off and burst into tears.

'Another competitor from Brook Farm Riding School eliminated,' said Dudley Diplock.

'Teach them to fall off there, don't they?' said a wag.

The crowd guffawed. Jake gritted his teeth. He was aware of Tory standing beside him and, sensing her sympathy, was grateful.

'It's your turn next,' said Jake, going up to Fen and checking Dandelion's girths. 'Take the double slowly. Everyone else has come round the corner too fast and not given themselves enough time. Off you go,' he added, gently pulling Dandelion's ears.

'Please, God, I'll never be bad again,' prayed Fen. 'I won't be foul to Sally-Ann or call Patty a drip, or be rude to Mummy. Just let me get around.'

Ignoring the cries of good luck, desperately trying to remember everything Jake had told her, Fen rode into the ring with a set expression on her face.

'Miss Fenella Maxwell, from Brook Farm Riding School,' said the radio personality. 'Let's have a round of applause for our youngest competitor.'

The crowd, scenting carnage, clapped lethargically. Dandelion, his brown and white patches gleaming like a conker that had been opened too early, gave a good-natured buck.

'Isn't that your little girl?' said Mrs Thomson.

'So it is,' said Molly Maxwell, 'Oh look, her pony's going to the lav. Don't horses have an awful sense of timing?'

21

The first fence loomed as high as Becher's Brook and Fen used her legs so fiercely, Dandelion rose into the air, clearing it by a foot.

Fen was slightly unseated and unable to get straight in the saddle to ride Dandelion properly at the gate. He slowed down and refused; when Fen whacked him he rolled his eyes, swished his tail and started to graze. The crowd laughed; Fen went crimson.

'Oh, poor thing,' murmured Tory in anguish.

Fen pulled his head up and let him examine the gate. Dandelion sniffed, decided it was harmless and, with a whisk of his fat rump, flew over and went bucketing on to clear the stile, at which Fen lost her stirrup, then cleared the parallel bars, where she lost the other stirrup. Rounding the corner for home, Dandelion stepped up the pace. Fen checked him, her hat falling over her nose, as he bounded towards the road-closed sign. Dandelion, fighting for his head, rapped the fence, but it stayed put.

'I can't bear to look,' thought Tory, shutting her eyes.

Fen had lost her hat now and, plaits flying, raced towards the triple. Jake watched her strain every nerve to get the take-off right. Dandelion cleared it by inches and galloped out of the ring to loud applause.

'Miss Fenella Maxwell on Dandelion, only three faults for a refusal; jolly good round,' coughed the microphone.

'I had no idea she'd improved so much,' said Tory, turning a pink, ecstatic face towards Jake.

Fen cantered up, grinning from ear to ear.

'Wasn't Dandelion wonderful?' she said, jumping off, flinging her arms round his neck, covering him with kisses and stuffing him with sugar lumps.

She looked up at Jake enquiringly: 'Well?'

'We could see half the show ground between your knees and the saddle, and you took him too fast at the gate, but not bad,' he said.

For the first time that day he looked cheerful, and Tory thought how nice he was.

'I must go and congratulate Fen,' said Mrs Maxwell,

delicately picking her way through the dung that Manners had not yet gathered.

'Well done, darling,' she shrieked in a loud voice, which made all the nearby horses jump. 'What a good boy,' she added, gingerly patting Dandelion's nose with a gloved hand. 'He is a boy, isn't he?' She tilted her head sideways to look.

'Awfully good show,' said Colonel Carter. 'My sister used to jump on horseback in Hampshar.'

Mrs Maxwell turned to Jake, enveloping him in a sickening waft of Arpège.

'Fen really has come on. I do hope she isn't too much of a nuisance down at the stables all day, but she is utterly pony mad. Every sentence begins, "Jake said this, Jake says that"; you've become quite an ogre in our home.'

'Oh, Mummy,' groaned Fen.

Jake, thinking how silly she was and unable to think of anything to say in reply, remained silent.

'How gauche he is,' thought Molly Maxwell.

The junior class, having finished jumping off, were riding into the ring to collect their rosettes.

'No. 86,' howled the collecting ring steward, 'No. 86.'

'That's you, Fen,' said Tory in excitement.

'It couldn't be. I had a refusal.'

'You're fourth,' said Jake, 'go on.'

'I couldn't be.'

'No. 86, for the last time,' bellowed the ring steward.

'It is me,' said Fen, and scrambling onto Dandelion, plonking her hat on her head and not wearing a riding coat, she cantered into the ring, where she thanked Miss Bilborough three times for her rosette. Success went to Dandelion's head and his feet. Thinking the lap of honour was a race, he barged ahead of the other three winners, carting Fen out of the ring and galloping half round the show ground before she could pull him to a halt in front of Jake. He shook his head disapprovingly.

Fen giggled. 'Wouldn't it be lovely if Africa got one too?'

23

3

The afternoon wore on, getting hotter. The Lady Mayoress, sweating in her scarlet robes, had a bright yellow nose from sniffing Lady Dorothy's lilies. The band was playing Land of Hope and Glory in the main ring as the fences for the open jumping were put up, the sun glinting on their brass instruments. Mrs Thomson and Mrs Maxwell moved their deck chairs to the right, following the sun, and agreed that Jake was extremely rude.

'I'm going to have a word with Joyce Wilton about it,' said Molly Maxwell.

'Horse, horse, horse,' said Mr Thomson.

'I can never get Fen to wear a dress; she's never been interested in dolls,' said Molly Maxwell, who was still crowing over Fen's rosette.

'I'm pleased Sally-Ann has not lost her femininity,' said Mrs Thomson.

'It's extraordinary how many people read *The Tatler*,' said Mrs Maxwell.

'Mrs Squires to the judge's tent,' announced the tannoy system.

'Miss Squires, Miss Squires,' snapped the hair-netted lady judge, stumping across the ring.

'Wasn't Dandelion wonderful?' said Fen for the hundreth time.

Tory could feel the sweat dripping between her breasts and down her ribs. She'd taken off her red jacket and hung her white shirt outside, over the straining safety pin.

Competitors in the open jumping were pulling on long black boots, the women tucking long hair into hairnets and

24

hotting up their horses over the practice fence. With £100 first prize there was a lot of competition from neighbouring counties. Two well-known show jumpers, Lavinia Greenslade and Christopher Crossley, who'd both jumped at Wembley and for the British junior team, had entered, but local hopes were pinned on Sir William's son, Michael, who was riding a grey six-year-old called Prescott.

Armoured cars and tanks had started driving up the hill for the dry shoot and the recruiting display. Soldiers, sweating in battledress, were assembling 25-pounders in ring two.

'Christ, here comes Carter's circus,' said Malise Gordon to Miss Squires.

'Hope he can keep them under control.'

'My chaps have arrived,' said Colonel Carter to Mrs Maxwell. 'I'm just going to wander over and see that everything's all right.'

Jake gave Africa a last polish. Tory, noticing his dead white face, shaking hands and chattering teeth, realized how terrified he was and felt sorry for him. He put a foot in the stirrup and was up.

'If only I weren't so frightened of horses I might not be frightened of life,' thought Tory, cringing against the rope to avoid these great snorting beasts with their huge iron feet and so much power in their gleaming, barging quarters.

The band went out to much applause and, to everyone's dismay, came back again. Jake rode up to Tory and jumped off.

'Can you hold her for a minute?' he said, hurling the reins at her.

He only just made the Gents' in time.

Looking into the deep, dark dell of the Elsan, and catching a whiff of the contents, he was violently sick again. He must pull himself together or Africa would sense his nerves. Mrs Wilton wouldn't find out; the kids could cope in the gymkhana events for half an hour by themselves. He'd be all right once he got into the ring. He'd walked the course; there was nothing Africa couldn't jump if he put her

25

right. He leant against the canvas and wondered if he dared risk another cigarette.

Tory was not happy. Excited by the microphone and the armoured cars and the crowds, Africa pulled and fretted as she jogged up and down.

'Thanks very much,' said Jake, taking the horse from her.

Tory looked at his white face and chattering teeth and felt so sorry for him. 'I get just the same before dances,' she blurted out.

Jake smiled slightly.

'Take your partners for the torture chamber,' he said, mounting Africa again.

He rode very short, almost jockey length, crouching over the mare like a cat, settling down into the creaking leather. Africa, a netted cord of veins rippling under her shining coat, tugged at the reins, now this way, now that. Trying to catch Jake out, she danced over the grass, shying at the tea tent, the ladies' lavatory, the flags. Jake didn't move in the saddle.

Christopher Crossley, the good-looking boy on the chestnut with four white socks, cantered past, startling Africa who bucked and swished her tail. Jake swore at him.

'Jake rides lovely, doesn't he?' sighed Fen.

Even Tory's uncritical eye could see that he rode wonderfully lightly; his hands hardly touched Africa's mouth. Taking her away from the crowd, he popped her over a couple of practice fences.

Colonel Carter sat down beside Molly Maxwell, announcing that his chaps were itching to get started. At that moment a competitor on a huge grey paused in front of them to chat to some friends. The grey promptly stuck out its penis. Mrs Maxwell caught the Colonel's eye and giggled.

'Aren't horses rude?'

The Colonel gave a bark of embarrassed laughter. Mrs Maxwell found she couldn't stop giggling. Tears were making her mascara run.

The band were playing a selection from *The Merry Widow*.

'Delia, oh Delia,' sang Colonel Carter, brushing his khaki leg against her silken thigh.

'Will you be able to get out again this evening?' he asked.

Molly stopped giggling with a little hiccup. 'Oh, Tory'll babysit. That's one way she's useful. Oh dear, I don't mean to be bitchy.'

'You never say an unkind word about anyone.'

No, thought Molly, perhaps I don't.

The Colonel looked at his watch.

'Half an hour to blast off,' he said. 'I hope Malise Gordon gets his finger out.'

There were nine jumps in all: a brush fence, a stile, a gate, parallel bars, the road-closed sign put up to a nasty five foot, another brush with a pole on top, a water jump which had been drained by various dogs, a wall and a triple.

The two stars, Lavinia Greenslade and Christopher Crossley, stood side by side slightly apart from the other competitors.

'The jumps are much too low and flimsy,' said Lavinia. 'Bound to be loads of clear wounds. We won't get away for at least an hour and I did want to look in at Henwietta's dwinks party.'

'Not much competition anyway,' said Christopher, adding to the groom, who was holding his horse, 'Cindy, can you adjust that bandage?'

The first competitor trotted out, an enormously fat girl with a huge bosom.

'Give herself a couple of black eyes every time she jumps with those boobs,' said Christopher.

The girl went clear.

'I told you there were going to be loads of clear wounds,' said Lavinia petulantly.

'I can't see, I can't see,' said Fen in a shrill voice.

'You come through here then,' said a man on a shooting stick, making a gap in the crowd through which Fen dragged a desperately embarrassed Tory to the ropes.

A chestnut came in, ridden by a boy with a big nose who jabbed his horse in the mouth over every fence.

'Jumps well,' said Tory.

'Horse does,' said Fen. 'Rider should be shot. Bloody hell,' she added as he went clear. The man on the shooting stick who'd let Fen through looked at her with less indulgence.

Lavinia Greenslade was next, the grey peering seductively through the long forelock of its mane, Arab ears curling upwards like eyelashes.

'Her father spends a fortune on her horses,' said Fen. 'That one was third at the Horse of the Year Show last year.'

Sure enough, the grey bounced serenely round the course like a ping pong ball, followed by Sir William's son who also went clear.

To the course builders' relief a man came in on a horse wearing so much leather it looked like a bondage victim and proceeded to demolish the course completely. Fear travelled through the collecting ring and for a dozen rounds no one went clear. The wall, the principal bogey, had to be laboriously rebuilt each time.

Colonel Carter looked at his watch. Five minutes to go. Time and the Colonel waited for no Malise Gordon.

Lavinia's boyfriend, Christopher, then went in and killed the jinx by jumping a very fast clear round. Jake envied the casual way he threw his whip to his groom, slid off the horse and went back to the ringside to join Lavinia and watch the rest of the rounds.

The next competitor was an old woman in a hair net with raddled face, scarlet lipstick and withered cheeks embedded with rouge.

'She's only seven stone,' said the man who'd let Fen through.

'Half of that's make-up,' muttered Fen.

The old lady rode as though she was steering a Rolls Royce. Her cob went clear without any visible effort.

'Jake's after this,' said Fen, as a girl with a bun escaping

28

from her hairnet came in on a mangy brown mare and proceeded to scatter every fence. As she came to the wall the mare dug in her toes and skidded four feet into the wall; then, as the bricks collapsed around her, she bolted on to totally demolish the triple.

'Oh, poor Jake,' said Fen, as they waited and waited for the course to be repaired.

At last they called number 195. Out came Jake from the gap in the crowds, his face a grey mask. By contrast, Africa, who danced and plunged, merry eyes gleaming at the crowd, coat rippling like a furniture polish advertisement, looked the picture of joy.

'Jack Lovette,' said Dudley Diplock. 'From Brook Farm Riding School.'

'Not another one,' Malise Gordon groaned inwardly.

Tory could see Jake's lips constantly moving, as he reassured Africa.

'Only time he talks is to horses,' grumbled Fen.

Once in the ring, Jake found his nerves had gone. He shortened his reins and stood up in the stirrups. Africa bounded towards the first fence.

'Too quick,' muttered Fen.

But Africa was over safely and Jake's eyes were already trained on the post and rails ahead, which she cleared easily. At the gate, catching sight of a balloon in the crowd, she stopped concentrating and rapped her hock hard. The gate swung, but miraculously didn't come down.

'That'll teach her,' said Fen, as Africa dragged her leg for a couple of paces.

'Rides well,' said a voice in the crowd.

'Horse carrying a lot of condition.'

'Isn't that Jake Lovell?' said Molly Maxwell.

Africa slowed down at the wall, then changed her mind and cleared it with a violent jerky cat jump, which would have unseated most riders.

'Haven't seen that boy before,' thought Malise. 'Handles that horse very well. She's not at all an easy ride.' With increasing pleasure he watched Africa clear the post and

29

rails and the parallel bars and sail over the water jump and the wall.

But, as Jake turned her towards the triple, Malise realized it was unnaturally high. One of the arena stewards who'd been crossed in love, and in the beer tent all afternoon, had just seen his beloved saunter past on the arm of a rival and had put the top bar up to six feet.

Malise Gordon stepped forward to protest but it was too late. Africa had turned and was approaching the triple at a steeplechaser's pace, her feet drumming on the ground, fighting for her head.

'Steady, darling,' crooned Jake.

The top bar, white against pitted grey-green turf, was higher than Africa's ears. For a second she hesitated, caught on a short stride, then, like a helicopter, rising off her hocks, she made a colossal jump. It seemed to the gaping crowd that she had taken off like a bird into the sky and bore no relation to the white poles below her.

'Christ,' said Malise.

At the same time Sir William's binoculars fastened on Africa. He checked his programme. From Brook Farm Riding School, of all unlikely places. She might do very well for Mikey next season.

The crowd gave a long sigh of rapture and sent up a great cheer.

Colonel Carter looked at his watch.

'Bloody good round,' said Christopher Crossley.

Jake jumped off Africa, patting her, determined not to betray the surge of exultation that was sweeping over him.

'That's it,' Malise Gordon told the arena party. 'Restrict it to six jumps, raise the pole over the first jump and the gate, put another row of bricks on the wall and put the triple at five feet. Buck up, or Carter will start letting off his guns.'

'That's seven clear rounds,' said Fen, counting on her fingers.

Colonel Carter heaved himself out of his deck chair.

'Are you off?' said Molly.

'Enemy wouldn't wait, would they? The men will start the display in ten minutes,' he said, striding past Malise.

'Don't be bloody silly,' snapped Malise. 'If you fire a single shot before the last horse has jumped, you'll cause chaos – and accidents.'

'Quarter of an hour; should give you ample time.'

'I'll send someone to give you the O.K.'

Colonel Carter ground his big yellow teeth. He was tired. Last night, with Molly, had been wonderful but rather exhausting. He hadn't had much sleep; the effects of Sir William's hospitality at lunchtime had worn off and, worst of all, he resented Malise's complete refusal to take his display seriously.

In ring three, near the chestnut trees, the gymkhana events were already starting, with a burst of music for musical chairs.

'Can you help me saddle up Swindle, Mr Lovell?' said Pattie Beasley.

'Give me quarter of an hour,' said Jake.

The horses waited in the collecting ring, maddened by flies, the heat and the rumble of approaching thunder.

'If you win, will you tell Mrs Wilton?' asked Fen.

'God, no. If she knew how good Africa was, she'd persuade Bobby to sell. Wish I could buy her myself, but I'd have to win the pools or marry an heiress.'

'Marry Tory,' said Fen with a giggle. 'She's going to be frightfully rich one day, and you could keep lots of horses, and I could come and live with you.'

'Fen,' said Tory, going crimson.

She was a champion blusher, thought Jake.

Fen watched Sally-Ann Thomson bumping off to take part in the musical chairs.

'Good thing Mrs Wilton's in Brighton,' she said. 'She'd be jolly cross if she knew you weren't keeping your eyes on her darling pupils.'

* * *

31

Mrs Wilton eased her car through the traffic. It had been a most unsatisfactory day. Her rich homosexual uncle, irritated by the heat and the refractoriness of his male hairdresser friend, had been so quarrelsome at lunchtime that she had walked out in a huff. One look at Brighton beach, packed with trippers avid for a day in the sun, and she had decided to drive back home to avoid the rush hour traffic. The journey, in fact, had been so easy that she decided to look in at the Bilborough Show. It never hurt to turn up unexpectedly; it kept Jake up to the mark. She rummaged in her bag for lipstick and applied it without even looking in the mirror.

Colonel Carter's blood pressure rose with the temperature. Bugger Malise Gordon. He would not only lose the respect of his soldiers, dying of the heat in their battledress, but also of the sizeable crowd, who'd turned up at five to witness some bangs and were now drifting away.

'People are getting bored with waiting, sir,' said his adjutant.

'Take this to Colonel Gordon,' said Colonel Carter, handing him a note:- 'The guns will be fired at 17.20 hours. Carter.'

It was just like the Charge of the Light Brigade, thought the young soldier, as he returned two minutes later with the same bit of paper, on the back of which Malise Gordon had scrawled:

'Imperative to wait end of last round. Gordon.'

Colonel Carter tore up the note in a fury.

The girl with the big boobs had seven faults, Sir William's son had eight. The horse whose rider jabbed him in the mouth had had enough and refused the brush fence twice, the stile once, and was eliminated. The old lady covered in make-up went next; she took a brick off the wall and knocked the bar of the triple.

Mrs Wilton parked her car. It looked as though the open jumping was still going. Colonel Carter examined his watch.

Christopher Crossley was about to start his round.

'Shall we divide, Lavinia,' he said, 'if we both go clear?'

'Fire!' The word of command rang out on the midgy, steamy air. Crash went the twenty-five pounders, causing immediate pandemonium in the collecting rings, horses rearing, bucking, plunging and scattering the crowd.

Lavinia Greenslade's grey was barging about like a dodgem car with rabies. Jake jumped straight off Africa and was clinging on to her bridle trying to calm her.

White with anger, Malise Gordon left Miss Squires and the green baize table and sprinted across to ring two, where he was joined by Sir William asking, 'What the hell is going on?'

'That megalomaniac Carter,' said Malise, striding up to Colonel Carter.

'What the bloody hell are you playing at? Stop those guns at *once*!'

Colonel Carter's reply was drowned in another crash.

A horse that had dumped its rider bolted past them reins and stirrups flying, followed by the girl with the big boobs who was also being carted.

'Look at that,' said Malise. 'There'll be a serious accident in a minute.'

'Your people should be able to control their mounts,' said Colonel Carter. 'If you're incapable of keeping to a time schedule, you should accept the consequences.'

Another gun exploded.

'Think you might hang on five minutes, Carter,' said Sir William. 'Only three horses left to jump.'

'Hold your fire, Colonel,' said the Lady Mayoress, who had put her hands over her ears.

Carter decided he was outnumbered.

'All right, if you want to make a mockery of the whole display we'll wait another ten minutes.'

'Maniac,' said Christopher Crossley, whose horse was leaping around as though someone was burning the grass under its feet, its nostrils as red as a peony. Jake, who was trying to sooth a trembling sweating Africa, admired the way Christopher went into the ring, and jumped a beautiful round, only taking a brick out of the wall.

Lavinia Greenslade's grey, however, who'd been completely unhinged by the guns, crashed round the course, leaving it as though an earthquake had hit it.

Once again Jake had to wait until it was repaired, the strain telling on both his and Africa's nerves.

'Bad luck,' said Christopher Crossley, as Lavinia rode out, looking furious.

'I'm going to object,' she said.

Molly Maxwell joined Colonel Carter.

'Are you having a cease-fire?' she said with a giggle.

'Bloody Gordon, insisted on finishing his jumping.'

'You should have started half an hour ago,' said Molly. 'I wouldn't stand for that. Wellington would never have taken Waterloo that way.'

'Oh, my God,' gasped Fen, seeing Mrs Wilton pushing briskly through the crowd. 'Look who's over there, Tory. She'll go potty if she sees Jake. We'd better distract her. Hullo, Mrs Wilton, we thought you were in Brighton.'

'Decided to come back. Had a good day?'

'I was fourth in the Junior Jumping.'

'Your first rosette. Well done. Has anyone else done anything?'

Fen shook her head.

'Where's Jake?'

'Supervising the gymkhana events, I think,' said Tory desperately.

'Yes, he is. Come and find him, and on the way you can see how sweet Dandelion looks in his rosette,' said Fen, seizing Mrs Wilton's red hand. 'And then come and see Mummy. I know she wants to buy you a drink. You must be hot after your journey.' She looked a picture of guilt as the words came tumbling out.

'What happened in the open jumping?'

'It's finished,' said Fen.

The course had been set to rights.

'In you go,' said the collecting ring steward.

Jake rode quietly into the ring.

34

'That's a nice horse,' thought Malise.

'Oh there's one more competitor,' said Mrs Wilton.

'Come and see Dandelion,' said Fen desperately.

'Why, it's Jake,' said Mrs Wilton in tones of outrage, 'and he's riding Africa.'

Africa bounded up to the first fence, as tense as a catapult at full stretch.

The ten minutes were up. 'Fire!' said Colonel Carter for the second time.

The gun went off like a clap of thunder.

A dog bolted into the ring, barking hysterically, a child dropped its ice cream and let out a wail of rage. Africa went straight up on her hind legs, eyes rolling in terror, and dropping again, with a bound bolted towards the first fence clearing it by inches.

Jake sat down in the saddle and tried to hold her. Another gun went off. Africa crashed into the gate and sent the stile flying.

The crowd looked on, helpless. Tory and Fen watched, frozen with horror, as the maddened mare swung around the corner, with Jake hauling futilely on the bit, aware only of Africa's hooves thundering on the dry earth and the white terrified faces flashing past.

As she raced for the triple, ten yards off, another gun went off. Jake tried to check her, but she'd missed her stride and took it completely wrong, jumping sideways and catching her foreleg in the wing of the jump. The crowd gave a moan of terror.

Africa lay under three poles, legs flailing like a centipede, making desperate attempts to get up. Jake staggered groggily to his feet, stars in his head. Praying against hope that Africa hadn't broken a leg, he lurched towards her still holding onto the reins.

Another gun went off; Africa threw off the poles and struggled to her feet, standing trembling all over, holding up her off hind hoof.

Malise ran up.

'You all right?' he said.

Jake nodded. 'Not so sure about the horse; can't put her foot down.'

Malise took Africa's bridle, stroking her gently, then he led her forward a step. Africa hobbled, then stopped. Malise ran his hand down the foot; she winced, but let him touch it.

'Nothing broken. Might have pulled a tendon. Better get the vet.'

Another gun went off. Africa trembled violently but was finished.

'Sorry about that,' said Malise. 'She jumped very well in the first round. Look, sit down on the grass,' he added as Jake started to sway.

But the next moment Mrs Wilton rolled up, marching with a far more military stride than Colonel Carter.

'So this is what you get up to when I'm away,' she shouted. 'How dare you jump that horse, how *dare* you?'

Jake looked at her. Through a haze of pain he saw her red angry face like a baron of beef receding and coming towards him.

'Leave him alone,' snapped Malise. 'Can't you see he's in a state of shock.'

Mrs Wilton turned on Malise furiously.

Jake said nothing and, after another look at Africa's foot, led her hobbling out of the ring. Mrs Wilton followed him, shouting abuse. She wanted to sack him on the spot, but she couldn't afford to, as there'd be no one except that half-wit, Alison, who only worked part-time, to look after the horses. Grooms were so hard to get. She'd have to ask her copywriting brother to write a witty advertisement for *Horse and Hound*. She supposed it was her fault for being too lenient with Jake; she should never have offered him a drink in the evenings. As he came out of the ring, Fen rushed forward.

'Oh, poor Jake; are you all right? Are you concussed? Can you remember what day of the week it is and what you had for lunch?'

36

Next minute Mrs Thomson came roaring up.

'There was no one to help Sally-Ann in the bending. She's fallen off and hurt her arm. Oh, you're back, Joyce,' she added in relief. 'Things will go more smoothly from now on.' Tory felt so sorry for Jake, grey and shaking and the recipient of such a torrent of abuse from Mrs Wilton and Mrs Thomson.

Christopher Crossley passed them going into the ring to collect first prize. He pulled up his chestnut horse for a minute.

'That was bloody bad luck,' he said, 'and that's a very nice mare. If you ever want to sell her I'm in the North Hampshire telephone directory under Crossley. Those bloody soldiers should turn the guns on themselves.'

Jake nodded.

As they approached the horse lines, Fen gave a scream.

'Dandelion – he's not there!'

Rushing forward, she found his head collar still tied to the fence.

'He's a valuable horse now he's a prize winner,' she wailed. 'He's probably been kidnapped.'

After a nasty quarter of an hour, in which Mrs Wilton trailed after Jake, calling him every name under the sun, Dandelion was discovered in the brave new world of Lady Dorothy's vegetable garden. Having laid waste to the herbaceous border, dug holes in the newly sprinkled lawn, cut a swathe through the rose beds and de-formalized the formal garden, Dandelion was now imitating an untamed bronco, galloping about, snorting, showing the whites of his eyes, with a large carrot sticking out of his mouth like a cigar.

Every time Jake or Fen got close he whisked out of range, snatching bites to eat.

'He looks like the Hamlet advertisement,' said Fen, quite hysterical with giggles.

By the time Jake had caught him, abuse, from Lady Dorothy, Mrs Wilton and Mrs Thomson, was cascading over his head like Niagara.

At last it was time to go home. Africa had been checked by the vet, who said she was suffering a bad sprain, no more, and should be rested. Malise Gordon then hurried home himself because he was going to the theatre. Fen had come second in the potato race and was in a state of ecstasy. Miss Bilborough had a date with one of Colonel Carter's men. Dudley Diplock had been asked for his autograph three times, but had not been thanked for doing the commentary.

Back at Brook Farm Riding School, a still dizzy Jake was putting the ponies to bed.

'Hear you're in the dog house,' said Alison, the Irish girl who helped out at weekends. 'Old Ma Wilton's hopping. I knew she'd catch you out sooner or later.'

Jake didn't answer; he was putting a poultice on Africa. He'd already rubbed one of his gypsy medicines (ointment made from marshmallow flowers) gently into her leg. He was finally sweeping up at about nine-thirty, when Mrs Wilton turned up. Her faced looked unappetizingly magenta in the naked light bulb of the tack room and he could smell whisky on her breath.

'I want to talk to you, Jake,' she said, speaking slowly to show she was quite sober. 'Do you realize you've ruined the reputation of Brook Farm Riding School?'

'What reputation?' said Jake. 'You can't descend from the basement.'

'Don't be cheeky. No need to answer back.'

Jake swept up the straw on the floor. Phrases like 'absolute shambles', 'endangering best horse in the yard' and 'duty to our young pupils' flowed over his head. His face had taken on an almost Asiatic aloofness.

'Why can't he ever show any contrition?' thought Mrs Wilton. If he apologized just once it would make a difference.

The diatribe continued. 'Taking advantage', 'wonder who's employing whom', 'use my house as an hotel', 'after all I've done for you'. Jake mimicked her under his breath.

Oh, God, she was getting very close now; he hoped she

wasn't going to start anything.

'I'm very disappointed in you, Jake,' she went on. 'I really trusted you, gave you some responsibility and you just kick me in the teeth. Yet I still feel *deep down* that you really like me.' For a second her voice was almost obscenely conciliatory.

'No, I don't,' Jake said flatly. 'Deep down it's much worse.'

Mrs Wilton caught her breath. Next minute, vindictiveness was warming her blood. She played her trump card. 'You'd better get Africa's leg better; she won't be with us much longer.'

Jake looked up, eyes narrowed.

'That jolted him,' she thought.

'Sir William's just rung. I thought he was going to raise hell about Lady Dorothy's garden, but he only wanted to know how Africa was and if we'd be interested in selling. He wants her for his youngest son to hunt next season. She might do very well with a decent rider on her back.'

Turning, she walked unsteadily out of the tackroom. Jake felt suddenly exhausted, near to tears, overwhelmed with black despair.

Going out of the tackroom, he walked down past the loose boxes until he came to Africa. Even though she was feeding, she left her manger and hobbled over to him, whickering with joy, nuzzling at his pockets. He put his arms round her neck and she laid her head against his cheek. Soppy old thing; she'd stay like that for hours, breathing softly while he scratched her behind the ears.

In his mind, he jumped that beautiful first round again, reliving that wonderful, amazing last jump. What a star she was; he couldn't give her up, and he knew more than ever that the only thing he could ever be in this world was a show jumper. Working for Mrs Wilton for over a year, he was constantly aware of time running past, time wasted. He had left the orphanage at eighteen and spent two years in a racing stable. It was there he made the discovery that difficult horses became easy when he rode them, and that

39

he could communicate with them as he never could with people. Even having his first girl, and subsequently others, wasn't nearly as exciting as that sudden breakthrough when a horse that had been written off as hopeless became responsive under his touch. Finally there was the joy, over the past months, of discovering Africa and slowly realizing how good she was. It was worth putting up with the horrible little girls and their frightful mothers. No mother had ever protected and fussed over him like they did, he thought bitterly.

And now he'd blown it; it was only a matter of time before Mrs Wilton sacked him. He supposed he could get another job as a groom, but not as a rider. Africa nuzzled him gently.

'I'm still here,' she seemed to say.

'But not for much longer,' sighed Jake, 'although I'll fight like a bugger to keep you.'

Tory Maxwell lay on her bed, bitterly ashamed of herself for eating three helpings of strawberries and cream. She looked around her extremely tidy bedroom and wished she had a photograph of Jake. The scent of lilac and lilies of the valley kept drifting in from outside, as insistently he kept drifting into her thoughts. Not that he had noticed her. His eyes had flickered over her as a man flips past the woman's fashion page in his daily paper, knowing it has nothing to interest him.

Her mother had gone out with that monstrous murderer, Colonel Carter. After what he'd done to Jake, Tory couldn't bring herself even to talk to him. How *could* her mother sleep with him? She imagined him climbing on top of her like an ancient dinosaur.

Looking in the mirror, she tried on a different coloured lipstick and put her hands over the sides of her round face. If she were thinner, she might just be pretty. Out of the window, against a brilliant, drained sapphire sky, she could see the silver of a pale new moon, followed by a little star. 'Just like me following Jake,' she thought.

'Oh, please,' she prayed, 'give me Jake Lovell, and then I could buy him all the horses he wants.'

Colonel Carter and Mrs Maxwell were on their third gin and tonic in the bar of the Grand Hotel, Guildford. They had pulled Malise and Jake to shreds, had a good bitch about Sir William and Lady Dorothy and were in a mood of great mutual self-congratulation about having found one another.

'You're looking particularly lovely tonight,' said Colonel Carter.

He always says that, thought Molly, but then perhaps it's true. She caught sight of her glossy reflection in the rose-tinted bar mirror. What should she wear to get married in? Perhaps oyster silk with a matching hat; it couldn't be the same thing she wore to Tory's party.

In future the Colonel could cope with all her bills.

In the corner, the pianist, who had unnaturally vermilion hair, was playing 'Someone to watch over me'.

'Just a little lamb that's lost in the wood,' sang the Colonel.

It was nice to take an attractive woman out again. He had always been unfaithful to Jennifer, his wife, but it had been a shock when she died. She'd done everything for him.

'I was very lonely when Jennifer died,' he said.

'I was very lonely when Alastair died,' said Molly. No reason to add that she and Alastair had been divorced for six years before he was killed in that car crash. It was so much more romantic to be a widow than a divorcée.

The waiter presented them with a huge menu, which they studied with too much attention (Colonel Carter in particular noting the prices) for people in love.

'I'm glad I stood up to that bastard, Gordon,' he said.

'I wish I knew where I'd gone wrong with Tory,' said Molly Maxwell.

In the bedroom down the passage from Tory's, lay Fen. She'd been sent to bed in disgrace for cheeking Colonel Carter about frightening Africa with his twenty-five pounders. Her bed was full of biscuit crumbs and she was

41

reading *The Maltese Cat* for the hundredth time with a torch. She turned the torch on her rosettes, white and blue, then looking out of the window, caught sight of the new moon.

'Make me the greatest show jumper in the world,' she wished.

4

Sunday started badly for Tory Maxwell. Unable to sleep, she had heard the floorboards outside her room creaking as the Colonel crept out at dawn. But he was back by 12.30, spruced up in clean clothes, moustache brushed and bearing a bottle of gin, and he and Molly Maxwell sat out on the terrace drinking dry martinis while Tory cooked the lunch.

'As I have to fork out so much for this cookery and typing course,' said Molly, 'I might as well make use of her.'

'What a charming garden,' said the Colonel.

'The lawn needs mowing,' hinted Molly Maxwell. 'But I seem to have so little time this summer.'

The white sauce for the cauliflower went lumpy because Tory was trying, at the same time, to read a piece in one of the colour supplements on deb's delights. The piece included a profile of Rupert Campbell-Black. After three years in the Blues, he was now too busy making a name for himself as a show jumper to go to many deb parties, but whenever he did he caused a rumpus.

'You can say that again,' sighed Tory, adding more milk to the sauce. She had been a victim of Rupert's bitchy asides on numerous occasions. He had got that blank stare of complete indifference to perfection. The sight of his cold, arrogant face looking out at her made her feel quite sick. Particularly as her mother thought he was absolutely charming and kept nagging Tory to ring him up and make sure he'd got the invitation and was coming to Tory's drinks party.

Tory was dreading the party. She didn't think anyone

43

would come and she was sensitive enough to realize that, although some of the fathers and the young men flirted with her mother, the mothers thought her pushy and jumped up.

At 1.30, although Fen still wasn't back from the stables, they started lunch. Colonel Carter carved. Conditioned by wartime austerity, he cut very thin slices. Tory noticed he touched her mother's hand when he passed her a plate. She knew they found her presence a strain. Her mother found fault with everything. The white sauce was too lumpy and thin, the meat overdone, and the roast potatoes soggy. Molly, who wanted the Colonel to think she had an appetite like a sparrow, pushed hers to the side of her plate.

'I don't mean to nag,' she said to Tory 'but one day you'll get married and have to cook for some chap, and he'll expect decent grub.'

Some hope, thought Tory. As she cleared away in an excess of misery, she ate the two roast potatoes her mother had rejected and two more left in the dish. When her mother came in, weighed down by the gravy boat, as an excuse to powder her nose in the kitchen mirror, Tory had to swallow frantically.

Half way through the pudding, when Molly was grumbling that the meringue was just like toffee, Fen walked in with a filthy face and hands and the same shirt she'd been wearing the day before, so triggering off a storm of reproof which Fen accepted with equanimity. The Colonel droned on about bridge.

'Jolly good roast potatoes,' said Fen. 'Are there any more?'

'There were two in the dish,' said Molly.

Tory blushed. 'I threw them away.'

'I bet you ate them,' snapped Molly. 'Really, Tory. D'you want to look like a house for your dance?'

'Did you have a good ride, Fenella?' asked Colonel Carter.

'Not very,' said Fen. 'Jake was in a foul temper.'

'Nothing new,' said Molly. 'Would you like some Stilton, Bernard?'

'Hardly surprising,' said Fen, glaring at Colonel Carter. 'Africa might have been ruined for life.'

'Shut up,' snapped her mother.

'Malise Gordon dropped in to see if Africa was all right, but Jake says both he and Sir William are after her. It's a rotten shame. Jake's worked so hard on her; no one gets her going better than he does. And he's got the most awful lot to take out this afternoon – fat grown-ups who can't ride, and in this heat, they've booked for a whole two hours. I'm going back to help him after lunch.'

'You are *not*,' said Molly Maxwell firmly. 'You spend too much time hanging round that place. You're coming out to eat with the Braithwaites.'

'Whatever for?' wailed Fen.

'Because they asked us.'

'Tory as well?'

'No. Tory's got to do her homework and write her thank you letters.'

'It's not fair. I loathe Melanie Braithwaite. She's a drip and she's not my age.'

Molly Maxwell insisted on taking Fen with them, as otherwise she would have had to go back to the Colonel's house on the way home and spend an hour in bed with him. That was the tiresome thing about men, she thought. They always wanted bed all the time and she so much preferred the flirting and the wining and dining.

Tory watched Fen, scrubbed and mutinous in a new dress, being dragged off to the Braithwaites. She then wrote five thankyou letters in her round, careful hand, and then accepted four more invitations. Being fat and plain and no threat to prettier girls, and because many of the debs' mothers had known and liked her father, she was asked to quite a lot of parties. Each one spelled disaster.

'I'm like a terrible first night, but first nights are lucky enough to fold, while I have to flop on for ever,' she said to herself.

Letters finished, she started on her homework, gazing at a page of shorthand until the heavy and light lines swam before her eyes.

'We are in receipt of your favour, yours faithfully, yours truly,' she wrote.

Oh, she'd be faithful and true to Jake. Then she wrote 'Jake' in shorthand, the dark backward sloping J and light horizontal K on the line, with two little commas underneath to show it was a proper name. Then she wrote 'Lovell'; it was the same sign as Lovely. He was lovely, too. She tried to visualize his face, but she could only picture his body and a blur. She felt impossibly restless. The telephone interrupted her daydreams; perhaps by a miracle it might be him, but it was only her mother saying that the Braithwaites wanted to play bridge and had pressed them to stay on for an early supper, so they'd be home at about ten, and could Tory do Fen's packed lunch and see that she had a clean tunic and leotard for tomorrow? Poor trapped Fen, thought Tory.

The evening stretched ahead of her. Jake would be back from his ride now and settling the horses. The longing became too much for her. She'd nip down to the stables on the excuse that Fen might have left her whip behind.

Quickly, she washed her hair. Her mother liked it drawn back from her forehead, but today she was jolly well going to let it flop loose. If only she had a slimming black dress, but her mother said she was too young and anyway she couldn't go down to the stables dressed as though for a funeral. Ponchos were fashionable; as though they covered all the spare tyres; but when they slid down on the shoulders they showed her bra straps, and if she didn't wear a bra she flopped all over the place. If only she had a waist, she could wear a long skirt to cover her fat legs, but it made her look like a barrel. In the end she gave up and wore a navy blue T-shirt outside her jeans. Her hand was shaking so much she couldn't do up the clasp of her pearls, so she left them off. In a fit of loathing, she drenched herself in her mother's scent and, as it was drizzling slightly, borrowed her mother's white trench coat, with the belt trendily done up at the back. It didn't matter if it didn't meet over her bust.

As she passed the church, people were coming out of Evensong, putting up umbrellas. On the village green, cricketers huddled disconsolately into the pavilion, hoping the apricot glow on the horizon meant that the rain was about to stop and they could finish their game.

The Brook Farm Riding School tackroom was overcrowded but very tidy – saddles and bridles occupying one wall, food bins another, and medicines, principally Jake's gypsy remedies, yet another. Room had also been found for a few faded rosettes and old calendars. The order book was open. Sunday, full of bookings, had been crossed off. Monday was comparatively empty, except for a group of children who wanted to ride after school. Jake sat on a rickety chair, cleaning a bridle and reading the colour supplement piece on Rupert Campbell-Black. The bastard was obviously going to make it in show jumping, just when Jake's world seemed to be falling apart, throwing him straight down to the bottom of the ladder, without even being within clutching distance of the first rung. The two-hour ride had really taken it out of him; his head was pounding and every muscle in his body felt bruised by the fall yesterday.

After a night's rest and Jake's marsh-mallow ointment, Africa's limp was barely perceptible. Mrs Wilton had gloatingly told him of Malise's interest that morning and Sir William had just rung again. No one could do anything about it, as Bobby Cotterel was in France till the end of the week, but it was only a matter of time.

He heard a step and, looking up through the dusty cobwebbed window, saw Fen's fat sister approaching. That was all he needed. Now she was stopping to comb her hair. Then her great blushing face, like a dutch cheese, appeared round the door.

'Yes?' he said bleakly.

'Did, I mean, I was wondering,' she stammered, 'if Fen left her whip here?' The feebleness of the excuse made her blush even more. 'It was – er – one our grandmother – gave her for Christmas, so she was worried.'

'I haven't seen it. She's so scatty, she probably dropped it on the way home.'

How pinched and dark under the eyes he looked, thought Tory, the red check shirt and the black hair only emphasizing his pallor. Sympathy overcame her shyness. 'I'm so sorry about people wanting to buy Africa. Fen told me.'

Jake nodded. She shifted from one foot to another and Jake was enveloped in a waft of Molly's scent, which did not evoke happy memories.

'Is her leg better?'

'She's all right.'

Why was she hanging round like a great blancmange? Getting up, he ran the sponge under the tap and plunged it into the saddle soap, adding:

'The whip – it isn't here.'

Tory gazed at her feet, twisting a button on Mrs Maxwell's mac. Then she noticed what he was reading.

'Oh, there's Rupert Campbell-Black. Horrible man.'

Jake looked up, slightly more accommodating. Tory blushed again.

'I'm sorry. Is he a friend of yours?'

There was a pause.

'I hate his guts,' said Jake.

'Oh, so do I,' said Tory. 'He's so vicious and contemptuous and, well, bloody-minded. How did *you* come across him?'

'We were at school together.'

Tory looked amazed.

'Prep school,' added Jake. 'I was a day boy. Mum was the cook, so the headmaster let me in free.'

'Oh, goodness, he must have been an absolutely poisonous small boy.'

Taking a nail, Jake pushed out the saddle soap that had got stuck in the cheek-strap holes.

'Poisonous,' he agreed. 'He made Eichmann look like a fairy godmother.'

'He's so rich,' said Tory, 'that lots of mothers are after him, but he's only after one thing.'

'What's that?' said Jake, to embarrass her.

Tory swallowed. 'Well, bed and things. He's awfully promiscuous.' She pronounced it promise-kew-us. 'And he never answers invitations; just rolls up with his current girlfriend and leaves after half an hour if he's bored. He let off thunderflashes at Queen Charlotte's. Lady Surrey was livid.'

'He obviously hasn't changed,' said Jake. 'I should have thought Harrow or the army might have knocked it out of him.'

'I think it made him worse,' sighed Tory. 'He gets a little gang of cronies round him and manages to be even nastier.'

Nothing unites people like a good bitch. Jake let her rattle on as he put the bridle together again and hung it up. Then he went to re-apply Africa's poultice. Tory followed him, longingly watching the tender way his hands ran over the mare, caressing her polished shoulder and her sleek veined legs. Africa nuzzled him, breathing through her velvet nostrils with love and trust.

'She's so beautiful,' said Tory wistfully.

The swelling had practically disappeared. Jake re-did the bandages and re-adjusted her summer rug. He wished Tory would buzz off and leave him alone to nurse his misery. As he came out of the stable, shutting the door behind him, the rain stopped. He looked at her round, anxious face, her clean flopping hair and enormous bosom straining against the dark blue T-shirt. There was kindness in her eyes. He looked at his watch.

'Let's go and have a drink.'

Tory looked at him stupidly.

'A drink,' he repeated mockingly. 'The pubs are open. You're eighteen, aren't you?'

'Yes, of course I am. Gosh, thanks awfully.'

As they walked to the pub, Jake noticed the hawthorns were rusting slightly but still smelt like fresh soap, and the wet, hot nettles gave off a heady blackcurrant scent. The cricketers were running out onto the pitch, anxious to get all the game they could into the last half-hour.

49

It was the first time Tory had been taken by a man into a pub; in fact, the first time a man had voluntarily asked her out at all. My first date, she thought excitedly. An old woman was buying Guinness and putting it in a black canvas bag. In the corner, two men with sun-reddened faces, their wives wearing white orlon cardigans and lots of cheap jewellery, had decided to break their journey on the way back to London and were drinking Pimm's. What on earth was she going to drink? She hated beer, her mother said gin and orange was common and she knew Buck's Fizz involved champagne, which was expensive. Her mind was a complete blank. She looked desperately around.

'I'd like a Pimm's,' she said.

Jake sighed. He'd hoped she'd drink something cheap, like cider, or better still, orange juice. That meant he'd have to have beer instead of the double whisky he so badly needed.

Tory sat down, the furry moquette of the bench seat scratching her thighs. The pub was cool and dark and restful inside; the side door had been fastened back, and outside was a little garden full of wallflowers and irises and pale pink clematis scrambling over some rustic poles.

At first, the conversation was very stilted, but after a couple of Pimm's, Tory's tongue was loosened and suddenly, like a washing machine that's been tugged open half-way through its cycle, everything came gushing out. What a disaster she was at dances, how she hated her finishing school, how ghastly Colonel Carter was and how she couldn't get on with her mother.

'Mummy likes Fen, because she's pretty and funny and because she's so young, but I'm an embarrassment to her and living proof that she's over forty-five.'

'She made you go to all these dances because she's looking for a husband,' said Jake. 'D'you think she's found one?'

'Oh, I hope not,' said Tory. 'He's so phoney. He was hanging a picture for Mummy the other day and hit his thumb with the hammer and,' she went even redder, 'he said booger instead of bugger.'

Jake hadn't even brushed his hair before he came out, but it fell into place automatically. Tory ached to touch it. She felt as though someone had bewitched her, as though she was drowning and there was no coming up even for the third time. In a panic, she noticed he'd finished his drink. She'd been reading about Women's Lib and someone called Germaine Greer. It was all right for women to buy drinks these days. She got a fiver out of her bag and handed it to Jake.

'Go on,' she said with a giggle, 'we're all equal.'

Jake shrugged and went to the bar. The cricketers had finished their game and flocked into the pub, and the barmaid was serving them with huge jugs of beer to pass around, so it was a few minutes before Jake got served. Tory sat in a haze of happiness; the longer he took, the longer they'd have. She looked at him slumped against the bar. He was so thin beside the beefy cricketers; she wished she could feed him up; she was sure he wouldn't grumble about overdone beef and soggy potatoes. On the door near the Ladies, a group of men were playing darts. Oh, dear, Cupid had scored a double top, straight into her heart.

Jake returned with the drinks and a packet of crisps.

'I don't know why I've been telling you all these things,' said Tory. 'You're the one who needs cheering up. But you're such a good listener.'

'I get plenty of practice. When you've got to take stupid women on long rides you develop a listener's face. It doesn't necessarily mean you're listening.'

Tory's face fell. 'I'm sorry,' she said humbly, starting to eat the crisps. 'I didn't mean to bore you.'

'You haven't,' he said irritably.

'Who taught you to ride?' she asked.

'My father. He put me on a pony almost before I could walk.'

'How long ago did he die?' said Tory.

'I don't know that he's dead.'

Tory looked startled.

51

'He was a gypsy. He met my mother when he was hop-picking on part-time work. Her father was the keeper at the big house. He tried to settle down with my mother and get a steady job, but it was like caging a lark. One day, the wanderlust became too strong, so he walked out when I was about eight years old.'

'You must have missed him.'

'I did.' The third pint of beer had loosened his tongue and the world seemed a more hospitable place.

'So did my mother. She cried a lot, behind locked doors, and my grandfather went through all the photograph albums cutting my father's picture out of the family groups.'

'So you might suddenly bump into him one day?'

'I doubt it,' said Jake, although he never passed a gypsy encampment or a fairground without having a look.

'Was he very good looking?'

'My mother thought so. Two years after he left she waved me off to school and said she'd be in to cook the school dinner later. Then she put some cushions in front of the gas oven and that was that. All I remember is that all the masters and boys were particularly put out because we were supposed to be having treacle pudding that day.'

He suddenly glared at Tory, whose eyes had filled with tears. What the hell was he telling the soppy cow all this for? He hadn't talked about his mother for years.

Tory couldn't bear it. He'd lost his mother and his father and now he was going to lose Africa.

'Do you think Bobby Cotterel will really sell her?' she asked.

' 'Course he will; doesn't give a damn about her. He was grumbling the other day because Mrs Wilton was threatening to put up the livery fees.'

The pub was filling up now and becoming noisy and clamorous. Tory looked at an obscene, pink pile of sausages, greasily glinting under a cover on the bar. How lovely to see food and for once not feel hungry.

'What will you do if Africa goes?'

'Get another job.'

'Around here?'

'No, up north probably. I doubt if Mrs Wilton will give me a reference.'

'Oh, you mustn't,' said Tory, aghast. 'I mean – it's so cold up north. I must go to the loo.'

She had difficulty negotiating the way to the Ladies', cannoning off tables and cricketers like a baby elephant.

'Oh, hell,' thought Jake, as she narrowly missed a flying dart, 'she's pissed.'

Tory collapsed on to the loo and realized with the shock from the cold slab under her bottom that the seat cover was still down. She lifted it up. 'If I can manage to go on peeing for over twenty seconds, Jake will take me out again,' she said to herself. By wriggling she made it last for twenty-two.

When she found she had put her bag in the basin and washed her hands over it, she realized she was very tight. She couldn't bear Jake to go away. She pressed her hot forehead against the mirror. 'Gypsy Jake,' she murmured to herself.

Then it became plain that she must buy Africa. She had the money. Jake could pay her back, or she could be the owner and he the jockey. She had visions of herself in a big primrose yellow hat, leading Africa into the winner's enclosure with two mounted policemen on either side. She was a bit hazy about what went on in show jumping. She looked in the telephone directory, but there was no Bobby Cotterel. He must be ex-directory; but the Mayhews had had the house before Bobby Cotterel. She spent ages finding the M's. They did come after L, didn't they? Oh God, the page was missing, No, it was the first number on the next page. Sir Edward Mayhew, Bandit's Court. Her hand was shaking so much she could hardly dial the number.

'Hullo,' said a brusque voice.

She was so surprised she couldn't speak.

'If that's burglars,' said the voice, 'I'm here plus fifteen guard dogs and you can fuck off.'

Tory gasped. 'No, it isn't,' she said. 'Is that Mr Cotterel?'
She must speak very slowly and try to sound businesslike.

Jake, having finished his glass of beer and ordered a large
whisky, gazed at his reflection, framed by mahogany and
surrounded by upside-down bottles in the mirror behind
the bar. Totally without vanity, he looked in mirrors only
for identity. He had spent too many Sundays at the
children's home, with scrubbed face and hair plastered
down with water in the hope of charming some visitor into
fostering or adopting him, to have any illusions about his
attractiveness.

'Come here often?' said the barmaid, who worked in the
pub on Sunday to boost her wages and in the hope of
finding a new boyfriend.

'No,' said Jake.

He glanced at his watch. Tory had been away for nearly a
quarter of an hour now. He hoped the stupid cow hadn't
passed out. He'd need a fork lift truck to carry her home. He
went out to look for her. She was standing by the telephone
in the passage with her shoes off.

'That's fine,' she was saying in a careful voice.

If Bobby Cotterel had not come back a week early from
the South of France because it was so expensive, and been
promptly faced with a large income-tax bill, he might not
have been in such a receptive mood. Africa troubled his
conscience, like his daughter's guinea pig, whose cage, now
she'd gone back to boarding school, needed cleaning out.
He was not an unkind man. This girl sounded a 'gent', and
was so anxious to buy Africa for four times the price he'd
paid for her, and he wouldn't have to pay any commission
to Mrs Wilton.

'The livery fee's paid up for another three weeks,' he said.

'I'll take that over,' said Tory.

'No, I'll be happy to stand it to you, darling.'

'Can we come round and give you the cheque now?'

'Of course. Come and have a drink, but for Christ's sake
don't tell anyone I'm back.'

Tory had had her first date, and been called darling and

54

invited for a drink by Bobby Cotterel.

She turned towards Jake with shining eyes.

If she lost a couple of hundredweight, she'd be quite pretty, he thought sourly. What the hell had she got to look so cheerful about?

'You O.K.?'

'Wonderful. I've just bought Africa.'

'Whatever for? You don't like horses.'

'For you, of course. You can pay me back slowly, a pound a week, or we can go into partnership. I'll own her, you can ride her.'

A dull red flush had spread across Jake's face.

'You're crazy. How much did you pay?'

'I offered eight hundred and he accepted. He's just had a bill for his income tax. I said we'd take the cheque around now, before Mrs Wilton starts blabbing about Sir William and Malise Gordon.'

'Have you got that amount in the bank?'

'Oh, yes, I got £5000 on my birthday, and lots of shares.'

'Your mother'll bust a gut.'

'Hooray,' said Tory.

'She'll say I got you plastered.'

'No, you did not. I did it all off my own bat, like those cricketers in the bar.'

She cannoned off a hatstand as she went out of the door.

Jake was finding it impossible to clar..ber out of the pit of despair so quickly. He might at least say thank-you, thought Tory.

They walked to Bobby Cotterel's house and handed over the cheque. Armed with a receipt, he walked her home, both of them following the white lines in the middle of the road. Half-shafts of moonlight found their way through the beech trees on either side of the road, shimmering on their dark grey-green trunks. Fortunately the house was still dark.

'Oh good,' said Tory, 'I can put back Mummy's mac before she finds out it's missing. I'm going to London tomorrow. I've got two awful drinks parties, then a dance

55

on Wednesday, but I'll be home on Thursday. Mummy and Colonel Carter are going out to dinner. I've got to babysit. Perhaps you could come around, after they've gone out, and we can decide what to do.'

'I think it may be a bit more problematical than that,' said Jake.

He took the key, opened the door for her and turned on the hall light. Oh God, thought Tory miserably, there was Fen's whip lying on the hall table, beside a moulting bowl of pink peonies. Jake turned to her, a slight smile touching his lips. Was it contempt, or pity, or mockery?

'Thank you very much,' he said and was gone.

Fighting back her disappointment that he hadn't attempted to kiss her, Tory then reflected that she would probably have tasted of onion-flavoured crisps.

5

The drinks parties on Monday and Tuesday were bad enough for Tory. But the dance of Wednesday was a nightmare. At the dinner party beforehand, some sadist had seated her next to Rupert Campbell-Black. On his right was a ravishing girl named Melanie Potter, whom all the girls were absolutely furious about. Melanie had upstaged everyone by turning up, several weeks after the season began, with a suntan acquired from a month in the Bahamas.

Rupert had arrived late, parking his filthy Rolls Royce, with the blacked-out windows, across the pavement. He then demanded tomato ketchup in the middle of dinner, and proceeded to drench his sea trout with it, which everyone except his hostess and Tory thought wildly funny. Naturally he'd ignored Tory all the way through dinner. But there was something menacing about that broad black back and beautifully shaped blond head, a totally deceptive languor concealing the rampant sexuality. She wondered what he would have done if she'd tapped him on the shoulder and told him she was the owner of an £800 horse.

Then they went on to the dance and she somehow found herself piled into Rupert's Rolls Royce, driving through the laburnum- and-lilac-lined streets of Chelsea. She had to sit on some young boy's knee, trying to put her feet on the ground and all her weight on them. But she still heard him complaining to Rupert afterwards that his legs were completely numb and about to drop off.

The hostess was kind, but too distraught about gate crashers to introduce Tory to more than two young men, who both, as usual, danced one dance, then led her back

57

and propped her against a pillar like an old umbrella, pretending they were just off to get her a drink or had to dance with their hostess. Thinking about Jake non-stop didn't insulate her from the misery of it all. It made it almost worse. Obviously it was impossible that he should ever care for her. If no one else wanted her, why should he? Feeling about as desirable as a Christmas tree on Twelfth Night, she was sitting by herself at the edge of the ballroom when a handsome boy sauntered towards her. Reprieve at last.

'Excuse me,' he said.

'Oh, yes, please,' said Tory.

'If no one's using this,' he said,' could I possibly borrow it?' and, picking up the chair beside her, he carried it back across the room and sat down on the edge of the yelling group around Rupert Campbell-Black. As soon as they got to the dance, Rupert had abandoned his dinner party and, taking Melanie, had gone off to get drunk with his inseparable chum, Billy Lloyd-Foxe, who was in another party. Now he was sitting, cigar drooping out of his handsome, curling mouth, wearing Melanie's feather boa, while she sat on his knee, shrieking with laughter, with the pink carnation from his buttonhole behind her ear.

Later Billy Lloyd-Foxe passed Tory on the way to the lavatory and on the way back, struck by conscience, asked her to dance. She liked Billy; everyone did; she liked his turned-down eyes and his broken nose and his air of life being a little bit too much for him. But everything was spoilt when Rupert and Melanie got on to the floor: Rupert, his blue eyes glittering, swinging Melanie's boa round like the pantomime cat's tail, had danced around behind Tory's back, pulling faces and puffing out his cheeks to look fat like Tory and make Billy laugh.

Tory escaped to the loo, shaking. She found her dinner party hostess's daughter repairing her make-up and chuntering with a couple of friends over the effrontery of Melanie Potter.

'Her mother did it on purpose. What chance have any of

58

us got against a suntan like that? She turned up at the Patelys' drinks party wearing jeans. Lady Surrey was absolutely livid.'

At that moment Melanie Potter walked in and went over to the mirror, where she examined a huge love bite on her shoulder and tried to cover it with powder.

'You haven't got anything stronger, have you?' she asked Tory.

Humbly, Tory passed her a stick of Erace.

'Oh, how marvellous; that's amazingly kind. You were on Rupert's other side at dinner, weren't you?' she added, wincing as she blotted out the red oval of tooth marks. 'Isn't he a sod? I've just emptied a bucket of ice over him for biting me.'

She handed back the Erace to Tory and combed her platinum blond hair more seductively over one eye. 'He and Billy are taking me to Tramps now; why don't you come too? David Bailey's going to be there. Rupe wants him to photograph me.'

And when Tory refused, insisting she was going home now because she had a headache, she only just persuaded Melanie not to make Rupert give her a lift home.

Unfortunately, Tory found a taxi all too easily. When she got back to the flat, which Molly Maxwell had borrowed from a friend for the summer, it was only 11.30. She found her mother and the Colonel on the sofa. The Colonel was wearing a lot more lipstick than her mother.

Tory went to her room and as quietly as possible cried herself to sleep. She woke, as she had on the last four mornings, with a terrible sense of unease – that her mother would find out about Africa.

She came home in the evening to babysit and went up to her room to change and have a bath. It was still ludicrously hot.

'Don't use all the water,' called out her mother. Through the crack in the door Tory could see her lying on her peach chintz counterpane, rigid under a face pack.

Tory was undressed down to her bra and pants, and

59

hoping, as she'd hardly eaten since her evening with Jake, that she might have lost a bit of weight, when she heard the telephone ring and her mother answering it in a self-consciously seductive voice:

'Hello.' Then, more matter of fact, 'Oh hello, Mrs Wilton, how are you?'

There was a long pause, then Molly said.

'No, it couldn't possibly be her. Tory's terrified of horses. Maxwell's quite a common name, you know. Well, just wait while I shut the door.'

Tory felt as though icy water was being dripped slowly down her spine. She was tempted to climb out of the window down the clematis; instead she got into bed, pulled the duvet over her head and started to shake.

Five minutes later her mother barged in, ripping the bedclothes off the bed. She was still wearing her face pack like some malignant mime of catastrophe. At first she was so angry she couldn't get the words out.

'Did you or did you not ring up Bobby Cotterel on Sunday and buy Africa?' she spluttered.

'I don't know what you mean,' mumbled Tory.

'Don't lie to me; who put you up to it?'

'No one. It's my money. Why shouldn't I buy a horse if I want to?'

'And I can't afford to buy little Fen a little pony.' Molly spat out the 'little'. 'Get up, you fat lump.' She reached forward and tugged Tory to her feet by her hair.

'It was that little swine, Jake Lovell, wasn't it?'

'No, it wasn't.'

' 'Course it was.' Molly Maxwell was shaking Tory by the shoulders until she thought her head would snap off. 'He's obsessed with that horse, spends all his time on it. But he won't much longer,' she added, her eyes suddenly lighting up with venom. 'Mrs Wilton's just given him the sack.'

'Oh, no,' said Tory, aghast. 'It was nothing to do with him. I rang Bobby Cotterel. I did everything myself.'

'Why?' hissed Molly, powder from her drying, cracking facepack drifting down to the floor. 'You've got a crush on that boy. I saw you mooning over him on Saturday at the show. That's why you've been such a colossal flop at all those dances, not trying with all those suitable young men, because you've got hot pants for some common stable boy. Well, you won't get him by buying him expensive presents.'

Tory couldn't bear to look at her mother any more, the hideous contrast with the twitching, disintegrating white face and the angry red turkey neck. She gazed down at her mother's feet, noticing the newly painted scarlet nails, cotton wool keeping each toe apart.

'He's a friend,' she sobbed. 'Nothing more.'

'Well, he's not having Africa. He's going back.'

'He's a she and she's not.'

'Sir William and Colonel Gordon are both prepared to top your offer. I'm going around to see Bobby Cotterel to make him tear up that cheque.'

Molly pictured herself, in a new dress, rather low cut, driving up to Bobby Cotterel's house and pleading with him.

'My daughter's not responsible for her actions.'

And Bobby Cotterel, who she suspected was between marriages, would pour her a stiff drink and comfortingly say, 'Tell me all about it, preferably over dinner.'

She was brought back from her reverie by Tory sobbing, 'It's my money and I can do what I like with it.'

'And how are you going to look after a horse?' hissed Molly. 'It can't live in the potting shed, and now Jake Lovell's lost his job, he'll be moving on.'

Tory was in such despair she hardly heard her mother's tirade about all the expense and trouble she'd gone to to give Tory a season until, catching sight of her face which resembled a dried-up river bed, in the mirror, Molly realized she had better get her pack off. Tugging open the door, she found Fen, who'd been listening avidly at the keyhole and nearly fell into the room on top of her. Fen gave a giggle and, waving in time with a half-eaten frozen lolly, started singing:

'My mother said that I never should play with the gypsies in the wood.'

'Shut up,' screeched Molly. 'It's your fault too for always hanging round the stables. You're not going down there tonight. Go to your room, do your homework and don't talk to Tory. I must ring Bernard. I can't possibly go out and play bridge after all this.'

'Want to bet?' said Fen, as her mother went into the bedroom, slamming the door behind her. Immediately they heard the ping of the telephone, followed at intervals by other pings.

Molly couldn't get through to Bobby Cotterel but, if she couldn't get him to tear up the cheque, there was always the possibility of re-selling Africa to Sir William or Malise.

That had possibilities too, she reflected. She'd like to meet Sir William again and for Malise Gordon she still had the hankering of the summarily rejected. She saw herself with less make-up and a higher neckline than for Bobby Cotterel, and Malise's hawklike face softening, as he took her hand, saying:

'When I first met you at Bilborough, I thought you were just a lovely face.'

After all, Colonel Carter hadn't popped the question; it would be good to make him jealous.

As Tory predicted, the Colonel talked her mother into going out for dinner.

'Bernard's friends have gone to a lot of trouble cooking and they'd be so disappointed if we cried off at the last moment,' she told Tory coldly, as if she was making a supreme effort to go out. Not that she'd enjoy a second of it, with all this worry (as well as Bernard's friends' cooking) on her plate.

Tory was still sitting on her bed, in her bra and pants as though turned to stone.

'Do you hear me, Tory? I'm putting you on your honour not to talk to Fen and not to telephone anyone or put a foot outside the house while I'm away.'

She said it three times, but she wasn't sure it had registered.

62

Jake sat in the tackroom, chain-smoking and watching the nearly full moon peering in through the window. Round and pink, with turned down eyes in an anxious chubby face, it reminded him of Tory. Poor kid, he hoped that cow of a mother wasn't giving her too bad a time. He'd like to have got in touch with her to find out the score, but he didn't dare ring the house. Africa was much better; he'd turned her out for a few hours and just laid down thick clean straw in her loosebox next to the tack room. He was just going to fetch her when he heard a step outside, and Tory came timidly through the door. Christ, she looked all blotchy like a swede that's been beaten up by the frost. The next minute, she was sobbing in his arms.

'I'm so sorry I got you sacked.'

'Doesn't matter. I was going to leave anyway. Plenty more fishwives in the sea.'

'But you haven't anywhere to go.'

'Mrs Wilton can't chuck me out till she's found someone else; she's too idle, and it's too late to put an ad in *Horse and Hound* this week, so I've got a bit of time. Did your mother give you a hard time?'

Tory nodded. 'She's determined to give Africa back, or sell her.'

She was shaking so violently, Jake sat her down on the rickety chair and made her a strong cup of coffee with four tablespoons of sugar. She didn't normally take sugar, but she found the sweetness comforting.

Jake lounged against the food bin, watching her.

'Look,' he said, dropping his half-smoked cigarette down the sink, 'why did you buy me that horse?'

Tory lowered her eyes, 'Because I like you,' she whispered.

Jake took her hands, which felt damp and chilled.

'How much?' he said gently.

Tory glanced up. He was so beautiful with his thin watchful face and his glinting earrings.

'Oh, so very much,' she said.

63

And suddenly, like a horse that's been locked up in a stable for a long time and sees the door opening on to a huge field of clover, the idea that he'd been battling against all week, overwhelmed him. A rich wife, that's what he needed. Not very rich, but enough to buy him a few horses and give him a start, so he could get to the top and wipe that self-satisfied smile off Rupert Campbell-Black's face.

And rather in the way a swimmer holds his nose and plunges into the water and finds it pleasantly warm, his arms were suddenly full of Tory. She was kissing him, sucking at him like a great vacuum cleaner – Christ, she'd pull his teeth out soon – and her arms had him in a vice and the huge friendly breasts were pressing against him.

'Oh, Jake, oh, Jake.'

Without fumbling, he undid the buttons of her dress and switched off the light, and they were on the bed of deep clean straw, with the light of the moon now filtering in through the skylight. He unfastened her bra and the splendid breasts overflowed, soft and sweet-swelling, like a river bursting its dam.

For a small, slight man, Jake was sexually well-endowed, but he spent enough time fingering a spot which Tory afterwards discovered was her clitoris, and she was so slippery with longing that she hardly felt any pain after that first sharp thrust inside her. She'd always heard it was awful the first time, but despite the scratching of the straw on her bare back she felt only ecstasy.

'Now I know why it's called a loose box,' said Jake, extracting himself and wiping her with a handful of hay from the rack.

'Any minute Africa'll wander in and say, who's been sleeping in my bed,' said Tory with a giggle.

'Not much sleeping,' said Jake.

He rested his head on her breasts. Actually she was much less fat without her clothes on; rather splendid, in fact.

'I didn't hurt you too much?'

'No, no. It was lovely.'

'And you do like me?' he said.

Tory nodded in the dark, then kissed him passionately, adoringly uncritical, like a dog greeting a returning master.

'Enough to marry me?'

Tory gasped, and stopped kissing him.

'I know I can make big money out of horses, once I get started,' Jake said. 'I just need a break.'

'I'll help you,' said Tory in excitement. 'I've got £5,000 a year.' Admittedly a lot of that had gone on Africa and been given to her mother for new clothes and the cocktail party. But if she married Jake, she wouldn't have to go to her own cocktail party or to any more dances.

Five thousand a year, thought Jake. That must mean at least £100,000 in the bank. If only he could get his hands on that, they could buy a place and a dozen horses.

'We've got to find somewhere to live,' he said. 'There's no point in getting anywhere too small. We need stables and at least fourteen acres; the house needn't be big.'

'I could paint it,' said Tory.

'And I could build the jumps,' said Jake.

She could feel him hot with excitement beside her.

'The only trouble is that I've only got about £1500 in the bank at the moment. That won't buy us a house, and everything else is tied up in trust till I'm twenty-one.'

Back came the black gloom, the pit, the despair; the stable door was locked and bolted on him again. It wasn't going to be any good after all. Jake slumped back on the straw.

Then he realized that Tory was full of plans to break the trust.

'The capital's mine. After all, Daddy left it to me. It's just sitting there, and there's a whole lot more to come when Granny dies.'

It was as though she was talking about having a good crop of runner beans in the garden and another crop coming up in a few months.

'I can't just take your money,' he said.

'Of course you can,' she said. 'I'm only crying because

I'm so happy. We'll go and talk to Granny Maxwell. She'll help us.'

They tried to keep their visit to Granny Maxwell secret. Tory arranged to go and see her the following Saturday. Alison, the stable girl, would lend them her car to drive up to Warwickshire. Molly, however, distrusting Tory's almost too passive acquiescence, guessed something was up and intercepted a letter from Tory to Jake which fell out of Fen's pocket on the way to the stables.

The letter spoke of them marrying, as well as the visit to Granny Maxwell, and the scenes that followed were terrible. Molly's hysteria knew no bounds. How could Tory be ungrateful and stupid enough to throw herself away on this penniless, illegitimate nobody? In fact, Molly suddenly realized that she would no longer have her daughter as an unpaid babysitter, cook, cleaner, shopper and errand runner. She would have no one on whom to vent her rage, to grumble to and about, no one so easy to cadge money off. She was in danger of losing her whipping boy and she didn't like it one bit.

She despatched a reluctant Colonel Carter to have a blimp-to-man talk with Jake. But, as Jake saw the Colonel as that monster who'd nearly destroyed Africa, the meeting wasn't a success. 'Dumb insolence,' were the Colonel's words for it. 'Fellow just gazed out of the window and read the paper upside down. Anyway, how can you expect a chap who wears earrings and hair over his collar to see reason?' Molly felt the Colonel had failed her. Malise Gordon would have had much more success.

In the face of Tory's intransigence, Molly buried her pride and rang Granny Maxwell, her ex-mother-in-law, who she'd always hated and suspected of plotting against her.

'Yes, I can see he doesn't sound very suitable,' said Granny Maxwell, 'but I prefer to judge for myself. Tory is bringing him down to meet me on Saturday.'

And Molly, for once, curbing the fountain of invective surging up inside her, felt silenced and snubbed.

Fen, although horrified at dropping the letter, was thoroughly over-excited by the whole thing.

'I wish I was old enough to marry him. You are lucky, Tory. Have you mated with him yet? I can't think why Mummy minds so much about his being intermediate.'

The heatwave continued, making the long drive up to Warwickshire sweaty and unpleasant. The sun blazed down on the top of the car, until Tory longed to escape down some woodland glade or picnic in a field by a winding river. The white chestnut candles lit up the valley, the bluebells making an exquisite contrast to the saffron of the young oaks. Cow parsley rampaged along every verge, but Jake was not interested in scenery. He seemed to find Alison's car difficult to drive and kept grinding the gears and stopping in fits and starts. Probably hasn't had much practice, thought Tory, watching his bitten-nail hands clenching the wheel. He answered all her questions in monosyllables, so she fell silent. She was dreading the meeting with her grandmother, who could be very rude and difficult. She couldn't see Jake getting on with her if he was in this mood. And if she won't help us, thought Tory in panic, perhaps he won't want to marry me after all. Then again, what did she know about this strange taciturn young man with whom she was hoping to spend the rest of her life? At least she'd shed nine pounds since she met him, and now could get easily into a size 16 skirt.

Dozing, then waking up, she realized they'd just gone through Cirencester. She looked at the map. 'Aren't we a little off course?'

'No,' said Jake curtly, putting his foot on the accelerator.

Climbing to the top of a very steep hill, he pulled into the side of the road saying: 'Get out for a minute.'

They had a magical view across the valley to where a golden-grey manor house lay dreaming against its pillow of beech woods. In front was lush, stream-laced parkland dotted with big shell-shaped trees, under which horses sought the shade, swishing their tails against the flies. To the left, a good deal of building and excavations were going on. But here, one large flat field had been left unploughed; on it every kind of coloured jump was set up. Jake studied the place at length through binoculars.

'Where are we?' asked Tory. The last signpost had been buried in cow parsley.

'Penscombe.' Jake suddenly looked drawn, a muscle was flickering in his cheek. 'Rupert Campbell-Black's place.'

Going back to the car, he scooped all the rubbish off the floor and from the ashtrays, which brimmed with cigarette butts, and tipped it over the wall into Rupert's land. One of the workmen, looking across, shook his fist at their departing car.

'Serve him right,' said Tory, with a giggle. But when she looked at Jake she saw he was not smiling.

Tory's grandmother lived sixty-five miles on in an equally beautiful but more sheltered position. Gabled and russet, the house peered out from its unkempt mane of Virginia creeper like a Yorkshire terrier.

A troupe of pekes and pugs came yapping round the side to welcome them. Despite the beauty of the day, they found Granny Maxwell sitting in the drawing room, watching racing on the television. She was also trying to read *Horse and Hound*, Somerville and Ross and a gardening book at the same time, with three pairs of spectacles hanging round her neck like trapezes. She had a strong face, broad-browed, hook-nosed, the peaty-brown eyes glittering imperiously beneath their black brows, the wrinkles deeply etched round the wide mouth. On her head she wore a grey-green curly wig, slightly askew and held on with sellotape.

'You're wearing your nightgown, child,' she said, looking at Tory's floating white dress. 'I like your blue pants.'

Then she held out a wrinkled, black-nailed hand to Jake.

'I assume this is Mr Wrong,' she added, with a cackle of laughter.

'Granny,' said Tory, blushing.

Jake grinned.

'Sit down, sit down; no, not in that chair,' she said, as Jake was almost bitten by an ancient, rheumy-eyed Jack

68

Russell already sprawled on it.

All the other pekes and pugs lay at her feet snuffling and panting. She wore an ancient cardigan, a lace shirt, obviously for the second or third day, and a tweed skirt with a droopy, descending hem.

She and Lady Dorothy must go to the same tailor, thought Jake. But aquamarines and diamonds flashed on the grimy hands as she talked, and the pearls round her neck were each as big as a mistletoe berry.

'I suppose you want a drink; young people drink at the most extraordinary hours these days. There are some tins of iced beer in the fridge, Mr Lovell. Unless you'd like something stronger? Then, go and get them, Tory.'

The room had the glorious, overcrowded look resulting from an exodus from a larger country house. Jake's hands rested on the rough carved mane of a lion. The carpet was the blurred pink and green of an Impressionist painting.

As Tory went out, Granny Maxwell studied Jake, who was surreptitiously looking at the horses circling at the start. At least he didn't fidget.

'Epsom,' she said, handing him the paper, 'I've had a bet in this race. Any tips for the 3.30?'

Jake glanced at the runners

'I'd have a fiver on Mal le maison.'

'I'm surprised you haven't chosen Marriage of Convenience. Or how about Fortune Hunter?' she added maliciously. 'He's 100–1.'

Jake looked at her steadily.

'I'll stick with Mal le maison,' he said flatly. 'And if I wanted to pick an outsider, I'd choose Whirlwind Courtship.'

'You haven't known Tory long, have you?'

'Not very long, but I like outsiders.'

At least he's not frightened of me, thought Granny Maxwell; that in itself is a novelty. Old and bored and waiting for death, she was aware that her family only came to see her when they were in financial trouble. She sometimes felt she was only kept alive by feuds and tyranny.

Tory came back with the cans of beer and a glass, and was immediately sent up to talk to Mrs Maggs, who was sorting out the hot cupboard.

'She's made you lardy cake and gingerbread men for tea. She thinks you're still eight. You look very tired, child,' she added in a gentler voice, 'and you've lost a lot of weight.'

She turned to Jake. 'Bring your glass of beer and walk round the garden,' she said, struggling to her feet. She walked very stiffly and had to be helped over the step. One hip was obviously very painful.

'Rheumatism,' she explained. 'It's difficult to be a very nice old woman when everything hurts.'

Having picked several heads off a coral pink geranium, she set off along the herbaceous border. It was the most glorious, overparked garden; peonies jostled with huge oriental poppies, lupins and irises. Catmint, not yet out, stroked their legs as they passed.

The pack of dogs, some on three legs, panted after them grumbling and yapping.

'This is what I call a beautiful garden,' said Jake.

'As opposed to what?'

'To Tory's mother's. All the flowers seem to stand in their own patch of earth there, in serried ranks. Thou shalt not touch.'

'Like a park,' said Granny Maxwell.

A bird flashed by, yellow as Laburnum.

'Yellowhammer,' said Granny Maxwell.

'Golden oriole, I think,' said Jake. 'Very rare in these parts; it must be the heat.'

Suddenly a jaunty mongrel with a tight brindle coat came bounding across the lawn and was greeted by much yapping and every sign of delight by the pack, particularly a little blond peke, who wagged her tail and kissed him. Granny Maxwell turned to Jake.

'We used to call them "butcher's dogs" in my day, because they followed the butcher's van. Owners get very fussed when mongrels try to mate with their pedigree dogs. I imagine that's why my daughter-in-law is making such a fuss about you. I made a fuss when my son threw himself away on Molly. Her father was a hairdresser. Remember that, if you ever think about her.'

'I try not to,' said Jake.

'She never got over being the toast of Hong Kong.'

'Now she's the sliced bread of Bilborough.'

Mrs Maxwell gave a cackle of laughter.

'Tell me about yourself. You had polio as a child?'

He nodded. 'When I was six I was in hospital for eighteen months, learning to walk again. It left me with a wasted leg.'

'And a raging desire to prove yourself, presumably,' said Granny Maxwell dryly. 'And your father was a gypsy?'

Jake nodded.

'My mother's family tried to re-settle him, but he missed the wandering life and the horses. He was a genius with horses. So he pushed off soon after I came out of hospital.'

'And your mother committed suicide. You blamed yourself for that, I suppose?'

'I think she was let down by some chap who she took up with after my father left, but I didn't know that at the time.'

'What happened after she died?'

'The school where I went free as a day boy made me board. I hated it, so I ran away and joined a group of gypsies. They taught me all I know, to poach and to look after horses and train dogs. There was an old grandmother there; she taught me about all the medicines she'd learnt from her great-grandmother.'

He took Granny Maxwell's arm and guided her down some stone steps to a pond filled with irises and marsh marigolds. She caught her breath at the pain.

'An infusion of the leaves of Traveller's Joy works wonders for rheumatism,' he said. 'I'll make you some up to try, or if you prefer, you can carry the skin of a dead frog against your skin.'

Granny Maxwell watched the dogs lapping out of the pond. The mongrel got into the water, drinking, paddling and making a lot of splashing.

'I always feel very badly about the gypsies,' she sighed. 'It's one of the great unnecessary tragedies of progress.

They should never have been forced into compounds to settle and sell scrap metal. But it's always the same story today of harassment from the police and from farmers. Before the war they always used to park in our fields for the seasonal piece work. My father often kept them employed from March until Christmas.

'I miss the sight of their fires at twilight, with that marvellous smell of rabbit stew, and the gaudy washing on the line, and the shaggy horses and silent, lean dogs. They knew a thing or two, those dogs.'

Jake didn't say anything, but felt an emotion, almost love, stronger than he had ever felt for another human being.

'How long were you with the gypsies?'

'Three years. Then I was picked up by the police and put in an orphanage.'

'Can't have been much fun.'

'It was better than prep school. The kids were less vicious. They even accused me of having a posh accent.'

They walked back across the burnt lawn.

'We need rain badly. And what about this horse Tory appears to have bought?'

When he spoke about Africa, his face took on a tinge of colour.

'She's just the best horse I've ever ridden; she's got so much potential and such a lovely nature.'

'Are you sure you don't love her more than Tory?'

Jake thought for a minute, frowning, then he said:

'I'm not sure, but if I take care of Tory as well as I look after Africa she won't do too badly. Anyway, she couldn't be worse off than she is at the moment with that bitch of a mother. She'll have a nervous breakdown if she has to go to many more of those smart parties. It's like putting a carthorse in a hack class, then beating it if it doesn't win.'

'And I gather Molly has a new boyfriend, some Colonel?'

'He's a jerk; they don't want Tory.'

'Why are they so reluctant to let her go, then?'

'Molly likes something to sharpen her claws on. Tory's

her cat-scratching board.'

She bent down to pull a bit of groundsel, then asked Jake to uproot a thread of bindweed that was toppling a lupin.

'It's hell getting old. I can only prune sitting down now. And what's in it for you?' she asked.

'I couldn't marry her if she weren't rich. I've got to get started somehow. And I think Tory and I could make each other happy. Neither of us has ever really had a home before.'

That was the nearest he was going to get to placating her.

'Aren't you banking too much on that horse being a winner? She might break a leg tomorrow.'

'I'll get more horses. This is only the beginning. To make it work as a show jumper, you've got to have at least half a dozen top horses and novices coming on all the time. The gypsies taught me how to recognize a good horse, and I can ride them, and I've got patience.'

'Let's go and watch the 3.30,' said Granny Maxwell.

Mal le maison was second, Whirlwind Courtship nowhere. That's torn it, thought Jake. At that moment, Tory came in with a tray.

'Are you ready for tea yet, Granny?'

'Put the tray down on this table in front of me, thank you, and sit down. I have something to say to you both.'

For a minute she looked at them both with speculative eyes.

'I'm not going to give you any money. Young people should get along by themselves. Tory has a considerable income and you'll soon save enough to buy and sell a few horses.'

Jake's face was expressionless. That was that. His hopes crashed.

'I've no intention of breaking the trust,' Granny Maxwell went on, picking up the blond peke and rolling it onto its back, 'until I see if you're capable of making Tory happy. In three years' time, she'll get the money anyway. However . . .'

Jake stiffened, fighting back hope, as with maddening

73

deliberation Granny Maxwell poured tea into three cups, and went into a long "would anyone like milk, sugar or lemon" routine, and then handed out plates, and asked whether anyone would like a sandwich.

'However,' she repeated, 'Mr Binlock is retiring to a cottage in the middle of June, which means the Mill House at Withrington – that's about twenty miles north of here – will be empty. You can have that.'

Tory turned pale. 'But Granny, it's got stables and fields,' she stammered.

'Exactly, but it's tumbledown and very damp. I hope you haven't got a weak chest,' she added to Jake, 'but it's yours if you want it.'

'Oh, Granny, darling,' said Tory, crossing the room and flinging her arms round her grandmother.

'Don't smother me, child, and there's no need to cry. And as you don't appear to have any transport, I'll buy you a decent horse box for a wedding present.'

Jake shook his head. 'I can't believe it,' he said.

'There's one condition,' Granny Maxwell went on with a cackle of laughter. 'That the first time you appear at Wembley, you buy me a seat in the front row. I'm a bored old woman. In time, if you do well, I might buy a couple of horses and let you ride them for me.'

'If you really are going to buy us a horse box,' said Jake, 'I'd better learn to drive properly and take a test.'

6

Six long months after she arrived in London in 1972, Helen
Macaulay met Rupert Campbell-Black. Born in Florida,
the eldest daughter of a successful dentist, Helen was
considered the brilliant child of the family. Her mother, a
passionate Anglophile and the daughter of a Presbyterian
minister, was constantly reminding people of her English
ancestry. In fact, a distant connection had come over, if not
on the *Mayflower*, perhaps by the next boat. Mrs Macaulay
glossed over this fact and from an early age encouraged the
young Helen to read English novels and poetry and admire
all things English. Later, Helen majored in English
Literature at the university at Tampa, where she was
confidently expected to get a brilliant degree.

Deeply romantic on the one hand, Helen was also
repressed by the rigid respectability of her family. The only
proof that her parents had ever copulated at all were the
four Macaulay daughters. Helen had never heard her
mother and father row, or seen either of them naked. Her
mother, who always insisted on women doctors, never
mentioned sex, except to imply that it was degrading and
wicked. Neither of her parents ever told her she was
beautiful. Work to keep sin at bay, feel guilty if you slack,
was the Macaulay motto.

Until she was nineteen, Helen never gave her parents a
moment's trouble. She worked at school, helped her mother
in the house, never had acne or gained weight, and never
answered back. At Tampa, at the beginning of the seven-
ties, however, she came under the influence of the women's
movement – anathema to her mother, who believed a

woman's place was in the home. Her mother did, however, support the feminists' view that a woman should never allow herself to be treated as a sex object, nor be admired for her body rather than her mind.

To her parents' horror, Helen started getting caught up in student protest movements, demonstrating against the Vietnam war and joining civil rights marches. Even worse, she came home in the vacation and said disparaging things about Richard Nixon. But far worse was to come. During her third year, Helen flunked out with a nervous breakdown, pregnant by her English professor, Harold Mountjoy.

Heavily married, but accustomed to the easy conquest of female students, Harold Mountjoy was quite unprepared for the torrent of emotion he unleashed in Helen Macaulay. It was Jane Eyre and Mr Rochester, Charlotte Brontë and her professor all over again. Except that Helen was a beauty. Only a tremendous earnestness and dedication to study had kept her on the straight and narrow so long at Tampa. On campus she was known as the fair Miss Frigidaire. Harold Mountjoy set about de-frosting her. Seeing her huge hazel eyes fixed on him, like amber traffic lights, during lectures he should have read caution. Instead, one day after class, he kept her back to answer a complicated question on Browning's Paracelsus.

Discussing ambition in life, Harold had lightly quoted: 'I am he that aspired to *know*, and thou?' To which Helen had instantly, almost despairingly, quoted back: 'I would *love* infinitely, and be loved!'

Harold Mountjoy realized he was on to a good thing and asked her for a drink. Secret meetings followed; self-conscious letters weighed down by literary allusions were exchanged, and finally Helen's virginity was lost in a motel twenty-five miles from the campus, followed by fearful guilt, followed by more motels and more guilt. Under Harold's radical guidance, Helen embraced radical causes and in the vacation shocked her parents even more.

Finally, towards the end of the summer term, Helen

fainted in class. Her room-mate, who, despite Helen's attempts at secrecy, had regularly been reading her diary, went to the head of the faculty. He, in turn, was highly delighted, because for years he had been looking for an excuse to dump Harold Mountjoy, whom he regarded as not only immoral but, far worse, intellectually suspect. Helen's parents were summoned. Appalled, they removed her from college. Her father, being a dentist, had the medical contacts to organize a discreet abortion. Helen and Harold were forbidden to see one another again. Harold, clinging to his job, terrified his wife would find out, complied with the request. This was the last straw for Helen. Losing her virginity had meant total commitment. She had expected Harold to tell her to keep the baby and to divorce his wife.

Desperately worried about her, her parents, who were kindly if rigid people, packed her off to England in the hope that this other great imagined love of her life would distract her. She was to stay for at least a year. Helen rang Harold Mountjoy in despair. He urged her to go. They would both write. In time they would meet again. There was a possibility he'd get over to England in August. At last Helen agreed.

The head of the faculty wrote to his London publishers, giving Helen an excellent reference and praising her diligence, and they agreed to give her a job, reading manuscripts, writing blurbs and copy-editing. He also fixed her up with digs with a female author in Hampstead.

So Helen pieced her broken heart together and came to England in October, unable to suppress a feeling of excitement that she would soon be able to visit St Paul's, where John Donne had preached, and Wimpole Street, where Robert Browning had courted Elizabeth Barrett. She might even get up to the Lakes to see Wordsworth's cottage, or Haworth, home of the Brontës.

Sadly, England proved a disappointment. Accustomed to year-round Florida sunshine, Helen arrived at the beginning of the worst winter for years. She couldn't believe how cold it was.

By day she froze in her publishing house, by night she froze at her digs, which were awful. The female author was an ancient Lesbian who watched her every move. Upstairs was a lecherous lodger who made eyes at her at meal times and kept coming into her room on trumped-up excuses. The place was filthy and reeked of a tom cat, which her landlady refused to castrate. The landlady also used the same dishcloth to wash up the cat's plates and the humans' plates. The food was awful; they seemed to eat carbohydrates with carbohydrates in England. She found herself eating cookies and candy to keep out the cold, put on ten pounds and panicked.

At the weekends she froze on sight-seeing tours, shivering at Stratford, at the Tower and on the train down to Hampton Court and in numerous art galleries.

The English men were a bitter disappointment, too. None of them looked like Darcy, or Rochester, or Heathcliff, or Burgo Fitzgerald or Sebastian Flyte. None of them washed their hair often enough; she never dared look in their ears in the subway. They also seemed de-sexed by the cold weather. They never gazed or whistled at her in the street. Anyway, Helen was not the sort of girl who would have picked up men. As the days passed, she grew more and more lonely.

Harold Mountjoy was another disappointment. After one letter: 'Darling girl, forgive a scribbled note, but you are too precious to have brief letters. It would take a month to tell you all I feel about you, and I don't have the time', he didn't write at Christmas or remember her birthday or even Valentine's Day.

Finally, at the beginning of March, Helen decided she could bear her digs no longer. On the same day that her landlady used a cat-food-encrusted spoon to stir the beef stew with, and the tom cat invaded her room for the hundredth time and sprayed on her typewriter cover, she moved into Regina House, an all-female hostel in Hammersmith, which catered exclusively for visiting academics, and was at least clean and warm.

Nor was her job in publishing very exciting. The initial bliss of being paid to read all day soon palled because of the almost universal awfulnes of the manuscripts submitted. To begin with, Helen wrote the authors polite letters of rejection, whereupon they all wrote back, sending her other unpublished works and pestering her to publish them; so finally she resorted, like everyone else, to rejection slips.

Her two bosses took very extended lunch hours and spent long weekends at their houses in the country. One of the director's sons, having ignored her in the office, asked her out to dinner one evening and lunged so ferociously in the car going home that Helen was forced to slap his face. From then on he went back to ignoring her.

The only other unmarried man in the office was a science graduate in his late twenties named Nigel, a vegetarian with brushed-forward fawn hair, a straggly beard, a thin neck like a goose and spectacles. For six months, Helen and he had been stepping round each other, she out of loneliness, and he out of desire. They had long political arguments and grumbled about their capitalist bosses. Nigel introduced her to Orwell and bombarded her with leftist literature.

He was also heavily involved with the anti-fox hunting movement and seemed to spend an exciting resistance life at weekends rescuing foxes and hares from ravening packs of hounds, harassing hunt balls with tear gas, and descending by helicopter into the middle of coursing meetings. He was constantly on the telephone to various cronies named Paul and Dave, arranging dead-of-night rendez-vous to unblock earths. Often he came in on Monday with a black eye or bandaged wrist, after scuffles with hunt supporters.

One Friday, towards the end of March, he asked Helen out to lunch. He was wearing a yellow corduroy coat, a black shirt, had clean hair and looked less unattractive than usual. Inevitably, the conversation got around to blood sports.

'They think we're all lefties or students on the dole living in towns,' he said, whipping off his spectacles. 'But we come from all walks of life. You see, the fox,' he went on in his flat Northern accent, 'beautiful, dirty, hard-pressed with so many people after him, hounds, foot-followers, riders, horses, terriers, he needs us on his side to tip the balance a little.'

Helen's huge eyes filled with tears. For a moment, in his blaze of conviction, Nigel reminded her of Harold Mount-joy. He speared a piece of aubergine farcie with his fork. 'Why don't you come out with us tomorrow? We're driving down to Gloucestershire to rot up the Chalford and Bisley. It's the last meet of the season. Dave's got hold of a lot of thunderflashes; it should be a good day.'

Helen, unable to face another weekend on her own, trailing round galleries or visiting the house of some long-dead writer, said she'd love to.

'And afterwards, we might have dinner in Oxford,' said Nigel. 'They've opened a good vegetarian restaurant in the High.'

And now she was rattling down the M4 to Gloucester-shire and wondering why the hell she'd agreed to come. The dilapidated car was driven by a bearded young zoology graduate named Paul, who had cotton wool in his ears and was already losing his hair. Beside him sat Nigel. Both men were wearing gumboots and khaki combat kit, and khaki, she decided, simply wasn't Nigel's colour.

Even worse, she had to sit in the back with Paul's girlfriend, Maureen, who was large, dismissive and aggres-sively unglamorous, with dirty dark brown hair, black fingernails and no make-up on her shiny white face. Between her heavy lace-up boots and the bottom of the khaki trousers were two inches of hairy, unshaven leg. She was also wearing a voluminous white sheepskin coat which stank as it dried off. It was rather like sharing the back with a large unfriendly dog. Even worse, she insisted on referring to Helen as Ellen.

Taking one look at Helen's rust corduroy trousers tucked into brown shiny boots, dark green cashmere turtleneck jersey and brown herring-bone jacket, she said, 'I don't

80

expect you've ever demonstrated against anything in your life, Ellen.'

Helen replied, somewhat frostily, that she'd been on several anti-Vietnam war marches, which launched Maureen, Nigel and Paul into an unprovoked attack on America and Nixon and Watergate, and how corrupt the Americans were, which irritated Helen to death. It was all right for her to go on about corruption in America, but not at all O.K. for the Brits to take it for granted.

Sulkily, she buried herself in a piece in the paper speculating as to whether Princess Anne was going to marry Captain Mark Phillips. She'd been following conflicting reports of the romance with shamefaced interest. Mark Phillips was so good-looking, with his neat smooth head, and gleaming dark hair, so much more attractive than Nigel and Paul's straggly locks. In America, hair like theirs had long gone out of fashion, other than for ageing hippies.

They were off the motorway now, driving past hedgerows starry with primroses. Buds were beginning to soften and blur the trees against a clear blue sky. Flocks of pigeons rose like smoke from the newly ploughed fields. Helen felt tears stinging her eyes once more.

'Spring returns, but not my friend,' she murmured, thinking sadly of Harold Mountjoy.

'I suppose foxes do have to be kept down somehow,' she said out loud, feeling she ought to contribute something to the discussion. 'They do kill chickens.'

'Rubbish,' snapped Maureen. 'These days, chickens are safely trapped in battery houses.'

'And Ellen,' said Paul earnestly, 'only five per cent of foxes ever touch chicken.'

Helen had a sudden vision of the five per cent sitting down to coq au vin with knives and forks.

Now Maureen, Paul and Nigel were slagging someone they referred to as R.C.B.

'Who's R.C.B.?' asked Helen, and was told it was Rupert Campbell-Black, the one the Antis hated most.

'Male chauvinist pig of the worst kind,' said Maureen.

81

'Upper class shit who makes Hitler look like Nestle's milk,' said Paul.

'Always rides his horses straight at us,' said Nigel. 'Broke Paul's wrist with his whip last autumn.'

'Remember that hunt ball when he smashed a champagne bottle on the table and threatened you with it, Nige?' said Maureen.

'What does he do?' asked Helen.

'Show jumps internationally,' said Paul, 'and allegedly beats up his horses. But he's so loaded, he doesn't need to do anything very much.'

Helen noticed the curling copies of the *New Statesman* and *Tribune* on the back seat and a tattered copy of Bertolt Brecht in the pocket of Maureen's coat. These are people who care about things, she reproved herself, I must try to like them better.

'What do we do when we get there?' she asked.

'The basic idea, Ellen,' said Maureen, 'is to copy everything the huntsmen do. We bring our own horns – Paul here actually plays the horn in an orchestra – and use them to split the pack. We've perfected our view halloos, and we also spray the meet with a special mixture called Anti-mate, which confuses the hounds.'

Nigel looked at his watch, which he wore ten minutes fast on the inside of his wrist. 'Nearly there,' he said.

Helen got out her mirror, added some blusher to her pale, freckled cheeks, ran a comb through her gleaming dark red page-boy, and rearranged the tortoiseshell headband that kept it off her forehead.

'You're not going to a party,' reproved Maureen.

Defiantly, Helen sprayed on some scent.

'Nice pong,' said Paul, wrinkling his long nose. 'D'you know the one about the Irish saboteurs, Ellen? They spent all day trying to sabotage a drag hunt.'

'Don't tell ethnic jokes, Paul,' said Nigel, smiling as widely as his small mouth would allow.

They were beginning to overtake riders and horses hacking to the meet. A pretty blonde on an overexcited chestnut waved them past.

'You've no idea how we're going to cook your goose later, my beauty,' Nigel gloated.

Soon the road was lined with boxes and trailers, and Paul drove faster through the deep brown puddles in order to splash all those riders in clean white breeches standing on the grass verge. Now he was fuming at being stuck at ten m.p.h. behind a huge horse box which kept crashing against the overhanging ash trees.

The meet was held in one of those sleepy Cotswold villages, with a village green flanked by golden grey cottages, a lichened church knee-deep in daffodils, and a pub called the Goat in Boots. A large crowd had gathered to watch the riders in their black and scarlet coats saddling up, supervising the unboxing of their horses and grumbling about their hangovers.

'What a darling place,' said Helen, as the sun came out. The Antis, however, had no time for aesthetic appreciation. Paul parked his car on the edge of the green and, getting out, they all surged forward to exchange firm handshakes and straight glances with other saboteurs. Both sexes were wearing khaki anoraks or combat kit as camouflage, but with their grey faces and long straggly hair and beards, they couldn't have stood out more beside the fresh-faced, clean-cut locals.

'Here's your own supply of Anti-mate,' said Nigel, dropping two aerosol cans into the pockets of Helen's coat, 'Spray it on hounds or riders, whenever you get the chance.'

Helen thought irritably that the cans would ruin the line of her coat, and when Nigel insisted on pinning two badges saying 'Hounds Off Our Wild Life' and 'Only Rotters hunt Otters' on the lapels of her coat, she wondered if it was necessary for him to take so long and press his skinny hands quite so hard against her breast. Perhaps she'd have to use the Anti-mate on him.

Two sinister-looking men walked by with a quartet of small bright-eyed yapping dogs.

'Those are the terriers they use to dig out the fox,' whispered Maureen.

Helen also noticed several magenta-faced colonels and braying ladies on shooting sticks giving her dirty looks. A group of men in deerstalkers and dung-coloured suits stood grimly beside a Land Rover.

'They're paid by the hunt to sabotage us,' explained Maureen indignantly. 'Given a chance, they'll block the road and ram us with that Land Rover.'

Helen was beginning to feel distinctly uneasy. She edged slightly away from the group of saboteurs, then said to herself firmly, 'I am a creative writer. Here is a golden opportunity to study the British in one of their most primitive rituals.'

Listening to the anxious whinnying from the boxes, she breathed in the heady smell of sweating horse, dung and damp earth. The landlord of the pub was dispensing free drinks on a silver tray. His wife followed with a tray of sandwiches and sausage rolls. Helen, who had had no breakfast, was dying to tuck in, but felt, being part of the enemy, that she shouldn't.

Nigel and Maureen had no such scruples.

'Good crowd,' said Nigel, greedily helping himself to three sandwiches, 'Oh dear, they're ham,' he added disapprovingly, and, removing the fillings, he dropped them disdainfully on the ground where they were devoured by a passing labrador.

Suddenly, as the gold hand of the church clock edged towards eleven o'clock, there was a murmur of excitement as a dark blue Porsche drew up.

'There he is,' hissed Maureen, as two men got out. Helen caught a glimpse of gleaming blond hair and haughty, suntanned features, as the taller of the two men vanished in a screaming tidal wave of teenagers brandishing autograph books. Others stood on the bonnets of their parents' cars, or clambered onto each others' shoulders trying to take photographs or get a better look.

'Worse than that Dick Jagger,' snorted an old lady, who'd been nearly knocked off her shooting stick by the rush.

A girl stumbled out of the melée, her face as bright pink as the page of the autograph book she was kissing. Half a minute later she was followed by her friend.

'He used this pen,' she sighed ecstatically. 'I'm never going to use it again.'

Gradually the crowd dispersed and through a gap Helen was able to get a better look. The man had thick blond hair, brushed straight back and in two wings above the ears, emphasizing the clear, smooth forehead and the beautiful shape of his head. His face, with its Greek nose, high cheek bones and long, denim-blue eyes, was saved from effeminacy by a square jaw and a very determined, mouth.

Totally oblivious of the mayhem he had caused, he was lounging against the Porsche, talking continuously but hardly moving his lips, to a stocky young man with light brown curly hair, a broken nose, sleepy eyes, and a noticeably green complexion. The blond man was signing autograph books so automatically and handing them onto his companion, that when the queue dried up, he held his hand out for another pen and a book.

'What a beautiful, beautiful guy,' gasped Helen.

'Yes, and knows it,' snapped Maureen. 'That's R.C.B. and his shadow, Billy Lloyd-Foxe.'

The landlord pressed forward with the tray.

'Morning Rupe, morning Billy. Want a hair of the dog?'

'Christ, yes.' Reaching out, the stocky light-brown-haired boy grabbed two glasses, one of which he handed to Rupert. Then, getting out a tenner and two flasks from his pocket, he handed them to the landlord, adding:

'Could you bear to fill them up with brandy, Les? I'll never fight my way through Rupe's admirers.'

'Bit under the weather, are you, Billy?' said the landlord.

'Terrible. If I open my eyes, I'll bleed to death.'

A groom was lowering the ramp of a nearby box and unloading a magnificent bay mare, sweating in a dark blue rug edged with emerald green with the initials R.C.B. in the corner, and looking back into the box, whinnying imperiously for her stable companions. Rupert turned around.

'How is she, Frenchie?'

'Bit over the top, Sir,' said the groom. 'She could use the exercise.'

He swept the rug off the sweating, shuddering mare and slapped on a saddle. Suddenly she started to hump her back with excitement, dancing on the spot as the hunt arrived in a flood of scarlet coats, burnished horses and jolly, grinning hounds, tails wagging frenziedly, circling merrily, looking curiously naked without any collars.

Helen felt her heart lift; how beautiful and glamorous they all looked.

'Little people get on big horses and think they're gods,' said Nigel thickly in her ear. 'Those hounds haven't been fed for three days.'

But Helen was gazing at Rupert Campbell-Black, who was taking off his navy blue jersey and shrugging himself into a red coat. Goodness, he was well constructed. Usually, men with such long legs had short bodies, but Rupert, from the broad flat shoulders to the lean muscular hips and powerful thighs, seemed perfectly in proportion.

Just as he and Billy mounted their horses the local photographer arrived, pushing his way through the ring of admirers.

'Hullo, Rupert, can I have a photograph of you and Billy?'

'O.K.,' said Rupert, gazing unsmiling into the camera.

'I'm not looking my best,' grumbled Billy. 'I haven't washed my hair.'

'Good chance for publicity,' said Maureen sententiously, and barging her way through, she handed Rupert an anti-hunting leaflet.

'Thank you very much,' he said politely. 'Can I have one for Billy?'

Maureen turned round to face the camera between them.

'Can I borrow your lighter, Billy?' said Rupert. Next minute he had set fire to the two leaflets and dropped them flaming at Maureen's feet.

'You're not even man enough to read them,' she said furiously.

Rupert looked her up and down. 'It's rather hard to tell what sex you are,' he drawled, 'but you're certainly not good looking enough to hold such extreme views. Go away, you're frightening my horse.'

The crowd screamed with laughter. Maureen flounced back to Helen. 'The bastard, did you hear what he said?'

Over Maureen's head, for a second, Rupert's eyes met Helen's. Then he looked away without interest. They're right. He's poisonous, she thought.

At that moment a beautiful, but over-made-up woman, her black coat straining over a splendid bosom, trotted up to Rupert with a proprietorial air.

'Darling, how are you feeling? I actually made it.'

Simultaneously the landlord arrived with the two filled flasks. As he handed one of them to Rupert she grabbed it, taking a large swig.

'Don't drink it all,' snapped Rupert.

'Darling,' she said fondly, screwing back the top, and handing it to him, 'You can come home later and drink as much of ours as you like.'

Rupert put a long booted leg forward and pulled up the mare's girths.

'I don't know if I'll need Monty as well,' he said to the groom. 'With these bloody hunt saboteurs about, we may not get much action. If you lose us, wait at the Spotted Cow.'

The next moment the hunt clattered off. Helen was amazed to see Nigel suddenly leap out of a hawthorn bush and squirt the hounds with Anti-mate. Next minute a little girl had rushed up and kicked him so hard on the ankles that he dropped the aerosol can with a yell.

'Stop it, you horrid man,' she screamed.

Rupert Campbell-Black, who was passing, grinned down at her:

'Well done, angel. I'll marry you when you grow up.'

The saboteurs leapt into their five cars.

'Keep your eyes peeled for foxes,' hissed Paul. Nigel was still grumbling about his ankle.

Hurtling down a country lane, sending the catkins shivering, they found hounds being put into the palest green larch covert. The saboteurs parked above it and the next moment a posse, including Nigel and Paul, vaulted over the fence and, armed with Anti-mate, disappeared after them. Judging by the expletives and the shaking of fists, they were causing havoc in the woods. The master decided to move on.

'Out of my way,' he said bossily to a group of girl riders. 'you're not with the Pony Club now. I expect you've only come out to gaze at Rupert Campbell-Black.'

The saboteurs moved off in search of fresh sport. Stopping in a layby to spray pepper, they got stuck in the mud. Two footfollowers, not realizing who they were, pushed them out.

The next two hours were like being at a race meeting, permanently under starter's orders. Every time the hunt picked up a scent the Antis managed to foil them.

Later, Maureen and Helen hung over a gate watching a sluggish stream choking its way through overhanging osiers and pussy willows. Fat celandines were pushing their way through the dead leaves. Helen gloried in the spring sunshine beating through her dark green jersey.

'Are the saboteurs anti-fishing as well?' she asked.

'Oh, yes,' said Maureen earnestly. 'Our more extreme members feel it's cruel to the worm.'

Helen's stomach gave an ominous rumble.

'I'm starving,' said Maureen. 'Thank God I had a cooked breakfast. We're all rendez-vousing at the Spotted Cow at one o'clock.'

Helen, who had had no breakfast and only scrambled eggs the previous night, had visions of gins and tonics and pub steak and kidney pudding. The ploughed brown fields in their evenness reminded her of mince. Perhaps there'd be shepherd's pie for lunch.

But in the end, they only stopped at the village shop to buy oranges and some Perrier.

'Can't squander the saboteurs' funds on food and drink,' said Nigel, offering her his bottle of Perrier.

Helen suddenly thought how much she'd prefer to share a flask of brandy with Rupert Campbell-Black. If she'd been out with him, she figured, he'd have made sure she was properly looked after.

The saboteurs were parked outside the Spotted Cow as the hunt came past, looking understandably bootfaced after such an abortive morning.

'Pull the choke out,' whispered Paul. 'It'll muddle the hounds.'

On the other side of another wood, the hats of the riders could be seen moving ceaselessly back and forth.

Another posse of saboteurs moved in from the right, view-hallooing to distract the hounds and throwing in a couple of fire-crackers, which set the already excited horses plunging.

'Pa, pa, pa, pa,' came the tender melancholy note of the horn.

'Oh, good. I mean, oh dear!' said Helen, 'They've found a fox.'

'That's Paul,' said Maureen smugly. 'He can blow a horn as well as any huntsman.'

Two women supporters in green quilted coats and tweed skirts parked nearby and got out of their car.

'Bloody Antis,' said one, incongruously smoothing a wildlife sanctuary sticker on her windscreen.

'Have you heard how the Paignton-Laceys' dance went?' said her friend.

'Fiona's not up yet this morning, but I saw Primrose, who said it was frightfully good. More chaps than girls for a change. Rupert Campbell-Black disgraced himself as usual. Got off with Gabriella. Evidently they disappeared for hours and hours. Charlie got quite frantic. They've only been married a year.'

'Better than Marcia's dance,' said the first one. 'Evidently he got simply plastered and docked the tails of all the yew peacocks; I mean they've taken literally hundreds of years to grow. I'd have sued the little beast.'

'He gets away with it,' said the first one, 'because he is so frightfully attractive.'

Suddenly she gave an enraged bellow as Nigel and Paul, spattered with mud, their hands cut and bleeding from the undergrowth, tore up the hill with the heavies hot on their trail, and leapt into the car.

Taking off, Paul shook off the heavies, finally stopping at the edge of a beech wood looking down a valley. In the back, Nigel was noisily sucking an orange. Getting out of the car, Helen caught her breath, for there, slowly riding up the hill, came Rupert Campbell-Black, his gleaming bay mare and his red coat the only splashes of colour against the greens and browns. Gaining the top of the hill he paused, trying to work out which way hounds might run. The sun, which had been hovering in the wings like an actor waiting to make an entrance, broke away from the clouds, warming the brown fields. Nigel got out of the car, wiping his hands on his trousers.

'To one who has been long in city pent,' he said pompously as he edged towards Helen: 'Tis very sweet to look into the fair and open face of heaven.'

Helen, who privately thought it would be much sweeter to look into the fair and very close face of Rupert Campbell-Black, edged away again.

'I think they're going to draw this covert,' said Nigel, vanishing into the beech copse, followed by Paul.

A hound spoke. Then the triumphant chorus rang out and there was the wild cry of the true horn. Suddenly, with the master cheering them on the line, hounds streamed down the valley in a dappled cloud. Then came the field, galloping, jumping, barging through gates with a clash of stirrups. There was Rupert, looking in a completely different class to the others, riding so easily and fluidly, almost nibbling his horse's ears as he seemed to lift her over a huge hedge.

'Wire on the other side,' he yelled back to Billy, who gathered his black cob together and cleared it just as easily. There was a clattering of hooves as they jumped into the road and out again, and set off towards the beech copse, which had been liberally sprayed with pepper and Anti-mate. As they entered the copse, Nigel and Paul stood on a nearby fence and started to blow a horn concerto, utterly muddling the hounds who, distracted by the pepper and the Anti-mate, charged around, frenziedly zigzagging back and forth, whimpering with frustration as they tried to pick up the scent.

Helen suddenly felt furious with Nigel and Paul. What right had they to spoil everyone's day? She and Maureen were standing in the field skirting the copse when suddenly Nigel came hurtling out of the wood, followed by Paul. The next minute Rupert Campbell-Black galloped around the corner, riding straight at them, his eyes blazing.

'He won't touch the girls,' screamed Nigel, promptly plunging his horn down Helen's new dark green cashmere jersey, stretching the neckband, and disappearing over the hedge. 'Chivalry will prevent him,' he called over his shoulder.

Chivalry prevented Rupert doing no such thing. He rode straight up to Helen, reined in the plunging mare and, before Helen could stop him, leaned over, put a warm hand down the front of her jersey and retrieved the horn.

'A good-looking Anti,' he said in mock-wonder. 'I never expected to see one. What's a pretty girl like you doing, getting mixed up with a desiccated creep like Nigel?'

'How dare you?' gasped Helen, hand to her breast as though she'd been violated.

'How dare *you*?' said Rupert. 'This is private property. You're trespassing. I'd go back to London and not get involved with a lot of rent-a-crowd lefties.'

'All right, Helen?' asked Nigel, emerging from the undergrowth.

'She's not getting much help from you, you little rat,' said

91

Rupert. 'She's got a very good body, though.'

Blushing crimson, hopelessly aware how unbecoming it was with her red hair, Helen gazed fixedly at Rupert's highly polished boot.

'Don't you insult my girlfriend,' said Nigel, striding up, slipping in a cowpat and putting his arm round Helen's shoulders.

Equally furiously, she shrugged him off.

'On the contrary,' said Rupert, pocketing the horn, 'I was being excessively polite, telling her she's the only decent-looking girl I'd ever seen out with the Antis.' He nodded in Maureen's direction. 'What d'you use that one for, breaking down lift doors?'

For a second he made the mare plunge towards Nigel, who retreated into the hedge, then, wheeling round, he was off.

'I'll get even with you,' screeched Nigel.

As they set off again, Helen sat in the back, stunned. Rupert was simply the most wrong but entirely romantic person she'd ever met. She was appalled how violently she felt attracted to him. She could still feel the warmth of his leisurely hand and remember the way the brilliant blue eyes had moved over her, assessing, absorbing data like a computer.

'My only love sprang from my only hate,' she whispered.

As Rupert cantered back to join the despondent remains of the hunt, Gabriella, who'd earlier helped herself to his hipflask, caught up with him.

'Coo-ee, darling, where *have* you been?'

One of the added irritations caused by the saboteurs, thought Rupert, was that it had been impossible to shake Gabriella off. Last night, belonging to someone else, with her magnificent white bosom rising out of plunging black lace, she had been a far more desirable proposition. He had taken her in a cordoned-off bedroom, hung around with tapestries. In the middle, a long line of footfollowers had actually conga-ed unknowing through the room, whooping and yelling and reducing them both to helpless laughter.

Today, red-veined from an excess of wine, with her make-up running, her hair coming down in a lacquered mass and her bulky thighs in too-tight breeches, she had lost all her charm, though none of her ardour. Rupert had a sudden yearning for the whippet-slim Anti, with her hair the colour of the bracken still strewing the rides.

'What a bloody useless day,' he said.

'It could be improved dramatically,' said Gabriella, riding her horse alongside him. 'Why don't we slip home? Charlie's gone shooting.'

'Probably like to count me as part of the bag,' said Rupert, looking at his watch. 'It's only a quarter to three. Worth giving it another hour.'

He was relieved to see Billy emerging from the wood, his head buried in his horse's neck to avoid the branches.

'I feel better,' said Billy. 'I've just been sick behind a holly bush. Have you got any brandy left, Rupe?'

'Not much,' said Rupert, handing him the flask. 'Better finish it.'

Rupert's fiendish behaviour was soon relayed with relish to the rest of the Antis. Helen, unable to work up any indignation at all, picked a bunch of primroses and wrapped them in a paper handkerchief dipped in a puddle.

Briefly, Paul and Nigel had lost the hounds, but had found them again in full cry within the walls of some huge estate. Unable to get at them physically, the saboteurs launched their toughest offensive. All hell broke loose as smoke bombs and thunderflashes exploded, fog-horns wailed and horns and whistles were blown.

'Jesus Christ! Some buggers are shooting in the covert. Pull hounds out,' yelled a huntsman.

Helen hid behind an ash tree, saying her prayers as the saboteurs charged about, yelling, screaming, slipping on wet leaves, tripping over bramble cables and the long silver roots of beech trees. Hounds had gone to pieces. All Helen could hear was whimpering. Nigel shimmied up the wall to look.

'Master's lost control,' he said happily.

93

To the left, the Land Rovers with the heavies were moving in threateningly. Paul seized Helen, bustling her into the front of the car.

'Let's beat it,' he said.

'Where are Maureen and Nigel?'

'Mo's in one of the other cars,' Paul put his foot down on the accelerator, 'and Nigel's got some ingenious plot of his own, but my lips are sealed. He's taken Fiona's car; said he'd join us later.'

It had started to spit with rain. Old ladies hurried home, putting on head scarves. Women rushed out into the cottage gardens, taking in washing.

'You're not wearing your safety belt, Ellen,' said Paul. 'Wouldn't want an attractive young lady to come to any harm.'

Turning on Radio Three, he accompanied a Beethoven sonata in a reedy tenor. Helen had a feeling he was glad they'd shed the others.

'I know you're Nige's girl,' he said throatily.

'I am not,' said Helen tartly. 'There is nothing between us.'

'That makes a difference. Didn't want to tread on anyone's corns. I happen to be playing at a concert at the Festival Hall next Saturday. Wonder if you'd care to come. We could have an Indian afterwards.'

Helen, who hated curry, said she'd look in her diary, which he seemed to regard as a satisfactory answer. As he rabbited on about the orchestra and the paper he was writing on shrews, Helen found it was unnecessary to make any other comment than the occasional 'um'. Breathing in the apricot dusk, she wondered what Rupert Campbell-Black was doing now.

Rupert and Billy hacked back to their horsebox through the pouring rain, discussing which horses they should take to the Crittleden Easter Meeting, which started on Friday. Billy, who'd put his collar up and turned his hat back to front to stop the rain running down his neck, was trying to light a cigarette.

'Did you see the girl with the Antis?' asked Rupert, in that deceptively casual way that meant he was interested.

'Bit thin,' said Billy.

'Marvellous face, though. Doesn't sound English. How the hell did Nigel get hold of her?'

'Perhaps she likes his mind.'

'Hardly likely to be anything else.'

Rounding the corner, fifty yards away, they saw Nigel busily letting down the tyres of Rupert's horsebox. Riding on the verge, he hadn't heard them coming.

'Leave this to me,' said Rupert softly.

Sliding off the mare, throwing the reins to Billy, he sprinted down the road and, taking a flying leap, landed on Nigel with a crash, knocking the breath out of his body. Next minute he had dragged him up a grassy side lane and was systematically beating him to a pulp. It was Billy who dragged Rupert off.

'For God's sake, that's enough. You don't want to be done for murder.'

At that moment Frenchie, the groom, woke up from sleeping off his lunch and appeared out of the front of the horsebox, rubbing his eyes.

'Where the hell have you been?' snarled Rupert. 'Getting pissed as usual, I suppose. Here, take the horses and get me some rope.'

Pulling off his hunting tie, he stuffed it into Nigel's mouth, then systematically stripped off Nigel's clothes, looking down with distaste at the white skinny body. As Rupert tied his hands and feet with spare head-collar ropes, Nigel gave a groan and started to wriggle.

'Think he'll be all right?' said Billy.

'Sadly, yes, the little shit,' said Rupert, giving him a kick in the ribs. 'It'll take him half an hour to wriggle down the road. It'll still be light; someone'll pick him up. Pity it's such a warm night.'

He picked up Nigel's combat jacket and removed his address book from the inside pocket. As he flipped through it, they hitched a lift in the horsebox back to the blue Porsche.

'How riveting,' said Rupert. 'He's got Fiona's telephone number, and mine, the little bastard, and yours too. What did he call that girl? Helen, I think. Here's one. Helen Macaulay, Regina House, W.14. Where the hell's that?'

'Shepherd's Bush or Hammersmith.'

'Frightfully unsmart,' said Rupert. 'I wonder if that's her.'

Helen got in around midnight. The walnut and cottage cheese paté and the vegetable curry had been disgusting. She'd hardly eaten anything, but, still dazed by Rupert Campbell-Black, had drunk more cheap elderberry wine than was good for her.

Maureen had glared at her all evening; Nigel had never turned up and Paul had somehow engineered that he drop her off at Regina House after dropping off Maureen at her digs.

'I won't come up for a coffee, Mo. I expect you're tired,' he said.

Helen suspected that Maureen, standing in her furry coat like a disgruntled Pyrenean mountain dog, was no such thing. Outside Regina House Paul said, 'May I kiss you, Ellen?' and lunged goatily. His beard tickled, he had B.O. and his breath smelled of curry. Helen lost her temper.

'You're too sanctimonious for words, right. You had a glorious day playing cops and robbers and feeling smug to boot, and what's more I'd like to report you to the RSPCA for being horrible to hounds.' Leaping out, she slammed the car door in his face.

Now she sat in her room feeling ashamed of herself and gazing at Harold Mountjoy's photograph, which seemed to have lost all its appeal. She noticed the spoilt, slightly weak expression, the hair carefully combed forward to cover the lined forehead and crow's feet round the eyes.

'My only love sprang from my only hate,' she whispered. She'd never see Rupert again. He obviously had millions of girls after him and, anyway, he was thoroughly spoilt. She looked at the primroses in the tooth mug with the ochre centres and pastel petals. She'd have to put him in her novel, then she could dream about him. Slowly she undressed, gazing at her body in the mirror. She'd never really studied it before, and yet he'd said it was beautiful. She found she'd put her nightdress on inside out; that was supposed to be lucky. She could do with some luck. She jumped at a sudden pounding on the door. It was the Principal of the hostel in a camel hair dressing gown, hair in a net.

'Telephone,' she snapped. 'Person says it's an emergency. Can't see how it can be.'

Helen sighed; it must be Nigel. Perhaps he'd been arrested and needed bailing out, or was grumbling because Paul had driven off without him. At least he couldn't accuse her of getting off with Paul.

In the telephone booth someone had left a copy of Lorca. Helen picked up the receiver: 'Hullo.'

'May I speak to Helen Macaulay,' said a voice. She'd recognize that clipped, light drawl anywhere. Her palms went damp, her knees turned to jelly.

'This is she.'

'Well, this is the enemy speaking – Rupert Campbell-Black.'

'How did you get my number?'

'It's a long story.'

'Is Nigel all right?'

'As right as he ever could be. What are you doing tomorrow?'

'Going to church in the morning.'

In the background she could hear the sounds of music and revelry.

'Shut up, you maniacs,' yelled Rupert. 'Look, I'll take you to church, then I'll give you lunch. I'll pick you up at half past ten.'

She liked the way he pronounced it: 'H'pp'st'n'.

7

Oblivious to the continued grumbling of the head of the hostel who was still hovering in the hall, Helen fled upstairs to her room and rushed to the mirror, just to reassure herself that she was still there and that such a thing could have happened.

'He called,' she whispered, 'he really called.'

With all those girls chasing after him, he'd bothered to get her phone number from Nigel. Then she buried her face in the primroses, breathing in their faint sweet smell, before collapsing on to the bed.

She must pull herself together. Rupert was a terrible rake, who attracted females far too effortlessly, no doubt leaving a trail of destruction in his wake, like Macheath. And what about the dreadful sexist things he'd said to Maureen, and what about married Gabriella, with whom he'd vanished for two hours at the ball? Perhaps she shouldn't go; her heart hadn't mended after Harold Mountjoy; a second break would be far more difficult to repair. But the thought of not seeing him made her faint with horror. She felt quite out of control, swept along like a branch chucked into a raging torrent.

Besides, there was no way she could get in touch with him to say she had changed her mind; and would she ever be any good as a writer if she didn't experience life?

It had been a very long day. If she didn't want black circles under bug eyes the next morning, she ought to get some sleep, but instead she sat down at her typewriter and covered six pages of foolscap describing the day. These she slotted into a folder marked 'England 1973'. Then she cleaned her teeth for two minutes, using dental floss between each tooth, and sank to her knees to say her prayers. A convinced conservationist who believed in husbanding nature's resources, she was horrified, when she got to her feet, to see that she'd left the tap running.

She woke in wild excitement. But elation soon gave way to panic as clothes littered the normally tidy room.

On and off, and on and off went the grey angora dress, which went best with her hair, but might be too hot if they went to a crowded restaurant. On and off went the crocus yellow silk shirt which brought out the colour of her eyes, but, worn with a grey suit, made her look too much like an efficient secretary. The rust suit was too autumnal, the steel blue wool dress was lovely, but she was perspiring so much with nerves she might have great embarrassing dark circles under the arms. Finally she settled for the kilt and matching beret and green velvet coat she had bought from the Scotch House, worn with a frilly white shirt.

Then, what about make-up? She knew you shouldn't wear much for church, but too much for God would be too little for Rupert. Really, it was very hard dressing for both, like having God and the Devil to dinner. Perfume was wrong for church, too Delilah-ish, so she settled for pouring half a bottle of cologne over herself instead. Much against her principles, she'd taken one of the tranquillizers she'd been given when she split up with Harold Mountjoy. It was having no effect at all. When she found herself rubbing deodorant into her cheeks and moisturizer under her arms, she realized she was really over the top.

She was ready by 10.15, waiting in the dark polished hall. Various dowdy lady academics were milling around, getting ready for outings to museums or galleries. If only one of them would tell her she looked nice; but lady academics don't notice such trivialities.

She took a surreptitious glance in the full-length mirror and suddenly decided that she looked ludicrous in the matching tartan beret and kilt, just like an air hostess. Racing upstairs, she changed back into the grey angora

99

dress. Oh God, there was lipstick on it. She covered the mark with a pearl brooch, which looked ridiculous just above her left nipple. Her newly-washed hair was all over the place from so much dressing and undressing. She rammed it down with a grey velvet hairband.

She couldn't stop shaking. It was now twenty-five to eleven. At first the minutes crawled by, then they started to gallop. He couldn't be coming; it was 10.50. Perhaps she'd heard him wrong, but she was sure he'd said half past ten. She tried to read a long analysis of the Watergate crisis in the *Sunday Times*, but the words kept blurring, so she gave up and gazed at some horrible shocking pink hyacinths that were twitching outside in the cold wind.

Perhaps, in her state of cardiac arrest, she'd given him the wrong directions to Regina House, saying left when she meant right. It was two minutes to eleven; she musn't cry, it would make her mascara run, but what did it matter when he obviously wasn't coming anyway? It was just some diabolical plot to raise her hopes and then dump on her from a great height because she was part of the saboteurs.

The club secretary had just pinned the lunchtime menu on the board and several of the inmates surged forward, trying not to look too eager, watering at the mouth at the prospect of roast beef and treacle pudding to liven up their uneventful lives. In utter despair, fighting back the tears, Helen turned to stumble upstairs, but just as the hall grandfather clock struck eleven the front door pushed open and Rubert walked in, coming towards her with that lovely loping athlete's stride. Unlike most people, he didn't automatically lower his voice when he entered an institution.

'Darling, darling, I'm desperately sorry. I had to look at a horse in Newbury on the way up; the traffic was frightful,' he lied. 'Are you all right? Did you think I wasn't coming?'

He walked up to her and, taking her hand, kissed her on the cheek.

Helen gazed up at him, unable to get a word out. Overnight, she'd changed him, in his red coat, into some

100

kind of devil, and here he was turning up, looking just the sort of preppy young man of whom her parents would approve. The severity of the impeccably-cut dark suit, striped shirt and blue tie only served to set off the dazzling good looks. A shaft of pale sunlight coming through the window gilded the smooth blond hair. It was as though a light had been turned on in the dark hall. Even the dingy academics gathered around the notice board changed the object of the salivating, gazing at him unashamedly.

'You want to go to church, don't you?'

Helen nodded, still speechless.

'Well, it's not too late. We'll probably miss the B film and the ads, but get in for the big picture,' he said, putting his arm through hers.

'I've never been to Hammersmith before,' he said, opening the car door for her.

'It's a fascinating ethnic cross-section,' said Helen earnestly.

In the back of the Porsche, sitting muddily on a huge pile of unopened letters, newspapers and old copies of *Horse and Hound*, sat a grinning black labrador.

'This is Badger,' said Rupert. 'He's the only being in the world who thinks I can do no wrong.'

'Badger thumped his thick black tail joyfully, scattering the letters, and, leaning forward, gave Helen a great slobbery kiss.

'Don't pre-empt me, Badger,' said Rupert, driving off so fast that the dog nearly fell off the back seat.

Badger insisted on coming today,' Rupert went on, 'to see if you were as pretty as I said you were.'

Embarrassed, Helen said, 'Don't you ever open your mail?'

'Not if I can help it. It's always people wanting my money or my life.'

He drove her at great speed to the Guards' Chapel. Immediately they'd crept into a back pew, Helen sank to her knees. Rupert, sitting sideways to accommodate his long legs, noticed she really prayed, eyes shut, lips moving.

Confessing in advance the sins she's going to commit later this afternoon, he thought dryly. While she was kneeling, he examined the freckled hands with their slender wrists and colourless nail polish, the small beaky nose, the very clean ears, the lipstick drawn not quite to the edges to disguise a large mouth, the frightful Alice band holding back the gorgeous, dark-red hair – it was the colour of drenched fox rather than bracken. Wondering if she had a ginger bush, he felt the stirrings of lust. He'd tank her up at lunchtime and take her back to his mothers's house. As she sat up, he noticed the perfect ankles, slightly freckled beneath the pale tights.

'Nice scent,' he whispered.

For a second she looked at him, her huge wide-apart yellow eyes flecked like a Conference pear, then smiled shyly.

'Christ, she's adorable,' he said to himself.

He had deliberately not picked up a hymn book on the way in so he could share hers. As their hands touched she jumped as though burnt, then, realizing she was over-reacting, tried to relax.

'Forty days and forty nights, tempted and yet undefiled,' sang Rupert loudly and quite out of tune.

During the sermon, Helen found her thoughts straying as she glanced at the crimson and gold banners topped with little gold lions with crowns on their heads, and breathed in the scent of a nearby arrangement of white lilac and narcissi. Among the congregation were several greyhound men in dark suits, with lean, carved features and very straight backs, accompanied by conservatively dressed women with good enough cheekbones to get away with turbans or hats with no hair showing. The altar was draped with purple for Lent. Helen was horrified to find herself wondering whether a dress in that colour would suit her. She must concentrate.

Rupert had no such intentions. After staring at the priest for a few minutes with half-closed eyes, he extracted a paint chart out of his pocket and studied the colours, finally marking a Prussian blue square with a cross. Then he produced yesterday's evening paper and, folding it up into a small square, started to read the racing results.

'Hooray,' he whispered, 'I've won £50 – it'll pay for a lunch.'

Helen tried to ignore him and stared stonily in front of her. But as the sermon droned on a loud snore suddenly rent the air. Rupert had fallen asleep and the next moment his head had flopped on to her shoulder. Several of the greyhound men, and a woman in a red turban like piped fish paste, glanced around in disapproval. Helen nudged Rupert sharply in the ribs. He woke up with a start, glanced round in bewilderment and then grinned at her totally without contrition. The smile suddenly softening the arrogant dead-pan features and creasing up the long blue eyes, reduced her to complete panic. Harold Mountjoy had never affected her like this.

She was relieved when the organ galloped through the last hymn and they surged out into the sunshine. Rupert nodded to several of the congregation, but didn't stop to talk until one of the greyhound men called out to him.

Rupert stopped, said, 'Hullo, Tommy,' and introduced Helen.

After the inevitable brisk swapping of mutual acquaintances, Tommy said, 'You've been doing very well; meant to come and buy you a drink at Olympia. Look,' he added, lowering his voice, 'there's a horse that might interest you at the barracks. Bought him in Ireland just before Christmas – make a top-class Puissance horse.'

'Can I come and look at him after lunch?'

'About four.'

Helen wondered if she were included in the invitation and was shocked by her relief when Rupert said, 'We'll be there.'

Before lunch he insisted on taking Badger for a walk in the park. It was a perfect spring day. Thickening crimson buds fretted a love-in-the-mist blue sky. The banks were

103

draped with crocuses of the same lenten purple as the altar cloth. A host of golden daffodils, retarded by the bitter winter, had just reached their prime and nodded their pale heads in approval. Helen longed to dawdle. But there was no chance of wandering lonely as a cloud. Rupert, with his brisk military walk, set off at a cracking pace. Helen, her high heels pegged by the soft grass, was soon panting to keep up.

'Did you buy the horse you looked at this morning?' she asked.

'It was a retired racehorse,' said Rupert. 'After flattening four fences it suddenly decided to stage a comeback and carted me half-way to London. Couldn't stop the bugger and I'm pretty strong.'

'What happened?'

'Fortunately the London–Newbury express thundered straight across our bows, the horse decided he wasn't ready to be strawberry jam and skidded to a halt. Must say I was shit-scared.'

Brought up that no gentleman swears in front of a lady, Helen wished he would not use such bad language.

'I'm starving,' he said. 'Let's go and have some lunch.'

'Will it be very smart?' asked Helen.

'Not until we get there,' said Rupert.

The restaurant, despite being sandbagged up to the gutters against IRA bomb attacks, was extremely smart inside with cane chairs and tables, a black and white check floor and a forest of glossy tropical plants, emphasizing the jungle atmosphere. From the kitchen came a heady waft of garlic and herbs and from the dining room the same swooping My dear-punctuated roar of a successful drinks party.

The head waiter rushed forward.

'Meester Campbell-Black,' he said reproachfully, 'You deedn't book.'

'I never book,' said Rupert.

'But I 'ave no tables.'

'I'm sure you can find us one, nice and private. We don't want people bothering us.'

'And you cannot bring dogs in 'ere. The health inspectors, they will shoot me.'

'Badger's different,' said Rupert, 'He's a guide dog for the blind drunk. Now, buck up, Luigi, don't keep us waiting.'

Sure enough, within half a minute, Luigi beckoned. It was quite an experience walking through a restaurant with Rupert and Badger. Every head turned, necks cricked, nudges were exchanged, as people looked first at him, then at Helen, trying to work out who she was, if anyone. The restaurant seemed to be packed with beautiful people, the girls all wearing fashionable flared trousers down to the ground with never a boot showing, their red nails tapping on their slim thighs, smoothing back their streaked hair and calling 'Hi, Rupe' as he passed.

Luigi installed them at a table divided from the rest of the restaurant by a dark green wall of tropical plants. Immediately Helen fled to the Ladies. She felt so drab in her grey dress, with her pale church face gazing back from the mirror. Savagely, she ringed her eyes with pencil, added a coral splodge of blusher to each cheekbone, painted her mouth to match and emptied so much Miss Dior over herself that it made her sneeze.

Back at the table, Rupert had ordered a bottle of Dom Perignon and removed his tie. Badger, lying at his feet, thumped his tail. Breathing in the newly applied Miss Dior, Rupert noticed the additional make-up. All good signs.

'I haven't been in London on a Sunday for ages,' he said. 'It's nice, and it's the first time I've had a chance to look at you properly – that's even nicer. You're really an astonishingly beautiful girl. What the hell were you doing with Nige?'

'We work together.'

'In publishing?'

'I read manuscripts and write blurbs. Actually,' she blushed, 'I'm also working on a novel.'

'Can I read it?'

'It's only in draft form.'

'Well, you must put me in it, then. I'll be Prince Charming. Nigel can be the toad. You're not really his girlfriend?'

'No, I am not,' said Helen with some asperity. 'He just asked me out with the Antis yesterday. How did you get my phone number?'

'Well, Billy and I found Nigel letting down the tyres of our lorry, so I shook him till his lentils rattled, then left him trussed up like a Christmas turkey and appropriated his address book. What did you think of your day out?'

'Very cruel. All those people tearing after a poor defenceless fox, ripping it apart for fun.'

'Have you ever seen a chicken coop after a fox has been, all with their heads bitten off and left? Foxes kill for the hell of it, too.'

'The fox doesn't get a chance,' protested Helen, 'with you blocking up their earths and digging them out with terriers after they've gone to ground.'

Rupert shrugged his shoulders. 'Farmers wouldn't let us hunt across their land if we didn't.'

He filled her glass, although she'd only drunk half of it, looking at her meditatively.

'Hunting's like adultery,' he said. 'Endless hanging about, interspersed with frenzied moments of excitement, very expensive and morally indefensible.'

'Why d'you do it, then?' asked Helen primly.

'Hunt or commit adultery? Because I enjoy them both. I fancy other people's wives from time to time. I enjoy riding hell for leather across country. It's one of the best ways of teaching your horses to jump anything; or stop an older horse getting stale. Horses love it, so do hounds, so do the people doing it. You just don't like to see people enjoying themselves.'

'It's still wrong for people to get all dressed up for the pleasure of killing something,' said Helen, hotly.

'Darling love, the saboteurs had far more fun than we did yesterday. Billy, my mate, always says if ever they abolish hunting he's going to join the Antis.'

106

Helen, remembering how she'd attacked Paul last night, had to concede he was right.

'But Nigel does have principles,' she protested. 'He's a strict Vegan.'

'Farts all day in the office, I suppose,' said Rupert, yawning.

Helen blushed, but refused to be deflected.

'Nigel,' she went on earnestly, 'has not eaten anything that moves for ten years.'

'Not even jelly?' asked Rupert.

Helen tried to look disapproving and giggled. 'You're impossible.'

'Impassible, am I?' said Rupert, mocking her pronunciation. 'Well, you certainly won't get past me in a hurry.'

Luigi arrived with the menu. Helen noticed there were no prices.

'What are you going to eat? I'm sure Luigi can flambé you some nut cutlets, but why not be really decadent and have a large rare steak?'

Luigi particularly recommended the scampi served with a cream pernod sauce or the filets of wild duck with juniper berry sauce.

'No, I don't want any of your mucked-about rubbish, Luigi. My guest would like . . .' He turned to Helen.

'Oh, pâté, and a small steak and a green salad.'

'And I'll have smoked salmon, and grilled lamb chops, very rare, with some fried potatoes, and can you bring an extra steak for Badger? He likes it well done, and we'll have a bottle of No. 6, and another bottle of this while we're waiting.'

While he was ordering, she admired the beautifully lean curve of his jaw. Unlike most Englishmen, and particularly one who spent so much time out of doors, there was no red tinge to his complexion which, even without the suntan, would have been pale olive. Glancing around, he caught her gazing at him. 'Well?' he said.

'You're very tanned.'

'Skiing last month.'

'I hear you're an expert at horse-back riding.'

Rupert grinned. 'You could call it that. The show jumping season's about to start in earnest. It's Crittleden next weekend. Why don't you come down on Saturday?'

He was touched to see how thrilled she was.

'I'd just love to. I'd so enjoy seeing one of your performances.'

'With any luck you might be seeing one of those before that,' he said, smiling at her with those wicked, dangerously direct eyes. Helen chose to ignore the innuendo. Was it Badger or Rupert under the table, pressing against her leg?

'How did you get into that terrible coven?'

Helen looked disapproving.

'Regina House is a very distinguished institution. It was founded to accommodate women of substance.'

'Oh, that's what's the matter with them,' said Rupert. 'I thought they all looked like that frightful harridan that was out with you yesterday, the one with more spare tyres than the Firestone factory.'

Under the influence of the wine, Helen found herself more and more at ease, minding less and less about his flip remarks. As their first course arrived, she found herself telling him about her first digs and the unfixed tom and the lecherous lodger.

'I gained ten pounds.'

'Well, it seems to have gone in the right places,' said Rupert, gazing at her breasts. He ate very fast, finishing his smoked salmon before she was a quarter way through her pâté.

'This is excellent paté.' She pronounced it 'part-*ay*'. He wondered idly if her accent would get on his nerves. 'I'm afraid I can't finish it, I'm awfully sorry.'

Off her grub, thought Rupert; another good sign.

'Now is the time for all good dogs to come to the aid of the part*ay*,' he said, spearing it with his knife and handing it under the table to Badger, who gobbled it up with more thumping.

As their second course arrived, she tried to steer the conversation on to more academic lines. Did he enjoy reading?

'Not a lot. The best book I've read in years is *The Moon's a Balloon.*'

'Do you go to the theatre a lot?'

'Well, I went once,' said Rupert.

Helen determinedly didn't look shocked. Writers had to accept all kinds of people.

Rupert was picking his chop bones now, tearing the meat off with very strong white teeth; particularly good teeth, she noticed, for an Englishman.

'Have you any siblings?'

'What?'

'Brothers and sisters,' she explained.

'Only one. A brother, Adrian. Very bright. My mother's favourite. He runs an art gallery.'

'Oh, which one?' asked Helen eagerly.

'The Bellingham; specializes in modern stuff.'

Helen said she'd been there often.

'Awful tripe, don't you think?' said Rupert. 'Adrian gets frightfully miffed when I tell him Badger could do better with his tail dipped in a paint pot.'

All these remarks were drawled out with a completely deadpan face. She couldn't tell if he was sending her up.

'At least you must go to the cinema?'

'No,' said Rupert. 'Quite honestly, if you've got nearly thirty horses, as Billy and I have, many of them novices that need bringing on, or top-class horses that need keeping up to the mark, you don't get much time for anything else. We've got a man and three girl grooms, but we still get up at 6.30 and seldom leave the yard before nine or ten at night. Horses still need looking after at weekends. And you've got to keep looking at other horses all the time in case you miss something. Nearly all the year round we're travelling non-stop from show to show all over the world. You don't get to the top by going to French films or hanging around art galleries.'

'I'm sorry,' said Helen, feeling corrected. 'Do you do the same sort of thing as Mark Phillips?'

'He events, I show jump. Ours is the serious stuff; eventing's for gifted amateurs.'

'Do you know Mr Phillips?' Helen felt ashamed for asking.

'Yes, he's a very nice bloke.'

'Will he marry Princess Anne?'

'So he tells me,' said Rupert, filling up her glass. Helen tried not to betray how impressed she felt.

She couldn't eat any more of her second course than her first. Rupert gave her steak to Badger.

'It's so expensive, it's awful,' said Helen in distress.

'It isn't offal, it's steak,' said Rupert, again imitating her accent.

'Did you go to Eton College?' she asked.

'No, Harrow.'

'Lord Byron went there,' said Helen excitedly. 'He was an extraordinarily fine poet.'

'Pulled some amazing girls too.'

'His letters are fascinating.'

'Supposed to have had his half-sister.'

Luigi brought brandy for Rupert and coffee and chocolate peppermint creams for Helen.

'No, thank you,' she said. 'I've given up candy for Lent.'

'I've given up women,' said Rupert, taking her hand, 'except you.'

Almost on cue an exquisitely beautiful girl with long, blue-black hair barged into their jungle glade.

'Rupert Bear,' she screamed, 'what are you doing, skulking away like a babe in the wood? Aren't you frightened of all the wild animals?' she added to Helen.

But before Helen could answer, the girl had rattled on.

'Nicky Cripps is absolutely livid with you, Rupe. He booked this table weeks ago and you just pinch it from under his nose. Aren't you going to offer me a drink, Rupert Bear, just for old times' sake?'

'Beat it,' said Rupert icily.

'Oh, well, I'll have to help myself,' and, picking up Rupert's glass of brandy with a shaking hand, she drained it. Suddenly there was a tremendous thump from under the table and Badger emerged grinning, pressing his black face into the girl's crotch.

'Hullo, Badger,' she said in a choked voice. 'You've always been keener on me than Rupert Bear is.'

Glancing at Rupert's face, Helen tried to lighten the atmosphere.

'Why do you call him Rupert Bear?' she asked.

The girl looked at her pityingly. 'Don't you know? Rupert B-A-R-E, because he spends so much time with his clothes off.' Reaching over, she picked up the cross that hung round Helen's neck. 'And don't think that'll keep you safe. You won't be able to ward him off any more than anyone else, and afterwards he'll spit you out like a grape pip.'

Rupert got to his feet. 'Get out,' he said in a voice that made Helen shiver. 'You're drunk and you're boring us.'

The girl gave a sob and fled. Helen escaped to the loo. She felt quite sick. Her face was flushed, her eyes inflamed.

As she slapped on some make-up, two girls came in, heading for the loos, shouting to each other over the partition.

'Bianca's just had a showdown with Rupert Bear,' said the first. 'And all in front of his new girlfriend.'

'She won't be new by next week,' said the second, 'she'll be an Ex like the rest of us.'

As she emerged from the loo, Rupert, having paid the bill, was waiting for her.

'What's the matter? You're shaking.'

'I want to go home.'

'Don't be silly.' Taking her hand, he led her back to the car.

'Now, what happened?'

'Two girls were talking in the john.'

'What did they say?'

Helen told him.

Rupert took her hands again, holding them tightly.

'Look, I'm sure it upset you, and what Bianca said too. But if you and I are going to have anything going together, and I feel we can, you must shut your eyes and ears to gossip. If you're any kind of celebrity, which I suppose Billy and I are, people will always bitch about you. If they don't know you, they make it up; if they catch you snapping at a traffic warden because your mother's just died, they'll assume you're always bloody-minded. I had a brief walk-out with Bianca. I broke it off. I've even had girls accusing Billy and me of being queer because I haven't made a pass at them. You listen to me, not anyone else. Is that clear?'

Helen nodded, speechless.

'You're terribly sweet.' Leaning forward, he kissed her very gently. At first she resisted, then, as her lips parted, he drew away.

'Come on, we've got to see that horse.'

8

'Jesus, Tommy,' he said a quarter of an hour later, as a huge black horse with a white face clattered out of the stable, tugging a helpless, terrified trooper on the end of a rope, 'are you trying to sell me an elephant?'

'He's a good horse,' said Tommy. 'Jump the Harrods building with all four feet tied together.'

Going up to the plunging animal, ignoring its rolling eyes and snapping teeth, Tommy caught the other side of the head collar. Together, he and the trooper managed to steady him.

'Come and have a look,' he said.

From a safe distance, Helen watched Rupert's practised hands moving over the horse, running down a leg here, picking up a hoof there, examining his teeth, looking at him from front and back.

'Lovely courageous head,' said Tommy, dodging hastily sideways to avoid a diving nip.

'What's his background?'

'Dam was an Irish draught mare, father was clean bred, won a few races in Ireland. We got him from Jock O'Hara.'

'Doesn't usually miss a good horse,' said Rupert, walking around him again.

'His wife was having a baby at the time. He was a bit more abstracted than usual.'

'And he's being discharged? What's wrong with him?'

'Well, quite honestly, he's a bit of a bugger; run away with nearly every trooper in the regiment, fidgets on parade, breaks ranks, naps on duty and won't obey orders.'

Rupert laughed. 'And you're suggesting I buy him?'

'You could always sort out difficult horses and I promise you he can jump. He carted a trooper in the King's Road last week. A milk float was crossing the road; old Satan stood back on his hocks and cleared it by inches. Several witnesses saw him. That has to be some horse.'

'O.K.,' said Rupert, taking off his coat, 'tack him up.'

A trooper stood nervously in the centre of the indoor school, waiting for Rupert's orders. Tommy and Helen, to her relief, watched from the gallery. At first, Satan walked around as though butter wouldn't melt in his mouth; only his eyes rolled and his tail twitched. His white face and the one white sock that came above knee and hock gave him a comic appearance. Rupert pushed him into a canter; with his huge stride he circled the school in seconds. Then, suddenly, the horse seemed to gather itself together and, as they rounded the top end, he humped his back in a series of devastating bucks which would have unseated any rodeo rider.

Helen gave a gasp, putting her hands over her eyes.

'It's all right,' said Tommy. 'He's still there.'

'O.K.,' said Rupert to the trooper, 'put all the fences up to four foot-six.'

Tommy got out a silver cigarette case and handed it to Helen, who shook her head. 'Watch this,' he said.

As Satan bucketed towards the upright, Rupert put him at exactly the right spot and he cleared it by a foot. It was the same with the parallels.

'Put them up to five foot-six,' said Rupert.

'Known Rupert long?' asked Tommy.

'No,' said Helen, 'and it won't be much longer at this rate,' she added nervously as Satan thundered towards the upright, then put in a terrific stop. The next moment Rupert was beating the hell out of the horse.

'Poor Satan,' murmured Helen.

Rupert turned him again. Satan cleared the upright, then, careless, stargazing at some pigeons in the roof, he rapped the parallel so hard that only Rupert's immaculate riding held him together and saved them both from

114

crashing to the ground.

'Put it up to six foot,' said Rupert to the white-faced trooper.

'Crazy,' agreed Tommy, 'but he always liked riding something over the top.'

This time Rupert cantered down quietly and Satan cleared the upright with several inches to spare. Rupert pulled him up. Coming out of the school the horse appeared positively docile. Sliding off, Rupert reached for his coat pocket which was hanging on the door and, taking out a packet of Polos, gave a couple to Satan, who looked at him suspiciously, then ate them, curling his upper lip in the air.

'I think we'll get along,' he said. 'I'll buy him, Tommy. You'll discharge him as uncontrollable, will you? And I'll have a word with Colonel Cory up at Melton Mowbray.'

Helen was ashamed how much the sight of Rupert mastering that huge, half-wild horse had excited her. He might not have heard of François Truffaut or Kandinsky, but when it came to horses he was obviously a genius. Suddenly, she felt a spark of pure envy; however much she slaved at her novel, she could never display such joyful, spontaneous talent as Rupert.

The sun was going down now, firing the barracks windows. Dog walkers were hurrying home from the park. As Rupert sorted out the details of the sale with Tommy, Helen did her face yet again. She turned on the car radio and found the middle movement of Schumann's Piano Concerto. Listening to the rippling, romantic music she looked uneasily at the pile of mail on the back seat. Many of the envelopes were mauve, or peppermint green, or shocking pink. Someone had addressed a letter: 'To Rupert Campbell-Black, the handsomest man in England.'

And so he was, thought Helen, as he walked back to the car, Badger at his heels. He looked very happy.

'That is one hell of a good horse. I reckon I could take him to the Olympics if he doesn't kill me first. Let's go and have a drink at my mother's house.'

'That'd be nice,' said Helen. Privately, she didn't feel

quite up to meeting Rupert's mother. She'd have to talk out of the corner of her mouth to hide the drink fumes.

Rupert listened to the Piano Concerto for a minute. 'I suppose this is the sort of music you like?'

'Yes,' said Helen. 'Are your parents happily married?'

'Yes,' said Rupert.

'How lovely,' said Helen.

'But not to each other. My mother's on her third marriage. My father on his fourth.'

'Were you very traumatized when your parents split up?' she asked.

Rupert looked surprised: 'Not at all. I stayed with Mummy and Nanny.'

'But you must have had endless replacement parents?'

'What?'

'Step-mothers and -fathers.'

'Oh, legions.'

'Weren't they very unkind to you?'

'I was very unkind to them. I was a little sod when I was young. They got their own back by never taking me out when I was at school.'

'So you never went out?' said Helen, her eyes filling with tears.

'Nanny came down by train occasionally and brought me fruit cakes. I spent most leave-outs and a lot of the holidays with Billy's family.'

'What about Adrian?'

'Oh, he was my mother's darling – far too delicate and sensitive to go to boarding school.'

Rupert spoke without bitterness or self-pity. He was not given to introspection and never considered anything his parents had done might have affected his behaviour in life.

Helen, who'd studied psychology, felt differently. Still hazy and emotional from an excess of champagne, she was flooded with compassion for poor, poor Rupert. Parents who'd never loved him, step-parents who neglected him, a mother who preferred his younger brother. No wonder he felt the need to beat other riders all the time; and to seduce

116

women to bolster his self-confidence; then, unused to a loving relationship, break it off the moment things became heavy. I could change him, she thought expansively. I could arrest the rake's progress and show him what real love is like.

Rupert's mother lived in one of those large white Georgian houses looking on to an emerald green railed-in square. The garden was filled with grape hyacinths, scillas and white daffodils. An almond tree was already scattering pink petals on the sleekly shaven lawn. Every window was barred. Rupert opened the door with several keys and sprinted in to switch off the alarm.

'Well, your mother certainly won't get burglarized,' said Helen.

'No, but you're just about to, my treasure,' said Rupert under his breath.

They went into the drawing room. As Rupert switched on the lights, Helen gave a cry of pleasure.

'What an exquisite room.'

There were pale primrose walls and carpets, old gold watered silk curtains, and sofas and armchairs covered in faded pale blue and rose chintzes. Two tables with long, pale-rose tablecloths were covered in snuff boxes. The walls were covered in portraits of handsome arrogant men and beautiful women, their faces lit up by fat strings of pearls. Orchids in pots added to the exotic atmosphere. On the draped grand piano were photographs – one of Rupert's mother as a deb and others of several men in uniform who were presumably replacement fathers. There was also a picture of Rupert on a horse being handed a cup by Princess Margaret. What caught the eye was a photograph of an extraordinarily beautiful youth, very like Rupert, but more fragile of feature.

'That's my kid brother,' said Rupert. 'What d'you want to drink?'

Helen shook her head. As Rupert poured himself a large glass of brandy, Helen caught sight of a study next door, the walls lined with books, all behind grilles.

117

'May I look?'

'Of course. Most of those on the left are first editions.'

Helen gave a cry of excitement: 'Why, here's Keats' *Endymion*, and Shelley's *Prometheus Unbound*, and *Mansfield Park*. Oh, wow! Your mother must be a very cultured woman.'

This seemed to amuse Rupert. 'She's never read any of them.'

'But that's awful. Is there a key?'

'Somewhere, I expect.'

She got to her feet reluctantly. On the study desk was a huge pile of letters.

'Doesn't your mother open her mail either?'

'It's a family failing.'

'Will she be home soon?'

'She's not here,' said Rupert, draining his glass of brandy. 'She's in the Bahamas escaping from the taxman.'

Helen looked at him, appalled.

'I must go. If I'd known she wasn't going to be here, I'd never have come.'

'You haven't come yet, sweetheart,' said Rupert softly, taking her in his arms, 'but you soon will, I promise.'

She was almost overwhelmed by the warmth and sheer power of him, so different from Harold Mountjoy, who'd been a bit of a weed.

'No,' she yelped.

'Yes,' said Rupert into her hair. 'You need some material for your "narvel".'

'You shouldn't have pretended your mother was here.' She struggled to get away from him.

'I didn't. Anyway, all's fair in love and war and I don't imagine it's going to be war between us,' and he bent his head and kissed her. For a few seconds she kept her lips rigid, then, powerless, she found herself kissing him back, her hands moving up to the sleek, surprisingly silky hair.

Rupert pulled her down on the faded rose-pink sofa.

'I haven't stopped thinking about you for a moment since I first saw you,' he said. He was running his hands over her

118

back now, assessing the amount of underwear, planning where the next assault should come from. There were no zips on the grey dress which would have to come over her head, which might frighten her if removed too soon. Over her shoulder he met the jovial eyes of one of his forebears. 'Atta boy,' he seemed to say.

'No,' said Helen, trying to prise off the hand barnacled over her left breast.

'You're repeating yourself, angel. You must realize I'm unfixed, like your landlady's tom cat.'

Through her dress he expertly undid her bra with his left hand. The thumb of his right hand began to strafe her nipple.

'No, I'm not like that.'

'Like what?' whispered Rupert. 'D'you want to spend the rest of your life behind bars, unopened like those first editions?'

Helen burst into tears. At first she was crying so hard, Rupert couldn't understand what she was saying. Then the first storm of weeping gave way to shuddering sobs and gradually the whole story came pouring out. How respectable her family were, what a terrible shock it had been when she became pregnant by a married man and flunked her finals. How her parents had been real supportive sending her to Europe to get over it all.

'This afternoon you appeared to be getting over it very well,' said Rupert. 'Perhaps I should send your father a bill. What did you say this married man was called?'

'Harold Mountjoy.'

'Should have been called MountHelen.'

Helen sniffed. 'He's a very distinguished writer,' she said reprovingly. 'I'm surprised you haven't heard of his work.'

'You must know I haven't heard of anyone,' said Rupert.

'I loved him,' said Helen. 'I thought he loved me. But he only wrote once. He forgot Christmas, my birthday, Valentine's Day.'

'Mothering Sunday?' asked Rupert grinning.

'The pregnancy was terminated,' said Helen with dignity.

'I promise I won't let you get pregnant,' said Rupert gravely.

'That's not the point. I don't want to be treated like a sex object.'

'Because you object to sex?'

'Oh, don't be so flip,' wailed Helen.

Rupert got out a blue silk handkerchief and wiped away the mascara that was running down her cheeks. He had enough experience of women to realize that if you backed off and were kind and considerate on a first occasion, they dropped into the palm of your hand on the next.

More important, he suddenly felt terribly tired. Phenomenally strong, he could go for long periods without sleep, but he realized that, apart from a two-hour marathon in the four poster with Gabriella on Friday night, he hadn't been to bed for three days. He had to drive home to Gloucestershire that night, a dealer was coming to see him first thing in the morning, and he wanted to buy Satan quickly before the Army started producing all kinds of red tape. He also had a string of novices to take to an indoor show the following evening.

'All right,' he said, getting to his feet, 'go home to your narvel. Let me put on a jersey and I'll drive you back to your coven.'

Helen felt absolutely miserable, convinced that she'd lost him. The sun had set and the trees and the houses, losing their distinctive features, were darkening against a glowing turquoise sky. Rupert didn't speak on the way to Regina House, nor did he say anything about taking her to Crittleden. Let her work up a good lather of anxiety, he thought. Helen got lower and lower. Perhaps he was hurt by her saying she couldn't sleep with him because she didn't love him, but she felt it was just too soon.

All the lights were on in Regina House as they drew up. A blackbird was singing in a nearby plane tree. Helen sat for a second, overwhelmed with tiredness and despair, tears about to spill over again. The women's movement was always urging one to be assertive and make the running, but in practice it wasn't easy.

'I'm sorry,' she said in a choked voice, 'I didn't mean to give you a hard time.'

Rupert yawned.

'On the contrary, sweetheart, it was me intending to give *you* a *hard* time.'

He got out of the car, but before he could open the door for her she had scrambled out, standing up so they faced each other a foot apart.

'Good night,' he said brusquely, intending to get back into the car and drive straight off.

But suddenly the bells of a nearby church, carried by the west wind, drifted through the muzzy grey twilight. Rupert shivered, suddenly reminded of the desolation of Sunday nights at school, summoned by bells to Evensong, followed by cold ham and bread and marge for supper, and everyone else coming back feeling homesick from days out with their parents. Rupert had never really had a proper home to feel sick about.

'I w-will see you again, won't I?' she stammered.

Her face with its huge, brimming, mascara-smudged eyes, had lost all its colour in the dusk. He took it in his hands.

'Of course you will, my little red fox. I've let you escape this time, but I'll get you in the end. Try and go to ground, you'll find the earth blocked; disappear down another earth, I'll get the terrier men to dig you out.'

His white teeth gleamed. As he bent and kissed her, Helen trembled with fear and longing.

'Don't listen to Nige,' he said, getting back into the car. 'He's not my greatest fan. I'll ring you later in the week about Crittleden,' and he was gone.

Helen stood in the twilight, listening to the bells, thinking about weddings and the attraction of opposites.

Rupert drove down the M4 thinking about Satan. He toyed with the idea of stopping off at the Newbury turn to see a married girlfriend whose husband was away, but he was too tired. At Exit 15 sleep overcame him and the moment he was off the motorway he pulled into a layby, climbed into the back and, hugging Badger for warmth, fell asleep.

The Frogsmore Valley is considered by many to be the most beautiful in the Cotswolds. On either side, fields checkered by pale stone walls and dotted by lush woodland and the occasional farm, fall steeply down to jade green water meadows, divided by the briskly bustling Frogsmore stream.

At the top of the valley, curling round like a horseshoe, lies the ancient village of Penscombe. Here, for the past hundred and twenty years, the Campbell-Blacks had made their home, alternately scandalizing and captivating the local community by their outrageous behaviour. On Rupert's twenty-first birthday, a month before he came out of the Army, his father, Edward Campbell-Black, had made over to him the house, Penscombe Court, and its surrounding 200 acres. The motive for this altruistic gesture was that Edward had just further scandalized the community by leaving his wife and running off with the beautiful Italian wife of one of his Gloucestershire shooting cronies. On reflection too, Eddie decided he was bored with running the estate at a thumping loss, and his beautiful Italian prospective bride decided that neither of them could stand the bitter west winds which sweep straight off the Bristol Channel up the Frogsmore Valley to howl round Penscombe Court throughout the winter. So they decamped permanently to the South of France.

Young Rupert further scandalized the community by moving back into the house with his friend Billy Lloyd-Foxe and a floating population of dogs and shapely girl grooms. Even worse, hell-bent on making the place profitable, Rupert promptly dug up the famous rose garden and the orchard, built stables for thirty horses, turned the cricket pitch, where the village used to play regularly, into a show-jumping ring and put up an indoor school beyond the stables to buttress them from the bitter winds.

Gradually over the next four years, the chuntering subsided as Rupert and Billy started winning and were frequently seen on television clearing vast fences and being awarded silver cups by members of the Royal family. Journalists and television crews came down and raved about the charms of the village and the valley. Suddenly Penscombe had two local heroes and found itself on the map.

Penscombe Court was, fortunately, situated on the north side of the valley, half a mile from the end of the village, so any late-night revelry was deadened by surrounding woodland and didn't keep the village or the neighbouring farmers awake too often. Rupert was generally considered capricious and arrogant, but Billy, who loved gossip and spent a lot of time in the village shop and the pub chattering to the locals, was universally adored. Any inseparable friend of Billy, it was felt, couldn't be all bad; besides, the locals had known Rupert since he was a child and had seen stepparents come and go with alarming regularity and, being a tolerant and generous community, felt allowances should be made. They also realized that Rupert, like the rest of his family, was indifferent to public opinion, so that their disapproval would not make a hap'orth of difference.

Just before midnight Rupert woke up from his nap in the layby and set off for home. He never saw the signposts to Penscombe without a leap of joy and recognition. As he drove along the top of the south side of the valley, Badger woke up and started snuffling excitedly at the crack of an open window. Ahead in the moonlight gleamed Penscombe church spire. Although it was after midnight, Rupert looked across to the north side and cursed in irritation to see half the lights in the house blazing. Billy must have gone to bed plastered without switching them off.

As he stormed up the drive through the chestnut avenue planted by his great-grandfather, he could see the pale green leaves opening like parachutes. Behind white railings, three dozing horses in New Zealand rugs blinked as he

123

passed. The car crunched on the gravel in front of the house. There was a great baying and yapping. As Rupert opened the front door, two Jack Russells, a Springer spaniel, a yellow labrador and a blond mongrel with a tightly curled tail threw themselves on him in delight, growling and fighting each other. Finally they all started rubbishing Badger, jealous because he'd been the one to go on a jaunt. Rupert kicked them gently out of the way. His suitcase was still lying in the hall where he'd left it that morning. In the drawing room the fire was going out, Sunday papers half-read and a pile of entrance forms lay scattered over the sofa. One of the dogs had shredded his hunting tie on the rug in front of the fire.

'Jesus,' said Rupert, slamming the door shut.

In the kitchen he found Billy trying to read *Horse and Hound*, clean the brown tops of a pair of black boots, drink whisky and fork oysters out of a tin, all at the same time.

'Hi,' he said, looking up. 'How did it go? Have you joined the Antis?'

Billy was not a handsome young man, for his nose was broken and his sleepy dark brown eyes were seldom visible because they were always creased up with laughter, but he had a smile that could melt the Arctic Circle. Rupert, however, was not in a mood to be melted.

'This place is a tip,' he snapped, pointing to the sink which was piled high with plates, glasses and dog bowls. 'Can't you even put things in the washing-up machine?'

'It's full,' said Billy calmly.

'Or in the dustbin,' went on Rupert, pointing to the empty tins of dog food and milk cartons littering the shelf.

'That's full too,' said Billy.

'And one of your dogs has crapped in the hall.'

'It was one of your dogs,' said Billy without rancour. 'Anyway, I've been bloody busy.'

'Drinking my whisky and reading the Sunday papers.'

'The hell I have. By the way, there's a nice piece about you in *The Observer*.'

'What did it say?'

'Oh, some sycophantic rubbish about you being the best rider in England.'

'Don't try to placate me, and why's the telephone off the hook?'

'To stop Bianca, and Gabriella, and goodness knows who else ringing up.'

Rupert replaced the receiver. Five seconds later the telephone rang.

'See what I mean?'

Rupert picked it up. Both of them could hear squawking. Putting the receiver in a nearby cupboard, Rupert shut the door.

Billy grinned: 'Anyway, I repeat, I've been bloody busy.'

'Doing what?'

'Taking care of the entire yard single-handed. I've even sold a couple of horses for you.'

'How much d'you get?'

'Ten grand for Padua and eight for the grey with the ewe neck.'

'Not enough,' said Rupert, looking slightly mollified.

'Never is for you, and I worked everything we're going to need tomorrow. Admittedly I was so hungover first thing I saw four ears every time I looked down a horse's neck.'

He speared up another oyster. 'And I think I've sorted out why The Bull keeps stopping. He's terrified of water.'

'So am I,' said Rupert, 'unless it's got whisky in it.'

He picked up the bottle and, not finding any clean glasses in the cupboard, poured it into a tea cup.

'Where the hell was Diane today?'

'Said she's got the curse, soldiered on for a couple of hours, then collapsed into bed.'

'Rubbish,' said Rupert. 'She had it a fortnight ago. She'd have stayed working if I'd been here. And Tracey?'

'It's her day off.'

'And Marion?'

'Gave in her notice and flatly refused to work. She was pissed off because you forgot to take her to some party on Saturday night. She's been ringing Sits Vac in *Horse and*

125

Hound all day and left them deliberately lying on the table for us to find.'

He handed the magazine to Rupert.

' "Cheerful, capable groom",' read out Rupert incredulously. 'Cheerful! Christ! She's about as cheerful as Blackpool lights during a power cut. "Experienced girl groom required for hunters and stud work. Opportunity to further breeding knowledge". She doesn't have anything to learn about breeding either. Oh hell, let her go, I'm fed up with her tantrums.'

'You cause most of them,' said Billy reasonably. 'You know perfectly well that Mayfair and Belgravia, not to mention The Bull and Kitchener, will all go into a decline if she leaves. And we can't afford that at the beginning of the season.'

He held out his glass for Rupert to fill up.

'And just remember how tremendous she is with customs men. They're so transfixed by her boobs they never bother to even glance at our papers.'

'Are you after her or something?' said Rupert.

'No, my heart belongs entirely to Mavis,' said Billy, looking down at the blond mongrel who was now curled up on his knee, slanting eyes closed, head resting on his collarbone.

'Oh, all right,' said Rupert, 'I'll go and see her in a minute.'

'She'll be asleep by now.'

'Not her, she'll be tossing and turning with desire and frustration.'

From the pantry next door the washing machine was thundering to a halt. Wiping the boot polish off his hands on to Mavis's blonde coat, Billy set her gently down on the floor. Opening the machine, he removed a tangle of white ties, shirts, breeches, socks and underpants and threw them into the drier.

Rupert looked disapprovingly round the kitchen which was low-beamed with a flagstone floor and a window looking over the valley. A bridle hung from a meat hook;

every shelf seemed to be covered with spilling ashtrays and unopened bills.

'We must get a housekeeper. I'm fed up with chaos.'

'It's pointless,' said Billy. 'You'd only employ pretty ones, then you couldn't resist screwing them and they'd get bolshy. Mrs Burroughs is coming in the morning. She'll tidy the place up.'

'I want it straight at weekends. Perhaps we ought to get Nanny back.'

'She'd have a heart attack at the goings-on. Perhaps you ought to get married. Wives are supposed to do this sort of thing. How was your red-headed Anti?'

'Interesting. Very uptight.'

'Not the easy lay you expected?'

'You've put your finger on the spot,' said Rupert, draining his whisky, 'which is certainly more than I did. She's rather sweet, but frightfully intense; kept wanting to talk about books and the theatre.'

'Must have taxed your brain. Are you going to see her again?'

'I might. I don't like unfinished business. By the way, I bought a bloody good horse today from the barracks. No one was about, so Tommy let me try him on the Q.T. Never seen a big horse so good in front. Despite his size he jumps like a pony. Need some sorting out though.'

'Don't make me tired. I've done enough sorting out for one day,' said Billy, picking up the yellow mongrel. 'Mavis and I are off to bed. See you in the morning.'

'I'll go and placate Marion,' said Rupert.

He went upstairs, brushed his teeth and his hair, then took the dogs out.

At the end of the lawn two black yew trees crouched like great gelded tomcats. Behind the house rose the wood, stretching for half a mile. Four vast Lawson cypresses rose in front of the bare beech trees like spires of a cathedral. Moonlight flooded the valley, silvering the lake and blanching the first daffodils. On the opposite side a car driving along the top towards Penscombe lit up the trees lining the road like a firefly. Rupert felt his heart expand with pride and love. This was his home and his land to do what he wanted with. He must keep on winning to keep it going, to make it better and better.

The dogs weaved about lifting their legs on rose bushes and young trees. From the stables he could hear the occasional snort and stamp, and resisted the temptation to go and wake the horses up. As he expected, the light was still on in Marion's flat over the tackroom. He shut the dogs in the house. Marion took a long time to answer the door. She was pale and puffy-eyed, but nothing could disguise the voluptuousness of her body, nor the length of leg revealed by the clinging nightshirt with the baleful figure of Snoopy on the front.

'What d'you want?' she asked in a choked voice.

'You,' said Rupert.

'Bastard.' Snoopy rose and fell as her breast heaved.

'That's no way to address one's boss.'

'You're not my boss any more. I've given in my notice. Didn't Billy tell you?'

'Yes,' said Rupert moving towards her and putting a hand between her legs. 'And I haven't accepted it.'

'Don't touch me,' she sobbed.

But as he splayed out his fingers and increased the pressure she collapsed into his arms.

9

Helen found the next week extraordinarily trying. She could think of nothing but Rupert, which made sleep, work and very existence impossible.

In the evenings at Regina House she read endless love poetry and played Schumann's Piano Concerto, being the only music she and Rupert had in common, over and over again, very quietly with her door an inch open, in case she missed the telephone ringing downstairs.

By day she had to put up with Nigel. He limped in after lunch on Monday with a black eye and two cracked ribs. She was appalled by his detailed account of the brutality of the beating up. But when he started describing how he'd been tied up and left naked behind a hedge she suddenly remembered Rupert's remark about trussing a Christmas turkey and had to gaze out of the window so Nigel wouldn't see her laughing. Fortunately, the self-obsessed Nigel mistook her shaking shoulders for sobbing.

She now realized how difficult it must have been for Juliet loving a Montagu while living in the Capulet camp. She found herself jumping and blushing scarlet as Nigel, who was suffering from acute telephonitis, exchanged lengthy indignation meetings on Rupert's dreadful behaviour with Dave and Paul and Maureen, and evidently every other saboteur in and around the country. There was brave talk of taking Rupert to Court, but as the other Antis pointed out, Rupert, being as rich as Croesus, would employ the best lawyer in town and as Nigel had been letting down Rupert's tyres, witnessed by Rupert and Billy and later the groom, he was on weak ground.

'Even worse, Helen,' Nigel added, his piggy unblacked eye gleaming behind his thick spectacles, 'R.C.B. appropriated my address book.'

'Oh dear,' said Helen, starting guiltily, 'will he find any important numbers?'

'Crucial,' said Nigel sententiously. 'That book contains the numbers of every resistance fighter in the UK, people who are believed to belong to the hunting fraternity, but who are really one of us and supply us with vital information. Fiona Westbury, the daughter of Saturday's master, is a classic example, and the secretary of the Chairman of the British Field Sports, who's been one of us for years. With that book in his hands, R.C.B. can smash our entire network. I'm sure he beat me up because he was so anxious to get his hands on it.'

'Rather like Watergate,' said Helen, again fighting a terrible desire to giggle.

As the week crawled by, she was filled with an increasing restlessness and sat at her typewriter playing he loves me, he loves me not with the raindrops cascading down the window from the incessant April showers, quite incapable even of typing 'Dear Sir', because the only sir who was dear to her still hadn't rung.

She'd learnt from the paper that the Crittleden meeting started on Good Friday and lasted over the Easter weekend.

On Thursday at lunchtime, in anticipation of seeing Rupert, she went out and spent nearly three weeks' salary on the softest beige suede midi dress. Coming through the door of the office, she found Nigel holding out the telephone receiver and looking bootfaced.

'Some man with a foreign accent asking for you, says it's personal.'

Helen felt her knees give way, her cheeks flame. She could hardly cross the room, then found herself positively winded by the thud of disappointment because it was Paul on the other end.

'I put on a French accent to deceive Nigel,' he said,

laughing heartily. 'How about that concert on Saturday night?'

Almost in tears, Helen had told him she was going away for the whole weekend.

'That's a shame,' said Nigel as she came off the telephone. 'I was going to a CND rally in Hyde Park on Sunday. I hoped you'd accompany me.'

'And I was hoping to see R.C.B at Crittleden,' Helen wanted to scream at him, 'but I don't think that's going to happen either.'

She spent a miserable Good Friday going to the three-hour service, praying for resignation and trying not to ask God to remind Rupert to ring.

On Saturday afternoon she went downstairs and, sitting on a hard-backed chair in the television room, tried to watch Crittleden, but had to wait until some Charlie Chaplin film had finished on the other channel before she could switch over. By this time the BBC had left Crittleden and gone over to some extremely noisy motor race. Seeing the pained expressions on the lady academics' faces, Helen explained that a friend of hers was jumping at Crittleden, which should be on any minute.

At last they went over to the show ground. It was pouring with rain and it was not until the last five riders, none of them Rupert, had demolished the course, that the announcer told them that the winner was a German rider who had produced the only clear. An Irishman was second with four faults, and Rupert Campbell-Black for Great Britain was third with eight faults. Billy Lloyd-Foxe and three other riders had tied for fourth place with twelve faults apiece.

After the incessant rain, said the announcer, the Crittleden Arena was like a quagmire and any rider who got round was to be congratulated. Through the downpour the German rider came into the ring, followed by the Irish rider in his holly green coat. Helen's heart started thumping, her mouth went dry, as Rupert followed them on a huge chestnut. The black collar of his red coat was turned up, his white breeches splattered with mud.

As they lined up, a man in a tweed suit and a bowler hat came out holding an umbrella over an attractive, middle-aged blonde in a dark grey suit, who delicately picked her way through the mud. Another bowler-hatted man in a tweed suit followed them, carrying a huge silver cup and shielding a tray of rosettes from the rain under his coat.

'Here comes Lady Pringle, a fine horsewoman in her own right, to present the prizes,' said the announcer. Helen could see Rupert chatting and laughing with Billy and, as Lady Pringle reached him, he took off his hat and, bending down, kissed her on both cheeks.

'Lady Pringle and Rupert Campbell-Black are obviously old friends,' said the announcer as she handed him a lemon yellow rosette, 'and she's obviously delighted to have a British rider in the first three.'

'Isn't that the young man who picked you up last Sunday?' said one of the female anthropologists, changing her spectacles to have a better look. But Helen had fled upstairs to sob her heart out on her bed. How could Rupert look so cheerful and carefree when she'd been going through such hell waiting for him to call?

'Lady Pringle, indeed,' she sobbed and, taking the photograph of Rupert which she'd surreptitiously cut out from one of Nigel's *Horse and Hounds* out of her diary, she tore it into tiny pieces. He was nothing but a stud.

She was crying so hard, at first she didn't hear the knock on the door.

'Telephone,' said a voice.

When she got downstairs it was Rupert.

'Angel, I'm sorry I haven't rung before. I left your number at home and I've only just remembered the name of your coven. We've been up at the South Lancashire Show and the lorry blew out on the way down, so we only arrived in time for the big class.'

'How did you get on?' asked Helen. She was damned if she was going to let him know she'd been watching.

'Not bad. I was third, Billy fourth. We had to unload the horses straight out of the lorry, and the going was terrible, bogs in front of every fence. Are you coming down?'

'I d-don't know,' said Helen, thinking of her swollen eyes and lack of sleep. 'I can't tonight.'

'Come down tomorrow. I'd come and collect you, but I've got classes in the morning. Get a taxi.'

'But it's miles,' said Helen, appalled thinking of all the money she'd squandered on the midi dress.

'It's only an hour from London. I'll pay,' said Rupert. 'Come to the main entrance. I'll leave the cash and a ticket with the man on the gate.'

Rupert's estimate of the time it would take to drive down to Crittleden was very different from the taxi driver's. No doubt he shifted that Porsche at 120 miles an hour the moment he got on the motorway, thought Helen, as she nervously watched the fare jerk up and up. £25–£35! She was sure the driver wouldn't take an American cheque and she couldn't ring up her bank as it was Sunday. Scrabbling round in her purse she only found £1.30. Perhaps he'd accept her gold watch until she could find Rupert. Even worse, two miles from Crittleden they ran into a huge traffic jam. A glorious mild day had followed yesterday's downpour. Every young green leaf and blade of new grass sparkled with raindrops and all the people who'd given the Show a miss yesterday seemed to have decided to go today. For the thousandth time Helen checked her face in the mirror. Her hair had gone right, the suede dress brought out the amber of her eyes, but she still looked tired.

'Got him bad, 'ave you?' said the taxi driver as the third application of Miss Dior in ten minutes fought with the diesel fumes. She'd looked rich enough when she'd got into the car; that dress must have cost a packet, and Americans were rarely short of a few bob.

'Been to Crittleden before?'

Helen shook her head. 'One of the show jumpers has invited me. You may have heard of him, Rupert Campbell-Black.'

'Rupert Campbell-Black,' said the driver. 'I know Rupert, 'ad him in the cab, and his mate, Billy Lloyd-Foxe.

'E's a lad, is Rupert. Did you see him at the 'orse of the Year Show in one of the novelty classes on the last day? Dressed up as Miss World, wiv coconuts in his dress. They fell out as he rode over the jumps, brought the 'ouse down. 'E's a lad, is Rupert. I got 'is autograph for my missis; she's mad about Rupert, she is.'

And Lady Pringle and Gabriella and Bianca too, thought Helen bleakly.

At last they reached the main gates.

'Help,' thought Helen in panic. There seemed to be half a dozen men in yellow coats on the gate.

The taxi driver had no such reserve. Winding down the window he shouted: 'I've got a lidy here for Rupert.'

Immediately one of the yellow-coated men leapt forward and peered into the cab.

'Might 'ave guessed it,' he said with a gap-toothed grin. 'Rupert certainly goes for lookers,' and getting a sheaf of tenners out of his pocket he handed them to Helen. 'I think he's given me most of his winnings yesterday. If you hang on quarter of an hour, mate, I'll get you a fare back to London.'

After Helen had paid the taxi-man sixty pounds, which seemed an appalling amount of money, the man in the yellow coat took her off to find Rupert. It was so muddy she was thankful she'd worn boots.

'I'm a bit late,' she said.

'Not surprised in that traffic. Got a good crowd here today, although it looks like rain later.' He pointed to indigo clouds which were beginning to mass on the horizon above the pale acid-green elm wood.

They found Rupert in the practice ring, cantering very slowly round on a magnificent bay gelding, totally oblivious of the crowd, mostly nubile teenagers, who were gazing at him.

The man in the yellow coat was about to call out when Helen stopped him. 'I want to watch for a second,' she said. 'Thank you so much.'

Rupert was wearing green cords tucked into gumboots, a

dark blue quilted waistcoat over a dark blue jersey, and no hat.

'I told you he was lovely,' said a teenage girl eating an ice cream.

'I never thought he'd be that lovely,' said her friend.

'That's his groom, Marion,' said the first girl, pointing to a sulky-looking blonde who was standing by the practice fence. 'She was interviewed in *Honey* about what it's like working for Rupert. She said he doesn't get enough sleep.'

At a word from Rupert the sulky blonde, who was wearing a red T-shirt with 'I only sleep with the best people' printed across her bosom, put up the pole to five foot. Rupert cleared it effortlessly.

'Wish I was the horse,' said the girl with rippling hair.

Helen had had enough.

'Rupert,' she called as he came past.

It was some comfort that he seemed so pleased to see her. Instantly sliding off the bay gelding and handing him to the sulky blonde, he ducked under the railings to join her. Immediately the autograph hunters surged forward.

'Bugger off,' snapped Rupert. 'Can't you see I'm busy?' and, putting his arm round Helen's shoulders, he pushed impatiently through the crowd.

'How are you?' he said.

'Wonderful,' said Helen, suddenly realizing she was.

'You certainly look it,' he said, running his hand down her suede arm. 'I adore that dress. It's the same texture as Belgravia when he's just been clipped, but I don't like that bloody Alice band,' and, removing it from her hair, he tossed it into a nearby dustbin.

Helen gave a cry of protest and ran towards the bin to find the hairband nestling among the remains of hamburger buns and Kentucky fried chicken.

'That was my favourite hairband,' she said, outraged.

'And your last one,' said Rupert.

And he turned her round to face him, running his hands through her red mane so it fell tousled and shining over her forehead and round her face.

135

For a second she gazed at him mutinously, then she laughed.

'Christ,' said Rupert. 'I'd forgotten how beautiful you were,' and drawing her towards him, he kissed her full on the mouth, in front of the crowds.

'We can't here,' she said, pulling away, blushing furiously.

'We can absolutely anywhere,' said Rupert. 'Come on, let's go back to the caravan and have a drink.' He looked at his watch. 'I've got a class in an hour and a half.'

On their way they passed the stables. Horses lolled their heads over the half-doors, gnawing at the wood, flattening their ears at each other and at passers-by.

A crowd of people were hanging round one box stable. 'That's Belgravia,' said Rupert.

As he went towards the half-door the crowd dispersed to a respectful distance, but the horse rolled its eyes and took a threatening nip at Rupert's sleeve.

'Ungrateful sod,' said Rupert, punching him gently on the neck. 'He doesn't like me; I mean hard work to him. You'd better be on form this afternoon.'

Leaving the horses, they walked through the mud up the hill to the caravan village in which the riders lived during the show. Rupert's was easily the biggest caravan and the only one painted dark blue piped with emerald. In the window hung a string of rosettes.

'We had a good morning,' said Rupert.

Inside the caravan Badger thumped his tail joyfully and, wriggling up to Helen, goosed her briskly. On the table sat Billy Lloyd-Foxe. Mavis, the yellow mongrel, sat perched on his knee being fed pieces of Easter egg. On the bench seats sat a mousy-haired man with big ears and his mouth open, a fat man with short legs, and a pretty brunette with a note-pad. They were all watching yesterday's competition on the video machine. Billy's horse was coming up to a big oxer and scattering poles.

'Freeze it,' said the fat man. 'You went in too close, Billy.'

'Not enough impulsion,' said Rupert. 'Got to jump an

136

extra foot in mud like that. I wish you'd all stop cluttering up my caravan. This is Helen Macaulay.'

They all stared at her.

'This,' continued Rupert, 'is my unstable companion Billy Lloyd-Foxe.'

Billy grinned. 'Hi. I saw you across a crowded meet, but sadly Rupe got in first.'

'This is Joanna Battie from the *Chronicle*, who's interviewing Billy,' said Rupert introducing the dark girl, 'and Humpty Hamilton.' The fat man nodded. 'And this is Ivor Braine, singularly misnamed because he's so thick.' The man with big ears opened his mouth even wider.

Rupert got down two glasses and another bottle.

'I wish you'd stop feeding that bloody dog my Easter egg. She'll get spots.'

'And turn into a Dalmatian,' said Billy. Mavis was now lying on her back, with her legs apart, and her head on his shoulder. 'Wish I had this effect on women,' he went on, smiling at Helen.

Once Helen had been given a drink they all ignored her and went back to watching the video, tearing everyone's round to shreds, which gave her a chance to look at the caravan. It was extremely luxurious with an oven, a fridge, a washing machine, bench seats, a double bed that folded up completely and a great deal of cupboard space.

At the end of the tape Rupert switched over to racing, picking up the paper in order to look at his horoscope.

'Good day for shopping,' he read. 'Perhaps I'd better buy that grey gelding. "Evening starred for romance." ' He grinned at Helen. 'I should bloody well hope so.'

At that moment Marion walked in, still looking sulky. She was chewing gum, which gave her a particularly insolent air.

'Have you rung Ladbroke's?' asked Rupert.

'I haven't had time,' snapped Marion.

'Better buck up. You'll miss the first race.'

'Put a fiver each way on Red Chaffinch,' said Billy.

'Come on, William,' said Joanna Battie, picking up her

notebook. 'This is going to be a bum interview. Isn't there anyone, or anything, you dislike in show jumping?'

'You should have interviewed Rupert,' said Billy, undoing the purple paper from one of the chocolates inside the egg and giving it to Mavis.

'I'll tell you what's wrong with show jumping,' said Rupert, filling up Helen's glass. 'Why don't the big shows provide the stabling free for the top riders? Cattle and sheep never have to pay a penny for accommodation. They ought to waive our entrance fees too, and pay us appearance money. Our names go on every press release. The crowds have come here to watch Billy, Humpty, Ivor and *mostly* me.'

'You're so modest,' said Joanna.

'And another thing,' said Rupert, warming to his subject, 'French, German and Irish riders get a grand every time they win abroad. We don't get a bean. We'll never smash the Kraut ascendancy until they start paying us decent money.'

'Do you agree with this, Billy?' asked Joanna.

'Well, I don't feel as strongly as Rupert. Probably because I'm not a member of the British team.'

'And because you never worry about money,' snapped Rupert. 'People who claim not to be interested in money are always bloody good at spending other people's.'

'If you want to be a top show-jumper,' said Billy, winking at Helen, 'you don't need to ride well, just be Olympic level at bellyaching.'

Marion came off the telephone to Ladbroke's.

'You haven't met Helen Macaulay, Marion,' said Rupert, a slight note of malice creeping into his voice.

'I've met her namesake,' said Marion sourly. 'Arrived Friday morning; bitten me three times already.'

'My namesake?' asked Helen, bewildered.

'The black horse I bought at the barracks. He's been showing Marion who's boss. I decided to call him Macaulay.'

Helen blushed crimson. 'Oh, how darling of you.'

138

'Are you going to make us something to eat?' said Rupert.

'Haven't got time,' said Marion. 'Class starts in three-quarters of an hour. I've got to help Tracey tack up Belgravia and The Bull. There's smoked salmon in the fridge and brown bread in the bin,' and she flounced out of the caravan, slamming the door behind her.

'What a lovely nature that girl's got,' Humpty said, getting up. 'We'd better go, Ivor. Thanks for the drink.'

'I'll come with you,' said Joanna. 'You'll want to get changed. I presume you're all going to Grania Pringle's party tonight. O.K. then, I'll have half an hour there with you, Billy. Good luck both of you.'

'Do you want me to go out while you change?' asked Helen.

'As long as you don't mind underpants,' said Rupert.

'I'll make you some sandwiches'. She went to the fridge which was packed with an upmarket medley of pâté, smoked salmon, smoked turkey and several bottles of champagne. She also noticed a great many empties already in the trash can.

'Bread's in the bin on the right,' said Rupert. Lifting her hair, he planted a kiss on the back of her neck, then when she swung round, he kissed her on the mouth, his hands feeling for her breasts. Helen tried to leap away but she was rammed against the oven.

Rupert laughed and let her go. 'Mustn't raise my blood pressure too much before a class.'

As Helen spread unsalted butter on slices of bread and placed smoked salmon, red pepper and a squirt of lemon on top, she allowed herself the brief fantasy of living with Rupert in the little caravan like a couple of gypsies, cooking him ingenious dinners on the stove each night, shutting out the rest of the horsey world except Billy. Billy, she decided, was real nice.

'How's Nige?' asked Rupert.

'Very overadrenalized,' said Helen, cutting the crusts off the sandwiches, 'and overly concerned that you've

139

appropriated his address book and now have access to all the names and addresses of the saboteur underground.'

'The only name and *add*-ress I was after,' said Rupert, mimicking her accent again, 'was yours. After that I threw the book into the Thames, so no doubt a lot of fishes are about to reveal the Antis' darkest secrets in the *Angling Times*.'

Helen turned round with the plate of sandwiches to find Billy already dressed in breeches and shirt, tying his white tie, and Rupert wearing nothing at all. She nearly dropped the sandwiches on the floor. Shoving the plate down on the table, she turned back to tidy up and found herself putting the crusts in the fridge.

'Very good sandwiches,' said Rupert. 'D'you want some, Billy?'

'No thanks,' said Billy, lighting a cigarette. 'It never fails to amaze me how you can eat before a big class. I'm about to throw up last night's dinner.'

'Nigel had two broken ribs, a black eye, and multiple bruises,' said Helen reprovingly.

'You ought to have brought me a colour photograph,' said Rupert, who was pulling on his boots.

There was a bang on the door. It was Humpty Hamilton.

'We can walk the course in five minutes,' he said. 'It looks a sod.'

'I'm definitely going to ask Lavinia Greenslade out tonight,' said Billy, shrugging into his red coat.

'You'll have to take her parents along as well,' said Rupert, seizing a couple more sandwiches as they went out of the caravan.

Helen, as a result of three glasses of wine and no sandwiches, was feeling very unsteady. She was glad Rupert
took a firm hold of her arm.

'Can you remember where I'm jumping?' he asked Billy.

'Fifteen,' said Billy, 'I've got to wait until thirty. I'm last.
Christ, look at that upright.'

They left Helen in the riders' stand while they walked the
course. She saw Joanna, the deadpan girl from the *Chronicle*,
pointing her out to some of the other journalists who
laughed and shrugged their shoulders. She wished she'd
brought a coat; the suede dress wasn't very warm.

She watched the riders splaying out over the emerald
green arena. There were a few girls in black or very dark
navy blue coats, several Irish riders in Army uniform or
holly green, but the majority wore coats as red as an
Armistice Day poppy. Some of them were pacing out the
number of strides between jumps, like seconds in a duel,
others put their hands up to rattle a pole to check how firm
it was in the cup, others stood eyeing a turn or an angle,
seeing how safe it was to cut a corner or come in sharply.

Several riders climbed up the famous Crittleden bank,
like a turned-out avocado mousse, to examine the fence
half-way across on the top. The jumps were absolutely
colossal. Humpty Hamilton, looking stouter than ever in a
quilted waistcoat, couldn't even see over half of them.

And there was Billy, pulling on yet another cigarette,
gloomily examining the water jump, while Mavis, thirsty
from all that Easter egg, drank frantically, trying to lower
the water level.

141

The indigo clouds had rolled away, leaving the softest pale blue sky above the acid green wood which had only a few sad grey streaks where the odd tree had died of Dutch elm disease. On the hill she could see the gleaming armadillo of parked cars and the caravan village.

Mostly her eyes were drawn to Rupert, who seemed to be spending more time ribbing his fellow competitors than studying the course. Unlike the others, he didn't look bandy-legged or stout, or diminished by not being on a horse. All round the ring, crowds were gathering with binoculars. Helen reluctantly imagined every eye was on Rupert.

Two men in check suits and bowler hats, flushed from lunch, were going up into the judges' box.

As the riders came out joking and laughing on the nervous high before a big class, the cameramen went in, most of them in jeans, gathering round the water jump. A large lady with a huge bust strode round the course with a tape measure, checking the height of each jump.

Tracey and Marion rode down to the collecting ring, one on the dark bay, Allenby, nicknamed The Bull, the other on the chestnut, Belgravia.

'God, I hate Rupe before big classes,' said Marion. 'He's so picky, checking and re-checking everything. Stop it, you monster,' she snapped, as Belgravia, oated up to the eyeballs, fidgeted and spooked at everything he passed, scattering the crowd with his huge feet and quarters.

'Seems on top of the world,' said Tracey.

'Wish I was,' said Marion gloomily. 'You haven't seen Rupe's new girl friend.'

'What's she like?'

'Not really his type: red-headed, breedy-looking, quivering with nerves rather like Belgravia. I suppose he is mad about chestnuts and she's mad about him, but trying desperately to hide it.'

'Sounds like all the rest,' said Tracey.

'Even worse, she's called Macaulay.'

'Blimey,' said Tracey, leaning forward and giving the

last bit of her Wimpy bun to The Bull. 'He's never done that before. Don't worry, I expect she'll go the way of all the others. He can't be that smitten if he was fooling about with Grania Pringle last night.'

Helen was joined by Rupert, Billy and Mavis in the riders' stand.

'I wish you'd leave that dog behind, Billy,' said a steward fussily.

'She brings me luck.'

'Can't see why she can't bring you luck in your caravan.'

The first riders were crashing their horses over jumps in the practice ring under the oak trees. Members of the public leaned forward to pat their equine heroes as they passed in their coloured rugs.

'What was the course like?' asked Helen.

'Bloody. You can park a double-decker bus between the parallel bars,' said Rupert. 'There are only two and a half strides between the double, and the wall isn't as solid as it looks. If you catch it on the way up, you're in dead trouble.'

'Zee vater must be at least six metres,' said a German rider gloomily. Billy looked green and lit another cigarette.

A man in a felt hat, with long sideboards and a raffish face, stopped on the way to the commentary box. 'Hullo boys,' he said in a carefully modulated put-on voice. 'Are you going to show them how to do it again today, Rupert?'

'I might if you don't describe me as our most brilliant young rider as I come into the ring, in which case I'll knock up a cricket score.'

The raffish man laughed. 'I'd better get upstairs, we're on the air in two minutes. How did the course walk?'

'Not very good. I don't like banks in the high street or in a jumping ring, but it may ride better than it walks,' said Rupert.

Surely ride and walk aren't transitive verbs, thought Helen. 'Who's that?' she asked as he moved on.

'Dudley Diplock – does all the commentaries. He's a pratt, knows bugger-all about show-jumping.'

Everything went quiet as the first rider came in –

yesterday's winner, Ludwig von Schellenberg on Brahms, a splendid horse, impeccably schooled.

'He's the one to watch,' Billy told Helen. 'He's the best rider in the world, and was virtually unbeaten last season.'

'Kraut horses learn obedience the moment they come out of the womb,' said Rupert.

British spirits were not raised, however, when the mighty Ludwig had a most uncharacteristic twelve faults.

'Shows how bloody difficult the course must be,' said Rupert.

'We'll all be up in the fifties,' said Billy.

'And here comes the despair of the Pony Club,' said Rupert, as Ludwig was followed by Humpty Hamilton on Porky Boy.

Humpty certainly rode in a very unorthodox fashion, pouter pigeon chest stuck out, hands held high, feet pointing down like a dancing master, showing a great patch of blue sky as he rose nearly a foot and a half out of the saddle over every fence. Nevertheless he acquitted himself well over the punishing course, and only had two fences down and a foot in the water for the same number of faults as Ludwig.

After that everyone went to pieces. Disastrous round followed disastrous round, slowing the proceedings up because the course had to be re-built every time.

Rupert got to his feet:

'I'd better go and show them how to do it,' he said.

He kissed Helen on the cheek. 'I won't be long, darling.'

Without his red-hot presence beside her, Helen suddenly felt cold. A brisk wind was unfurling the flags and spreading out the horses' tails. On television it had looked like a game for children with toy horses and toy fences. The camera had caught nothing of the colossal height of the jumps, the pounding hooves, the heroic splendour and sheer size of the horses thundering about like some Battle of Borodino. Suddenly Helen felt scared for Rupert.

'Aren't you terrified?'

'Terrified,' said Billy, clutching Mavis for comfort and

144

lighting another cigarette, 'particularly as Malise Gordon has just arrived and parked himself below us.'

'Who's he?'

'One of the selectors and the new Chef d'Equipe. He manages the British team and goes abroad with them to keep them in order.'

'What's he like?' said Helen, admiring the taut aquiline features, the high complexion and the dark hair greying at the temples. 'He looks kind of attractive.'

'Bit of a tartar, stickler for discipline, always has spats with Rupe – well, you can never exactly tell what Rupe's going to do next. Going to bed sober, early and alone has never been his strong point. Although I'm sure,' Billy added hastily, worried that he might have hurt Helen, 'now he's met you, he'll mend his ways. Mind you, it's getting to the stage when Rupe's so good, Malise can't afford to leave him out.'

Helen watched Rupert saunter across the concrete below them, then vault over the fence into the collecting ring. Goodness, he must be fit. He walked up to Marion and Belgravia, bending down to adjust the bandages on the horse's front legs.

'Is he that good?' Helen longed to talk about him.

'Christ, yes. Doesn't have any nerves, cool as an icicle before every class, and he's so fast and he meets every fence just right. Knows what risks he can take too. And he's got the killer instinct. Even in novice classes he's always out to win.'

Ivor Braine was in the middle of a good round. The television man ran nimbly after him with the boom, recording the grunts and snorts of his horse.

'Sounds like a live sex show,' said Billy. 'We always say it's Ivor's Dumbo ears that carry him round.'

Ivor was followed by a handsome Frenchman in a blue coat with a crimson collar, who proceeded to demolish the course. As he came thundering down to the water the horse jammed on its brakes and the Frenchman took a leisurely somersault through the air, landing with a huge splash.

145

'*Il est tombé dans l'eau*,' said Billy. 'I know that's going to happen to me and The Bull. Now they'll have to rebuild the course and Belgravia won't like the wait.'

In the collecting ring the horse was plunging round, eyes rolling, nostrils flaring, flecks of foam going everywhere.

A colossal cheer went up as Rupert erupted into the ring through the red brick arch. In the private boxes people came out on to the balconies to watch, clutching their gins and tonics. Helen was sure she could detect some Beatle-screaming. Belgravia stood still just long enough for Rupert to take his hat off, fidgeting and stamping to be allowed into action.

Humpty Hamilton sat down beside Helen.

'Belgravia looks completely over the top. Is it true, Billy, his half-brother was second in the Grand National?'

Belgravia gave three colossal bucks. Rupert laughed and didn't move in the saddle. As the klaxon went off with its eldritch screech the horse bounded forward.

'Complete tearaway,' muttered Humpty. 'Steerable, but not stoppable.'

'That horse would benefit from some dressage,' thought Malise Gordon disapprovingly. 'If it weren't for Rupert's colossal strength, he'd be quite out of control.'

Over the brush sailed Belgravia, over the post and rails, over the rustic poles, driven on by Rupert's erotic pelvic thrusts. When he came to the massive upright he flew over it as though it was a tiny log.

At the gate with Crittleden written across it in large red letters he came in too fast, slipped, just righted himself, and rapped the fence hard as he went over. For a second it swung back and forth, making Rupert's fans gasp, Rupert didn't even bother to glance round. With his long stride, Belgravia managed the double in three strides. Now he was rounding the corner. Next moment Helen saw Belgravia's pricked ginger ears appearing over the top of the bank, then his lovely head with the white star, and then Rupert. They were on top, popping over the little fence, then tobogganing down the other side, Belgravia on his haunches. Only

146

Rupert's superhuman strength again stopped the horse running into the fence at the bottom. He was over; the crowd gave a cheer. Over the wall and the combination, which caused him no trouble. Then he kicked Belgravia into a gallop and sailed over the water, yanking him back to get him in line for the final triple.

'Too fast,' said Billy in anguish. 'He's going to hit it.'

Helen shut her eyes, listening to the thundering hooves, waiting for the sickening thud of falling poles and the groans of the crowd. Instead there was a mighty roar of applause. Helen opened her eyes.

'Ouch,' said Billy.

Looking down, Helen realized she'd been gripping his arm.

'I'm real sorry.'

'Be my guest. Brilliant round, wasn't it?'

'Wonderful.' Helen watched a delighted Rupert letting his rein go slack and walking Belgravia out of the ring, slapping his lathered neck, pulling the ginger ears with joy. Belgravia's coat, dark, bronzed and shiny with sweat, looked like uncooked liver.

'That puts me in joint second, which means £500, but there are still fifteen to go,' said Humpty.

Helen noticed the arrogant way Rupert ignored the cheers. Sliding to the ground, he patted the horse once more and turned towards the riders' stand. Stopped by admirers on the way, in an exultant mood, he was prepared to sign autographs.

'Once you get a clear, people realize it can be jumped and you'll probably get a lot more,' said Billy. 'If I watch any more rounds I'll start getting the heeby-jeebies.'

He lit another cigarette. Mavis closed her slanting eyes to avoid the smoke.

'How long has your mount suffered from hydrophobia?' asked Helen.

'What?' Billy looked alarmed.

'Been frightened of water.'

'Oh, ever since I had him. I think he might have nearly

drowned in some tiny river when he was a foal because it really scares him. Last week I managed to get him over a six-foot stream at home, but he trembled for ages afterwards. I just don't know how he'll go today. He's such a good horse,' he went on, his face lighting up. 'So kind, and such a trier, he'll get himself into all sorts of trouble rather than duck out, and he's so bright. Over and over I put him wrong and he just brakes at the last moment and sails over, and he's so cheerful, never moody, and so gentle, a child could lead him up to London on a piece of string like a little dog.'

Helen smiled. 'I think Mavis is getting jealous,' she said.

'Oh, Mavis knows she's my favourite dog, and there goes my favourite girl,' said Billy, as a blonde with a pink and white complexion on a grey horse waited to go into the ring.

'Look at her bloody father telling her to give it a whack at the water, and her mother telling her not to. Poor girl's in such a muddle. I could sort her out,' he said longingly. 'Good luck, darling,' he called down. Lavinia looked up, waved her whip and smiled. Her parents looked simply furious.

How nice he is, thought Helen, and he's Rupert's best friend. There couldn't be much wrong with Rupert if he inspired friendship like this. In anguish, Billy watched poor Lavinia, after a nervous, tentative round, meet the same fate as the Frenchman, flying through the air into the water.

'At least she won't have to wash her hair before she goes out with you this evening,' said an amused voice. It was Rupert. He was eating an ice cream.

'Congratulations,' said Helen.

'Bloody well done,' said Billy.

'That should wrap the whole thing up,' said Rupert, shooting a sideways glance at Billy. 'Don't imagine there'll be any more clears.'

'Thanks a lot,' said Billy. 'I've still got to jump. Oh, look at poor darling Lavinia coming out in tears.'

'She looks like a seal,' said Rupert. 'She may just be dwipping water, not cwying. Lavinia,' he added to Helen, 'can't say her "R"'s.'

'It was a good round until she came to the water,' protested Billy.

'That girl couldn't ride in a taxi with the door shut,' said Rupert. 'They ought to pay her disappearance money.'

Billy got up. 'Can you hold Mavis for me?' he asked Helen.

'Good luck,' said Rupert.

As he went downstairs the dog whined and strained after him.

'Shut up,' snapped Rupert. Mavis gave him a cold stare, then climbed on to Helen's knees and settled down with a sigh of deep martyrdom.

Helen, though not wild about dogs, was grateful for the warmth. Seeing she was shivering, Rupert put his red coat round her shoulders. The heat still left from his body was like a caress. Riders kept returning to the stand, many of them on twelve faults. Everyone congratulated Rupert. He was in tearing spirits until Malise Gordon came over and sat down on his other side. Rupert was about to introduce Helen when Malise said, 'Not a bad round, but a bit hit and miss.'

Rupert's lips tightened, his face suddenly expressionless.

'Belgravia could do with a lot more work on the flat,' went on Malise, 'and a lot less corn.'

'He never felt in any danger to me,' said Rupert coldly.

'You were very lucky at the gate, and at the rail after the bank, and you came in much too fast at the triple. That's a good horse, but you won't get him out of trouble every time.'

Rupert stared stonily ahead.

'We ought to be thinking of him in terms of the Olympics or the World Championships,' said Malise in a slightly more conciliatory tone.

'Belgravia'd be the ideal horse,' said Rupert, relenting slightly too. 'In the World Championship,' he explained to Helen, 'the four finalists have to jump each other's horses. Belgravia's such a sod, no one would have a hope on him.'

149

'Hardly cricket,' said Malise.

' 'Course it isn't,' said Rupert insolently. 'I thought we were talking about show-jumping.'

'By the way,' asked Malise, 'have you come across a rider called Jake Lovell? He's been jumping on the northern circuit. I think he's very good.'

Rupert paused for a second. 'No. Is he good enough to make the British team?'

'He will be in a year or two.'

'You'd do much better with Billy,' said Rupert quickly.

'Billy has yet to convince me he has the killer instinct,' said Malise, standing up. 'I'll probably see you at Grania's.'

Helen could see exactly why he and Rupert struck sparks off each other.

Down in the collecting ring Billy went up to Lavinia Greenslade and commiserated with her.

'Same thing's bound to happen to me,' he said. He was just about to ask her out when her mother came up. 'Wish you wouldn't call out to Lavinia just as she's going into the ring,' she snapped. 'Completely put her off her stroke.'

'Sorry,' muttered Billy.

Winking at Lavinia, he walked over to The Bull who whickered with joy and stuck his nose inside Billy's coat. Built like an oak tree with a vast girth, short, wide-apart well-shaped legs and surprisingly small feet, it was the wide forehead and rather small eyes that made him look like a bull. The wide blaze down his forehead gave him an added appearance of placid contentment.

'How is he?' he asked Tracey.

'Gorgeous,' said Tracey. 'Always is. Didn't Rupert jump champion?'

Billy rode off, trying to control his nerves. Rupert had been so cockahoop, he felt needled into producing something better. Other riders, having finished jumping, were all too ready to offer him advice. But it was no good listening to other people at this stage; he'd only get muddled. Over the years he'd schooled himself to tackle the problem by himself. In the ring you were on your own.

The German number two rider, Hans Schmidt, came out. An Irish rider was next, then Billy.

'How did you get on?' he asked Hans.

'Von stop at zee vater,' said the German despondently, 'and zee gate and zee wall down, puts me in second place viz Ludvig and Humpty.'

'Bloody good,' said Billy.

'Zee Bull looks vell, put on a lot of condition.'

'Thanks,' said Billy.

The collecting ring steward called his number. Good lucks came from all round. Billy was very popular.

As he waited for the Irishman to come out, a little girl bent over and stroked The Bull's nose.

'Good luck, Bull,' she said shyly.

Billy smiled and thanked her, wishing the butterflies in his stomach would go away. He couldn't even remember which fence to jump first. The Bull, however, showed no such fears, striding out briskly, ears pricked, tail up, merry eyes sparkling, taking everything in.

'Take your hat off, Billy,' whispered a ring steward.

The crowd roared with laughter as Billy started and hastily whipped off his hat, damp curls sticking to his forehead. Malise stopped talking to Grania Pringle in the President's box.

'I want to watch this round,' he said. 'Must say The Bull looks marvellous.'

'More than can be said for Billy,' said Grania. 'He's pea green.'

'Take it slowly,' Billy told himself over and over again. If you can go clear, even with time faults, you'll be second. 'You're the best, you're the best,' he whispered to The Bull as he leaned forward and started cantering as the klaxon went.

The Bull bucketed over the first three fences, giving huge scary leaps with inches to spare, then he settled down, trundling merrily along, little legs going like pistons, meeting everything just right.

151

'God, that horse has improved,' said Malise, as he flew over the double. 'Billy's really been working on him.'

Helen held her breath as The Bull scrambled up the bank which, after much use, was extremely slippery. On the top Billy steadied him. Just for a second The Bull looked dubious. The crowd crossed their fingers in case he stepped back which would have constituted a stop, costing Billy three faults, but he popped over, tobogganed down the other side and took a huge jump out over the tiny rail, snorting with disapproval, ears flat, tail swishing.

'Didn't enjoy that,' laughed Humpty. 'Look at his old tail going. Who did you say his dam was, Rupert?'

'Probably a cow,' said Rupert.

Helen giggled.

The combination, three good solid fences, held no fears for The Bull.

'He's faster than you,' said Humpty with some satisfaction.

'I know,' said Rupert coldly.

Now it was only the water, and the final triple. Turning The Bull, Billy thundered down, his red coat like a spot of blood against the dappled crowd.

'Come on, Billy,' howled Rupert.

Ahead Billy saw the water glinting as wide and as blue as the Serpentine. On each side huddled the photographers, waiting for the third ducking.

'Go on, go on,' Billy whispered, 'you're a star, you can do it, we can do it.'

He felt The Bull tense. He's probably thinking it's twenty feet deep, thought Billy. Just for a second the horse hesitated. Then suddenly he seemed to relax and put his trust in Billy.

'If you think it's O.K.,' he seemed to say, 'let's give it a whirl.' People who were close swear to this day that The Bull closed his eyes. Standing back, he took a mighty leap off his hocks, soaring about six feet in the air, and landed three feet beyond the tape on the other side. People claim it was the longest jump they had ever seen. As he landed, the ring erupted in a bellow of cheers: 'Go on Billy, you can do it, go on.'

He had only the triple to jump and that had caused no problems to anyone. But to the crowd's amazement, Billy suddenly pulled The Bull up, hugging him, patting him, running his hand up and down his mane, and telling him what a king he was.

'You've got one more fence to jump,' yelled the photographers.

'You've missed the last fence. Go back. You've still got time,' shouted the ring steward who'd reminded him to take his hat off.

'I know,' said Billy, and, raising his whip to the judges to show he was retiring, he cantered slowly out of the ring in front of the stunned crowd.

Rupert met him in the collecting ring, absolutely white with rage.

'Bloody maniac, what the fuck are you playing at? You've just chucked away £1,000 or £750. It was only you and me in the jump-off.'

'I know,' said Billy, 'but he was so frightened, and he jumped the water so bravely, I thought I'd call it a day, so he could remember how good he'd been.'

Rupert looked at him incredulously. 'You must be crazy.'

Billy slid off The Bull, burying his face in the brown shiny shoulder, hugging him, patting his chest.

'Good boy, clever boy.'

Rupert suddenly realized Billy's eyes were filled with tears. Tracey rushed up and, removing the rug which she'd been wearing round her shoulders for warmth, put it over The Bull.

'What happened?' she said in concern. 'Did he hurt himself?'

Billy shook his head.

'No,' he said in a choked voice, undoing a packet of Polos, all of which he gave to The Bull. 'I was so pleased with him, winning didn't seem to matter any more.'

153

Rupert sighed. 'I'm afraid Malise Gordon will feel differently,' he said. 'I hope you realize you've blown your chances of going to Rome.'

He put an arm round Billy's shoulders. 'All the same, it was a bloody good round. You were up on the clock on me.'

Marion came up with Belgravia. 'They want you in the ring, Rupert.'

As Rupert rode off to collect his first prize, Billy turned to Tracey.

'I'm sorry,' he said humbly. 'Perhaps I shouldn't have done it.'

' 'Course you should. He's got years ahead. Look how pleased he is.'

The next minute they went slap into Malise who took Billy and The Bull aside.

'That was a bloody silly thing to do,' he said.

Billy hung his head.

'I'm sorry, but it's the first time he's ever jumped water and it was such a tremendous jump.'

'Well, don't do it again.' Malise patted The Bull. 'I must say he looks terrific. So don't get carried away and over-jump him in the next three weeks. I'll certainly be needing him for Rome, if not for Madrid.'

Billy looked up incredulously.

'What did you say?'

'Don't go blathering it around to everyone, but I'd like you to bring him to Rome.' He gave The Bull another pat and stalked off.

'Whatever did he say to you?' said Tracey. Then, seeing there were tears in Billy's eyes again, 'Did he bawl you out?'

'No, yes, no, I don't know,' said Billy in a dazed voice. 'I think I'll ride The Bull back to the stable myself.'

After winning a major competition, Rupert was usually in a manic mood. But today he felt that Billy had somehow stolen his thunder. Malise Gordon's remarks had niggled him . He resented the implication that Belgravia's win had been a matter of luck. If Billy hadn't pulled The Bull up in that stupid fashion, Rupert would have been able to prove

Malise wrong by trouncing Billy in the jump-off against the clock. Anyway, he'd like to see Malise or anyone else controlling Belgravia. And all that fuss about dressage, it was no more than bloody Come Dancing.

He was further irritated that Billy, despite having chucked away £750 prize money without a thought, was behaving as though Malise had kissed him under the mistletoe. Rupert loved Billy, but he was constantly irked by Billy's hazy assumption that the Lord or Rupert Campbell-Black would provide. Like many generous people, Rupert liked to have the monopoly of the expansive gesture. Billy's £750 could have gone a long way towards repainting the yard. It never occurred to Rupert that Billy might have beaten him.

After the competition, the heavens opened and journalists and other riders crowded into Rupert's caravan to get out of the rain. But after drinking Rupert's health in Rupert's champagne out of the huge silver cup he had just won, they were far more interested in talking about The Bull's amazing jump and Billy's retirement. Rupert loved Billy, but he did not like playing second fiddle. He might have been indifferent to public adulation, but he liked it to be there, so he *could* be indifferent to it.

Leaving them all gassing together, he took half a bottle of champagne into the shower. As the drumming of raindrops on the caravan roof drowned the noise of the hot water, he was gripped by the lust that always overwhelmed him after a big class. Normally he would have screwed Marion in the back of the horsebox, but he doubted if she would oblige with a quickie with Helen around. Anyway, he didn't want Marion; he was amazed by his violent craving for Helen. He must get her into bed soon. Only that could restore his *amour propre* and remove the ache from his loins. He'd already told Billy to find somewhere else to shack up for the night as he needed the caravan for Helen and himself. But, although he knew she was hooked on him, he was by no means sure she was going to be a pushover. He'd have to make her jealous. He knew Grania Pringle would oblige.

155

Helen, in fact, was feeling absolutely miserable. She knew Rupert was busy, that this was his world, but he had this ability to be all over her one moment and virtually oblivious of her the next. Since he'd won the cup, he'd been completely withdrawn. And now all these people were guzzling his drink, talking shop and ignoring her. Only the German, Hans Schmidt, who had rather mad arctic blue eyes, had made any attempt to chat her up.

But he hadn't seen any of the German movies she so admired and when she got him on to writers it was even worse.

'I just adore Brecht,' she said with enthusiasm.

'I too am a great admirer of breasts,' said Hans, brightening perceptibly and gazing at her bosom.

'No, Brecht, the writer.'

'Ya, ya,' said Hans. 'Small breasts, big breasts, it's quite all right viz me for zee ladies to like other ladies' breasts.'

Helen went pink and hastily started talking about Gunther Grass. She thought she was making progress. The German seemed most interested until he suddenly said, 'Vot is zis grass? Is it some kind of hay which Rupert feed his horses?'

So she gave up and he turned back to Humpty Hamilton who was having an argument with the man from the *Daily Telegraph* about dust allergy.

Billy still being interviewed by Joanna Battie from the *Chronicle*, who was showing all the intensity of someone who realizes they've stumbled on a really good story, could do little more than smile apologetically and shove the bottle in Helen's direction from time to time.

Unaware of the taciturnity and habitual suspicion towards outsiders of all show-jumping people, Helen felt she must have lost her sex appeal. Nor did she realize they were too wary of Rupert to chat up one of his girlfriends.

She longed to be able to shower and change before Lady Pringle's party. She'd never met a member of the British aristocracy before and wondered if she ought to curtsey, and how she should address her. Her mother always emphasized the importance of using people's names when you talked to them. Was it Milady, or your gace, or what? She'd liked to have asked Joanna or Marion, who had just returned exhausted from settling the horses, but they both looked at her with such hostility. To hell with them all, she thought, helping herself to another drink. 'I am a writer, I must observe life and listen to British dialogue.'

One of the journalists was ringing his newspaper on Rupert's telephone.

'I'm sure he was half-brother to Arctic Prince,' said Humpty.

'He was own brother,' said Ivor sullenly.

'Half-brother.'

'Own brother. I ought to know, I rode the horse.'

'I must use the telephone next to ring my news desk,' said the man from the *Telegraph*.

At this moment Rupert came out of the shower, a dark blue towel round his hips, blond hair dark and otter sleek. Helen felt her stomach give way.

'I want to change, so would you all fuck off?' he said coldly.

'Don't mind us,' said Humpty. 'You never have before. Wasn't Polar Pete half-brother to Arctic Prince?'

'I don't care. Get out – *all* of you. And get off my telephone, Malcolm.'

He ripped the telephone wire out of its socket.

'I was on to the news desk, singing your praises,' said Malcolm indignantly.

'I don't care. Beat it.'

Grumbling, they all dispersed into the sheeting rain, running with their coats over their heads, until only Billy and Helen were left. Rupert re-plugged the telephone. It rang immediately. At a nod from Rupert, Billy picked it up. Rupert came over and kissed Helen. He tasted of toothpaste and smelt faintly of eau de cologne. In the safety of Billy's chaperonage, she allowed herself to melt against him, kissing him back until she could hardly stand. Rupert put a hand on her breast.

'I can feel your heart,' he said softly, 'and it sure is racing.'

'Ahem,' said Billy. 'Sorry to interrupt, but it's Dick Brandon. He wants to drop in for a drink.'

'Hell! Oh, all right, tell him to come over. Go and have a shower, darling, the water's baking.'

'Will it be very fancy tonight?'

'Not particularly.'

'Shall I wear pants?'

Rupert's eyes gleamed. That *was* getting somewhere. 'Certainly not,' he said.

Helen was relieved to find that the shower, unlike the showers at Regina House, gushed out constant hot water. But there was no lock on the door and Helen imagined Rupert barging in, so she showered with frantic haste. She put on a black silk jersey dress with a discreetly low back and pale grey tights which stuck to her legs because they were still wet.

Outside, she found that the double bed had been let down from the wall. Joining the two bench seats, it formed a huge area. On top of the dark blue duvet lounged Rupert, wearing a striped shirt and grey trousers. Perching on the edge of the bed were Billy and a man in a light check suit with an expansive red-veined face, bags under his eyes and blond hair going grey. They were three-quarters of the way down another bottle of champagne. Rupert's eyes were beginning to glitter slightly.

'Well, if the horse is so bloody good, I can't see why you're selling her,' said Brandon.

'She's not quite up to my weight and she's too sensitive for me. You know what I feel about mares.'

Suddenly they all noticed Helen standing there, white skin flushed from the shower, brilliant red hair falling over her forehead, the perfect contrast to the black dress. The man in the check suit whistled.

'Oh boy,' he said. 'Come here, sweetheart.'

As she came towards him, he ran his hand down her pearly grey stockinged leg as if she were a horse.

158

'Now this I'm really prepared to offer for.'

Rupert laughed and, reaching out for Helen, pulled her down beside him, offering her his glass to drink out of. Then he ruffled her hair, gazing into the huge shy bruised eyes.

'I'm afraid this one's definitely not for sale, Dick,' he said.

'Christ, Rupe is a lucky sod,' thought Billy. 'She gets more stunning by the minute.'

II

Another bottle of champagne was consumed and the rain had stopped before they set out for Grania Pringle's party. The setting sun was firing the puddles and bathing the dripping trees with a soft pink light.

Rupert and Billy, both already slightly tight and in raging spirits, walked on either side of Helen, putting their inside arms through hers and lifting her over the muddier ground.

'Where my caravan has rested,

Flowers I leave you on the grass,' carolled Billy in a quavering baritone as they walked past the caravan village. Mavis ran on ahead, picking up her blonde feet like a hackney pony, delicately tiptoeing along the runnels of the puddles.

On the way they stopped to check the horses, who were dozing in nine inches of wood shavings. The Bull was looking out of his box and Mavis scampered up and licked him on the nose. Helen couldn't help noticing how both The Bull and Kitchener whickered with pleasure to see Billy, nudging at his pockets for Polos, but both Belgravia and Mayfair and the younger novice horses flattened their ears and backed off as Rupert approached.

'Got to show them who's boss,' said Rupert lightly, but, adding that it was getting chilly, he put an extra rug on Belgravia.

'Don't forget the anti-freeze,' said Billy, and promptly burst into song again. Then he said,

'I'm going to make the most enormous play for Lavinia Greenslade tonight.'

160

'Wavish her in the whododendwons,' said Rupert. 'Like hell you will. I'll give you a tenner if you get to first base.'

The Pringles lived in a large Georgian house behind the Crittleden elm wood, looking over a lake and a cherry orchard whose white blossom was now tinged almond pink by the last rays of the sun.

Helen gave a gasp of pleasure.

'Loveliest of trees, the cherry now,' she gushed expansively, 'Is hung with bloom along the bough.'

'Hung with bloomers,' said Rupert, deliberately mishearing her. 'Sounds just like Nanny. What were those bloody great things she insisted on wearing winter and summer?'

'Directoire knickers,' said Billy.

'That's right. When she hung them on the line on washday we always thought they'd carry the house away like an air balloon.'

They both collapsed with laughter.

In order not to be a spoilsport, Helen tried to join in.

From the noise issuing from the front door the party was obviously well under way. As Helen changed out of mud-spattered boots into black high-heeled shoes, a handsome blonde, scent rising like incense from the cleavage of her splendid bosom, came out to welcome them.

'Rupert, darling, how lovely to see you.'

She gathered him into a braceleted embrace. Over his shoulder her sootily mascaraed eyes appraised the rest of them, affording Helen and Mavis about the same amount of enthusiasm.

'That's Grania Pringle,' thought Helen. Close up she didn't look very lady-like.

'Must you bring that creature in here?' she said to Billy.

'Love me, love my dog,' said Billy unrepentantly. 'Sorry, Grania, but she howls the caravan down if I leave her behind.'

'Well, I don't have any difficulty loving you, but I do draw the line at Mavis.'

'You haven't met Helen Macaulay,' said Rupert,

161

extracting himself from her clutches. 'She comes from Florida where tomatoes, she informs me, are their tertiary industry.'

'Tomatoes,' said Lady Pringle. 'How extraordinary. Your mother gave me a marvellous recipe for tomato provençale last time I saw her, Rupe. We all stank of garlic for weeks afterwards, but it was simply delicious.' She turned back to Helen, 'Are you a horsey gel?'

'No thank God,' said Rupert, 'she works in publishing. And she's absolutely fed up with Humpty Hamilton and Ivor Braine and Billy gassing about blood lines all afternoon. Have you invited any intellectuals for her to talk to?'

'Only Malise Gordon,' said Grania. 'He writes books, frightfully clever chap, you must meet him. But he's rather hemmed in by Lavinia Greenslade's parents, who are twying to persuade him to take Lavinia to Wome.'

'Must be mad,' said Rupert. 'She couldn't even stay on the wocking horse at Hawwods.'

'Shut up,' said Billy, grinning.

'Billy's rather a fan of Lavinia's,' explained Rupert. 'He's longing to wape her.'

'And Lavinia's Daddy will be so cwoss, he'll come and wun me over in his Wolls Woyce,' said Billy.

Grania screamed with laughter. She was already beginning to get seriously on Helen's nerves.

'You boys are awful. Come and have a drink.'

'If Greenslade *mère* and *père* are bending Malise's ear, that means Lavinia must be unchaperoned for a second and I'm off,' said Billy, and vanished into the crowd in the next room.

'I'm afraid I've hidden the whisky, Rupert,' said Grania. 'You know what pigs this lot are, but you'll find some in the decanter in the library and there's another bottle in the kitchen cupboard.'

Whisky, however, was only for Rupert. Helen had to make do with a glass of very indifferent sparkling wine. The next moment Grania had swept her away from Rupert and thrust her into a loudly arguing group consisting of several show jumpers and Joanna Battie.

'Now then, Joanna,' said Grania briskly, 'you can't monopolize all these delicious chaps. This is Helen Macaulay, boys; she's frightfully clever and works for a publisher in London. Now I know all you show-jumpers are writing your autobiographies, so why don't you get her to publish yours? Come along, Rupert, my sister's dying to meet you.'

And off she swept, leaving Helen scarlet with embarrassment. 'Hi again,' she mumbled to Joanna. 'Are you all writing books?' she asked the ring of men.

'Too busy keeping them' said a man with brushed-forward hair and a pale, pinched, disapproving face who was drinking tomato juice. 'Joanna's the writer round here, aren't you, Joe? Except she gets it all wrong.'

'Never met a journalist who got anything right,' grumbled Humpty Hamilton. 'Last week the *Telegraph* said Porky Boy was out of Sally in our Alley. I mean, everyone knows Windsor Lass was his dam.'

'Oh, shut up, Humpty,' snapped the man with brushed-forward hair. 'You told us that yesterday.'

'You should come off the wagon, Driffield,' said Humpty. 'It's making you very bad-tempered.'

'I've lost twelve pounds, which is more than I can say for you, Humpty. You look five months gone in that sweater.'

'How much d'you reckon Rupert weighs?' said Ivor Braine, who was gazing at Helen with his mouth open.

'Helen should know,' said Joanna acidly.

'About twelve stone, I should think,' said Humpty.

'And eleven stone of that is pieces of paper with girls' phone numbers on,' said Joanna.

Helen flushed. She hated Joanna, and her flat little voice, and hair drawn back from her forehead. She was more deadpan even than the show-jumpers.

'How long have you been reducing for?' she asked Driffield.

'About a month.'

'You must have terrific control.'

163

'No!' he cut right across her, 'that's wrong, Humpty, he went clear.'

'No he didn't, he had four faults, and he was at least a quarter of a second slower than Rupert against the clock.'

Helen gritted her teeth. Across the room, as the horsey chat ebbed and flowed endlessly round her, she could see Rupert talking to Dick Brandon, hemmed in by women, all braying like Grania. Every few minutes, she noticed, Grania fed in another one and saw to it that Rupert's glass of whisky was constantly topped up. Every so often he looked across and mouthed 'All right?' to Helen and pride made her nod back.

She was certain Grania had deliberately thrust her into a group of small men. She topped all of them in her high heels. Separated from Rupert, she wanted him to be able to see her as the centre of attention, being madly chatted up, but among this lot she felt about as attractive as a spayed Great Dane among a lot of Jack Russells. She bent her legs slightly.

Now they were discussing who'd bought what horses during the winter and which looked as though they were going to be the most promising novices. Hans Schmidt, wearing slightly too fitted and too bright blue a blazer, came up, clicked his heels, and kissed Helen's hand.

'Ha, Mees Helen of Troy,' he said.

Helen turned to him gratefully, but next minute he was caught up with the others, discussing some potentially unbeatable Hanoverian mare.

Over in the corner Billy was hanging over the back of an armchair shared by Mavis and Lavinia Greenslade. After her dunking in the water she'd re-washed and curled her hair. A belted peacock-blue dress showed off her tiny waist. Her small hand rested on Mavis's head. Billy and she'll have very curly-haired children, thought Helen. She wished Rupert would look after her like that. She must pull herself together and try and be more extrovert.

The group had moved on to discussing the best routes to take to the next show, which was in the West country.

'The A40's much quicker,' said Humpty Hamilton.

Suddenly they were joined by an amazing woman of about sixty. Squat, with a discernible black moustache on her upper lip, she was wearing a hairnet, a red flannel nightgown, bedroom slippers, and looked, thought Helen, not unlike President Nixon in drag.

'Hullo, boys,' she said in her deep voice. 'If we don't get something to eat soon, you'll have to carry me home.' She was just about to move on when she caught sight of Helen, gave her the most enthusiastic eye-meet she'd received all evening and joined the group.

'Who's that?' whispered Helen, holding out her glass to a passing waitress.

'Monica Carlton,' whispered Humpty. 'Law unto herself, breeds Welsh cobs, always comes to parties in her nightgown, then can get absolutely plastered and doesn't have the hassle of undressing when she gets back to her caravan.'

'While that waitress is here, she might as well fill me up too,' said Miss Carlton, thrusting her glass at Humpty. 'You look familiar,' she added to Joanna Battie.

'We met at Olympia last Christmas,' said Joanna. 'I write for the *Chronicle*.'

'Dreadful rag,' boomed Miss Carlton, retrieving her full glass. 'Still, it comes in useful for wiping up puppies' widdle.'

Helen giggled. Scenting enthusiasm, Miss Carlton turned towards her. 'You're a lovely little thing,' she went on. 'We certainly haven't met. I'd have remembered you.' She looked Helen up and down approvingly. 'Don't belong to any of these boring little farts, do you? Might have guessed it; too good for any of them.'

'I resent that,' said Humpty. 'The amount of times I've given you a fireman's lift home after parties, Monica.'

'Well, perhaps you're better than some. Now, where are you from, my beauty?' she said, turning her full attention on Helen. 'Are you going to be here tomorrow?'

'I don't know,' stammered Helen.

'Well, if you are, I'll take you for a spin round the countryside in my trap. You'd enjoy that. My two chaps travel at a spanking pace.'

And she was off, describing the merits of her two cobs who, it seemed, had won prizes at every show in England. As she talked, her eyes wandered over Helen's body and the hand not clutching a glass squeezed Helen's waist on every possible opportunity. Around them, Helen was vaguely aware of all the show-jumpers creasing themselves with laughter. None of them was prepared to rescue her.

'Everyone all right?' It was Grania flitting past.

'Just admiring your antiques,' called out Helen desperately. 'I'm a real Chippendale freak.'

'Oh, you Americans are always mad about old things; you *must* meet my husband. I see you've already met naughty Monica.' She patted Miss Carlton's bristly cheek. 'Grub's up downstairs, by the way.'

'Thank God for that,' said Humpty. 'I'm starving. Come on everyone.'

Rupert caught up with her just as she was entering the dining room. 'All right, darling? Sorry to neglect you; I'm in the process of selling a horse.'

'I'm fine,' said Helen, hardly able to trust herself to speak. 'Just fine.'

'You must be starving. I'll get you a plate.'

But the next moment he'd been lassooed by a large woman in red, asking him what had happened to some horse she'd sold him last year. Next minute the crowds had closed around him. Turning around, Helen saw Miss Carlton bearing down on her with two huge plates of chicken and rice. 'Coo-ee,' she shouted.

Desperately, Helen fled in the other direction where she could see Billy and Mavis and Lavinia sharing another armchair. She'd just have to play gooseberry.

'Please,' she rushed up to them, 'can I talk with you? Rupert's with some woman, and Miss Carlton's on the warpath.'

'Of course.' Billy got to this feet. 'You haven't met

Lavinia, have you? Are you having an awful party?'

'I haven't seen much of Rupert,' she said, trying to keep the bitterness out of her voice.

'I know. I'm sorry. He's still haggling with Dick Brandon and it's the first real show of the season. No one's seen each other all together for ages, if you know what I mean. They've got a lot to catch up on.'

'Oh, Billy, darling,' said Lavinia, 'I've forgotten to put any Fwench dwessing on my lettuce. Can you get me some, and do see if there's any more of that delicious garlic bwead.'

For a second Helen's eyes met Billy's, but both of them managed not to giggle.

'Well, if Monica comes up, you must protect Helen.'

'He's weally nice, isn't he?' said Lavinia dreamily. 'Mummy doesn't approve because he's such a fwiend of Wupert's. Not but what Wupert isn't very attwactive,' she added hastily, 'but Mummy thinks Wupert leads Billy astway. Is this your first date with him?'

'No,' said Helen, finding herself chewing and chewing on the same piece of chicken, 'my second.'

'Goodness,' said Lavinia, her china blue eyes widening, 'that must be a wecord.'

Billy came back and they were joined by Humpty and Ivor Braine with a bottle of red.

'I say, Helen,' said Humpty, going rather pink, 'you certainly made a hit with Monica.'

'Oh dear,' said Helen, blushing.

'Thinks you're the prettiest filly she's seen in years,' said Ivor and roared with laughter. 'Going to take you in her trap tomorrow, she says.'

'Well, don't get twapped in her twap,' said Lavinia. 'She chased me round the tackwoom once.'

'Better watch out. She breeds her own Welsh cobs; they say she doesn't even need a stallion,' said Billy.

'Well at least she's better than Driffield,' grumbled Ivor. 'Since he's given up booze he's got so bad-tempered.'

'The big fairy,' said Humpty. 'Let's chuck him in the lake after dinner.'

167

Next moment Hans joined them carrying a plate of trifle.

'Mind my dog,' said Billy, as the German prepared to sit heavily on the sleeping Mavis.

Hans rolled his eyes in the air. 'Always zee same, zee English, zee dog sleep in zee chair or zee bed, zee husband sleep on the floor. You are American, Fraulein Helen. Are zey not crazy people? Why not come back to Germany wiz me?'

'I say, Hans off,' said Humpty. 'You'll have to fight a duel with Monica.'

'You might also have Rupert to contend with,' said Billy, giving Mavis the rest of his chicken.

'No, Rupert is no problem. I can beat him any day of zee week, how do you say it, against zee cock? But Monica, she is different proposition, she is Superman. If Monica stake a claim, I can only love you from afar.'

Helen felt suddenly happy. She hadn't been a flop after all. In their clumsy way they were paying her attention, accepting her, ragging her as they ragged each other.

'Oh blast,' said Lavinia, 'here come Mummy and Daddy. They've been talking to Malise an awfully long time. Talk to me like mad, Helen. And, Billy, you turn away and talk like mad to Humpty and Hans and Geoff. Then perhaps they won't suspct anything. Where did you get that lovely dwess, Helen?'

'Bus Stop,' said Helen. 'My mother doesn't really approve of me wearing black.'

'Nor mine,' said Lavinia. 'If you're here tomowwow you must come and have a cup of tea in our cawavan. It's not gwand like Wupert's."

Once again, Helen felt overwhelmed with pleasure, particularly when Driffield suddenly brought her a plate of fruit salad.

'This moment must go down in history,' said Humpty. 'It is the first time Driffield has ever done anything for anyone else in his life. Where's Joanna? She must put it in the *Chronicle*.'

'Are you feeling all right, Driffield?' said Billy.

'He's dwunk too much tomato juice,' said Lavinia.

Driffield went scarlet and looked irritated and pleased at the same time. They were all laughing. Then Helen looked across the room and her happiness evaporated. There was Rupert standing by the sofa signing autographs for some girl and still talking to Dick Brandon, who was sitting down. Beside Brandon sat Grania talking to another woman. Helen watched frozen as she saw Grania slide her hand up and down the inside of Rupert's thigh, those beautiful brown muscular thighs she'd seen earlier. Rupert did not move. Grania carried on. Leaping to her feet and spilling the fruit salad mostly over the carpet and Mavis, Helen fled from the room.

'Darling!' yelled Rupert as she passed. He caught up with her in the hall.

'Where are you off to?' Then, seeing her stricken face, 'What's the matter?' and, taking her hand, he pulled her into a nearby room which turned out to be an office with desks and ledgers and a calendar of spiky-legged race horses on the wall.

Rupert leant against the door.

'Now, what's the matter? I thought you were having a good time.'

Helen backed away until she found herself sitting in a wire basket.

'I'm fed up with all these people treating you like public property,' she said.

Rupert shrugged. 'Come back to the caravan now and I promise you my undivided attention until morning.'

'Like hell! In five minutes someone'll be banging on the door trying to sell you a horse, or asking for your autograph for their great aunt.'

Rupert laughed. 'Temper, temper. I'm sorry about all these people.'

'It was positively obscene, all those women hanging round you like wasps round a molasses tin.'

Rupert felt a surge of triumph. It had worked. She really was jealous.

169

'I'm fed up with them all. Gabriella, and Bianca, and that obnoxious Joanna,' she emphasized all the 'a's, 'and Marion looking daggers at me all afternoon, and worst of all Grania; if she's a Lady, I'm the Queen of Sheba.'

'Don't be silly. No one ever suggested she was. Her father made his fortune flogging laxatives. Do you honestly think I fancy her? She's like some geriatric canary.'

'You didn't think so two minutes ago when she was running her hand up and down your thigh like an adrenalized tarantula.'

'I was hemmed in. Autograph hunter to the right, prospective buyer to the left, I couldn't just prise her off. It might have distracted Dick Brandon. Do you realize I've just made twenty grand?'

'Bully for you; you've also just lost a girlfriend.'

He put his head on one side and grinned at her.

'A girlfriend, have I just?' he said mockingly. Then his voice softened. 'Don't be such a crosspatch,' and he came towards her, pinning her against the table so she couldn't escape.

'Now *you're* hemmed in, and don't you like it?' he said, drawing her towards him until he was holding her tight against his body, which was so smooth and hard it seemed to curve into hers like expensive soap.

For a second she melted, her longing for him was so strong, her relief to be in his arms. Gently he pulled down the shoulder of her dress and began to kiss her along her collar bone.

The other hand glided over her bottom: 'Chicken, you *are* wearing pants.'

'I am not, I'm wearing a dress.'

'What's this then?' he pinged the elastic.

'Panties,' said Helen quickly.

Rupert sighed. 'There is a language barrier,' he said.

Helen suddenly twigged. 'You thought I'd go to a party without panties?' she said in a shocked voice.

'I hoped you might, seeing as how you're going to take off

170

all your clothes for me later this evening.'

'No,' said Helen, struggling away. 'I'm not going to be another of your fancy bits, just to be spat out like chewing gum when the flavour's gone.'

Rupert started to laugh. 'Fancy bit, what an extraordinary phrase. Sounds like a gag snaffle. And I don't like chewing gum very much. Nanny always said it was common.'

'Why do you trivialize everything?' wailed Helen. 'I just don't want to be rushed.'

'Oh really,' drawled Rupert. 'Would you rather we made a date for the year 2000? Would January 5th be O.K., or would the 6th suit you better? I'm afraid I can't make the 7th. Perhaps you could check in your diary.'

'Oh, stop it. I just don't believe in jumping into bed with people who don't give a damn for me.'

'You haven't given me much chance. You can hardly expect me to swear eternal devotion on the second date.'

'I don't,' sobbed Helen, 'I truly don't. I just don't want to get hurt again. Harold Mountjoy . . .'

'Oh dear, now we're going to be subjected to another sermon on the Mountjoy. Is that it? You only go to bed with married men? If I get married to someone else, then can I fuck you?'

'Please don't use that kind of language.'

'What's wrong with the word fuck? That's what we're discussing, aren't we? Stop being so bloody middle-class.'

'I am middle-class.'

'Personally I think prick-teaser is a much worse word than fuck. Why the hell did you come down here, then?'

'I wanted to see you.'

'You can, all of me. Come back to the caravan.'

'No!' screamed Helen. 'I'm going back to London.'

'How?' asked Rupert.

'Where's the nearest railroad station?'

'About ten miles away. And, frankly, I'm not going to drive you. Nor am I going to lend you one of my horses, although I suppose you could borrow a bike from one of

Grania's children. Or perhaps Monica could whizz you home in her trap.'

Helen burst into tears. Running to the door, she went slap into Grania Pringle.

'Oh, there you are, darling. I've been looking for you everywhere, Rupert. Can I borrow you for a sec?'

Helen gave a sob and fled down the passage. She locked herself in the john. Twice someone came and rattled the door, then went away again. The party was still roaring away downstairs and, from the shouts and catcalls, seemed to be spilling out into the garden. Feeling suicidal, she washed her face and combed her hair.

Creeping out into the passage she saw the huge red nightgowned back of Monica Carlton. She was talking to Mrs Greenslade. Terrified, Helen shot into reverse, taking the nearest door on her left.

Helen pushed open the door and found herself in a library where the only gaps in the walls not covered with books were filled with vast family portraits. In one corner on a revolving stand stood a globe of the world with the map of America turned towards her, the states all blurred together and sepia with age. A fire leaping in the grate gave off a sweet, tart smell of apple logs, reminding her of her grandmother's house in the mountains, and filling her with such homesickness that she had to choke back her sobs and blow her nose several times on an overworked paper handkerchief.

Drawn instinctively towards the bookshelves, she was half-way across the room before she realized a man was sitting in an armchair in front of the fire, reading.

'I am sorry,' she said with a gulp. 'I didn't mean to disturb you.'

'You're not. I'm hiding.'

'From Mrs Greenslade?'

'Et alia. We weren't introduced this afternoon. Malise Gordon.'

He put out his hand.

'Helen Macaulay,' she mumbled.

'Sit down. I'll get you a glass of Algie's brandy.'

'Please don't bother.'

He didn't answer and went over to the drinks trolley. He was wearing a pinstripe suit, thread-bare but well-cut across the shoulders, with turn-ups and a fob watch. She noticed the upright, military bearing, the thin mouth, the eyes, courtesy of British Steel Corporation. He was the kind of Englishman one used to see in old war movies, Trevor Howard or Michael Redgrave, who hid any emotion behind a clipped voice, a stiff upper lip and *sang froid*.

'What were you reading?' she asked.

'Rupert Brooke.'

'Oh,' said Helen in surprise, 'how lovely. There's one Rupert Brooke poem I really love. How does it go?

"These laid the world away",' she began in her soft voice, ' "poured out the red
Sweet wine of youth; gave up the years to be
Of work and joy, and that unhoped serene,
That men call age; and those who would have been
Their sons, they gave, their immortality." '

Her voice broke as she was suddenly stabbed with grief at the thought of Harold Mountjoy's child that she had lost.

'It's so beautiful, and so sad,' she went on.

For a second the colour seemed to drain out of Malise Gordon's face. Then he handed Helen the glass of brandy.

'How extraordinary,' he said. 'I was just reading that poem. My father was at school with Rupert Brooke.'

'What was he like?'

'Oh, awfully nice, according to my mother.'

'Your father must have some marvellous stories about him.'

'Probably did. Unfortunately he was killed in 1918 in the last advance of the war.'

'That's just terrible. You never knew your father. Did you go to Rugby too?'

He nodded.

'I so enjoy the Rugby poets.' said Helen. 'Walter Savage Landor, Clough, Arnold, they have a deep melancholy about them which I find very appealing. I did the Victorian poets for my Major. I think Matthew Arnold is by far the most interesting.'

Seeing her curled up on the sofa, having kicked off her shoes, the firelight flickering on her pale face, Malise thought she was the most beautiful girl he had ever seen. Her ankles were so slender, he wondered how they could

174

bear the weight of her body, or her long slender neck the weight of that glorious Titian hair. Quivering with misery, she was like a beech leaf suddenly blown by the gale against a wall; he had the feeling that, at any moment, the gale might whisk her away again. He would like to have painted her, just like that, against the faded gold sofa.

'Where is Rupert?' he asked.

'Being enjoyed by his adoring public. Actually, he's just been "borrowed" by Lady Pringle.'

'She's never been very scrupulous about giving people back.'

'She's kinda glamorous, but very old,' said Helen. Then, realizing that Grania must be younger than Malise Gordon, added hastily, 'for a woman, I mean – or rather a Lady.'

'Hardly,' said Malise, echoing Rupert.

'Oh, I know about the laxatives,' said Helen, 'but all these ancestors?' She waved a hand round the walls.

'All fakes,' said Malise, cutting the end off a cigar. 'I restore pictures as a sideline. Grania's great-grandmother over there,' he pointed to a bosomy Victorian lady, 'was actually painted in 1963.'

Helen giggled, feeling more cheerful.

'You and Rupert just had a row?'

Helen nodded.

'What about?'

'He wants to go to the max.'

Malise raised his eyebrows.

'In England I think you call it the whole hog.'

'Ah, yes.'

'He's so arrogant. He ignores me all evening, selling some horse, then expects me to go meekly back and spend the night in his caravan. I said I was going back to London, so he told me to find my own way. I just don't know what to do.'

'I'll take you. I'm going back to London tonight.'

'But I live in Shepherd's Bush; it's way out. Rupert claims he's never heard of it.'

175

'Rupert on occasions can be very affected. It's about a mile from my flat. It couldn't be easier to drop you off.'

Cutting through her stammerings of gratitude, he started to ask her about herself, about America, her family, her university, her ambitions to be a writer and her job. He even knew her boss.

'Nice chap. Never read a book in his life.'

'But no one seems interested in books over here,' sighed Helen, picking up the Rupert Brooke. 'This is a first edition and they haven't even bothered to cut the pages. I don't understand the British, I mean they have all this marvellous culture on their doorsteps and they're quite indifferent to it. Half the office hasn't even been inside St Paul's, and John Donne actually preached there. Rupert's mother has shelves full of first editions. No one ever reads them. She keeps them behind bars, as though they were dangerous animals full of subversive ideas. They never even know who's painted their ancestors.'

'Unless it's a Gainsborough they're going to flog at Christies for half a million,' said Malise. 'Then they're fairly sharp.'

'That lot out there can't talk about anything but horses,' said Helen bitterly.

'You mustn't blame them,' said Malise. 'For most of the season, which goes on sadly for most of the year now, they're spending 24 hours a day with those horses, studying them, schooling, worrying about their health, chauffeuring them from one show to another. That lot you met next door have battled their way to the top against the fiercest competition. And it hasn't been easy. We're in the middle of a recession; petrol prices are rocketing; overheads are colossal. Show-jumping's a very tough competitive sport and only a few make it, and unless they keep on winning, they don't survive.'

He got up and walked over to the globe and spun it round, pointing to the tiny faded pink shrimp that was England.

'Most of them would never have left the villages they

176

were born in if they hadn't been brilliant horsemen. Now, as a result of this brilliance, they are kings to the public, household names, ambassadors to their country all over the world. Rome today, Madrid tomorrow, New York the day after, constantly on television; yet most of them haven't an "O" level between them.

'Often you'll hear the winner of a competition gabbling to his horses all the way round, coaxing him over those huge jumps. Yet, ask him to describe that round in a television interview afterwards and he'll be completely tongue-tied. They're physical people, and they think in physical terms, and they're far more at home with horses than they are with humans, and they distrust anyone with any kind of learning, because it makes them feel inadequate. But don't underestimate them. Because they lack the gift of tongues, it doesn't mean they don't feel things deeply.'

He paused, frowning at her, then smiled.

'I'm sorry, I didn't mean to lecture you. I know what you've been going through today. Ever since I was appointed Chef d'Equipe last year I've been trying to break down these barriers of suspicion. You simply can't apply Army discipline and expect them to jump into line. They are all deeply individualistic, chippy, very highly strung. Despite their deadpan exteriors, they get terribly het up before a big class. But once they accept you, you're in for keeps unless you do something very silly.'

He thought it was time to change the subject. 'Is your firm publishing any decent books this summer?'

And they went back to talking about literature, which Malise enjoyed because she was so adorably pompous and earnest, and because he could see how she was relaxing and gaining confidence, and just watching that exquisite face gave him pleasure. He was tempted to ask her to sit for him.

'I wish I could meet someone like Rupert Brooke,' she was saying. 'I guess he can be regarded as the most charismatic personality of his generation.'

Malise Gordon winced and put another log on the fire. 'I wish *your* generation wouldn't so wilfully misuse words.'

177

Helen laughed. 'I guess then that Rupert was the most glamorous character of his generation.'

'Taking my name in vain,' said a voice. Rupert was standing in the doorway, his face quite expressionless.

'No,' said Malise Gordon. 'We were discussing another Rupert – a poet.'

'Quite unlike me,' said Rupert lightly. 'Helen knows I'm an intellectual dolt, don't you darling?' He turned to Helen, still smiling, but she knew beneath that bland exterior he was angry. 'I wondered where you'd got to.'

'Talking to me, since Grania – er – borrowed you.'

'How nice,' said Rupert. 'So no doubt you've discussed every exhibition and play and foreign film on in London. Perhaps you've even graduated to Henry James.'

'We hadn't got round to him yet,' said Malise.

'That'll have to wait till next time,' said Rupert. 'Come and dance,' he added to Helen. It was definitely an order. But before she could move, a sound of screams, whoops and catcalls rent the air, drowning the deafening pounding of music. The noise was coming from outside. Malise drew back the heavy dark green velvet curtains. A group of men were running through the moonlit cherry orchard carrying something that was wriggling frantically, like a sheep about to be dipped.

'They're throwing Driffield in the lake,' said Rupert.

'Isn't that lake polluted?' asked Helen in worried tones.

Rupert laughed. 'It soon will be, if they throw Driffield in.' He took Helen's wrist. 'Come on, darling.'

Malise took his watch out of his waistcoat pocket.

'We ought to head for home,' he said.

'*We?*' asked Rupert, his fingers tightening on Helen's wrist. Then she said, all in a rush,

'Colonel Gordon's going back to London tonight. He's very kindly offered me a lift.'

'That's ridiculous.'

'There isn't anywhere for me to sleep.'

'Grania'll give you a bed. Party's hardly got going yet.'

'Events would bely that,' said Malise, as bellows,

178

guffaws and sounds of splashing issued from the lake. 'I hope Driffield doesn't catch cold. It's hardly the weather for midnight bathing. As for Grania putting Helen up, I'm sure every bed and sofa in the house is already heaving with occupants. Shall we go?' he turned to Helen.

She nodded, unable to speak. Part of her longed to stay with Rupert. She'd never seen anyone so angry. His blue eyes narrowed to slits, his face pale as marble. He picked a white narcissus out of the flower vase, examining the crinkly orange centre.

'I'll drive you back to Vagina House,' he said.

'Don't be silly,' said Malise crushingly, 'you've got classes early tomorrow and you've had far too much to drink. Police always patrol the Worthing–London road at this hour of night. Not worth risking your licence. You can't afford to be off the road for a year.'

'I am quite capable of driving,' said Rupert through gritted teeth.

'And then you'd have to turn round and drive all the way back. Be reasonable.'

Rupert turned to Helen. 'You really want to go?'

'I guess so.'

Looking down, Rupert found he had shredded the narcissus. One petal was left. 'She loves me not,' he said.

'I'll get my coat,' said Helen.

Fleeing from the room, she nearly fell over Monica Carlton, fast asleep in her red nightgown, propped against the gong. On her lap lay a plate of chocolate mousse which Mavis was busy finishing up.

In the room where she'd left her coat and boots a couple were heaving on the bed.

'Billy, we must be careful,' said a voice. 'Mummy will be fuwious if she catches us.'

Billy was going to win his tenner, thought Helen. As she grabbed her belongings and let herself out of the room, Mavis shot through her feet to join in the fun.

Outside she found Hans Schmidt swaying in front of her.

'Fraulein Helen,' he said triumphantly, 'come and dance

179

wiz me.' He was just about to drag her off in the direction of the music when Malise and Rupert came out of the library, both looking wintry. To make matters worse, Hans insisted on coming out to the car with them and roaring with laughter when he discovered what was going on.

'You are losing zee touch, Rupert,' he kept saying.

'Fuck off,' snarled Rupert. Then, as Helen got into the car, 'Your things are still in the caravan.'

'Only my suede dress,' said Helen.

'I'll get Marion to post it on to you,' said Rupert and, without even saying goodbye, turned on his heel and stalked back into the house.

'There's absolutely no need to cry,' said Malise, as the headlights lit up the grass verge and the pale green undersides of the spring trees. 'That's definitely thirty-love to you.'

'D'you think he'll ever call me again?' said Helen with a sniff.

' 'Course he will. It's a completely new experience to Rupert, not getting his own way. Very good for him.'

Malise slipped a Beethoven quintet into the stereo. Helen lay back, revelling in the music and thinking how much Rupert would hate it. Ahead along the winding road she watched the cats' eyes light up as their car approached.

'All right?' said Malise.

'Sure. I was thinking the cats' eyes were like girls, all lighting up as Rupert approached.'

'And Rupert never dims his headlights,' said Malise.

'Is it worth it? Me going on with him, that is if he does ring me?'

'Depends if you've reached the stage when you can't not. In which case any advice I give you will be meaningless.'

'Explain him to me,' pleaded Helen. 'All I hear is gossip from people who hardly know him.'

'I've known his family for years. Rupert's mother was exquisitely beautiful but deeply silly. She couldn't cope with Rupert at all and abandoned him to a series of nannies, who all spoilt him because they were frightened of him, or felt sorry for him. He learnt far too early in life that, by making himself unpleasant, he could get his own way. The only decent relationship he had was with old Nanny Heald, and she was his father's old nanny, so she didn't look after Rupert very long. Rupert's mother, of course, was besotted with Adrian, Rupert's younger brother, who was sweet, curly-haired, plump, easy going, and who, of course, has turned into a roaring pansy.

'As a result I don't think Rupert really likes women. He certainly doesn't trust them. Subconsciously, I think he enjoys kicking them in the teeth, just to pay them back as a sex for letting him down when he was a child. He's bright, though, and enormously talented. Funnily enough, the one thing that might save him could be a good marriage. But she'd have to be a very remarkable girl to take the flak.'

As they reached the motorway, he put his foot on the accelerator.

'Wouldn't it be easier,' he said, 'to find a respectably rising barrister or some bright young publisher?'

Helen shrugged. 'I guess so, but he is kind of addictive. You take a lot of trouble with all these guys. Have you got kids of your own?'

'We've got a daughter. She events.'

'Oh,' said Helen, 'that's what Mark Phillips does, as opposed to Rupert.'

'That's right.'

'Any sons?'

'No.' There was a pause. Then he said in a measured, deliberately matter-of-fact voice. 'We had a boy. He was killed in Northern Ireland last year.'

'Oh,' said Helen, aghast, 'I'm desperately sorry.'

'He drove into a booby trap, killed outright, which I suppose was a mercy.'

'But not for you,' said Helen. 'You weren't able to say goodbye.'

'Oh hell,' she said to herself, 'that's why he was reading that Rupert Brooke poem. And I came barging in with all my problems.'

'Were you very close?' she asked.

'Yes, I think so. The awful thing was that I'm not sure he really wanted to go into the Army at all. Just felt he ought to because my father had a dazzling war and . . .'

'And you got an MC, Billy told me.'

'But Timmie was really rather a rebel. We had an awful row. He'd got some waitress pregnant, felt he ought to marry her. He didn't love her, he just had principles. We tried to dissuade him. His last leave was all rows, my wife in hysterics.'

'What happened to the baby?'

'It was a false alarm, which made the whole thing more ironic. Now I wish it hadn't been. At least we'd have something of him left.'

They had reached London now. When they got to Regina House he got out as well. A few stars had managed to pierce the russet haze hanging over London. Lit from behind by the street light, there were no lines on his face.

Helen swallowed, took a deep breath to conquer her shyness and stammered, 'I always dreamed English men would be just like you, and it's taken me six months in this country to find one,' and, putting her hand on his shoulder, she kissed him quickly on the cheek. 'Thank you so much for my lift. I do hope we meet again.'

'Absolutely no doubt about that,' said Malise. 'Young Rupert'll be on the warpath in no time. But listen to an old campaigner: play it cool, don't let him have it all his own way.'

Malise let himself into his Lowndes Street flat and switched off the burglar alarm. It was a cheerless place. His wife had conventional tastes, tending to eau de nil wallpaper, overhead lights, and Sloane Square chintz. She was away in the country, eventing with their daughter. The marriage had not been a success. They had stayed together because of the children, but now there was only Henrietta left. In the drawing room, on an easel standing on a dust sheet, was an oil painting of a hunting scene Malise was restoring. He could finish it in two hours. He didn't feel tired. Instead, he poured himself a glass of brandy and set to work, thinking about that exquisite redhead. She was wasted on Rupert. He was not entirely sure of his motives in whisking her back to London. Was it a desire to put Rupert down, or because he couldn't bear the thought of Rupert sleeping with her tonight, forcing his drunken hamfisted attentions on her? For a minute he imagined painting her in his studio, not bothering to turn on the lights as dusk fell, then taking her across to the narrow bed in the corner and making love to her so slowly and gently she wouldn't realize it had been miraculous until it was all over.

He cursed himself for being a fool. He was fifty-two, thirty years her senior, probably a disgusting old man in her eyes. Yet she had stirred him more than any woman he had met for years.

She'd have done for Timmie. He picked up the photograph on the piano. The features that smiled back at him were very like his own, but less grim and austere, more clear-eyed and trusting.

Were Rupert and Billy and Humpty merely Timmie substitutes? Was that why he'd taken the job of Chef d'Equipe? After six months he was surprised, almost indignant, at the pain. Putting the photograph down, he slumped on the sofa, his face in his hands.

As Helen let herself into Regina House the telephone was ringing. 'Shush, shush,' she pleaded, and, rushing forward, reached the receiver just before the Principal of the hostel, furious and bristling in her hair net.

'It's one o'clock in the morning,' she hissed, 'I won't have people ringing so late.'

But Helen ignored her, hunching herself over the telephone to ward off the outside world. Praying as she'd never prayed before, she put it to her ear.

'Hullo,' said a slightly slurred voice, 'can I speak to Helen Macaulay?'

'Oh yes, you can, this is she.'

'Bloody bitch,' said Rupert, 'waltzing off with the one man in the room I can't afford to punch on the nose.'

Helen leant joyously against the wall, oblivious of the gesticulating crone in the hair net.

'Are you O.K.?' Rupert went on.

'Fine. Where are you?'

'Back in my horrible little caravan – alone. I've got your dress here, like a shed snake-skin. It reeks of your scent. I wish you were here to fill it.'

'Oh, so do I,' said Helen. Again at a distance, she felt free to come on more strongly.

'Look, I'm on the road this week and most of next. I haven't really got myself together, but I'll ring you towards the end of the week, and I'll try and get up to London on Monday or Tuesday week.'

'Rupert,' she pleaded, 'I didn't want to go off with Malise. It was just that you seemed so otherwise engaged all evening.'

'Trying to make you jealous didn't work, did it? Won't try that again in a hurry.'

13

For the next few weeks Rupert laid siege to Helen, throwing her into total confusion. On the one hand he epitomized everything she disapproved of. He was flip – except about winning – spoilt, philistine, hedonistic, immoral, and very right-wing – eating South African oranges just to irritate her, *and* in the street, which her mother had drummed into her one must *never* do. The few dates they were able to snatch in between Rupert's punishing show jumping schedule and Helen's job always ended in rows because she wouldn't sleep with him.

On the other hand she had very much taken to heart Malise's remarks about Rupert's disturbed childhood and the possibility that he might be redeemed by a good marriage. Could she be the one to transform this wild boy into the greatest show jumper of his age? There was a strong element of reforming zeal in Helen's character; she had a great urge to do good.

Princess Anne had also just announced her engagement to Mark Phillips and every girl in England was in love with the handsome captain, who looked so macho in his uniform and who, despite being pretty unforthcoming when interviewed on television, was obviously a genius with horses. Princess Anne looked blissfully happy. And when one considered Rupert was just as beautiful as Captain Phillips, and extremely articulate when interviewed about anything, did it matter, pondered Helen as she tossed and turned in her narrow bed in Regina House, reading A E Housman and Matthew Arnold, that she and Rupert couldn't talk about Sartre and Henry James? He was young. He could learn. Malise said he was bright.

Anyway, all this fretting was academic because Rupert hadn't mentioned marriage or said that he loved her. But he rang her from all over Europe and managed to snatch an evening, however embattled, with her about once a fortnight, and he had invited her to fly out to Lucerne for a big show at the beginning of June, so she had plenty of hope to sustain her.

Meanwhile the IRA were very active in London, exploding bombs; everyone was very jumpy, and her mother wrote her endless letters, saying that she need no longer stay in England a year, that things sounded very hazardous, and why didn't she come home. Helen, who would have leapt at the chance all through the winter, wrote back saying she was fine and that she had a new beau.

Rupert sat with his feet up on the balcony of his hotel bedroom overlooking the Bois de Boulogne. After a class at the Paris show that ended at midnight the previous night, he was eating a late breakfast. Wearing nothing but a bath-towel, his bare shoulders already turning dark brown, he was munching a croissant with apricot jam and trying to read *War and Peace*.

'I can't understand this bloody book,' he yelled back into the room. 'All the characters have three names.'

'So do you,' said Billy, coming out on to the balcony, dripping from the bath and also wrapped in a towel. He looked at the spine of the book. 'It might help if you started with Volume I, not Volume II.'

'Fucking hell,' said Rupert, throwing the book into the bosky depths of the Bois and endangering the lives of two squirrels, 'that's what comes of asking Marion to get out books from the library.'

'Why are you reading that junk anyway?'

Rupert poured himself another cup of coffee. 'Helen says I'm a philistine.'

'She thinks you're Jewish?' said Billy. 'You don't look it.'

'I thought it meant something to do with Sodom and

186

Gomorrah until I looked it up,' said Rupert, 'but it just means you're pig ignorant, deficient in culture and don't read enough.'

'You read *Horse and Hound*,' said Billy indignantly, 'and your horoscope and the racing results, and Dick Francis.'

'Or go to the the-*at*re, as she calls it.'

'I should think not after that rubbish she dragged us to the other night. Anyway, you went to a strip club in Hamburg last week. I've heard people call you a lot of things, but not stupid.'

He bent down to pick up his hairbrush which had dropped on the floor, and winced. 'I don't know what they put in those drinks last night but I feel like hell.'

'I feel like Helen,' said Rupert. 'I spent all last night trying to ring her up. I got hold of the London directory, but I couldn't find Vagina House anywhere.'

'Probably looked it up under "cunt",' said Billy.

Rupert laughed. Then a look of determination came over his face. 'I'll show her. I'll write her a really intellectual letter.' He got Helen's last letter, all ten pages of it, out of his wallet. 'I can hardly understand hers – it's so full of long words.' He smoothed out the first page. 'She hopes we take in the Comédie Française and the Louvre, and then says that just looking at me elevates her temperature. Christ, what have I landed myself with?'

'Don't forget to put "Ms" on the envelope,' said Billy.

'Marion even got me a book of quotations,' said Rupert, extracting a couple of sheets of hotel writing paper from the leather folder in the chest of drawers. 'Now, ought I to address her as Dear or Dearest?'

'You "Darling" her all the time when you're with her.'

'Don't want to compromise myself on paper.' Rupert picked up the quote book. 'I'll bloody outquote her. Let's look up Helen.' He ran his fingers down the Index. 'Helen, here we are, "I wish I knew where Helen lies", Not with me, unfortunately. "Sweet Helen make me immortal with a kiss." That's not going nearly far enough.'

'Are you going to buy Con O'Hara's chestnut?' asked

Billy, who was trying to cut the nails on his right hand.

'Not for the price he's asking. It's got a terrible stop. "Helen thy beauty is to me." That sounds more promising.' He flipped over the pages to find the reference. ' "Helen thy beauty is to me . . . Hyacinth hair." Hyacinths are pink and blue, not hair-coloured. Christ, these poets get away with murder.'

'Why don't you just say you're missing her?' asked Billy reasonably.

'That's what she wants to hear. If I could only bed her, I could forget about her.'

'Sensible girl,' said Billy, 'Knows if she gives in she'll lose you. Hardly blame her. You haven't exactly got a reputation for fidelity.'

'I have,' said Rupert, outraged. 'I was faithful to Bianca for at least two months.'

'While having Marion on the side.'

'Grooms don't count. They simply exist for the recreation of the rider. Helen's not even my type if you analyse her feature by feature. Her clothes are terrible. Like all American women, she always wears trousers, or pants, as she so delightfully calls them, two sizes too big.'

'Methinks the laddy does protest too much. Why don't you pack her in?'

'I'm buggered if I'll give up so easily. I've never not got anyone I really wanted.'

'What about that nun in Rome?' said Billy, who was lighting a cigarette.

'Nuns don't count.'

'Like grooms, I suppose.'

' "Sweet Helen, make me immortal with a kiss",' read Rupert. ' "Her lips suck forth my soul. Come, Helen, come, give me my soul again." '

'That's a bit strong,' said Billy. 'Who wrote that?'

'Chap called Marlowe. Anyway it's not my soul I want her to suck.'

Billy started to laugh and choked on his cigarette.

Rupert looked at him beadily. 'Honestly, William, I

don't know why you don't empty the entire packet of cigarettes on to a plate and eat them with a knife and fork. You ought to cut down.' He returned to the quote book. 'This bit's better: "Thou art fairer than the evening air, clad in the beauty of a thousand stars." That's very pretty. Reminds me of Penscombe on a clear night.' He wrote it down in his flamboyant royal blue scrawl, practically taking up half the page.

'That'll wow her. Anyway, I should be able to pull her in Lucerne. She's coming out for a whole week.'

'D'you know what I think?' said Billy.

'Not until you tell me.'

'Unlike most of the girls you've run around with, Helen's serious. She's absolutely crazy about you, genuinely in love, and she won't sleep with you not because she wants to trap you, but because she believes it's wrong. She's a middle-class American girl and they're very very respectable.'

'You reckon she's crazy about me?'

'I reckon. Christ, Rupe, you're actually blushing.'

Rupert soon recovered.

'What are we going to do this evening?' he asked.

'Go to bed early and no booze, according to Malise. We've got a Nations' Cup tomorrow.'

'Sod that,' said Rupert, putting his letter into an envelope. 'There's a stunning girl who's come out from *The Tatler* to cover the – er – social side of show-jumping. I would *not* mind covering her. I thought we could show her Paris.'

'Sure,' sighed Billy, 'and she's brought a dog of a female photographer with her, and guess who'll end up with her? I wish to Christ Malise would pick Lavinia for Lucerne.'

'Not while he's imposing all this Kraut discipline and trying to keep his squad pure, he won't,' said Rupert. He looked at his watch. 'We've got three hours.'

'I'm going to give The Bull a work out.'

'Tracey can do that. Let's go and spend an hour at the Louvre.'

After a couple of good classes in which they were both placed, Rupert and Billy felt like celebrating. Pretending to go to bed dutifully at eleven o'clock, they waited half an hour, then crept out down the back stairs, aided by a chambermaid. It was unfortunate that Malise, getting up very early to explore Paris, caught Rupert coming out of the *Tatler* girl's bedroom.

In the Nations' Cup later in the day Rupert jumped appallingly and had over twenty faults in each round. In the evening Malise called him to his room and gave him the worst dressing-down of his life. Rupert was irresponsible, insubordinate, undisciplined, a disruptive influence on the team and a disgrace to his country.

'And what's more,' thundered Malise, 'I'm not having you back in the team until you've learnt to behave yourself.'

Helen sat in the London Library checking the quotations in a manuscript on Disraeli before sending it to press. Goodness, authors are inaccurate! This one got everything wrong: changing words, leaving out huge chunks, paraphrasing long paragraphs to suit his argument. All the same, she was glad to be out of the office. Nigel, having recently discovered she was going out with Rupert, made her life a misery, saying awful things about him all the time. In the middle of a heatwave, the London Library was one of the coolest places in the West End. Helen was always inspired, too, by the air of cloistered quiet and erudition. Those rows and rows of wonderful books, and the photographs of famous writers on the stairs: T. S. Eliot, Harold Nicolson, Rudyard Kipling. One day, if she persevered with her novel, she might join them.

Being a great writer, however, didn't seem nearly as important at the moment as seeing Rupert again. She hadn't heard from him for a fortnight, not a telephone call nor a letter. Next Monday she was supposed to be flying out to Lucerne to spend a week with him, and it was already Wednesday. She'd asked for the week off and she knew how Nigel would sneer if she suddenly announced she wouldn't be going after all. And if he did ring, and she did go, wasn't she compromising herself? Would she be able to hold him off in all that heady Swiss air? God, life was difficult. A bluebottle was bashing abortively against the window pane. At a nearby desk a horrible old man, sweating in a check wool suit, with eyebrows as big as moustaches, was leering at her. Suddenly she hated academics, beastly goaty things with inflated ideas of their own sex appeal, like Nigel and Paul, and even Harold Mountjoy. She wanted to get out and live her life; she was trapped like that bluebottle.

'Have you any books on copulation?' said a voice.

'I'm afraid I don't work here,' said Helen. Then she started violently, for there, tanned and gloriously un-academic, stood Rupert.

Her next thought was how unfair it was that he should have caught her with two-day-old hair, a shiny face and no make-up. The next moment she was in his arms.

'Angel,' he said, kissing her, 'did you get my letter?'

'No, I left before the post this morning.'

'Sssh,' said the man with moustache eyebrows disapprovingly. 'People are trying to work.'

'Are you coming out for a drink?' said Rupert, only slightly lowering his voice.

'I'd just love it. I've got one more quote to check. I'll be with you in ten minutes.'

'I'll wander round,' said Rupert.

Helen found the quotation, and was surreptitiously combing her hair and powdering her nose behind a pillar when she heard a loud and unmistakeable voice saying:

'Hullo, is that Ladbroke's'? My account number's 8KY85982. I want a tenner each way on Brass Monkey in the two o'clock at Kempton, and twenty each way on Bob Martin in the two-thirty. He's been scratched, has he? Change it to Sam the Spy then, but only a tenner each way.'

Crimson with embarrassment, Helen longed to disappear into one of the card index drawers. How dared Rupert disturb such a hallowed seat of learning?

'Funny places you work in,' he said, as they went out into

the sunshine. 'I bet Nige feels at home in there. Come on, let's go to the Ritz.'

They sat in the downstairs bar, Helen drinking Buck's Fizz, Rupert drinking whisky.

'Don't go and get tarted up,' he said, as she was about to rush off to the powder room. 'I like you without make-up sometimes. Reminds me of what you might look like in the mornings.' He ran the back of his fingers down her cheek. 'I've missed you.'

'And I've missed *you*. How was Paris?'

'Not brilliant.'

'I read the papers. Belgravia was off form.'

'Something like that. I bought you a present. They're all the rage in Paris.'

It was an ivory silk shirt that tied under the bust, leaving a bare midriff.

'Oh, it's just gorgeous,' said Helen. 'I'll just never take it off.'

'Hm, we'll see about that.'

'Such beautiful workmanship,' said Helen, examining it in ecstasy. 'It'll be marvellous for Lucerne. I've bought so many clothes. I do hope the weather's nice.'

Rupert's fingers drummed on the bar. He beckoned for the barman to fill up his glass.

'There isn't going to be any Lucerne.'

'Why ever not?' Helen was quite unable to hide her disappointment.

'I've been dropped,' said Rupert bleakly.

'For a couple of bad rounds in a Nations' Cup? That's insane. It wasn't your fault.'

'Well, it was actually. Malise told us to go to bed early. I never sleep before a Nations' Cup, so I took Billy out on the tiles. We got more smashed than we meant to. Next day, every double was a quadruple.'

'Oh, Rupert,' wailed Helen, 'how could you when you were jumping for Great Britain? Surely you could have gone to bed early one night? And to involve Billy. Malise must have been *so* disappointed.'

Rupert had expected sympathy, not reproach bordering on disapproval.

'Poor Malise, who's he going to put in your place?'

'I don't know, and I don't want to talk about it.'

Helen could see he was mad, but could not stop herself saying, 'I'm just so disappointed. I so wanted to go to Lucerne.'

'We'll go some other time. Look, I'm off to the Royal Plymouth tomorrow morning. It's an agricultural and flower show with only a couple of big show-jumping classes a day, so I shan't be over-occupied. Why don't you take the rest of the week off and come too?'

Helen was sorely tempted.

'When were you thinking of leaving?'

'Now. I want to avoid the rush-hour and I've got a lot to catch up on tonight after three weeks away.'

'I can't'.

'Why not?'

'I've got an editorial meeting at three o'clock, and I've got to get this manuscript off to the press by Friday. I was planning to have everything clear before Lucerne.'

'And I've screwed up your little jaunt. Well, I'm sorry.' He certainly didn't sound it. Helen warmed to her subject.

'And I do have some sort of responsibility towards my colleagues, unlike you. To go and get drunk before a Nations' Cup is just infantile. And Malise said you could be the finest rider in Britain if you took it a bit more seriously.'

'Did he indeed?' said Rupert, dangerously quietly. Draining his glass and getting a tenner out of his notecase, he handed it to the barman. 'Well, it's no bloody business of yours or his to discuss me.'

He got to his feet. Helen realized she'd gone too far.

'Malise and I only want what's best for you,' she stammered.

'Sweet of you both,' said Rupert. 'Have a nice meeting. It's high time you took up with Nige again. You two really suit each other.'

And he was gone.

Rupert returned to Penscombe at eight o'clock the following morning, just as Marion and Tracey were loading up the lorry for the four-hour drive down to Plymouth. He looked terrible and proceeded to complain bitterly about everything in the yard; then went inside to have a bath and emerged twenty minutes later looking very pale but quite under control.

'What's up with him?' said Tracey.

'Had a tiff with the flame-haired virgin, I should think,' said Marion.

Her suspicions were confirmed when Rupert started to quibble about the order in which the horses were being loaded.

'Who are you putting next to The Bull?'

'Macaulay. I thought it would settle him.'

'Don't call him that. I'm not having him named after that bitch any more. He can go back to being Satan. Suits him much better.'

With Billy driving, Rupert slept most of the way down to Plymouth. The showground was half a mile outside the town. It was a glorious day. Dazzling white little clouds scampered as gaily across a butcher-blue sky as boats with coloured sails danced on the sparkling aquamarine ocean. The horses, clattering down the ramp, sniffed the salty air appreciatively. Once in the caravan which Marion had driven down, Rupert poured himself a large measure of whisky.

'Tears before sunset,' said Marion to Tracey.

On their way to the Secretary's tent to declare, Billy was telling Rupert about Ivor Braine's latest ineptitude.

'He was popping out to the shops, and I asked him to get me a packet of Rothman's. I said "If you can't get Rothman's, get me anything", and he comes back with a bloody pork pie.'

Billy suddenly realized he had lost his audience. Glancing round, he noticed that very still, watchful, predatory expression on Rupert's face, like a leopard who's just sighted a plump impala. Following Rupert's gaze, he saw a suntanned blonde in a pale pink sleeveless dress. Probably in her mid-thirties, she was laying out green baize on a table.

'Gorgeous,' murmured Rupert.

'Married,' said Billy.

'Good,' said Rupert. 'I'm fed up with born-again virgins.'

The blonde looked up. She was really very pretty, Billy decided.

Rupert smiled at her. She smiled back, half-puzzled, assuming, because his face was so familiar, that they'd met before. On the way back from declaring they found her lugging a huge challenge cup out from the car. Other cups were already lined up on the table.

'Let me,' said Rupert, sprinting forward and seizing the cup.

'Oh,' she jumped, 'how very kind. Oh, it's you.' Suddenly, as she realized who Rupert was, she blushed crimson. 'I expect you'll win it later.'

'Hope so,' said Rupert, setting it on the green baize. Then he looked at the inscription. 'This one's actually for lightweight hunters. I'm certainly a hunter,' he shot her an appraising glance, 'when the prey's attractive enough. But not that lightweight.'

She seemed to think this was very funny. It was nice to have someone who laughed at his jokes.

'Shouldn't your husband be helping you unload this stuff?' He handed her another cup.

'He's away in Madrid. Some trouble over an order. He had to fly out this morning.'

Better and better, thought Rupert, running his eye over the outline of her round, tight buttocks, as she peered into the back of the car.

'Blast,' she said. 'I picked a big bunch of sweet peas for the table. I must have left them in the porch.'

'They might have slipped under the front seat,' said Rupert, affording himself another good view.

'No.' She emerged, flushed and ruffled. 'Oh, dear, and I

was going to tie them up with ribbon, as a bouquet for the Mayoress.'

'I'll drive back and pick them up for you.'

'You can't. It's awfully sweet of you, but it's twenty miles.'

Rupert patted her arm. 'Leave it with me. I'll find you a bouquet.'

He went back to the caravan and had another couple of stiff whiskies and then went on the prowl. He peered into the horticultural tent; it was dark and cool, and smelled like a greenhouse, the huge flower arrangements making a rainbow blaze of colour. Up at the far end he could see a group of judges poring over some marrows, handling them like vast Indian clubs.

It didn't take him long to find what he was looking for: a deeply scented bunch of huge, dark crimson roses, with a red first-prize card, and a championship card beside them. Without anyone noticing, he seized the roses and slid out of the tent. No one was about except a large woman in a pork pie hat giving her two Rotweillers a run.

Back at the caravan he put the roses in a pint mug.

'Where did you get those?' demanded Billy, who was pulling on his breeches.

'Never you mind.'

'Inconstant Spry,' said Billy, as Rupert arranged them, then poured himself another whisky.

'You better lay off that stuff,' warned Billy. 'And don't get carried away. We've got a class in three-quarters of an hour.'

'Here you are,' Rupert said to the pretty blonde.

'Oh, they're lovely,' she said. 'Ena Harkness, I think, and they smell out of this world. You didn't go and buy them?'

Rupert smirked non-committally.

'You did, and you've even beaten the stems so they won't wilt. I've got some ribbon in the glove compartment. I'll hide them in the shade for the moment. I must repay you. Come and have a drink after you've finished your class. My name's Laura Bridges, by the way.'

Rumour raced round the collecting ring as the riders warmed up their horses.

'I hear Rupert's been dropped,' Driffield said to Billy with some satisfaction.

'Is it twue Malise caught him in bed with a weporter from *The Tatler*?' giggled Lavinia. 'He is awful.'

'For Christ's sake, don't say anything to Rupe,' said Billy. 'He's not in the sunniest of moods.'

'What about that gorgeous redhead?' said Humpty. 'I wouldn't mind having a crack at her myself.'

'Nor would I,' said Driffield, 'but I gather she doesn't put out.'

'Shut up,' said Billy. 'Here he comes.'

As Rupert cantered up on Macaulay, scattering onlookers, Humpty said, 'That horse is new.'

'Where d'you get him?' sneered Driffield. 'At a pig fair?'

Everyone laughed, but the smiles were wiped off their faces half-way through the class when Rupert came in and jumped clear. He had reached that pitch of drunkenness when he rode brilliantly, total lack of inhibition giving an edge to his timing. He also made the discovery that Macaulay loved crowds. Used to the adulation of being a troop horse through the streets of London, he really caught fire and become a different animal once he got into the ring and heard applause.

'If you're going to be that good, perhaps it's unfair to call you Satan again,' Rupert said as he rode out, patting the horse delightedly.

Over the crowd he could see that the Mayoress had arrived and, surrounded by officials, was progressing towards Laura Bridges' green baize table, no doubt to receive her bouquet. Vaulting off Macaulay, he handed him to Marion and ran off to have a look.

Mr Harold Maynard, horticultural king of Plymouth, had won the rose championship at the Royal Show for the past five years. Going into the tent, confident he had swept the board for the sixth year, he was thunderstruck to find his prize exhibit missing. He was about to report the loss to the show secretary and get it paged over the loudspeaker, when he suddenly saw his lovingly-tended Ena Harkness roses, now done up with a scarlet bow, being handed over to the Mayoress by a curtseying Brownie.

'What very choice blooms,' said the Mayoress, who prided herself on being good with kiddies. 'I've never seen roses so lovely.'

With a bellow of rage, Mr Maynard pushed through the crowd and seized the roses.

'How dare you steal my Ena Harkness?' he shouted.

The Mayoress swelled. 'They've just been presented to me by this young lady.'

'And where did you get them from?' Mr Maynard turned furiously to the quailing Brownie.

'Mrs Bridges gave them to me,' she whispered.

'And who may she be?' roared Mr Maynard, brandishing the roses like a policeman's truncheon.

'I'm me,' said Laura Bridges, 'and don't shout at that poor child.'

Rupert arrived to find Laura Bridges, Harold Maynard, a number of Harold's horticultural chums from the allotments, several show officials and the Lady Mayoress in the middle of a full-dress row. The Brownie was bawling her head off.

'What's up?' he said.

'This lady's stolen my Ena Harkness,' bellowed Mr Maynard, glaring furiously at Laura Bridges.

Next minute, Rupert had grabbed him by his coat collar. 'Don't you speak to her like that, you revolting little shit. She did *not* steal them, and you bloody well apologize.'

'Those are my roses, and don't use foul language. I'm calling the police,' yelled Mr Maynard.

'You are bloody not,' said Rupert and, picking Mr Maynard up he hurled him backwards into the nearby horticultural and produce tent. A second later four of Mr Maynard's chums from the allotments had landed on

Rupert. Shaking them off, he dived into the tent after Mr Maynard, picking up a lemon meringue pie and smashing it in his red roaring face. Turning, Rupert started pelting Mr Maynard's cronies, who were trying to storm the tent in pursuit, with iced cakes. Next minute a Bakewell tart flew over their heads and hit the Mayoress slap in the face. Just as the allotment contingent were advancing on Rupert, menacingly brandishing huge marrows, reinforcements arrived in the form of Billy, Humpty, Ivor Braine and Driffield, who, picking up everything they could find, hurled them at Mr Maynard's chums. Carrots, turnips, cabbages, rhubarb pies and fairy cakes flew through the air.

'What the hell's going on?' Humpty asked Billy. 'We've got to jump off in a few minutes.'

The next minute a vast Black Forest gateau, hurled by Mr Maynard and meant for Rupert, hit Humpty in the middle of his forehead. Roaring like a little bull, rubbing cream out of his eyes, Humpty jumped on Mr Maynard, hammering him with his fists. Driffield, behind the safety of a long white table, was lobbing sponge cakes into the mêlée, stopping to take a bite from time to time. Three of the allotment chums had Billy on the ground now and were belabouring him with vast parsnips.

'Stop it, you wotten cowards,' screamed Lavinia Greenslade. 'Thwee against one isn't fair.' And, having kicked them all in the bum, she picked up a chair and bashed it over their heads.

Suddenly there was the wail of police cars.

'We better beat it,' said Humpty reluctantly.

'Come on,' said Driffield, stuffing pieces of shortcake into his pockets and running towards the tent opening. But they were too late, for the next minute the tent had filled with policemen. Slowly show-jumpers and horticulturalists picked themselves off the floor.

'Now, who started this fight?' said the Sergeant, getting out a notebook. 'Morning Mr Lloyd-Foxe, morning Mr Hamilton.'

For a minute no one said anything. Then, from the

corner, pulling himself up by the trestle table, Rupert staggered to his feet.

'I did, officer,' he said, weaving towards them. 'But *he* provoked me,' and picking up the last prize-winning fruit cake, he flung it at Mr Maynard. Unfortunately it missed, knocking off a policeman's helmet.

'Book him,' said the Sergeant.

'You can't,' said Humpty in tones of outrage, wiping chocolate icing out of his hair. 'He's got to jump off.'

A noisy argument ensued, only ended by the police threatening to book all the show-jumpers.

'You can't do that,' said the show Secretary in horror. 'The public have come specially to see them. They've got two more big classes after the jump off.'

'Well, I'm booking him,' said the Sergeant, slapping handcuffs on Rupert. 'Never heard such abusive language in my life.'

On the way out, Laura Bridges stopped him.

'I'm so sorry. It was all my fault.'

Rupert grinned. 'Don't give it a thought, sweetheart.'

'I'll get you out of there,' promised Billy.

'Not now,' said Humpty. 'Bail him out after the classes.'

In the early evening Billy and Laura Bridges, who'd pulled every string in the book, arrived at the police station. The police agreed to let Rupert go as long as he appeared in Court first thing tomorrow. They found him sobering up in the cells and playing poker with a couple of constables who happened to be show-jumping fans. The story had made the late editions of the evening papers and the show ground and the front of the station were swarming with press. Rupert was smuggled out of the back door.

Despite the heat, he was shivering like a rain-soaked puppy. He looked terrible.

'Better come home with me,' said Laura. 'Keep the press out of your hair and at least give you a decent night's sleep.'

Billy, who wanted to see Lavinia, went back to the show ground.

In the car, Rupert lay back and shut his eyes.

'How d'you feel?'

'Bit of a headache. Don't know if it's hangover or flying marrows.'

'Presumably you did take those roses from the tent?'

'Yes.'

She patted his knee. 'It was very sweet of you.'

'Can I go and have a bath?' he said when he got to her house. 'Just to wash the rainbow cake out of my hair.'

Downstairs, changed into a sweater and jeans brought by Billy, he found her in the kitchen. She had changed too, into a long pale blue cotton dress with a halter neck, which showed off her beautiful brown shoulders.

'When did you last have something to eat?' she asked.

'I don't remember.'

She gave him a glass of ice-cold milk. 'Do you good,' and got a large piece of steak out of the larder.

'You can put this on your eye if you like, or I can grill it for you.'

Rupert decided he was very hungry.

'Two newspapers rang for you while you were in the bath,' she said, as she switched on the grill. 'I said you'd gone to stay with friends in Exeter.'

Rupert went up to her, dropping a kiss on the bare shoulder.

'What a very very nice lady you are.'

They ate outside in the dusk, hardly talking, but allowing the silence to be companionable. Afterwards Rupert wandered into the drawing room and examined the photograph of the man on the desk.

'Your husband?'

She nodded. 'My Charlie.'

'Good-looking bloke. You happy with him?'

'Very.'

She also had three children. The last had just gone to prep school. 'I love them, but you've no idea the bliss, after thirteen years of marriage, of having the house to ourselves.'

She was swinging gently on the hammock seat. Every

time she came forward her blonde hair gleamed in the light from the window. Rupert longed to sit down beside her, but thought the swaying back and forth might make him sick.

'Ever get bored with each other sexually?'

She shook her head.

Reaching down, he took her hands, pulling her to her feet. She felt so honey-soft and nicely fleshed. His hand crept round to the back of her neck where the halter was knotted.

'I'm not sure you should,' she said. 'After that fight you can't be feeling very well.'

'I know the one thing that'd make me better.'

Slowly he unknotted the halter, allowing her dress to slither to the ground. Underneath she was quite naked. On her warm golden breasts there were delicate blue lines. She had full thighs, and round curving hips. In a few years her body would collapse like a peony. Now it was superb. And, knowing it, she gazed back at him without embarrassment.

Rupert pulled her towards him.

'I want to give you the best time in the world,' he murmured. 'Tell me what turns you on.'

At three o'clock in the morning the telephone rang.

Laura stretched out an arm.

'Charlie, darling, where are you?' she asked with simulated sleepiness. 'Oh, that's lovely. You can get a flight to Plymouth. I'll come and meet you. What an hour! You must be exhausted. Yes, I've been fine. The show was a great success. Love you, darling, all news when I see you. Bye.'

'Where is he?' asked Rupert.

'Madrid. He'll be back in three hours. He's got his own plane.'

Rupert laughed. 'Good thing he didn't parachute in unexpectedly.'

'I'll drive you back to the show ground on the way.'

Rupert snuggled up against her splendid breasts. 'Come on, we don't want to waste any time.'

* * *

It was another beautiful day. An innocent cerulean sky hung over the deep green fountain of the oak trees. As they left the house dawn was just breaking. Rupert breathed in a smell of dust, roses and approaching rain.

'Laura,' he said, as they reached the outskirts of Plymouth, 'I was at a pretty low ebb when I met you yesterday. You've been very good to me. Feel I ought to write Charlie a thankyou letter.'

'Have you got a steady girlfriend?' she asked. 'Apart from the multitudes, I mean.'

'We've just packed it in.'

'Why?'

'She's too serious-minded, and she won't sleep with me.'

Laura braked at the lights. 'Must be crazy. You're the eighth wonder of the world.'

'I am when I'm with you.' He put his hand between her legs, pressing gently. 'That must have been one of the most glorious fucks I've ever had. If I wasn't absolutely knackered, I'd drag you back to the caravan for another go. D'you ever get away to London, or Gloucestershire?' he asked, as she drew up at the show ground.

'Sometimes, usually with Charlie.'

'There'll be next year's show.'

'Charlie'll probably be here next time.'

He took her face in his hands and kissed her.

'We'll get together again sometime. I won't forget you in a hurry.'

Laura watched him walking across the dew-laden grass, with that lovely athlete's lope, red coat slung over his shoulder. As he turned and waved, she thought it was a very good thing Charlie was coming back. The boy was quite irresistible. Underneath the macho exterior, he was very vulnerable. I could straighten him out, she thought wistfully.

Rupert headed for the stables. He couldn't ever remember having been so tired in his life. Due in Court at nine, he must get a couple of hours' sleep beforehand. He hoped the press weren't going to make too much of a meal of it. He might even get suspended for a year. Malise would be charmed.

No one was about yet. Belgravia and Mayfair were lying down. Macaulay, however, who missed life at the barracks, welcomed any interruption and stuck his head out, nudging Rupert for Polos.

'From what I can remember,' Rupert told him, 'you jumped bloody well yesterday. Over the next few months you and I are going to raise two hooves to Malise Gordon, until he can't afford not to have us back in the team. We'd better think up a new name for you; perhaps we ought to call you Bridges.'

But as he walked wearily towards the caravan, remembering the day he had bought Macaulay, he felt kneed in the groin with longing for Helen. It must be tiredness that made it hurt so much. His resistance was weakened. Bloody hell, there was a light on in the caravan. Billy must have gone to bed drunk. He found the key behind the left front wheel, where it was always left. He let himself in cautiously. Billy might be shacked up with Lavinia.

For a minute he thought he was hallucinating. For there, lying in the double bed, apparently naked, dark blue duvet over her breasts, lay Helen. There were huge circles under her eyes, and she'd obviously been crying. She looked waif-like and terrified. Not a muscle flickered in Rupert's face. For a few seconds he gazed at her.

'How did you get in here?' he said coldly.

Then, as the tears began to roll down her cheeks, he crossed the caravan, taking her in his arms. After Laura's opulent curves she felt as frail as a child.

'Sweetheart, it's all right.'

'I'm so desperately sorry,' she sobbed. 'I know you g-got drunk, and into that dreadful fight, because I was real mean to you the day before yesterday.'

'You weren't.'

'I was too. You were down because you'd been dropped, and all I did was come on sanctimonious and blame you. I

204

should have been supportive and kind. You're right; I am a prude. I don't love Harold at all. I love you and and it's stupid to pretend I don't.'

She was crying really hard now. Rupert got out his handkerchief, then not able to remember whether he'd used it to clean up Laura Bridges, shoved it hastily away and grabbed a handful of Kleenex from the box on the side.

'You can make love with me whenever you want to,' she said.

'Only if you want to,' he said gently.

'I do,' her lip trembled, 'more than anything else in the world. I'm just so scared of losing you.'

Rupert tightened his grip on her. 'You're not going to.'

'I want you so much *now*,' she pleaded.

'Christ,' Rupert said to himself, 'I come home smelling like an old dog fox, and I'm so pooped I can't do a thing.'

He took her hands. 'I respect you far too much to force you,' he said gravely.

'You don't have to be kind. I really want it.'

'It wouldn't be right.' Then he had a brainwave. 'Why don't we get married?'

'Married?' she whispered incredulously.

'Why not? It's different.'

'Are you sure you're not still . . .'

'Drunk? Not at all, I haven't had a drop since yesterday lunchtime.' He pulled off his boots, then collapsed into bed beside her.

Then, removing his signet ring, he slid it on to her wedding-ring finger. 'That'll have to do, 'til I get you an engagement ring.'

She gazed at it, speechless, turning it over and over.

'You really mean it?'

'Really.' He lay back and laughed. 'I was so mad at you yesterday morning, I even changed Macaulay's name. Now you'll be changing yours, perhaps I'd better call him Campbell-Black. Christ, you're beautiful. I can fall asleep for the rest of my life counting freckles.'

Next minute he was fast asleep.

He was woken by Helen an hour before the Court case.

'My God,' he said, startled. Then, seeing his signet ring on her finger, he gradually brought the last few days' events into focus.

'Rupert,' she said, frantically twisting the ring around and around, 'when you came in this morning you asked me to marry you. But honestly, I'll understand if you've decided against it.'

'Darling.' As he pulled her into his arms he could smell toothpaste and clean scented flesh. She must have been up for hours. 'Of course I meant it. There's only one obstacle.'

'What's that?' she said, going pale.

'I don't remember you accepting.'

Helen flung her arms round his neck, kissing him fiercely. 'Oh, yes, please. I promise I'll be supportive. I'll learn about horses and be a real help in your career.'

Rupert looked alarmed. 'You don't have to go that far. I must go and have a pee.'

When he came back her arms closed round him like a vice. He pushed her away. 'Wait. I want to look at you first.'

She was so so shy, hanging her head, as he admired the slender arms, the tapering waist, the jutting hip bones. Very gently he stroked the little snow-white breasts.

'They're beautiful,' he murmured.

'Too small,' she muttered. 'I wish I had a wonderful forty-inch bust, the kind like pillows you could fall asleep on.'

'Nanny always claimed it was much better for one's back to sleep without pillows,' said Rupert. Then, realizing it was not the time for jokes, he kissed each chestnut nipple, waiting for them to stiffen under his tongue.

With a colossal feeling of triumph he pushed her back on to the bed and began to move downwards, kissing her ribs, then her belly.

'No,' she gasped, grabbing his head.

Firmly he removed her hands. 'Shut up. You're mine now, to do exactly what I like with.'

206

Feeling her quivering frantically with desire, he progressed down to the ginger bush. Then, suddenly, he encountered a sticky, lacquered mass, like a hedgehog.

'What the bloody hell?' he yelled. 'Are you trying to poison me?'

'It's only vaginal deodorant,' stammered Helen.

'It is bloody not, sweetheart, you've used hair lacquer by mistake.'

Picking her up screaming, he carried her into the shower and held her under until he washed it off, then threw her dripping on to the bed.

'Now, let's get one thing straight. I like the taste of you. And I don't want it diluted by any damned deodorants. I'm going to wipe out that New England puritanism if it kills me.'

In Court he got off with a hefty fine. His lawyer, used to Rupert's scrapes, had travelled down overnight. Mr Campbell-Black, he said, had had a row with his girlfriend the day before, which had upset him so much he'd proceeded to get drunk. Now the row was made up and he and his girlfriend were planning to get married. His client was very sorry. It wouldn't happen again. The press were so captivated by the news that they concentrated on the engagement rather than on the fight.

Later, between classes, Rupert bumped into Laura who introduced her husband, Charlie. Conversation was very amicable. As Charlie moved on to talk to some friends, Laura said in a low voice: 'I'm so glad you're getting married to her.'

Rupert grinned. 'Will you sleep with me again as a wedding present?'

Laura looked reproving. 'Your new wife wouldn't like that very much.'

'Ah,' said Rupert lightly, 'she'll have to take me as she finds me, if she can find me.'

I4

Nearly two years later Helen stood in the middle of her
bedroom at Penscombe, tearing her hair and trying to
decide what she should pack for Rome and then Madrid.
She and Rupert would be away for nearly three weeks, so
she would need at least three cases to carry all the different
clothes for sight-seeing, swimming, sunbathing, watching
Rupert in the ring, and for the string of parties and dinners
which always coincided with international shows abroad.
She had started a hundred lists, then scrumpled them up.

But even clothes littering every available surface
couldn't detract from the beauty of the room with its high
ceilings, huge Jacobean four-poster, old rose walls, pale
yellow and pink silk striped curtains and fluffy amber
carpet. On the dressing table and beside the bed were great
bunches of yellow irises. The general effect of a sunrise
provided the perfect foil for Helen's colouring. Or so the
woman from *House and Garden* had said last week when she
came down to photograph the house and the dramatic
changes Helen had made to it.

On the primrose-yellow silk chaise-longue lay a copy of
this months's *Vogue*, with a photographic feature on the new
beauties. Most beautiful of them all was undoubtedly Mrs
Rupert Campbell-Black, showing Helen, huge-eyed, swan-
necked, her Titian hair spread by a wind machine, Rupert's
diamonds gleaming at her ears and throat. Also on the
chaise-longue were guide books for Rome and Madrid and
Italian and Spanish phrase books. Helen took her trips
abroad very seriously, sight-seeing and trying to learn as
much of the language as possible. Beside the books lay

Helen's journal. It was the same dark green notebook she'd had in Regina House. She was ashamed that since she'd married Rupert she'd filled in less than a half of it, only sketchily recording events in what had certainly been the most exciting years of her life. But she'd been so busy living, she didn't seem to have had much time to write about it.

She remembered the day Rupert had asked her to marry him. In the afternoon she'd been sitting in the stands with Doreen, Humpty Hamilton's even fatter, bouncier wife, mother of two children, watching Rupert and Humpty jump in a class. Helen, delirious with happiness, couldn't resist telling Doreen she was engaged. Doreen Hamilton was delighted at the news and promptly bore Helen off to the bar for a celebration drink, then offered her a word of advice.

'If you marry a show-jumper,' she said, 'involve yourself in his career as much as possible and travel with him as much as you can, even if it means sleeping in lorries, or caravans, or frightful pokey foreign hotels. And if he suddenly rings up when you're at home and says come out to Rome, or drive down to Windsor, or to Crittleden, always go – at once, even if you've just washed your hair and put it in curlers, or you've just got the baby to sleep. Because if you don't, there'll always be others queuing up to take your place.'

Helen, cocooned in the miracle of her new and reciprocated love for Rupert, was unable to imagine him loving anyone else, or any girl queuing up for fat little Humpty, but she had heeded the advice and gone with Rupert to as many shows as possible. Not that this involved much hardship; his caravan was extremely luxurious and when they went abroad Rupert insisted on staying in decent hotels or with rich jet-set friends who seemed to surface, crying welcome, in every country they visited. But it meant she always had to look her best.

Going to the window, with its rampaging frame of scented palest pink clematis, she gazed out across the valley, emerald green from weeks of heavy rain, remembering the first time she'd seen the house. Rupert and Billy, having both won big classes on the final day of the Royal Plymouth, decided to stay on for the closing party that night. After intensive revelry, Rupert suddenly turned to Helen and said, 'I think it's time you had a look at my bachelor pad,' and they loaded up the horse box and set out for Gloucestershire, Rupert driving, Helen sitting warm between the two men. 'An exquisite sliver of smoked salmon between two very old stale pieces of bread,' said Billy.

Helen went to sleep and woke up as they drove up the valley towards Penscombe. The sun had just risen, firing a denim-blue sky with ripples of crimson and reddening the ramparts of cow parsley on either side of the road. Suddenly the horses started pawing the floorboards in the back and Mavis and Badger, who were sprawled across Billy's and Helen's knees in the front, woke up and started sniffing excitedly.

'Ouch,' said Billy as Badger stepped heavily across him. 'Get off my crotch. Why the hell don't you get his claws cut, Rupe?'

Helen looked across the valley at the honey-gold house leaning back against its pale green pillow of beech trees.

'What a beautiful mansion,' she gasped. 'I wonder who lives there?'

'You do,' said Rupert. 'That's your new home,' and he and Billy laughed to see how speechless she was.

'I can't believe it,' she whispered. 'It's so old and so beautiful. It's a stately home.'

'You may not find it quite so splendid when you get close to,' said Rupert, slowing down as they entered the village.

He took the lorry straight round to the stables, where Marion and Tracey, who'd driven home the night before with the caravan, were waiting to unload the horses. Leaving Billy to check everything was all right, Rupert whipped into the house, collected a bottle of champagne and two glasses and took Helen out on the terrace.

Below them lay the valley, drenched white with dew, softened by the palest grey mist rising from the stream that ran along the bottom. On the opposite hillside, the sun was filtering thick biblical rays through the trees, which in turn cast long powder blue shadows down the fields. And, sauntering leisurely down one of these rays like horses of the dawn, came three of Rupert's sleek and beautiful thoroughbreds, two greys and a chestnut. Tossing their heads, they broke into a gallop and careered joyously down the white valley, vanishing into the mist like a dream.

Leaning on the stone balustrade on the edge of the terrace, Helen gazed and gazed. Behind her the wood was filled with bluebells; thrushes were singing out of a clump of white lilacs to the left. Badger, after the long journey, wandered around lifting his leg on bright yellow irises, before happily plunging into the lake.

'It's the most beautiful place I've ever seen,' she breathed. 'You're not a closet Earl or anything are you? I feel like King Cophetua and the Beggar Maid.'

'King who?' asked Rupert, hitching a hip on to the lichened balustrade and edging open the champagne with his thumbs. The cork flew through the air, landing in a rosebush.

'Is it all yours?'

'As far as that village on the right.' He filled a glass and handed it to her.

'Anyway it's yours too now, darling, every inch of it.'

Looking up, she saw he was smiling. Even an eighth of an inch of blond stubble, and a slight puffiness round the wickedly sparkling eyes, couldn't diminish his beauty.

'Just as every single inch of you belongs to me from now on,' he added softly.

Then she realized it was not King Cophetua he reminded her of, but the Devil tempting Christ in the wilderness, saying, 'All this will I give you.'

Just for a second she had a premonition of unease. Then Rupert chinked his glass against hers and, draining it, said, 'Let's go to bed.'

211

'We can't,' stammered Helen. 'What will everyone think?'

'That we've gone to bed,' said Rupert.

Upstairs he pulled the telephone out, but didn't bother to lock the door.

'Well, at least I'm going to draw the curtains,' said Helen.

'I wouldn't,' said Rupert.

But the next minute she'd given the dark red velvet a vigorous tug and the whole thing descended, curtain rail and all, on her head in a huge cloud of dust. In fits of laughter, Rupert extracted her.

'I told you not to pull it!' Then, seeing her hair covered in dust, 'My god you've gone white overnight. Must be the effect of saying you'll marry me.'

He pulled her into the shade of the great ancient four-poster and began unbuttoning her shirt. Next minute she leapt out of her skin as the door opened. But it was only Badger, dripping from the lake, trying to join them in bed.

'Basket,' snapped Rupert. 'And you might bloody well shut the door,' he added, kicking it shut.

After Rupert had come, with that splendid driving flourish of staccato thrusts which reminded Helen of the end of a Beethoven Symphony, he fell into a deep sleep. Helen, lying in his arms, had been far too tense and nervous of interruption to gain any satisfaction. Looking around the room, she took in the mothy fox masks leering down from the walls, the Munnings and the Lionel Edwards, and surely that was a Stubbs in the corner, very much in need of a clean. All the furniture in the room was old and handsome, but it too was desperately in need of a polish, and all the chairs and the sofa needed re-upholstering. There were angora rabbits of dust on top of every picture, and sailors could have climbed up the rigging of cobwebs in the corners. Judging by the colour of the bed linen, it hadn't seen a washing machine for weeks. Helen began to itch and edged out of Rupert's embrace. She was touched to see a copy of *War and Peace* by the bedside table. At least he was trying to educate himself. Writing 'I love you' in the dust, she wandered off to find a bathroom.

She found the john first, and was less touched to find a framed photograph on the wall of Rupert on a horse, being presented with a cup by Grania Pringle. Along the bottom Grania had written, 'So happy to mount you – love Grania.' That's one for the jumble sale, thought Helen, taking it off the wall.

The bathroom made her faint. A great white bath, standing six inches off the ground on legs shaped like lion's paws, was ringed with grime like a rugger sweater. Above it, a geyser on the wall spat out dust and then boiling water. The ceiling was black with dirt, the paint peeling like the surface of the moon. On another beautiful chest of drawers, which was warping from the damp, stood empty bottles, mugs and two ashtrays brimming over with cigarette stubs.

Having found a moderately clean towel and spent nearly an hour cleaning the bath, she had one herself, then set out to explore the house, finding bedroom after bedroom filled with wonderful furniture, carpets and china, with many of the beds recently slept in but not made. At the end of the passage she discovered a room which was obviously Billy's. On the chest of drawers was a large photograph in a frame of Lavinia Greenslade, and an even larger one of Mavis. There were glasses by the bed and drink rings on everything.

A bridle hung from the four-poster. There were sporting prints on the wall and more framed photographs of horses jumping, galloping, standing still and being presented with rosettes. On the chest of drawers was a pile of unopened brown envelopes and more overflowing ashtrays.

Descending the splendid staircase with a fat crimson cord attached to the wall to cling on to, she admired a huge painting of Badger in the hall. Underneath it two Jack Russells were having a fight. She found a pair of Springer Spaniels shut in the drawing-room. Every beautiful faded chair and sofa seemed to be upholstered in dog hair. On the wall was a large lighter patch where a painting had been sold. The rest of the walls were covered, among other things, by a Romney, a Gainsborough, a Lely and a Thomas Lawrence. Next door, behind the inevitable wire cages, was the library. No wonder Rupert was indifferent to culture; it was all around him, to be taken for granted. For a minute, looking at more cobwebs and dust, she thought she'd strayed into Miss Haversham's house.

Then she trod on something that squelched.

'Oh my God,' she screamed.

'What's the matter?' asked Billy, coming through the door, holding a pile of entry forms and a cheque book.

'One of those damned dogs has gone to the bathroom in the living room.'

She couldn't understand why Billy laughed so much.

'It's not funny,' she said. 'I've never seen such a dump. Doesn't anyone ever clean it? It's an arachnephobe's nightmare. Marion and Tracey must be the most awful slobs to let it get into such a state.'

'Suppose it is a bit of a mess,' said Billy apologetically. 'But we're not in the house much during the day and one never notices dust at night. We had a char. She wasn't very good, but Rupert kept her on because she made him laugh. He said she had charisma. Then he came back and found her in one of the spare room beds drinking gin with the electric blanket on. After that even he had to sack her, so we haven't had anyone for about six weeks.'

'Doesn't look as though you've had anyone for six years,' said Helen, scraping her shoe on the gravel outside.

'Come and look at the stables; that should cheer you up. Is Rupert asleep?'

Helen nodded.

'I know it's a mess,' he said putting his arm through Helen's and leading her across the lawn, passing over-grown shrub roses that hadn't seen a pruner in years and pink scented peonies collapsing on the grass. 'But we're so frightfully busy, we haven't really got time to organize the house. That's why Rupert desperately needs a wife,' he went on, squeezing her hand. 'Not only are you the most adorably beautiful girl we've ever seen, but we really need

214

you to look after us.'

'Thanks,' said Helen. 'So in fact I'm really marrying two riders, four grooms, thirty horses, a million dogs and a stable cat. I feel like Milly in *Seven Brides for Seven Brothers*. But it's such a beautiful house, and it could be made so gorgeous.'

'And I'm quite confident you'll be able to do it,' said Billy happily.

The stables were built of the same honey-coloured stone as the house, the doors painted the same dark blue Rupert had chosen on the colour chart in church on their first date. Horses looked out inquisitively, eager for any diversion. Brick-red geraniums bloomed in blue and white striped tubs. There was not a blade of straw or a speck of dust anywhere. In the centre was a circle of grass beautifully mown round an ancient mulberry tree. It was like a toy stable.

Billy introduced her to the junior grooms, Susie and Janis, two more pretty shapely blondes. Tracey and Marion, having the afternoon off, had collapsed into bed, Marion, Helen suspected, to cry her eyes out. She hadn't addressed a word to Rupert since she heard he was getting married.

Billy led her into the tackroom, which was beautifully kept. The tack was dark and gleaming, the bits shining, every inch of wall lined with rosettes. Helen breathed in the smell of leather, linseed oil, saddle soap. 'But I don't understand,' she said. 'It's as neat as a new pin here. Why is the house such a mess?'

Billy shrugged. 'This is where the action is. If I were you I'd move into Macaulay's box. At least you'd get clean straw and regular meals.'

After a good night's sleep, Helen felt more able to cope. Next day she went back to Regina House and the office. Despite Rupert's outraged protests, she felt she ought to get things straight and tidy up. Nigel, when he heard she was going to marry Rupert, was even more outraged.

'You'd think Rupert was General Franco or Oswald

Mosley,' she grumbled.

'Jolly nearly,' hissed Nigel. 'I'm ashamed of you, Helen.'

The next day the IRA blew up a shop and then a hamburger bar in London, not far from Helen's office. Rupert was at a show in the West Country, but he was on to Helen immediately.

'Are you all right, darling? Christ, I've been worried. Look, I'm not leaving you in London any more. You must move in at once. I can't bear another night away from you.'

'But what am I going to do with myself all day?'

'You can organize my life.'

'Can I re-decorate your house?'

'If it makes you happy, as long as you let me burn your entire wardrobe, and promise never to buy any more clothes without my coming too. I haven't got a show next Monday,' he went on. 'I thought we might get married.'

And so they were married at Gloucester Registry office. Helen wore a grey silk suit chosen by Rupert. Billy and Humpty were witnesses.

They set off to Yorkshire on their honeymoon, staying in an old pub in the middle of the moors. On the Tuesday Rupert went to look at a horse which he decided not to buy. On Thursday he said he was fed up with the pub and knew a better one over the Pennines.

As they were driving there Helen suddenly noticed AA signs and advertising posters: 'The great Lancashire Show starts today.' She said idly to Rupert, 'Is Billy going?'

'Yes,' said Rupert, leaning across and kissing her, 'and so are we.'

When they reached the show, there were Billy and Tracey looking sheepish, and Marion looking bootfaced, and, surprise surprise, Mayfair and Macaulay and Rupert's riding clothes. Helen looked down at the huge unusual ring of sapphires and emeralds which Rupert had given her as an engagement ring and remembered what Doreen Hamilton had said about being a show-jumper's wife, and laughed instead of cried.

'Darling Mother,' she wrote home that evening, 'I got married on Monday. My husband is called Rupert Campbell-Black. He is real handsome and very famous in England, because he is a stadium jumping star. In England it is called show-jumping, and a big sport rather like baseball. He has the most beautiful stately home near Shakespeare's birthplace, you will just go crazy about it. It is so old, and the village he lives in looks as though none of the houses have been touched since Elizabeth Ist's day. I enclose photographs of the house and of Rupert. I know you wanted me to get married in Florida and in white, Mother, but I promise you I am truly truly happy. I never believed being in love could be like this. Rupert had a very traumatic childhood, I'm surprised he hasn't been in analysis for years, but he is very normal. His mother lives in the Bahamas and is on her third husband, and his father is on his fourth wife.

'I haven't met them yet. But soon I'm going to meet Rupert's old Nanny, who is really the person who brought him up, and gave him security. He thinks the world of her. I'm going to make him happy. I love him so much I long to have you meet him, but the summer is Rupert's busy time. At the moment he is at shows all the week and at weekends, but I promise the first weekend we get free, we'll fly out and see you. All love, Helen.'

Rupert's meeting with Helen's parents didn't take place until August and was not a success. The plan was that Helen should fly direct to Florida and Rupert, having looked at some horses in Kentucky, should join her a couple of days later. As it was in the middle of the show-jumping season, Helen explained, he would only be able to stay for the weekend before flying back to Europe for the Dublin Horse Show, where, having been forgiven at last by Malise, he had been picked to jump for Great Britain, but at least it would give her parents the chance to meet him.

Arriving home, Helen was appalled to find her mother had arranged a full-scale wedding party, with 300 guests to meet Helen's handsome English husband, with even a minister coming to the house to perform a service beforehand, in which the happy couple would be blessed.

'I just don't feel you're married after a registry office ceremony,' said her mother.

'Rupert'll absolutely freak out,' protested Helen. 'He hasn't brought a cutaway, or even a dinner jacket.'

'He can always hire one, or borrow one from Father,' said her mother.

With a growing feeling of apprehension, Helen watched the preparations. In fact, her mother was so well organized that on Friday afternoon she and her four daughters were able to slip down to the beach below their house for a couple of hours' sun. Helen's three sisters, all lithe and beautiful, awaited Rupert's arrival that evening with intense excitement. They were amazed at the change in Helen. She looked so beautiful and happy, and so much more self-assured.

'Look at that dreamy yacht,' said Esme, the younger sister, as a big boat with bright blue sails crowded with bronzed, half-naked people tacked close to the shore. The next moment one of them had jumped ship. Wading through the shallows carrying a case, he turned as he reached the sand and, brandishing it, shouted, 'Thanks for the lift.'

'Are you ready for that?' said Milly, the second sister, in wonder.

'It's Rupert,' gasped Helen.

He was as blond and as brown as a beach boy, and he was wearing nothing except a rather small United States flag draped round his loins.

'Jesus,' said Claudia, the third sister.

'Don't swear, Claudia,' said Mrs Macaulay.

Helen hurtled down the beach, flung her arms round Rupert's neck and only just stopped the American flag tumbling to half mast.

'Darling, we were expecting you tonight.'

'I got a lift with some chums. I missed you.'

On Palm Beach, home of the beautiful, he was still the

218

most beautiful of all.

'Mother, this is Rupert,' said Helen.

Mrs Macaulay was vain enough not to be very pleased at having to meet her new son-in-law when she was scarlet and sweating from the heat. She would have preferred to have parted the wistaria on the terrace, welcoming him in a pretty dress, hair newly set, make-up light but perfect. But she knew one must behave like a lady at all times, so she radiated graciousness.

'Hi, Rupert,' she said, holding out a hand slippery with sun-tan oil and trying not to look at the American flag. 'I'm so pleased to welcome you as our son. I hope you'll call me Mother.'

Rupert, in fact, never managed to call her anything. He didn't even kiss her; both felt it would have been too sweaty an embrace. He looked at her handsome, rigid, determined face with the greying red hair. He took in the well-controlled figure in its skirted bathing dress, he noticed the gold cross hanging between the crepey breasts, and he shuddered and vowed he would never let Helen get like that. Mrs Macaulay averted her eyes and noted Rupert was not wearing a wedding ring. Father must find him one before tomorrow.

'I'm not going to hire a morning coat,' snapped Rupert, when at last he and Helen were alone in their bedroom, 'nor am I going to be blessed by some Yankee poofter. We were married in England; that's enough for me.'

'Hush darling, they'll hear you, and it's worth it for all the wedding gifts.'

'Not if you look at them closely. Six magazine racks, two sets of monogrammed highball glasses, twelve egg cod-dlers, a dozen staghorn steak knives. Jesus! Two sets of glasses with polo players on. Polo, I ask you.'

'Oh, that was darling great-aunt Grace. Doesn't know the difference between show-jumping and polo. She was doing her best. There's a lovely dinner service, and some beautiful cachepots, and glass. The problem is how to get them all home.'

'We'll have to hire a plane and hope it crashes on take-off.'

Helen giggled, but she felt defensive about her parents and their friends. If only he would behave for the wedding, she knew everyone would love him. Rupert went moodily to the window.

'God, I miss Badger. Why don't your parents have a dog? I am not going through with this party. If I do I'll wear a suit.'

'All right,' said Helen soothingly. 'But please, darling, be nice just this once. Mother's been arranging it for weeks and Milly's going to sing "What is Life to Me Without You". Mother's been coaching her for weeks, and Dad's even been out and bought himself an Ascot and some striped pants. All you've got to do is show up and be polite.'

Rupert behaved rather well during the service. Later everyone crowded on to the lawn, and after champagne had been drunk for an hour or so, the most distinguished male relation rose to praise Helen, and to welcome Rupert to the family. Afterwards there was a pause.

'Speech, speech,' shouted all the relations and friends and the large sprinkling of Mr Macaulay's patients, flashing their beautifully capped teeth. Rupert, wearing a dark suit and not wearing the wedding ring his father-in-law had pressed on him that morning, rose to his feet.

'My heart is in my mouth at this wonderful party,' he said charmingly, 'but as my Nanny always told me not to talk with my mouth full, I'm not going to say anything, except to thank Mr and Mrs Macaulay. I could tell jokes about gay Irish dentists, but I don't think my father-in-law would like that. Thank you all for your wonderful presents,' and with that he quietly slid under the table.

'But you weren't even drunk,' said Helen, still furious, as their plane took off for England.

'I know, but I was bored. I'm sorry, darling, but the only relations I like are sexual relations.'

'And you've left Aunt Martha's paintings behind.'

'I know,' said Rupert. 'I was terrified they might frighten

the dogs.'

Rupert's parents both wrote Helen delightfully vague letters. Rupert's mother sent her a diamond brooch with a broken clasp, Rupert's father a jar of caviar. Both promised they'd be over sometime – probably when they want to borrow money, said Rupert – and wished them every happiness.

Helen's meeting with Rupert's old Nanny was hardly more successful.

'What shall I wear?' she asked Billy beforehand.

'A skirt with horizontal stripes. All Nanny cares about is good childbearing hips.'

Nanny's cottage in Wiltshire had been bought and furnished by the Campbell-Black family. They had filled it with pieces from their various houses which were far too large. It was an obstacle race to get across the sitting room. Nanny, almost the largest thing in the cottage, stood six feet tall, with big ears, a whiskery seamed face, a boxer's jaw and shrewd, tough little brown eyes like Henry the Seventh. She was wearing a shiny high-necked navy blue dress with a white collar, which gave the impression of a uniform. Although it was a very hot day, she was watching fireworks on a black and white television with the central heating at full blast and none of the windows open. Perhaps years of Campbell-Black austerity and indifference to the cold had unhinged her, thought Helen. Every surface in the room was covered in photographs of babies in long white dresses. The only others were of Rupert at every stage of his career, as a solemn blue-eyed baby, at St Augustine's, Harrow, in the Blues, and, mostly, of him show-jumping. Otherwise there was no evidence that she was remotely pleased to see him.

She hardly thanked him for the half-dozen bottles of her favourite, disgustingly sweet sherry that he brought her. Pouring out three glasses, she gave much the smallest to Helen.

'Isn't Helen beautiful?' said Rupert.

Nanny looked Helen up and down and sniffed. 'Very beautiful face,' she said.

'She's got a beautiful figure too,' protested Rupert, laughing. 'I know you'd have only been happy if I'd married some Flanders mare producing sons every eight months.'

Nanny snorted and proceeded to tear Rupert off a strip for hell-raising in Paris and getting arrested at Plymouth and getting married without a proper wedding. Rupert accepted it with amazing mildness.

'I'm sorry we didn't ask you to the wedding; we didn't ask anyone. I couldn't face all my step-parents muscling in on the act. And my mother would have been bored to have been reminded of all her weddings.'

'Who's your father married to at the moment?' said Nanny.

'Some Italian whore,' said Rupert.

'I suppose you had to get married?' asked Nanny.

'No, we did not.'

'Whatever happened to Bianca? And Melanie Potter? She was a bonny girl.'

'She's married with two daughters. I told you last time.'

Nanny knew everything about him, and every round he'd jumped in the last two years.

'Your mother remembered my birthday,' she said accusingly. 'More than you did, and so did your brother Adrian. I hear he's got a girlfriend.'

'Are you sure?' said Rupert in amazement. 'I don't think so.'

'Never knew he was bi-spectacled,' said Nanny.

Helen didn't dare look at Rupert.

'Helen's American,' said Rupert.

'So I read,' said Nanny. 'Never thought you'd end up with a foreigner. I've read about Watergate,' she added, as though Helen were personally responsible.

Helen was so hot she took off her jersey, revealing her slender brown arms and waist.

'Not much of her, is there?' said Nanny. 'Anorexic, I suppose.'

Finally, when Helen thought she'd faint from the heat, she said, 'I think we ought to go, Rupert.'

Nanny was not at all upset; she didn't even come to the door. Desperate to get out into the fresh air, Helen made her goodbyes and fled, but not before she heard Nanny say, 'Got money, I suppose? Only reason for marrying a foreigner really.'

'Isn't she a gem?' said Rupert on the way home.

'She's a Machiavellian old monster,' said Helen.

'Doesn't mean it; she's nearly eighty. All the same I can't wait for you to have a baby so we can get her out of mothballs to look after it.'

It was plain, in fact, as the months went by, that Rupert and Helen were very different. Rupert was spoilt, easily irritated and didn't flinch from showing it. His ambition in life was to get his own way and beat the hell out of the opposition. He had many moments of frustration and boredom in life, but very few of self-doubt.

Helen, on the other hand, was riddled with self-doubt. She believed that one should not only constantly strive to improve oneself and others, but that work would indeed keep the devil at bay.

To begin with, therefore, she made heroic efforts to interest herself in horses and learn to ride, but she was too tense and nervous and the horses sensed this, and the way she always caught her breath got on Rupert's nerves. Then Marion (Helen never knew if it were deliberate) put her up on one of the novices, who carted her through a wood with low-hanging branches and finally deposited her on the tarmac of the village street. Helen bruised herself very badly and after that gave up trying to ride.

She still took an interest in show-jumping, however, reading every book on the subject, scanning the papers for horsey news. She even started reading dressage books and discussing her theories wth Rupert, trying to show him where he was going wrong. Rupert was not amused. He did not want gratuitous advice that Macaulay might go better in a running martingale, or Belgravia might profit from learning to execute half-passes.

'When all's said and done,' he told her sharply, 'I'm riding the fucking horse, not you, so belt up.'

Helen, during the long, long hours that Rupert and Billy were occupied with the horses, turned her attention to the house and soon had the place swarming with builders, plumbers, electricians and painters.

'You'd think they were building the Pyramids,' grumbled Rupert.

But gradually the damp and the dry rot were eradicated, and a new heating and wiring system installed. Pastel colours replaced the crimson and dark green wallpapers and old brocades. Tattered silks and moth-eaten tapestries were succeeded by new pale silks, glazed chintz and Laura Ashley flower prints.

Helen also employed a decent cleaner, Mrs Bodkin, paid her well and managed to keep her. Mrs Bodkin admired Helen. She found her formal and distant and not given to gossip, but she was kind, straight, listened to Mrs Bodkin's problems and was prepared to muck in with the cleaning.

She certainly needed to. Rupert and Billy were appallingly untidy. Both dropped their clothes where they took them off, never brought a cup or glass downstairs, and, if they couldn't find a boot jack at the front or back door, trailed mud all over the hall and the new carpet, followed by a convoy of dogs with dirty paws.

The dogs drove Helen increasingly crackers, shedding hair, barking, fighting, claiming Rupert's attention. Also, the colder the winter got, and the last one was a killer (you could skate on the water in the john) the more the dogs tried to climb into bed with them. Rupert, who fell asleep the moment his head touched the pillow, didn't notice or mind Badger lying across his feet, or a Springer spaniel curled up in the warmth of his back. Helen, a nervy insomniac, was kept awake night after night, shoving the dogs out of bed and listening to them licking themselves or scratching interminably in creaking baskets.

As the winter got colder, and the winds blew off the Bristol Channel, and the central heating was not yet installed, poor Florida-reared Helen developed a hacking cough. Rupert, who like most very healthy people, lacked sympathy with illness, suggested she should get a job coughing between movements on Radio 3.

And that was another problem. Culturally they were so different. Every time she wanted to listen to classical music, Rupert turned on Radio One. Every week she determinedly read the *Times Literary Supplement*, *Encounter* and *New Society*. She started to read the *New Statesman*, but Rupert cancelled it; he was not having subversive Trotskyite rubbish corrupting the dogs, he said.

Then there was the matter of the Augustus John drawing. Helen, having spent a long time deciding what would really please Rupert for a wedding present, blued her entire savings on a drawing of a horse by Augustus John.

Rupert was enchanted.

'I think that was the old roué who had a walk out with my grandmother.'

He was studying the drawing in great detail when the doorbell rang. It was a man about the washing machine. When Helen returned quarter of an hour later, Rupert had propped the drawing on the sofa and was looking at it with satisfaction.

'That's better.'

'What?' said Helen. Then, noticing a pencil and rubber in Rupert's hand, gave a gasp of horror. 'What *have* you done?'

'Re-drawn the near side hock. Chap simply hadn't got it right.'

'But you can't tamper with the work of great artists,' said Helen, appalled.

'I can, when they can't draw,' said Rupert.

Although he insisted on buying her a completely new wardrobe, making her look, he'd told Billy, like the aristocrat she plainly isn't, on the whole he approved of the changes she made to the house. But he drew the line at mats under glasses to stop the drink rings, and he tore down the net curtains in the first floor bedrooms and the downstairs loo, and he threw all the artifical flowers she bought to brighten up the dark hall into the boiler.

Their worst row was triggered off, however, when Helen introduced discs into the lavatory cisterns to disinfect the water and dye it blue. Rupert came roaring into the kitchen, one of the blue discs in his hand, dripping dye all over the floor.

'What the fuck is this?' he howled. 'Have you gone mad? Are you trying to poison my dogs?'

'They shouldn't drink out of the john,' screamed Helen. 'Then they go and lick everyone. It's disgusting. They've got water bowls in the kitchen, and a water trough, and a lake in the garden. Why do they bother with the john?'

'Because they always have. I'm not having you introducing any more of your dinky little American ideas. It'll be chiming doorbells and musical lavatory paper next. I want the water clear by the time I get home, and if any of the dogs get ill, I'll report you to the RSPCA.' And he stormed out, slamming the door. Helen and Mrs Bodkin removed the blue discs.

Poor Helen tried and failed to impose gracious living on Billy and Rupert. She yearned for candlelit dinners with the silver out, damask napkins, intelligent conversation and lingering over coffee and liqueurs. But, looking after horses, there was no guarantee what time Rupert and Billy would get in. After three attempts at boeuf en croute that turned out tougher than a tramp's boots, Helen found out that all they really wanted was sausages and mash, or Irish stew on their knees, slumped in front of the television. Usually they argued across the programme about the day's events, or some horse they were thinking of buying. Rupert bolted his food, hardly noticing what he ate. She was often tempted to offer him Chappie and Winalot. Often they were so tired, they fell asleep in the middle of a meal.

But however much Rupert fell asleep over the television,

he always woke up and wanted sex when they went to bed, and again in the morning, and often popping in, if he wasn't at a show, in the middle of the day. 'I'm happy as long as I'm mounted,' he used to say, 'and you're so compulsively rideable, my darling.'

If they ever had a row, Rupert had to make it up because he wanted to sleep with her. If she found his demands excessive, and she frequently didn't achieve orgasm herself, she never said so. But after nearly a year she still grabbed a towel when he walked into the bedroom and found her naked. She always locked the lavatory door, and she only really liked sex if she'd just had a bath. She was embarrassed by his unashamed delight in her body. She still couldn't convince herself that he really enjoyed doing those things he insisted he liked doing long enough to make her come, so she often wriggled away pretending she had, then felt desperately ashamed of faking. But she found him irresistible and she needed his constant assaults as evidence that he still doted on her.

For there was oodles of competition. Wherever they were, girls ran after Rupert, clamouring for his autograph, mobbing him at parties, even pulling hairs out of his horses' tails as souvenirs, until they were almost bald. And although she got kudos, wherever she went, as Rupert's beautiful wife, and there was a great feeling of mutual congratulation in being such a handsome couple, it was Rupert people really wanted to see.

Marion troubled her too. She longed for Rupert to sack her (as he was always threatening to do) but was too tactful to say anything. But she remembered Marion's reddened eyes, particularly after their wedding. She tried to be particularly nice to the girl, giving her a beautiful black cashmere jersey for her birthday, which Marion never wore, and was constantly urging Rupert to ask her to dinner and suggesting handsome young men to meet her. But Marion politely refused and kept her distance, gazing at Helen with the hostile sombre eyes of a prisoner of war.

Billy explained to Helen that Marion was so good with

the horses that it was worthwhile putting up with her moods. Billy was such a comfort. He'd offered to move out when Helen and Rupert got married, but neither of them could bear to lose him. After all, he and Rupert had been inseparable since they were eight, and they were business partners, and Rupert needed someone to talk horses with. As the weeks passed Helen decided Billy was simply the nicest person she'd ever met. He was so kind, funny, easy-going and, she flattered herself, just a tiny bit in love with her. If she had a row with Rupert, Billy stuck up for her. If Rupert was irritable because the horses were going badly, she could dump on Billy, knowing she wasn't being disloyal, because Billy understood Rupert and loved him, at the same time as knowing all his faults. It was a very happy arrangement. Billy obviously wasn't serious about Lavinia Greenslade and wouldn't get married for years.

Rupert sometimes complained of being gentrified, but he and Billy soon found it a boon that the house was run like clockwork, that their suits and red coats were always back from the cleaners, that there were always enough clean white shirts, ties and breeches, that their boots were mended, that the house was ordered and tidy, that entry forms were filled in, that fan mail was answered, and endless requests to speak or open fêtes and supermarkets were politely refused by return of post.

This left Rupert and Billy to concentrate on the horses, which they certainly needed to do. The three-day week brought extra costs. Petrol prices in particular shot up. There were forecasts of economic doom for years to come and, with the Socialists coming to power, there was more chilling talk of a wealth tax, which would cripple Rupert's income. It became increasingly vital to win and win. And they did. There was no doubt that since Rupert married Helen he and Billy had calmed down, and were now both regular fixtures in the British team.

So now Helen, on the eve of leaving for Rome and Madrid, gazed out on the green valley. She was really looking forward to the trip. For the first time she felt she could leave the house without the workmen doing something frightful. She loved going abroad, picking up antiques and pieces for the house, visiting galleries and museums, learning new languages. Also it meant a holiday from all the dogs in the bed, and as Rupert was far less famous abroad they weren't constantly besieged by groupies (or 'Rupies' as Billy called them). And Malise Gordon was there. She always enjoyed spending time with him. They often went to galleries and museums together when they were away, making Rupert slightly edgy. He was jealous of something that Malise and Helen shared that he couldn't give her, so he continually mocked it.

Helen turned back to all the beautiful clothes Rupert had bought her. She realized above all that it was important to him that other men admired and fancied her, but like Meissen china in a glass case, the admiration had to be kept at a distance. Last year in Rotterdam, when a rather inebriated Dutchman asked her to dance in a nightclub, it had only been Billy's half nelson that had stopped Rupert knocking him across the room. A slightly more persistent admirer at one of the Dublin Horse Show balls had been less lucky and ended up with a fractured jaw.

15

Jake Lovell rode across his fields at a leisurely pace. When he came to a hedge or a wall he popped the grey gelding over it, but he was in no hurry. He'd already worked all the novice horses that morning, and the Grade A horses were having a rest after a three-day show. Besides, it was a beautiful day and the cuckoo was yelling its head off in the hazel wood nearby. Wolf, Jake's shaggy adoring lurcher, was chasing rabbits but never letting his master out of his sight for very long, and Jake wanted to think.

It was nearly five years since he had married Tory, and Granny Maxwell had given them the Mill House at Withrington. And although they had been years of hard work and struggle, Jake knew they had been the happiest in his life. The Mill had been in a dilapidated state when they moved in, but gradually he and Tory had painted the rooms, and gradually they had scraped together enough money to pull down the old stables and build new ones, so they now kept a dozen horses.

There had been terrible setbacks. Two Mays ago he'd been selected to ride for Great Britain for the first time, but the day he was due to leave, Africa stepped on a rusty nail, which put her out of action for several months. One of the young novices, a really promising grey thoroughbred, had jumped out of its field, escaped on to the motorway, been hit by a lorry and had to be destroyed. Then, as Tory had inherited the bulk of her capital by then and Africa was out of action, Jake had spent rather too much money on a top-class horse to fill the gap, which had broken its leg and had to be put down at the first show he took it to.

Things had not gone according to plan in other directions either. At the start of their marriage, Tory had worked as a secretary to a local solicitor, her salary being the main contribution that had saved her, Jake and the horses from starvation. For months they seemed to live on pork pies and baked beans bought with her luncheon vouchers. But within a year and a quarter she was pregnant, and in July of the following year she produced a son. They called him Isa, short for Isaac, after Jake's lost gipsy father, and Jake, who'd been very apprehensive, not particularly liking children and feeling most unready to be a father, found himself utterly besotted with the child. Perhaps it was because little Isa was his only blood relation, or because the boy was so beautiful, with his huge black eyes and white blond hair; or because he was so sturdy and merry and placid and seemed positively to thrive in a cold damp house, and being permanently carted from show to show in a carrycot.

Jake was also pleasantly surprised to find how easy it was to be married to Tory, who was the ideal show-jumper's wife. She never made him feel guilty if he were late back from shows or up all night tending a sick horse. When he came in she always provided him with good food, a sympathetic ear, and sex if he wanted, but was never offended if he didn't. She understood his terrible nerves before big classes, and why often, if he were sorting out his relationship with a particular horse, he could be withdrawn and taciturn. She coped with all the paperwork, paying bills and sending off entry forms. When they married, she'd been terrified of horses, but Jake had helped her to overcome this, and although she'd never be much good as a rider, she soon picked up the rudiments of feeding and looking after a string, fussing over each animal as though she was its mother. So all the horses were happy and the yard ran like clockwork even when he was away.

She was also passionately proud of everything he did and nailed up every new rosette with joy, so a whole wall of the tackroom was now covered. Most important of all, she understood that his character was like a stray dog's rescued from Battersea Dogs' Home. Constantly moving from one show to another satisfied some nomadic gipsy wanderlust in his blood, but he only felt safe doing this knowing he had a safe, loving home to come back to. Like many wanderers, only by going away would he test that home would be still there when he returned.

Two years before he had had a special stroke of luck. He had gone to a horse sale in Warwick, not one of his favourite pastimes. He tried not to be anthropomorphic about horses, but sales always reminded him of the children's home. All those horses, bewildered, frightened, displaced, often coming from cosseted homes or, after years of hard work, to be sold to the knacker's yard, or to people who didn't know how to look after them, or who would abuse their willing natures.

The mare he'd been tipped off about went for more than he could afford, but suddenly he heard a horse squealing his head off. Get me out of this horrible place, he seemed to be saying. Wandering down the horse lines, Jake found a half-starved, dirty, flea-bitten grey gelding, standing about 16.3, with a wall eye, big feet, a coarse head, huge ears flapping like a mule's, and ribs sticking out like a plate rack. He had to be the ugliest horse Jake had ever seen. He was obviously starving. But Jake looked at his teeth and was surprised to see the horse was only six or seven. He looked a hundred, but his legs were clean and strong, and when he was petted and scratched behind the ear, he stopped screaming and accepted Jake's attention with obvious pleasure.

'What's his history?' Jake asked the dealer who trotted him up and down.

'Some old nutter bought him as a pet for his wife, who had one foot in the grave anyway. They called him Sailor. One day the horse stopped suddenly in the yard and she fell off, catching her head on the mounting block, and croaked two days later. The old nutter was heart-broken, but too mean to have the horse put down, so he left him in a tiny yard, virtually starving him to death.

'Finally the old nutter died. When they discovered his body, they found the horse. The only thing he had to drink out of was a rusty bucket, with two inches of rainwater filled with dead wasps. As you can see, it's a case for the RSPCA, but you can't prosecute a dead man.'

For a second, Jake felt choked with rage.

'Poor old sod,' he said stroking the ugly grey head, 'had a bad time, have you?'

He had to pay £150 in order to outbid the horse-meat dealers, which he could ill afford at the time. Once home, he stuffed Sailor full of food and, during the day, turned him out with Africa. After three months he took him hunting and had one of the best days of his life. Sailor still looked like nothing on earth – it was always impossible to get any condition on him – but he could jump anything you put him at and keep going all day. And Jake experienced a surge of excitement he had not felt since he first jumped Africa.

Jake had had many arguments with Granny Maxwell because he refused to overface his horses and did not bring them on fast enough. But there was no need to bring Sailor on slowly. By the end of the next season he had been placed in every class he entered and had lifted himself to Grade A. The Northern show-jumping fraternity, who were a hard-boiled bunch, not easily impressed, laughed at Sailor when they first saw such an extraordinarily unprepossessing horse, but stayed to pray once they had seen him jump.

He was also the cleverest horse in the yard and, when he was bored, would unbolt his stable door and wander over to the house, putting his flea-bitten head in through the kitchen window, hoping for an apple or a piece of chocolate – always milk, he wouldn't touch plain – but just as happy with a petting. He never strayed beyond the yard. It was as though he couldn't believe his luck in having found a good home. He was also the gentlest horse, devoted to Africa, and Wolf the lurcher, and Tory's Jack Russell, Horace, who could lead him in from the fields tugging at the headcollar rope with his teeth. He was also a marvellous babysitter. Tory found she could leave baby Isa in Sailor's box, playing round the manger, clinging on to Sailor's legs and often pulling himself up by the horse's rather skimpy tail. If he fell over and cried, Sailor would nudge him gently, breathing on him, until he laughed and got up again.

Today, on this ravishing day, Jake was hacking Sailor round the fields just to check that all the fences were safe. He had a feeling things were at last coming good for him. Africa was fit again and jumping like a kangaroo. She had won two big classes in Birmingham last week, even beating the mighty Humpty Hamilton against the clock, and Sailor had been placed three times. It had helped this year that he could at last afford to take on a full-time groom, a girl called Tanya, who was as good at riding as at stable management. The idea was that Jake could now concentrate on schooling and competing, but he still found it hard to delegate believing that no one understood or could look after his horses as he could.

Over the past four years he had travelled the Northern and Midland circuits, never venturing South, because it was expensive in petrol, because he hated staying away from home for the night, and because some niggling fear told him that he and his horses weren't yet quite ready to beat the hell out of Rupert Campbell-Black.

Rupert had never been far from his thoughts, however. He had watched him obsessively whenever shows were televised, and read every word about him in the papers, as one outrageous scrape followed another. In fact Jake suspected he had only been picked for the team the May before last (when he'd had to drop out because Africa was unfit) because Rupert and Billy had both been dropped for hell-raising in Paris, and then later getting into some frightful fight at the Royal Plymouth.

Soon afterwards, as though realizing he'd gone too far, Rupert had suddenly married a gorgeous American red-head, who seemed to have had a dramatic effect on his behaviour. Gone were the days of womanizing and wild drinking. Rupert appeared less and less often in the gossip pages and more and more on the sports pages, cleaning up at shows all over Europe, appearing as a regular fixture in the British team, and even being tipped as a Probable for the Olympic Games the following year. Jake gnashed his teeth. He had a feeling that Rupert was pulling further and further away from him, that he would never catch up now.

Still, it was too nice a day to worry about Rupert. Ahead, flanked by pale green willows, he could see the Mill House, its ancient red brick weathered to strawberry roan, tossing its shaggy mane of white roses, which no one had time to prune. It was a long low house. He, Tory, little Isa and Tanya the groom lived on the left-hand side. The right contained the old mill, with its store rooms and huge stone wheel which, fifty years before had been turned by a fast-rushing stream which still hurtled under the house, through the garden and eventually into the River Trent.

Behind the house, hidden from view, were the stables, and beyond that a ring of oak trees with huge acid-green lichened trunks, which protected them all from the vicious North winds.

Jake's ambition this year was to build an indoor school. There were too many days in winter, with the dark mornings and long nights, or when it was frosty, wet or slippery underfoot, when it was impossible to work the horses outside. He'd eaten into Tory's capital so much, he'd have to get a loan from the bank. But ever since the three-day week and the socialists coming to power and the economic gloom, the banks had clamped down and were only lending money at colossal interest. He didn't want to sell more shares at the moment, as they'd have nothing to fall back on and nothing to secure any further borrowing they might need.

He was so deep in thought that it was a few seconds before he realized that Sailor had pricked up his lop ears, Wolf was bounding forward, and Tory was shouting from the house. Popping Sailor across the stream, he cantered up the lawn, which was more of a hayfield these days, as no one had time to mow it.

'Telephone,' she yelled. 'Hurry!'

She was standing by the willow tree, which permanently dangled its leaves in the stream. Eight months pregnant with their second child, she was about as fat now as she had been when he first met her. Her face was pink with excitement.

'Who is it?' he said, sliding off Sailor.

'Malise Gordon, ringing from London. I'll take Sailor.'

Jake handed her the horse and ran into the house as fast as his limp would allow. He mustn't sound too eager. Probably Malise only wished to say he was coming North on a recce, to watch Jake at some show. The telephone was in the hall, which Tory had painted duck-egg blue last February. Damp patches were already showing through. One day they might be able to afford a carpet.

'Hello,' he said curtly.

'Hello, how are you?' said Malise in his brisk military tones, not stopping for an answer. 'You had a good show at Birmingham, I hear. Glad Africa got her form back. Humpty was very irritated to be beaten, but very impressed how she was going.'

'Thanks,' said Jake, feeling Wolf curl up around his feet as he leafed through the neatly typed envelopes on the hall table. Tory had been busy sending off entry forms to the various show secretaries.

'You can't hide your light under a bushel for ever,' said Malise in a slightly hearty voice. 'You ought to try some shows further South.'

'I thought of having a crack at Crittleden in July, and perhaps Wembley in October.'

Malise laughed. 'I was thinking of *much* further South. How about coming to Madrid?'

It was a moment Jake had dreamed about for so long. His throat went dry and he had to clutch on to the rickety table for support.

'Madrid?' he croaked.

236

'Yep, sorry it's such short notice. Ivor Braine's horses have all got the cough, and Driffield broke his arm over the weekend, so I thought you might like to go in his place.'

Jake didn't answer, his mind careering from terror to elation.

'Hello, are you still there?'

'Just,' said Jake. 'I'd like to.' Then, as an afterthought, 'Thanks very much.'

'The rest of the team'll be coming on from Rome,' said Malise, 'except for Humpty, who's flying from Heathrow and sending his groom down by train with the horses. It's a bugger of a journey, takes three or four days, so I suggest you put your groom and your horses in Humpty's box. His groom, Bridie, can collect yours on the way and they can travel as far as Dunkirk together, then take the train the rest of the way. You can fly out to Madrid with Humpty,' he went on, 'and meet the horses there. No point both you and the horses arriving exhausted.'

'No,' said Jake sharply, 'I want to travel with the horses.'

'I really wouldn't recommend it.'

'Anyway I can't spare my groom. Tory's about to have a baby and she can't look after the yard on her own.'

'Are you sure? You really won't enjoy that flog.'

'I don't mind.' Jake had never been abroad and the thought of letting his precious horses out of sight for a second on foreign soil filled him with horror.

'And you'll bring Valerian and Africa?' asked Malise.

'Valerian's been a bit pulled down by some virus. I've got a much better horse. He was placed in three classes at Birmingham.'

'OK,' said Malise, 'you know your own horses. If we need you for the Nations' Cup you can jump Africa.'

In the kitchen Jake found Tory talking to Wolf, who was sitting on the kitchen table. She was also opening a bottle of champagne.

'Where did that come from?' he said, shocked at such extravagance.

'Granny Maxwell gave it to me just before she died. She

237

said I wasn't to open it until you were selected. She had faith in you too. Oh, Jake,' she put down the bottle and flung her arms around his neck and he could feel the tears on her cheeks. 'I'm so so proud of you.'

In the week that followed, Jake was almost too busy to be nervous. Although Tory repeatedly nagged him, he'd never bothered to get a passport, thinking it was tempting providence until he was actually picked. Now all sorts of strings had to be pulled by the BSJA and trips taken to the passport office. Africa and Sailor had to have passports too, which included a drawing of the horse. However many times Jake re-drew Sailor, he still looked like an old Billy goat. They also had to have blood tests, and their health papers had to be stamped. Then shows had to be cancelled and Jake and the horses had to be packed for. With a four-day journey there and possibly back, he would be away for nearly three weeks. He would liked to have rung Humpty and asked his advice about foreign customs and what to wear, but he was too proud. Meanwhile the village dressmaker sat up late every night making him a red coat.

He tried the coat on the night before he left, wishing he was taller and broader in the shoulders. At least he didn't have a turkey red face that clashed with it, like Humpty.

Tory was putting Isa to bed. Wolf, the lurcher, sat on his curved tail, shivering on Jake's suitcase, the picture of desolation. Normally he went with Jake to every show, but some sixth sense told him he was going to be left behind tomorrow.

Next minute Isa wandered in, in blue pyjamas with a Womble on the front and a policeman's helmet on his head which he wore all day and in bed at night. His left wrist was handcuffed to a large teddy bear. He was at the age when he kept acquiring new words, and copied everything Jake and Tory said.

'Daddy going hunting,' he announced, seeing the red coat.

'Not exactly,' said Jake. 'I'm going away for a few days to Spain, and you must take care of Mummy.'

'Will you be back before Mummy gets her baby out? Will you bring me a present?'

Jake turned so he could look at the coat from the back. He wished he knew how hot it would be in Spain.

'What d'you want?'

'Nuvver lorry.'

'You've got about ten,' said Jake. 'For Christ's sake, don't touch that briefcase.'

'What's this?'

'Spanish money.'

'Where is Pain?' said Isa, ignoring Jake and spreading out the notes.

'Over the seas. I said *leave* that case alone.'

Normally he hated snapping at Isa, but last-minute nerves were getting to him.

'Daddy have a whicksey,' said Isa, who regarded a stiff drink as the cure to all grown-up ills, 'and get pissed up.'

'I said *go* and find Mummy.' Jake retrieved the notes and the health papers.

'Mummy's crying,' said Isa.

Jake felt a burst of irritation. He felt guilty about leaving her, but what else could he do? She wanted him to get on; what the hell was she crying for? He found her in the bathroom bending her bulk down slowly to retrieve plastic ducks, boats and sodden towels. Her swollen ankles were spilling over her slip-on shoes. She had had those shoes since he married her.

'What's the matter?' he snapped.

'Nothing.' She concentrated on squeezing out a flannel.

'What the hell's the matter? I can't help going.' His guilt at leaving her made him speak more harshly than he'd meant to. 'It's not going to be much fun for me; 1500 miles on the train in the blazing heat with two horses.'

It was part of the bargain of their marriage that she never clung to him or betrayed her desperate dependency.

'I'm sorry,' she mumbled. 'I'm over the moon that you're going. I don't know what's the matter with me.'

Her lip trembled. Jake put his arm round her, feeling the

239

solid shape of the baby inside her, pressing against him. For a second she clung to him, lowering her guard.

'It's just that I'm going to miss you so much.'

'It'll go very quickly,' he said. 'I'll ring you the moment I get to Madrid.'

Next minute they heard a terrific banging, and Wolf barking. Looking out, they saw Tanya, obviously having to stand on a bucket, peering out of the tiny high tackroom window.

'Will someone come and rescue me? Your wretched son's just locked me in.'

And yet next morning, getting up at first light, with the rising sun touching the willows and the milk-white fields, the Mill House looked so beautiful that Jake wondered how he could bear to leave it. Tanya had already been up for two hours getting the horses ready. She had even borrowed two milk churns from a nearby dairy to carry water, in case Jake ran out on the train journey.

'I'm sorry you're not coming,' he said.

'You can take me next time.'

'If there is a next time,' said Jake, lighting a cigarette.

'Nervous?'

Jake nodded.

Africa heard Humpty's lorry before Jake did. She had changed over the years, growing stronger, more muscular, and filling out behind the saddle. She was more demanding and less sociable, and could be moody and impatient, especially if she was in season. Now, aware that something was up, she darted to her half-door to look out, eyes bold, ears flattened, pawing at her straw, stamping with her forelegs. The other horses put their heads out of the boxes, ready to be jealous because they were not included in the trip. Only Sailor stayed in his box, calmly finishing off his feed. Sailor calmed Africa down. But Jake was her big love.

Both Tory and Tanya felt a stab of relief that Bridie, Humpty's groom, wasn't at all pretty. Plump, with mouse brown curls, she had a greasy skin and a large bottom.

240

'Just my luck to be stuck for four days with that,' thought Jake.

Inside the lorry they could see Humpty's three horses, with the resplendent Porky Boy on the outside, coat gleaming like a conker. By comparison, Sailor, shuffling up the ramp, looked as though he was going on his last journey. At least Africa, in her dark beauty, whinnying and prancing up the ramp, slightly redeemed the yard.

'Well, I don't think you need have any worries about Jake getting off with that,' said Tanya, as the lorry heaved its way over the bridge, rattling against the willow branches.

'The forecast's awful,' Bridie told Jake cheerfully. 'I'm afraid it's going to be a terrible crossing.'

In fact the entire journey was a nightmare. The horse box moved like a snail. A storm blew up in mid-Channel and the boat nearly turned back. Jake spent the entire journey trying to calm the horses. The crossing took so long they missed the train at Dunkirk and had to wait twelve hours before they caught another one, which took them to the Spanish border quite smoothly. There they got into trouble with both French and Spanish customs, who took exception to Jake's emergency passport. Jake, speaking no languages at all, and Bridie, who only had a few words of Spanish, found themselves shunted off to a siding for a day and a half, fast running out of food. Bridie, who was quite used to such delays, whiled the time away reading Mills and Boon novels and being chatted up by handsome customs officials who didn't seem remotely put off by her size.

Jake nearly went crazy, pacing up and down, smoking packet after packet of cigarettes, trying to telephone England.

'If you're abroad, there are always hold-ups,' said Bridie philosophically. 'You'll just have to get used to them.' He's as uptight as a tick that one, she thought. Any minute he'll snap.

At last Jake got on to Tory, who managed to trace Malise in Rome, who pulled more strings and eventually arranged for them to take the next Madrid-bound train. In the ensuing wait, Jake started reading Mills and Boon novels too, not realizing that only now was the real nightmare about to begin.

Their transport turned out to be cattle trucks, with Humpty's three horses and Bridie in one, and Jake, Africa and Sailor in another. There were no windows in the trucks, just air vents and a sliding door. 'Porky Boy won't like this,' said Bridie. 'He's used to a light in his box.'

After lots of shunting and banging back and forth, until every bone in Jake's body was jarred, they were then hitched to a Spanish passenger express. Once the train started there was no communication with the outside world. No one to talk to, just total blackness and occasional flashes as stations flew past. The whiplash effect was appalling. Jake knew exactly what it was like to be a dry martini shuddering in a cocktail shaker.

As they slowed down outside a big station, Jake heard crashing and banging from Bridie's truck next door.

'Porky Boy's gone off his head,' she yelled. 'I can't hold him still enough to dope him.'

Risking his life and eternal abandonment in the middle of Spain, Jake leapt out of his truck and ran along to Bridie's, only making it just in time, and narrowly avoiding being crushed to death by a maddened Porky Boy. Somehow, with the torch between his teeth, he managed to fill the syringe, jab it into the terrified plunging animal and cling on, soothing and talking to him, until he calmed down.

Bridie was tearful in her gratitude. Frantic about Africa and Sailor, Jake then had to wait until the milky white light of morning revealed rolling hills, dotted with olive trees, flattening out to the dusty, leathery plains around Madrid, before the train slowed down enough for him to get back to them. He was so proud. Africa had a cut knee where she had fallen down, and both were obviously saddened by his absence, but delighted to welcome him back. They swayed from side to side keeping their footing. If they could, he thought, they would have got out and pulled the cattle trucks themselves.

When they finally reached Madrid, the trucks were pulled into the passenger station. Jake and Bridie found the platform packed with chic Spanish commuters, soberly dressed for the office, and looking with astonishment on two such travel-worn wrecks and their shabby horses.

After such a hellish journey, Jake was prepared for hen coops in which to stable the horses. But the Madrid show ground turned out to be the last word in luxury, with a sumptuous club house, swimming pools and squash courts, and a huge jumping arena next to an even bigger practice ring containing more than fifty different jumps.

'Humpty says it's worth coming to Madrid just to practise over these fences,' said Bridie as she unloaded a stiff, weary, chastened Porky Boy.

Even better, each foreign team had been given its own private yard with splendid loose boxes. Next door, the victorious German team had just arrived from Rome and were unloading their huge horses and making a lot of noise. Jake recognised Ludwig von Schellenberg and Hans Schmidt, two riders he'd worshipped for years. Tomorrow, he thought with a thud of fear, he'd be competing against them.

He was distracted from his fears by another crisis. The loose boxes were all bedded with thick straw, which was no good for greedy Sailor, who always guzzled straw and blew himself out. Jake had run out of wood shavings on the journey down. How could he possibly explain to these charming, smiling but uncomprehending Spaniards what he wanted? Bridie's dictionary had 'Wood' but not Shavings'. He felt a great weariness.

'Can I help?' said a voice.

It was Malise Gordon, who had just flown in from Rome, his high complexion tanned by the Italian sun, wearing a lightweight suit and looking handsome and authoritative.

Jake was never so pleased to see anyone.

Immediately Malise broke into fluent Spanish and sorted everything out.

'You look absolutely shattered,' he said to Jake. 'Sorry it was a bloody journey, but I warned you. Still, it was as well you were there to look after Porky Boy last night. Are your horses O.K.?'

While the Spanish grooms put down the wood-shavings for Sailor, Jake showed Malise Africa's knee, which mercifully hadn't swollen up.

'Where's your other horse?'

'Here. They've got his box ready.'

Sailor, a messy eater, had tipped all his feed into the wood shavings and was busily picking it out. He gave Malise a baleful look out of his wall eye. After the four-day journey he looked perfectly dreadful.

'Christ,' thought Malise, 'we'll be a laughing stock entering something like that.' But, he supposed, in the remote chance of Jake having to compete in the Nations' Cup, he could always ride Africa. Anyway, the boy looked all in. No point in saying anything now.

'I'll take you back to the hotel. You'd better get some sleep.' Malise looked at his watch. 'It's only ten o'clock now. The rest of the team won't arrive till this afternoon. I suggest we meet in the bar around nine p.m. Then we can have dinner together and you can meet them all.'

To Jake, who had never slept in a hotel, the bedroom seemed the height of luxury. There was a bathroom with a shower, and a bath and a loo, and free soap and bubble bath, and a bathcap, and three white towels. In the bedroom there was a television, a wireless, a telephone and a huge double bed. He was dying for some coffee but he didn't dare pick up the telephone in case they couldn't understand him. French windows led out on to a bosomy balcony which looked over a park. To the left, if he leaned out, he could see a street full of shops and cafés with tables outside. Already smells of olive oil, pimentos and saffron were drifting up from the kitchen. Drawing the thick purple

245

curtains and only bothering to take off his shoes, Jake fell on to the surprisingly hard bed. The picture on the wall, of a matador in obscenely tight pink trousers shoving what looked like knitting needles into the neck of a bull, swam before his eyes and he was asleep.

Despite his exhaustion, however, he only slept fitfully. His dreams of disastrous rounds kept being interrupted by bursts of flamenco music or the screams of children playing in the park. By six the city had woken up and stretched itself after its siesta and Jake decided to abandon any hope of sleep. Outside, the streets were packed with cars rattling over the cobbles, hardly restrained at all by lights or frantically whistling policemen. Tables along the pavement were beginning to fill up, crowds to parade up and down. Looking across at the park, he saw a small child racing after a red ball, then tripping over a gambolling dog, falling flat on his face and bursting into noisy sobs. Next moment a pretty dark-haired mother had rushed forward, sworn at the dog and gathered up the child, covering him with kisses. Jake was suddenly flattened with longing for Isa and Tory. He was desperate to ring home, but he didn't know how to, nor yet did he dare pick up the telephone and ask for some tea.

Instead, raging with thirst, he drank a couple of mugs of water out of the tap, then unpacked, showered and, wrapped only in one of the white towels, wandered out on to the balcony. Instantly he stepped back, for there on the next balcony was a beautiful girl painting her toenails coral pink and soaking up the slanting rays of the early evening sun.

She was impossibly slender, with long legs and arms, which, despite being covered in freckles, were already tanning becomingly to the colour of weak tea. She wore a saffron yellow bikini and her hair was hidden by a big yellow towel. Beside her lay the catalogue of some art gallery, a Spanish dictionary, what looked like a book of poetry and a half-finished glass of orange juice. Obviously she could make Reception understand her. The whole

246

impression was of a marvellously pampered and overbred race horse. As she stretched luxuriously, enjoying the sensation of being warm and alive, Jake felt a stab of lust. Why didn't one ever see girls like that in Warwickshire? He wished she would pick her nose or scratch her crotch; anything to make her more normal and less desirable.

Suddenly there was a commotion in the corridor. The girl jumped up. A man's voice could be heard shouting in the passage, 'O.K., we'll see you in the bar about nine.'

The girl in the saffron bikini could be heard calling out in an American accent, 'Darling, it's so good to see you.'

There was a long pause. Then he heard the man's voice more clearly. It was a flat distinctive drawl which he would recognize anywhere and which made his knees disappear and the hairs prickle on the back of his neck.

'Bloody awful journey,' said the voice. 'Lorry kept overheating. We've been on the road for nearly thirty-six hours.'

'Sweetheart,' said the girl, 'I'm so sorry. You must be exhausted.'

Another pause followed, then the voice said sharply, 'I don't care how fucking exhausted I am, get that bikini off.'

The girl started protesting, but not for long. Next moment there were sounds of lovemaking, with the bed banging against the wall so hard that Jake felt he was back in the cattle truck. Mercifully it only lasted five minutes. Any more evidence of Rupert's superstud servicing would have finished Jake off altogether. Almost worse was the splashing and laughter as later they had a bath together. It was still desperately hot. Jake made his bed neatly and, soaked with sweat, had another shower and changed his shirt, for something to do. He'd have liked to have washed some underpants and shirts and hung them out on the balcony, but he could imagine Rupert's derisive comments. Later he heard them having a drink on the balcony.

'Better get a few quick ones under my belt, so Malise doesn't think I'm alcoholic.'

By nine o'clock Jake was so crucified by nerves and

waiting that he couldn't bring himself to go downstairs, until Malise rang up from Reception saying they were all in the bar, and had he overslept? Malise met him as he came out of the lift. Noticing the set face, the black rings under the eyes, the obvious tension, he said, 'Don't worry, they're all very unalarming.'

There they were – all his heroes. Humpty Hamilton, puce from the heat, drinking lager. Lavinia Greenslade, whom he remembered from the first Bilborough Show. She was even prettier now that she'd lightened her hair, and wore it shorter and curlier. On either side, like two guard dogs, sat her mother, who wore too much cheap jewellery, and her father, who had ginger sideboards and a stomach spilling over his trousers. They didn't smile. Lavinia was too recent a cap herself for them to regard any new member of the team with enthusiasm. Billy Lloyd-Foxe had filled out and broken his nose since prep-school days, but looked more or less the same. He was laughing with a most beautiful red-headed girl, who was wearing black flared trousers and a white silk shirt tied under her breasts and showing off her smooth bare midriff. By her freckled arms and her coral pink toenails, Jake identified the girl on the balcony. Rupert had his back turned as he paid for a round of drinks and signed an autograph for the barman, but Jake immediately recognized the back of that smooth blond head and the broad blue striped shoulders. He felt a wave of horror and loathing.

'This is Jake Lovell,' said Malise. 'I'm sure he knows who all of you are.'

Rupert swung round, smiling. In his brown face his eyes were as brilliantly blue as a jay's wing.

'Hi,' he said. 'Welcome to alcoholics not at all anonymous. I hear you had a worse journey than us, which seems impossible. What are you going to drink?'

Jake, who'd rehearsed this moment so often, and who was prepared to be icily aloof, found himself totally disarmed by such friendliness and muttered he'd like some Scotch. Billy got to his feet and shook Jake's hand.

'You've been cleaning up on the northern circuit. Don't venture up there often myself, too easy to get beaten.'

'That was a good horse you were jumping at Birmingham,' said Humpty, patting the empty seat beside him, 'What's she called, Australia?'

'Africa,' said Jake.

'Looks almost clean bred. Who was her sire?'

'Don't know.'

'And her dam?'

'Don't know that either.'

'Oh, shut up, Humpty,' said Rupert, handing Jake a very large glass of whisky, which made Malise frown slightly.

Rupert lifted his glass to Jake. 'Welcome to the British squad,' he said. 'Hope it's the first of many.'

'Thanks,' said Jake. He took a slug of his whisky, which was so strong it made his eyes water. He put his glass down at once, so they shouldn't see how much his hand was shaking.

'Lavinia's been capped for Great Britain six times,' said her mother defensively.

'Oh, please, Mummy.'

'You should be proud of the fact,' went on her mother. 'The only girl in the team.'

'What about Driffield?' said Rupert. 'I've always thought his sex was slightly in question.'

'No, it isn't,' said Humpty. 'I've shared a room with him.'

'That's enough,' said Malise.

'Did you get to the Prado this afternoon?' Helen asked him.

Malise shook his head.

'I spent a couple of hours there,' she said. 'The Velasquez are out of this world. Such power. I only managed to do two rooms, but I also looked at the cathedral. The nave is just wonderful.'

Rupert stifled a yawn. 'I prefer navels,' he said, running his hand over his wife's midriff. Then, pushing down her black trousers, he fingered her belly button. 'Particularly yours.'

It was definitely a gesture of possession and he smiled across at Jake with that bullying, mocking, appraising look that Jake remembered so well.

Humpty turned back to Jake. 'By the way, thanks for looking after Porky on the way down. Bridie said he might have damaged himself and her very badly if you hadn't stepped in.'

'The train driver ought to be shot,' said Jake.

'Spaniards don't like animals,' said Humpty. 'Porky's highly strung of course, but so was his dam.'

And Humpty was off on a long involved dissertation on Porky Boy's breeding. Jake appeared to listen and studied the others. Mr and Mrs Greenslade were discussing what horses Lavinia ought to jump, across Lavinia, who was gazing surreptitiously at Billy. Billy was arguing fairly amicably with Rupert about whether a particular mare was worth selling and how much they'd get for her. Helen and Malise, having exhausted Velasquez, had moved on to Spanish poetry. She was an astonishingly beautiful girl, thought Jake, but too fragile for Rupert. Jake couldn't imagine him handling anyone with care for very long.

'I just adore Lorca,' Helen was saying. 'He's so passionate and basic; that poem that starts "Green, Green, I want you Green".'

'Sounds like Billy,' said Rupert, 'only in his case it's Gweenslade, Gweenslade, I want you Gweenslade.'

'Shut up,' hissed Billy, shooting a nervous glance in the direction of Lavinia's mother.

'Not unless you buy me a drink,' said Rupert, handing Billy his empty glass.

'O.K.,' said Billy, getting up. 'Who needs a refill?'

'Jake does,' said Rupert.

Unable and not particularly wanting to get a word in edgeways while Humpty talked, Jake had had plenty of time to finish his whisky. Having not had anything to eat for at least thirty-six hours, he was beginning to feel very tight. But before he could protest, Rupert had whipped his glass away and handed it to Billy.

'Not as strong as the last one, then,' said Malise firmly. 'That was a quadruple.'

'He's not eighteen you know,' said Rupert softly.

'How old are you?' asked Humpty.

'Twenty-six,' said Jake.

'Same as me and Rupe,' said Billy, hailing the waiter.

'It's funny we haven't heard of you before,' said Lavinia. 'Awfully womantic, to be suddenly picked out of the blue like that.'

'I started late,' said Jake.

'But I'm sure I've seen you before,' said Billy, puzzled, as he handed double whiskies to Jake and Rupert.

'Pwobably in *Horse and Hound*, or *Widing* magazine,' said Lavinia.

No it wasn't, thought Billy to himself. There was something about Jake that made him feel uneasy, layers of memory being slowly peeled back like an onion, not very happy memories, the kind you tucked into a corner of your mind and tried to forget.

They dined in a taverna a couple of streets away. The walls were covered in fans and castanets and pictures of ladies in mantillas. In a corner a fat tenor in a rather dirty white frilly shirt, and with greasy patent leather hair, was dispiritedly strumming a guitar. The owner rushed out, shaking hands with Malise, Humpty, Rupert and Billy and showing them their signed photographs on the wall, then going into a frenzy of ecstasy over Lavinia's blonde beauty. Redheads were less rare in Madrid than blondes, and Helen was a little too thin for Spanish tastes.

Jake was beginning to feel distinctly odd. He must get some food inside him. He found himself with Lavinia on his left and Mr Greenslade on his right. Bottles were put on the table and Rupert immediately filled everyone's glasses. Completely incomprehensible menus came round.

'What's gazpacho?' he asked Lavinia.

'Tomato soup,' said Rupert.

That sounded gentle and stomach-settling.

'And polpi?'

'Some sort of pasta,' said Rupert.

'I'll have that,' said Jake.

Suddenly he noticed Billy's hand caressing Lavinia's thigh under the table, where her mother and father couldn't see. The waiter arrived for their order. Firmly Jake said he'd like gazpacho and polpi.

'I'd like a large steak and chips,' said Humpty.

'So would I,' said Billy, 'but not chips, just a salad – my trousers are getting disgustingly tight – and Mediterranean prawns to start.'

'You shouldn't drink so much,' said Rupert, filling up his glass.

Helen turned to the waiter and started to address him in Spanish.

'Oh, for Christ's sake,' said Rupert irritably, 'they all speak English.'

'Spanish is the native language of approximately 200 million people throughout the world,' said Helen, flushing slightly. 'That can't be all bad.'

'At least she can translate your horoscope in the Spanish papers,' said Billy.

'And jolly useful at Customs,' said Mrs Greenslade, who admired Helen.

'We've got Marion for that,' said Rupert. 'She's got big boobs, which is more a language the Customs officers understand.'

Apart from his hand stroking her thigh, Billy was studiously avoiding Lavinia for the benefit of her parents, so she turned to Jake.

'How did you get on in Rome?' he said. 'I haven't seen any papers.'

'I got a second and a third. Wupert did best. He won two classes and got a clear wound in the Nations' Cup. But we were still thwashed by the Germans and the Fwench. I don't think we'll ever beat them. Ludwig and Hans Schmidt are like computers: they just pwogwamme their horses and wound they go.'

Jake was eating bread, desperate to mop up some alcohol. The fat flamenco singer, after a lot of stamping, launched into some mournful ditty.

'Sounds like Grand Hotel,' said Rupert.

Now he'd had a lot to drink, Jake found his eyes continually drawn to Rupert, like a rabbit to a snake. He still felt the same sick churning inside. Rupert's whiplash tongue was still there. Soon he knew he'd be the recipient. He realized again what an evil man Rupert was behind his offhand jokey exterior.

It was very hot in the restaurant. Jake was drenched with sweat.

'OK?' asked Malise. 'Grub should be up in a minute. That's one of the maddening things about Spain: no one dines before ten o'clock. At least we get a nice late start.'

'I'm going to spend tomowwow morning sunbathing,' said Lavinia.

'You are not,' said her father, 'You'll sort out that stop of Snowstorm's. We're not risking him ducking out again.'

At last food began to arrive. A plate of soup was put in front of Jake. A great waft of garlic made him feel distinctly queasy. God knows what was in it. Little bits of fried bread, green peppers and cucumbers floated on top.

'This is a most interesting paella,' Helen was saying as she speared a large mussel. Feeling slightly sick, Jake took a mouthful of soup and only just avoided spitting it out. It was stone cold and heavily garlicked. He put his spoon down and took a huge gulp of wine, then a piece of bread to take the taste away.

What was he to do? Was it some diabolical plan of Rupert's, telling the waiter to bring him cold soup, so he could laugh like a drain when Jake ate it?

'What's the matter?' said Malise.

'Nothing,' said Jake. He mustn't betray weakness. He took another mouthful and very nearly threw up. Glancing up, he saw Rupert eyeing him speculatively.

'Gazpacho good?' he asked.

'It's stone cold, if you want to know,' said Jake. 'They've

forgotten to heat it up.'

Rupert grinned. 'It's meant to be,' he said gently. 'I should have warned you. It's a Spanish national dish, no doubt enjoyed throughout the world by approximately 200 million people.'

Jake gripped the sides of the plate. For a second he felt such a wave of hatred he nearly hurled it in Rupert's face.

'I'll have the gazpacho,' said Billy, leaning over, whipping away Jake's plate and handing him the Mediterranean prawns in return.

'Then you'll sleep alone,' said Rupert.

'It seems I have no other choice,' said Billy, smiling blandly at Mrs Greenslade, and squeezing Lavinia's thigh a bit harder.

Rupert started discussing bullfights with Humpty Hamilton.

'We'll go to one later in the week.'

'I'm not going,' said Lavinia. 'I thinks it's vewy cwuel.'

'Have you ever seen one?' asked Rupert.

'No.'

'You're just like Helen. She was out with the Antis when I first met her.'

She looks like a fox, thought Jake, beautiful, nervous, wistful, with those haunted yellow eyes, a tamed fox that might bolt at any minute.

'The El Grecos are wonderful,' she was saying to Malise. 'You look like an El Greco yourself, kind of lean and distinguished.'

Malise, Jake noticed, blushed slightly and looked not unpleased.

'I'm going back tomorrow morning. Why don't you come too?' she went on.

'Tomorrow, my angel,' said Rupert with a distinct edge to his voice, 'you are going to spend the morning in bed with me.'

The second courses were arriving. Jake felt the mayonnaise and prawns mixing unhappily with the whisky and wine in his stomach. Pasta was just the thing to settle it.

Next moment a plate was put down in front of him. He nearly heaved at the sight; it was full of octopus.

'I didn't order this!'

'Si, senor, polpi.'

Jake turned dark red. 'You said it was pasta,' he hissed at Rupert.

'How silly of me,' drawled Rupert. 'Of course, polpi, octopus. I'd forgotten. What a pity you didn't ask Helen or Malise.'

'You're a shit, Rupert,' said Billy, 'Look,' he added to the waiter, 'take this back and get some risotto, or would you rather have a steak?'

Jake shook his head. He was feeling awful.

'I think I've had enough.'

'Have some of my wice and chicken,' said Lavinia, tipping it on to his side plate. 'It's weally good, but I'll never get thwough it all. Did you know there were two men in the Spanish team called Angel and Maria?'

Dinner dragged on. Jake was dropping now. He picked at the rice Lavinia had given him but didn't manage to finish it. Once again he was overwhelmed with such homesickness he almost wept. If he was home now, he'd probably have just come in from a show. Tory would be waiting and together they'd go up and gloat over the sleeping Isa.

'Anyone want pudding?' asked Malise.

'I'd love some berries,' said Helen. 'Have they any fresh berries?'

'In English you specify them,' said Rupert through gritted teeth. 'Strawberries, raspberries, gooseberries.'

'I'm sure there are some strawberries,' said Malise, smiling at Helen.

'What about you, Jake?'

Jake shook his head and got to his feet. 'Thank you for dinner. I'm off to bed,' he said. 'Can I settle up with you in the morning?'

'This is on the BSJA,' said Malise.

'Well, thanks,' said Jake.

255

'Sleep well,' said Malise. 'Order breakfast from Reception. They all speak English, and for Christ's sake don't drink the water in the taps.'

'You going to bed?' said Rupert in surprise. 'Sorry about the polpi and the gazpacho. New boy's tease you know.'

'I know,' said Jake bleakly, 'only too well.'

Looking at the set white face, in a flash Billy remembered. Lovell, J. Of course! He knew he'd seen him before. He was the gipsy boy at St Augustine's, Gyppo Jake, whom he and Rupert had bullied unmercifully until he ran away. It was the one thing in his life he'd always been ashamed of. He wanted to say something to Jake, to apologize for the teasing at dinner, but it was too late. He'd gone.

Outside Jake took a taxi down to the show ground. Fortunately he'd remembered his pass and the guards let him in. He realized he was very drunk.

The Great Bear overhead kept disintegrating and reforming, like a swarm of illuminated gnats. Crossing the exercise ring, he threw up behind a large Spanish chestnut. As he covered it with sand, he hoped one of Rupert's bloody horses would slip on it tomorrow.

Bastard, bastard, bastard, he hadn't changed at all. New boy's tease indeed. Nausea overwhelmed him again. He leant against an oak feeling dizzy. Finally he made the stables. It was a comfort that Africa and Sailor were so pleased to see him. Blinking sleepily, they smelt of hay and contentment. One arm round each of their necks, he clung on to them, desperate for reassurance. They were *his* horses from *his* yard.

'Tomorrow,' he said, 'we'll go out and lynch him.'

Jake never knew if it was a result of meeting Rupert again, or because he drank too much tap water, but in the early hours of the morning he was laid low with a vicious attack of gyppy tummy. For the first few days of the show, it was all he could do to struggle up and crawl down to the stables to look after Africa and Sailor. Later in the day, he was either eliminated or knocked up a cricket score of faults in every class he entered. The jumps were huge and solid, with the poles fitting deeply into the cups, and the competition was fierce. Both Africa and Sailor were out of sorts after the long journey. Jake was so strung-up, he transmitted his nerves to the horses, who jumped worse and worse as the week went on.

To make matters worse, none of the classes started before three o'clock in the afternoon, with an evening performance beginning at 11 p.m. By the time the final national anthem had been played it was three a.m. and usually four o'clock before Jake fell into bed, to wake like a stone at six in the morning, his usual time for getting up, after which he couldn't get back to sleep again.

A doctor was summoned and gave him pills and advised forty-eight hours' rest. But for a workaholic like Jake, this was impossible. He couldn't bear to be parted from his horses, his one link with home. He had no desire to sightsee with Malise or Helen, or lounge round the pool sunbathing with the others and be confronted with the contemptuous bronzed beauty of Rupert Campbell-Black.

So while the others relaxed and enjoyed themselves, Jake didn't miss a round jumped by another rider, or a work-out

in the warm-up area. He was learning all the time, but not to his advantage. There were too many of his heroes around to influence him, and he got increasingly muddled as first he tried to ride like the Italians, then like the dashing Spaniards, then like the mighty Germans.

The rest of the team, except Rupert, tried to be friendly and helpful. They were all relieved he was not the white-hot saviour predicted by Malise, but as one catastrophic round followed another and he became more monosyllabic and withdrawn, they gave up.

Rupert, on the other hand, was openly hostile. On the morning after they arrived in Madrid, he was riding round the practice ring when Billy said, 'You know that new chap?'

'The great gourmet and conversationalist?' said Rupert scornfully.

'Don't you recognize him. He's the same Gyppo Lovell who was at St Augustine's with us.'

'Can't be.'

'Bloody is. Don't you remember his mother was the cook. Mrs Lovell? She did herself in.'

'Hardly surprising after producing an undersized little runt like that. Didn't he become a boarder?'

'Yes,' said Billy bleakly. 'He was in our dormitory. We gave him such hell he ran away.'

'Perhaps we should repeat the experiment. With any luck he might do it again.'

'You didn't help much last night,' snapped Billy. 'Making him order octopus. Poor sod, he's never been abroad before.'

'Certainly doesn't know how to behave in a hotel,' said Rupert. 'I caught him making his bed this morning.'

For a few minutes they rode on in silence, then Billy said, 'I feel I ought to make it up to him somehow for being such a shit at St Augustine's.'

Rupert started to play on an imaginary violin. 'Don't be so bloody wet. Little creeps like that deserve to be hammered. How the hell did he get started anyway?'

'Well that's the interesting part. D'you remember a hugely fat deb named Tory Maxwell?'

Rupert shuddered. 'Only too vividly. Maxwell big as a House – unable to turn round without the use of tugs.' He glanced sideways at Billy, relieved to see he had made him laugh. 'And quite rich.'

'That's the one. Well, Jake Lovell married her and evidently used all her cash to get started.'

'No wonder he's undersized; squashed flat in the sack. Must be like going to bed with a steam roller. Who told you all this?'

'Malise. Last night. He thinks Lovell's brilliant.'

'Well, he's wrong. Lovell's just about as insipid as the mince his mother used to cook. And, what's more, he kept Helen and me awake all night throwing up.'

To rub salt into Jake's wounds, all the other members of the team were jumping well and in the money, particularly Rupert who won a Vespa on the third day and insisted on roaring round the show ground on it, to everyone's amusement and irritation. Jake's was the only part of the British tackroom without its share of rosettes.

Rupert never lost an opportunity to put the boot in. On the third day, just before the competition, he persuaded Marion to hide all Jake's breeches and his red coat and fill up his trunk with frilly underwear.

Marion was only too happy to oblige. Wandering round, heavily curvaceous in pink hot pants and a sleeveless pink T shirt, she was the toast of the show ground, always followed by a swarm of admiring tongue-clicking Spaniards, and the recipient of endless bonhomie from the other male international riders.

Jake, resentful that Rupert not only had an exquisite wife but a spectacular groom, ignored Marion, a reaction to which she was unused.

'He went bananas when he found his clothes missing,' she told Rupert gleefully. 'He's not as cool as he makes out.'

Although Marion soon returned his clothes, what upset Jake more was that the yellow tansy flower he always wore

in the heel of his left boot to bring him luck had somehow vanished. Without his talisman, his luck was bound to plummet and as a result he lost even more confidence.

Most of all he was upset by Rupert's constant cracks about Sailor – that he must be a mule or a camel, and no wonder he'd frightened them at the customs; they must have thought were letting a dinosaur into the country. Jake felt very protective towards Sailor, whom he loved very deeply, and his heart blackened against Rupert.

On the fifth day Malise announced the British team: Rupert, Billy, Humpty Hamilton and Lavinia, with Jake as reserve. In the evening he took Jake out for a drink and explained there was nothing else he could do on Jake's current form.

'Don't worry,' he said, spearing an olive out of his very dry martini. 'This often happens to new caps.'

'Not as badly as this,' said Jake, gazing gloomily into a glass of soda water. He still felt too sick even to smoke. His eyes seemed three inches deep in his face. His face was grey and seamed with exhaustion; he must have lost half a stone.

'It's a vicious circle,' said Malise gently. 'Everyone talks about the killer instinct and being hungry enough to go out and win, but you're so snarled up inside you're frightening the hell out of your horses. I know the fences seem huge and you're worried about overfacing them, but you *must* be more aggressive. The only way to tackle those fences is to attack. Be accurate, but ride on all the time. Those big heavy poles are so firm you can afford to clout them. Africa should be able to sail over them anyway.'

Jake's face registered no emotion. A fly was buzzing round their heads. Malise flicked it away with a copy of *The Times*.

'Spanish fly,' said Jake suddenly, with the ghost of a smile. 'S'pposed to be good for sex, isn't it?'

Malise laughed. 'Never tried it myself, more Rupert's province. Expect you're feeling homesick too, missing Tory and the baby, and you're pulled down looking after the horses by yourself. It's amazing how your first win will

buck you up.'

'If I ever do win.'

'My dear boy, I've seen you on form. I know you're good. You've just got to calm down.'

Jake suddenly felt an emotion close to adulation. He could imagine following Malise into battle without a qualm. If only he'd had a father like that, or even a father like Mr Greenslade, who bossed you around all the time because he minded about you. There he was buying himself a drink at the bar, and about to come and join them.

'I'm going to be very unorthodox,' said Malise. He handed Jake a bottle with some red pills in. 'Those'll make you sleep; put you out like a light. Don't tell the rest of the team I've given them to you. They'll play havoc with your reflexes, but you're not jumping tomorrow or in the Nations' Cup, and a couple of good nights' sleep'll put you right for the Grand Prix on Saturday. And don't tell me you don't approve of sleeping pills. Nor do I, except in an emergency. Tomorrow you're not going anywhere near the stables. Marion and Tracey will look after Africa and Sailor. You can go on the sight-seeing jaunt with the rest of the team.'

After fourteen hours sleep, Jake woke feeling much better. He didn't know whether Malise had had a word with them, but all the team were particularly nice to him as they set off out of Madrid in an old bus, across dusty plains, like the hide of a great slaughtered bull, then through rolling hills dotted with olive trees and orange groves. The road was full of potholes, sending sledgehammer blows up Jake's spine as the back wheels went over them. Rupert sat next to Helen with his arm along the back of the seat, but not touching her because it was too hot. Billy sat in front, talking constantly to them, refereeing any squabbles, sticking up for Helen. Lavinia Greenslade sat with her father. Humpty sat with Jake and talked non-stop about Porky Boy.

Only Rupert didn't let up in his needling. Every donkey or mule or depressed-looking horse they passed reminded him of Sailor or 'Jake's Joke', as he now called him.

They lunched at a very good restaurant, sitting outside under the plane trees, eating cochinella or roast sucking pig. It was the first square meal Jake had been able to keep down since he arrived. While they were having coffee, a particularly revolting old gipsy woman came up and tried to read their fortunes.

'Do tell your ghastly relation to go away, Jake,' said Rupert.

Helen, beautiful, radiant and clinging, was surprised Rupert was being so poisonous to this taciturn newcomer. She tried to talk to Jake and ask him about his horses, but, aware that he was being patronized, he answered abruptly and left her in mid-sentence.

Afterwards they went to a bull farm and tried playing with the young bulls and heifers with padded horns and a cape. Rupert and Billy, who'd both had a fair amount to drink at lunchtime, were only too anxious to have a go. Humpty, who'd eaten too much sucking pig ('You might pop if a horn grazed you,' said Rupert), refused to try, and so did Jake.

Side by side, but both feeling very different emotions, Jake and Helen watched Rupert, tall and lean, a natural at any sport, swinging away as the little bull hurtled towards him. Determined to excel, he was already getting competitive. Billy, fooling around, couldn't stop laughing, and was finally sent flying and only pulled out of danger just in time by Rupert. In the end Rupert only allowed himself to be dragged away because they had to be in Madrid to watch a bullfight at six. Before the fight, they were shown the chapel where the matadors pray before the fight.

'Do with a session in there before tomorrow afternoon,' said Billy. 'Dear God make us beat the Germans.'

The bullfight nauseated Jake, particularly when the picadors came on, riding their pathetic, broken-down, insufficiently padded horses. If they were gored, according to Humpty, they were patched up and sent down into the ring to face the ordeal again. They were so thin they were in no condition to run away. The way, too, that the picadors were tossing their goads into the bull's neck to break his muscles reminded Jake of Rupert's method of bullying.

The cochinella was already churning inside him.

'I say, Jake,' Rupert's voice carried down the row, 'doesn't that picador's horse remind you of Sailor. If you popped down to the Plaza de Toros later this evening, I'm sure they'd give you a few pesetas for him.'

Jake gritted his teeth and said nothing.

'That's wight,' whispered Lavinia, who was sitting next to him. 'Don't wise. It's the only way to tweat Wupert.'

Jake felt more cheerful, particularly when, the next moment, Lavinia plucked at his sleeve saying, 'Can I wush past you quickly? I'm going to be sick.'

'I'll come with you,' said Jake.

Neither of them was sick but on the way home enjoyed a good bitch about Rupert. The rest of the team went out to a party at the Embassy. Jake followed Malise's advice and went to bed early again.

On the morning of the Nations' Cup, Jake woke feeling better in body but not in mind. The sight of fan mail and invitations so overcrowding Rupert's pigeon hole that they spilled over into Humpty's and Lavinia's on either side gave him a frightful stab of jealousy.

Then in his own pigeon hole he found a letter from Tory, which filled him equally with remorse and homesickness. 'Darling Jake,' she wrote in her round, childish hand, 'Isa and Wolf and all the horses and Tanya and most of all me (or should it be I) are missing you dreadfully. But I keep telling myself that it's all in a good cause, and that by the time you get this letter, you'll have really made all the other riders sit up, particularly Rupert. Is he still as horrible or has marriage mellowed him? I know you're going to do really well.'

Jake couldn't bear to read any more. He scrumpled up the letter and put it in his hip pocket. Skipping breakfast, he went straight down to the stables. He wanted to work the horses before it got too punishingly hot.

Walking into the British tackroom, he steeled himself for whatever grisly practical joke was on the menu today, but he found everything in place. Because it was Nations' Cup Day, everyone was far too preoccupied. The grooms were tense and abstracted, the horses edgy. They knew something was up. Jake worked both the horses and was pleased to find Sailor had recovered from the bout of colic he'd had earlier in the week, and Africa's leg was better.

Back in the yard he cooled down Sailor's legs with a hose, amused by the besotted expression on the horse's long speckled face. Nearby, Tracey was washing The Bull's tail. Beyond her, Rupert's groom, Marion, was standing on a hay bale to plait the mighty Macaulay's mane, showing off her long brown legs in the shortest pale blue hotpants and grumbling about the amount of work she had to get through. Macaulay was so over the top that, rather than risk hotting him up, Rupert had decided to ride Belgravia in the parade beforehand and only bring out Macaulay for the actual class. This meant Marion had two horses to get ready.

Jake, who'd been carefully studying Rupert's horses, thought they were getting too many oats. No one could deny Rupert's genius as a rider, but his horses were not happy. He had surreptitiously watched Rupert take Mayfair, Belgravia and Macaulay off to a secluded corner of the huge practice ring and seen how he made Tracey and Marion each hold the end of the top pole of a fence, lifting it as the horses went over to give them a sharp rap on the shins, however high they jumped. This was meant to make them pick up their feet even higher the next time. The practice, known as rapping, was strictly illegal in England.

Jake, however, was most interested in Macaulay. He was a brilliant horse, but still young and inexperienced. Jake felt he was being brought on too fast.

In the yard the wireless was belching out Spanish pop music.

'I do miss Radio One,' said Tracey.

The Italian team came past, their beautifully streaked

hair as well cut as their jeans, and stopped to exchange backchat with Marion and Tracey.

As Jake started to dry Sailor's legs, the horse nudged at his pocket for Polos.

'How long have we got?' Tracey asked Marion.

'About an hour and a half before the parade.'

'Christ,' said Tracey, plaiting faster. 'I'm never going to be ready in time. Give over Bull, keep still.' The Bull looked up with kind, shining eyes.

'You want a hand?' asked Jake. 'I've nearly finished Sailor.'

'You haven't,' said a voice behind him.

It was Malise Gordon, looking elegant, even in this heat, in a pale grey suit, but extremely grim.

'You're going to have to jump after all,' he said. 'That stupid idiot, Billy, sloped off this morning with Rupert to have another crack at bull-fighting and got himself knocked out cold.'

Tracey gave a wail and dropped her comb. The Bull jerked up his head.

'It's all right. He'll live,' said Malise irritably. 'The doctor doesn't think it's serious, but Billy certainly doesn't know what day of the week it is and there's no chance of him riding.'

Tracey burst into tears. Marion stopped plaiting and put her arms round Tracey, glaring at Jake as though it was his fault.

'He's got a head like a bullet; don't worry,' Marion said soothingly.

'Come on,' said Malise, not unkindly. 'Pull yourself together; put The Bull back in his box and get moving on whoever Jake's going to ride. Africa, I presume.'

Jake shook his head. 'Her leg's not right. I'm not risking it. I'll ride Sailor.'

For a second Malise hesitated. 'You don't want to jump The Bull?'

Catching Tracey's and Marion's look of horror, Jake shook his head. If by the remotest chance he didn't let the

265

side down, he was bloody well not having it attributed to the fact that he wasn't riding his own horse.

'All right, you'd better get changed. You're meant to be walking the course in an hour, but with the General coming and Spanish dilatoriness it's impossible to be sure.'

Luckily Jake didn't have time to panic. Tracey sewed the Union Jack on to his red coat. Normally he would have been fretting around, trying to find the socks, the breeches, the shirt and the white tie which he wore when he last won a class. But as it was so long since he had won anything, he'd forgotten which was the last set of clothes that worked. His face looked grey and contrasted with the whiteness of his shirt like a before-and-after Persil ad. His hands were trembling so much he could hardly tie his tie, and his red coat, which fitted him before he left England, was now too loose. Then suddenly, when he dropped a peseta and was searching for it under the forage bin, he found his tansy flower, slightly battered but intact. Overjoyed, he slipped it into his left boot. Aware of it, a tiny bump under his heel, he felt perhaps his luck might be turning at last.

Rupert arrived at the showground in a foul temper. He'd just had a dressing-down from Malise for going bull-fighting on the morning of a Nations' Cup. He was worried about Billy and he realized, with Billy gone, that their chances of even being placed were negligible. Normally he didn't need to distance himself before a big class, but Helen's chatter about El Grecos and Goyas, and her trip to Toledo, 'with the old houses silhouetted against the skyline,' got on his nerves and he'd snapped at her unnecessarily.

She'd hoped to win him over in a new dress – a Laura Ashley white smock dotted with yellow buttercups, worn with a huge yellow straw hat – but he had merely snapped, 'What on earth are you wearing that for?'

'It's the latest milkmaid look,' said Helen.

'I don't like milkmaids, only whisky-maids; and you're going to obscure about fifteen people's view in that hat. No, there isn't time to change; we're late as it is.'

'God, it's hot,' said Lavinia Greenslade, as they sweated in the unrelenting sun, waiting for the go-ahead to walk the course. Her eyes were swollen and pink from crying over Billy's concussion. It had taken all Malise Gordon's steely persuasion, coupled with her parents' ranting, to make her agree to ride.

The rotund Humpty was sweating so profusely that great damp patches had seeped through his red coat under the arms and down the spine.

'Wish we could jump in our shirt sleeves,' he grumbled.

'Not in fwont of the Genewal,' said Lavinia. 'He's weally hot on pwotocol.'

Jake clenched his teeth together, so the others couldn't hear them chattering like castanets. Walking the course didn't improve his nerves. The fourteen jumps were enormous – most of them bigger than he was – with a huge combination in the middle and a double at the end with an awkward distance. You could either take three small strides between the two jumps or two long ones. He tried to concentrate on what Malise was saying as they paced out the distances.

In a Nations' Cup, four riders on four horses jump for each country, jumping two rounds each over the same course. There is a draw for the order in which the nations jump. Today it was France, Italy, Spain, Germany then Great Britain last, which meant that a French rider would jump first, followed by an Italian, then a Spaniard, a German and finally a British rider. Then the second French rider would jump followed by the second Italian, and so on until all the riders had jumped. Each nation would then total the scores of its three best riders, discarding the worst score. The nation with the lowest number of faults would then be in the lead at half time. The whole process is then repeated, each rider jumping in the same order. Once again the three lowest scores are totted up and the nation with the lowest total over the two rounds wins the cup. If two countries tie there is a jump off. Nations' Cup matches are held all over Europe throughout the Summer and Autumn and the side that notches up the most points during the year is awarded the President's Cup. For the last two years this had been won by Germany.

Malise gave the order for the British team to jump: Humpty, Lavinia, Rupert, Jake.

'If you get a double clear,' Humpty told Jake as they came out of the ring, 'you get a free red coat.'

'Can't see myself having much chance of wearing out this one,' said Jake.

He thought so even more a few seconds later as Lavinia gave a shriek of relieved joy, bounded towards Billy, as he stood swaying slightly at the entrance to the arena, and flung her arms round him.

'Lavinia,' thundered her mother and father simultaneously.

Lavinia ignored them. 'Are you all wight? You shouldn't have come out in this heat. Does your poor head hurt?'

Billy was deathly pale, but he steadied himself against Lavinia and grinned sheepishly at Malise. 'I'm terribly sorry.'

'T'riffic,' said Rupert. 'You can ride after all.'

'No he can't,' said Malise firmly. 'Go and sit in the shade, Billy, and take my hat.' He removed his panama and handed it to Billy.

'For Christ's sake,' snarled Rupert, hardly bothering to lower his voice, 'even concussed, Billy's more valuable than Lavinia or Jake. They simply haven't the nerve when the chips are down.'

'Thank you, Wupert,' said Lavinia, disengaging herself from Billy. 'If it weren't against the intwests of my countwy, I'd hope you fall off.'

'Are you implying my Lavinia isn't up to it?' said Mrs Greenslade, turning even redder in the face.

'Yes,' said Rupert unrepentantly. 'And Jake even less so.'

'Shut up, Rupert,' said Malise, losing his temper. 'You're behaving like a yobbo.'

'Well, if you want us to come bottom yet again, it's up to

you,' said Rupert.

'I'm honestly not up to it,' said Billy placatingly. 'I can see at least six of all of you.'

Fortunately an ugly scene was averted by a loose horse pounding through the collecting ring, his lead rein trailing and flysheet slipping. Whickering with delight, he shoved the rest of the British team summarily out of the way and rushed straight up to Jake, burying his nose inside his coat and nudging him with delight. It was Sailor; his feet were oiled, his coat polished, his thin mane coaxed into plaits, his sparse tail fell jagged from a tube of royal blue tail bandage.

The next minute Tracey joined them, panting and laughing.

'The moment he saw you he broke away from me.'

'Amazing that someone finds you attractive,' said Rupert.

'That's enough, Rupert,' said Malise icily. 'You'd better warm up before the parade, Humpty.'

18

The General, in true Spanish tradition, was late. So the parade started without him. The Germans came first. The famous four, Hans, Manfred, Wolfgang and Ludwig. Olympic gold medallists who had not lost a Nations' Cup competition for two years, they had reason to be proud. They rode with a swagger on their equally famous horses: four beautiful Hanoverian geldings, with satin coats, elegant booted legs, arched necks, and chins apparently soldered to their breast bones. As they passed, their grooms gripped the fence and cheered. They were followed by the French, beautifully turned out with the lighter and less obedient horses, and then the Italians in their impeccably cut coats with the blue collars, riding with slapdash elegance, two of them smoking. Then there was a great ear-splitting cheer, sending a great communal waft of garlic up from the crowd, as the Spanish team came in. Beautiful riders on beautiful, powerful horses, their manes flowing free, but somehow not co-ordinated like the Germans. The crowd, however, thought they were the greatest, and screams and shouts of 'Magnifico' and 'Olé' followed them all round the ring.

The British team came last. Rupert rode on the magnificent Belgravia, chestnut coat gleaming in the sunshine. Not having been ridden in at all, (Marion hadn't even had the time to walk him around), he was boisterous and uncontrollable, and the crowd, particularly the women, marvelled how this handsome Englishman hardly moved in the saddle, as the horse bucked and violently shied beneath him. On his left was Humpty on Porky Boy, then

270

Lavinia on the grey Snow Storm, whose coat was already turning blue with sweat, and then Sailor, shuffling along, looking on his last legs, as though he could hardly stagger as far as the grandstand. The crowd laughed, barracked and pointed.

Jake gritted his teeth. He'd show them.

The wait that followed was interminable. The teams lined up in front of the grandstand and all, except Lavinia, removed their hats as each country's National Anthem was played. The band knew their own National Anthem and, confident the Germans would win, had been practising Deutschland, Deutschland all week, but when they got to Great Britain, they launched into the Star Spangled Banner, which everyone thought very funny except the moustachioed bandmaster, who turned an even deeper shade of purple.

The horses meanwhile were going mad in the heat, except Sailor who stood half asleep, one back leg bent, hanging his head, twitching his flea-bitten coat against the flies, and occasionally flattening his ears at Belgravia, who was still barging around like a bee-stung bronco. Jake tried not to look at the jumps. All the women in the audience fanned themselves with their programmes. Medallions, nestling in a thousand black hairy chests, glittered in the sunlight.

In the riders' stand, next to the collecting ring, Helen comforted a disconsolate Billy. 'You'd be mad to jump,' she said.

'Must say I've got the most awful headache. Jake's horse looks like I feel,' said Billy.

As the teams came out of the ring, Sailor bringing up the rear, shuffling along, head hanging, Helen looked at Jake's set face. She hadn't seen him smile once since he'd arrived. The knight of the sorrowful countenance, she thought.

'He's like Don Quixote,' she said to Billy, 'and that poor beaten-down old horse looks like Rosinante.'

Billy wasn't interested in literary allusions.

'What a bloody stupid thing to do,' he said. 'Malise is livid.'

'Doesn't look it,' said Helen, watching Malise, in dark glasses, with a gardenia in the buttonhole of his pale grey suit, completely calm as he went from one member of the team to another, steadying their nerves, encouraging them.

'Lavinia's not wearing anything underneath that black coat,' sighed Billy.

As the British team filed into the riders' stand, Malise gave Helen the jumping order on a clipboard so she could keep the score. The General still hadn't arrived, but it was decided to start. The arena went very quiet as the white doors opened and the first French rider came in and took off his hat to the judges. As he went past the start, the clock started ticking. It was soon obvious, as he demolished jump after jump, sending poles and bricks flying, that this was a far from easy course. The Italian who came on second was also all over the place and notched up twenty-eight faults.

'Viva España!' screamed the crowd as the first Spanish rider came in. Although they had applauded the earlier riders politely, they cheered their own hero unrestrainedly.

'Doesn't look very magnifico to me,' said Rupert, as the horse went head over heels at the rustic poles, crashed through the wall and the final double, losing his rider again, and having to be led out impossibly lame.

'I've seen enough,' said Humpty, running down the steps and out to the collecting ring to scramble on to Porky Boy as the first German rider rode leisurely into the ring. Hans Schmidt was the second best rider in the German team, but his dark brown horse didn't like the course any more than the others and came out, most unusually with twelve faults.

As he walked out, ruefully shaking his blond head and muttering *dummkopf*, he was practically knocked sideways by Humpty bouncing into the ring. The merry Porky Boy, ears pricked and fighting for his head, his black tail swishing back and forth across his plump cobby quarters, bucketed towards the first fence. The crowd was amused by him and his rider, who rose so high out of the saddle over the bigger jumps that it seemed he would never come down again. But he got around with a very creditable twelve faults.

Now it was time for the second Frenchman to jump.

No one went clear, as round followed round and disaster followed disaster. Several horses overturned and were eliminated. A Spanish horse burst a blood vessel and had to be destroyed later in the day. Despite Rupert's gloomy prognostications, Lavinia jumped well for only twelve faults, which meant the Germans and the English were level pegging on twenty-four faults at the end of the second round, with the other nations trailing well behind. The next German, Manfred, got eight faults, the best round so far. He was followed by Rupert, who did not jump well. Macaulay, like Belgravia, overoated and insufficiently ridden in, had been frightened in the collecting ring by three loudspeakers crackling fortissimo above his head. An enormously powerful horse, it took all Rupert's strength to stop him running away in the ring. By some miracle they went clear until they got to the upright, where Macaulay, put wrong, hit it sharply.

For a second the pole bounced agonizingly in the cup, then fell. Unbalanced, and taking off too early, Macaulay also had a foot in the water. Rupert came out of the ring looking bootfaced.

'He's dying to beat the hell out of that horse,' said Jake to himself. He watched Helen, beautiful in her yellow hat, biting her lip with disappointment as she entered eight faults by Rupert's name. Jake didn't want to be around when Rupert came back. He'd seen enough rounds anyway.

Riding around the collecting ring, he felt sicker and sicker, trying to remember the turns and the distances between the jumps. But his mind had suddenly gone completely blank, as though someone had pulled a lavatory chain, draining all the information out of his head, leaving an empty cistern.

He wished he could slip into the matadors' church to pray. He listened to the deafening cheer as the last Spanish rider went in and groan follow groan as he demolished the course.

Now it was time for the mighty Ludwig von Schellenberg, the greatest rider in the world, to go into the ring and show everyone how to do it, which he did, jumping clear. But so carried away was he by the poetry and stylishness of his round that he notched up one and a half time faults.

He came out grinning and cursing. Now, as luck would have it, as Jake was due to jump, the last rider in Round One, the General chose to arrive and everything ground to a halt while two lines of soldiers with machine guns formed a guard of honour and the band played the Spanish National Anthem several times, and dignitaries were introduced with a lot of bowing and shaking of hands, and the General was settled in his seat.

'This is a bugger,' said Malise, after Jake had been kept waiting twenty minutes. 'I'm very sorry. They'll call you any minute. Just aim for a steady clear, take it easy and ride at the centre of the fence.'

Up in the riders' stand Helen was doing sums.

'If the Germans count Ludwig's, Manfried's and Hans's rounds, and drop Wolfgang's, that puts them on twenty-one and a half,' she said. 'We've got Rupert on eight, Humpty on twelve and Lavinia on twelve; that makes thirty-two.'

'We won't get lower than that this half,' said Rupert. 'Jake's bound to be eliminated.'

Ludwig von Schellenberg came into the riders' stand. 'You look beautiful, Mees Helen, in that hat,' he said, clicking his heels as he kissed her hand.

'She's a Mrs not a Miss, you smarmy Kraut, and keep your hands off her,' said Rupert, but quite amiably. Ludwig was one of the few riders he liked and admired.

'Number 28,' called the Collecting Ring Steward.

Jake rode quietly into the ring. During the long wait he had counted Sailor's plaits, found there were fifteen, his unlucky number, and had quickly undone them, so Sailor's sparse mane crinkled unbecomingly like Harpo Marx's hair.

As the horse shuffled in, flea-bitten, head hanging,

Ludwig laughed and turned to Rupert: 'Do you get your horses from zee knacker's yard now?'

'May I be Franco with you?' said Rupert. 'That is the ugliest horse anyone's ever seen.'

Helen looked at Jake and repeated her remark about the knight of the sorrowful countenance to Malise, but Malise wasn't listening either; he was praying.

The audience was losing interest. There hadn't been enough clear rounds, the Germans were so far ahead it didn't look as though anyone, and definitely not the Spaniards, would catch them up. The General was talking to his Energy Minister about oil prices. No one was paying much attention as Sailor cantered towards the first fence.

Tilting at windmills, thought Helen, filled with compassion.

'Never get over it,' said Rupert.

But suddenly this extraordinarily ugly animal shook himself like an old music hall actor who realizes he's got a capacity crowd, gave a snort of pleasure and took hold of the bit.

'Christ, look at that,' said Humpty Hamilton as Sailor cleared the first fence.

'And that,' said Billy as he cleared the second.

'And that,' said Malise, resisting a temptation to crow, as he cleared the third.

'And that,' said Helen.

'Jesus, he can really jump,' said Billy. 'Look at the way he tucks up his feet.'

The crowd, bored by Spain's poor performance, suddenly diverted by this extraordinary horse, laughed at first then started to clap and cheer.

'He's going to get time faults if he's not careful,' said Mrs Greenslade, as Jake checked Sailor before the combination, but, pop, pop, pop, over he went.

'Christ,' said Humpty. 'That horse must have some good blood in him.'

'Who is zees horse, Malise?' said Ludwig. 'It is not permitted, I think, to jump mules. I shall lodge an objection.

Sailor was over the water. Now there was just the double left.

As he turned sharply to make up time, the sun shone straight into Jake's eyes, dazzling and blinding him. He had to leave it all to Sailor. The British team held its breath as the horse came trundling down, carefully positioned himself and cleared both parts beautifully. As he shambled out of the ring to deafening cheers, some people in the riders' stand could have sworn he winked his wall eye. Jake, his face blank, leaned forward, pulling Sailor's ears, running his hand repeatedly up and down the horse's curly mane.

'Beginner's luck,' said Rupert.

'That horse isn't a beginner,' said Billy. 'He looks like an Old Age Pensioner.'

'He's got half a time fault,' said Helen, putting C for Clear by Jake's name. 'That puts us in the lead.'

In the collecting ring, Sailor philosophically accepted the ecstatic embraces of Bridie and Tracey, but was more interested in getting his three Polos reward from Jake, who in his turn was trying to hide his elation. Having automatically checked Sailor's legs for any swelling or tenderness, he loosened his girths and put on his fly sheet.

'Well done,' said Malise. 'It's hard to believe that horse hadn't walked the course himself.'

And as Humpty, Billy, Lavinia and both her parents surged round Jake to offer their congratulations, Malise added, 'Delighted he's come good. Completely justified your faith in him. Get Tracey to walk him round in the shade and keep him quiet, and come and have a Coke or something.'

But Jake couldn't bear to leave Sailor. Using a bucket of water brought by Tracey, he sponged the horse's head, throat and neck and between his back legs to cool him down. Putting a hand over Sailor's eyes, he sprayed his head and ears with fly spray and as it wasn't wise for the horse to take in quantities of water, he washed his mouth with a sponge to refresh him.

'Belgravia'd have your hand off if you did that,' said Marion, who was walking a sweating Macaulay round the paddock. 'He jumped well,' she added, nodding at Sailor.

Was this the first round in peace talks? thought Jake, Marion, one of the Iron Curtain satellites, temporarily making diplomatic overtures towards the West.

'Thanks,' he said.

The second half of the competition was much tougher. The delays had got to the horses and frayed the riders' nerves. The heat was stifling, the flies even worse. Sipping an ice-cold Pepsi in the competitors' stand, Jake tried to keep calm.

'It's the first time for ages the Germans haven't been in the lead after the first half,' said Mrs Greenslade. 'But they're tremendously good at coming from behind.'

'Sounds fun,' said Rupert, glancing at Helen, who went pink.

The Germans, in fact, came back fighting. Humpty jumped well, but could only manage eight faults. Lavinia had four, to her parents' ecstasy.

'Bloody boo sucks to you, Wupert,' she said as she came out of the ring.

But the first two Germans had only four faults each.

Then Manfred came in and got only eight faults.

'Rupert's got to go clear,' said Billy, looking at Helen's marks and counting on his fingers. 'God, I wish I'd taken 'O' level maths.'

Down in the collecting ring, Malise told Rupert the same thing: 'Macaulay's a big brave horse. He can do it, if you keep calm and put him right.'

But Rupert was still raging with Jake and Malise, and with Lavinia for being so smug about getting four faults.

Macaulay was a big, brave horse, but he'd suffered when Rupert was angry before, and he sensed Rupert was angry now and it unsettled him. Putting him over an unnecessarily high practice fence, Rupert had banged his fetlocks badly. Macaulay was a brave horse, but he didn't like being pushed around.

Rupert jumped clear until he came to the seventh fence, a huge oxer, then he turned Macaulay too sharply, put him at the fence wrong, pulling him up a stride too early. Despite a huge and heroic jump, Macaulay couldn't make it and had the pole down. This unsettled him for the combination. Fighting for his head, he almost ran away with Rupert and had all three elements down, then put a foot in the water, finishing up with twenty faults.

The British team groaned. This was the round they'd have to drop. It would be too much to expect Jake to repeat his brilliant first round. They had been so near beating the Germans; now victory was slipping away like a sock in a gum boot. Rupert rode straight out of the ring, ignoring the cries of bad luck spoken in five different languages, straight past Marion, out of the collecting ring and back to the stables.

Ludwig came in, stepped on it and, as expected, went clear without a time fault. It was all up to Jake. If he went clear, they would win by half a time fault. The volatile crowd were disappointed not to have a Spanish win, but they admired the courage of this gipsy boy and his hideous horse, and adopted him as their own. 'Magnifico,' they cried half in irony as he came into the ring.

'We're bloody well going to do it,' whispered Jake into Sailor's ear as he leaned forward and shortened his reins. Sailor gave three bucks to show he hadn't fallen asleep and the crowd roared their appreciation.

Off Sailor went towards the first fence, and Billy, despite a blinding headache, felt that rare surge of pleasure which transcends any kind of jealousy when a new star is born.

'You're right,' he said to Malise. 'He's brilliant.'

Malise, unable to speak because he felt so nervous and choked with emotion, merely nodded.

Suddenly Billy felt someone tugging his sleeve. It was Marion. One look at her horror-stricken face and he followed her down the steps.

'What's the matter?'

'It's Rupert. He's killing Macaulay.'

'Where is he?'

'Back at the stables in the box. He's bolted the door.'

As Billy sprinted the three hundred yards back to the stables, he was aware of a huge cheer that seemed to raise the sky. Jake must have gone clear.

Marion ran beside him, sobbing.

'The bastard, the bastard. It was his fault.'

'Go and saddle up Belgravia quickly. Rupert'll have to ride him in the parade.'

The white hot stone of the stables seemed to burn Billy's eyes. For a second he felt dizzy and thought he was going to faint. Then he heard the terrified screaming of a horse, and the sickening thud of a whip on flesh. He streaked across the yard. Both the half-doors of Macaulay's box were shut.

'Rupert, let me in.'

'Fuck off.'

'Bloody well let me in,' shouted Billy, pushing his huge shoulders against the door.

'Mind your own fucking business.'

Billy stepped back and ran at the bottom half-door. It began to give. Then he hurled his shoulders at it, nearly taking his head off as it caved in. For a second, after the dazzling sunlight, he couldn't see a thing. Then he gave a flying leap and landed on Rupert, winding him and rolling him on the ground.

'Fucking horse,' gasped Rupert. 'Give me that whip or I'll use it on you.'

'You bloody won't.' Billy scrambled to his feet.

Macaulay was a pitiful sight. Cowering in the corner, the lather turned red with blood, he had weals all down his shoulder, and one across his face just above the nostrils which were extended and as red as a poppy. His eyes were rolling in terror, his veins swollen, his sides heaving.

'You poor bastard,' said Billy, going up to him. The horse cringed away in terror. 'It's all right,' he said, catching his bridle. 'It's all over.' Rupert got to his feet, his face murderous. 'Give me that whip, I haven't finished.'

279

'You put him at it wrong,' said Billy quietly. 'You were a stride off; no horse could have jumped that fence. It's all right, boy.' He stroked Macaulay's trembling neck. 'It's all right. You stupid bugger,' he added over his shoulder, 'you could be prosecuted for this.'

'I'll deal with my horses as I choose,' snarled Rupert. He was about to make a dive for the whip when they heard a clattering of hooves outside. It was Marion with Belgravia.

'Go on,' said Billy. 'Don't you realize we've won? Jake went clear.'

'So what?'

'You've got to go and collect the cup. You won it too, you know. You only got eight faults in the first round. Go on, Belgravia's waiting.'

'I'm not going.'

'Stop behaving like a teenager,' said Billy echoing Malise. 'Do you want everyone saying you're a stinking loser?'

For a second he thought Rupert was going to take a slug at him. Instead he ducked out of the half-door and vaulted on to Belgravia's back.

'Here's your hat,' called Billy after him.

Marion took it and handed it up to Rupert.

'You're a bastard,' she hissed. 'I'm giving in my notice.'

Mr and Mrs Greenslade, Malise and all the grooms were cheering like schoolboys as the British team rode into the ring. Even Helen, now over the disappointment of Rupert's twenty faults, was jumping up and down and waving her yellow hat in the air. Sailor, the hero of the afternoon, walked on the outside, wall eye looking suspiciously at the crowd but accepting the deluge of cushions, flowers and handkerchiefs that descended around him with equanimity. Jake managed to catch two pink carnations and threaded them into Sailor's browband.

As they lined up in front of the General's box, a cushion flew through the air, and Rupert had to duck to avoid it. Jake turned to him. 'Rather reminds me of pillow fights in the dormitory of St Augustine's,' he said softly.

Rupert gave him a look of pure loathing which would have withered most people, but Jake was beyond withering.

'They were also very keen at St Augustine's on people being good losers,' he said, and laughed in Rupert's face.

The British team stood in front, with the other teams fanned out behind them. Jake choked back the tears as the Union Jack rose in a series of jerks up the flag pole, and the National Anthem was played for the second time that afternoon, very badly and this time in a minor key.

'God jolly well ought to save our Queen fwom foweign bands,' said Lavinia.

Afterwards, they had to walk rather apprehensively between an avenue of machine guns and meet the very distinguished General, who, despite his great age and the punishing heat, rose to his feet and congratulated them in perfect English. Rupert he appeared to know already, and enquired after his beautiful mother. But before Rupert could reply, a second commotion that afternoon was created by Sailor, who, dragging the unfortunate official who was trying to hold him, refused to be separated from Jake and, undeterred by the armed guard, followed his master half-way up the stairs.

Fortunately the General had a sense of humour and allowed two of his minions to help him down the stairs to pat Sailor on the nose. Jake smiled. The General smiled, Sailor nudged the General in the pocket as though checking if he were armed too, and the photographers went wild.

'Sailor among soldiers,' said the headlines next morning and the press went wild because it was the first time anyone had beaten the Germans for two years. The Germans, who were all very sporting, came up and shook Jake by the hand.

'I think we will have to pull the stocking up, no?' said Hans.

'Are you thinking of selling that horse?' said Ludwig.

As they finally galloped round the ring, rosettes streaming, sashes across their left shoulders, Jake clutched a solid silver bear, the symbol of Madrid, his prize as leading rider.

'I don't care what you say,' said Humpty, swelling his chest at each cheer, 'that horse must have some good blood somewhere.'

'I must telephone Tory,' said Jake as they rode out of the ring. 'God, I hate those telephones.'

'Mummy'll do it for you,' said Lavinia. 'She speaks Spanish.'

Billy was waiting for them.

'Well done,' he said to Jake. 'Good thing I got concussion. I'd never have pulled off a double clear.'

That night at dinner they went over every fence in every round and the Nations' Cup was filled and drunk out of again and again. And everyone, even Billy who'd deadened his headache with four Anadin, was relieved that Rupert and Helen excused themselves from the celebration on the very genuine excuse that the General had asked them to dinner.

Much later, not entirely sober, Jake went down to the stables to check on his horses. Earlier he'd added salt and electrolytes to Sailor's feed to make him drink because he'd been very dehydrated after sweating so much in the afternoon. Now he found his water bucket was empty, and kicked over. Jake filled it up again. Rather laboriously he re-poulticed Sailor's legs to take away the aches brought on by such strenuous jumping.

Then he went and looked at his darling Africa, walking her up and down. Her leg was better; she'd be O.K. for the Grand Prix tomorrow. He couldn't resist going into the tackroom and shining his torch on the red rosette he'd won earlier, rubbing its shiny ribbon along his face, kissing the hard cardboard centre.

'Maudlin idiot,' he told himself, but he was still walking on air.

As he came out he saw a light in Rupert's box. Creeping towards it, he looked over the half-door and found Marion re-dressing Macaulay's weals. Jake winced in distaste. His shoulder looked as though someone had been playing noughts and crosses with a knife.

Macaulay saw him first and cowered into the corner. Marion swung round, instinctively pulling the rug over the damage.

'What the hell are you doing here?'

'Looking at my horses. I suppose that's Rupert's work?'

For a second Marion hesitated between discretion and outrage. Outrage won. 'Of course it was, the bastard.' She peeled back the rug and went on applying cream to the wounds.

'I've got some better stuff for that,' said Jake. Returning to his trunk in the tackroom, he got out a jar of ointment, which had turned liquid in the heat.

'What's that?' said Marion suspiciously.

'An ancient Romany recipe,' said Jake, opening the jar. 'Steady boy, I'm going to make you better.' Gently he began to rub the ointment into the weals.

Macaulay trembled and flinched but did not move away; he seemed to understand that Jake was trying to help him.

'He'd never let Rupert do that,' said Marion.

'Who stopped him?'

'Billy did.'

'Malise know?'

'No, and with Rupert's luck he won't find out. Macaulay'll be in his box tomorrow. Rupert's riding Belgravia in the Grand Prix, and Mayfair in the class before. The day after, we're flying back to England first thing. He's a lovely horse, but Rupert's ruined him. He'll sell him on now. Can't bear to be faced with anything that makes him feel guilty. Helen'll go mad. Macaulay's the only horse she's interested in, because he named him after her.'

Having treated the last cut, Jake patted the horse. Then, perhaps because he was more than a little drunk, he said, 'Leave him to rest; come and have a drink.'

Marion looked at Jake's expressionless face. He was like one of those birthday cards left blank so you could write your own message. 'All right,' she said. 'I'm sorry I nicked your breeches.'

'That's O.K. I knew Rupert put you up to it.'

'He's really got it in for you.'

'Makes two of us. I've really got it in for him.'

They never got to the bar.

'Rupert would really fire me if he could see me now,' said Marion.

'Well, he'll certainly hear you if you don't keep your voice down; they're in the next-door bedroom.'

Marion laughed. 'I gave in my notice today anyway.'

'You going to leave?' asked Jake, unbuttoning her white shirt.

'I've given it in so often he probably didn't believe me.'

Accustomed exclusively over the last five years to Tory's bulk, Jake could hardly believe the slenderness of Marion's thighs or the springy breasts which didn't collapse under her armpits when she lay down. For a few minutes he stroked her body as wonderingly as if she were a £50,000 thoroughbred, and when he kissed her he was enchanted by the skill and enthusiasm of her response. They broke away. She smiled at him, touching a gold ear ring.

'Are you really a gipsy?'

'Half,' said Jake.

She ran her tongue along the lifeline of his hand. 'I'm crossing your palm with saliva.'

It was a feeble joke but they both had to bury their faces in the pillow to muffle their laughter. Both got an extra buzz from knowing how angry Rupert would be if he could see them. Jake was small, thin and not very handsome but his hands had a magical effect on Marion, soothing away all the tensions and frustrations she'd been bottling up since Rupert married Helen. Rupert's love-making was aggressive, like a power drill – her Campbell-Black and Decker, she used to call him. She enjoyed it only because Rupert was so wildly attractive and she melted at his slightest touch. Jake was gentle, considerate, yet seemed by comparison extraordinarily detached.

In fact Jake was extremely attracted to Marion and very glad he was able to prevent himself coming too soon by working out a plan of action.

Afterwards, when they lay sated in each other's arms, Marion said, 'That was wonderful. Who would have thought it? You're not looking for a groom, are you?'

'I couldn't pay you as much as Rupert, and you'd distract me too much.'

'You totally ignored me all week.'

'That was deliberate. I hated you for being part of Rupert's entourage and you're so goodlooking you irritated the hell out of me.'

'Prettier than Helen?'

'Much.' He knew that was the judgement that would win her over.

'I wish Rupert thought so, the bastard.'

'Is he faithful to her?'

'At the moment. I think he's rather captivated by the idea of his own fidelity. It's such a novelty. But they've hardly had a night apart since they've been married, and she sticks like a leech. Wait till she gets pregnant and can't go everywhere with him. That's when the trouble's going to start. He can't do without it.'

'Nor can I, by all events,' muttered Jake.

'Look,' he said, pushing her hair back from her forehead, 'you're fond of Macaulay aren't you?'

'Yes, I love him.'

'All you have to do is to let me know when Rupert's selling him.'

'He'd never sell him on to you.'

'Perhaps not, but someone else could buy him for me.'

'He's too strong for you. Rupert can only just hold him, and he's a sod in the stable.'

'I don't control horses by brute strength,' said Jake, 'and my guess is that he won't jump for Rupert any more.'

'Have you got a nice wife?' asked Marion, hoping he'd make love to her again.

'Very,' said Jake.

'Rupe said you married her for money.'

'Doesn't stop her being nice.'

'Don't you feel guilty?'

'No,' said Jake. 'This is my reward for a double clear.'

19

A month later Jake Lovell drove through the warm June evening doing sums. Late the previous night, Marion had rung him from a call box to tip him off about a horse called Revenge.

'He's a sod, but a brilliant one, and you'd better hurry. Rupert's after him too.'

Wasting no time, Jake had driven all the way down to Surrey to look at the horse, and he liked what he saw. Jake was seldom cheated when buying a horse. His stint with the gipsies had stood him in good stead. They taught him that dealers often disguise lameness, deliberately laming the opposite leg by shoeing it wrong, that they put black marks on a horse's teeth with hot wires so it'll pass for a six-year-old, or even shove mustard up its rectum so the animal prances along with its tail up in a travesty of high spirits. They had also taught him never to be carried away by a horse's looks.

He had to confess, however, that Revenge was the handsomest horse he'd ever seen, a showy red chestnut with a zigzag blaze, a mane and tail that looked as though they'd been dipped in peroxide, and an air of intense self-importance. He had been bought by a doting millionaire for his daughter, when she suddenly decided she wanted to take up show-jumping. Revenge had turned out far too strong for her. Allowed to get away with murder, he had learnt to buck and spin at the same time, and tried to drag Jake off under some low-hanging oaks at the top of the field. On the other hand, he had jumped a line of large fences without effort, landing like a cat, and showing not only an ability to get himself out of trouble, but incredible powers of acceleration.

Jake ached all over where the horse had had him off three times, but he still wanted him. Unfortunately, George Masters, the dealer, wanted £5000, which Jake hadn't got. He'd just sold two of his best novices in order to put down the deposit on the indoor school. The balance on this would be owing by the end of the summer.

Darklis, the new baby girl, was adorable, but she meant more work for Tory. Isa, jealous and playing up, needed extra attention, which meant Tory had less and less time for the horses. Tanya, the one groom, was hopelessly over-worked. Jake desperately needed another groom, but to pay her he needed to go to more shows and win more money. To do that he needed another Grade A horse to fall back on when either Sailor or Africa were unfit. There's a hole in your bank balance, dear Jake, dear Jake, he told himself.

So deep was he in thought on the way home that he suddenly realized he'd taken the wrong turning and was driving through Bilborough. There was Bilborough Hall, russet and mellow in the evening sun, scene of his first show on Africa. If he competed there now, as a member of the British show-jumping team, would he be invited to lunch up at the house with the nobs? There was Brook Farm Riding School. He felt a sick churning relief that he no longer worked for Mrs Wilton. There was the village green, and the church and Molly Maxwell's house.

Molly Carter she was now, the Colonel's Lady. Diplomatic relations had been resumed between Molly and Tory after Isa was born, but they were still uneasy. Jake had never forgiven the Colonel for firing his guns. Molly had never forgiven Jake for running off with her daughter, and even worse, making her happy.

Molly's marriage to Colonel Carter had not been happy. He was hardly back from his honeymoon at that hotel in Brittany that served English food, before he realized what a bitch she was. Too old and too proud to split up, they were locked together in mutual enmity. The Colonel's retirement from the City had thrown them even more into one another's company. Molly took refuge in endless bridge. The Colonel tried to control Molly's spending and dickered with the stock market. Fen had been shunted off to boarding school when she was eleven, and was discouraged from visiting Jake and Tory in the holidays because of Molly's quite unfounded suspicions that Jake would probably seduce her.

Driving slowly past the house, Jake could see his mother-in-law playing bridge with three other harpies in the drawing-room. The house had a burglar alarm now, and a yellow rose growing over the porch, and a swimming pool round the back, so the Colonel could do his ten lengths every morning, like an old walrus.

Jake suddenly felt hungry. He hadn't had any lunch and, with a hundred and fifty miles to drive home, he decided to drop into the next pub. Being early evening, he found it half-empty, but as he ordered a pint of beer and a pork pie, he heard a familiar bray of laughter. Not turning, he edged down the bar. There, in the mirror behind the bottles, he could see his step-father-in-law, arched rather like a golden retriever over a brassy blonde, who certainly wasn't his mother-in-law.

In amusement, Jake watched the Colonel putting his hand over the blonde's hand and lifting it with a clash of bracelets to his lips. Stupid old goat, he thought. Picking up his pint, he catfooted towards the table.

'Hello, Bernard,' he said softly.

Colonel Carter dropped the blonde like a wasp-filled pear and turned puce. Suddenly the ring on his paisley scarf seemed very tight.

'Hullo, Jake,' he said with a great show of heartiness. 'Long time no see. What are you doing in this neck of the woods?'

'Looking for a horse.'

'You've been doing very well this year. Getting your name in the papers. Even saw you on the box the other night. Going to Crittleden, are you? Sailor still going strong?'

'Of course he is,' said the blonde. 'He did well in Madrid, didn't he? Double clear indeed, and Billy getting concussed, naughty boy. Macaulay was off form, though. I think that Rupert Campbell-Black's dead cruel.'

Jake found himself gazing into the heavily blue-mascaraed eyes of the true show-jumping groupie. She was showing a lot of crinkly bosom in a shiny blue and white dress, her shoe straps were biting into her fat ankles and she enveloped Jake in wafts of cheap scent, but her face was kinder than Molly's.

'Aren't you going to introduce us, Bernard?' she said.

'Well, as you obviously know, this is my son-in-law, Jake Lovell,' said the Colonel even more heartily, 'and this is Vivienne, a great friend of my late wife, Jennifer.'

Vivienne didn't look as though she'd be the great friend of anybody's wife, thought Jake.

'Aren't you going to join us?' she said.

'All right, just for a minute, as long as Bernard doesn't mind,' said Jake maliciously. 'How's Fen?'

'Not too good really,' said the Colonel. 'Very moody, never brushes her hair, fights a lot with Molly, litters her clothes around the place. Moll sold her pony last week.'

Then, seeing the expression on Jake's face, he added defensively,

'Wretched animal kept jumping out of the field. Had to go and collect it in the middle of the night.'

'Probably lonely. Does Fen know?'

'Not yet.'

'Break her heart,' said Jake.

'Poor little soul,' said Vivienne.

'How's she getting on at school?'

The Colonel shook his head. 'Refuses to work. Just draws horses and gazes out of the window. Wrong place for her, really. They don't have riding there. But Molly insisted.'

'Don't know why people have kids, then send them away,' said Vivienne, enjoying her disapproval of Molly. Then, turning to Jake: 'Pity she can't live with you if she's so horse mad.'

Jake, who'd been thinking the same thing, was biding his time. Fen was only thirteen, but was already showing distinct promise. If he could get her under his wing, he could mould her the way he wanted to, and she'd be very useful helping with the horses. They might even to be able to avoid getting a second groom.

'What d'you like to drink?' he asked.

'My round really,' said the Colonel, not getting up.

'I'd like a gin and Cinzano, Jake, with lots of ice, thanks,' said Vivienne, hastily seizing the opportunity, used to the Colonel's meanness.

'If you twist my arm, I'll have a whisky and soda,' said the Colonel, who'd been drinking a half-pint before.

'Attractive, isn't he?' Jake heard Vivienne say as he went to the bar.

'Shame about the little girl. Ought to go and live with them.'

'Molly worries about what her friends think,' mumbled the Colonel. 'Likes to appear the devoted mother.'

'On the other hand,' said Vivienne slyly, 'Fen'll soon be old enough to be competition. Won't be much fun when Molly's menopause clashes with Fen's adolescence.'

The Colonel didn't think so either.

'Tell us about this horse,' said Vivienne. when Jake returned with the drinks.

'He's called Revenge,' said Jake, 'and he's got acceleration like a Ferrari, and Christ he can jump, but he's got a very bad temper and has learnt some bad habits.'

'How much do they want?' asked the Colonel.

'Five thousand. I'm just wondering how the hell to raise it.'

He looked speculatively at the Colonel and then at Vivienne.

'That's awfully cheap,' said Vivienne: 'Three good wins and you'll get your money back.'

The Colonel suddenly felt heady. His masculinity had been badly dented by Molly; she was always accusing him of being an old woman about money. He'd show her. It was time the lion roared.

'I'll buy it for you, Jake,' he said. 'Fun to have a flutter.'

Vivienne clapped her fat hands together with more jangling.

'Oh, what a good idea. You can split the prize money.'

Jake didn't react, determined not to betray his excitement. 'Horse'll take a bit of sorting out; not going to hurry him; probably won't see any return for your money for a year or so.'

'Go on, Bernard, it'll give you an interest. You've always wanted to own racehorses.'

'What'll we tell Molly?' asked Jake flatly, 'She wasn't ecstatic last time a member of her family bought me a horse in a pub.'

'That I bumped into you,' said the Colonel, 'decided to help you out.'

For a quarter of an hour they discussed technicalities. Rupert might well go higher. If so they'd scrap the whole idea.

Jake looked at his watch. It had Donald Duck on the face, and had been a birthday present to Isa that Tory had thought the child was too young for.

'Ought to get back; Tory's keeping supper.'

'Bye-bye Jake. Can I have your autograph?' said Vivienne.

'Nice lady,' said Jake, as the Colonel walked him out to the car.

'Old friend,' mumbled the Colonel.

'Friend of Molly's, too?' asked Jake.

'Needn't mention her to Molly, need we?'

'I never met her,' said Jake. 'You saw me going into the pub and you stopped to say hello and we had a drink together.'

'Good man,' said the Colonel, patting Jake rather gingerly on the shoulders. 'Always felt sorry about that Tory business. Worried about Fen too. You'd be doing her a kindness.'

Jake fingered the Colonel's cheque in his pocket.

'I'll think about it.'

Jake waited until morning to ring up Masters. He didn't wish to appear too keen. He offered £4000.

'You must be joking,' said Masters. 'Anyway Rupert Campbell-Black's coming to look at him at eleven. He was the first one after the horse, so I ought to let him have a butcher's.'

'The butcher's is where that horse will end up if you don't curb its nasty vicious habits soon,' said Jake. 'Four grand is my offer and I'm not topping it. If Rupert offers more, let him have it. I'm going to see another horse over Cheltenham way this afternoon and I want to know if I've got the spare cash to buy it, so I'd be grateful if you'd let me know what Rupert says one way or the other.'

'I'll ring you the moment I hear,' said Masters placatingly. 'Don't rush into that other deal too quickly.'

Jake then had to spend the morning biting his nails. It was all nerve, allowing the elastic to go slack so the other person started pulling on it. When Masters rang back, he made Tory say he was out and would ring back, which he didn't. Then Masters rang again.

'That shit Campbell-Black never turned up, never bothered to ring. The horse is yours if you want it.'

'Four thou,' said Jake.

'Four thousand five hundred.'

'Four two-fifty.'

'Done.'

'I'll come and collect him now.'

It was another hot wearying drive and it took three stable lads, George Masters and Jake all their persuasive power and a lot of bad language to get Revenge into the lorry, by which time the horse was drenched with sweat. As Jake drove away he could hear him stamping and kicking in rage, and wondered if he'd been mad to buy him.

Two miles on, he was driving along a narrow country lane, brushing the buttercups and the elder flowers, when

293

suddenly a dark blue Porsche hurtled round the corner and only just avoided a head-on collision by skidding onto the verge and nearly removing a wild rose bush.

The driver, a blond man wearing dark glasses, swore and hurtled on. There was no mistaking Rupert, but Jake didn't recognize the brunette beside him. Maybe she was the reason Marion had rung him up.

'When you get there, mate, you'll find the cupboard's bare,' and he threw back his head and laughed. Revenge renewed his kicking and stamping.

'And you'd better be nice to me, boy,' he called back to the horse. 'You've no idea how lucky you are not to go to that bastard.'

And all the way home, as the dead gnats peppered the windscreen, he kept laughing to himself, until at last, as the sun was setting, he saw the gleaming willows and red pink walls of the Mill House and felt as always that wave of joy at coming home. Christ, he was tired. Darklis was still on four-hourly feeds, so they weren't getting much sleep. Tomorrow he had to get up early to drive up to a show in Yorkshire, and then the next week on to the Royal at Stoneleigh.

Tory came out to meet him, with Wolf bounding ahead.

'You got him? You must be exhausted.'

When they lowered the ramp, Revenge was cowering in the corner, shivering as though in a fever, despite the heat of the evening.

'Poor old boy, he must have had a bad time. But isn't he beautiful?' said Tory.

As Jake went towards him, Revenge bared his teeth and darted at Jake like a cobra.

'He's a bugger,' said Jake. 'No one's to go near him for the next day or so but me.'

Having tied him up securely, Jake rubbed him down, put on a sweat rug, watered and fed him. But the horse didn't seem remotely interested in food and, once he was let loose, proceeded to pace round and round his box.

'Leave him,' said Jake. 'He'll settle down.'

'Thank God for Tory,' he thought as he went into the house.

Everything was tidy. The toys that had strewn the hall when he left that morning were now all put away. The only evidence of babies was a pile of fluffy nappies folded in the hall. A smell of shepherd's pie drifted enticingly from the kitchen.

'How's things been?'

'Fine really, except for Isa posting all the entry forms down the loo. Fortunately I'd typed them, rather than filling them in in ink, so they didn't run. They're drying off in the hot cupboard.'

'By the way,' she said, after she'd given him a glass of beer (they were still too poor to drink wine, except for special occasions), 'Fen's here.'

He looked up. 'Run away from school?'

'Yes. She discovered Mummy'd sold the pony.'

He found Fen, still dressed in her school uniform, slumped sobbing on the bed.

'How could she do it? She forgets my birthday, then next day, she sells Marigold. She won't even tell me where she's gone.'

'Probably to a good home. We'll find out,' said Jake, 'and she *was* too small for you.'

'I know. I really have tried not to put on weight so I wasn't too heavy, but she was the only thing I'd got. I loved her so much.'

Jake patted her shoulder. For a second she was crying so hard she couldn't get the words out. Then she said, 'I can't stand school any more. It's a horseless, dogless desert, going on and on.' She reached out for Wolf who'd climbed on to the bed, trying to lick her tears away. 'And I can't live with Mummy any more. I hate her and I loathe him. Please don't send me back.'

Jake was shocked by her appearance. Last time he'd seen her, a year ago, she'd been a little girl. Now she was a teenager with lank greasy hair, spots and a pasty skin flecked with blackheads. Although she was terribly thin, he could see the first swell of breasts beneath the grass-green school sweater.

'Please let me come and live with you,' she sobbed. 'I won't be a nuisance. I'll babysit and I'll get up early, and work at night and at the weekends.'

Jake stroked her hair. 'I'll talk to Tory. Come downstairs and have something to eat.'

'I can't, truly. I'd be sick. Oh, Jake, I'm so sorry. You must be knackered, and to be faced with me after that drive. But I keep thinking of Marigold.' Her face crumpled again. 'How lonely and bewildered she'll be.'

'I'll go and ring your mother,' said Jake.

'Fen's here,' she heard him say on the downstairs telephone. 'No, don't talk to her tonight. She's fast asleep; must have walked most of the way.'

Jake overslept next morning. Pulling on his clothes, he went downstairs to see how Revenge had survived the night. As he put on his shoes in the kitchen, he could hear Africa knocking her water bucket about and Sailor pawing the door and neighing, 'Where's my bloody breakfast.'

'All right, all right,' grumbled Jake, 'I'm coming.'

Outside he froze with horror. Both halves of Revenge's door were open. Isa, fascinated by the horses, had developed a dreadful habit of standing on a bucket and letting himself into the boxes. Heart hammering, Jake ran across the yard as fast as his limp would allow. Inside he found Fen, her arms round Revenge's neck, feeding him carrots and kissing him on the nose.

'Good boy, good boy. You'll love it here and you're going to become a great and famous showjumper. Jake'll see to that.'

'Fen,' said Jake, desperately trying to keep his voice steady, 'come out of there.'

She looked up at him with an angelic smile. 'He's so sweet. Can I ride him later?'

Revenge glared at Jake, raised a threatening front hoof,

and then darted his big white teeth in the direction of Jake's arm.

'Stop it,' said Fen firmly, taking his head collar and giving it a shake. 'That's bad manners. You don't bite your master.'

Revenge debated the matter for a minute, rolling his eyes and looking boot-faced.

'No,' said Fen, even more firmly, 'you're just showing off. You're an old softy, really.'

Revenge, deciding that perhaps he was, butted Fen in the pockets in search of more carrots.

'What's his name?' she asked.

'Revenge.'

Fen grinned. 'Revenge is sweet, he really is.'

At that moment Jake decided to keep her.

'If you're so taken by him, you'd better feed him and skip him out.'

'What's he been eating?' said Fen.

'Stable boys, mostly,' said Jake, 'but I think we'll try and wean him off that habit.'

Rupert drove home in a blazing temper. He'd tried everything to make Masters tear up the cheque, but when the man insisted he'd given the buyer a receipt, and refused to name him, Rupert lost his temper and an undignified shouting match ensued.

On the way home Rupert took it out on Sarah, the brunette he'd met at a show earlier in the week. He'd been furious with himself for bedding her that morning. He'd been on the way home from a dinner in London and had rung Helen to say he'd be late home, as he was making a detour to Surrey to look at a horse. The detour had also taken in Sarah's flat. He hadn't enjoyed screwing her at all and he'd fallen asleep afterwards, which made him impossibly late for his appointment with Masters. He'd taken a stupid risk too. Masters might easily have rung home and Helen smelled a rat and been hurt unnecessarily. He didn't feel particularly guilty about being unfaithful, but enraged that, through his stupid dalliance, he'd lost a really good horse. He'd have to get his spies out and track Revenge down. By the time he had chewed up a few more people, he might go even cheaper. Since Madrid, Macaulay had been a write-off, losing all his form and confidence. He'd have to go too, he thought, as he dropped Sarah off.

'When'll I see you again?' she called after him anxiously.

But Rupert had driven off without a word. Even the sight of Penscombe in the height of its summer beauty didn't soothe him. Helen's clothes, her endless schemes for the garden – a lilac walk here, a little heated swimming pool there, a 17th-century stone nymph there – cost a fortune. Billy worked hard, but he cost a fortune too, always buying other people drinks and feeding Mavis chicken. The whole shooting match is dependent on me, Rupert thought sulkily. I've got to win and win to support it.

He drove straight around to the stables where he found Billy working one of the novices in a nearby field. He admired Billy's patience, but why was he resting The Bull and Kitchener this week and not at a show, winning money?

Billy pulled up and rode towards him, wiping the sweat from his forehead.

'Did you get him?'

'Already sold on.'

'Shit, that was bad luck. Who got him?'

'Wouldn't say.'

'Might have been more trouble than he was worth. This is going to be a very good horse, by the way.'

'Good. It's about time he started paying his way.'

He found Marion in the tackroom, cleaning a saddle. She didn't look up. Still sulking, thought Rupert. For a second he admired the unsupported breasts in the tight blue T shirt, and the succulent thighs in the denim skirt, which was only just buttoned up enough to hold it up.

'Didn't get him,' he said. 'He was sold on.'

'Who to?' Marion bent over the pommel, so Rupert couldn't see how much she was blushing.

'Masters wouldn't say.'

'Just as well. I quite like having two arms and legs.'

'Particularly when they're such sexy legs.'

She looked up: 'Wasn't aware you'd noticed them recently.'

'I always notice them.'

'How was Sarah?' It was an inspired guess, but it hit home.

Rupert didn't flicker, then, unable to resist a joke, added, 'Rather like Coventry Cathedral – ravishing from the outside, but very disappointing once you got inside.'

Marion started to giggle. 'You are frightful.'

He went up behind her, stroking the back of her neck. She leant against him, furious with herself for feeling faint with longing.

'Rupert, darling,' called a voice.

'In here,' said Rupert, moving away from Marion to examine the diet charts.

It was Helen, also in navy blue, in a dress which must have cost fifty times more than my skirt and T-shirt, thought Marion. Helen was looking rather pale, her newly washed hair falling to her shoulders, subtly smelling of Miss Dior, her blue high heels catching in the ridges of the floor.

She's as out of place here as a tiger lily in a cabbage patch, thought Marion.

'Darling, how did you get on?'

'I'm coming in,' said Rupert. 'I'm filthy. You can bring me a drink in the bath.'

He was reading *Horse and Hound* in a foot of hot, scented water when she walked in. Funny, he reflected, how even after two years she averted her eyes.

'Nice dress.'

'It can go back if you don't like it.'

'I do. You can take it off in a minute.'

'Here's your drink,' she said hastily, hoping to distract him.

Rupert took a deep gulp and went on reading Audax on the Derby.

'Why don't you come and soap my cock?'

Helen blushed. 'Billy'll be in in a minute.'

'So what? Not in here he won't. Come on.'

Helen sat on the loo seat and took a birdlike sip of her drink.

'Why are you drinking vodka?' demanded Rupert. (She usually had sherry.)

'It's Perrier, actually.'

'What on earth for?'

'I went to see Dr Benson today.'

He looked up sharply. 'You ill?'

'No,' she took a deep breath, 'I'm going to have a baby.'

'You what?' The next moment he'd reared out of the bath like a great dripping whale and taken her in his arms, drenching her.

'Oh, darling,' he said in a choked voice, 'are you sure?'

'Positive – Rupert, you're soaking me.'

'Christ, that's fantastic. I can't believe it.'

'It's wonderful, isn't it?'

'You must rest. You mustn't carry anything heavy. Are you sure you're up to carrying that glass of Perrier? When did you think you were? Oh, sweetheart, you should have told me.'

'I wanted to be sure.'

'I thought you were on the pill.'

'I stopped taking it.' Tears suddenly filled her eyes. 'I was real scared after the termination,' she almost gagged on the word, 'I wouldn't be able to conceive. Then I started feeling vile in Madrid.' She sat down on the loo seat.

'You never told me.' Still dripping, he crouched beside her, kissing her again and again.

She was so pleased he was pleased, but she wished he'd get dressed. This rampant nakedness seemed incongruous somehow with the momentousness of the occasion.

Finally he stood up. 'My father'll be knocked out. What shall we call him – Eddie?'

'He might be a girl.'

Rupert started doing his sums. 'When he's 24, he'll be

able to ride in the 2000 AD Olympics.'

He went to the bedroom window and opened it. 'Billy, Billy.'

'Put something on,' urged Helen, wrapping a towel around him.

'Billee.'

Next minute Billy appeared at the edge of the lawn, still riding the grey.

'Yes?'

'For Christ's sake, come here.'

'Not across the lawn,' wailed Helen. 'Mr Higgins'll do his nut.'

'Helen's going to have a baby!'

Billy threw his hat high up in the air and rode through some delphiniums.

'Fantastic.'

'You can be fairy godfather,' said Rupert, 'and just think what a wonderful opportunity it'll be to get Nanny back to look after him.'

Over my dead body, thought Helen.

At that moment one of the Jack Russells wandered into the bedroom and sicked up a few frothy blades of grass on the carpet. 'And the dogs are going to be kept outside once the baby comes,' she said to herself, 'I'm not having them in the nursery.'

20

Fen never dreamt she'd have to work so hard. Jake's indoor school was finished by the autumn, which meant, even as the days drew in, that she was able to get up at five in the morning and work the horses for two hours before school. Then she would come home, grab a quick bite to eat, dash off her homework, then back to the indoor school until late in the evening. Often she fell asleep at her desk. Her form mistress rang up Tory and complained. Fen was not stupid, just exhausted and totally unmotivated. It was the twentieth century; people didn't send children down the mines any more. Her complaints fell on deaf ears. Tory remonstrated gently with Jake and tried to get Fen into bed by ten, but it was often midnight before they finished.

Jake was a very hard taskmaster. As Fen was tall for her age, it was pointless to waste time learning to ride ponies. She must go straight on to horses, and as she'd be competing initially against children who'd been riding the circuit since they were seven, there was a lot of ground to catch up.

Fen found it hard to be patient. She only wanted to jump and jump, but Jake insisted she do the groundwork first, hardly letting her ride across the yard without coming to see if she were doing it properly. To straighten her back and deepen her seat, he gave her daily lessons on the lunge, without reins and stirrups, with her arms behind her back, and a stick through them to keep her shoulders straight. Cold weather didn't deter him. Sometimes they worked outside, with everything frozen, and the snow hardening to a sheet of ice. With the wind up their tails, the horses would give a series of bucks and, stirrupless and reinless, Fen would fly through the air and emerge from the shrubbery like a snowman.

Day after day she came in with raw bleeding knees and elbows, every bone in her body aching. Seldom did she complain, she was so frightened of being sent back.

On the whole she was happy, because she felt she was getting somewhere. Like Jake, she loved the cosy family atmosphere created by Tory. She adored the children, Wolf and the cats and the horses, and hero-worshipped Jake. Revenge, however, was her special pet. She spent any free moments in his box, talking to him, calming him. In a way they were learning the ropes together. Like her, when he arrived, he was miserably displaced, suspicious of everyone. Gradually they got their confidence back.

Revenge was never worked in the same field twice. Horrendously highly strung, he was a picky eater, hated any box but his own and was liable to kick any strange stable to pieces. He also fell madly in love with Africa, following her everywhere, to Sailor's irritation, and yelling his head off if she went to shows without him. Jake brought him on with infinite slowness, never overfacing him, retiring him over and over again, going for slow clears to give him confidence, never exciting him by jumping him against the clock.

Revenge still put in the odd huge buck and had a piece out of Fen if he'd got out of bed the wrong side. But she defended him to the death.

'He's really a kind horse,' she would explain, 'he always waits when he's bucked you off.'

Tory and Fen got on well, but there were undeniable tensions. Although she helped out in the stables, Fen made a lot of extra work at home. She was extremely untidy, dropping her clothes as she stepped out of them, forgetting to bring her washing down, spending hours in the bathroom washing her hair, gazing at her face in the steaming mirror and leaving the bath filthy and the plughole blocked with hair. She was also terribly dreamy and, when she

303

wasn't with the horses, her nose was always buried in some technical horse book or riding magazine, and if there was washing-up she always managed to find something to do in the stable. Tory tried not to resent Fen nor to mind her teenage moods, nor to feel jealous that Jake and she spent so much time together.

Fen adored Jake, but, unlike Tory, she saw his faults. Tory spent hours making quiches and chicken pies for Jake when he was away at shows, which he seldom touched because he got so nervous, and which Tanya, the groom, usually finished up so Tory wouldn't be hurt. Jake never laughed at Tory's jokes, seldom reacted, often didn't answer. She noticed how Tory ended so many sentences with 'Isn't it', to evoke some sort of response, how she never answered Jake back. Jake and Fen on the other hand had blazing rows.

One grey day towards the end of November, Fen was particularly tired. Her form mistress had sent her out of the class and the headmistress had come past and shouted at her. Her period was due any minute, her spots were worse than ever and she felt fat and edgy. Jake was in a picky mood. Tomorrow he and Tanya were off to Vienna and Amsterdam for two big shows. Everything had to be packed up and ready. It was so mild that Tanya had tied Revenge up in the yard to wash his tail. The dead dry leaves were swirling around his feet.

She had just finished, and Fen, who had fed all the other horses, had Revenge's feed ready, when she suddenly remembered she hadn't added any vitamins or chopped carrot to encourage him to eat. Putting the bucket down beside Sailor's door, she rushed back to the tackroom and here got sidetracked by the latest copy of *Riding* which had a piece on her hero, Billy Lloyd-Foxe. Alas, Sailor who was on a diet and incurably greedy, seeing the bucket, promptly unbolted his door. Having wolfed all Revenge's feed, he was discovered by Jake smugly licking his lips.

Jake hit the roof. 'Fen!' he bellowed.

'Yes,' she said nervously, coming out of the tackroom

with a carrot in one hand and the magazine in the other.

'Can't you fucking concentrate for one minute?' said Jake furiously. 'Filling your stupid head with dreams of Wembley, and lining up above Rupert Campbell-Black, with the Queen telling you what a star you are. Well, you'll bloody well never get there unless you pull your head out of the clouds.'

'I'm sorry.'

'What's the use of saying sorry? Sailor's just eaten Revenge's food. You're bloody useless.'

Fen lost her temper. 'I hate you; you're a slave driver.'

Dropping *Riding* and the carrot, she raced across the yard, untying Revenge's head collar. Leaping on to his back, she clattered across the yard, clearing the gate out to the fields, thundering across them, clearing fence after fence, making for the hills.

'Come back,' howled Jake. 'That horse is valuable.'

'I don't care,' screamed Fen, picking up Revenge as he stumbled over a rocky piece of ground, galloping on and on until she'd put four or five miles between herself and the Mill House.

As she passed a cairn of rocks, she realized how dark it had got. Then, suddenly, like a blanket, the mist came down. Tugging Revenge around, she retraced her steps. She came to a fork in the pathway. There was boggy ground to the right. She turned left, the path turned upwards and upwards. It must lead somewhere. Then she went rigid with horror as she realized they were on the edge of a ravine and had nearly tumbled over. She gave a sob of terror as she realized she was totally lost. Gradually the enormity of her crime hit her. Revenge didn't even belong to Jake; he was Colonel Carter's and potentially the best horse in the yard, clipped and out in the cold in the middle of winter.

'I don't know what to do,' she cried, flinging her arms round the horse's neck, shuddering uncontrollably in her thin, mist-soaked jersey. 'Oh, God and Rev, please help me.'

For a few seconds Revenge snatched at the short grass.

Then he sniffed the wind and set off purposefully. Fen tried to check him, terrified of more ravines, but he was quite determined. They came to marshy ground. Fen, petrified of getting bogged down, could feel his hoofs sinking in, and hear the sucking sound as he pulled them out. She jumped as tall rushes brushed against her legs. Now he was splashing through a little stream. On he plodded, avoiding rocks and boulders, checking carefully for holes. Fen tucked her frozen hands in his blond mane, clinging to him for warmth, letting him carry her. He couldn't know the way; he'd never been that far from home. They'd never find it.

The mist seemed to be clearing. She could see trees below, and, oh God, surely that was the same cairn of rocks? They were going round in a circle.

She gave a sob of despair as Revenge turned and started picking his way delicately down a steep hill. It seemed to go on for ever; any minute she'd fall off him and tumble crashing to the bottom. Then suddenly the mist seemed to slide away and dimly she could see lights ahead.

Jake, back at the Mill House, was frantic. He'd been out on one of the novices, scouring the countryside for Fen, shouting, calling, finding nothing. No sound had come back through the thick blanket of fog. Every time he saw a car snaking along the road, he waited for a squeal of brakes and terrible screams.

He came home again. There was no news.

'Bloody stupid girl. Christ, why did she do it?'

Tory took a deep breath. 'You're too tough with her, Jakey. She's only thirteen.'

'No time to be superstitious,' snarled Jake, and rode off into the night.

Tory sighed and went back into the house. It was nearly nine o'clock. Darklis was crying, woken up no doubt by Isa, who was worried about Fen. She had just settled them, when from the yard she heard Africa give her deep whiney. All the other horses immediately rushed to their half-doors, peering out at the clouds rolling back on a beautiful starlit night. The dry leaves circled and rustled,

306

whipped by the wind. The horses turned to prowl around in the straw, then came back to the door and listened again, each knuckering more excitedly.

Suddenly Tory heard hoof beats. Africa sent out a joyful neigh into the darkness. The other horses whinnied, snorting and pawing at their doors. Revenge didn't whinny back; his task wasn't over yet. Five minutes later he walked into the yard.

Tory ran out. 'Oh, thank God you're home.'

Fen burst into tears. 'Rev did it. He bought me back. I'm so sorry, so terribly terribly sorry.'

Rushing out of the tackroom, Tanya caught her as she fell off the horse. 'You're frozen, pet. There, don't cry. You're safe.'

'Rev did it,' mumbled Fen.

Revenge didn't want a hero's welcome. He stumped past the other horses without a glance, making disapproving noises about stupid teenagers who got lost and made him late for supper. He smelt of mist, sweat and exhaustion, and went straight to his box and, with a long groan, folded up and began to roll, his feet shadow-boxing the air.

'Where's Jake?' muttered Fen, through frantically chattering teeth.

'Out looking for you. Go in and have a bath.'

Even after a bath she was still cold. She put on her nightgown and three jerseys over it, looking around her little room. The green-sprigged Laura Ashley wallpaper, put up especially by Tory, was already covered in posters of Billy Lloyd-Foxe and Ludwig von Schellenberg. The shelves brimmed over with every horse book imaginable, and her collapsing Pullein-Thompson novels. Every shelf was crowded with china horses which took Tory so long to dust. On her dressing table was the hedgehog which Jake had made her from teasels for her last birthday. They had been so good to her and she'd kicked them in the teeth.

Jake would be quite right to pack her back to her mother and the Colonel. She picked up Lester, her battered teddy bear, named after Lester Piggott, cuddling him for comfort.

Her heart sank even further at the sound of horse's hoofs on the bridge, muffled by the willows – Jake coming home.

He'd be insane with rage. He had a five o'clock start in the morning. His best horse had been sabotaged. Looking through a crack in the curtain she saw him slide off the big black gelding, hand him to Tanya and go into Revenge's box. Leading him out, he examined his legs, making Tory walk him up and down.

Fen trembled, terrified he'd find something wrong. But he merely nodded curtly and turned towards the house. Fen crept away from the curtain. Next moment she heard him coming up the stairs, and the boards creaking outside her room. I'm not going to cry, she thought desperately, he's bored by tears.

'I'm so sorry,' she stammered.

'I should think so,' he said bleakly. 'Of all the bloody irresponsible things to do. You could have killed yourself and the horse.'

'I didn't think.' She hung her head.

'Time you started. Can't afford passengers.'

'Please don't send me back.' A tear splashed on to her hands. If she had looked up she would have seen his face soften.

It would make her swollen-headed if he told her that the only reason he was so harsh with her was because he knew how good she could be. He put a hand on her shoulder.

'It's all right, no harm done. Rev's O.K. Must like it here. After all, he came home.'

Fen looked up, eyes streaming. 'He did; he was so clever. I was completely lost. He brought me home like Lassie.' There was a pause.

'When d'you break up?'

'The eighteenth.'

'Well, you can leave two days early and come to Olympia with me.'

She gazed at him unbelievingly.

For a minute she couldn't speak, then she flung her arms round Jake's neck. 'Oh, Jakey, thank you,' she sobbed, 'I love you so much.'

Helen had honestly intended to go to the Olympia show. She still had some Christmas shopping to do. She'd catch up on a few matinées in the afternoons and spend the evenings watching Rupert. Friends who'd gone skiing had lent them a penthouse flat, overlooking Holland Park, just a few minutes from Olympia. She was touched and a little ashamed by Rupert's delight that she would be with him. It was the first show she'd been to for ages. She'd been so sick with the baby and felt so tired, and after a tidal wave of Rupert's female fans sent her flying and nearly trampled her to death at the Royal International back in July, she'd decided to give shows a miss.

Rupert had been competing abroad for much of the last five months, and during the separations she'd been very lonely and spent many restless nights worrying she might miscarry or the baby might be deformed. She took her pregnancy very seriously, eating the right food, resting, going religiously to ante-natal classes and giving up drink completely. So those jolly re-unions after Billy and Rupert came back from successful shows, when even Helen got mildly tight, were things of the past.

She steeled herself not to mind when Rupert was away. She missed him, but subconsciously she built up other resources. She spent a fortune on baby clothes and another fortune on a new nursery suite, decorating the baby's room daffodil yellow and white and putting in an oven, a washing machine, a dryer and a small fridge next door, with a room for the Nanny, all done up in Laura Ashley, beyond that.

She also liked being able to watch all the egghead programmes she wanted on television, to listen to classical music all the time and not to have to cook huge meals when she was feeling sick.

Then Rupert would come home, bringing not tenderness but silver cups and suitcases of dirty washing. Invariably on his return he wanted a sexual marathon, and although her gynaecologist had reassured her that sex couldn't harm

309

the baby, Rupert's lovemaking was so vigorous that she was terrified she'd miscarry and found herself tensing up and going dry inside.

She also had the feeling Rupert wasn't being supportive enough. He flatly refused to go to ante-natal classes or be present at the birth.

'It's too Islington for words,' he said, by way of excuse. 'I've pulled calves, I've pulled foals, but I'll be buggered if I'll pull my own baby. I've found you the best gynaecologist in the country, booked you into a private room at Gloucester Hospital. Let them get on with it.'

He also laughed his head off when he found her listening to Beethoven and Vivaldi in order to stimulate mentally the baby in the womb.

'D'you want to give birth to a string quartet?'

Throughout November and December he'd been away on a successful but punishing round trip to Geneva, Vienna and Amsterdam, which left only a hectic twenty-four hours at home before setting out for Olympia. Even so Rupert found time for sex. He'd won a polaroid camera as one of his extra prizes at Amsterdam and was determined to take photographs of Helen in the nude.

'Your boobs are so fantastic since you got pregnant.'

Helen, conscious of her swelling stomach, couldn't get into the swing of things at all. Nor did she like being photographed first thing in the morning without any make-up on.

'It's not your face I'm interested in,' said Rupert, laying each photograph on the dressing table so they gradually took on colour and shape, until he got so turned on he had to make love to her.

Afterwards she came out of the bathroom, wrapped in a towel, to find a naked Rupert joyfully poring over the photographs.

'For goodness' sake put them away. Mrs Bodkin might see them,' she pleaded.

'This one's much the best. Come and look.'

Helen approached cautiously; then embarrassment turned to rage as she realized he was admiring not her naked beauty but a photograph of Badger, lying grinning upside down in his basket, now banished to the landing.

'I must show Billy,' said Rupert.

'Why not take one of Mavis too?' snapped Helen.

She was fed up with those wretched dogs and horses. It wasn't a question of playing second fiddle; she wasn't even in the orchestra.

Later Rupert and Billy had a session with their secretary, Miss Hawkins, catching up on the mail and checking that entry forms had been sent off for the next few months. When Helen came down with some washing she found the dark blue diary for the next year on the kitchen table. They must have been working out the first six months' show dates. Fondly she turned to March 7th, the most important entry of all, the expected date for the birth of the baby. But instead, to her fury, she found Antwerp, Dortmund, Milan scrawled across the first eighteen days in March, with red Pentel arrows stretching from page to page indicating they wouldn't be returning to England between shows. Helen couldn't believe it. Rupert intended to be away for the most momentous event of his life. She stormed into the drawing-room, where Rupert was pouring himself and Billy pre-lunch drinks.

'Billy, will you please leave the room,' she said in a dangerously quiet voice. 'I want to speak with Rupert.'

'Yes, sir, certainly sir,' said Billy, grinning and making himself scarce.

'What on earth's the matter?' asked Rupert. 'Not sulking about Badger's picture, are you? D'you want a drink?'

'You know I haven't touched liquor since I became pregnant. I'd like to know the meaning of this.' She flung the diary at Rupert. 'Look at March.'

Rupert opened it. 'Well? Oh, I'm sorry to be away three weeks on the trot, but they're all good shows and I'll be home a lot in January and February.'

'Haven't you any idea what else is happening in March?'

Rupert look blank. 'Can't think.'

311

'Our baby is to be born.'

Rupert grinned in dismay. 'Oh, Christ, angel, I'm frightfully sorry. It completely slipped my mind. Don't worry, I can hop on a plane the minute you go into labour, or if you really think it'll arrive on the 7th,' he glanced at the diary, 'I could fly out late to Antwerp. They don't have the big prize money there till the third day.'

Helen, for the first time since they were married, went berserk, screaming abuse at Rupert, her red hair flying like a maenad, her face scarlet.

Rupert looked at her in amazement. 'Are you sure you haven't been drinking?'

The next minute she was hurling ornaments at him. The altered Augustus John went flying through the air and hit the wall with a splintering crash. Then she started on the bookshelf. *Burke's Landed Gentry* nearly landed on target, followed by *Ruff's Guide to the Turf*, followed by bound volumes of *Paradise Lost*, and Dante's *Inferno*. Gibbon's *Decline and Fall* fell at Rupert's feet. Rupert, laughing and dodging out of the way like a boxer, annoyed her even more. As the top shelf was emptied, there was a knock on the door. It was Mrs Bodkin in her hat and coat, quivering with curiosity.

'Was there anything else?'

'Yes,' said Helen. 'Bring me a jug of orange juice, please.'

Two minutes later Mrs Bodkin puffed in with the jug and two glasses on a tray.

'Thank you. That'll be all, Mrs B. See you tomorrow,' said Helen, firmly shutting the door on her. Then, picking up the jug of orange juice, she hurled it in Rupert's face and collapsed sobbing on the sofa.

Nothing Rupert could say would placate her. If he wasn't going to be with her when the baby was born, she wasn't coming to his bloody show. She still refused to speak to him when he and Billy set off to London that afternoon. Rupert, who'd always believed that a room full of roses and a gold bracelet could placate any woman, was slightly surprised.

Olympia, the last show before Christmas, always has an end-of-term atmosphere. Most of the riders have a break afterwards until the middle of January. All the glamour of the sport is concentrated and enhanced by an indoor show. The collecting ring stewards and the stable manager in charge of the 150 loose boxes have increasing difficulty keeping high-spirited riders in order as the excitement mounts. Practical jokes and parties go on all week.

Neither Billy nor Rupert, however, were in a particularly festive mood as their lorry rolled into the horse-box park on the eve of the first day. Billy was fretting because he suspected Lavinia Greenslade had transferred her affections to a handsome French count named Guy de la Tour. Rupert was still smarting over Helen's intransigence. Christmas shopping traffic jams were driving him wild.

'Fuck the plebs, fuck the plebs,' he screamed, leaning on his horn.

Billy was further depressed to see a huge lorry carelessly parked like an acute accent, with Guy de la Tour, Republique Française in huge letters across one side.

'Let's go and get drunk,' said Billy.

Rupert's temper was not improved the following day when they walked past the exercise ring and saw Fen lunging Revenge.

'Nice horse,' said Billy.

Although Revenge had been transformed into a picture of hard muscle, health and well-being over the past six months, he was still unmistakeable with his strange zigzagging blaze and his two long white socks. For a second they paused to watch him.

'Don't recognize the groom,' said Billy.

'I say, darling,' shouted Rupert.

Fen swung round, turning crimson. She couldn't believe they were talking to her.

'What's the name of that horse?'

'Revenge.'

'Who does he belong to?'

'Jake Lovell.'

'Shit, that's where he's ended up,' said Rupert. 'The little bastard pulled a fast one on me. I wonder who tipped him off.'

'Dear God,' prayed Fen fervently, 'make my spots go, give me some decent boobs and don't let me fancy Rupert Campbell-Black.'

At the beginning of the week the collecting ring gossip was all of the two Italian horses who had escaped and had a lovely time galloping up and down the main road. Now it had switched to Guy de la Tour's romance with Lavinia and to Jake Lovell's new horse. Every time Revenge came into the arena, afternoon or evening, people rushed to the ringside to have a look. At the beginning of the show the lights and the crowds had upset him, and he went around star-gazing and leaping two foot above the jumps like a ginger, hairy-legged spider. After forty-eight hours, he settled down.

There had been a bad moment, however, on the second day. Jake put his foot in the stirrup and Revenge put in a hell of a buck, landing Jake on top of a steaming pile of dung.

'Found your own level, Lovell,' jeered Rupert as he rode past. Jake's reply was suitably obscene. It took all Fen's tact to calm him down.

'I'll soak your breeches in Napisan,' she said soothingly. 'All the stains'll come out.'

Nor were the fates being kind to Billy. Just when he was trying to woo Lavinia back, a local barber gave him a hideous, far-too-short haircut.

'I got so engrossed in *Playboy*, I forgot to watch him,' moaned Billy afterwards.

Even worse, Billy turned The Bull too fast into the Combination on the second night, forcing him to put in a stop. Billy sailed over his head, landing on a pole and knocking out his two front teeth, which further damaged his beauty. There wasn't time to have them capped. He'd have to wait until after Christmas.

With no sign of Helen, Rupert's eye started to rove. Every day there were novelty events – the Army did a display of tent pegging, lady clowns did dressage. The Pony Club put on a demonstration of Snow White and the Seven Dwarfs. First amused by the fact that Snow White's horse had diarrhoea, Rupert's eye then fell on a ravishing girl playing Grumpy named Tiffany Bathgate. During the week he'd bought her drinks and chatted her up. He even bought her a £150 gold watch from the Garrard's stand as a Christmas present, which she permanently showed off on her wrist like a dog holding out a sore paw.

By the final night Fen was absolutely knackered. She hardly had the energy to wash her hair for the party that night. Living on junk food all week, her spots were worse than ever. She longed and longed to be a rider or at least one of the élite bunch of grooms who all knew each other, swapped endless gossip and who had found time to go shopping and come back with pretty clothes from Biba and Bus Stop. She admired from afar the handsome Guy de la Tour, he who had so captivated Lavinia. Love had made Lavinia prettier than ever. She had cut off her long bubble curls and now, with her hair as short as a boy's, looked the epitome of French chic. Already half the show-jumping groupies, who hung around the place in breeches hoping someone might mistake them for a competitor, had followed suit and lopped off their long rippling manes as well. Fen also noticed Billy looking absolutely miserable. She felt so sorry for him, although he had cheered up a bit earlier that evening when he and Rupert won the fancy dress relay.

Billy with a pipe in his mouth and a Gannex mac had dressed up as Harold Wilson, while Rupert cavorted around in high heels, a red dress and a blond wig, with orange peel in his teeth, as Marcia Falkender. It had brought the house down.

Now all the grooms were getting their charges ready for the last event, the Radio Rentals Grand Prix. Fen, with both Sailor and Revenge to do, had her work cut out. Cries of 'Give me the body brush', 'Anyone seen my sponge?' 'Christ, they're calling us already' were coming from all sides.

'In the bleak mid-winter frosty wind made moan,' sang the loudspeaker. Now the band were playing Hi Ho, Hi Ho for the Pony Club demo. Rupert and Billy sat side by side in the riders' stand, their long legs up on the backs of the seats in front, watching Grumpy.

'Isn't she gorgeous?' said Rupert smugly. 'She's coming out with me tonight.'

'How old is she?' asked Billy.

'Sixteen, or so she claims.'

'Shouldn't be playing Grumpy, she's grinning like a Cheshire cat,' said Billy, as Tiffany Bathgate cantered by, pony tail swinging. 'I'll report her to the District Commissioner.'

'She's bringing Dopey with her,' said Rupert. 'Meeting me at the flat. Just imagine having the two of them.'

'You ought to be ashamed of yourself,' snapped Billy.

'Why don't you come too?'

'I'm going to the party afterwards: I must talk to Lavinia. She's been avoiding me all week. Her parents are wild about Guy because he's a count.'

'A cunt,' said Rupert.

'That too,' said Billy.

'I wonder if Greenslade père realizes Guy hasn't a bean,' said Rupert. 'He needs the Greenslade cash to keep his place going in France. "I cannot afford to 'eat the underrooms," he told me last night. Do you think I should give Helen an English setter puppy for Christmas?'

'No,' said Billy.

Snow White and her entourage cantered out of the ring, with Grumpy blatantly grinning at Rupert, as the arena party put the finishing touches to the jumps for the Grand Prix. Now the rose red curtains which parted theatrically to admit each competitor were clashing with the scarlet coats of the riders, as they walked the course to a jazzed-up version of 'Oh Come All Ye Faithful'.

The collecting ring was very hazardous. Belgians crashed their horses over the jumps crying 'Numero Huit, Numero Sept' to their grooms and discussing where they were going for dinner. Rupert was having a row with an Irish rider (nicknamed Wishbone, because of his long bow legs) because they had both tried to jump the upright at the same time.

Fen walked her two horses around the outside, keeping out of trouble, Sailor calming Revenge, who looked as beautiful as Sailor looked ugly. Fen was still shaking from her first encounter with her mother and Colonel Carter since she left home. As owners, they'd come to the show to watch Revenge. Molly had been 'absolutely livid' with Bernard when she discovered he'd blued £5000 on a horse for Jake, behind her back. She'd denied him her bed for more than a month. But gradually she was beginning to appreciate the kudos of being a winning owner. Everyone was tipping Revenge as an Olympic probable. Molly was already planning her wardrobe for the next Games in Colombia the following August. She enjoyed sitting in the riders' stand and talking about 'My horse' in a loud voice. Molly was also very relieved that Fen appeared to have totally lost her looks.

Certainly it had been Jake's show. Africa, Sailor and Revenge had all won big classes. You couldn't get into the lorry for silver cups. Sailor grew in popularity, the crowd were wild about the 'Old Mule', with his mangy tail and his drooping head, who caught fire in the ring. Whenever he left the lorry now Jake was mobbed by autograph hunters. And Fen told him someone had written 'I love Jake Lovell'

317

on the wall of the Ladies, and underneath lots of people had written 'Me, too'. Joanna Battie had interviewed Jake for the *Chronicle*, gushing over his romantic gipsy looks. Jake pretended to disapprove, but secretly he was delighted and had re-read the piece several times. He had even been interviewed by Dudley Diplock as he came out of the ring. The fact that he hardly got a word out didn't seem to matter. He smiled, and when Jake smiled publicly, which was about once every five years, the world melted.

The bell rang, the riders left the arena. In the distance you could still hear the mournful cry of the men on the gate trying to flog programmes to last-minute arrivals. The arena was flooded with light for the television cameras. As Rupert mounted Belgravia, he spat out his chewing gum.

'I want it,' said a besotted teenager, rushing forward. A deafening cheer lifted the roof off as Rupert rode into the ring.

'I can't help it,' thought Fen. 'He's vile, but he is attractive.' Rupert jumped an untroubled clear and rode out as Ivor Braine rode in. The collecting ring steward, who had a headache from drinking too much at lunchtime, was shouting at late arrivals.

'I'm going to report Rupert Campbell-Black to the BSJA for calling me a fart,' he grumbled. 'And you're late, too,' he said to Humpty, who was supposed to be jumping next.

'Get out of my way then, you little fart,' said Humpty. 'You're a worse nagger than my wife.'

Humpty also went clear.

Billy, waiting to jump, felt near to suicide. Lavinia was still avoiding him. Now Count Guy was in the collecting ring, crashing over the practice fence, pretending not to understand the collecting ring steward, who was now castigating *him* for being late.

'That man is a preek,' he drawled to Lavinia, as he rode towards the rose-red curtains.

'*Bonne chance*, my angel,' said Lavinia, blowing him a kiss.

Count Guy's dark brown stallion, however, took a dislike

to the curtains and shied into a group of officials in pinstripe suits, dislodging for a moment the complacency of their smooth flushed faces, as they scuttled for cover. Then with a flurry of Gallic expletives, Guy rode into the arena and proceeded to lay waste the course.

'Oh, bad luck, darling,' said Lavinia as he came out, shrugging dramatically, reins dropped, palms of both hands turned to heaven.

'Fucking frog,' muttered Billy as he passed him on the way in. But he was so upset, he jumped badly and notched up twelve faults.

'I've got a splinter,' grumbled Marion.

Ignoring her, Rupert went back to the riders' stand to watch the rest of the rounds. As he listened to a group of German riders chattering behind him, his thoughts contentedly drifted towards Tiffany Bathgate who, with her dumpy friend, would at this moment be washing themselves (as well as they could in the Olympia showers) for him. There were two bottles of champagne in the flat fridge. Perhaps he should offer them a proper bath when they arrived. Goodness knows where that might lead.

The next moment the two girls were forgotten, as Jake and Revenge came in, jumping unevenly but very impressively. Revenge was fooling around between fences, but when he jumped he really tucked his legs up.

'I want that horse,' thought Rupert grimly. 'He's got everything I like: brains, temperament, good looks.'

He was suddenly aware that the woman on his right was making a lot of noise.

'Do you remember me?' she said, turning to Rupert.

'I never forget a face like yours, but I'm terrible at names,' said Rupert. It was his standard reply.

'I'm Molly Carter, Maxwell that was. Tory, my daughter, was doing the season in 1970. You were *such* a deb's delight. All the mums were in love with you too.'

'Tory. Of course I remember. Very shy, treated every man as though he was going to chuck snowballs with stones in at her.'

'She married Jake Lovell, you know. It was a bit of a shock at the time, but he's done awfully well.'

'Helped by Tory's money, of course,' said Rupert.

'Oh, of course. He'd never have made the grade without her.' She gave a little laugh. 'And my husband's been helping him out recently.'

'Really,' said Rupert, his brain beginning to tick.

'Revenge is our horse.'

Not by a flicker of a muscle did Rupert betray how interested he was. 'Your horse?'

'Jake was short of cash last June and desperate to buy Revenge in a hurry. Some other buyer was after him, so Bernard put up the money. I was livid at the time, but he seems rather a good investment. Won twice as much as he cost already. Jake is rather maddening, though.'

'Yes?'

Under Rupert's blue gaze, Molly was becoming indiscreet.

'He could have won a lot more, but Jake keeps retiring the horse because he doesn't want to push him. Feels he's not ready to jump against the clock.'

'Rubbish,' said Rupert. 'When a horse is as good as that you've got to press on.'

'Really?' said Molly. 'Oh, do look, the Princess has arrived. I love her dress.'

Everyone stood up with the usual clattering of seats. The band played the National Anthem. Round followed round, but only Ludwig and Jake on Sailor jumped clear.

'Helen's having a baby in March,' said Rupert, getting to his feet. 'So we're not going out much, but we must all have dinner sometime.'

'That would be lovely,' said Molly, giving him their telephone number. 'Bernard usually goes to London on Wednesday morning to see his stockbrokers, but I'm always there.'

'I'll remember that,' said Rupert pointedly.

Molly smirked to herself as he walked down the steps. She'd always thought Rupert was most attractive. Nice that she hadn't lost her touch.

Six riders had to jump off. Jake took one look at the course. For an indoor arena with limited space it was enormous, ending up with an upright of 5 ft 8 ins.

'I'm not jumping Revenge,' he said to Colonel Carter.

'Don't be bloody silly, man. There's £4000 at stake.'

'I don't care. It's too much to ask an inexperienced horse. He jumped a beautiful round earlier. Let's leave it at that.'

The Colonel looked thunderous.

'Only tell how good he is if you have a go.'

'He's had a tough week.'

Molly's face was twitching. 'I think you're being very foolish, Jake. I've just been talking to Rupert Campbell-Black, Bernard, and he said he'd certainly jump Revenge against the clock.'

'All the more reason for me not to,' snapped Jake.

'Quite right,' said Fen crossly. 'He's a young horse; set him back months if he lost his confidence.'

'Really, Fenella,' said Molly, 'no one asked your opinion.'

Rupert rode past on the way into the arena.

Stupid pratt, he thought, listening for a second to the splendid row.

'That *bloody* little man,' whispered Molly to Rupert, 'he's absolutely refusing to jump him.'

Rupert shrugged. 'Well, you know what I feel.'

'He'll be sixth anyway,' said Jake. 'That's £500. I said I'd train him my way. You'll have to lump it.'

Rupert rattled everyone by setting a virtually unbeatable time of 29.3 seconds.

'Such a good rider,' said Molly to Colonel Carter and, lowering her voice, 'You've no idea what sense he talked.'

No one could beat Rupert's time. Ludwig was a second slower, Lavinia had a fence down, Humpty couldn't catch him, nor could Hans Schmidt.

'I think that's £4000 in the bag,' said Rupert to Billy. 'I might even take the girls to Annabel's.'

Jake felt sick. Looking at the six jumps he wondered how

the hell he could beat Rupert's time. Then, when he came to the rustic poles, where everyone else had gone round the wall, he cut in from the other side, jumping the fence sideways as he turned. The crowd gave a shout and, suddenly aware of a knife-edge finish, bellowed him home. He cleared the last fence and looked at the clock. He'd done it. A fifth of a second faster than Rupert. He hugged Sailor, who gave three huge bucks, nearly unseating him. The crowd went mad.

'Well done, my friend,' said Ludwig, clouting Jake on the back. It was his biggest win yet. Everyone – except Rupert, Molly and Colonel Carter – surged forward to congratulate him.

The arena was now pitted with holes like a beach after a hot bank holiday. Several women in fur capes and ball dresses carrying rosettes and the huge silver cup walked out, tiptoeing to avoid any droppings as the winners came in, Jake riding Sailor and leading Revenge. The Princess smiled and said she'd been following Sailor's career and she was sorry she hadn't got any Polos, and hadn't Revenge jumped well? Jake felt very happy.

Back in the collecting ring the Yuletide spirit was relentlessly reasserting itself. Two Welsh cobs were being harnessed to a sledge which was being loaded up with Christmas trees by a man in a red coat. Helen's old admirer, Monica Carlton, in a tricorn hat and a frockcoat, was putting on a false moustache.

The band played 'All The Nice Girls Love a Sailor', as Sailor cantered the lap of honour under the spotlight, as proud as a butler with the family silver. Jake went deliberately slowly, knowing that Rupert would have difficulty holding Belgravia.

'For Christ's sake, get a move on,' snarled Rupert, cannoning into him.

'It's all very well,' thought the Colonel darkly, 'Jake gets £4000 plus £250 out of that. I get a measly £250.'

Rupert came out of the ring, looking at his watch. Tiffany Bathgate would be at the flat in half an hour; he'd better step on it. Then he glanced across the collecting ring and his blood froze, for, picking her way towards him, very pale but unspeakably beautiful, a fur coat hiding any trace of pregnancy, was Helen. As usual, she made everyone else look commonplace. Rupert was off Belgravia in a second, handing him to Marion, taking Helen in his arms.

'Darling, I'm so sorry. It was all my fault,' she said.

'No, it was mine,' said Rupert, holding her against him, his brain racing.

Looking down, he saw how the fox fur coat set off the red hair and the huge eyes that were already filling with tears.

'I missed you so much,' she said, 'I nearly went to the apartment and waited for you as a surprise.'

Rupert felt dizzy with horror. That would have been a fine welcome for Tiffany Bathgate and Dopey.

'What would you like to do?' said Rupert, his ingenuity working overtime. 'There's a party, if you're not too tired, then we could have some supper.'

Anything to keep her away from the flat until the coast was clear.

'I'm a bit tired, but I don't want to be a party pooper.'

'I'll just go and see what Billy's plans are,' said Rupert. 'Have a word with Malise. And here's Humpty and Ivor. I won't be a second.'

'Hullo, stranger,' said Humpty, kissing her. And as they all gathered round to welcome her, she suddenly realized how nice they were and how wrong she'd been to build them up as obsessed, insensitive monsters.

Rupert went over to Billy, who had just bought himself a treble whisky from the bar.

'Helen's arrived.'

'I saw. Fine mess you've got yourself into. I don't know why you're looking so cheerful.'

'I love my wife,' said Rupert blandly. 'Look, you must go and wait at the flat and divert those schoolgirls. Take them out to dinner, explain that Helen's turned up.'

'Why the fuck should I? I *must* talk to Lavinia.'

'The party'll go on for hours. She'll be much more

receptive after a few drinks. Look, I'll pay. But I promised Tiffany a night out (and in) so be a love and give them a whirl, and tell Tiffany to keep herself on ice for the next time.'

Billy looked mutinous.

'You don't want to ruin my marriage,' pleaded Rupert. 'You can't upset Helen at this stage. She oughtn't to be under any stress with the baby coming.'

Billy sighed. 'O.K. I'll intercept them, then take them straight back to wherever they are staying and come on to the party.'

Billy was knocked sideways by the smell of warm scented flesh, newly washed hair and radiantly expectant youth. The two girls were bitterly disappointed, and also well below the age of consent. Tiffany slipped up later by saying she would be doing her 'O' levels in two years' time. In the end, Billy was too kind to dump them. He gave them a slap-up dinner with lots of champagne, most of which he drank himself, and when he saw Tiffany dolefully looking at her gold watch, said,

'It wasn't an excuse, honest. Helen really did turn up.'

'You will give him my phone number, won't you?' she said.

Back at Olympia, lights had been turned out in the stables. Horses dozed in their loose boxes. An egalitarian Christmas drunk was running up and down, pinching hay out of Belgravia's hay net and distributing it among horses that hadn't got any.

The party was soon well under way. This year Humpty was acting as host; everyone turned up at his caravan with bottles. Predictably, Driffield arrived with a bottle of Airwick.

'Thought you needed it, Humpty,' said Driffield, splashing whisky into his glass. 'Place smells like a wrestler's armpit.'

Heavy drinking stepped up the high jinks. For his

officious behaviour during the week, the collecting ring steward was dumped in the water trough. Later, a pretty waitress from the Olympia Bar, well primed by the rest of the British and German teams, asked Humpty if she could actually meet Porky Boy. She'd heard he liked Maltesers and she'd specially bought some. Only too happy to show off his favourite asset, a blushing Humpty led her off to Porky Boy's box, followed at a safe distance by the other riders. The waitress looked into the box first.

'Oh dear,' she said, turning to Humpty, 'he seems to have shrunk.'

Rushing forward to defend his beloved, Humpty discovered to his horror that instead of Porky Boy, one of the grey Shetland ponies that had pulled Snow White's wedding coach was calmly guzzling Porky Boy's hay. For a second Humpty was speechless.

'Dear me,' said Rupert, looking over the half-door, 'poor old Porky. You haven't put him in the washing machine, have you? I'm sure his label said Hand Wash.'

'You have been geeving heem too streect a diet, my friend,' said Ludwig. ' 'E 'as faded away.'

'Perhaps Porky's been using Pond's Vanishing Cweam,' said Lavinia.

Everyone screamed with laughter.

Humpty exploded. 'Who's stolen Porky Boy?' he bellowed. 'Someone's stolen my horse. Don't you all laugh at me. I'm going to call the police.'

He was just dialling 999 in the nearest telephone box when suddenly Porky Boy emerged from behind a bank of wilting poinsettias, looking very put out at being deprived of his supper, and proceeded to rush back to Humpty straight through the stand of some enraged British Field Sports ladies, who were putting green rubber trousers into cardboard boxes.

Humpty then jumped on Porky Boy and chased Rupert, Ludwig and Hans round the stands and into the arena. Ivor Braine was happily getting drunk with Wishbone, the sandy-haired Irishman.

'Get it down, lad, it'll do thee good,' Ivor was saying, as he filled up the Irishman's glass.

Dudley Diplock was grumbling to Malise about the fact that they no longer televised the presentation of the prizes.

'It's what the public like to see.'

But Malise wasn't listening. He was looking at Helen Campbell-Black, who was being pinned against a pile of straw bales by Monica Carlton, who was still wearing her moustache and tricorn hat.

'Excuse me,' said Malise and went over to rescue her.

'Oh, shove off, Malise,' said Monica. 'I get little enough chance to talk to this exquisite creature.'

'So do I,' said Malise. She looks ill, he thought, and supposed it was the tired last months of pregnancy.

Fortunately Monica soon got sidetracked by the pretty waitress.

'Are you O.K.?' Malise asked Helen, slightly lowering his voice.

'Fine,' she said brightly.

'I like to take a fatherly interest in the wives of my team,' he said, in what he knew was an unnaturally hearty voice.

'I wish Rupert would take a fatherly interest in our baby,' said Helen bitterly.

'It's probably jealousy,' said Malise, 'and apprehension. He sees the looming challenge to his own identity and privacy. I know I felt the same, but I became positively doting once they arrived.'

'I sure hope so,' sighed Helen.

They watched Lavinia and Count Guy, arm in arm, working their way through the crowd towards them.

'Like Lavinia's new baronet,' said Monica Carlton, twirling her moustache. 'Pity she's chucking herself away on that frog.'

'I didn't know,' said Helen, startled. 'Is it serious?'

'I think so,' said Malise.

'Oh, poor Billy,' said Helen in distress. 'I don't think Lavinia would have been quite right for him, but then I don't think anyone would be special enough for Billy.'

'Might just be the making of him,' said Malise. 'He's too soft, too protected by your husband, drinks too much, too.'

'We're just going,' Lavinia said to Helen, adding fondly, 'Guy doesn't like parties over here because he hates not being able to talk Fwench, but I just wanted to intwoduce him.'

'Ah, la belle Hélène,' said the handsome Count softly.

He took Helen's hand, pressed it to his lips, then gazed into her eyes.

'Everyone speaks of your great beauty, but none did you the justice. Now I understand why Rupert keep you hidden away.'

'When's your baby due?' said Lavinia, rather pointedly.

And when Helen told them, Guy, not appearing to mind in the least not talking French, proceeded to express amazement that Helen was still so slim, and launched into a long dissertation on what she ought to eat, and how his Aunt Hortense had just had her sixth child, and how he hoped Helen would come and stay in his château when the next Paris show was on.

'Must go and have a word with Jake Lovell,' said Malise.

'I thought you wanted to *aller*, Guy,' said Lavinia petulantly. 'We're getting married,' she told Helen.

'Oh I'm so pleased for you both.'

'Come *on*, darling,' said Lavinia, dragging the reluctant Guy away.

Helen wished she could go too. She was feeling absolutely shattered. Nearby, Wishbone was trying to sell Humpty an Irish horse.

'But who's he by?' Humpty kept saying.

'Ah,' said Wishbone, smiling engagingly, 'who would you like him to be by?'

Malise found Jake in a corner, talking to Hans and Ludwig. Beside them Fen had fallen asleep on a hay bale.

'That's a very good horse of yours, Jake,' said Malise.

'Vitch von?' said Hans Schmit. 'Zay are both top hole.'

'Revenge,' said Malise. 'You ought to be thinking of him in terms of the next Olympics.'

'Not enough mileage,' said Jake flatly.

'I disagree. I saw that horse when he was carting Annie Buscott all over the place. The improvement's been remarkable.'

Jake blushed slightly.

'Olympics aren't till September,' said Malise.

'What about Sailor?' said Jake quickly.

'Great Nations' Cup horse, not sure if he's Olympic stature. No, don't look boot faced. I know how you feel about Sailor, but his wind isn't that good, and in a high altitude country like Colombia, he won't be very happy. Africa's a great horse too, but I notice she likes soft going more and more these days. I only discovered this evening that Revenge is owned by your father-in-law.'

'Taking my horse's name in vain,' said Colonel Carter, who'd been eavesdropping. 'Think he's got Olympic potential?'

'Well, I certainly wouldn't rule him out.'

'What are you going to do with him now?' Colonel Carter asked Jake. He'd had enough to drink to become bullying.

'Turn him out for a couple of months. He needs a break.'

'Well, don't leave him out too long,' said Malise. 'He needs the experience; but I congratulate you, Jake, He's a credit to you. So's she.' He looked down at the sleeping Fen. 'Been watching her in the practice ring. Living with you full time, now, is she?'

Jake nodded.

'She'll be knocking on the front door herself in a few years' time,' said Malise.

Jake made sure Fen was asleep, then said, 'She's a little cracker.'

The party dragged on. Wishbone and Ivor were singing 'Danny Boy' when Billy finally arrived at two in the morning. Rupert buttonholed him immediately. 'Everything O.K.?'

'Fine,' said Billy. 'I've delivered them safely back. You can go home now.' He helped himself to the last four fingers of whisky with a trembling hand.

'How was little Tiffany?' asked Rupert.

'Upset; but not nearly as much as me. I've just seen Lavinia necking in the street with Guy de la Tour. She's certainly out for the Count.'

'So will you be if you keep on drinking. Helen and I are off. Come with us.'

'Did Lavinia say anything?' said Billy.

Rupert looked at him straight. 'Yes, I'm afraid she said she and Guy are getting married. Look, I'm sorry, but you can do better than her.'

As Billy was leaving, he bumped into Malise.

Seeing Billy's face, Malise said, 'Why don't you come back to my flat for a cup of coffee?'

'Terribly kind, but I think I'd rather be by myself.'

'Are you sure? Where are you going?'

'Don't know really – bit of a shock – I was going to ask her to marry me, you see, when this Guy suddenly turns up.'

He was very drunk, but despite the awful haircut and the missing front teeth, he had a stricken dignity. Tenners were falling out of his overcoat pockets. Malise gathered them up.

'My fancy dress winnings,' explained Billy.

'I'll look after them for you,' said Malise. 'Come on, where are you staying?'

'Addison Gardens, with Rupert.'

As they passed the men's lavatory, they could hear Ivor supervising Wishbone being sick. 'Get it oop, lad, get it oop. It's all right as long as tha' knows the way it's going.'

'I'll walk you up there.'

'Please, I'd rather be alone,' said Billy.

'All right,' said Malise. 'Look, Lavinia's a nice girl, and I can't imagine she and Guy will last very long, if that's any comfort to you. But I honestly think you can do much better than that. As Helen said earlier, you're special.'

Billy shook his head. 'I loved her, but I suppose they'd have been frightful in-laws. Good night.'

It was bitterly cold outside. Programmes, crisp packets, streamers, old number cards and wisps of straw were whipped round his feet by the icy wind.

'In the bleak mid-winter,' Billy sang, 'frosty wind made moan.'

His voice broke and tears poured down his cheeks as he set out unsteadily in the direction of Addison Gardens.

22

Back at the Mill House, good as his word, Jake turned his horses out for a rest. It pleased him to see them really enjoying their grass. Even Revenge dropped his belly like an old hunter. In February, a programme was announced for Olympic possibles. The riders mustn't overjump their horses and they must take part in the Olympic trials at the Bath and Wells Show and Crittleden in June. The probable team would then be chosen for a trial over the huge, demanding fences at the Aachen Show in Germany in July, after which the Olympic team – four riders and a reserve – would finally be selected.

Officially, the Olympic Committee told Jake, they were interested in both Sailor and Revenge. Unofficially, Malise rang Jake and asked him if, in the event of one of the other riders, say Rupert, being selected without a decent horse, would Jake be prepared to jump Sailor and lend Revenge to Rupert. The answer was an extremely curt negative. If Revenge made sufficient progress to be selected, over Jake's dead body would he let anyone else ride him, particularly Rupert. Malise appreciated his sentiments and reported back to the Olympic Committee, who felt somewhat differently. Colonel Roxborough, the Chairman, Master of the Westerham, a bronze medallist before the war, who'd never moved an inch to get any of his five wives, was not the only member who felt Jake was behaving in a thoroughly unsportsmanlike fashion. After all, Belgravia and Mayfair, who'd both been overjumped, were not as good as they used to be, and Macaulay, after a dazzling start, had suddenly lost form altogether.

The Committee were heartened, however, by Billy Lloyd-Foxe at last hitting top form. Trying to forget Lavinia, avoiding parties where he might bump into her and cutting down on his drinking, he had concentrated on his horses, with dramatic results. The Bull, and often Kitchener, were in the money at every show they went to, and both were regarded as Olympic possibles.

Among the other possibles were Humpty, Driffield, Ivor Braine and Lavinia de la Tour, who had married Guy in March. Billy managed to be abroad for the wedding, but sent them a king-size duvet as a wedding present, adding a wry little private note for Lavinia: 'If I can't spend the rest of my life lying on top of you, at least my present can.'

As a newly wed, no doubt subjected to endless demands by Guy, Lavinia lost form. It was agony for Billy to see her with Guy on the circuit, but he found his heart didn't ache quite so much if he was beating the hell out of both of them.

In March, while Rupert was driving from Dortmund to Vienna, Helen went into labour. As his lorry was snow-bound on a mountain road, no one managed to contact him for thirty-six hours. Flying straight back to Gloucestershire, he found that Helen had nearly died after a long and very difficult birth, and that the baby was in the intensive care unit. Seeing her paler than her white pillow, her red hair dark with sweat and grease, Rupert was overwhelmed with remorse. How could he have done this to her?

'I guess Nanny was right about good child-bearing hips. I'm sorry, darling,' he said, taking her hand.

Not by a single word did she reproach him, but he saw the hurt in her huge eyes and knew that his absence would be held against him later. As he sat with her in her private room, various doctors came and talked to him, and nurses popped in to have a gaze. Actually the Sister in charge was frightfully pretty, but after three hours Rupert was rigid with boredom, and turned on the television. It was Benny Hill, who always made him laugh, but when he looked around and saw Helen was crying, he turned it off.

He was delighted to have a son, particularly after his

smooth and expensive GP friend, Dr Benson, had turned up and assured him that both child and mother should pull through.

'But I really think you should stick around for a bit, Rupe. She's had an awful time and kept calling out for you all the time.'

'I appreciate your advice,' said Rupert coolly.

'You can do better than that,' said Benson, equally coolly. 'You can act on it, unless you want Helen to wind up in a bin.'

Rupert rang Billy and told him he wouldn't be coming to Vienna and would he bring back Rupert's horses.

'What's the baby like?' asked Billy.

'Got red hair, so we know it's Helen.'

Then Rupert sat down and wrote letters, putting baby Marcus Rupert Edward down for St Augustine's and Harrow. Looking at the tiny baby, with his sickly face like a howling lemon and the bracken-red stubble of hair, it seemed impossible that he would ever attain such heights.

In the evening, Rupert went home to Penscombe and slept for fourteen hours, but after that scrupulously visited Helen every day. She seemed pathetically grateful for the attention, but was distressed that she was unable to breast-feed.

'What the hell does it matter?' asked Rupert. 'How do you think Cow and Gate became millionaires? I thought you wanted your figure back.'

He was further irritated that Helen had struck up a friendship with another mother called Hilary Stirling. In her early thirties, Hilary denied her unquestionable good looks by wearing no make-up and scraping her dark hair into a bun. A passionate supporter of the Women's Movement, a bra-less, undeodorized vegetarian, with unshaven legs and armpits, she had just had her second baby, Kate, named after Kate Millett, by natural child-birth – 'A wonderfully moving experience,' she told Helen.

Hilary's husband Crispin, who appeared to do every-thing in the house – cook, clean *and* look after Germaine

333

(their first child) – had been present at the birth. He was very earnest, with long thinning hair and a straggly beard, and came to visit Hilary in hospital with Germaine, now aged eleven months, hanging from his neck in a baby sling. Helen thought him extraordinarily unattractive, but at least, unlike Rupert, he had been caring and supportive.

It suddenly seemed to Rupert that every time he rolled up to see Helen, bringing bottles of champagne, gulls' eggs, smoked salmon and armfuls of spring flowers from the garden, that Hilary was sitting on Helen's bed, breast-feeding her disgusting baby and flashing her goaty armpits.

Admittedly she was ultra-polite. 'It's so kind of Helen to let me take refuge in her private room, although we personally wouldn't dream of using anything else but the NHS.'

Admittedly, she immediately made herself scarce, despite Helen's protestations. 'I'll leave you, dear. You see little enough of Rupert *alone* as it is. I'll come back after he's gone.' But every word was spat out with contempt.

Helen thought she was wonderful.

'She's a very talented painter. Look at this little sketch she did of me this morning.'

'Looks as though you've been peeling onions.'

'Oh, Rupert, don't be silly. She's real clever too; got several degrees.'

'And every one below zero,' snapped Rupert.

In between visiting Helen, he had not been idle. He worked the novices and kept up his search for an Olympic horse, which included dining with Colonel Carter and even forcing himself to flirt with the appalling Molly.

After a fortnight, Helen was allowed home and baby Marcus was installed in Rupert's old cradle, newly upholstered in white frills, in his beautiful buttercup-yellow nursery, next to Rupert and Helen's bedroom, with Rupert's old Nanny, who had already settled in to look after him, sleeping in the room on the other side.

Rupert thought this was insane.

'How can Billy and I wander around with no clothes on if

Nanny's two doors down? Billy might easily come home plastered and wander into her room by mistake. The baby ought to be on the top floor with Nanny, like Adrian and I were.'

'But I'd never see him,' protested Helen. 'I want him near me. You can't expect poor Nanny to stagger along the passage and down two flights of stairs every time he cries.'

Helen grew stronger physically, but sank into post-natal depression. She had ears on elastic. Every time a lamb bleated out in the fields she thought it was Marcus crying and raced upstairs. Rupert had the lambs and ewes moved to another field out of earshot. But Helen was still impossibly jumpy. Rupert was hustling her to sleep with him again and was furious when, egged on by Hilary, she refused. A power struggle, too, was developing between her and Nanny. If Marcus cried in the night, often they hit head-on over the cradle, like shiny red billiard balls. Nanny insisted on putting Marcus in long white dresses and refused to have anything to do with disposable nappies. She also wanted a strict routine – you had to show the baby early on who was master. Helen, again egged on by Hilary and Mrs Bodkin, believed that babies should be fed on demand and cuddled a lot. If they couldn't sleep you took them into bed with you, whereupon Nanny launched into horrific tales about ladyships in the past who'd done the same thing and suffocated their babies.

One day when Rupert was away Marcus wouldn't stop crying, his frame wracked, his little lungs bawling the house down. How could such a tiny thing make so much noise?

'Leave him. He'll exhaust himself,' insisted Nanny.

Helen, terrified of losing Marcus, and utterly fed up with this whiskery old boot hanging over him and calling all the shots, summoned the doctor.

Dr Benson, who was more than a little in love with Helen, was delighted to confirm her fears. 'Baby's hungry; needs more food.'

Afterwards there was a stand-up row and Nanny packed her bags.

Terrified of Rupert's wrath, Helen rang up Hilary, who offered only praise.

'Best thing you've ever done. Don't let that MCP talk you around.'

Later, Rupert walked into the nursery to find Helen changing a nappy and, with a look of horror, walked out again. Really, he was the most unrole-reversed guy.

With a hand that trembled slightly, she powdered Marcus and rather clumsily put the disposable nappy inside the Harrington square. She fastened the two blue safety pins, tucked him into his cradle and gave him a kiss. With a gurgle of contentment he fell asleep immediately, obviously not missing Nanny.

Rupert was waiting outside.

'Why the hell are you doing that? Is it Nanny's afternoon off?'

Helen took a deep breath.

'I gave her notice this morning.'

'You what?' thundered Rupert. 'Where is she?'

'Gone.'

'You sacked Nanny without asking me?'

'It's nothing to do with you,' said Helen, losing her temper. 'You're never here, never take any interest in Marcus.'

'Balls. I haven't been away from home for more than a night since you had him.'

'You've only been back three weeks,' screamed Helen, going into her bedroom.

'You turned her out, just like that?'

'She's out of date.'

'She was my Nanny and my father's before that. We're healthy enough. Can't be much wrong with her.'

'Why don't you put her in the antiques fair then? I'm not having her upsetting Mrs Bodkin and, anyway, Hilary figures for successful parenting . . .'

'Don't you quote that bloody dyke at me. Successful parenting, my arse, and who's going to look after the baby now?'

'He's called Marcus, right, and I am. Most mothers do look after their kids, you know. I don't want Marcus growing up caring more for Nanny than me, like you did.'

'And how d'you intend to get away? It's Crittleden next week, Rome the week after.'

'Tory Lovell takes her baby with her.'

'Christ, you should see it. Caravan festooned with nappies, Tory shoving distilled suede boot into some bawling infant, who spits it all out, then bawls all night, keeping every other rider awake.'

'Well, I'll stop at home then,' sobbed Helen.

Suddenly from next door there was a wail.

'Go and see to him,' snapped Rupert. 'Now aren't you sorry you sacked Nanny?'

Fortunately Billy chose that moment to arrive back from Vienna, trailing rosettes, bringing Rupert's horses and panting to see the new baby, so the row was temporarily smoothed over.

'What a little duck,' he said, taking a yelling Marcus from Helen. 'Isn't he sweet? Look at his little hands. No, shush, shush sweetheart, that's no way to carry on, you'll upset your mummy.'

Amazingly, the next minute, Marcus shut up, gazing unfocused at Billy, enjoying the warmth and gentle strength.

'Isn't he a duck?' he said again.

'You'd better take over as Nanny,' said Rupert with a slight edge in his voice. 'Then we won't have to fork out for an ad in *The Lady*.'

Helen thought for the millionth time how glad she was Billy hadn't married Lavinia Greenslade. He was such a comfort.

'You will be godfather, won't you?' she said.

Billy blushed. 'Of course, although I'm not sure I'll be able to point him in a very Christian direction. Who else have you asked?'

'Only my new friend Hilary, so far,' said Helen, shooting

a defiant glance at Rupert. 'I can't wait to have you two meet. I'll know you'll enjoy her.'

Every night for the next week they were woken continually by Marcus crying, driving Rupert to frenzies of irritation.

'That's my night's sleep gone,' he would complain, then drift off to sleep two minutes later. Helen would get up, feed Marcus, soothe him to sleep and lie awake for the rest of the night.

In April, Billy and Rupert set off for Crittleden, leaving Helen and Marcus alone in the big house, except for one of the girl grooms, whom Rupert had insisted sleep in. Resentful of Rupert, Helen poured all her love into the delicate little boy. Thank goodness Hilary lived only a few miles away, so they spent alternate days together, discussing books, plays, paintings, their babies and, inevitably, Rupert.

Jake Lovell was having his best year yet. His horses couldn't stop winning. Revenge, brought in from grass, fat, mellow and almost unrecognizable, was now fit and well-muscled again. Even Jake realized his Olympic potential, but in four years' time.

Tory and Fen, however, were wildly excited when a form arrived for Jake asking him to fill in his measurements for an Olympic uniform, which included a blazer and trousers for the flight and the opening ceremony. Aware that forms had been sent to all the other possibles, Jake had no intention of tempting Providence by returning the form until his selection had been confirmed after Aachen. He was appalled when he discovered that Tory, with her usual efficiency, had filled in the form and posted it.

Despite this tempting of Providence, the first Olympic trial at the Bath and Wells Show went well. Both Sailor and Revenge jumped accurately and were only beaten by seventeen-hundreths of a second against the clock by The Bull. Humpty was fourth, Driffield fifth, Ivor Braine sixth, Rupert a poor seventh, not even getting into the jump-off. The rest were nowhere.

Before the second trial in June at Crittleden, Jake was a good deal more edgy. Colonel Carter was never off the telephone, throwing his weight around, trying to organize Revenge's career, until Jake lost his temper and told the Colonel to get stuffed.

More sinister, Jake noticed an unfamiliar missel-thrush singing in the willow tree nearest the stables, the day before they were due to leave for Crittleden. Jake chased it away, but it came back and went on singing. When he lived with the gipsies a missel thrush had sung all day outside the caravan of the old gipsy grandmother. One day she was in rude health, the next she had died. Jake believed in omens. All day he worried about the children, Isa and little Darklis, who at thirteen months had grown into the most enchanting black-haired, black-eyed gipsy girl, the apple of Jake's eye.

He even went and fetched Isa from the playgroup himself. He didn't tell Tory of his fears. They had decided not to bring the children to Crittleden, as Jake and Fen needed a good night's sleep before the trial, and children around might be distracting.

'Are you sure you don't mind not coming?' Jake asked Tory.

'I can watch you on television,' she said. 'Anyway I'd be so nervous for you, I'd wind you up. I know you're going to make it.'

Jake hated leaving them all. Whenever would he get over this crippling homesickness every time he went away? As they left on the hundred and fifty mile drive it was pouring with rain and the missel-thrush was still singing. It was even wetter and colder at Crittleden. Jake and Fen spent a lot of time blocking up holes in the horses' stables.

On the way to the Secretary's tent to declare for the next day, Jake bumped into Marion, fuming as usual with Rupert.

'He's only got Mayfair in the running now. He used the tack rail on Belgravia so much, one of his legs went septic, so he's off for a fortnight. Rupert's talking of using electrodes on Mayfair; the horse is a bundle of nerves.'

'And Macaulay?' said Jake.

'Sold on to an Arab sheik Rupe met playing chemmy at the Claremont. So he's off to some Middle East hellhole, poor sod. You know what that means?'

'Yes,' said Jake bleakly. 'He'll cart the Sheik's son and heir once too often and end up in the stone quarries. Can you get me the address?'

Marion said she'd try, but Rupert had been very cagey about this deal because Helen, who was in an uptight state, might be upset if she found out the horse had gone.

'Not that she's showing any interest in anything except Marcus at the moment.'

Jake shook his head. 'Why d'you stay with Rupert?'

Marion shrugged. 'I guess I'm hooked on the bastard, and at least I can make the lot of his horses a little easier.'

All the next day the rain poured down like a waterfall. The riders put up the collars of their mackintosh coats and shivered. As he finished walking the course, Jake was accosted by a reporter from the local evening paper.

'This is the toughest course ever built at Crittleden, Jake. Anything to say?'

Jake kept walking. 'I'm sorry I can't talk to you before a class.'

'But I've got a deadline,' wailed the reporter. 'Arrogant sod,' he added furiously.

But Jake didn't hear, and when he passed Humpty and Driffield he barely nodded, trying to cocoon himself, to get a grip on his nerves. He found Fen holding Revenge and Sailor – three drowned rats. Sailor, who loathed the cold, looked more miserable and hideous than ever.

'You O.K.?' he asked Fen.

She nodded. 'What's the course like?'

'Not O.K.,' said Jake. 'Dead and holding. It'll put five inches on all the fences.'

Smug in the covered stands after a good lunch, the Olympic Committee smoked their cigars and waited. Jake, who had a latish draw, watched one rider after another come to grief, which did his nerves no good. He noticed that the dye of his cheap red coat was running into his breeches. If he survived this ordeal, he'd bloody well buy himself a mackintosh coat.

Only Porky Boy and The Bull went clear. Revenge went in at number 20 and, despite having to carry two stone of lead because Jake was so light, he jumped strongly and confidently, with only a toe in the water for four faults. Jake felt passionate relief that he wouldn't have to jump again. But in one of the boxes, from which Colonel Carter would not emerge because Molly didn't want her newly set hair rained on, Jake could see them both looking disappointed.

Rupert went in next, jumping a very haphazard clear, and came out looking none too pleased; he was followed by Driffield, who, despite Olympic-level bellyaching before-hand, had only four faults.

Sailor looked even more fed up as Fen took off his rug. But he nudged Jake in the ribs, as if to say, 'I don't like this any more than you do, so let's get on with it.'

'I heard Rupert saying it's like a skating rink in the middle on the far side of the rustic poles,' said Fen, 'so jump to the right.'

'Yes sir,' said Jake, trying to stop his teeth chattering.

'Your breeches look like a sunset,' said Fen.

'Hope that's not symbolic of my career,' said Jake.

Sailor was cold and it took him the first four jumps to warm up. He gave Jake a seizure when he rapped the double very hard. But fortunately, though the pole trem-bled, it didn't come out of the cup and Jake managed to steer him clear of the skating rink at the rustic poles. Although Jake was aware what a tremendous effort Sailor had to make at each fence, carrying so much lead, he completed the course without mishap.

Jake's heart filled with gratitude. What horse could be more gallant? As he patted him delightedly and gave him half a packet of Polos, he wondered if subconsciously he was holding back Revenge because he *so* wanted to take Sailor to Colombia.

'Keep him warm and under cover,' he said to Fen and went off to check the jump-off course. He found all the clear-round riders having a frightful row with the Crittleden judges.

'For Christ, sake,' said Rupert, 'we've gone clear. Isn't that enough for the buggers? It's like jumping out of quicksand.'

'Porky Boy might easily slip,' said Humpty.

'It's a sod of a course,' agreed Billy.

But the judges were adamant: the Olympic Committee wanted them to jump again. This time Porky Boy had three fences down, Rupert and Driffield two and Jake and Billy one each.

'Can't ask us to go again,' said Billy, grinning at Jake. 'At least that's a grand in each of our pockets.'

'Sailor's finished,' said Jake. 'Couldn't even jump over a pole on the ground.'

Billy nodded. 'Don't worry, they're not that crazy.'

But once again the Olympic Committee, or rather Colonel Roxborough, who had once won a bronze medal, wanted a duel to the death.

'Seems a bit extreme when Jake's horse is carrying so much lead,' protested Malise. 'They really are ghastly conditions.'

'Could be just as ghastly in Colombia,' said the Colonel. 'Are we conducting an Olympic trial, or are we not? You couldn't divide a gold medal.'

Malise had to go down and tell Billy and Jake they had to jump again, knowing he must not transmit the grave doubts he felt.

'I'm retiring Sailor,' said Jake.

'Then you'll scupper your Olympic chances,' said Malise. 'Just take it very slowly.'

Sailor was too exhausted even to look appalled as Jake rode him through the driving rain back into the collecting ring. Jake couldn't bear to watch Billy, but he heard the subdued cheers as he rode out with twelve faults.

Rain was dripping in a steady stream from Malise's hat as he walked up to Jake.

342

'Now, I mean it, take it really slowly.'

'He's got no bloody choice after what you've put him through,' snapped Fen.

Malise knew he should have slapped her down, but she was speaking the truth.

Jake hated having to ask Sailor to do it. He felt like a murderer as he cantered slowly into the ring. Tory must be watching at home and worried too. If only that bloody missel-thrush had shut up. Rain at fifty degrees was making visibility almost impossible.

'I'm sorry, boy, I'm sorry.' He ran a reassuring hand down Sailor's dripping grey plaits.

There were only seven fences. Sailor managed the first and second, but the ground was so churned up that he slipped on take-off at the third, the wall, and sent all the bricks and nearly himself flying. It was like riding on a kitchen floor after you've spilt hot fat. Frightened now, Sailor knocked down the oxer and rapped the upright, which trembled, but as in the first round, didn't fall. Perhaps they were in luck after all. Somehow he nursed Sailor over the rustic poles; now he was coming down to the combination. By some miracle, despite a nasty skid, he cleared the three elements. Now it was only the parallel. Ears flattened against the rain, tail swishing in irritation, Sailor looked for a second as though he was going to stop.

'Go on, baby, go on,' muttered Jake.

Sailor made a mighty effort, girding his loins, then with an extra wiggle, threw himself with a groan over the fence.

Only eight faults. They had won. Despite the deluge, the crowd gave him a tremendous cheer as Jake pulled Sailor to a walk, patting him over and over again. Then just in front of the selectors' box, like some terrible nightmare, Sailor seemed to stop, make an effort to go on, then physically shrink beneath Jake and collapse in the mud. Jake, whose good leg was trapped beneath him, took a few seconds to wriggle free. Scrambling up, covered in mud, he limped over to Sailor's head, cradling it in his arms. Sailor just lay there. Then he opened his wall eye, tried to raise his head, gave a half-choked knucker and his head fell back.

'Sailor!' whispered Jake. 'It's all right, sweetheart. You'll be O.K. in a minute. Where's the vet?' he howled, looking around frantically at the horrified blur of the crowd.

The next minute the vet ran on to the course through the torrent of rain, carrying his bag.

'Quickly; it must be his heart; do something,' pleaded Jake.

The vet opened Sailor's eye and shook his head. 'I'm afraid I can't. He's dead.'

'He can't be,' said Jake through pale trembling lips, 'He can't be, not Sailor,' and suddenly, his face crumpled and tears were mingling with the rain drops.

'Sailor,' he sobbed, kneeling down, putting his arms round Sailor's neck, 'Don't die, please, you can't, don't die.'

In an instant the immaculate Crittleden organization swung into gear. The tractor and trailer were chugging through the mud from the collecting ring and the arena party ran on, putting eight-foot screens round Jake and the horse, and the loudspeaker started booming out music from 'South Pacific.'

The crowd stood stunned, not moving. Colonel Roxborough descended from the stands, Malise ran in from the collecting ring, but Fen got there first, flinging her arms round Jake and Sailor, cuddling them both, sobbing her heart out too.

'Any hope?' asked Malise.

The vet shook his head. 'Heart attack, I'm afraid.'

Fen turned round. 'It's your fault,' she screamed at Malise and Colonel Roxborough, 'your bloody bloody fault. Jake didn't want to jump him. Now what have you proved?'

Malise went up and put his hand on her shoulder. 'Awfully sorry, very bad luck, might have happened at any time.'

'Don't touch me,' hissed Fen, shaking him off. 'You're all murderers.'

Malise went over to Jake, who was still cradling Sailor's head in his arms, crying great strangled sobs. 'It was the missel-thrush,' he kept saying over and over again. He seemed almost deranged.

'Come on, Jake,' said Malise gently. 'Bloody bad luck, but let's get him out of the ring.'

It took three of the arena party to pull Jake off, and the rest of them to get Sailor into the trailer.

Half the crowd and all the grooms were in tears. The riders were visibly shaken. The organizers were in a tizzy about who'd won.

'It's in the FEI rules, Jake wasn't mounted when he left the ring,' said Grania Pringle, who was about to present the prizes.

'Then Billy's got to get it,' said Colonel Roxborough. 'Let's get on with it, get people's minds on to something more cheerful. Bloody good thing it happened today. Just think if he'd collapsed in Colombia. That's what Olympic trials are for.'

Grania Pringle turned on him, her beautiful make-up streaked with tears. 'Bloody well shut up, Roxie. Don't be so fucking insensitive.'

As the tractor came out with its grisly burden Billy, near to tears himself, rode up to Jake: 'Christ, I'm sorry. Of all the ghastly things to happen. We all knew how you felt about him. But I'm not taking first prize, Malise. Jake won it. He must have it.'

'Very kind of you, Billy, but we have to abide by the rules.'

He looked at Jake. It was hard to tell now which was downpour or tears. The rain had washed all the mud from the white shrunken face.

'Bastard,' he spat at Malise, and turned in the direction of his lorry. Suddenly he turned back. 'Where are you taking Sailor?' he demanded.

'Don't worry your head about that,' said Malise. 'Get out

of those wet clothes.'

'You're not taking his body away for cat food.'

'He won't go for cat food,' said Malise reasonably. 'They'll take him to the Hunt kennels.'

Jake shot him a look of pure hatred. 'As if that were any better. Take him to my lorry.'

Fen dried Revenge off and fed him, while Jake loaded the two novices into the box. She couldn't bear to watch them loading Sailor, so she went and rang Tory to tell her they were coming home. As she came out of the telephone box, Malise was waiting for her. She was about to walk past him when he said, 'Look, I know how you both feel.'

'I should doubt it,' said Fen coldly. 'And don't try telling Jake it's only a horse. He loved Sailor more than any human.' She added suddenly, with a wisdom beyond her years, 'He felt they were both ugly, both laughed at, both despised and rejected. Together they were going to show the world.'

Malise looked at her thoughtfully. 'He's very lucky to have you. Can't you stop him driving in this condition? It's simply not safe.'

'You didn't worry too much about Sailor's safety, did you?' snapped Fen. 'So I don't think you're a very good judge. And in this condition, which you put him into, all he needs is Tory.'

Jake didn't speak a word on the way home. Fen found it unbearable the way Revenge kept nudging Sailor's body, waiting for his wise old friend to scramble, grumbling, to his feet and tell him not to worry. They reached The Mill House at midnight. Jake drove the box straight around to the orchard. The rain had stopped, leaving a brilliant clear night. Moonlight flooded the dripping apple trees and the grave, which had already been dug for them by the next-door farmer. He stayed to help them unload Sailor, which was a good thing, as he was stiff and cold now, and terribly heavy. It was so bright you could see the flecks on his fleabitten coat, his mane still neatly plaited. Jake wrapped him in his white and maroon rug and patted him goodbye.

Jake's face was set and expressionless as he covered the body with earth, pressing it down neatly. Later, when he'd unloaded and settled the other horses, he made a cross and put it on the grave.

By a supreme effort, Tory managed not to cry in front of him, and when they finally fell into bed around four o'clock he just groaned, laid his head on her warm, friendly breasts and fell asleep.

Next day he spent a long time digging up wild flowers to plant around Sailor's grave. Outwardly he appeared calm, but Tory knew he was bleeding inside. In the afternoon Malise rang up. Jake refused to talk to him.

'How is he?' asked Malise.

'All right,' said Tory, 'but he won't talk about it.'

'Well, it might cheer him up to know he and Revenge have been selected to go to Aachen. Probably he's suffering from shock. He'll be O.K. in a day or two.'

He rang up again two days later. 'Just confirming Jake and Revenge are available for Aachen.'

'Well, it's a bit awkward,' said Tory.

'Let me speak to him.'

'I'm afraid he doesn't want to talk to you. And he's completely gone off the idea of going to the Olympics.'

'But that'd give him an interest, best possible therapy,' said Malise. 'He can't deprive his country of a horse like that.'

Colonel Carter was less reticent. He rang repeatedly, complaining about Jake refusing to take Revenge to Aachen and poor Tory, who had to field the calls, received a torrent of abuse.

'It's preposterous. Fellow's a milksop, blubbing in the ring. Suppose he's lost his nerve.'

For once Tory lost her temper. 'Don't you realize they've broken his heart?'

The village sent a wreath to put on Sailor's grave. Letters of sympathy poured in. 'We all loved him,' wrote one woman. 'To us Sailor was show jumping.' 'I'm sending you my pocket money,' wrote one little girl. 'I expect the other

347

horses are missing him, and you might like to buy them some Polos.'

On the Thursday morning after Sailor's death Fen, having spent two hours on the novices in the indoor school, was just munching a piece of toast and marmalade, and dashing off an essay on Mercutio before racing off to school, when Wolf started barking frenziedly and she heard the sound of wheels on the bridge. Going out, she found a plump blonde with a sweet round face, and two tough-looking men getting out of a horse box.

'Yes?' she said.

They all looked faintly embarrassed, then the girl said, 'I'm Petra, Rupert Campbell-Black's new groom. We've come for the horse.'

'What horse?'

'Revenge.'

Whimpering, Fen bolted back upstairs to wake Tory and Jake. Jake, unable to sleep, had only dropped off with the aid of a sleeping tablet at six o'clock. He came down zombie-like, eyelids swollen, eyes leaden with sleep, wearing only jeans. Noticing his sticking-out ribs, Fen thought how much weight he'd lost recently.

'What did you say?'

'They've come for Revenge.'

'Don't be bloody silly,' said Jake, going to the open back door. 'Bugger off, all of you.'

The girl went very pink. 'We understood you'd been told.'

'What?'

'That Rupert Campbell-Black bought Revenge yesterday.'

Jake went very still. 'Are you certain?'

She nodded, pitying him. Jake had long been one of her heroes.

'I don't believe it,' snapped Jake. 'Just one of Rupert's silly games. I'll go and ring up Bernard.'

The Colonel was out. Molly answered, hard put to conceal her elation.

348

'Bernard's been trying to get through to you for three days, Jake.'

'Is it true?'

'Yes. Rupe's been after Revenge for months.'

It was 'Rupe' now, was it? Jake leant against the hall table, suddenly dizzy with hatred.

'I'll buy him. Offer him to me.'

'I hardly think you can top Rupe's offer.'

'How much?'

'Forty-five thousand pounds,' said Molly maliciously.

'You're crazy. He'll ride that horse off its feet in six months.'

'Well, that doesn't really matter, now that Bernard's got the cash,' said Molly. 'Anyway, I'm sure Rupert won't. He's taking him to the Olympics. Bernard's set his heart on that. We tried to talk to you last night to say the deal had finally gone through, but you wouldn't come to the telephone. Oh, Bernard's just come in. Have a word with Jake.'

The Colonel picked up the telephone. ' 'Fraid it's true, Jake. Had the feeling you were a bit chicken about the Olympics, bit out of your depth really. He who dares wins you know. Campbell-Black's man enough to have a go.'

'He's a sadist,' said Jake.

'Rubbish. He's a brilliant horseman with a lot of experience Not fair to Revenge to hold him back.'

Jake hung up and rang Malise.

'Rupert's told me. I tried to dissuade him, but the deal had gone through. I'm awfully sorry, Jake, but there's not much I can do. It's Carter's horse.'

Jake got dressed and went out to the yard, to find Fen standing outside Revenge's box with a 12-bore in her hands and Wolf snarling beside her.

'Keep away from that door,' she hissed. 'This is our horse. If you lay a finger on him I'll blast you full of lead.'

'You've been watching too many Westerns, love,' said the taller of the two men, but he backed away slightly.

Jake strolled across the yard. 'Put that gun down, Fen.'

'No! He isn't their horse to take.'

'I'm afraid he is,' he said. 'Bernard's sold him to Rupert.'

It was too much for Fen. Revenge was her baby, the horse she'd transformed from a nervous, napping wreck to a loving, happy and willing horse. She dropped the gun with a clatter and rushed up to the men. 'Please don't take him away,' she sobbed. 'We lost Sailor last Saturday. Please don't take away Revenge, too.'

'I'm sorry, love, I know it's hard, but orders is orders.'

Jake turned to Tanya. 'Go and get Revenge.'

It took only a few minutes to put one of Rupert's rugs and a head collar on Revenge. Jake went to the book they kept in the tackroom, describing each horse's likes and dislikes, and the training and the feed he'd been getting, and which of Jake's medicines he needed. Numbly he wondered whether to give it to Rupert. It would certainly help the horse. Then, he thought, sod it, and, tearing out the page, he crumpled it up and threw it in the bin.

It gave him a terrible pang to see how merrily and confidently Revenge bounced up the ramp of the lorry, thinking he was going to a show. He'd been such a devil to box when he'd arrived. He looked worth every penny of £45,000 now.

Jake went up and stroked him and gave him a handful of stud nuts. It gave him an even worse pang to think how Revenge would react when he got to the other end and didn't find Fen to welcome him. He couldn't look as the lorry drove off over the bridge, through the fringe of willows.

Africa was the first to notice Revenge's absence. She'd been looking out for Sailor since Jake came back, leaving her manger after a quick mouthful, coming to the half-door with a puzzled expression on her black face and calling out for him. Now Revenge was gone too, she was irritated and nervy, circling her box, picking up straw, letting it hang from her mouth like the village idiot. Jake went up and put his arms round her neck, fighting back the tears. 'I miss them too,' she seemed to be saying with her wise kind eyes, 'but you still have me; please love me because I'm the one who always loved you best.'

And suddenly Jake felt ashamed. Africa, the goodest, truest, gentlest of them all, and he'd been neglecting her recently, because Sailor and Revenge seemed so much more important. He went into the tackroom, looking at the rows and rows of rosettes. Across the yard in the sitting room, lovingly polished by Tory, were all his silver cups. Pride of place had been given to the cup he'd won at Olympia with Sailor. Then, he'd been king of the castle. Now he was at the bottom of the heap again, with only Africa and half a dozen novices to his name. He looked up at the cupboard on the opposite wall where, well out of reach, he kept all his poisons: belladonna, henbane for galls, hemlock, and the ground-down toadstools, which if sparingly administered could cure colic or purge a sick horse to recovery.

In an old silver snuff box he kept warty caps. One spore of the fungus would attach itself to Rupert's throat, giving all the symptoms of consumption, but causing death in a few weeks. It was a nice thought. But he preferred to beat Rupert in other ways.

He went upstairs to Fen's room, noticing the threadbare landing carpet. Tory was desperately trying to comfort her. Poor little Fen; first Marigold, then Revenge. He put a hand on Tory's cheek and stroked it. She looked up startled, blushing at the unexpected tenderness, relieved he wasn't as shattered as she'd expected.

'Fen,' he said, 'I've got an idea. I think it's high time Africa had a foal.'

Fen didn't react. She just lay there, slumped, her shoulders heaving.

'And it's high time you had your own horse,' he went on. 'Think I've found one for you. She's only five, and roan, not a colour I like, but her mother was a polo pony, so she turns on a sixpence and she jumps like a cricket already.'

Almost blindly Fen reached out for Jake. 'It's so terribly, terribly kind of you,' she sobbed, 'but it's no good. I can't stop thinking about Revenge.'

23

The more Rupert rode Revenge the better he liked him. He'd never sat on such a supple, well-schooled animal. It was like playing a Stradivarius after an old banjo. They clicked the moment he got on the horse's back. It was easier for Revenge to carry Rupert's twelve stones than Jake plus two unmoveable stones of lead. The horse also loved jumping against the clock. He had already won one class at the Royal Highland, where he had trounced all the other possibles. Now he was in Aachen with the probables, for the final trial, and attracting a huge amount of interest from the world's press. How would Gyppo Jake's horse go with Rupert over such huge fences?

Rupert, in fact, had received a lot of flak. After Sailor's tragic death, the public felt it was very unfair on Jake that the other horse he'd spent so much time bringing on should be snatched from under his nose. As soon as Marion heard that Rupert had appropriated Revenge, she handed in her notice, properly this time, then went straight to Fleet Street and told them exactly how much Rupert had paid for the horse, an offer the frightful Colonel couldn't refuse, and then went on to give them some choice titbits about the cruelty of Rupert's training methods. The *News of the World* felt the material was too hot to print but *Private Eye* had no such scruples. Rumours were rife.

No one could get any comment from Jake on the subject, so the reporters besieged Rupert.

'Well, I'll concede Jake Lovell's a good trainer,' he said diplomatically, 'but the horse needed an experienced rider on his back. Winning's about taking chances. Jake wasn't

even prepared to take the horse to Colombia. As for the cruelty charges, they're too ridiculous to discuss. Horses won't jump if they don't want to.'

And now it was the eve of the trials and Rupert knew perfectly well that if Revenge beat the rest of the international field as well as the English probables tomorrow and was picked for Colombia, people would conveniently forget how the horse had been acquired. Helen was so wrapped up in little Marcus that she hardly appreciated the furore. Rupert had hoped she might leave Marcus with Mrs Bodkin and fly out to Aachen, but she was still looking desperately tired and said she didn't feel quite confident enough to leave him.

Rupert, however, was finding consolation in his new groom, Petra, whom he had nicknamed Podge. He was glad Marion had gone; he was fed up with her tantrums and her beady eyes following him all the time. Podge, on the other hand, with her chunky body and legs, though not as upmarket or as handsome as Marion, had a nice smooth skin and was always smiling, and she adored the horses, almost more than she worshipped Rupert. Naturally, Revenge was homesick at first; any horse coddled as Jake's were would feel the draught when he left the yard. But Podge had made a huge fuss of the horse and after a few days kicking his box out and spurning his food, he had settled in.

It was the eve of the Aachen trials and, having seen the horses settled, Rupert and Billy took a taxi back to their hotel. There was something about a hotel bedroom that made Rupert want to order a bottle of champagne and a beautiful girl to drink it with.

'What shall we do tonight?'

Billy pushed aside Rupert's clothes, which littered both beds, and collapsed on to his own bed.

'Go to bed early. I'm absolutely knackered.'

'Ludwig's having a barbecue at his house.'

'I don't want a hangover tomorrow.'

'But just think of all that Kraut crumpet.' Rupert went to

the window and gazed down the tidy village street, then said casually,

'Thought I might take Podge.'

'Oh, for Christ's sake, leave her alone. You know how it rotted up your relationship with Marion. Pity there isn't a Gideon bible, then I could read you the seventh commandment all over again.'

'Well I'm not getting much joy out of my wife at the moment. She's temporarily closed, like the M4.'

Billy put his hands over his ears. 'I don't want to hear. You know I adore your wife.'

The telephone rang. Rupert picked it up.

'Hullo, darling. I was just talking to Billy about you.' Next moment the lazy smile was wiped off his face.

'It's Marcus,' sobbed Helen. 'He's been hospitalized. He can't breathe and he's gone purple in the face. Oh Rupert, I know he's going to die. Please come back.'

'I'll be on the next plane. You're at Gloucester Hospital? Don't worry, darling, he'll pull through. The Campbell-Blacks are very tough.'

He rang Malise in his room, who came over straightaway.

'You must go back at once.'

'I'm sorry. Helen's in a frightful state.'

'Hardly surprising. They're terrifying, these illnesses of little children. I remember going through them with Henrietta and,' he paused, 'with Timmie. I hope everything'll be all right. Give Helen our love and sympathy.'

Rupert was lucky enough to get a plane at once and he reached the hospital by midnight. He hadn't bothered to change; he was still wearing boots, breeches and a tweed coat over his white shirt and tie.

'My name's Campbell-Black,' he said to the receptionist. 'My wife came in this afternoon with our baby, named Marcus. He may be in the operating theatre.'

His hand shook as he brushed his hair back from his forehead. The girl looked down her list, wishing she'd bothered to wash her hair that morning. She remembered

Rupert from earlier in the year, when he'd caused such a stir when Helen had the baby.

'Marcus's in the children's ward on the fourth floor.'

The lift was occupied with a patient coming back from the operating theatre. Rupert ran up the stairs. The sister met him in the passage.

'My son, Marcus Campbell-Black,' he panted, 'he was brought in this afternoon.'

'Oh, yes.' With maddening lack of haste the sister went back into her room to check the chart.

'He's in Room 25.'

'Is he, is he?' Rupert choked on the words, 'going to be all right?'

'Of course he is. He had an attack of croup.'

'What's that?'

'No one quite knows why it comes on. The baby goes blue and can't breathe. Parents invariably think he's swallowed something and is choking to death. All he needs is to inhale some moisture. We're keeping him in the humidifying tent for tonight. Dr Benson says he'll be as right as rain tomorrow.

'Are you all right?' she asked staring at Rupert's horrified expression. 'It must have been a terrible shock for you. Mrs Campbell-Black will be so pleased you've come back. She was very upset, but Dr Benson's given her something to calm her down. Can I get you a cup of tea?'

And she brought me all the way back for this, thought Rupert, in the middle of the final Olympic trial. In Room 25, he found Marcus lying happily in a huge cellophane tent, inhaling friar's balsam from a humidifier. Helen was sitting on the edge of the bed wiggling Marcus' toes. She got up and ran to Rupert.

'Oh, I'm so glad you came. I was so frightened. I thought he was going to die.'

Rupert patted her shoulder mechanically. Nanny would have recognized croup, he thought darkly. Behind her on the bed, he could see his son and heir pinkly gurgling, digging his pink starfish fingers into his shawl and felt a

355

black rage.

'Look,' said Helen fondly, diving under the tent and holding Marcus up in a sitting position. 'He can hold his head up now. Don't you want to cuddle him?'

'I'm sure he ought to be kept quiet,' said Rupert.

He listened while she poured out her worries and tried not to contrast the innocent fun he'd be having in Aachen, getting slightly tight with Billy at Ludwig's barbecue, with the terrifying world of children's illness and the dark claustrophobic intensity of Helen's love.

'I'm sorry I brought you back,' she said. 'I was so terrified you might find him dead. I needed you so badly. I'm sorry I've been offish lately, but it must be worth coming all this way just to see him. He's so cute, isn't he? Do you think he's grown?'

'I need a drink,' said Rupert. At that moment Benson walked in.

'Hullo, Rupert,' he said heartily. 'You must have been worried stiff, but, as you can see, he's all right. Nothing to worry about. You need a drink? Come on, I'm sure Matron's got something tucked away.'

Benson obviously wanted a heart-to-heart. Matron only had sweet sherry, but at least it was alcohol. Immediately Benson launched into the subject of Helen.

'Bit worried about her. Only twenty-four. Very young to cope on her own with a big house and a young baby. She misses you, you know.'

'I miss her,' said Rupert, somewhat shirtily, 'but Christ, she won't come to shows with me. I got her a marvellous nanny and she promptly sacked her. I asked her to come to Aachen. I've got an Olympic trial tomorrow. I'll have to fly back in the morning.'

Benson looked pained. 'So soon?'

'I do have a living to earn.'

'I know,' said Benson soothingly. 'I do think it would help if you could get a nanny: a young cheerful girl, who Helen wouldn't feel threatened by. Then in time she'd feel confident enough to leave Marcus.'

'She needs a holiday.'

'Best holiday she could have would be for the baby to get well and strong. But I'm afraid all the indications are that he's going to be an asthmatic.'

'Christ, are you sure?'

'Pretty certain. We'll do some tests while he's in here. And you know that's not a condition helped by the mother's anxiety. With any luck he should grow out of it, or at least be able to handle it, as he gets older.'

Rupert drained the glass of sherry, pulling a face.

'Want another?' asked Benson,

Rupert shook his head. He felt absolutely shattered. He had been up at five that morning.

'What's your schedule?'

'Well the trial's tomorrow, then the International in London. Then, if I'm picked for Colombia, a brief rest for the horses before we fly out.'

'And after that, you could take her and Marcus away for a long holiday?'

Rupert shook his head. 'Virtually impossible in the middle of the season. Horses lose their precision if you rest them too long.'

Benson nodded. 'Appreciate your problem. I've got patients on the tennis circuit. Has she got a friend she can stay with?'

Rupert thought of Hilary. He guessed she had been stirring things.

'Not really. I'll have to find her a nanny. Can I take her home this evening?'

'Good idea. The child's in no danger now. Do her good.'

Helen was aghast when Rupert told her he'd be flying back in the morning. She lay in the huge double bed, with that pinched defiant look of roses touched by the frost in December. Then, as Rupert joined her, she lay back, staring at the ceiling, wanting to be soothed and comforted and told she was being splendid.

Rupert comforted her in the only way he knew, by trying to make love to her. After a few minutes she started to cry.

'Christ, what's the matter now?'

'I'm too worried about Marcus. I can't switch off, and now you're going back.'

'Darling, the trial's tomorrow afternoon.'

'Horse, horse, horse.' She was suddenly almost hysterical. 'Surely Marcus is more important than a horse trial?'

It was a debatable point, thought Rupert, but he merely said, 'Benson says there's nothing to worry about.'

Rupert left at nine o'clock and ran into bad weather, arriving only just in time to walk the course. Once again he contrasted Podge's lovely smiling welcome with Helen's set, martyred face as she'd said goodbye that morning.

'How's Marcus?' asked Podge. 'Oh, I'm so relieved he's O.K. We was all so worried. Revvie and I missed you. He was restless last night, so I slept in his box – 'spect I look like it.'

'Lucky Rev,' said Rupert. 'He looks in the pink anyway.'

'He's great, on top of the world. You'll just have to sit on his back.'

What a contrast to Marion, thought Rupert.

For the first time in his life he was suffering from nerves. It must be tiredness. He longed for a stiff drink, but Podge had made him a large cup of strong black coffee instead. He knew the world's press was watching as he rode into the ring.

His fears were groundless. Revenge jumped like an angel, literally floating over the vast fences. After the trial, the selectors went into a huddle. Elated, almost sure of a place, Rupert went off to ring Helen, now back in the hospital with Marcus. He carefully spent five minutes asking how they both were before telling her Revenge had come first, beating even Ludwig, going like a dream and muzzling any critics.

'I'm very glad for you,' said Helen in a tight little voice.

'Who's that in the background' said Rupert.

'Hilary and the kids,' said Helen. 'She's driving Marcus and me home from hospital and staying the night. She's being so supportive.'

As he came off the telephone, a German reporter accosted him.

'Meester Black, it is unusual for zee English to beat zee Germans in this country, no?'

'No,' said Rupert coldly, 'I think you're forgetting the last two world wars,' and stalked off.

Feeling utterly deflated, he went back to the stable where an ecstatic Podge was chattering to Revenge as she settled him for the night.

'Didn't you do well, darling? It's Colombia here we come. We'll have to make you a sun hat to keep off the flies.'

'Don't count your chickens,' said Rupert, checking Revenge's bandages.

'You look really tired,' said Podge, then, blushing, added, 'I bet you didn't eat last night, nor this morning. I made you a shepherd's pie for tonight. It's not very good and I'm sure you'd rather go out with Billy.'

Rupert pulled the half-door behind him:

'I'd much rather stay in, right in,' he said softly, drawing her towards him, 'and I absolutely adore shepherd's pie.'

'Oh, we can't,' squawked Podge, 'not here, not in front of Rev.'

'Want to bet?' said Rupert, pushing her against the wall.

Jake Lovell heard the news on the tackroom wireless as he was filling in the diet sheets. Fen, who was cleaning tack, didn't dare look at him.

'After a successful trial in Aachen, Germany,' said the announcer, 'the following riders and horses have been picked for the Olympics in Colombia. Charles Hamilton and Porky Boy, Billy Lloyd-Foxe and The Bull, Rupert Campbell-Black on Revenge.' Fen gave a gasp of horror. 'Brian Driffield on Temperance with Ivor Braine as reserve.'

Fen went over and put her arms round Jake. 'I'm so, so sorry,' she said. 'It was you who made him a great horse. Rupert just had to get on his back.'

Molly Carter, delighted that Revenge had been selected,

felt a trip to Colombia would be in order.

'We must give a celebration party for Rupert and Helen before he leaves. 'Phone him up, Bernard, and fix an evening he's free, and then we can invite everyone else. And do ask him about hotels in Bogota, and say to make sure we get tickets to watch Rev.'

Colonel Carter came off the telephone, magenta in the face. 'Most peculiar. Rupe says Revenge belongs to him now, and there is no possible way he's coming to any party.'

'Oh, Bernard,' snapped Molly. 'You know what a tease Rupert is. He must have been joking. I'll ring him up.'

'Rupert,' she said archly, two minutes later, 'Bernard must have got the wrong end of the stick. We want to give a little celebration party for you.'

'Well, you can count me out,' said Rupert curtly. 'I never mix business with pleasure and you and the Colonel were strictly business, believe me,'

'You can say that?' spluttered Molly. 'After all we've done for you?'

'Yes,' said Rupert. 'Go and spend your forty-five grand on buying a few friends. It's the only way you'll get them,' and hung up.

Billy couldn't believe he'd been selected for the Olympics. For days he floated on a cloud of bliss. He felt sorry for Lavinia – not being picked. But it would make things much easier in Colombia if she wasn't there to upset him.

All the team had been much too superstitious to fill in their clothes measurement forms, so there was a last-minute panic to get the uniform in time. Rupert made a terrible fuss about the clothes.

'I am *not* going to wear a boating jacket with a badge on,' he said disdainfully, throwing the royal blue Olympic blazer across the room. 'And these trousers make us look like Wombles.'

Billy didn't care. He was so enchanted to be in the team, he'd have worn a grass skirt, if necessary.

The only blot on the horizon was the tension in Rupert's marriage. Billy didn't like Hilary one bit. He thought she was bossy, strident and disruptive, and having a very bad effect on Helen. She was always around the house these days, breast-feeding her baby in the drawing room, or shovelling brown rice down little Germaine. Despite disapproving of Rupert's stinking capitalist habits, she had no compunction about drinking his drink or using his washing machine all day. You couldn't get a pair of breeches washed these days for revolving nappies.

The excuse for Hilary's presence was that she was doing a painting of Helen. Like the sketch she had done before, she made Helen look the picture of victimized misery — Belsen thin, her face all eyes, tears streaking her wasted cheeks. Rupert, who, like most rich people, detested free-loaders, grew so irritated that, after half a bottle of whisky one night, he crept in and painted a large black moustache and a beard on the picture, with a balloon coming out of Helen's mouth saying: 'Monica Carlton had me first'.

Billy fell about laughing, Helen was absolutely livid. Hilary merely looked pained, assumed a They-know-not-what-they-do attitude and started another painting. So Rupert achieved nothing.

One evening when she was giving Marcus his late bottle, Billy tackled Helen.

'Angel, I don't want to interfere, but I think you ought to come to Colombia.'

'I can't leave Marcus.'

'Well, bring him.'

'He's too little. He'd never cope with the climate.'

Billy tried another tack. 'I know Rupe seems very tough on the outside, but he needs the applause, most of all from you. He's too proud to plead, but I know he's desperate for you to go. Hilary could look after Marcus.'

Helen cuddled Marcus tighter, a look of terror on her face. 'When Marcus had croup the other day and I thought he was dying, I made a pact I'd never leave him.'

'You do have a husband as well.'

But Helen wouldn't be persuaded.

The last show before the Olympics was the Royal International. Rupert and Billy left The Bull and Revenge to enjoy a well-earned rest in Gloucestershire, and drove up to London with Kitchener and Belgravia and a handful of novices. On the Wednesday, Billy and Kitchener won the King George V Cup, an all male-contest and one of the most prestigious in the world.

The following evening, while the women riders were competing for the Queen Elizabeth Cup, all the British Olympic team, except Rupert, who had other unspecified plans, went out on the tiles together. They started in a West End pub called the Golden Lion. Ivor, Billy and Humpty had all bought rounds of drinks and were deliberately hanging back to see if they could make Driffield put his hand in his pocket.

'That's mine,' said Billy, as the barman tried to gather up the second half of Billy's tonic. 'I'm hoping someone is going to buy me the other half.'

Looking pointedly at Driffield, he put the tonic bottle into his breast pocket. He was still coming down to earth after his win. Everyone was hailing and congratulating him on that and on getting picked to go to Colombia. Looking around the bar, he was aware of some wonderful girls in summer dresses eyeing him with considerable enthusiasm. He wished he could ask one of them out. It was a glorious July evening. The setting sun was lighting up the dusty plane trees in the square, the door of the bar was fixed open and people were drinking in the streets.

'I'm thirsty, Driff,' he said.

'I'm thirsty, too,' said Humpty.

'I didn't know you were thirty-two,' said Ivor, surprised. 'I thought you were only thirty, Humpty.'

'I was saying I was thirsty, Driff,' said Billy, winking at the others.

He flicked his still-lit cigarette end in the direction of the open door, but it missed and landed in the lap of a girl in a cyclamen pink dress who was sitting on a bench nearby.

'Oh, Christ!' Billy bounded towards her. 'I'm frightfully sorry,' but as he leaned forward to remove the cigarette end, the tonic from the bottle in his pocket cascaded forward, all over her dress.

'For God's sake, look what you're doing,' said her companion.

'Oh, hell,' said Billy, 'I'm dreadfully sorry.'

The girl burst out laughing. 'It really doesn't matter; it'll dry in a sec. It's so hot, it's nice to have an impromptu shower.'

Billy looked into her face and his heart skipped several beats. She was certainly one of the prettiest girls he'd ever seen. She had a smooth brown skin with a touch of pink on each high cheek-bone, slanting dark brown eyes, a turned-up nose, a mane of streaky tortoiseshell hair and a big mouth as smooth and as crimson as a fuchsia bud. Her pink dress showed at least three inches of slim brown thigh and a marvellous Rift valley of cleavage.

Billy couldn't tear his eyes away. 'I'm most awfully sorry,' he repeated in a daze.

'It couldn't matter less,' said the girl, highly delighted at the effect she was having on him.

Billy pulled himself together. Getting out one of Rupert's blue silk handkerchieves, he started to wipe away the ash, but it all smeared into the tonic.

'Oh, dear, that's much worse. Look, let me buy you another dress.'

'There's no need for that,' snapped her companion. He was about thirty-five, with a pale sweating face that was even more rumpled than his grey suit.

'Then let me buy you a drink – both of you. What would you like?'

'You've caused quite enough trouble already,' the man said. 'Why don't you buzz off?'

'Don't be beastly, Victor,' said the girl, in her soft husky voice. 'We'd *love* a drink.'

The man looked at his watch. 'We'll be late. The table's booked for nine and they don't like to be kept waiting.'

'They'll wait for me,' said the girl blandly.

'Anyone would,' said Billy. 'Have a quick one.'

But the man had got to his feet. 'No, thank you *very* much,' he said huffily.

'I must have a pee,' said the girl. 'You go and get a taxi, Vic.'

There was a great deal of Ally Ooping and badinage from the rest of the riders, as Billy waited for her to come out. What would Rupert do in the circumstances? he wondered. Probably accost her and get her telephone number, but he couldn't do that with the frightful Victor hovering.

As she came out he caught a heady new waft of scent. She'd teased her tortoiseshell hair more wildly and applied more crimson lipstick. He wanted to kiss it all off. Perhaps that luscious mouth would pop like a fuchsia bud. He took a deep breath. 'I don't mean to be presumptuous, but you're the prettiest girl I've ever seen.'

'That's nice,' she said.

'My name's Billy Lloyd-Foxe.'

'The great show jumper,' she said mockingly. 'I know. You won the King's Cup yesterday.'

He blushed scarlet. 'I'd adore to see you again.'

As she smiled, he noticed the gap in the white, slightly uneven teeth, the raspberry pink tongue of the good digestion.

'You will.' She patted his cheek with her hand. 'I promise you. Oh, look, Victor's managed to get a taxi. How extraordinary.' She ran out into the street and he hadn't even asked her name. Nil out of ten for initiative. If Rupert had been here he would have lynched him. On the other hand, if Rupert had been here, the girl would have gone off with Rupert instead.

Billy spent the rest of the week at the International, feeling horribly restless, praying the girl from the Golden Lion might turn up. After Lavinia, he'd vowed he'd never let another girl get under his skin, and here he was, moping around again. Even in the excitement of setting out for Colombia, he was unable to get her out of his mind.

In the weeks leading to the Olympics, Jake Lovell sank into deep depression. Then, unable to face the razzmatazz and hysterical chauvinism of the actual event, he flew off to the Middle East to try and find Macaulay. He had located the Sheik, but when he got there, after a lot of prevarication, he discovered that Macaulay had indeed blotted his copy book by savaging the Sheik himself, and had been sold on less than six weeks before to a dealer who kept no records and couldn't or probably didn't want to remember where Macaulay had gone.

Jake went to the British Embassy, who were very unhelpful. With a big oil deal going through, they didn't want to rock the boat. After repeated nagging, they sent Jake to Miss Blenkinsop, who ran a horse rescue centre in the capital, and, as far as Jake could see, was a constant thorn in the authorities' flesh, as she waged a one-woman battle against appalling Middle Eastern cruelty and insensitivity towards animals.

Miss Blenkinsop was a gaunt, sinewy woman in her late fifties, totally without sentimentality, and with the brusque, rather de-sexed manner of someone who has always cared for animals more than people.

She gave Jake a list of sixty-odd addresses where he might find the horse.

'Hope your nerves are strong. You'll see some harrowing sights. Arabs think it's unlucky to put down a horse, so they work them till they drop dead, and they don't believe in feeding and watering them much either. Horse has probably been sold upcountry. You've as much chance of finding him as a needle in a haystack, but here are all the riding schools and the quarries, the most likely spots within five miles of the city. I'll lend you one of my boys as interpreter. He's a shifty little beast, but he speaks good English, and you can borrow my car, if you like.'

For Jake it was utter crucifixion. He was in a bad way emotionally anyway, and he had never seen such cruelty. Like some hideous travesty of Brook Farm Riding School, he watched skeletons, lame, often blind, frantic with thirst, shuffling around riding school rings, or tugging impossibly heavy loads in the street or in the quarries, being beaten until they collapsed, and then being beaten until they got up again.

For five days he went to every address Miss Blenkinsop had given him, bribing, wheedling, cajoling for information about a huge black horse with a white face, and one long white sock. No one had seen him. Sickened and shattered, he returned every night to his cheap hotel where there was no air conditioning, the floors crawled with cockroaches and drink was totally prohibited. As the coup-de-grâce, on the fifth night, he couldn't resist watching the Olympic individual competition on the useless black and white hotel television. As Billy rode in, the picture went around and around, but sadistically, it held still for Rupert and Revenge, who produced two heroic rounds to win the Bronze. Ludwig got the gold on his great Hanoverian mare, Clara; Carol Kennedy, the American number one male rider, got the silver.

Black with despair and hatred, Jake went up to his cauldron of a room and lay on his bed smoking until dawn. He had nearly run out of money and addresses. Today he must go home empty-handed. Around seven, he must have dozed off. He was woken by the telephone.

It was Miss Blenkinsop. 'Don't get too excited, but I may have found your horse. He's been causing a lot of trouble down at the stone quarries.' She gave him the address.

'If it is him, don't bid for him yourself. They'll guess something's up and whack up the price. Give me a ring and I'll come and do the haggling.'

At first Jake wasn't sure. The big muzzled gelding was so pitifully thin and so covered in a thick layer of white dust as he staggered one step forward, one step back, trying to shift a massive cartload of stone, that it was impossible to distinguish his white face or his one white sock. Then the Arab brought his whip down five times on the sunken quarters, five black stripes appeared and with a squeal of

366

rage, Macaulay turned and lunged at the driver, showing the white eye on the other side.

'That's my boy,' thought Jake with a surge of excitement. 'They'll break his back before they break his spirit.'

Miss Blenkinsop had a hard time making the Arab owner of the quarry part with Macaulay. Although vicious, he was the strongest horse they'd ever had and probably still had six months' hard labour in him, but the price the hideously ugly Englishwoman was offering was too much for him to refuse. He could buy a dozen broken-down wrecks for that.

When Jake took Miss Blenkinsop's trailer to collect him, Macaulay was too tall to fit in. So Jake led him very slowly back through the rush-hour traffic.

Macaulay twice clattered to the ground with exhaustion, and several times they narrowly missed death as the oil-rich Arabs hurtled by in their huge limousines. But Macaulay displayed no fear, he was beyond that now, and most touchingly, he seemed to remember Jake from the time he'd treated his lacerations after Rupert's beating-up in Madrid. When Jake came to fetch him, his lacklustre eyes brightened for a second and he gave a half-whicker of welcome.

That night, after he had made the horse as comfortable as possible, Jake had supper with Miss Blenkinsop. She drew the curtains and produced an ancient bottle of Madeira. After two glasses, Jake realized he was absolutely plastered. After Arab food, the macaroni cheese she gave him seemed the best thing he had ever eaten.

Jake always found it difficult to express gratitude, in case it was construed as weakness.

'I don't know how to thank you,' he finally mumbled.

'Don't bother,' said Miss Blenkinsop. 'Do something about it. Spread the word when you get back to England. We need cash, not sympathy, and a law banning the exporting of all horses to the Middle East.'

'If I can get Macaulay back on the circuit,' said Jake, 'the publicity for you will be so fantastic, the money'll start flooding in.'

'He's in a very bad way. Think you'll be able to do it?'

Jake shrugged. 'He's young. My grandmother cured a mare with a broken leg once, bound it in comfrey and she went on to win four races. I'm going to have a bloody good try.'

For a second he stared at his glass, miles away, then he said, 'I had a horse called Sailor once. He was near death when he arrived, but he did pretty well in the end.'

Even when Jake and Macaulay got back to England, the news that Great Britain had won the team silver medal, Billy clinching it with a brilliant clear, didn't upset him very much.

24

Kings, they came home. After a gruelling thirty-hour journey from Colombia to Stansted Airport, The Bull and Revenge, accompanied by Tracey and Podge, had a good night's sleep at Colonel Roxborough's yard. Next day they drove the horses in the lorry to Heathrow to meet Rupert and Billy. They had quite a wait, because of scenes of hysterical excitement at the airport. Press and television cameras were everywhere; police had to keep back the huge crowd. Britain hadn't notched up that many medals at Colombia not to be very proud of her show-jumping bronze and silver.

At last, they all set off for Penscombe, at around four o'clock in the afternoon, in tearing spirits, sharing several bottles of champagne on the way. Tracey was soon laughing like a hyena. Only Podge was sad. In a couple of hours she would have to give most of Rupert back to Helen, but there'd be other shows, she tried to tell herself. Outside Cirencester, Rupert was stopped by a policeman for speeding, who solemnly got out his notebook, then asked for their autographs. Every time people saw their lorry with the lettering 'Rupert Campbell-Black and Billy Lloyd-Foxe, Great Britain' they started cheering. Even Rupert was thrown by the welcome as they neared home. As they entered Chalford there were crowds all along the route, cheering, waving British flags and holding up placards saying 'Well done, Billy and Rupert.' 'Three cheers for Bull and Revenge.'

Rupert looked at Billy. 'Shall we ride home?'

Billy nodded, too moved to speak.

The horses were still tired, but delighted to be out of the lorry and in familiar territory. The Bull proceeded to stale and stale in the middle of Chalford High Street to the delighted screams of the crowd and the photographers.

And they were cheered all the three miles home, Rupert and Billy riding in front, followed by Tracey and Podge in the lorry, hooting victory salutes on the horn. Two miles out, Henrietta, one of the junior grooms, arrived with an ecstatic Badger and Mavis, red, white and blue bows attached to their collars. Billy scooped up Mavis on to the saddle in front of him, where she ecstatically licked his salty face. After that, The Bull had to guide himself home because Billy needed one hand to clutch Mavis and the other to wipe his eyes. The Bull didn't care. With garlands of flowers round his massive neck, he must have put on a stone between Chalford and Penscombe with all the sweets, carrots and sugar that were fed him along the route.

To Rupert, Penscombe had never looked so lovely as on that golden September afternoon, with the valley softened and blurred by a slight blue mist, and great pale cream swathes of traveller's joy. There was the weather cock glinting on Penscombe church. And suddenly towards them came the village band, sweating in their red tunics, playing 'Land of Hope and Glory' somewhat out of tune.

'This is really too much,' said Billy, half laughing and half crying, as the band shuddered to a straggly halt in front of them, then turned round, striking up 'Rule Britannia' to lead them in. The village was decked out like a Royal Wedding: every house had put out the flags, a huge streamer stretched across the village street saying 'Welcome Home our Four Heroes.' Photographers ran along the pavement, snapping as they went. By the War Memorial the mayor was waiting for them. Shaking them both by the hand, he read a speech of welcome that Revenge tried to eat. Rupert was looking everywhere for Helen. Can't even bother to come and meet me, he thought, savagely.

And suddenly, there she was on the pavement, in a yellow sleeveless dress, holding Marcus in her arms, looking apprehensive and not at all sure of her reception. In an instant, Rupert was off Revenge and kissing her passionately, but not too hard in case he squashed Marcus, and the photographers went crazy.

'Show us your medals, Rupe,' they yelled.

So Rupert, ultra-casual, got them out of his hip pocket and hung them round Marcus's neck. But when he tried to pick up the baby and cuddle him, Marcus arched his back rigidly and started to yell, so Rupert handed him back to Helen. Helen looked up at Rupert incredulously. Hilary had spent so much time putting the boot in that she had imagined some devil would roll up. She'd forgotten how beautiful he was, even after a long drive and an even longer flight. As he came through those hysterically cheering crowds, laughing and joking, he seemed like a god again. It was only just coming home to her, the magnitude of his achievement.

She picked up the bronze and the silver medals and examined them wonderingly.

'You made it, you honestly made it. Oh, Rupert, I missed you so much,' and suddenly she knew she was speaking the truth as she realized she'd kept him at a distance since she got pregnant, and maybe it was her fault.

'Did you?' said Rupert, his face suddenly serious.

'Horribly. Can we really try and spend some time together, and make a go of it?'

Rupert kissed her again. He felt ridiculously happy.

'As long as you give Thrillary the bullet.'

Helen looked disapproving, then giggled. 'We're not quite so close. She is rather overly directive.'

'She's more of a male bloody chauvinist pig than I am,' said Rupert.

Next day, after all the excitement, Billy was ashamed to find himself overwhelmed with a feeling of restlessness and anticlimax. After checking the horses, he decided to give himself a day off and spent most of the morning opening mail. As a result of his silver medal, there were countless offers of free stud nuts, tack, rugs, breeches. A lorry manufacturer was offering him a large sum of money to do a press campaign. Several television companies were waving fat fees to make films of his life.

'I shall have to turn professional,' he told Miss Hawkins, their secretary, half-jokingly.

Perhaps the depression was caused by the fact that everyone in the world seemed to have written to congratulate him – except that wonderful girl he'd seen at the Golden Lion. He hoped each letter might be from her, but as he didn't know her name he couldn't identify her anyway. For the thousandth time, he kicked himself for not being more forceful at the time.

'Some man from the Press named Jamie Henderson's written to ask if he can come down and interview you,' said Miss Hawkins. 'I pencilled in next Sunday. I thought you could take him up to the pub for lunch, as he's coming all the way down from London. It's the only day you've got really. You'll be off to Athens, Portugal and Germany the next day.'

She was highly delighted that Billy was for once getting as much attention as Rupert. 'His Lordship still in bed?' she went on in surprise. 'Are those two having a second honeymoon?'

When his depression didn't lift in the days that followed, Billy thought it might well be due to the fact that Rupert and Helen suddenly seemed to be madly in love again. Helen had agreed to get a nanny; Rupert had agreed to come home more often, and for them to do more things together. Billy was happy that they were happier, but it only emphasized his own isolation. What was the point of being a conquering hero if you didn't make any conquests?

The Sunday Jamie Henderson was due, Billy rose early because it was so hot, worked all the horses that needed it, then hacked The Bull out because it was such a beautiful day. The stream at the bottom of the valley was choked with meadowsweet, and as he rode home he could hear Badger howling at the church bells.

As part of their new togetherness campaign, Helen and

Rupert were just leaving to go out to lunch with Marcus as Billy walked in through the front door.

'We'll be at the Paignton-Lacey's,' said Helen, 'so you and this press man will have the house to yourselves. There's no need to lunch out. There's cold chicken and potato salad in the larder, and I've washed a lettuce. All you've got to do is pour French dressing over it. And don't leave the butter in the sun,' she added.

'This baby needs more luggage than a horse,' said Rupert, tramping out to the car with a blue plastic chamber pot in one hand, a packet of disposable nappies in the other and several bottles under his arm. 'One never gets enough to drink at the Paignton-Laceys'.'

Billy took the carry cot from Helen and put it in the back. As he waved them off to the accompaniment of Marcus yelling and Vivaldi on the car radio, Rupert looked at him and raised his eyes to heaven.

Billy had a bath and put on a clean shirt and a pair of jeans. He was nervous, for he never knew what to say to reporters. Sitting outside with a jug of Pimms, he read the Sunday papers, which were still full of Olympic news. There was a nice picture of him in the *Sunday Express*, and a piece in the *Telegraph* with a headline about Rupert's shadow coming out of the shadows. He was pleased about that too. He took off his shirt; might as well try to top up his Olympic tan.

In no time at all he seemed to have finished the jug. The valley looked even more beautiful now. The apples were reddening in the orchard, the dogs panted on the lawn, insects hummed in the Michaelmas daisies. September was such a lovely month; why wasn't there someone here to share it with him?

He watched an emerald green Volkswagen pause on the road running along the top of the valley towards Penscombe. He looked at his watch; Jamie Henderson was late.

The door bell rang, followed by a frenzy of barking. Then a voice said, 'All right, down. I'm a friend, not a foe.'

Billy went down into the hall. After the dazzling sunshine

it took a few seconds before he could distinguish the figure in the doorway. Dressed in white hotpants and a red shirt, her hair streaked by the sun, her long, long legs and body rising up to the wonderful breasts, like a trumpet, stood the girl from the Golden Lion.

'I've brought you some freesias,' she said. 'They should have been Sweet Williams.'

Billy opened his mouth and shut it again.

'I must be dreaming,' he said slowly. 'Please don't let me wake up.'

She came towards him and gave him the gentlest pinch on his bare arm. 'You're awake all right. Didn't I promise we'd meet again?'

'I know, but I never believe in good fortune. Come through to the kitchen and I'll get you a drink. I made a jug of Pimms, but I drank it all waiting for some boring reporter who's supposed to be interviewing me.'

'That's me.'

'I don't expect he'll take long. What did you say?'

'That's me – Janey Henderson.'

'Oh, my God, our secretary put down Jamie. I was expecting a fella. Are you really a journalist?'

She nodded and turned her palms towards him. 'Look, I've got Biro marks on my hands.'

He got an apple, some cucumber and an orange, and started chopping them up. Janey admired the broad mahogany-coloured back.

'You're very brown. I suppose that was Colombia. Congratulations by the way, I watched you on telly.'

'Wasn't me, it was The Bull. I was so shit-scared, my mind went a complete blank. He just trundled me around. Just getting some mint.' He stepped out of the kitchen windows, raided the herb bed and came back.

'Look, I can't believe this. Are you really a journalist?'

Janey grinned. 'Rather a good one.' She took the mint from him and started to strip off the leaves and put them in the jug.

'Oh dear,' said Billy. 'Should I have heard of you?'

374

'Not really, if you've never seen my paper. They want me to do a big piece on you.'

'I don't read enough,' said Billy apologetically. 'Helen, Rupert's wife, is always accusing us of being intellectual dolts.'

'You can read the instructions on a Pimm's bottle and that's enough for me.'

'Shall we go outside?'

Janey considered. She didn't want to get flushed and shiny.

'We can pull the bench into the shade,' said Billy.

'They wanted me to bring a photographer but I said it would cramp my style.' The way her eyes wandered over his face and body when she said it, made him feel hot and excited.

She sat in the shade, Billy in the sun. They talked about The Bull.

'Honestly, I worship the ground he trots on,' said Billy. 'He's such a trier and he's got such a beautiful mouth.'

'So have you,' said Janey.

Billy didn't know what to do with his mouth now.

'Is it true that you're thinking of turning professional?'

Billy nodded. 'I've had my shot at the Olympics, so there's no excuse really not to. I can't go on living with Rupert forever. I'm twenty-seven now.'

'Don't you find it difficult, the three of you?'

'Easy for me; must be hard for them sometimes.'

'They don't mind you coming in late, bringing back girls?'

'Haven't been many of them lately.'

Janey looked at him until he dropped his eyes.

'What about Lavinia Greenslade?'

Billy filled up her glass before answering.

'I was very cut up when she married Guy. But at least I had something to get stuck into with the horses. Since we split up, I've had my best season.'

'Are you getting over her?'

Billy ate a piece of apple out of his Pimm's. 'Yup. I got over her in the Golden Lion about six weeks ago.'

'It was six weeks, three days to be exact.'

Billy sidled down the bench and took her hands. 'I didn't know how to find you. Every time anyone interviewed me in Colombia, all I wanted to say was that I'd got a message for the girl in the Golden Lion (you look a bit like a lion), and would she please come back. I spent more time thinking about you than worrying about the next day's rounds.' Then an awful thought struck him. 'You're not married or engaged, are you?'

Janey shook her head. 'The ash came out of the dress, by the way.'

Reluctantly, Billy let go of her hands. 'Do you interview lots of people?'

'Robert Redford last week, Cassius Clay the week before that.' Billy felt quite faint with horror.

'You didn't meet *them* first in a pub?' he asked.

They finished the Pimms and they talked and talked. Billy had never felt such a strong sexual attraction to anyone. She was so glowing and she had a special way of swivelling her eyes and gazing up at him from under her eyelashes that made him quite dizzy with longing.

It was so hot, they had lunch in the kitchen. At first he sat opposite her, then he came and sat beside her.

'Do you have hundreds of brothers and sisters?'

'Yes. I'm the youngest. They're all married. My mother despairs of getting me off the shelf.'

'That's ridiculous. How old are you?'

Janey paused for a second. 'Twenty-four.'

Neither of them ate much lunch, but they finished one bottle of Muscadet and started on a second.

'I hope this piece is going to be O.K.,' sighed Janey. 'My shorthand keeps misting over. How long have you lived here?' she asked.

'Since I was twenty-one, although before that I used to come here sometimes in the school holidays. I adored the place even then. If Rupert and I had fights, I used to wander off down the valley. There's a secret glade with a pond where I used to look for the kingfisher.'

'What's he like?'

'Rupert? Oh marvellous. I know him so well, it's like a marriage.'

Janey put the top on her biro and, putting her notebook away, then said in a deceptively casual voice, 'What's his own marriage like, off the record?'

'Very happy,' said Billy firmly. He knew that journalists, were always trying to catch him out over Rupert.

'Must be under terrible pressure, now she's got a baby and can't go everywhere with him, with girls mobbing him wherever he goes.'

'They've got it worked out, and if you met Helen, she's so stunning, no one would want to wander from her. Anyway, it's always a honeymoon whenever he comes home.'

Oh, dear, he hoped he hadn't landed Rupert in it, but somehow he wanted to convince Janey that marriage to a show-jumper wasn't impossible.

'Can we go and see The Bull?'

'Can you ride?' said Billy, gathering up the fruit from the Pimm's jug.

'I've tried, but I can't stay on when they start running.'

Billy grinned. 'I'll teach you.'

They seemed to have spent an awfully long time over lunch. The sun was already dropping, shining into their eyes. The Bull was delighted with the Pimm's fruit.

'Why don't we go and look at your secret glade?' said Janey.

'All right,' said Billy. 'Let's leave your notebook in the tackroom. You're not going to need it.'

There wasn't a breath of wind, but the great heat of the day was beginning to subside; smoky-grey ash trees seemed to shiver in the stillness. The cows were lying down and the young horses in the big field were trying to crowd into the shed to get away from the flies.

As they walked up the fields their hands occasionally brushed. Janey felt the corn stubble bristling against her sandals. As the path narrowed she moved in front. Billy admired the length of her smooth and Man-tanned legs. The softness of her upper thighs, beneath the white shorts, made his throat go dry.

'I always come up here when I am very happy or when I am very sad – when I was dropped from the British team, when I was picked for the Olympics.'

Janey gave him another sidelong glance and picked a blackberry.

'Which do you feel now?'

'Not sure. That's up to you.'

She didn't answer. They had dropped down now to a little spring, crowded with forget-me-nots and pink campion, which had almost dried up, she noticed.

'Unlike me,' thought Janey, who could feel herself bubbling between her legs.

They came to a gate. On the right was a mossy old walk, skirting a poplar grove.

'Hell,' said Billy, looking down the path. 'It's overgrown with nettles. You'll get stung,' he added, as Janey clambered over the gate. 'I'll carry you.'

'No,' squeaked Janey, pulling away from him.

If only she'd stuck to her diet last week and been down to her target nine stone, she'd have let him. But nine stone seven was too heavy; he'd rupture himself.

'We'll go back,' said Billy reluctantly.

'No,' said Janey. 'I need to see this enchanted glade where you seduced all those Pony Club groupies and Lavinia Greenslade.'

Billy, construing this as rejection, was suddenly cast down. She was coming here so she could get some good quotes. Janey ran down the path. Thirty yards down on the left she found a willow-fringed pool with its green banks completely secluded in the green gloom. She'd forgotten how much nettles hurt. 'Ow, ow, ow,' she moaned, collapsing onto a bank, tears stinging her eyelids, white spots jumping up on her brown legs.

'Oh, angel,' said Billy,' 'you should have let me carry

you. Your poor beautiful legs. Let me get some dock leaves.'

He picked a handful, green and smooth, dipping them in the pool.

'Christ it hurts,' said Janey through clenched teeth.

He lay down on the bank beside her.

'There,' she said, pointing to the outside calf of her right leg and the inside of her ankles.

'That's better, a bit higher.'

Billy, crooning with contrition, moved the dock leaves up to her knees.

'I shouldn't have let you come down here.'

'Oh, yes, you should,' said Janey softly. 'A bit higher.'

His hand had reached the inside of her left thigh now. His fingers were so gentle, she could feel the damp cool of the dock leaves against her burning red legs.

'Higher,' she whispered.

As though acting on their own, Billy's fingers crept up, and dropped the dock leaves as he met a fuzz of damp pubic hair dividing around the skimpiest of pants. He looked up, and found her smiling at him through her tears.

'Enter these enchanted woods, you who dare,' she said mockingly. 'Go on, that's the only way you can cure the hurt.'

'Oh, Christ, Janey,' he muttered, feeling the moisture between her legs. The next minute he had moved up the bank beside her, putting his arms around her, and kissing her almost reverently, and she was kissing him back, her tongue expertly caressing his tongue and the inside of his lips. His hand found the wonderful generous breasts, with the nipples hard as hazelnuts, and he felt her draw in her stomach as his hand crept downwards. She had exactly the right amount of flesh on her. Her hands were caressing his bare back, her fingers burrowing in his hair.

'Jesus,' he said to himself incredulously, 'this amazingly beautiful girl really wants me. Oh, please God, don't let me botch it up by coming too quickly.'

He undid the buttons of her shirt with trembling hands

379

and buried his face in the billowy cleavage, breathing in her scent.

'My nettle stings at the top need a bit more attention,' Janey said, with a gasp of laughter, so he slid his hand underneath her pants, finding her clitoris, which was as hard as her nipples.

'Oh, please go on, please, please,' she moaned, then shuddered and gave a long contented sigh, and he felt her throbbing to stillness.

'Come inside me, I want you,' she said a moment later.

'Not yet.' His experience of outdoor screwing was that one always got worried about keepers crashing through the bracken and came too quickly. But she wouldn't listen to him, sitting up with her breasts tumbling, undoing his belt with practised skill. Jeans were really hell to get out of, he thought, like getting a woman out of a roll-on, and his cock stuck out through the hole in his pants, so he had difficulty getting them off too.

After all her London lovers, Janey suddenly realized what a marvellous body Billy had, with the broad shoulders, flat stomach and the incredibly muscular buttocks and thighs, from riding so much.

'God, you're strong,' she said.

Billy laughed. 'You should try Rupert. When he squeezes a horse with his legs you can hear it groan.'

'I'll never last a second,' he warned, as he was sucked into the warm spongy whirlpool, feeling her vaginal muscles gripping him, feeling her hands caressing his buttocks, moving with him.

'I'm sorry. I can't help it. I've got to come.'

For a few seconds he lay on top of her, feeling the delicious warmth. Then he rolled off, pulling up a handful of grass to wipe her dry.

Janey grinned. 'I hope there aren't any nettles in it.'

'Are they still murder?'

'Much better. I'm beginning to understand about the pleasure–pain principle. Maybe de Sade had a point.'

He brushed a green beetle out of her hair. 'Sorry I came so quickly.'

'I should have been offended if you hadn't. Wouldn't have said much for my sex appeal. Anyway, I'd already come once when you were stroking me, so I could afford to be generous.'

Billy looked down at his flaccid cock. 'A bad workman blames his tool,' he said.

He lit them both cigarettes to keep off the midges. Janey lay on her elbow, looking up at him through half-closed eyes.

'How come you sell yourself so short when you're such a megastar?'

Billy shrugged: 'I've always hunted in pairs with Rupe.'

'So?'

'No one's likely to look at me when he's around, so he usually gets the girls.'

'That's not what I heard.' Janey combed her hand through his black chest hair. 'I think you're stunning.'

'And I don't meet many girls like you. I didn't want to rush my fences.'

He put out a hand to bracket one of the brown breasts. 'You're so beautiful.' He felt his cock rearing up like a kit: 'I think I might hit better form this time, or are the midges eating you?'

'I'd much rather something else ate me.'

Billy looked at her lascivious face, mascara-smudged under her eyes, crimson lipstick kissed away. Slowly she edged up the bank, until her bush was level with his face.

'Oh' she murmured, as he rolled over and got to work, 'Oh, sweet, sweet William, this is definitely the lap of honour.'

Billy laughed and carried on.

By the time they set off back to the house a huge red setting sun was spiked on the poplar copse like a balloon about to pop. Pigeons flapped towards the wood.

'Helen and Rupert are back,' said Billy. 'Come and say hello.'

Janey shook her head. 'I must get home.'

'But you can't,' he said, appalled. 'You've only just come.'

Janey giggled. 'You can say that again. I'm not up to meeting anyone at the moment. Anyway, they're virtually in-laws.'

'You can't just go.' Billy looked like a small boy left behind by his parents after the first day out from prep school. 'I'm going to Lisbon tomorrow,' he went on. 'We haven't talked about anything. Why don't you come with me?'

'I've got to work.'

'Will you write to me? I'll be back for the Horse of the Year Show on the first of October.'

'I'll be back from America about the third or fourth. You can leave a number with the Features desk.'

'Please don't go. I can't bear it.'

'It's been so perfect,' she said. 'I don't want to come in and make polite conversation, I must get back to London and write it all down before I forget it.'

'Not all of it.'

'No, the glade's our secret. See you at Wembley.'

And with that he had to be content.

He couldn't go straight into the house. He walked round in a daze, watching the sun set and the stars come out. He couldn't believe it, just as when he was a small boy he couldn't believe anyone as dazzling as Rupert could choose him as a friend.

He walked into the kitchen to find Helen rather ostentatiously clearing away the remains of lunch and heating a bottle for Marcus.

'I'm sorry, Helen, lunch was marvellous.'

'Badger didn't think so. He's just thrown up most of the chicken and potato salad on our bedroom carpet. You left the larder open and the fridge and the freezer, and the butter in the sun. Are you in love or something?'

The next day they set off for Portugal, Greece, then Germany, then back without a break for the Horse of the

Year Show at Wembley. It was the longest four weeks of Billy's life. When he couldn't get Janey on the telephone he nearly flew back. He discussed her endlessly with Rupert.

'You know I'm hopeless at playing the field. I want to marry her.'

Rupert looked thunderstruck. 'You can't marry her. You don't even know her.'

'I've spent a whole day with her.'

'You haven't even screwed her yet?'

'I have, too,' said Billy sulkily, 'and it was marvellous.'

Rupert looked even more disapproving. 'Then she's just a whore, going to bed with you on the first date. It wasn't even a date. She came to interview you, wormed it all out of you. You wait until her piece appears. "Billy Lloyd-Foxe is not only a silver medallist, he also gets the gold in the sack." '

'Oh, fuck off,' said Billy furiously. 'Why d'you reduce everything to your own disgusting level?'

25

The moment Billy got back he rang the news desk at Janey's paper, to be told that she was away. Her interview with Jack Nicholson had taken longer than expected – Billy wondered miserably what form it had taken – and she was expected back sometime that week.

Now it was the fifth day of the Horse of the Year Show and there was no sign of her. He must have passed the competitors' board fifty times a day in the hope of a message. Every time he saw a tawny mane of hair in the crowd his stomach disappeared. His fears that she'd only been nice to him because she wanted some good quotes were multiplied when he talked to Joanna Battie and Dudley Diplock.

Did they know her? he asked.

' 'Course I do,' said Joanna. 'She's her paper's star writer, hang-gliding one week, going into battle in a tank the next, interviewing Prince Charles the next. Pretty high-powered stuff.'

'Very pretty,' said Billy.

'Very,' said Dudley with a wolfish laugh. 'Puts herself about by all accounts. Fleet Street claims she got to the top on her back.'

'On her front,' said Joanna. 'Janey's too much liberated to accept the missionary position.'

Billy felt quite sick. 'Are you sure?'

'Well, let's say she's a bloody good journalist and, like most of them, she's not too particular how she gets her information. They pay her well. I reckon she's on twenty thou a year, don't you, Joanna?'

384

After a sleepless night, Billy talked to Rupert as they exercised the horses. Rupert was reassuringly outraged.

'For God's sake! Remember the things they've said about you and me in the past, even implying we're a couple of fags. You know it's all fairy tales. They make it up to excite themselves. Christ, Revenge is sluggish. I'm going to have to nail up his box during the day to stop the public stuffing him with goodies.'

At that moment Humpty Hamilton came waddling past in a pale blue quilted waistcoat. 'Hi, Sweet William,' he said and waddled on, roaring with laughter.

Next to come by was Driffield. 'Hullo, great lover,' he sneered. 'Seen the paper?'

Finally, as Billy was handing The Bull back to Tracey, Lavinia rode into the practice ring. 'Hullo, Sweet William,' she said, an acid note creeping into her voice. 'You *have* made a conquest.'

Heart thumping, Billy ran to the news stand.

'Hi, Sweet William,' said the man behind the counter, handing him a newspaper. 'You've boosted my sales so much this morning you can have it for free.'

Billy retired behind a pillar. Janey's piece was in the middle, opposite the leader page, with a huge heading 'Sweet Sweet William' and a picture of Billy taken from an extremely flattering angle.

'When I went to see Billy Lloyd-Foxe,' Janey had written, 'I took him a bunch of freesias. They should have been Sweet Williams, since he is easily the nicest man I have ever met.' Then there was a lot of guff about his Jean Paul Belmondo looks, and his clinching the team silver and winning the King's Cup. Then it ended:

'We all know of his sympathy with animals, his brilliant horsemanship, and his ability to smile even in the bitterest defeat. Last year he admits he was heartbroken when his long-standing girlfriend, Lavinia Greenslade, married French hearthrob, Guy de la Tour. Since then the only female in Billy's life has been Mavis, his blonde mongrel, who follows him everywhere, bestowing a slit-eyed expression of marked disapproval on any lady intruder.

'Billy lives with Helen and Rupert Campbell-Black, and his soothing, easygoing presence must a be a great help in sustaining a somewhat volatile marriage. But Billy, with characteristic modesty, says he owes everything to Rupert (including money, he adds with a smile). He also has the highest praise for his chef d'equipe, martinet Malise Graham, and of course The Bull – who eats the fruit out of the Pimm's jug – with whom he jumped a final clear in the team event to clinch the silver for Britain. He may only have got a silver, but he's got a heart of gold. I haven't heard a bad word about him on the circuit. After seven hours in his company, all I can say is please give me back my heart, Billy. Our offices are open to accept parcels twenty-four hours a day.'

Billy read it incredulously over and over and over again. It was a love letter. He rushed to the telephone. There was still no answer at Janey's flat. The Features desk said she'd got back last night and was racing to finish the Nicholson piece and had probably switched off her telephone. Billy couldn't bear it. He had to see her. He told Rupert he was going into London for a couple of hours.

'Well, don't be too long,' said Rupert, grinning. 'You're obviously better in the sack than I thought. And what's this about my "somewhat volatile marriage"? What does "volatile" mean – that I'm always out on the tiles?'

Billy took a taxi to Janey's flat. It was a long time before she answered. Compared with her glamorously tawny appearance before, she looked pale and black under the eyes and rather unadorned like a sitting room the day after the Christmas cards are taken down.

'Billy,' she said, 'how lovely to see you.' She didn't sound as though it was at all.

'I'm sorry to barge in, but I've missed you like hell.'

She backed away nervously. 'Darling, I'm terribly sorry, I can't stop. The office want Jack Nicholson by tomorrow lunchtime, so I'll have to work all night.'

'Surely you can stop for five minutes.'

'I can't, honestly. I've got complete brain freeze, I've just got to crack it.'

'The piece you wrote about me, it was so kind, and ludicrously flattering.'

She smiled, looking suddenly more like the Janey who'd come down to Penscombe. 'Did they run it today? They must have held it back for the Horse of the Year. I filed the copy weeks ago.'

And perhaps she feels quite differently about me now, thought Billy. He was dying to ask about Jack Nicholson. Instead he said, 'It's the last night tomorrow. Will you have dinner with me afterwards?'

'I don't know. I'm supposed to be dining with some MP as a preliminary interview. What time d'you finish?'

'About eleven, but I'm off to Washington, New York and Toronto on Monday, and I must see you.'

'You must go now, but I really will try and make it tomorrow.'

'I'll leave a ticket at the gate. Janey, I love . . .'

But she'd shut the door on him. Billy was filled with black despair. She hadn't seemed pleased to see him, dismayed in fact, and rather guilty and not looking him in the eye. If she'd filed that copy weeks ago, she was bound to have met someone else in America.

Back in her flat, Janey Henderson felt equally suicidal. Her vanity wouldn't allow her to explain to Billy that she'd already been home for forty-eight-hours on a crash diet, in order to look ravishing for him on Saturday night. He'd caught her at the worst possible moment – she'd been writing and hadn't got dressed or had a bath or used deodorant for two days. Her body had that rank smell of fear and sweat that always drenched her when she was wrestling with a piece. She was convinced her breath smelt from her all-meat diet. She hadn't shaved her legs since she'd last seen him, her hair was filthy, she was sure she had scurf and she couldn't meet his eyes because he'd caught her with unplucked eyebrows and no make-up. Also her ginger cat, Harold Evans, had been sick in the bathroom that morning and she hadn't had time to clean it up. The flat looked like a tip because her char had walked out while she was away and the neighbour who'd come to feed Harold Evans had failed to change his earth box – hardly a lovers' bower.

Janey knew she ought to go back and wrestle with Jack Nicholson. Instead she re-read the proof of the piece on Billy. She had actually lied to him and had only telephoned the corrections through the previous night. It really was rather good, and he looked even more gorgeous just now in a battered Barbour. He must have masses of girls after him. She mustn't seem too keen. She'd lusted and lost too often over the last ten years. She was, in fact, twenty-nine. That was another lie she'd told Billy. Would he ever trust her when he found out?

Janey Henderson came from a respectable upper-middle-class family. Her father had been in advertising, her kind easy-going mother had stayed at home, brought up the children and encouraged them to have careers, but never taught them how to do anything around the house. Janey, the baby of the family, had been the most successful. She possessed a strong sex drive which led her into trouble, but was bourgeois enough to be paranoid about being talked about. Used to adoration at home, she expected it from her lovers and in order to keep them happy she would tell lies and, when they rumbled her and grew angry, she tended to move on to another one, who could be fooled for a few weeks that she was absolutely perfect. Her father doted on her and, if she had any troubles with landladies or bills or angry bosses, she'd run to him. In the old days he had always bailed her out, but since his advertising agency had folded in the economic collapse of 1973, he suddenly found himself very short of money.

Janey Henderson was attracted to power. As a journalist, she had racketed around and met endless stars. She had mixed with the rich and famous and longed to live like they did. She was a good, if sloppy, writer, an inspired listener who was able to sift out the minutiae that mattered. A

388

teenager in the swinging sixties, she had enjoyed the fruits of the permissive society and benefited in her career from the rise of the women's movement. She had also seen her girlfriends trying to do their own thing, raising their consciousness and their husbands' blood pressure, finally walking out on these husbands and then being absolutely miserable as single parents. At twenty-nine, Janey realized there was nothing one needed more than a good man. She wanted to settle down and have children. She had seen Rupert's beautiful house and assumed that servants and land and unlimited Pimms were all the normal perks of a show-jumper's life. Janey also longed to be a more serious writer. If she married Billy, she could be more selective, producing one piece a month instead of two or three a week, and could even write books.

Janey Henderson pondered on these things. The sight of the blank page in the Olivetti and the mess in the flat brought her back to earth. There was no MP to be interviewed tomorrow night. If she had to hand in copy at lunchtime, she reckoned it would take her till late evening to clean the flat and make herself look ravishing.

Harold Evans was weaving furrily round her ankles, demanding lunch.

'I must take you away from all this squalor, Harold,' said Janey, picking him up. 'How would you like to live in Gloucestershire?'

Back at Wembley, Billy was inconsolable, despite the fact that Rupert had good news of a possible sponsor. 'He approached me to test the water. I said you'd need at least £50,000 a year to stay on the road.'

'What a lot of money – what does he make?'

'Cat food.'

'The Bull won't have to eat it, will he?'

'No, but he might have to change his name to Moggie Meal Charlie, or something.'

'Christ, what's this sponsor like?'

'Oh, frightful. Thatched hair, jangling initial bracelets,

frilled duck-egg-blue evening shirts, firm handshakes, fake American accent, and calls you by your Christian name every second sentence.'

'What's his name?'

'Kevin Coley. Rather suitable under the circs. Puts a lot of himself into his products.'

Billy grinned. 'What's in it for him?'

'Social mountaineering. He's made his pile and now he wants upmarket fun and some smart friends. He thinks you have tremendous charisma.'

'Glad someone does,' said Billy gloomily. 'He won't much longer if The Bull goes on knocking down fences.'

'I think you should talk to him,' said Rupert. 'Fifty grand a year's not to be sniffed at. Your mother's not likely to croak for at least twenty years. And I thought you wanted to marry that girl?'

'After today, I don't think she'll have me.'

Billy was sure that Janey wouldn't turn up the following night. Even his horoscope was ambiguous: it warned Pisces subjects to watch out for fireworks, and make travel plans in the evening.

It had been the Germans' Wembley. Hot-foot from the Olympics and their double gold, they had jackbooted their way through the week, winning every big class except the *Sunday Times* Cup, which had gone to Rupert. On the last night the crowd was really hungry for a British victory. The big class was the Victor Ludorum, a two-round competition in which riders with double clears jumped off against the clock for £6000. Rupert jumped clear in the first round and so did Billy, although he was very lucky. The Bull rapped every fence and had the upright swinging back and forth like a metronome on lente, but he didn't bring it down and the crowd went wild.

They had given him and The Bull a colossal welcome whenever he'd come into the ring that week. But each time Dudley Diplock had announced them as 'that great Olympic combination – Billy Lloyd-Foxe riding The Bull' the little horse had raised two hoofs at the commentary box and knocked up a cricket score. He was tired after a long season. Tonight, however, he felt more bouncy. 'You've got to win,' Billy urged him, 'to impress Janey, if she comes.'

Now Billy sat in the riders' stand, biting his nails, watching Rupert jump his second round. Revenge was also a bit tired. He flattened twice and had eight faults at the combination and a brick out of the wall. As he came out of the ring, Rupert patted Revenge consolingly, determined to refute any charges of cruelty, knowing the television cameras were still on him.

Billy met him in the collecting ring.

'Just wait till I get this bugger back to his stable,' said Rupert. 'I'm going to beat the hell out of him.'

'He's had a long year,' protested Billy. 'Think how well he did in the *Sunday Times* Cup.' He did hope the honeymoon between Rupert and Revenge wasn't over.

As he mounted The Bull to warm him up over a couple of practice fences, he could hear Dudley Diplock waxing lyrical over 'Ludwig's second clear'.

'That's that Dudley Moore,' said a fat woman who was leaning over the rail to her friend. 'He's done the commentary here for years.'

Billy felt desperately low; Janey was obviously not coming. His mind was a complete blank. He couldn't remember the course, or how many strides there were between any of the fences. The Bull clouted the practice fence.

'For God's sake pick your bloody feet up,' snapped Billy with unusual irritation. The Bull looked martyred and limped a few paces. As Billy turned him to jump it again, he heard a voice calling:

'Hullo, William.'

And there she was. Her lovely hair all tortoise-shell and lion-like as it had been at Penscombe. She was wearing a black and grey-striped silk rugger shirt with a white collar and very tight black trousers.

Billy found it impossible to wipe the silly grin off his face as he trotted across the collecting ring towards her. 'You made it! God, that's wonderful! And you look bloody marvellous. Was the MP furious you ditched him?'

'Livid.'

'I don't blame him.'

'I heard Rupert's out already,' she said. 'I've just passed a stand absolutely hung with whips, spurs, boots and strange leather devices, exactly like a tart's store cupboard. I don't know *what* you get up to in show-jumping, really I don't.'

Billy laughed.

Janey patted The Bull. 'I'm sorry I was a bit offish yesterday, I'm always awful when I'm working.'

'Did you finish the piece?'

'Yes.' She shot him a sly look. 'It wasn't nearly as complimentary as the one about you.'

'Number 43,' shouted the collecting ring steward. 'Where's number 43?'

'Billee, they're calling you!' shouted Hans Schmidt.

'For the last time, number 43.'

'I think they're calling you,' said Janey.

Billy came down to earth. 'Oh my God, so they are. Don't move, I won't be long.'

'I want to watch you.'

'Stop coffee-housing,' said Rupert, 'and get into the ring.'

'Oh, thank goodness. Rupe, this is Janey. Will you get her a drink and look after her till I get back?'

'How d'you do?' said Janey. 'I hear you had two legs out of the combination. It sounds awfully rude.'

'Oh, please,' Billy prayed as he rode into the ring, 'don't let her fall for him.'

He must concentrate. But joy seemed to surge along the reins and The Bull bounced round the course rapping nothing and the crowd went berserk as Billy pulled off the only British double clear.

'Well done,' said Janey, who was sitting in the riders' stand with Rupert, clutching a large vodka and tonic. 'You were marvellous, and you got a bigger ovation than the

Rolling Stones.' She giggled. 'I asked Rupert who that fat man in the ring with a tape measure was. He said he's the course builder. I said, how did he know he was coarse. You do have the *most* extraordinary terminology in show-jumping. What on earth's a rustic pole?' She'd obviously made a hit with Rupert, who generally didn't like people taking the piss out of the sport.

There were six riders in the jump-off. Three Germans, Wishbone, Count Guy and finally Billy. Ludwig went first and jumped a very fast clear. From then onwards, there were no clears until Hans Schmidt came in.

'They're so controlled, those German horses, you'd never think they could motor,' said Janey.

'Look at his stride – twice as long as The Bull's,' said Rupert.

Hans, incredibly, knocked two seconds off Ludwig's time, cutting every corner.

'Billy won't make it?' asked Janey.

'I don't think so. The Bull simply isn't fast enough.'

Hans came out, a broad grin on his round face. 'Beat zat,' he said, as Billy rode into the ring.

'And here comes Billy Lloyd-Foxe on The Bull, our Olympic Silver medallist riding for Great Britain,' said Dudley, trying to be heard over the cheers.

'Must be hell having to jump while you're having a shit,' said Janey.

The cheers continued as The Bull circled, his fluffy noseband like a blob of shaving cream, cantering along on his strong little legs, bottom lip flapping, ears waggling, taking in the applause. Billy gave him a pat. He was a mediaeval knight jousting for Janey's hand.

'If he wins, everything'll be all right and he'll ask me to marry him,' said Janey, crossing both fingers. As the bell rang the cheering started; as he rose to the first fence it increased, and it increased in a steady crescendo as he cleared each fence, riding for his life. As he turned for the last two fences, the double and then the huge wall, Billy glanced at the clock, realizing he was in with a chance. The cheer rose to a mighty roar and the whole crowd rose to its feet as one to bellow him home. The Bull was over the double and hurtled over the wall, nearly crashing into the side of the arena, before Billy could pull him up.

The ten-thousand crowd turned to the clock. Billy turned around, putting his hands over his eyes. As he took them away a mighty roar took the roof off. He had won by a tenth of a second. The scenes that followed were worthy of a cup final. People were leaping over the stands into the arena, rushing forward to cheer and pat The Bull. Spectators were throwing hats, cushions, handbags into the arena.

Rupert looked at Janey and saw all her mascara had run.

'Wasn't he wonderful?' she said.

'You do love him, don't you?'

She nodded, getting out a paper handkerchief.

'Well, mind you look after him.'

Billy and The Bull got another deafening round of applause as they came into the ring to collect their rosette. Then the band played Little White Bull, and The Bull, very smug after all the attention, bucketed round the ring twice, deliberately keeping within the circle of the spotlight. Afterwards, Billy came up to see Janey. 'You were so wonderful,' she said. 'I've never been so proud in my life. What an absolutely sweet horse he is.'

From all sides, people were congratulating Billy, but he had eyes only for Janey. 'Look, I've got to go back into the ring for the personality parade. Will you be all right? How did you get on with Rupert?'

'Great, but he's not nearly as attractive as you.'

Billy blushed. 'He must have been pulling his punches.'

The cavalcade that brings the Horse of the Year show to an end must be the most moving event in the equestrian calendar. Among the celebrities were little Stroller and two of the police horses who'd displayed exceptional bravery in an I.R.A. incident, followed by ponies, hacks and hunters, the heavy horses and, finally, the Olympic team. Then Malise, not without a tremor of emotion in his voice, read out Ronald Duncan's beautiful poem: 'To the Horse', and Janey found herself in floods of tears again. What a wonderful, dashing, romantic, colourful world she was moving into, she thought, after three large vodka and tonics on an empty stomach.

As Billy came out to the collecting ring, a man came up to him whom he instantly recognized from Rupert's description as Kevin Coley.

'Bill Lloyd-Foxe?' he said, pumping him by the hand. 'Kev Coley.'

Billy was almost blinded by his jewelry.

'I think Rupe's spoken about me.'

'Of course,' said Billy, trying not to laugh. 'He was *most* impressed.'

'So was I, by tonight's win. Great stuff, Bill, great stuff. I'm ready to talk terms. Why don't we have dinner together?'

Billy's heart sank. 'Well, actually, I've got someone with me.'

'Bring her too,' said Kev expansively. 'My wife Enid's up in the stands. The girls can chat while we talk business.'

Suddenly they were interrupted by an old lady, tears pouring down her face. 'Oh, Mr Lloyd-Foxe, I read in the paper you were thinking of turning professional. You won't sell The Bull, will you?'

Billy smiled. 'Of course not.'

'I've bought him some Polos.' She got a dusty packet covered in face-powder out of her bag.

'Gosh, that's terribly kind of you,' said Billy.

'Don't you worry your head, ma'am,' said Kevin Coley. 'If Bill turns professional, he'll never have to sell The Bull.'

Billy found Janey in the lorry, repairing her face. Tracey had already hung the rosettes up on the string across the window.

'Darling, I cried my eyes out – it was so choke-making.' She mustn't hug him too hard or her new trousers might rip.

'Sweetheart, do you mind if we go out to dinner with a man who wants to sponsor me?'

'No, yes, I do. I want to be alone with you and see the conquering hero come.' Putting her hand down, she touched his cock.

Suddenly Billy realized that if he married this wonderful girl, he could sleep with her every night for the rest of his life.

'We can do that later on,' he said. 'It just means that if I pull this deal off, I can ask you to marry me.'

Rupert joined them, wearing a dark suit, and smelling of aftershave.

'I hear you've met up with Medallion Man,' he said, then in an undertone to Billy, 'Do you mind frightfully saying that I had dinner with you all tonight if Helen asks? I am sure she won't.'

'Where are you off to?' said Billy.

'Well, do you remember a little unfinished business called Tiffany Bathgate?' and added, as Billy looked disapproving, 'and anyway, I thought I'd make myself scarce, in case you and Janey wanted to use the lorry later.'

At four o'clock in the morning, Billy lay in Janey's arms in the double bed in her flat. They had just made love and he was thinking how beautifully she kept the place. There were clean dark-blue sheets on the bed, and three bunches of freesias on the bedside table had driven out any smell of cat. What a glorious, talented creature she was.

'Ouch' he said, trying not to wake her as Harold Evans kneaded his stomach.

'Billy,' she said, 'there's something I've got to tell you. Promise you won't hate me for it?'

Billy's heart sank. The lovely irridescent soap bubble was about to burst. 'I'm twenty-nine, not twenty-four,' she went on.

Billy started to laugh with sheer relief. 'Is that all? I wouldn't have minded if you'd said forty-four. Are you sure you won't find it infra dig to marry a younger man?'

26

Billy found himself very nervous about telling Helen he was getting married. Rupert had been no problem. In fact Rupert and Janey both experienced passionate relief that they enormously liked but didn't fancy one another; they were too alike, perhaps. And Rupert, having set up the sponsorship which enabled Billy to marry Janey and start his own yard, felt he had masterminded the whole affair, which mitigated any jealousy.

Nothing would happen in a hurry, anyway. Billy would have to find somewhere to live and, although it might be difficult to go on being partners if Billy were a professional, Rupert was sure they could work something out. Although it would be a struggle financially, Rupert wasn't prepared to turn professional until he'd had another stab at a gold medal in Los Angeles in four years' time.

Helen, however, was shattered when she heard the news. Without Billy the precarious balance of their marriage would surely be destroyed. He was so sweet to Marcus and he could always jolly Rupert out of a bad mood by making him laugh. Nor did the two women really take to each other. After Billy and Rupert returned from their American trip, Billy brought Janey down for the weekend. Both girls were set back on their heels by the glamour of the other. Janey never expected Helen to be that beautiful. Helen didn't expect Janey to be that sexy. Janey had never worn a bra and her clothes were always a little too tight, because she kept falling by the wayside on her diets, and her shirts and dresses were always done up a button too low. Helen's were always buttoned up to the neck. After six years in Fleet

Street, Janey was virtually unshockable and during dinner on the Friday she arrived, kept both Rupert and Billy in stitches, providing wildly inaccurate low-down on the sex lives of leading public figures.

Helen had taken great trouble to cook a superb dinner: crab pancakes in cheese sauce, gigot of lamb, and the most perfect quince sorbet. It was a good technique if one wanted to establish a reputation as a brilliant cook, reflected Janey, to serve very small helpings as Helen did, so everyone wanted seconds. Janey, not having eaten all day, was starving, and had thirds of everything, praising Helen like mad. Everyone drank a lot. Janey got happily tight.

How nice, thought Rupert, to find a woman with such an appetite. He'd never admired Lavinia; she was a drip. Janey was fun and tough. She would be good for Billy.

Between Helen and Janey there was also professional jealousy. Janey asked Helen about her novel. Helen said it was coming on very very slowly.

'I'm an academic, you see, and I'm not prepared to put up with anything second-rate.'

'Why don't you try journalism?' asked Janey.

Helen said she didn't really feel she could bring herself to do anything like that. She'd never read the *Post*, but she'd heard it was very sensational.

Janey registered the snub and said that, in her experience, writers who were any good, wrote.

'I've got a book coming out in the Spring,' she said. 'A collection of interviews. I just got the piece I did on you in at the end, darling,' she added to Billy.

She and Billy were so in love, they couldn't keep their hands off each other. Helen wistfully tried to remember the time when she and Rupert were like that. The attempt at a second honeymoon after the Olympics had not lasted very long.

Marcus was brought down and admired and fed. How can such good-looking parents produce such a hideous baby? thought Janey. But realizing it would endear her to Helen, she asked if she could give Marcus his bottle.

'Billy tells me you're getting a nanny.'

'Well, a girl,' said Helen. 'It'll mean I can spend more time with Rupert.' She must try to like this self-confident, sexy creature. 'I'm so pleased you're getting married to Billy,' she said when they were alone. 'He's so darling, but he's kind of vulnerable too. You will look after him, won't you?'

'Strange – Rupert said the same thing,' said Janey. 'I actually hope *he's* going to look after me.'

Everyone else thought Janey was marvellous; the dogs, the grooms, Marcus, Miss Hawkins, Mrs Bodkin, for whom Janey left a fiver. There was a bad moment, however, when Janey was changing for dinner on Saturday night and couldn't be bothered to go down the passage to the loo. Instead, she got a chair and was crouching over the basin having a pee, when Helen walked in to turn down the beds. Helen was shocked rigid and even more annoyed that Rupert thought it was very funny. Janey, sensitive as radar, realized Helen didn't approve of her.

'She's a bit lined-skirt-and-petticoat, or half-slip, as she'd call it, isn't she?' she said to Billy. 'I bet she makes love in long rubber gloves.'

Billy laughed, but he refused to bitch about Helen.

'We really must look for a house very soon,' said Janey.

Rupert persuaded Helen to give a party at Penscombe for Billy and Janey. As she'd done up the house so beautifully, he said, it would be nice for everyone to see it, and they hadn't had a party since their marriage. She wouldn't have to do any work. They'd get in caterers, and as the drawing-room wasn't big enough for dancing, they'd hire a marquee. The party would be held in the middle of December just before the Olympia Christmas show, so all the foreign riders would be in the country.

There were frightful arguments over the guest list; all the show-jumping fraternity had to be asked.

'But not Malise, Graham, or Colonel Roxborough. I don't want any grown-ups,' said Rupert.

'Oh, we must have Malise,' protested Helen. 'He's so civilized.'

'He wasn't very civilized when Ivor Braine took the wrong course in the Nations' Cup last week. If he comes, he'll start telling me to go to bed early because I've got a class next year.'

'You ought to ask him,' said Billy. 'He'd be awfully hurt.'

'Oh all right, but I'm not asking Jake Lovell. His fat wife wouldn't get through the door.'

By the time they'd included Janey's Fleet Street friends, and most of the celebrities she had interviewed, who knew Rupert and Billy anyway, as well as all Rupert's smart friends, the numbers were up to 300. Rupert flipped through the final selection.

'I've slept with practically every woman on this list. Gives me a feeling of *déjà vu*,' he said to Billy.

'You haven't slept with Hilary.'

'*She's* not coming!'

'Bloody is. According to Mrs B., she's been round a lot recently.'

Rupert, furious, stormed off to find Helen.

'Either that woman doesn't come to the party or I don't.'

'All your friends are coming,' said Helen. 'I don't see why I shouldn't have *one* of mine.'

'She'll bring that disgusting baby, and start whipping out a triangular tit in the middle of the party.'

'Hilary is not just a good painter, she's a highly intelligent, concerned human being.'

'Crap,' said Rupert. 'All right, I'll ask all the grooms then.'

'You can't,' said Helen aghast. 'They can never hold their drink.'

A week before the party, while Rupert and Billy were in Amsterdam, the au pair, Marie-Claire, slipped on the yellow stone steps in the hall and landed painfully on her coccyx. The next day Hilary slipped carrying Germaine but managed to keep her balance. Helen suddenly decided to carpet the hall and the stairs a pale avocado green, to match the pale pink and green peony wallpaper. The carpet men worked overtime, the dogs sat in a martyred row on the tintacked underfelt, and everything was finished and tidied away by the eve of the party, when Rupert and Billy were due home.

Helen had just got Marcus to sleep when they arrived and woke him up with all the din of barking, neighing, shouting and the banging-down of lorry ramps. Why the hell did they make so much noise? She had to spend a quarter of an hour soothing and rocking Marcus back to sleep, and went downstairs to the kitchen just as Rupert was coming in through the back door. There was snow in his hair.

'Hello, darling,' he said kissing her. 'You all right? I see the marquee's up. Everyone's coming: the Germans, the French team, the Italians, all the Irish – it's a complete sell out.'

'Go and get a drink. There's a surprise for you in the hall,' said Helen.

Rupert went out – there was a long pause. The new carpet was so soft, Helen didn't hear him come back. His face was expressionless.

'Do you like it?'

'I didn't know Marcus could be that sick,' said Rupert. 'That carpet is exactly the same colour as regurgitated Heinz pea and bacon dinner. What the fuck have you done?'

Helen bridled. 'It's called pistachio.'

'Pissed-tachio after everyone's spilt red wine over it tomorrow night,' said Rupert.

'The steps were a death trap,' snapped Helen.

'Pity your friend Hilary didn't fall down them more often. That's Cotswold stone you've just covered up!'

'Those steps were dangerous. Marcus'll be walking in a few months.'

'He'll walk right out of the house when he sees that carpet.'

'Well, everyone thinks it's very pretty.' Helen's voice was

401

rising. 'Mrs Bodkin, Marie-Claire.'

'That's only because you pay them. Who else? Thrillary I suppose. Expect it's her idea: matches her complexion.'

It was, in fact, a great party. Rupert and Billy mixed a champagne cocktail to start off with, which, with one and a half hours solid drinking before dinner, got everyone plastered. Janey, looking sensational in see-through black, was such a hit with all the foreign riders that Billy put her on a leading rein and, screaming with laughter, towed her around after him. Their happiness was totally infectious. Even Driffield couldn't find anything to grumble about.

Only Helen, in priceless ivy-green silk, a boat-shaped neckline showing off her slender white shoulders, seemed tense. She was not a natural hostess and she was only too aware of all the Biancas and Grannias and Gabriellas of Rupert's past. Nor could she bear to see drink rings spreading like Olympic symbols on her furniture, and cigarette ash and wine stains on her new carpet.

Rupert tried to persuade her to enjoy herself. But once dinner was over, he felt he could relax his duties as host. People knew where they could get a drink. From then on, he was seen coming off the dance floor with one beauty after another.

Hilary arrived late. Armed with a carrycot, she marched down the hall, sending international show-jumpers flying, and up the stairs.

'Straight up to my wife's bedroom,' said Rupert sourly.

Next moment Helen went past with a baby's bottle.

'Is that for Hilary?'

'Marcus is crying.'

'You should have sent him to Mrs Bodkin. Where the hell's Marie-Claire?'

'She disappeared into the shrubbery with one of the French team two hours ago and hasn't been seen since,' snapped Helen. 'I told you the drink was too strong.'

Upstairs, Helen collected Marcus and went into the bedroom, where she found Hilary combing her hair.

'Oh, you look beautiful,' she gasped.

Hilary had been to the hairdressers and had her dark hair set in wild snaky curls round her face. She had rouged her cheekbones and kohled her eyes and was wearing a red and black gipsy dress with a flounced skirt and hooped earrings.

'I never dreamed you could look so wonderful,' Helen said in genuine amazement.

'I wanted to prove to your bloody husband I wasn't a complete frump,' said Hilary. 'I've even shaved under my armpits.' She held up her arms, showing not a trace of stubble. 'And I absolutely hate myself.'

'Well, I sure appreciate you,' said Helen.

Hilary, drenching herself in Helen's Miss Dior, said, 'How's it going? Sounds wild enough.'

'I'm not great at parties.'

'Rupert shouldn't subject you to them. What did he say about the carpet?'

'He hated it.'

Why did the conversation always return to Rupert? wondered Helen.

The excitement had stepped up when they went downstairs. Ludwig was blowing a hunting horn. Billy, plastered and blissful, was necking on the sofa with Janey, Mavis curled up beside them, looking resigned.

'Come and dance, Helen,' said Humpty Hamilton, who was wearing one of Rupert's tweed caps back to front.

'You haven't met Hilary, have you?' said Helen.

At that moment Rupert came off the dance floor with a ruffled blonde.

'Evening' he said to Hilary without any warmth.

'Doesn't Hilly look lovely?' said Helen.

Rupert looked her up and down. 'Rather like one of Jake Lovell's relations.'

Next moment a very drunken Hans staggered up and bore Helen off to dance. 'What a beautiful place you have 'ere, Mees Helen. What a beautiful woman you are,' he sighed. 'Lucky Rupert.'

In front of them, in the crepuscular gloom, she could see

Count Guy, wrapped like a wet towel round Marie-Claire. So it was that member of the French team, she thought, wondering if she ought to stop them.

'Poor Laveenia.' Hans shook his head. 'I bet she weesh she marry Billee now. But what a beauty he's got heemself. What a beautiful girl.'

'Yes, she's very nice.'

'Did you know Ludwig's geeving Billee a horse as a vedding present? A very good one: Mandryka.'

Count Guy's arm was up to his elbow down Marie-Claire's dress. Really, she couldn't be a very suitable person to look after Marcus, thought Helen. Over in the corner, she saw Hilary dancing with Malise. They were talking intently. That was good; they'd get on together.

The party ground on. The local MFH, trying to find his way home, drove over the ha ha. Podge was sick in the flower bed. Helen was dancing with Billy, his hair all over the place.

'It's a wonderful party, Angel. I can't tell you how grateful I am. You've made Janey so welcome, she can't get over it. I say, there's Hilary doing the tango with Ludwig. She's looking really very sexy this evening, and you know I'm not her greatest fan.'

Billy went back to Janey. As an excuse to escape from the party for a second, Helen decided to check if Marcus was OK. There were wine stains all over her beautiful carpet. Why couldn't they all go, so she could get the place straight again? In the hall Rupert was talking to Hans and a couple of Italians. When he'd drunk too much, he seldom betrayed it, but his eyes tended to glitter. Now they were like sapphires under a burglar's flash light.

'Where are you going?' he said, not turning around.

'Just to check Marcus.'

'If he doesn't shut up, I'll come upstairs and ram a cricket stump up his arse.'

Quivering with rage, Helen fled upstairs. How could Rupert say terrible things like that, just to get a laugh, when Marcus was so darling? Despite the din, he was still fast asleep.

Whoops and yells from downstairs made her rush out onto the landing. Hanging over the stairs, she heard Rupert saying to a rather pale Podge, 'Go on darling, go and get him.'

'Mrs C—B won't like it.'

'She'll have to lump it.'

Podge opened the front door. Helen could see a flurry of snowflakes and she was gone.

'You can't, Rupert,' said Janey, half-laughing. 'Don't be a sod, not on Helen's new carpet. It's taken quite enough punishment as it is.'

Helen went back and turned off Marcus's light. What could they be talking about? She powdered her nose and combed her hair. Oh God, she was tired. If only she could go to bed and read *Mansfield Park*. Then she heard more cheers and a commotion downstairs. For a minute she thought she must be dreaming, for there was Revenge in the hall, and Rupert was jumping onto his back, riding into the drawing room to colossal cheers and screams of laughter. Blazing with fury, she ran down the stairs.

'What the hell are you doing?' she screamed. Over the laughter, no one heard.

'Twenty-five pounds you can't jump that sofa,' said Count Guy.

'Done,' said Rupert and the next moment he'd cleared it, narrowly missing the chandelier.

'Rupert!' screamed Helen. 'What are you doing on that horse?'

Everyone suddenly went quiet.

'No party's complete without Revenge,' said Rupert, and popped him back over the sofa.

'Get him out of here,' she screamed hysterically. 'Out, out, out!'

'All right,' said Rupert, but as Revenge came into the hall, unnerved no doubt by the occasion, he crapped extensively, which was greeted by howls of mirth.

'I think he's trying to say he doesn't like your new carpet,' said Rupert. Helen gave a scream of horror and fled upstairs, throwing herself down on her bed, sobbing her heart out. How could he do this to her, how could he, how could he?

Malise met Hilary at the bottom of the stairs. They had already had a long discussion about the Campbell-Black marriage and knew whose side they were on.

'Go to her,' said Malise. 'At once. I'll see someone clears up this mess.'

Hilary found Helen a sodden heap on the bed. 'I can't bear it, I can't bear it. Why does he humiliate me like that?'

'I don't know, dear,' Hilary stroked her hair. 'He's a monster, as I keep telling you. You're exhausted. Take a couple of Mogadon and go to sleep. I'll help you get undressed.'

Just as she had got a still sobbing Helen out of her clothes and was fetching her nightgown from under the pillow, Rupert walked in.

'Get out,' he said to Hilary. 'I might have guessed you'd be here.'

'I've just given your wife a couple of sleeping pills. Now leave her alone.'

'She can't go to sleep. She's the hostess.'

'You stop being a hostess after something like that. How could you do that to her? You're the most uncaring man I've ever met.'

'It was a joke and for a bet,' said Rupert tonelessly. 'All the mess has been cleared up. There's not a mark on the carpet. Now get out.'

'Please stay,' sobbed Helen.

'I'm not leaving till you fall asleep, dear,' said Hilary.

'Oh, for Christ's sake,' exploded Rupert, storming out of the room.

Helen, surprisingly, was so exhausted she fell asleep almost immediately. Hilary stayed a few minutes, folding up her clothes and tidying the room and her own appearance. Switching off the light, she quietly closed the door, then, moving down the landing, checked first Marcus and then Kate. Out on the landing she found Rupert, waiting with a glass in his hand. His hatred was almost palpable.

'They're all asleep, no thanks to you,' she said.

Downstairs they could hear a tantivy. The band was playing the Post Horn gallop. Rupert stooped to pat Badger, who was trembling. He hated rows and was rising like a soufflé out of one of the Jack Russells' baskets.

'Why do you drool over that dog and neglect Helen? What's she ever done to you?'

Rupert stood up. 'She was perfectly happy before you came along and started breast-feeding her this feminist crap.'

'That's not true. She was nearly dying when I first met her, and you weren't even there.'

'I happened to be trapped in one of the worst blizzards of the winter; not much I could do about it.'

'You grumble that she has no friends, and then when she finds one, you insult her. You always treat me as though I don't exist.'

'Perhaps you don't. I detest women that come on like Supergirl, and you detest me,' he said coming towards her, breathing in the hot feral sweat of her body, 'because your pratt of a husband couldn't even satisfy a hamster.'

'Don't you dare say anything against Crispin!' screamed Hilary.

'You have to go round poisoning other people's marriages,' Rupert went on. 'Well, bloody well stay away from Helen.'

'She needs a few allies.'

'Not like you, she doesn't.' He was taunting her now. 'I know what your game is. You liked undressing her, didn't you? She's beautiful, isn't she? And you've been running after her as fast as your unshaven legs can carry you, you bloody dyke. Well, she won't enjoy it, she's not very keen on that sort of thing.'

Next minute Hilary had slapped him very hard across the face. Without a thought, Rupert hit her back, even harder. She burst into tears and, somehow, a second later she was in his arms and he was kissing her, forcing her

407

mouth open. Frantically she struggled, flailing her fists
against his back, so much broader and more muscled than
Crispin's. Suddenly she relaxed, mouth separating, and
was kissing him back even more fiercely.

'I hate you,' she sobbed.

'You don't. You want me like hell. You've wanted me
ever since you saw me at Gloucester Hospital. That's why
you've been smarming over Helen all this time.'

'You're a brute.'

'Of course.' He took her hair and yanked her head back
so he could kiss her again. Fingers splayed on her back, his
thumbs caressed her shaven armpits. 'That's a great
improvement,' he said softly. 'It was getting so long, you
could have plaited it.'

He drew back the landing curtain. The snow was three
inches thick on the window ledge and still coming down.

'We mustn't,' she said, pulling away from him. 'It's so
unsupportive.'

'Not nearly as unsupportive as you're going to be,' he
whispered evilly. 'I'm going hunting tomorrow. Get rid of
Crispin after lunch. He can take Germaine tobogganing for
an hour or so.'

27

Unable to face the hassle of a big wedding, Billy married Janey in Gloucester Registry Office at the beginning of January, thus forfeiting the large number of wedding presents which are so useful to a couple setting up house. Rupert was best man. Helen was disappointed that they didn't even bother to have the marriage blessed in Penscombe church, but Billy felt, that first year with Janey, that the gods were blessing him anyway. Never had he been so happy.

Just before they married, Janey negotiated a fat deal with her paper that she would write a series of racy interviews around the world, which enabled her to travel with Billy on the circuit, all expenses paid. From Antwerp, to Paris, to Madrid, to Athens, to New York her portable typewriter gathered airline stickers, as she talked to Presidents, rock stars and distinguished tax exiles.

Often there were tensions when she had to file her weekly piece. A sweating, tearful, teeth-gritting Janey, bashing away at her typewriter in some foreign hotel bedroom, wasn't conducive to Billy getting any sleep before a big class. Nor did Janey, hopelessly unpunctual, endear herself to other members of the team by making them late for dinners and parties. Billy was too besotted to notice. His horses were going well. Mandryka, the dark brown Hanoverian Ludwig von Schellenberg had given as a wedding present, upgraded himself incredibly quickly and was showing all the makings of being as great a horse as The Bull, or Moggie Meal Al, as he was now re-named. Billy winced, but not much. At £50,000 a year from Kevin

Coley, it was worth wincing for. Anyway he was still the same Bull in the stable.

In fact, in that first year of marriage, Janey and Billy were extremely rich. Janey's salary, plus expenses, plus Billy's steady winnings, plus Kevin's sponsorship, added up to nearly £100,000 a year. And although Billy was always buying Rupert drinks and gave Helen his winnings for housekeeping (when he hadn't spent them celebrating), gas, electricity, telephone and heating bills at Penscombe were invariably picked up by Rupert.

When they were in England, Billy and Janey lived with Helen and Rupert and muttered vaguely about househunting. In the end it was again part of Rupert's colossal generosity towards Billy that he let them have Lime Tree Place, an enchanting but dilapidated 17th-century cottage on the Penscombe Estate, which had just become vacant, on condition they pay for doing it up. Planning permission had to be obtained to extend the kitchen and build on a dining room, two more bedrooms and a nursery. Being twenty-nine, Janey hoped to start a baby almost immediately. In time, they would turn the mouldering, moss-encrusted outbuildings into stabling for a dozen horses. Helen came down to the cottage and talked a lot about closet space and knocking down walls, and, inspired by the beauty of Penscombe, Janey felt there was no need to spare any expense.

For Janey and Billy, that first year seemed effortless, because at home they were backed up by Helen's clockwork domestic routine which ironed Billy's breeches, washed his shirts, remembered to get his red coats and dinner jackets back from the cleaners; and by Miss Hawkins, who saw that Billy's entry forms were sent off and bills were paid and appointments put in the diary.

For Janey's liking, they had spent rather too much time with Kevin and Enid Coley, who flew out to several of the foreign shows and were always hanging about at Wembley, Crittleden and Olympia.

Billy made excuses for Kevin, saying he was merely

proud that Billy's horses were going so well and particularly that Moggie Meal Al came second in the European championships in Paris. And if Kevin did tell Billy how to ride and Malise exactly how to run the British team, Billy felt Malise was perfectly capable of taking care of himself. Janey was rather less tolerant. As a wedding present, the Coleys gave them a vast china poodle lifting its leg on a lamp post. Janey wrote Enid a gushing letter of thanks and put the poodle in the cellar.

There were also too many invitations to visit Château Kitsch, as Janey called Kevin's mock Tudor castle in Sunningdale, where there was lots of horseplay and one was likely to be pushed into the heated swimming pool at any moment. But on the way home, they enjoyed lots of giggles about the electric toadstools that lit up on either side of the drive at night, and the huge luminous Moggie Meal Cat symbol outside the front door which winked and miaowed when you pressed the door bell, and the button in Kevin's den which had merely to be pushed for the entire leather-bound works of Dickens and Scott to slide back, revealing a bar offering every drink known to man.

Janey, reared in Fleet Street, could drink even Billy under the table. Looking out of the window one evening, Helen saw them coming up the drive hysterical with laughter, as Billy pretended to lift his leg on every chestnut tree.

'Billy's being Kevin's china poodle,' explained Janey. 'Christ, my feet are killing me. We ran out of petrol and had to walk from Stroud.'

Helen had mixed feelings about Janey. In the end you couldn't help liking her. She was fun and marvellously iconoclastic about show-jumping, but she was a bit too easy to talk to. Any secret confided, would be round Penscombe and Fleet Street in a flash. And Janey was so messy, wandering round the house with her cat, Harold Evans, riding like a parrot on her shoulder, eyes screwed up against the cigarette smoke, spilling ash and leaving a trail of dirty cups and, after midday, glasses.

Helen, so fastidious, couldn't bear the fact that Janey

411

kept pinching her perfume and make-up and borrowing her clothes. There was an embarrassing occasion when Helen and Rupert were away for the weekend and Janey borrowed one of Helen's dresses to go out to dinner with the Coleys and split it, not even down the seam, so it was beyond repair.

Even worse was the time Helen came downstairs, ashen, because her mink coat, given her by Rupert on their second anniversary, was missing. She was about to ring the police, when Janey suggested they look round the house first.

'Isn't this it, bundled up in the downstairs loo?' Janey announced rather casually two minutes later. 'Mrs Bodkin must have brought it down for re-furbishing – ha ha, that's a joke – or something.'

It was unfortunate that Janey had left three toffee papers, and a programme for a Michael Frayn play that had been on in Bath, in the pocket. Helen was very upset, but too nice to shout at Janey. Instead she went to church and asked God to make her more tolerant.

Occasionally, Janey cooked, but made such a mess in the kitchen that it took Helen twice as long to clear up afterwards, and she wished Janey wouldn't take books out on her library tickets, read them in the bath and forget to return them, or even worse, lose them abroad. Helen, who'd never kept a library book too long, and always renewed them, was upset and bustled.

In a way, Billy and Janey's presence helped Rupert and Helen's marriage. Rupert tended not to be so intolerant if the others were there; but in another way their happiness showed up the flaws.

Rupert was wildly jealous of the love Helen lavished on Marcus. 'I'm so enjoying him,' she kept saying. ('As though Marcus was a quadruple vodka and tonic,' said Janey.) He was also envious of the relaxed hedonistic relationship Billy had with Janey. When had Helen ever got tight with him. When had they last been hysterical with laughter? He heard the giggles and gasps of pleasure issuing from their bedroom. Mrs Bodkin was always finding empty bottles under the bed.

Janey, Helen thought, brought out the worst in Billy. She encouraged him to drink more, bet more, always dine out rather than eat at home. Billy, more emotional and physically less strong than Rupert, couldn't cope with such excess.

The blatant sexuality of the relationship unnerved Helen too. Billy and Janey were always sloping off to bed. You only had to look at Janey's washing on the line. Mrs Bodkin's mouth disappeared in disapproval at the black and scarlet crotchless knickers, the cut-out bras, the G-strings, suspender belts and fishnet stockings. Janey, careless and thoughtless, left her vibrator in their unmade bed, which was found by Mrs Bodkin.

'Billy's got a bad back. It's for massaging his spine,' explained Janey, airily. Mrs Bodkin was not convinced; Janey was a minx.

Helen and Janey's attitudes to each other were ambiguous. Janey was jealous of Helen's beauty. Helen even looked gorgeous in a bath cap, and Billy would never say a word against her. Helen, spurred on by Janey's fame and journalistic success, started working on her novel again.

'She talks as though she's writing *Hamlet*,' grumbled Janey. It irritated the hell out of Janey that Helen was always slightly dismissive of Janey's journalism. She never commented on Janey's pieces even if they were spread across two pages of the paper. Even when she produced her much-praised interview with Kissinger entitled 'You're only as good as your last peace', Helen only said, when pestered, that she didn't feel Janey had quite captured the full weight of Kissinger. It was part of her puritan upbringing that you must never praise if you didn't admire. But in this instance, duty became a pleasure.

'She doesn't mean it bitchily,' Billy kept protesting.

'Oh, she does, Buster, she does,' said Janey grimly.

Helen, in fact, was jealous of Janey for being so sexy. Occasionally she worried that Billy, Rupert and Janey spent so much time abroad together. Rupert did little to

413

dispel this fear. It diverted any suspicions she might have had about him and Hilary.

Show-jumping and Rupert changed during the mid-seventies. As the sport became more popular and sponsorship increased, so did the prize money. Before, the show-jumping season had lasted from April to October; now, riders could jump all the year round and, because of the number of indoor evening shows, they were kept busy by night as well as by day. When he started in the sport, Rupert would buzz off to Argentina to play polo, or go racing at Longchamps or skiing at Klosters. Now, show-jumping had become an all-consuming passion. Always on the circuit, he was jumping his horses so hard, he wore them out in a year or so and, as a result, was endlessly searching for new ones. If he was at home he was training horses or selling them on. Horses took over his life, so determined was he not to turn professional.

Podge travelled with him, adoring, satisfying his physical needs, suffering but not sulking if something better took his fancy. And on the rare occasions he was back in Gloucestershire, there was Hilary, ranting, cantankerous and insatiable, but exerting a horrible fascination over him.

After the party for Janey and Billy, Helen retreated into herself, becoming more and more houseproud, 'spending her time rubbing female fingerprints off Rupert,' said Janey. Helen spent a great deal of money on clothes and at the hairdresser's, and did a lot for charity. Hilary didn't help. For her own good reasons, she kept urging Helen to walk out on Rupert.

'You are a talented writer, inhibited by a fascist pig – virtually a one-parent family. What support does he give you, looking after Marcus?' she demanded.

'Unlimited funds,' Helen had to admit truthfully.

'Our parents' generation sacrificed their careers for marriage,' went on Hilary. 'You mustn't make such sacrifices. It is impossible to be happily married, a good mother and have a career.'

414

Helen hoped she was a good mother. She was certainly an adoring one. Marcus was walking now and his first words were 'Mummy'. And he had several teeth. He had grown into a beautiful child, shy, with huge solemn eyes, and a riot of Titian curls which Rupert was always urging Helen to cut. Marcus was wary of Rupert, who was not amused by jammy fingers on clean white breeches, or by the fact that Marcus screamed his head off if ever Rupert put him on to a horse. Calm and sunny when his father was away, Marcus picked up the vibes from Helen and became whiney and demanding on his return.

Another bone of contention was the dogs. Having read articles in *The Guardian*, Helen was terrified Marcus would catch some obscure eye complaint from them. She wanted them kept outside. Rupert flatly refused. The dogs had been there before she had, he pointed out coldly. In fact, since Marcus was born, he reflected, the dogs were really the only things pleased to see him when he came home. Both he and Helen festered inside with a sense of grievance.

Billy was saddened by the increased deterioration in Rupert's marriage, and discussed it at length with Janey. One hot evening at the end of July, on the eve of their departure for Aachen they lay in bed at Penscombe sharing a bottle of Moet.

'How on earth,' said Janey, 'can anyone as beautiful as Helen be so uptight? If I had those kind of looks . . .'

'You do,' said Billy, snuggling up against the spongy cushion of her bottom, feeling for her breasts.

'D'you think I'd look nice with my hair up, like Helen?' asked Janey.

'I'd rather you shaved your bush.'

'D'you think they'll split up?'

'No. I think underneath they still love each other. Besides, Helen's too scared of the outside world, and Rupert doesn't believe in divorce. Marriage is for children, and having someone to run your house. You get your fun elsewhere.'

'I hope you don't feel like that!'

'No,' said Billy, sliding his hands down over the smooth folds of her belly.

Janey pressed her stomach in. 'I must lose weight. Do you think he's gone off her physically?'

'Hard to tell. He nearly killed an Italian diplomat who made a pass at her a couple of years ago. She's one of his possessions; he's very territorial.'

'Do you think he's good in bed?'

'Cock like a baseball bat. Used to bat bread rolls across the room with it when we were at school.'

'Lucky Helen.' Janey sat up, excited at the thought.

'Am I big enough for you?' asked Billy anxiously. Janey climbed on top of him, holding on to the brass bedstead, causing frightful creaking. 'Quite big enough. Look how good I am at rising at the trot.'

28

Hilary, in fact, was Rupert's first serious affair since he had met Helen, and it was a complete love-hate relationship. Despite her protestation that all men were beasts, Hilary herself was an animal in bed – insatiable, almost a nymphomaniac. She didn't bathe enough, she was a slut, she had a bad temper, and Rupert had to keep kissing her to shut her up, and later cut her nails himself to stop her lacerating his back. He detested her hypocrisy in still going on being a friend to Helen.

It was the one affair about which he never boasted to Billy, knowing how appalled Billy would be. Making love to Hilary was like eating a pork pie when you were desperately hungry, then discovering by the date on the discarded wrapping, that it should have been eaten a month before.

'If you ever breathe a word about this to Helen I'll throttle you,' he frequently warned her, and she knew he wasn't joking. This, however, did not prevent her from rocking the boat. The night before Rupert was due to leave for Aachen he'd stood her up and she had rung up Penscombe in a rage, screaming at Rupert down the telephone. Rupert, who was in bed with Helen at the time, reading his horoscope in *Harper's*, held the receiver to his ear for a minute, then said calmly, 'Have a word with Helen about it. She's just here.' And Hilary was forced to pull herself together and issue an impromptu invitation for Helen and Rupert to come to a dinner party in three weeks' time, which meant she had to go to all the expense of giving one.

For Hilary, despite her ranting, was mad about Rupert

and grew increasingly strident as he showed no inclination to move in with her. Part of the fascination for him was that they saw so little of each other, perhaps a couple of hours a month.

Hilary was sure she could nail him if they had a little more time together. While Rupert was in Aachen at the end of July, she flew out to Germany, leaving the children with the long-suffering Crispin. Her excuse was that she needed to be alone to paint. After Aachen, Rupert sent Podge home with Billy and the horses, saying he was off horse-hunting and would be home in a day or two. He had been very short-tempered with Podge all week, because he felt guilty and nervous about Hilary coming out. Together, he and Hilary drove to a hotel in the Black Forest, chosen by Hilary. Their stay was a disaster. Having screwed her, Rupert found it a nightmare to have to make conversation to her at dinner, or walk with her in the forest, or be greeted by her carping, rather common voice when he woke in the morning. After forty-eight hours, they had a mighty row and returned home on separate planes.

Podge, meanwhile, had returned home twenty-four hours earlier with Billy and Janey to find England in the grip of a drought. Day after day the sun blazed down; young trees and flowers withered; Penscombe's green valley turned yellow; the streams dried to a trickle; leaves were turning. In Gloucestershire people were forbidden to water the garden or wash their cars, and there was talk of standpipes and water rationing.

When they got back, Janey and Billy collapsed into bed for sixteen hours to get over the journey. But Podge and Tracey still had to get up at six next morning after four hours' sleep, because the horses had to be looked after. When a telephone message came through that Rupert was coming back that evening, Podge re-doubled her efforts. Usually, to re-establish his ascendancy as master of the house and the yard, he came home in a picky mood, criticizing everything she'd done and then biting her head off for sulking. By late afternoon, the relentless heat showed no sign of letting up. Most of the horses were inside to avoid the flies, and were let out at night. Arcturus, a grey Irish-bred stallion, was Rupert's latest acquisition. He showed potential, but had blotted his copy book by jumping sloppily at Aachen. Wearing only a black bikini and espadrilles, her sweating hair in a pony tail, Podge chattered away to him as she strapped his dappled coat to firm up his muscles.

'Bugger off, sweetheart,' she said, as Arcturus nudged her lovingly in the back. 'Your master's coming home tonight, and he'll want you looking lovely. Hope he's cheered up and not cross with us any more, Arcy. You didn't mean to hit that last triple, and I didn't mean to bugger up the map-reading on the way out. He can be 'orrible, Arcy. If he wasn't so lovely when he was being lovely, I don't s'pose we'd put up with the 'orrible bits.'

'I don't expect you would,' said a voice behind her, 'but I'm in one of my lovely moods today.'

Arcturus jerked up his head as Podge jumped out of her skin, dropping the whisp and going crimson. 'I didn't think you was coming back till this evening,' she muttered.

'Obviously not, or you'd be properly dressed.'

'Sorry.' She picked up the straw whisp and attacked Arcturus's already gleaming flanks again. 'But it's been ever so 'ot.'

'You look very fetching,' said Rupert, pulling her pony tail. 'I just don't want Phillips getting ideas.' Phillips, the undergardener, had an unrequited crush on Podge. 'You're my property,' added Rupert.

Podge was filled with a happiness so intense, that tears stung her eyelids.

'Hey,' said Rupert, giving her pony tail another gentle tug, 'you don't seem very pleased with me.'

'I am, I am.' She brushed away the tears with the back of her hand, leaving a smear of dirt across her face. 'I just thought you was cross with me, and if I got everyfink perfect for when you got back, you wouldn't be.'

'Everything looks fine,' said Rupert. 'I'm going to

change. Finish off Arcy and then we'll walk up the fields and see Gemini's foal.'

He sauntered off, followed by Badger and two of the Jack Russells.

Podge's hands shook as she filled the haynet and Arcturus's water bucket. Then she shot up to the loft and frantically washed her face. Oh, that awful muddy smear down one side. And she'd wanted to wash her hair before he got back. It must still reek of Billy and Janey's chain-smoking on the drive home. She had a frantic shower, twice washing under her arms and three times between her legs, and making herself sneeze by shaking on so much talcum powder. She'd just pulled on a faded orange T-shirt and skirt which clung to her wet body, when she heard Rupert yelling from downstairs. As she came backwards down the ladder out of her attic flat, Rupert was waiting, sliding his hands up under her skirt, his thumbs biting into her plump bottom.

'Don't,' she shrieked.

He was wearing nothing but a pair of old jeans and he smelt of an expensive French aftershave which she couldn't pronounce. Suddenly she had difficulty breathing.

'Not here,' she gasped. 'What about Phillips and Mrs Campbell-Black?'

'In London. Come on. Why'd you change? You looked sexy in that bikini.'

'Too fat,' muttered Podge, pulling on gumboots.

'What the hell are those for?'

'Adders,' muttered Podge. 'Phillips killed one by the tennis court last week. And nettles and thistles.'

As they walked up the scorched fields, Rupert carrying the Hasselblad camera he'd won in Aachen, the chestnut trees were raining down orange leaves, the thistles were turning to kapok, and the little copse of hornbeams Rupert had planted earlier in the year had already died. There were huge cracks in the ground. In the distance they could hear the jangle of a fire engine.

'If we don't get some rain soon, we're going to be in

trouble,' said Rupert. 'Going'll be murder at Crittleden.'

The nettles on the way down to Billy's secret pond, which used to reach to four feet and close over the top, were shrunk to a pathetic eighteen inches and no threat to Podge's legs today. The pond was almost empty. Sweat was running in rivulets between Podge's breasts and down her sides. She felt her heart pounding.

'Which horses are you taking to Rotterdam?' she asked.

'You asked me that five minutes ago. You're not concentrating,' Rupert said mockingly. As they reached the bottom of the path, he took her hand and turned right.

'Gemini's in the oak meadow,' said Podge quickly.

'We'll go and see her later,' said Rupert. 'I've got more pressing plans for you.' He put his arm round her waist, then moved it upwards, till his hand squeezed her left breast. 'Very pressing.' Then he let her go.

They reached the stream that ran down the valley with water meadows on either side. It was greener here, the stream choked with figwort and forget-me-not. A circle of ash trees formed a sun trap. No one could see them from the road.

'What happens if someone walks across the fields?'

'Private property. I'll have them for trespassing.' Rupert raised his hand and smoothed the sweat from her face. 'I've missed you, Podge,' he said gently. 'Get your clothes off.'

An expression of doubt flickered in her eyes, but she took off the orange T-shirt so that her breasts fell out full, pointed and sloping downwards.

'Lean against that tree,' said Rupert, adjusting his camera for the light.

Instinctively, Podge put her hand up to loosen her hair.

'No, leave it tied back. I want to see the expression on your face.'

'I haven't any make-up on.'

'Suits you. Put your arms above your head and lean back against the trunk. Beautiful. Christ, you've got gorgeous boobs. Now turn sideways. Keep your arms up, lovely.' He took another picture, then came over, running his hands

421

over her breasts, then kissing her. He tasted of toothpaste and animal health and wonderful digestion. Putting her arms round him, Podge kissed him back so violently, they nearly toppled over.

'Steady,' he whispered. 'I haven't finished yet.'

He undid the drawstring of her skirt and she stepped out of it, then he pulled her pants off. The mouse-brown bush was flattened and he ran his hands through it to fluff it up. Then he spread the pink lips. A shiny snail's trail was trickling down both thighs.

'All right, keep your legs apart. Don't be shy, sweetheart. If you knew how fantastic you look. Now turn around. Don't tense your bum up. Relax.' She heard two more clicks. She waited, clinging on to the ribbed surface of the tree, throat dry, heart crashing against her ribs. Then she felt a warm hand on her back. Rupert wasn't even sweating.

'Lovely arse,' he said softly, running his fingers down the cleft before he came to the sticky warmth between her legs.

'Christ,' he said, his hand like a burrowing ferret. 'You are the most welcoming thing.'

He thought of Hilary's tantrums, of her vacuum-cleaner kisses, her sharp teeth and scraping hands. He thought of Helen's cool distaste and he compared them with Podge's ecstatically grateful gentleness.

'Why don't you take *your* clothes off?' she said, turning around and kissing him passionately, as she fumbled with the zip of his jeans and then his pants. Then, sinking to her knees, she buried her face in the blonde hair of his groin, sucking him as pleasurably as a child with a lolly.

'Steady, sweet. I don't want to come yet.'

As he turned to remove his trousers, she seized the camera. 'Now it's my turn to photograph you!'

Giggling hysterically, she photographed him as he was turning, then caught him again as he was coming towards her half-laughing, half-angry.

The next moment he'd caught up with her, pushing her down on the grass, parting her legs and kissing her damp bush. She writhed, tensed, gave a gasp of pleasure and came. So blissfully quickly, thought Rupert. Recently, Hilary seemed to come later and later, like the Christmas postman. He turned over, lay back and pulled Podge on top of him, feeling her muscles, so tight but so oily, gripping him, breasts swaying like party balloons when the front door opens. Really, she was gorgeous.

The sun had disappeared behind the ashwood by the time they had finished, sated with pleasure and exhaustion. Podge rinsed herself out in the stream, startling several minnows. As they walked home up the sun-drenched valley, Rupert picked grass seed out of her hair.

'There isn't time to see Gemini's foal,' he said. 'I've got to go and give the prizes at Cheltenham Flower Show.'

They were greeted in the yard by Tracey and Phillips. 'Mrs Campbell-Black's just rung from London,' said Tracey. 'I couldn't find you. Will you ring her back?'

'Just been up to Oak meadow to photograph Gemini's foal,' said Rupert coolly.

'That's funny,' muttered Phillips, bitter with jealousy, to Rupert's departing back. 'The grass was so poor, we moved them up to Long Acre this morning.'

Rupert went off to Rotterdam two days later. The day before he was due back, Helen drove into Cirencester to shop and bumped into Hilary in the market, crossly buying cheese for the dinner party she'd been forced into giving the following night.

'Rupert is going to be back, isn't he?' she demanded. 'Not that he's a great asset at dinner parties, always making fascist remarks and falling asleep. But I've got ten smoked trout and I don't want my numbers messed up.'

Helen, who found herself increasingly irritated by Hilary, said you could never be sure with Rupert, but she thought it'd be 99 per cent certain.

'Well, make sure he's there,' said Hilary. 'No, about an inch more Dolcelatte, please.'

Hilary had realized by the time she got back from the Black Forest, how much she was going to miss the excitement Rupert provided in her drab life. She must get him back. It would be too cruel if he didn't turn up tomorrow night.

Leaving her, Helen popped into the chemist to pick up the rolls of film she'd found lying around on Rupert's dressing table. He'd actually taken some of Marcus last time he was back and she was dying to see them. Mr Wise, the chemist, had popped out and hadn't checked the photographs as he normally did. He always liked to look through the Campbell-Blacks' folders; they often contained pictures of famous people and interesting places abroad.

The drought didn't seem to be deterring the trippers at all. Stuck in a holiday traffic jam on the way back to Penscombe, Helen couldn't resist looking at the photographs. That was a gorgeous one of Marcus, but she wished Badger wasn't licking his face, and a lovely one of the rose bower, and a rather boring one of the Jack Russells and Arcturus. Why must Rupert always photograph animals? That was lovely of the herbaceous border, and the valley; how yellow it was now. That must be Gemini's foal. She'd finished one folder and shook the photos out of the next. The first thing she saw was a plump, topless girl. Mr Wise must have given her the wrong set of photographs. Here was another one of her full length, legs apart, in the most disgustingly provocative pose. Helen looked closer, and stiffened. The girl looked like Podge. She looked at four more pictures, all disgusting. Yes, they were definitely Podge. The next one, taken at an angle, half cut off the man's head, but the rest of him looked decidedly familiar. The next, also naked, was definitely Rupert, full frontal and roaring with laughter.

A second later, Helen had rammed the Porsche into the car in front with a sickening crunch. She banged her head hard, and the bonnet of the car just buckled up like the face of a bulldog in a cartoon film.

'Why don't you look where you're going?' yelled the driver of the car in front. He found Helen crying hysterically, trying to collect together the scattered photographs before anyone could see them.

Rupert flew in from Rotterdam around six the following evening, tired but once again victorious. He'd left the grooms to bring back the horses. Phillips met him at the airport in Helen's Mini and gleefully told him that Mrs Campbell-Black had pranged the Porsche the previous afternoon. Serve the bastard right, he thought, as he saw Rupert's look of fury. Shouldn't go down in the woods with Podge.

Helen walked up and down her bedroom, wondering how the hell to tackle Rupert. By some miracle, in four years of marriage, she'd never actually caught him being unfaithful. She'd suspected other women – Marion, Janey, Grania Pringle, several of Rupert's ex's, but never in a million years Podge, with her fat legs, her cockney accent and her plain homely face. It had come as a terrible, terrible shock. Helen couldn't stop shaking. It was so revolting too, taking photographs of her in one of their own fields, where anyone might have walked past. She wished she had a girlfriend to pour her heart out to, but Janey was still on the way back from Rotterdam with Billy, and, anyway, Janey wasn't safe. She thought of ringing Hilary, but Hilary would just say, 'I told you so'. She still had a blinding headache from yesterday's shunt in the Porsche, and a huge bruise on her forehead beneath her hair.

The usual frantic barking told her Rupert was home. For once, instead of going to the stables, he came straight upstairs into the bedroom.

'I hear you pranged my car. Are you all right?'

'Perfectly, thank you.' Helen gazed out of the window, quivering with animosity, refusing to look around.

'How the hell did it happen?'

'I was in a jam, looking at some of your photographs just back from the drug store.' She swung around, handing him the folders. 'They're kind of interesting. Have a look.'

Casually Rupert picked them up. When he was feeling trapped, his eyes seemed to go a darker, more opaque, shade of blue and lose all their sparkle.

'I thought I'd taken some nice ones of Marcus. That's good, and so's that, and there's a gorgeous one of Badger, and Arcy. Christ, he's a good-looking horse. Pity you shut your eyes in that one.' He gave a low whistle. 'Who's that?'

'You know perfectly well,' screamed Helen. 'It's that slut, Podge.'

'Phillips must have borrowed my camera. God, she's got quite a shape on her.'

'It was you who took them,' hissed Helen, 'and your hand is remarkably steady, which is more than can be said for Podge's when she took photos of you.'

Rupert flipped through the photographs, playing for time.

'Who's that headless chap? Got a cock like the Post Office tower.'

'It's yours,' said Helen in a choked voice, 'and I guess you can't deny the fact that the next one is you.'

'I'm afraid it is,' said Rupert. Then he committed the cardinal sin of starting to laugh.

Helen lost her temper. 'How dare you go to bed with her!'

'Who says I've been to bed with her?'

'Don't be ridiculous. And I suppose Janey and Billy know all about it. How could you, how *could* you?'

Rupert scratched his ear, looking at her meditatively. 'Do you really want to know?' he said softly

'Yes, I bloody well do.'

'I fucked her because she was at home when I got back, and she wanted me.'

Helen flinched.

'And she's a bloody miracle in bed.'

'And I'm not, I suppose?'

'No, you are not, my pet. If you want the truth, you're like a frozen chicken. Fucking you is like stuffing sausage meat into a broiler. I'm always frightened I'll discover the giblets.'

Helen gasped, unable to speak.

'You never react, never display any pleasure, never once in four years of marriage have you asked for it. If I want you, I have to sit on the street with a begging bowl, and I'm bloody fed up with it. Every time you part your legs a degree, you behave as if you're bestowing a colossal favour. It's not your fault. Your bloody mother instilled it into you. "Behave like a lady at all times." My God.'

Helen gazed at him, too stunned to say anything, just watching him strip off his clothes in front of her, down to the lean, beautiful sun-tanned body that was so terribly reminiscent of the photographs. For a terrifying moment she thought he was going to pounce on her, but he merely went off into the shower, to emerge five minutes later dripping and rubbing his hair dry with a big pink towel.

'Have you got the message?' he said. 'I don't get my kicks at home so I get them elsewhere.'

'You've got to fire her,' whispered Helen, through white lips. 'I can't go on meeting her, knowing this, having seen those disgusting pictures.'

'What's disgusting about those pictures? Kodak obviously enjoyed them. She's got a nice body and, what's more important, she's not remotely ashamed of it. You could pick up a few tips from her.'

He went into his dressing-room and got out his dinner jacket and a white dress shirt.

'Where are you going?' Helen asked numbly.

'Out to dinner. It's Hilary's dinner party, remember? You insisted I should be back on time.'

No one could dress more quickly than Rupert when he chose.

'You can't go out to dinner after this,' Helen whispered in bewilderment.

'Why not? The drink's free. It's much better than staying here and listening to the hysterics that you're about to give way to any minute. I don't like having books thrown at me and that scent bottle's dangerously large. Don't you think you'd better get changed, too?' He was frowning in the mirror now, as he tied his tie.

'Aren't you even going to apologize for you and Podge?'

Rupert flicked the bent tie expertly through the gap. 'Why should I apologize for your inadequacies?'

Now he was brushing his still damp hair with silver brushes, back over the temples, and in two wings over the ears. He picked up his jacket. 'Don't bother to wait up for me. I'll tell Ortrud, or whatever her name is this week, you've got a migraine.'

Helen simply couldn't believe that he could treat an act of such magnitude so lightly. And the terrible things he had said. Was she really that awful in bed? Was it all her fault? The moment he'd gone, she threw herself down on the bed sobbing her heart out. Not for the first time she wished she hadn't put Marcus's nursery next to their bedroom. Within seconds there was thumping on the door and cries of 'Mummy, Mummy.' Helen gritted her teeth. Where the hell was Ortrud? The thumpings grew more insistent. 'Mummy, why are you crying?'

Helen put on her dark glasses and opened the door. Marcus almost fell inside. He was wearing blue and white striped pyjamas and clutching a stuffed purple skunk Rupert had brought him from Aachen.

'Mummy crying,' he said doubtfully.

Helen picked him up, revelling in his newly bathed softness.

'Momma's got a sore head.' She banged her hand against her temple, then the skunk's head against the window. 'Mummy go bang in car. That's why she's crying.'

Marcus seemed to accept this. Helen looked nervously for the thin trickle of mucus from his nose that always heralded an asthma attack (usually triggered off by Rupert's presence), but there was no sign.

'Story,' said Marcus pointedly.

'I can't face it,' thought Helen. 'Ortrud,' she screamed down the stairs. But Ortrud, on hearing that Helen would be staying in, had pushed off to the Jolly Goat in Stroud to meet her friends.

Rupert, having vented his wrath on Helen because he felt so guilty, was not enjoying Hilary's dinner party. Hilary, despite her arbitrary comments to Helen about even numbers, was delighted he had come alone.

'What's the matter with her?' she asked.

'Migraine,' said Rupert tersely.

'You mean a row,' said Hilary, out of the corner of her mouth. 'Have some of Crispin's elderflower wine to cheer you up.'

Rupert looked round dismissively at the earnest women, their bulges concealed beneath ethnic smocks, and their bearded husbands looking self-conscious in dinner jackets. If it hadn't been Hilary and Crispin's wedding anniversary they would have refused to dress up. Everyone, except Rupert, brought presents.

Hilary put him on her right at dinner. There wasn't even a decent-looking woman for him to flirt with or make eyes at across the table. The dinner was disgusting – smoked trout, then jugged hare, of all unbelievable things in August. With Hilary's slovenly cooking, it was probably jugged hairs as well.

'What's the matter? You're not your usual dazzling self,' said Hilary in a low voice, letting her hand brush against his as she passed the redcurrant jelly. Rupert didn't return the pressure.

'What's really the matter with Helen?' she asked. 'She was all right yesterday.'

'She's all wrong now,' said Rupert. He turned to the German woman with plaits round her head on his right.

'It must be a lonely life working with horses,' she said to him.

'No,' said Rupert. 'It's very overcrowded.'

What an idiot he'd been to shit on his own doorstep. He'd have to sack Podge now, and Arcy and the other horses who were absolutely devoted to her would be upset at the height of the season. Grooms weren't hard to find, but ones as good as Podge virtually impossible. Why the hell, too, had he ever embarked on an affair with Hilary? She revolted him now. She insisted on lingering for hours over coffee. 'I hate breaking up the ambience.'

Rupert grew increasingly restless as the dwindling candlelight flickered on the shiny unpainted faces. The woman on Rupert's right went off to the loo. Crispin was out of the room making more coffee, no doubt caffeine-free.

429

Hilary's lugubrious paintings glared down from the walls. Hilary could bear it no longer.

'Helen's found out about *us*, hasn't she?'

Rupert's eyes narrowed. 'Who?'

'*Us*, you and me of course.'

Rupert laughed. 'No, about someone else, actually.'

'I don't understand.'

'Helen found out I was knocking off someone else.'

'A long time ago?'

'No, ten days ago.'

Hilary gasped. 'You bastard. You rotten bastard,' she hissed. 'You're deliberately winding me up. I don't believe you.'

'What are you two looking so secretive about?' Crispin appeared at their side. 'Sorry I was so long, dear, I was changing Germaine. More coffee, Rupert?'

Rupert looked at Crispin's hands. He bet he hadn't washed them. 'No thanks.' He got to his feet. 'I must go. Been a lovely evening, but I got up at four o'clock this morning and I don't like to leave Helen too long.'

'He never minded in the past,' said Hilary, to herself furiously.

'Why don't you ring up? She's probably fast asleep. Pity to break up the party.'

'What party?' said Rupert, so only she could hear him. 'Our particular party is over, my darling.'

'What happened to your Porsche?' asked Crispin, watching Rupert curl his long legs into Helen's Mini.

'Helen had a prang yesterday.' Then he was gone.

He was home by a quarter to twelve. Ortrud's light was on, so was Podge's, over the stables. Probably the whole household knew he'd gone out after a screaming match with Helen. He wandered down to the stables. It was still impossibly hot. A full moon upstaged the crowded stars. The horses were moving restlessly. Arcturus came to the half-door. Rupert gave him a carrot he'd pinched from Hilary's crudité dish on the way out.

'Wish I was a stallion like you,' he said.

Arcy rolled his eyes and took a nip at Rupert, who cuffed him on the nose.

'One day, when you're famous,' he told the horse, 'you'll be encouraged to fuck any mare you like. Why can't I?'

Rupert knew Podge would be waiting up for him, but he went straight back to the house. He didn't fancy sleeping in the spare room. It was supposed to be haunted and he wasn't tight enough not to mind.

After finally settling Marcus, Helen had had a bath, bathed her eyes, washed her hair and put on the plunging, black silk, Janet Reger nightgown Rupert had given her for Christmas, but which she had never worn because she had no cleavage. Now she lay in the big bed without the light on, with the moonlight pouring in through the windows. As Rupert tiptoed past the door she called out to him. He entered cautiously, waiting for abuse, his hair gleaming as silvery as one of his hair brushes.

'I'm sorry,' she said in a choked voice. 'It's all my fault.'

Rupert, completely wrong-footed, was unbelievably touched.

'I understand exactly why you went for Podge,' she went on. 'I'm hopeless in bed. It's just my upbringing that makes me so dreadfully inhibited, but I love you so so much. I can't bear the thought of losing you. I'll try and make as many overtures as Rossini.' She was trying to make a joke, but her voice cracked. Rupert sat down, pulling her against him.

'No, it's my fault,' he said, stroking her bare arms. 'I'll get rid of Podge tomorrow, pay her off. Then so you never have to see her again. I suppose it's my upbringing, too. Fidelity wasn't the family's strong point, but I love you.'

'I'll go and buy black sexy underwear, like Janey's and read sex books and learn how to drive a man to the ultimate of desire.'

'You do already. Have I ever not wanted you? I just got tired of trying to fuck someone who didn't want me.'

That night Tabitha was conceived.

431

29

Gradually Billy's and Janey's cottage got into shape. And although Billy drew the line for a time at a swimming pool or a tennis court, the place seemed to have every other luxury.

'If I have a fantastic season and you write your arse off, we should be straight by the end of next year, give or take a few bottles of Bell's,' Billy told Janey when they moved in in October. But he never expected the bills to be quite so astronomical. Having no wedding presents, he and Janey had to buy everything from garlic crushers to washing-up machines. Billy's mother was very rich and could have helped out. But she didn't like Janey, who described her as an old boot with a tweed bum, or, in kinder moments, as 'the Emperor Vespasian in drag'. Mrs Lloyd-Foxe had the big nose and thick grey curls that look better on a man. She thought Janey was tarty and agreed with Helen that Janey wrote very over-the-top articles in the paper. Last week Janey had written about her marriage, giving rather too many intimate details. Most people, including Billy, thought it was very funny. Mrs Lloyd-Foxe did not.

'How's dear Helen and darling little Marcus?' she asked, every time she rang Janey, knowing it would irritate her.

Mrs Lloyd-Foxe had daughters, who seemed to lay babies with the ease that chickens produce eggs. It was up to Janey, her mother-in-law implied frequently, to produce a son as soon as possible. 'Then there'll be a little Lloyd-Foxe to carry on the line.'

Helen, feeling slightly sick, but much happier after her rapprochement with Rupert, was thrilled she was having another baby. Janey wanted to be pregnant, too and hadn't taken the Pill since she'd been married to Billy. But each month it was just the same. She went to see her doctor, who said it was very early days and suggested she had her tubes blown.

'You've also been racketing round the world a lot,' he told her. 'Why don't you stop work for a bit, play house, look after Billy and get in a nesting mood? Try to confine intercourse to the middle of the month, between your periods.'

Janey, in fact, was bored with racketing around. She was fed up with living out of suitcases, interviewing pop stars and heads of state. She wanted to stay at home and watch the lime trees round the cottage turn yellow, and go out mushrooming in the early morning.

There was also the matter of her expenses, which were colossal, and which had very few bills to back them up, because Janey had lost them. There had been too many dinners for ten at Tiberio's or Maxim's, with Janey and Billy treating the rest of the team. The show-jumping correspondent, jealous of her pitch being queered by Janey, had sneaked to the sports editor about unnecessary extravagance. The editor, Mike Pardoe, nearly had a coronary when he saw the total and summoned Janey from Gloucestershire.

Pardoe had once been Janey's lover. As she looked at his handsome watchful, wolfish face, Janey thought how much much nicer Billy was.

'These expenses are a joke,' said Pardoe. 'How the hell did you spend so much money in Athens? Did you buy one of the Greek islands?'

'Well, the copy was good. You said so.'

'It's gone off recently. Most of it seems to have been written with your pen dipped in Mouton Cadet and from a hotel bedroom. I want you to come back to Fleet Street where I can keep an eye on you and put you on features I need. You're a good writer, Janey, but you've lost your edge.'

'I want to write a diary from the country, rather like *The*

433

Diary of a Provincial Lady,' protested Janey.

'Who the hell's interested in that?'

Janey was livid. She looked at Pardoe's fridge, laden with drink, and the leather sofa, on which he'd laid her many years before, and which had just been upholstered in shiny black. She didn't want to go back to that wild, uncertain pre-Billy existence, where you shivered on the tube platform on the way to work, in the dress you'd worn the night before and everyone knew you hadn't been home.

She went off and lunched with a publishing friend and told him she wanted to write a book on men and where they stood at this moment in the sexual war. 'I'm going to call it *Despatches from the Y-Front.*'

'Good idea,' said the publishing friend. 'Make a nice change from all this feminist rubbish pouring off the presses. Take in the lot: divorcees, adulterers, house husbands. Is the post-permissive male better in bed? Make it as bitchy, funny and as contentious as possible. I'll give you a £21,000 advance.'

Tight after lunch, Janey went back to Pardoe and handed in her notice.

'You'll be back,' he said. 'If you ever finish that book, which I very much doubt, I might serialize it.'

'I doubt it,' said Janey, 'because you'll certainly be in it, and you'll be too vain to sue.'

Janey was not that worried about how long she'd take over the book. Her father had supported her mother. Why shouldn't Billy support her? Billy came back from Hamburg to be told Janey had resigned, but was being paid a big advance to write a book.

'I'm going to be a proper wife, like Helen,' she went on.

Billy said he preferred improper wives and, although he liked the idea of her living in the woodcutter's cottage, like Little Red Riding Hood, he did hope too many wolves wouldn't turn up dressed as grandmothers. He was also slightly alarmed that, along with the £50,000 bill from the builders, there was a tax bill for £10,000 and Janey's VAT for £3,000. Suddenly there didn't seem to be anything to pay them with.

'Give the bills to Kev,' said Janey, airily. 'That's what he's there for.'

But all worries about money were set aside with the excitement of moving in and the furniture looking so nice on the stone floors and lighting huge log fires in the drawing room and cutting back the roses and honeysuckle which were still in flower and darkening the windows. Then there was the bliss of waking up in their *own* bed in their *own* room, looking through the lime trees at the valley. How could they not be happy and prosper in an enchanted bower like this?

Janey missed Billy when he started going off to shows without her, but she was enjoying getting things straight, and it was heaven not having to get up at 5 o'clock in the morning to drive off over mountain passes or break down on icy roads. The winter that followed was very cold, and the wind whistled past their door straight off the Bristol Channel, but Janey merely turned the central heating up to tropical and thought idly about her book. The muse must not be raped; she must be given time to yield her secrets.

Rupert missed them both terribly when they moved out. All the fun seemed to have gone out of the house. He was making heroic attempts to be a good husband and Helen was trying equally hard to be more sexy. But when you were feeling sick and heavy with pregnancy, it wasn't easy. Badger missed Mavis most of all, and spent days down at the cottage whenever Rupert was away. When Rupert arrived to fetch him, he would lie in front of the fire in embarrassment with his eyes shut, pretending that, because he couldn't see Rupert, he wasn't there.

As an ingratiating gesture, Janey invited Kev and Enid Coley to her first dinner party. The huge china poodle was unearthed from its home in the cellar, dusted down and put in its place of honour in the drawing-room. Unfortunately Janey had sprayed oven-cleaner all over the inside of the cooker the day before and had forgotten to wash it off, so when she removed the duck from the oven, the kitchen was

435

looded with toxic fumes and the duck was a charred wreck, the size of a wren. So everyone screamed with laughter and Billy was sent off to Stroud to get a Chinese take-away. Just as well, perhaps. When Billy checked the mustard Janey'd put on the table, he discovered it was the horses' saffron anti-fly ointment.

'Janey's very attractive,' commented Enid Coley on the way home, 'but I'm not sure she's a homemaker.'

By the time Christmas came, things were very tight. The Bull bruised a sole before the Olympia show and Billy didn't have a single win with the other horses. He sent a Christmas card to his bank manager and decided he'd have to tap his parents, who'd invited them down for Christmas.

'Only for a couple of days,' Janey told Mrs Lloyd-Foxe, firmly. 'We can't really leave the horses.'

The visit was not a success. Janey, who always left shopping until the last moment, was forced to spend an absolute fortune on Christmas presents, which shocked Billy's frugal parents, who gave them a hideously ugly piece of family silver, instead of the cheque they had anticipated.

The Lloyd-Foxes lived in a house called The Maltings, which was so cold that Janey couldn't bring herself to get up until lunchtime, and then only to hog the fire. Billy's mother was not tactful. She came back incessantly to the subject of babies. It was so sad at bridge parties not to be able to boast of a little Lloyd-Foxe baby in the offing. She was so pleased dear Helen was being sensible and having a second child.

'I'll iron Billy's shirts for him,' she said, coming into the bedroom and picking them off the floor. 'I know how he likes them, and I'll make you an apple pie to take back to Gloucestershire. He so loves puddings.'

'She'll get it in her kisser if she doesn't shut up,' muttered Janey.

Out of sheer irritation, Janey left her room like a tip, with the fire on, and didn't bother to make the one bed they'd slept in, out of the two single beds. Billy was the only form of central heating in the house. And as, at noon and six o'clock, Janey moved towards the vodka, Billy's mother's jaw quilted with muscles. She was very tired with cooking and she could have done with a little help and praise from Janey. Finally, on Boxing night, Billy asked his father for a loan.

Mr Lloyd-Foxe hummed and hawed and said it had been a bad year with the squeeze and, although he had twenty thousand to spare, he had divided it between Billy's sisters, Arabella and Lucinda.

'I feel they need it more than you and Janey do, as you're both working.'

Janey didn't even bother to kiss her mother-in-law goodbye, and it was only after they'd left that Mrs Lloyd-Foxe discovered Janey had painted the letter 'L' out of the The Maltings sign on the gate.

After Christmas the bills came flooding in. Billy, who'd never paid a gas or telephone or electricity bill in his life, had no idea they'd be so high. He also read his bank statement, which was infinitely more scarlet after Janey's Christmas shopping spree.

'Did you honestly spend £60 on that cushion for my mother?'

'Pity I didn't hold it over the old monster's face,' said Janey.

The tax man and the builders were also hustling for payment. Another shock was that the £21,000 advance on the manuscript was divided into three: £7,000 on signature, £7,000 on delivery and £7,000 on publication.

'How soon do you think you'll deliver?' asked Billy.

The original date had been March, but Janey, who'd only made a few random notes, said there wouldn't be a hope before the summer, which meant that Autumn publication was very unlikely.

Janey had no idea, either, of the astronomical cost of running and travelling a string of horses, nor was she any good as a back-up team. She kept forgetting to post entry forms, which meant Billy drove 200 miles to a show to find he wasn't eligible to compete. Often, fast talking got him in, sometimes, it didn't. Billy was one of the best riders in England, but he was not a natural jockey, like Rupert. He had to work at it and keep schooling his horses to get really good results. Nor did Janey understand Billy's temperament: that he lacked self-confidence, and needed to be kept very calm before a big class. Rows and requests for money sapped his concentration. He needed to distance himself and, with a lovely wife in a warm bed at home, he tended to spend less time in the indoor school at night and to get up later in the morning.

In March, he came home from a three-week trip abroad. He'd missed Janey desperately and deliberately rang her at Southampton to say he'd be home in time for dinner, adding, rather plaintively, that he hadn't eaten all day. As he settled the horses at Rupert's, a marvellous smell of boeuf bourgignon drifted out of the kitchen, and he wondered if Janey would be cooking something nice for him. As he came up to the front door he tripped over a pile of milk bottles. The place stank of cat, not rabbit stew, and as he took the last finger of whisky to the sink to fill the glass up with water, he found it full of dirty dishes. The washing-up machine had broken, explained Janey; the man hadn't come to mend it yet. As he went back into the drawing room, he noticed the drink rings on the Georgian table Helen had given them as a wedding present. The place looked rather as Penscombe used to before Helen came and tidied it up. Somehow, these days, mess got on his nerves. He had had a bad week, hardly in the money at all. He tried to ignore the pile of brown envelopes unopened on the hall table. There was no more whisky; only vodka, but no tonic.

'Drink it with orange squash.'

'I'm starving.'

'I'm sorry, darling. I forgot to get anything in, and it was too late by the time you rang. Let's go out.'

'Too bloody expensive. I'll have some cornflakes.'

Billy's stomach was churning painfully. He wondered if

438

he were getting an ulcer. He had an early start in the morning. He went upstairs; the hot cupboard was bare, and there was nothing in his drawers.

'Have I got any clean shirts or breeches?'

'Oh, Christ,' said Janey, clutching her head, 'I left them in the launderette in Stroud. The washing machine's up the spout, too.'

'What time do they open?'

'About 8.30.'

'I've got to leave at six.'

'I'm sorry, darling, truly I am. Look, give me your breeches and shirts and I'll wash them by hand. Then we can dry them in front of the fire, and I'll get up early and iron them.'

'It's all right. I'll borrow some from Rupert. I'm only away for a couple of days this time.'

'I'm desperately sorry,' said Janey, suddenly catching sight of two unposted entry forms in her out-tray and shuffling them under a pile of papers. 'I'm going to mix you a nice drink.'

After two glasses of vodka and orange squash, which didn't taste so bad after all, Billy felt fortified enough to open the brown envelopes.

'Janey, darling,' he said, five minutes later, 'we shall simply have to pull our horns in. These bills are frightful.'

'Can't you take a trip to Château Kitsch? Harold Evans caught a finch in the herb garden today and came in with his mouth full of chives and parsley. He's also got a liver complaint.'

Billy looked up, alarmed. 'Have you taken him to the vet then?'

Janey giggled. 'No, he's complaining there's not enough liver.'

Billy grinned, but was not to be deflected.

'Sweetheart, we must try and cut down. We don't need a swimming pool. We simply can't afford the deposit, or even less, to pay for it when it's finished.'

Janey pouted. 'It'll be so nice for you to flop into the pool

439

when you come back from shows.'

'There's only about three months a year warm enough to do that in Gloucestershire.'

'I've been trying to economize. Mrs Bodkin's got flu, and I took her a bunch of daffodils without leaves today, because they were 20p cheaper.'

'But we haven't been really living it down, have we? There are five half-opened tins of cat food gathering mould on top of the fridge and Mavis really doesn't need half a chicken every day. She's getting awfully fat.'

'Well, Badger often drops in for lunch. You know how Helen starves those dogs.'

'I think we ought to cut down Mrs Bodkin to half a day a week,' said Billy, ignoring Janey's frown. 'And give up Miss Hawkins. You could do my fan mail.'

'Do your fan mail?' said Janey, outraged. 'What about *my* fan mail?'

'Just for a little, till we get straight.'

Janey started to get angry and hysterical. 'I've got to finish this book. It's got to be handed in by July. I haven't got time for anything else. I'm writing every day. I get up at eight and I've only just finished this evening. Stupid not to grab inspiration when it takes you.'

She didn't point out that most of that day had been spent drinking coffee, and later whisky, with one of the builders. After all, she rationalized, she had to get the rough-trade view for her book somehow.

'I know, darling,' said Billy soothingly. 'All I'm saying is that we must not do any more to the house at the moment.'

'Go to Kev,' said Janey, emptying the last of the vodka into his glass. 'Kev will provide, the great ape. I'm going to make you some scrambled eggs.' She went towards the kitchen. 'I say,' she popped her head round the door a moment later, 'Helen gave me a chapter of her novel to read today.'

'Any good?'

'She can't write "Bum" on a wall. She said, "Janey, I want you to be real honest with me," which meant she

440

wanted me to lie convincingly. She told me a much funnier thing today. She's got frightfully thick with the new vicar, and evidently when Rupert flew back from Geneva for the night last week, he found the vicar holding a Lenten meeting in the drawing room, with everyone, including Badger, meditating with their eyes shut.'

Billy laughed. 'Rupe told me.'

He wandered into the kitchen, trying not to notice the mess or the way Janey threw the eggshells into a huge box, where they joined about a hundred other eggshells. That must account for the odd smell. He picked up a jar of coffee on the dresser and looked at the price. 'Christ, coffee's expensive. I'm going to drink liquor in future.'

Janey came and put her arms round him: 'I do love you,' she said. 'Don't worry about money, I've got a lovely bottle of St Emilion.'

After three huge vodkas and a bottle of St Emilion, the problem didn't seem so bad. Billy would ride with panache, Janey would write like a maniac while he was away. They would soon get out of their mess.

Spring came, more longed-for than ever after the hardness of the winter, and the woods were filled with violets, anemones, primroses and bird song. Chaucer's people thought about pilgrimages; Janey thought about new clothes. The wild garlic made her feel homesick for drunken lunches in Soho. She knew marriage to Billy was far more precious and durable, but she missed the jokes and the gossip. She lived on the telephone to her mother. She was finding it increasingly difficult to buckle down to her book. She was used to the weekly clapping of journalism, the steady fan mail, people coming up to her at parties and saying, 'You were a bit near the knuckle last week.'

In the country, there was no second post, no *Evening Standard*, no Capital Radio; she found it difficult to get used to the slow rhythms. Gloucestershire was a soporific county and she found herself falling asleep in the afternoon. She had her fallopian tubes blown, which was not really painful, but affected her more than she expected. She sank into

441

despondency; and to pre-menstrual tension was added post-menstrual depression, when she found she wasn't pregnant.

One afternoon Billy's mother dropped in with a bridge friend. The cottage looked awful. There was no cake, only some stale bread, no jam and a teapot already full of leaves. Mrs Lloyd-Foxe followed her into the kitchen.

'Any news?' she asked. Janey shook her head, but was so upset that she burnt the toast.

'What a beautiful view,' said the bridge friend, looking out of the window.

'The only views I like these days,' said Janey, 'are my own.'

The bills poured in. Janey's tax bill arrived and Billy realized that, as her husband, he was liable for an extra £15,000, with a further £3,000 owing to VAT-man.

Every time Janey went shopping, wherever she looked, baby clothes seemed to be mocking her. She seemed to be alone in a world of mothers. She took her temperature and wrote it down on the back of a Christmas card every day, and Billy was supposed to leap on her when her temperature went up. But invariably she'd mislaid the card or Billy wasn't there on the right day.

In May, Helen gave birth to a daughter, whom they called Tabitha. Rupert was present at the birth, and although to Helen, he seemed to spend more time making eyes over his white mask at the pretty nurses, and seeing how all the machinery worked, he was at least present if incorrect. And from the moment he set eyes on Tabitha and she opened her Cambridge-blue eyes, Rupert was totally enchanted. She was indeed the most angelic baby. She gurgled and laughed, and, almost immediately, she slept through the night; and, if she woke, it was Rupert who got up without a murmur, displaying a sweetness and patience Helen had never seen before.

Where Rupert was concerned, it was the great love affair of the century. Here was someone he could love unstintingly, and who adored him back. Later her first word was 'Daddy', and, when she took her first steps, they were towards Rupert. And almost before she could walk she screamed to be put on a pony, and screamed even louder when she was lifted off. Rupert would do anything for her, bathing her, playing with her for hours, watching as she slept, plump, pink-cheeked, blonde and ravishing in her cot. Delighted at first with Rupert's delight, Helen gradually became irritated by it, drawing even closer to Marcus, who couldn't understand at two, why his father didn't dote on him and bring him presents and cuddle him on his knee. As a result, when Rupert wasn't around, he would punch and pinch little Tab and fill her cot with toys. One day Rupert caught him trying to suffocate Tab with a pillow and gave him a back-hander which sent him flying across the room. Two hours later, Marcus had one of his worst asthma attacks. He recovered, but by that time Rupert had moved on to another show.

The christening upset Janey very much. She was a godmother, but it was such a tribal affair, such a ritualistic celebration of fertility. All the Campbell-Blacks were there in force, going into ecstasies over such a ravishing baby. Mrs Lloyd-Foxe sent Tab a beautiful silver mug. Janey got drunk afterwards and spent all night in floods of tears. Billy was in despair. 'We've only been married a year and a half, darling. I'll see a doctor. It might be my fault.'

30

All the riders were now revving up for the World Championship, which was being held at Les Rivaux in Brittany in July. Only six British riders would be selected to go. Considering Billy a certainty, Kevin Coley had reserved a big tent at Les Rivaux and was intending to make a party of it, flying out all his important customers for a jolly.

As it was only May, Billy wasn't too worried about qualifying. He was bound to hit form soon. The Bull had got over a virus complaint and was back on the circuit. Another key event, from Kevin Coley's point of view, was Westerngate, a big show in the Midlands, towards the end of May. The Moggie Meal factory was just a few miles outside Westerngate, and Kevin Coley had a tent at the show, where all his senior staff were expected to turn out in their best clothes and mingle with important customers.

The highlight of the day for all of them was to meet Billy and watch his horses, Moggie Meal Al, Moggie Meal Kitch (Kitchener) and Moggie Meal Dick (Mandryka), jumping. They were also keen to meet Billy's beautiful and famous wife, Janey, whom many of the wives had thought a scream when they read her pieces.

Westerngate was about eighty miles north of Penscombe. Billy was expected to be on parade all three days of the show, and Kevin and Enid Coley were naturally disappointed that Janey was working on Thursday and Friday, but were very much looking forward to seeing her on Saturday for lunch.

'Do I have to come?' grumbled Janey.

'It *is* important,' urged Billy. 'They're our bread and

butter.'

'Marg and sliced bread, if you ask me. I hate to leave the book,' she lied, 'when it's going so well.'

'I'll come home on Friday night and collect you,' said Billy, 'and we can drive down in the morning. But we'll have to leave early; I've got a novice class around eleven-thirty.'

On the Monday before the show, Billy had gone to Kevin to ask for an advance of £20,000 to keep some of his creditors at bay. Kevin thought for a minute. 'Yes, I'll help you out, Billy.'

'That's terribly kind of you,' said Billy, heaving a sigh of relief.

'It isn't kind, it's fucking generous. But I'm not going to help you out that much. I'm only going to give you £2,000, or you'll lose your hunger.'

Billy's heart sank.

'You'll have to win the rest. Cut down on the booze and lose some weight. It's a tough world. I'm counting on you for the World Championship. I've booked that tent for Les Rivaux, so you'd better start winning, and qualify.'

Billy wished Kevin hadn't booked the tent; it was tempting providence.

Bad luck seemed to pursue him. He had such a hangover at Fontainebleau, he forgot to check if Tracey had screwed in Kitchener's studs. Kitchener went into the ring and promptly slipped on take-off, putting him out for the whole season, which left Billy with only The Bull and Mandryka. Janey was sympathetic when he rang, but she was four days late with the curse, and cocooned in secret expectations.

On Wednesday night, Billy came home from Fontaine-bleau and found Janey had put three pairs of breeches and four white shirts in the washing machine with one of her scarlet silk scarves, so they came out streaked red like the dawn. Billy was very tired or he wouldn't have hit the roof.

'I can't think what you're worrying about. I'm not complaining,' Janey shouted back at him, 'and I've ruined

445

a perfectly good scarf. I've been so busy, you're lucky to have your shirts washed at all. Why don't you go out and win something, then you could afford to send them to the laundry?'

Billy felt that terrible clawing pain in his gut that was becoming so familiar these days. A large glass of whisky seemed the only answer.

Going upstairs in the faint hope of finding some clean shirts, he saw instead the beautiful new iron bedhead above the spare-room bed.

'Where did that come from?'

'I bought it weeks ago.'

'And paid for it?'

'Not yet.' Janey didn't meet his eyes.

'Why d'you buy bloody bedheads when I can't afford boots?'

'Why don't you buy cheap vino instead of paying £3 a bottle? Why are you always buying drinks for people, giving them the shirts off your back, even if they are streaked red like the dawn? As I said, why don't you win something? I'm fed up with playing second fiddle to a string of bloody horses.'

Billy went back upstairs. When she joined him, he was lying in bed wearing pyjamas buttoned up to the neck. Even though his face was turned to the wall she caught a waft of bad digestion and drink fumes.

'Billy,' she said apologetically. He didn't answer, but she knew he was awake. Nothing, however, could dent her happiness. She was eight days late. She woke up in the night and Billy was so still she thought he'd committed suicide, so she woke him up in a panic and, half-asleep, he instinctively put his arms round her, forgetting the dreadfulness of the row.

He left before she woke in the morning to go to Westerngate, but returned on Friday night in better spirits. The Bull had come second in a big class, so perhaps his luck was turning.

Janey was delighted. 'Who beat you?'

446

'Jake Lovell, of all people. He's back on the circuit.'

'Who's he?'

'You know Jake. Oh, I'd forgotten. You probably never met him. He was a cert for the Colombia Olympics, with two top-class horses. Then one had a heart attack at Crittleden. Appalling bad luck. Should never have been jumped. And then Rupert set his heart on the second.'

'And got it, no doubt,' said Janey. 'He always gets anything or anyone he wants.'

'Yes, he did. It was Revenge actually. Belonged to Jake's stepfather-in-law. Rupert made him an offer he couldn't refuse; left Jake without any horses. Now he's really back on form. I'm glad. I always felt bad about that business.'

Cheered up by Billy's second, they got mildly tight together. 'I'm so pleased you're coming tomorrow,' said Billy. 'They're all dying to meet you. I want to show you off.'

Janey didn't feel like being shown off. She felt fat and bloated; perhaps it was the first stirrings of pregnancy. In anticipation of maternity, and to cover the bulges, (she was ten days late now), she was wearing one of Billy's streaked shirts and nothing else.

'Do you like short hair?' she said, pausing at the *Daily Mail* fashion page.

'I do on Mavis. Can I shave your bush tonight?'

It was all rather erotic. Billy had bought her a porn magazine to read and laid her on a towel on the bed and used his razor and masses of soap and hot water. Wincing in case he nicked her, she read a story about a Victorian maid and her boss, which was too absurd for words and full of misprints and anachronisms, which she kept reading out to Billy:

' "I want to lock your bunt," said the vicar, his hot six rearing up.' But it soon had her bubbling over inside; the libido was an awfully bad judge of literature, Janey decided.

'Christ, you look fantastic,' said Billy as he rinsed away the last soap and hairs. Janey peered at herself. 'Rather like

447

an old boiler chicken.'

'It'll be fantastic going down on you. Did you ever allow any of your other boyfriends to do this to you?' asked Billy, as he leapt on her. 'Can we play for a long time?'

Janey, however, having come quickly herself, wanted to get it over with. She was suddenly tired and wriggled frantically trying to bring him to the boil, and then exciting him with a story of how Pardoe took her in the back of his Jaguar one summer night.

Janey fell asleep immediately afterwards. Billy lay awake and fretted. Mandryka had put in a nasty stop yesterday. He must get to Westerngate early and sort it out. Janey woke up in the morning with a hangover, feeling Billy's prick nudging her back, his hand stroking her shaven flesh.

'What time ought we to leave?'

'Ten at the latest. I haven't declared and I promised Kev we'd be there for pre-lunch drinks.'

Janey didn't want sex but, to get herself in a more receptive mood, she fantasized she was a schoolgirl in a gym tunic, being ticked off by a very strict headmaster in a dog collar. Next moment the headmaster's wife walked in and they both decided to have her.

'Shall I tell you a story to excite you?' asked Billy.

'I'm fine,' said Janey, who was deep in headmasters. 'Nearly there.' The next moment, pleasure flooded over her. She longed to go back to sleep.

'You look so fantastic,' said Billy, 'how about soixante-neuf?'

Janey couldn't face a huge cock down her throat. 'I can't Billy, not with a hangover. Please stay inside me. I want to feel you coming.'

Afterwards they both fell asleep. When they woke it was five to ten.

'What are you doing?' said Billy, when he went into the bathroom five minutes later.

'Washing my hair.'

'But you can't, we've got to leave *now*.'

'You'll just have to drive a bit faster, or go without me.'

448

'I can't,' he said aghast. 'They're expecting you. Your hair looks fine. It's only a show. It's you they want to see, not your hair.'

'I know what they'll all say, "Not as attractive as her photograph, nothing to look at in the flesh",' snapped Janey, who was now upside-down, head in the bath, rubbing in shampoo 'I do have a public image to keep up. It was you who wanted bloody sex.' They didn't leave until after eleven.

'Revving up is actionable,' hissed Janey, coming out of the house.

'So is being an hour late,' snapped Billy.

'And my fringe has separated.'

Billy didn't think that a striped rugger shirt with a rather dirty white collar, flared jeans and an old denim jacket were suitable, but he didn't complain, as he would have had to wait another twenty minutes. Rancid with ill temper, they drove all the way to Westerngate with Janey trying to do her face, snapping at Billy every time he went round a corner. The traffic was terrible. They were held up for thirty-five minutes by a couple of gays unloading some carpet into an antique shop in Broadway High Street.

Billy kept looking at his watch. 'Kev's going to flip his lid. I'm going to be too late to declare.' His stomach was killing him.

They arrived at half-past one. Billy went straight off to try and square the secretary, leaving Janey to park the car in the sponsors' car park. There was the Moggie Meal tent. There was the awful cat winking on the flag. Oh God, here was Kevin Coley, coming towards her, wearing a suit the colour of a caramel cup cake. He looked simply livid.

'Hi, Kev,' she said casually. 'The traffic was awful.'

'Where the hell is Billy? He's been late once too bloody often and they've put their foot down. They've closed the declaration. They're already walking the course. That means he'll probably be dropped for the Royal and for Aachen, and it's too bloody near the World Championships.'

449

'He's gone to talk to the stewards now. They'll let him in. The crowd have come to see The Bull.'

'Don't you bank on it. Everyone's been waiting for you, too. We held lunch until a quarter of an hour ago. It's not bloody good enough.'

It was with great difficulty that Janey stopped herself shouting back at him. Matters were hardly improved when Billy turned up, abject with apologies, and said they were going to allow him to jump, and he had better go and walk the course.

'See you later, darling,' he said to Janey. 'Go and have some lunch.' Face set, she ignored him.

Kevin Coley took her arm, none too gently. 'You'd better come along to the tent and repair some of the damage. And smile, for Christ's sake. You're being paid for it.'

In the tent, they found customers and staff stuffing roast beef and lobsters. Most of them were already tight. Kevin clones were everywhere, with thatched hair and lightweight and light-coloured suits. The wives also all seemed to wear beige or pastel suits. Many wore hats on the back of their heads, with too much hair showing at the front, and high heels which kept catching on the raffia matting and sinking into the damp earth beneath.

Enid Coley, in a brown check suit and yellow shirt with a pussy-cat bow, was not the only one who looked disapprovingly at Janey's jeans and rugger shirt. 'I don't care, I don't care,' thought Janey. 'I'm eleven days late, and I'm going to have a baby.' The little Coley children or the Sprats, as Billy called them, had all been at the bottle and were rushing around being poisonous. 'I'll never let my children grow up like that,' Janey thought to herself. Kevin put her between two directors' wives who were eating strawberries and cream.

'The gardens aren't as good as the ones at Buckingham Palace,' said one.

'No,' said the second, 'although I didn't really notice the ones at Buckingham Palace the first time I went.'

Next moment Helen walked into the tent looking like a

450

million dollars in an off-white canvas suit and flat dark brown boots.

'I'm real sorry I couldn't make lunch. You did get the message, didn't you? But with young kids, it's so difficult to get away,' she said to Kevin and Enid, who looked as though they'd been kissed under the mistletoe. Enid, pink with pleasure, took Helen on a tour of the more important clients. Helen was so nice to all of them. Then suddenly she saw Janey and her face lit up.

'Janey, how lovely. I didn't know whether you'd be able to get away.'

'We were just saying the BSJA ought to club together and buy you a bra, Janey,' said Enid Coley.

Later, Janey sat in the riders' stand with Helen watching the big class. She had been pleased with her rugger shirt and jeans until she saw Helen's suit, which was French and cost at least £300. When they had walked through the crowds earlier, all the men had stared at Helen, so Janey had taken her dark glasses off, so people could see her sexy, slanting eyes, but they still looked at Helen, so she took off her denim jacket to show off her splendid bosom, but they still looked at Helen. Why the hell couldn't Billy be as rich as Rupert, so she could afford decent clothes? She was still furious with Kev, who was sitting on her other side. In the next-door stand, he had booked seats for all his frightful clients, who clapped and shrieked when riders fell off, and cheered before rounds were finished, and stood up and took pictures all the time, to the rage of the people sitting behind them.

'Isn't Kev hell?' she whispered to Helen. 'I bet he streaks his chest hair.'

'I think he's charming,' said Helen, in surprise.

Billy's stomach was killing him, like a giant clenching a huge fist in his gut. The only answer, as Kevin was safely in the riders' stand, was to nip into the bar for a couple of quick doubles.

'Those hangover pills you gave me aren't doing much,' he grumbled to Rupert, when he got back to the collecting ring.

451

'I should think not,' said Rupert. 'They're for backache. D'you know, I really think Tab is very bright. She smiled at me today. They don't usually smile till three months.'

'Lucky you. Janey's not smiling at me.'

Suddenly, Billy thought of the shaved bush under those jeans and, overwhelmed with lust, he waved at Janey. Janey ignored him.

It was a tough course. Ludwig went clear. Two Americans, just arrived and accustoming themselves to European fences in anticipation of the World Championships, went clear. The usual mighty roar of applause went up as Billy and The Bull rode into the ring. All Kevin's guests stood up to take photographs.

'My husband may not be the most successful, but he's certainly the most popular rider in England,' said Janey, shooting a venomous look at Kevin, who was tugging at his goal-post moustache and twisting his initial bracelet.

'Come on, Billy. Come on The Bull,' yelled the crowd. They too refused to adopt Moggie Meal Al.

'I can't bear to look,' said Janey, and didn't, continuing to talk to Helen about straight-legged jeans.

Billy was clear and jumping beautifully, until he came to the penultimate fence, when a great cheer went up from the Moggie Meal contingent and distracted The Bull, who jumped the wing instead of the fence and, catching his front leg, went head over heels. The Moggie Meal supporters let out piercing shrieks and started clicking their cameras frantically.

Billy was unhurt and managed to hang onto the reins, getting up and running like mad after a thoroughly rattled Bull. Nearly crashing into a flag, Billy picked it up and waved it in mock fury at The Bull, who backed away in terror. Billy started to laugh, threw down the flag, snatched up a handful of grass and gave it to The Bull, reducing the crowd to fits of laughter. Vaulting on to The Bull's back, he cantered out of the ring, grinning broadly.

'That's two grand up the spout,' thought Janey. 'I don't

know what he's got to look so cheerful about.'

Billy came into the stand, kissed Helen hello and sat down between her and Janey.

'Sorry, Kev,' he said.

Janey caught a waft of whisky and hoped it didn't reach Kevin. After two minutes, Billy got to his feet.

'Who'd like a drink?'

'Not for me,' said Kevin Coley pointedly.

'Nor me,' said Helen, standing up. 'I must go and ring Bergita. Has anyone got any change?'

'Be my guest,' said Kevin Coley, going pink again as he handed her the coins.

'That's what I call a real lady,' said Kevin as Helen made her way along the row, thanking everyone for getting up.

'As opposed to me,' muttered Janey to herself, crossly.

'Pity she doesn't come to shows more often. But then she's such a caring mother,' Kevin went on.

Janey looked stonily down at the collecting ring, where a black-haired rider was walking towards a girl groom, with long mousy hair, who was leading a large grey horse.

'Who's that? He's attractive,' she said to Billy.

'That's Jake Lovell,' said Billy. 'I was telling you about him last night. And that groom's his sister-in-law, Fenella Maxwell. She won a novice class this morning and she's only sixteen. She's bloody good. Jake's trained her really well. Isn't she pretty?'

'She's certainly a most attractive young lady,' said Kev.

'I'm surprised you can tell for the spots,' said Janey.

'Miaow,' said Kevin.

'Oh, go eat your own product,' snapped Janey.

She went downstairs to the loo. She really must stop being a cow. Glancing at her reflection under the fluorescent lighting, she thought how awful she looked, piggy-eyed and shadowed. She did hope she wasn't going to be one of those women who felt sick for nine months. As she sat on the loo, she felt the sudden cold on her shaven bush. Just to convince herself, she slipped her finger between her legs, then pressed it against the white gloss lavatory wall. She couldn't believe it. She reached further into her vagina, pushing against the neck of the womb. She pressed the white wall again. It was unmistakeable: a second dark red finger print. She gave a groan, tears spilling out of her eyes. She was wracked with despair. Oh, God, the red badge of discouragement. It was so ironic. Before she was married, the red finger print was all she craved; she'd been so terrified all the time of getting pregnant. Now she knew why it was called the curse, the curse of not having babies. She leant against the wall and cried and cried.

Twenty minutes later she came out of the loo, huddled behind her dark glasses. Kevin was waiting outside. 'Where the hell have you been? Billy was looking for you. He's just about to jump Moggie Meal Dick. He told me to tell you. What's the matter?' He lifted off her dark glasses. 'Why are you crying?'

'Nothing, it's nothing.'

'Worried about money?'

Her lip trembled. 'I thought I was pregnant. I was ten days late, you see. I've just discovered I'm not.'

'Been trying long?'

'About eighteen months. Since we married, really.'

'May not be your fault.'

Janey gave a bitter laugh. 'Billy's mother thinks it is.'

Kevin looked at her thoughtfully.

'Enid's got a first-rate gynaecologist. I'll tell her to give you a ring.'

Mandryka got four faults and was out of the running. Rupert was first, Jake Lovell second. It was noticed that both men stared stonily ahead, not exchanging a single word, as they lined up for their rosettes.

Helen drove home with Rupert. 'I really do think Janey should look after Billy better. All his boots need heeling. He was wearing a filthy shirt and Kevin said she made him really late today.'

Rupert shook his head. 'There's no doubt that William has made a marriage of inconvenience.'

454

Billy went abroad again. He was very loath to leave Janey when she was so depressed, and also miss the opportunity of sleeping with her in the middle of the month when she was at her most fertile. He was tempted to fly back for the night, but he simply couldn't afford it. Janey promised him she'd try not to worry and would concentrate on her book.

Concentration was not easy. The tax man dropped in, so did the builders and the VAT bully boys, all wanting money. Janey explained that Billy was away and that she wasn't entitled to sign cheques unless he was here, but fear came in great waves. She hadn't liked the way the VAT man looked at her furniture. The days were so long too. She got up early, which meant she was starving by midday, and started misery eating. Having worked until six in the evening, she was shattered and ready to dive into a quadruple vodka. Evenings yawned ahead.

She went to see Helen and grumbled how bored she was. Helen suggested she did something for charity. Why didn't she join the local Distressed Gentlefolk's Committee? Janey went sharply into reverse, saying that that would be carrying coals to Newcastle, and she was only bored because she had so much work to do.

The third day after Billy left, Janey tried and failed to write a chapter on schoolboys. She didn't know any schoolboys; all her brothers were older. She ought to go to Eton or Harrow or the local comprehensive and talk to some, but research took time and was invariably expensive.

She wrote down all the men she'd been to bed with, rather too many of them, hoping this might give her inspiration. It didn't. Then she tore the list up in case Billy found it and was upset. The house looked awful. She went from room to room trying to find some free table space. She'd written in the bedroom and the kitchen and the drawing-room and even the dining room, and left them all in a mess – everywhere except the future nursery. She was not going in there; it made her cry.

The garden looked so pretty, full of hollyhocks and roses, and honeysuckle hanging heavy on the warm June air. The lime trees were in yellow flower, filling the air with sweet heady scent. The lime tree bower my prison, she thought to herself. She looked again at her contract and trembled. 70,000 words, it said. She hadn't really produced any of them, and her publisher kept ringing and saying he'd be only too happy to come down and discuss what she'd already done.

She wished she were in Athens with Billy. It was no good trying to work. She'd go out and weed the front garden and think about married men. But after she'd weeded up two snapdragons she decided she'd better just think about weeding. Perhaps her subconscious would start working overtime.

Mavis sat, aggrieved and shivering ostentatiously, behind her. Going outside meant walks, not weeding. Harold Evans came out and rolled in the catmint. Mavis gave half-hearted chase, and Harold shot up a tree, tail flushed out like a lavatory brush.

After half an hour, Janey peered in at the kitchen clock. Two minutes past six. Hooray, it was drinks time. She went in and poured herself some vodka. An inch up the glass, two inches? Oh well, it was mostly ice. She couldn't be bothered with lemon, but splashed in some tonic.

God, what a wasted day. She tried to think about men in a two-career family. Not easy, really. She and Billy could do with a wife each to look after them. She looked round the kitchen and shuddered at the mess. She'd really clear up before Billy came home. She picked up the paper. There was a brilliant piece by one of her rivals, which depressed

456

her even more. At least there was a Carry On film on television to cheer her up.

She heard the sound of voices, but it was only two farm labourers going past the gate, tired and red from the sun, returning home to supper and a pint of beer, perhaps, because they'd earned it. How lucky they were. The despair of another wasted day overwhelmed her.

After three vodkas, she was starving. She made a herb omelette with six eggs, throwing the eggshells into the cardboard box which she still hadn't emptied. She meant to share the omelette, which turned into scrambled eggs, with Mavis, but Mavis didn't like herbs, so Janey ended up eating the lot. The boring pan had stuck; she'd clean it later. She ran her hands through her hair. A snow of scurf drifted down. She hadn't washed it since Westerngate. God, she was going to seed. She bolted all the doors and, having poured herself another vodka, was just about to turn on the television when the door bell rang. Who the hell would call at this hour of the night? It was bound to be some rapist out in the woods or, even worse, the bailiffs. She'd ignore it. Mavis was barking her head off and and the bell rang again. Terrified, she unbolted the door and opened it an inch on the chain.

'Who's that?' she said, peering through the gap. Next moment she was assailed by Paco Raban.

'It's me, Kevin.'

She could see his medallion catching the light.

'Come in,' she said weakly. 'I thought you were the VAT man or a rapist. Probably both, knowing my luck.'

Relief that he was neither gave way to panic. Which was the least sordid room to take him into?

'I'm working,' she said, plumping for the drawing room. 'I'm afraid I only tidy up before Billy comes home.'

'So I see,' said Kevin.

The drawing-room faced north and was cold. There were dead flowers, the skeleton of a three-month-old fire, coffee cups and dog and cat plates. Janey shivered.

'Let's try the kitchen.'

457

Kevin followed her, wrinkling his nose. He looked quite amazing in a black velvet suit, a white silk shirt slashed to the navel, three medallions and his blond hair newly washed.

'You look different,' she said.

'I've shaved off my moustache.'

'That's right,' muttered Janey fuzzily. 'It's right that a goal-post moustache should come down in the summer.'

'I've just left your husband in Athens this morning. I had to attend a function in this area. Thought I'd look in.'

'How is he?' said Janey, her face brightening.

'Bit choked. Moggie Meal Al seems to have lost his confidence since he hit the wing at Westerngate. Moggie Meal Dick keeps four-faulting.'

'Which one's he?'

Kevin frowned. The frown deepened as he saw the mess of cups and dirty milk bottles, the sink full of dishes.

'I've been working so hard,' Janey explained again.

Kevin looked pointedly at the half-full glass, still with unmelted ice cubes.

'What would you like to drink?' she said.

'A dry white wine, please.'

'Well, be a duck and get it from the cellar. I must go to the loo.'

Upstairs she looked at herself in despair. Her hair looked like a mop, her face was red, her eyes tiny from drinking and lack of make-up. Old trousers and a shrunk T-shirt made her bum and boobs look huge. Scraping a flannel under her armpits, spraying her crotch with scent, she slapped on some liquid foundation and failed to pull a comb through her tangled mane. She went to the typewriter and wrote: 'Men shouldn't drop in,' with one finger.

Downstairs, Kevin, up from the cellar, was holding a bottle and looking boot-faced. 'I gather you don't like our wedding gift.'

Janey went white. 'Oh, no, no, no! We just put it there because, er, Billy's mother came to dinner and she had a poodle which, er, died, and we thought she'd be upset.' She

458

shrugged helplessly. It had been worth a try.

Then there was the hassle of finding a corkscrew and a clean glass, and then a basin that wasn't full of dirty dishes to wash it in.

'There's a basin in the downstairs loo,' said Janey. Then, worried she might have forgotten to pull the chain, she seized the glass and rushed off. But it was all right. She had.

'Why d'you buy Whiskas instead of Moggie Meal?' said Kevin, looking at another of Harold's plates, which was gathering flies.

'I'm sorry, Kev. I know I'm a lousy wife, but I'd just learnt the names of Billy's horses when you changed them all, and the village shop's run out of Moggie Meal. I get so bombed when I'm writing and I haven't eaten all day.'

Kev raised an eyebrow at the remains of scrambled egg in the pan.

'How's the book going?'

'All right. I'm up to "Married Men".'

'Based on Billy?'

'Billy's too nice. Most married men I know are like babies – into everyone.'

She wondered if he used hot tongs as well as a blow dryer, and had got that butterscotch-smooth tan out of a bottle. He was in good shape though, his flat stomach emphasized by the big Gucci belt.

She was dying to get herself another drink, but he was only a quarter way down his. Kevin didn't drink much; it made his accent slip. She felt mesmerized by his flashing gold cufflinks and medallions.

'Don't you get frightened when you're here alone?' he asked.

'I've got a panic button wired up to Rupert's house, and a burglar alarm, but since Harold kept setting it off I gave up using it.'

'You were pretty scared when I arrived.'

'I thought you were the bailiffs. Please don't come home, Bill Bailiff,' she giggled lamely.

Kevin got up and walked round the kitchen. 'This place

459

is a tip and you look frightful. I'd never allow Enid to let herself and our place go like this.'

Janey felt livid.

She got up and poured another drink, but nothing came out. 'It helps if you unscrew the top of the bottle,' said Kevin.

'Do you honestly think,' Janey went on furiously, 'that if you walked into Solzhenitsyn's house, he'd be dusting or putting cups in washing machines or making chutney? You bet there's a Mrs Solzhenitsyn playing the Volga boatman to calm his nerves and bringing in the samovar and caviar butties every ten minutes, and typing his manuscript, as well as keeping his house clean. Christ!'

'Enid looks after me.'

'You bet she does! Because you're so jolly rich she doesn't have to work. She doesn't have a money problem in the world, any more than Helen does. So they can spend all day washing their hair and waxing their legs and thinking about paintwork and getting your underpants whiter than ever.'

'My mother went out to work, and she cleaned the kitchen floor every day.'

'So what?' snapped Janey. 'She wasn't a writer. Writers think about writing all the time, not cleaning tickets, and if they're worried about money all the time, they can't write.'

'It'd be better,' said Kevin, 'if, instead of writing rubbish about the opposite sex which makes you restless, you scrapped that book and spent more time looking after Billy. He looked like a tramp in Athens, breeches held together with safety pins, pink shirts, dinner suit covered in stains, holes in his shoes.' He picked up a pile of envelopes, flipping through them. 'These envelopes should have been posted weeks ago. You're a slut,' he went on, turning to face her, 'and you're overweight. If you were my wife, I'd send you straight off to a health farm.'

'Ridiculously bloody expensive,' said Janey, blushing scarlet. 'I'd rather buy a padlock for the fridge. I am trying to write a book.'

'You drink too much. So does Billy. It's impairing his judgement. If he's not careful, he won't be selected for the World Championships.'

'I expect he's fed up with being hassled by you.'

'That's not the way you should talk to your husband's sponsor,' said Kevin, getting to his feet and putting down his half-finished drink. 'Well, I'm off.'

Janey was shaken. She was so used to rows with Billy ending up in bed that she couldn't cope with the progression of this one.

'Aren't you going to finish your drink?'

'No, thanks. Get some sleep, and when you're sober we'll do some straight talking.'

'It's hardly been crooked talking this evening,' said Janey sulkily, following him unsteadily to the door. In the doorway he turned, shoving his fist against her stomach, just a second before she hastily pulled it in.

'God, that zip's taken some punishment! I'll come back on Thursday and take you out to dinner,' he said.

It was all Billy's fault, thought Janey, as she shaved her legs three days later, for telling Kev to drop in on her. Beastly jumped-up creep. The bath looked as though a sheep had been sheared. Not a follicle of superfluous hair was left on her body. Her bush had started to grow again like a badly-plucked chicken, so she'd even shaved that too. She hadn't had anything except three grapefruit and two bottles of Perrier since she'd last seen Kevin. She'd cleaned the house and washed her hair and painted her nails and rubbed body lotion in all over, even into the back of her neck. She couldn't tell Billy about Kev because he hadn't rung, which boded ill too. He always rang if he won.

Oh, well, she'd be a good wife, and nice to Billy's sponsor and at least Kev would be useful for her chapter on arrivistes. Janey detested Kevin Coley, but she cleaned the bedroom most thoroughly of all, putting roses on one bedside table and the Moggie Meal Sponsored Book of Pedigree Cats beneath the Bible on the other. She felt much thinner but her nerves were jangling from so many slimming pills. Nothing was going to happen tonight, she kept telling herself, but she hadn't felt so jumpy since she'd gone to Wembley for her first date with Billy. Kev hadn't said what time he was coming. Probably he had high tea and would arrive at five.

He turned up at eight. When she answered the door he said, 'Sorry, must have come to the wrong house,' and turned back down the path.

'Kevin, have you been drinking?'

He turned, grinning. 'Is it really you? You look quite different from the lady I saw three days ago.' He stared at her for a minute. 'Wow,' he said, sliding a hand round her waist. 'You look delightful, quite the old Janey.'

For a second he fingered the spare tyres above her straining white trousers. 'You could lose another stone and a half without missing it, but you're on the way and the place smells fresher too.'

No one, reflected Janey, would be able to smell anything except Paco Raban.

'I'm only coming out with you to research my chapter on married men,' she said.

He had a buff-coloured Mercedes. Frank Sinatra's Songs for Swinging Lovers was belting out of the tape machine. Christ, he must be old to like that kind of music, thought Janey. That brushed-forward hair must cover a multitude of lines. The village boys, idly chatting and guffawing in the evening sun, stared as they passed. That'll reach Mrs Bodkin and probably Helen, by tomorrow, thought Janey.

'Lovely properties,' remarked Kev as they drove along, 'lovely old Cotswold places.'

He was wearing a white suit and a black shirt and a heavy jet medallion. You'd get a black eye if he kept it on in bed, Janey was appalled to find herself thinking. Interesting that he'd made such an effort for her. Beyond seeing that his suits were reasonably well cut in the first place, Billy didn't think about clothes. He was without vanity; that was one of the things she loved about him.

Kev took her to a very expensive restaurant in Cheltenham. The menus had no prices and, although he showed off and was very rude to waiters, snapping his fingers, complaining the wine wasn't cold enough and sending food back on principle, they treated him with undeniable deference.

'How do you keep so fit?' she asked, looking at his waistline.

'I exercise a lot. Enid and I have joined the country club. You have to be elected. I play a round of golf whenever feasible. I jog at weekends. I exercise with weights in the morning.'

Janey giggled. 'Do you swing Enid above your head?'

'Don't be silly,' said Kevin coldly.

For the first course Janey lapsed and had huge sticks of asparagus dripping in melted butter.

'Naughty,' chided Kevin. 'At least 300 calories.'

'I don't care,' said Janey, lasciviously taking an asparagus head in her mouth. 'I'll go back to grapefruit tomorrow.'

Kevin had melon and left the maraschino cherries, followed by steak, well done, with runner beans and a green salad. Janey noticed he left the spring onions. She felt a great weariness, probably because she hadn't had enough to drink. She was fed up with talking about product attributes and growth potential. Then suddenly when she thought the evening was beyond redemption, he ordered another bottle of Sancerre, and some of his cronies came over, plainly impressed by Janey.

'I'm taking care of her while Billy's abroad,' said Kev, and winked.

Suddenly Janey was enjoying herself. There was nothing like the high that went with the possible beginning to an affair. Kev kept looking at her, holding her eyes a second longer than necessary, as though he was caressing her. He was so tough, and positive, and knew exactly where he was going.

'D'you want to go somewhere and dance?' he said, as he signed the bill.

She shook her head, ashamed of the hopeless desire that was sweeping over her. As they left the restaurant, she swayed and he caught her arm.

'Sorry Kev. Don't ask a girl to drink and diet.'

It had been a clear hot day, followed by a dewy short night. They'd been haymaking. The fields had that mingled honey scent of mown grass and drying manure. As they drove home she said, 'You'll be the first man since Billy.'

'So I should hope.'

'It'll be like losing one's virginity all over again.'

Kevin put a perfectly manicured hand on her thigh. The diamond in the centre of the thick gold ring on his third finger glittered in the moonlight.

'I've wanted you since the first night we met, but you've always been so bloody superior.'

'Not a lady like Helen?'

'You're a snob. She'd never have sneered and put me down the way you have.'

'I'm sorry. I suppose I hated Billy being dependent on someone else.'

He removed one of the two bracelets on her right wrist and threw it on her lap. 'And don't jangle.'

'You jangle enough,' she said.

When they got back to the cottage, Mavis followed her round like a disapproving duenna. Kevin went to have a pee. Janey went into the kitchen. It was so hot, she opened the fridge and, getting a piece of ice out of the tray, ran it over her tits to make the nipples stand up. Then she poured herself a huge drink to steady her nerves. The next minute Kev walked in and took it from her and poured it down the sink. 'You don't need that sort of booster any more,' he said.

'I hate him,' she said to herself. 'He's everything that darling Billy isn't.'

Mavis, who'd done sterling service as a hot water bottle all winter, was outraged when Kevin tried to shut her out of the bedroom.

'She always comes in,' protested Janey.

'Not anymore, she doesn't,' said Kevin, booting her with his foot.

'You would get on well with Helen,' sighed Janey.

'I don't approve of pets in bedrooms. Ouch!' howled Kev as Mavis bit him sharply on the ankle.

It took all Janey's self-control not to giggle. There was no plaster in the house, but finally Kev, stripped off except for one of Billy's handkerchiefs tightly bound round his ankle, climbed into bed.

'I hope your alarm clock works,' he said. 'I've got a meeting in Bristol at nine-thirty.'

Janey looked at him through half-closed eyes. 'Are you sure you don't want to send me back because I'm not at room temperature?'

She put her hand on his cock, which was inching upwards and was about to add that in terms of growth potential he was not bad himself, but she didn't think he'd be amused. He made no comment about her shaved bush until afterwards.

'You do that?'

'No, Billy does.'

'Relationship still very much alive, then?'

'Yes,' said Janey.

It was very nice to be made love to by someone so scented and powdered and tasting of Gold Spot (which Janey was less keen on), but all the perfumes of Arabia couldn't conceal the feral whiff of the jungle killer. Beneath his trappings, Kev was a wide boy, a thug as ruthless as Rupert.

She was ashamed of betraying Billy by sleeping with Kev in their bed. On the other hand, it was bliss not to have to get up and go home dribbling afterwards. Kev had only brought a slimline briefcase with him. Inside was a clean shirt, a toothbrush and toothpaste in a case, and a disposable razor. He's everything that Billy's not, thought Janey once again. Perhaps that's why I fancy him and that's what I really need.

Billy rang up next day. Things weren't thrilling. He was

missing her. He'd be back on Sunday.

'Did Kev ring you? Good. Mandryka got a third yesterday, but The Bull's a bit stale. I'm going to rest him next week before the World Championship. How's the book going?'

'Fine,' said Janey, who hadn't touched it. She felt guilty but safer. Kev wouldn't let her starve.

'By the way, where were you last night?' asked Billy.

Janey's mind galloped. 'I had dinner with Helen.'

'That's nice.'

Putting down the telephone, she rang Helen and suggested they had supper at the local bistro. Before she went out she was fortified by a telephone call from Kev. She'd been waiting all day, wondering if he'd ring. She found she couldn't eat anything, so pushed her food around her plate.

'You're not pregnant, are you?' asked Helen.

'No, no. I was so disgustingly fat, I took the opportunity of Billy's being away to go on a diet. Now my stomach seems to have shrunk, thank God.'

'Don't talk to me about reducing,' sighed Helen. 'Rupert's given up liquor until after the World Championship. He's lost ten pounds and he looks great but, golly, it makes him mean.'

For once, Helen unbent a bit. Rupert had bought her a gym tunic and wanted her to dress up as a schoolgirl.

'But I can't. I've got knobbly knees and I'm terrified he's going to start fancying the real thing.'

Janey, remembering Billy's tales about Tiffany Bathgate, rather thought Rupert already had.

'I wish Billy'd occasionally look at another woman,' she said idly. 'It'd be such fun getting him back.'

Janey was doing no work on her book but the house looked absolutely marvellous. Although women deny it, they very seldom have a new man in their lives without idly thinking what he'd be like to marry. Janey Coley sounded perfectly dreadful; it really wouldn't do.

On Saturday morning, Janey steamed open their bank statement, was appalled at what she saw, hastily stuck it up again and went out and bought a pair of white dungarees, a white canvas skirt and two striped T-shirts. The weather was so lovely, she lay in the sun. She could always tell Billy she'd been typing in the garden.

Kev came and screwed her on Saturday afternoon. Both of them were sober and the pleasure was even more intense. Janey'd lost eight pounds and was beginning to feel beautiful again. Afterwards they lay in each other's arms.

'Did Billy ring you?' asked Kevin.

'Yes, not much joy. Sometimes I wish he wasn't such a good loser.'

'He's a loser,' said Kevin brutally. 'Let's make no bones about it.'

'How are we all going to cope at Les Rivaux? Billy's so sweet, he won't suspect anything, but I'm not so sure about Enid.'

Suddenly she was startled out of her wits by the door bell. It was a member of the Tory party, canvassing for a by-election.

'I'm just changing to go out,' Janey called out of the window, 'but you can rely on my vote.'

'Got to get that bloody man Callaghan out somehow,' said Kevin.

Next time the bell went Kev had to unplug himself. Janey staggered to the window. This time it was the Labour Party.

'No, you don't need to convince me; you can rely on my vote,' she said.

'That's done it,' said Kev, getting up. 'I've got to go anyway.' Janey was appalled at how miserable she felt. They had a bath together.

'Too small, really,' said Kev as he dried himself. 'You ought to come in my jacuzzi at Sunningdale. You will, one day.'

Feeling happier, Janey put on her new white dungarees, which just covered her boobs, and nothing else. Her newly washed hair divided over her brown shoulders. As she made the bed, she instinctively removed hairs, looking for

Kevidence, she told herself with a giggle. She persuaded him to have a drink before he went. They were in the drawing room when they heard a step outside. Janey went to the window. 'Expect it's the Liberal Party. Oh my God, it's Billy.'

'It's all right,' said Kev calmly. 'Billy told me you were depressed and to drop in to cheer you up. I just happened to be in the area.'

Janey patted her hair frantically in the mirror.

'Do I look as though I've just got out of bed?' she asked.

Kev laughed. 'You always do anyway.'

Billy was absolutely thrilled to see them both. He'd always been worried that they got on so badly and this would certainly make things easier. He looked awful: thoroughly tired out, his hair a tangled mess, eyes bloodshot. He smelt of curry and drink. He needs some Gold Spot, thought Janey.

'How did the last days go?' asked Kevin.

'Bloody awful. The competition's so hot because everyone's over for the World Championship. You're lucky if you get in the money at all. Here's some Arpège for you, sweetheart.' He also put down a bottle of duty free whisky.

'Your wife's been on a diet,' said Kev. 'Doesn't she look great?'

'Sensational,' said Billy. 'So does the house.' He looked around. 'Really lovely. You must have worked hard. I'm filthy. I must go and have a bath and change.'

'Have a drink first,' said Janey, sloshing three fingers of whisky into a glass. She was nervous Kev might have left some of his jewellery in the bedroom. Billy accepted it gratefully; anything to postpone the opening of the brown envelopes and his bank statement. They discussed the World Championships – he would either jump Mandryka or The Bull.

'The Bull – I mean Moggie Meal Al – is a bit stale. I'm going to rest him for the next fortnight.'

32

The gods that had blessed Billy during the first year of marriage seemed to withdraw their sponsorship during the second. The following week, Billy rang, jubilant from a show in the South, saying he'd just come first in a big class and won a £5,000 car. He was going to pop up to London in the morning for a ten o'clock appointment with Enid's gynaecologist, who'd been making some tests, then pop back to the show, compete in the afternoon, then drive the car straight home afterwards. Tracey would drive the lorry and, as the car was still being run in, he was afraid they'd both arrive in the middle of the night.

'But I really feel my luck's turning, darling.'

Janey spent the afternoon in bed with Kevin, so she was glad Billy was going to be late. At midnight the telephone rang. It was from a call box.

'Billy!'

'Yes darling.'

'Where are you?'

'On the Penscombe–Birdlip road.'

'Are you all right?'

'I don't know. I was driving home when a wall jumped out and hit me.'

'Christ.'

'I'm afraid I was a bit over the limit, and I think the car's a write-off.'

'Stay where you are,' said Janey. 'I'll come and get you.'

She drove in her nightie, frantic with worry. The first thing she saw was a concertinaed pile of scrap metal. God knows how Billy had escaped alive. Then she saw Billy sitting on the wall, singing.

> 'Billy Lloyd-Foxe sat on a wall,
> Billy Lloyd-Foxe had a great fall.
> All Kevin's horses and all Kevin's men
> Couldn't put Billy together again.'

He was absolutely plastered. She must get him home before the police came along and breathalysed him.

'Billy Lloyd-Foxe sat on a wall,' he began again.

'Shut up and get in the car.'

She had to help him in; his legs kept giving way. When they got home she helped him upstairs. He collapsed on the bed, white and shaking. There was a huge bruise on his forehead.

'Must have a pee.'

He got to his feet and, staggering towards the wardrobe, opened the door and was about to step in.

'Bill-ee, the loo's the other way.'

'Oh yes.' He took two steps back, one forward, and veered off towards the loo.

'I didn't know anyone could pee that long,' said Janey when he came back.

'I've done one minute, fifty-five seconds before now. Rupert timed me.' He collapsed on the bed again. She knelt down beside him.

'What's the matter?'

He looked at her, not focusing. 'I went to the doctor.'

'And what did he say?'

'That it's me, not you. I've got a zilch sperm count. He showed me it under the microscope. Not a tadpole in sight.'

He hung his head. 'He said we should think seriously about adoption.' Janey put her arms around him.

'Oh, angel, I'm so sorry. But it doesn't matter. Of course we can adopt.'

'But I wanted you to have my babies. You wanted one so badly and I can't give you one. Christ!'

She felt desperately sorry for him, but she couldn't help feeling relief in a way for herself, and boo sucks to his bloody mother. She put him to bed and within seconds he had passed out. He woke with a most appalling headache and went to the doctor, who said he had concussion as well and he should rest for a week. Billy ignored him. The following morning he set off with Rupert for Aachen.

Janey rang Kevin as soon as he'd gone and, feeling disloyal, told him about the car and the sperm count. In a way, she felt she'd been dealt a marked card. She'd married Billy thinking he was a star and the star had almost immediately started falling out of the firmament. That she'd contributed almost entirely to this fall didn't enter her head. She forgot how miserable she'd been, racketing from lover to lover in Fleet Street, waiting desperately for telephone calls, often spare at weekends. She remembered only the fun and excitement. Kevin's propaganda was soft-pedalled but lethal.

'Honey, Billy is simply not macho enough for you. You're like a beautiful lily. You'll only thrive if tied to a very strong stake. He's too weak, too Piscean. He's totally dominated by Rupert. He simply can't cope on his own. He's never going to get himself out of this mess. He's over the top. Everyone's saying so.'

By contrast, Kev was so positive, ordering her about, paying restaurant bills with wads of fivers. She even suspected he put her on expenses.

Billy rang her from Aachen. He sounded depressed and slightly tight. 'Darling, please don't worry about babies. I promise I'll sort us out after the World Championships. I miss you horribly. I wish you were here.'

Janey proceeded to plead with him not to ring her until he got home. 'I hate to hear you so down. It really upsets me, puts me off work. I know you'll get in the money soon.'

Feeling faintly guilty, Janey then left Mavis with Mrs Bodkin and flew off to Spain with Kev. Billy was due back on Sunday. She'd be home by Saturday lunchtime. She spent a fortune on clothes and having her hair streaked beforehand. She felt, subconsciously, that if she made the financial situation worse, some kind of confrontation would be triggered off. Kev had never mentioned any permanent

471

relationship – he was too fly for that. But the affair was certainly hotting up.

Billy got home at midday on Saturday, his heart like lead. There was no barking. Janey must have taken Mavis for a walk. He had difficulty opening the front door for letters on the doormat. He was so tired, it took him a little while to realize that among them were his own letters and postcards from Aachen. And there was the telegram he'd sent yesterday saying he was coming home early, unopened.

The house was very tidy. Harold Evans weaved furrily round his legs. But there was no sign of Janey anywhere. He felt faint with horror. Perhaps she'd been murdered or kidnapped. He poured himself a large whisky and telephoned Mrs Bodkin.

'She's gone away, researching for her book in Norfolk,' she said, 'and staying with her mother. She's coming home today. I've got Mavis. She's been as good as gold. D'you want to come and pick her up?'

Relief gave way to a dull anger. Mrs Bodkin looked secretive and over-excited when he arrived, her mouth disappearing in disapproval. She loved Billy; he was as nice a gentleman as you could find, and so thoughtful. But he should never have married that trollop.

After two more drinks back at the cottage, he heard a car draw up. There was Janey running up the drive in a faded purple T-shirt and sawn-off pink trousers. Her tortoiseshell hair was incredibly bleached by the sun (Billy didn't recognize streaking) and she was browner and thinner than ever. His stomach twisted with desire and the pain of his ulcer. All he could think of was how much he'd like to fuck her.

'Darling, how lovely! You said you weren't coming back until tomorrow,' cried Janey. 'Must have a pee.'

She didn't look as though she'd been staying with her mother, thought Billy. She never bothered to wear make-up or scent when she went down there.

'I bought you some Norfolk strawberries, darling,' she lied. Actually, she'd bought them in Cheltenham on the way from the airport, in case she needed an alibi. They went back into the house.

'Sweetheart, you look awfully pale,' said Janey, suddenly noticing. 'What's happened?'

'I sent you this telegram. You haven't read it.'

He turned away, fighting a terrible desire to break down and cry. Janey opened it with shaking hands. Had she heard something about her and Kev? Smoothing out the paper, she read: 'Mandryka broke leg. Had to be shot. Coming home. Love Billy.'

She turned in horror.

'Oh, my angel, I'm so sorry.' She went over and put her arms round his shaking shoulders. 'What happened?'

'It was my fault. He missed his jerk, hit the top pole smack, got caught up in the rest of the poles, and that was that. It was horrible.' His face worked like a little boy about to cry. 'He was such a great horse. I know he was bad-tempered, but he could be so brave.'

'Come to bed,' she said gently. 'I'll take care of you.'

Upstairs he rolled on top of her, took her perfunctorily, then immediately fell asleep.

'There's no choice,' said Billy, facing the ruins of his career next morning. 'It's The Bull for the World Championship. At least Kev's keeping away and not breathing down my neck at the moment. Christ knows what he'll say about Mandryka.'

He was away the next two days, jumping the Grade B and C horses at Crittleden. Janey spent the second afternoon in bed with Kevin, where they did more talking than copulating. Billy, said Kevin, had been drunk in Aachen when he jumped Moggie Meal Dick. That was why he put the horse wrong at the fence where he broke his leg. Everyone was talking about it.

He was gone long before Billy got home, giving Janey plenty of time to wash off scent and make-up, get back into her old clothes and be sitting dutifully at her typewriter.

'Good day?' she asked.

'Not bad. Here's *The Tatler*. Rupert gave it me. There's a

473

picture of Tab and Helen. I think Rupe's bought up every copy, he's so chuffed.'

Billy went upstairs and changed into his dressing gown, secured with his old Harrovian tie; the belt had been lost years ago. As there was no sign of dinner, he poured himself a drink and then started opening the new pile of brown envelopes. He started to tremble. He knew Janey had been depressed about babies and probably needed to cheer herself up, but these bills for clothes were ludicrous. And how the hell could she have spent £50 at the hairdressers? She hadn't even had a haircut. He poured himself another drink and sat down on the sofa.

'Darling, we must talk about money.'

Janey, however, was deep in *The Tatler*. 'Oh look, there's Mike Pardoe, and there's Rupert's mother. She is amazingly well preserved. She must be over fifty.'

Billy tried again. 'I've just been through the returned cheques. The bank say they're going to bounce anything more we submit. Soon, I won't be able to feed the horses.'

'Oh, dear,' said Janey in mock horror. 'Of course the horses always come before everything else.'

'How long d'you think it'll be before the book's finished?'

'How can I tell? Oh, that is a sweet one of Tab, and Helen looks marvellous. She is so *bloody* photogenic. And there's Caroline Manners. What an incredibly plain child.'

'You said July, last time I asked.'

'More likely October.'

'So it won't be published this year?'

'Nope. Oh, look, Henrietta Pollock got engaged. Poor man.'

Billy's heart sank. He was hoping to keep the manager sweet by a promise of £14,000 by Christmas.

He tried again. 'We simply can't go on like this. We've got an overdraft of £30,000. We owe the tax man twenty grand and the builders fifty grand and the VAT man's threatening to take us to court, and you spend £50 at the hairdressers, and £250 on clothes, expecting me not to notice. D'you take me for a complete fool?'

'Not complete. Pity you pranged the car. Oh, there's Ainsley Hibbert. She's gone blonde. Not a bad guy with her, too.'

'Janey, have you listened to a word I've said?'

'Yes, I have. We owe rather a lot of money: about £100,000, in fact. You'll have to tap darling Mumsie, won't you? She won't let poor Billy starve.'

Billy was having difficulty keeping his temper.

'If the book's not going to be finished yet, could you do some journalism, just to pay the more pressing bills?'

Janey got up. 'I must go and put on the parsnips.'

'I don't want any dinner. If you honestly think I can eat . . .'

'It doesn't seem to stop you drinking. Why don't *you* go out and win something? It's awfully boring being married to a failure.'

Billy put his head in his hands.

'Why d'you always try and make me feel small?'

'You are small,' said Janey. 'You told me you'd lost a lot of weight recently.'

'For Christ's sake, can't you take anything seriously? If we really try, I know we can get straight.'

'Borrow something from Rupert.'

'He's pushed himself, at the moment.'

'Paying for the new indoor swimming pool,' said Janey, walking out of the room.

Two minutes later Billy followed her, putting his arms round her. 'Angel, we can't afford to fight.'

Janey laughed bitterly. 'I should have thought that was the only thing we *could* afford to do.'

The telephone rang. Billy went to answer it. 'Oh, hullo. Yes, I see. I quite understand. It was very good of you to let me know. Good luck, anyway.' Very slowly he put the receiver down; as he turned he seemed to have aged twenty years.

'That was Malise. I've been dropped for the World Championships. He wanted me to know before I read it in tomorrow's papers. They've selected Jake Lovell instead.'

What, thought Janey, was Kev going to say, stuck with a tent in Les Rivaux and all his male customers revved up for a stag freebie full of Oh la la's?

33

Although there was colossal prestige in being picked for the
Olympics, it meant one only competed against amateurs.
The competition the riders wanted to win almost more,
therefore, was the World Championship, which took place
every two years, midway between the Olympic games, and
which was open to amateurs and professionals alike. The
Championships were also considered more of a test of
horsemanship, because in the last leg the four finalists had
to jump a round on each others' horses.

As well, more and more show jumpers were forced to
turn professional. 'Vot is zee point,' as Ludwig told Dudley
Diplock in an interview, 'in competing at zee Olympics,
when so many of zee best riders are banned, and only
votching zee event on television?'

It was with considerable trepidation, at six-thirty a.m.
on a Tuesday in mid-July, that Jake set off with Fen and
Tanya for Les Rivaux in the lorry, to take the ferry at
Southampton. The lorry had been loaded up with hay,
hard feed and woodshaving bedding the night before. Tory
was to follow later with the car, the caravan and the
children. Everything was planned to the last 't' – including
a large jar of lemon sherbets for Macaulay. Even so it
turned out to be a nightmare journey. The temperature was
up in the eighties. Cow parsley along the motorway verges
had given way to hogweed, holding its flat disks up to a
cloudy grey sky, through which the sun shone opaque like
an Alka Seltzer. Jake drove, Tanya map-read, Fen kept
them both supplied with cups of black coffee.

As they neared the coast, the sky darkened. At the port

Fen lost the horses' health papers and the entire lorry had to be turned out, before she found them where they should have been all the time, in the horses' passports. By now, they had missed two ferries and the horses, picking up the vibes of anxiety, were stamping and restless. After a further delay, despite blackening skies and large, white-tipped agitated waves, the ferry decided to sail. A storm blew up in mid-Channel, bucketing the boat from side to side and throwing Fen's new pony, the young and comparatively inexperienced Desdemona, into such a panic she nearly kicked the box out.

Fen, having had repeated strips torn off her by Jake for losing the health papers, was further upset by two lorry-loads of little calves on the boat, mooing piteously, with their pathetic faces peering out between the slats. In turn, she went and tore a strip off their driver for not giving them any water.

Finally, they reached the French port at seven o'clock and set off for Les Rivaux. Jake was going mad at being stuck behind juggernauts, but this was Fen's first trip to France and she couldn't contain a surge of excitement, as the sun came out and they drove past orchards, poplar-lined rivers and a ravishing château, half-hidden by trees, its reflection glimmering in a lake. She was bitterly disappointed that her hero, Billy Lloyd-Foxe, hadn't been selected. He'd bought her a drink at Westerngate; not that that meant much, for he'd been buying everyone drinks. But perhaps she might meet some handsome Frenchman at the World Championship who'd sweep her off to his château and make fantastic love to her behind peeling grey shutters. Her dreams were rudely shattered by a loud bang. The lorry swerved terrifyingly. Somehow, Jake managed to steer it into the slow lane and, despite frenzied screeching of tyres from all sides, avoided a crash. They had blown a tyre, causing the most frightful traffic jams, which resulted in apopleptic Frenchmen, no doubt missing their dinners, leaning continually on their horns, which did nothing to improve Jake's nerves.

Eventually, just as the breakdown van arrived and towed them into the side of the road, a vast dark blue juggernaut with the familiar emerald green words 'Rupert Campbell-Black, Great Britain' on the side, flashed past, blowing a derisive tantivy on the horn and making no attempt to stop and help.

It was three o'clock in the morning, and many more cups of black coffee later, before they finally rumbled into the horse-box park to find, as a final straw, that two of their boxes had been appropriated by Rupert's horses and a third by a horse belonging to someone named Dino Ferranti.

'He's the American number three,' said Jake.

Fen loved Jake, despite having so many strips torn off her that she was practically fleshless. She knew this kind of hassle was the last thing he needed before a championship. He was all for putting the horses in other stables and sorting it out in the morning, but Fen, seething with protective indignation, was determined to drag Rupert's new groom, Dizzy, out of bed.

It wasn't hard to find Rupert's caravan, even though it was parked some way from the others under an oak tree. Every light was blazing and such sounds of laughter and revelry disturbed the hot summer night that even the stars looked disapproving.

Throwing open the door, she found Rupert, Ludwig and a languid very good-looking boy with streaked blonde hair, lazy grey eyes, and an olive complexion playing strip poker. Dizzy, wearing only a G-string, was stretched out on one of the bench seats. Another beautiful dark-haired girl was sitting on Rupert's knee, wearing one of his striped shirts and nothing else. Ludwig was down to his underpants, a riding hat and one sock. The languid boy was just in jeans and Rupert, who was off the drink and smoking a joint, was the only one fully dressed. They were all high as kites, laughing uproariously and half-watching a blue film on the video, in which a plump redhead was doing unmentionable things to a supine Father Christmas.

Having glanced at the film, Fen went crimson, and

looked back at the table, hastily averting her eyes as one of the brunette's breasts fell out of the striped shirt.

'*Bon soir*,' said Rupert. '*Asseyez-vous*. It's 50p in the back stalls.'

'Come on, honey,' drawled the handsome boy in a strong Southern accent, his eyes crossing like a Siamese cat. 'Come and sit on ma knee.'

'No, you come and neck wiz me,' said Ludwig, getting to his feet and clicking his bare and socked heels together.

'You're all disgusting,' stormed Fen. 'And what's more,' she said turning on Rupert, 'you and some creep named Dino Ferranti have stolen our stables.'

'Aw c'mon, honey, come over here,' said the American boy, holding out long, sunburnt hands.

'Well, you'd better find somewhere else to put your donkeys,' said Rupert. 'You haven't met Dino Ferranti, have you?'

'No, nor do I want to,' said Fen, losing her temper. 'Look,' she screamed, waving the papers under Rupert's nose, '*numero quatre-vingt et un, deux, trois, quatre*. It's as plain as the *nez* on *votre visage*.'

'We didn't realize they were your stables,' said Dizzy, pouting.

'I suppose you're too thick to read, like most of Rupert's grooms.'

'Temper, temper,' said Rupert.

'You bloody well come and shift them. If you'd had the decency to stop and help on the motorway, we'd have arrived at the same time as you and there wouldn't be this stupid muddle. I've never met anyone so deficient in team spirit.'

'What d'you want me to do?' asked Rupert. 'Start singing Forty Years On? Billy's the singer, and he's not been selected, thanks to your fucking brother-in-law.'

Fen didn't rise. She turned and went down the steps.

'All right, if you won't move your horses, I'll let them out.'

'Don't play silly games,' snapped Rupert. 'You'll regret

it. Come on Dino, it's your deal.'

'Who's that? She's kinda cute,' drawled the American boy, taking a swig out of the whisky bottle and handing it to Ludwig.

'Jake Lovell's sister-in-law,' said Rupert.

'Wass he like?'

'Hell. He's got a chip or, as my wife would say, a French Fry on his shoulder. His lack of charm seems to have rubbed off on her.'

Five minutes later, Dino lost the round and had to take off his jeans. Getting up to unzip his flies, he looked out of the window.

'Beautiful night,' he drawled. 'Moonlight's bright as day. Look, there's the Big Dipper. Ah don't know if Ah'm imagining things, but Ah just saw a grey horse trotting past the window.'

Ludwig got unsteadily to his feet and peered out.

'It's Snakepit and zee other horse,' he said. 'Zee leetle Maxvell ees taken zem avay. You better pull zee thumb out, Rupert.'

Dino Ferranti started to laugh. 'Well, I'll be damned.'

In a flash, Rupert had tipped the brunette onto the floor and was out of the caravan, streaking across the grass in his bare feet.

'Come back,' he bellowed to Fen.

Fen trotted on, keeping a safe distance ahead of him. 'Not till you promise to get your horses out of our stables.'

Despite the month off drink and two miles jogging every morning, Rupert couldn't catch up with her. His language deteriorated.

'Tut Tut,' said Fen, 'and in front of a lady too. If you don't promise, I'll let them loose in the forest. They need a break. Can't be much fun being owned by a revolting bully like you.'

For five minutes, which seemed an eternity to Rupert, she cantered slowly ahead until she was under the dark brow of the forest.

'Well?' she said.

Rupert agreed. 'All right, we'll move them. Now give them back to me, you little bitch.'

'And have you run me down? I'll take them back and tie them up *outside* your stables.'

'I'll sue you for this.'

'We could sue you for pinching our stables,' and making a wide circle, she galloped off, yelling over her shoulder, 'I hope you sleep horribly.'

For grooms there is no lying-in. Two and a half hours later, Fen had to stagger out of bed to feed and skip out the horses. Having not eaten the day before, after being sick on the boat, she felt desperately hungry. On the way back to the lorry for some breakfast, she bumped into Humpty's groom, Bridie. After swapping notes about their respective horses, they decided to go and have breakfast together.

'Going's bloody hard,' said Bridie, gazing at the ground, which was splitting and cracking like a great brown jigsaw. 'No sign of rain, either; not going to suit Lord Campbell-Black.' She lowered her voice. 'He's been overjumping all his horses. I saw them at Crittleden last week. They'd just come on from the Royal and from Aachen. Arcturus was lying down in his box, so exhausted I thought he was dead. It was sheer exhaustion. They haven't had a break since January. Arcy can't move unless he's drugged up to the eyeballs. When the effect wears off he's in agony.'

'Who's Rupert going to jump in the Championship?'

'Snakepit,' said Bridie.

Fen groaned. 'Trust Rupert to put in a sod.'

'Needs two people in the stable, one to groom, one to keep an eye on him. He's got a terrible cow kick. Already killed one of Rupert's Jack Russells.'

'Perhaps he won't make the final.'

'On current form he can't fail.'

They went into the breakfast tent. Fen was piling apricot jam on to her fourth croissant when Bridie asked her if she'd seen Dino Ferranti.

'I met him briefly last night,' said Fen coldly.

'Don't you think he's devastating?' sighed Bridie. 'Those

482

snake hips and those terrific shoulders, and that angelically depraved face. And he dresses so well.'

'He was half-naked when I saw him,' said Fen.

After that the whole story came out.

Bridie looked at Fen in awe.

'You didn't let out Rupert's horses?'

'Yes, I did.'

'And rode Snakepit.'

'Yes.'

'Probably didn't play up because you weren't frightened of him. Mind you, I think Rupert's devastating, too. If he lifted a finger in my direction I'd go.'

'I wouldn't. I think he's hell.'

Four hours later Ludwig and Dino Ferranti, both in dark glasses and both with fearful hangovers not improved by the midday sun, tottered down to the stables to work their horses. They paused at the sight of Isa Lovell, not a day over six, cantering Macaulay round the practice ring.

'OK, Fen,' he shouted in a shrill Birmingham accent, 'put it up,' and, cantering towards the upright, cleared 5ft 3ins without any trouble.

Dino Ferranti had the puffy eyes of the heavy sleeper, but at this moment he couldn't believe them.

'Look at that!'

'I'd rather not,' said Ludwig. 'With kids zat good, I'm not going to be World Champion much longer.'

They stopped and watched for a few minutes, as the child put the horse over several more jumps.

'That's the girl from last night,' said Dino.

'Ha,' said Ludwig. 'Mees Maxwell, Jake Lovell's groom. Maybe that's zee horse Jake's going to jump. Looks very familiar. No, it can't be.'

'Looks bloody well,' said Dino.

Les Rivaux is one of the most beautiful seaside ports in Brittany. The showground is about a mile outside the town, half-ringed, on the inshore side, by the forest in which Fen had threatened to let Rupert's horses loose. In front lies the

483

sea. On the day of the first warm-up class of the show, it lay like a film of mother of pearl on the platinum-blond sand.

'Too many foreigners,' said a large English lady tourist disapprovingly, as two Italians nearly fell off their horses at the sight of Rupert's groom, Dizzy, riding past in a tight turquoise T-shirt and no bra.

Les Rivaux was already swarming with Dutch riders in leather coats, Portuguese with hot eyes and chattering teeth, Argentinian generals, Americans in panamas and dark glasses, all gabbling away in different languages, all lending a Ritzy, illicit flavour to the show ground. The weather was still muggy and hot and, although the swallows were flying low and the cows lying down, there was no sign of rain to soften the punishingly hard ground.

A large crowd gathered to watch this first event, a small speed class in which most of the riders had entered the horses they would later jump in the World Championship. In the big afternoon class, they would jump their second horses.

Rumours had already begun to circulate round the showground that Jake Lovell was jumping one of Rupert's old horses. Jake was not to be drawn, nor was Fen, and when Rupert first saw Tanya leading Macaulay and Desdemona quietly round the Collecting Ring that morning, he stared for a minute at the familiar big black horse with dinner-plate feet and the ugly white face, but made absolutely no comment.

It was a mark of Rupert's nerve that it had no effect on his riding. He continued to bitch and mob up the other riders, which was always his way of psyching himself up before a class, then produced a round that threw everyone else into a panic. Not only was his speed faster than light, but, from the way he had to exert every ounce of brute strength to keep Snakepit on course, the horse was obviously a devil to ride.

Guy de la Tour, the star on whom the French crowd had pinned their hopes, jumped a slower but stylish clear to a storm of bravoes. He was followed by Ludwig, recovered from his hangover, but who, despite Clara's long legs, couldn't catch Rupert. Speed was not Macaulay's strong point; he was too careful and jumped too high. Jake was very happy with a slow clear, putting him in 11th place.

As the Americans were hot favourites for the Nations' Cup, there was a lot of interest in how the horses would react to a French course. Neither the number one male rider, Carol Kennedy, nor the number two, the red-headed Mary Jo Wilson, had found their form yet, and notched up eight and four faults respectively.

Interest was therefore centred on Dino Ferranti, riding a young liver chestnut thoroughbred called President's Man. Dino had never competed in Europe before, but even Fen, who'd had another row with him in the practice ring because his groom dismantled the upright when she was about to jump it, had to admit he was a glorious rider. For the purist, he lounged in the saddle like a cowboy and sat a little too far back, but he was so supple he seemed made of rubber, and was able to throw his weight completely off the horse while it was in the air, yet somehow touch down smoothly as he landed.

Loose mane and long tail flying in the American fashion, President's Man loped round the course like a cotton-tail rabbit. There was consternation and raised eyebrows all round when the clock said he was three seconds faster than Rupert.

'Well done,' said everyone as he came out.

'That's very lucky to win the first class in the show,' said Humpty. 'That is a handsome animal. Who's he by?'

'Great, our first win,' said Mary Jo, rushing up and hugging Dino. 'That's Rupert second, Ludwig third and Guy fourth.'

'Do you mind?' said a shrill voice, barging through the circle of mutual admiration. 'I haven't been in yet.'

'*Soixante-six,*' called the collection ring steward. '*Numero soixante six.*'

'*Je suis ici,*' shouted Fen, ramming her hat down over her nose and galloping into the ring. Desdemona was only 14.3, little more than a pony. Her father was a thoroughbred, her mother a polo pony, and she was fast and nippy, with amazing acceleration between fences, but, like her mistress, her courage at this stage was much greater than her technical skill.

Laughing and joking, Ludwig, Dino, Rupert and Guy had their backs to the ring, all admiring the comely Mary Jo. Suddenly they heard cheering from the crowd and, turning, saw the little roan mare flying round the ring. She turned in the air over the stile, whipped over the double and took the wall at full gallop, clearing it by inches. Jake put his hands over his eyes as she thundered down towards the combination.

Looking in wonderment through splayed fingers, he saw her pop, pop, pop over the three fences like a ping-pong ball. Knocking a tenth of a second off Dino's time, she had to gallop half way round the ring before she could pull up. Pink in the face with elation, she made a discreet but perfectly noticeable V-sign at the group round Mary Jo as she came out of the ring. Darklis and Isa were yelling like savages.

Jake bawled her out for 'bloody irresponsibility'. 'You could have brought her down at any moment.' Then his face softened, 'But it was a great round.'

They were calling for the winners. Fen stuck her nose in the air and rode into the ring. Dino caught up with her. In a white stock, black coat and the tightest of white breeches, with her newly washed hair tucked into a net, she was almost unrecognizable as the angry child who'd barged into Rupert's caravan the previous night.

'Lady, ah sure underestimated you.'

Fen ignored him.

'You look real pretty when you're mad, but ah sure wish you'd smile.'

'I will when they give me my rosette.'

'Ah thought you were Jake Lovell's groom.'

'So I am, so are Isa and Darklis. We all muck in. Everyone's everything.'

'Are you going to ride that pony in the World Championships?'

Fen patted Desdemona lovingly. 'No. I'm too young.'

'Thank Christ for that,' said Dino, looking them up and down. 'I guess it's only a matter of time, though.'

News of Rupert's strip poker party and Fen's moonlight flit with his horses, spread round the ground like wildfire, only rivalled as gossip by stories of Billy's drinking, and speculation as to whether Jake's horse, now registered as Nightshade, was really Macaulay. Then, an Italian rider found a bucket of bran in his horse's stables, not put there by any of his entourage, and immediately everyone started panicking about sabotage. Security was tightened up all around. The Americans and the Germans hired security guards with rotweillers. Even Rupert went so far as to employ a man to sleep all night outside Snakepit's box.

'Terrified Fen'll let him out again,' said Dizzy.

'I bet you wouldn't have taken him,' she added to Fen, 'if you'd known what a sod he can be – only equalled at the moment by his master. I don't know what the hell's the matter with him.'

Rupert was missing Billy. In every major competition he'd ever jumped, Billy'd been there to fool around with, bounce ideas off and talk out problems. Rupert was too proud to go to Malise for advice. He'd lecture him and then be irritated if Rupert didn't follow the advice. Helen was too ignorant and not really interested.

Hyped up to a peak of physical fitness, Rupert longed to swim in the sea, but thought it might put his eyes out for the Nations' Cup tomorrow. He longed for a drink, but he'd vowed not to touch a drop till the championship was over. French girls mobbed him, if anything, more than English ones, but he was finding easy lays less and less satisfactory, and Helen's arrival the following day would put the kibosh on that. He was also livid with Helen for not bringing out the children. Lavinia de la Tour had offered them the run of Guy's château, thirty miles away, but Helen was too nervous about French food and water and rabid dogs and the effect of the heatwave on Marcus's delicate skin. Tab, whom Rupert was dying to show off, Helen felt, was too young.

Rupert had never suffered from nerves before, but he didn't want to ride Macaulay in the final. He'd watched the gypsy rabble of the Lovell gang – those beautiful children, with their frightful Birmingham accents and their fearlessness, swarming all over Jake's horses, polishing and plaiting them up, kissing them, playing round their feet as though they were big dogs. He'd never seen horses so relaxed or children so happy. He compared Marcus's cringing terror and he vowed Tab would never grow up like that.

He was drawn to Dino Ferranti, whom he'd met while jumping on the Florida circuit, as he was drawn to Ludwig, as the rich, beautiful and successful are invariably drawn to one another.

Dino reminded Rupert a little of Billy. They were both easy-going and had the same sense of the ridiculous. But at twenty-six, Dino was tougher and more ambitious. He was vainer than Billy too, with his pale silk shirts, his beautiful suits, his expensive cologne and his ash-blond hair that fell perfectly into place, however much he ran his hands through it. But beneath that almost effeminate languor, Dino had a will of iron, and physical strength like Rupert that allowed him to be in the thick of a party until five o'clock in the morning, yet still able to wipe the smile off the opposition next day.

Dino's grandfather had been an Italian immigrant who loved messing around with flowers and had started a small perfume factory. He produced a scent called Ecstasy, which became as famous and enduringly popular as Joy, Arpège or Chanel No. 5. His son, Paco, had a shrewd head and capitalized enough on his father's talent to become a millionaire, as President and founder of Ferranti Inc, which made all kinds of scents, colognes, soaps and aftershaves, which sold worldwide. Later he diversified and started an engineering business. His three elder sons all went dutifully into the company. But Dino, his favourite, the youngest and most beautiful, rebelled. From an early age, he was only interested in horses, riding his own ponies and, even though he was beaten for it, his father's race horses. Assuming he would grow out of this obsession, Paco let his son ride as much as he liked, feeling deeply relieved when Dino reached six feet by the time he was seventeen, obviously too tall for a flat-race jockey. At six foot two, he was too tall for a jump jockey and turned instead to show-jumping, but there was no way he could make big money out of the sport in America. His brothers complained he always smelled of the stables and flew off to further the cause of the Ferranti empire whenever he came home.

Deciding to cut his losses, Dino enrolled at Massachusetts Institute of Technology to major in business economy. When he took his freshman exams, his papers were exemplary until the last exam, when, such was his despair, he staggered in dead drunk in a dinner jacket just as everyone was picking up their pens. Waving a half-empty gin bottle, he proceeded to offer it round to other shocked and frantically shushing candidates, before passing out at his desk.

Such was the brilliance of his other papers, all straight As, that the examiners overlooked such a lapse. Dino was elected president of the next year's class. Paco was so delighted that the day Dino was due to come home for the vacation a plane landed on the campus airstrip – Paco's reward for his son's success.

Dino promptly flew home, kissed his mother and, having thanked his father, asked for a private word in the library.

'Dad, business isn't for me.'

Paco was astounded. 'But you're doing so well.'

'I didn't want to embarrass you by having a Ferranti fail, and I guess I hate losing too, but I don't want to spend the rest of my life in an office. You've got other sons to do that. I'm going to jump horses.'

Paco sighed. 'Still, still. Why can't you do both?'

'Because horses need you twenty-four hours a day, just as a successful business does. I'm a great rider, I know it. I want to be up there competing against the best in the world. It is the only life I want to lead.'

'Are you asking or telling me?'

'Telling,' said Dino gently. 'If you're prepared to help me, I'll be eternally grateful. If not, I'll make it on my own.'

'You can't make a living out of it.'

'In Europe, I can.' He saw the sadness in his father's eyes. 'I'm not a loser. I won't starve. I'd never forgive myself if I didn't try.'

Paco looked at his favourite son reflectively. 'All straight As – all but one, when you were loaded. I never guessed how much you were hating it. That takes guts. Maybe you'll make a go of it. I'll make a bargain with you. I'll help you out for the first five years, so you can stay in the States.'

Five years later, almost to the day, Dino arrived in Les Rivaux.

The World Championships start with a Nations' Cup. The twenty riders in this event who have the least faults go through to the next leg, which consists of three gruelling individual competitions. The four riders who average out the least faults in these go through to the final. A compulsory rest day follows. Then the final takes place in which each of the four riders jump their own horse, and then in turn the horses of the other three riders.

Great Britain had patchy fortunes in the Nations' Cup. Rupert produced two dazzling clears on Snakepit. Humpty, trying to impress a new sponsor, jumped disastrously with over twenty faults in both rounds. Driffield went clear, then went to pieces in the second round. Jake had eight faults in the first round, then went clear.

The Americans jumped brilliantly; so did the Germans, putting them first and second, with the British a poor third. This meant four American riders, four Germans, Rupert, Jake, Wishbone, Piero Fratinelli, the Italian No. 1, a couple of Mexicans and, to the ecstasy of the French crowd, Guy de la Tour, went through to the semi-final.

By the third and final competition of the semi-final,

Ludwig and Rupert were so far ahead on points that they virtually only had to stand up to get into the last four. The class consisted of ten enormous fences, with a jump-off against the clock. Rupert got eight faults, Ludwig twelve, which ensured them a place in the final. Dino went clear. Only Jake and Count Guy were left to jump.

'It'll be you, me, Ludwig and Guy,' Rupert said to Dino as he came out of the ring. 'One from each country. Very suitable.'

Jake was so incensed by Rupert's contemptuous assumption that there was no likelihood he would make the final, that he was prepared to carry Macaulay over the fences if necessary.

'You must win this class, even to qualify,' said Malise, giving Macaulay a pat as Jake rode off into the ring.

Macaulay was obviously determined to give all his supporters a heart attack. Fooling around, pretending to shy at the crowd, bucking and getting up to all sorts of antics between fences, he nevertheless went clear, kicking up his heels in a sort of equine V-sign.

Everyone got out their calculators, trying to work out whether he was in or not. In came Guy, who was ahead of both Dino and Jake on points. Laughing, handsome, he was turned on by a big crowd, particularly of his own people. He could feel the waves of love and admiration wafting over like a hot blow dryer.

Coming up to the penultimate fence, a huge upright which had unsettled everyone except Macaulay, Guy's spectacular black gelding, Charlemagne, gave it a mighty clout. Everyone held their breath, but the pole stayed put. Alas, Guy made the mistake of looking round, like Orpheus, and the Eurydice he lost was his place in the championship. His concentration snapped and he put Charlemagne wrong at the combination. The horse hadn't enough impulsion to get far enough over the first element and demolished the second and the third. The crowd groaned. All round the course, riders and their retinues were frantically tapping their calculators.

'It's worse than A-level Maths,' grumbled Fen.

Next moment, Malise came up to Jake, with a barely suppressed expression of delight on his face.

'You're in,' he said.

Americans were crowding around Dino, punching him on the arm.

'We're in, we're in.'

No one dared show any elation in the face of such bitter French despair. Financially and, from the point of view of national morale, it was essential that the host nation had at least one rider in the final. The crowd were too stunned to clap. The commentator was too stunned even to translate into English his announcement that Rupert, Dino, Ludwig and Jake would go through.

Dino and Jake decided not to jump off. They wanted to rest their horses for the final. They rode into the ring together. Twenty thousand francs would be divided between them, but not the huge vase that went to the winner. It looked just like an urn.

'Oh, my God, we can't exactly break it in half,' said Dino.

'You better keep it, Jake. I'm sure it's to put your ashes in.'

'Hell,' thought Rupert, 'I'm going to have to ride that black bugger after all.'

34

It was one thing to get through to the final but quite another to have to think about it for the next two days. Ludwig was lucky. The German team liked each other, ate, drank, sightsaw, sunbathed and worked their horses together. All were firmly rooting for Ludwig. A German victory was all that mattered. Dino received the same support from the American team.

Malise sighed and wished he could unite the British in the same way. But Rupert, Humpty and Driffield were all individuals motivated by self-interest and ambition and frantic jealousy. Nor could you expect any solidarity from Jake Lovell, a loner who liked to keep to himself at shows. At earlier shows, Billy had kept everyone sweet, particularly Rupert. Now he was absent, tempers and hatreds flared up. Driffield's persistent grumbling was getting on everyone's nerves. Humpty was in despair, knowing his newly acquired sponsors would be far from happy he hadn't made the final. Rupert and Jake made no secret of their mutual animosity. It was ironic, thought Malise, that each would get more of a kick from finishing in front of the other than winning the championship.

Determined to create some sense of union, however, Malise insisted the entire team and their wives, including Fen, went out to dinner that night to celebrate having two British riders in the final. Tomorrow was a compulsory rest day, so it didn't matter if they suffered a few hangovers.

Jake promptly refused, on the grounds they couldn't get a babysitter. Alas, they got back to their hotel to find the patron's wife, who had given them frightful rooms overlooking a noisy main road, had suddenly discovered from the evening paper that she had as a guest a potential World Champion. Nothing, she insisted, was too much for Monsieur Lovell. She and her husband would immediately move out of their quiet bedroom overlooking the courtyard, so Jake and Tory could have the double bed and ensure two good nights' sleep before the great ordeal.

All this was overheard by Malise, who was staying at the same hotel. Perhaps, he asked, Madame would be prepared to babysit that evening.

To Jake's fury, Madame was only too 'appy. Darklis and Isa would have dinner in the kitchen and watch *The Sound of Music* on television. It is arguable whether Monsieur or Jake felt more like strangling Madame at that moment.

By the time their rooms had been sorted out, Fen, Jake and Tory were the last to arrive for dinner. The restaurant at the end of the town took up the entire ground floor of an 18th century château on the edge of an estuary. Gleaming virginia creeper jacketed the walls and threatened to close the shutters. Pale crimson geraniums cascaded into the khaki water.

'Smell that wine and garlic,' sighed Fen ecstatically. 'Oh, cheer up, Jake. At least it'll be a change from hamburgers and Mars bars.'

Malise, suntanned and elegant in a cream linen suit and dark blue spotted tie, and Colonel Roxborough, sweating in grey flannel, rose to welcome them. But not before Rupert had turned to Humpty saying, 'Here comes Prince Charmless and the two ugly sisters.'

'Rupert,' implored Helen, blushing scarlet. 'Hi, Jake. Congratulations. I was so excited when I heard you were in.'

'As the actress said to the Bishop,' said Rupert. 'You're privileged, Jake. You must be the only person who's excited my dear wife in years. I certainly don't.'

Helen had arrived at Les Rivaux after a long, long detour to visit some cathedral, so she had missed seeing Rupert go through to the final. They'd had a row because she refused to sleep with him, insisting she must wash her hair before dinner.

'That's not true. I'm over the moon about you making the final. It's just marvellous to have two British riders there.'

'Must be difficult for you, Helen. Do you support us or the Yanks?' asked Humpty.

'Particularly when you see Dino Ferranti,' said Humpty's wife, Doreen. 'He's out of this world.'

'Come on, sit down,' said Malise. 'You go next to Doreen, Jake, and Fen can go between me and Rupert, and Tory on Rupert's other side.'

'Tory's going to need a long spoon,' said Fen, glaring at Rupert.

'*Touché*,' he said, and laughed.

'What's everyone going to have to drink?' said Colonel Roxborough. 'Still on the wagon, Rupert?'

'Only till Saturday. Then I'm going to get legless. Christ, I'm starving.'

He looked across at a side table where a waiter was slicing up a long French loaf with a bread knife. 'Just imagine that that was one's cock,' he said with a shudder.

Thinking she must make some attempt at conversation, but feeling eighteen and a fat deb again, Tory asked Rupert how Tabitha was.

'Fine,' said Rupert and proceeded to ignore her totally, talking across to Colonel Roxborough about Count Guy's *débâcle* and staring at a luscious brunette at a table nearby.

Jake longed to rescue Tory but he was trapped by Doreen Hamilton. Insulated by successive waves of exultation and apprehension at making the final, he looked at the slice of lemon in his gin and Schweppes, counting the pips: I will win, I won't, I will. Must have the best of three. There were two pips in Mrs Hamilton's lemon: I will, I won't. Despondency struck. Then he looked across at Colonel Roxborough's glass, two slices, two pips on the top: he bent his head; three on the bottom, which added up to an uneven number. Relief overwhelmed him; he would win.

Doreen Hamilton looked at him oddly. 'What *are* you doing?'

Jake grinned. 'Counting lemon pips. Odd numbers I win, evens I don't.'

'That's cheating. You start with an odd, so there's more chance of ending on an odd. Tell me,' she lowered her voice, 'how is Macaulay going to behave when Rupert gets on his back.'

'Very badly, I hope.'

Rupert was making no secret of the fact that he found the company boring.

Doreen's incessant chatter gave Jake plenty of opportunity to look around. Helen, with her sadness and red hair, reminded him of autumn. He noticed the rapt expression on Malise's face as he talked to her. So that was the way the wind blew. She'd be much happier with Malise, thought Jake. He'd look after her, but he was far too upright and old-school-tie to make a play for her.

'Soupe de Bonne Femme.' Driffield was looking at the menu. 'What's Bonne Femme?'

'Good woman,' said Rupert. 'Of absolutely no interest to anyone.'

At last the food, and several bottles of wine, arrived.

'I'm sure this octopus comes out of a tin,' grumbled Driffield.

'I wish I'd chosen hors d'oeuvres like you, Fen,' said Humpty, looking disconsolately at his piece of *pâté* the size of a matchbox.

'I must say I'm terribly hungry,' said Fen, spearing an anchovy.

Rupert was eating cepes. He glanced up and caught Fen looking at him. 'A franc for your thoughts.'

'I was hoping one was poisonous.'

'Even if it were I'd be OK for the final, have no fear. Do you honestly think Hopalong Chastity stands a chance against me?'

'He'll beat the pants off you,' snapped Fen, 'and don't call him that.'

496

'Hasn't got the big-match temperament. He'll go to pieces.'

'He beat you at Olympia.'

'This is the big time.'

For a second he stared straight into her eyes, and suddenly it was as though he was putting a spell on her.

'You're going to be a knockout in a couple of years,' he said, lowering his voice.

'Big deal for an ugly sister.'

'You heard, did you? I'm sorry.'

Almost matter-of-factly, as if he were examining a horse, he ran an appraising finger down her cheek. She winced away, aware of the bumpiness of her complexion.

'Those spots would go with regular sex, and you'd soon lose that puppy fat,' he said. 'You ought to come and work for me. I'd let you ride in all the senior classes. You're ready for it. That was a stunning win at the beginning of the week. Jake's holding you back.'

'Like Revenge, I suppose. I don't forget so quickly,' she said, her colour mounting.

'Revenge won two medals,' he said. 'I'm quite serious. You and I'd make a great team, in bed and out.'

He was speaking almost into his buttonhole, so none of the table except she could hear.

'What about Helen?' hissed Fen. 'I suppose she doesn't understand you.'

For a minute the candlelight flickered on the predatory, cold, unsmiling face. Then he laughed, making him human again.

'On the contrary, I don't understand her. She uses much too long words.'

Fen gave a shriek of laughter. Then, as the smile faded and he went on staring at her, she was appalled to feel her stomach curl, overwhelmed with a squirming, helpless longing for him.

Her plate of hors d'oeuvres was taken away, hardly touched.

Humpty looked reproachful. 'What a waste!'

497

Nor could she eat her chicken Kiev.

Jake, deep in conversation with Doreen and Colonel Roxborough about other people's horses, had also drunk a great deal more than he'd eaten. Suddenly, he glanced down the table and saw little Fen staring at Rupert. She was curiously still. He'd seen that look in frightened mares confronted by stallions, terrified yet sexually excited. He'd felt the same terror, without the excitement, when Revenge was taken away from him. Rupert was not going to take Fen.

He stopped eating his steak, fingering his knife. Helen had noticed it too. Suddenly she stopped talking to Malise about Proust.

'It's like asking me to go over to the Russians,' Fen was saying furiously, 'and furthermore, I don't like the way you treat your horses.'

'You've absolutely no idea how I treat my horses. You just listen to gossip.'

'You're only sucking up to me because you think I'll be so overwhelmed by your glamour, I'll give you a lot of tips about how Jake rides his horses.'

But it was the helpless snapping of courtship.

Desperately, Helen turned to Tory. 'What's the name of the horse Jake's riding in the final?' she asked.

'Christ, she ought to know,' thought Fen. 'She's married to a finalist.'

'He's called Nightshade,' mumbled Tory nervously.

'But in the stable we call him Macaulay,' said Fen.

'How weird,' said Helen. 'Rupert had a horse called Macaulay once, named after me. Macaulay was my maiden name.'

Rupert's face was a mask.

'It's the same horse,' said Fen, slowly spitting out every word.

'It can't be,' said Helen bewildered. She turned to Rupert. 'He died of a brain tumour. You said he did.'

'I did not,' said Rupert in a tone that made Fen shiver.

Everyone was listening now.

'I sold him to that Sheik Kalil, who bought half a dozen horses a couple of years ago.'

'And you bought him from Kalil?' Helen asked Jake.

'No,' said Jake flatly, 'I found him in the stone quarries.'

'He was pulling a cart loaded with bricks,' said Fen, 'and he was starving. They don't feed horses out there, or water them, just drive them in the midday sun till they collapse. Then they whip them till they get up again.'

A muscle was flickering in Rupert's cheek.

'You've been listening to fairy stories again,' he said to Fen.

'We've got photographs,' hissed Fen, her fury fuelled by guilt and anger because she found him irresistible. 'Jake saved his life. I know you all sneer at all the medical knowledge he picked up from the gipsies, but it bloody well works. And it worked on Macaulay. He was just skin and bone held together by weals. He could hardly walk. It's taken Jake two years to get him right.'

Helen looked appalled. 'Is this true, Rupert?'

Rupert shrugged his shoulders. 'How should I know? If you're prepared to accept any cock-and-bull story. I run a yard on a very tight budget and I can't ensure every horse I sell on is going to be mollycoddled for the rest of its life.'

'You sold him to the Middle East,' said Fen, knocking over her wine glass as she jumped to her feet. 'You must have known what would happen. You ought to be bloody well ashamed of yourself.'

Bursting into tears, she fled out of the restaurant.

There was a stunned silence. Rupert picked up his knife and fork and went on eating his steak.

'What's up with her?' said Driffield, looking at the puddings on the menu.

'Perhaps she's eaten something that doesn't agree with her,' said Ivor.

'Adolescent girls,' said Colonel Roxborough. 'Up one moment, down the next. Over emotional. My daughter was like that. It's their age. How old is she?' he asked Tory.

'Sixteen,' muttered Tory, staring at her plate. She

detested scenes and she felt desperately sorry for Fen, but need she have gone quite so over the top?

'Probably tired,' said Malise.

'Needs a good night's sleep,' said Doreen Hamilton comfortably.

'Needs a good screw,' said Rupert.

He hadn't noticed that Jake had got to his feet and had limped down the table until he was directly behind Rupert.

'What did you say?'

Rupert didn't turn his head. 'You heard.'

'Yes, I heard.' Jake's eyes glittered like deadly night-shade berries, his face ashen against the tousled black hair.

'You leave her alone, you bastard.'

'You're hardly in a position to call me that. At least my parents were married to one another, in church too, unlike yours.'

'Rupert,' exploded Malise.

'You leave my parents out of this,' hissed Jake. 'I'm warning you – keep away from her.'

'Why?' drawled Rupert. 'Have you got the hots for her? If you read your prayer book you'd realize that sort of thing's very frowned on. Thou shalt not covet thy neighbour's wife's sister and all that.'

The next moment, Jake had grabbed Rupert's shirt collar with one hand and snatched up the bread knife from the side table with the other.

Jerking Rupert towards him, he held the knife against Rupert's suntanned neck.

'Keep your foul mouth shut,' he gritted. 'If I catch you putting one of your filthy fingers on her, I'll run this through you, you fucking sadist,' and very slowly he drew the blade across Rupert's throat. No one moved, no one spoke. Everyone's eyes were mesmerised by the knife blade glinting in the candlelight.

Then Helen gave a strangled sob.

'Jake,' said Malise quietly, 'give me that knife.'

'It's all right, Colonel Gordon,' said Jake, without

looking in his direction. 'This time it's a warning, Rupert, but you heard me: you stay away from her. Next time you won't get off so lightly.'

He threw the knife down so it fell across Fen's red wine stain, giving an illusion of spilt blood, then limped out of the restaurant.

'Are you all right?' gasped Helen.

Rupert sprang to his feet, ready to give chase. But Malise was too quick. Leaping up, he blocked Rupert's path.

'No,' he said sharply. He might have been speaking to a rabid dog about to pounce. 'Stay – here. It was *all* your fault.'

Rupert looked at him incredulously.

'That man has just tried to kill me.'

'There's a simple remedy to that,' said Malise. 'Don't wind him up.'

'Bloody bad form,' said Colonel Roxborough. 'Fellow can't hold his drink. Let's have some brandy. Think we all need it.'

'I want some *crêpes suzette*,' said Driffield.

Rupert sat down, his face absolutely still.

Malise looked round. 'None of this is to go any further than this table. We don't want the press getting hold of it. Rupert was simply taking trouble to be nice to Fen; she overreacted because she's protective about Macaulay. Jake overreacted because he's protective about both her and the horse. Isn't that true, Tory?'

Blushing scarlet, Tory mumbled that Jake was probably uptight about the final and she better see where'd he got to, and, thanking Malise for a lovely dinner, she stumbled out of the restaurant, knocking over a chair as she went.

'Tory the elephant packed her trunk and said goodbye to the circus,' said Rupert.

Fen didn't stop running until she got to the stables. It was dark now, a huge full moon with a smudged apricot-pink face gazed down at her reproachfully. How could she

501

have let herself go like that?

She went straight to Macaulay's box. He was enchanted to see her and nuzzled her pockets enquiringly as she sobbed into his solid black neck. 'Oh Mac, I'm sorry. I shouldn't dump on you when you've got so many worries of your own, but I'm in such a muddle. I should never have said all those awful things. Malise'll never pick me for the team now.'

Gradually her sobs subsided as Macaulay stood in silent, titanic sympathy.

'You're such a duck,' she said in a choked voice. 'Please buck that pig off the day after tomorrow.'

She heard a step outside. Jake, Malise, Rupert? She couldn't talk to anyone. She melted into the dark of the box behind Macaulay. The top half-door was stealthily opened. Behind Macaulay's stalwart frame she couldn't see who it was. Then she heard the sound of something hitting the water bucket. Then the door was shut and bolted.

'Hell.' She was locked in for the night.

Next minute the ever-greedy Macaulay had shot towards the door and she heard the sound of munching. Desperately she snatched the bucket from him.

'No, darling, you mustn't eat it. We don't know what it is.'

Snorting with exasperation, Macaulay pursued her around the box.

Suddenly the top half of the door was opened again.

'Who is it?' she said in terror.

'What the hell are you doing here?' said Jake.

'Talking to Mac.'

'Disturbing his beauty sleep more likely. You OK?' he added more gently.

'Yes, but look what someone's put in his box.' She held up the bucket.

Jake lit a match and then whistled. 'Jesus Christ!'

'What is it?'

'Beet, unsoaked,' he said grimly. 'Someone's trying to nobble him.'

'Rupert,' said Fen.

Jake shook his head. 'He's still in the restaurant. Might be one of his supporters, but I don't think it's Rupert's form. Too easily traced, and he's just longing for a chance to make me look silly in the final. More likely some Kraut fanatic or one of the Yanks. Brits don't knobble Brits. All the same, we'll have to take turns to sleep outside the box. I'll stay here tonight. You go back and share our double bed with Tory.'

'You ought to get a decent night's sleep.'

'I'm so bloody tired, I'd sleep on a bed of nails.'

Back in their hotel, still wearing a pale-grey silk petti-coat, Helen Campbell-Black removed her make-up with a shaking hand, turning her head to catch different reflections in the three-sided mirror. Rupert was already in bed, watching a tape of Clara jumping on the hired video machine. Every so often he froze the film so he could study the angle of Ludwig's body or the position of his hands. Each fence was played over and over again. Then he got up and strolled naked across the room, changing the tape to one of Dino jumping President's Man in Florida. The horse was young and inexperienced, giving each fence at least a foot, because he hadn't yet learnt to tuck his legs under him. Manny, as Dino called him, would need much more riding in the Final. Rupert could see Dino carefully positioning him at each fence. Pity there wasn't any film of Hopalong jumping Macaulay.

As Helen picked up a different jar to remove the make-up round her eyes, she caught a glimpse of Rupert in the mirror, with his back to her. He must have lost ten pounds. He'd always had a marvellous physique, but now he was fined down to a leaner, even more muscular hardness. He seemed to burn with excess energy and restlessness. I must be married to the most desirable man in the world, she thought despairingly, so why do I feel so undesiring? Since the affair with Podge, she'd tried so hard to make advances, to be more imaginative, but it was as though he pressed the

503

freeze button on her each time, turning her to stone, robbing her of any spontaneity.

Was he attracted to Fen, she wondered, or had he just been baiting Jake? She knew Jake pulling a knife wouldn't put him off in the least. Malise had dismissed the incident as a drunken brawl, but she was frightened by the obsessive black hatred in Jake's eyes.

She delayed getting into bed as long as possible, praying that Rupert might fall asleep. But when she finally came out of the bathroom, he had turned off the television and was lying on the bed, looking at the latest photographs of the children she'd brought from England. He flipped past the ones of Marcus with hardly a glance, but examined every angle of Tab's sweet pink face. Perhaps Tab would be the one female in his life he could love unstintingly without despising her or himself.

'Take your nightdress off,' he said, without even looking up.

Helen sighed and complied.

Rupert pulled her towards him, not even bothering to kiss her. I'll be so dry inside, she thought in panic, and he's so huge it's going to hurt. Instinctively her mind and her body went rigid. His cock reminded her suddenly of the grey stone gargoyles jutting, hard and ugly, out of the walls of the cathedral.

'What's the matter?' Rupert prised her legs open with his hand.

'Jake pulling that knife, I can't get it out of my mind.'

'What aspect of it?' he said mockingly. 'Were you turned on by such a macho display on Jake's part, or the thought of being a rich widow?'

'Oh, stop it,' sobbed Helen.

'Or were you jealous of Fen?'

'She's only a child,' gasped Helen, as his fingers moved up inside her. 'It's not fair.'

'To her or you?' said Rupert. 'Look, do you honestly think I'm going to chat up a fat pustular schoolgirl for any other reason than to rile Hopalong Chastity? And I

504

certainly succeeded. None of the Lovell contingent'll get any sleep tonight.'

'And what about Macaulay?'

'You never bothered about him when I had him. Any solicitude after he's sold on seems a bit out of place.'

He took her then. Helen lay back, quite unable to participate. It was over in a couple of minutes and she was certain he'd been thinking about Fen.

Tense and miserable, she knew she should drop the subject, but she couldn't help warning Rupert to stay away from Fen. Jake was obviously unbalanced about her. When he didn't answer, she thought he was really taking in what she said. It was five minutes before she realised he was fast asleep.

Rupert was right. None of the Lovell contingent slept. Fen, lying on one edge of the bed, couldn't stop thinking about Rupert. 'My only love sprang from my only hate.' she whispered to herself, as Helen had five years earlier. Tory lay on the edge of the other side. She was worried about Jake. A row like that was the last thing he needed before the final. She felt even more guilty that she was suddenly racked with jealousy of Fen, her baby sister, who was growing more beautiful every day. Rupert, who had never treated Tory with anything but contempt, had really taken the trouble to chat up Fen, and she too had seen the black hatred in Jake's face when he held that knife to Rupert's throat. She tried to tell herself that Jake was fiercely protective of anything he owned, particularly his family. She tried to suppress the thought that Jake was falling in love with Fen.

Jake, after an hour's deep sleep, was woken by the barking of the rotweiller guarding Ludwig's horses. Hatred of Rupert, churning around and around in his head, prevented him dropping off again. Next morning, despite all Malise's stipulations, the story of the knife was all around the show ground.

Grooming the horses next day, Fen found she had never been the recipient of so much chatting up. The public flowed by to get a glimpse of a possible future champion. Suddenly, every German, American and English groom or rider seemed to have time to stop and gossip, and ask her how she and Macaulay were getting on, what he was like to ride, what sort of temperament he had. Watching the Lovell children swarming all over him, they could be excused for thinking he was as mild as an old sheep.

Dino Ferranti rolled up about midday.

'Hi,' he said.

'Buzz off,' said Fen, applying the body brush with more vigour.

'That is a cute horse, and you sure have a cute ass when you're grooming him. How's he feeling today?'

'Just fine,' snapped Fen.

'I really like him. Jake's smart; doesn't jump him that often, does he? Pulls him out for the big event. I never heard of him before this week.'

Fen turned, pink from exertions and anger. 'Don't smarm over me just because you want information about Mac. I'm not telling you anything about him.'

'Honey, you're over-reacting. I admire your boss. How'd you like to have dinner with me tonight?'

'No, thanks.'

'We won't mention Macaulay once, right. I just need an attractive girl to help me relax.'

'Why should I help you relax? You're the opposition.'

He really is attractive, she thought reluctantly, lounging against the door, with that wide untroubled smile and the marvellously relaxed, elongated body. He shook his head.

'You ought to get out. There's more to show-jumping than the inside of a tack-cleaning bucket. You ought to have some fun. Anyway,' he added slyly, 'I am just dying to hear what happened last night. Did Jake really pull a bread knife on Rupert? You must be the most fought-over girl in France.'

'Shut up,' said Fen, blushing to the roots of her sweating hair. 'I don't want to discuss it. Now, please go away.'

Later in the day all the finalists tried to relax. Leaving Helen to visit the house in which Proust spent his childhood, Rupert went racing with Count Guy and Lavinia, and had three winners, which seemed a good omen. The copy of the *Evening Standard*, specially flown in for Patrick Walker's horoscope, also predicted Scorpios would have an exciting and successful weekend. So he felt he could legitimately relax. The German team swam and sunbathed together. The Americans took a plane to Paris and went sightseeing. Jake took Tory, Fen Tanya and the children for a picnic in the Brittany countryside, finding a perfect place shaded by a glimmering silver poplar copse by the side of a meandering river. Tory and Tanya slept, the children swam and made daisy-chains with Fen. Jake wandered off with binoculars, revelling in the wild flowers and butterflies. He found a very rare orchid, stocked up on the medicine cupboard and also, to his joy, discovered a clump of tansy, so he had a fresh lucky sprig to put in his left boot for tomorrow.

Night fell. Jake and Tory were safely tucked up at the hotel. In a sleeping-bag outside Macaulay's box, Fen took up her position with Lester the teddy bear. It was quiet and very hot. All she could hear was the occasional stamp of a horse and the sound of Rupert's bodyguard pacing up and down outside Snakepit's box. The indigo sky was over-crowded with stars. Too many, like my spots, thought Fen. They suddenly seemed to have doubled. It must be the curse coming. Perhaps that was why she was so jumpy.

Now she was alone she could think about Rupert – and Dino. She was in such a muddle. Jake had kept her so busy over the past three years that truthfully there had been no time for men in her life, except for her long-distance crush on Billy Lloyd-Foxe. Now she was assailed by all kinds of longings and despairs. If only she were Helen, able to roll up at the championship with gleaming hair, bathed, in a beautiful uncreased dress after eight hours of sleep. She hated Rupert, and Dino, who had only asked her out because he wanted to pump her, but it made her realise how much she was missing by devoting herself so exclusively to horses. If only she felt tired. She stiffened as a step approached. Then she caught a waft of scent. It was Dino.

'Couldn't sleep. No point in jumping rounds in my head, so I just came by to check no one's been after Manny.'

'They haven't,' said Fen.

'D'you want a drink?' He produced a flask from his pocket. 'It's only Bourbon. I've only had two drinks all evening. Christ, I'd like to get looped. May I talk with you for a few minutes?'

He slid down the stable wall beside her, sitting with his long legs bent at an acute angle. In the faint light, she could see the perfect profile.

'Are you nervous?'

He nodded. 'Sounds kinda girl scout, but I don't want to let the team down – they've been so great – or the horse, or my Daddy or Mumma. They were great, too, to back me. I guess none of us needs the money like Jake. How come he hates Rupert so much?'

Fen explained about the bullying at school and the barrage of insults and the annexing of Revenge, and the cruelty to Macaulay.

'Guess that's enough to be going on with,' said Dino, handing her his Bourbon flask. He noticed with a flicker of encouragement that she didn't bother to wipe the neck before she drank.

'Jake's terribly torn,' explained Fen. 'He wants to beat Rupert so badly, but he's crucified at the thought of what it might do to Macaulay's confidence having Rupert on his back again. It must be hell, like going to a wife-swapping party on one's honeymoon. Bad enough the thought of one's darling wife sleeping with three other men, but even worse if she enjoyed it more than she did with you.'

Dino laughed. 'Yeah, that just about sums it up. I'm kind of ambivalent about Rupert, too. I really like the guy. He makes me laugh, but that was before I met his wife.'

'What about her?' Fen tried to sound casual.

'Well, she's so beautiful; I mean, seriously beautiful. The

way he carries on with girls. They were coming out of his ears on the Florida circuit, and boy, they threw themselves at him. I figured he'd made some kind of marriage of convenience to some dog. Then I had dinner with them this evening. I mean, how could you cheat on that? Christ, I'd never let her out of my sight, and he treats her like shit, putting her down all the time. I was appalled. Doesn't she have anyone on the side? She could get anyone.'

Fen suddenly felt horribly depressed. Because Rupert was so unfaithful to Helen, one tended to write her off as a sexual threat.

'I've never heard anything about other men. I think she's too frightened of Rupert, and so are the men. One of the Italian team kept her too long on the dance floor once and his hands started to travel, and Rupert hit him across the room.'

'That figures – like Hamadryad baboons.'

'Like what –?'

'Huge baboons that live in the desert in Abyssinia. They're more interested in fighting off other male baboons than in screwing their wives. In fact they neglect their wives when there's no one to fight off. I'm telling you, I'm going to be in Britain for Crittleden and I am going to make one helluva pitch. She doesn't deserve that kind of treatment.'

'I wonder if Jake's getting any sleep,' said Fen.

'Shouldn't guess so. It's like Henry V on the Eve of Agincourt. I'd better go and get some insomnia. Night, honey, this time tomorrow we'll be bombed on euphoria or despair.'

Lying awake at the hotel, Jake looked at his watch – three o'clock. Within fourteen hours, he'd know if he'd pulled the mightiest from their seats. His good leg ached because it hadn't been relaxed with sleep. He kept breaking out in a cold sweat at the thought of riding Snakepit. He knew he wasn't strong enough to hold him. If he fell off and wrecked himself, there wasn't anyone to ride the horses. He also knew Tory had been awake all night beside him. Thank God she knew when to keep her trap shut.

509

'Tory,' he said, reaching out for her.

'Yes.' She put her arms round him. 'Do you want to talk, or turn on the light and read?'

She could feel him shaking his head in the darkness.

'It's going to be all right. Horses always go well with you. You're going to win.'

'I wish I was riding Sailor.'

'He'd have looked after you, but he might have looked after the others a bit too well. Macaulay hasn't got such a conscience.'

She slid her hand down the empty hollow of his belly and touched his cock.

'Would that help?'

'It might, but I won't be much use to *you*.'

'I don't need it.' The bedsprings creaked as she clambered down the bed, then he felt the warm soft caress of her lips and the infinite tenderness of her tongue. Because he knew she liked doing it, there was no hurry, no tension.

'I was so right to marry you,' he mumbled.

Tory was filled with an overwhelming happiness. In the eight years of their marriage, he'd probably paid her as many compliments, but when they came they were worth everything. She felt bitterly ashamed that she had wasted so much emotion being jealous of Fen.

Rupert got up and dressed.

'Where are you going?' said Helen.

'For a walk. It's hot. I can't sleep.'

'Oh, darling, you must rest. Shall I come with you?'

'No, go back to sleep.'

A quarter of an hour later he paused beside Fen, her long hair fanning out, already slightly damp from the dew, teddy bear clutched in her arms. He toyed with the idea of waking her, but she needed sleep. He'd put her on ice for a later date. As he pulled the sleeping bag round her, she clutched the teddy bear tighter, muttering, 'Don't forget to screw in the studs.'

When he let himself into the lorry, Dizzy hardly stirred in

her sleep, smiled and opened her arms. Rupert slid into them.

Ludwig von Schellenberg had such self-control that he willed himself into eight hours' dreamless sleep.

35

World Championship day dawned. There were a couple of small classes in the morning to keep the rest of the riders happy, but all interest was centred on the four finalists. Each box was a hive of activity of plaiting and polishing and everyone giving everyone else advice. It was hotter than ever. In the lorry, Jake watched an Algerian schools programme on television, trying to steady his nerves, and wondered if there was any hope of his keeping down the cup of tea and dry toast he'd had for breakfast. Tory was frying eggs, bacon and sausages for the children (it didn't look as though anyone would have time to cook them a decent meal before the evening) and at the same time ironing the lucky socks, breeches, shirt, tie and red coat that Jake had worn in each leg of the competition. The new tansy lay in the heel of the highly polished left boot. Jake had seen one magpie that morning, but had been cheered up by the sight of a black cat, until Driffield informed him that black cats were considered unlucky in France. Milk bottles, tins, eggshells in the muck bucket were beginning to smell. Fen was studying a German dictionary.

'It doesn't give the German for "whoa." You'll have to fall back on *Dummkopf, Lieberlein* and *Achtung*.'

'Or *Auf Wiedersehen*,' said Jake, 'as Clara bucks me off and gallops off into the sunset.'

'The American for whoa, must be Starp, Starp,' she went on.

'You remember that red T-shirt you wore when Revenge won at Olympia?' said Jake.

'I've got it here,' said Fen.

'D'you mind wearing it this afternoon?'

Fen did mind very much. It was impossibly hot and she'd got very burnt yesterday, and the red T-shirt would clash with her face. But it was Jake's day; she mustn't be selfish.

'Of course not,' she said.

Jake was encouraged by the number of telegrams. British hopes rested with Rupert, but Jake had generated an enormous amount of good will. People were obviously delighted to see him back at the top again. There were telegrams from the Princess and one from the Colonel of the Regiment at Knightsbridge Barracks, who'd somehow discovered that their old horse Macaulay had ended up with Jake. The one that pleased him most was from Miss Blenkinsop in the Middle East. He knew that she, as much as he, enjoyed the sheer pleasure of showing the world that he could succeed with a horse Rupert had thrown out. Every time Macaulay won anything, he'd religiously taken 10% of the winnings and posted them to Miss Blenkinsop for her Horse Rescue hospital. If he won today, she would get £1000.

If he won. 'Oh my God,' he said, and bolted out of the caravan, through a crowd of reporters, and into the lavatory, where he brought up his breakfast.

'Why don't you bloody well go away?' shouted Fen to the reporters. 'You know you won't get any sense out of him before a big class.'

In the end they had to be content with interviewing Darklis, who sat on a hay bale, smiling up at them with huge black eyes.

'My Daddy's been thick four times this morning. He doesn't theem to like French food. I love it. We've had steak and chips every single night.'

At last there was the course to walk, which made Jake feel even worse. It was far bigger than he'd imagined. The water jump seemed wider than the Channel. The heavy, thundery, blue sky seemed to rest on the huge soaring oxblood-red wall, and Jake could actually stand underneath the poles of the parallel.

Malise, walking beside him, winced at the French marigolds, clashing with purple petunias and scarlet geraniums in the pots on either side of each jump. How could the French have such exquisite colour sense in their clothes and not in their gardening?

A couple of English reporters sidled up to them. 'Did you really pull a knife on Rupert, Gyppo.'

'Bugger off,' said Malise. 'He's got to memorize the course. Do you want a British victory or not? That's tricky,' he added to Jake, looking at the distance between the parallels and the combination. 'It's on a half-stride. The water's a brute. You'll get hardly any run in there. You'll need the stick.'

'Macaulay never needs a stick,' said Jake through frantically chattering teeth. The sheer impossibility of getting Snakepit, let alone President's Man, over any of the fences paralysed him with terror.

Rupert walked with Colonel Roxborough, wearing dark glasses, but no hat against the punishing Brittany sun. He seemed totally oblivious of the effect he was having on the French girls in the crowd. The German team walked together, so did the Americans. Count Guy, in a white suit made by Yves St Laurent, was the object of commiseration. Over his great disappointment now, he shrugged his shoulders philosophically. At least he didn't have to jump five rounds in this heat and his horses would be fresh for Crittleden the following week.

In the Collecting Ring, Ivor Braine had been cornered by the press and was telling them, in his broad Yorkshire accent that he was convinced Jake had been brandishing a knife because the steaks were so tough.

'I wish Saddleback Sam had made it,' said Humpty for the thousandth time.

Driffield was busy selling a horse at a vastly inflated price to one of the Mexican riders.

'Wish it was a wife-riding contest,' said Rupert. 'I wouldn't mind having a crack at Mrs Ludwig, although I would draw the line at Mrs Lovell.'

Once again he wished Billy were there. He'd never needed his advice more, or his silly jokes to lower the tension. Obviously drunk at ten o'clock in the morning, Billy had already rung him to wish him luck.

Rupert had asked after Janey. Billy had laughed bitterly. 'She's like a wet log fire. If you don't watch her all the time, she goes out.'

Next week, reflected Rupert grimly, he was going to have to take Janey out to lunch and tell her to get her act together.

Despite the lack of a French rider in the final, all the publicity had attracted a huge crowd. There wasn't an empty seat or an inch of rope unleaned over anywhere. Malise sighed. If there was a British victory, all the glare of bad publicity of the feuds between riders might be forgotten. He watched Rupert, cool as an icicle, putting Snakepit over huge jumps in the Collecting Ring. Jake was nowhere to be seen. He was probably being sick again.

At two o'clock, each of the four finalists came on, led by their own band. Ludwig came first, to defend his title on the mighty Clara, yellow brow-band matching the yellow knots in her plaits. Her coat was the colour of oak leaves in autumn, her huge chest like a steamer funnel. Unruffled by the crowd, her eyes shone with wisdom and kindness.

Then came Dino on the slender President's Man, who looked almost foal-like in his legginess. The same liver chestnut as Clara, he seemed half her size. Dino lounged, totally relaxed in the saddle, like a young princeling, his olive skin only slightly paler than usual, hat tipped over his nose, as though he was taking the piss out of the whole proceedings.

Then Rupert, eyes narrowed against the sun, the object of whirring cine cameras and cheers from the huge British contingent, motionless in the saddle as the plunging, eyerolling Snakepit shied at everything and fought for his head.

And, finally, Jake, his set face as white as Macaulay's, who strutted along, pointing his big feet, enjoying the cheers.

515

Like a council of war, the four riders lined up in front of the President's box, the bands forming a brilliant scarlet and gold square behind them. Les Rivaux can seldom have produced a more breathtaking spectacle, with the flags, limp in the heat, the scarlet coats, the plumes of the soldiers, the gleaming brass instruments, the grass emerald green from incessant sprinkling, the forest, which seemed to smoulder in its dark green midgy stillness, and in the distance the speedwell-blue gleam of the sea. The bands launched into the National Anthem, each crash of cymbal and drum sending Snakepit and President's Man cavorting around in terror. Macaulay and Clara stood like statues at either end of the row.

Fen, body aching from grooming, fingers sore from plaiting, her red T-shirt drenched with sweat, waited for Macaulay to return to the collecting ring. She was far more nervous than usual. She had a far bigger part to play. With the three other grooms she would spend the competition in the cordoned-off part of the arena and change Jake's saddle on to each new horse. Nearby was Dizzy, bra-less and ravishing in a pink T-shirt, her newly washed blonde hair trailing pink ribbons. One day I'm going to look as good as her, vowed Fen. Then she squashed the thought of her own presumption and had another look at the vast fences. How absolutely terrifying for Jake. The field emptied, large ladies bustled round with tape measures, checking poles for the last time.

'I've bet a hundred on Campbell-Black,' said the Colonel in an undertone to Malise. 'I reckon it'll be a jump-off between him and Ludwig, with the American third and Lovell nowhere. He simply hasn't got the nerve.'

Helen, seeing the riders in their red coats, was reminded of the first day she'd met Rupert out hunting.

'Dear God,' she prayed, 'please restore my marriage and make him win, but only if you think that's right, God.'

Tory, in the riders' stand, with Darklis and Isa, prayed the same for Jake, but without any qualification.

'I wonder when Daddy's going to be thick again,' said Darklis.

Then a hush fell as in came Ludwig. As he rode past the President's box and took off his hat, the rest of the German team, who'd all been at the champagne, rose to their feet, shooting up their hands in a Heil Hitler salute, to the apoplexy of Colonel Roxborough, who went as scarlet as his carnation.

The only sound was the snort of the horse, the thunder of hoofs and the relentless ticking of the clock. Girding her great chestnut loins, a symbol of reliability, Clara jumped clear.

Malise lit a cigar. 'At least we know it's jumpable,' he said.

Dino came in, talking quietly to the young horse.

'That's a pretty horse,' said Malise.

'And a pretty rider,' thought Helen, who was sitting near him.

Being so much slighter, President's Man seemed to go twice as fast. Dino's thrusting acrobatic style and almost French elegance and good looks soon had the crowd cheering. He also went clear.

Then came Rupert, hauling on the plunging Snakepit's mouth, hotting him up so he fought for his head all the way around. By some miracle of timing and balance, he too went clear, and Snakepit galloped out of the ring, giving two colossal bucks and nearly trampling a crowd of photographers under foot.

'God help those who come after,' sighed Malise.

'I'm not taking a penny less than £30,000,' said Driffield.

Fen gave Macaulay a last-minute pat and a kiss.

'Good luck. Remember you're the greatest, and remember what you've got to avenge.'

Jake looked suddenly grey. 'I can't go in.'

'Yes, you can. You're doing it for Macaulay and Miss Blenkinsop.'

'I'm going to throw up.'

'No you are not. Keep your mouth shut and off you go.'

'*Numero Quatre*,' called the collecting ring steward irritably.

Jake rode into the ring, obviously quite untogether. He might never have been on a horse in his life. He had the first fence down; and the second he took completely wrong, Macaulay stumbled and nearly came down on the hard ground. Then he hit the third.

'Twelve faults. He's been nobbled,' thought Tory in despair.

'He's blown it,' drawled Dino.

'Oh, my God,' said Fen. In anguish she watched the tenths of seconds pirouetting on the clock as Jake pulled Macaulay up to a standstill, stroked his neck, spoke to him and started again.

'Can't even ride his own horse,' said Rupert scathingly. 'It was a freak he got to the final anyway.'

'He's bound to get time faults,' said Colonel Roxborough.

Jake set off again in a somewhat haphazard fashion and cleared the rest of the ten fences, but never really connected all the way round, notching up 3½ time faults.

He shook his head as he rode up to Fen.

'A great start, huh?'

'Competition's young, you wait,' she said, giving Macaulay a lemon sherbet. Then, when Jake had dismounted, she removed the saddle, which had to be put on Snakepit, the horse Jake was riding next.

'You've got three minutes to warm him up,' she said looking at her watch.

'Needs cooling down, if you ask me.'

Ludwig's groom came over to collect Macaulay, who went off looking very put out, turning his head continually to gaze back reproachfully at Jake. Jake went up to Snakepit, who flattened his ears and rolled his eyes.

'Now you'll get your come-uppance,' Dizzy hissed at him.

In the roped-off arena, Macaulay did several wild jumps, nearly unseating Ludwig. He didn't like the discipline of the German rider. He went into the ring, a mulish, martyred expression on his white face.

'Look at the old moke,' giggled Fen. 'Isn't he lovely?'

Despite his disapproval, however, Macaulay gave Ludwig a good ride and went clear.

'Interesting what that horse can do when it gets a proper rider on its back,' said Rupert.

Dino went in on Clara. He was very nervous and gave Clara very little help, but each time he put her wrong she was so well trained she got him out of trouble, rising like a helicopter off her mighty hocks.

Jake didn't want to watch Rupert on President's Man. He was getting acquainted with Snakepit. He spent several minutes rubbing his ears, smoothing his sweating, lathered neck, talking to him softly and giving him pieces of sugar. Faced with the challenge of a new horse, he was too interested to be nervous.

Next minute he was up, determined not to hang on the horse's mouth. He went on talking to him. Snakepit was so short in front it was like sitting on the edge of a cliff, a cliff that might crumble any minute and turn into an earthquake. He rode quietly round for one of the two minutes left, stroking and still talking, then put him over a jump, letting him have his head. Suddenly, Snakepit seemed to sweeten up.

'What d'you reckon?'

'Very good,' said Fen. 'Must be a nice change for him, like a weekend on the Riviera after working in a factory.'

Cheers from the ring indicated Rupert had gone clear on President's Man, urging him on by sheer brute force and driving power. The horse, however, was upset.

Jake rode Snakepit into the ring. Snakepit tugged at the bridle and found no one hauling him back, so he stopped pulling and gave Jake one of the easiest rides of his life.

As they came to the upright Jake, out of sheer nervousness, hooked him up a stride too short, but Snakepit, revelling in his newfound freedom, made a mighty effort and cleared the fence easily.

519

'Bloody hell,' said Rupert. 'He'd have stopped if I'd done that to him.'

'Looks a different horse,' said Malise in a pleased voice. Having insisted that Jake was selected, he was desperate for him to ride well.

The Colonel grunted. 'Still going to win my bet.'

At the end of the second round everyone was clear except Jake, who was on 15½ faults. The crowd was beginning to get bored. They wanted trouble, crashes, upsets and falls. It was Ludwig's turn to ride Snakepit.

'I vas in two brains vether to ride heem. I've got a vife and children,' said Ludwig to Jake, 'but after your round, I doubt if I'll have any trouble wiz him.'

Snakepit, however, thought otherwise. He didn't like the harsher, more rigid style of the German, who, like Rupert, wouldn't give him his head. He deliberately knocked down the upright and kicked out the second part of the combination.

Rupert had no trouble going clear on Clara.

Jake, who was warming up President's Man, couldn't resist having a look at Dino on Macaulay.

'The American chef d'equipe told him to give Mac a good whack at the water,' said Fen gleefully, 'and Dino's neglected to take off his spurs too.'

'Jesus, it's like riding a charging elephant,' muttered Dino to himself. 'Hasn't he got any brakes?'

Macaulay lolloped crossly into the ring, with a mulish expression on his face. 'I'm not a seaside donkey giving rides,' he seemed to say, as he ran out at the upright. Then, having been given a clout with the bat, he jumped it, then proceeded to bring the wall tumbling down.

'Joshua at the battle of Jericho,' said Fen. 'Oh goodee, Dino's whacked him again.'

Coming down to the water Macaulay ground to a halt, them jumped the small brush fence with no effort at all, landing with a huge splash in the middle of the water, absolutely soaking Dino. Then he put his head down and started to drink. The crowd, particularly the Lovell children, screamed with laughter.

Dino finished the course and rode out grinning. 'I didn't expect an impromptu shower,' he said to his team mates.

'That round's probably lost him the championship,' muttered Fen. 'He's a good loser.'

President's Man was frightened, puzzled and muddled. Having been broken and trained by Dino, he'd seldom carried other riders. But now he liked the gentle hands and the caressing singsong voice of the man on his back. Trying to imitate Dino's acrobatic style, Jake managed to coax a beautiful clear out of him.

'Bloody hell,' said Dino, shaking his head. 'You'd figure Manny'd want to avenge me after what Macaulay did to me.'

It was the start of the last round. The excitement was beginning to bite, the crowd had woken up.

'This is a gymkhana event,' grumbled Colonel Roxborough. 'I'd never have let my Baskerville Boy go in for this.'

'Rupert's on zero, Ludwig's got eight faults, Dino eleven, Jake fifteen and a half, but he's got the easiest round to come,' said Malise, who was busy with his calculator.

Ludwig rode in first on President's Man. The young horse was really tired and confused now. He had jumped his heart out for three clears and he'd had enough. Like Snakepit, he preferred the gentleness of his last rider. Despite brilliant tactics from Ludwig, he knocked up eight faults.

'Glory alleluia,' said Fen, rushing up to Jake as he mounted Clara, 'Ludwig's got half a fault more than you now.'

Riding Clara was like driving a Lamborghini. With the slightest touch of the leg she seemed to surge forward. Jake had never known such acceleration. He felt humble to be riding such a horse. The crowd were growing restless again. With three clears under his belt, Rupert was obviously going to walk it.

'Oh dear, oh dear,' said Fen with a total lack of sympathy. 'Snakepit's carting Dino.'

Snakepit, thoroughly over the top, galloped around the

ring, taking practically every fence with him, notching up twenty-four faults.

'Actually he did bloody well to stay on,' Fen conceded, as Snakepit carried him unceremoniously out of the ring.

'I think I've won my bet,' said Colonel Roxborough.

'Looks like a British victory,' said Malise, wishing he felt more elated.

'Rupert used to own that horse,' said the Colonel smugly. 'He'll find him a piece of cake.'

Macaulay thought differently. Rupert had decided not to warm Macaulay up. The horse had already jumped three rounds and anyway, when Rupert had gone up to him, Macaulay had promptly flattened his ears, given a furious squeal of rage and recognition and struck at him like a cobra. Rupert only just jumped out of the way in time.

'Don't look,' said Fen to Jake. 'It'll only upset you. Concentrate on Clara.'

'I think Rupert needs our help,' said Colonel Roxborough.

Humpty, Malise, Driffield, Colonel Roxborough, Dizzy and Tracey all stood round Macaulay's head, holding on to his bridle for grim death as he stood at the entrance to the arena.

They blocked Macaulay's view as Rupert got onto his back, but he knew instantly. He seemed to tremble in terror, his ears glued to his head, his eyes seemed all whites in a white face.

But with six of them hanging on, he could do nothing.

'In you go,' said Colonel Roxborough. 'Good luck.'

They all jumped away as Macaulay shot forward. The moment he got into the ring, he went up on his hind legs, huge feet shadow-boxing, his white face suddenly a mask of malevolence. Then he came down.

'Oh, look,' said Fen in ecstasy. 'He's not going to fail us.'

Taking no notice of Rupert's brutally sawing hands, Macaulay went into a rodeo act, bucking and bucking and cat-jumping and circling in the air, frantic to get Rupert off.

'He ought to join the Royal Ballet,' said Fen.

Ivor's mouth was open so long a fly flew in. Even Driffield stopped selling his horse.

'Do something,' said Helen frantically to Malise. 'He's going to kill him.'

'With any luck,' muttered Fen.

'Dear God,' said Jake in misery, 'I should never have subjected Macaulay to this.'

It was amazing that Rupert stayed in the saddle so long. Macaulay's mouth was bleeding badly now, bits of red foam flying everywhere. It was quite obvious to the crowd that the great black horse, like a maddened bull, had only one aim in life – to get the rider off his back.

Rupert plunged his spurs in and brought his whip with an almighty thwack down on Macaulay's quarters.

'You can't shift me, you black bugger,' he said through gritted teeth.

'*Oh la la, quelle domage,*' said Fen happily. 'Oh, *bien fait, Macaulay.*'

Dino shot her a sidelong glance. 'You're being kind of unsporting,' he drawled, as a final maddened buck sent Rupert flying through the air. It was lucky he let go of the reins. A second later, Macaulay had jammed on his brakes and swung round in pursuit. Rupert had never run so fast in his life. As he dodged behind the wall, Macaulay followed him, squealing with rage, teeth bared. The crowd were in an uproar.

'Stop him,' screamed Helen. 'Someone do something.'

Rupert had shot into the oxer now, hiding behind the brush part, peering out from a lot of sky blue cinerarias like Ferdinand the Bull. Macaulay was too fly to be thwarted. He cantered round to the other side, where Rupert was only protected by a large pole, and went for him, darting his head under the pole, only missing him by inches.

Rupert ran out of the oxer, belting towards the combination, taking refuge in the third element, which was a triple, only two hundred and fifty yards from the collecting ring.

'I don't know why he doesn't take up athletics,' said Fen. 'He'd certainly qualify for the Olympics.'

Malise strode up to the French Chief Steward.

'You must send in the arena party to head him off,' he said.

'And get them keeled?' said the Steward. 'He is still within the time limit.'

The squeak of the elimination hooter went off at that moment, making everyone jump out of their skin. Macaulay was prowling around and around the triple, darting his head at Rupert, tail swishing furiously, quivering with rage.

'That horse doesn't seem very keen on Rupert,' said Ivor Braine.

'Hardly surprising,' said Humpty. 'It used to belong to him.'

Four gendarmes entered the ring, gingerly fingering their pistols. Macaulay turned, revving up for another charge. Rupert snatched up one of the poles. It was extremely heavy, like a caber. As Macaulay advanced, Rupert brandished it at him.

The collecting ring steward rushed up to Jake. 'I theenk, Meester Lovell, you better go and collect your horse.'

At that moment Macaulay reared up, striking at Rupert, only missing him by inches, knocking the pole from his hands.

Rupert backed away; he had no protection now.

Jake walked into the ring, a small figure, totally insignificant without a horse.

'Watch this,' said Fen to Dino.

As Macaulay turned to go in for the kill, Jake put his fingers to his mouth and whistled. Macaulay stopped in his tracks, looking wistfully at Rupert for a second, then, turning, trotted back across the arena, whickering with pleasure, nudging Jake in the stomach, licking his face. The crowd, having been frozen with terror, suddenly burst into a huge collective roar of laughter.

'Well done,' said Jake softly and, not even bothering to take hold of Macaulay's bridle, he walked out of the ring. Macaulay trotted after him, giving him great sly digs in the ribs as if to say, 'Didn't I do well?'

Malise turned to Colonel Roxborough. 'Even the ranks of Tuscany could scarce forbear to cheer.'

'I've just lost a hundred and we've lost the championship. I don't know why you're looking so bloody cheerful.'

'Tarry a little,' said Malise.

Rupert came out of the ring, his face like marble. Helen rushed forward. 'Darling, are you all right?'

'No, I am bloody not,' spat Rupert, pushing her out of the way. 'I'm going to object. That was deliberate sabotage on Jake's part.'

The reporters surged forward, clamouring for a quote.

'What are you going to do, Rupe?'

'Lodge an objection. That horse should be put down instantly. It's a total delinquent. Jake put it in deliberately to fuck me up.'

He was so angry he could hardly get the words out. The collecting ring was in an uproar.

Malise elbowed his way to his side.

'I'm going to object,' said Rupert.

Malise shook his head. 'Can't make it stand up. Macaulay's no more difficult a horse than Snakepit. He was all right with all the other riders. He's like a lamb with the Lovell children.'

'Well, Jake trained him to do it, then. You saw how he called the bugger off when he wanted. He tried to kill me the other night, and he tried to kill me now.'

The reporters were avidly writing down every word.

'The competition isn't over, Rupert,' said Malise, lowering his voice. 'Jake's got to ride Clara.'

'To hell with him,' snarled Rupert. 'If the jury won't accept an objection, I'll have the law on him for attempted murder.' And he stalked off in the direction of his lorry.

Jake rode Clara into the ring, holding his hands up high, sitting very straight in the saddle, trying to copy Ludwig's style of riding.

'It seems a shame to ask you to beat your master,' he said.

'Oh Clara, please do a cleara,' said Fen.

The crowd had witnessed near tragedy and then high comedy. The commentator had to put everyone back on course. Ludwig had sixteen faults after four rounds, Dino had thirty-five; Rupert Campbell-Black had been eliminated. Jake, after three rounds, was half a fault lower than Ludwig. He could not afford a single fence down if he was to win. He kicked Clara into a canter. Over the first fence she sailed, over the second, over the third. She gave the parallel a clout but the bar didn't budge. Ludwig, smoking frantically, stood with his back to the arena, the rest of the German team giving him a running commentary.

Fen, eyes tight shut, was slightly moving her lips.

'What are you doing?' asked Dino.

'Asking God to help Jake,' said Fen, not opening her eyes.

'Rather unfair to Jake,' said Dino. 'I guess he can do it by himself.'

Malise suddenly turned to Driffield. 'For Christ's sake, stop selling that horse and come and watch this.'

Alone in the ring, it was as though Jake was in another world. He was only conscious of the joy of riding this beautiful, beautiful horse, thinking he could clear the stands, even the Eiffel Tower, on her. He turned for the water.

'Come on *Lieberlen*, or *Dummkopf*, I forget which it is.'

Clara took a great leap, happy to have an expert on her back. Jake was aware of the blue water going on for ever and the anxious, upturned faces of the photographers. But he found the perfect stride and was safely over. The crowd couldn't forbear a cheer, then shushed themselves. The three elements of the combination, then the huge triple and he was home. Overcome with nerves, he made Clara take off too early at the first element. She only just cleared it, so he turned her to the left at the next element, giving her room for an extra stride and placing her perfectly at the last element.

He was over.

'Magic riding,' raved Malise. 'Oh, come on, Jake.'

Unable to restrain itself the crowd broke into a huge roar. The triple seemed to rush towards him. He lifted the mare up and up. The poles flew beneath him.

'That'll do,' he thought in ecstasy. 'I'm World Champion.'

All around the thunderously cheering arena, Union Jacks were waving as he rode out of the ring, patting the gallant mare over and over again.

'He won,' screamed Fen, hugging Tory and then flinging her arms round Dino and kissing him.

Dino, taking advantage, kissed her back. 'That's almost worth only coming third,' he said.

All the British team, except Rupert, were going mad with excitement. Malise and Colonel Roxborough were throwing their hats in the air. Jake came out of the ring and slid off Clara into Tory's arms. For a second they clung to each other, not speaking. He could feel her hot tears on his cheek and the thunder of congratulatory hands raining down on his back.

A magnum of champagne was thrust into his hands. He opened it and soaked everyone around, then they all had a swig.

There was no sign of Malise or Rupert. They were closeted with a member of the international jury, Rupert shouting in only too fluent French and Malise trying to pacify him. But there was no case, said the Frenchman. There was nothing in the rules about not putting in a difficult horse. Macaulay plainly hadn't liked Rupert, but he'd behaved with all the other riders, and Snakepit certainly hadn't been an easy ride for anyone, except Jake. Jake was undeniably the winner and they'd better get on with the presentation. Muttering that he was going to report Jake to the BSJA, Rupert stormed out of the tent.

'Where are you going?' said Malise.

'Not back into the ring to get the booby prize,' snarled Rupert.

'My dear boy,' said Malise gently, drawing him aside,

527

'I'm sorry. It was bad luck. You've had a great disappointment and probably a very frightening experience.'

'Balls,' said Rupert. 'I've been robbed.'

'You must have beaten Macaulay severely for him to go for you like that.'

'He was my horse. What fucking business is that of anyone's?'

'The RSPCA for a start, and the FEI, not to mention the BSJA. It won't do your image any good, nor will a lot of emotive stuff about selling Macaulay to the Middle East, and him starving and ending up in the stone quarries.'

'If you believe that story.'

'I do,' said Malise, 'and it could ruin you. The press are longing to get you, and you know what the English are like about cruelty to animals. It'll take a lot of guts, but go back into the ring and keep your trap shut. Bet you'll get a lot of marks.'

Back came the bands, but this time the four horses were too tired to be disturbed by the drums and the cymbals. Ludwig shook Jake by the hand. 'Well done, my friend, well done.'

'Clara was the best-trained horse. You should have won it,' said Jake.

'You fought back from a terrible start; zat is more important.'

Dudley Diplock ran up to Jake. 'Seuper, absolutely seuper,' he cried, giving Macaulay a wide berth. 'Can I interview you immediately after the presentation?'

Rupert rode in last. The crowd gave him almost the biggest cheer in sympathy. He was handsomer than Robert Redford, he had jumped three spectacular clears and certainly most of the women in the audience had wanted him to win.

Jake rode forward, leaving the other riders lined up behind him, and removed his hat as the band played the National Anthem. His hair was drenched with sweat and there was a red ring on his forehead left by his hat. In a daze, he was given an assortment of rosettes, so you could hardly see Macaulay's white face for ribbons. There was also a purple sash, which clashed with Jake's scarlet coat, and a huge laurel wreath for Macaulay's neck, which he tried to eat. Then, to Jake's intense embarrassment, one beautiful girl in matching green suits after another came up and presented him with prize after prize: a gold medal, a Sèvres vase, a Limoges tea set, a silver tray, a magnum of champagne, an enormous silver cup and, finally, a cheque for £10,000.

There was nothing except one rosette and much smaller cheques for the others.

'Can't we each have one of those girls as consolation prizes?' said Dino.

Even when Prince Philip came up and shook him by the hand, Jake was too euphoric even to be shy and managed to stumble a few sentences out. Aware that the place was swarming with photographers and television cameras, Macaulay resolutely stuck his cock out and refused to put it in again.

'Just like Rupert,' said Fen.

As Jake came out of the ring, he was cornered by Dudley Diplock. 'May I personally shake Macaulay by the hoof. How the hell did you get him to do it?' he added, lowering his voice. 'I've been waiting ten years for someone to give that shit Campbell-Black his comeuppance. The whole show-jumping world will club together and give you a medal.'

Gradually it was dawning on Jake that most people seemed more delighted Rupert had lost than that he had won. After the television interview with Dudley, which was not very articulate but so full of euphoria and gratitude to Macaulay and Tory and all the family and Malise, that it charmed everyone. Malise joined them. Neither he nor Jake were demonstrative men, but for a second they hugged each other.

'You were brilliant,' said Malise in a strangely gruff voice. 'Sorry I didn't get to you earlier but I've been with Rupert. He wanted to object.'

'Nothing to object about,' said Dudley.

'Quite,' said Malise. 'But that's never deterred him in the past. Fortunately, they weren't having any of it. But he has been badly humiliated, so I think the less crowing about that side of it the better. Come on,' he added to Jake, 'everyone's waiting to talk to you.'

'Who?'

'The world's press, for a start.'

'I want to ride Mac back to the stable. I've got nothing to say to them. I won. Isn't that enough?'

Malise looked at him. Was there a flicker of pity in his eyes? 'It won't have had time to sink in,' he said, 'but things are never going to be the same again. You're a superstar now, a world beater. You've got to behave like one.'

On the way, they passed Helen Campbell-Black; she was crying. Both Malise and Jake hoped that Rupert wasn't going to take it out on her. As they fought their way into the crowded press tent, euphoric English supporters, stripped to the waist, including Humpty, Ivor Braine and Driffield, were already getting plastered.

'Fucking marvellous! You beat the bugger,' said Driffield, thrusting a glass into Jake's hand, while Ivor overfilled it with champagne.

'Three cheers for the champion,' said Humpty. 'Hip-hip-hooray.' Everyone joined in. The noise nearly lifted the roof off.

'Lovell for Prime Minister,' yelled an ecstatic British supporter. Opening another magnum, he sprayed the entire press conference with champagne.

Jake was carried shoulder-high to the table with the microphones. He collapsed into a chair and was bombarded with questions. He answered the foreign ones through an interpreter.

He was extremely happy, he said, but very, very tired. One didn't sleep much before a championship. He'd won because he was very lucky. Macaulay was a great horse, perhaps not in the class of any of the other horses, but he had been rested all year. Clara was the best trained horse.

She didn't knock down a single fence, she ought to get a special prize.

Everyone was still clamouring for information about Macaulay.

Jake said carefully that he'd always liked the horse, and when Rupert sold the horse on, he'd tracked him down and bought him.

'Did you deliberately put him in to sabotage Rupert?' asked *Paris Match*.

Jake caught Malise's eye. 'Of course not. I'd no idea how he'd feel about Rupert.'

'Did you know Rupert had sold the horse because he was vicious?' asked Joanna.

Jake looked up, the sombre black eyes suddenly amused. 'Who's vicious?' he said. 'Rupert or the horse?'

Everyone laughed.

Later a celebratory party went on until four o'clock in the morning, but Rupert and Helen gave it a miss and flew home.

Soon all that was left of the World Championship was a few wheel tracks and a bare patch at the corner of the collecting ring, where all week ecstatic grooms had snatched up handfuls of grass to reward their successful charges, as they came out of the ring.

36

A week after the riders came back from the World Championship, Billy went up to London to speak at the Sports Writers' Association Lunch. If they'd known I was going to be dropped, they probably wouldn't have asked me, he thought wryly. Janey needed the car to go shopping ('Only food from the market; it's so much cheaper,' she added quickly), so she dropped Billy off at the station. He couldn't face *Horse and Hound;* it'd be too full of the World Championship, so he bought *Private Eye,* which always cheered him up, except when they were foul about Rupert. As he sat on the station platform, he turned to Grovel. He read a marvellous story about a member of the Spanish Royal family's sexual perversions, and another, even more scurrilous, about a trade union leader and a pit pony. Then his heart stopped beating. The next story began:

'Ex-slag-about-Fleet Street, Janey Henderson, sacked for the size of her expenses, is now trying to write a book about men. Despite encyclopaedic knowledge of the subject, Janey felt the need for further research and recently returned from four days in Marbella with loathsome catfood tycoon, Kevin Coley. Meanwhile her amiable husband, Billy Lloyd-Foxed (as he's known on the circuit), is forced to turn a blind drunk eye. Coley is his backer to the tune of £50,000 a year.'

Billy started to shake. It couldn't be true, it couldn't – not Janey. She'd always laughed at Kev. *Private Eye* got things wrong; they were always being sued. He read it again. The words misted in front of his eyes. He didn't even hear the train come in. The ticket collector tapped him on the shoulder. 'You want this one, don't you, Billy?'

'Yes, no, I don't know. No, I don't.'

Running, pushing aside the people coming off the train, he rushed out of the station, flagging down the first taxi. 'Take me home.'

'All right, Mr Lloyd-Foxe.'

No one was there. Janey was still out shopping. He pressed the LR button on her telephone to find out the last number she'd rung. It was Kevin Coley's, at head office. Hating himself, he looked in her top drawer. Janey had started a letter which she'd crumpled up.

'Darling Kev, I won't see you to-day, so I'm writing. God, I miss you, I'm just coming down to earth after Marbella. Can't you think of somewhere nice and far to send Billy?'

He gave a moan of horror. His legs were trembling so much he could hardly stand. The bottle clattered against the glass and the whisky spilt all over the carpet. He drained it neat in one gulp, then he ran all the way to Rupert's. He found him in the yard, selling a horse to an American. One look at Billy's face and Rupert said to the buyer,

'Sorry I've got to go. If you're interested in the horse, give me a ring later.' Then, putting a hand on Billy's shoulder, he led him inside. As soon as the drawing-room door was shut behind them Billy said,

'Did you know Janey was being knocked off by Kevin Coley?'

'Yes.'

'How the hell?'

'Helen saw them lunching together in Cheltenham, and Mrs Bodkin's been chuntering. And Mrs Greenslade said in Les Rivaux that she saw them coming off a plane.'

'It's all over *Private Eye*. Why the hell didn't you tell me?'

'I thought Janey'd come to her senses,' said Rupert, pouring him a large drink. 'Christ, if you'd have told Helen every time I'd had a bit on the side, she'd be back in America. Probably doesn't mean a thing to Janey. She's just a bit bored.'

'With one bounder, she was free,' said Billy miserably. 'She's been so cheerful in the last three weeks. She was so down before, I thought it was because the book was going well. It must have been Kevin. What the hell do I do?'

'Punch him on the nose.'

'I can't, at £50,000 a year. Very expensive bloody nose.'

'Find another sponsor.'

'Not so easy. I'm not the bankable property I was two years ago.'

'Rubbish. You're just as good a rider. You've just lost your nerve.' Rupert looked at his watch, 'Aren't you supposed to be making a speech in London?'

Billy went white, 'I can't.'

'You bloody well can. Don't want to go ratting on that. They'll say you've really lost your nerve. I'll drive you up.'

Billy somehow survived the lunch and making his speech. Paranoid now, he imagined all the audience there looking at him curiously, wondering how he was coping with being cuckolded. The journalist in the front row had a copy of *Private Eye* in his pocket.

Even worse, that evening he and Janey had to go to some dreadful dance at Kev's golf club in Sunningdale. Billy didn't say anything to Janey. He had a faint hope, as he had when he was a child, that if he kept quiet and pulled the bedclothes over his head, the nasty burglar might assume he was asleep and go away. Janey, he noticed, didn't grumble at all about going, as she would have done once, and looked absolutely ravishing in plunging white broderie anglaise.

She was easily the most beautiful woman in the room. All the men were gazing at her and nudging Kev for an introduction. Billy wondered how many of them had read *Private Eye*, and proceeded to get drunk.

Enid Coley was made of sterner stuff. Having tried to fill up Janey's cleavage with an orchid and maidenhair fern wrapped in silver paper, which Janey rudely refused to wear, she waited for a lull in the dancing. Then she walked up to Janey, holding a glass of wine as though she was going to shampoo her hair, and poured it all over Janey's head.

534

'What the hell d'you think you're doing?' demanded Billy.

'Ask her what *she's* been doing,' hissed Enid. 'Look in my husband's wallet, and you'll see a very nice picture of your wife. Since you've been away she's been seducing my husband.'

'Shut up, you foul-mouthed bitch.'

'Don't talk to me like that. If you weren't so drunk all the time, you might have done something to stop it.'

Taking Janey, dripping and speechless, by the hand, Billy walked straight out of the golf club. It was not until they were ten miles out of Sunningdale that she spoke. 'I'm sorry, Billy. When did you know?'

'I read *Private Eye* at the station.'

'Oh, my God. Must have been terrible.'

'Wasn't much fun.'

'Beastly piece, too. I wasn't sacked. I resigned. Kev, in fact, was rather chuffed. He's never been in *Private Eye* before.'

Billy stopped the car. In the light from the street lamp, Janey could see the great sadness in his eyes.

'Do you love him?'

'I don't know, but he's so macho and I'm so weak. I guess I need someone like him to keep me on the straight and narrow.'

'He's hardly been doing that recently,' said Billy. 'Look, I love you. It's *my* fault. I shouldn't have left you so much, or let us get into debt, or been so wrapped up in the horses. It must have been horrible for you, with no babies, and struggling to write a book on no money. I'll get some money from somewhere, I promise you. I just don't want you to be unhappy.'

On Monday, Kevin Coley summoned Billy. 'I've had a terrible weekend. I haven't slept a wink for worrying,' were his opening words.

'I'm so sorry. What on earth's the trouble?' asked Billy.

'I knew I had to break the news to you that I can't go on sponsoring you. My only solution is to withdraw.'

'Pity your father didn't do that forty years ago,' said Billy.

Kevin missed the joke; he was too anxious to say his piece. 'The contract runs out in October and I'm not going to renew it. You haven't won more than £3000 in the last six months. I'm losing too much money.'

'*And* fucking my wife.'

'That has nothing to do with it.'

'Then I tried to hit him,' Billy told Rupert afterwards, 'but I was so pissed I missed. He's talking of sponsoring Driffield.'

'Oh, well,' said Rupert, 'I suppose one good turd deserves another.'

Winning the World Championship had transformed Jake Lovell into a star overnight. Wildly exaggerated accounts of his gipsy origins appeared in the papers. Women raved about his dark, mysterious looks. Young male riders imitated his deadpan manner, wearing gold rings in their ears and trying to copy his short, tousled hair style. Gradually he became less reticent about his background and admitted openly that his father had been a horsedealer and poacher and his mother the school cook. Sponsors pursued him, owners begged him to ride their horses. His refusal to turn professional, his extreme reluctance to give interviews (I'm a rider not a talker) all enhanced his prestige. The public liked the fact that his was still very much a family concern, Tory and the children helping out with the horses. Fen, under Malise's auspices, won the European Junior Championship in August, and, although still kept in the background by Jake, was beginning to make a name for herself.

Most important of all, Jake had given a shot in the arm to a sport that, in Britain, had been losing favour and dropping in the ratings. The fickle public like heroes. The fact that Gyppo Jake had trounced all other nations in the World Championship dramatically revived interest in show-jumping.

Wherever Jake jumped now, he was introduced as the reigning World Champion, which was a strain, because people expected him to do well, but also increased his self-confidence. For the rest of the year, and well into the Spring, he and Macaulay stormed through Europe like Attila the Hun, winning every grand prix going. Two of his other novices, Laurel and Hardy, had also broken into the big time. Laurel, a beautiful, timid, highly strung bay who started if a worm popped its head out of the ground in the collecting ring, was brilliant in speed classes. Hardy, a big cobby grey, was a thug and a bully, but had a phenomenal jump. Both were horses the public could identify with.

But it was Macaulay they really loved. While other riders changed their sponsors and were forced to call their horses ridiculous, constantly changing names, Macaulay remained gloriously the same, following Jake around without a lead like a big dog, nudging whoever presented the prizes and responding with a succession of bucks to the applause of the crowd.

In November, Jake was voted Sportsman of the Year. Macaulay came to the studios with him and excelled himself by sticking out his cock throughout the entire programme, treading firmly on Dudley Diplock's toe and eating the scroll that was presented to his master. For the first time, the public saw Jake convulsed with laughter and were even more enchanted.

Enraged by his humiliation in the World Championship, and the appalling publicity he received over selling Macaulay to the Middle East, Rupert decided to up sticks for a couple of months. Loading up six of his best horses, he crossed the Atlantic and boosted his morale by winning at shows in Calgary, Toronto, Washington and Madison Square Garden.

Helen had always sighed wistfully that her parents had never had the opportunity to get to know their grandchildren. Rupert took her at her word. Flying the whole family out, plus the nanny, he dumped them in Florida with Mr and Mrs Macaulay, while he travelled the American circuit and 'enjoyed himself', as, Mrs Macaulay pointed out sourly. Staying with her parents with the two children shattered one of Helen's illusions. Even if things got too bad with Rupert, she could never run home to mummy anymore. The whole family were glad to get back to Penscombe in November.

Two weeks after Rupert left for America, Billy had gone on a disastrous trip to Rotterdam, where he had fallen off, paralytically drunk, in the ring and sat on the sawdust, laughing, while one of his only remaining novices cavorted round the ring, refusing to be caught. The English papers had been full of the story. Billy got home to find that Janey had walked out, taking all her clothes, her manuscript, Harold Evans and, worst of all, Mavis. Billy had stormed drunkenly round to the flat, where she was living with Kev, and tried to persuade her to come back. She had goaded him so much, and become so hysterical, that finally he'd blacked her eye and walked out with Mavis under his arm.

A week later he received an injunction from Janey's solicitors accusing him of violent behaviour and ordering him to stay away. Next day, The Bull, who'd been lacklustre and off form for weeks, had a blood test. Not only was he anaemic but had picked up a virus, said the vet, and should not be jumped for three months.

Billy took refuge in the bottle, selling off his novices and pieces of furniture to quieten his creditors, and to buy more whisky, refusing to see anyone. He also sacked Tracey, because he couldn't afford to pay her any more. She refused to go. No one else could be permitted to look after The Bull. She'd live on her dole money, she said, and wait until Billy got his form back.

Rupert was shattered, when he got home, to find Billy in such a state. Typically, whenever he'd spoken to Rupert on the telephone from America, Billy had pretended things were all right and he and Janey were ticking along. Now, sitting in a virtually empty cottage, surrounded by empty bottles, he had gone grey and aged ten years. Immediately,

Rupert set about a process of, as he called it, re-hab-Billy-tation, ordering Helen to get Billy's old room ready at Penscombe, packing Billy off to an alcoholics' home to dry out and searching for a new sponsor.

Helen, while sorry for Billy, could not help being secretly delighted. She had never really approved of Janey. Now with Billy back in the house, they would have fun together like the old days.

But it was not the same. It was like sending your son off to the wars all youthful, glorious and confident in his plumed uniform, and having him come home in the royal blue suit and red tie of the wounded, hobbling around on a stick. Billy talked incessantly about Janey, Mandryka and his failures. He didn't drink any more. He was quiet, sad and pathetically grateful. Helen once again marvelled at Rupert's kindness and gentleness.

One evening in early December, when she'd been talking to Higgins the gardener, Helen heard shouting from the indoor school. Peering around the door, she found Billy walking around the wilful eight-year-old bay thoroughbred named Bugle, which Rupert had picked up in America. Unable to get a tune out of him, Rupert had handed him over to Billy. Now he was haranguing Billy because of his reluctance to take Bugle over a line of jumps, all well over five foot.

Billy was shivering like a whippet on a cold day. 'I simply can't do it yet, Rupe,' he groaned. 'Give me a few more weeks.'

'Get moving and get over those bloody jumps,' yelled Rupert. 'This is not a holiday camp.'

'Oh, Rupert, don't force him,' Helen began.

'And you can bugger off,' said Rupert, turning on her furiously.

Helen retreated to the drawing-room and tried to read the *Times Literary Supplement*. Twenty minutes later, Rupert walked into the room, ashen and trembling even more than Billy had been.

'What's the matter?' asked Helen, in horror.

Rupert poured himself three fingers of neat whisky which

539

he drained in one gulp.

'He jumped them,' he said. 'He jumped them beautifully and all clear, half a dozen times. I'm sorry I shouted at you, but I just can't afford to let him see how scared I am for him.'

The problem was to find Billy a sponsor. Janey's departure, the failure of the horses and the heavy drinking had been so widely publicized that Billy would have to show himself in the ring, sober and successful, before anyone would come forward.

'You can ride for me for the rest of the year,' said Rupert.

'I have my pride,' said Billy, 'and I've bummed quite enough off you and Helen.'

Billy made his comeback at the Olympia Christmas show, not the best occasion to return, with the merry-making and hell-raising, and the memories it evoked of both Lavinia Greenslade and Janey. All the other riders and grooms were very friendly and welcomed him. But he knew that, behind his back, they were saying how much he'd aged, that he'd lost his nerve and would never make the big time again.

Never had he been more desperate for a drink than half an hour before the first big class. Rupert, who'd been watching him like a warder, frog-marching him away from the bars, had just been called away to do a quick television interview. Tracey was walking Bugle around the collecting ring. Inside the ringside bar, Billy could see Christmas drinkers knocking back doubles, slapping each other on the back, guffawing with laughter. Surely one drink wouldn't hurt, one quick double to steady his nerves. If he was this strung up, he'd transmit his fears to young Bugle. Rupert gave him pocket money now. Easing his last fiver out of his breeches pocket, he was just going into the bar when a voice said, 'Hullo, Billy. How lovely to see you back.'

For a second he didn't recognize the plumpish but ravishingly pretty girl, with the long, light-brown hair tied back with a black velvet ribbon, like the young Mozart.

'It's Fen, Fenella Maxwell. How are you?' Stepping

540

forward, she kissed him on both cheeks. 'Are you in the next class?'

He nodded.

'So am I. Malise has persuaded Jake to let me jump. I'm absolutely terrified.'

'Makes two of us,' said Billy, still staring at her.

'Rupert says you're riding a super new horse.'

'Yup, he's super all right. Whether I'll be able to get him around is another matter.'

Suddenly they were surrounded by a group of ecstatic teenagers. 'It's Fen,' they screamed, pushing Billy out of the way. 'Can we have your autograph? How's Desdemona?'

As she signed their books, with a new and rather flashy signature which she'd been practising during the long journeys in the lorry, she saw Billy sliding away.

'Here,' she said to the teenagers, 'don't you want his as well?'

The teenagers looked enquiringly at Billy, then politely handed him their books.

'Who's he?' muttered one of the teenagers, as they wandered off, examining Billy's signature more closely.

'Billy someone,' said her friend, also examining the autograph. 'Didn't he used to ride The Bull?'

'He's the best rider in England,' Fen shouted after them.

Billy shook his head ruefully. Fen tucked her arm through his. 'I told you it was high time you came back,' she said. 'Let's go and walk the course.'

The course seemed enormous. Billy sat in the riders' stand clutching a Coke and wondered how the hell the riders could coax their horses over such enormous fences. To Rupert's intense irritation, Jake Lovell jumped a beautiful clear on Macaulay, as did Fen on Desdemona.

'That yard simply can't put a foot wrong at the moment,' said Malise. 'High time you were back to redress the balance, Billy.'

Despite the heat and stuffiness of the arena, Billy began to shiver. He could feel his white shirt drenched beneath his red coat. In the old days, there had been excitement and nerves, not this cold, sickening sensation of leaden nausea. Could everyone see? As he mounted Bugle, he noticed two young riders with Jake Lovell haircuts, swapping stories. Once they had looked up to Billy and would certainly have watched him jumping on a new horse. Now they nodded briefly, carrying on with their conversation.

He jumped one practice fence and, nearly falling off, left it at that. Oh God, they were calling his number. Rupert's face swam in front of him.

'I think I've got a sponsor interested. A Victor Block from the Midlands. He's the Cutie Cup Millionaire; makes bras and corsets. You may have to change Bugle's name to Cutie B Cup, but he's worth a lot of bread and he's up in the stands, so don't have three stops at the first fence.'

'If I ever get to the first fence,' said Billy in a hollow voice.

'For Christ's sake, hurry up, Billy,' snapped the collecting ring steward. 'Don't spend so long in the bar next time.'

As he rode into the ring, panic assailed him. He should never have agreed to ride. The saddle was hard and unfamiliar, his legs felt cramped and powerless, refusing to meet the leather and blend into it, his hands on the reins were numb and heavy, without any flexibility. In the old days he'd fallen into the rhythm of any horse's stride. Now he humped along like a sack of cement.

'And here comes Billy Lloyd-Foxe on Dougall. Se-uper, absolutely se-uper, to see you back, Billy. Let's all give Billy a big hand.'

The applause, albeit tentative, unnerved the inexperienced Bugle. The first fence loomed up higher and higher. Desperately Billy tried to balance himself, hands rigid on the reins, interfering with the horse, pulling him off his stride. Bugle rapped the pole; it swayed but didn't fall.

'Oh, God,' groaned Tracey, her nails digging into her palms. 'Oh, don't let him be over the hill.'

'Is this the bloke you want me to sponsor?' asked Victor Block. 'Doesn't look much cop to me.'

'You wait,' said Rupert, trying not to show his desperate anxiety.

542

Bugle approached the second fence, battling for his head. Billy felt the horse steady himself, judge the height, rise into the air and, making a mighty effort, twist over the fence.

'Forgive me,' said Billy in wonder, sending up a prayer of thankfulness.

Now his hold on Bugle's neck was relaxed, the bay's pace increased, covering the churned-up tan with long lolloping strides. Suddenly, Billy felt the blessed sustaining confidence start to come back. Fence after fence swept by. He was riding now, helping rather than hindering. Bugle was jumping beautifully. Billy's heart swelled in gratitude. He was oblivious of the cheering gathering momentum. He took off too far away from the wall, but it flashed, oxblood red, beneath him and Bugle cleared it by a foot.

'What a horse, what a horse.' He had to steady him for the last double and nerves got to him for a second, but he left it to Bugle to find his stride. Over and clear. A huge roar went up.

Billy concentrated very hard on Bugle's perfect black plaits to stop himself breaking down, as he circled the horse before riding him out of the ring. On the way he passed Guy de la Tour who was smiling broadly.

'Well done, mon ami, well done,' and riding up to Billy he shook him by the hand, and then, leaning over, kissed him on both cheeks. The crowd broke into a great roar of approval. Billy the prodigal had returned.

Mr Block turned to a jubilant Rupert. 'Happen you're right. I'll sponsor him. But I'll have to organize the money side, so he can get on with the riding.'

In the jump-off, Jake went fastest, with Rupert second, Guy third and Fen fourth. Billy, anxious not to hurry a young horse, was fifth. As Jake rode back into the ring to collect his rosette and cup, followed by the rest of the riders, Rupert turned to Billy.

'I had to get you back on the circuit,' he said. 'One of us has got to break the run of luck of that murdering gipsy bastard.'

37

All runs of luck come to an end. After a brilliant March, in which he swept the board in Antwerp, Dortmund and Milan, Jake rolled up for the Easter meeting at Crittleden, a course which had never really been lucky for him since Sailor's death. It had rained solidly for a fortnight beforehand and the ground was again like the Somme.

In the first big class, Macaulay, who was probably a bit tired and didn't like jumping in a rainstorm, slipped on take-off at the third element of the combination. Hitting the poles chest on, he somersaulted right over. Jake's good leg was the padding between the ground and half a ton of horse. Spectators swear to this day that they could hear the sickening splinter of bones. Without treading on Jake, Macaulay managed to scramble to his feet immediately and shake himself free of the debris of wings and coloured poles. Most horses would have galloped off, but Macaulay, sensing something was seriously wrong, gently nudged his master, alternately looking down at him with guilt and anguish, and then glancing over his shoulder with an indignant 'Can't you see we need help?' expression on his mud-spattered white face.

Humpty Hamilton reached Jake first.

'Come on, Gyppo, up you get,' he said jokingly. 'There's a horse show going on here.'

'My fucking leg,' hissed Jake through gritted teeth, then fainted.

He came around as the ambulance men arrived. Normally a loose horse is a nuisance at such times, but Macaulay was a comfort, standing stock still, while Jake gripped onto his huge fetlock to stop himself screaming, looking down with the most touching concern. He also insisted on staying as close as possible, as Jake, putty-coloured and biting through his lip in anguish, was bundled into an ambulance.

Fen took one look at the casualty department at Crittleden Hospital and rang Malise, who was in London.

'Jake's done in his good leg,' she sobbed. 'I don't think a local hospital should be allowed to deal with it.'

Malise agreed and moved in, pulling strings, getting Jake instantly transferred to the Motcliffe in Oxford, where the X-rays showed the knee cap was shattered and the leg broken in five places. The best bone specialist in the country was abroad. But, realizing the fate of a national hero rested in his hands, he flew straight home and operated for six hours. Afterwards, he told the crowd of waiting journalists that he was reasonably satisfied with the result, but there might be a need for further surgery.

Tory managed to park the children, and arrived at the hospital, out of her mind with worry, just as Jake came out of the theatre. For the first forty-eight hours they kept him heavily sedated. Raving and delirious, his temperature rose as he babbled on and on.

'Were any of his family in the navy?' said the ward sister, looking faintly embarrassed. 'He keeps talking about a sailor.'

Tory shook her head. 'Sailor was a horse,' she said.

'When can I ride again?' was his first question when he came around. Malise was a great strength to Tory. It was he and the specialist, Johnnie Buchannan, who told Jake what the future would be, when Tory couldn't summon up the courage.

Johnnie Buchannan sat cautiously down on Jake's bed, anxious not in any way to jolt the damaged leg, which was strapped up in the air.

'You're certainly popular,' he said, admiring the mass of flowers and get-well cards that covered every surface of the room and were waiting outside in sackfulls still to be opened. 'I haven't seen so many cards since we had James Hunt in here.'

Jake, his face grey and shrunken from pain and stress, didn't smile. 'When can I ride again?'

'Look, I don't want to depress you, but you certainly can't ride for a year.'

'What?' whispered Jake through bloodless lips. 'That'll ruin me. I don't believe it,' he went on, suddenly hysterical. 'I could get up and discharge myself now.' He tried to rise off the bed and remove his leg from the hook, gave a smothered shriek and collapsed, tears of pain and frustration filling his eyes.

'Christ, you can't mean it,' he mumbled. 'I've got to keep going.'

Malise got a cigarette from the packet by the bed, put it in Jake's mouth and lit it.

'You nearly lost the leg,' he said gently. 'If it hadn't been for Johnnie, you would never have walked again, let alone ridden. Your other leg, weakened by polio, would never have been able to support you on its own. You've got to get your good leg sound again.'

Jake shook his head. 'I didn't mean to sound ungrateful. It's just that it's my living. This'll ruin me.'

'It won't,' said Johnnie Buchannan. 'If it knits properly, you'll be out of here in five or six months and can conduct operations from a wheelchair at home. If you don't play silly buggers, and take the physio side of it seriously, you could be riding again this time next year.'

Jake glared at them, determined not to betray the despair inside him. Then he shrugged his shoulders. 'All right, there's not much I can do. You'd better tell Fen to turn all the horses out. They could use the rest.'

'Isn't that a bit extreme?' said Malise.

'No,' said Jake bleakly. 'Who else can ride them?'

For a workaholic like Jake, worse almost than the pain, was the inactivity. Lying in bed hour after hour, he watched the leaves slowly breaking through the pointed green buds of the sycamores and the ranks of daffodils tossing in the icy wind, and fretted. He had no resources. He was frantically homesick, missing Tory, the children, Fen and the horses and Wolf the lurcher. The anonymity of the hospital sickeningly reminded him of the time when he had had polio as a child and his mother seldom came and visited him, perhaps feeling too guilty for never bothering to have him inoculated.

For a fastidious, reserved and highly private person, he couldn't bear to be totally dependent on the nurses. He was revolted by the whole ritual of blanket baths and bedpans. Lying in the same position, his leg strapped up in the air, he found it impossible to sleep. He had no appetite. He longed to see the children, but with the hospital eighty miles from home, it was difficult for Tory to bring them often; and when she did Jake was so ill and tired and weak he couldn't cope with their exuberance for more than a few minutes, and was soon biting their heads off. He longed to ask Tory to come and look after him, but he was too proud, and anyway she had her work cut out with the children and the yard.

The Friday morning after the accident, Fen had been to see him. Such was his despair, he had been perfectly foul to her and sent her away in tears. Wracked with guilt, he was therefore not in the best of moods when Malise dropped in during the afternoon, bringing three Dick Francis novels, a biography of Red Rum, a bottle of brandy and the latest *Horse and Hound*.

'You've made the cover,' he told Jake. 'There's an account of your accident inside. They say some awfully nice things about you.'

'Must think I'm finished,' said Jake broodingly. 'Thanks, anyway.'

'I've got a proposal to make to you.'

'I'm married,' snapped Jake.

'It's about Fen. If you're grounded, why don't you let her jump the horses?'

'Don't be bloody ridiculous. She's too young.'

547

'She's seventeen,' said Malise. 'Remember Pat Smythe and Marion Coakes? She's good enough. What she needs is international experience.'

'I don't want her overfaced. Anyway she's daffy. She'd forget her own head if I wasn't there to tell her what to do.'

'It's not as though your horses were difficult,' said Malise. 'Macaulay dotes on her. She's ridden Laurel and Hardy, and Desdemona's been going like a dream.'

'No,' said Jake, reaching for a cigarette.

'What is the point? You've brought all those horses up to peak fitness and you've got two grooms who need wages. Why throw the whole thing up and just lie here worrying yourself sick about money? Let her have a go. She's your pupil. You taught her. Haven't you got any faith in her?'

Jake shifted sideways, giving a gasp of pain.

'Pretty grim, huh?'

Jake nodded. 'Can you get me a drink?'

Malise poured some brandy into a paper cup.

'It'll give you an interest. She can ring you every night from wherever she is.'

'And where's that going to be?'

Malise poured himself a drink, to give himself the courage to answer. 'Rome. Then she can fly back for the Royal Windsor, then Paris, Barcelona, Lucerne and Crittleden.'

'No,' said Jake emphatically.

'Why not?'

'Too young. I'm not letting a girl her age abroad by herself, with wolves like Ludwig, Guy and Rupert around.'

'I'll keep an eye on her. I'll personally see she's in bed, alone, by eleven o'clock every night. She needs a long stint abroad to give her confidence.'

'How's she getting to Rome? In Rupert's private jet, I suppose.'

'Griselda Hubbard's got a lorry which takes six horses. She can easily take two or three of yours.'

'Griselda Hubbard,' said Jake outraged. 'That's scraping the barrel.'

548

'Mr Punch has turned into rather a good horse,' said Malise.

'But not with Grisel on him. Fen's far better than her.'

'Exactly,' said Malise. 'That's why I want to take her.'

Back at the Mill House, Fen was battling with blackest gloom and trying to cheer up Macaulay. It was nearly a week since Jake's fall, but the horse still wouldn't settle. He wouldn't eat and at night he walked his box. Every time a car came over the bridge, or there was a footstep in the yard, he'd rush to the half-door, calling hopefully, then turn away in childlike disappointment. Since Jake had rescued Macaulay from the Middle East they hadn't been separated for a day. Fen had tried to turn him out with the rest of the horses, but he'd just stood shivering by the gate in his New Zealand rug, yelling to be brought in again. Poor Mac, thought Fen, and poor me too. She'd thought about Dino Ferranti so often since the World Championship, hoping so much that she'd bump into him on the circuit this summer. And now Jake had ordered the horses to be turned out, and there'd be no going abroad, and she'd be stuck with taking Desdemona to a few piffling little local shows that Jake considered within her capabilities.

A rather attractive journalist whom she'd met at Olympia had rung up that afternoon and asked her if she'd like to sail over to Cherbourg for a party on the Saturday night. She'd had to refuse, just as she kept having to refuse dates and parties because there was always some crisis cropping up with the horses. And now Jake was in hospital, she had ten times as much responsibility. She'd been up all last night with Hardy, who, having gorged himself on the spring grass, suddenly developed a violent attack of colic. Brought into the stable, he had promptly cast himself and been so badly frightened when he couldn't get up, that Fen had had to call out the vet. It was some compensation that morning that a recovered Hardy, instead of taking his usual piece out of her, had butted her gently with his head and then licked her hand in gratitude.

Added to this, Jake had been perfectly bloody when she'd visited him in hospital. She knew he was depressed or he wouldn't have been so awful, but sometimes it was difficult to make allowances. And, finally, it was Sarah, the new groom's third night off that week. She was very good at her job, Sarah, and extremely attractive, with long black hair which never got greasy and a flawless creamy skin which never got spots. She was also quite tough. She had turned down a job with Guy de la Tour because it was underpaid. At his stable you were expected to work twenty-four hours a day, seven days a week, the only compensation was being screwed by Count Guy when he felt like it. Instead she had taken a job with Jake.

'Your brother-in-law,' said Sarah, 'may be moody, and prefer four-legged creatures to anything on two legs, but at least he pays properly and gives you plenty of evenings off.'

'Not if you're family, he doesn't,' thought Fen gloomily, as she watched Sarah, tarted up to the nines, drive off to a party in her pale blue sports car.

Once again, Fen repeated Dino's words, 'There is more to life than the inside of a tack-cleaning bucket!' She was fed up with bloody horses. She wanted some fun.

A delectable smell of chicken casserole drifted out from the kitchen. Looking at her watch, she was surprised to see it was half past nine. Inside, she found Tory stacking up a pile of envelopes. She had spent the evening cancelling shows and wondering which bills to pay first.

'Poor lovie, you look shattered,' she told Fen. 'Let's have a drink before dinner.'

'Can we afford it?' said Fen, looking at the bills.

'I think so,' said Tory. 'At the moment, anyway. It just infuriates me that, having paid for all that foreign stabling in advance, we won't be able to use it.'

Having opened a bottle of red wine and filled two glasses, Fen slumped in the armchair by the Aga. Although it was the end of April it was still cold. Wolf, the lurcher, who was missing his master even more than Macaulay, leapt onto Fen's lap for comfort.

'Poor old boy,' said Fen, cuddling his shivering, shaggy body.

'How's Mac?' said Tory, draining the broccoli.

'Still off his feed. His whole routine's been disrupted. Ouch,' she screeched, as Wolf, hearing the sound of a car on the gravel, leapt off her knees, scratching her thighs with his long claws. Next moment, he was through the back door and had rushed off, barking frantically, into the yard.

'Who the hell could that be?' said Fen.

'Wolf obviously knows him,' said Tory. 'He's stopped barking.'

'May I come in?' said Malise.

'Oh hell,' muttered Fen,' he'll think we've eaten and stay gassing for hours.'

'Hullo,' said Tory, blushing with her usual shyness. 'You've come at the right time. We've just opened a bottle.' She filled up another glass.

Malise sat down at the long scrubbed table, enjoying the warmth, admiring the children's paintings and the newspaper photographs of the horses on the cork board, alongside this year's already substantial number of rosettes for which there was no longer space in the tackroom. He looked at the pile of envelopes.

'You've been busy.'

'Cancelling shows,' said Tory. 'Hoping we might get some of our money back. Why don't you stay for supper?' she stammered. 'We've got masses.'

'I'm sure there isn't enough,' said Malise.

'Tory always cooks for five thousand and it's always marvellous,' said Fen.

Malise suddenly realized he hadn't eaten all day.

'Well, it'd be awfully nice.'

'It's only chicken,' said Tory apologetically.

'I'll get it out,' said Fen. Typical Tory, she thought, as she got four huge baked potatoes and a large blue casserole out of the oven.

'Nice kitchen,' said Malise as he put butter in his baked potato. 'How's Macaulay?'

'Devastated,' sighed Fen. 'He even misses shows. Every time the telephone goes in the tackroom, he starts cantering around the field.'

'This is excellent, Tory,' said Malise. 'I hadn't realized how hungry I was. By the way, I've just been to see Jake.'

'Oh, how kind. How was he?'

'Pretty miserable still; frustrated, bored.'

'And still in a lot of pain?' asked Tory.

'Yup, but at least I gave him something to take his mind off his leg. You'd better get the horses in tomorrow, Fen. He's agreed you can jump them.'

'Poor Jake,' said Fen. 'I drove over to see him this morning. He looked awful. What did you say?' She stopped with a piece of carrot on the way to her mouth.

'He's going to let you ride the horses.'

'Where?' stammered Fen.

Malise laughed. 'Rome, Paris, Windsor, Barcelona, Crittleden, Lucerne just for starters.'

Fen opened her mouth and shut it again. Then she turned to Tory. 'Is this true?'

Tory laughed and hugged her. 'If Malise says so, it must be.'

'But we can't afford it.'

'Of course you can. You'll be jumping as a member of the British team, so those expenses'll be paid, and if I'm anything to go by, you'll be in the money very soon.'

Fen looked at him incredulously. 'Thank you,' she said in a choked voice. Then, jumping to her feet and falling over Wolf, she ran out into the yard, muttering that she must go and tell Macaulay.

'Oh, please, God, forgive me,' she prayed as she buried her face in Macaulay's neck, 'I didn't mean it when I said I wanted to give up show-jumping.'

The following day, Fen loaded up Macaulay in the trailer and drove to Oxford. Without asking anyone's permission she unboxed him in the Woodstock Road and rode him across the emerald-green, billiard-table-smooth hospital lawn and, cavalierly trampling a bed of dark red wallflowers underfoot, banged on the window of Jake's room.

Jake, sunk in the depths of gloom, thought he was hallucinating when the great white face with the white eye peered through the glass at him. Fortunately it was a slack period. Matron was at lunch, patients were resting and comely Sister Wutherspoon, who was a show-jumping fan, pushed Jake's bed so it was flush to the opened window. The reunion touched everyone. At first Macaulay couldn't quite believe it, pressing his face against Jake's shoulder, whickering in ecstasy, then licking his pyjama jacket and his face with a great, pink, stropping tongue. For a minute Jake couldn't speak, but at last his face took on some colour as he fed Macaulay a whole pound of grapes and a bar of chocolate and an apple. Word soon spread round the hospital. A crowd of nurses had soon gathered in the room to pat and even take photographs of the World Champion, thrilled to see the delight on Jake's face. They had all been worried about his slow recovery and his black depression. In the middle the matron walked in and everyone melted away. Fortunately she was also a show-jumping fan.

'We really don't allow visitors out of hours, Mr Lovell, but I suppose we can make an exception in Macaulay's case.'

After twenty minutes, Fen put Macaulay back in the trailer and came back to talk to Jake, thanking him over and over again for letting her go, promising to ring him every night.

'When are you off?'

'Friday morning. Grisel's collecting me.'

She saw him again once before she left, on the way home from a day trip to London. He was so busy giving her last-minute instructions, he didn't notice she never took the scarf from her head.

'Rome's tricky,' he said. 'You'll find the fences coming off the corners very fast, and at dusk the trees around the arena throw shadows across the poles, which make it very easy to

553

make mistakes. Macaulay's eyesight's not brilliant. If you're in any doubt, don't jump him. You won't like Rome: lots of wops with machine guns pinching your bottom. Don't carry money or your passport in your bag, the muggers are frightful, and put any winnings in the hotel safe at once.'

'If there are any,' said Fen in a hollow voice.

'I gather Billy Lloyd-Foxe is back in the team, too,' said Jake. 'If you have any problems, go to him rather than Malise. He has to ride the horses. He knows what he's talking about.'

'I've been very wicked,' said Fen, when she got back to the Mill House three hours later and found Tory in the kitchen darning Fen's lucky socks. 'I've bought three pairs of trousers, three shirts, two dresses and a bikini. I promise I'll win it all back. And I passed a poster of Janey Lloyd-Foxe in the tube, telling me to read her column every week, so I drew a moustache on her and wrote "bitch" underneath.'

'I hope no one saw you,' said Tory in alarm. 'Let's see what you bought.'

'And I went to the hairdresser,' said Fen casually. 'I covered it up with a scarf, because I thought Jake might freak out. It's gone a bit flat.'

She removed the scarf. Tory just gaped at her. Fen had gone out that morning with dark mouse hair trailing almost to her waist. Now it was streaked white blonde and no longer than two inches all over her head. Tendrils curled round her face and down to a point at the nape of her neck. She had been on a crash diet for the last ten days since she heard about the trip, and now weighed no more than eight stone. As a result of so many salads, the spots had gone for good, the new hairstyle emphasized the emerging cheek bones, the brilliant, slanting, aquamarine eyes and the long slender neck.

'I'm sorry,' Fen hung her head, 'but I thought it would be easier to keep like this.'

Certainly it won't be easier to keep men at a distance, thought Tory. Malise was going to have his work cut out as a chaperone. Suddenly, with a flash of equal pain and pleasure, she realized that Fen was no longer a child, a little sister. Almost since this morning she'd grown up into a beauty.

'It's gorgeous,' she said in awe. 'The hair's heaven.'

Fen grinned with relief. 'Griselda won't be able to keep her hands off me!'

38

Fen had seldom met anyone she disliked more than Griselda Hubbard. Having told Fen to be ready at 5.30, she rolled up, while it was still dark, at 4.45, just as Fen was feeding Desdemona and Macaulay. Refusing to come in for a cup of coffee, she sat drumming her fingers on the wheel of her vast eight-gear juggernaut, gazing at the immaculate yard as though it was a pigsty, forcing Fen into a complete panic and sabotaging all her down-to-the-last-minute organization. Macaulay loathed getting up early, at the best of times. There was no way you could hurry him over his breakfast or Sarah over blow-drying her hair.

'It'll dry all crinkly if I leave it,' was her only answer, in reply to Fen's frantic pleas.

'What on earth's that?' said Griselda, as Fen installed a huge sweetshop jar of lemon sherbets, taking up a large corner of the very limited cupboard space.

'Macaulay's reward if he jumps well.'

'You're optimistic,' said Griselda dismissively. She was bull-terrier solid rather than fat, with huge fleshy thighs stretching a maroon track suit, and a hard face with short-permed dark hair, small beady eyes, and more than a suggestion of moustache on her upper lip. She might have been any age between thirty and forty-five but in fact was only twenty-eight.

'I am not sitting next to her,' muttered Sarah.

Georgie, Griselda's girl groom, as thin and wiry as Griselda was solid, had a pointed nose, watery blue eyes and a long beige plait down her back. There was a lot of fuss about loading. Griselda had four horses, with her star, Mr

556

Punch on the outside.

'I'm not having that brute next to Punchie,' she said, as Fen started to lead Macaulay up the ramp.

'He wouldn't hurt a fly,' protested Fen.

'Punchie is not a fly,' said Griselda, 'and that's not what Rupert Campbell-Black says. Put Desdemona next to Punchie.'

'Desdemona gets scared. It's easier if she's between Mac and Hardy, and Mac goes in first.'

'Look, if you hitch a lift with me,' said Griselda, 'you abide by my rules.'

Handling the monster lorry like a man, Griselda calmly knocked down two of Tory's carefully nurtured lilac trees on the grass verge by the gate. Fen shivered for Desdemona and Macaulay's safety, as Grisel overtook juggernaut after juggernaut on the motorway. She got to the ferry two hours early, which meant lots of hanging around. Fen insisted on feeding her horses at the docks, which, to Griselda's intense irritation, had Mr Punch and the rest of her horses clamouring for their lunch too. To upset Fen, there was the inevitable lorry-load of bewildered, thirstily bleating little calves. The driver said they were destined for the pot.

'Why can't they bloody kill them in England?' said Fen.

'EEC Regulations,' said the driver.

'Don't be so sentimental,' said Griselda. 'You eat meat, don't you?'

When they were at sea they had lunch in the restaurant. Grisel ordered a huge steak. 'I need my fuel. I'm the only one doing any work.'

Fen, who was starving, ordered a grilled sole, which seemed less bloodthirsty. The moment it arrived, Grisel made a point of asking her to go down to the hold and check the horses.

Throughout the three-day journey, she treated Fen with even more contempt than the grooms, insisting she map-read, then hitting the roof when Fen gazed out of the windows at the pink and white apple blossom and, wondering how she would put Desdemona at all the fences that flashed past, twice navigated Grisel on to the wrong motorway.

Every sixty miles or so, Griselda ordered Sarah or Fen to make her yet another cup of strong black coffee with three spoonfuls of sugar.

Jake always stopped to water and graze his horses on the way. Griselda believed in pushing on. 'We'll never make Fontainebleau by nightfall if we bugger around blowing them out with grass. Who'd like a lemon sherbet?'

'They're Macaulay's,' snapped Fen.

'He'll hardly get through that lot. No wonder he's so podgy.'

'Certainly likes her pound of flesh,' muttered Sarah to Fen, 'although why she should want any more flesh defeats me, the ugly cow.'

'She's supposed to have a boyfriend,' said Fen.

'Must have picked him up at St Dunstan's.'

Finally, two days later, with the Ave Maria ringing out all over the city, they drove into Rome. Fen was knocked sideways by the beauty of the churches, the statues, the lakes reflecting the yellow and turquoise sky and the great hump-backed dome of St Peter's. The streets swarmed with people parading up and down, gossiping and showing off their new clothes. The traffic was terrifying. Griselda, however, drove the lorry on undaunted, on the principle that if she crashed into a Ferrari it would come off worst. Sarah, sitting by the window, was the object of repeated wolf-whistles.

'I always felt I'd like to end my days in Rome,' she said smugly.

'You probably will if Griselda doesn't drive more slowly,' said Fen. 'Oh look at that beautiful park over there.' Through the gap in the houses she could see a rustic amphitheatre circled with umbrella palms.

'That's the show-ground,' said Sarah. 'It's supposed to be the most beautiful in the world.'

The stables, part of a military barracks, were splendid, with big roomy boxes, enabling the horses to look out into the yard.

'There's Snakepit and The Bull,' said Sarah. 'So Rupert and Billy are already here.'

Fen suddenly felt nervous and wondered what they'd think of her new hair.

'Hullo,' said Dizzy, coming out of Snakepit's box. 'We flew out. We were lucky. Have you had a frightful journey?'

'Marvellous,' lied Fen, because Griselda was in ear-shot.

'Where are the team staying?' Griselda asked Dizzy.

'The Apollo; just round the corner.'

'Well, I'm off,' said Griselda. 'I expect you'll want to settle your horses, Fen. Can you carry my cases to the taxi rank, Georgie? And mind you brush out the horse area, and clean up the living area.'

'Bitch,' said Fen, glaring at Griselda's solid, departing back, with Georgie running after her, buckling under the cases. 'We're getting home some other way,' she added to Sarah, 'even if we have to carry the horses.'

Having examined the loose boxes for sticking-out nails and jagged edges of wood, they put down wood shavings and fed and watered the horses. Macaulay, however, had a more pressing need. Dropping down, folding like a camel, he rolled and rolled.

'God, I'm so tired. I could sleep on a clothes' line,' said Fen.

'Where shall we have supper?' said Sarah.

'There's a nice trattoria round the corner,' said Dizzy.

'Can I come with you?' asked Fen.

'No, you can't,' said Driffield, who'd been checking his horses. 'You're staying at the Apollo with the team and you'll be expected to dine with them, too. Come on, we'll share a taxi.'

'Pay for it, you mean,' said Fen under her breath, knowing Driffield's meanness. 'You can sleep in the hotel room alternate nights, and I'll sleep in the lorry,' she said apologetically to Sarah.

'Malise won't put up with that,' said Driffield. 'You've made the grade now, dear, and you'll have to behave like

559

one of us.'

The Hotel Apollo was a sprawling yellow villa, its stuccoed walls peeling. The walls of the lobby were decorated with friezes of Apollo in various guises, cavorting with bathing nymphs, bemused maidens and hairy-legged flute players. There was a rackety lift, but Fen preferred to climb a huge baroque staircase to her room on the second floor, which turned out to be the height of luxury.

Meanwhile, downstairs in the bar, Malise, hiding his disappointment that Helen hadn't made the trip to Rome this year, was giving Billy and Rupert a pep talk. 'I need your help, chaps,' he said, with unusual heartiness. 'Fenella Maxwell's not eighteen yet. Tory and Jake are in a panic she's going to get seduced by some wop. I promised them we'd keep a close eye on her.'

'Tory's overreacting,' said Rupert. 'I can't actually envisage Fen having to fight them off.'

'Poor old Jake,' said Billy, looking down at his glass of coke. 'Bloody bad luck when he'd just battled his way to the top.'

'I must send him a Please-Don't-Get-Well card,' drawled Rupert. 'He tried to kill me last year, remember?'

'Pity he didn't succeed.' said Driffield nastily.

Billy thought wistfully of the old days, when pre-dinner drinks were the nicest part of the day, to celebrate or cheer you up after a lousy round. You'd start with a pint of beer because you were thirsty, and after that you had several large whiskys, with increasing merriment in anticipation of some exotic food, heightened by plenty of wine and several brandies afterwards. Life had seemed framed in a halo, studded with buttercups. Now all meals had a terrible sameness, with people getting sillier or more aggressive. The first wild agony of losing Janey had given way to a dull numbing loneliness. He had become aware of the appalling sameness of the show-jumping circuit, the faceless bedrooms, the endless travelling. Before, it had been redeemed by hell-raising with Rupert, or living it up with Janey.

Everywhere he went, he was reminded of her and the good time they had had, and every night he watched the other riders ring home to check up on their families and report the latest success. He had no one to ring now, no one who gave a stuff if he won or lost, except his creditors, whom he was gradually paying back. The money from each small win was sent to Mr Block, who kept what was necessary for Billy's livelihood, took his cut and passed the rest on to the tax man. In fact, if he could get back on form and notch up about five really good wins, he could discharge the whole debt. Once Janey had filed for divorce, Billy's mother, making no secret of her relief, had come to his aid, not giving him a huge sum, but enough to settle the most pressing bills. Rupert had been wonderful. Looking across at him, a fond father showing photographs of the twelve-month-old Tabitha to Malise, Billy felt a wave of passionate gratitude for his support and kindness. Never once had Rupert tried to persuade him to have a drink, as other people constantly did.

Malise's voice broke into his thoughts.

'Hope you don't mind coming here again too much,' he said in an undertone. 'I'm fond of this place, even if it is a bit quaint.'

Billy smiled. 'Of course not.' That was all part of the act, to be cheerful, never to show the cracks in his heart.

He pointed to one of the more grotesque figures portrayed in the frieze round the walls of the bar.

'What did that poor chap do?'

'Raped Apollo's mother. He was pegged down so that birds could peck continually at his liver.'

'Sounds like mine in the old days,' said Billy.

'Another Coke?' asked Malise.

'No, I'm fine.' Billy looked across at Griselda Hubbard, massive in a red track suit. What a disgustingly ugly pig she was, and already bad-mouthing poor little Fen.

'She's a hopeless map-reader and kept making the most ridiculous fuss about stopping to graze and water the horses. If I'd listened to her we'd still be in France. Jake's

561

mad to let her ride the horses when she's so soft. They'll be walking all over her in a week or two, and she's no sense of hierarchy, treats her groom like an equal, even a superior. She'll have both her and the two horses tucked up in her hotel bedroom watching telly at any minute.'

'I hope we can get English food here,' grumbled Driffield, brandishing an empty glass and looking around, hoping someone would buy him a drink.

Rupert was discussing declining television viewing figures with Malise. 'They ought to sack Dudley; he's such a pratt. What we need on the circuit is crumpet.'

'Who's talking?' sneered Driffield.

'Not groupie crumpet, competing crumpet, some good-looking riders,'

'Like Lavinia,' said Malise.

'She was never good enough, or pretty enough,' said Rupert.

'Ahem,' said Billy.

'Anyway, she married a frog. I am talking about someone like Ann Moore or Marion Coakes; someone every little pony-mad girl can identify with. It's the pony-mad girls that make up the audiences and bring in their parents.'

'What about Fenella Maxwell?' said Malise.

'Well, if she shed about a stone and a half, most of which is spots.'

'Thank you, Rupert,' said a shrill voice.

Everyone turned round.

'Mamma Mia,' said Billy.

'Christ,' said Rupert. 'You *have* grown up.'

Fen stood staring at them, eyes widened like a faun, drained sea-green shirt tucked into drained sea-green Bermuda shorts, espadrilles on the end of her long smooth brown legs. Her spiky blonde hair was still wet from the shower. Not a spot spoiled her smooth, brown cheeks, just a faint touch of blusher. She looked like a wary but very beautiful street urchin.

'Oh, God,' thought Malise, 'how am I going to chaperone *that* in Rome?'

As it was very late, they went straight in to dinner. Ivor Braine and, amazingly, Driffield made concerted efforts to sit next to Fen. Ivor just crumbled Gristiks and gazed at her with his mouth open. All the team, except Griselda, who was obviously feeling upstaged, were incredibly nice, asking her about Jake's leg and the horses and how the glamorous Sarah was settling in. The waiters, flashing teeth and menus, kept filling her glass with Chianti. Not having touched a drop since she'd started dieting, she suddenly felt very light-headed.

'I'm starving,' she told Driffield. 'I don't think I could ever look at a grapefruit or a lettuce leaf again.'

'How much have you lost?'

'Not enough for Rupert.'

Across the table, Rupert laughed and raised his glass to her.

'I overestimated. You look delectable. Don't lose an ounce more.'

'I'm going to have fettucine,' said Griselda sourly, "followed by abbacchio al forno.'

'What's that?' said Ivor.

'Roast baby lamb, cooked whole,' said Griselda, watering at the mouth.

'Probably one of those lambs that came over on the ferry,' thought Fen savagely. 'Bloody carnivore.' Suddenly she felt less hungry.

'What's ucelletti?'

'Little song birds roasted on a spit,' said Griselda. 'They're very good.'

'God, this is a barbaric country,' said Billy. 'I'm surprised they don't casserole all those stray cats hanging round the street.'

'Not enough meat on them,' said Rupert.

Next moment a messenger arrived at the table with two telegrams for Fen. One was from Jake and Tory and the children. When she opened the other, she gasped and went bright scarlet, but failed to shove it back into the envelope quickly enough to stop Driffield reading it.

' "Congratulations",' he read out, ' "and good luck. Look forward to seeing you this summer. Dino Ferranti." Consorting with the enemy, are we? You could do a lot worse for yourself. Evidently his father's as rich as Croesus.'

'It's nothing,' stammered Fen. 'We just met briefly at the World Championship. I wonder how he discovered I'd been selected.'

Rupert was looking across at her with a dangerous glint in his eyes. 'The sly fox,' he said, 'must have been working overtime at Les Rivaux. As well as making a play for you, he was running like mad after Helen.'

'Not nearly as much as Macaulay was running after you,' began Driffield, then stopped when he saw the blaze of anger on Rupert's face. 'Sorry, dangerous subject.'

'Dino,' said Rupert, leaning over to fill up Fen's glass, 'even pursued Helen when we were in America. While she was staying with her mother, he was evidently never off the telephone, pestering her to go out with him.'

Fen felt her happiness evaporate. Seeing her face, Billy said quickly, 'Never met Dino. Can't imagine him pestering anyone. He sounds far too laid back.'

Dinner seemed to go on for hours. Fen found she couldn't finish her spaghetti.

'Is Billy all right?' she said to Driffield in an undertone. 'He seems to have lost all his sparkle and his hair's even greyer than it was at Olympia.'

'Hasn't really had a good win since then,' said Driffield. 'Malise is only keeping him in the team for sentimental reasons.'

'He's still so attractive.'

'Who is?' asked Rupert. Throughout dinner his eyes had flickered over Fen. He was the only man she'd ever met who could stare so calculatingly and without any embarrassment, as though he was a cat and she a bird's nest he was going to raid in his own good time.

'No one,' she said quickly. She turned to Ivor. 'Tell me about your new horse. Is he really called John?'

'I think you've lost your audience, Ivor,' said Rupert, five minutes later. Fen had fallen fast asleep, her head on the red raffia table mat.

39

Three days later, Fen had reached screaming pitch. The week had been one succession of disasters. She remembered Jake warning her that his first show with the British team had begun catastrophically, but nothing could have been as bad as this. She didn't even dare ring him at the hospital.

On the first day, she'd entered Desdemona in a speed class for horses who had never jumped in Rome before. The little mare had gone like a whirlwind, treating the course with utter disdain, sailing over fences she couldn't see over, whisking home in the fastest time by a couple of seconds. Fen was so enchanted by such brilliance she promptly jumped off and flung her arms around Desdemona's neck, to the delight of the crowd.

The British team were less amused.

'You berk,' said Rupert, as starry-eyed she led Desdemona out of the ring, 'you've just lost yourself a grand.'

'But she won,' gasped Fen.

'She may have done, but you disqualified her by dismounting before you left the ring.'

'Oh, my God,' said Fen. 'Oh, Des, I'm sorry. I didn't think. What on earth will Jake say?'

'Shouldn't tell him. Least said, soonest sewn up,' said Ludwig cheerfully, who, as the new winner, rode grinning into the ring to collect his prize money.

In the big class later in the, day Fen made two stupid mistakes, putting Macaulay out of the running. Then on the second day in the relay competition, because Rupert always paired with Billy and Ivor with Driffield, Fen was stuck with a reluctant Griselda.

'I'll show her,' fumed Fen, waiting on Desdemona, holding her hand out ready for the baton, as Griselda cantered up to them after a clear and surprisingly swift round on Mr Punch. Desdemona, however, had other ideas. Mr Punch had nipped her sharply several times on the journey out and, at the sight of him thundering down on her, she jumped sharply out of his way, causing Fen to drop the baton.

'What dreadful language,' said Rupert, who was standing nearby, grinning from ear to ear. 'What a good thing all those nice Italian spectators can't understand what Griselda's saying to Fen.'

Determined to redeem herself in the big class in the evening, Fen rode with such attack that when Macaulay decided he didn't like the jump built in the shape of a Roman villa and started to dig his toes in, Fen shot straight over his head, covering herself in bruises.

The previous day, Malise had organized some sightseeing. They went to St Peter's and saw the statue of St Peter, with the stone foot worn away by the kisses of the pilgrims.

'I came here with Janey,' Fen overheard Billy saying to Rupert. 'I swore that by the end of our life together I'd have kissed her more than the pilgrims had kissed that foot. Perhaps that's why she pushed off.' He was trying to make a joke of it, but Fen could sense his despair.

Being superstitious, all the riders wanted to visit the Trevi fountain.

'Isn't it beautiful?' said Fen, admiring the bronze tritons, the gods and goddesses, the wild horses and the leaping glistening, rushing cascade of water.

'Only thing missing is Rossano Brazzi,' said Driffield.

'Who's he?' asked Fen.

'He was in *Three Coins in the Fountain*. Christ, you must be young. Do you think,' he added, looking at his loose change, 'an Irish penny would work?'

'No, it's bad luck,' said Rupert, chucking in a fifty pence piece. 'I expect you'll sneak back at dusk and fish that out, Driffield.'

Fen threw in a ten-pence piece.

'Please, Fountain,' she prayed, 'when I come back, let it be with a really nice man who loves me as much as I love him.'

Opening her eyes, she found Billy beside her. He had also tossed 50p into the fountain, watching it float down, to land on the bronze and silver floor. His lips were moving, his face haggard, his hair even greyer in the sunlight.

'He's wishing he'll come back to Rome with Janey,' thought Fen. 'Oh poor, poor Billy.'

Back at the show in the afternoon, she hadn't fared any better. And now she'd been packed off to bed at eleven o'clock, with soothing reassurances from Malise that she was not to worry, she'd soon find her feet and to get a good night's sleep. How could she possibly sleep with all that din and merrymaking in the streets below?

Her mood was not helped by the fact that Sarah and Dizzy had been asked out by two American tennis stars, over for the tournament which ran concurrently with the horse show. Both grooms had come and had used Fen's room to bath and wash their hair and change, then had gone off in raging spirits looking gorgeous.

Fen went out on the balcony. Here I am in the most beautiful city in the world, she thought, with the Spring in its green prime, with the streets and parks filled with lovers kissing, holding hands, necking in traffic jams, lying on the grass. Everywhere she went, gorgeous Italian men, with hot, pansy-dark eyes, followed her, wolf-whistling and pinching her bottom, but Rupert and Billy and Malise chaperoned her so fiercely she wasn't allowed near them. Only that evening at a drinks party she'd been chatted up by a fantastic-looking French tennis player, who was just asking her out to dinner when Rupert came up and told him to piss off.

'What's that you say?' asked the Frenchman.

So Rupert told him in French, even more forcibly, and the Frenchman had gone very white and backed off. That was another thing. Rupert had made terrific verbal passes

568

at her at the World Championship, but now he was treating her as though she was a very boring nine-year-old child he was expected to look after. And that night, no doubt, he and Billy had gone off on the tiles.

She knew she ought to undress and try to sleep. But it was so hot and stuffy she stayed on the balcony watching the lights twinkling in the grounds of the Villa Borghese. Even the moon was wrapped in a gold lurex shawl of cloud, as though she was going out for the evening.

'Nothing in excess,' Apollo's motto, was carved over the door at the entrance to the hotel. I'm obviously not going to get a chance even to have anything in moderation, Fen thought sulkily.

'Please Apollo,' she pleaded, 'I promise I won't be excessive. Just let me have a bit of fun.' As if in answer to her prayer, the telephone rang. Fen sprang on it. '*Buona Notte*.'

'Hi,' said a soft voice, 'is that Fen?'

'Who's that?' she squeaked, her heart hammering.

'It's Dino, Dino Ferranti.'

Fen sat down suddenly on the bed.

'Hullo, hullo,' he said when she couldn't speak. 'Fen?'

'Yes,' she stammered. 'Oh, how blissful to hear you.'

'I sure missed you, baby. Did you get my telegram?'

'Oh, yes. It was so sweet of you. How did you know?'

'I've had my spies out. How are you getting on?'

'Not great, I haven't won a thing.'

'Don't worry, it's a helluva course. Has Rupert been leaping on you?'

'On the contrary, they're all treating me as though I was a typhoid carrier.'

'This is a godawful line,' said Dino.

'Where are you?'

'In Rome.'

'Rome!' She knew she should be cool, but she couldn't keep the squeak of delight out of her voice.

'Just dropped by to look at a horse. I'm flying out tomorrow. I guess it's late, but you wouldn't like to come out, would you?'

'Oh, yes, please.'

'I'll pick you up in half an hour.'

She'd never washed her hair or bathed so quickly. Thank God, she hadn't worn her new pink dress and pink shoes yet. She'd been saving them for a special occasion. 'Everything in excess,' she told her radiant reflection as she sprayed duty free scent, bought on the boat, everywhere: in her shoes, behind her knees and ears and on her bush.

She hoped Dino wouldn't go off her because she'd cut her hair. She wished she had time to paint her toe-nails.

She decided not to take the lift, in case she ran into Malise. Instead crept down the huge staircase, clinging onto the banisters for support. Her knees kept giving way. In two minutes she'd see Dino.

Blast! There were Rupert and Driffield in the lobby, apparently examining some expensive jerseys in a glass case. She shot back upstairs, peering through the banisters. Hell! They were still there. She'd just have to brazen it out. Why shouldn't she go and have a drink with Dino? She reached the bottom of the stairs and was just tiptoeing across the marble floor to the front door, when Rupert and Driffield turned around, both doubled up with laughter.

'What's the matter?' asked Fen, walking past them, her nose in the air.

'April fool,' said Rupert.

Ignoring them, Fen walked on.

Catching up, Rupert tapped her on the shoulder. 'April fool.'

'I don't know what you're talking about.'

'I sure missed you, kid. This is Dino Ferranti.'

Fen looked at him, bewildered.

'Is he here already? Where is he?'

Rupert looked down at her, his eyes narrowed to slits, that mocking cruel smile on his beautiful face.

'In America, as far as I know.'

'He's not,' said Fen patiently. 'He's in Rome. I've just talked to him on the telephone.'

'And he's come to look at a horse and all the British team are treating you as if you were a typhoid carrier.'

The colour drained from Fen's face.

'It was you,' she whispered.

'Sure was. Don't you think I've picked up quite a good American accent from my wife?'

Fen looked at him with contempt. 'You bastard. How could you?'

Rupert shrugged. 'New girl's tease.' He ruffled her hair. 'Come on, I'll buy you a drink.'

'You bloody won't,' and, bursting into tears, she ran back upstairs. As she panted, sobbing, up to the second floor Rupert came out of the lift.

'Come on, it was a joke.'

'Not to me, it wasn't.' She fled down the passage, but as she scrabbled desperately in her bag for her key, Rupert caught up with her.

'Angel, I'm sorry. I didn't realize it would upset you that much.'

'Go away,' she sobbed. 'I hate you.'

'Shush, shush,' he said, taking her in her arms. 'You'll wake up Griselda from her ugly sleep.'

'Stop it,' she said, hammering her fists against his chest as tears spilled down her cheeks. But he was far too strong for her.

Next moment he was kissing her quivering mouth. For a second she clenched her teeth together. Then, suddenly aware of his warmth and vitality, she melted and began to kiss him back. Her hands, against her will, crept up over the powerful shoulders, her fingers entwining in the sleek thick hair.

'What the hell are you two doing?' said a voice.

Fen nearly went through the ceiling. Rupert didn't move.

'What does it look as though we're doing?' snapped Rupert.

He stopped kissing Fen, but still shielded her in his arms. 'Look, Malise, this is entirely my fault, not Fen's. I enticed her out as a practical joke, pretending to be someone else.

571

Then I followed her upstairs and – er – forced my attentions on her.'

'She didn't appear to be putting up much resistance,' said Malise coldly.

'That's my irresistible charm.' said Rupert. Releasing Fen, he opened her door and gave her her bag which had fallen on the carpet. 'Go to bed, darling. I'll sort this out.'

Malise, in a dinner jacket, had been to the theatre. Rupert and he glared at each other.

'Well,' said Rupert softly, 'what are you going to do about it?'

'Nothing, this time,' said Malise, 'but you can thank your lucky stars, albeit interpreted by Patric Walker, that I caught you outside the bedroom. If this happens again, I'll leave you out of the team for the rest of the year.'

Rupert looked unrepentant. 'She's so adorable, it's almost worth it,' he said.

Billy, who'd forgotten to declare for the following day and had just returned from the show offices, was absolutely livid when he heard what had happened.

'You rotten sod,' he shouted at Rupert. 'Didn't you see the way her little face lit up when the cable arrived? She's obviously mad about him. How could you do such a fucking awful thing to her? You don't understand anything about people's feelings. You're like a bloody boy scout in reverse. You have to do a bad deed every day,' and he walked into his bedroom, slamming the door. Immediately he dialled Fen's number.

'If that's Rupert, you can bugger off.'

'It isn't. Are you O.K.?'

'Perfectly,' said Fen in a choked voice.

'Do you want a shoulder to cry on?'

'And get into more trouble with Malise! No, thank you very much,' said Fen with a stifled sob, and hung up.

By morning, misery had hardened into cold rage against Rupert. How could she have betrayed Jake and let herself kiss him back like that and, even worse, have enjoyed it? She was a nymphomaniac virgin. She went out to work the horses, boot-faced, with dark glasses covering her swollen eyes.

Malise came down to watch her, asking her to come and have a cup of coffee with him afterwards.

Perhaps he'll even send me home, she thought miserably.

But Malise merely wanted to tell her that she hadn't been picked for the Nations' Cup. Ivor Braine had pulled a back muscle, so the team would be Rupert, Billy, Driffield and Griselda.

Hanging her head, Fen reminded Malise of a snowdrop.

'I'm sorry I've been so hopeless.'

'You haven't. You won that class the first day.'

'You don't want to send me back because you've made a ghastly mistake?'

'You have the self-confidence of a snail,' said Malise. 'You obviously don't rate me as a chef d'equipe if you assume I'd select someone who was no good.'

Fen sprinkled chocolate on her cappucino.

'Wherefore rejoice,' she said moodily, 'what conquests brings she home?'

'Oh, you will. Look, you're a very, very good rider; better, dare I say it, even than Jake when he jumped that first earth-shattering double-clear on Sailor in Madrid. But it's all strange. Macaulay's strange, you haven't got Jake to mastermind your every move, Griselda's bitching; and Rupert and everyone else are letching.'

Fen flushed and bit her lip.

'Rupert really wouldn't do for you,' he said. 'I realize he's attractive. But Helen's had so much of that to put up with, and you know how Jake detests him.'

'I didn't want — it wasn't like that,' stammered Fen.

'I don't want excuses,' said Malise, 'Rupert accepts full responsibility, but that still doesn't alter the fact that you shouldn't have been out of your room, in a party dress, an hour after you'd been sent to bed. Now, d'you want to come and have a look at the Sistine Chapel?'

There were two big classes that afternoon: the first a knock-out competition, the second a Puissance, sponsored by one of Italy's leading car manufacturers.

'Macaulay's in a foul mood,' Sarah told Fen when she got to the show ground. 'He's just sulking in his box.'

'He's fed up with not winning,' said Fen. 'I'm going to jump him in the Puissance.'

Sarah looked horrified. 'Are you sure that's wise? Jake's never jumped him in a Puissance, and high-jumping really isn't his forte. The ground's absolutely rock hard.'

'I don't care,' said Fen. 'Get him ready.'

The knock-out competition before the Puissance consisted of two U-shaped courses each of nine jumps, lying side by side. The riders raced up the outside of the Us, then around the top and came side by side down the inside of the Us. Riders going around the right-hand U had to wear a primrose-yellow sash to distinguish them. Twenty-four riders started. Fen had a walkover in the first round. Apart from that she had a tough draw, which included Guy de la Tour, Ludwig and Rupert. In the other draw was Piero Fratinelli, son of the car firm and darling of the crowd.

Her first battle was against Griselda, whom she had great delight in beating by a couple of lengths. This was just Desdemona's sort of class. She was nippy, lithe as a cat; her father hadn't won the Cesarewitch for nothing.

Count Guy, whom she rode against next, had had rather too many glasses of wine at lunchtime and carelessly had the first fence down, so Fen was able to conserve Desdemona's energy and coast to an easy clear. Ludwig put out Rupert; Piero Fratinelli sadly put out Billy. But Fen had no time to feel sorry before she had donned the yellow sash and was back in the ring, competing against Ludwig.

'He's taken one prize off us this week, and he's not going to do it again,' Fen said to Desdemona.

The handsome Ludwig was already in the ring, exchanging badinage with the rest of the German team who, already knocked out, were sitting in the riders' stand. He turned, giving Fen a dazzling but slightly patronizing smile.

'Ah, Mees Fenella, I vill really haf to try. You look very nice in zat yellow sash.'

574

'Yes,' muttered Fen, 'and I'm jolly well going to wear it again in the final.'

Ludwig got away a fraction after. Fen, who streaked ahead, nibbling at Desdemona's ears, racing her like a gymkhana pony, rocketing over the jumps without any regard for safety. On the U-turn her hat flew off.

'Oh, Christ,' thought Billy, in anguish. 'I hope she doesn't fall on her head.'

Ludwig, on his big striding horse, was gaining on her. Neck and neck they came down the centre.

'Go on, Des,' screamed Fen.

Desdemona saw the collecting ring. Her blood was up. Flattening her pink ears in fury, she edged past the post a nose ahead of Ludwig.

'Photo feenish,' chorused the German team from the stands.

'It's ours,' said Rupert, grinning and making a V-sign at them.

Piero beat Wishbone, to the delight of the crowd. The stadium was like a cauldron. Fen kept the primrose-yellow sash and the right side. She had to wait, riding Desdemona around and around, while Piero got his breath back.

'No. 31,' said the collecting ring steward.

'Good luck,' said Rupert, handing her hat. 'At least we know you're not swollen-headed.'

Ignoring him, Fen rode into the ring, where Piero was sitting on the huge, dark bay thoroughbred, Dante, who had been purchased for millions of lira and who was hardly sweating.

How ever much she polished Desdemona's coat, she'd never got her that shiny, thought Fen wistfully, but the little mare stepped out proudly, ears pricked and flickering at the cheers.

David and Goliath, thought Billy, as Piero looked down at Fen, and smiled as he took off his hat to the judges. Fen bowed beside him. Then with a supremely Latin gesture, Piero picked up Fen's hand and kissed it.

'Bella bella bella,' roared the crowd.

'She's gone scarlet, bless her,' said Driffield fondly.

Billy looked at him in amazement. Christ, even Driff was smitten.

Piero and Fen lined up, Desdemona snatching at her bit and casting disapproving glances at Dante: don't you dare cheat now. The red flag dropped: they were off.

'Come on, angel,' cried Fen, as they threw themselves over the first three fences. Reaching the bend, she saw a huge black shape already swinging around. He was ahead of her.

'Go on, Des,' screamed Fen, bucketing over the fences like a runaway Ferrari. The crowd were going berserk. 'Piero, Piero, Piero,' the cry rose to a tremendous roar. Piero, ahead by a fence, looked round to make sure of his lead. Fen picked up her whip and gave Desdemona a jockey's swipe down her steaming flank. Outraged, the mare shot into overdrive. At the same time, the dark bay, Dante, caught a pole with his off hind. As it fell Fen drew level. She was over and clear; she'd made it. Desdemona, livid at being whacked, went into a succession of outraged bucks which nearly unseated Fen.

'I'm sorry, angel,' she said, pulling her up. 'I needn't have done it but I daren't risk it. You are a total star.'

She hoped the crowd weren't going to lynch her for beating their hero, but Malise's face told her everything.

'You've broken your duck. Brilliantly ridden.'

'Terrific,' said Billy, hugging her. 'She went like a dream.'

'Not bad for a beginner,' said Rupert. 'Are we friends again?'

'No,' said Fen and stalked off to warm Macaulay up for the Puissance.

That evening, when she got back to the hotel Fen rang Jake.

'I suppose you've won a class at last,' he said sourly, 'or you wouldn't be ringing.'

'Co-rrect,' said Fen. 'I made such a cock-up of things

earlier in the week, I didn't dare. Desdemona won the knock-out. I beat Ludwig, then Piero in the final.'

Jake grunted. 'How's Macaulay?'

'Wonderful. Actually I've got good news and bad news about him.'

'For Christ's sake. He's all right, isn't he?'

'Well, the bad news is, I entered him in the Puissance.'

'You what?' Even at a thousand miles away, she quailed. 'But the good news is, he won.'

For two minutes Jake called her every name under the sun. Then he asked, 'How high did he jump?'

Fen giggled. 'Seven foot two, easy peasy. He could have gone higher; and, oh Jake, he was so delighted to be in the money again. You know how he adores winning. He bucked after every jump and insisted on doing two laps of honour and ate the President's carnation. But he's really well,' she added hastily. 'I hosed down his legs myself and put on cooling linament, and I'll walk him round in an hour or two, but it really bucked him up.'

'How much have you won?'

'Well, I haven't worked it out yet; you know my maths. About £3000, I should think. But the best news is I won a little car as well, so I'll be able to whizz you around all over the place when you come out of hospital. How are you, anyway?'

Jake didn't want to talk about himself, but she could tell by the sound of his voice how thrilled he was.

40

There was a drinks party at the British Embassy that night, and for once the team weren't under Malise's ever-watchful eye. A complimentary ticket from the Minister of the Arts to hear Placido Domingo as Othello at the Teatro dell Opera had been too much for him, but he'd had tough words with the team beforehand.

'This is the first Nations' Cup in the series. If we win, it'll be a colossal boost to morale. So there's to be no heavy drinking and I want everyone in their rooms by midnight. You'll be the only one completely sober,' he added to Billy, 'so I'm relying on you to look after Fen and see she's in her own bed and not Rupert's by eleven o'clock.'

Billy shook his head. 'If you honestly think Rupert'll take any notice of me.'

Rupert arrived at the party in a new suit – pale blue and made for him by one of Italy's leading couturiers, who normally only designed clothes for women, but who had succumbed because he rightly felt Rupert would be such a good advertisement for his product.

Anyone else would have looked a raving poofter, thought Billy, particularly wearing an amethyst-coloured shirt and tie. But such was Rupert's masculinity, and the enhanced blueness of his eyes, and the lean, broad-shouldered length of his body, that the result was sensational.

All the girls at the party were certainly falling over themselves to offer him smoked salmon and asparagus rolls and fill up his glass with champagne.

'They're all convinced I'm an American tennis player,' he said, fighting his way through the crowd to Billy. 'I've already been complimented three times on my back hand and my serve. The only thing I want to serve here,' he said, lowering his voice, 'is Fenella Maxwell.'

'Oh, for Christ's sake,' snapped Billy.

'She wants it,' said Rupert softly. 'She was like a mare in season last night. Besides I've a score to settle with Hopalong Chastity.'

'Poor sod's in hospital with a smashed leg. Isn't that enough for you?'

'William, he's tried to kill me twice, once with a knife, once with Macaulay. I intend to get my own back.'

He glanced across the room to where Fen was talking to the Italian Minister of the Arts, who was about three times her age. She looked pale and tired.

'Look at her being letched over by that disgusting wop. I'll just make her jealous by chatting up those two girls over there and I've got her on a plate.'

'You conceit is unending. Christ, I wish I could have a drink.'

'Those two look as though they might have some dope at home. Come on.'

The girls were certainly very pretty – one blonde, one redheaded.

'You must be tennis players,' giggled the redhead. 'You look so incredibly healthy.'

'No,' said Rupert, unsmiling.

'What do you do then?'

'I ride horses,' said Rupert; then, after a pause, 'extremely successfully.'

The conversation moved on to marriage.

'Billy is separated and gloriously available,' said Rupert. 'I am married and ditto.'

'Doesn't your wife mind?'

'No.'

'Does she work for a living?'

'No, nor does she smoke, drink or fuck.'

The girls laughed uproariously. Billy turned away. Outside it was dusk. A stone nymph in an off-the-shoulder

579

dress reclined in the long grass, set against a blackening yew tree. Fireflies flickered round a couple of orange trees in tubs. Water from a fountain tumbled down grey-green steps between banks of pale-lilac geraniums.

I can't bear it, he thought miserably, and toyed with the idea of asking Fen to come and have dinner with him alone. She didn't look very happy, particularly now the blonde was obviously getting off with Rupert. She and her friend were secretaries at the Embassy, the blonde was saying; they loved the life in Rome.

Her redhead friend joined Billy by the window.

'I'm sorry about your marriage,' she said. 'I'm separated myself. No one who hasn't been through it knows how awful it is.'

Billy mistook the brimming tears of self-pity in her eyes for pity of his own plight.

'When did you split up?' he asked.

'Six months ago,' she said, and she was off.

Fifteen minutes later they were interrupted by Driffield, looking like a thundercloud.

'Crippled lame,' he said in disgust. 'Horse can't put his foot down. Vet's just had a look; thinks it's an abscess.' He grabbed a glass of champagne from a passing tray. 'Where's Malise?'

'Gone to the opera.'

'Bloody fairy.'

'My God,' said Griselda, joining them. 'That means Fen will have to jump. That's all we need.'

'She jumped bloody well this afternoon,' said Driffield.

'I'd better go and tell her,' said Billy. But, glancing across the room, he saw she'd disappeared. He tried the other rooms, fighting his way through the yelling crowd, then he tried the garden, hearing laughter from behind a rose bush.

'Fuck off,' said a voice as he peered around. Two elegant young men were locked in each other's arms.

Fen's coat wasn't in the cloakroom. Yes, said the attendant, a girl in a pink dress and pink shoes had just left with the Minister of the Arts. He assumed she was his daughter.

'She isn't,' said Billy bleakly.

'Lucky chap,' said the attendant.

Billy returned to Rupert and told him what had happened. Rupert, who'd already drunk a bottle and a half of champagne, shrugged his shoulders. 'Oh well, she won't come to any harm with him. He looked past it. Anyway these 'ere,' he jerked his head in the direction of the two secretaries. 'look very accommodating. We'll all have dinner, then go back to their place.'

'I don't want to,' protested Billy. 'I must find Fen.'

'She'll go back to the hotel early,' said Rupert. 'She heard Malise's pep talk. She was as contrite as anything this morning.'

At dinner, the girls got sillier and sillier, and Billy's despair deeper. Back at their flat he went to the bathroom to have a pee. The spilt talcum powder, the chaos of make-up, the tights and pants dripping over the bath, the trailing plant gasping for water and the half-drunk gin and tonic reminded him poignantly of Janey. He longed to go back to the hotel. The redhead was pretty, but it was obvious she would much rather be in bed with Rupert. 'Your friend's a one, isn't he?'

On the walls of her room were posters of Robert Redford and Sylvester Stallone. The bed was very narrow.

'I don't usually do this on the first night,' she said slipping out of her pale yellow dress with a slither of silk. Her body wasn't as good stripped; her breasts drooped like half-filled bean bags.

'I'm awfully sorry,' Billy said later, looking down at his flaccid, lifeless cock.

'Don't you find me attractive?' said the girl petulantly.

'It's because you're so beautiful you've completely overwhelmed me,' lied Billy. 'And I've got a big class tomorrow, which never helps.'

With his hands and his tongue he had given her pleasure, but, rejected by her husband, she needed confirmation that

581

men still found her irresistible. Billy could feel her being 'frightfully understanding', but he could imagine the whispering round the Embassy tomorrow.

'My dear, he couldn't get it up at all. No wonder his wife walked out.'

By a quarter to twelve Rupert was ready to go home too.

'We'd love tickets for tomorrow,' said the blonde as they left. 'You will ring, won't you?'

'I nearly couldn't perform,' said Rupert in the taxi. 'She just lay back stark naked on the bed and said, "Come on Campbell-Black, let's see if you're as good as they all say you are." Must be hell to be impotent.'

'I hope to God Fen's back,' said Billy.

But to his horror her key, No. 88, was still hanging at the reception desk.

'Jesus,' said Rupert, 'there's Malise getting out of a cab. Go and tell him about Driffield. I'll get the key and whizz up and wait in her room. You join me when the coast's clear.'

'Good opera?' Billy asked Malise.

'Magical,' said Malise. 'I cried nonstop through the last act.'

He didn't even seem to notice that the hall clock said half past twelve.

'First Edition's unfit,' said Billy. 'Vet says it's an abscess.'

'Hell,' said Malise. 'Fen'll have to jump. Does she know?'

'We didn't tell her,' said Billy, 'in case we raised her hopes and you wanted Driff to jump Anaconda.'

Malise shook his head. 'Macaulay's the better bet. You saw Fen safely into bed, did you?'

Billy nodded, blushing slightly. 'Must be asleep by now.'

'Good man. I'll tell her in the morning.'

With a growing sense of outrage, Billy and Rupert sat in Fen's room, Rupert drinking weak brandies from Fen's untouched duty-free bottle, Billy drinking one disgusting cup of black coffee from the sachets after another.

582

At three-thirty, they heard a commotion outside.

'*J'ai perdu mon clef*, key, you know; what St Peter, the one with the kissed foot, had in abundance,' said a shrill voice, 'so if you'd be so very kind as to let me into my room.'

In a flash Rupert was at the door, where he found Fen and a sleepy-looking maid in a dressing-gown.

'*Grazie*,' he said to the maid and pulled Fen inside. 'What the bloody hell have you got to say for yourself?'

Fen's hair was tousled, her brown skin flushed. Her eyes glittered, red-irised and out of focus. She was wearing an exquisite, grey, silk shirt which just covered her groin, and carrying her pink dress.

She gave a low bow.

'*Buona notte, senors*; or should it be *buon giorno*, I forget. I sheem – hic – to have got myself into the wrong room.' She backed towards the door.

'Come here,' hissed Rupert. 'Where the hell have you been?'

'Do you really want to know? I've been having fun. When in Rome, get done by the Romans.' She opened the door into the passage, swinging on the handle.

Rupert caught her by the scruff of the neck, frog-marched her back into the room and sat her down on the bed. Then, locking the door, he pocketed the key.

'Now, come on. Out with it.'

Fen looked at them owlishly. 'I've been out with the Minister of the Arts, such charm and such finesse. He said I was a work of art myself and he bought me thish lovely shirt from Pucci.'

She stood up, pirouetted round and collapsed onto the bed again.

'And I regret to tell you I lost my virginity. And it's no point going to look for it at the Loshed Property Offish; it's gone for good. One should be in the hands of an eckshpert the first time, don't you think? "I jumped seven foot two this afternoon, so it's but a tiny leap into your ancient four poster, Mr Minister," I said.'

Billy felt a great sadness.

'You little slut,' said Rupert slowly. 'You just picked him up and went to bed for a sixty-thousand lire shirt.'

'Better than nothing, which I'd have got from you lot. Anyway.' said Fen, suddenly furious. 'If I'm a slut, what the hell d'you think you are, going to parties, picking up awful typists, and all those horrible things you said about Helen? How can you behave like that when you've got a beautiful wife, and lovely children? You're the most immoral man I've ever met.'

There was banging on the next-door wall. Someone shouted in German.

'Oh, shut up,' said Fen, banging back again.

Her eyes lit on the brandy. 'I want another drink.'

Billy got to his feet. 'You've had enough,' he said flatly. 'Come on, get to bed. I'll help you undress.'

Fen swayed away from him. 'No no, I can't be undressed twice in an evening.' Then she swayed back towards him.

'Darling Will-yum, don't look so sad. True love will suddenly come to you as it hash to me.' She stood on tiptoe trying to kiss him, but the effort was too much for her. She collapsed back on the bed and passed out.

'It's not funny,' said Rupert.

'I know it isn't,' said Billy.

'What the hell are you doing?' said Rupert, as Billy started unbuttoning the shirt.

'Shame if she puked over her Pucci,' said Billy.

'Lovely body,' said Rupert. 'Reminds me of Saville Minor. I suppose we can't take advantage?'

'No, we can't,' said Billy, tucking her into bed.

Through nightmares of pain and torture – was someone acupuncturing her brain with red hot pokers? – Fen could hear bells. They must be ambulance bells, taking her to hospital to die.

But it was the telephone. She reached out, dropped it and picked it up.

'Morning, Fen, sorry to wake you,' said a brisk voice. 'Have you had a good night?'

'Yes,' she croaked.

'Congratulations, anyway, on your first cap. Driffield's out. You'll be jumping today.'

'I what?' stammered Fen in horror.

'Makes you speechless, does it?' Malise laughed. 'See you down at the stables in about an hour. Then we can put Macaulay over a few practice fences.'

Fen put the telephone down and groaned. She got up, rushed to the loo and was sick.

'Why doesn't someone turn down those bloody bells?' she croaked. 'They can't be Christians to make a din like that.'

Her breeches, which she'd taken to the launderette the previous day, were still hanging over the balcony. She winced with pain as she opened the shutters. The sunlight hit her like a boxing glove. She staggered back to the bed and, picking up the telephone, dialled Billy's number.

'Billy, it's Fen – I think. Get me an ambulance.'

He laughed. 'Is it that bad?'

'I've never known pain like it.'

'I'll be with you in a couple of minutes.'

He found her white and shuddering. 'Here lies one whose name is writ in Krug,' she moaned. 'Take me to the nearest pharmacia and tell me the Italian for Alka Seltzer. I've got to jump, Billy. More likely, to jump over that balcony.'

'Drink this. It's disgusting, but it should help.' He handed her some Fernet Branca in a toothmug.

'Ugh, it is disgusting. I'm going to throw up.'

'No, you're not. Keep your head up, take deep breaths.'

'Do you think there's any hope of the arena party going on strike?' said Fen.

Billy looked at the bruises on her thighs, wondering if they were the result of amorous pinches from the Minister of Arts. Fen seemed to read his thoughts and blushed. 'I got them falling off Macaulay.'

She was not helped by a sudden heatwave hitting Rome. As she tottered the course beside Billy three hours later, the temperature had was in the nineties. The sun seemed to be beating down only on her head. There was no shade. The coloured poles danced before her eyes.

'Where did you go last night, Fen?' said Griselda bullyingly, as they examined a vast wall.

'I don't remember the name, but I had shellfish,' said Fen faintly.

'Hum,' said Griselda in disbelief.

'This course is designed to make riders think every inch of the way,' said Malise, as they examined the huge water jump floating with water lilies, known as the bidet. 'It's going to take very accurate jumping. The stile's only four and a half strides before the combination. Macaulay'll probably do it in four, Fen. Are you feeling all right?'

'Fine,' said Fen, clinging onto the wing of the fence. 'It's just the heat.'

'Poor kid, suffers from nerves as badly as Jake,' thought Malise, looking at her green face.

Eight teams came out for the Nations' Cup. Fen, after the previous day's triumph, got a rousing cheer as she rode in the parade, flanked by Rupert and Billy.

The playing of each National Anthem seemed to go on for ever.

'It's you, not our gracious Queen, that needs saving today,' said Rupert out of the corner of his mouth.

Great Britain's fortunes were varied. Rupert jumped an effortless clear which brought more rousing cheers – even from the most partisan crowd in Europe.

Waiting, pouring with sweat, teeth chattering, wondering whether to be sick again, Fen felt too ill even to be pleased that Griselda had nearly fallen off at the bidet and had notched up twelve faults. She came out furiously tugging Mr Punch's head from side to side.

Britain was in third place when Fen went in.

'Go for a steady clear,' said Malise. 'I'd like to drop Griselda's round.'

Fen felt like a Christian after the Roman emperor had made that terrible thumbs-down sign of death. Alone in the ring, under those towering stands which had just become a sea of faces, she could feel the lions stealthily padding towards her.

Macaulay, who always felt a great responsibility for the rider on his back, understood that Fen needed help. Watching his earnest white face appearing over each jump, Billy realized he was taking Fen around. He was about to take five strides after the stile, then changed to four, bouncing easily over the combination, but causing Fen to lose a stirrup. Slowing fractionally so she could find it again, he rounded the corner. For a minute Fen looked perplexed, then she turned him sharp right towards the huge yellow wall. A million times afterwards she relived that moment. She seemed to hear a shout from the collecting ring, but it was too late. Gathering Macaulay together, she cleared the wall, then looked around in bewilderment for the next jump. In front, a triple was facing backwards with a red flag on the left. Excited officials were waving their arms at her; the crowd gave a groan of sympathy. And suddenly it dawned on Fen – she'd taken the wrong course.

Head hanging, fighting back the tears, white-faced, she cantered out of the ring.

'Fucking imbecile,' said Rupert.

'You've ruined our chances,' said Grisel, her mouth full of hot dog.

Fen slid off Macaulay, loosening his girths, giving him his lemon sherbets, whispering, 'I'm sorry, I'm sorry,' over and over again.

'Bad luck,' said Sarah, 'you were going so well.'

Malise came up. 'I hope that won't happen in the second round,' he said bleakly.

'I must not cry, I must not cry,' said Fen, and fled to the loo, where she was sick for the fifteenth time that day.

On her return, she found everyone more cheerful, particularly Mr Block, Billy's sponsor, who'd flown out to watch the Nations' Cup. Billy and Bugle had gone clear, bouncing over the fences like a Jack-in-the-box. At the end of the first leg the Germans were in the lead, the Italians second, and the English and the Swiss tying for third place.

Fen couldn't face the riders' stand. She sat on an upturned bucket, under the thick canopy of an umbrella pine, with her head in her hands. Macaulay, led by Sarah, came up and nuzzled her.

'Poor old boy,' said Fen listlessly. 'It's bloody hot.'

Macaulay looked longingly as an ice-cream seller came by.

'Oh, get him one,' Fen told Sarah. 'He deserves it.'

At that moment Rupert came up, keeping his distance because Macaulay promptly rolled his eyes and stamped his foot threateningly. 'I hope you'll know better in future than to get plastered and seduced by geriatric wops,' said Rupert viciously.

Already the sun was beginning to slant sideways through the pines, throwing treacherous shadows across the fences, particularly the parallel.

On his mettle, Rupert jumped just as brilliantly in the second round. He was unlucky to hit the second pole of the parallel and notch up four faults. He came out in a furious temper.

'Horse was going superbly, but he simply couldn't see what he was jumping at the parallel. I'm going to object.'

Nor did the Germans or the Italians fare any better. The unaccustomed hot weather and the punishing course were tiring them all out. Griselda finished her second hot dog and rode off into the ring.

'How the hell can she stuff herself like that before a class?' said Fen.

'Her nerve ends are so coated with fat they don't function properly,' said Sarah. 'Oh, whizzo, she's fallen in the bidet. Look at her covered in water lilies.'

'You're being very unpatriotic,' reproved Billy. 'She is on our side.'

He put a hand on Fen's forehead. 'Are you feeling any better?'

'Not after that frightful cock-up.'

He shrugged. 'Happen to anyone.'

Having fallen off, Griselda went on to notch up a further four faults.

'Just get around this time. That's all that matters,' said Malise, as Fen went in. She had never felt so ill in her life.

'Keep the white flag on your left, keep the white flag on your left,' she said to herself over and over again.

Somehow she got over the first seven fences, including the bogey parallel. But as she approached the combination a child at the edge of the crowd let go of her gas balloon and, with bellows of misery, watched it float out like a spermatozoa just in front of Macaulay. For a second he glanced at it, confused, put in a short stride, found himself under the fence and took a colossal cat jump which nearly unseated Fen. Losing her reins, but clutching on to his mane for grim death, she managed to stay on as he cleared the second element, but her foot went straight through the iron. His last huge leap over the final element completely unseated her and she went crashing to the ground, but, with her foot trapped, was dragged, bumping horribly, for several yards before Macaulay, realizing what had happened, jammed on his brakes. Two officials ran up and disconnected her. Blood was pouring from her nose on to her white shirt, tie and breeches. Staggering to her feet, she looked dazedly round for Macaulay.

'I must get back on; got to finish.'

There he was, looking apologetic and worried. His white face seemed to come towards her and go away. Stumbling over to him, she tried to clamber on, but as he was 17.2 it was like climbing the Matterhorn.

'Give me a leg up,' she screamed to the steward. 'I'll run out of time.'

The stewards, in broken English, told her she mustn't jump and looked desperately around for the first-aid man. Just as he came running on, she somehow managed to get her foot in the stirrup and heaved herself up, blood still streaming from her nose.

Heedless to the cries to stop, she turned to the last row of jumps.

589

'Get her out of the ring,' said Billy, as white as his shirt. 'She'll kill herself.'

The crowds were screaming in horror. Fen had lost so much blood it seemed that she was dressed all in red. Somehow she cleared the next two fences. She looked around, bewildered and swaying. There was only the oxer left. Fortunately Macaulay took charge. He could see the collecting ring and he wanted to get back there as soon as possible. Trotting briskly around the oxer, with Fen clinging round his neck, he carried her carefully out of the ring.

Malise, Billy and Rupert rushed forward.

'It's only a nosebleed,' muttered Fen into Macaulay's blood-soaked mane. 'You were right about there only being four and a half strides between the stile and the combination.' As they lifted her off, she fainted.

'Get an ambulance,' said Billy in anguish. 'We must get her to hospital. I'm going with her.'

'Don't be so fucking silly,' said Rupert and Malise in unison. 'You've still got to jump.'

They decided to keep Fen in hospital overnight. After they'd cleaned her up, it was found she was only suffering from a severe nosebleed and slight concussion. Later, when Billy turned up to visit her, he found her in a clean white nightgown, slumped in bed, red-eyed, with her swollen face turned to the wall.

'Fen, it's me, Billy.'

'Is Macaulay all right?'

'Blooming. I saw he got his five lemon sherbets. I've brought you these.'

He held a bunch of yellow roses in front of her face.

'Thanks.' She hunched up her shoulders, pulling the sheet up over her eyes. Billy put the roses in the washbasin and sat down on the bed.

'How are you feeling?'

She looked round, her eyes swollen with crying, her lips puffy and bruised where she'd hit the ground, her face covered in bruises.

'Terrible.'

Billy smiled. 'You look as though you've just done ten rounds with Henry Cooper.'

'It's very kind of you to come and see me, but I want to be on my own.'

'Just wanted to see if you were all right.'

'Perfectly,' she snapped.

Billy got to his feet. As he reached the door she gave a strangled sob. Billy sat down again and took her in his arms.

'I'm so ashamed,' she wailed, burying her face in his

shoulder. 'Such an awful thing to do. But I was so fed up with being chaperoned and everyone treating me like a baby. In fact, a baby would have behaved with more responsibility. Getting eliminated twice in a Nations' Cup, I've let you all down: Macaulay, Jake, Malise, all the team, Great Britain.'

'Fen,' Billy stroked her hair, 'can I tell you something?'

'No, I want to talk. I lied to you last night. I was just boasting because I was drunk and fed up. Umberto, that's the Minister of the Arts, was awfully sweet, but his boyfriend died two months ago and he misses him terribly. All he wanted to do was to talk about him. He did the talking. I was listening, and you tend to drink a lot when you're listening. He didn't lay a finger on me except for kissing my hand. But when I got back Rupert was so bloody censorious, just assuming I'd been behaving like a whore, after all he'd been up to – and I was jealous of you chatting up that beastly redhead – I just lost my temper. But I promise I didn't sleep with him.'

For a minute Billy couldn't speak for relief.

'So I don't want Malise calling Umberto out, or anything.'

'He's hardly likely to after Umberto gave him a ticket to hear Placido Domingo,' said Billy.

'Don't make jokes,' sobbed Fen. 'It's not funny.'

'So you're still intacta.'

Fen nodded dolefully. 'Not much else to boast about, with cock-ups in every other direction.'

'Except from Umberto.'

'Oh, shut up,' sniffed Fen.

Suddenly she realised he was still wearing boots and breeches spattered with her blood. He'd taken off his white tie and exchanged his red coat for a dark-blue jersey with a hole in the elbow, but he'd forgotten to take off his spurs.

'You came straight from the show. You shouldn't have bothered. I'm sorry about your breeches.'

'Fenella,' said Billy gently, 'if you'd keep your trap shut for one second, I've got something for you.'

592

He put his hand in his pocket, then dropped a red rosette and a little silver model of the she-wolf suckling Romulus and Remus.

'W-what's this?'

'We won.'

'But how could we? Griselda was on twelve and I was eliminated.'

Billy grinned. 'The Germans went to pieces and I jumped another clear.'

Fen opened her mouth and shut it again; then she flung her arms round his neck. 'But that's wonderful, *and* with Mr Block watching. Oh, I'm so, so pleased.'

'Malise is going round like the Cheshire cat that's just wolfed the canary.'

Fen picked up the rosette. 'Is he still livid with me?'

'On the contrary. He now thinks you were very brave to jump at all. Rupert told him you'd swallowed a bad oyster last night and soldiered on because there wasn't anyone else to jump.'

'Rupert did?' said Fen incredulously. 'That was extraordinarily kind of him.'

Billy laughed. 'Rupert loves winning, so now Malise thinks you've been very plucky.'

'I haven't,' muttered Fen. 'I've been an idiot.' She looked at the rosette again; it matched the spattered blood. 'I had no part in getting this. I don't deserve it.'

'You deserved the one at the beginning of the week which Ludwig got, so this one makes up for it.'

But the tears were starting again.

'Angel, please don't cry.' He pulled her into his arms again, letting her tears drench his shirt. He was so warm, so comforting and rocklike, she couldn't bear him to go.

A nun came in, saying time was up and that Fen ought to rest.

Billy looked up. '*Duo momenti, grazie.*' He turned back to Fen. 'I'll come and collect you tomorrow morning.'

'Could you bring me some clothes to wear, preferably a yashmak?'

'And tomorrow night I'll take you out to dinner and treat

593

you like a grown-up.'

It was a very pale, subdued Fen that came out of hospital next morning. Billy brought her some clothes, but what he'd thought in his haste was a dress turned out to be a cotton nightgown with the pink panther on the front. Her lips and nose were still swollen and blackened.

'Don't look at me, I'm so ugly.'

The nuns bundled her bloodstained clothes into a carrier bag. 'I hope we don't get arrested,' said Fen.

'I'm afraid the taxis are on strike,' said Billy, putting his arm through hers, 'so we'll have to bus back to the Villa Borghese.'

'Ooch,' said Fen, as a passing Italian pinched her bottom.

The bus came crashing along, fighting for survival in the surging thrusting jam of cars.

'It's illegal to hoot in Rome,' said Fen.

'Bad luck for owls,' said Billy, as they fought and pummelled their way into the bus. For at least ten seconds they were separated, then Billy fought his way back to her.

'You O.K.?'

'I need a pencil sharpener for my elbows, and I've been goosed by six men.'

'You mean geesed.'

The bus doors closed, shooting another ten people into the body of the bus and ramming Fen against Billy. She arched away from him in embarrassment, but it was no good, the crowd pushed her forward again and she lost hold of the bus strap, cannoning into his arms, which closed round her.

'I'm going to complain to Sardine's Lib,' she mumbled in embarrassment.

'I'm not,' said Billy. 'Relax.'

Looking up, Fen saw the tenderness in his eyes and looked away quickly. But once again there was something so comforting and solid about him that she let herself relax for the rest of the ride, praying he couldn't feel her heart hammering.

'He loves Janey,' she told herself furiously. 'He's just being kind.'

The rest of the day seemed to pass in a dream. Everyone except Griselda was incredibly nice to her. Malise let her jump Desdemona in a small class to get her nerve back and was highly delighted when she came fourth. With a sense of unreality, she sat in the riders' stand beside Mr Block to watch the Grand Prix, which ended up with a jump-off between Piero, Rupert, Ludwig, Wishbone, Billy and Griselda. Billy, galvanized by the previous day's double clear, seemed to have got all his old fire and confidence back. Riding as though he'd got a spare neck in his pocket, he knocked three seconds off everyone's time. Rupert was second.

'Why the hell did I bring you back, when all you do is beat me?' grumbled Rupert as they rode into the ring.

Back at the stables, everyone was beginning to pack up. Griselda watched Georgie working and grumbled, 'I've got a bloody trek home, being mis-directed by that stupid Maxwell child. Let's hope Malise has learnt his lesson and leaves her out of the team.'

Billy, who was hosing down Bugle's legs, looked up angrily. 'She's already been selected for Paris and Lucerne.'

'Oh, Christ, don't say I've got to put up with her for the rest of the month. I must get Malise to make other travelling arrangements for her.'

Rupert, who was feeding popcorn to Snakepit, looked across at Billy and raised his eyebrows.

Billy nodded.

'He already has,' said Rupert. 'I've sold a couple of horses this week, so we're taking her back.'

'What about Sarah?' said Griselda, in tones of outrage.

'Very pretty,' said Rupert. 'She can have my bed in the lorry any time, as long as I'm allowed to share it with her.'

Griselda looked absolutely furious. 'The sneaky little thing, actually making other arrangements without telling me. Who's going to share the petrol and pay for the tolls on the autostrada? Trust her to pull a fast one without telling me.'

'She doesn't know she's coming with us yet,' said Billy sweetly, 'but knowing how much you and Georgie like the lorry to yourselves, I know she wouldn't like to cramp your style.'

'Well, on your heads be it if she misroutes you into Rumania,' said Griselda crossly.

Billy said goodbye to Mr Block, who was flying back to London.

'Well done, lad,' he said, pumping Billy's hand. 'I'm highly delighted with the way things have gone. We're on our way.'

Then Billy found Malise. 'Look, I know I ought to foot the bill for dinner tonight, and I'm very happy to, and I'd really like to be with you all, but I thought I'd take Fen somewhere quiet,' he blushed. 'I think she needs cheering up.'

Because he knew she was ashamed of her battered face, Billy took Fen to a little dark cave of a restaurant, where they sat in an alcove away from everyone else. She was still feeling fragile, so he ordered her a plain rice risotto with a knob of butter and parmesan, and fed her spoonfuls as though she was a child.

'I'm so proud of you,' she said for the hundredth time. 'But this isn't much of a celebration for you, with me off my food, and both of us drinking Coke.'

Billy put his hand over hers and it felt so right, he left it there.

Afterwards they wandered through the cobbled streets of Rome, past shadowy ruins and floodlit fountains, until they found a secluded stone bench to sit on. There, Billy kissed her very, very gently on her poor sore mouth.

'I'm so glad you didn't go to bed with that wop the other night.'

He ran his hand down her cheek. It was such a relief not to have to duck her head out of the way so he shouldn't feel her spots.

596

'Oh, Billy, I've had a crush on you since I was thirteen.'

'On me?' he said, amazed.

'Yes, millions of girls have as well, but you're too modest or too nice to realize it. It's the general consensus of opinion that Rupert's for flings, but you're the one they want to marry. Not that I'm proposing or anything,' she added, blushing furiously.

Billy kissed her again. She was not quite sure what one did with one's tongue, so she copied him.

'You're so sweet,' he murmured, 'but I'm too old and battered and bitter for you. You don't need third-hand goods.'

'Rubbish,' protested Fen. 'What about antiques? They're third- and fourth- and fifth-hand, and they're infinitely more precious than anything new.'

They walked back to the hotel through the warm, scented night, Fen's espadrilles crunching on the gravel.

As he opened her bedroom door for her he said, 'I'll knock on your door in twenty minutes, when the coast's clear.'

Frantically, Fen bathed and cleaned her teeth and sprayed on scent. Despite the warmth of the night she couldn't stop shaking. If only she had bigger boobs. Janey was so gloriously top heavy. She looked at Lester the teddy bear, and turned his face to the wall. 'I don't want you to be corrupted.'

Overwhelmed with shyness, conscious of her swollen face, she turned off the lights before she let Billy into the room.

'Do you think we'll ever find the bed?' he said, as he drew her, frantically trembling, towards him. 'Hey, hey, there's no need to be frightened.'

'That's what they always say about adders. Look, I know I'm not as sophisticated, or as beautiful, or as witty, or as clever, or as sexy as Janey. Anyone would be a letdown after her.'

'Hush,' he said, stroking the nape of her neck. 'Who's making comparisons?'

'I am, because everyone you go to bed with must remind you of her and it must hurt.'

Billy found the bed and pulled Fen down beside him.

'It's certainly not hurting at the moment. You're the one it might hurt.'

'I've ridden for so long, I don't think I've got a hymen any more. I've never been able to find it.'

Her little hands were tentatively moving over his chest.

'Still scared?' he whispered. Then, when she didn't answer, he kissed her upper lip. 'I'll take things very, very slowly. We've got all night.'

He was thinking so much about not rushing her, or scaring her, that he hardly worried about his own perform-ance. But he felt an amazing happiness when her hands travelled cautiously down his stomach and she said: 'Oh feel:. isn't it lovely, and so strong, like the leaning tower of Pisa? Is it nice if I run my fingers round the rim?'

'Bliss,' mumbled Billy.

'And does that hurt?'

'If you stroke them gently like that, it's heaven.'

She was so excited that neither of them ever discovered whether she had a hymen or not. Twined round him like a monkey, riding him so lightly, she exhorted him to please go on, go on. In the end he forgot to be gentle, driving into her with all his strength.

'Oh, it was magic, magic,' she whispered afterwards.

'Are you sure? Are you really sure?'

'Didn't hurt at all,' she said, snuggling into his arms.

'Look,' said Billy, 'the British flag is creaking up the pole.'

Suddenly she heard him singing, slightly shakily, 'God save our gracious Queen, Long live our Noble Queen,' until there was furious banging on the wall.

Fen gave an ecstatic sigh. Billy's singing again, she thought.

To Billy, the following weeks came as a revelation. While Janey had exuded sex appeal, he always had the feeling that, although she enjoyed sex, it was more for her own

598

gratification and her own ego. He was never irresistible to her. With Fen he felt he held the key to paradise. She quivered with excitement whenever he touched her. She wanted to touch him all the time, she adored everything about him and everything he did to her was perfect. She was the most unselfish person he'd ever been to bed with, always thinking of his pleasure before her own, massaging his back when he was tired, happy to stroke and caress him for hours.

They talked horses endlessly, but unlike other riders, she was prepared to spend hours discussing how his horses might be improved, not permanently waiting to engineer the conversation on to her own.

Having stabled Macaulay and Desdemona at Fontainebleau, they stayed an extra day there, wandering through the forest and enjoying a magnificent French dinner in the evening, to make up for not being able to eat anything except risotto in Rome. Then they flew home to take Laurel and Hardy, and a couple of Billy's new horses bought by Mr Block, to Windsor. Then on to Paris, Barcelona and finally Lucerne, where at each place the British riders were invincible. Bugle was jumping brilliantly, so were Desdemona and Macaulay. It was also perfectly apparent to the rest of the team what was going on between Fen and Billy.

'You pipped me to the post,' said Rupert ruefully, but he couldn't help being glad to see Billy so happy.

Malise, turning a blind eye, was delighted too. He was very fond of Billy and had hated to see him so down and lacking in confidence. He was also thrilled by the success of the team. Billy and Fen were obviously madly in love. They were discreet in public, but you only had to see the way he carried her cases for her and she turned to him for advice, and how they drifted together and always seemed to be echoing each others thoughts and laughing at private jokes. Fen had cheered up the team too. Humpty had replaced Griselda for Lucerne, and he and Ivor and Driffield were all mad about Fen. She was their team mascot, and as a team they had never been more united. They had not lost a Nations' Cup this year.

Fen lay in a bubble bath. A champagne cork ricocheted off the steaming walls of the bathroom in their hotel at Lucerne.

'To your first Grand Prix,' said Billy, filling up a tooth mug and handing it to her.

'I can't drink the whole bottle,' protested Fen as Billy put down the loo seat and sat on it, watching her.

'What's the matter?' he said. 'Aren't you glad you've beaten everyone?'

'It feels like the end of the holidays.'

He came and knelt down beside her, soaping her breasts and kissing her damp neck.

'Sweetheart, it's only the beginning. We may be going home, but I'll be seeing you at Crittleden next week, and then at the Royal and the Royal International.'

Fen looked down. The soap was beginning to disperse the bubbles.

'I know, but it won't be the same.'

'It'll be even nicer, I promise. Come on; we'd better buck up. Malise wants to leave to go out to dinner in twenty minutes.'

She didn't tell him that that afternoon a telegram had arrived at the hotel for him from Janey, congratulating him on yet another double clear in the Nations' Cup. Rupert had torn it up before Billy saw it.

'Last thing he needs at the moment, and don't you go telling him either,' he'd said to Fen.

She hadn't said anything, but it terrified her. Throughout the past month Fen and Billy had avoided talking about Janey. She felt like a broken ankle that didn't hurt if you didn't walk on it.

As well as her Grand Prix money, Fen, as leading lady rider of the show, had won a full-length fur coat. She disapproved passionately of fur in principle, but when Billy had dried her after her bath, she couldn't resist putting it on as a dressing gown, feeling the silk lining caressing her hot naked body.

Billy stopped in the middle of knotting his tie and came towards her.

'God, that's sexy. Just looking at you gives me a hard-on.'

He took her face between his hands. She was so beautiful. All the bruising and swelling had gone.

'You don't realize what you've done to me,' he said. 'Given me back my faith in life. I never believed I could wake up in the morning again with such a ridiculous sense of excitement.'

Fen parted the fur coat, so she could feel his cock nudging against her belly button. She laid her head against his chest.

'I'm not saying this to make you feel old, but I've never had a real father. My own father died when I was eight, but he divorced Mummy long before that and Colonel Carter was a twerp and, although Jake's been wonderful, he's *not a cuddler*; too austere. Apart from dogs and horses and guinea pigs and hamsters, you're not only the first father, but the first thing I've ever been able to love.'

Looking down, Billy realized he must never, never let her be hurt.

'I know I'm carry-cot snatching, but I can't help it,' he muttered into her hair.

Anxious to get back to Tabitha, Rupert flew home to Penscombe after the Lucerne Grand Prix. Over a year old now, Tab could walk several steps, but usually crawled forward with a curious sideways gait like a crab, with one leg sticking out. She was wearing blue pyjamas; the top had fallen off one shoulder. She was so enchanted when he walked through the door, she could hardly get a word out.

'My darling angel,' said Rupert, extracting her from a swarm of excitedly barking dogs and holding her above his head until she crowed with laughter. She was so pink and blonde and beautiful.

'Daddy's brought you lots and lots of presents.'

601

The best present for Tab was obviously seeing her father again. She snuggled up to him like a kitten.

Helen came into the hall warily, holding Marcus by the hand.

'Hullo, darling,' she said kissing him. 'Had a good trip?'

'Great. We won the Nations' Cup and Billy's really back on form. Christ, he's jumping well.'

'I'm so glad. Not back on the booze, is he?'

'No, no. He's utterly bombed on Perrier and love.'

'Love?' said Helen, surprised.

'Little Fenella Maxwell. Best thing that ever happened to him.'

'But she's not eighteen yet; just a child.'

'So's he. She mothers him like an old mare. They're really sweet together, and at last he's got someone who can talk to him about horses.'

'Unlike me,' thought Helen bitterly. 'I'm having lunch with Janey tomorrow,' she said.

After the 400-mile drive from Lucerne, Billy and Fen stayed near the coast and took a lunchtime ferry the next day. The grooms had lunch. Billy booked a berth for three hours and took Fen to bed, dreading the separation ahead as much as she was. They reached Gloucestershire, about sunset. It was one of those magical evenings when they had both the lorry windows open and the air was heavy with the scent of elderflowers and wild roses.

Fen sat glued against Billy, hand on his thigh, any pretence that they weren't having an affair abandoned. It was only ten miles to Penscombe now. Once there she would borrow one of Rupert's trailers and drive Macaulay and Desdemona on to the Mill House, arriving about midnight.

Tracey was fast asleep on one of the bunk beds. Sarah was emptying out the fridge. Billy and Rupert's horses were beginning to stamp and whinney as they recognised the familiar scents of home.

'Will you do me a great favour?' said Billy, staring fixedly at the road ahead. She could feel how tense he was.

'Of course.'

'Will you stay the night with me at the cottage, then I'll drive you back in the morning?'

Fen was almost speechless with happiness. Billy needed her, he really needed her. She reached up and kissed his cheek. 'I was wondering how on earth I was going to drag myself away from you this evening.'

'I rang Mrs Bodkin from Lucerne and told her to clean the place up and make the bed. I'm a big boy now. I can't go on living with Helen and Rupert for ever, and anyway,' he looked at his watch, 'I haven't fucked you for at least seven hours. Will you mind a few of Janey's things lying around?'

'Not if you don't,' said Fen.

She rang Tory from Rupert's tackroom. 'I've got as far as Rupert's. I'm utterly jiggered. Helen's asked me to stay the night. Do you mind awfully? Billy, or someone, will drive me back in the morning.'

'I'll be punished for lies like that,' she said to herself as she put down the receiver.

It was dusk by the time they'd settled the horses. All that was left of the day was a saffron glow on the horizon. Billy, who knew the path along the edge of the woods, led the way, holding her hand, with Mavis racing in front chasing rabbits. He longed to kiss her, but both were conscious of not having cleaned their teeth since morning. The night was so warm they could smell the honeysuckle and syringa a hundred yards away.

'What an adorable place,' said Fen, in ecstasy. 'Gosh, you're lucky to live here.'

In the gateway Billy put his arms round her, holding her like a balloon that might float away at any moment.

'It's all right,' she said softly. 'I'm here to look after you.'

As he opened the front door, Mavis shot ahead, squeaking with excitement. He turned on the light and went into the kitchen, dumping the cases. Fen followed him. 'It looks lovely,' she said.

'Mrs B's been working fantastically hard,' said Billy.

'Christ, I wish we could have a drink.'

'I'll make some coffee,' said Fen, picking up the kettle.

'Are you hungry?'

She shook her head.

'Then let's go to bed. I need to lay you and the ghost.'

Fen went into the hall. Behind the door opposite, she could hear excited squeaking and scrabbling.

'Mavis must have shut herself in.'

She opened the door and switched on the light, then gave a gasp of horror. In front of the fire, thin, beautiful and menacing in a black sleeveless T-shirt and the tightest black leather trousers, stood Janey.

'Hullo Fen,' she said with a twisted smile. 'It's been amazingly kind of you to look after Billy in my absence, but I'd like him back now.'

Fen gave a sob and turned on her heel, bumping into Billy as he came out of the kitchen.

'You look as though you've seen a ghost.'

'No, I've seen a real live person. Go into the drawing-room and see.'

As she fled down the garden path she heard Billy calling her to come back, but she kept on running along the woodland path. Once she stumbled and fell over, cutting her hands but not even feeling the pain. She didn't stop until she reached Rupert's front door. It was open. The dogs surged forward, barking. Rupert came out of the kitchen, a large whisky in one hand, a letter in the other.

'Hullo, duck. Had a tiff?' Then he saw her dirty grazed hands and her stricken face. 'Angel, what's the matter?'

'It's J-Janey, she was waiting for us at the cottage.'

'Fucking hell, how did she get in?' He led Fen into the kitchen and poured her a large drink.

'I don't want anything.' Her face crumpled.

'Oh, sweetheart, I'm sorry. He won't take her back.'

'He will, I know he will. He only had me as a stop-gap.'

'Rubbish, I've never seen him happier.'

'I can't bear it, I simply can't bear it.'

Helen, who'd been tucking the children up, heard the

commotion and came downstairs. Walking into the kitchen, she found a blonde in Rupert's arms.

'Oh, I do beg your pardon,' she said with heavy sarcasm. 'I didn't mean to interrupt.'

'Don't be stupid, it's Fen. That bitch Janey's come back.'

Fen turned to Helen. 'I'm so sorry to bother you,' she sobbed, 'but I didn't know where else to go.'

The telephone rang. Still with one arm round Fen, Rupert picked it up.

'Yes, she's here. Well, not brilliant. What the fuck's going on? Good, see you. He's coming over,' he said replacing the receiver. 'Now dry your eyes and have that drink.'

Billy was over in ten minutes. Rupert left them alone. Fen looked up, her eyes spilling over with tears. 'Oh, Billy.'

'Darling Fen.' He drew her towards him. 'I never dreamed in a million years she'd come back.'

'You must talk it over with her. She's still your wife.'

'I don't know if I want her back. I'm so much better without her.'

'There's something you should know. Janey sent you two telegrams, one in Paris and one in Lucerne. Rupert tore them up.'

Billy digested this. Then he said bitterly, 'That was only when I started winning again. Janey likes hitching her wagon to a star. Whether she'll be so amused by a star on the wagon, I doubt.'

His hold tightened on her. 'I'll go back and have it out with her. Will you stay here? Rupert'll look after you and I'll come and see you in the morning. I just want you to know you're the sweetest thing I've ever been lucky enough to meet in my life.'

Meanwhile Rupert had gone onto the terrace and had found Helen watching the stars come out, the faint reflection of the half-moon mingling with the water lilies strewn across the lake.

'How the hell did Janey know Billy was coming home tonight?'

605

'Well, I may have told her. I don't think I did. I had lunch with her yesterday. She was wearing Billy's Old Harrovian tie. I certainly told her Billy was real happy with Fen.'

Rupert turned on her in fury. 'You did what?'

'Well, she was so worried, she said it was so much on her conscience. Billy being on his own and drinking and doing so badly.'

'She knew bloody well he was doing well; she sent him telegrams.'

'Then she looked really sad, and said she did hope some day he'd find someone nice – so I told her about Fen.'

'She was fishing, you stupid bitch.'

'Rupert, please, don't talk to me like that.'

'You've only done Billy the worst turn ever. He'd just struggled out of the quicksand; now you've pushed him back again.'

At that moment, Billy came out on the terrace.

'Will you look after her?'

'You should be doing that,' snapped Rupert, 'and kicking out that slut.'

Rupert stayed up half the night talking to Fen, who was almost crazy with grief.

'I'm sorry to be so boring but I love him so so much. I saw her. I know she wants to come back, and she's so winning, and Billy's too straight not to let her. It's funny, I wanted to fall in love so badly – but I never dreamed it would hurt so much. Life's not like the Pullein-Thompson novels is it? They always have happy endings.'

Helen couldn't sleep. Why did Rupert always have more time for other people – Fen, Billy, Tab – than he did for her? On the other hand she knew she was being punished.

'Dear God,' she prayed, 'what have I done? I told Janey about Fen, not because I wanted to reassure her, but because I wanted to put her down.'

42

Next day the rain came, stripping off the last pastel frivolity of the blossom, segregating the fluffy white heads of the dandelion clocks, bowing down the cow parsley, muffling the cuckoo, and turning every show ground into a quagmire. To Fen, it seemed she was permanently soaked to the skin, always cold, shivering with misery, particularly at night without Billy to love and warm her. Lester, the teddy bear, was re-instated and soaked with tears, like her pillow, as, night after night, she cried herself to sleep. By day, work was the only anodyne. She begged Malise to excuse her from the huge nine-day show at Aachen on the grounds that Billy would be in the team, probably with Janey in tow. Instead Malise left Billy out, giving him a few weeks' sabbatical to sort out his marriage. Billy, after all, had turned professional and was no longer eligible for Los Angeles, and Malise was determined to get his Olympic squad into shape in plenty of time. On present form, Fen, Rupert and Ivor Braine were certain to be part of the team. The fourth place he still hoped to keep open for Jake, provided his leg mended in time.

Fen tried to hide her heartbreak from Jake when she visited him in hospital on her return from Lucerne.

'Look what we won,' she said brightly, tossing a carrier bag full of rosettes onto the white counterpane.

Jake took one look at her face.

'Who is it, that bastard, Campbell-Black? I said it would happen. I'll bloody kill Malise when I see him.'

Fen went over to the window, fighting back the tears.

'It wasn't Rupert at all. It was Billy.'

'Billy!' For a moment Jake was dumbfounded.

'What happened? You're not . . . ?'

'No, nothing like that. Janey came back.'

'Christ. I suppose the bitch found out he was going well and didn't want to miss out.'

'Something like that.'

Jake loved Fen, but so angry was he with Billy and Janey, and so horrified to see Fen's haggard face, that he took it out on her. He hated himself. He wished he had words to comfort her, but he just wanted to hit out at a world that seemed so manifestly unfair to both of them.

Fen let him rage until he'd run out of reproof and expletives, then collapsed sobbing on the bed.

'I couldn't help it, Jake. I didn't mean to fall in love.'

Jake patted her shoulder. 'Sorry I came on so strong. I just hate you being hurt. Should never have let you go.'

'Haven't you ever been in love or hurt by a woman?'

'Never – by a woman.' (Not since his mother had committed suicide, anyway.)

'Not even Tory?'

'Tory couldn't hurt a fly button.'

Gradually the rosette board filled up the kitchen, as one show followed another – Aachen, Calgary, Wolfsburg. Funnily enough, it was Rupert who saved her in those first weeks. In the evenings abroad, he wouldn't let her slink back to the lorry to cry her eyes out, but dragged her out to dinner with the team. In his mind she was part of Billy, and therefore to be protected, cherished and occasionally bullied. He had never really had a woman friend before. Women in his book were to be pursued, screwed and discarded. Repeatedly, he was on the brink of taking her to bed, because he wanted to and he thought it might blot out the pain, then some rare altruism stopped him.

Fen was confused. Accustomed to hate Rupert, she now discovered in him an unexpected gentleness, particularly in the way he talked about Tabitha.

Billy tackled Rupert the moment he came back to England.

'How's Fen?' was his first question.

'I took her out to dinner last night.'

'With the team?'

'No, by myself.'

'What the bloody hell for?'

'She needed cheering up.'

'What form did the cheering up take – horizontal?'

'She wanted to talk. She's still mad about you.'

'Oh, God,' said Billy, trying not to feel pleased.

'But the only way out of this stupid impasse is for her to find someone else.'

Billy was appalled how much the thought upset him, but he said, 'You may be right.'

'Damn sure I'm right. Particularly if you persist in this bloody-fool belief that Janey's the best thing for you.'

Billy wasn't sure. The night he'd got back to the cottage and found Janey there, they had screwed all night, blotting out all feelings of guilt and remorse. Next day, he'd insisted on driving Fen, white, silent, stunned, back to the Mill House, feeling her almost disintegrating in his arms as he said goodbye to her, saying he'd always adore her – which was a different word than love.

When he got back, Janey'd been through his wallet and found Fen's photo and was in hysterics.

Billy tried to reason with her. 'I never looked at another woman the entire time we were married. Then you file for divorce. I was trying to get over you.'

'Why didn't you come round and murder Kev?'

'I'm not like that. I missed, the only time I took a slug at him.'

'Was she better in bed than me?'

'She was different,' said Billy tactfully.

'Did you screw her in our bed?'

Billy shook his head.

'But you were coming back to.'

'Look, you'd have thought I was a frightful drip if I hadn't.

609

Billy *had* changed, thought Janey. The drink blotches, the red face, the sour whisky breath had gone. He was brown, lean, well-muscled, tougher, more irritable, but infinitely more attractive.

'You mustn't see her any more,' said Janey, pouring herself another glass of vodka, hardly graced by tonic.

'How can I not see her? We're in the same team. If I worked in an office, or was an engineer or an architect, I could try and find another job in another part of the country, but show-jumping's the only thing I can do. I was totally impotent after you left me. She picked me up from the gutter. She gave me back my confidence, my nerve, my sexuality. I've won £20,000 in the last month.'

'What d'you want me to do, ask her to move in?'

'I'm just trying to say it isn't as simple as that. You can't just waltz out of my life for nearly a year and expect things to be exactly the same.'

'I've finished my book,' said Janey, 'and I've been offered £30,000 for the serial rights. And my publisher has commissioned another book, so you won't have to struggle quite so hard, darling.'

She's not listening, thought Billy in despair. She never listens, except when she's on to a good story.

Hysterical scenes followed. Janey steamed open letters, counted the Kleenex – 'Perhaps she's used one' – examined the hairs in the bath: 'That's thicker and curlier than mine.'

'That's pubic hair, for Christ's sake,' said Billy.

Janey's attitude was totally irrational. On endless occasions she had deceived him, betrayed him, made a fool of him, but it was part of her abyss of insecurity that she simply couldn't believe that he wasn't sloping off to see Fen when he got the chance.

Nor was it just her insane jealousy of Fen; she was paranoid about the rest of the world. What did Billy's mother, Helen, Rupert, Malise think about her behaviour? Janey liked a place in the sun and a lot of spade work would be required to win back these people's approval.

Everyone was laying bets that the reconciliation wouldn't last.

Fen didn't see Billy again until the Crittleden meeting at the end of July. Rupert had warned her that Janey was coming, so in order to upset herself as little as possible, Fen arrived only just in time to walk the course for the big event, the Crittleden Gold Cup, worth £15,000 to the winner. She found the show ground in an uproar. Always with an eye to publicity, Steve Sullivan, who owned Crittleden, had introduced a new fence which all the riders considered unjumpable. Called the moat, it consisted of two grassy banks. The horses were expected to clamber up the first bank, along the top and halfway down the other side, where they were expected to pop across a ditch three foot deep, on to the second bank, which they again had to scale, ride along the top and down the other side. Here they had to jump a small, three-foot rail a couple of strides away.

Worried that all the show-jumpers might load their horses up into their lorries and drive ten miles down the road to Pripley Green, where there was another big show taking place, Steve Sullivan had only put up details of the Gold Cup course an hour before the competition. When the riders saw the moat was included, all hell broke loose.

'I'm not jumping that,' said Rupert.

'Nor am I,' said Billy.

'If they jump the moat, they'll bank the other fences,' said Ivor Braine.

'Remember the bank at Lucerne?' said Humpty. 'They had an oxer immediately afterwards. All the horses treated the oxer like a bank and fell through. One of the Dutch horses had to be shot. I'm not risking Saddleback Sam.'

'That ditch is three foot deep,' said Billy. 'If a horse falls in, it'll put him off jumping water for life.'

'It's a very gentle slope down,' protested Steve Sullivan. 'It's not slippery. They'll jump it easily, won't they Wishbone?' he added, appealing to the Irishman.

'Sure. I can't see the thing giving much trouble,' said Wishbone.

'There,' said Steve. 'I took my old mare across it the other night. She jumped it without turning a hair.'

'She's due to be turned into cat food at any minute,' snapped Rupert. 'Doesn't matter if she breaks a leg. These are top-class horses. I'm not risking £100,000 for a bloody moat.'

He went off and complained to Malise who came and examined the course.

'Seems perfectly jumpable to me; an acceptable hunting fence.'

'These aren't hunters,' said Rupert.

Billy conferred with Mr Block.

'I haven't spent eight months getting Bugle right to have him smash himself up in one afternoon. D'you mind if I pull him out?'

'Do what you think best, lad,' said Mr Block. 'Don't like the look of it myself. First hoss'll be all right, but once the turf gets cut up, it'll be like a greased slide in the playground.'

Steve Sullivan's sponsors, Fuma, the tobacco giants, however, had put a lot of money into the competition and wanted a contest. The telephones were jangling in the main stand. Steve suggested putting up a big wall which the riders could jump instead, as an alternative to the moat.

'Not a fair contest,' said Rupert. 'Walls aren't the same as banks.'

'Handing it on a plate to a little horse,' said Humpty. 'Little horses only need two strides between the bottom of the bank and the rail.'

Count Guy declared the moat *vraiment dangereuse*. Ludwig agreed: 'It ees your Eenglish obsession with class, haffing a moat, Steve. Where is zee castle, zee elephant and zee vild-life safari park?'

Steve Sullivan was sweating. He'd never faced a mutiny before. The riders were all standing grimly on the bank, hands on their hips.

Fen, meanwhile, had been quietly walking the rest of the course. It was a matt, still day, overcast but muggy, the

612

grass very green from the recent storms. Midges danced in front of her eyes. Finally she reached the moat and stood banging her whip against her boots, looking at them in disapproval, hat pulled down over her nose.

All those grown men, including Griselda, making such a fuss, she thought. It was a tabby cats' indignation meeting. Rupert walked up and kissed her. 'Hi, angel, you've arrived just in time to join the picket line. We're going to give Steve his come-uppance.'

At that moment a television minion, wearing a white peaked cap and tight pink trousers, rushed up. 'Boys, boys, we simply must get started,' he cried, leaping to avoid a large pile of mud. 'Motor-racing's finished, and so has the Ladies' Singles, and they're coming over to us at any minute.'

'Go back to your toadstool, you big fairy,' said Rupert.

'But a very rich fairy, you butch thing,' giggled the minion. 'Are you going to jump, that's what we need to know?'

The riders went into a huddle.

Fen stood slightly apart. She had caught sight of Billy. For a second they gazed at each other. He noticed how thin she'd got, her breeches far too large, her T-shirt falling almost straight down from collar bone to waist. Fen moved quickly away, stumbling into a fence, sending the wing flying. As she picked herself up, she heard Rupert say to the BBC man, 'OK, you're on. We'll all jump.'

Fen fled back to the collecting ring under the oak trees where she found Desdemona being walked round by Sarah.

'What's happening?' she asked.

'Bloody storm in a challenge cup,' said Fen. 'We're all going to jump, but, from the nasty gleam in Rupert's eye, I know he's up to something.'

'You'd better ring Jake.'

'No, he's bound to tell me not to jump.'

The crowd seethed with rumour and counter-rumour. They had seen the riders gathered round the moat. This was about the most testing competition of the year. Many of them had travelled miles to watch it. The arena nearly boiled over with excitement and a huge cheer went up as Rupert, the first rider, came in. Theatrically, with much flourishing, he took off his hat to the judges and cantered the foaming, plunging, sweating Snakepit around and around, waiting for the bell which was waiting for the go-ahead from the television cameras.

He was off, bucketing over the emerald green grass, jumping superbly, clearing every fence, until he came to the moat.

'He'll show them how to do it,' said Colonel Roxborough.

'I think not,' said Malise bleakly.

The entire riders' stand rose to their feet, holding their breaths, as Rupert cantered up to the huge bank, then at the last moment, practically pulled Snakepit's teeth out and cantered around it, ignoring the shouts of 'wrong way', and cantering slowly out of the ring.

There were thirty-five horses entered for the class. The next twenty riders deliberately missed out the moat, or retired before they reached it. For the first few rounds the crowd scratched their heads in bewilderment, then, as they realized they were witnessing a strike, the deliberate sabotaging of a class, the bewilderment turned to rage and they started to catcall, boo and slow-hand clap. In the Chairman's box, with its red carpet and Sanderson wallpaper, Steve Sullivan was having a seizure.

'Bastards, bastards! All led by the nose by that fucker, Campbell-Black.'

Malise watched the spectacle with the utmost distaste.

'Behaving like a bunch of dockers and car-workers,' said Colonel Roxborough apoplectically, slowly eating his way through a bunch of grapes in a nearby Lalique bowl. 'Most jump jockeys would like Bechers out of the National. They don't go on strike.'

'Can't you put the screws on Billy, Mr Block?' pleaded Steve.

'I troost Billy's joodgement when it comes to hosses,' said

614

Mr Block. 'There'll be another class next week.'

Malise went down to the collecting ring. Billy, having followed the other riders' example, had just come out of the ring, to loud booing from the crowd. He avoided Malise's eye.

Only Driffield, Ivor and Fen, of the British riders, were left to jump.

'You're making complete idiots of the judges and the crowd,' said Malise furiously to the British squad. 'If you don't like the course don't jump it, but don't resort to these gutter tactics. D'you want to kill the sport stone dead?'

With £15,000 at stake, Driffield was sorely tempted.

But then Count Guy and Ludwig both went in and retired, and who was he to argue with the experts? Dudley Diplock was in despair in the BBC commentary box. Telephones were ringing on all sides.

'Can't we go back to tennis?' he pleaded into one receiver. 'Or motor-racing or cricket? There must be a county match somewhere.'

Another telephone rang. 'You sit tight, Dudders,' said the sports editor. 'It's a bloody good story, the news desk have been on to say, "Be sure to interview Campbell-Black afterwards. He seems to be the ringleader".'

Driffield retired.

'Your turn now, darling,' said Rupert to Fen. 'Jump as far as the bank. Don't worry about the crowd – only Italians throw bottles – and then retire. The BSJA can't suspend all of us.'

Jake lay in his hospital bed, waiting for a telephone call. He had checked with the switchboard five times. The telephonist was a friend of his. They had given him a direct line, but no call had come through. He was livid with Fen. Perhaps she'd seen Billy – he'd caught a glimpse of him walking the course – and been too distracted to ring. And now she was obviously going to join the strike organized by Rupert. The moat looked very dangerous. He'd be furious if she did jump, furious if she didn't. He got the Lucozade bottle off the bedside cupboard and poured himself a large whisky into a paper cup.

The nurses gathered round the bed. 'We've just heard on the radio that they're all on strike.'

'Poor old Dudley,' said Jake, and couldn't help laughing, even though Matron had just walked into the room.

'Well. this is simply the blackest, most extraordinary day in show jumping,' said Dudley desperately, 'and here comes little Fiona, I mean Fenella, Maxwell, on Esmeralda, I mean Desdemona, a really super little mare, who's been jumping brilliantly all summer. I wonder if she's going to strike like the other riders.'

The crowd were in an uproar, booing, yelling, screaming.

'Jump, jump, jump,' they yelled, stamping their feet in the stands and slow-handclapping.

'All this must be upsetting to any horse, particularly a young horse like Esmeralda. Now what's Fiona going to do?' said Dudley.

Fen raised her whip to the judge, then took one look at the mass of jeering yelling faces. The next minute a beer can landed at Desdemona's feet.

'If you'd stop making this ghastly din,' she screamed at the faces 'I'd like to try and jump this course.'

Only a handful of spectators heard her, the rest thought she was hurling abuse and stepped up the catcalling. Another beer can landed at Desdemona's feet. Fen turned, shaking her fist.

'Is she going to be all right?' said Billy in anguish.

'I'm sure she's tough enough to cope,' said Janey, shooting him a furious glance.

Fen could hardly hear the bell. Fuelled by rage, stroking Desdemona's neck, she set off. Over the wall, over the oxer, over the parallels, over the rustic poles, over the road jump, just avoiding two more beer cans, then over the gate. She rounded the corner, away from the collecting ring, riding towards the moat, but instead of circling it like the other

616

riders, she dug her heels in. Desdemona bounded up the grassy hillock. The first thing the riders saw were her roan ears, then her face and her forelegs arriving on the top.

'Bloody hell,' snarled Rupert.

'Traitor,' thundered Griselda.

'Blackleg,' said Driffield.

'Scab,' said Humpty.

'She'll get the £15,000,' said Driffield, in anguish.

'She's not over yet,' said Billy.

'Stupid exhibitionist,' said Janey. 'Serve her right if she kills herself.'

As Fen reached the top the crowd went silent, as if a radio had suddenly been switched off. As the little mare trotted along the top, picked her way fastidiously down the other side and paused above the water, Fen allowed her to have a good look.

'Constitutes a stop,' said Griselda.

'Didn't take a step back,' said Billy, as Desdemona bounded gaily across to the other bank, slightly unseating Fen, who had to cling onto her mane as she scrambled up and over the other bank. By some miracle she came down the other side, collected and popped easily over the rail. For a second the crowd were totally silent; then they let out a huge heartwarming cheer.

'Bloody marvellous,' said Billy. 'Oh, well done, pet.'

Rupert and Janey turned on him in unison. 'Whose side are you on?'

'The side of guts and great horsemanship,' said Billy sulkily.

'You little beauty,' whispered Steve Sullivan.

The Colonel ate the last black grape, pips and all. 'That girl will go to Los Angeles, or I'll have something to say about it!'

'I agree,' said Malise.

'Se-uper, absolutely se-uper,' shouted Dudley from the commentary box. 'Oh, well done, Felicity. Brilliantly ridden.'

Jake suddenly found he was clinging on to Matron's hand as, with a huge roar that grew to a crescendo, the crowd cheered Desdemona home. In a businesslike manner she cleared the rest of the jumps. 'What a fuss about nothing,' she seemed to be saying, and cantered out of the ring with a buck and a whisk of her tail.

Jake turned to Matron, grinning from ear to ear. 'Christ, did you see that? Have a drink.'

'You know you're not allowed alcohol in hospital, Mr Lovell.'

'To hell with that,' said Jake, reaching for another paper cup with a shaking hand and pouring the remains of the whisky into it.

'Oh, well, cheers,' said Matron, tapping her cup against his.

'No one speak to her,' ordered Rupert.

'Send her to Coventry,' said Janey.

As Fen came out, a crowd, noticeably short of other riders, swarmed round her. Desdemona disappeared under a deluge of patting hands.

Sarah fought her way towards them.

'Oh, Des, oh, Fen, oh, well done. I was so scared.' She wiped away the tears. 'No one will ever speak to us again.'

Fen looked up at the riders' stand and saw the rows of stormy faces looking down at her.

'Picket line looks fairly grim,' said Fen flippantly. 'Coventry, here we come.' But her heart sank.

'Bloody hell,' said Billy, getting to his feet, 'don't be so petty.'

'Sit down,' thundered Rupert.

'Don't you dare speak to her,' squealed Janey furiously.

Ignoring the cries of protest, Billy walked down the stone steps, vaulted over the collecting ring rail and fought his way to Fen's side.

'Well done, beauty. Showed us all up.'

Fen started, turned pale, gazing down at his dear, familiar face with the turned-down, smiling eyes and the

618

sun catching the greying hair. Never had the temptation been so strong to jump off Desdemona and collapse into his arms.

'Oh Billy,' she croaked, 'I miss you.'

He didn't have time to answer.

Dudley Diplock came rushing up, brandishing a microphone. The crowd separated to let him pass, deferring to television, then, gathering behind him, waving at the cameras, trying to get in shot. Journalists crowded around.

'Good on you, Fen.'

Another huge cheer came from the ring. Fen swung round in the saddle. Wishbone had jumped the bank, but had the stile down. Fen was still in the lead. Ivor was about to go in.

'If you can jump it, Fen,' he said adoringly, 'reckon I can have a go.'

After that the rest of the riders jumped the moat without mishap.

Hans Schmidt jumped clear on his new horse, Papa Haydn, and in the jump-off was a tenth of a second faster than Fen. But, although he got the £15,000 and the cup, he removed the oak-leaf wreath of victory from Papa Haydn and put it round Desdemona's neck. The crowd roared their approval.

'I take zee money,' he said, kissing Fen, 'but you take zee laurels.'

She was cheered around two laps of honour.

Dudley collared her again. 'What made you jump it despite the other riders?'

Fen grinned. 'I don't like a lot of men telling me what to do. I think they behaved like a load of drips.'

'Fighting talk,' said Dudley. 'You're not worried you've made yourself very unpopular?'

Fen shrugged. 'They could have jumped it if they'd wanted to.'

'Jake told you to have a go, did he?'

'I didn't ring him,' confessed Fen. 'I was terrified he'd tell me not to. Sorry, Jake,' she said into the camera.

'I'm sure you all know,' said Dudley, 'that Fiona's

619

brother-in-law, World Champion Jake Lovell, is in hospital recovering from a nasty broken arm.'

'Leg,' said Fen gently.

'Leg; and we all wish you better, Jake, and hope to see you back soon. This must be the best possible pick-me-up.'

'That deserves another drink,' said Matron. 'We seem to have exhausted your whisky, Mr Lovell. I think I've got a drop of brandy in my office.'

Janey had been drinking all day and, when she and Billy got back to the lorry, she headed straight for the vodka bottle.

'Why the hell did you insist on rushing up and congratulating her in front of all the press and television cameras?' she asked.

'What *will* people think?' said Billy, trying to make a joke.

'They'll think you're still having it off with her.'

'They will if you go on yelling like this.'

'I suppose you were making a date with her in that brief, poignant moment.'

'I was not.'

'Or saying how much you missed her.'

'I merely told her she jumped well. She deserved it. I hate packs ganging up because they haven't got enough guts to savage someone on their own. I did it many years ago to Jake, and I've been bitterly ashamed of it ever since, and I'm not going to do it again.'

'I suppose you fancied her like mad when you saw her.'

He looked at her face, red, shouting and featureless with rage.

'Oh, for Christ's sake,' he snapped, 'you buggered off for nearly a year.'

'I knew it wouldn't be long before you threw that in my face again.'

'I'm not,' said Billy wearily, 'but if I can forget about Kev why can't you forget about Fen?'

'I left Kev because it was over, because I was bored with him. You were in full flood with Fen. How do I know it's over, that you don't lie beside me at night hankering for her boy's body?'

Billy filled up the kettle from the tap and turned on the gas. He was so slow lighting a match that he nearly blew his eyelashes off. Even the gas ring was against him. He was tired, he was hungry, he longed for a drink. He was depressed by the knowledge that Bugle could have jumped the moat and he'd have been fifteen grand richer. None of this would matter if Janey would meet him one tenth of the way.

'How do I know it's all over between you and Fen?' She burst into noisy sobs.

Billy went over and hugged her.

'You'll have to trust me; it's you I love, always have loved. I shacked up with Fen because I was dying of loneliness, and you won't help either of us by regurgitating her memory every five minutes.'

'I know,' sobbed Janey. 'I don't know why you put up with me.'

A new syndrome, which Billy imagined Janey'd picked up from Kev, was the mood of sweetness and light, followed by heavy drinking, followed by the hurling of abuse and china, followed by flagellating herself into a frenzy of self-abasement. Billy found it exhausting. He'd had a shattering year. He sometimes wondered if his shoulders were broad enough to carry both their problems. Holding her heaving, tearful, full-blown body, breathing in the vodka fumes, Billy looked out of the window at the Crittleden oaks, tall against a drained, blue sky and was suddenly overwhelmed with longing for Fen, for her merryness, innocence and kindness. She'd looked so adorable, flushed and defiant, with her wary greeny-blue kitten eyes, waiting for the other riders to turn on her. The whistling of the kettle made them both jump.

43

'How many miles to Coventry?' sighed Fen.

'Threescore miles and ten.

Will I get there by candlelight?

Yes – but don't come back again.'

It was the last night of the three-day East Yorkshire Show. Fen lay in bed with Lester, the teddy bear, slumped beside her, listening to the rain irritably drumming on the roof of the lorry. Sleep had evaded her again, and even the new Dick Francis had failed to distract her. She put it down and reached for her diary with the tattered photograph of Billy tucked in between September and October. He was laughing, his eyes screwed up against the Lucerne sun.

Next week was Wembley. It had been a desperate six weeks for Fen. After Crittleden, as good as their word, the British riders had sent her to Coventry. At every show she attended people who'd been her friends cut her dead or deliberately turned their backs. She knew Rupert was behind it. He'd gone out of his way to be kind to her after she'd split up with Billy, and she'd defied him publicly and humiliatingly, which had been a terrible blow to his ego. As the majority of riders were either frightened of Rupert or jealous of Fen's meteoric rise, they were only too happy to follow his lead.

Things were not all Campbell-Black, however. Jake's leg was mending at last; he was expected to be out of hospital soon after Wembley and riding again by the spring. And if the Crittleden victory had enraged the riders, it had enchanted the public. News of the victimization had reached the press, who were all on Fen's side. Overnight the telephone started ringing, with newspapers, magazines and television companies clamouring for interviews. Invitations flooded in for her to speak at dinners, open supermarkets, address pony clubs, donate various items of her clothing to raise money at charity auctions. Everywhere she was mobbed by autograph hunters. Her post was full of fan mail from admiring men and little girls, who wanted signed photographs or help with their ponies.

For a public, hungry for new idols, Fen fitted the bill perfectly. With her slender, androgynous figure with its suggestion of anorexia, jagged cabin-boy hair, and gamin, wistful, extraordinarily photogenic face, she was a true child of her time. Just as the public was drawn to Jake because he was mysteriously enigmatic, they loved Fen because she couldn't hide her feelings. She was either furious or suicidal or ecstatic, and her naturally friendly nature endeared her to everyone.

Fen was flattered by the fame and adulation, but all her energies were centred on the horses; all she cared about was Billy.

The horses were going superbly, except for Hardy who was growing more ungovernable. He was too strong and fly, and ever since he'd run away with her at the Royal and Lancaster early in the month, jumping right over two rows of girl guides sitting quietly by the ringside, Fen had been frightened of him, and he knew it. If he got any worse, he'd be a serious danger to Jake when he started riding again.

The horses occupied her more than full time, and it was only on the endless drives, or when she fell into bed, usually long after midnight, that she allowed herself to think of Billy.

Rumours filtered through on the groom grapevine that all was not well in the Lloyd-Foxe household. Tracey told Dizzy, who told Sarah, who told Fen, of endless rows into the night, of Janey opening Billy's suitcase on the motorway and throwing all his clothes out of the window, because she thought he was driving too fast, of Janey storming out of a BSJA party because she heard Fen was coming, of Billy looking white and strained, and uncharacteristically snapping at the grooms.

So Fen lived on the crumbs of hope. She knew Billy would make every effort to save his marriage, but she couldn't help counting the days to Wembley in October, when they would all be under the same roof for a week.

The following evening a very tired Billy arrived home from the Lisbon Show. It was the first show to which Janey had not accompanied him since they got back together. She had stayed at home to write a piece on international polo players. At first, Billy found it a relief to be away from the rows and hysterics, but it was not long before the old demons started nagging him. He had forgiven Janey totally for going off with Kev, but he couldn't stop the sick, churning fear which overtook him when he rang home and she wasn't there. He hated the idea of her being closeted with handsome polo players. He remembered how she'd first interviewed him. He could hear her now:

'In the last chukka, how amazing! You *are* brilliant, and what amazing right arm muscles. Let me feel them. You have to be so brave to play polo.'

He and Rupert had reached Penscombe as a great red September sun was falling into the beech wood. The trees had hardly started to turn, but there was already a ring of lemon-yellow leaves round the mulberry tree in the centre of the yard and a wet leaf smell of autumn in the air. Having supervised the unloading and settling-down of his horses, Billy decided to walk the half-mile home through the dusk. He needed a few minutes to prepare himself for Janey. What sort of mood would she be in? Would she have missed him? Would she have ransacked his drawers, frenziedly searching for evidence? He dreaded Wembley, because Fen's presence would trigger off more abuse.

Dew was already whitening the grass, the blue smoke from a hundred bonfires was blending with the damp vapours rising from the stream at the bottom of the valley.

A blackbird was scolding as he approached the cottage; the golden dahlias in the front garden were already losing their colour in the fading light. The sick feeling of menace overwhelmed him once more. There were no lights on in the cottage.

Oh God, where was she? She knew he was coming home this evening. He broke into a run, slipping on the wet leaves and the mud. He banged the gate noisily behind him. That should give the polo player a chance to leap for his breeches. He *mustn't* think that. Next moment Mavis hurtled down the path, greeting him in ecstasy. The front door was open. Janey must have gone out in a hurry. Despairingly, he dropped his case on the yellow flagstones in the hall, so he had two hands free to stroke Mavis's joyful, wriggling body.

'Billy, darling is that you?' called Janey.

Overwhelmed with relief, he could only croak out, 'Yes.'

'I'm in the drawing-room.'

He found her sitting at her typewriter, wearing only his sleeveless Husky and a pair of scarlet pants.

'I thought you weren't here,' he muttered.

She got to her feet and ran to him.

'Oh, darling, I'm sorry. The piece was going so well, I couldn't be bothered to put the light on.'

'You'll ruin your eyes,' said Billy. 'Sorry to interrupt. Why don't you keep on working?'

'Course not, now you're back. How d'you get on?'

Billy unzipped the holdall, produced a handful of rosettes and chucked them down on the table.

'Brilliant,' said Janey, sorting them out. 'Two firsts, three seconds, a third, a fourth and two fifths.'

'The first was the Grand Prix, and there's lots of loot, a lovely kitchen clock and a television set and a very obscene china bull with a huge cock. I left it at Rupert's. I'll bring it down in the morning.'

Watching her poring over the rosettes, her breasts falling forward, strands of bush escaping from the red satin pants, Billy felt his own cock rising and wished he didn't always

625

want her so much. Sex had not been brilliant lately because Janey had so often fallen asleep drunk, but if they could avoid a row before they went to bed, he might get to screw her tonight.

Janey looked up, misconstruing the expression on his face.

'Sorry I look so awful, but I took Mavis for a walk in the woods at lunchtime and my trousers got drenched, so I took them off and couldn't be bothered to find any more.'

'You look lovely.'

'I've been a good little wife,' Janey went on. 'There's a casserole bubbling in the oven. I've ironed all your shirts; not very brilliantly, I'm afraid; some of the collars curl worse than Mavis's tail, and I've got your dinner jacket back from the cleaners.'

Billy was pleased she was in high spirits; then he felt a lurch of fear. The last time he'd seen her in this manic mood, floating-on-air, that inner-directed radiance that had nothing to do with him coming home, was when she was starting her affair with Kev. He desperately wanted a huge drink to blot out the terrors.

Janey read his thoughts. 'Let's have a drink.'

He followed her into the kitchen, which looked amazingly tidy. Janey got down two glasses and, instead of reaching for the vodka for herself, got a carton of orange juice out of the fridge. Filling the glasses, she handed one to him.

'Aren't you drinking vodka?'

'Nope. I've got something to celebrate.'

'You've sold the book in America?'

'Nope, I'm coming off the booze for a few months.' She chinked her glass against his. There was no mistaking the sparkle in her eyes. Billy couldn't bear to look at her any more. He went to the dresser and started flipping through his pile of mail.

'Seven and a half months, in fact,' said Janey.

'What?'

'That's the time I'm giving up booze for.'

626

'Whatever for?' said Billy wearily.

'I'm going to have a baby.'

Billy dropped the pile of letters.

'Your baby,' said she softly. 'Our baby.'

'How d'you know?' he muttered. There had been so many false alarms.

'James Benson confirmed it today.'

'Is he sure?'

'Absolutely.'

Billy turned incredulously.

Then she ran to him, flinging her arms round him, burying her face in his shoulder.

'Oh, Christ,' he said, 'how wonderful. Oh Christ, how wonderful. Where can I hug you that I won't hurt it?'

'Anywhere you like. It's only six weeks old.'

'Why didn't you tell me you were going to Benson?'

'I didn't want you to get too excited. I told myself if I could manage to keep my trap shut until I'd had the test, it'd be all right. It's like you not drinking until all the bills are paid off.'

'They are now. Lisbon wiped out the lot. Oh, angel, I'm so happy.'

'Are you sure?' she said in an uncertain voice. 'You don't f-feel,' she stumbled over the word, 'I've done it to trap you into staying with me?'

She took his face in her hands and found it was wet with tears.

'I was so miserable about the low sperm count,' he muttered. 'I felt such a shit not being able to give you a baby. Oh, darling, I'm so happy. It's the best news I've ever had. Can we ring my mother and tell her? She'll be beside herself.'

'D'you think?' asked Janey doubtfully. 'She hasn't paid the subscription to my fan club for a long time.'

'Course she will.'

'Oh, and I told Helen,' said Janey. 'She rang this afternoon, and I was so excited I had to tell someone.'

'Was she pleased?'

'Ish. You know Helen,' she said, ' "It'll be a real positive experience for you, Janey. After all, you're still just at prime child-bearing age." The silly cow.'

Billy grinned. 'I still can't take it in. God, it's wonderful.'

The telephone went. Billy leapt on it.

'Hi. Guess what? Oh, you know,' he said, sounding a little deflated. 'Helen must have told you. Isn't it? I haven't come down to earth yet.'

'Rupert is terribly pleased,' said Billy as he put down the receiver. 'He wanted to bring a magnum of Krug over, but I said it'd be wasted on us, so he suggested some extra strong grass that Guy had sold him.'

Janey giggled. 'No, that's all behind us. We're responsible parents-to-be now. Let's go and have a fuck instead.'

Fen and Sarah arrived at Wembley just before midnight on Sunday. Fen was utterly shattered. She hadn't eaten or slept properly for weeks. Jake could only help so much, as though by remote control. She'd had a bad fall from Hardy and her back still ached. The very thought of jumping the four horses all week, in big classes that went on late into the evening, filled her with exhaustion.

Next morning, on her way to declare, she looked through the red curtains and saw Billy walking the course for a novice class. He was wearing old green cords and a tweed coat and laughing at some crack of Rupert's. He looked so happy and carefree and so much younger. Her heart twisted with longing. I'm not cured, she thought in panic. In the secretary's tent she found Humpty and Griselda, who both turned their backs on her. Oh, God, how long was this stupid pantomine going on?

Early in the evening, when she was least expecting it, she bumped into Billy. He was very friendly, but shifty somehow, not meeting her eyes and firing questions about Jake and the yard, asking after Laurel twice and congratulating her in a hearty, most unBillyish way. He seemed almost in a hurry to get away from her, which left her far more uneasy and depressed than the other riders shunning her.

She wandered down to the stables. Macaulay's top door was shut to stop his adoring public feeding him and tugging souvenir hairs out of his mane. She slid into the box and shut the doors quickly behind her. Macaulay whickered with pleasure but didn't get up, so she sat down on the straw beside him, stroking his mane, still crinkly from the afternoon plaits.

There were two classes that evening – a fancy dress pair relay and then the *Sunday Times* Cup, worth £10,000. She hadn't entered the relay because she was scared no one would want to be her partner. Outside, she heard shrieks of laughter. Standing up, she peered through the crack in the box, and saw Billy and Rupert teetering past wearing fishnet stockings, three-inch heels, and coats and skirts with coconuts heaving in their twin-sets. Rupert, immaculate in a blond wig, was Mrs Thatcher; Billy, wearing a mop on his head, was Shirley Williams. Then they were gone, and next door she could hear Sarah getting Hardy ready for the *Sunday Times* Cup. Fen sighed and sat down beside Macaulay again. She was just nodding off when she heard hoofs clattering outside, and an excited voice saying:

'Guess what? Gossip, gossip, gossip,' It was Dizzy.

'What?' said Sarah, coming to the door.

'Where's Fen?' asked Dizzy.

'In the lorry, I think. I haven't seen her for some time. Come on, out with it.'

'Janey Lloyd-Foxe is pregnant.'

Fen's hand tightened convulsively on Macaulay's mane.

'Jesus,' said Sarah. 'When did you find out?'

'Well Count Guy, Billy, Rupert and Driff were all declaring. And Count Guy was ribbing Billy, saying he'd heard some *très interessant* rumours, and Billy went all scarlet and pleased and admitted Janey was having a baby. Count Guy was tickled pink, of course. He didn't like Billy being separated from Janey, in case he started running after Lavinia again. Anyway, they were busy congratulating

629

each other when bloody Driffield said, "Who's the father? Kevin Coley?" The next minute Billy let him have one on the jaw – wham – sending Driff flying across the tent. Then Billy jumped on Driff with his hands round Driff's neck, howling, "Take it back, you effing bastard," and other pleasantries.'

'Golly,' said Sarah.

'Rupert and Count Guy dragged Billy off and Driffield said he'd get Billy suspended. "No, you won't", said Rupert. "There's nothing in the BSJA rules about eliminating a competitor before an event, only during." '

Both grooms started to giggle.

'Anyway,' Dizzy went on, 'Malise made Driffield apologise. Driff said it was only a joke and Billy, Rupert and Guy turned on their booted heels and stalked out undeclared, and had to come back five minutes later when Driffield had gone. So it looks as though Driff, not your poor boss, is going to be the next candidate for Coventry.'

'Christ,' said Sarah, 'Fen'll go bananas when she hears. He must be mad about Janey to punch Driff. I'm glad someone has at last; he's such a poisonous little toad.'

'I thought Billy couldn't have kids,' said Dizzy. 'Do you think it *is* Kev's?'

Like a sleepwalker, Fen came out of Macaulay's box.

'Fen,' gasped Dizzy, backing into the patiently waiting Arcturus. 'We didn't realize you were there.'

'Obviously not,' said Fen, 'or you wouldn't keep Rupert's horse hanging round in the cold. All you bloody well do all day is gossip.'

Not even bothering to close Macaulay's door, she walked unsteadily away from them. 'Billy's going to have a baby,' she muttered over and over again through trembling lips. She had no idea where she went, but she ended up in the lorry, locking the door behind her.

A few minutes later she heard pounding on the door.

'Fen, it's Sarah. They're walking the course.'

'I don't care,' sobbed Fen. 'Leave me alone.'

'Please – I'm sorry about your overhearing everything,

but Hardy's all ready and I know you wanted to jump him in this class.'

'Go away, for Christ's sake.'

'Let me in. I want to look after you.'

Fen didn't answer. She lay on her bed, sobbing convulsively, shuddering like a palsied dog. She couldn't cope any more. There was no future, nothing, nothing. The light had gone out at the end of the tunnel; both ends were blocked up; there was no hope. 'Oh, Billy, oh, Billy,' she groaned.

Then she heard someone fiddling with the door handle, then voices, then more fiddling and the door was forced open and the inside of the living area was flooded with light.

'Go away,' Fen screamed. 'I can't take it. I simply can't take it.'

Then she saw a man's figure framed in the doorway.

'Billy,' she croaked, in an insane moment of hope. 'Oh, Billy.'

'Afraid not, sweetheart,' drawled a voice. 'You'll just have to put up with second best.'

It was Dino Ferranti.

Fen slumped back on the bed. 'Leave me fucking alone.'

'You can't fuck alone. It's a physical impossibility,' said Dino, sitting down on the bed and drawing her close to him. 'There, honey, hush, hush.' He stroked her hair, damp with tears, feeling her drenched shirt and jersey against him, horrified by the fragility of her body.

'I love him so much I don't know what to do.'

'Hush, don't try to talk.' Gradually he managed to calm her.

'What am I to do?' she repeated shakily.

Dino pulled off a piece of kitchen roll, dried her eyes and held out another piece for her to blow her nose with.

'There are still twelve riders to jump before you. You're gonna get dressed and jump that course.'

'I am bloody not.'

'Sure you are. Just figure if this had happened in L.A. You couldn't just not jump. Every round's a dress rehearsal for that day, right?'

'Los Angeles is ten months away,' snapped Fen. 'I'm having difficulty getting through the next five minutes.'

She was shivering violently now.

Dino poured her a glass of brandy.

'Have a slug of this.'

'I don't want it.'

'Yes, you do. Open your mouth.' He almost forced it down her throat.

'Bastard,' said Fen, but she drank it.

'Now get out of those clothes.' Like a father, he removed her shirt and tie, which were streaked with lipstick and mascara.

'That's my lucky shirt and tie,' moaned Fen, covering her breasts with her arms.

'Haven't brought you much luck today,' said Dino. 'Try another combination.' He held out a clean shirt for her.

'I am *not* going to jump,' said Fen mutinously. 'Not on Hardy. He's a nightmare and I haven't walked the course.'

'You've got time to watch the last three rounds,' said Dino. 'Come on, put your jacket on and borrow my shades.'

'I hate you,' said Fen. 'I truly, truly hate you.'

For a moment, as he stood behind her while she checked her appearance in the mirror, she was struck by the contrast between her waiflike figure, white face and swollen eyes, and Dino, brown as peanut butter, ridiculously elegant in a black silk shirt and pale grey suit. He'd streaked his hair pale grey since she'd last seen him.

'Talk about Beauty and the Beast,' she said.

News of Janey's pregnancy and Billy punching Driffield had spread rapidly around the showground.

Fen came out of the lorry to find the place swarming with reporters. Dino despatched them ruthlessly. No, Fen couldn't speak to anyone, nor could she sign autographs. With his arms round her, he forced a gangway through the crowd.

'Who's that with her?' asked the man from the *Express*. 'Face is familiar.'

'Think he's an actor,' said the girl from the *Mirror*.

By some miracle they had time to watch a couple of rounds.

'Watch the wall,' warned Sarah. 'There's been a lot of mistakes there, and the combination's on a funny stride. People have been taking three strides, then changing their minds and asking the horses off too early, then hitting the third element.'

'I suppose you know *all* about it,' snapped Fen at Sarah.

'I'm awfully sorry, Fen,' said Sarah in an undertone. 'I'm so glad you made it.'

'I wouldn't have,' said Fen, casting a venomous glance at Dino, 'if Mussolini here hadn't come jackbooting round. Why can't I go into a decline in peace?'

Mary-Jo Wilson, the number one American girl rider, auburn-haired and extremely attractive, was in the ring. She took a brick out of the wall and had a pole down at the second element, then crashed through the third. The crowd gave a groan of sympathy.

'What did I tell you?' said Dino. 'Hi Mary-Jo,' he shouted as she came out of the ring.

'Dino!' Her face lit up. 'I didn't know you were in Europe.'

'How many clears?' Fen asked Sarah.

'Only four.'

Dino removed his dark glasses from a protesting Fen.

'But my eyes are still red.'

'Just fantasise you're a white rat.'

She rode through the cherry-red curtains into the brilliantly lit arena.

'And here comes Fenella Maxwell,' said Dudley Diplock, in ecstasy. 'Hot from her brilliant second in the Crittleden Gold Cup, on Hardy.'

The crowd, who'd been bitterly disappointed when Fen hadn't appeared at her appointed place in the class and had assumed she'd scratched, gave a cheer of delighted surprise.

'Bloody unfair,' grumbled Griselda. 'Why should they waive the rules for her?'

'Because she's a star,' said Billy. 'She's the one they've come to see.'

It is the mark of a great athlete that the mind can transcend adversity, and somehow heighten the performance. After two shaky jumps, which had her fans gasping and nearly stripped the paint off the poles, Fen clicked into automatic pilot. Hardy, given his head and showing his true quality, went clear. The crowd went berserk. Their idol hadn't failed them. Crittleden wasn't just a flash in the pan.

'Thank God I didn't walk the course,' said Fen as she came out. 'I'd have been so terrified I'd never have crossed the starting line.'

'You made a cock-up at the first two fences,' said Dino.

'Don't come on like Jake,' said Fen icily. 'I'm going back to the lorry.'

'No, you're not,' said Dino, catching her by the scruff of her neck. 'You've got to jump off.'

He took her up into the riders' stand to watch the first rounds. From all sides people hailed him.

'Where are zee horses?' asked Hans Schmidt.

'Arriving the day after tomorrow. I might jump Manny in the Victor Ludorum.'

At that moment Billy's number was called. Behind Fen and Dino, Janey Lloyd-Foxe was holding court, looking ravishing in a red wool Laura Ashley smock.

'You'd think she was eight months pregnant,' muttered Fen savagely. Janey was talking to Doreen Hamilton, speaking more slowly than usual so that Fen could hear every word.

'Yes, Billy is absolutely over the moon. The night I told him, he couldn't sleep for excitement. It's going to be a terrific incentive to his career. He says he's jumping for two now. He's treating me like glass. Won't even let me pick up a duster.'

'Never been her forte anyway,' said Fen to herself, her

634

knuckles white where she clutched her whip.

'When's it due?' asked Doreen.

'June. Billy'll be at the Royal and the International, but he says he'll probably cancel both.'

The jump-off course was a blur before Fen's eyes.

'Oh, here comes my darling,' said Janey as Billy, the first to jump off, cantered into the arena, a huge grin spread across his face. 'Don't you think prospective fatherhood suits him?'

Dino put a hand on Fen's knee. 'Ignore her,' he said. 'She's only trying to wind you up.'

Bugle put in an incredibly fast time. Janey went into noisy ecstasy.

'Never seen him ride before,' said Dino. 'He's bloody good. No one's going to be able to cruise after that.'

He was right. Both Ludwig and Wishbone clocked up slower times. In came Rupert to the usual ecstatic, school-girl screams. The whole of the pony club stand, hopeful of losing their virginity in such a glorious cause, rose to their feet to cheer.

'Extraordinary that someone so good-looking should be such a bastard,' said Dino. 'Like a blackbird singing the most exquisite song and dumping on you at the same time. Jesus, look at that acceleration. He ought to have starting gates.'

As Snakepit stampeded the course, the jumps hardly seemed to exist. He skimmed them effortlessly like a pebble flicked in ducks and drakes.

'He's improved a whole lot since the World Champion-ships,' said Dino, as Rupert thundered home two seconds faster than Billy. 'Pow, you can't help admiring him.'

'I can, only too easily,' said Fen.

Joyously raking his hand down Snakepit's steel-grey plaits, Rupert shot out through the red curtains, sending Hardy flying.

'Why don't you look where you're going, clumsy oaf?' snarled Fen.

'Because I don't like what's in my way,' snapped Rupert,

635

'and if Svengali Lovell can tell you how to beat that time, I'm a Dutchman.'

'Unfair to Dutchmen,' Fen shouted back over her shoulder. 'Some of them are rather nice.'

'Remember, if you're going too fast, accelerate,' Dino called after her.

Suddenly, Fen remembered Rupert in Rome sneering at her disastrous performances in the Nations' Cup, saying that women always crack under pressure.

'To hell with Rupert,' she said to herself, 'to hell with Janey Lloyd-Foxe and her beastly baby. If I'm going to commit suicide this is as good a way as any.'

Having bowed briefly to the Princess in the royal box, she turned Hardy round and thundered through the start at a gallop. Hardy, who was used to being checked all the time and fighting for his head, was puzzled for a minute, then rose to the challenge. Over the first fence she was up on Rupert's time, throwing herself over, her hands nearly touching Hardy's noseband. Over the parallel bars and, with an amazing flying change, she jumped the gate almost sideways.

God, thought Dino, suddenly terrified, she's taking me literally. Scorching over the upright, bucketing over the walls, Fen was already looking ahead to the combination. She was coming in too fast; she was going to crash. She knew a terrifying moment of fear, then Hardy took over and executed a trio of perfect jumps and hurtled Fen through the finish. From the earsplitting cheers of the crowd, who had risen to their feet, she knew she had beaten Rupert's time. The problem now was stopping. At the side of the arena a bank of blue hydrangeas came to meet them. Hardy skidded to the right, sliding along on his back legs for five seconds before coming to a halt.

Fen sauntered out of the ring, pleased that for once even Dino seemed shaken out of his customary cool.

The next moment Ludwig clapped his hand on her back.

'Brilliant. I haf never seen a round like zat.'

Count Guy followed suit, and suddenly all the British

riders, except Rupert and Griselda, were shaking her hand and hugging her. She was home from Coventry at last.

Was it all worth it? wondered Fen, as she accepted her red rosette from the Princess, with the huge, silver cup sparkling even more dazzlingly as it reflected the lights. Wás it worth the lack of sleep, the setbacks, the heartbreaks, for this moment of glory? She admired the Princess's perfect ankles in flesh-coloured tights as she walked back to the Royal box. Then there was a terrific roll of drums which nearly sent Snakepit and Rupert into orbit, leaving a gap between Fen and Billy, who was third. Turning, Fen looked him straight in the eye. With a supreme effort, far greater than winning the cup, she managed to smile. 'I'm so pleased about your baby,' she said.

Then, before he had time to answer, the arena was plunged in darkness and Fen and the dappled grey Hardy were illuminated by the spotlight. She was aware that no one was leaving, there was no crashing of seats or banging of exit doors, or feet running down the concrete steps, just a long silence followed by the most almighty cheering, and, as the band struck up 'I want some red roses for a blue lady', everyone started singing and clapping in time. Then the other riders filed out and she was alone and spotlit in the ring, sending Hardy into his wonderful, effortless, long striding gallop, and the crowd cheered so loudly that she went round again. Billy may not love me, she thought, but they do. Why can't I go on riding around this ring for the rest of my life?

Dudley captured her in the collecting ring, brandishing his microphone like a furry, black iced lolly:

'Se-uper, absolutely se-uper. You sorted out the girls from the boys today.' He roared with laughter. He'd had too many in the whisky tent. 'And Harvey went se-uperly. You *must* be pleased.'

'He did, and I am.'

'Must be a cert for L.A. now.'

'You can't look beyond tomorrow with horses,' said Fen.

'Must be difficult to choose between him and Esmeralda.'

Fen looked broodingly at Dudley for a second.

'*She's* called Desdemona, and *he's* called Hardy, and why don't you remove your silly hat when you're talking to a lady, Dudley. Although, knowing you, you probably think I'm a gentleman.'

Oh, Christ, she thought, I shouldn't have said that.

Out of the corner of her eye, beyond the Shetland ponies and the famous ex-racehorses who were lining up for the personality parade, she could see a pack of reporters hovering.

'Well done, Fen, wizard round. Let's have a jar later in the week,' bellowed a voice, and there, leering above her, almost sending Dudley flying, was Monica Carlton bowling past with her Welsh cobs.

'One door shuts, another door opens,' said Fen, giving Monica a weak smile. Dudley was flapping around saying goodnight to the viewers and reminding them to switch on tomorrow for the Puissance. Fen tried to dive behind a coster's van, but the reporters were old hands. Next moment they'd ringed her like a lasso, blocking her escape on all sides.

'What d'you think about Billy Lloyd-Foxe's wife having a baby?'

'I'm very pleased for him.'

'Nothing else to say?'

'If it grows up like Billy, it'll be a wonderful child.'

'But not like Janey?'

'I didn't say that.' Fen looked desperately round for help. 'I hardly know Janey.'

'You were very fond of Billy, weren't you?'

'It's difficult not to be,' said Fen, bursting into tears. 'He hasn't an enemy in the world.'

All she could see was their avid searching eyes and their frantically scribbling biros.

'Why can't you leave me alone?' she sobbed.

A shadow fell across the note books.

'Pack it in,' said Dino coldly and, taking the couple nearest Fen by their coat collars, he yanked them out of the way. 'Bugger off and fuse your own typewriters with your lousy copy. You heard what the lady said – leave her alone.'

44

Back in the lorry, Dino peered unenthusiastically into the fridge. 'One black avocado, half a can of beans, a pork pie that ought to be on superannuation. You have two choices,' he said to Fen. 'You can cry yourself to sleep, right, or come out to dinner with me. I'm starving.'

'I'm not hungry and I ought to ring Jake.'

'Sarah called him. He said, what the hell were you doing risking Hardy's neck, then exhausting him, showing off in that double lap of honour.'

Fen pulled a face. 'And that's all the bloody praise I get.'

Dino took her to an Italian restaurant off High Street, Kensington, which stayed open late. Outside, Fen could see dusty, yellowing plane trees fretted by raindrops, and lovers under pulled-down umbrellas hurrying to catch the last tube. Imprisoned in Wembley, with its heat, airlessness and tensions, she'd forgotten an outside world existed. At the next-door table a couple were holding hands. Taking in the merry din, the bottles of chianti, the photographs of the Colosseum on the wall, the solicitous waiters, Fen was reminded of the night in Rome with Billy, when her face was all bruised and he'd fed her risotto with a spoon. She wanted him so badly it took her breath away.

'What are you thinking about?' demanded Dino.

'That I ought to be in the intensive-care unit, not wasting your money.'

'It is *my* money,' said Dino, grabbing the menus. 'I'll order for you.'

'Grapefruit bolognese'll do me fine,' said Fen, emptying

half a glass of wine in one gulp.

'How come you speak Italian so well?' she said when he'd finished ordering.

'Because I *am* Italian, I guess.'

'You're American,'

'Only by adoption. I'm just a simple, lousy, Latin lover at heart.'

'Why have you streaked your hair grey?'

'Well, hearing you were heavily into older guys, like Billy, I figured I stood more of a chance if I looked more mature. Besides,' he grinned, 'I thought it suited me.'

'It does,' admitted Fen. 'You look too bloody glamorous for words, but it's too early to make jokes about my broken heart.'

Dino put a suntanned, beautifully manicured hand over hers. 'How come you didn't acknowledge my telegram?'

'I wasn't sure it was from you.'

'It said it was, didn't it?'

'You don't know the terrible thing Rupert did to me in Rome.'

Just for a second his hand tightened painfully on hers.

'No, not that,' said Fen. 'I'd been packed off to bed ludicrously early and was sitting there, dying of boredom, when Rupert rang up, pretending to be you, and asked me out to dinner.'

'Did you go?'

'Did I? I've never got bathed, washed my hair and dressed quicker in my life. Then I found Rupert and Driffield killing themselves at the bottom of the stairs.'

Dino looked half-smug, half-sympathetic.

'That was a lousy trick. Were you disappointed?'

'Shattered. After that, I thought the telegram was probably one of Rupert's vile little practical jokes too, so I never wrote and thanked you.'

'If you had, I'd have been over much sooner.'

'And I might never have got involved with Billy. D'you think I'll ever get over him?' she added dolefully.

'Sure you will. Just stick around.'

The waiter arrived with their first course: half a dozen Mediterranean prawns each and a huge bowl of mayonnaise, strongly flavoured with garlic.

Dino ordered another bottle, and started stripping the prawns with incredible dexterity, then dipping them in the mayonnaise and passing them to Fen.

'Mm, they actually are delicious. Do you undress women as expertly?'

'Far more expertly, and I don't pull their heads and legs off, either.'

Fen paused for a minute, thinking how amazingly attractive he was; if you liked that sort of thing, she told herself hastily.

'Did you ever get Helen Campbell-Black into bed?'

Dino grinned. 'We had lunch several times, but she never had more than one course and left half of that because she was always wanting to rush me off to some art gallery. I said, "Honey, I am not into culture, I'm only into sex." '

'You didn't manage to divert her into some large double bed?'

He shook his head. 'She was running scared the whole time. Whenever I put my hand on her back to guide her across the road, she shot into the oncoming traffic. If you try anything further, a burglar alarm goes off.'

'In Rupert's lorry?'

'No, in her head. She's so beautiful you want to gaze and gaze, but I guess she's like a Ming vase: beautiful but empty.'

'Goodness, I've eaten all those prawns,' said Fen.

'Good girl.' Dino ran his hand down the inside of her arm, caressing her gently, almost abstractedly as if she were a dog. 'Funny, I fancy you. I always have.'

Fen jumped away. 'You mustn't say things like that. I'm not ready for propositions.'

'Wasn't a proposition. Just a statement of fact.'

'Even though I'm not as beautiful as Helen?'

Dino looked at her meditatively. 'You could gain some weight,' he said, 'but you'll do.'

Fen noticed he was beginning to squint slightly. He must be desperately jet-lagged.

'How's Manny?'

'Awesome; much better than me. He's grown so much and filled out. He was winning a lot earlier in the year. Then my daddy had a cardiac arrest in July. He's better now, but I was off the circuit for some weeks.'

'Why have you suddenly come over here at the end of the season?'

'To work with this guy whom I reckon is the best coach in the world. I'm going to stable the horses at his barn for a few months, take in a few shows in Europe, then have a stab at the World Cup in April. Then back to the States for the run up to the Olympics. I guess I want a gold as much as you do.'

'Who is this coach? Do I know him?'

'No one knows him very well. He's kind of unapproachable.' Dino smiled confidingly. 'Actually, I fancy one of his female jockeys. I figured if I was living there with permanent access, I might stand a better chance.'

Fen slumped in her chair, utterly deflated. She looked down at the tiny lamb cutlets that had just arrived and removed the blackened sprig of rosemary that lay across them. She was utterly heartbroken over Billy, but no girl likes an attractive re-boundee whipped from under her nose before she's even had a moment to try and re-bound on to him. It would have been useful to have Dino in England if anyone asked her to bring a man to a party or to some official dinner. Moodily she poured too much salt on to the side of her plate, watching it turn green in the mint sauce.

'No, I don't want any more to drink,' she said sulkily. 'I've got a class at nine tomorrow.'

Dino took no notice and filled up her glass.

'Did you meet this girl on the circuit?' she asked.

'Last year at the World Championship.'

Fen glanced up suddenly and was amazed to see he was laughing.

'Jesus, you're thick, Maxwell. You may win trophies at

shows, but you've got the perception of a blindworm.'

'I don't understand,' stammered Fen.

Dino took her hand again, turning it over, gently tracing the heart line with his thumb.

'I saw Jake this afternoon. He figures you've done a fantastic job, but it might help to have another guy around the barn to jump some of the horses. In return, he's going to help me with Manny when he comes out of hospital.'

Fen suddenly felt near to tears again. 'So he thinks I can't cope?'

'On the contrary, he thinks you're too good to waste. He wants a gold for you, too. He's only helping me because he knows there's no way I can beat you.'

Fen sat on Jake's hospital bed a fortnight later. 'It is absolutely infuriating,' she grumbled, 'but the entire household: Tory, the children, the grooms, the horses, even Wolf, are madly in love with Dino Ferranti. It's a good thing you're coming home next week to restore normality before they all defect to America with him.'

She got up and wandered restlessly around the room, looking at the inside of the hundreds of get-well cards, eating grapes, trying not to be upset by Jake's hisses of pain as, with contorted, sweating face and gritted teeth, he battled on, endlessly bending and stretching to strengthen the muscles of both broken and wasted legs. She couldn't help noticing how fragile and lacking in muscle they looked and wondered if he would ever ride again, let alone make the big time.

'The physiotherapist warned you not to overdo it,' she said reprovingly.

'Physiotherapists aren't interested in medals;' said Jake, pushing his drenched fringe out of his eyes.

'Tory's planning a surprise Thanksgiving Dinner for Dino, so he won't feel homesick,' Fen went on. 'Sarah is actually putting on make-up first thing in the morning for the first time in history. Any minute Desdemona will start curling her pink eyelashes. I can't think why he has to be so bloody charming all the time. Goodness, you've got a card

644

from the Princess! You are a star. Are you looking forward to coming home next week?'

'Of course,' panted Jake, leaning back for a second against the bedhead.

'We're all longing to have you,' said Fen.

Neither statement was strictly true. Jake, having dreamed of nothing but getting out of hospital for five months, was now thrown into a blind panic at the thought of facing the outside world. Learning to walk again was really taking it out of him – crashing over all the time, dragging himself up again, black with despair that neither of his legs would ever be strong enough to support him, and terror whether he'd ever have the guts to get on a horse again.

Night after night, he dreamed of tumbling poles and colossal horses crashing from great heights on to his legs, splintering them to spillikins, and woke up sobbing and screaming, until the night-nurse arrived to calm him down. After his early animosity, he felt an almost slavish gratitude to the nurses and the Matron, who had all taken such a personal pride in getting him right. When they weren't too busy on the wards, particularly at night, they would spend hours talking to him and he found himself unbending as he never did at home or with the other riders. There was one blonde nurse for whom he had a special fondness: Sister Wutherspoon, who brought him fresh eggs from the country and always popped in to show herself off, radiant and scented, before she went out on dates. Jake suppressed a faint suspicion that she might return his interest. Desirable nurses were not attracted to bad-tempered cripples like himself.

Finally, he didn't feel up to facing the whole slog of running the yard, driving miles to shows, raking the country for new horses. He longed for the children but didn't know if he could cope with the decibel level of their shrill demands, or with the doglike devotion of good, shiny-faced Tory, heaving her eleven-stone bulk round the Mill House, as she waited on everyone.

All he wanted to do was to spend two months soaking up the sun on some Hawaiian beach, with Sister Wutherspoon in a grass skirt ministering to his every need. Grass skirts would be no good in Warwickshire; Macaulay would eat them. He was glad Dino was going to be there to shoulder some of the responsibility.

Fen, on the other hand, was in a muddle. Having run the yard virtually single-handed for five months, she was close to collapse, but she had been buoyed up by her hopes of Billy coming sweet, and by the feeling that she was being indispensable and splendid. Now Dino had moved in and taken over at least half of the reins. Everyone seemed happier and she couldn't help being jealous. She felt she'd been demoted from head girl to the upper fourth and when Jake came home, she'd be back in the kindergarten.

She was irritated by the way everyone deferred to Dino. She couldn't fault him as a worker. Despite the very late hours he kept, he got up at six like everyone else and spent at least seven or eight hours in the saddle, working not only his own horses but all of Jake's novices. He had strange ideas about feeding his horses, arriving with a trunk full of vitamins and additives, but he was out of bed in a flash if there was any trouble with a sick horse in the night.

And, despite his languid, playboy image, he was amazingly domesticated. Fen nearly fainted one evening when she came home from an interview in Birmingham with ATV, to find him ironing his shirts.

'What are you doing?' she asked in amazement, 'Tory can do those.'

'Why the hell should she? She's exhausted.'

Fen watched the expert way he slid the iron along the folds of the blue, silk sleeve into the cuff. 'Where d'you learn to do that?'

'At college. All the money went on the horses. I couldn't afford to send shirts to the laundry. I hate crumpled shirts, so I figured I better learn to iron.'

'You'll make a wonderful wife someday,' said Fen.

At that moment Darklis appeared in a pink nightgown, looking disapproving.

''Lo Fen. We saw you on the telly. Are you coming, Dino? You promised to read *Green Eggs and Ham*. Dino's going to take me to Disneyland,' she added to Fen. 'Come on, Dino.'

'I'll be up when I've finished this lot,' he said, refusing to be bullied.

In the hall Fen met Tory wearing a dressing gown, pink from a hot bath.

'I've just left 'Diana' Ferranti slaving over a hot iron,' said Fen.

'Isn't he marvellous?' sighed Tory. 'I had a blinding headache and he just took over. He's cooking supper too. Gosh, it smells good. So nice to have a man who can tell the difference between rosemary and basil. Jakey wouldn't notice if you gave him dog biscuits.'

'I'm beginning to think Dino's more interested in Basils than Rosemarys, anyway,' said Fen pointedly.

She went out to the yard to check the horses. It was a very cold, starry night. An early frost had lurexed the cobbles in the yard and starched the golden willow spears which rustled underfoot and already clogged the stable gutters. As she adjusted a rug here and checked a water bowl or bandage there, Fen brooded on Dino's deficiencies. In some painful way he reminded her of Billy. But while Billy was like a dog: loving, dependent, enthusiastic, Dino was feline, cool and detached. He was far tougher and more critical than Billy. He saw Fen's faults only too clearly. But whereas Jake would bite her head off, Dino tended to mob her up.

Only last week he had caught her shouting at Sarah for giving Hardy, who was supposed to be on a diet, the wrong feed. When he told her to pack it in, she started shouting back at him, whereupon he calmly bundled her into a loose-box and shut both doors on her until she cooled down.

'How can I have any authority with the grooms if you take the piss out of me all the time?' she complained furiously afterwards.

'They have to humour and nurse you before big classes, so bloody well treat them properly at home.'

Most irritating of all, despite saying how much he fancied her during dinner after the *Sunday Times* Cup, he hadn't lifted a long, suntanned finger in her direction since he arrived at the Mill House. Perhaps living in such close proximity had put him off. Not that she cared a scrap; she was still hopelessly hooked on Billy. But she was irked that girls with soft caressing American accents always seemed to be ringing Dino up, and twice since he'd been living there, he'd disappeared off in his car after work and not returned until dawn was breaking. Occasionally Fen cried herself to sleep and wondered if Dino, who occupied the blue room at the end of the passage, ever heard her as he tiptoed past to bed.

All in all, for a man who was supposed to be staying in England because of her, he was behaving in an odd way. Standing in Desdemona's box, ruffling her coat which had thickened from being turned out during the day, she gave her the last glacier mint.

Looking out of the half-door she saw a small pale sliver of new moon curling itself round the weather cock. Turning the 50p piece in her pocket, she sighed, realizing there was no point wasting a wish on Billy any more.

'Please moon,' she said, 'give me a gold.'

A week later Jake came home. It was a perfect October afternoon with all the trees, silhouetted, against a rain-heavy navy blue sky, turning colour. There was not a speck of dust anywhere in the yard or an inch of tack unpolished. Only Dino's horses and four of the novices who were still going to shows were in their boxes. The rest of the horses were out in the different fields which checkered the hill behind the stables.

But they sensed something was up. They had been restless all day, snapping and shrieking at each other, not settling down to serious grazing, but hanging round the gates. Only now, just before Jake was due, had they all galloped off out of sight to talk to Macaulay, Africa and Africa's foal, who were grazing in the top field. Darklis and Isa weren't back from school yet, although a huge banner saying 'Welcome Home, Daddy,' which they'd painted with Sarah and Dino's help, hung from the two largest willows across the gateway. Above the murmur of the mill stream Fen heard the sound of a car on the bridge. Sarah darted forward to remove a couple of willow leaves which had floated down into the yard. Then Wolf, who'd also been jumpy all day, gave an excited bark. As the car drove into the yard he leaped forward, scrabbling hysterically at the paint with his paws.

'Welcome home,' cried Fen, running forward. 'Steady boy.' She caught Wolf's collar before opening the car door. 'You don't want to send your master flying.'

But when he realized it truly was Jake, Wolf remained motionless for several seconds as though he'd been stunned. Then he put back his head and let out a series of spine-chilling howls. Jake noticed tears were coursing down the lurcher's rough brindled cheeks.

'Come on, boy,' said Jake gently as the dog crept forward, laying his head on his master's knee, tail rammed between his thin trembling legs, as though he couldn't believe such a miracle. No one spoke as Jake stroked Wolf's head over and over again, smoothing away the tears. Then, as he struggled out of the car, Dino went forward to give him a hand.

'Hi,' he said. 'It's so good to have you home. Even the sun's come out to welcome you.'

Jake nodded, face impassive, not trusting himself to speak.

'Come inside and rest, darling,' said Tory.

'I want to see the horses.'

'You must take it slowly,' she pleaded. 'Today's been such a strain.'

'Pass me my crutches,' snapped Jake.

'Here they are,' said Fen.

649

As he stumbled painfully across the cobbles, slipping and once falling to his knees, Fen was about to rush to help him.

'Don't,' said Dino sharply, grabbing her arm.

He tried not to show how shocked he was by Jake's appearance in the sunlight. Grey with exhaustion, desperately thin, he'd had to make two extra holes in his belt to keep his trousers up.

'Oh, God,' said Fen, as he stumbled again.

'He's got to do it on his own,' said Dino.

After what seemed an eternity he reached the gate, leaning on it, gasping, to recover his breath. Laboriously he managed to open it and stagger inside, leaning back against it for support. The field sloped up to the skyline, dotted only by a few orange beeches and lemon yellow ashes. Not a horse in sight. Jake put his hand to his mouth and whistled. There was a long pause. He was about to whistle again when suddenly over the brow of the hill they came, black, dark brown, chestnut, bay, grey, roan. Some of them jumped over fences from nearby fields, thundering down the hill, manes and tails flying. It was like the last furlong of the Derby as they hurtled towards Jake. Hardy came from the back, elbowing, nipping, shoving the others out of the way, squealing jealously. Already plump from their rest, they had never moved faster in the height of their fitness as they stampeded the gate.

'They'll kill him,' whispered Sarah.

'They're going to crush him to death,' cried Tory in anguish.

'Get him out of there,' urged Fen. 'Oh, Dino, do something.'

But miraculously, about ten feet away, they jammed on their brakes and, although the ones behind cannoned unceremoniously into the leaders, they all slithered to a halt, not even touching the tips of Jake's shoes. They stood there, gazing at him goofily. Then, with a thunder of whickering, they edged forward and with the utmost gentleness started to nudge and nuzzle his face, his hands and his coat, occasionally getting jealous, flattening their ears at each other and giving each other a nip or a squeal. Hardy, true to his character, stropped Jake all over with his tongue, then gave him a sharp nip on the sleeve of his coat, just to show he was still boss.

'I've never seen anything like that before,' said Dino, looking down and seeing tears pouring down Fen's cheeks. Finding her hand in his, he gave it a gentle squeeze. Fen looked down, started, blushed scarlet and snatched her hand away to wipe her eyes.

'Someone's missing,' said Sarah.

'It's the big fellow,' said Dino.

Next minute they saw Macaulay standing on the crest of the hill, like Bambi's father. Jake gave another whistle and the next moment Macaulay came crashing down the hill like an out-of-control steam roller, so fast that all the other horses parted in self-preservation to let him through. When he reached Jake, he chased all the others away with enraged squeals, instantly returning to press his great white whiskery face against Jake's. Jake put his arm round Macaulay's neck, clinging on for support, his shoulders shaking.

'D'you think he's O.K.?' said Fen in dismay.

'Leave him,' said Dino. 'He's best alone with the horses.'

45

Having dreaded Jake's return, Fen found it easier than she'd expected, because he and Dino got on so surprisingly well. Dino was unruffled by Jake's black moods and biting sarcasm, and didn't take them personally.

'The guy's in a lot of pain,' he told Fen. 'Got to get his act together. He needs to jackboot around a bit to regain his self-respect.'

Together they worked on the horses, and on Hardy and Manny in particular, with Jake giving orders, stumbling around the yard, first on two crutches, then one, and by the end of November with a walking stick. He also plugged relentlessly away at the exercises. Mr Buchannan was delighted with his progress and said, with any luck he'd be riding by February.

At night after supper, instead of collapsing in front of the television, Jake and Dino would talk over a bottle of wine until they dropped. Dino asked most of the questions, but while Jake gave Dino the benefit of all his gipsy secrets and remedies, Dino was able to counter with information on the latest medical and dietary breakthroughs in the States. Soon all Jake's horses were taking extra vitamins. 'They all rattle as they go past,' said Fen crossly.

Dino also encouraged Jake into a new régime to get him back into peak condition. Fen was staggered to see Jake, who seldom managed more than a cup of the blackest, sweetest coffee for breakfast, actually sitting down to slices of apple, dried apricot, prunes and sticks of carrot, followed by one of Dino's multi-vitamin cocktails.

'All the same, Dino's just picking Jake's brains,' said Fen

indignantly, as she dried up one evening. 'You wait till America gets the team gold and Dino the individual. Then you'll be sorry.'

'Don't be mean, Fen,' said Tory gently. 'Dino's doing it for Jakey's sake as well. He looks so much better and it does him so much good to feel needed.'

Fen was also finding Jake's criticism very hard to take. After all, she'd made more money during the last year than he ever had and she was fed up with Dino sticking up for Tory. She was only drying up tonight because Dino'd torn another strip off her for treating Tory like a slave.

'You all just leave her with the dishes. Why the hell doesn't Jake buy her a dishwasher?'

'But she's quite happy,' protested Fen.

'You talk as though she was some retarded kid in a mental institution.'

Dino had been particularly touched by Tory's surprise Thanksgiving Dinner.

'Where did you get this pumpkin pie recipe?' he said, amazed. 'It's better than they make at home.'

Tory went pink. 'I rang up Helen Campbell-Black,' she stammered.

Fen and Jake looked at her incredulously. She must adore Dino to seek advice from the enemy camp.

The only thing that cheered Fen up during those weeks was her own increasing success. She had two good wins at home shows. All the papers regarded her as a cert for L.A. Her fan mail grew bigger. She was expected to have instant opinions as magazines called daily, asking her for her views on men, clothes, slimming, food. Hardly a day passed without some journalist coming down to Warwickshire to interview her. You couldn't walk past a magazine rack without seeing her face peering out. Fen was not conceited by nature but she couldn't help brooding on the admiration of the outside world, compared with the distinct lack of reverence with which she was treated at home. Jake and Dino believed there was a job to be done and she was there to get on with it.

One afternoon in late November, Fen and Sarah had been hacking out, getting Desdemona and Macaulay fit for Olympia. As they rode into the yard they found Dino, who'd just had a strenuous session in the indoor school, cooling off Manny in the yard.

Next minute Tory came out of the kitchen door, her hands covered with flour.

'Oh, Dino, someone named Mary-Jo rang. She's staying at the Dorchester. Can you ring her?'

'Sure, I'll do it now.' He handed the horse to Louise, his groom, and walked into the house.

'Lucky Mary-Jo,' sighed Sarah.

'Who's she?' asked Tory. 'She asked after Jake's leg and sounded awfully nice.'

'Mary-Jo Wilson, I should think,' said Fen, sliding off Desdemona. 'The American girl wonder. Lots of red hair tucked into a bun and perfectly tied stocks, with diamond tiepins, and a white carnation in her buttonhole. Too bloody poncy for words, if you ask me. I'm sure she rides side-saddle in bed.'

'But jolly attractive in a Helen Campbell-Black sort of way,' said Sarah, not without malice. 'Dino obviously likes redheads.'

'Well, she sounded sweet,' repeated Tory, without any malice at all.

Dino came back into the yard. 'Sorry it's short notice,' he said to Tory, 'but I won't be in for dinner tonight.'

'Shall I keep something hot for you?' said Tory.

'I'm sure Mary-Jo's doing that already,' snapped Fen, then immediately wished she hadn't.

Dino shot her a sour look. 'It'll make a nice change,' he said evenly, and went off to supervise Manny's feed.

'Why are you so foul to him, Fen?' said Tory reproachfully.

'Because he's so bloody swollen-headed.'

'His head's not the only thing that'll be swollen when he sees Mary-Jo,' said Sarah with a giggle.

'Don't be disgusting,' snapped Fen.

654

She felt impossibly bad-tempered, particularly when Dino came back in time for breakfast the next morning, spent all day yawning, and was so untogether Hardy had him off three times.

A week later Dino boxed up his horses and took them off to a show in Vienna, where there was a World Cup qualifier. Fen was so certain he'd taken Mary-Jo that she rang up the Dorchester, to be told that Miss Wilson had checked out the morning Dino had left and wasn't expected back until December 12th, the day Dino was due home. Fen spent the next few days imagining Dino waltzing around and around a Viennese ballroom to the Blue Danube with Mary-Jo in his arms.

Dino returned as expected on the 12th after a very successful show. Manny had obviously improved dramatically under Jake's tuition. He had qualified for the World Cup, won a big class on the third night and come second in the Grand Prix. Jake was delighted. That's what he gets a kick out of, thought Fen. He really likes improving horses at home better than jumping them at shows.

Dino brought toys for the children, silk scarves for the grooms, a beautiful black sloppy sweater for Tory, which covered all her bulges, and a new bit which they were all raving about on the continent for Jake. But nothing apparently for Fen. That's because I was so horrible before he left, she thought miserably, escaping to the yard. It was a very cold night. The water trough was already frozen and a thin sheet of ice lay over the cobblestones. In the tackroom she found a drooping Louise hanging up Dino's tack, which she'd been cleaning on the drive home.

'You must be knackered, poor thing.'

Louise nodded. 'Sure, but it was a great show. You always feel less bushed when you win.'

Fiddling with the striped handle of a body brush, Fen casually asked, 'How did Mary-Jo do?'

'Not bad,' said Louise, as though it was the most natural thing in the world for Mary-Jo to have been with them. 'She's having problems with Melchior. He keeps kicking out fences; but Balthazar jumped real super and qualified for the World Cup. She's worried she won't make the team for L.A., particularly as Dino must be a dead cert now. But the competition's so hot and she's twenty-six already and by the next games she'll probably be tied up with babies. Pity she can't come down here for a week or two and work with Jake. Not that the American coaches aren't great, but Jake does have the edge with difficult horses.'

'I can't think why he doesn't apply for the job as American chef d'equipe,' snapped Fen and, chucking down the body brush, she stalked out into the bitterly cold night, wandering around in jersey and jeans, oblivious of time and temperature. Tory's voice brought her back to reality. In the kitchen she found Dino, changed into a grey cashmere jersey and grey cords, drinking a large whisky and soda and telling Tory about Vienna. Rosettes and photographs were spread out all over the pine table.

'It's so beautiful. We went to one cemetery where all the great musicians are buried: Mozart, Brahms, Beethoven, Haydn. The most moving thing of all was Schubert's grave. Look.' He handed the photo to Tory. 'On the headstone they've carved a picture of him arriving in heaven and an angel putting a laurel wreath on his head – because no one recognized his genius on earth.'

'Unlike you,' said Fen acidly. 'Everyone appreciates you, Dino.'

'Not everyone.' Dino's face was expressionless, but he quickly gathered up the photographs.

'Lovey, you look frozen,' said Tory. 'Have a hot bath. I'm just off with Isa to see Darklis' play. Dinner's in the oven. Goulash and baked potatoes. And there's an apple pie in the larder if you want it.'

Jake was away in Ireland for two days to look at some horses. It had been regarded as a great step forward that he felt well enough to go. Fen, however, couldn't face dinner alone with Dino and Louise.

'Thanks.' She walked through the kitchen. 'I'm not hungry at the moment. Wish Darklis tons of luck.'

In her bedroom she slumped on her bed. Fighting tiredness and misery, she drew the blue and white gingham curtains. The tops were still off the shampoo and conditioner she'd used to wash her hair for Dino's return; the wet towel was still on the bed, the hair dryer plugged in. Despite switching on the fire she couldn't stop shivering and decided to have a bath. She'd just stripped off when there was a knock on the door.

'Who is it?' She grabbed the wet towel.

'Me.' Dino came into the room, shutting the door behind him.

Fen turned away towards the mirror. 'I'm about to have a bath.'

'I've fixed you a drink.' He put a large vodka and tonic down on the dressing table. There was a pause as he picked up the Mrs Tiggy-Winkle with a teazel face, a mob cap and a pink dress which stood beside all the china horses on the bookshelf.

'That's kind of neat.'

'Jake made it for me years ago.'

She sat on the dressing-table stool, thin bare shoulders rising out of the dark red towel, slanting eyes suspicious.

Dino noticed the plugged-in hair dryer.

'Going out?'

She shook her head. 'My hair was dirty.'

The room was warming up now. Why couldn't her teeth stop chattering?

'I've got a present for you,' said Dino, easing a black square box out of his hip pocket and opening it. Fen gasped as he took out a gold chain, with an F exquisitely set in pearls and emeralds on the end. He hung it around her neck, fumbling over the clasp, with hands that were not quite steady.

'Well,' he said.

Looking up at his reflection, she noticed his suntan was fading and the Siamese-cat eyes were squinting slightly as they always did when he was very tired.

'It's lovely,' she whispered, fingering the F. 'It's the

657

loveliest thing anyone's ever, ever given me. I'll never take it off. Thank you so much. I thought,' her voice shook, 'you'd deliberately forgotten me because I'd been such a bitch.'

She stood up to turn round, but Dino gripped her bare arms, dropping a slow infinitely measured kiss on her left collar bone. Suddenly her stomach started to curl and a pulse to beat insistently between her legs.

'How could I forget you?' he said ruefully. 'I never think of anyone else.' He was nuzzling at the side of her neck now, softly kissing the lobes of her ears. 'And, quite frankly, if I don't unzip my flies and climb inside you soon I'm going to end up in the funny farm.'

'Truly? You're not just being kind?'

'Kind? Christ, I've backed off enough.'

He turned her around. She gazed up at him, troubled, trembling. 'I'm not sure, Dino. I've been so hurt, I've only got a little bit of heart left.'

'I've got more than enough heart for both of us. I won't hurt you, sweetheart. I'm going to make you better.'

Slowly he drew back her clenched arms which were holding the towel up and put her hands round his neck. Beneath her fingers she could feel the power of his shoulder muscles.

'Go on, kiss me,' he whispered.

As she tentatively put her lips up, he kissed her back so gently she thought she'd faint with joy; first her top lip, then the bottom, then sliding his tongue between her teeth. One hand was cupping her left breast now, moving slowly and lovingly, the harbinger of pleasure.

'Darling little Fen, tell me what turns you on.'

'You do,' she moaned. 'Oh, please go on.'

But as he pulled her down on the bed and began to kiss her in earnest, sliding his hand over her body, she caught a glimpse of Billy's photograph beside the bed. Then she thought about Janey and then about Mary-Jo Wilson, who last night had been lying beside Dino submitting, no doubt ecstatically, to the same expert caresses. She couldn't stand

658

it. This time she wanted a man who was all hers, one whom she didn't have to share.

Violently, she pulled away from him.

'Hey, what's the matter?'

'You are. You're so bloody promiscuous, smarming all over me one minute, then rushing up to London at the drop of a telephone receiver to push off to Vienna with Mary-Jo. Guess who's coming for Dino? You bet your sweet life Mary-Jo is.'

For a second Dino's hand clenched on her shoulder. Then he looked around the room at the posters of Snoopy and the china horses and Lester the teddy bear and the pyjama case in the shape of a camel, and then at the tattered photograph of Billy Lloyd-Foxe in the leather case.

'You're still a kid, aren't you?' he said bitterly. 'I guess you're just about adult enough to sleep with an old teddy bear like Billy Lloyd-Foxe.'

'Bastard,' hissed Fen, and the next moment she'd slapped Dino's face very hard. 'Just shut up about Billy.'

Dino shrugged. 'And you resort to blows like a kid. Unfortunately, I happen to be a grown-up boy. I had my twenty-first birthday five years ago and I've got the appetites of a normal guy. If you think I'm going to remain celibate while you keep putting another battery in the stupid flashlight you're carrying for Billy you've got another think coming.'

'It's not a stupid torch,' screamed Fen. 'You're just like Rupert and Jake. None of you understand the meaning of the word love.'

'All I can promise,' said Dino, 'is that I want you more than any girl I've ever met, but I'm a hedonist, not a medieval knight keeping myself pure for some unobtainable lady love, nor do I like sleeping alone. The central heating in this house leaves a lot to be desired. So if you won't put out I'm going to find my entertainment some place else.'

And with that he left her. The next minute she heard his car door bang and the crunch of wheels on the gravel.

Bursting into tears, she threw herself down on the already sodden bed.

46

The next few days were awful. Fen and Dino hardly exchanged a word. Fen got up before dawn. Dino changed his routine, got up after lunch and spent his evenings working the horses in the indoor school. It seemed impossible in such a small house that they could avoid meeting. Dino was polite but unsmiling; he no longer mobbed her up.

On Friday morning Fen, Dino, Louise and Sarah were due to get up at 3.30 a.m. for a 4.30 departure for a show in Amsterdam. On the Thursday before that, the *Sunday Express* sent a photographer and a reporter down to the Mill House to interview Fen. In the evening she had to go to a dinner at the Savoy where she was being nominated for one of the Sporting Personality of the Year awards. The organizers were sending a car for her, which, at the end of the evening, would whizz her back to Warwickshire to catch three hours sleep before leaving for Amsterdam.

The *Sunday Express* reporter was a charming middle-aged roué, who thought Fen was gorgeous and buttered her up to mountainous heights in the hope of possible indiscretions. After lunch cooked by Tory, the photographer took pictures of Desdemona and Macaulay from flattering angles, as they were still a bit podgy from their six weeks' rest, later photographing the yard and the house and the kitchen, with Tory cooking at the Aga and Fen pretending to fill in entry forms against a background of rosettes.

'I'm thinking of getting a secretary to cope with all my fan mail,' said Fen, who'd had three glasses of wine at lunch.

'I'm not surprised,' said the *Express* reporter. 'Every little girl in England dreams of being like you.'

'I hope to Christ they don't behave like her,' said a voice, and Dino wandered in, unshaven, yawning, bloodshot-eyed and poured himself a large whisky.

'Is that your breakfast?' snapped Fen.

'No, the first one was my breakfast,' said Dino. 'Hi,' he added to the reporter and wandered off in the direction of the stables.

'That's Dino Ferranti, isn't it?' asked the reporter, refilling Fen's glass. 'Good-looking bloke, despite the stubble. More like a rock star. He your latest?'

'Hardly,' snapped Fen, 'He's working with Jake. Honestly, if I were cast away on a desert island I'd rather be propositioned by a gorilla!'

'You'd be wasting your time,' said Dino, coming back into the room. 'Gorillas are mostly gay. Anyone seen this week's *Horse and Hound*?'

'And don't bloody eavesdrop,' said Fen, 'Let's go into the sitting-room. We'll be more private.'

It was already dark when she waved them goodbye. Outside, the lorry was waiting, already filled with petrol, water and human and equine supplies. She'd better step on it. The car was picking her up at five-thirty. Sitting at the kitchen table she found Dino, Tory and Sarah checking the list of what they were taking to Amsterdam. Fen looked at her message pad – ATV, *Woman's Own* and Malise Gordon had rung. Picking up the telephone, she suddenly noticed black fur all over her pale pink angora jersey, which was drying on a towel on top of the Aga.

'Bloody hell,' she said, dropping the receiver back on its cradle.

Tory looked up, alarmed. 'What's the matter?

'My pink jersey. I've got to take it tomorrow and you can't even keep the bloody cats off it.'

Dino looked up from a pile of horses' health papers.

'Pack it in,' he said softly. 'Tory's cooked lunch for your press admirer, which you haven't even had the manners to thank her for. She's done all our ironing for tomorrow and seen everything's back from the cleaners, as well as providing enough food for us for a month. She doesn't actually have the time to police your pale pink sweater,' he really spat out the Ps, 'against marauding tom cats.'

Fen lost her temper. 'I ran this bloody yard single-handed for five months and now I don't get any proper back-up,' she screamed and stormed out of the kitchen. Ten minutes later she was back with dripping hair: 'Who's been using my hairdryer?'

'I did,' said Tory apologetically, 'on Darklis.'

'Well, you've fused it. How am I expected to dry my hair?'

'Why don't you go stick your head in the oven,' said Dino, 'and preferably don't light the gas! You're getting much too big for your £500 boots. We all know you're England's answer to show-jumping and the role model for the entire schoolgirl population, and we're fed up with it. You know perfectly well you wouldn't speak to Tory like this if Jake was here.'

'*Were* here,' screamed Fen, '*were* here. "If" takes the subjunctive,' and she stormed out of the room again.

'Oh, dear,' said Tory, in distress, gazing at the last orange rays of sunset. 'Oh, dear, oh, dear.'

Fen was in such a rage that she went off to London without saying goodbye to anyone. She wore a black, backless taffeta dress she'd bought in Paris the previous summer and never worn, with high-heeled black shoes, black stockings and Dino's necklace at her throat. As she walked into the pre-dinner drinks party, which was choc-a-bloc with every sporting celebrity, commentator and journalist you could imagine, a few heads turned in her direction. She drifted over to Dudley Diplock, propped up against the fireplace, who was already three-parts cut, and gave the room the benefit of her back view. The dress was so low it almost gave her a cleavage at the back. When she turned around five minutes later, everyone was gaping at her. It was one of those evenings when her looks really worked, perhaps because she was giving off such wanton promise, or because she longed to forget Dino and everything at home.

'What does F stand for?' asked a famous tennis player.

'Fuckable,' said Fen sweetly, 'and it's spelt out in emeralds and pearls.'

'You can say that again,' said the tennis player as everyone laughed.

Soon the journalists were hovering round her. They kept asking her about Billy and Dino, but she cracked back that she was married to her career and had no intention of getting a divorce. She had a good deal to drink and had some difficulty negotiating even the short walk into the dining room. She found herself sitting between a famous footballer with permed blond hair and a fake suntan, named Garry, and an Olympic shotputter whose arm muscles bulged through his dinner jacket, whose stomach folded over the table, and who lifted Fen above his head to loud cheers when she complained she couldn't see the Princess.

The first course, because most people were in some sort of training, was Parma ham and melon, which Garry the footballer thought too outré for words.

'You got a boyfriend?' he asked Fen.

'Nope.'

'Fort as much. Riding an 'orse is a substitute for sex.'

'What an original thing to say,' said Fen politely, moulding her uneaten roll into pellets and chucking them at Dudley.

'Stands to reason. Funny thing, most of them look like 'orses, but you don't.'

'You're talking garbage,' said the shotputter.

'Why don't you come home with me?' said Garry the footballer. 'Wife's staying with her mother. I'd give you more fun than an 'orse.'

'You reckon?' said Fen.

Suddenly all the flashbulbs exploded as the photographers clustered round a late arrival, a tall, dark, very broad-shouldered man wearing a dirty bomber jacket, a dark blue shirt, no tie, jeans and sneakers. He was extremely good looking in a brutal, suntanned, heavy-eyelidded way, and appeared not remotely embarrassed to be the only man in the room not wearing a dinner jacket. The plane from Rome was late; he hadn't had time to change.

At the sight of him the convoy of waitresses, rushing in like some musical comedy act, nearly dropped the massive oblong silver plates of beef they were bearing aloft. One comely brunette was so excited she gave the shotputter five slices of beef as she gazed entranced. Others dived for the kitchen and within seconds, six plates of Parma ham and melon were pressed on the new arrival from all sides, followed by several very large glasses of Bacardi and soda, which he lined up in a row in front of him, laughing all the while, showing beautiful big white teeth with several gold fillings. In the mat of black chest hair hung a gold St Christopher.

'Who's that?' said the shotputter.

'Enrico Mancini,' said Fen. 'The fastest driver on earth.'

'Certainly be'aves like it,' said Garry disapprovingly. 'I don't like racing drivers. Fink they're God's gift. Not much skill in driving around and around the same track.'

He's coarser looking than Rupert, thought Fen, watching Enrico Mancini joking with a couple of television commentators, but he behaves with the same certainty that he owns the earth. He was forking up Parma ham very fast now, his eyes raking the room for crumpet or cronies.

'Lovely beef,' said Fen. 'I don't know how they cook it on such a large scale.'

She took a big slug of red wine and, looking across at Enrico Mancini, found he was staring at her. Christ, he was taking the skin off her face. She looked hurriedly away, then glanced back five seconds later. He was still staring, gazing with peculiar intensity through a pot of yellow chrysanthemums. Her beef had lost all its appeal. She took another slug of wine. Putting her elbow on the table, it slid off as though it was greased. When she looked back again he'd moved the flowers and was smiling at her, lounging lazily in his chair. Then he blew her a kiss. Fen blushed, then found herself smiling.

'Eat up your beef, Fenella,' said the footballer. 'You'll never get to Los Angeles that way.'

'No, thanks, I'm full,' said Fen, putting her knife and fork together.

'Shame to waste it,' said the weightlifter, forking up the slices of beef. Dudley Diplock swayed over to have a chat, launching into a long story about Colonel Roxborough.

'How wonderful,' said Fen after five minutes, when it was obvious some response was expected.

'I said he'd had a stroke,' said Dudley.

'Oh, dear, I'm sorry. I misheard you. Who did you say?'

'Colonel Roxborough. But he's expected to pull through.'

Fen could see Enrico Mancini writing a note on the back of a place card.

'I reckon you've got a good chance of getting the woman's award tonight,' said Dudley.

'How dreadful for the family,' said Fen, who thought they were still on Colonel Roxborough's stroke.

'The award, Fen! If you do, we'll have a chat straight to camera immediately afterwards. Good luck.'

'Thanks, Dudley,' said Fen. Her glass seemed to be full again and someone had brought her a large brandy and the pretty brunette waitress, with some disappointment, Fen thought, was handing her a card.

On the back of Enrico Mancini's place card was written, 'Will you come out with me afterwards?'

Fen looked up. Enrico was still staring at her with that knowing, speculative, supremely confident smile. He raised his eyebrows. Fen shook her head, mouthing: 'I can't'.

'Black or white,' said the waitress.

'White. No, sorry, I mean black.'

'Must go to the toilet,' said the footballer.

Fen had broken off some frosted grapes and was putting them in her bag, wrapped in a paper napkin, for Darklis and Isa, when she felt a warm hand travelling the length of her back, lasciviously fingering her spine.

'There is no such word as "can't", said a husky Latin voice. Spinning around, she saw Enrico had taken the footballer's seat.

He had eyes the colour of black treacle and an incredibly sensual mouth shaped rather like a car-tyre. I wonder if he changes it after three laps when it gets worn out with kissing, thought Fen with a giggle.

'Why d'you laugh?' he said softly, 'I don't find you funny.'

'I don't find you funny either,' stammered Fen. 'I'm just nervous.'

'With good cause,' said Enrico. 'You won't escape. I have wanted you for a very long time.'

'About an hour,' said Fen, looking at her watch.

'No, no, I see you on television in May in Rome with Desdemona, when you beat my friend Piero Fratinelli. His father makes my car. Then later you fall off Macaulay and got on again with the concussion. I said I must meet this girl. She is not only beautiful but brave. I am more attracted by courage than beauty in a woman. You and I will be magnificent in bed.'

'You saw me in Rome?' said Fen amazed.

'Of course. That ees the only reason I come here tonight. They told me you'd be here. Shall we go?'

'We can't,' said Fen.

His eyebrows were so black and his hair so thick and his face so strong and commanding. Oh, heavens, thought Fen in panic, how can I not go to bed with him?

'Why not?'

'Well, it's a bit rude, before the speeches and the awards.'

'I will give you my own personal award,' said Enrico, staring at her breasts. 'Much better than some stupid prize.'

'Besides I've got to go straight back to Warwickshire at eleven o'clock. I'm leaving for Amsterdam at four-thirty.'

Enrico looked at his massive digital watch, pressing knobs. 'How many miles?'

'More than a hundred and twenty.'

'At night, that takes me one hour and ten minutes, no

more. We leave London at three. That gives us four hours if we leave now. Not long, but quite long enough for the first time, which should be brief, passionate, exquisite and leave one hungry for the next.'

Fortunately there was a roll of drums and it was announced the awards would begin in two minutes. Fen staggered off to the loo. She looked pretty abandoned; her hair was all over the place. Overwhelmed by frantic excitement, she tipped half a bottle of Diorissimo over her body and wandered back to the table, to find Garry having a frightful row with Enrico for stealing his seat. Fen collapsed into hers as the lights dimmed. Garry, who was even more drunk than Fen, was removed, complaining bitterly, to a chorus of shushes. Enrico poured Fen another glass of wine.

'What does hedonistic mean?' she asked the shotputter.

'Haven't a clue.'

'Nor have I, but I think I'm about to be it.'

She hardly heard a word of the speeches as, in the dim twilight of their corner, she felt Enrico's hand running all over her back, firm, warm, powerful hands with splayed flat fingers and pudgy balls to the thumbs. Now they were inching round underneath the front of her dress.

'You mustn't.'

'I must,' he said, leaning across her to stub out his cigar.

'Ouch,' squealed Fen as he bit her shoulder.

Now his free hand was moving downwards, slipping into the cleavage of her buttocks. She leapt away as the lights blazed on. The Princess, to thunderous applause, was presenting the award for the male personality of the year to yet another famous footballer, who was saying he was 'absolutely over the moon, definitely' and holding up his prize like a football cup.

When the Princess started reading out the female nominations Enrico started kissing Fen. Enjoying the frantic swordplay of tongue and saliva, she could feel the stubble of his cheeks. He had a zoo-like, unwashed smell. He was just like a stallion. Unheeding, she kissed him back.

His hand was between her legs now. If the lights hadn't blazed on again she had a feeling he would have taken her there and then in that dark corner.

The huge cheers seemed to be getting louder. Someone was tapping her on the shoulder.

'You've been nominated,' whispered the shotputter.

'Fuck off,' growled Enrico.

Fen wriggled away from him just as the spotlight found her.

'Come here,' said Enrico.

Next moment there was a burst of cheering and Dudley Diplock was crying, 'Well done, Fen. Go on. You've won.'

Everyone seemed to be helping her through the tables as she frantically straightened and pulled down her dress and wiped away the mascara, smudged under her eyes.

'Oh, she's crying, bless her,' said a fat woman, 'She's only eighteen and so unspoilt.'

Fen fell up the stairs and was picked up by Dudley.

'Hullo again. Congratulations,' said the Princess, laughing.

Fen clutched the trophy, which was a model of a silver pen writing on a silver page. Finally the deafening cheers were silenced. Fen took the microphone, grinning fatuously.

'Honestly, I had no idea. I can't tell you how knocked out I am. Thank you, sports writers, for this stunning award. It was all due to the horses. I've just got good ones and my brilliant brother-in-law, Lake Jovell,' no, that wasn't right, 'I mean Luke Jovell,' she opened her hands despairingly, 'I'm sorry, I'm a bit over the top. It's excitement and all your wonderful hospitality.'

Everyone laughed and cheered.

Dudley collared her for an interview, but all she could think about was being in bed with Enrico. She could see him at the table, fingers drumming impatiently. He was not a man who would be kept waiting very long.

As she left she tapped one of the BBC minions on the shoulder.

'Could you tell the car that's supposed to be taking me

back to Warwickshire that I won't be needing it.'

'Right ho, dearie.'

'Should I ring home? They're expecting me back by one o'clock.'

'No,' said Enrico.

His flat was all white, with shagpile carpet as thick as a hayfield, huge white sofas and walls lined with mirrors. Everywhere there were photographs of Enrico, winning races or being photographed with Presidents and Kings.

'This is small place,' he said, adjusting the dimmer switches. 'In Rome I haf really nice apartment.'

In the drawing-room he took off her dress, then her tights and her pants. Then he turned the spotlights on her, so that she was reflected a hundred times in the mirrored walls, as though taking part in some vast orgy. She wished her face wasn't so pink and weathered rather like a toffee apple compared with her slender, white body. At first she covered her breasts and her bush with her hands, but she was too drunk really to mind.

'I'm awfully rusty,' she mumbled. 'Can we have a long warm-up first?'

Enrico shook up a bottle of Moet Chandon, then opened it, spraying it all over Fen's body and into every crevice. Then he picked her up and carried her into the bedroom where, on a huge oval bed, he proceeded very slowly and thoroughly to lick every drop off until Fen was a squirming, ecstatic bundle of desire. God, she thought, he had a cock like a salami. A lot of junk is talked about the size of the male member having no importance in sex. And when a man is as magnificently endowed as Enrico, as skilful in manipulation, and of such unquestionable sex appeal, and the girl in question is as well lubricated as one of Enrico's engines, the result is bound to be ecstatic. For Fen it was the most glorious hour of her life. 'Talk about a one night stunned,' she muttered afterwards.

Hazily she looked at the clock beside the bed, red eyes flickering like hers. 'My God, it's a quarter to three. We must go,' she said, leaping to her feet.

Enrico put out a hand. 'Stay with me. Give Amsterdam a miss.'

'I can't. The lorry's loaded. The tickets booked. I must go.'

Enrico leaned over, kissing her and running his hand down her body.

'You are like little schoolboy, no? Next time I bugger you.'

'Not sure,' muttered Fen, wriggling away. 'I *must* be home by four.'

The motorways were deserted. She was almost more turned on by his handling of his Ferrari and the subdued dragon roar of its engine. He didn't seem to be driving fast at all and it was only as he overtook other night flyers that she looked at the speedometer and realized they were travelling at more than 120 mph. They hardly spoke. One big hand rested between her thighs.

How long would she be in Amsterdam, he asked, and where was she staying? He would be in New York when she got back, but he would be back in London for the last day of the Olympia show, when he would come and watch her. She was to leave some tickets at the box office.

He had her home by five past four; it would have been four o'clock if he hadn't spent five minutes parked on the bridge, with the engine growling, leisurely kissing her goodnight, his tongue tickling her epiglottis.

' 'appy treep, my darling,' he said as he dropped her off at the front gate. Thank God Jake's still away, thought Fen. As she walked up the path, high heels crunching on the frozen grass, the owls were hooting and the dog star was just sinking into his kennel behind Pott's meadow.

All was activity in the yard. She could see Sarah and Louise putting on bandages and tail guards, changing rugs. In the lorry Tory was making a last-minute check.

She crept unnoticed into the kitchen and went slap into Dino, still wearing the same check shirt, jeans and sweater he'd had on when she left. He plainly hadn't been to bed and was absolutely white with anger.

'Where the hell have you been?'

'I haven't been to hell at all; rather the reverse.' She realized she was still tight. 'I've just been finding out what hedonism is and I do agree it's much better than celibacy.'

For a second, she thought he was going to hit her.

'Why the fuck didn't you call? All the kids, Tory and the grooms saw you winning the award. They were so excited they had a bottle of champagne ready to welcome you when you got back. Not that you looked as though you needed it from the way you fell up the stairs. Then you just disappear. Don't even bother to cancel the car.'

'I did. I told a BBC man.'

'Probably pissed, like you. Anyway he never passed on the message. No one got any sleep or knew whether to load up the horses. We were all worried stiff.'

Enrico, thought Fen dreamily, was stiff but not worried. The grandfather clock in the hall struck the quarter hour.

'We're leaving in fifteen minutes,' said Dino.

'I'll be ready. Don't worry.'

At that moment Tory came in. 'Oh Fen, where have you been?'

'I got diverted,' said Fen, weaving joyfully towards the door, 'highly diverted. I'm sorry to have caused so much trouble.'

Never had her bed looked so inviting. She'd only had time for a lightning shower and a change when she heard the lorry revving up. Bloody hell! Dino was just doing that to wind her up. Sweeping everything on top of her dressing table and the contents of her washbasin into a holdall and throwing Lester on top, she fled downstairs.

47

It was not an 'appy treep. Fen's hangover descended like a million thunderbolts just as they reached Southampton. The crossing was frightful and she spent the entire time commuting between the hold, where she comforted a terrified Hardy until the petrol fumes overcame her, and the ladies' loo. Her face, as a result of Enrico's stubble, was blotched like salami.

Dino, Louise and Sarah, blisteringly unsympathetic, went off to a huge lunch and didn't even buy her a brandy to steady her stomach. As the lorry, which seemed so pedestrian after Enrico's Ferrari, steadily ate up the miles, she was overcome by the depression that goes with extreme tiredness. It had all been a dream. She should never have let Enrico take her to bed on the first night. She would never see him again. It was eleven o'clock when they reached Amsterdam; midnight before the horses were stabled and fed and they reached the hotel. Louise was sleeping in the lorry, Sarah, Fen and Dino in the hotel. Dino pointedly carried Sarah's suitcase but not Fen's. The manager came out to welcome them in perfect English. 'Miss Maxwell, Mr Ferranti, you must be very tired. Would you like something to eat? We can make some sandwiches.'

'I'd sure appreciate a drink,' said Dino, stretching after the long drive. 'We'll be down in a minute.'

The porter took them upstairs. He reached Fen's room first and threw open the door. Fen was knocked sideways by the most heavenly scent. She could hardly get inside for the flowers – roses, gardenias, stephanotis, banks and banks of freesias and hyacinths. It was like suddenly coming out of a freezing cold night into a heated conservatory.

'How gorgeous,' she gasped.

'My God,' said Sarah. 'Someone must have denuded every flower shop in the low countries. Not Interflora, but Entireflora, ha ha. Who on earth are they from?'

Fen took a card out of the tiny envelope lying on the bed.

'Adorable Fen, you were magnificent, I die till Monday week, all my love E.'

'I say,' said Sarah, snatching the card.

'Don't,' screamed Fen, trying to snatch it back and keep the silly grin off her face.

'Who the hell's E?' asked Sarah. 'Prince Edward, Edgar Lustgarten, Ethelred the Unready, Edward Fox, 'Enry Higgins, Eamonn Andrews? Go on, who is he? Who is E?'

'I'm not going to tell you,' said Fen. 'My trap is shut.'

Dino appeared at the door, 'If we're going to catch the restaurant before it closes . . . Christ.'

'Fen has a new boyfriend,' giggled Sarah. 'His name begins with E.'

'Stands for excessive, extravagant and extremely silly,' snapped Dino.

'No, it doesn't,' said Fen, putting a freesia behind her ear and waltzing round the room. 'It stands for 'edonism.'

Throughout the show, Fen jumped atrociously. Her mind was simply not on the horses. She couldn't eat, she couldn't sleep at night, as she inhaled the heavy scent of the flowers, which brought back the powerful disturbing image of Enrico. No man had any right to be that attractive. He had discovered erogenous zones she didn't know existed. She kept looking at her watch, surprised that only a minute had passed.

On Saturday night he telephoned her from New York. The manager brought the telephone to the table where she and Dino and Louise were having a very scratchy dinner, attempting to celebrate Dino's win in a big class that evening. The line was awful.

'I cannot wait to have you in my arms, Cara,' said Enrico

and, proceeding to tell her all the unmentionable things he was going to do to her when they met again, Fen was surprised the telephone didn't turn blue. Fen in turn went redder and redder, acutely aware of Dino listening in stony silence.

Fen got an earful from Jake when she got home. Even though they arrived back after midnight, he had her up at crack of dawn the next morning, insisting she jump a new and extremely difficult novice round the indoor school, with her arms folded, stirrups crossed and reins knotted. She fell off four times and ended up on the floor screaming at Jake.

'You're not going to make a bloody fool of yourself at Olympia,' he said.

'I suppose Tory and Dino have been sneaking.'

'They didn't need to. One of the Olympic scouts was in Amsterdam. He said if Jesus Christ had ridden that donkey into Jerusalem the way you were riding Laurel and Hardy all week, he deserved to be crucified.'

The end of term jollities of the Olympia Christmas show were lost on Fen this year. Parties were held every night in lorries and on trade stands. Dino went to all of them, each with a different girl and deliberately got drunk. Fen went to none, because she wanted to look beautiful for Enrico, which was difficult, with the long hours and the airlessness of Olympia and because sleep, when she finally got to bed, again evaded her because of the din outside.

Gossip circulated as usual. Rupert Campbell-Black had acquired a new wonder horse from America called Rock Star, which was reputed to have cost him 200,000 dollars. His marriage, on the other hand, was in trouble. Helen had managed to do her Christmas shopping without visiting Olympia once. The Lloyd-Foxes, by contrast, were blissfully happy. Janey had embarked on a book on postnatal depression called *The Blues of the Birth*. Jake's leg was mending, but no one thought he would make Los Angeles. Fen was showing a dramatic loss of form, and so was Dino Ferranti. Wishbone, despite being in the Whisky 'Tint' every day, had been placed in every class.

The days crawled by. Not eating properly, Fen was appalled to see that she was getting spots again. Not knowing where she was staying, Enrico sent flowers to her care of the BSJA tent and lots of giggling ex-debs carried them down to Fen's lorry, which now, according to Dino, looked like a hearse.

At long last it was the final day of the show and Enrico was due that evening.

'What d'you think?' said Fen, teetering on one of the bunks in the lorry so she could see her bottom half in the mirror opposite. She was trying on a new pair of white sharkskin breeches, specially made for her.

'Brilliant,' said Sarah, who was cleaning Hardy's bridle, 'I've never seen anything so sexy. They make your legs go on for ever, but you *must* wear pants underneath.'

'No. It'll ruin the line.'

'It'll ruin your reputation if they split.'

Fen bent down, straining the breeches to the limit, and extracted a riding coat from the tissue paper in the cardboard box.

'Now what d'you think of these together?' she said triumphantly, when she'd shrugged her way into it. The coat was dark purple instead of the regulation black or midnight blue, lined with rose-pink silk, tightly fitting and only just skirting the top of her hip bones. It made the perfect foil for the white breeches.

Sarah whistled. 'You'll never get away with that. It's a bum freezer. Colonel Roxborough will have another stroke.'

'You wait,' said Fen, 'I bet it starts a trend. Everyone'll be wearing them in a few months.'

'Not if you've got a bum Griselda's size,' said Sarah.

'But it does look sexy!'

'Incredibly. But you look more like a page in *Figaro* than a show jumper, and I don't think the BSJA will like it.'

As long as Enrico does, that's all that matters, thought Fen. 'I still think you ought to wear pants,' said Sarah,

'What else did you get?'

Faintly embarrassed by such extravagance, Fen produced a pale blue flying suit with zips everywhere and a pair of matching pale blue leather boots.

'Gorgeous,' sighed Sarah enviously. 'You must have blued your entire year's winnings. Goodness, I must go and get Hardy ready.'

'Where's Dino?' said Fen idly, suddenly wanting confirmation that her new riding clothes weren't over the top.

'Playing poker with Ludwig, Rupert and Billy. I don't think he went to bed at all last night.'

Fen needn't have worried. Her new clothes caused an instant sensation, setting every photographer snapping and all the riders wolf-whistling; except Dino and Grisel, who both looked extremely disapproving.

'Playing Buttons in the Christmas pantomime?' was Dino's only comment.

Just as she was walking the course for the last class of the show, in despair that he wasn't going to turn up, Enrico arrived and caused an even bigger sensation. Wearing a red shirt, a black coat with a huge astrakhan collar and half an inch of stubble on his chin, he was accompanied by a girl and a man. The girl, deeply tanned with her streaked blonde hair scraped back into a bun, was wearing huge gold hoop earrings and the sort of long squashy fur coat destined to put her straight on to the hit list of the Animal Rights Movement. The man, also blond, was wearing dark glasses, a pale blue flying suit identical to Fen's and carrying a pale blue handbag.

Hell, thought Fen, that means I can't wear my flying suit tonight – we'd look like hers and hers. Enrico, who had found the tickets Fen had left for him at the box office, was making a lot of noise settling in. All the fresh-faced pony club girls, the horsey ladies and the fathers in their Barbours with three whiskys under their belts, were looking at him in amazement.

'Look, there's Enrico Mancini,' said Rupert. 'Who's that bird with him?'

677

'Anna-Fabiola Caraccio,' said Dino. 'She's a friend of Mary-Jo's; and with them is that fag designer, Ralphie Walcott.'

E for Enrico, thought Dino. That was it. That explained the booming exhaust on the bridge. He watched Fen go crimson, giving Enrico a fleeting wave and mouthing that she'd be over to see him as soon as she'd jumped the first round.

Damn, damn, damn, damn, thought Dino, his heart twisting with misery.

For once, Fen was glad she was drawn first. Even though she'd hardly taken in the course when she walked it, she managed to transmit her elation to a rather jaded Hardy, who went around without touching a fence, to the noisy delight of the crowd. Hardly bothering to pat him, Fen threw her reins to the waiting Sarah and ran off. Dino, watching from the riders' stand, saw Fen mounting the steps, her spiky blonde hair gleaming, turning every head with those shiny tight white breeches. He saw Enrico get up and kiss both her hands and her lips and then, because the people behind were complaining they couldn't see Driffield jumping, watched him sit down and pull Fen onto his knee.

'I though you weren't coming,' said Fen.

'Carissima,' purred Enrico, sounding rather like one of his own engines, 'the traffic was terrible; all those stupid peoples looking at the lights. Then we have to queue at the entrance. Ralphie 'ere 'ad his 'andbag searched. 'Ave we missed a lot? That was a beautiful round; you look so sexy in those trousers.' He ran his hand up her inner thighs till it came to rest on her crotch.

Noticing disapproving glances from all around, particularly from the Royal Box, Fen wriggled away.

'We're going to a party,' said Enrico. 'Don't change. Just come like that. Can you leave now?'

'Not really,' said Fen, feeling flustered, 'I've got another round to jump and I might be in the jump off.'

'Give it the miss,' said Enrico, putting his hand back onto her groin.

'I can't, really,' said Fen, thinking of the money she'd spent that morning. 'Too much at stake.'

'Don't be seely, Enrico,' said the beautiful girl. 'Haff some self-control. You wouldn't stop in the middle of a Grand Prix.'

'Those trousers – they turn me on so much,' complained Enrico.

Wishbone had just come in, but no one sitting near Fen and Enrico was watching him at all. Crimson with embarrassment, Fen escaped back to the riders' stand.

'Vroom, vroom,' teased Rupert. 'You are flying high. Enrico's got an even worse reputation than I have. Watch out he doesn't give you the big E.'

Dino, having kicked Manny with unaccustomed viciousness as they went into the ring, jumped appallingly and knocked up such a cricket score that he didn't even qualify for the second round. Only sixteen riders went through. Fen, going first, went clear again. Instantly she went off to placate Enrico. She was appalled to find him creating yet another disturbance, infuriating everyone by coming out in the middle of Billy's round.

'You have finished, no,' he demanded.

'No, I'm terribly sorry, not yet. I should be through in about three-quarters of an hour, but I've got to jump off and then change.'

'Don't change a theeng. I want you like that,' said Enrico, stopping to give her a lingering kiss.

'For Christ's sake, get a move on, Rico,' snapped Ralphie, who was still trapped in the row and being told from all sides to sit down.

'You go on to the party,' said Fen. 'I'll meet you there.'

'Ees better,' said Enrico. 'Give her the address, Ralphie.'

'Are you sure it's not smart and I can wear this?' asked Fen.

'Si,' said Enrico, his hand on her crotch again. 'Come and come and come as you are.'

In a turmoil, Fen went back to the collecting ring. The

second round over, the arena party rushed on with brushes to smooth the tan. The band played carols.

'Oh, come all ye unfaithful,' sang Rupert.

'Where's Dino?' said Fen. Looking at the jump-off course, she suddenly felt nervous and uncertain, needing his advice.

'Disappeared somewhere,' said Sarah. 'He seemed terribly choked about his round.'

Fen cantered Hardy around the collecting ring, trying to get him on his toes. It was like sitting on a log. For once he wasn't even fighting for his head. As her number was called, she saw Dino go into the riders' stand. He was wearing a suit, his hair wet from the shower. He must be angry if he didn't even come and wish her good luck. There was £10,000 at stake.

Going first, her only answer was to put in such a fast clear she'd frighten the others into making mistakes. There was no doubt Hardy was exhausted. For once she had really to push him on for all her worth. She cleared the first four fences without too much difficulty, then pulled him too sharply into the triple. Unable to make it, and to avoid crashing into the wing, he ran out. Yanking him back, she rode straight at the jump from three yards away and just cleared it. Only the combination was left, but Hardy was all to pieces now. He took off too early at the first element and Fen had to hurl herself forward in a supreme effort to keep her weight off him and not jab him in the mouth. Alas, the effort was too much for her new breeches. As she flew through the air she was aware of a dreadful ripping sound and the sharkskin split right down the back. There was nothing she could do; she was going too fast. She had to jump the remaining two elements, splitting the breeches further each time until her entire backside was exposed with no long coat to cover it.

As she whipped through the finishing line, the entire riders' stand stood up, cheering. The crowd were in an uproar, half drunken guffaws, half wails of embarrassment and sympathy. The photographers had no such scruples and rushed forward, an excited, snapping, leaping pack.

Frantically tugging Hardy to a standstill in front of a bank of pink chrysanthemums, Fen put her hands down to assess the damage and, encountering so much bare flesh, clapped her hands over her eyes, leaving Hardy to trot around the ring, reins flapping.

Next moment the course builder was rushing towards her with a coat. But Dino was too quick for him. Vaulting over the hedge of red poinsettias in front of the riders' stand, he sprinted across the tan, captured a somewhat bewildered Hardy and, tearing off his grey jacket, put it around Fen, leading her, sobbing, out of the ring.

Reporters converged on them from all sides.

'Great viewing,' said Rupert, who was about to jump and was laughing his head off. 'Now I know why that fence is called the combination. Nanny used to wear combs that split up the back like yours.'

'Fuck off,' snapped Dino.

Pulling Fen off Hardy, whom he left to Sarah, he hustled her through the crowd. Before she knew it she was back in the lorry.

'Bloody little fool,' he yelled, slamming the door behind them. 'Why the hell didn't you wear panties?'

Fen looked at him aghast, her eyes full of tears, not even able to speak. So he answered for her.

'Because you wanted to excite the hell out of your new boyfriend, right? Well, he's no bloody good for you, I can tell you here and now.'

'How d'you know?'

'Used to screw an old girlfriend of mine. Gave her crabs in fact, just proving that Latins are lousy lovers.'

'That's not funny,' sobbed Fen.

'I'm amazed he asked you out a second time,' he went on furiously. 'Fuck 'em and forget 'em, that's his motto. Bloody Mafia thug. Do you honestly think he's the way to get over Billy? Couldn't even wait for you to finish your class, could he?'

'He had to go to a party.'

'You bet he did, and by the time you got there he'd have picked up another bit of trash.'

'You're just jealous,' screamed Fen, 'because he's so attractive.'

Fighting to control his temper, Dino took a deep breath. 'All I'm saying,' he said in a calmer voice, 'is that the guy is bad, mad, stupid, cruel and insensitive. But if you insist on finding that out for yourself, don't come whining to me when he ditches you. Now, you'd better get changed. You must be fifth and you've got to collect your money.'

'I am not going back into that ring.'

'Don't be such a drip. Go back in and laugh it off, and that mob'll eat out of your hand. You've bared it, now you've got to grin. And then we're going home.'

'I'm bloody not,' said Fen. 'I'm going to join Enrico at that party. Then I've got a broadcast at the BBC first thing tomorrow morning. I'll make my own way home.'

There was a bang on the door. It was Louise.

'Fen, Sarah says they're waiting for you.'

'I'm not coming, and you can get out,' she added to Dino. 'I want to change.'

'You need to change,' said Dino brutally, 'back into a decent human being. You were a really sweet kid when I first met you. I wonder whatever happened to her.'

'Get out,' screamed Fen, 'out of my life.'

As soon as he'd gone she gave way to tears. Horrible man, how dare he say those awful things? She couldn't wait to reach Enrico to be soothed by his admiration and distracted from her misery and humiliation by his lovemaking. But what the hell could she wear? Her breeches were only fit for the bonfire, she couldn't turn up in the same flying suit as Ralphie. She only had a pair of black jeans and a white shirt, and she was far too drained to wear white. Rifling through Sarah's drawer, she unearthed a black T-shirt. It'd have to do. She'd settle for looking pale, interesting and understated. Enrico had liked her in black last time.

She knew she ought to have gone back into the arena. She

ought to ring Jake and to check that Hardy was all right, but all she could think of was getting to that party before Enrico whizzed on to another one. She didn't believe Dino. She was sure he was jealous, but he'd sown a whole seed packet of doubts.

The repeated hammerings on the door distracted her. Party eye make-up only seemed to emphasize the tiredness of her eyes. She now had three spots instead of two and make-up failed to disguise them. Obsessed that her breath might smell because she'd eaten so little recently, she cleaned her teeth until her gums bled, then cheered herself up by making a Dracula face in the mirror.

Outside the lorry, she went slap into a swarm of reporters, who peppered her with questions about Dino, Enrico and her breeches. Without Dino, it was almost impossible to throw them off and she was forced to run out of Olympia into the homegoing crowd, who all stared and pointed at her. With so many Christmas parties around, it was impossible to find a taxi. Not knowing London well, Fen started to walk in the direction of Eaton Square, which was the address Ralphie had given her. It was bitterly cold. Half an hour later, frozen stiff, her feet like blocks of ice in her high- heeled shoes, she reached Knightsbridge and found a cab.

She hardly had time to cover her red nose and her three spots, which had re-appeared, when the cab pulled up. Her heart sank when a spectacular but utterly stoned girl opened the door. Her bright pink hair matched her trousers. Her sequinned waistcoat only just covered her nipples.

'Hi,' she said vaguely.

'Is Enrico here?'

The girl gave a silly laugh. 'Somewhere he is. Come in.'

Having repaired her face as best she could, Fen went into a big, dimly-lit room. People with glazed expressions were having off-centre conversations. Everyone was very done up and glamorous. Fen recognized several well-known actresses. Two women were necking in a corner, a man in a ballet skirt and a tweed coat was asleep on the sofa. There was no sign of Enrico.

She found him in the next room, in a corner, with Fabiola on his knee, one hand inside her shirt, the other half way up her thigh. He was talking to two other girls. Heart hammering, Fen walked over.

'Hullo Enrico.'

'Fenella.' At least he tipped Anna-Fabiola off and came towards her. For a minute, she was wrapped in warm masculine reassurance as he held her to his chest. But she could also smell stale sweat and there was garlic and whisky on his breath when he kissed her.

He let her go and led her back to Anna-Fabiola, who smiled vacantly. The two girls who'd been vying for his attention looked at Fen as though she was something the cat couldn't even bother to bring in. She desperately needed a drink.

'What happened to your breeches?' said Enrico. 'I wanted to 'ave you like that.'

'They split in the jump off,' said Fen miserably. 'In front of 10,000 people. It was awful.'

But Enrico wasn't interested. He was talking to Ralphie, who'd just wandered over with his flying suit undone almost to his crotch, so as to display a pink, hairless chest. In the end Fen was forced to find her own drink. When she came back Enrico had undone all the buttons of Anna-Fabiola's shirt and was playing with her breasts.

'Isn't she lovely?' he said to Fen. 'Wouldn't you like to play with her, too?'

With a sob Fen turned away. Suddenly she wished she was going home in the lorry with Dino and Sarah, home to reality and sanity. She was exhausted, sober, desperately in need of comfort and bitterly aware that she was looking her worst and couldn't compete with any of the girls hanging around Enrico. She was amazed when he followed her, taking her upstairs and opening and shutting several doors, before he found an empty bedroom. There was no lock on the door.

'We can't' said Fen, aghast. 'Someone might come in.'

'Let's hope they will,' said Enrico. 'You are very sexy, Cara. You need to be shared.'

Next moment he was undressed, lying on his back, his chest matted with black hairs like an ape, his cock rising like some grotesque Italian pepper-grinder. The smell of unwashed body assailed her as she knelt over him. She suddenly remembered Dino's warning about crabs. When Enrico seized her head, forcing it down, she nearly threw up.

'Go on, little schoolboy, you make love to me this time.'

His hand was fingering her bum crack. Appalled, she wished she could ram her tail between her legs, like Wolf. It was all horrible, with none of the ecstasy of the last time. She longed to run away but she had nowhere to go. There were no trains to Warwickshire at this hour. Anyway, she had to do the broadcast. There was a bang on the door. Fen snatched the sheet round her. It was Ralphie and Anna-Fabiola.

'Come and join us,' said Enrico, holding out his arms.

Leaping out of bed, Fen snatched up her clothes and fled past them. She spent the night, shivering, on a tiny sofa in some maid's room, which actually had a lock on the door. All she could think about was getting back to the Mill House to tell Dino what a fool she'd been.

Somehow she got herself together and to the BBC by ten o'clock in the morning. It was a children's programme; she couldn't let them down. She was met by a very embarrassed producer who said that, as Doctor Seuss was in town, they'd had to completely re-jig the programme and, very sadly, wouldn't be needing her after all. Of course, she'd be paid all expenses and her fee and she must come another time; they'd be in touch. Fen knew perfectly well he was lying, that he'd seen the story and the photographs of her breeches splitting in all the morning papers and was terrified she might corrupt the young.

All the way home in the train, Fen died of shame as she huddled behind dark glasses, coat collar turned up, watching businessmen glued to and gloating over her photograph. The headlines were predictable: 'Bottoms Up' said *The Sun*, 'Cheeky Fen' said the *Mirror*.

Tory met her at Warwick station, looking very red-eyed. Fen thought it was because she'd been behaving so badly.

'I'm sorry I didn't ring,' she stammered. 'I meant to, but I was so choked about my breeches splitting. When did the others get back?'

'About three in the morning,' said Tory, starting up the Land Rover.

Wolf, in the back, crept forwards wagging his tail and putting his rough face against Fen's cheek. At least she had one friend. For a mile or so they didn't speak. It was a mean, grey day. The only colour came from the last red beech leaves and the blond grasses edging the road.

'Was Dino in an awful bate?' mumbled Fen.

There was a pause.

Then Tory said, 'He's gone.'

'Gone?' said Fen, 'Where?' Suddenly she felt as though she'd jumped out of a plane and her parachute wasn't opening.

'Back to America.'

'But he can't have,' whispered Fen.

'He left this afternoon, loaded up the horses and everything.'

'But whatever for?' said Fen, aghast.

'He didn't say,' said Tory, bursting into tears.

'Did he – did he leave any message for me?'

'Only to say he'd probably see you in Los Angeles.'

'Nothing else.'

'He gave me a washing-up machine,' sobbed Tory. 'It arrived half an hour after he'd gone.'

48

Back in November that same year, Helen Campbell-Black sat in James Benson's waiting room, flipping through the houses for sale in *Country Life*, and idly wondering how much Penscombe was worth. Glancing at her gold watch, she decided there wasn't really time before her appointment to rush to the john for yet another quick clean-up. It seemed ludicrous, after having two kids, that she was still desperately embarrassed by anything down there. She shifted slightly on the leather sofa. The irritation was really awful and not helped by her worrying about it all the time. Outside the waiting room, a group of starlings, ravenous after a week of hard frosts, were jostling each other around the bird table. A thrush darted forward, warily grabbing a crust that had fallen on the starched white grass and carrying it off to the safety of a nearby ash tree. Helen admired his speckled breast and bright eyes. How odd that the bird and the complaint between her legs should have the same name.

'What a beautiful woman,' thought the nurse, as she showed Helen into the consulting room. If there was one patient likely to make Dr Benson flout the Hippocratic oath, it was she. He always insisted on seeing Helen on the last appointment before lunch, so he could spend more time with her. And although he was supposed to be a friend of the husband's, he never referred to him in any other way than as 'that shit Campbell-Black.'

This morning's examination did nothing to revise Dr Benson's opinion, but as he ushered Helen back to her chair his face was as bland as ever.

'I'm afraid you haven't got thrush,' he said. 'It's the clap.'

'I beg your pardon?'

'The clap. Gonorrhoea.'

For a second he thought she was going to faint.

'What!' she gasped.

'Gonorrhoea,' he said gently.

'But I can't have, I mean, I haven't, I wouldn't sleep with anyone but . . .' her voice trailed off.

'I'm sure not, but, whatever you've heard to the contrary, it really isn't caught from lavatory seats.'

'So in fact . . .' she began.

'When did you last have intercourse with Rupert?'

She tried to pull herself together, trying to remember. 'About a fortnight ago.'

'That was probably it, although it could have lain dormant longer. Don't worry. It's easy to cure.'

Helen started to cry. Benson went to the cupboard and poured her a large gin and tonic, even adding ice and lemon. It was several minutes before she could bring herself to drink it, as though she was terrified of contaminating the glass. Dr Benson longed to take her in his arms and comfort her, but he could still hear his secretary typing outside and, with four children at public school, he could ill afford to jeopardize a brilliant career.

'I can't believe it,' Helen said in a choked voice. 'I feel so polluted, and where can Rupert . . .?'

'Have got it from?' Benson shrugged. 'Some passing scrubber on a trip abroad.' Then, seeing the anguish in her face. 'You know – far from home, missing you, needing to celebrate a victory. Won't have meant a thing to him. He'd better come and see me the moment he gets back. He'll have to be off sex for a bit, too.'

'I can't believe it,' Helen said again, gazing into space, shaking violently.

Benson was surprised. He only saw a reaction like this when he told parents their children had some fatal disease or had to break the news to a patient that they had cancer.

'You'll need a course of penicillin injections. Nothing to worry about.' He turned to his desk. 'And I'm going to give you tranquillizers and some sleeping pills to tide you over the next few days. Cheer up. It happens to the best people.'

'I feel so contaminated,' whispered Helen. 'How could Rupert do it?'

'Probably didn't know. Come on, we'll organize the jabs and then I'll buy you lunch.'

'No,' Helen leapt up, cringing away from him, 'I couldn't force myself on anyone, knowing this.'

Helen had to wait until late the following night to confront Rupert, although the entire household was aware something was up. The grooms, Mrs Bodkin, Charlene the Nanny, all knew that Mrs C-B had gone off to see handsome Dr Benson and had returned white-faced, had locked herself in her bedroom and had given way to hysterical sobbing.

'Didn't touch any lunch or dinner,' said Charlene, the Nanny. 'Didn't even come and say goodnight to the children.'

'Might be a hysterectomy, might be cancer of the womb,' said Mrs Bodkin, in excitement.

'Might be another baby,' said Dizzy, 'Which means she can't walk out on His Nibs for another nine months.'

'If it is, I'm off. I'm not looking after three children,' said Charlene. 'What d'you think it'd be like working in public relations?'

Rupert got back from Hamburg about nine o'clock. He realized something was up when Helen didn't come down and say hullo, although far off were the days she'd charged down the stairs to fling herself into his arms. He dumped his case in the kitchen.

'All dirty washing,' he said to Charlene, who had positioned herself at the kitchen table, it being the best place to hear any excitement, and was reading the *Daily Mail* and eating a yoghurt.

'Look what I bought for Tab,' said Rupert, proudly producing an exquisite German doll in national costume.

'According to the instructions on the box she does almost everything except say "Oooh" at the moment of orgasm.'

'Beautiful,' said Charlene. 'What did you get Marcus?'

'Sweets,' said Rupert blandly. 'I must have left them in the lorry. I suppose I better give them to him in the morning.'

'Bastard,' Charlene said to herself.

'Where's Helen?'

'In her room.'

'She all right?'

'Not in carnival mood.'

'Know what it's about?'

'She's been a bit jumpy all week. Went to see Dr Benson yesterday and came back in a frightful state.'

'Oh dear,' said Rupert pouring himself a large whisky, 'I'd better go and see her.' Then his eye was caught by a recipe on the cork board in Helen's writing entitled: How to make Prawns and Kiwi fruit in Pernod-flavoured Mayonnaise. Getting out his fountain pen, he wrote 'Oh, please don't'.

Charlene giggled, so Rupert proceeded to tell her how his new horse Rock Star had gone. 'He really is world class. If I can't get a gold with him I might as well retire.'

When he went upstairs an hour and several whiskies later, he found the bedroom door locked.

'Let me in.'

'Go away,' screamed Helen.

'I'll break the door down, or shoot it out if you'd prefer.'

After a long pause she unlocked it.

'Christ, you look as though a train's hit you.' He'd never seen her look so ill.

'I went to James Benson yesterday.'

'So I hear. Are we expecting quads?'

'Don't you dare be flip,' she hissed. 'I've got gonorrhea.'

'Really,' drawled Rupert, his dark blue eyes suddenly taking on that opaque look. 'You must be more careful who you leap into bed with in future.'

'Stop it, stop it,' screamed Helen. 'You know perfectly

well I haven't slept with anyone but you.'

'I don't know that at all,' said Rupert coldly. 'I see little enough of you, and your extreme reluctance to come on any of my trips abroad would rather suggest the contrary.'

'You bastard,' yelled Helen. 'You caught it from one of your disgusting whores.'

'Oh, come on. You've got absolutely no proof. I've certainly got the clap. I was treated for it in Hamburg – those German clinics are like Sainsbury's on a Saturday morning – but I caught it from you.'

'Don't put that number on me. I've never looked at another man since I married you.'

'What about Dino Ferranti?' said Rupert softly. 'He's been in England for six weeks. Rumour has it he spends most of his nights on away fixtures.'

'I haven't been near Dino or anyone else,' said Helen. 'You gave it me and you know it. I'm leaving you and I'm taking the children.'

'You can take Marcus,' yelled Rupert, 'but if you lay a finger on Tab, I'll fight you in every court in this country.'

This was the final straw. Maddened, Helen tried to lash out at him, but Rupert dodged back and only the ends of her long colourless nails caught his cheek. The next moment the door opened.

It was Marcus, red hair ruffled, eyes huge with terror, pyjama-top falling off.

'Thtop thouting, Daddy, please thtop thouting.'

Tabitha toddled in after him, wearing only the top half of her pyjamas, nappy discarded.

'Daddy, Daddy,' she squealed in delight, running to-wards him, 'Daddy home,' then seeing blood on his face, 'Daddy got a hurt.'

'Poor Daddy's indeed got a hurt,' said Rupert, pulling a couple of paper handkerchiefs out of the box on Helen's dressing table to stem the bleeding. Then, gathering Tab up in his arms, he walked out of the room.

'I'm beginning to think you and Badger are my only fans.' Helen, with a superhuman effort, pulled herself together. 'Daddy has cut himself shaving,' she explained to Marcus. Everyone loved everybody, she went on. She was absolutely fine. Anything to ward off an asthma attack. But thin mucus was trickling from his nose, a sure sign that one was on the way. He was having difficulty in breathing. Oh God, it was her fault for locking herself in her room and not coming to say goodnight. He must have heard her crying.

'Relax, Marcus, please.'

Soon she had laid him face down across her lap, tapping his frail ribs with cupped hands to force the mucus out of the bronchial tubes as the physiotherapist had taught her. He had swallowed so much phlegm, eventually he threw up all over her and the carpet. By the time she had got him to bed and calmed him down, read him a story and cleaned up the mess, it was long after midnight.

The light was on in Rupert's dressing room. On the bed she found Rupert fully dressed, stretched out fast asleep with the sleeping Tab in his arms. Photographs of Rock Star were scattered all over the bed and the floor. In their blond beauty and their carefree abandonment, they were so alike. When Helen tried to take Tab back to her own bed the child went rigid in her sleep and clung on, so Helen left them.

Back in her bedroom, she wearily took a couple of Mogadon pills and tried to think rationally about her marriage. She was trapped, trapped, trapped. She longed to leave Rupert, but where could she go? Certainly not home to her parents. The tensions of those two months in Florida last summer had put paid to that, and how could she ever afford Marcus's colossal medical bills in the States? And if she walked out, taking the children, they would have to give up so much: Penscombe, the valley, the swimming pool, the camp up in the woods, the tennis court, the horses, the skiing, the jet-set existence, the fleet of servants, not to mention the library and the pictures, which they would probably appreciate later. All this for life in a one-bedroom flat. Janey at least had a career and could support herself; Helen had nothing. Her novel, to be honest, was merely a series of jottings. She poured everything out in her journal, sometimes leaving it around in the hope that Rupert might read it, and realize how unhappy she was. But he only read Dick Francis and *Horse and Hound*. Maybe he was as unhappy as she was and only bullying Marcus to work off his frustrations.

Yet she was only twenty-seven. Was this emotional dead-end really all there was to life? Admittedly there were times of comparative contentment when Rupert was away, which was, after all, eleven months of the year, interspersed with periods of desperation like the present one, when he humiliated her publicly by chasing other women, and now giving her the clap.

She was only twenty-seven. She longed for love but, having been married to Rupert for six and a half years she felt she had become what he kept telling her she was: boring, prissy, brittle and frigid. He had so sapped her self-confidence that she didn't think she'd ever be able to hold another guy. She knew she attracted people like Malise, Dino and James Benson, but was sure they would all lose interest once they got her into bed.

Zonked by sleeping pills, Helen didn't come down until eleven o'clock the next day. She found Marcus guzzling German chocolates, sweet papers everywhere.

'Where did you get those from?' she said furiously.

'Daddy bought them for me.'

Helen went storming into the tackroom. 'You've given Marcus candy.'

'You're always reproaching me for not giving him presents. The one time I remember, I get it in the neck.'

'You know the kids aren't allowed candy except after lunch. How can I raise them when you spend your time undermining my authority?'

'What authority? Producing a whining, sickly little milksop.'

'That's because he's terrified of you.'

The marriage limped on for a few more weeks. Helen continued to paint the house different colours, spending a fortune on wallpaper and fabrics. 'One day I'm going to

693

wake up and find I've been completely reupholstered in Laura Ashley,' grumbled Rupert.

As Dr Benson had predicted, Helen and Rupert recovered from the clap. Rock Star continued to sweep the board and provide a powerful new interest for Rupert, achieving almost a walk-over at the Olympia Christmas Show.

The following Sunday, the last before Christmas, Janey and Billy lay in bed reading the papers.

'Christ,' said Janey. 'Have you seen this?'

'Hell,' said Billy. 'D'you think it's true?'

'I'm sure, and checked for libel, or they wouldn't risk it. Helen's going to do her nut.'

The Campbell-Blacks were having roast beef for Sunday lunch. Rupert was just carving second helpings when he was called away to the telephone. Helen cleared away the children's plates, helping them to apple pie and cream, and then settled down with the Sunday papers to wait until Rupert came off the telephone. She glanced at the one on the top of the pile. It was an awful rag, but you had to read it. Some starlet named Samantha Freebody was naming her loves on page 6, the little tramp. Helen read about the antics of several deviant vicars and lascivious witches, then turned to page 6 and froze, for there, confronting her, was a large picture of Rupert lying on a beach in bathing trunks, eyes narrowed against the sun, glass in his hand, palm trees in the background.

'One of my most thrilling affairs,' Samantha Freebody had written, 'was with international showjumping ace, Rupert Campbell-Black. I was filming in Portugal and he came out for five days as part of the British showjumping team. We met at a party. I was swept off my feet by his blond, blue-eyed good looks, and his air of tremendous self-confidence. He'd had a good win in the show ring that day and, having met me, was keen to keep on riding all night. At first I resisted his advances; I didn't want to appear cheap. But a tide of champagne and euphoria swept us down to the beach and at two o'clock in the morning we

694

made passionate love under the stars, until the warm waves washed over us. For the rest of the five days we were inseparable, loving each other all night. By day I would go and watch him in the ring. After five days we decided to end our idyll, he had other shows to go on to. I had to finish my movie. He was married, his wife expecting her second baby. It was only fair to give him back to her, but I really enjoyed the novelty of our naughty, racy lovemaking.'

'Can I get down?' said Marcus for the second time.

'May I?' said Helen automatically, getting up and lifting Tab out of her high chair. 'Go and watch television, darlings.'

Upstairs she locked herself in the loo and threw up and up and up. Rupert was waiting as she came out.

'What on earth's the matter? You sound like Jake Lovell before a big class.'

'Look at this,' croaked Helen, handing him the paper.

Rupert skimmed through it without a flicker of expression. 'Load of rubbish; don't believe a word of it.'

'The dates tally. You were in Portugal just before I had Tab.'

'Just ignore it,' said Rupert. 'That girl's publicity mad.'

'I don't understand you,' screamed Helen. 'You go berserk if anyone criticises the way you ride.'

'I ride for a living. That's what matters. I don't fuck for a living.'

'Could have fooled me. She obviously does.'

'I wonder how much she got,' said Rupert, picking up the paper again.

'Aren't you even going to sue?'

'What's the point?' Rupert shrugged, 'If you leave mud to dry, you can brush it off. What did you do with the roast beef? I want a second helping.'

'You can honestly eat having read that?' said Helen, appalled. 'And how am I supposed to cope? Mothers sniggering at the playgroup. Mrs Bodkin, Charlene and the grooms all talking their heads off.'

'I'm sure they'll enjoy it enormously.'

'How can I ever hold my head up in the village shop again?'

'Ask them to deliver,' said Rupert.

Matters were not improved a week later when a leading columnist in the *Sunday Times* took Samantha Freebody to the cleaners for naming names.

'How must Rupert Campbell-Black's unfortunate wife and children feel?'

The answer was much, much worse. Everyone who hadn't seen the original piece, rushed off to the library to read it. A couple of days later Janey rang up Rupert to wish him a Happy New Year.

'And for God's sake hide *Private Eye*,' she went on. 'You've been nominated White's Shit of the Year.'

'Thank God it's 1980 now,' said Rupert. 'Apart from buying Rocky, 1979 hasn't been the greatest of years.'

In the evening Rupert found Helen in the drawing-room writing letters. He wished she wouldn't always wear her hair up these days, like a confirmed spinster.

'Applying for a new husband?' he said.

Helen gritted her teeth and didn't answer.

Rupert crossed the room, and kissed the nape of her white neck. 'I'm sorry I gave you the clap and went to bed with Samantha Freebody. I am totally in the wrong. There is absolutely no excuse. But the more you reject me and take no part in what I do, the worse it becomes. Come on, get up.'

The sudden unexpected overture totally disarmed her.

'There, there,' he said, drawing her against him, 'it's all right. Shall we have another try? I'm going to cancel the next two shows and take you abroad. Charlie Masters has offered us his house outside Nairobi. We can lie in the sun and I'll give you the honeymoon you never had.'

'And I will heal me of my grievous wound,' quoted Helen sadly.

'Grievous womb?' demanded Rupert. 'You been to see Benson again?'

Helen shook her head, smiling faintly.

'That's better,' said Rupert. 'It seems an awfully long time since you smiled.'

'What about the children?'

'They're not coming,' said Rupert firmly, 'nor are the dogs; just you and me on our own. And I'll start off tonight by taking you out to dinner.'

The door bell rang. It was Janey. Billy had gone to some evening show in Warwickshire and she was at a loose end.

'Come and have a drink,' said Rupert. 'Helen and I are having a rapprochement.'

'About time,' said Janey.

She was full of gossip and in high good humour. Evidently Fenella Maxwell had gone into a complete decline since Dino Ferranti had walked out. Fen didn't seem very good at holding men, she added with satisfaction. Janey had lapsed in her resolution to give up drink while she was pregnant, but at least she had cut down and was only drinking wine.

Helen could hardly believe her ears half an hour later when she heard Rupert saying to Janey, 'Why don't you come out to dinner with us?' She went upstairs and sat on her bed in a rage for ten minutes. Then she steeled herself to be tolerant. After all Janey *was* on her own.

Downstairs, she found Tabitha had invaded the drawing-room, reducing the place to chaos. Every ornament had been moved, Janey's handbag had been upended and a flotsam of bus tickets, old telephone numbers, biros, defunct mascara wands and dirty combs lay scattered over the floor. Then she started screaming for sweets and for Daddy to read her a story. On being told Daddy was going out, the screaming re-doubled. Picking her up under one arm, Rupert took her upstairs for Charlene to sort out.

'That child is more destructive than a JCB,' said Janey, re-loading her bag. 'Don't ever worry that Rupert will leave you for another woman. No stepmother would take on that monster.'

Helen was appalled how pleased she was because Janey

697

was bitching about Tab.

Rupert hadn't bothered to book, but as usual the best table in the restaurant was rustled up straight away. Everyone was staring and nudging: 'Look who's just walked in. It is, isn't it? He's even better in the flesh.' Helen wished she had washed her hair.

'Where are you going for your second honeymoon?' asked Janey.

'Kenya,' said Helen.

'Some golfing friends of my parents have just gone there on safari. They're called Dick and Fanny, can you imagine!'

Janey could always make Rupert laugh, thought Helen, with a stab of envy.

'Have you heard the latest Samantha Freebody story?' Janey went on, squeezing lemon on her smoked salmon. 'What's the difference between Samantha Freebody and a Kit Kat?'

'What?' asked Rupert.

'You can only get *four* fingers in a Kit Kat.'

Rupert howled with laughter, and Helen, although blushing furiously, joined in.

'Billy bumped into her at the opening of some sports centre last night,' Janey went on. 'He was going to cut her dead when she accosted him and said: "You've got a hole in your jersey!" and Billy replied quick as a flash, "You've got a hole between your legs, but the difference between us is I don't write about my hole all over the papers." She's so publicity mad, the old slag heap, Billy says she'd turn up for the opening of an envelope.'

Somehow by bringing the whole awful business into the open, Janey was making things much better, thought Helen. Now she was attacking Rupert.

'You're a monster to Helen. You treat her appallingly.'

'I don't remember you treating Billy all that well in the past,' said Rupert coldly.

'That was only once. I just needed to prove that Billy was really the only man for me. I'm with him for keeps now.'

Janey was being real nice, thought Helen, so upfront and supportive. It was such a novelty to be talked about and defended and argued over that Helen drank more than usual.

While they were having coffee she went to the loo.

'All right?' they both said solicitously when she came back.

'Rupert's just suggested that Billy and I fly out to join you in Kenya for one of the weeks,' said Janey.

'But, but, I thought it was supposed to be a honeymoon,' stammered Helen.

Rupert didn't quite meet her eyes.

'All honeymoons should be spent in duplicate,' said Janey. 'Helen and I'll come if you and Billy promise not to talk about horses.'

49

Charlie Masters' house, a few miles outside Nairobi, was perfect. Open balconied, it had papyrus walls, leopard skins on the floor, a vast sunken bath, comfortable beds, and a fleet of smiling African boys who could not only cook but didn't turn a hair at any outlandish English antics.

The garden, lushly crowded with jacaranda, flame trees and a sweet-smelling tangle of herbaceous plants, also contained a tennis court and a swimming pool ringed with palm trees. All around lay the bush, and Helen had the feeling that the house was only here by the courtesy of nature and that any minute the jungle might take over. From the start, the holiday was a disaster. With Billy and Janey around, she and Rupert never had a moment to themselves. Billy and Rupert tended to play tennis or swim all morning, followed by a large lunch and lots of alcohol. Then sleep or sunbathing, followed by more tennis and swimming, followed by a large dinner, more drinking and a trip round the Nairobi night clubs. Billy was drinking again, not to excess, but on holiday he reckoned he was justified in coming off the wagon.

Helen, exhausted and emotionally bankrupt, wanted to sleep, be cherished and made love to in the gentlest way and to talk through her and Rupert's problems. She tried to persuade Rupert to dine alone with her, but the others seemed always to come along too. She was deeply embarrassed, too, by the way Rupert and Billy wandered round the garden with no clothes on, their cocks wiggling like those rubber devils that hang from driving mirrors. She was sure Janey only wore a bikini because she was pregnant.

Helen worried too about the children — well, mostly Marcus, and insisted on telephoning home every day from the local post office, which was extremely time-consuming and irritated the hell out of Rupert.

Finally, being Rupert, as soon as he and Billy hit Kenya, people discovered they were there and old friends started ringing up and inviting them to parties. Newspapers wanted to interview them, Kenyan television wanted to send down a crew. The alacrity with which Rupert welcomed every diversion made it obvious that he didn't want to get away from it all in the least.

After one long, boozy lunch, when Rupert and Billy had gone out on safari, Helen unbuttoned slightly to Janey.

'I simply don't know what to do. Our marriage is in smithereens. Rupert simply doesn't want to spend time with me. I feel everything I do gets on his nerves.'

Janey poured herself another glass of wine. 'Want one?'

Helen shook her head. 'Oh, all right, just a small one.'

They took their glasses out onto the terrace. A shower of rain had rinsed the earth, and a rainbow arched over the jacaranda trees.

'I think you're too subservient,' said Janey. 'I mean Billy was lovely but pretty casual before I took off with Kev.'

'Billy was always very caring,' said Helen.

'But he was always happy to booze with his chums rather than come home to me. Why don't you try making Rupert jealous? He was jolly broody over Dino Ferranti. Even talked to Billy about having your telephone tapped.'

Helen looked amazed. 'He had no cause. There was nothing between Dino and me except a few lunches.'

'Ha,' said Janey. 'Rupert is aware how fragile a thing possession is. He can't imagine anyone having lunch with anyone else's wife without evil intent. He thinks everyone is like himself.'

'But what can I do? We can't go on like this.'

'Don't shove off until you've found someone else. If you're going to be virtually a single parent, why not get paid for it? If you left Rupe you wouldn't be able to buy dresses like that, or do up the house every two years. It's very cold outside the marital cage.'

It was so oppressively hot that they returned to Janey and Billy's bedroom. Sitting on the bed, Helen appeared to let off a huge fart. Crimson, she jumped to her feet. 'That wasn't me.'

Janey laughed. 'You've sat on my vibrator.'

Helen took a slug of wine.

'If your sex life's so good,' she said, 'why d'you need a vibrator?'

'Oh they're lovely,' sighed Janey, 'and they do jazz things up. Billy's wonderful, but not absolutely infallible.'

Outside, the crickets were shrilling their permanent burglar alarm, the frogs croaked in lazy lechery.

Janey peered at her smooth brown face in the mirror. 'God, I look like a hag. Look at all these wrinkles.'

'You haven't got any,' said Helen, 'and now you've given up smoking, you won't get all those little lines around your mouth.'

'I'm bound to get them as punishment for all the men I've sucked off,' said Janey ruefully.

Helen turned away, shocked. What an appalling thing to say. She'd only sucked Rupert off once and been so revolted she'd never done it again. She realized in despair how many light years sexually she was behind Janey. She must try and catch up. Blushing even further, taking another huge gulp of wine and gazing at the eyeless African mask on the wall, she asked, 'Do you – do you really enjoy doing that to men?'

Janey shrugged. 'Well, it's an acquired taste. Whisky and dry martinis don't taste very nice the first time. It's all right if you swallow it fast. I said to Billy the other day, "It's a pity one can't have it with tonic, or better still with ice and lemon"! The trouble with sex is that all sorts of things are wildly exciting in fantasy, but no good when they happen. I get frightfully turned on by the thought of being buggered, even whipped. But when darling Billy tried it, I didn't like it at all.'

That evening they all went to a party which continued in

a state of rampage and carousal until 8 o'clock in the morning. Neither Rupert nor Billy felt like playing tennis the next morning, so they lazed round the pool.

Helen was wearing dark glasses, a large hat to prevent her freckles spreading, and a lime green bathing suit. She's so thin now, she's really better covered up, thought Janey critically.

Every day Janey'd start on another diet, and abandon it by lunchtime, when Rupert opened a bottle and the smell of Abdul's cooking drifted out from the kitchen. But her skin was turning as golden as a peach. She was four months pregnant, and Billy liked her plump, anyway.

Helen, having finished yesterday's *Guardian*, was reading *Crime and Punishment* with effort. Janey was reading *Vogue*. Rupert was flipping through *Horse and Hound* for mentions of his name. Billy was reading through a pornographic novel, skipping until he came to the sex bits. Jomo, the African boy, was steadily but unhurriedly sweeping up jacaranda petals and bird droppings. Morning glory spread in a sapphire haze over the tennis court wire, vying with the sky in blueness.

'Have you ever tried that?' said Billy, handing the book to Rupert.

'Once in Solihull during the Royal.'

'Let me see,' said Janey.

'No you can't,' said Billy, 'or you'd go back to bed for the rest of the morning. And you've only got another week to get brown.'

'Billy never finished *Histoire d'O*,' said Janey, peeling a piece of loose skin off her heel. 'He kept having to take me upstairs between pages.'

Rupert got up to pour himself a drink. He was broad-shouldered, bronzed and rippling fit as any of his horses, thought Janey. She lifted her thighs slightly off the lilo, so the flesh fell downwards and they looked thinner.

'Bikinis are awfully stupid things,' said Janey. 'You look as though you'd got one on when you take it off.'

'Take it off then,' said Billy idly, not looking up from his

703

book.

Janey encountered a searching look from Rupert.

'All right,' she said and removed her bikini. Her breasts had a soft, honeyed ripeness, her round belly swelled like a fig and her bush was shaved, leaving her as smooth as a pink snooker ball. Helen, rigid with shock and envy, couldn't take her eyes off her. Billy looked up and found Rupert staring at Janey with an erection like a steeple. Next moment Billy found he had an erection like a steeple too.

'Christ, it's like a cathedral city round here,' he said, rolling over and returning to his book.

Without turning his head, Rupert said to Helen, 'Take your bathing dress off, too.'

'I can't. I burn so easily.'

'Use plenty of oil,' said Janey, her breasts moving as she handed Helen the Ambre Solaire.

'I'm fine,' snapped Helen.

'Take it off,' repeated Rupert, with a distinct edge to his voice.

'No! What would Jomo think? It's all right for Janey; she's a guest. I'd never be able to look Abdul in the face again when I discussed desserts.'

She turned back to *Crime and Punishment* and read a whole page without taking in a word. Abdul seemed to take an enormously long time clearing up ashtrays and taking orders for drinks.

I can't do it, I can't, thought Helen in panic, I can't take my clothes off in front of them and besides, said an inner more truthful voice, my boobs aren't as good as Janey's.

Janey didn't bother to dress for a late lunch, which started with salad Niçoise. A large piece of tunny fish fell on her left breast. Rupert removed it with a spoon, Everyone, including Abdul, giggled immoderately, except Helen, who was a tight knot of embarrassment inside. Realizing this, Billy tried to persuade Janey to get dressed. But the atmosphere was getting more and more highly charged.

'I'm going to have a siesta,' said Janey, who'd been exchanging lingering glances with Rupert. Inside, seeing her flushed face and bloodshot eyes, she felt irritated at how awful she looked and wondered how she could have flirted so much with him.

The next minute Billy had come up behind her, catching her oiled breasts in his hands, kissing the back of her neck, slipping his hands between her legs, which seemed even more oiled.

'Christ, you're excited,' he said.

Instantly they were on the bed, not bothering to close the windows or the door.

Helen went into her bedroom next door. Despite the oppressive heat, she was trembling violently. She could hear Janey's cries and moans and hastily shut the window. Rupert came in, red-faced and hard-eyed.

'God, it's hot in here. Why the hell have you shut the window?' Opening it, he paused for a few seconds, listening to Janey and Billy, a half-smile on his face. Helen was desperate for him to make love to her gently and tenderly, not because she really wanted it, but because she'd seen the intense, predatory way he'd suddenly started looking at Janey. She'd die if he had an affair with her.

'Rupert, I do love you.'

'Why don't you show it, then?'

'It's so hard when you're always so angry with me.'

'Oh, for Christ's sake.' He walked out, slamming the door.

He returned when it was dark and Helen was changing for dinner, grabbing her irritably. Helen shrunk away. 'I've just taken a bath and the Mountleys are coming to dinner.'

'So the Campbell-Blacks aren't coming, hurrah, hurrah. Why the hell did you ask them?' Then answered for her. 'Because they've already asked us twice and you can drop literary names all evening.'

Professor Mountley was in his fifties, an American who taught English Literature at Nairobi University. His English wife, a little younger, was a show-jumping groupie.

'She knows even more about my bloody horses than I do,' said Rupert.

Rupert mixed white ladies and they all sat on the terrace,

gazing at the green pigeons and the enormous stars and listening to the rustle of night creatures; frogs bubbling like a cauldron, the hysterical chatter of baboons and the water pump sound of approaching lion.

'I'm beginning to understand why evacuee children were so frightened of cows in the war,' said Janey.

'Nice to be here,' said Professor Mountley, raising his glass to Helen.

'Nice to be still here,' said Janey. 'I'm sure some leopard is going to gobble me up.'

'Did you know warthogs lead exemplary married lives?' said Mrs Mountley.

'No wonder there aren't any in Gloucestershire,' said Rupert.

Rupert and Billy were drinking steadily, Janey only less so because it might be bad for the baby, and because she didn't want to get too flushed. After long lovemaking, a sleep, three Alka Seltzers and a bath, she was feeling wonderful. She was wearing a frangipani flower in her hair and a white, ruffled, slightly transparent shirt, through which could be glimpsed her rosily sunburnt breasts. Conscious of Billy's adoration, the Professor's admiration and Rupert's blatant lust, she was getting thoroughly over-excited.

Before dinner, Helen had gone in and offered her a choice of blue or lime-green caftans. Being pregnant, she said, Janey might find them more comfortable. ('Comfortable indeed,' Janey had snorted to Billy. 'Shapeless and ugly, you mean.') If she wasn't aware of Helen's lack of malice, she'd have thought she was doing it on purpose.

'Billy's been reading all about orgies today ' she said to Professor Mountley at dinner.

'Janey!' said Helen furiously.

'We call it group therapy in the States,' said the Professor, with a nervous laugh.

Soon they were all discussing orgies.

I can't bear it, thought Helen. I wanted a nice civilized evening discussing *Crime and Punishment* with the Professor and all anyone can talk about is sex. They were all

Philistines. Earlier in the week she'd lent Janey her precious copy of *A Hero of Our Time*, and Janey had dropped it in the bath. Rupert was talking to Janey in an undertone. Frantically she tried to lip read what they were saying.

Billy, sensing her distress, patted her arm. 'Everything's under control.'

The Mountleys left around midnight, when everyone was still sitting round the table. The Professor was very reluctant to go, but Mrs Mountley had recently become a grandmother and felt things were definitely getting out of hand.

Helen, having seen them off, stood on the balcony breathing in the heady smell of warm earth, frangipani, dust and burning charcoal. Beyond the garden she could see the gleaming eyes of waiting animals. But the animals inside the house frightened her much more. Determined to break the spell, she went back into the dining room.

'Don't know about you, but I'm absolutely exhausted.'

Rupert looked up, a long cigar clamped between his white teeth.

'Let's have another drink,' he said, getting up and filling everyone's glasses with brandy, 'and then let's go to bed,' he paused, 'together.'

Helen laughed nervously. 'Together?'

'Sure – why not?'

Janey got up, her eyes glittering. 'Do we use your bedroom or ours.'

'I'd prefer a home fixture,' said Rupert. 'And besides, our bed is bigger.'

He strolled over to Janey and began to kiss her. Frozen with horror, Helen watched him take her pink breast out of the white shirt and gently stroke it, then he undid the zip of her trousers. Helen shot a panic-stricken look at Billy, only to see him watching with fascinated pleasure.

Janey ran laughing into the bedroom. Giving a view halloo, Billy followed her. Rupert turned to Helen, holding out his hand.

'Come on, darling, or you'll miss the first act.'

Helen looked at him aghast. 'We can't! what about the servants?'

'I sent them home hours ago.' He grabbed her arm.

At the bedroom door she baulked. Billy, already undressed, was sitting on the bed drinking brandy, watching Janey and wearing Helen's sun hat. He was roaring with excited laughter and had a huge erection. Janey was standing in front of the mirror, tossing her hair back, spraying Helen's most expensive scent over her boobs and jiggling them so they caught the light. Helen turned to bolt, but Rupert's vice like grip on her arm tightened.

'No you don't. Don't be a fucking spoilsport. We might finally find out what turns you on.' Shoving her towards the bed, he turned the key and pocketed it. Turning to Billy, he added, 'It's harder than getting Snakepit into the lorry.'

Billy took off the sun hat and turned to Helen.

'Come on, lovie, it'll be fun. No one's going to eat you.'

'Everyone's going to eat her,' said Rupert and, pulling down Helen's pants and lifting her dress and her pink silk petticoat, he kissed her bush. As she wriggled frantically away, his hand clamped down on her bottom.

Across the room her eyes met Janey's, which were mocking and slightly contemptuous.

'Come and help me undress her,' Rupert said to Janey.

As he peeled off the black dress and the petticoat, Janey undid the pink bra.

'Lovely underwear,' she said. 'Did you get it at Janet Reger?'

Helen covered her pitifully small breasts with one hand, clasping the other over her bush.

'I can't, I can't,' she pleaded to Rupert in panic. 'I truly can't.'

'Don't be so bloody wet,' he hissed. 'Do you want to make me look a complete idiot. Here she is, all yours,' he added and, scooping her up, dropped her on the bed between Janey and Billy. The fastest trouser-dropper in the business, next minute he was on the bed beside Janey.

From then on it was a heaving anthill of legs and arms.

Helen lay beneath Rupert, her eyes glazed, her hair coming down, as responsive as a corpse, aware that Rupert was fondling Janey's breasts at the same time. Janey, determined to put on a virtuoso performance, climbed on top of Billy, bucking like a bronco, arching her back in pleasure, writhing and wriggling against Rupert's hands.

Then they changed over and, despite shutting her eyes, Helen knew Billy was inside her. He was much solider and heavier, yet gentler than Rupert.

'I'm not hurting you, am I angel?' he breathed in her ear, running his hands over her body. 'You're so beautiful. Please enjoy it.'

Helen didn't respond, lying rigid with horror, her teeth clenched, eyes closed. Billy, her dear, dear friend. How could he do this to her? But Billy was watching Janey bucking on top of Rupert. God, she looked wonderful! He was so proud of her!

'I'm coming,' cried Rupert suddenly, his face contorting.

'So am I,' said Janey, screaming and threshing.

She might be faking, thought Billy, but it's a lovely performance, and next moment he'd shot into Helen. Looking down, he saw two tears welling out of her closed eyes and coursing down her cheeks.

'Don't cry, angel. Please don't cry.'

More tears welled.

'Oh Christ,' he thought. 'We shouldn't have forced her.' He rolled off, gathering her against him. Rupert gave Janey a long, long kiss, then eased out of her and said in an undertone, 'See if you can get Helen going.'

'Move over,' Janey said to Billy, pushing him to the left of the bed. 'Our turn now.' She trailed her fingertips up Helen's thighs. Helen gave a moan of terror, shrinking away from Janey, eyes darting frantically for a way of escape. But, like bookends, Rupert and Billy blocked her exit.

'No, no, no,' she sobbed, as Janey's insistent fingers started burrowing inside her, as she felt Janey's breasts flopping on her stomach and Janey's tongue on her breasts.

'Jesus,' Billy muttered to himself, 'I'll be off again in a minute.'

'Please don't be frightened, Helen,' whispered Janey, as she caressed and stroked. 'We're all having such a good time, we want you to enjoy it too.'

I can't go on forever, thought Janey, five minutes later. No wonder Rupert complains she's frigid. She needs 24 hours defrosting. Rupert, bored with a spectator role, crawled down the bed and entered the slippery warmth of Janey from behind, so he could watch Helen. She looked like a martyr at the stake. Putting his hand around, he found that, despite Janey's ministrations, she was as dry as a marathon runner's throat.

She's useless, he thought.

Suddenly, with Rupert behind Janey, Helen saw a way of escape. Shoving Janey to the left, she wriggled away from her and, before any of them had realized it, had jumped off the bed and stumbled across the room. In Rupert's pocket she found the key.

'Come here,' he snarled.

For once she was in luck. In his excitement, Rupert hadn't locked the door properly. Crying hysterically, she managed to slip out, slam the door and turn the key, just as he crashed against it. She longed to run away into the night, but on the terrace the moon had gone in and everywhere was as black as ink. She heard the dry cough of a leopard and decided to settle for the third bedroom. There were no sheets on the bed. Huddled under the counterpane, gazing unseeingly at the bookcase, she shuddered until dawn. If her sleeping pills hadn't been in the bathroom cupboard, which could only be reached by going through the bedroom, she would have taken the lot. Any minute she expected an enraged Rupert to appear and drag her back to the torture chamber.

But the others were enjoying themselves.

'The grown-up has gone to bed now,' said Janey.

'All hands on dick,' said Rupert, filling up the glasses.

Playing games of their own, they carried on till morning.

50

Ringing home next day, Helen discovered that Marcus was in bed with tonsilitis and a temperature of 103. She was so riddled with guilt that she felt so relieved there was a really good excuse to fly straight home by herself.

In recent months the tonsilitis attacks had been getting closer together. The antibiotics were having less effect and Marcus was looking so waiflike that Helen accepted James Benson's recommendation that he should have his tonsils out at once.

'They're as big as billiard balls. Marcus'll be much better shot of them. It won't cure the asthma, but all the illnesses he's having as a result of the infected tonsils are pulling him down. There's a very good man at the Motcliffe in Oxford. He'll only be in hospital for four or five days.'

'Can I go in with him?'

'I honestly don't recommend it. You've been under a lot of strain recently.' Privately Benson thought he'd never seen her look so ill. 'Leave him with experts who see this operation fifty times a week.'

'You're saying I'm no good as a mother,' said Helen, beginning to shake.

'No, no,' said Benson reassuringly. 'I'm saying you're too good.'

'It's certainly been a stressful year. D'you think that's making his asthma worse?'

Benson shrugged. 'Probably. Children are like radars, Marcus must realize how unhappy Rupert's making you.'

Thank God we didn't take the kids to Kenya, thought Helen, with a shudder.

711

'Rupert wouldn't want me to go in with him.'

'Well, don't. By all means visit him during the day, but go home and get a good night's sleep every night.'

The night before Marcus was due to have his tonsils out, at the beginning of March, Helen and Rupert went to a big ball in London to raise funds for the Tory Party. It was the sort of invitation that Rupert would normally have refused; but, surprisingly, he was rather a fan of Mrs Thatcher, the new Prime Minister, and felt she needed every bit of help if the Tories were to stay in power.

'You wouldn't be able to afford to have Marcus's tonsils out privately if the Socialists brought in a wealth tax.'

They went very grandly to the ball with several ministers and their wives. Helen found the evening a nightmare. Hollow-eyed, thinner than ever, her black ball dress had had to be taken in yet again. She knew she was being a damper on the evening, but all she could think about was Marcus in his white hospital bed and the surgeon's knife going into his little throat in the morning. All around her, every table seemed filled with ravishing, chattering women flirting with bland smooth-haired men. At the same table a be-diamonded brunette with a roving eye, who'd already had a long amorous dance with Rupert, was surreptitiously holding hands with one Tory minister and at the same time, making animated conversation to his wife.

'The whole world's at it,' thought Helen, in despair.

There was Rupert coming off the dance floor, looking around for fresh talent. Goodness, he was going up to Amanda Hamilton, the much-admired wife of the Minister for Foreign Affairs. Now she was smiling up at him and he was taking her on to the floor. She must be forty, but very attractive in a determined sort of way – driving her husband Rollo on from success to success, knowing everyone, rigidly governed by the social calendar.

Rupert had actually met Amanda Hamilton before, at a party last June, and had promptly asked her out to lunch.

'No, I can't,' she had replied in her shrill, piercing voice. 'Next week's Ascot.'

'The week after then.'

'No, that's tennis.'

Rupert was slightly taken aback, until she explained that Wimbledon went on for a fortnight and she had to be in her seat on the centre court by two o'clock every day.

After that, she explained patiently, there would be a trip to America with Rollo, then Goodwood, and then Scotland.

Now, holding her in his arms in the twilight gloom, as the band played This Guy's in Love With You, Rupert admired her rounded, magnolia-white shoulders. A side door suddenly opened to admit a couple to the dance floor, and Amanda Hamilton's Scotch-mist-soft complexion was briefly illuminated. She didn't duck her head, for her unwrinkled, untroubled beauty had no need of dimmer light.

'How was Wimbledon?' asked Rupert.

'Very exciting. He's spoilt, that American who nearly won, but my goodness he can play tennis. I rather admire that kind of drive. It seems odd that no one minds painters or musicians or actors having tantrums, but tennis players, who are, after all, kind of artists, are expected to behave themselves. He's rather like you, in fact. You've had a bad press recently, haven't you?'

'You noticed?' said Rupert.

'Fighting with judges, frolicking with starlets, beating up your horses.'

Rupert shrugged.

'D'you beat your wife too? Is that why she looks so miserable?'

Rupert glanced at Helen, who was still sitting frozen, gazing into space.

'What do you think?' he said.

'She looks as though the dentist is filling her back teeth, having forgotten to give her an injection.'

Rupert grinned.

'I don't think it's funny. Why are you consistently so foul to her when she's so beautiful?'

'She's given me up for Lent.'

713

'Don't blame her, with you running after everything in skirts – or trousers – these days. Girls don't seem to wear skirts anymore.'

'You seem to have been taking a great interest in my career.' His hand was beginning to rotate very gently on her back.

'It amazes me that someone with such dazzling qualities should be quite happy about presenting such an appalling image to the outside world.'

'I know what my friends think. Other people don't matter.'

Amanda Hamilton shook her head so the pearl combs gleamed in her dark hair.

'One day you might get bored with riding horses and want to try your hand at something more serious.'

'Like taking you to Paris.'

'Rollo was saying the other day that one felt rather insulted if Rupert C-B *hadn't* been to bed with one's wife.'

Rupert tightened his grip, his hand moving upwards until he encountered bare flesh.

'I'd hate to insult Rollo,' he said softly.

'He could do you a lot of good. Have you ever thought of going into politics?'

'No.'

'You'd be very good. You've got the looks, the force of personality, the magnetism, the wit.'

Rupert laughed. 'But not the intellect. My wife says I'm a dolt.'

'You've got commonsense, and I've heard you're a very good after-dinner speaker.'

'I speak much better during dinner – and to one person, preferably you. When are you going to dine with me?'

'We're off to Gstaad tomorrow. Oh, listen, the music's stopped.' She clapped vaguely and turned towards her table.

Rupert grabbed her arm. 'Wait. It'll start up again in a second.'

'No,' said Amanda, with gentle firmness, 'We've danced

quite long enough. Go back and look after your poor little wife. You must both come and dine with us when Rollo gets back from Moscow next month.'

'No, thank you. I've got absolutely no desire to get better acquainted with your husband.'

Amanda smiled and patted his cheek.

'Think about politics as a career. I mean it seriously.'

Rupert stared at her unsmilingly.

'*Seriously*,' he emphasized the word, 'I'm only interested in getting a gold at the moment.'

Two days later, Jake Lovell walked down the long corridors of the Motcliffe Hospital to say hullo to the matron and in the hope of catching a glimpse of the angelic Sister Wutherspoon. By some stupid Freudian misreading of the diary, or perhaps because he was so anxious to get the go-ahead to ride again, he had arrived for his appointment with Mr Buchannan five hours early. Mr Buchannan was operating, said the secretary, and couldn't possibly see him before four o'clock.

The day had already been full of omens. It had snowed heavily since lunchtime the previous day and he and Tory had had to dig out the car that morning. Two magpies had crossed his path as he was leaving Warwickshire. An odd number of traffic lights had been green on his way through Oxford. He'd taken fifty-one strides from the car park to the front door. There were eleven people in the lift. His horoscope said the aspects for Venus were good and this was a make-or-break day. He hoped to hell it wasn't the latter. He'd had enough of breaks. He vowed that if Johnnie Buchannan told him he could ride again, he'd make the Olympic team. The individual event on September 8th was exactly six months away.

The nurses on the ward greeted him like a long-lost brother.

'My, we *are* walking well. You'll be beating Seb Coe in the 800 metres at this rate.'

It was very warm in the hospital. Outside, the snow was

still falling thickly, blurring the outlines of the trees, laying a clean sheet over the lawn. Orange street lights glowed out of the gathering whiteness. Feeling totally blanketed against reality, Jake asked after Sister Wutherspoon.

'She's having two days leave,' said Joan, Sister Wutherspoon's spotty, fat friend, 'but she was absolutely furious to miss you. She left you her number in case you felt like ringing her at home,' she added, excited at the prospect of matchmaking.

Jake pocketed the number. He had five hours to kill. He might as well ask her out to lunch. On the way to the telephone he passed by some of the private rooms and heard an unearthly animal screaming like a rabbit caught in a snare. The screams increased, growing more terrible.

Anxious to disassociate himself, Jake walked on. Rounding the corner, he was sent flying by what seemed like a huge bear jumping out of a room at him.

'What the fuck?' he snapped.

Then he realized it was a woman in a huge blond fur coat, tears streaming down her face. She looked half crazy with terror.

'I'm sorry,' she stammered. 'I don't know what to do. Marcus. Such terrible screaming. Something must have gone wrong.'

Jake realized it was Helen Campbell-Black.

'Where is he?' he said over the screaming.

'In there. He's just had his tonsils out. They said not to visit till later, but I wanted to be here when he came back from the theatre.'

Jake took her arm. 'Let's go and see him.'

Marcus was still screaming. He was as pale as his pillow; his white nightgown, like a shroud, was splattered with blood. Jake stroked the child's red hair gently.

'He'll go to sleep soon.'

'Can't they give him something to stop the pain?'

'He'll just have had a huge shot of morphine. Every time he swallows, it must be like an axe on his head.'

Gradually the screams subsided into great wracking sobs,

716

until finally Marcus fell into an uneasy whimpering sleep.

'He'll be O.K. now,' said Jake, straightening the sheet.

'Are you sure? W-why did he scream so much?'

'They have to wake them up immediately after the operation to make sure everything's all right. We went through the same thing with Darklis and Isa. They were both perfectly O.K. when they came around later. Darklis was as cheerful as anything, eating ice cream and raspberry jelly by the evening. When she woke up, she asked, "When am I going to have my tonsils out?" '

Helen looked at him stunned, as though only half-listening to what he was saying.

'W-why it's Jake, isn't it? Jake Lovell?' she said slowly. 'I didn't recognize you.'

'You weren't exactly in a recognizing mood.'

Suddenly she jumped out of her skin at the sound of more screaming coming down the corridor.

'Don't worry,' he said soothingly. 'It's only another child coming back from the operating theatre. They all sound like that.'

Woken, Marcus started crying again. Helen rushed to his side. 'Oh, please don't, angel.'

In a few seconds he'd fallen back to sleep again. They waited for quarter of an hour. Every noise seemed magnified a thousand times – a car horn outside, a nurse laughing in the passage, even the snow piling up on the window ledge outside, but Marcus didn't wake. Jake looked at his watch:

'Come on. I'll buy you a drink.'

'I can't leave him.'

'Yes, you can. I'll have a word with my friend, Joanie. If he makes a squeak they'll ring us at the pub and you can rush back.'

Outside, the snow was still falling – heavy flakes like goose feathers, bowing down the privets in the hospital garden, settling on the collar of Helen's fur coat, forming points on the toes of her tan leather boots, clogging up her eyelashes. Jake walked slowly. It was treacherous underfoot. He couldn't afford to fall over, today of all days. They had only got as far as the car park when she broke down again.

'I can't go. I'm sorry.'

He led her to his Land Rover, sitting her down on a nose-band and a copy of *Riding* magazine. Snow curtained all the windows. All Jake could do was say, 'There, there,' gently, almost absent-mindedly, patting her shoulder.

Gradually the first wild intensity died down, subsiding into a succession of wrenching, despairing sobs.

'I'm so sorry,' she kept saying. 'I'm such an idiot. Please, please forgive me.'

'If we don't both want to die of hypothermia,' he said, 'we ought to find that pub.'

She suddenly realized that he was only wearing a Barbour, his shoes were soaked and his teeth chattering.

'I'm so sorry,' she said again in a trembling voice. 'I can't go to a pub looking like this.'

He handed her her bag. 'Well, powder your nose, then.'

In the pub Jake found Helen a seat by the fire and went off to order treble brandies. Looking in the bar mirror he could see her vacantly gazing into space, twisting her fingers around and around. Christ, he thought, she's the one who ought to be in hospital. He took the brandies back to the table, holding one out to her. It was a second before she took it.

'I'm a trusty St Bernard struggling through the snow to bring you sustenance,' he said.

She didn't answer.

'Come on, it'll really help.'

He noticed how loose her expensive boots were around her legs, and that her skirt, which was only held up by a brown suede belt, was on an extra notch. She took a gulp, made a face, choked and then took another gulp. She wished the taste didn't remind her so much of that last night in Kenya.

'Where's Rupert?'

'Gone skiing.'

'Needn't have bothered. Plenty of snow here. When's he

coming back?'

She shrugged her shoulders. 'Five days – a week.'

'And you're left to cope with all this?'

Helen held out thin, shaking hands to the fire.

'I ought to go back,' she said restlessly.

'No, you ought not. They'll ring if he wakes.'

'Poor little guy, he's been so ill,' she said. 'He was so excited about coming into hospital. All the gifts and everyone for a change bothering about him rather than Tab – except Rupert, of course.'

'He ought to be in a ward. Other children'd take his mind off his sore throat. Darklis and Isa didn't want to come home.'

People kept coming in, stamping the snow off their feet. On the other side of the fireplace a couple of undergraduates in college scarves were eking out Scotch eggs and pints of beer. Helen's hair glowed in the firelight; it was the only bright thing about her. Suddenly there were tears trickling under her dark glasses again.

'Oh God,' she muttered in a choked voice.

'Don't worry.'

'I haven't got a tissue.'

One by one Jake removed all the paper napkins on the nearby tables and handed them to her. The waitress, trying to keep the tables for people having lunch, clicked her tongue disapprovingly as she replaced them.

'Do you want a menu, sir?' she asked, pointedly.

'Yes, later, but for the moment, can you get us two more very large brandies?' He gave her a fiver, adding, 'Keep the change.'

The waitress looked at Helen curiously. Must have been a death at the hospital, she thought. Then she looked at Jake. He was familiar, with his dark brooding eyes. She was sure she'd seen him in *Poldark* or *Jamaica Inn*.

'Who's that by the fire?' she asked the other barmaid. 'What was he in?'

'I think he's got a group. No, he's a show-jumper! I know. He's the one that broke his leg. Dr Millett was telling

719

us. They thought they was going to have to amputate, but he put up a real fight and pulled through. What's his name, Rupert Lovett, Jack Lovett?'

'Jake Lovell,' said the first barmaid, picking up the soda syphon.

'Here you are, Mr Lovell,' she said, putting down the brandies on the table. 'How much soda would you like? Can I have your autograph for my niece? She loves horses.'

Jake scribbled his name on the back of her bill pad and turned back to Helen. He felt a certain academic interest in why she was in such a frightful state. He'd never admired her looks, too thin, breedy and rarefied, and in his eyes she was always contaminated by being part of Rupert. But today he was drawn to her, as he had been drawn to Macaulay, and to all other things terrorized by Rupert. Being out of the circuit for nearly a year, he was not *au fait* with the gossip. He'd read about Samantha Freebody, of course, but that was too long ago to have such a traumatic effect.

'He's a beautiful child,' he said.

Helen gave the ghost of a smile. 'And he's extra bright. He's starting to read and he's not four yet.'

'Rupert got him on a horse yet?'

'He's allergic to horses.'

'Lives in the wrong house, doesn't he? Sure he's not allergic to his father?'

'Rupert thinks he's a wimp,' she said bitterly. 'Can't wait for him to go to prep school.'

'Where's he going?'

'St Augustine's – if Rupert gets his way.'

'Christ, don't send him there,' said Jake, appalled.

'What was Rupert like at school?' asked Helen.

'Same as he is now – Torquemada.'

She looked up with a start of recognition.

'Have you always hated him?'

'For over twenty years.'

'He had an awful childhood,' said Helen. 'His mother didn't really love him.'

720

'A woman of taste,' said Jake.

The waitress came up, all smiles now.

'Are you ready to order? And could I have your autograph for our manager's daughter?'

'Steak and kidney, chips and cauliflower cheese,' said Jake.

'I don't want anything,' protested Helen.

'Don't be silly, and bring a bottle of red,' he added to the waitress. 'You need food,' he said a minute later. 'I used to try and go without it until Dino Ferranti converted me. He always said that most depression is caused by tiredness and lack of food.'

'I liked Dino,' said Helen. 'He was fun.'

'We all liked him,' said Jake. 'Fen misses him like hell, but she's too proud to admit it.'

Then lunch arrived and Jake tucked in in the way that only really thin people do. Helen suddenly found she was hungry after all. It was real steak and kidney and there was wine in the gravy.

Jake nodded approvingly: 'How's Rocky?'

'Rupert figures he's the best horse he's ever ridden.'

'Paid enough for him.'

'How's Macaulay?'

Jake's face softened. 'He is something else. After Sailor died I vowed I'd never get so fond of a horse again. But Macaulay really gets to me. If he could read, he'd go around on his own. He's not really a world class horse, but he's such a trier and he's got so much heart.'

'He's not overly fond of Rupert.'

Jake grinned. 'That's another thing we've got in common.'

After a good start Helen didn't manage to finish her lunch. Quite pink now from her thermal underwear, she looked as though she'd got a temperature.

'I ought to go back.'

'I'll ring and check,' he said.

When he came back she'd disappeared. He thought she'd bolted until he saw her shopping basket, with the

721

copy of *The Brothers Karamazov* and *The Guardian*. When she returned, he noticed she'd toned down the flushed cheeks and tidied the rumpled hair. He knew it wasn't for his benefit. Just the instincts of a woman who liked looking perfect all the time.

'He's fine,' he said, getting up. 'Out like a light, still. No one expects him to wake for several hours.' He filled up her glass.

'You have been kind,' she said slowly. It was as if she was noticing him as a person for the first time.

'Why are you here anyway?'

Jake told her.

She was stricken with remorse. 'It's such a crucial day for you. I'm so sorry. I've been so obsessed with my own problems, I didn't even think of anyone else. Are you hoping to go to L.A.?'

Jake touched wood. 'Yes, if Johnnie Buchannan gives me the go-ahead today. I've got just six months to get fit.'

'Will you take Macaulay?'

'I'd like to, although potentially Hardy's a better horse. He's been going well with Fen, but he's still very spooky and erratic. Christ, if only I had a year.'

Looking at him, Helen suddenly saw coming alive that single-minded, driving fanaticism, which had to be there: the fuel of Olympic fire.

'Buchannan warned me I might never ride again. I promised that he mended me, I'd bring him home a medal. Fighting talk, huh?'

He stopped suddenly, flushing slightly, hearing his own obsession, wanting to disguise it.

Helen looked at the black hair, the thickly lashed dark eyes and the thin, watchful face. Suddenly she winced and clutched her temples.

'What's the matter?'

'I get this pain. It seems to start as a headache, then becomes toothache, then often reappears as earache.'

'Neuralgia,' said Jake. 'Caused by tension.'

He felt so sorry for her. She reminded him of a vixen

722

escaping from hounds, lying in the bracken taking a brief panting respite to get her breath back. In a minute she'd be running again, waiting, terrified, for the kill. But Rupert hadn't killed her. He'd totally destroyed her self-esteem.

As they came out of the pub it was still snowing, shortening the visibility, so they could only see the vague outlines of the towers of Oxford.

'Beautiful city,' said Helen softly. 'Home of lost causes, and forsaken beliefs, unpopular names and impossible loyalties.'

'Pretty impossible to be loyal to Rupert,' said Jake dryly.

Underfoot it was freezing so hard that he ought to have been more frightened of falling over. But, in vino, he crossed the snow without a slide or a stumble.

Helen was amazed that Marcus recovered so quickly. Driving in on the fifth day to take him home, she found him playing with the most exquisite model circus. There were clowns, little dogs with ruffs, a ring master and even a ballerina in a pink tutu, who slotted into a cantering horse with a pink plume. All the nurses were gathered around playing with it.

'How darling,' said Helen in delight. 'Who gave you that?'

'Dake did.'

'Dake?' said Helen, puzzled.

'Dake with the sore leg. It's better now. Want to see Dake.'

'Who can he mean?'

'Jake Lovell,' said Sister Wutherspoon warmly. 'He popped in last night on his way back to Warwickshire and brought the circus with him. Marcus was a bit restless; excited about going home. Sister Tethers, who was on duty, had a very sick child to look after. Jake stayed playing with Marcus for hours.'

'How very kind,' said Helen. 'How very, very kind.'

'Mr Buchannan gave him the go-ahead on Monday evening. I still don't think he's come down to earth.'

723

'Oh, I'm so pleased,' said Helen, 'and he still remembered Marcus.'

'Want to see Dake,' said Marcus.

The winter seemed to go on and on, but at last the snow melted; aconites and snowdrops appeared and Helen watched Rupert's dogs trampling over her crocuses, snapping off their fragile heads, and found she minded less than on other years.

As she went for long solitary walks in the woods, her thoughts strayed far too often to Jake Lovell. Over and over again she got out the road atlas and realized how far he'd driven through the snow to give Marcus the circus. She remembered how unembarrassed he'd been by her tears and how cold he'd got sitting in the car, just patting her shoulder.

As she watched the spring emerge with aching slowness she wondered how she could thank him for lunch and for the circus. She didn't want to write in case some secretary opened the letter. He might have told Tory about lunch, but if he hadn't, it might make things awkward. Personal letters were so obvious when they arrived at a private house. She remembered so many arriving for Rupert over the years, usually in gaudily-coloured envelopes, sometimes with SWALK on the back, and how she'd longed to steam them open. Janey, she knew, would have had no such scruples.

Chatting to Janey in the kitchen one day, and leafing through the latest issue of *Horse and Hound*, with a shock of recognition she came across a picture of Jake. The caption underneath said he would be making his comeback at the Crittleden Easter meeting, and how glad readers would be to see this brilliant but very private rider back on the circuit. He had evidently recovered from one of the worst accidents in show-jumping history and had learned to walk by sheer guts and determination. The story went on to praise his staunch, close-knit family and to explain that Jake had not achieved the international fame of other British riders because, before the World Championship, he preferred to jump in this country and get home to his family in the evening. Malise Gordon was quoted as being absolutely delighted. If all went as planned, he hoped Jake would be offering himself for selection for Los Angeles.

'Good that Jake Lovell's back, isn't it?' she said to Janey.

'I shouldn't imagine Rupert thinks so.' Janey took the magazine from Helen. 'I've always thought he was very attractive. All that Heathcliff gipsy passion kept under such perfect control. He's much more self-confident too. I saw him interviewed on the box last night about his comeback and he actually managed to string a sentence together. And, instead of looking sulky and defensive, he was rather cool and detached.'

Helen found her voice thickening, as it did when she asked if she could cash a cheque at the village shop. 'Have you ever heard any gossip about other women?'

'No, he's squeaky-clean reputation-wise. You only have to look at Tory to see he hasn't got very high standards.'

'I guess he's only interested in getting to the top,' said Helen.

'Perhaps,' said Janey thoughtfully, 'but there's something irresistible about men who are impossibly hard to get, which is not something one can say about your dear husband.'

It was strange, reflected Helen, that, after that unspeakably dreadful last night in Kenya, she and Janey could still be friends. Janey had an amazing ability to swan in, not attempting to justify or apologize for appalling behaviour, which made it possible. Rupert, however, she could not forgive. They both moved around the house not communicating, like goldfish in a bowl.

The week before Easter brought the first sunshine for days. Helen went around the house turning off lights that weren't on, because the rooms were suddenly so unexpectedly bright. Out in the fields she noticed little red buds on the wild roses and larks singing in the hazy drained-blue sky, thrashing their bodies like moths against non-existent windows. Perhaps I could escape, thought Helen, listening to the larks' strange whistle; perhaps I too am thrashing against a window that isn't really there.

Next day the vicar came to tea, to talk about raising money for the church spire. Afterwards Rupert walked in from the stables, to find Helen and he praying together in the drawing-room.

'Christ,' he said in horror, and walked out again.

The vicar, who had a white beard and stank like a polecat, scrambled creaking to his feet.

'I wish we could make some progress with your husband,' he said with a sigh. 'I feel he is very troubled.'

'I don't think he'd see it that way,' said Helen hastily, 'but thank you very much.'

Carrying the tea things into the kitchen, she found Rupert and Tab eating an Easter egg and reading *Dandy* together.

'Flappy Oyster,' said Tab.

She shouldn't be eating Easter eggs before Easter Sunday, thought Helen, appalled, but she didn't say anything.

Rupert looked up. 'Has your friend from Hollywood gone?'

Burying her face in the washing-up machine, as she stacked the cups and saucers, Helen said, 'I thought I might come to Crittleden on Saturday.'

'The anniversary of your first show,' said Rupert. 'That's rather touching.'

'I'm having lunch with the Godbolds,' said Helen, putting all the knives in the wrong way up, 'so I can come on afterwards. I also thought I might fly out to Rome for a couple of days.'

Rupert looked slightly startled. 'Whatever you like,' he said.

For the first time in years Helen felt excited and took ages planning what she was going to wear to Crittleden. Despite the lack of sun April had been very dry, so she wouldn't have to wear gumboots. She settled for a pin-striped suit, a white silk shirt and a charcoal grey tie and a grey trilby.

After a lightning lunch at the Godbolds, where she ate nothing, she arrived at Crittleden just as the riders were walking the course for the big class. There was Rupert fooling around with Wishbone and Billy, and there was Jake, still limping quite badly, walking beside Fen. He looked small and pre-occupied and very pale. Neither of them were speaking. Fen was only an inch or two smaller than he was.

Jake felt nausea creeping through his stomach as he made his way towards the collecting ring. People nodded and waved and clapped him on the back, but he hardly noticed them. Why the hell hadn't he chosen a smaller show to make his comeback?

A little girl rushed forward for his autograph. 'Later,' he snapped.

Lack of sleep and food had made him dizzy. Everything seemed unreal. For the past week he'd hardly slept, dozing off, then waking up with the sensation of falling, then lying awake, jumping fences in his head, seeing them growing higher and impossibly higher, as the long hours crept towards dawn and cigarettes piled up in the ashtray.

The sky was getting greyer. He began to shake.

'Are you all right?' said Sarah. 'Don't worry. You've been jumping super at home. Mac'll take care of you.'

Macaulay tried to knock Jake's hat off to cheer him up and was sworn at for his pains. When Jake was mounted, Macaulay tried again, just a little buck that in the old days would have made Jake laugh – but which today nearly put him on the floor and produced another torrent of abuse. To further shatter Jake's confidence, Rupert was crashing Rock Star over the practice fences, putting him wrong, so he hit his forelegs hard and would be certain to pick them up when he went into the ring. God, he was a beautiful horse in the flesh, thought Jake; a chestnut stallion showing all the compressed power of his American breeding, with curving muscles like coiled steel cables.

Jake jumped a couple of fences, then, having been nearly sent flying by Rupert, retreated to the outer field, desperately trying to get his nerves under control. Suddenly he passed Helen Campbell-Black, looking like a city gent, ludicrously out of place in a pin-striped suit.

'Hi,' she said, smiling and coming towards him.

Jake nodded curtly and, circling, rode back to the arena.

Fen was waiting for him: 'You're on,' she said. 'Good luck.'

'Good luck,' called voices on all sides.

In the old days he had usually been all right once he got into the ring, the nervous tension a necessary preliminary to the class itself, heightening awareness, but that was when his body was fit and flexible, not frozen with fear. Now he was like a child at his first gymkhana. What if he really was jinxed? Sailor had died here. Last year he had smashed up his leg. These things went in threes. What had the fates in store for him today?

Macaulay, aware of his master's terror, heard the bell and suddenly decided to take matters into his own big hoofs. Bucketing towards the first fence, he cleared it easily. Somehow, clinging onto his mane, Jake stayed in the saddle. It was a very hit and miss business. The crowd had their hearts in their mouths all the way round. No one cheered, for they didn't want in any way to distract Macaulay, but as he cleared the last triple with a flourish they broke into a roar that seemed to part the grey clouds and bring out the sun, putting a sparkle on everything.

Fen found herself hugging Malise in the collecting ring. 'He did it,' she gulped, 'he really did it. It's going to be all right.'

As Jake rode towards the exit, deadpan as ever, the cheers mounted and all the people in the boxes came out on to the balconies to bellow their approval. Helen joined in the applause politely. She felt absurdly deflated. Jake had hardly noticed her and then cut her dead.

'Great round,' said Malise.

Jake shook his head. 'It was bloody terrible and you know it, but at least I, or rather Macaulay, got around.'

Everyone was congratulating him. It amazed him. They were so thrilled to see him back. But he couldn't take the hero worship and the enthusiasm just yet. He wanted to be alone with Macaulay to thank him. Riding quietly out of the collecting ring he saw Helen Campbell-Black. Aware that he'd snubbed her earlier, he rode towards her.

'Hullo,'

She looked up: 'Oh, hi,' she said, ultra casually.

There was a long pause.

'He jumped well,' she stammered, 'I'm so happy for you.'

'How's Marcus?' said Jake to the top of her trilby.

'He's real fine, so much better. Look, I've been meaning to thank you for ages for lunch and for Marcus's circus. You were so kind driving all that way.' She was really gibbering now.

'That's all right,' said Jake.

After another long pause she looked up and they gazed at each other.

'I've got your handkerchief, too,' she said, colour mounting in her face, 'and Marcus plays with his circus the whole time. He just adored you.'

Jake said nothing, but went on staring down at her.

As Macaulay sidled beneath him, Helen put up a trembling hand to stroke the horse's black neck.

'Are you going to Rome?' she asked, desperate for something to say.

'No. Are you?'

'Yes.'

'Don't go.'

'W-what?' She looked at him in amazement.

'I said, don't go. Make some excuse. When's Rupert leaving?'

'Lunchtime on Monday week. He's flying out.'
'Right. You'll be home in the afternoon?'
'Yes.'
'I'll ring you there.' And he was gone.

Helen was thrown into complete panic. Had she dreamed it? Could Jake really have said that? From that Saturday at Crittleden to the Monday nine days later, when Rupert left for Rome, she went through every fluctuation of excitement, worry, terror and disbelief.

She was completely inattentive at committee meetings and at parties. When the parties were boring she could think of nothing but Jake. Yet when Amanda Hamilton invited them to dinner on the Saturday and Helen, radiant in russet taffeta, was chatted up by two rather glamorous Tory MPs, she hardly missed him at all. Amanda had been particularly nice to her, soliciting her aid to persuade Rupert to go into politics.

Perhaps if he did, thought Helen, things would be different. He'd be in England most of the time and there wouldn't be any of those punishing three-o'clock-in-the-morning departures, and by using his brain he might have less of a chip about her apparent intellectual superiority.

Rupert was highly relieved that Helen wasn't coming to Rome. Amanda Hamilton was going to be out there for the Rome tennis tournament, staying with friends. He was making no progress with Amanda. Like a do-it-yourself cupboard, he told Billy, she was taking far longer to make than one would expect. Pathological about adverse press, she even refused to lunch with him. But she fascinated him more than any woman he'd met for ages, and he was determined to get her into bed before long.

When Rupert's car refused to start on Monday, Helen drove him to the airport. As she drove slowly back to Penscombe, admiring the wild cherry blossom and the pale green spring leaves, she reflected that it was a good thing she'd be out when Jake rang, just to show she wasn't that keen.

731

Walking into the house she buried her face in a huge bunch of white lilac which filled the entire hall with its scent. Marcus rushed out to meet her and show her the pictures of the fair he'd painted at play school.

'Any messages?' she called out casually to Charlene, who was in the kitchen.

'No. Oh, I tell a lie, Mrs Bacon rang about jumble.'

'No one else? Are you sure you didn't go out or into the garden?'

'I've been here all afternoon.'

Helen was totally thrown. She'd been so certain Jake was going to crowd her, that she had a tiger by the tail. Why the hell couldn't Mrs Bodkin throw away dead flowers, she thought, as she wandered restlessly round the drawing-room, moving ornaments, even snapping at Marcus. She tried to read. Half an hour passed. Then Malise rang, hoping to catch Rupert before he left. Janey rang for a gossip and the headmistress of Marcus's play group rang about their summer bring and buy. Helen was uncharacteristically terse with all of them. Then Charlene's mother rang and gossiped to Charlene for twenty minutes. Helen couldn't even accuse her of wasting money as it was an incoming call. Perhaps Jake was in a call box trying to get through; perhaps he'd lost the number. Oh, the nightmare of being ex-directory. Unsupervised by Charlene, the children swarmed into the drawing-room. The next moment Tab had put jammy fingerprints all over the apricot silk curtains.

'Charlene,' screamed Helen, 'for God's sake, get off the telephone.'

Charlene flounced in, looking martyred. 'It's Gran. She's got cancer of the bowel.'

'Oh God,' said Helen, mortified. 'I'm so sorry.'

The telephone rang. Helen sprang to it.

'Hullo.'

'Helen?'

'Yes.'

'It's Jake. Sorry I couldn't ring before. The class went on and on.'

There was a pause. Mindlessly she watched Tab stumping towards the table with the long pale blue cloth, on which stood all Helen's favourite ornaments.

'Look, I know it's short notice, but I'm coming your way tomorrow. Can we lunch?'

'I don't know. Tab, leave that tablecloth alone. *Alone*, I said.'

'Shall I pick you up?'

'No.' It was almost a scream. '*Tab – I said, put it down!*'

'You know the Red Elephant at Willacombe?'

'Yes.'

'I'll see you there at one o'clock.'

'O.K. – hey wait.'

But he had replaced the receiver.

Leaping forward, Helen retrieved a Rockingham Dalmation from Tab's predatory fingers.

'I said, "Don't touch".'

Picking up the child, she was suddenly overwhelmed with happiness, swinging her around and around, covering her with kisses until she screamed with delight.

'Weeties,' said Tabitha, sensing weakness.

'Oh, O.K.' said Helen, 'if you really want all your teeth to fall out.'

Looking in the diary after a sleepless night, Helen saw to her horror that she was supposed to go to a fund-raising lunch for the NSPCC. As Vice-President for the local area, she was expected to play a leading part and make a rousing put-your-hand-in-your pocket speech after lunch.

The President was very put out when Helen rang and said she couldn't make it. Charlene had to go to an unexpected funeral, she explained, so she had to stay home and look after Marcus and Tab.

'Surely one of the grooms can do that? I mean, we are expecting you. You're on the poster and you're such a draw. They're all looking forward to meeting you.'

'I'm sorry, Davina, but I really can't leave them.'

'What about Janey Lloyd-Foxe?'

'She's away.' Horrifying how easy she found it to lie. 'Honestly, I'd never forgive myself if Marcus had an asthma attack.'

The President was not so easily defeated. She rang back at half past eleven, just as Helen was having a bath.

Charlene answered the telephone before Helen could reach it.

'Hullo, Mrs Paignton-Lacey, Mrs C-B's in the bath.'

'Give it to me.' Dripping, Helen snatched the telephone.

'D'you always have a bath in the middle of the morning? Who was that answering the telephone?'

'Charlene.'

'I'd thought she'd gone to a funeral.'

'She's just leaving.'

'Hmm, well I've sorted out your problems. Angela Pitt's nanny's a state-registered nurse and she's quite happy to bring Angela's smalls over to you and look after your smalls.'

'That's very kind,' said Helen, realizing the bedroom door was still open and Charlene was probably hovering, 'but I'm afraid the answer's no.' She kicked the door shut.

'But that's absurd. Surely a state-registered nurse is better.'

'At looking after Marcus rather than his own mother?' snapped Helen. 'Since we're talking about cruelty to children, I figure my first duty is towards my own kids. I appreciate your help, Davina, but please don't try and run my life,' and she hung up.

Looking at herself in the bedroom mirror, she was suddenly elated and amazed by her own defiance. Suddenly, however, panic assailed her. What if Davina rang again and got Charlene after she'd left, or if Marcus really had an asthma attack? Whimpering with terror, she rang the Red Elephant. Could she leave a message for Mr Lovell? After a long pause, the manager said there was no one booked in the name of Lovell, although they had four Mr Smiths and five Mr Browns who'd booked tables for lunch. Helen rang off. Perhaps he wasn't going to show up at all.

Mrs Campbell-Black, reflected Charlene, as she listened to Helen singing I'm in the Mood for Love in the bath, was behaving in a very odd way. Yesterday she'd unloaded all Badger's tins of dog food from the supermarket into the dish washer and put a packet of Tampax in the fridge. Even when she came out of the bath and found Tabitha trying on lipsticks and dropping one on the pale gold carpet, she didn't fly off the handle as she normally would.

And now she was walking into the kitchen in a new silver flying suit and shiny black boots, with her hair trailing down her back in one long red plait.

'You look fantastic,' said Charlene, in genuine amazement. 'Like an astronaut. You ought to go to the moon.' (She's over it already, she thought to herself.)

'Do you really like it?' asked Helen, shyly, desperate for reassurance.

'Gorgeous. Makes you look so slim. You'll be wasted on the NSPCC,' Charlene added slyly. And asphyxiate them too with all that expensive perfume, she reflected. Mrs C-B must have bathed in it.

Marcus wandered in. 'Mummy pretty. Going out?' His face fell.

'Only to a lunch to make money to help kids who aren't as lucky as you. I must go. I won't be late.'

God will smite me down for such terrible lies, she thought.

Terror increased on the drive to the restaurant as she passed two NSPCC stalwarts driving like mad in the other direction – late for their one glass of sherry. She glanced in the driving mirror, hoping she wasn't getting too flushed. She was so nervous, she'd been rushing to the loo all morning. It would be terribly difficult to pee wearing this flying suit; she'd have to take the whole thing off. There was the Red Elephant. She couldn't see Jake's Land Rover anywhere.

He was waiting in the bar, three-quarters the way

735

through his second whisky. For a minute she thought he was going to kiss her on the cheek, then he settled for shaking hands.

'D'you want a drink here, or shall we go straight in?'

All along the bar sat businessmen, gawping, finding her face vaguely familiar, trying to identify her.

'Let's go straight in.'

Rupert could never enter a restaurant without turning the whole place upside down so Helen was amazed that Jake slid in so quietly. They reached their table in a corner without anyone recognizing him. There was a bunch of dark purple irises in a royal blue vase.

'It's not considered good form, but would you rather sit with your back to the room?' Jake asked.

Helen nodded.

At her request for a glass of white wine, Jake ordered a bottle and another whisky for himself. Helen found herself quite unable to meet his eyes. It had been so easy to talk before because it had been just a monologue, with her pouring out all her woes. Now, sitting opposite, conversation was incredibly heavy going, like chopping up raw swede with a blunt knife.

Marcus was much better. Darklis and Isa were well. Both of them felt it bad form to mention Tory or Rupert. Helen was reluctant to ask Jake about his horses in case she betrayed her total ignorance. Jake felt the same about films, plays and books. The weather had been perfect, so that only lasted them thirty seconds. A kindly waiter arrived with the menus. Helen randomly chose whitebait, which she hated, and grilled lamb cutlets with courgettes.

She hadn't actually looked him in the face yet. White wine didn't seem to jolly her up at all. Desperate for something to say, she boasted she'd met half the Tory shadow cabinet at dinner on Saturday. Then thought what a fatuous thing to have done. Jake was bound to be wildly left wing. Conversation didn't improve with the arrival of food. There were long silences. Jake, unsmiling, said very little. Helen was beginning to rattle. Gloom swept over her;

she had no charm; she was boring him as she bored Rupert and obviously Dino. She looked down at the silver bodies of the whitebait in their coats of batter and could see their glassy little eyes staring at her.

Suddenly Jake leaned across, took her knife and fork, and put them together and beckoned the waiter: 'Could you take the plates away, and bring our next course; but there's no hurry.'

'Anything wrong, sir?'

'Nothing. We just weren't as hungry as we thought.'

Helen gazed down at her hands, which were frantically pleating the white tablecloth.

'I'm sorry,' she mumbled. 'What a dreadful waste.'

Jake stretched out his hand and very gently began to stroke her cheek. For a second she shied away, then gradually relaxed under his touch.

'There,' he said softly, 'there. It's all right, pet. I'm just as scared as you are.'

'Are you?' she glanced up, startled.

'More so, I should think. I was so terrified you'd say no. I couldn't work up the courage to ring you until six o'clock. I hung round the phone box, steeling myself.'

'And I figured you weren't going to call.'

'And I thought you'd probably cry off this morning, so I booked in under the name of Smith, and went out first thing, so you couldn't reach me.'

'And when I got cold feet and rang up to cancel and found you hadn't booked, I got in a blind panic because I thought you weren't coming.'

They both found they were laughing. Then she told him about the hassle with Davina and the NSPCC.

'What was *your* excuse?'

'I said I was going to look at a horse. Tory looked at me as though I was barking. We haven't got enough cash for a three-legged donkey at the moment.'

'And I left all that whitebait.'

'Doesn't matter. Nice treat for the restaurant cats. D'you mind if I smoke?'

As the match flared, she noticed the beautiful, passionate mouth, with the full lower lip and for the first time realized his eyes were not black but a very dark sludge green matching his shirt.

'Have you really got gipsy blood?'

'Sure. My father was pure Romany. I ran away back to the gipsies when I was six. After my mother died, I tried to find him, and lived with the gipsies for three years before the social security people caught up with me and slapped me in the children's home.'

'So you've really had no family life to speak of?'

'I've got one now, and when I see what Tory's mother did to her, I reckon I was well off.'

'What was it like living with the gipsies?'

'Cold, sometimes, and always with the feeling of being moved on by the cops. But I enjoyed it, I learnt a lot. They taught me to recognize a good horse, and treat all nature as a medicine cupboard. Which reminds me.' He put his hand in his pocket and produced a bottle of grey-green liquid.

'For you. For neuralgia.'

Helen took it wonderingly. 'You remembered. What is it?'

'Extract of henbane. Deadly poisonous, neat. Crippen used it to murder his wife.'

Helen looked slightly alarmed.

'But that's very diluted. It's a marvellous sedative and a painkiller. Try it, but keep it in a safe place.'

Helen was so moved and touched, she had to make a joke out of it.

'D'you eat hedgehogs as well?'

'No,' he said coldly, 'nor do I tie them on top of poles, like your husband.'

Oh dear, thought Helen, I've upset him.

Then he said, 'Did you know hedgehogs' prickles go all soft when they're with kind people?' and suddenly smiled.

God, he's attractive, thought Helen. She felt as if she were on top of a snowy mountain, perched on a sledge, with her hands and feet tied, hurtling into the unknown with no

738

way of stopping or steering.

'Do you tell fortunes?'

He shrugged. 'A little. It's really a con trick. The hand betrays the calling: if it's rough, or pampered, or the nails are bitten. You look more for the face behind the eyes, the droop of the mouth.'

Helen held out her hand. Her engagement ring, far too loose, had fallen underside down. For a second the huge sapphires and emeralds on her third finger caught the light, then fell back into place. Jake examined the palm for a second.

'It tells me a small, dark stranger has entered your life.'

'You think so.'

'I know.'

'Is he going to remain there?'

'That's up to you.' He ran his finger lightly along the heart line, 'Whatever you may think to the contrary, you're extremely passionate.'

Neither of them made much headway with their second course, but finding so much to talk about now, they drank their way through a second bottle of wine.

'Were you really intending to ask me out at Crittleden?'

'No, I was far too pre-occupied about riding again.'

'What changed your mind?'

'I suddenly wanted you like crazy.'

Helen blushed. 'Ever since you bought me lunch at the pub, I've kept thinking about you. I thought it was gratitude, now I'm not sure.'

Jake undid one of the zips on her flying suit: 'Pretty. Does this lead anywhere?'

'Only a pocket.'

'Nice. I'd like to live in your pocket.'

Looking down at his hand at her collar bone, involuntarily Helen bent her head and kissed it, then went crimson.

'I didn't mean to do that,' she said, appalled.

'I know you didn't. I willed you to.'

Still they lingered, oblivious of the yawning waiters looking at their watches, ostentatiously re-laying tables on either side of them. Seeing her slowly relax, and those huge eyes losing their sadness, Jake couldn't tear himself away. He'd always thought her very over-rated as a beauty. Now she seemed to blossom in front of him – lovelier every second.

In the loo, Helen was amazed to see her own face. She couldn't believe she hadn't turned into someone else. It took hours to get her flying suit half off and have a pee. She kept undoing the wrong zips. She realized she must be very tight. She was appalled, looking at her watch, to see it was a quarter to four.

She was glad that, in her flat boots, she was at least an inch shorter than Jake. As they walked to her car, he put a hand on the back of her bare neck under her hair, warm and reassuring. It was nice walking beside someone the same size. Rupert always dwarfed her.

'I must go back,' she said wistfully. 'I'm dreadfully late.'

As he opened her door he said, 'Drive a couple of miles down the road towards Penscombe. There's a little wood on the left. Wait for me there.'

The wood was full of primroses and violets. For a dreadful moment she'd thought she'd found the wrong copse or that he wasn't coming. Then at last he appeared over the hill, stuck behind a trundling farm tractor carrying bales of hay. Taking both hands off the wheel, he raised them in a gesture of despair.

He was out of the car in a second, leading her into the wood, beech husks crunching beneath their feet. Then, as Helen tripped over a bramble cable, Jake caught her, drawing her behind a huge beech tree, laying her against the trunk, taking her face between his hands, examining every freckle and eyelash and yellow fleck in her eyes.

'Even Helen of Troy couldn't have been as beautiful as you,' he whispered and kissed her very gently on the lips. Helen was very glad the beech tree was holding her up. No one had ever melted her in this way. She had no desire to fight him off, just a longing that he would go on holding her for ever. But as they broke for breath, some deathwish prompted her to ask,

'It's not because I'm Rupert's wife?'

For a second his face was black with rage, just like the time he'd pulled a knife on Rupert.

'I don't want anything of Rupert's,' he said through gritted teeth, his hands biting into her arms until she winced. 'Get this absolutely straight. Rupert poisons everything he touches. It's a measure of what I feel for you, that I still want you *despite* the fact you're his wife.'

This time he kissed her really hard and she kissed him back, half-longing that he'd push her down and take her on the beech husks. But he led her back to her car, his face shuttered.

'You're not cross?' she stammered. 'I've had such a good time today. Living with Rupert makes you sceptical, I guess, so you question everyone's motives.'

'Well, don't question mine. Where you're concerned they're quite straightforward. I just can't stand that shit having anything to do with you.'

He opened the door and, as she got in, leaned over to slot in her safety belt, kissing her briefly on the forehead.

'You know this is only the beginning?'

'Is it?' Helen was overwhelmed by a great happiness.

He nodded. 'But we can't afford to rush things. I've got too much to lose.'

'You mean Tory and the children.'

'No,' he said slowly, 'I mean you. I don't want to panic you. Drive carefully. I'll ring you tomorrow afternoon.'

It was a good thing there weren't any traffic cops lurking as Helen floated home. She got lost twice and bought peace offerings of freesias for Charlene and sweets for the children. Really, she was going to the dogs in grand style. She came through the door singing with happiness at five past five.

'So sorry I'm late. Lunch went on and on and on. Everyone was rabbiting on about sponsored swims and bring and buys. What are you having for supper, darlings? Beefburgers and French fries. How yummy.'

741

Normally Helen would have freaked out at junk food, thought Charlene, putting the freesias in water, and she certainly didn't get like that over a thimbleful of sherry and one glass of hock.

In the evening Charlene went to a wine bar with Dizzy, who this time hadn't gone to Rome.

'Promise, promise, promise, you won't tell anyone?'

'I promise.'

'Goodness,' said Dizzy in awe, a quarter of an hour later. 'I wouldn't have thought the old thing had it in her. Are you sure?'

'Well, she certainly wasn't preventing cruelty to children. Mrs Paignton-Lacey dropped off the minutes for the last meeting on the way home, two hours before Mrs C-B got back.'

'Christ,' said Dizzy. 'Well done, her. About time someone gave Super Bastard the run around. I wonder who he is.'

'Must be pretty special. She came back floating above ground like the hovercraft. She was never like that after lunching with Ferrantic.'

52

Helen sent Charlene and the children out for a picnic the following afternoon so she could talk to Jake without being overheard. But gradually as the minutes ticked by, she felt her happiness subsiding like a tyre with a slow puncture. Three, four, five, six, struck the grandfather clock in the hall. It was no longer afternoon. The children came home, tired and fractious and, sensing her sadness and inattention, played up even more. Helen looked at the chaos of toys lying around the nursery, counting 'he loves me he loves me not' as she put them away. The last piece of Lego was back in its box, and came to 'he loves me not'. Jake must have gone off her. Perhaps Tory had kicked up a fuss when he got home and he'd decided the whole thing wasn't worth the hassle.

The evening passed with agonizing slowness. She couldn't settle to anything. She was appalled how suicidal she felt. She couldn't have got that hooked that quickly. This is only the beginning, he'd told her. A small dark stranger has entered your life. How could he hurt her like this? How could he reduce her to such ridiculous uncertainty and despair?

At midnight she took the dogs out for a last walk. As if to mock her, it was the most perfect evening, with a gold, almost full moon, with a hazy halo of apricot pink. Along the edge of the wood the huge Lawson cypresses rose like cathedral spires, taking on an almost sculptured quality. As she walked across grey, shaven lawns, past silent statues, the last of the daffodils gave a flicker of light. The reflection of the moon in the lake was rippled first by a wakeful carp, now by Badger drinking. Her shadow was tall and very black on the lawn. It was so light she could see the blue and green stones in her engagement ring. Was there after all to be no small escape, no respite from her marriage?

Despairing, she turned back. Glancing up at the golden, lit-up windows of her bedroom she could see the rose and yellow silk curtains of the huge four-poster in which she would soon lie alone. As she came into the house the telephone was ringing. After midnight, so it must be Rupert. He never had any sense of time. Steeling herself, she picked up the receiver.

'Helen! Can you talk? It's Jake.'

She burst into tears. It was a minute before he could get a word in. 'Hush. I'm sorry, pet. Please don't cry; it breaks me up. I couldn't ring before. Hardy cast himself this afternoon. Had the most frightful colic. The vet's been here since two o'clock. He's just finished operating. He'd swallowed a nail and we thought we'd lost him.'

'Oh God, that's awful. Is he going to be O.K.?'

'He's still out like a light; but the vet reckons he'll pull through.'

'I'm so sorry. You must have been frantic.'

'I couldn't get to a telephone. It's in the tackroom and the vet and Fen were in Hardy's box next door the whole time. Look, I can't talk long; the vet's still here, but I must see you tomorrow, if only for five minutes.'

'It'll be hard for you to get away if he's still sick. I'll come over your way.'

'That would help and, pet, please don't cry any more.'

They met the next day, literally for a quarter of an hour. Jake looked desperately tired; he hadn't been to bed. Hardy was very shaky on his legs, he said, but well enough to bite the vet that morning, so it looked as if he would pull through. Watching his face as he talked about the horse, Helen felt deeply ashamed. He really loves him, she thought, as Rupert was incapable of loving a horse; in fact, anything. Last night he must have suffered just as much as she had waiting for him to ring, and she'd greeted

744

him with hysterics.

They walked through the beechwoods, breathing in the wild garlic, Wolf bounding ahead and Jake picking up the bluebells the dog had knocked over so Helen could take them home for a few more days of life.

They sat on a fallen log. Helen hung her head, clutching the bluebells. She'd put her hair up today. Jake slowly took out every hairpin so it cascaded down her back in a shining red mass.

'Don't put it up any more. It reminds me of what you were like before I started to –' he paused – 'to know you.'

Then he said more briskly, 'Look, we've got to get one thing straight. You've been married to a show-jumper for quite long enough to know that things happen with horses, that it's impossible even to say I'll turn up or telephone at a particular time with a hundred per cent certainty.'

'I know,' she said in a trembling voice, 'but I've got so little self-confidence.'

'I know that,' he said putting his hand under her chin and forcing it upwards. 'And I want to give some back to you, but only if you give me a chance and realize from the start that if I ever don't ring you, or don't turn up, it's because I can't. Even though I was demented with worry over Hardy last night, a hundred times I nearly risked it and picked up the phone, which would have been madness, because any minute Tory could have picked it up in the kitchen. It's difficult enough for us to find time to see each other without complicating things. All right, end of lecture, I'm not going to kiss you because I must have smoked a hundred cigarettes in the last twenty-four hours and I don't want to put you off even before we've got started.'

'You couldn't, truly you couldn't.' She threw herself into his arms, half crying, half laughing.

He held her for a long time, not speaking, just stroking her hair. Then he said, 'I'm off to the Bath and Wells tomorrow for three days. Why don't you drive over? We could have dinner.'

'That would be just lovely.'

'Or I could book a room in one of the nearby hotels.'

He felt her stiffen.

'I don't know.'

How could she explain that he was so desperately important to her that she couldn't bear him to go off her so soon? She knew he would, once he realized how hopeless she was in bed.

'Why not?'

'I don't know you well enough.'

He laughed. 'There's no more satisfying way of getting to know someone better.'

He rang the next day to tell her the name of the hotel and what time he thought he'd get there. He didn't mean to bully her, but he felt privately it was vital to bed her as soon as possible. Not just because he wanted her like hell, but because he felt he'd never make any real progress in restoring her self-confidence until he got to grips with her particular hang-ups. On several occasions he'd heard gossip that she was frigid. He didn't believe it. Frigid was a gross over-simplification, a term often used scornfully by men about women who no longer loved them physically. He believed Helen had been very badly frightened, but was not frigid.

He wished he could spend hours in her box, talking to her, soothing her, making her feel secure. But he had so little time. If he was going to be picked for Los Angeles he couldn't let up for a second. And so he insisted on her meeting him that night at the hotel.

Helen sat alone in her bedroom at dusk. There was no wind. Outside, sheep were calling to lambs, baby house martins under the eaves were squeaking peremptorily for their parents to catch insects more quickly. The white cherries shone luminous in the half light. The rank, peasant smell of wild garlic in the wood threatened to extinguish the sweet delicate scent of the pink clematis, which swarmed round the bedroom window. Her pink track shoes were yellow with buttercup pollen, from wandering aimlessly through the fields all afternoon blowing dandelion clocks.

This time tomorrow she thought, I'll be in bed with Jake.

She had never been so frightened in her life. She wished she could pray, but how could she ask God to help her be better in bed with someone who wasn't her husband. She still hadn't planned her alibi for tomorrow night. Charlene was already going out, so she'd have to ask one of the grooms to baby-sit. Always before, she'd left a telephone number where she could be reached, but she could hardly give them the number of the Nirvana Motel. And how was she going to smuggle her suitcase out to the car? She'd have to send the children out for yet another picnic.

Even worse, she'd been sitting on her bed, trimming her bush with nail scissors, when Charlene had walked in with some ironed clothes and Helen had hastily to pretend she was cutting her toenails. Anyway, what was the point of trimming her bush when the thing it covered was the trouble? Over and over again, Rupert's words came back to haunt her:

'You're just like a bloody frozen chicken. Every time I put my hand in there I expect to pull out the giblets.'

And she was so thin now, it would be like going to bed with an Oxfam ad. She had a blinding headache so she took some of Jake's medicine. Gradually the pain eased and she felt calmer. Maybe if he could cure her head, he could melt the ice of her frigidity as well.

But it was as if some malignant fate were at work. Just as she was leaving Penscombe the following day, she discovered she'd got her period. She'd been so pre-occupied, she'd completely forgotten she was due.

She glanced at her watch. It was too late to ring Jake at the show. She could ring the Nirvana Motel and leave a message saying she couldn't make it, but that left her with the appalling prospect of not seeing him. She'd have to go, perhaps have a quick drink – he wouldn't want her in this state – and then come home.

It was so hot, she wore only a yellow sleeveless dress, yellow sandals, and a white silk scarf to keep her hair from

747

tangling. As she drove very fast to meet him, she was so wracked with stomach cramps she hardly noticed the beautifully green bosky evening or the cow parsley frothing along the verges, or the smell of wild garlic, stronger than ever, like some rampant Dionysian presence pursuing her.

Waiting for Jake, she sat trembling in the hotel foyer, trying to make herself look as inconspicuous as possible. Pretending to read the evening paper, the hall porter watched her idly. You could always tell the first time they came here, he thought, they never stopped fiddling with their hair, squirting on perfume, glancing in their hand mirrors, then fearfully up at the door. Suppose he didn't turn up; supposing someone they knew walked in. He'd even seen wives sitting here waiting for their lovers when their husbands walked in with someone else. He had another look at Helen. This one was a looker all right, but she'd go through the ceiling with nerves in a minute. Oh, now she'd dropped her bag all over the floor. He moved forward to help as Helen fell on her knees, frantically scrabbling up banker's cards, keys, loose change, lipsticks and stray Lillets. At that moment, Jake sauntered through the door, his coat slung over his shoulder. He looked suntanned and happy and not remotely embarrassed.

'Hello, darling,' he said, pulling her to her feet, and kissing her on the cheek. 'Did the babysitter arrive? I've had the most bloody day at the office. And I'm afraid my father rang to say he wants to come and stay next week.'

Just like any other married couple, thought Helen in admiration, and she had great difficulty not giggling when he signed them both in as Mr and Mrs Driffield.

'No, we'll manage,' he said to the porter when he offered to carry their cases up to the fourth floor; adding in an undertone as they got into the lift, 'I'm buggered if I'll tip him for nothing.'

When he opened his case in the bedroom, all it contained was a toothbrush, toothpaste, a bottle of gin and a large bottle of tonic.

'I think that covers all eventualities,' he said, as he

fetched two glasses from the bathroom. Then, seeing the expression of misery on her face, he put them down on the dressing table and took her in his arms, trying to still the desperate trembling.

'Pet, please, you look as though you're going to the electric chair.'

Helen burst into tears. It was some seconds before she could speak, and then he spoke for her. 'You've got the curse.'

'How d'you know?' she said incredulously.

'I knew you had it coming. All week you were very edgy, and the day before yesterday your breasts were swollen and you had huge circles under your eyes. Fen always says just before the curse is the only time she has decent boobs.'

Helen was amazed that he should be so observant. Smoothing her hair very gently behind her ears, he removed her earrings. 'Now, will you please stop crying. We don't have to do a thing if you don't want to.'

He poured half and half gin and tonic into the glasses and handed her one. 'You got a pain?'

She nodded.

'Well gin's the best for that. Take a big slug of it. Come on, lie down,' he said, removing her yellow high-heeled sandals. 'Just relax. We've got hours.' He lay down beside her, draining half his drink.

'You don't have to stay,' Helen stammered. 'You might not want to – if there's no sex.'

For a second his face blackened. 'What the fuck is that supposed to mean? D'you honestly think I only want you for sex?'

'I don't know. It's all Rupert wants.' Somehow the words spilled out before she could stop them.

'How many times,' he said wearily, 'do I have to remind you, I'm not Rupert?'

'I know you're not,' she said in a trembling voice, 'but it wouldn't make any difference if you were, or if I didn't have a period. I'm no good to you. I'm hopeless at sex. I'm frigid.'

'Who said so?'

'Rupert did. He says I'm simply not interested in it.'

'Not interested in him, you mean.'

Despite the heat he could feel the gooseflesh on her arms.
She was still shuddering violently, her teeth chattering.

He reached for her glass, making her take a big gulp, and
then a second and a third.

'Come on, now, tell me all about it.' Then it all came
pouring out – the humiliations, the taunts, Rupert's always
insisting on sex whenever he came home, despite the
endless infidelities, then the clap and, finally, Samantha
Freebody.

'That's not all, is it?' said Jake. 'What happened in
Kenya?'

'How'd you know anything happened?' whispered
Helen.

'Second sight. Come on. We can't afford to have any
secrets.'

He made her take another slug of gin.

'I can't talk about it,' she whispered.

'Go on. It'll help, I promise.'

So she told him, often crying so hard he couldn't hear the
words, about the foursome with Billy and Janey.

'Afterwards, Rupert made me feel as though I'd let him
down, paid him the ultimate insult by not joining in. I
couldn't. I'm simply not made that way.'

Jake tipped her head back, swept the sodden hair away
from her forehead and dried the tears with his handkerchief.

She heaved a long sigh. 'I'm so sorry to bore you.'

Jake held her tightly. 'Poor baby, poor poor little baby.
You did end up in the wrong yard, didn't you?''

Her yellow dress had no zip, so Jake was able to slide it off
over her head, before laying her back on the counterpane.

'Still got the pain?'

'A little.'

'I'll bring you something for that next time. The gin'll
start working soon.'

750

Beneath the coffee-coloured silk petticoat, he could feel her stomach muscles tightly knotted. But gently, as he stroked them with those magic hands that could calm the most frightened horse, she began to relax. She was so tired, after nights of not sleeping, that the singsong voice and the stroking hands and the gin were making her drowsy. Almost before she knew it, he had slid off her petticoat and unhooked her bra. Then he was kissing her mouth and, almost in spite of herself, she was kissing him back, gently at first, then more and more fiercely, and still his hand continued to stroke her belly.

'You're so beautiful,' he murmured.

'I'm so thin.'

'No, you're perfect.'

After Tory's bulk, he found Helen's fragility incredibly erotic. For once he felt like a great hunk of man, all-powerful by comparison.

And she looked so unbelievably touching, with her damp cheeks and wide yellow eyes smudged with mascara, and her hair falling in a long red tangle over one shoulder. As he kissed her again, his hand slid downwards, caressing all the time, circling the pubic hair then sliding under the pants to find the clitoris, stroking it with the utmost delicacy. Helen tensed and then relaxed.

'She's not frigid,' he thought in triumph. Slowly, slowly like a moth emerging from a chrysalis, she seemed to yield to him. Then she gave a deep sigh of contentment.

After a minute she opened her eyes and smiled.

'Frigid, eh?' he muttered into her hair.

'That was so lovely,' she gasped.

'Wasn't it?' He grinned down at her, looking absurdly pleased with himself.

'But you haven't had any sex at all,' she said suddenly distressed.

'Doesn't matter. I can wait till next time. It'll be worth waiting for.'

The unselfishness, the insight, the kindness put the seal on her love for him.

'That was the most wonderful sex I've ever had,' she said.

'For me, too,' he said, kissing the hollows of her throat.

Three days later, he had her for the first time in a meadow on the edge of Bifield woods, near the old gipsy encampment, where his forefathers must often have taken his foremothers. A heavy shower of rain had flattened the grass for them and dispersed the regiments of insects, but it was still very hot. Their lovemaking was rapturous. They fitted together perfectly and despite anything he might say to the contrary to Helen, Jake experienced a feeling of pure triumph: that this was Rupert's wife lying beneath him and reduced to a quivering jelly of ecstasy. Once again he had succeeded where Rupert had failed.

Meanwhile, in Rome, at almost the same time, Rupert Campbell-Black was experiencing an almost identical moment of triumph, as he lay on top of Amanda Hamilton for the first time. Rock Star had had a glorious double clear in the Nations' Cup, making up for Fenella Maxwell's indifferent form and clinching the victory for Great Britain. Today, Amanda was actually missing the final of the men's doubles in order to play mixed singles with him. Full-breasted, narrow-hipped, long-legged, her body was superb for a woman of forty. Only a slight creeping on thighs and breastbone betrayed her age. Her string of pearls was still round her neck. In out, in out, superbly in control, Rupert drove her towards orgasm.

Suddenly her face contorted with concentration, then she gave a cry of ecstasy.

'At last.'

'My darling,' said Rupert, smiling tenderly.

'I've suddenly worked it out,' said Amanda. 'It was *your* cousin, Charlie Cameron, who was married to Rollo's niece-in-law, Antonia Armitage. Before she was married to him, she was Antonia Luard.'

If it had been any other woman, Rupert would have hit her.

53

For the first four weeks Helen and Jake enjoyed an unnatural freedom. Rupert and Fen were travelling abroad with the British team, following the same route from Rome, Fontainebleau, Paris to Lucerne along which, the previous year, Fen had cavorted so joyously with Billy. Now Fen did no cavorting. She went to bed early, listened with both ears to Malise's advice, worked her horses diligently, but still showed an alarming lack of form. Each day she grew more panicky that she wouldn't be selected for L.A. and would never see Dino again. That was her sole ambition.

In England, however, Jake was on sensational form. Macaulay, blissful to have his master on his back again, was jumping superbly. Hardy, recovered from the operation and still erratic and cantankerous, had some brilliant days. Wherever Jake went, he annihilated the competition. But he was still nagged by the worry that the selectors had forgotten him because he'd been off the circuit so long. How much more would he have to achieve before they began to sit up and take notice?

Almost, but not entirely, taking the edge off his anxiety was his obsession with Helen. Travelling the British circuit, he was away from home three or four nights a week. Sarah was abroad with Fen. Hannah, Jake's new young groom, had a convenient crush on one of the Irish riders, spending most nights sleeping under haycocks or in the back of the Irish boy's lorry. Helen, with a Volvo at her disposal, whizzed up numerous motorways and spent as many nights as possible with Jake, stretched out in his lorry or on a duvet in the back of the Volvo. Sometimes they went to hotels.

Often, despite Jake's reluctance, Helen paid. If she had the money, why not? From the moment she committed herself to Jake she felt absolutely no guilt about being unfaithful to Rupert or spending his money.

She did feel guilty about neglecting the children, but she was so happy whenever she returned, radiant and talkative, and so loaded down with guilt presents, even choc drops for Badger, that everyone flourished. Helen, being an emotional tyro, was blissfully unaware that everyone in the household knew someone was up and were having bets on who he was.

On the 28th of May Jake returned to the Mill House, having spent three days at the Great Cheshire Show, where he had won every big class by day and spent his nights making love to Helen. In three days' time, which was also the first day of the Lucerne show, the Olympic Committee would announce ten short-listed riders from whom the final five would be selected in mid-July. Jake arrived home absolutely shattered. His mended leg ached badly, but that was probably due more to an excess of sex than to show-jumping. As he climbed out of the lorry, the sun was setting. Tory ran out of the house to welcome him. With her bulk and her round shining face, she seemed, after Helen's slenderness, like a Matrioska doll that has suddenly gone two sizes up. He hoped her elation might be due to the news that he'd been selected, but it was purely because she was so thrilled to see him. He was so tired, he kept giving the wrong answers to her questions. As he went into the kitchen, the children surged forward in their pyjamas to welcome him, hugging and kissing him, bombarding him with questions about the trip. Realizing he couldn't cope with the din, Tory sent them off to watch television. Jake poured himself a drink.

'How did Fen do in the Nations' Cup?'

Tory had prayed he wouldn't ask. She didn't want him upset so soon after he'd got home.

'They dropped both her rounds.'

'Shit. What happened?'

'She was in floods when she rang. I don't think it was

anything Desdemona did wrong. Fen said it was her fault. She'll probably ring you after the Grand Prix.'

Jake dropped a couple of ice cubes in his whisky and went out into the yard, watching the horses being put to bed. Macaulay, having rolled and wolfed his dinner, was already dragging up the straw, preparing to lie down. Hardy was still restless. It always took him a long time to settle back, even into his own box. As Jake progressed down the line, each horse came to the half-door to welcome him. Tonight, for once, they didn't cheer him up. Why hadn't he heard from Malise?

He went into the tackroom.

'Supper,' called Tory from the kitchen door.

'Won't be a minute,' Jake called back. Next moment he'd picked up the tackroom telephone. As he waited for Helen to answer he noticed the peeling paint on the door. If Charlene answered, he would put the telephone down.

'Helen, it's Jake.'

'Darling.' It was worth the risk to hear the ecstasy in her voice. 'Where are you?'

'At home. I can't talk. I just want you to know I miss you like hell.'

Suddenly he saw Tory appearing in the doorway. 'I'll call you tomorrow, bye.'

'Darling,' said Tory, 'I could have made that call for you.'

'Think I left my wallet in Humpty's lorry. I had a drink with him at lunchtime.'

'Your wallet's in the kitchen, silly,' said Tory. 'You *must* be tired. It's so sweet you've got that photograph of me from the colour supplement tucked inside it. It's an awful picture. I look so fat. D'you really miss me when you're away?'

'Course I do.'

The photograph in fact was part of a feature on show-jumping wives that had just appeared in the *Sunday Times* colour magazine. On one side of the page were two photographs: one of Tory looking fat, pink and eager, nailing up rosettes in the kitchen, the other of Janey Lloyd-Foxe, managing to look absurdly sexy in a maternity smock. The other side of the page was devoted entirely to a photograph of Helen on the terrace at Penscombe, gazing wistfully down the valley, looking unbelievably beautiful. It was taken before she met Jake and was the reason he had sloped up to the newsagent to scrounge another copy.

In the kitchen, Jake thanked God that Hannah, Isa and Darklis were having dinner with them. The children, allowed to stay because it was Sunday tomorrow, were arguing who was going to sit next to him.

'You can both sit next to Daddy,' said Tory, putting a long loaf of garlic bread on the table.

Darklis had painted a picture at school which she showed proudly to Jake.

'It's you and Macaulay at Los Angeles, Daddy.'

Both he and Macaulay were standing on the rostrum wearing gold medals with balloons coming out of their mouths saying 'God save the Queen'.

'I think you're being a bit premature, but thank you,' said Jake.

As Tory served out beef cooked in beer and the children both helped themselves to too much mashed potato, and Hannah brandished the rosettes they'd won this week, which tomorrow would be nailed to the cork board, Jake wondered if the last month with Helen had been all a dream.

Suddenly the telephone rang. For a mad moment of panic he thought it might be Helen ringing back. It was Malise, calling from Lucerne.

After two minutes, Tory put Jake's dinner in the oven. After ten minutes, Tory gave the rest of the beef out in second helpings, knowing Jake wouldn't want any more.

'Yes,' he said, his back hunched over the telephone, with a curious stillness. 'Yes, I see, O.K. Yes.'

'We're going to need another bottle,' said Hannah.

'I don't know if we've got one,' said Tory. 'What for?'

'To celebrate, or to cheer ourselves up.'

At last Jake came off the telephone. He looked like a thundercloud. Then he smiled and put his arms round Tory.

'Fen was third in the Grand Prix.'

'Oh, thank goodness for that,' said Tory.

There was a long pause. They all waited. 'And I've been short-listed for L.A. He wants me to fly out to Lucerne with Hardy and Macaulay tomorrow.'

Tory woke up at four in the morning and, reaching out for Jake, found the bed empty. He was in the study. Cigarettes were piling up in the ash tray. Outside, it was already light, blackbirds were bustling importantly across the lawn, like clerics in a cathedral close.

'Darling, what *are* you doing?'

'I couldn't sleep.'

'Too excited?'

He shook his head ruefully. 'Too much to think about.'

He'd waited so long for that telephone call, despairing that it would ever come. Now it had and he ought to be overjoyed, but all he could think was that he wouldn't see Helen for at least a fortnight. The prospect appalled him.

By morning, he had the whole thing in perspective and was quite matter-of-fact when he rang her. Helen sounded absolutely shattered and made no attempt to keep the disappointment out of her voice.

'I'm thrilled for you, darling, but we won't be able to have that week in Yorkshire. I can't bear it.'

'I'll only be away ten days.'

'But that's an eternity and then Rupert'll be back for the Royal and the Royal International. Can I see you this afternoon?'

'It's a bit tricky.' He sounded detached, as though he was already in Lucerne, 'I've got a hell of a lot to do. We're desperately short-staffed anyway, with Fen and Sarah abroad and all the papers to get in order.'

Being superstitious, he hadn't brought anything up to date in case he wasn't selected.

'I'll ring you later,' he said.

Jake didn't get a moment to ring until seven o'clock. Everyone was in the yard or in the kitchen, so in the end he was reduced to pretending he needed some cigarettes from the pub. Then the pub call-box was out of order, so he had to use the one in the High Street to the fascination of all the locals. Helen was in a frightful state.

'Sweetheart, I've been frantic. I figured something must have happened.'

'I'm sorry. I've been hellishly busy.'

'Am I going to see you this evening?'

'I can't.'

'I'll come over to you.'

'I haven't had a night at home for days. I've got a hell of a lot still to do. We're leaving first thing.'

Next moment he jumped out of his skin as a neighbour tapped on the window, wanting to congratulate Jake on being short-listed.

'What are you doing in a call box, anyway?' he asked.

'Ours is out of order,' said Jake.

'Come and use ours then.'

'I've nearly finished,' Jake banged the door shut. 'Darling, I'm sorry, someone banged on the window. Look, I'll ring you as soon as I get to Lucerne.'

'I can take a hint,' said Helen in a tight voice. 'You've only got time for your bloody horses.'

'Don't be such a bitch.'

'I thought you were different,' sobbed Helen, 'but you're behaving just like Rupert.'

'Hardly surprising, if you carry on like this.'

But she slammed down the telephone.

The locals drinking outside the pub were highly diverted to see Jake come out of the telephone box, wander up the street away from his own car, nearly get run over crossing the street, then wander back into the telephone box again.

Jake was very restless at dinner, snapping at the children, hardly eating anything.

'You all right?' asked Tory, as she cleared away.

'I'm sorry.' Jake put an apologetic hand on her back. 'It's just nerves, I guess.'

'And tiredness,' said Tory, throwing the remains of his ham and baked potatoes into the muck bucket. 'You're jolly well going to bed early.'

'I will, I promise, but I met Hugh Massey in the street. He says he's got a video of last year's show at Lucerne. He promised to show it to me.'

'Don't be long,' she said.

Pretending to collect his car keys, Jake went upstairs. Darklis caught him in the bathroom.

'Why are you cleaning your teeth, Daddy?'

'Because I got a bit of ham stuck,' lied Jake.

In disgust Darklis gazed at her face in the bathroom mirror.

'I don't think anyone will marry me when I grow up.'

'I'll marry you, sweetheart,' said Jake, dropping a kiss on her head.

'You've already got a woman,' said Darklis gloomily.

'I've got two,' thought Jake wryly.

Helen was waiting in the car park of the Goat and Boots, three miles away. She got into his car and they drove half a mile into the country and turned off the road. Helen fell into his arms.

'I'm so sorry, I'm desperately sorry. Please don't ever let me behave like that again. I just couldn't bear the thought of your going away.'

'Hush, pet, hush.' Gradually he calmed her.

'Now,' he said, 'I'm going to talk and you're going to listen. We've got to face the fact that I'm going to be horrendously busy for the next two months. For one thing, we desperately need the cash. Fen's been off form and she needs sorting out. I've still got a long way to go with Hardy. I've got to kill myself to get a place in that team. To be selfish, if I'm not selected I don't want to reproach myself for the rest of my life for having blown it because I didn't work hard enough. I'm not a natural, like your husband. Ever since I've been in show-jumping it's been one hell of a struggle to keep going. Fen, the children, the grooms, and

759

most of all Tory, have had to make colossal sacrifices. After that last fall I've crawled back from the gates of hell. But only because they made it possible. I owe it to them all to get to L.A. and I want to go.' His voice softened, and he put up his hand to stroke her cheek, which was wet with tears. 'Until I met you, I thought I wanted it more than anything else. Allow me three and a half months until the Games are over. There, that's the longest speech I've ever made.'

'I'll put up with anything,' said Helen, in a trembling voice. 'I just thought you'd gone off me.'

Jake laughed. 'You're like Macaulay, desperate for reassurance.'

'That's the difference between us,' said Helen slowly. 'My marriage is absolute purgatory. Yours is perfectly O.K. We're batting from different strengths.'

There was a pause. Jake was too truthful to disagree with her.

'Shall I fly out to Lucerne?' she asked with a sudden surge of hope.

'No, I don't want any distractions.'

And with that she had to be content.

Rupert rang the following evening. He was half-way to Lucerne.

Rocky, he said, had won the Grand Prix on the Saturday.

'How's Fen getting on?' asked Helen.

'Disastrously. I can't think why Malise doesn't pack her off back to Junior classes. Mind you, he's really gone off his head now. He's just sent for Jake Lovell. "Jake Lovell," I said to him, "couldn't get a jump in a brothel." '

Lucerne was a show of mixed fortunes for Jake. Macaulay, who hadn't flown since Jake brought him half starved back from the Middle East four years before, obviously thought he was being taken back to the stone quarries and completely freaked out on the flight. Sweating as though in the highest fever, his huge body quivering with terror in the tiny crate, his anguished eyes imploring Jake not to desert him, he reminded his master of nothing so much as Helen. It took all Jake's skill and patience to stop him kicking the plane out.

Arriving in Lucerne, Macaulay was pathetically pleased to see such old friends as Fen, Sarah and Malise. He was further comforted to see Desdemona in situ, and dragged Jake half way across the yard to check if it were really her. Touching her nose, exchanging breaths, Macaulay was still rigid with disbelief. Only when Desdemona reached up to rest her roan face against his still sweating neck, protective and defensive, did he begin to relax. But he never really recovered his form all week.

Bearing in mind that there would be a punishing flight to the Olympics and Macaulay was not all that sound in the wind, and a clean-winded horse was essential for the Los Angeles smog, Jake, after long discussions with Malise, decided to pull him out of the contest. He was heartbroken. Most of all he had wanted to win a medal on Macaulay, but his horses always came first, and Jake was not prepared to put the big fellow through the traumas of another plane journey. He'd already made plans to box him home.

Which meant everything rested on the sleek but irritably twitching grey shoulders of Hardy, who was magnificent on his day, but perfectly capable of carting Jake or kicking every fence out if he so chose. In Lucerne, after a sulky start, he came second in two classes, and jumped an exemplary clear in the first round of the Nations' Cup. In the second he put in a dirty stop at the water, leaving Jake sitting in the exquisite model lake with a stream of expletives on his lips and a bridle in his hand, while Hardy cavorted round the ring like Tinkerbell, refusing to be caught. Having learnt to duck out of his bridle, Hardy suddenly decided what fun it was, and did exactly the same thing in a speed class the following day.

All this provided wonderful fuel for Rupert, who proceeded to put the boot in on every occasion. Although Fen got very hot under the collar and snapped back at Rupert, Jake refused to rise. He got a quiet satisfaction from the thought of how much better he'd been riding Rupert's wife at home, and a further laugh when the post arrived one morning and Rupert actually handed him an envelope containing a passionate love letter from Helen. Thank goodness, she'd had the foresight to type the envelope and post it in London.

Finally, Hardy put a muzzle on all his critics by coming second to Ludwig in the Grand Prix. But all in all, Jake did not feel the week's adventures had enhanced his Olympic prospects.

After Lucerne, it was back to the Royal in Birmingham, then out to Aachen, then more shows in England and finally Crittleden at the end of July, after which the team would be announced.

All this made Jake very uptight and, although he missed Helen appallingly, he had plenty to occupy his mind. Helen, on the other hand, had nothing. She thought about Jake obsessively. It was as though he was the same television programme permanently in front of her eyes. His face haunted her dreams. At night she tossed and turned, longing for his hands on her body.

She had even convinced herself that Jake would make a much better father for the children, particularly Marcus. Rupert had come home from Lucerne and taken both children to the fair. Here he had insisted on riding on all the most frightening things. Tabitha adored every minute of it. Marcus was absolutely terrified and ended up being sick on the top of the big wheel, soaking not only Rupert's trousers but the couple immediately below them, who took it in very bad part. Rupert returned home in a blazing temper, with Marcus white and shaking and Tabitha in high glee telling everyone what had happened. That evening Marcus had his worst asthma attack ever.

As Helen soothed him to sleep in the early hours of the morning, she found under his pillow one of the little dogs with a ruff from the circus Jake had given him.

'Want to see Dake again,' murmured Marcus slowly,

'Like Dake very much.'

'Oh so do I, darling,' sighed Helen.

A week later Janey gave birth to a beautiful, dark-haired boy who weighed seven pounds and happily looked exactly like Billy. They called him Christopher William, soon abbreviated to Christy, and both parents absolutely doted on him.

Watching Billy in his new-found role as an adoring father, Helen brooded all the more on Rupert's lack of interest in Marcus.

On the other hand, she had reason to be grateful to little Christy. As a devoted godmother, she was provided with the perfect alibi. Afternoon or evening, she merely had to tell Charlene she was popping along to see Janey and the new baby. Then, having dumped a bunch of flowers and a glossy magazine and cooed for two minutes, she could rush off to see Jake.

During the Royal Show, she and Jake were able to snatch an afternoon together. Leaving Rupert safely competing in a couple of classes, Jake left Birmingham and drove the eighty odd miles over to Penscombe. Charlene had taken the children to a birthday party, so they had the house to themselves.

Jake was very jumpy. He hated making love to Helen on Rupert's territory. He thought of the Mill House with its damp, peeling paint, torn wallpaper and messy, homely rooms which had suffered eight years of wear and tear from children and animals. Then he looked at this ravishing house, and the green valley, and the tennis court, and the swimming pool, and the garden in its rose-scented mid-summer glory. The blatant perfection of the whole thing depressed him. And yet, overwhelming all this was his desperate need to see Helen again, and again, though he hated to admit, the buzz of actually making love to her in Rupert's huge four-poster. He was amazed how passionate and totally uninhibited she'd become.

'I never thought I'd like it that way,' she said. 'The only

problem with soixante-neuf is that neither of you can tell the other how marvellous it is while you're doing it.'

'Let's do it straight next time, so you can,' said Jake.

'Bighead,' said Helen, rolling on to her front.

Lying on top of her, Jake slowly returned to earth, kissing her freckled shoulders, gently nibbling the lobes of her ears.

Helen, who'd buried her face in the pillow, said in a muffled voice, 'Jake – I love you.'

There was a long pause, a horse whinnied from the valley, a dog barked in the distance. Then Jake said, 'I love you, too.'

Lying beside her, smoking a cigarette, not worrying about the smell of tobacco because Rupert wasn't due back until the following day, he said, 'I've never said that to anyone in my life before.'

'Not even to Tory?'

He shook his head.

'Why did you marry her, then?'

'Because she was rich and she bought me my first horse.'

'Didn't you love her at all?'

'Not in the way I love you. As I said, she's been a very good wife, but we're all inclined to take her for granted. Dino brought her out. He really bothered with her, and she adored him.'

'Dino was also very fond of me,' said Helen, her face suddenly sulky. Jake sat up and looked down at her, grinning.

'I do believe you're jealous of Tory.'

Then, seeing the pain and misery in her eyes, he pulled her into his arms. Clinging to him fiercely like a child begging for a bedtime story to ward off the terrors of darkness, she said, 'Tell me about the gipsies.'

He settled her into the crook of his arm.

'Well, if a woman's unfaithful to her lover he cuts off her ear or her nose, or scars her cheeks, so you'd better be careful. If your wife's unfaithful you tie her to a cartwheel and thrash her, or shave her head.'

'Golly,' said Helen nervously, 'how primitive.'

'Then if you want to marry a girl you send her a spotted handkerchief. If she's wearing it next time you meet her, you know she's willing to marry you.'

Helen was amazed how much it hurt her to ask, 'Did you give one to Tory?'

'Yes. It was very cheap, red cotton. All I could afford at the time. She still keeps it in her jewel case, but it's terribly faded.'

He looked at his watch. 'Christ, I must go.'

'Oh, please not.'

'I've got a class at seven. I've got to walk the course and it'll take me an hour to get back in the rush-hour traffic. I'll have to drive like hell as it is.'

'Am I jeopardizing your career?'

'Yes,' he said, kissing her.

Next minute the door bell pealed and the dogs went into a frenzy of barking.

'Christ, who's that?'

Helen snuggled up to him. 'Lie still. It might go away.'

The doorbell rang again, the barking increased.

Naked, Helen crept down the passage and, hidden by the clematis which swarmed over the spare room window, peered out. A minute later she was back in her bedroom, giggling. Jake was already getting dressed.

'All I can see is a straw hat.'

'Well, you'd better go and re-direct it,' said Jake.

Wrapping herself in a big rust-coloured towel, Helen went downstairs.

In the doorway she found two elderly women fanning themselves. One was carrying a camera.

'We thought for an awful moment you were out,' said the first, who was wearing the straw hat.

'I was in the bath,' said Helen. 'Can I help you?'

'We've come to interview you for *Loving Mother* Magazine. Miss Taylor here,' the woman in the straw hat waved in the direction of the woman with the camera, 'is going to take the pictures.'

'Oh, my goodness.' Helen froze with horror. She

765

remembered they'd rung and made an appointment weeks ago, and Jake must have rung straight away afterwards and she'd forgotten to put it in the diary. Suddenly she could feel Jake's sperm trickling down her legs and backed away hastily, ramming her legs together, hoping they couldn't smell all the sex and excitement.

'You'd better come in,' she said weakly. 'You must forgive me. I had a panic getting Rupert off to a show this morning,' she lied. 'Usually, I'm so punctilious about these things.'

Miss Crabtree gave a jolly laugh. 'Oh the needs of the great man must take preference.' She stepped into the hall. 'What a lovely home.'

Helen's mind was racing. How the hell was she going to smuggle Jake out? Then she had a brainwave. 'Come on to the terrace; the view's so lovely. Would you like a drink?'

Miss Crabtree consulted her watch. 'Well, it's only half past four. We'd love a cup of tea.'

'Of course. A cup of tea.' Helen fled into the kitchen, put the kettle on and rushed up the back stairs, half hysterical with laughter and terror. She found Jake dressed and trying to make his cigarette butt disappear down the loo.

'Have you got rid of them?'

'No; they've come to interview me about being a devoted wife and mother.'

Jake grinned. 'They'd better come and interview me.'

'Shut up. I've got them safely on the terrace. You steal out by the back door.'

Tugging on a dress and a pair of pants, she flung her arms around his neck. 'Ring me this evening.'

Tearing downstairs, she rang Charlene. She could hear tumultuous party noises in the background.

'Bring the children back at once. Someone's come to photograph them.'

'I can't in the middle of tea, and then there's the conjuror and Tom and Jerry.'

'Well bring them back as soon as possible.'

They were nearly out of Earl Grey and the only biscuits

were shaped like animals and topped with different coloured icing. All the cups were in the dish-washer, which wasn't turned on. She'd have to have a word with Charlene; things were getting awfully slack.

She was just drying the cups when Miss Crabtree wandered into the kitchen.

'It's rather hot out there, so I thought I'd come and help you. They're so lovely and cool, these old houses.'

Any moment, thought Helen in panic, Jake would come down the back stairs into the kitchen, and where the hell had Miss Taylor gone?

'How old are your children?'

Helen dragged her mind back.

'Um – four and two.'

'What a lovely age.'

'They'll be back soon. They've gone to a party. I thought we could talk in peace first.'

'I hope you don't mind. Miss Taylor's gone upstairs to find a toilet.'

Helen gave a whimper of horror. 'Oh dear. I hope there's a clean towel up there.' She was just rushing out of one kitchen door when she heard steps on the back stairs.

'Why don't you go and sit in the drawing-room,' she pleaded to Miss Crabtree. 'It's awfully cool in there. I'll bring the tea in.'

'It might help if you put some tea in the pot,' said Miss Crabtree with a jolly laugh, not budging an inch.

Tripping over Action Man and an ancient teddy bear, placed on the stair to be taken up to the nursery, Jake fell into the kitchen. To Helen's amazement, he was carrying a bucket and a J cloth. She gazed at him despairingly.

'All right, Mrs C-B,' he said, putting on a strong cockney accent. 'I've finished. I've done all the upstairs winders, even that little blighter on the top landing. Fort I'd swing to my death.'

'Oh-oh,' Helen mouthed ineffectually. 'Oh, how much is that?'

Jake scratched his head. 'Fifteen pounds,' he said.

'There's a lot of winders.'

Helen got a fiver and a tenner out of the house-keeping pot.

'Here you are. Thank you so much.'

Miss Crabtree, who'd taken matters into her own hands, had made the tea.

'Would you like a cup?' she added to Jake. 'Cleaning windows is an awfully thirsty business, although . . .' her voice trailed off. He didn't seem to have cleaned the downstairs windows at all.

'No, thanks,' said Jake. 'I'll be off.'

'There are quite a few smears here,' said Miss Crabtree bossily.

'Only did the top two floors,' said Jake. 'I leave the bottom to Mrs Bodkin. When do you want me again? In a monf's time?'

Helen nodded, not trusting herself to speak.

'Well, cheerio, then.' Jake nodded to Miss Crabtree.

'I'll see you out,' mumbled Helen.

Quite helpless with laughter, they collapsed outside the back door.

'I'd no idea you were such a good actor,' she said, as he shoved the money back into the pocket of her dress.

Jake kissed her again. 'I'll ring you after the class is finished tonight.'

In the kitchen Miss Crabtree was joined by Miss Taylor.

'What a lovely house. Where's our hostess?'

'Saying goodbye to the window cleaner. They're awfully un-class conscious, aren't they, the Americans? I mean she's just as charming to him as she is to us.'

54

As 'the day of the last Olympic trial at Crittleden approached, Jake grew more and more nervous. Hardy's off days were fewer and Fen had had some good wins on Desdemona. But equally Griselda Hubbard had hit amazing form, and two young short-listed riders, Ralph Naylor and Fiona McFadden, had both jumped brilliantly under pressure at Aachen and several newspapers were agitating for their inclusion in the team. Rupert and Ivor Braine had been so consistent all year, so they were virtually certain of a place.

Fen was terribly down because Joanna Battie had written a bitchy piece headlined: 'Fen – resting on her Laurel,' pointing out that she hadn't had a decent win on Laurel since the previous year at Wembley, and that Desdemona was too small for an Olympic course. Knowing how desperate Fen was to go, Jake felt almost more apprehensive for her than for himself.

Rupert, on the other hand, was irritated because Helen refused to make up her mind whether or not she was going to Los Angeles. She used as an excuse the Los Angeles smog being bad for Marcus' asthma, but in reality she wanted to see if Jake were selected. If he wasn't, she'd stay behind. Rupert, who was trying to persuade Amanda Hamilton to fly out for a few days, wanted a decision one way or the other.

The course for the final trial was unnecessarily huge. There were a number of very unhappy rounds before Jake came in. Griselda was on twelve, Ivor eight. Fen had one stop, because she'd come in too fast, and two elements of the combination down. Everyone was grumbling that the combination was unjumpable. Then Jake rode in and proved them wrong by going clear. Thus encouraged, Rupert, Wishbone and Ludwig went clear. But in the final jump-off, Jake really set Hardy on fire on the long run-up to the last fence to score the fastest time.

'Well done,' said Fen, desperately trying to be enthusiastic. 'You must be picked after that.'

Jake shook his head. He was horribly afraid it wouldn't be good enough. They wanted dependability at the Olympics. The selectors locked themselves away. The riders waited and waited for the promised announcement. After an hour biting their nails, Jake and Fen, who were jumping at Stoneleigh early the following morning, decided to push off. If they were selected they'd hear soon enough. If they weren't it didn't matter anyway.

The jams were terrible. They seemed to get caught up in all the holiday traffic. Nobody talked very much. After an hour's delay on the M4 they decided to cut across country. Bored with tapes, Sarah turned on the lorry radio.

Fen looked miserably out at the great rolling cornfields, deepened to red gold by the rain. When would she ever see Dino again. When would she ever be happy? Idly she listened to the eight o'clock news. Mrs Thatcher, the Prime Minister, would be spending a few days up at Balmoral, staying with the Queen during the summer recess. The Russians had launched another satellite. The unemployed had risen by 20,000 as a result of school leavers.

'The Olympic Show-Jumping Committee tonight announced their team for Los Angeles,' said the announcer.

Everyone stiffened. Fen grabbed Sarah's hand, crossing her fingers on the other. 'Oh, please, please God.'

'The five riders and their horses include: Rupert Campbell-Black and Rock Star, Griselda Hubbard and Mr Punch,' Sarah gave a groan. 'Ivor Braine and John.' The announcer rustled his notes, 'Jake Lovell and Hardy and Fenella Maxwell and Desdemona.'

Giving a whoop of joy, Jake nearly drove off the road.

The car behind them was trying to overtake and hooted furiously.

Speechless, Sarah and Fen hugged each other, then Sarah hugged Jake. Then they all started shouting at the tops of their voices and bellowing. 'California here we come.'

Jake drove to the next village where they found an off-licence and bought a bottle of wine.

'Have one on the house,' said the landlord, putting another bottle in the carrier bag. 'I've just heard it on the radio. Congratulations.'

They pulled up on the edge of a field and drank the Muscadet out of mugs, allowing the horses to graze, and watching the sun set.

'Here's to you,' said Sarah. 'I'm so proud of you both.'

Next moment Fen had stumbled to her feet and was hugging Desdemona.

Jake saw that her shoulders were shaking. He put an arm round her. 'What's the matter?'

'Nothing. I'm just so happy.'

'There's no need to cry then.'

'I'm going to see Dino again.' Half-laughing, half-crying, she rubbed away the tears, streaking her face with grimy hands. 'I expect he's got a million other girlfriends by now, but at least I'll get the chance to say I'm sorry.'

'Missed him that much, have you?'

Fen nodded. 'There's never a moment when I'm not missing him. But you wouldn't understand that, never having been in love.'

After the team announcement Malise wrote to all the five riders, confirming their selection. They would be expected to jump together once more as a team at the Dublin Horse Show, the first week in August, then rest their Olympic horses until they flew them out to Los Angeles at the end of the month.

Leaving Rocky at home to rest, Rupert flew the rest of his Grade A horses over to France for the Deauville and Dinard

Shows, and was due home on Monday night. He had been deeply scathing of the rest of the Olympic team.

'A schoolgirl, a cretin, a riproaring dyke and a crippled gipsy. I'll have to carry the lot of them,' he told Amanda Hamilton.

Nor was he particularly pleased when Helen decided that she would be coming to Los Angeles after all.

Helen sat on the terrace, drinking white wine, breathing in the night-scented stock and reading George Herbert in the fading light:

'Who would have thought my shrivel'd heart
Could have recovered greenness.'

Who indeed? She had never believed, after Kenya, that she would ever be happy again, that she would be totally wiped out by love for Jake, that the only person she wanted to be in the world was the second Mrs Lovell. Not that Jake was showing any inclination to make her so. She knew that he loved her, except in her frequent moments of panic, and with that, until after Los Angeles, she would have to be content.

As Rupert was not due back from Dinard until the next day, and Charlene and the children were away for the night, Jake said he might pop in – but only might – she mustn't expect him. On the eve of departure for Dublin, he was frantically busy loading the lorry. Rupert, taking the easy way, was flying over and letting the grooms do the driving.

Helen hadn't done anything except wash her hair and have a bath earlier. She'd learnt superstition from Jake. If she tarted herself up, he wouldn't make it. Watching a half moon sailing like a moth up the drained blue sky, she gave a cry of joy, for there, clearly visible, moving along the top road towards Penscombe above the honey-coloured stone wall, was Jake's car.

Rushing upstairs to the bedroom, she cleaned her teeth, splashed on cologne and, tugging off her pants, leapt into the bath. Holding up the skirt of the yellow dress, she'd worn the night he'd first made love to her, and which she knew he liked, she hastily showered between her legs, shivering with excitement as the hard jet of water flattened her bush and seeped into her vagina.

Leaving two dusty footprints in the bath, she leapt out and combed her hair. Since Jake had told her he liked her just as much without makeup, she felt secure enough not to bother with that all the time, either. Stretching voluptuously, she went to the window, and then stiffened with horror, for there, as usual coming too fast along the road and only five minutes behind Jake, was Rupert's blue Porsche.

Next minute she heard the crunch of wheels on the gravel and the dogs barking and tore downstairs. Opening the door she collapsed gibbering into Jake's arms.

'What's the matter?'

'Rupert's just behind you. I've seen him on the road. What can we do?'

'Nothing,' said Jake, his brain racing. 'Go and wash that scent off. We have to brazen it out. Pretend I just dropped in.'

'Better come out on to the terrace,' said Helen. 'It's getting dark out there and he won't be able to see how much we're blushing.'

Jake followed her out, running his finger down her spine.

'Anyway, if he finds out, he finds out. He's got to know sometime,' he said. Helen went very still. Turning around, she looked straight into Jake's eyes. 'Has he?' she whispered.

Jake gazed back at her steadily, no shiftiness in his eyes now.

'Yes,' he said. 'You know he has to, sooner or later. It'd just be easier after LA.'

Helen moved towards him. 'Do you really mean that?'

'Yes, I think I always have. I just haven't said it.'

He only had time to hold her briefly before there was a second crunch on the gravel and more barking.

'I can't face him,' said Helen, in sudden panic.

'I'll sort him out. Just get me a drink – Scotch; a

quadruple, and as soon as possible.'

Helen fled to the kitchen, her bare feet making no sound on the carpet.

Bang. Rupert slammed the front door behind him. He was not in a good mood. He'd specially come back to spend the night in London with Amanda and, after two admittedly splendid hours, she'd pushed off to Sussex, saying she had to drive her daughter to some dance.

'Helen,' he shouted, 'Tab, I'm home. Where the hell is everyone?'

Jake waited on the terrace.

'Helen,' Rupert shouted again, more irritably.

'She's in the kitchen,' said Jake.

'Who's that?' Rupert came out onto the terrace, then stopped in his tracks, looking at Jake with slit eyes. His hair was bleached by the French sun, and he was wearing a blue T-shirt, with 'I Love LA' in red letters across the front. Inspiration suddenly came to Jake.

'Beautiful place you've got here,' he said. 'I'd only seen it from the road.'

'There are perfectly good gates at the bottom of the drive. I'm sure you don't need me to show you the way to them,' said Rupert coldly.

'I dropped in,' said Jake, 'on the off-chance you might be back. I got a letter from Malise this week. I decided, as we've both been selected and I want the team gold as much as you do, we'd stand a better chance if we buried the hatchet, at least temporarily.'

He held out his hand.

Rupert, for once at a loss for words, looked down at the hand, which was completely steady. He thought of his own humiliation in the World Championship. He thought of Fen defying him at the Crittleden strike. He thought of Jake in the dormitory at St Augustine's, a terrified little boy, cringing away from the lighted matches. Now, here he was waving white flags and offering peace initiatives.

The hand was still there. Briefly Rupert took it.

'All right. I don't trust you a fucking inch, Gyppo, but for

774

the sake of the team gold we'll suspend hostilities till after the games. Then,' he added smiling, 'I'll smash the hell out of you! We'd better have a drink. Helen,' he yelled.

'Yes,' said Helen faintly.

'She was getting some ice,' said Jake. 'Probably hovering to see if I was to be allowed a drink.'

'You were lucky to catch me. I wasn't planning to come back tonight at all. What d'you want?'

'Scotch, please.'

At that moment Helen came through the door, clutching a tray with one already poured glass of whisky, the whisky decanter, a second empty glass and the ice bucket. She looked at them both with terrified eyes, like a rabbit caught in the headlights, not knowing which way to bolt.

'Hi,' said Rupert. 'We've decided not to kill each other. You've met Helen before, haven't you?'

As Jake took his glass from Helen to stop the frantic rattling, he wondered for a second if Rupert was speaking ironically. Then decided that such was his egotism and contempt for Jake that he couldn't possibly envisage anything between him and Helen. All the same it was a good thing there was *only* Helen's glass, half-full, on the terrace wall.

Jake took a huge gulp of whisky and nearly choked. Christ, it was strong, and thank God for that.

Rupert poured two fingers into his own glass.

'I'm giving up after Dublin,' he said. 'I want a stone off before the games.'

'I can't afford to lose it,' said Jake. 'How was Dinard?'

'Bloody good.'

'And Rocky?'

'Bloody good, too. I keep thinking he's going to jump off the top of the world. I'm scared he's going to peak too early.'

In a daze, Helen poured herself another glass of wine. I cannot believe this, she said to herself. Here are two men, who I know detest each other beyond anything, talking not just politely but with enjoyment. Not by a flicker of an

775

eyelid did Jake betray any nerves or the slightest interest in her, but continued to discuss the team, their weaknesses, the strength of the opposition at the games and which riders they had to watch. He asked Rupert's advice about the LA climate, and possible breathing and fitness problems. After Dublin, Rupert explained, he was flying Rocky straight out to LA to give them both time to get adjusted to the climate. This would certainly give him the edge over the other British riders, who wouldn't be leaving until a fortnight later.

If Rupert's in LA, thought Helen, that'll give Jake and me a safe fortnight. She marvelled at his quick-wittedness. She never dreamed he would use the excuse of coming, to make peace. She was overwhelmed with gratitude that he had averted a scene. She wished she could remember his exact words before Rupert arrived, but she'd been in such a panic. When he said Rupert would have to find out sometime, did he mean that he was going to commit himself to her and leave Tory; or merely that, by the law of misfortune, Rupert would rumble them sooner or later? She felt sure he had meant the former. Watching his face, dark, intense, growing more shadowed as the sun slipped behind the beeches, yet suddenly illumined gold as a chink was found between the leaves, Helen could only read one emotion; passionate interest in what Rupert was saying. Bloody, bloody horses, she thought; will I ever get away from them?

Jake tried to leave after the second drink. He was already slightly tight and, on an empty stomach, might easily make some false move. He glanced at his watch and put his glass down: 'I must go. Sorry to barge in on you like that. Goodbye, and thanks,' he added casually to Helen.

Rupert went to the door with him. A desire to show off overcoming natural antipathy, he said, 'Like to see the yard?'

'O.K.' said Jake, 'Just for two minutes.'

An hour later, Helen heard his car drive away and Rupert came through the front door.

'I'm starving. Shall I go and get a take-away?'

'I want to be taken away,' thought Helen in desolation. She had been so happy when Jake had turned up and now she had no idea when she'd see him again, particularly as he was going to Dublin first thing in the morning.

She couldn't resist discussing him with Rupert.

'Wasn't it amazing his coming here?'

'He was certainly impressed by the set-up,' said Rupert, picking up his car keys. 'Said he'd come to bury the hatchet; bury it in my cranium more likely. Don't trust the bugger an inch. Suspect he came to have a gawp, as much as anything; to see if he could pick up a few tips. Asked me the way back to Warwickshire. Hadn't a clue where he was. I told him the Sapperton way. He was so pissed, with any luck he'll run into a wall. Do you want Chinese or Indian?'

The following Friday, Helen slumped in total despair at the breakfast table, two hands gaining warmth from a cup of black coffee. She had only heard from Jake once since he'd been in Dublin and that was only a two-minute call before someone interrupted him. He said he'd ring back and hadn't. He'd obviously got cold feet.

'Letter for you, Mrs C-B,' said Charlene, handing her a bulky envelope: 'Postmarked Dublin. You'd better watch out it's not a letter bomb.'

Helen was about to tell her not to be nosy, then she recognized Jake's black spiky handwriting. Inside the envelope, was folded a large, dark-blue, silk spotted handkerchief.

'That's lovely, Mrs C-B,' said Charlene. 'Navy goes with everything.'

Helen went white and upended the envelope. There was nothing else inside. The spotted handkerchief – Jake was telling her he wanted her for good.

'She seemed absolutely dazed,' Charlene told Dizzy afterwards.

Then she jumped to her feet laughing.

'I'm going to Dublin,' she said. 'I want to watch – er – my

husband in the Aga Khan Cup.'

The Aga Khan Cup – a splendid Trophy – is presented to
the winning side in the Nations' Cup at the Dublin Horse
Show. All Dublin turns out to watch the event and every
Irish child that's ever ridden a horse dreams of being in the
home team one day. For the British, it was their last chance
to jump as a team before LA. All the riders were edgy;
which of the five would Malise drop? In the end it was
Griselda, who pulled a groin muscle ('shafting some
chambermaid,' said Rupert) but who would be perfectly
recovered in time for LA.

On the Thursday night the British team had been to one
of those legendary horse-show balls. Unchaperoned by
Malise (who was unwisely dining at the British Embassy)
and enjoying the release from tension after being selected,
they got impossibly drunk, particularly Jake, and all ended
up swimming naked in the Liffey. Next day none of them
was sufficiently recovered to work their horses.

Jake, who didn't go to bed at all, spent the following
morning trying to ring Helen from the Press Office. He had
huge difficulty remembering and then dialling her number.
A strange bleating tone continually greeted him. Dragging
Wishbone to the telephone, he asked, 'Is that the engaged
or the out-of-order signal over here?'

'Sure,' said Wishbone soothingly, ' 'tis somewhere between the two.'

'Christ,' yelled Jake, then clutched his head as it nearly
exploded with pain.

Half of him was desperate to talk to Helen and find out
how she'd reacted to the blue spotted handkerchief he'd
sent off to her the other day, when he was plastered. The
other half was demented with panic at what he might have
triggered off. None of the telephones seemed to work.
Wishbone, who was talking to a man in a loud check suit,
who seemed to know every horse in the show, bought Jake
another drink.

'Drink is a terrible dirty ting,' he said happily, 'but the

only answer is to drink more of it.'

Jake looked at his watch and wondered if he'd ever totter as far as the ring.

'We'd better go and walk the course,' he urged Wishbone. 'We'll be very late.'

'Stop worrying,' said Wishbone. 'We haven't got a course yet,' He jerked his head towards the man in the loud check suit, who was busy buying yet another round. 'He's the course builder.'

All in all the British put up a disgraceful performance. A green-faced tottering bunch, they staggered shakily from fence to fence, holding on to rather than checking the spreads, wincing in the blinding sunshine, to the intense glee of the merry Irish crowd, who had seen visiting teams sabotaged before.

Ivor fell off at the first and third fences, and then exceeded the time limit. Fen knocked every fence down. Rupert managed to get Rocky round with only twenty faults, his worst performance ever.

Jake, waiting to go in by the little white church, was well aware, as Hardy plunged underneath him, that the horse knew how fragile he felt.

'For Christ's sake, get around,' said Malise, who was looking extremely tight-lipped, 'or we'll be eliminated from the competition altogether.'

Suddenly Jake looked up at the elite riders' stand, which is known in Dublin as the Pocket. He felt his heart lurch, for there, smiling and radiant, was Helen. She was wearing a white suit, and her hair, which she'd been in too much of a hurry to wash, was tied back by a blue silk spotted handkerchief. His challenge had been taken up.

'Oh, good, Helen's come after all,' said Malise, sounding very pleased and beetling off to the Pocket. 'Good luck,' he called over his shoulder to Jake.

Concentration thrown to the winds, Jake rode into the ring. Somehow he managed to take off his hat to the judges and start cantering when the bell went, but that effort was too much for him. Hardy put in a terrific stop at the first fence and Jake went sailing through the air. The next moment Hardy had wriggled out of his bridle and was cavorting joyously round the ring until he'd exceeded the time limit.

Jake just sat on the ground, sobbing with helpless laughter. When he finally limped out of the ring Malise was looking like a thundercloud.

'There is absolutely nothing to laugh about.'

'You don't think he'll unselect us?' said Fen, in terror.

Jake shook his head, then winced. But all he could say to himself joyfully over and over again was, 'She's here and she's wearing the handkerchief.'

The Irish won the Aga Khan Cup.

'There's absoutely no point in talking to any of you,' said Malise, furiously. 'But I want everyone, grooms, wives, hangers-on included, to come to my room at nine o'clock tomorrow. If any of you don't show up, you're out.'

The only answer seemed to be to go on to another, even more riotous ball, where reaction inevitably set in.

'The hair of the dog is doing absolutely nothing to cure my hangover,' Fen grumbled to Ivor, as he trod on her toes round the dance floor. 'Really, if Rupert doesn't get his hand out of the back of that girl's dress soon, he'll be tickling the soles of her feet.'

The music came to an end.

'I'm going to bed.'

'Don't,' said Ivor. 'I'll have no one to dance with.'

'Go and talk to Griselda,' said Fen, kissing him on the forehead. She couldn't cope with the frenzied merriness. Nights like this made her longing for Dino worse than ever. She drifted rather unsteadily across the ballroom and out through one of the side doors, looking for Jake to say goodnight. A couple of Irishmen called out to her, trying to persuade her to come and dance, then decided not. There was something about Fen's frozen face these days that kept men at a distance, the way Helen's used to.

She wandered down a passage and into a dimly lit library, which was empty except for one couple. They were standing under a picture light, talking in that intense, still way of people who are totally absorbed in one another. They were about the same height. Fen's blood ran cold. She must be seeing things.

The man was comforting the girl.

'Be patient, please, pet.'

'It was a crazy idea to come,' she said in a low voice. 'I can't bear not being able to be with you all the time or to go to bed without you tonight.'

The man was stroking her face now, drawing her close to him. 'Sweetheart, just let me get Los Angeles over, and then we'll make plans, I promise.'

'You really promise?'

'I promise. You know I love you. You've got the handkerchief.' He bent his head and kissed her.

Fen gave a whimper and fled. Forgetting her coat, she ran out of the building and through the streets, desperate to escape to her hotel room. Helen and Jake – it couldn't be true. That explained why he'd been so differently recently. Remote and unsociable one moment, then wildly and uncharacteristically manic the next, and terribly absent-minded. He'd hardly have minded if she'd fed Desdemona caviar.

Fen had always hero-worshipped Jake and regarded his marriage to Tory as the one safe, good constant she could cling on to and perhaps one day emulate. Now her whole world seemed to be crumbling. What about Tory? What about Isa and Darklis? And more to the point, what the hell was Rupert going to do when he found out? Nothing short of murder.

55

Everyone, albeit a little pale and shaking, was on parade for Malise's meeting next morning. No one was was asked to sit down. Malise, immaculate as usual, in an olive-green tweed coat and cavalry club tie, glared at them as though they were a lot of schoolboys caught smoking behind the pavilion. Yesterday's blaze of temper had given way to a cold anger.

'At least we can go to the games knowing we haven't peaked yet,' he said. 'I have never seen such an appalling demonstration. You rode like a bunch of fairies. I doubt if any of you had more than an hour's sleep beforehand. You've made complete idiots of the selection committee.'

'Three days in the glasshouse,' muttered Rupert.

'And you can shut up,' snapped Malise. 'Your round, bearing in mind the horse you were riding, was the worst of the lot. They say a lousy dress rehearsal means a good first night, but this is ridiculous.'

Then he smiled slightly, and Fen suddenly thought what a fantastically attractive man he was for his age.

'Now,' he said, 'if you can find somewhere comfortable to park yourselves, I'll show you some clips from earlier Olympics.'

Refusing a seat, Jake lounged against the door so he could look at Helen, who was sitting in one of the chairs, with Dizzy perched on the arm. She was pale and heavy-eyed, with her red hair drawn off her face and tied at the nape of the neck by the blue spotted handkerchief. To Jake, she had never looked more beautiful. He felt simply flattened by love. He could hardly concentrate on the clips of straining javelin throwers, and sprinters crashing through the tape, and muddy three-day-eventers, and Anne Moore getting her silver.

Malise switched off the video machine.

'I don't think I need to tell you much else. If you do get a medal, particularly a gold, it will be the greatest moment of you life, make no mistake about that. And if you don't get that medal because you were not quite good enough on the day, or because your horse wasn't fit, or because your nerves got to you, that's all well and good. But if you can look back afterwards and say, I failed because I drank too much, or didn't train or stayed up too late or didn't work my horse diligently enough, you'll regret it for the rest of your life.'

'He might be echoing Jake,' Helen said to herself.

He looked round at the five riders. 'You're probably the oldest Olympic squad we've ever fielded, except for Fen, which means we can offer a wealth of experience; but the heat may get to you. It also means this may well be your last chance of a crack at the Olympics.'

He turned to the grooms and to Helen and to Griselda's rather mild father, who was sharing the arm of a chair with Ivor's mother. 'I'd like to say the same to the families and grooms and wives for the next month. Try to be totally unselfish. You will find the riders tricky, irascible and demanding. As the competition gets nearer, this may take the form of increasing detachment as they try to distance themselves. This you must put up with. They need to keep calm, for in this way the horses will stay calm. Don't make unnecessary demands. Wives and families, if they're not coming to LA, shouldn't expect regular telephone calls. Times are cockeyed. Security will often make it difficult to get to a telephone.'

Malise looked over to Jake.

'I'm sorry Tory's not here,' he said with a smile, 'but she's the one person I know who doesn't need to hear any of this. She's always given you exemplary back-up.'

Helen bit her lip. She felt an agonizing stab of jealousy.

She must try not to hassle Jake.

'All right, that's all,' said Malise briskly, 'except I want to come home with two golds.'

Having redeemed himself and his country by winning the Grand Prix on Saturday night, Rupert flew Rocky direct to Los Angeles the following day, which would give them both nearly a month to get used to the climate.

A fortnight later, he flew back to England on the excuse of having his Olympic uniform fitted and sorting out business matters, but in reality to see Amanda Hamilton. He was meeting her at her house in Kensington. This he regarded as a major breakthrough and also that he'd been able to drag her down from Scotland in the middle of August, when she should be making shooting lunches for Rollo and entertaining his cabinet colleagues.

As he drove past pavements pastel with tourists and looked at the expanse of female leg and the briefness of skirts and shorts, Rupert reflected how strange it was that his sexual energies had become almost entirely concentrated on Amanda. The fact that she often didn't bother to dress up or wash her hair or put on make-up when she saw him, only increased his interest. As did the fact that she was always busy with her children or her committees or Rollo's career and had very little spare time for him. He'd had to fight every inch of the way. Used to girls who were only too available, who were always bathed and scented and dolled up to the nth degree and quivering with anticipation, Rupert found her an amazing novelty. They knew all the same people and were governed by the same rules. She was also the first woman he couldn't bully.

The house in Rutland Gate was burglar-alarmed up to the eyeballs. Amanda's excuse to Rollo had been Great Aunt Augusta's eightieth birthday party, which had taken place at lunchtime. Amanda would spend the night in London and fly north next morning.

It was always a good idea, she explained to Rollo, to pop in on the servants unexpectedly and keep them on their toes.

The servants, a Filipino couple, who'd left a member of the Royal family because there had been too many riding boots to clean, were very put out at Mrs Hamilton's arrival. They'd planned to have a party in the basement that night, but were slightly appeased when Amanda told them to carry on and that she wouldn't be needing dinner.

After dining in Barnes, which was safe, according to Amanda, because 'one never saw anyone one knew in the suburbs', and which didn't take long because Rupert wasn't drinking, they crept into the house unnoticed. Downstairs, the party was in full swing.

'Will Rollo have me for breaking and entering?' said Rupert, removing his tie.

Amanda didn't laugh. 'You know he can't afford any scandal,' she said, putting her diamond earrings in her jewel case. 'Is Helen flying back to LA with you next week?'

'Yes', said Rupert. 'I think she must have been to some marriage guidance counsellor, who's told her to take an interest in my career.'

'Good,' said Amanda, feeling the earth of the plants by the window.

'Why do servants never understand about watering?'

'Why "good"?' snapped Rupert from inside his shirt.

'You don't want a messy divorce at the moment. You'll go down much better with the party if you have a beautiful and adoring wife.'

'I go down brilliantly anyway,' said Rupert, leaping on her.

'It does seem rather awful doing it in Rollo's bed.'

'Not nearly as awful as not doing it.'

Afterwards, she lay in Rupert's arms thinking but not telling him how lovely it was to have a whole night together. Against her better judgement she was becoming increasingly fond of him. Rupert was spoilt and perfectly disgraceful, but he made her laugh and then of course he was terribly attractive.

'If you get a gold, will you retire?'

'Nail my whip to the wall you mean? I might. I can't go on riding horses for ever.'

'What are you going to do about Helen? I really do mean it. You don't want a divorce if you're going into politics.'

'As long as I can have the dogs and Tab and the house, I wouldn't mind. Helen can have Marcus and the first editions and the Van Dyck.'

'Will you promise to think seriously about politics after LA?' urged Amanda. 'The PM was very charmed by you. If Sir William goes to the Common Market there should be a safe seat in Gloucestershire in the Autumn. You can't play around forever. An ageing playboy is a pathetic sight,' she went on, lying back on the pillow. 'Gradually he starts drifting down to girls who are less pretty, and instead of making them on the first night it takes three nights, or they decide after one night they don't like him. You're thirty-one now.'

'And you think that's going to be my fate?' said Rupert, coldly.

Amanda Hamilton looked at the beautiful, depraved face and the marvellously lean, muscular, suntanned body, and her face softened.

'No, not for a long time, but I don't think an unhappy marriage, coupled with an intellectually undemanding career, are doing you any good.'

Rupert took her face between his hands. 'I suppose you'd never think of divorcing Rollo? You and I'd be marvellous together.'

Amanda blushed. 'I'm far too old for you and there's Rollo's career and anyway we've got four children to educate. They'll probably all go on to a university.'

'I'll educate your children,' said Rupert. He glanced at the silver-framed photograph on the mantelpiece of Amanda's eldest daughter, Georgina, and was about to say he wouldn't mind teaching her the facts of life at all, then thought better of it. Amanda didn't like those kinds of jokes.

By now, Rupert wanted her again and, getting out of bed, prowled the room looking for novelty. He could take her sitting in that pink, buttonback chair, then his eye lit on the huge mirror over the mantelpiece.

'What are you doing?' asked Amanda. 'That looking-glass is 17th century. It was a wedding present from Rollo's grandmother. Been in his family for years.'

'I want to see us,' said Rupert, gasping under the huge weight of the mirror. He balanced it on the padded arms of the chair, which he'd pulled alongside the bed.

'Can you see yourself now?' he asked Amanda.

'Not a thing.'

'I'll tip it forward a bit.' Rupert piled up pale blue and lilac silk cushions behind the mirror.

'For God's sake, be careful,' said Amanda, but she was diverted by what she saw.

The old glass was very flattering and gave a dusky warmth to her body and a golden glow to her face. She liked the way her breasts fell and the lovely curve of her waist into her hips.

'Christ, that's marvellous,' said Rupert, getting on to the bed behind her. He was so dark-tanned it was almost like going to bed with a black man. Fascinated, she watched his long fingers stroking her belly, then sliding into the dark bush.

'Look how beautiful you are,' he said softly, spreading back the butterfly wings of her labia. Next moment he had lifted her buttocks and driven his cock into the warm, sticky cave of her vagina.

Amanda gasped.

'Nice, isn't it?'

Now he was lifting her right leg, holding back the inside of her thigh so she could see the long length of his cock driving into her. It was like an express train going into a tunnel.

Madly excited, Amanda bucked back against him, feeling his fingers stroking her faster and faster.

'Come on, darling, come on.'

As they both came they were aware of a mighty crash. Amanda gave a shriek as, lurching forward, the mirror hit the wooden handles of the chair and crashed to the ground in a thousand pieces.

'Now see what you've done,' she said furiously. 'Rollo will murder me.'

Next minute she heard voices. Drunken, excited Filipinos were storming up the stairs.

'Move the chair back and get into the bathroom,' snapped Amanda, sliding into her nightie.

'All right, Conceptione,' Rupert heard her saying. 'I'm afraid the mirror fell off the wall – the string must have rotted.' Hastily, she shoved Rupert's glass of coke behind a cache-pot. 'Bring me a Hoover. No, I'll clear it up. I'm fine. You go back to your party.'

Three minutes later Rupert heard the noise of the Hoover. Still pushing it around the floor, Amanda opened the door to the bathroom. 'You can come out now.'

Rupert could tell she was absolutely livid.

'I'll pay for it,' he said.

'The money doesn't matter,' she wailed. 'Think of the seven years' bad luck. Think of Georgie's O levels and the next election.'

Rupert looked out through the lift-gate bars on the window at the yellowing grass of Kensington Gardens.

'What about my gold?' he thought broodingly.

As soon as Jake returned from Dublin, Olympic panic set in. The telephone never stopped ringing with officials, press, horsiana manufacturers and potential sponsors, who'd heard he and Fen might go professional after the games.

Because they were not rich like Rupert, they had to keep taking the rest of the horses to shows right up to the last moment. In between, there were endless medical tests for both horses and riders, and Jake and Fen had to rush up to London to get their Olympic uniform fitted, then on to Moss Bros. to choose coats and breeches.

Fen was livid she wasn't allowed to wear a dark blue coat. 'Black's so hard,' she grumbled. 'Anyway, I'm not going to a funeral.'

'You may well think you are,' said Jake, 'when you see the size of the fences.'

Jake was so ludicrously busy he had no time to see Helen, which, despite Malise's strictures, drove her so frantic she even rang him at the yard.

'It's me, darling. Why haven't you called? Pretend this is a wrong number and call me back as soon as you've got a moment.'

It was almost a relief when she and Rupert flew off to Los Angeles, giving him a breathing space in which he could concentrate on the job in hand. But if he worked flat out during the day, he still spent his few hours in bed worrying about the future.

Their finances were still in a precarious position. The bank manager needed the Mill House and the yard and Tory's shares as security. He was very proud of Jake and his incredible come-back and often dropped his name at the golf club, but Jake knew this amiability would vanish overnight if he got into financial trouble.

Now he had been picked for the Olympics he was an infinitely more bankable proposition, particularly as half a dozen potential sponsors were pestering him. But he didn't like any of them and he knew they'd cool off if he came home without a medal. Anyway, he'd seen the appalling pressures sponsors had put on Billy, Humpty and Driffield – having to take days off to open factories and turn up at parties and chat up important clients before a big class. Jake knew he didn't have the easy kind of charm or placid temperament to cope with such an invasion of his privacy. He was terrified of no longer being his own boss. It would be back to Brook Farm Riding School and Mrs Wilton. If the sponsors owned the horses they might take them away, as Colonel Carter had taken Revenge.

More than anything he wanted to get a gold and beat Rupert. But now just as much, he wanted Helen, her cool slender body and the extraordinary white-hot passion he inspired in her. When he was with the horses or the family he could switch off and forget about her. But at night the pain of longing came back more intensely than ever.

But, how the hell could he support two households? If Helen ran off with him, Rupert would see she was left penniless. Even if she got a writing job she'd have to employ someone to look after the children (if Rupert let the children go, which was unlikely). And if Jake walked out on Tory he would lose the children, Fen and the Mill House, not to mention Tory and her incredible back-up. He'd have to find another owner. And how would he divide the horses? Would he get Macaulay's front half, Tory the back, like a pantomime horse?

Finally, Helen worried him. She said she was prepared to live on nothing, but she'd had six years with Rupert, with daily women to clean her beautiful house, nannies for the children, and gardeners to tend those exquisite flower beds, not to mention champagne and flowers at every four-star hotel she stayed at. How would she cope with poverty? She had compared herself with a pot plant, wilting unwatered in a greenhouse, while the rain fell on the sweet earth outside. But equally, how would a pot plant fare when faced with the winds and snows of the outside world?

He had tried to discuss this with Helen, but she was so insecure she always misconstrued this as backing off. None of this had he thought through when, tanked up with champagne, he had posted her the blue silk handkerchief from Dublin.

On the day before he left for Los Angeles, as if in answer to a prayer, he had a telephone call from Garfield Boyson, who owned a huge video empire. Boyson was amiable, intensely tough, a lifetime lover of horses and rich enough not to be worried about money.

'I'm driving through your village at lunchtime,' said his crackling voice from a car telephone. 'How about a drink?'

'Too busy,' said Jake: 'We're leaving tomorrow.'

'You'll not be too busy for this,' said Boyson. 'See you at the Stirrup Cup in half an hour.'

Sloping off to take leave of Mrs C-B, thought Fen sourly, as Jake disappeared without explanation. Village boys stopped to admire Boyson's gleaming Rolls-Royce, his chauffeur nodding in the late August sunshine. Inside the bar a bench seat was tightly clamped round Boyson's vast bulk. As he downed a treble whisky and clawed up potato crisps, his eyes, almost entirely hidden by rolls of flesh, were shrewd and kindly.

'Hullo lad, what'd you like?'

'Tomato juice. I'm working,' said Jake pointedly. He lit a cigarette.

'You should give up that habit,' said Boyson. 'LA's lousy for people with bad chests.'

'So I've been told.'

'Worcester sauce?' asked the barmaid. 'Oh it's you, Jake. Didn't see you come in. How's it going?'

'Spare,' said Jake.

The barmaid looked at the wall where was proudly hung one of Macaulay's World Championship rosettes.

'Hope we get one from Los Angeles to join it,' she said.

Jake turned to Boyson. 'Well I'm sure you didn't ask me here to tell me to give up smoking.'

Boyson laughed fatly. 'I didn't. Sit down, lad. I've watched your career for some time. Admired your guts, the way you fought back. Admire that sparky sister-in-law of yours.'

'Men tend to.' Unsmiling, Jake looked at his watch.

'Rupert's right about you,' said Boyson. 'Said you were as short on charm as you were on inches.'

'Thanks,' said Jake, draining his glass and getting to his feet.

'Sit down,' said Boyson, waving a fat ringed hand. 'One thing I don't want is a PR man. I'll not ask you to chat up customers and open shops. Just like to make things easier.'

'What d'you get out of it?'

'Well, not to pussyfoot around. My name in front of your horses. Boyson Macaulay. Boyson Hardy. Doesn't sound bad.'

'No!' said Jake.

'Wait a minute. For that I'd pick up your bills and your travelling expenses and give you a new lorry with my name on it. Noticed yours was falling to pieces at Crittleden. I'd even buy you some horses.'

'And when we start losing?'

'We'll draw up a watertight three-year contract. All riders lose form, so do horses. I know all that. But you've always worked with second-class horses, making them into top-class ones. I'd like to see what you could do with a horse like Rocky or Clara.'

Boyson had ordered more drinks, exchanging Jake's tomato juice for a large whisky. Jake drained it without noticing.

'You'd start ordering me about, expecting me to ride your way.'

'I wouldn't. I might argue with you occasionally, but you'd be the boss. I don't expect you to tell me how to run my company.'

'What sort of terms were you thinking about?'

'About 75 grand a year, and extra of course for the box and any horses.'

Jake's brain reeled. This was really the big time, he thought excitedly, although his face didn't flicker.

'Not much for horses.'

'Might be more – if you'd agree to another thing.'

'What?'

'I've got a lad of fifteen; nice boy, but I didn't marry his mother, if you know what I mean.'

'Only too well. I had the same problem.'

'I know. That's one of the reasons I thought you and I might get on. He's crazy about horses, wanted to be a flat race jockey, but he's grown too big. You could do with a third jockey in your yard, take the pressure off. He's a good lad; admires you no end; got your picture on his wall; says you're the only rider worth bothering about.'

'What if he's no good?'

'He is,' said Boyson. 'Believe me. His mother died

recently. He needs a family.'

'I'll think about it,' said Jake.

'Go to Los Angeles first. I know you've had a lot of expenses. The yard'll be virtually out of action for a month. Horses may take time to get their form back, so don't worry your head about how you're going to pay for it all. Come home with a medal and we're in business.'

'And if I don't?'

'We'll have to think again.'

'I don't like bribery, Mr Boyson.'

'Garfield to you, and I don't like failures.'

'Why don't you sponsor Rupert then?'

'Because he hasn't kept his nose clean – too many scandals; can't understand it with that beautiful wife.'

'And I'm squeaky clean,' said Jake, getting up.

'Well, at least you're discreet,' said Boyson. 'I haven't been able to find anything on you.'

They left England on a perfect day. Tory was helping Fen with her packing upstairs. Jake was in the kitchen checking papers. Sarah had left from Stansted airport with Hardy and Desdemona two days before. The horses would be out of quarantine and into their Olympic quarters by the time Jake and Fen arrived.

Tory, going down to the kitchen, found Wolf on the stairs, swallowing miserably, knowing he wasn't included.

'Nor am I, darling,' she said, stroking his rough brindle head. 'We'll have to look after each other.'

Jake looked out of the window at the soft russet stables. The willows round the mill-pond were already touched with yellow, and the mill stream dried to a trickle. Last night he'd watched a rippling arrow of migrating wild geese spread out across the sky. Now the house martins were taking up their positions on the telegraph wire.

'Look at those birds all in a row,' said Darklis. 'What are they doing?'

'They're practising leaving,' said Jake.

Perhaps that's what he ought to be doing. The martins

would be gone by the time he came home. With an aching feeling of sadness and anticipated homesickness, he gazed at his tawny fields and his stables, with the horses looking out of the half-doors, all knowing something was up; apart from Macaulay, who had turned away, sulking.

If only he could have afforded to take Tory and the children. If he accepted Boyson's sponsorship he'd be able to do things like that. Tory wouldn't have to work herself into the ground; she and the kids could have new clothes. Then in his pocket he felt the tansy that Helen had had specially made for him in gold – for luck. He'd given Helen the handkerchief; there was no way he could go back now.

Tory came into the kitchen.

'Fen's ready. You ought to be off soon,' she said. 'I wish you'd have some lunch. I've made you a quiche, and some sandwiches for the journey. I splurged and put smoked salmon in them.'

He shook his head, half-smiling. 'We get dinner at the hotel tonight.' They were flying at crack of dawn tomorrow. He turned to Darklis. 'Go and tell Fen we're leaving in ten minutes.'

As soon as she'd gone, he drew Tory close to him, cradling her round, tired, kind, unmade-up face between his hands, smoothing back the lank mousebrown hair she'd had no time to wash.

'Don't,' she mumbled into his shoulder. 'I look so awful. I'm going on a crash diet. I'll be thin when you come home.'

He put his arms round her, feeling her comforting solidity.

'I won't expect you to ring,' she said in a not quite steady voice. 'Malise has told me what lines from LA are going to be like. Just ring if you can, but we'll all be thinking of you.'

For a second they clung together. Suddenly he wished she was his mother, wise and everloving, that he could always come back to, even though he was committing himself to Helen. With an uneasy premonition, he thought this might be the last time he saw her.

'Wish you were coming.'

794

'I wish I was, too. Take me next time.'

'I love you,' he said truthfully and for the first time. He'd just have to sort everything out after the games.

As they went out into the yard he saw she was crying. To distract him she said, 'You must go and say goodbye to Macaulay.'

Macaulay had his back to the door. As Jake approached he flattened his ears. Jake went into the box. 'I'm sorry, boy, – I know how you feel. I'm as disappointed as you are.'

56

'We'll be landing in twenty minutes,' said the air hostess. 'Can I have eight autographs for the crew?'

Fen fled to the loo, desperately tarting up, in case, by some miracle, Dino had come to meet her at the airport. When she came back they were still flying across the desert and Ivor was still struggling with the quick crossword in the *Daily Mirror*, which he'd started the moment they left Heathrow. Jake seemed increasingly uptight. Perhaps he was wondering if Helen would meet them.

Suddenly there was Los Angeles and Fen's tiredness seemed to disappear as she looked down at the great turquoise expanse of ocean and the platinum blond beaches. She could even see the flecking of the breakers. Now they were flying over a vast checkerboard of streets, houses, gardens and brilliant blue swimming pools, and skyscrapers glittering in the midday sun, and the great network of freeways superimposed like arteries. The horizon was bordered by a thick, muzzy, browny-grey smog curtain.

Jake fingered his gold tansy, trying to keep his nerves in check. This is Dino's country, thought Fen in ecstasy. I've finally made it.

'I can see Robert Redford and Donald Duck,' she cried, leaning across Ivor.

'Where, where?' he said, gazing out of the window.

'Go back to your crossword,' she said soothingly. 'You might even finish it by the time we get through customs.'

As they stepped off the plane the heat from the scorching Californian sun hit them like a knock-out punch.

'We'll be microwaved,' moaned Fen.

'We'll never jump in this,' said Jake to himself.

Customs seemed to take longer than the flight. Waiting for them outside, wearing nothing but sneakers, jagged denim shorts and a baseball cap was Rupert. He was so brown he almost made the black ground staff look white.

'Welcome to LA,' he said mockingly. 'As part of Malise's new solidarity drive, and because Big Mal himself is in a meeting, I've come to welcome you all. Security is a nightmare.'

'Did the horses travel all right?' asked Jake.

'Eventually. The crates didn't fit, and they had to wait for hours to load, and the flight took thirty-three hours.' Then, seeing Jake's look of utter horror, he went on, 'But they're all fine and out of quarantine. Hardy's already bitten Malise, so he must be feeling O.K.'

'Can we go straight to the stables?'

Rupert looked surprised. 'If you feel up to it.'

Fen sometimes wished Jake wasn't quite so conscientious. She was dying for a bath and a change, in case she bumped into Dino.

As they drove along in the car Rupert had hired, not a breath of wind stirred the palm trees as they flashed past.

'Is this the roosh hour?' asked Ivor nervously.

'This is nothing,' said Rupert briskly, passing a Cadillac on the inside, then nipping outside a Pontiac. 'Once you've negotiated the rush hour, the individual competition will seem like falling off a log.'

'How far are the stables from the Olympic village?' asked Jake.

'Well that's another slight problem,' said Rupert. 'About ninety minutes drive on the Olympic bus.'

'Shit,' said Jake, exchanging looks of horror with Fen.

'I'm lucky,' said Rupert, not without a certain complacency. 'Helen and I are staying with chums in Arcadia, so I'm only five minutes from the show ground.'

'Nice house?' asked Fen, aware that Jake was beginning to look really fed up.

'Terribly quiet,' said Rupert, blithely. 'Only thing you can hear at night is the occasional splash as an overripe avocado pear falls into the swimming pool.'

No one could fault the stables. They were huge and airy, with push-button doors, air conditioning in the boxes, and water playing on the roofs all day to keep the temperature at 65 degrees. They were also banned to the press. The grooms slept in dormitories overhead.

Sarah, who'd dyed her hair red, white and blue, was thrilled to see them. 'The talent is fantastic,' she said to Fen. 'I've just been asked out by a Mexican rider named Jesus.'

Desdemona was even more delighted to see Fen. She looked so small in the huge box. As she cuddled her and checked her for bumps and bruises, Fen, trying to keep her voice steady, asked,

'Has the American team arrived yet?'

'Mary-Jo and Lizzie Dean arrived this morning. But Carol Kennedy and Mr Ferranti,' Sarah winked at Dizzy, who was looking over the half-door, 'aren't due until tomorrow night.'

'Hi, Fen,' said Dizzy. 'Evidently Dino's swept all before him this year. Manny hasn't had a fence down in three months. He's hot favourite for the Individual Gold.'

'So eat your heart out, Mr Campbell-Black,' said Sarah.

'Don't be unpatriotic, dear,' said Dizzy.

Both of them had already acquired golden suntans. Dizzy was wearing Union Jack shorts. They made Fen feel drabber and tireder than ever. At that moment Malise rolled up, svelte as usual in a cream suit and a panama with an old Rugbeian hat-band.

'You've made it. Don't hang about here too long. You need some sleep. When you're ready I'll take you back to the Olympic village and we'll sort out your security chains. Better sleep in them. After tomorrow you won't be allowed anywhere without them.'

After an hour and a half's drive back to the Olympic village in a non-airconditioned bus, which just dumped

798

them outside the male and female sectors, Jake could see exactly why Rupert had found a house in Arcadia. Having been issued with his security chain, which contained his name, a photograph, nationality, and the classes for which he was entered, he had to fight his way through the tightest security cordon. It took ages to find his room, as the guards on each floor all had to check where he was going. Finally tracking it down, he discovered he was sharing not with Ivor but with two weightlifters, who were fortunately out on the town. Apart from three beds, the room included three small chests of drawers, a wardrobe, a shower, a gas ring and a fridge. He supposed they daren't provide an oven in case someone put his head in it.

He was pouring with sweat, but it wasn't just the heat. Looking outside, he was suddenly aware of the number of security vans prowling around between the scorched yellow lawns with their sprinkling of palm trees, and the helicopters and aeroplanes overhead, all part of the largest security operation ever mounted in peacetime.

The tough guys on the gate, with their guns and their German accents, the bare institutional corridors, the guards seated on every floor, the smell of fear, the anonymity, all unnerved him, and reminded him of the children's home.

Overwhelmed with homesickness and claustrophobia he started to unpack. Underneath the beautifully ironed shirts and his new red coat, he found a pile of telegrams and good luck cards he hadn't seen. There was also a letter from Tory.

'Darling, I'm missing you almost before you've gone. When you get this, you'll be in LA on the way to the greatest adventure of your life. Please don't be scared, and *please* eat properly. Don't worry, remember you're still the World Champion and the greatest rider in the world. Give a kiss to Hardy. The presents are from the children. All my love, Tory.'

One parcel contained a black china cat with a horseshoe around its neck. The other a toothbrush which had a glass bubble on the end containing a tiny model of Mickey Mouse, and a bell which rang when you cleaned your teeth.

One of the telegrams was from Garfield Boyson, another from Eleanor Blenkinsop. Feeling much happier, Jake undressed, showered and fell into his first dreamless sleep in weeks.

'It's too awful,' grumbled Fen the next morning. 'I'm sharing with Griselda and an enormous lady discus thrower of very questionable sexuality who snored all night. The corridors are swarming with security guards. I could do with one in the room for protection, except there isn't room for the three of us as it is. Griselda is already making eyes at a beefy cyclist in the next room, and on the other side there are three event riders who keep saying "Must go and ring Mummy." ' She giggled. Nothing really mattered today except that she would see Dino.

They were cheered up by more telegrams downstairs, although Jake was slightly daunted to find three long, rather hysterical letters from Helen, saying how much she was missing him, and would he make contact as soon as possible. Then they explored the Olympic village. Jake was appalled by the sheer noise and size. There were sports shops, hairdressers, cinemas and theatres, saunas, swimming pools, even a disco, and endless souvenir shops and televisions everywhere. He'd expected a kind of monastic retreat. It was going to be about as easy to distance oneself here as in a monkey house.

Fen was almost more appalled in the souvenir shop to see posters of Dino on sale. In one he had a terrific suntan, looked too ludicrously glamorous for words and was wearing a pale grey shirt. In another he was jumping Manny, wearing the US red coat with the sky blue collar. In horror she watched two American girl gymnasts buy copies of both.

'Look,' said Jake to distract her, 'there's Sebastian Coe.'

'And there's Daley Thompson,' said Fen, in awe.

Then they went to a meeting called by Malise. The plan, he said, was that from tomorrow the team would rise at four in the morning, drive down to the stables and work the horses from six to eight, then leave them to rest during the punishing midday heat. Then the grooms would walk them around to loosen them up for an hour or so in the cool of the evening. During the day the riders' time would be more or less their own, except for the odd meeting or press conference. Beach barbecues, endless parties, trips to Disneyland, Hollywood or Las Vegas were also on offer. Malise wanted them to relax, enjoy themselves, stick together and save the adrenalin for the competitions. It was now Saturday. The opening ceremony was on Sunday, the individual competition a week on Monday and the team event the Sunday after that.

That evening, Malise continued, the Eriksons, with whom Rupert and Helen were staying in Arcadia, had invited the British and the American teams to a barbecue at their house. This information threw both Fen and Jake into a panic. Jake was longing to see Helen, but he didn't want a hassle. Dublin had been a nightmare, worrying all the time whether Rupert suspected anything. He didn't want Los Angeles to be a repeat.

Fen, having showered about fifty times, couldn't put on her make-up. She was shaking so much her eyeliner kept leaving her eyelashes and shooting up the lid. She totally gave up on lipstick. She wore new, baggy, pink-striped Andy Pandy dungarees and a pale pink T-shirt.

Griselda, who was exchanging even hotter glances with the next-door cyclist, cried off the evening, saying she was still jet-lagged. Luckily, after two more stints on the non-air-conditioned bus, Malise had hired a car to drive the team about. As the Eriksons' house was only five minutes from the stables, they decided to check the horses on the way to the barbecue. Shadows of palm trees were beginning to stripe the road, but it was still punishingly hot. Even Desdemona seemed listless.

'Probably still suffering from travel sickness,' said Malise, reassuringly.

Perhaps Dino would be suffering from jet-lag too,

thought Fen, and wouldn't feel like a party. But next minute she saw Carol Kennedy going past in dark glasses, so Dino must at least have arrived. Frantically she checked her face in the depths of Desdemona's box.

Outside, she met Rupert, who pulled out the front of her voluminous dungarees, peered inside and asked if she was 'reduced to wearing Tory's cast-offs,' which did nothing to increase her self-confidence.

'Come on,' he said. 'Malise is champing for the off. Not that he'll get any dinner before midnight, Suzy Erikson is so disorganized.'

As they reached Malise's hired car, Fen said,

'There's Mary-Jo.'

Mary-Jo was wearing a white T-shirt with 'Carol Kennedy for President' printed in large blue letters across the front. 'Wait,' she called out to them. Close up she looked red-eyed and distraught.

'My dear child,' said Malise concerned. 'What's the matter?'

'It's Dino,' she sobbed.

'What's happened to him?' said Fen, in horror.

'Manny went ape on the plane. They think he may have been stung by something. It was Dino's plane. He was driving it. He wanted to crash land in the desert, but he was transporting Carol's horses as well and there was the chance he might have killed the lot of them, the terrain was so rocky, so he had to shoot Manny.'

'Christ,' said Rupert, appalled. 'Surely they could have tranked him?'

'They tried. It didn't make any difference.'

'Where's Dino now?' asked Malise.

'Dropped off Carol's two horses and then flew Manny's body back home.'

'Who's he riding now?' asked Jake, looking absolutely shattered.

'Nothing,' sobbed Mary-Jo. 'That's what makes it so awful. Manny was our star horse, right, but he was really Dino's only horse. His father'd been ill and he was letting the yard run down.'

'Won't he come to the games at all?' whispered Fen.

'He told Carol he couldn't face it, not after all those years and years of hard work. And he just adored Manny. I tried to call him at his place just now, but his mother said he was too upset to talk to anyone.'

'Surely he can ride someone else's horse?' said Rupert. 'He's easily your best rider.'

Mary-Jo allowed herself a faint smile.

'Thanks,' she said.

'Well, almost,' said Rupert.

'Dino wouldn't do that to anyone – take their horse off them at this stage, knowing how much work they'd put in.'

'Seems crazy to me,' said Rupert. 'If I was your chef d'equipe I'd put him on one of Carol's horses.'

'I'm awfully sorry,' said Malise. 'I'll write to him tomorrow. It's heartbreaking.'

'But extremely fortuitous for us,' said Rupert in an undertone, as Mary Jo moved out of earshot to tell Ludwig and Hans.

'That was totally uncalled for,' snapped Malise. 'Dino was definitely in the running for the Gold.'

'Exactly,' said Rupert. 'We had better go and have some dinner.'

'I think I'll go back to the village,' said Fen, in a high flat voice. 'Jet lag's suddenly got to me. After all, it is four in the morning in England.'

'Oh, come on, darling,' said Rupert. 'Come and see this amazing place. They've even got jacuzzis in the dog kennel. A couple of Bloodies and a good steak and you'll feel on top of the world.'

'Honestly, I'm jiggered,' said Fen, who'd gone terribly white.

'Are you sure?' said Jake, who also seemed stunned by the news about Manny, 'I'll come back with you.'

'No, I'll be fine.'

Back at the Olympic village, Fen had to climb four flights of stairs, because some Ghanaian athletes, who'd never

803

been in a lift before, were spending all day riding up and down. Despite her talk of jet lag, Griselda, thank God, was not in the room. As she slumped on the bed, Fen felt the Games had lost any importance. If she blew it next Monday, or the following Sunday, what did it matter.

Poor Dino, she kept whispering, oh poor, poor Dino. In a daze she got out her writing case. Donald Duck paper didn't seem suitable, nor a postcard of an athlete running with the Olympic torch. She tore a page out of her diary, headed December – appropriately wintry, some day in the future, when life didn't matter any more.

'Dearest Dino,' she wrote, 'I just heard about Manny. I can't think of anything to say except I'm sorry. I loved him too. I know what you're going through. I can't think of anything to say about my behaviour last winter, except I'm sorry too about that. With all my love, Fen.'

Walking down the four flights of stairs again, she posted the letter before she had time to change her mind.

The Eriksons lived in a beautiful ranch-style house, which had once been an avocado farm, now converted into the most exquisite garden, with clematis, morning glory and bougainvillaea growing up every tree. Behind reared the mountains, snow-capped and often blacked out by thunderstorms or rain storms, but seldom affecting the perfect weather in the valley.

Rupert went into the house and kissed his beautiful hostess, with whom he had once been on intimate terms. She was wearing a sopping wet yellow bikini and drinking a Margarita.

'Helen's by the pool,' said Suzy Erikson.' Have you any idea how many are coming so I can warn Annunciata?'

'Well, the American team aren't coming,' said Rupert, 'Nor are either of our women riders, although you'd hardly call Griselda a woman!'

Then he told Suzy about Dino. She was shattered.

'Oh, poor Dino, and bang goes our chance of a Gold. That's tough, that's real tough.'

'What is?' said Helen, from the doorway.

She was wearing the briefest of dark blue bikinis that she would have thought absolutely shocking eight months ago in Kenya, and a blue spotted silk scarf tying back her hair. It was the first time Rupert had ever known her tanned; it brought out the amber of her eyes and the wonderful slenderness of her body.

'What's tough?' she said.

'Your lover's had an accident,' drawled Rupert.

'What d'you mean?' said Helen, aghast. 'What are you talking about?' She gripped on to the door handle for support, her knuckles whitening. Fortunately Rupert had turned to the drinks tray and was pouring out some Perrier.

'His prize horse threw a fit on the plane and had to be shot – so I'm afraid he's not coming to the Games. Tough, huh?'

'Is he hurt?' said Helen, trying to keep her voice steady.

'Nothing broken except his heart, according to Mary-Jo.'

Helen, as though sleepwalking, found one of the leather sofas flanking the fire and sat down very suddenly on it.

'Could I have a drink, please?'

Her mind was galloping: where was Jake? Had he flown home already, without getting in touch? Did horses mean that much to him? Her heart seemed to be crashing against her rib cage.

'I guess Manny was insured,' said Suzy Erikson, examining her back view in the long mirror. 'I wonder if I ought to get my bottom lifted.'

'Only by me,' said Rupert, putting a hand under her buttocks.

'If he's not coming,' said Helen shakily, 'Fen'll have to jump.'

Letting go of Suzy, Rupert looked at her irritably. 'Are you that out of touch? Since when did Fen ride for the American team? I'm talking about Dino Ferranti, your admirer, remember? What d'you want to drink?'

'Oh, poor, poor Dino,' said Helen, shaking like a leaf at

the terrible gaffe she'd nearly committed.

Rupert and Suzy were having drinks by the pool when Jake, Malise and Ivor arrived. Several other handsome, golden-tanned Californian couples had also turned up. A splendid blonde was gambolling in the blue-green water. Helen was lying in a hammock, still in her bikini. She wanted Jake to see how good she looked.

'Hi, Ivor.' She got out of the hammock and kissed him. 'How was the flight?'

Ivor went scarlet and mumbled something about it being 'Joost fine'. Then Helen kissed Malise, which gave her the perfect excuse to kiss Jake too. Putting her face against his cheek on the side away from Rupert, she whispered, 'I love you' in his ear. The smell of hot flesh, suntan oil and Femme sent his senses reeling.

He was astonished afresh by her amazing beauty. All his doubts fled. How could he ever live without her? He felt as though he was walking straight through the celluloid of a Hollywood soap opera and plucking out the heroine. He had little time to talk to her, however. Malise, who wanted to quash a romance which he had grimly suspected was developing in Dublin, sat down on the hammock and proceeded to monopolize Helen. Ivor was soon frolicking in the pool and roaring his head off, playing with the blonde and a large yellow rubber duck. Jake was saved by his host, Albie, an English expatriate mad about show-jumping, who seemed to know every horse Jake had ever owned.

More people arrived, all very beautiful. Jake wished Californians weren't so tall; they made him feel like a midget. Rupert, not drinking, was working off his excess energy in a mixed four on the floodlit tennis court.

'You are horribly unchivalrous,' grumbled the brunette playing against him, as she leapt out of the way of one of his thunderbolt serves. 'Gentlemen are supposed to ease up when they serve to a lady.'

Jake would like to have swum but he felt far too pale and puny to take his shirt off in this company, let alone display his scarred and wasted legs. Helen was still trapped by

Malise and now, as well, by some film director.

'Must go and check everything's O.K. in the kitchen,' said Albie. 'Come and meet Paul and Meryl. He writes screenplays. She acts in them.'

Paul and Meryl were polite, but obviously much more interested in ensuring Meryl got the biggest part and Paul's screenplay was not tampered with. Others joined them. Jake felt gauche and out of place. This lotusland depressed him utterly, knowing he could never conjure up paradises like it for Helen.

Wandering into the drawing-room, he picked up the latest copy of *Horse and Hound*, wondering whether to get a taxi back to the village. Malise didn't look like shifting for hours and there was no sign of dinner.

'Is the heat getting to you?' said Suzy Erikson, curling up beside him on the leather sofa.

'A little.'

'Why don't you swim?'

'I'd rather watch.'

'You would, wouldn't you? You're the stillest man I've ever met.'

'Besides,' he added wryly, 'I've got a lousy physique.'

Suzy ran her eyes over him. 'I wouldn't say that. You've certainly got something.'

'An empty glass for a start.'

'Let me freshen it.'

'No, thanks, I've got to get up at four o'clock tomorrow morning to exercise my horse.'

'What d'you do after that?'

'Our time is pretty much our own.'

'Then I'll come and pick you up and drive you into the mountains.'

'The entire team?'

'No, just you,' she said softly.

'You're making a pass at me?'

'Right. Haven't you heard how up front Californian women are? And I find you very attractive . . .'

'I'm married,' said Jake.

807

'Your wife can't be very smart letting you come over here on your own.'

'She would have come if we could have afforded it.'

'Feeling homesick, huh?'

Jake shrugged. 'A little.'

'I'm real good at curing that. I'd really like to spend some time with you.'

With a glorious feeling of irresponsibility, Jake looked at the depraved little face with its gleaming cat-like eyes, and long, dark hair as coarse and shiny as Macaulay's mane. She had changed out of her bikini and beneath the pale beige string vest the curvy body, with its high full breasts, was perfectly visible. He suddenly thought how nice it would be to take off into the mountains with her, over the hills and far away, and junk all his problems.

'That,' he said, 'is one of the nicest offers I've ever had, but I've actually come to LA to jump fences, not into bed with beautiful ladies. That's my chef d'equipe out there and he's very hot on abstinence.'

Suzy laughed. 'He hasn't had much success with Rupe.'

'Rupert's different. He doesn't suffer from nerves. I've got to distance myself.'

'I've got a marvellous shrink, if you've got anxiety problems. He claims you've got to be filled with both anger and calm.'

'He should start with Hardy, my horse,' said Jake.

'Suzy,' said a sharp voice, 'Annunciata wants to know whether you want to start with the Gambetta?'

It was Helen.

'Oh, you tell her. You're so good at that sort of thing.'

'No, you tell her,' snapped Helen. 'People are starving.'

When Suzy had left the room Helen brought Jake another whisky: 'Lousy hostess. Can't even freshen people's drinks. That woman's a nympho.'

'Shame,' said Jake. 'I thought it was my personal magnetism.'

'What did she want?' said Helen, quickly.

808

'To take me to the mountains.'

Helen went white.

'And I refused very politely,' Jake went on, 'because there's only one woman I want to take anywhere. You look so beautiful, it's a shame to spoil it by sulking.'

'You were flirting with her.'

'I was putting Malise and Rupert off the scent, and you weren't doing so badly on the hammock.'

'Where's Fen?'

'Shattered about Dino.'

Helen then told Jake about mistaking Dino for him.

'You can't imagine how I overreacted. It was awful. I so nearly gave us away.'

'How did Rupert react?'

'I'm not sure. If anything, I guess he thinks I'm upset because Dino's not coming.'

'Well let him go on thinking that. All the same, we must be careful.' He told her about the possibility of the Boyson sponsorship. 'It would go half-way to solving all our problems. But I must keep my nose clean until the contracts are signed.'

'But we can meet during the day. Rupert's out so much.'

He shook his head. 'Too risky. Everyone knows your face over here. The place is swarming with press, desperate for a new angle. I don't want it to be us. You've just got to hack it until after the games.'

Helen's lip quivered. 'I don't think I'll survive.'

'You've got to,' he said more sharply than he intended. 'There's too much at stake – our whole future.'

A shadow fell across them. It was Rupert. Before either of them could say anything he shouted down the hall, 'For Christ's sake, Suzy, can't we have dinner? I'm going to pass out.'

'If you want instant Guacamole, go jump on an avocado in the garden,' said Suzy, wandering in, waving a three-pronged fork. 'There's steak, swordfish, salmon, smoked chicken and red snapper, so you won't go hungry. It'll be ready in two minutes.'

'I suppose we could always barbecue Jake,' said Rupert.

Jake got to his feet. 'You did that once already,' he said in a voice that made Helen shiver. 'At St Augustine's, if you remember,' and he limped out to talk to Malise.

'You were so vile about that guy before he arrived, I knew I'd find him attractive,' said Suzy.

Having finally fallen asleep at 3. a.m. Jake had to get up, jangling with nerves and hangover, an hour later. Speeding along the fast lane reserved for car pools, Malise, not used to fierce power braking, kept producing appalling screeches like a butchered pig, every time he tried to slow down. Even worse, sitting between Jake and Fen, taking up almost the entire back-seat, Griselda grimly ate her way through two huge fried-egg sandwiches.

As Jake gave Hardy the gentlest of workouts in the already punishing heat, he realized Rupert's horse Rock Star was hardly sweating. And while Jake felt dislocated and woolly headed from lack of sleep, Rupert, despite his late night, seemed utterly together. By leaving ahead of the pack, not only had he acclimatized his horses to the heat and humidity, but also adjusted his time clock as well.

Fen walked Desdemona beside Jake.

'She's very down,' she said.

Like her mistress, thought Jake, noticing her swollen eyes but making no comment. Ivor was worried about John.

'It's like sitting on a dead log.'

All around them other nations were crashing their wringing wet horses over massive combinations on what was plainly very hard ground.

Later in the day, Malise called another meeting. Rupert rolled up in a pale blue track suit, like Rock Star, hardly sweating after a four-mile jog along the beach.

'The great problem with the Olympic Games is peaking too soon,' said Malise. 'Now you're in LA you feel you must be doing something to prepare yourself and your horse. You see other teams popping their horses over all sorts of different kinds of fences, and think they've got inside information, but you can be sure no one will know anything until we walk the course on Monday week. If I were you I'd concentrate on work on the flat, and jump your horses as little as possible. Let them rest, relax and enjoy yourselves and have fun.'

'I'd rather have Fen,' said Rupert, who'd also noticed her red eyes.

As they came out of the meeting they bumped into Ludwig and Hans, who'd just been looking at the Olympic swimming pool.

'Did you know it vos specially built for zee Oleempics?' said Hans.

'So was that girl,' said Rupert, as a spectacularly blonde and voluptuous Roumanian athlete loped past them without a backward glance. 'Bet I can bed her before the games are over.'

'How much?' said Ludwig.

'Hundred bucks.'

'Done.'

The event that saved Fen from utter despair was the opening ceremony that afternoon. Everyone had been cynical about the American hype beforehand – particularly Rupert, who made Helen furious with his persistently disparaging remarks. But somehow, the Antony and Cleopatra set, the girls in hot pants with their silver balloons, the eighty-five males bashing away at *Porgy and Bess* on their grand pianos, and the President grinning like a telly puppet, the whole thing worked.

There was a big row beforehand. Rupert had removed the Olympic badge from his blue blazer and had had the trousers narrowed to drainpipe proportions. Fen had shortened her skirt. Griselda had put on so much weight that she kept popping buttons like Tom Kitten, and the skirt of her dress was so stretched there weren't any pleats left. Ivor had typically ordered trousers too small, so the turn-ups skimmed his ankles, and a blazer so big it hung like a peasant's smock.

'You're all a bloody disgrace, except Jake,' snapped

Malise. 'Let's hope you can lose yourselves among the rest of the British athletes.'

After all the razzmatazz, it seemed the athletes might be ignored, but on they came in, country by country, to tumultuous cheers from the amazingly over-adrenalized and happy crowd. There were Mexicans in big hats, and Africans in national costume, and the French incredibly chic in couture-designed clothes, and the English very formal, with the sexes sharply defined.

'You can tell Rupert's been in the army,' said Fen, watching his straight-backed march. Jake tried to disguise his limp as much as possible.

'Thank God we're jumping out in Arcadia and not in front of a crowd as big as this,' said Fen, looking at the endless pebbledash of faces.

Huge cheers greeted China and Roumania and everyone stood up. Then, on a note of crazy informality, the American athletes came on to an earsplitting roar. They all wore tracksuits, so, unlike other countries, there was no division of the sexes. Joyous as otters they swarmed, rowdy and exuberant, in total disarray. All carried cameras and were soon snapping away at one another and the other teams and the stadium, then fighting their way through to the other side of the parade to photograph Mom in the stands.

Even when the black athlete came on carrying the Olympic torch on the last lap, there was doubt whether she'd ever make it, as the US team swayed around her clicking away like pressmen.

'The Marx Brothers seem to have taken over,' said Rupert.

But finally the little flame, all the way from Greece, was lit and, after the endless speeches, the doves of peace fluttered into the blue in their thousands.

'I hope you'll take note,' hissed Fen to Rupert, 'and stop bitching at Jake.'

Then the beautiful girl singer stood up and started belting out 'Reach out and touch someone' and everyone was breaking formation and kissing each other and shaking hands. Fen found herself kissed by Ludwig, Count Guy and Rupert, and three times by Ivor.

'Oh, Christ, here comes Griselda,' said Rupert. 'I'm off. One must draw the line somewhere.'

'I told you not to wear mascara,' said Jake, as Fen wiped her eyes.

And suddenly it got to her – the Olympic ideal. Despite the sniping, the commercialism, the chauvinism and the heartbreak, here she was in Los Angeles, carrying her own torch for Britain in front of this wonderful, friendly, deeply moved, appreciative crowd.

For a few minutes her misery over Dino and over Jake and Helen was put aside as she suddenly realized the magnitude of her achievement, that at nineteen she'd been picked to ride for Britain. For without all the competitors, there would be no competition. And if there weren't people prepared to lose bravely and with a good grace, there wouldn't be any winners. True greatness was the ability to pick yourself up from the floor.

'Isn't this your best moment ever?' she whispered to Jake. He nodded, too moved to speak.

'It'll be even better when we go home with the team gold, and the gold, bronze and silver in the individual,' said Rupert. 'Oh, look there's my Roumanian,' and, shoving through the crowd, he grabbed her. For a second she gazed at him with her slant-eyed impassive Slav face, then the crowd shoved them together, and he was kissing her.

'First base,' said Jake, wondering if Helen was looking.

'Ludwig's going to lose that bet,' said Fen. 'Can't you hear the clang of iron curtains dropping?'

After the ceremonies they met Helen, who'd been watching with the Eriksons.

'Wasn't it wonderful?' said Fen. 'You must feel jolly proud to be American.'

Tolerant suddenly, because Dino not coming to the games had made her even more aware of the agonies of being in love, she moved aside to introduce herself to the

813

Eriksons and apologize for not being able to make it to the party, leaving Helen and Jake a moment alone together.

'I was watching you the whole time,' whispered Helen, her eyes glowing. 'Conscious of you every single moment, so proud that you finally made it here after all those setbacks, knowing you'd be thinking of me.'

Jake felt once again the great weight of her love.

57

They had eight days to kill before the Individual event. It was a bit like being on holiday, knowing war was going to break out any minute. Griselda sweated and became more and more bad-tempered. Fen wilted. Ivor fell asleep on the beach and woke up scarlet down one side of his face. Jake, being dark-skinned, fared better. For the first time in his life he was really brown. Suzy Erikson was constantly phoning him. Rupert went skiing, racing, surfing, pursued Miss Roumania, and played endless games of poker with Ludwig, Count Guy, Carol Kennedy and Wishbone to the despair of their chefs d'equipes, who felt that nations should stick together. At each game, honouring Dino's absence, they left an empty chair. But he didn't show up.

Fen kept hearing little bits of news of him. There was a huge piece headlined 'The Agony of Dino Ferranti' in the *Los Angeles Times* the day after Manny was shot. Carol Kennedy had also spoken briefly to him on the telephone. 'I guess he's still in shock,' he said. 'I offered him Whittier to ride, but he's simply not interested.'

Countless times a day Fen looked in her pigeon hole at the Olympic village, hoping that, among the telegrams and cards from wellwishers, there might be a letter from him.

Jake had frightful trouble sleeping in the Olympic village. The weightlifters were so fed up with his chain-smoking that they made him go outside and smoke in the passage. Often he didn't bother to go to bed at all, just staying up to watch television. Once Ivor discovered you could watch cartoons all night, Malise had great difficulty getting him to bed, as well.

Malise organized a team trip to Disneyland, and Fen had to hold Ivor's hand when he got scared in the haunted house and during the pirates' battle, and calm him down when he became overexcited after shaking hands with Mickey Mouse. In amazement, Fen gazed at the massive overweight Americans, stuffing themselves with hamburgers, hot dogs and ice cream, and exhorting her through capacious mouthfuls to 'Have a nice day'.

'Have you ever seen people so fat?' she whispered to Jake. 'D'you think Griselda's got any Los Angeles blood?'

'No,' said Rupert, overhearing, 'Griselda's far too unpleasant. They remind me more of your wife, Jake.'

Just for a second Fen thought Jake was going to spring at Rupert.

'Don't rise,' she pleaded, putting a hand on Jake's arm. 'He's only trying to wind you up.'

Everywhere they went they were mobbed by autograph hunters, mostly Americans who had no idea who they were, but who were currently obsessed by anything Olympic. Rupert, because of his dazzling looks, his beautiful American wife, and his earlier successes on the American circuit was the one whom they recognized. But not always.

'I know you,' screamed a crone with a blue rinse, as they were leaving Disneyland. 'You're in television?'

'No, I'm in shorts,' snapped Rupert.

Rupert kept up his jogging every morning and was soon joined by Miss Roumania. Progress was obviously being made. After a week he produced a pair of pale blue pants for Ludwig. 'That tag inside says "Made in Roumania".'

'How do ve know?' grumbled Ludwig. 'I don't speak Roumanian. It might say somezing quite different, like "Made in Los Angeles".'

'It's Miss Roumania who's being made in Los Angeles,' said Rupert.

'Vot is her English like?' asked Hans.

'Non-existent, thank God,' said Rupert. 'But she thinks our vicked capitalist vays are absolutely marvellous!'

The eight days dragged by. Gradually, Hardy and Desdemona seemed to be coming together, as Fen and Jake waited on tenterhooks to see which three British riders of the five would be selected to jump in the Individual. As Americans went on winning medals by the bucketful in every contest and the Star Spangled Banner was played over and over again, the commentators reached new levels of chauvinistic hysteria. They seemed hardly to recognize that other countries existed, so there was a hardening of purpose among the British team.

On Friday, to break the monotony, they had a mock competition – two rounds, then a jump off. Carol Kennedy, riding his dark brown mare, Scarlett O'Hara, beat everyone by five seconds in the jump off.

'Either he's an idiot or that mare is phenomenally fit,' said Rupert. 'If it's the latter, we're in trouble.'

Hardy, overfresh and full of himself from his long rest, knocked a fence down in the first round, but Jake was very pleased with him. Rocky jumped superbly. Apart from one silly mistake in the jump off, he didn't put a hoof wrong. Desdemona, also on tremendous form, came fourth, sailing over the fences with all her old bounce, somewhat reviving Fen's spirits.

'All right,' said Malise. 'That's the team for the individual: Rupert, Jake and Fen.'

Fen didn't dare look at Griselda.

Arriving at the stables on the Saturday, however, Fen found Sarah with a long face. Desdemona couldn't put her near hind down. She must have bruised it.

Fen, Sarah and Jake stayed up all night, poulticing her foot and trying to reduce the swelling, walking her out to test the stiffness under the huge Los Angeles stars. By morning Fen thought she was all right. The British vet and the American national vet thought otherwise, and went into a huddle with Malise. Fen felt her presence was purely incidental.

'She's stiff behind and there's swelling. I think she may have chipped a bone,' said the national vet.

'She needs at least a week's rest,' said the British vet.

'A week,' said Fen, aghast. 'That rules out the team event, too.'

'I guess so,' said the American. 'I'll have another look on Friday, in case you've wrought miracles, but I'm afraid tomorrow is definitely out.'

For Fen, who'd been up all night, it was too much.

'Fucking bureaucrats,' she screamed. 'You don't know a bloody horse from your elbows. Give her a shot of bute. She'll be fine. She's often stiff in the morning.'

The American vet, nettled, accused Fen of treating her horse like a machine.

Jake and Sarah took Fen's part, and a very undignified yelling match ensued, listened to with glee by all the surrounding grooms and riders, who were frantically translating for one another.

Finally Malise removed Fen by the scruff of the neck and took her off for a cup of coffee in a quiet corner of the British Supporters' Club.

'You must pull yourself together,' he told her.

'There's nothing left of myself to pull,' wailed Fen. 'Desdemona's O.K. She's my horse. I ought to know.'

'When you see the course tomorrow,' said Malise gently, 'you'll understand. You might get by in a Nations' Cup or in a Grand Prix, but Desdemona's forte is speed, not jumping huge, daunting fences, which she'd really have to stretch herself to get over. I know you love that pony, but I can't let you ride if you're going to be nervous about pushing her every inch of the way.'

'Everyone goes on and on about winning not being important and the taking part is all that matters. I'm not even allowed to take part.'

'You've got years ahead.'

'But I may never get a horse as good as Des.'

'If you don't ruin her tomorrow, you'll probably have a chance of another two cracks at the Olympics on her. How would you live with yourself if you jumped her and lost her for good, like poor Dino?'

At the mention of his name, Fen put her head down on the table and sobbed her heart out. 'I've tried, truly I have, I've tried to be cheerful. I've taken Ivor to Disneyland three times. But I did hope to see Dino. We were a bit close once.'

Malise patted her shoulder. 'I know how you were looking forward to seeing him, and now this. It's wretched.'

'Can I fly home?'

Malise shook his head. 'That's not part of the deal. You're still reserve. If anything happens to any of the others you'll have to jump their horses. I'll need your help tomorrow to see how the course is riding, to cheer us all up. Griselda isn't any good at that. She'll still be sulking because I haven't picked her.'

'You must be joking,' said Fen. 'I've been as cheerful as a corpse the last few months.'

'And I need you to look after Jake; keep him calm. D'you think he's missing Tory?' Malise raised an eyebrow. Fen had the feeling he was fishing.

'Yes,' she said. 'I'm sure he is.'

The same afternoon Rupert went racing with Ludwig and Guy. Jake broke his vow and, submitting to Helen's pleading, drove her into the mountains. Looking for wild flowers, he was reminded of the picnic he had had with Tory and the children the day before the World Championship. Then he had found the lucky clump of tansy. Now Helen's gold tansy in the breast pocket of his shirt was warding of evil.

Helen found Jake boringly worried about Fen.

'She's very young. She'll have other opportunities.'

'You don't think that when you're young,' said Jake, 'and she's had such a sod of a two years. Losing Billy, then being sent to Coventry, then losing Dino, and his not turning up at the games, and now this. She's very brave; makes very little fuss.'

I need you far more than she does, Helen wanted to shout. She was fed up with the entire Lovell family. She was jealous of Fen, and she was fed up with Suzy going on about how attractive Jake was, and assuming that he must be madly in love with Tory not to submit to Suzy's charms.

Not having been alone with Jake for days, she wanted to pour out her troubles. Now she was faced with his total detachment. He seemed to have cocooned himself against the outside world. He wasn't interested in the news, or plays or the concerts she had been to at the Hollywood Bowl, or even how appallingly Rupert was behaving. She failed to appreciate that the sensitivity with which he had listened to her and taken her to bed during the summer, had a flip side of terrible nerves and vulnerability to outside pressures before a big class.

Finally, when tired of walking, they collapsed on to the grass, he lay with his head on her belly, not speaking, just gazing up at the snowy peaks against the stormy dark sky, luxuriating in the cool air until he fell asleep. Unable to bear wasting precious time when they could be making love, Helen woke him up.

'Jake, d'you really love me?'

'Of course I do.'

'You're not showing it much at the moment.'

Jake sat up on his elbow, his eyes deeply shadowed in his tanned face.

'Can't you understand that the emotional cauldron of the Olympics either makes or breaks you? I can't afford distractions.' He took her hand and placed it on his breast pocket so she could feel the gold tansy. 'But I keep you next to my heart the whole time.'

'I hoped I'd inspire you,' she wailed.

'You do,' said Jake, then, remembering Dublin, 'but you also distract me. I don't want to spend tomorrow, when I should be concentrating on winning, worrying that I'm going to slip up or betray myself in front of Rupert.'

'Don't you even want me there?'

'Of course I do. Just don't expect me to wave and smile during the day. People say I'm rude and ill-tempered. I just want to go inside myself before a class. If I have to worry whether you're happy, it'll be one more pressure.'

Seeing her uncomprehending face, he said, 'There's so much at stake – our whole future.'

'I get so lonely at big classes,' said Helen petulantly. 'I'm almost glad Mother's coming tomorrow.'

She pulled Jake towards her. 'Please kiss me. I want you so badly.' But kissing was all he would do, which left her feeling profoundly uneasy. When Rupert had been mad about her in the early days, he'd always made love to her before and after and, frequently in the caravan, in the middle of classes.

On his way back from the races that evening, Rupert dropped into the Olympic village to collect his post and found a letter postmarked Perthshire. Ever-cautious Amanda had not used headed writing paper, but she apologized for being 'utterly bloody' about the looking glass and admitted that she was missing him very much, that they'd all be staying up to watch him tomorrow, and to wish him good luck. She'd be back in London in September.

Equally cautious, Rupert tore her letter up and was about to throw it in the litter bin when he pieced it together again to see if it were really true. He felt absurdly pleased, and wondered why the hell he'd been playing around with Miss Roumania. He had better go back to Arcadia and get some sleep. They were walking the course at 7.30.

Malise Gordon was not a religious man, but he prayed before the Individual that night. He must try and be a good loser and not make any of the three riders feel too awful if they made a cock-up, and try and keep them calm without transmitting any of his fears and worries. Ivor had a good horse and didn't usually suffer from nerves, but he lacked fire in his belly. Jake was desperately short of sleep and likely to crack. Rupert was far too confident and Rocky much too fresh. On the right day they were invincible, but Malise felt apprehensive. He felt ridiculously touched that Fen had sent him a good luck card with a black cat on it. 'To the best chef d'equipe in the world,' she had written inside. 'We'll live to fight another day, love, Fen'.

58

Jake slept fitfully, wracked by half-dreams. It was the opening ceremony and the singer turned into Helen, sobbing into a microphone that Jake didn't love her. Then he was in the ring with girths breaking and bridles coming off. Finally he dreamed that Hardy had a heart attack in the ring. Lying there in the blazing sun gathering flies, he suddenly turned into Sailor. Jake woke up screaming, crying his eyes out. The next minute one of the weightlifters was sitting on his bed, patting his shoulder with a huge hand, the other was lighting him a cigarette. Having notched up a silver and a bronze the day before, they could afford to be magnanimous. As it was half past three, they said, there was no point in Jake going back to sleep for an hour, so they might as well have a cup of tea and all chat to take his mind off things. Jake would rather have been left alone, but he was touched by their concern.

The weightlifters were dozing off as, with a feeling of unreality, Jake put on the new socks, the white breeches, the shirt and tied his tie with trembling fingers. He was all in white like a bride, until he pulled on the gleaming brown-topped boots, and shrugged his way into the new red coat, with the black velvet collar and the Union Jack on the pocket. The day had actually come, as it came to boys going back to prep school, or to men in the condemned cell.

'Good luck,' mumbled the weightlifters sleepily. 'We'll watch you on the box. Sock it to 'em.'

'Good luck,' said the wrestlers, when Jake collected Ivor. 'For Christ's sake, look after him.'

'Good luck,' said the dour security guard at the end of the

passage, smiling for the first time since they arrived. 'Have a good day.'

It was a good thing they started early for as the sun rose, pale saffron gilding the Santa Monica mountains, cars were already jamming the freeways, and a continuous stream of enthusiasts from every nation – but mostly America – clutching a selection of hats, thermos flasks, coolers, beer cans, sandwiches, transistors, and even portable televisions to sustain them during the long day, poured into the show ground. Ticket touts were everywhere, and to get to the stables, the team had to fight their way through autograph hunters and people peddling Coca Cola, chewing gum, hamburgers, hot dogs, and souvenirs.

'If someone else offers me a poster of Dino I shall scream,' said Fen.

By seven o'clock the stands were packed under a hazy, dove-grey sky, which indicated colossal heat to come. Many of the crowd didn't know one end of a horse from another, but, bitten by Olympic fever, they wanted to see America notch up yet another gold.

At seven-thirty, the riders and their chefs d'equipes walked the course, surging out over the rich brown tan. No one else, not even the press, was allowed into the arena. Royalty, however, brooked no such restrictions.

'Morning, Dudley,' Prince Philip called to Dudley Diplock, who was hovering at the entrance. 'Walked the course yet?'

'No, Sir.'

'Well come on, come on,' said the Prince, striding straight through the cordon of security guards, Dudley hopping after him.

'Look at that crowd,' said Ivor, in a hollow voice.

'Look at that course,' said Jake, as he gazed at the fences, whose massive size wasn't remotely softened by a riot of trees and flowers.

'Positively awesome,' breathed Carol Kennedy, as he looked at the combination. There were two unusual fences, one built with light and dark brown bricks in the shape of a

823

hot dog and another designed like a boat with sails at either end instead of wings, with the horses jumping over the bows.

'Holy Mother, that's a turrible thing,' said Wishbone, looking at the hot dog.

Even Rupert was curiously silent as they measured and re-measured the distances.

'You've all jumped higher than this,' said Malise, as they gazed at the massive oxer.

'But not every fence,' said Ivor.

Fen suddenly felt overwhelmed with shame that she should have wanted Desdemona to jump this course. It was simply too big and she couldn't see any way Hardy could get around. She felt horribly frightened for Jake. She wanted to be with him to bolster his confidence, but Malise told her to stick to the riders' stand, and watch her eyes out for the first dozen or so rounds and pass back any advice.

Jake, icy cold with chattering teeth, despite the heat, kept to himself and talked to no one. He had a very late draw, which was bound to tell on his nerves. Suddenly, he longed for Tory and her quiet sympathy and understanding, she who didn't mind if he bit her head off. Just as he was going through the security check into the stables he heard a cry and Helen bore down on him. She looked ravishing in a white grecian tunic and a big white hat with the blue spotted scarf round the brim. A few yards behind her was a large handsome middle-aged woman with a bulldog jaw.

'Darling,' Helen cried, 'I've been looking for you everywhere. I just wanted to wish you luck and have you meet Mother.'

Jake looked at her incredulously. 'What?'

'Meet Mother. I've told her so much about you.'

'Don't be so fucking stupid,' snapped Jake. 'I can't meet anyone at the moment,' and turned on his heel.

Helen was stunned. 'He's a bit uptight,' she told her mother. 'You can meet him later.'

Everyone crowded into the riders' stand to watch the first round. A hush fell over the arena. A ripple ran through the crowd as the first competitor came in. It was Hans Schmidt – his hat at its usual crooked angle, the jauntiness, belied by the determination on his face, Papa Haydn, the dark bay Hanoverian, totally under control. A groan went up from the German team, as he sent the second fence, a double of uprights, never a German forte, flying, then proceeded to hit the third fence and the fourth and, not getting up speed, had two toes in the water. Unnerved by such an uncharacteristically bad round, Papa Haydn demolished the sail boat and then the hot dog, took a pole out of the massive triple, which was sited away from the collecting ring, and hit the first element of the combination, for a final thirty-six faults.

'And he is ranked number five in the world,' said Wishbone in a trembling voice.

'First competitor nerves,' said Rupert.

The strain of waiting for the course to be re-built told on Count Guy, who came next, and who came to grief at the third fence, managed to clear the water, but was going so fast he couldn't pull up. He proceeded to kick out the sail boat, the hot dog, the massive oxer, and the two last elements in the combination. He was followed by a Japanese rider, who came in with a kamikaze attitude of finishing the course at all costs, and came out to loud cheers with an amazing total of fifty-five faults. One of the young Irish riders coaxed his ugly brown mare round on twenty-four to produce the best round yet. Dino's replacement, Lizzie Dean, couldn't carry the weight of expectation piled on her and notched up twenty faults.

'It obviously walked better than it rode,' muttered Ivor, who was as green as one of Suzy Erikson's avocadoes.

The heat blazed down, getting more and more murderous, as Spaniards, Swiss, Italians, Canadians followed one another. If they weren't unhinged by the course, they were distracted by the crowd who, every time anyone cleared a fence, uttered yoo-hoos and Tarzan howls, and yells of 'Keep it up, keep it up.'

Ludwig came in and roused a certain interest, when it was announced he had won the Gold at the last Olympics, and had been second in the World Championship. Clara looked a picture of health as she trotted into the ring, long ears shining, taking in the huge crowd. It was soon obvious that she was on form, as she delicately picked her way around the course, clearing the sheet of blue water by a foot, but managing to slow up and become the first horse to clear the sail boat. The yells and cheers that greeted this achievement, however, completely unsettled her. She rattled the hot dog badly, crashed into the oxer and kicked out the vast triple, finishing up with eight faults. All the other riders clapped sympathetically as Ludwig rode out, ruefully shaking his head. All the same, thought Fen, it's the best round yet. Clear rounds were obviously going to be impossible to come by. She tried to remember exactly how Ludwig had tackled the sail boat so she could tell Jake. As she watched the Mexican named Jesus come hopelessly to grief, she felt sicker and sicker with nerves for him.

Even worse, as Ivor went back to the stables to warm up John, someone moved up beside her and she found herself sitting next to Helen and Mrs Macaulay.

'This is Jake's sister-in-law, Fenella,' said Helen. 'This is Mother.'

Fen and Mrs Macaulay nodded at each other without warmth. Fen wondered if Helen had told her mother all about Jake. Helen looked at Fen's uncommunicative profile.

'Jake seems very uptight,' she said. 'I tried to have him meet Mother.'

'The only person he wants to meet at the moment is his maker.'

'He does suffer terribly from anxiety,' said Helen.

'He's missing Tory,' said Fen. 'He tried to ring her this morning, but all the lines were engaged.'

'I thought it was very much a marriage of convenience,' said Helen stiffly.

'Christ, no,' said Fen. 'He's mad about her. Look how berserk he got at Disneyland when Rupert made that crack about her being too fat.'

'And he doesn't play around?' Helen couldn't resist asking.

'Oh, no more than the average show jumper,' lied Fen airily. 'You know what they're like. Too many opportunities to expect total fidelity, but he always goes back to Tory.'

Seeing Helen's twitching, anguished face, Fen decided she'd gone too far. I'll go to hell for being such a bitch, she thought, but since Dino hasn't turned up and I'm out of the Olympics, I'm in hell anyway; so what does it matter?

'Oh look, here comes Mary-Jo,' said Mrs Macaulay. 'I'm sorry, Helen, but that's my girl. I refuse to root for Great Britain.'

For five minutes the huge crowd, who'd been getting up and down all morning, halted their pilgrimage for food and drink. Cheered on by their fervour and hysterical enthusiasm, and her own passionate desire to win, Mary-Jo and Balthazar went round for four faults, only hitting the hot dog, and going into the lead. Red as her red coat, grinning from ear to ear, throwing her hat in the air and catching it like a drum majorette, she galloped out of the ring, the crowd rising to applaud her.

Unable to face Mrs Macaulay's smugness, Fen asked Helen to keep her place and went downstairs to encourage Ivor, who was jumping in a couple of rounds. God, it was hot. As though you'd gone to sleep and forgotten to switch off the electric blanket. The officials in their coral blazers and white panama hats sweated, and coloured flags wilted against the snow-topped mountains.

She reached Ivor as a poor little Swiss girl rode past, crying her eyes out, four years of hope shattered by three refusals at the first fence.

Ivor didn't fare much better. Stricken with stage fright, he rode like a novice. Nor was he helped by the announcement that here was Ivor Braine from Great Britain on The John. The crowd, thinking it hysterically funny that someone should call a horse by their name for the lavatory, went into guffaws of laughter and catcalls. Offended and

827

thoroughly unsettled, John ground to three stops at the hot dog.

'Oh no, John, no, John, no,' said Rupert, and went off to crash Rocky round the practice ring, as usual getting Dizzy to arrange the jumps on exactly the wrong stride, so Rocky hit every one and hurt himself.

'Teach him to be careful,' said Rupert.

A mighty roar from the arena indicated that Carol Kennedy had gone in and was about to jump.

'Now that's an attractive man,' said Mrs Macaulay. 'There's something about American men.'

'He's gay, mother,' snapped Helen.

Despite being used to the frantic enthusiasm of American crowds, even Scarlett O'Hara was unnerved by the noise. She hit the hot dog, then looked as though she was going clear, but as she sailed over the last element of the combination, the crowd let out such a shout of jubilation that the mare assumed she had finished. It took all Carol's skill to get her straight for the huge double and she toppled the last pole. Still, he was second on eight faults with Ludwig.

'Isn't he a prince?' said the girl behind Helen, as Rupert waited to go in. 'I saw him on TV last night. You have to hand it to the British. They do have class.'

Quality in every line, Rocky was easily the handsomest horse in the contest. Under the gleaming amber coat his muscles rippled like serpents, and as he danced into the arena, long ears cocked to the unfamiliar sights and sounds, the blend of explosive power with natural grace was unforgettable.

'For Christ's sake, take it steadily,' warned Malise.

Rocky was the best horse in the contest, but he had never seen a crowd this big, nor heard so much noise, nor seen so many undulating rows of peaked caps, like a wriggling aviary.

His forelegs were sore where Rupert had crashed him over the jumps. His tail switched angrily; he was horribly hot, fed up and upset. As Rupert circled him twice to steady him, he humped his back and fought for his head.

That horse is over-fresh and insufficiently ridden in, thought Fen.

Two minutes later, Rupert rode out of the ring with an incredible twenty-eight faults. Everyone in the riders' stand and the commentary box was stunned.

'Talk about the Rocky Horror Show!' said Fen under her breath. Then, horrified by her own lack of patriotism, she shot a sidelong glance at Helen and Mrs Macaulay and was shattered to see neither of them was looking remotely upset.

'Must go and find Jake,' she said, getting to her feet.

'Wish him good luck,' said Helen. 'Don't forget to tell him,' she called after Fen.

Wishbone was just about to go into the ring. Nearly forty, he'd had a gruelling career, and everyone was taking bets on whether the drink or anno domini would get to him first. Today, despite three large whiskys, the heat didn't seem to affect him or his big bay gelding, Christy Mahon. They too got eight faults.

'Well done,' shouted Fen, as he came out of the ring. 'Bloody good round.'

She found Ivor, his face tear-stained, in the deepest of glooms. 'Where's Jake?' she asked.

'In the Gents, throwing up.'

'He's got to jump in twenty minutes. For God's sake, go and get him.'

Jake crouched over the lavatory, gazing miserably at the white bowl. Having had no breakfast and virtually no supper he was only throwing up bile now. He felt dreadful, shaking from head to foot. Oh God, he wished Tory was here.

Someone was rattling the door. It was Ivor.

'You O.K., Jake?'

Jake groaned.

'Fen thought this might help.' Ivor passed a brandy under the door.

'Take it easy,' said Malise's voice. 'In a few hours this'll be all over.'

'How soon have I got to jump?'

'About four to go.'

'Any clears?'

'No — Rupe knocked up a cricket score,' said Malise bleakly.

So it all depends on me, thought Jake.

He drained the brandy. Amazingly, it seemed to calm his nerves and take the edge off his fears. Outside, he found Fen.

'Now listen, they've all come unstuck at the hot dog. I think you ought to come off the corner earlier, giving Hardy a bit more time to size it up and take it in five strides.'

'He seems to have got out of bed on the right side. He's only given me one nip today,' said Sarah.

Hardy was not a handsome horse, but his chubby dappled quarters and shoulders shone like polished pewter, his tail was whiter than the snow on the mountains, and his plaits, threaded with red cotton, were the neatest in the contest.

For a second, Jake smiled at Sarah as she plugged both the horse's ears with cotton wool. 'You've done a good job on him,' he said. 'He looks great.'

'Good luck,' said Fen.

'I don't need to tell you this,' said Malise, 'but all our hopes rest on you now.

Giving Hardy a clap on the rump, Jake went off into the tunnel. Fen just managed to make her seat beside Helen as Jake rode into the ring.

'This is Jake, whom I was telling you about,' Helen said to her mother. 'He nearly quit because he had such a frightful smash last year.'

The crowd were tired. They had already sat through nearly three hours of jumping. They had seen all the Americans go and were already drifting away for their lunch.

It's actually happening, thought Jake, as he cantered towards the first huge fence. Feeling Hardy's irritation at having his natural ebullience curbed, he let him have his head. Hardy bounded over, he cleared the next and the next, and with a whisk of his hind legs flicked over the water with inches to spare. He's in top form, thought Jake joyfully. The sail boat caused him no problems. Following Fen's advice, he then took a very sharp turn off the corner, and taking five strides, rather than everyone's four, gathered sufficient momentum and bounded over the hot dog with ease.

He was the first horse to clear this fence, which caused such screams of delight, excitement and hysteria from the crowd that they pierced straight through the cotton wool in Hardy's ears, temporarily unhinging him. Breaking into a gallop he crashed through the huge oxer and and sent every brick of the wall flying.

'Shit,' said Helen.

'Helen Macaulay,' said her mother, appalled.

'I've been Campbell-Black for six years, Mother.'

'More's the pity.'

Fen decided she rather liked Mrs Macaulay.

Jake, meanwhile, had pulled Hardy almost to a standstill, stroking him and balancing him, the same way he had calmed Macaulay in the World Championship.

'Silly bugger's going to get time faults,' said Rupert.

'He knows what he's doing,' snapped Malise.

Jake kicked Hardy into a canter, and proceeded to bounce over the rest of the course, riding out to deafening applause.

'Well done. Marvellous,' said Malise, looking considerably more cheerful than he had ten minutes before. 'You've saved the day. You're on eleven.'

Only three rounds followed, two of them hopeless, but the British hopes were slightly dashed when a Nigerian on a huge black gelding went round at a gallop, a broad grin on his face. Despite shooting out of the saddle at every fence, and reducing the crowd to fits of laughter, he managed to clear everything except the water and the hot dog.

Malise got out his score sheet. 'That's Mary-Jo on four,

Carol, Ludwig, Wishbone and the Nigerian on eight, and you on eleven, Jake,' he said.

Then there was a gruelling, three-hour interval before the second round. Twenty riders went through. Ivor was out, Rupert had just scraped in, Jake was fifth. There would be fewer jumps, but they would be harder.

'Let's go and have some lunch,' said Malise.

'I'm going to stay behind and sort out Rocky,' said Rupert grimly.

'Must try and keep Wishbone out of the whisky tint,' said Paddy, his groom. Ivor couldn't speak for despair.

'Rupert was overconfident. You were underconfident. It happens to the best people,' Malise told him.

On the way to lunch Jake suddenly swayed, overcome by heat, lack of sleep and food and a large brandy.

'You won't be jumping for at least three hours,' said Malise firmly. 'Go and have a sleep on Sarah's bed.'

'Don't be bloody silly,' said Jake, mopping his dripping forehead. 'I couldn't possibly sleep.'

'Well, lie down then.'

Within seconds of stretching out on the tiny bed in the attic room over the stables, Jake was asleep.

The second round was much tougher. The temperature was up in the nineties, turning the Olympic stadium into a furnace. The horses having been warmed up, and jumped, and put back in the stables, thought that work was over for the day and couldn't understand why they were being pulled out again. Most of them were already tired.

Even the vast crowd seemed depleted, as spectators, escaping from the punishing heat, watched the competition on the closed-circuit televisions scattered round the halls.

Biting her nails, Fen watched rider after rider fighting their way through a forest of obstacles. Ludwig had worked Clara too hard in the interval and the great mare knocked up a cricket score.

Jake, having been woken up, was warming up Hardy as Mary-Jo entered the ring. From the arena he could see the stands heaving as the spectators stampeded to get back to their seats and cheer on their heroine. Mary-Jo was on four faults. Jake listened to the roars of applause growing to a crescendo, which must have been heard all the way to New York. Then there was a silence, and a terrible groan. Four faults, that meant she was on eight, then the cheers started again, rising and rising once more. He must concentrate on Hardy. Then suddenly there was a deafening bellow, which sent Hardy into a frenzy, despite the cotton wool in his ears.

Looking up at the stadium, Jake could see hats being thrown in the air, rising up above the back of the stand like popped corn. Unless Carol or Wishbone or the Nigerian went clear, Mary-Jo had got her gold. There was no way Jake could catch her. The cheering went on and on, until finally Mary-Jo came out of the tunnel, wiping away the tears, then disappearing into a shrieking crowd of well-wishers.

Carol Kennedy, on eight, went next and again was unlucky. He was jumping cleanly and steadily when the shadow of a helicopter above fell across the first element of the double, making it difficult to judge the distance. The gallant Scarlett O'Hara knocked down both elements, but otherwise went clear. The crowd were in ectasy, stamping their feet, crying: 'Yoo-Hoo-Hoo.' Carol was now on sixteen faults, with an excellent chance of the silver.

In rode Rupert. It was only a miracle that he could even get the bronze. He was still in a white-hot rage, determined to go clear and show everyone how the course should be jumped. Obviously terrified out of his wits, eyes rolling, frothing blood at the mouth, Rocky went clear until he came to the triple going away from the collecting ring, when he began to slow down. Rupert lifted his whip. Rocky took off too soon, and sent triple, horse and rider flying. Rupert hung onto the reins and appeared unhurt, but it was several seconds before he could mount the panic-stricken Rocky who, thoroughly unsettled, proceeded to notch up a further eight faults.

'Bad luck,' said Wishbone who was waiting to go in. But Rupert ignored him, riding straight past him with a pale, dangerous face. Wishbone had had enough whisky in the interval to give him courage, but rather too many for perfect judgement. He knew it was his last chance of a medal. The Irish didn't have enough riders here to make up a team, but he loved his old horse, and would dearly have loved to go home with a medal, so he crossed himself and prayed fervently to the Virgin Mary as he rode into the ring. The Virgin Mary was listening. Gently she guided horse and rider around the ring. Wishbone jumped like a man inspired, with only one fence down, putting him into second place.

The crowd erupted. Wishbone had entertained them with his antics for many years now. He was a very popular rider. They cheered and cheered. Ireland had got the silver, but America had the gold and bronze.

'They seem to have completely forgotten that there's still Jake and that Nigerian to jump,' said Fen furiously.

'Are you all right?' she said to Jake. 'It must be much worse when there's so much at stake.'

He nodded, not trusting himself to speak. If he got four faults he got the bronze; if he went clear, the silver. That was the message bleakly spelled out. With the crowd making such a din, there was no way he could get Hardy to concentrate.

'Take his cotton wool out,' he said to Sarah.

'Are you sure?' she said, horrified. 'He'll freak out.'

Malise came up and gave Hardy a last pat. 'They're obviously not going to shut up,' he said. 'I'd go in. Just trust to your instincts.'

If I get a medal, thought Jake as he waited, watching the mouthing ecstatic faces, I'll get £75,000 a year from Boyson. He thought of Tory and the children watching at home. He thought of Helen, who he'd been so foul to earlier.

'Go in, please,' said the ring steward in his coral blazer.

From then on Jake thought about nothing but Hardy. Riding slowly to the centre of the arena, he turned to the President's Box, where the President, who loved horses, sat with Prince Philip and Princess Anne, and he removed his hat to the judges, showing the sudden pallor on his suntanned face. Then he spoke to Hardy and Hardy put one foot forward and bowed low to the Prince and the Princess and the President and the crowd burst into ecstatic, charmed applause. They'd got their gold; they could afford to be generous. There was no way this gipsy and his tricks could beat their Mary-Jo.

'Isn't that darling?' said Helen to Mrs Macaulay.

Jake looked up at the cool, snow-tipped mountains beyond the stadium and the great blocks of faces watching him, and calmly he replaced his hat and waited for the crowd to settle.

Gradually the cheering decreased to a sizzle of excitement, like fat in a chip pan. Jake touched the Union Jack on his saddle cloth, then the tansy in his breast pocket. Hardy stood as still as a rock for once. He had heard the crowd in all its noise and glory, and it hadn't harmed him.

'Stupid exhibitionist,' said Rupert to Ludwig.

'Pity not to have any clears,' said Dudley Diplock.

Finally, when there was no sound at all except the clicking of cameras and the insect hum of a 100,000-strong crowd trying to be quiet, Jake kicked Hardy into a canter. Neither of them looked a bit tired. It was almost as though they were jumping an exhibition round. As they cleared the first two fences, then the third, then bounded joyously over the water, the crowd realized Hardy was enjoying himself and started to cheer and stamp and clap him on.

'They really like me,' Hardy seemed to be saying, as he picked his feet up and really bucketed over the hot dog with a jaunty whisk of his tail.

'This is the fence I hated last time,' he seemed to say, slowing up at the oxer. 'You like it this time, listen to the applause,' said Jake, as Hardy flew over like a swallow.

'He's a bit slow,' said Fen, sitting beside Malise on the edge of the riders' stand.

'Yes,' said Malise, 'but what a round; sheer poetry. Come on, Jake.'

As if Jake heard them, he stepped up Hardy's pace, and

came storming over the combination. Now it was the last double.

'I can't look,' said Fen. She waited, head in her hands for the sickening thud of poles. She heard a gasp, a long pause, an ecstatic scream from Helen on her right and then a mighty roar of applause.

'He's done it, the only clear,' shouted Malise, throwing his panama in the air. It fell and was trampled underfoot before he could even be bothered to retrieve it.

The crowd held their breath as everyone calculated. Jake glanced at the clock. He was just within the time. Even if the Nigerian went clear, he'd got the bronze. Dropping Hardy's rein on his neck, he raised both hands to heaven in a double salute and rode out through the cheering channel of spectators, grinning from ear to ear.

'Fucking marvellous,' screamed Fen, tears pouring down her cheeks, as she hugged Malise, his wet face glistening too in the bright sun.

'This is the most amazing turn-up for the books,' Dudley Diplock was gibbering from the commentary box. 'No one ever thought Gyppo Jake would make it back to the big time. This is little short of a miracle.'

'Let's go and congratulate him,' said Malise and Fen simultaneously, but Helen was too quick for either of them. Jumping over the row in front, she rushed out and down the steps and, red hair flying, she rushed to meet Jake.

'Oh darling, darling, darling,' she said, seizing his hand.

Jake looked down at her. Colour in his face now, dazzlingly happy, handsome as never before, all efforts at impassivity gone.

'We did it,' he said incredulously. 'We really did it,' and in the euphoria of winning, he bent down and kissed her, and she kissed him back, clinging on to him.

In the riders' stand, trapped by the crowd, Fen's eyes met those of Mrs Macaulay.

'Your brother-in-law,' said Mrs Macaulay accusingly.

'Yes,' said Fen, equally accusingly. 'My sister's husband.'

From the right she saw Rupert, white with rage descending on Jake and Helen. Fortunately, at that moment Sarah, in floods of joyful tears, and the rest of the British grooms swarmed round Jake and Hardy. Instantly they were joined by Wishbone and the American and German teams who were all patting him on the back and showering him with congratulations. Count Guy arrived with a magnum of Krug.

From then on, everything was a daze. Jake was terribly glad to see Malise looking so happy, and Fen jumping up and down, and he was both pleased and sorry when he heard the poor Nigerian, the last to jump, had been unable to cope with the strain and had knocked up twenty faults, which meant Jake had the silver and Wishbone the bronze.

Everywhere he turned there were photographers and people reaching forward to pat Hardy.

'I can't think why he isn't biting everyone,' crowed Sarah. 'Now he's a medallist, he's obviously turned over a new leaf.'

The jumps were cleared and the huge Clydesdales dragged on the winners' podium. Together, Mary-Jo, Jake and Wishbone rode into the ring, followed by their three grooms. Sarah got a special cheer for her beauty and her red, white and blue hair. Then the grooms took the horses as the riders mounted the podium. Jake found it difficult not to laugh as the girls carrying the boxes of rosettes, like flag-sellers, came out with their ludicrously stiff, wide-apart-legged walk.

He bowed his head as the President's wife hung the silver medal round his neck, touching it immediately, checking it was real. He thought his heart would burst with the wonder of the whole thing. Mary-Jo was crying unashamedly as the three flags climbed up the flagpole and the band played the Star Spangled Banner. Wishbone had no handkerchief, and had to blow his red-veined nose on his shirt tail.

'Well done,' said Prince Philip, shaking them all, but particularly Jake, by the hand. 'Only clear round,' he added. 'You must feel *very* proud.'

'Thank you, Sir.'

Jake was so dazed with emotion, he was glad to get back to Hardy, who was so festooned with long-tailed rosettes he could hardly see through them. He wanted to stay with him afterwards but he was swept off to a press conference. By the time the reporters had finished with Mary-Jo, Jake had consumed at least a bottle and a half of champagne.

'Pity you didn't get a gold, Jake,' said the *Los Angeles Times*.

'Frankly I'm bloody glad to have the silver. Being a gipsy, traditionally I cross people's palms with it. It's the right medal for me.' Everyone laughed.

'All the same,' he went on, looking at the forest of cameras and notebooks and tape recorders, 'it's a pity Dino Ferranti had to pull out, or Mary-Jo and I might easily have been a rung lower.'

'Do you think there's any reason you did so well?' asked the *Daily Telegraph*.

'I had a good back-up team,' said Jake, and proceeded to thank everyone from the family to Malise, to the nurses and doctors at the Motcliffe.

'What are your plans for the future?' asked the *New York Times*.

'I'm going to ring my wife and then go and get plastered.'

Dudley fought his way through the huge crowd of fans waiting outside. 'Congratulations, Jake. Brilliant, brilliant performance. We've kept a line open for you in the commentary box. We'd like to televise you breaking the news to Tory, if we may.'

'You may not,' said Jake. 'One doesn't often ring up one's wife to say one's got a silver. Some things should be done in private.'

Going into the commentary box, he slammed the door. 'Can I put a person to person call through to Mrs Lovell?' he said, picking up the telephone.

'Certainly, Mr Lovell,' said the switchboard girl. 'Congratulations.' He got through incredibly quickly.

'Oh Jakey, oh Jakey,' Tory was laughing and crying so

much he could hardly hear her. 'It's so wonderful. You both were so wonderful. The whole village have been here watching it. They've drunk us out of house and home and now they're having the most terrific party. We're all so proud of you.'

'Hardy was your baby,' said Jake. 'You sorted him out for me.'

'He jumped so brilliantly; and when he bowed; and the only clear too. Speak to the children.'

'How much did you win?' asked Isa.

'Can you take me to Disneyland?' said Darklis.

Jake asked if he could speak to Tory again. 'I miss you,' he said. 'D'you want to fly out for the team event?'

'Oh, I'd love to. Can we afford it?'

'I think so, now,' said Jake.

'Boyson just rang by the way,' said Tory. 'He said you'd kept your side of the bargain, he'd be keeping his. Oh, listen, listen, can you hear?' she said in a choked voice. 'They're ringing the church bells, Oh Jakey, it's two o'clock in the morning. No one's asleep. They're cheering and dancing in the street, and the pub's open, and they're ringing the bells in your honour. Listen!'

Down the wires, Jake could hear the faint peal. He was so moved he couldn't talk any more. 'I'll ring tomorrow,' he said. 'I love you.'

'I love you,' said Tory.

'Everything all right?' said Fen as he came out of the box, wiping his eyes.

He nodded. 'Absolutely marvellous. They're ringing the church bells'.

Perhaps it'll be all right after all, thought Fen.

59

They gave him a ride in a police car, sirens blaring, to get him back to the Olympic village.

'I'm sorry,' said Jake at the gates, feeling dazedly for his security chain. 'I seem to have mislaid it.'

'All right, Mr Lovell, we know who you are,' said the security guard. 'Congratulations.'

The other British athletes were euphoric.

'Well done,' said Sebastian Coe and Daley Thompson, hammering him on the back.

The weightlifters hoisted him shoulder high and carried him around the village. Everyone bought him drinks. Jake looked in the mirror in the little room as he changed to go out to dinner. He found his security chain where he'd left it, around his neck, under his shirt.

'You are a superstar,' he said, jabbing his finger at his reflection, pleased that the two pointing fingers met every time, proving he wasn't drunk. He wished he could go out quietly and celebrate with Sarah and Fen; he didn't want the strain of behaving well. He wished Tory was here to share in the triumph, but he had never before known such personal happiness.

Determined not to betray his devastating disappointment, Rupert was in no mood for a victory celebration. He had wanted to leave showjumping in a blaze of glory, moving smoothly from the gold medallist's podium into politics and, possibly, Amanda's arms. Now, the months of train-ingand abstinence had gone for nothing. And although Rocky had jumped like a pig with chilblains, and Rupert

840

had beaten the hell out of him afterwards, a small voice inside told him it was not Rocky's fault.

When he had got back from Las Vegas, with the torn-up pieces of Amanda's letter in his pocket, he shouldn't have stayed up half the night talking to people at Suzy's dinner party. He was thirty-one, not eighteen anymore. Finally, letting himself into the bedroom at two in the morning and finding Helen breathing specially deeply, pretending to be asleep, Rupert – king of the catnappers – had been unable to sleep himself, lying awake and thinking about Amanda.

Now he was expected to go out and celebrate that little jerk's freak silver. Malise had rocketed him after the competition.

'These things happen with horses and the less said about your cock-up today the better. Now we've got to go all out for the team gold. You've got six days to get Rocky together, and I want you on parade at half past nine tonight.'

'What for?'

'To celebrate Jake's silver.'

'I've got a previous engagement,' said Rupert coldly. 'I'm taking Helen and her Mother to Ma Maison.'

'That's where we're all going.'

'Cost a bomb,' snapped Rupert. 'Hardly imagine the Olympic fund will stretch to that.'

'It's already been paid for,' said Malise, not without a certain quiet pleasure which he afterwards regretted. 'Garfield Boyson rang from England and guaranteed the bill in advance.'

Rupert's face took on that curiously dead expression that boded trouble. Garfield Boyson had already approached Rupert; in fact he was the only sponsor Rupert would have been prepared to work with. If Boyson had picked up his bills for the next two years, he would have been able to slack off and only enter for the big prestigious competitions, gradually devoting more and more time to politics. And now Jake had pinched the sponsorship from under his nose.

'I thought you weren't going to drink until after the team event,' said Helen as Rupert, hair still wet from the shower, but already dressed in a grey striped shirt and white trousers, poured himself four fingers of whisky.

'Hasn't done me much good so far,' said Rupert, adding a splash of water from the wash basin. 'Need something to get me through what's obviously going to be a fucking awful evening.'

Helen tried very hard to curb her elation. Rupert had told her Boyson was footing the bill this evening, which meant Jake must have got the sponsorship, which in turn must mean he could now afford to leave Tory and marry her.

'It should be fun,' she said. 'I've never been to Ma Maison. Mother's dying to meet all the team, and I know Malise will enjoy Mother.'

'Should do,' said Rupert. 'He got enough practice driving tanks in the war.'

Helen had her back to Rupert, but her slender right arm was crooked over her back, wrestling with the zip of her dress, which was catching in her hair.

'Let me.' Moving towards her, Rupert pushed the newly washed hair aside and pulled the narrow gold zip up to the nape of the neck. He looked at her reflection in the mirror, breathing in the waves of Femme from her warm, newly-bathed, hopelessly excited body. She was wearing a dress of dark gold silk, high necked, long sleeved, falling to the ankles, and clinging caressingly to every inch of her body. Her hair, long at the back, was drawn up at the sides by two gold combs. For a second, his long fingers clamped her waist, then they shifted up towards her breasts. He realized that, totally untypically, she wasn't wearing a bra or even a petticoat. Feeling her tense and draw away, he tightened his grip.

'Haven't seen that dress. When d'you get it?'

'Ages ago – not for a special occasion – I just liked it.'

'I'm sure – you look great in it – almost too great.'

'What's that supposed to mean?' she said defensively, 'Ma Maison's always crammed with movie stars and you're always accusing me of looking too straight.'

'Not this time I'm not.' Rupert glanced at his watch. 'In

fact if we miss pre-dinner drinks, we've got time to . . .' He
began to pull down the zip.

'No,' gasped Helen, shrinking away from him, almost
falling over the dressing table, knocking bottles on the floor
in her desperate haste to get away.

'I'm all made up and ready,' she said, trying to make a
joke of it, 'and I promised Mother we'd meet at 9.30. We
can't leave her stranded at the restaurant.'

'How's she getting there?' said Rupert. 'On her broom-
stick?'

Ma Maison, thanks to Boyson's munificence, had
pushed out the boat. On the British team table there were
silver plates, silver goblets for the never-ending bottles of
Krug, white roses and lilies, surrounded by silver leaves, in
the silver bowl at the centre of the table, with two silver
horses on either side rearing up from the silver, satin table
cloth.

Jake was given a hero's welcome when he arrived. It took
him ages to get across the restaurant as people pumped his
hand and wanted to touch his silver medal, glinting in the
candlelight. A group of English actors who'd witnessed his
victory that afternoon in Arcadia were now happily getting
plastered, insisting that he sit down and have a drink.

'Who were those people?' he asked Fen, when he finally
reached the British team table.

'Michael Caine, Susan George, Roger Moore, to name
three,' said Fen.

'Oh. I thought they seemed familiar.'

At that moment a beautiful girl came up and, tapping
Rupert on the shoulder, handed him a menu and a pen.
'Would you very much mind?' She gave him a dazzling
smile.

'Not at all,' said Rupert, picking up the pen.

'Asking Jake Lovell if I could possibly have his autograph?'

Jake was already very tight, cocooned in euphoria,
acknowledging the accolades with one part of his mind, but
with the other back in the ring, jumping every fence, feeling

great waves of love for that tricky, brilliant horse who'd finally confounded the critics and come up with the goods.

Fen on the other hand wondered how much longer she could keep going. She'd been up since four, supporting Jake all the way, yet still praying Dino might turn up. Now, looking at Helen shining with happiness, aware that both Rupert and Jake were steadily getting drunk, she was filled with a feeling of terrible doom.

'Can I sit next to you and can we go to Disneyland tomorrow?' asked Ivor.

At that moment Suzy and Albie Erikson arrived to make up the party.

'Darling,' said Suzy, kissing Jake on the mouth, 'you were just sensational. You've got no excuse to resist my advances now.'

Fen shot a glance at Helen. She was looking at Suzy with pure hatred.

'We've just had an earthquake warning,' said Albie cheerfully. It's going to start right here at this table, thought Fen.

The waiter poured out more champagne.

'To Jake,' said Malise. Everyone except Jake and Rupert raised their silver goblets.

'To Hardy,' said Jake, half-draining his goblet. Then, looking across at Helen, his eyes not quite focusing, he raised it to her, blew her a kiss and drained the rest.

Help, thought Fen. 'Do you think the course'll be as difficult on Sunday,' she asked Rupert, frantic to distract his attention. Glancing around, he saw how wan she looked.

'You O.K., duckie?'

She nodded. 'I'm sorry about Rocky today. You must be heart-broken.'

Rupert shrugged. 'D'you know who I miss most of all?'

'Billy,' said Fen. 'I miss him, too.'

Ma Maison came up with a special menu which Fen had patiently to explain to Ivor.

'Clear soup, that's for Jake's clear round, then Coquille

St Jake à la champagne – that's scallops, then Gâteau Hardy. For God's sake, stop gazing at Goldie Hawn, Ivor.'

As dinner progressed Rupert's anger channelled into anti-American asides to irritate both Helen and her mother. 'The Olympics have become a shambles,' he was saying, 'a laboratory war between East and West. The Americans have better drugs, better computers to detect minor faults, better shrinks to psych out the athletes. The whole spirit of amateurism has gone.'

Mrs Macaulay, who was discussing property prices with Albie, swelled like a bullfrog. Helen, toying with a piece of coquille, managed to engineer Malise on to the subject of Jake. 'Naturally I'm disappointed Rupe didn't get a medal, but if anyone deserved one, it was Jake.'

Malise nodded. 'It's a fairy tale, really, after that terrible fall.'

'You're fond of him, aren't you?'

Malise smiled deprecatingly. 'He's tricky and cussed, but you have to admire his integrity. Of course, he's fantastically lucky in his home back-up.'

'Isn't Tory kind of dull?'

'God no,' said Malise sharply. 'She keeps him calm. I must say I never expected him to get a silver. I thought he'd crack.'

'But he didn't. He managed without her,' said Helen, kneading her bread into pellets in her agitation.

'She's carried him through the last ten years,' said Malise gently.

A diversion had been created on the other side of the table. Joan Collins had arrived and was being embraced by Rupert.

'Helen, my dear.' Malise lowered his voice, 'I've known you long enough to give you a piece of advice. Don't play with fire – particularly Olympic fire. Cool it – until after the games.'

Helen blushed furiously. 'I don't know what you mean.'

'Yes, you do,' said Malise gravely. 'I've got enough headaches keeping this lot together, without you rocking the boat.'

Joan Collins, svelte in black lace, was progressing down the table. 'Hi Jake. We haven't met, but what a round! I was stuck in the studio, but we suspended shooting to watch the second half. All the Brits went wild.'

She turned to Helen. 'Darling, how are you?' Then her eyes lit on the gold dress. 'You meanie. I had my eyes on that. Saw it at Giorgio's yesterday. Then I found out the price. You're lucky to have a rich husband to pick up the bills. Let me know if you ever get tired of him.'

Helen went very still.

'I think she already has,' said Rupert. He looked across at Helen, his fingers drumming on the table, 'Oh, this old thing,' he said softly.

'Oh, shut up,' said Fen. 'It does suit her.'

Suzy, who'd been flirting outrageously with Jake, got up to go to the loo. Mrs Macaulay immediately took her place. Jake found himself getting the fifth degree. Her big red face seemed to have an extra pair of eyes in the middle of her forehead. Really, he must be extraordinarily drunk. As Mrs Macaulay questioned him about Tory, the children, the yard and the horses, it became plain to her that, despite the fact that Jake was obviously four parts cut and kept calling her Mrs Campbell-Black, his marriage was a good deal happier than Helen's was to that monster who was still badmouthing America.

'The television coverage is utterly one-sided,' said Rupert. 'American viewers are totally unaware of any foreign competition.'

Helen turned to Malise helplessly. 'Don't you find LA fascinating?' she said. 'It's such an eclectic mixture of the functional and the bizarre.'

'Don't talk crap,' snapped Rupert. Malise frowned. Mrs Macaulay went purple. 'That's no way to address a lady.'

'What makes you think she's a lady?' drawled Rupert. 'Certainly not her parentage.'

Mrs Macaulay rose to her feet. 'I'll not stay here to be insulted.'

'Why don't you leave then?' said Rupert.

Only Malise's blandishments, Helen's pleadings and the arrival of the Gâteau Hardy, a splendid ice cream cake in the shape of a grey horse, induced her to stay.

Rupert returned to attacking the American team. 'They're all robots, Mary-Jo's a robot, Carol Kennedy's a robot, Dino Ferranti . . .'

'He is not,' yelled Fen.

'Fancy him, do you? So does my dear wife. She is dear, too. At least you earn your keep. She's a parasite.'

'Didn't know Helen came from Paris,' said Ivor, in surprise.

Everyone laughed, which for a moment eased the tension.

'There's a marvellous concert at the Hollywood Bowl tomorrow,' Helen said to Malise, 'and tomorrow they're doing *Hamlet* in Russian. I'd love to go.'

'Count me out,' said Rupert. 'Why not *Black Beauty* in Urdu? The only use for the Hollywood Bowl is to be sick in it.'

Fen resisted the temptation to giggle.

'There's a very naughty movie on at the Rialto,' said Suzy who, irritated to find she'd been ousted from her place next to Jake, wanted to get back in on the action. 'Why don't we all go tomorrow night?'

'My wife is not interested in sex,' said Rupert flatly.

Jake had been watching Rupert for some time. His eyes narrowed and his right hand played idly with the knife he'd been given to cut the cake.

'I'm not surprised,' he said, 'being married to you.'

Rupert looked up. There was a long embarrassed pause. Then Fen said desperately, 'Ivor and I are going on a tour of movie stars' homes tomorrow. We're going to see Rudolph Valentino's grave, and . . .' Rupert put a hand on her arm. 'Shut up, darling,' he said softly. 'Jake was talking.'

'Why don't you give her a break for a change?' said Jake.

'What kind do you suggest, a broken jaw perhaps?'

There was another awful pause.

'Just because you rode like a costive chimpanzee today,'

said Jake 'and screwed up the chances of the best horse in the class, you don't have to take it out on her.' He was quivering like a leopard about to spring.

'Oh dear,' drawled Rupert. 'We have grown in status since we won our silver medal this afternoon, haven't we?'

'Shut up,' yelled Jake.

'Been at the human growth hormone, have we?' taunted Rupert. 'Little man has had a happy day and is now making a big big night of it. Gipsy, my arse! You're just a little suburban creep whose mother screwed around so much she couldn't remember who your father was.'

Jake picked up the knife.

'No,' thundered Malise.

Suddenly the whole restaurant had gone quiet.

'You little creep,' said Rupert gently. 'The only thing I'd use you for is to measure my tennis net.'

Helen leapt to her feet, knocking over her wine glass.

'Stop it,' she screamed. 'Just because you're jealous as hell of Jake, you have to spoil everything.'

'St Georgia to the rescue,' said Rupert.

'I'm going,' said Helen. 'Thank you Malise, I'm real sorry, everyone,' and she fled out of the restaurant, a shimmering column of gold, cannoning off tables, blinded by tears.

'Aren't you going to cut that cake?' said Griselda.

Rupert caught up with Helen outside the restaurant. They stood side by side, not speaking, while the doorman conjured up their car. Helen was amazed that Rupert could be so charming, when Michael Caine stopped on the way out and asked them to a party the following night.

'Shut up,' he snarled on the journey back when she asked him to drive slower, 'Let me get home in one piece. Then we're going to do some straight talking.'

At the Eriksons' house the servants had gone to bed. Drunk though Rupert was, he managed to switch off the burglar alarm, before going into the drawing-room and pouring himself a glass of neat whisky. Helen walked towards the stairs.

'Where are you going?'

'Bed. I've had enough of you for one day.' Careful, she told herself, careful. But all those things that Malise and Fen had said earlier about Tory and not rocking the boat had only made her more desperate.

'Come here,' said Rupert.

It was not a voice to disobey. Rupert once again had that curiously dead expression on his face that always heralded trouble.

She removed her gold high heels, which would impede a quick get-away, and sank into the white warmth of Suzy's sumptuous fake-fur sofa.

'You ought to be ashamed of yourself,' she said in a low voice. 'I guess they had a celebration dinner for you when you won your bronze.'

'Hey, wait a minute. You've got very protective about Jake Lovell lately, haven't you? Embracing him when he came out of the ring, sticking up for him this evening. What's going on?'

Helen took a deep breath, aware that she was pushing a huge boulder towards the edge of a cliff and that any minute it might roll over, crushing innocent people in its path.

'What's going on?' repeated Rupert.

One of Helen's combs had fallen out of her hair, which flopped forward over her face. Looking at the golden tanned face and the shimmering gold body and the mass of shining hair, Rupert suddenly thought she had never looked so desirable – almost wanton – despite her terror.

'You're looking very good. As I said earlier, you're looking much too good. Don't tell me you've got yourself a man at last?'

'Yes, I have,' said Helen, goaded.

'Who is it?'

'Jake,' whispered Helen, 'Jake Lovell.'

'What did you say?'

'You heard me.'

'Jake Lovell!' Rupert began to laugh, totally without

mirth. 'Are you trying to tell me you've been having it off with that pathetic little cripple?'

'Don't you dare call him that!'

'A cripple,' Rupert went on, 'a warped gipsy cripple. Doing our bit for the disabled, are we? It figures, I suppose it made you feel good. A pound in the collection box on Sunday, a day a month for the NSPCC, hawking a slit tin up and down the high street once a year for the Distressed Gentlefolk and leaping into bed with a cripple. Mrs Campbell-Black does so much for charity. You bet she does!'

'You're revolting,' screamed Helen. 'Pulling everything down to your own disgusting level.'

'It appears to be you who've done the pulling.'

'Even at a time like this, all you can do is to make jokes.'

'Oh, believe me, baby, I don't think this is funny.'

'I love him,' sobbed Helen, putting her face in her hands, 'and he loves me.'

Rupert filled up his glass. Then in an almost calm voice that made Helen's blood run cold, he said:

'How long has this been going on?'

'Since February, when Marcus was hospitalized. I was worried stiff. Jake came in to see the consultant about his leg. He was very caring and supportive. I sure needed it after the Kenya trip.' She looked up at him. He stared back, as though daring her to go further. Helen dropped her eyes first.

'So that's why you've been hanging around the circuit like a bitch on heat. How extraordinary. I was barking up quite the wrong tree, thinking you'd be turned on by Janey, wasn't I? Never guessed your particular buzz would be a crippled dwarf.'

'Jake is not a dwarf,' screamed Helen. 'He's five foot seven.'

'You've measured him have you – all over?'

For a few seconds he paced up and down the room, trying to calm the rage that kept boiling up inside him.

'And you had to pick the one man who's always been out

850

to get me. Remember when he tried to kill me before the World Championship? He doesn't give a stuff about you. He just wants to score off me.'

'He doesn't. He wants to marry me.'

The boulder was over the cliff now, crashing down, gathering force.

'Marry you?' said Rupert, genuinely amazed, 'How?'

'As soon as he can get a divorce.'

'And he's going to leave that fat, rich cow for you?'

'Yes,' sobbed Helen. If she said it, it must be true.

'And presumably that night when I came back from Dinard and he was there jawing about healing breaches and team solidarity, he'd merely come to fuck you – I beg your pardon – make love with you?'

Helen lost her temper. 'Yes, he had. What about you and Podge, and Dizzy and Marion, and Samantha Freebody, and the one that gave me clap, not to mention all the others? You've never been faithful to me for one minute.'

'Oh, yes, I was,' said Rupert, 'until you got involved with that snivelling child and refused to come abroad with me. He doesn't give a stuff about you,' he went on. 'Why did he nearly kill me at Disneyland for saying Tory was fat? Why was he on the telephone to her the moment he won that medal? You're not going to break up that marriage. Anyway, what's so special about him?'

'He's a better rider,' screamed Helen, leaping to her feet, 'and he's much better in bed.'

The next moment Rupert had hit her across the room. Then he picked her up and hit her again, so that she collapsed sobbing across the glass table, spilling Rupert's whisky over the white sofa.

'And what the fuck are you going to live on? He's got no money. He can't give you anything but Lovell, baby.'

'He's got the Boyson sponsorship,' croaked Helen.

'He had,' said Rupert, gathering up his car keys. 'That was on the condition he kept his nose clean. It's pretty murky now.'

'Where are you going?' whispered Helen through lips

which were already beginning to swell up.

'To find your lover and beat him up till he sees stars and stripes. Then I'm going to string him from the Hollywood sign by his precious medal ribbon.'

'No!' screamed Helen, 'No, please!'

But Rupert had gone. Next moment she heard the crunch of his car roaring off towards Los Angeles.

Trembling like a palsied dog she ran to the telephone, and after several false starts managed to get through to the Olympic village. One of the security guards answered. No, they couldn't possibly wake Jake in the middle of the night. He'd gone to bed and he was sharing a room with two weightlifters, both of whom had a competition tomorrow and needed their sleep. There was a 'Do not disturb' sign on the door.

'Please,' sobbed Helen. 'It's his wife. I must talk with him. There's been a terrible accident.'

The security man hummed and hawed. 'O.K., I'll go and wake him.'

It seemed an eternity as she stood watching the remains of the whisky drip onto the oyster carpet, before Jake picked up the telephone.

'Tory, darling, what's the matter? Are you O.K.? Is it one of the kids?' Helen could hear the terrible anxiety in his voice, which made her cry all the more.

'No it's not Tory, it's me, Helen. It was the only way I could have them fetch you.' She was so hysterical it was a minute before he could discover what she was trying to say.

'Steady, pet. Calm down. Tell me what's the matter.'

'Rupert knows everything. He's suspected us for ages.' That wasn't true, but somehow it made a better story. 'We gave ourselves away this evening. He's on his way to the village.'

'Did he hurt you?'

'No – yes – well a little. I'm O.K., but he says he's going to kill you.'

As though in a dream, Jake watched a group of English cyclists, drunk and stark naked except for their security chains, being humoured very kindly along the passage by some security guards. For a wild second he wondered whether to seek asylum. There were enough guards on duty even in the middle of the night to protect him from a regiment of Ruperts. But then Rupert would probably go back to Arcadia and kill Helen.

'I'm so sorry,' she sobbed. 'I didn't mean to shop you. I was so frightened.'

'Sweetheart, you must keep calm.' It was as though he was speaking to a child and watching himself in a black and white film, cushioned by drink, yet curiously sober. This wasn't happening to him.

'Are you still wearing that gold dress? O.K. Well get out of it and change into some day clothes. Pack a case, put in clothes to last you for a few days, bring your passport, bankers' and American Express cards, dark glasses and as much spare cash as you can get your hands on. I'll come and fetch you.'

'Jake, I'm sorry.'

'It's all right, but hurry.'

Rupert stormed into the Olympic village twenty minutes later, and was held up by a further ten-minute hassle with the guards, because he was, if not completely drunk, obviously in a very wild, excitable state. Finally they let him through and he proceeded to search every room on the third floor, until he found Jake's. The weightlifters, trying to get their beauty sleep, were not amused to be roused by Rupert, roaring around the room, searching under beds, in the shower, even in the fridge.

Then he looked in Jake's chest of drawers. His passport and washing things had gone, and all his clothes, except his red coat, his breeches, white shirts, ties, and boots, which still hung in the wardrobe. On the chest of drawers were framed photographs of Tory and the children. It was as though he'd left the most important part of his life behind.

60

Rupert returned to the Eriksons's house to find all the lights blazing and the place full of cops. Suzy and Albie, coming in tight and finding doors opened, chairs knocked over, whisky spilt, Helen's room ransacked and the alarm unset, had promptly assumed that they'd been burgled. Rupert ran upstairs, took in the chaos of clothes, jewels and papers. All his spare cash had gone. He went back to the drawing-room.

'There's only been one burglary in this house. Jake Lovell's walked off with my wife.'

'Are you sure?' said Suzy in amazement. 'He didn't seem remotely keen on her.'

'He's a better actor than she is,' said Rupert. 'It's been going on since February. We've just had true confessions time.' He looked at the carpet and the sofa. 'Sorry about the whisky.'

He was very pale, which gave the suntan an almost green tinge, but seemed totally in control.

'Annunciata seems to have pushed off, too,' said Albie, wandering into the drawing-room and pulling off his tie.

'Oh, no,' said Suzy, far more upset by that than by Helen's departure. 'I've got fourteen people for lunch tomorrow.'

'Only thirteen without Helen,' said Rupert grimly.

After the police had gone he told them what had happened. In a way their flip, brittle approach helped him to cling onto his sanity.

'I must say she has been looking sensational since Jake arrived in L.A.,' said Suzy, 'and she got mad whenever he talked to me. I'm sorry, Rupert. Being bored with your wife

854

doesn't necessarily mean you want someone else to take her off your hands, particularly when it's your worst enemy.'

She was amazed Rupert was so calm. She found it rather chilling. Perhaps he was still in shock.

Then he said, 'Can I use your telephone to ring a few people? It'll be midday Tuesday morning in England now.'

'Of course,' said Suzy. 'Go into the study.' She was dying to discuss the whole thing with Albie.

Hell-bent on vengeance like an army scorching the earth, Rupert rang Amanda Hamilton in Scotland. Fortunately, perhaps, he got Rollo and explained what had happened. Rollo was most sympathetic and fully appreciated that Jake and Helen might try to seize the children. He said it would be perfectly all right for Charlene to fly up to Scotland with Marcus and Tab until Rupert got back from L.A.

'I'm awfully sorry,' Rollo said again. 'Have a word with Amanda.'

Even thousands of miles away Rupert could almost hear Rollo putting his hand over the receiver while he briefed his wife.

Amanda sounded extremely shocked. 'Darling, I'm so sorry. Are you O.K.?'

'Fine,' said Rupert, 'but they could have timed it better, with the team competiton on Sunday. The press are going to have a field day. That's why I want to get Tab,' he paused, 'and Marcus, of course, out of the way.'

'Did you know yesterday? Was that why Rocky jumped so badly?'

'No,' Rupert interrupted her. 'That was my fault.'

Then he rang his secretary, Miss Hawkins, and told her to put a red alert on all banker's cards, Access and American Express, to order the bank to stop all cheques and to close all Helen's accounts at Peter Jones, Harrods, Hatchards and Cavendish House in Cheltenham. Anyone at home, he said, particularly Charlene and Mrs Bodkin, or any of the grooms or the gardeners, would be fired if they spoke to the press.

He went back into the drawing-room with a grim smile

855

on his face. 'That should clip their wings.'

'I suppose I'll have to wait till morning to try and trace Annunciata,' said Suzy petulantly. 'I expect she's moved in with that frightful boyfriend.'

Annunciata, in fact, was fed up with working for Suzy, fed up with the long hours, the untidyness (Suzy just stepped out of her clothes) and the meals demanded at all hours. She never knew how many people to cater for.

It was only a summer job anyway and she'd hardly had time to see any of the games, not even Mr Lovell winning his silver. After being woken up by the frightful row between Mr and Mrs Campbell-Black, Annunciata had crept upstairs and heard the whole thing, including hearing Rupert hitting Helen and storming off into the night, and a hysterical Helen ringing Jake Lovell. Annunciata had then appeared and asked Mrs Campbell-Black if she needed any help with packing.

'She even wanted to know if we had any tissue paper,' Annunciata told her beady American boyfriend on the telephone. 'She was very frightened but she still remembered to take the hot tongs and heated rollers and her hair dryer.'

The beady American boyfriend, deducing that Rupert would come roaring back to the house in a towering rage, advised Annunciata to move out pronto. After all, it was only a summer job and he was cute enough to realise that here was a story which, if Annunciata, lived up to her name, and related to a newspaper, would save her having to work for several years.

Tory, after the victory celebrations, fell into bed at five in the morning, but still couldn't sleep for happiness. After all that struggle, Jakey had got his silver. She'd never seen him as happy as he'd been at the press conference. And now, with the Boyson sponsorship, he'd be able to have the horses he wanted; he and Fen wouldn't have to work quite so hard and he'd have more time with the children, which he'd always longed for, and they wouldn't have to scrimp and worry all the time about where the next penny was coming from. She didn't even feel tired when she had to get up at seven and take the sleepy, grumbling children to school. All day, people kept ringing up to congratulate her and Jake. Flowers and telegrams arrived constantly. The village was in a state of total euphoria, already planning the Welcome Home celebrations.

Tory watched clips of Jake's silver four times on breakfast television, and in Olympic Round-up, *and* played it back on the video, as she washed up all the glasses from last night. She didn't bother with lunch. She'd been on a diet and had lost ten pounds since Jake left.

Singing at the top of her voice, she went to collect the children. Jake would be getting up soon, she thought fondly, with a terrible hangover.

On balance, she'd decided not to fly to LA. By the time she'd got everything organized it would be Friday. Then, after a night flight, there'd only be half a day before the team event. Then they'd be coming home again. There'd be other occasions.

Her mother had rung up and Tory'd been so happy she'd forgotten to be cool with her. After all, it was a long time since Colonel Carter had taken Revenge away. Surely yesterday's medal proved Jake was the greater rider than Rupert?

She even found time to go and give Macaulay two apples and tell him about his master's great triumph. Housework could go by the board today. It was a beautiful September afternoon. Just a touch of wind ruffled the mill pond and the hanging green willow curtains.

The children were very fractious when she picked them up from school. Darklis had lost one shoe, but at least it was better than two, she said. Isa had been beaten up in the playground for boasting about his father. Tory sent them off to watch television. Suddenly as she was cutting the fat off the lamb chops for their supper, she felt very tired. She'd have a large vodka and tonic when she'd put the children to bed. Then perhaps Jake would ring. Another wave of happiness overwhelmed her.

Then she heard the noise of argument from the sitting-room. Isa, to Darklis' rage, had switched on Ceefax over The Sullivans so that she could see the Olympic results.

'Mummy,' screamed Darklis. 'Isa's hitting me.'

'Stop it, Isa,' yelled Tory.

'I always get the blame,' shouted Isa. 'Mummy, come quickly. There's something about Daddy.'

Shoving the chops under the grill, Tory ran into the sitting-room.

'Silver medallist Jake Lovell,' she read over the soothing tones of The Sullivans, 'has disappeared from the Olympic village. Not seen since last night, he is alleged by the *Los Angeles Times* to have gone off with Helen Campbell-Black, wife of Rupert Campbell-Black, a fellow member of the British team and a bronze and silver medallist in 1976.'

Tory thought she must be dreaming. It couldn't be true. They'd made some mistake. Jake had only rung her last night and told her he loved her. There was a moth bashing against the television screen.

'What does it mean, Mummy?' asked Isa. 'Where's Daddy gone?'

'Nowhere, darling,' said Tory in a strange voice. 'It's some mistake. Daddy wouldn't do that.'

She cancelled the Ceefax titles with the norm button then, after a few seconds, switched on the Ceefax Olympic report again.

'Mummy,' complained Darklis. 'I want to watch The Sullivans.'

'Silver medallist, Jake Lovell,' Tory read again, 'has disappeared from the Olympic village.'

It was a few seconds before she realized that the telephone was ringing. She rushed to answer it. It must be Jake to say it was a hideous mistake.

'Mrs Lovell?'

'Yes.'

'It's the *Sun* newspaper here.' It was that thickened voice again with which they announced trouble or asked difficult

858

questions. 'Just wondered if you've got anything to say about your husband running off with Helen Campbell-Black.'

'I don't know what you're talking about,' said Tory and slammed down the receiver.

The telephone rang again. It was the *Mirror* with the same question. Then it was the *Sun* again. Tory took the receiver off the hook. She started to shake violently.

'Mummy Mummy, the oven's on fire.' Darklis, having wandered into the kitchen in search of a biscuit, found the neglected chops ablaze under the grill. The frozen peas had boiled down to a green scum.

'Mummy, Mummy,' yelled Isa, starting to cry, 'they're talking about Daddy.'

Martin Bell, gazing sternly out of the television screen, his light brown curls whipped by the Los Angeles breeze, was confirming that Jake had indeed disappeared from the Olympic village; so had Helen Campbell-Black from the house in Arcadia, where she had been staying with her husband. According to the *Los Angeles Times*, whose reporter had interviewed the maid, Helen had left after a row with Rupert, directly after a dinner at Ma Maison restaurant, held to celebrate Jake's silver medal. Malise Gordon, the British chef d'equipe, had appealed to Jake to return for the team competition.

Tory was brought back to earth by the doorbell. It was a neighbour, Mrs Irvine.

'I heard it on the radio,' she said. 'I'm so sorry for you. I'll get the children's supper and answer the telephone. You'll not want to be bothered.'

'I'm sure it's some mistake,' said Tory.

'The poor little soul didn't seem to have taken it in,' Mrs Irvine told her husband later, 'so I got the doctor.'

At that moment the doorbell went. It was the local stringer for the *Daily Mail*. After that they came like locusts, with their long-range cameras, trying to get in through the front door, the back door, even the windows, swarming through the village, attempting to bribe grooms, neighbours, trades people, desperate for information.

Tory tried to put a call through to L.A., but all lines were engaged.

'It's a bad dream,' she kept telling herself. Jake wouldn't go off like that, not when he'd asked her to come out to L.A., not with the team event on Sunday, which meant almost more to him than the individual, and which he knew meant infinitely more to Malise.

Alarmed by her calmness and refusal to accept the facts, the doctor gave her a sedative. It was not that Jake wouldn't leave her, she kept saying, but he'd certainly never leave the horses, or the children, particularly in the middle of the Olympics. It was a belief she had to cling on to.

Malise, however, rang at ten o'clock. 'I'm afraid we know nothing more at this end. What I imagine happened was that Jake and Helen may have walked out together; at least that's what she told Rupert. Tempers flared. Rupert was absolutely livid at not getting the gold. He'd been simply poisonous all evening, threatening to beat Helen up. She appealed to Jake for help and he probably felt he ought to remove her somewhere safe until Rupert cooled down.'

Malise, reflected Tory, as the truth began to sink in, sounded like a gynaecologist telling her she'd got a stillborn baby.

'I'm sure there's nothing to worry about,' he went on. 'I'm convinced he'll come back for the team event.'

But Jake did not come back. The Games were into their second week. The public were slightly bored with tales of derring-do and mega-achievement; they wanted a good scandal. Rupert, his beautiful American wife and her romantic gipsy lover were the perfect answer.

'For just a handful of silver she left him,' quipped the *New York Times*.

Everyone who knew Jake and Rupert re-kindled the old feud. Jake had been bullied at school by Rupert and had got his revenge twenty-two years later by trouncing Rupert at the Olympics and then running off with his wife.

It was the same in L.A. as at the Mill House. Once the *Los Angeles Times* had led on Helen's row with Rupert and her running off with Jake, the reporters were everywhere. Like some horror army of killer ants, they crept through seemingly locked doors, through windows, haunting the Olympic village, the Eriksons's house, the stables and the exercise rings.

Fen, as their prime target, had been absolutely knocked sideways by the news.

'I must go to Tory,' she pleaded with Malise on the Wednesday morning. 'She sounds absolutely terrible now it's really sunk in. The English papers are crucifying Jake. I can't leave her to face it on her own. Let me fly home.'

'You can't,' said Malise, surveying his shambles of a team. 'Unless Jake comes back you'll have to jump Hardy.'

Everywhere Fen went, people were bad-mouthing Jake. Everywhere, the press swooped on her. Every time she worked Hardy the exercise ring was crowded with photographers and curious onlookers.

Rupert was far less vulnerable. First, he was holed up in Suzy's house, which was electric-fenced and burglar-alarmed to the teeth. Secondly, you didn't try and interview a man-eating tiger. Rupert was in the kind of eruptive mood that kept even the press at a distance.

'Jake was just doing his bit for Britain,' he told Billy on the telephone. 'Unfortunately in this case, the bit happened to be Helen. Extraordinary. For seven years she never looked at another man. Then, according to Dizzy, for the last five months no one's been able to see her ears for skirt.'

'He sounds terrible,' Billy told Janey as he came off the telephone. 'Do you think I ought to fly out there? The Beeb have offered to pay my fare and give me a fat fee if I'll help Dudley do the commentary for the team competition.'

'No, you ought not,' snapped Janey. 'Rupert's had it coming to him for years. I am not going to be left alone with Christy when he's so little . . . nor,' she added to herself 'am I going to let you loose in L.A. with Fenella Maxwell.'

Twenty-four hours limped by with no sign of Jake. On

Thursday morning Fen was working Hardy in one of the big exercise rings. Normally the German team should have been using the ring at this time but they'd willingly swapped over with the British to fox the press and give Fen the chance of a little privacy. It was nearly ten o'clock and the sun was already scorching down. Hardy, missing Jake, was edgy and miserable. He had received so much adulation on Monday and Tuesday morning. Now, suddenly, no one wanted to admire the horse whose master had disgraced a nation.

As she slowly cantered him around on the left rein, Fen pondered the horrors of the last two days. Rumours seethed. Jake and Helen had been sighted in England, in all parts of America, on a flight to Bermuda. Jake had grown a moustache, was wearing a false beard. Helen had dyed her hair, blonde, brunette, even cut it all off. Last night Malise had made another stiff-upper-lipped plea on television for Jake to come back: 'We will jump as a team and conduct ourselves like gentlemen.'

'Is he referring to Griselda?' said Rupert.

Rupert still keeps up the stream of flip remarks, thought Fen, allowing no one to see his black despair and utter humiliation. Malise seemed terribly upset too. Fen herself had been in tears all night. She wished she could help Tory. Bloody Helen Campbell-Black, she thought savagely, not even able to hold off until after the games.

Fen's hair was wringing wet beneath her hat, as was her T-shirt. The reins slipped between her damp hands. Suddenly she was overwhelmed by longing for Dino. She had never needed him more. She could have lain down and slept for a year in his arms. But she musn't think of Dino or Helen; it only upset her. She must keep calm and psych herself into the right frame of mind for Sunday. Perhaps by some miracle Jake would come back.

'Oh Hardy, where's your master?' she sighed.

In the distance she could see the German team riding down from the stables in a cloud of dust to take over. She must make herself scarce before the press turned up. This afternoon, she thought wearily, she had to take Ivor to Disneyland again.

Catching her not concentrating, Hardy gave a whinny and a great whicker of joy and carted her across the ring.

'For God's sake, you disobedient bugger,' yelled Fen, hauling ineffectually on his mouth, 'where the bloody hell d'you think you're going?'

Hardy ground to a halt. Fen glanced up and gasped. For there, holding Hardy's dark blue sweat rug, tall and golden as a Lombardy poplar in autumn, stood Dino Ferranti.

'Hi, Hardy baby,' he drawled, putting up a not altogether steady hand to stroke the dappled face. 'I'm real glad you haven't forgotten me, just as I'm real glad your mistress's language is a lousy as ever.'

Dino had had a long and very trying nine months, but everything was compensated for when he looked up and saw the expression of incredulous, bewildered delight on Fen's face, the expression on which left him in absolutely no doubt about how she felt.

'You've gone blond again,' she muttered.

'I know. I didn't seem to score with grey hair.'

'Oh Dino, Dino,' she cried, and tumbled off Hardy into his arms. He kissed her so fiercely she had no doubt of his feelings towards her.

'Oh, I love you,' she bleated incoherently. 'I've missed you. I've been so so miserable.'

'Me too,' he groaned. 'Oh Christ, darling, we've been so dumb.'

As he held her tight, she could feel how much he was trembling and how his ribs protruded beneath the blue denim shirt.

'You've got so thin,' they both said simultaneously, and then started to laugh. Next moment Fen's laughter had turned to tears.

'It's so awful.'

'I know. I'm real sorry, sweetheart.' He took her face in his hands, kissing her forehead and her nose and the tears spilling out of her eyes before he found her mouth again.

863

'No, no,' she protested, when at last he freed her. 'It was so awful for you about Manny. Did you get my letter?'

'There was so much mail and I was so unglued I didn't even get around to looking at it until yesterday. Hell, I needed you so badly. But I guess I couldn't handle seeing you again in case you were still mad at me, or didn't feel the way I did. So I chickened out and went home to lick my wounds. Then I heard about Helen and Jake buggering off. I figured you might need me as much as I needed you. Right? So here I am.'

'Oh, I'm so glad,' said Fen, burying her face in his chest. 'I was so aching to see you, it was the main thing that drove me on to get selected. I thought I'd die when Mary-Jo said you weren't coming. You won't ever disappear again, will you? Life's so awful when you're not there.'

'You try getting rid of me.' He was about to kiss her again when he said, 'Ouch.'

Hardy, irritably trying to tell them they were hopelessly neglecting a silver medal winner, had nipped Dino on the shoulder.

Then all three jumped violently as a rousing chorus started bellowing, 'Vy vos zey born so beautiful, vy vos zey born at all.'

Swinging round, they found the entire German squad sitting on their horses, laughing their heads off. 'And about bloody time too, my friends,' said Ludwig.

At the entrance to the stables the inevitable jackal pack of reporters was hovering.

'Heard from Jake?'

'No,' snapped Fen.

'How's Tory bearing up?'

'Haven't talked to her today.'

'Where's he gone?'

'I don't know.'

Oh, the bliss of having Dino there once more, to get rid of them.

'Go on! Pack it in. Fucking get off our backs,' he said, hustling Fen and Hardy through the gates.

'Dino, Dino Ferranti,' said one of the reporters with quickening interest. 'You stayed at Jake's barn last fall, didn't you? What sort of guy was he?'

'The greatest,' snapped Dino. 'Not just as a rider but as a human being. If he walked out on the games, he must have had a good reason, O.K.? I guess he wanted to protect Helen from her bastard of a husband.'

On the way to Hardy's box, Dino started kissing Fen again.

'Give him to me,' said Sarah, grabbing Hardy. 'You are in no fit condition. Take her away, Dino. She deserves the afternoon off. Make a change from taking Ivor round Disneyland.'

Dino put his arm through Fen's. 'I'm staying at Carol Kennedy's place just up the road. Let's go there. At least we can be alone.'

'I ought to have a bath,' said Fen, suddenly aware of her sweaty hair and clothes.

'I'll give you one,' said Dino. 'It'll take hours.'

Fen blushed scarlet.

'Dino!' shouted a voice.

It was a middle-aged woman, with the kind of lean muscular body that looks better in breeches than in the summer dress she was wearing.

'We thought you weren't coming,' said her husband.

'Changed my mind.'

'We were real sorry about Manny.'

'Yeah, it was tough.'

There was a pause. The couple looked inquiringly at Fen, whose hand was still firmly held by Dino. Aware she must look hot and shiny from being kissed, she hung her head. Dropping her hand, Dino took hold of her hair at the back and very gently yanked her head upwards.

'You haven't met Fenella Maxwell,' he said in the most drawling voice, 'my future wife.'

Fen jumped out of her skin, then looked up at him with such startled, anxious eyes that he let go her hair and put a comforting arm round her shoulders.

'Truly?' she gasped.

'Very very truly,' Dino said, laughing.

'Your future wife,' said the woman in delighted surprise. 'Is that a fact, Fenella – er – Maxwell?'

'Jake Lovell's sister-in-law, you were too polite to say,' said Dino. 'She's with the British team.'

'Well, congratulations,' said the husband, pumping Fen by the hand. 'How long have you been engaged?'

Dino looked at his watch and laughed again. 'About fifteen seconds,' he said, 'perhaps sixteen by now.'

'Oh, wow! This may not be the best way of relaxing before a mega-competition,' said Dino, 'but it's certainly the nicest.'

He eased himself out of her and collapsed on to the flowered sheets. Carol Kennedy's house was near Suzy Erikson's. Out of the window they could see the mountains.

'I feel so relaxed I don't think I'll ever get up again,' said Fen.

'It sure went through the top of the Richter scale,' said Dino. 'Were you scared?'

'Not as much as I thought I was going to be.'

'Nor was I. It didn't matter if we bombed; we've got all our lives to get it right. Shall we have lots of kids? My Daddy's dying to be a grandfather.'

Fen rolled over. 'Are you sure you want to get married?'

'Don't you?' he said, appalled.

'Oh, yes, more than anything. I just don't want you to feel trapped.'

'I want to be trapped. You gotta make an honest man of me.'

He leaned on his elbow, running his hand down her body, stroking the hollow of her stomach.

'I'm going to feed you up.'

'I'm sorry I was so vile in England.'

'Well, I came on pretty hostile too. You were bent out of shape over Billy. I over-reacted and backed off too hard so as not to crowd you.'

'But all that stupid business with Enrico,' protested Fen. 'Ouch! That's my boob you've dug your nails into.'

'Anyone else, I wouldn't have minded, but he's such a bastard. No, that's not true. I'd have killed you if it had been anyone, I was so jealous.'

'I haven't been out with a single man since you left.'

'What about married guys?' said Dino. Fen giggled. 'Nor them, either. How about you?'

'Um – well I did try to screw my way out of it, but it didn't do any good. I knew I'd never love anyone else. I worked and worked. I had fantasies about getting the gold and dazzling you into loving me back.'

Fen snuggled up to him. 'You didn't need a gold. God, I feel guilty feeling so ridiculously happy, when everything else is so awful.'

She knew she ought to put a call through to Tory, but couldn't bring herself to burst the bubble of bliss just yet. She looked at the lean brown length of him, revelling once again in the thick blond hair, the Siamese-cat eyes, the wide, curling mouth. 'I never dreamed I'd end up with anyone as stunningly attractive as you,' she said humbly. 'In fact, your looks have definitely improved with age. D'you think I ought to ring Malise just in case he thinks his entire team is doing a disappearing act?'

'He knows.' Very gently Dino began to stroke the inside of her thigh. 'I wanted to test the water, so I made sure I bumped into him first this morning. He told me where to find you. He also reckoned,' Dino smirked slightly, 'you were going into a decline.'

'I was not,' said Fen indignantly. Then, as Dino moved his hand upwards and began to slide two fingers in and out of her, she gasped and said, 'Well, perhaps I was.'

'Come here,' said Dino, bending over to kiss her. 'I need a fix again.'

In the end it was he who made her ring Tory. She heard the operator saying the call came from L.A.

'Jake. Is that you?' Tory's voice trembled with hope.

'No, I'm afraid it's only me, Fen. You O.K.? No, I'm

867

awfully sorry, there's really no news of him this end. How are the children taking it?'

'We're managing very well,' said Tory, in an unnaturally bright voice. 'I just hope Jake isn't too shattered by the press furore to come out of hiding.' She started to cry.

'Oh, please don't,' said Fen, feeling her eyes fill with tears. 'Look, d'you remember Dino, Dino Ferranti? He turned up today. Have a word with him.' She handed the receiver to Dino.

Dino was immensely kind but very practical. Had she got enough food in the house? Was anyone helping her with the kids and the horses? Who was fending off the press?

'Everyone's being marvellous,' said Tory, 'but they're so embarrassed. They were so proud of Jakey and were planning this huge welcome-home bonanza. Now they don't know what to do.'

'Tell them to cheer for Fen. Angel, please don't cry.' He raised a palm upwards in a particularly Latin gesture of despair, then said, 'Listen, I'm going to get a night flight, right?'

'Oh no,' whispered Fen in horror. 'You can't do that. I need you.'

'I'll be with you sometime tomorrow,' he went on. 'Don't bother to meet me. I'll call from Heathrow. I'll sort everything out. Well, he might do still; we'll just cross our fingers.'

Putting down the telephone, he gathered Fen into his arms.

'I can't bear it, not so soon after I've found you. I need you as much as she does,' she sobbed. 'I'm sorry to be so selfish.'

Dino let her cry, stroking her hair, cradling her.

'It's the most awful thing I've ever had to do,' he said, 'but if I'm joining your family, right, I have a responsibility towards all of them. Things are simmering along at the moment, but if Jake doesn't show on Sunday, the shit is really going to hit the fan. He's already blown the monetary advantages of his silver. The press are gonna assassinate him for letting down his country and you've no idea of Rupert's capacity for vengeance. Every door'll be shut to him. He'll probably be suspended for ten years.'

'Oh, poor Jake,' said Fen in horror. 'Why *did* he do it?'

Dino brushed her damp hair and kissed her forehead. 'I guess he fell in love. We know how potent that is. Helen was suicidal, frantic to escape from Rupert. Jake momentarily wanted someone glamorous to complement his new star status, probably wanted to deal the coup de grâce to Rupert. Nothing like cuckolding your enemy. All the same, I figure Helen's to blame. However much Rupert hammers Jake for enticement, I guess it was Helen who pulled the plug out. She blew it to Rupert, knowing it would trigger Jake into leaving. But whatever happens, Jake's on a collision course. Rupert'll ruin them both.'

He glanced at her watch. 'I'd better book that flight.'

As he came off the telephone Fen put her arms round him. 'I didn't believe it was possible, but I love you about a million times more than I did an hour ago; all the same I wouldn't tell Tory about us yet. Other people's happiness tends to push you over the top.'

61

It was like the House of Atreus, as disaster after disaster hit the British team. Despite every effort, Desdemona was still not fit, which meant that, unless Jake came back, Fen would have to ride Hardy.

'He's a misogynist,' grumbled Fen next morning, after he'd had her off for the second time. 'I'll never get him out of the collecting ring in this mood.'

'Well, we've got to have someone whose round we can drop,' said Griselda, kicking Mr Punch on and clearing the combination on a perfect stride.

'Bitch,' thought Fen. 'May you be struck down by toads and pestilence.'

She spoke too soon. Coming back to the Olympic village that evening she found Griselda staggering out of the loo, as green as the elephant who ate the mushroom in the Babar books.

'I've vomited fifteen times,' she announced, collapsing onto her bed.

'Too many cyclists,' muttered Fen under her breath. 'Shall I get a doctor?'

'No,' groaned Griselda. 'I'll be O.K.'

By late evening poor Griselda's temperature had gone up to 104 and she was admitted to hospital with suspected food poisoning.

'And then there were three,' said Rupert next morning, as they had a final workout before the competition the following day. Despite his appearance of icy indifference, Rupert was in a terrible state. Rage against both Helen and Jake kept bubbling up inside him, corrosive as black bile.

Despite the quantities of whisky he'd shipped each night in search of oblivion, he had hardly slept since they'd gone. Drink had never affected his eye in the past, but watching Humphrey Bogart movies on television all night hadn't helped. In the relentless Los Angeles sunshine that morning, as he was cantering towards a huge upright, Jesus the Mexican decided to gallop across his path ten yards beyond the fence. Just for a second Rocky panicked, took off too early, clouting the heavy pole with his forelegs. Turning a somersault in the air, he crashed down with Rupert under him.

By the time Fen, Malise and Jesus the Mexican had reached them, Rocky had scrambled to his feet. Shaking himself gingerly, he decided he wasn't hurt and cantered off. Rupert tried to get up, groaned and fell back, clutching his shoulder.

'What is it?' said Malise, dropping to his knees.

'Shoulder,' said Rupert through clenched teeth. 'Dislocated. Get me to a fucking hospital at once and get it put back. Jesus!'

'*Si*,' said the Mexican, 'I am here.'

Just for a second a ghost of a smile flickered across Rupert's face.

'Not you,' he said. 'I was talking to an earlier model.'

Malise went with Rupert to the Casualty Department. He lay stretched out in the ambulance, his face grey-green, sweat beads drenching his forehead and upper lip, cursing quietly to himself the whole way. Just to look at the horrible angle of his arm made Malise feel sick.

'At least it's not fractured,' said the doctor, after the X-Ray. 'Pretty straightforward to put back. You'll just be out of action for a few days.'

Malise and Rupert exchanged glances. Rupert turned to the doctor.

'I don't want an anaesthetic.'

'Don't be ridiculous,' said Malise.

'I don't need one. How did they manage before they had chloroform? I don't want my reflexes fucked up for tomorrow.'

'You're not jumping tomorrow,' said Malise.

'What other alternative do we have?'

'Appealing to Jake to come back.'

'If he shows his face within fifty miles of the show ring he'll end up in here as well,' said Rupert. 'In the morgue.'

'Have you any idea how painful it will be without an anaesthetic?' said the doctor.

'Yes,' said Rupert. 'Our doctor at home put it back for me once when I was out hunting. I carried on for the rest of the day.'

'You were younger then,' said Malise.

'This is the second time,' said the doctor.

'I know,' said Rupert, throwing back his head and clenching his teeth. 'Come here, sweetheart,' he added to the beautiful nurse who was gazing at him with pity and admiration, 'and hold my hand.'

He was about to say he expected he'd do it a third time, but as the doctor got to work he fainted.

'At least the pain should take my mind off my erring wife,' he said when he came around. But despite repeated shots of morphine, he had never known such agony.

At five o'clock Malise called a press conference: 'The British team is down to three riders. One of them Rupert Campbell-Black, has been very seriously injured today but is determined to ride tomorrow. I want to make one more appeal to Jake Lovell to think seriously about coming back. Great Britain needs him. Rupert has agreed there will be no reprisals.'

Fen's night was scarcely better than Rupert's. She had thought that now Dino had re-appeared, everything would be easier. But she found herself even twitchier. Had he really been there at all? Did he really love her and want to marry her? She felt bitterly ashamed of the resentment she felt that he'd gone to look after Tory. If he really loved you, mocked a voice, as she got dressed at four o'clock in the morning, he wouldn't have been able to tear himself away. She'd been miserable for so long, she couldn't adjust to happiness. In a few hours she was going to face the worst ordeal of her life and she felt quite unprepared to cope with it. She must get herself into the right frame of mind. But Enrico had gone off her as soon as he'd got her into bed. Might not Dino?

'Tell me how stupid I am,' she said to Lester the teddy bear, as she tied her tie.

But Lester didn't answer.

'Have a nice day,' she said to him as she left the room. 'It's more than I shall have.'

Malise was standing by the car. Ivor was already in the back, looking green. 'I slept like a log,' he said in a surprised voice.

'Lucky you,' said Fen.

The press surged forward.

'Any news from Jake?'

'Nothing,' said Malise bleakly. 'We shall only be fielding three riders. It's too late for him to declare now.'

Rupert was glad when the night was over. He'd always assumed he would be able to withstand torture; now he wasn't sure. He wondered if the doctor had trapped a nerve when he'd put the shoulder back.

At five-thirty he had a bath. The hot water helped to relax him, but after a quarter of an hour he found he couldn't get out. The slightest move to raise himself produced absolute agony in his shoulder. Another half-hour passed, as he slumped between each thwarted attempt. He was terrified of slipping. With his left foot he pulled out the plug, waiting for the enamel surface to dry, so he might have more grip. It must be getting on for six-thirty. They'd be walking the course in an hour. He'd have to yell for Suzy, who probably had a hangover and wouldn't wake up. He was almost sobbing with pain and frustration. If only he could crawl to the bedroom, he could give himself another shot of morphine. Then he heard the doorbell go, then again. He made another attempt to get out. Then he heard Suzy's door open.

'Suzy,' he croaked. Then he heard voices in the hall.

Probably Malise, wondering where the hell he was.

'He's not in his room, so he must be in the bath,' Suzy was saying sleepily.

Thank God he hadn't locked the door. Suzy banged on it.

'Someone to see you, Rupe.'

'Who the hell is it?' he said.

'It's me,' said a blissfully familiar voice, and there in the doorway stood Billy.

For a second Rupert gazed at him, dumbfounded.

'Christ, do I ever need you!' he said in an unsteady voice.

'I know. I'm terribly sorry about Helen.'

'No, to get me out of this bloody bath,' said Rupert. 'But give me a shot of morphine first. It's on the chest of drawers in my bedroom.'

The sting of the needle entering his shoulder was the most wonderful sensation he could imagine.

'How the hell did you manage to get out of Janey's clutches?' he asked.

Billy grinned. 'I told her that sometimes water was thicker than blood.'

'Draw's good,' said Malise. 'We're fourteenth out of sixteen.'

All the other riders were tremendously sympathetic and friendly.

'They can afford to be,' said Rupert. 'They think we've had it.'

'Who are the favourites?' asked Fen.

'Americans, Germans, Swiss,' said Rupert. 'We're about a million to one. I've put a monkey on.'

'Don't let Fen see any of the papers,' hissed Malise. 'They've all crucified Jake.'

'Good,' said Rupert. Then, shooting a sidelong glance at Malise, he said, 'It's not the winning that matters, it's the being taken apart.'

It was a tremendous boost to the British team to see Billy.

'Can't you jump?' said Ivor.

'I'm going to sit in the commentary box with Dudley,' said Billy, 'and be wildly partisan.'

'At least you'll get the names right,' said Fen.

'I'm glad you think so, Fiona,' said Billy. 'How's Rupe bearing up?' he added in an undertone.

'He won't talk about either Helen or Jake except to make the odd flip crack. He probably will with you. I think he's going through hell, but I can't quite work out if it's violent possessiveness or murdered pride, or whether he's suddenly realized he loves her.'

At seven-thirty they walked the course. Everyone agreed it was the biggest ever built in show-jumping. Fen could walk straight underneath the parallel without bumping her head. Close up, for the first time she realized how huge the fences were.

'Can't think why they don't stage the Olympic swimming contest in the water jump,' she said.

Ivor's mouth was open wider than ever. 'It's even worse than the individual.'

In front sauntered the American team. In their white, short-sleeved shirts and breeches, showing off their mahogany suntans, long bodies and thoroughbred legs, laughing and exuding quiet confidence, they looked as though they'd been fed on peaches and T-bones all their life. The crowd gave them a colossal cheer of encouragement as they passed. The German team looked equally together as they goose-stepped out the distances. But for the first time Fen felt there was real solidarity between the British team.

The arena was like an oven already. By the time I go in, thought Fen, it'll be turned up to Regulo 10.

'That's going to cause the most trouble,' said Malise, looking at the fence constructed in the shape of a huge brown derby hat. 'It's so unfamiliar, you'll have to ride them really hard at it; then there's that big gate immediately after.'

'At least they've scrapped the hot dog,' said Ivor, in relief. 'All these flowers are giving me hay fever.'

Rupert broke off a frangipani and gave it to Fen.

'You'll be had up for demolishing the course even before you start,' she said.

Malise was right. The derby fence upset everyone. Ludwig, the German pathfinder, expected to go clear, was nearly brought down by it, and knocked up sixteen faults.

'Roll on ze next Olympics,' he said ruefully, as he came out of the ring. 'I am very bored of being ze good loser.'

Canadian, Australian, Italian and French riders all came to grief. Jesus the Mexican had a punishing fall. The first American rider, Lizzie Dean, came in and cleared the derby, but ran slap into the gate and had eight faults at the combination.

'I can't watch any more. My self-confidence is in tatters,' said Fen. 'The only good thing about this competition is Billy doing the commentary. He keeps saying "Hooray" every time a foreign rider kicks out a fence.'

'You'll be jumping in three-quarters of an hour,' said Malise. 'Better go and warm Hardy up. By the way, some flowers arrived for you. They're in the tackroom.'

He allowed himself a small smile as Fen bolted the 400 yards to the stables. The flowers were two dozen pale pink roses and the card inside said, 'To darling Fen, Good Luck, I love you, Dino.'

'How the hell did they get them delivered here?' she said.

'Carol Kennedy bought them,' said Sarah. 'He promised Dino he'd make sure you got them. Stop grinning like a Cheshire cat. This is no time to be worrying about the opposite sex.'

'Having got these,' said Fen, putting them in a bucket of water, 'I can now stop worrying about it.'

Because they were fielding only three riders, the British team started jumping with the second riders of the other teams. Among these, Hans Schmidt only had a couple of poles down for eight faults and Mary-Jo came in and showed everyone how to do it, with a glorious clear.

'That should encourage Ivor,' said Fen, who had jumped off Hardy for a second to watch him.

Ivor rode in blinking. Not a seat was empty. After Mary-Jo's gold earlier in the week, and her clear now, the huge crowd was at fever pitch.

'I always enjoy Ivor's intellectual approach to the sport,' said Rupert, from the shade of the riders' stand. 'Now Ivor has removed his hat, will he ever find his head again?'

After Tuesday's fiasco, Ivor started well and rode with colossal determination. The sailboat, the derby, the high gate, the huge wall, the massive blue water jump caused him no trouble at all. Then he unaccountably stopped twice at the parallels.

'That's that then,' said Rupert. 'Let's go and have a screw, Dizz.'

'For God's sake get your bat out, Ivor,' Billy was yelling in the commentary box, to the startled delight of the viewers. 'One more stop and the whole team's eliminated.'

Scarlet in the face, as if by telepathy, Ivor pulled his whip out of his boot, in which it was tucked, and gave John half a dozen hefty whacks.

'Good God,' said Malise.

The picture of injured pride, John heaved himself over the parallel, and, swishing his tail in rage, proceeded to go clear, except for bringing down the middle element of the combination.

'Absolutely marvellous. Well done, Ivor,' said Billy, excitedly from the commentary box. 'Do you know, he only paid £1000 for that horse?'

'Ten faults, plus one time fault. That's not at all bad,' said Malise.

Fen knew she should have some inner tap which could turn off all outside excitement and leave her icily calm. On Desdemona she'd always jumped best when she was angry. But Hardy needed to be kept serene. He seemed a little tired after his medal-winning adventures on Monday, which would at least make him jump more carefully and not start ducking out of his bridle. Following Jake's lead, she had removed the cotton wool from his ears and let him go to the entrance of the arena, so he could watch the preceding round. It was both inspiring and daunting. Carol Kennedy went clear, to colossal applause, which meant the Americans were on twelve faults at the end of the third round, and could probably scrap Lizzie Dean's round. The Tarzan howls and the waving American flags had Hardy hopping all over the place.

'The time is incredibly tight,' said Malise. 'Don't waste any of it in the corners. But remember, the important thing is to get round at all costs. If you're disqualified we're out.'

'You do say the cheeriest things,' said Fen.

'Good luck,' said Rupert.

Fen felt the butterflies going berserk in her stomach, as the terror finally got to her.

'I can't face it,' she said in panic. 'I simply can't jump in front of all those people.'

'Yes, you can,' said Rupert, putting his good left hand up to squeeze her thigh. 'Come on, darling, you'll float over them. Hardy's done it all before. Leave it to him.'

'Are you sure?' Suddenly she looked terribly young.

Rupert smiled. 'Quite sure.'

Out in the arena there was nothing like it. Nothing like the fear and the exposure in that blazing white hot heat, watched by 200,000 eyes and millions and millions of television viewers.

Billy, who by now was well stuck into the whisky, admired the slender figure in the black coat, her blonde hair just curling under her hat, one of Dino's pink roses in her buttonhole.

'This is certainly the most beautiful girl rider in the world,' he said. 'Riding Hardy, with whom her brother-in-law, Jake Lovell, did so brilliantly on Monday to get the silver medal. Now come on, darling.'

'I told you not to mention Jake,' hissed Dudley, putting

his hand over the microphone, 'and don't call Fiona "darling".'

The relief of the bell stopped all thought-process. Suddenly Fen's nerves vanished.

'It's you and me, babe,' she whispered to Hardy as he cleared the first four fences without any trouble, kicking up the tan, following the hoof prints of earlier riders. She steadied him for the derby. He didn't like it, then decided he did and took a mighty leap, clearing it by a foot. The yell of the crowd distracted him, the heat haze above the gate made judging the distance difficult. Fen asked him to take off too early, he kicked out the fence, and then toppled the wall after that, hurting himself, eyes flashing, ears flattened, tail whisking like an angry cat.

'Now she'll go to pieces,' thought Malise in despair.

But Fen held him together and drove him on, picking her way over the obstacles, not touching any of them.

'Look at him,' said Sarah in ecstasy. 'He's really, really trying.'

Coming up to the last fence, Hardy started showing off and gave a huge kick back. The crowd laughed. He kicked back again. Lazily whisking over the last fence, he gave it an almighty clout. For a second the pole shuddered, trembled on the edge, then fell back into the cup.

'God is on our side after all,' said Malise.

'Bloody good,' said Rupert, as Fen slipped off the huge horse, flinging her arms round Hardy's neck, and taking back all the beastly things she'd ever said about him.

'Until the next time,' said Sarah.

Now the last riders in each team had to jump. Peter Colegate, riding instead of Dino, knocked up a surprising fifteen faults, so his was the round the Americans dropped. Hans Schmidt went clear.

The round, however, the world was waiting for was Rupert's. Fen straightened his tie and did up one brass button of his red coat which was draped over his damaged right shoulder: 'Are you O.K.? Does it hurt horribly?'

'Yes, but I've just had another shot; I'm so spaced out I'll probably carry Rocky over the fences with one finger.'

Not by a flicker, as he rode into the ring, did Rupert betray his awareness that every camera in the world was trained on him to see what the effect had been of Helen pushing off. If the press had gone to town on Jake that morning, it was without Rupert's help. He had refused to say a word to them.

He held the reins lightly in his left hand. He carried no whip. The crowd, seeing that he was coming in to jump the most punishing course in history with one arm in a sling, roared their approval and encouragement.

Dropping his reins, he removed his hat. His blond hair glittered golder than any medal. The pain was agonising. Even the gentlest pop in the collecting ring had jolted his shoulder unbearably, but none of this showed in his face.

Rocky was a gallant and kind horse. Something was different today; perhaps it was the sympathetic, almost helpless way Rupert had jumped him earlier; perhaps it was because for once his master wasn't carrying a whip. Suddenly there was an expression of deep responsibility on Rocky's handsome, golden face.

'I will take care of you today,' he seemed to be saying. 'Just to make you feel a sod for all the times you've beaten me up in the past.'

Over the first two fences Rupert had the greatest difficulty balancing himself, then he settled in. Rocky was jumping carefully, only clearing each fence by an inch or so. Now he was thundering down to the water – and over. Now he was over the derby and the gate, now turning for the huge three-part combination.

'Undoubtedly Rupert is the best rider in the world,' shouted Billy jubilantly in the commentary box. 'Look at the power of those leg muscles; he isn't even shifting in the saddle. Go on, Rupe, go on.'

For a miraculous moment it looked as if he was going to go clear; then Rocky trailed a leg at the last fence and, unlike Fen, brought it down. Out he rode to almost the biggest cheer of the day.

Billy bolted out of the commentary box to congratulate him. 'Wait,' wailed Dudley. 'There are still the Japs and the Portuguese to jump.'

'That was absolutely brilliant,' said Billy, rushing up to Rupert. 'God knows how you did it.'

'Should have been a clear,' said Rupert, kicking his right foot out of the stirrup and wincing and biting his lip as he lowered himself down.

'Tremendous performance, Rupert,' said Malise, looking at his score sheet, 'The Yanks are on twelve, the Germans on sixteen, the Swiss on eighteen, the French on twenty. We're fifth with twenty-two,' he added with quiet satisfaction.

'You shouldn't be jumping, but I'm sure glad I saw you. Congratulations,' said a voice. It was the doctor from the hospital.

Rupert smiled, but the doctor, noticing his pallor and how much he was sweating, waved his medical kit. 'I thought you'd probably need something stronger to face this afternoon.'

'I need an enormous whisky,' said Rupert.

'Not too enormous,' said Malise.

62

Afterwards Fen couldn't recall if she ate any lunch. Ivor ate his way solemnly through two steaks without realizing it. Billy came too, cracking jokes with Rupert, keeping up everybody's spirits. They knew they wouldn't win, the margin was too big, but they were quietly elated. They had conducted themselves with honour.

Prince Philip, who was an old friend of Rupert's, came up and congratulated them.

'Really tremendous! Well done, all of you! Don't know why you bother to ride with any hands at all, Rupert.'

'I'd better go back and wind up Dudley,' said Billy, getting to his feet. 'He says I must be more enthusiastic about the other nations. Good luck, everyone. Take care of yourself, Rupe.'

Rupert raised his hand. He wished Billy could stay. He was beginning to feel desperately tired and the pain was really getting to him.

'Can you give me something?' he said to the doctor.

'It'd be better nearer your round or the effect might wear off. I daren't give you two shots or you'll pass out in the ring.'

When the riders came out for the second round, it was soon apparent that the first round had overstretched the horses. Despite menacing clouds on the horizon and the rumble of thunder, the sun was at its height, beating down on to the stadium at a heat of over 100 degrees.

Only the top ten teams went through, but it still meant nearly forty rounds for the crowd to watch. The Americans, who had been led to believe that their team couldn't lose, came back in anticipation of slaughter. Bored now by foreign rounds, screaming and hysterically cheering on their own riders, their chauvinism was only equalled by Billy's in the commentary box.

'He's a nice guy, he deserves it,' he said when Ludwig went clear, dashing British hopes, but he was unashamedly delighted when Mary-Jo put in an unexpected twelve faults, and Lizzie Dean hit two fences and put in a stop, and the early French and Swiss riders knocked up cricket scores.

Ivor came in so elated by his first round success that he only knocked up eight faults.

'Marvellous,' said Billy. 'That's really marvellous. Now, with all the second riders gone, Great Britain's edged up to third place, and the Germans are moving right up behind the Americans.'

As it became apparent that a duel to the death was setting in, people ran in from the halls and the stands filled up to bursting.

'I must have another shot,' said Rupert.

'You can't risk it,' said the doctor.

Carol Kennedy went clear again. Once again Fen had to follow him.

'The Americans are on thirty-one; we are on thirty,' Malise told her.

Fen's nerves were in tatters. Last time they'd had so little to lose; now they were in with a chance. If Hardy started kicking out fences, all was lost.

'Kiss me, Hardy, e'er I die of fright,' she said.

In England, they were televising only the second round of the competition. Dino checked the video for the hundredth time to see if there was enough tape for Fen's round.

'Tory, darling,' he called into the bedroom, 'Fen's about to jump. I think you ought to come and see it.'

He could hardly bear to watch her, she looked so small and defenceless as she rode into the ring. He had seen

Rupert patting her hand and giving her encouragement. The bastard looked so impossibly handsome and, with his dislocated shoulder, a more romantic figure than ever. And even worse, Billy Lloyd-Foxe was doing the commentary. What the hell was *he* doing in America?

'And here comes Fenella Maxwell, riding her second round for Great Britain,' said Billy. 'Only nineteen and easily our most brilliant and beautiful girl rider, and voted Sports Personality of the Year in 1979. Come on now, Fen, darling.'

'Oh, shut up, Billy,' howled Janey and Dino from different parts of England.

'Please don't cheer,' Fen prayed to the crowd as Hardy plunged all over the place. 'Please don't distract him. Let us get around. Concentrate, Hardy, my darling.'

Suddenly Hardy decided to behave, jumping over the fences as though they were fallen logs in the wood.

'I want to go clear, oh please, let me go clear,' prayed Fen, getting excited. But Hardy took such an unexpectedly huge jump over the wall that it didn't give him enough run into the water and he landed well in with a splash. Fen felt her face covered with tepid water. Hardy was drenched. He loathed getting wet. He lashed his tail, ears flattened.

'That's done it,' groaned Rupert. 'He'll never clear the upright; he's come in too close.'

Determined to prove Rupert wrong, Hardy did an incredible cat jump; up and up he went as though he was climbing a ladder. Then with a merry flick of his back feet he was over.

Dino put his arm around Tory.

'Go on, Fen,' yelled Darklis.

'Don't look around,' screamed Isa. 'Daddy'll murder you.' He stopped, remembering, and looked in embarrassed apology at his mother. 'I mean, for goodness sake, hurry.'

Fen thundered down to the last triple – she was over.

'Hooray,' yelled Billy, stamping his feet in the commentary box.

The applause was so deafening, Fen didn't realize she'd got a time fault.

Once again, everyone got out their calculators.

'That puts us on thirty-five, very much in contention,' said Malise. 'The Germans are on thirty-four, the Americans on thirty. But we can't afford any complacency. The Italians are on thirty-nine, with Piero Fratinelli to come.'

Rupert was seriously worried. The morphine wasn't having the desired effect this time. He hardly warmed up Rocky at all; every stride was agony. There was no point risking a fall and finishing himself off altogether over a practice fence. He sat in the tackroom on an upturned bucket, with his head in his hands. He daren't go near the First Aid Post in case they stopped him riding.

'You going to be able to make it?' said the doctor.

'Sure,' said Rupert, 'but I hope they bloody hurry.'

Hans Schmidt had eight faults.

'That's good for us,' Billy was saying in the commentary box.

Then, blighting everyone's hopes, Piero Fratinelli came in and jumped clear for Italy.

'That's not at all good for us,' sighed Billy. 'Good round though.'

He grinned across at Fen, who was biting her nails in the riders' stand, and mopped his brow.

In came Peter Colegate, who'd replaced Dino. The American crowd was in a state of hysteria. All across the stands US flags were being waved in encouragement, as the big striding bay thoroughbred, who'd won several races in his youth, ate up the course.

'I don't fancy anyone's chances against him if there's a jump off,' said Billy.

The thoroughbred's racetrack origins were his undoing, however. Picking up the tension from his rider, hearing the hysterical yelling of the crowd, he was reminded of his youth and, thundering towards the final fences, he cleared the pink wall with ease, then accelerated and flattened both parts of the double and, hearing the howl and groan of the crowd, only just scraped over the last massive triple.

'Hooray,' said Billy from the commentary box. 'That's absolutely marvellous for us, but admittedly not great for the Americans.'

Carol Kennedy turned to Fen, shaking his head. 'Our mutual friend would have gone clear.'

'What's the score?' Fen asked Malise.

'Italians forty, Americans thirty-eight, Germans forty-three.'

They looked at each other for a minute.

'That means if Rupert goes clear we get the gold, four faults we get the silver, eight faults we'll have to jump off, which will be too much for Rupert.'

Rupert rode into the ring.

'And here comes Rupert Campbell-Black on Popstar,' said Dudley. 'He has a dislocated shoulder, which was put back yesterday. The suspense is absolutely killing, but I think we are about to witness a great display of courage.'

'Courage is a quality the Campbell-Blacks have never lacked,' said Billy. 'One of Rupert's ancestors was on the King's side during the Civil War, and even though he was tortured by Roundheads, he never squealed.'

All the vengeful heat of the sun seemed to be concentrated on Rupert's black velvet hat. The coloured poles and the flower arrangements swam before his eyes. The officials in their coral blazers seemed to be dancing, the derby rising and falling by itself, the red and blue boat sailing away. The pain was excruciating now. If Rocky played up, he was doomed. Somehow he removed his hat, but, as Rocky sidled away, it took hours to get it back on again.

Where the hell was the first fence? For a panic-stricken moment he couldn't remember. He looked up at the sea of faces, curiously still for once, the peaks of their caps like a million beaks. He had a terrifying hallucination – they were going to swoop down and peck him to death. Everything went black, he swayed, then forced himself to look down at Rocky's blond plaits. His good hand was shaking violently

– like a wanking schoolboy. The thought made him laugh. Thank God, there was the first fence. He kicked Rocky into a canter.

'And there goes Rupert,' said Billy in a voice that was not quite steady. 'All our hopes go with him.'

Rocky, aware that his master was wildly untogether, jumped the first fence wrong, rapping it really hard, jarring Rupert's shoulder appallingly. To a man, the crowd winced. The next jump was almost as unhappy. Rupert lost a stirrup, his balance all awry. Then he jabbed Rocky's mouth over the sailboat and the horse pecked on landing.

'God, that must hurt,' moaned Billy.

Coming up to the derby, Rupert found his iron and somehow managed to stay on.

'Oughtn't he to retire?' said Fen in anguish. 'It must be killing him.'

Suddenly, with a relentless surge of courage, Rupert cleared the gate, and turned to the water, riding at it like a man possessed, clearing it by two feet. The crowd roared in ecstasy and then in apprehension. Rupert was beginning to do a bit too well. Suddenly an American victory was in jeopardy. Now he was turning towards the big combination: three vast brick-red fences with their clashing bright green pools of ferns. He left the first element to Rocky, who jumped it big, leaving him too close to the second element. With a brilliant shift in the saddle, Rupert swung Rocky to the right so he had more room and could get in an extra stride before clearing it, then swung him back again so he had the same extra diagonal. Rocky clouted the final pole, which was almost indistinguishable from the greenery filling the jump, but it stayed put.

The crowd burst into a spontaneous yell of applause.

'The Gods who live forever,' muttered Malise to himself, 'are on our side today.'

'That was the most glorious piece of riding,' said Billy. 'Oh, come on, Rupe. I can't bear to look any more. You take over, Dudley.'

There were only three fences between Britain and a

medal and, because of this, they all seemed higher than the grandstand.

Rocky was jumping majestically, but Rupert realized he must speed up. He couldn't afford time faults. Through a haze of pain the three fences receded and came towards him; he'd never judge the distances; he couldn't really gallop on with only one hand.

'He can either go carefully and risk time faults, or risk knocking them down,' said Billy. 'Knowing Rupe, I bet he chooses the latter.'

Rupert did. He came thundering down to the first fence.

'Oh, steady,' said Malise in anguish.

'Too fast,' gasped Fen. 'Oh God help him.'

Rupert was over the first fence, meeting it absolutely perfectly.

'We'll have to jump off for the bronze,' shouted Billy excitedly.

Rupert was somehow over the two treacherous uprights of the double.

'We've got the silver,' yelled Billy. 'Come on, Rupe, come on.'

Rocky gathered himself together, took a mighty leap and sailed through the air, over the triple and into the history books. Pandemonium broke out in the commentary box. Billy was hugging Dudley, both yelling at once. Dizzy burst into tears.

'I'm awfully sorry, Ma'am,' said Fen, realizing she was hugging Princess Anne. Suddenly she heard a hoarse strangulated sound behind her; it was Ivor, cheering like an old mule.

'We got the gold!' screamed Fen, jumping up and down. 'We got the gold!'

As Rupert rode out of the arena at a walk, the whole stadium rose to their feet to applaud him. The cheers went on for a full five minutes. Naturally disappointed the home team hadn't made it, the crowd were prepared to honour such a display of courage.

Rupert rode up to Malise. His face was expressionless.

888

'What price fairies now?' he said.

Malise grinned up at him. 'On the day, my fairies came good. Bloody marvellous.' Then, surprised at Rupert's lack of excitement, 'You went clear you know. We've got the gold.'

Rupert shook his head. A loudspeaker confirmed his victory. He stayed absolutely calm. He didn't smile or give Rocky great slaps of joy on the neck which was his normal practice. His hand didn't even tremble. He slid off the horse, gave him a quick pat, and leant his head for a second against the red-gold satin neck. Everyone swarmed round him, cheering and yelling.

'Great, Rupe, terrific, you showed them.'

Rupert broke away from them and stumbled towards the tunnel. Everyone followed him, cheering. Malise fought his way back to Rupert's side.

'Leave him alone,' he snarled at the pack, suddenly losing his temper. 'Can't you understand the strain he's been under?'

'It's all right,' he said gently to Rupert.

Rupert turned, his eyes streaming. 'A moron, a school-girl and a cuckold,' he said. 'We took on the whole bloody world.'

'And beat them,' said Malise.

Halfway down the tunnel Rupert slumped against the wall, shutting his eyes, battling to stop the tears.

'I'm sorry,' he mumbled. 'Been a bit of a strain the last few days. Too much dope, not much sleep. Oh, Christ.'

'Look,' said Malise, patting Rupert's good shoulder, 'over the years I've seldom seen eye to eye with you. But I have to hand it to you today. Without doubt you produced the finest and bravest display of riding I've ever seen. You made the other riders look like gymkhana kids. No one in that stadium or watching it on television will ever forget it.'

Rupert sniffed and wiped away the tears with the back of his hand.

'Think Jake would've beaten me?'

'My dear boy, today no one could have beaten you.'

Rupert stretched out his good hand and grabbed Malise's arm.

'I've always given you a hard time,' he said shakily, 'but I guess you're the best too.'

Odd, thought Malise, how the moments of greatest happiness come from the people you least expect.

Suddenly Rupert brightened perceptibly. 'I put a monkey on our winning,' he said. 'I must have made a fortune.'

Chestnut, dappled grey and dark bay, they walked proudly into the arena, ears pricked, eyes bright, knowing they were the best in the world. On their backs rode Rupert and Ivor in their red coats, with Fen in black in the centre. And realizing once again they were riding one man short, the magnanimous crowd cheered them to the top of the stadium. Everywhere, Union Jacks seemed to be waving.

'And straight against that great array.'

'Forth went the dauntless three,' thought Malise.

'Mummy,' said Georgina Hamilton in Scotland, 'you really must allow me to meet Rupert. I mean, he may be old and frightfully wicked, but he is phenomenally attractive. And they always say it's best to start with an older man.'

Tabitha, who'd been allowed to stay up, bounced on Amanda's knee.

'Daddy jump,' she said. 'Daddy jump well.'

'He did indeed, darling,' said Amanda. She turned to Rollo, trying to keep her elation within bounds. 'If that doesn't get Rupert a safe seat, nothing will.'

'He is stunning,' said Georgina. 'Oh, promise you'll introduce me.'

'It's a good thing,' thought Amanda, 'that Georgina is going back to boarding school next week.'

'Want Mummy. When will I see Mummy?' said Marcus for the hundredth time that day.

'I'm so proud of her,' said Tory. 'She rode so wonderfully well. It's so awful that such a marvellous victory should be blighted by the other thing. Jakey must be heartbroken not to be part of it.'

'He couldn't come back into that,' said Dino. 'I guess he didn't want to rock any more boats. If he's coming back, I figure it'll be later.'

Malise followed them with his military walk, marching on air. The crowd once again gave an extra cheer in appreciation of Dizzy and Sarah in their Union Jack shorts.

As she stood on the highest middle step of the podium, Fen was still smaller than Carol Kennedy.

'Dino will be very proud of you,' he said, kissing her.

'You'd have pulled it off if he hadn't dropped out,' said Fen.

Carol shrugged: 'You'd have pulled it off more easily if you'd had Jake.'

'We might not have,' said Fen. 'We were more of a team than ever before.'

The President's wife came forward in a pale blue dress and Fen bowed her head as the pink, blue and green ribbon was hung round her neck. As though it were in braille, she put her hand up to touch the gold, tracing the lady with her sheaf of corn on one side, the athlete borne aloft on the other.

'We got a gold,' she said incredulously.

'Team gold's the best,' said Rupert.

They watched the British flag slide up the white pole. A breath of wind stretched it out. Never had the National Anthem sounded so beautiful.

'God save,' began Fen, then found she couldn't go on. Tears splashed on to her high cheekbones. Rupert put his hand on her shoulder, squeezing it reassuringly.

When the music stopped she turned back to him, burying her face in his shoulder.

'What shall we do this evening?' he said.

'You ought to go to bed,' said Fen.

'How about a really marvellous fuck?' said Rupert.

Fen burst out laughing.

'I've always wanted you,' said Rupert, kissing her.

'Hey, lay off,' howled Dino, hurling a cushion at the television set.

'Lucky thing,' said Georgina Hamilton. 'She's very attractive. Mind you, I expect she'll console him now Helen's pushed off.'

Amanda Hamilton was surprised how much she minded that embrace. She knew it was victory euphoria, but Fen really was very pretty. Amanda caught a glimpse of herself in the mirror, and pulled in her tummy. She'd been eating too much porridge, and must go on a diet before Rupert got back.

'I've seen a lot of sights,' Malise told Prince Philip, wiping away a tear, as the riders galloped round the arena, their rosettes streaming like coloured meteors, 'when I went all through the war, but this is the greatest experience of my life. Makes you very proud to be British.'

'That was a staggering piece of riding by Rupert Campbell-Black,' said Prince Philip.

Jake Lovell, in a scruffy motel near Kennedy airport, and rapidly running out of money, decided not to have another cigarette, as he had only half a packet left. With Helen in his arms, he lay in bed watching television.

'Hardy was your horse,' sobbed Helen. 'You ought to have been up there getting a gold, too.'

'I'm on the winners' rostrum already. I've got you,' said Jake. But his heart was like lead. Helen must never realize the colossal sacrifice he had made, or she'd never forgive herself.

Dino tucked Tory up in bed, making sure that she took both her sleeping pills. Her apathy worried him; he felt it would be healthier if she raged against Helen and Jake. Then he put the children to bed. Darklis was so overexcited she wanted a story. Every time Dino tried to skip, or missed a word because he was tired, she corrected him. He found

Isa in floods of tears. Why had his father gone off with Helen? Why was the paper calling him a traitor and a deserter? What did treachery mean? Who would look after his mother now? Was it something that he, Isa, had done?

Dino comforted him as best he could. He didn't really know the answer to any of those questions either, but he knew Jake going off had nothing to do with Isa, and he was sure that once the Games were over, Jake would want to see him and Darklis again. At last Isa fell asleep.

It was two o'clock in the morning. The Mill House seemed bitterly cold after America. Dino supposed it was the changeover from Summer to Fall. Now, jet lag was catching up with him and he felt absolutely shattered. For the hundredth time he asked himself if he'd been insane to indulge in this quixotic gesture of rushing off to Europe to look after Tory.

He had avoided going into Fen's room because he was missing her so appallingly. Now, desperate for reassurance, he pushed open the door, breathing in the faint trace of her perfume and the mustiness of damp and dust and lack of use. All the china horses on the shelves and the teddy bears that used to fill up the entire window seat had been put away. Perhaps that was his fault for telling her during that terrible row she ought to grow up. He'd liked the room better as it was before -- except for the photograph of Billy Lloyd-Foxe, which had been removed.

Feeling he shouldn't be snooping, he opened the top drawer of the chest and found a small pile of newspaper cuttings and photographs held together by a pink plastic paper-clip. They were all of himself, making him feel slightly better. All the same, he'd been mad to leave her with Rupert and Billy. He went back into the sitting-room and opened a bottle of wine. He felt shattered but not really sleepy; his time clock was still up the creek.

Turning on the television, he stretched out on the sofa. They were now showing the press conference. Everyone cheered and whooped as Malise and the British team filed in. There was a tremendous popping of champagne corks.

Rupert, who sat next to Fen with his good arm along the back of her chair in a vaguely proprietorial way, did most of the talking. He looked great; the earlier tears might never have occurred. He must have lost another half a stone since Helen left him, but it merely made his arrogant, slightly depraved face more finely planed than ever.

'Now, none of us want to talk about my wife or Fen's brother-in-law, so no questions about that,' he said. 'I think we proved that we can win medals without the others. Ivor had the most difficult task, as the pathfinder. He jumped quite brilliantly. Fen had to jump on a different horse, and he can be a sod, I promise you. He's much too strong for her, but she kept him sweet, and I'd like to remind you that she's only just nineteen and jumping in her first Olympic competition.'

Fen blushed as a huge cheer went round the room.

'I'm incredibly proud of them,' said Malise. 'I think today they all moved up a gear, and that people will talk about Rupert's legendary second round as long as show-jumping lasts.'

'And it wasn't just us, either,' said Fen, holding out her glass for more champagne as the cheers subsided. 'It was Malise who kept us all calm when we looked like going to pieces, and Dizzy and Sarah, our grooms, and poor Griselda who's in hospital, and our families, who've had to put up with us being offish and totally self-obsessed for the last month . . . Also,' she added defiantly, 'there's my brother-in-law, Jake Lovell.'

Somebody booed, then everybody followed suit, stamping their feet, shouting 'Out, out, out.'

'No, shut up,' said Fen furiously. 'He taught me everything I know, and he made Hardy the horse he is; Hardy who got a silver and a gold, so we ought to thank him and give him credit as well.'

'Particularly,' drawled Rupert, 'for taking my wife off my hands.'

For a second there was an embarrassed pause, then everyone roared with laughter.

Rupert seized the champagne bottle, filling up his glass.

'In fact, the toast definitely isn't absent friends. We like the people who stuck by us, don't we, angel?' He stroked the back of Fen's neck. There wasn't a reporter in the room who didn't respond to his magnetism.

'We noticed you had Fen in a clinch on the podium,' said the man from the *Daily Mail*.

'Who can blame me?' said Rupert insolently.

Fen looked wary. 'Our horses are good friends,' she said.

'What about you two?' said the man from the *Daily Mirror*.

'This is quite unnecessary,' snapped Malise. 'They came here to discuss the gold medal.'

The man from the *Mirror* ignored him. 'Might be nice if you consoled Rupert,' he said.

'No, it would not,' said Fen furiously. 'I'm going to marry Dino Ferranti.' Then she clapped her hands over her mouth in horror.

Dino knew that, where Rupert was concerned, Fen was unfinished business. He trusted Fen, but for the last three hours he had been through all the agonizing jealousy of a man deeply in love.

'Yippee,' he shouted, 'Yippee.' Then, exactly on cue, he heard the bells pealing out in the village. He opened the window. It was a clear starlit night. Orion was climbing out of bed on the horizon, pulling on his boots. Not a breath of wind ruffled the curtains. The peal of the bells must be carrying miles down the valley. His darling, darling Fen had won the gold. The village hadn't known what to do; they had been shell-shocked by Jake walking out. Now they had another heroic exploit to celebrate. They could carry on with their Welcome Home celebrations. Not many villages in England could boast a silver *and* a gold.

Tory, woken by Dino's shout of joy, pulled the blankets and pillows over her head to blot out the sound of the bells, remembering in anguish how they had rung out for Jake only six nights ago. Oh God, please, please bring him back.

As the telephone rang, she experienced a frantic surge of hope, then the black, black despair overwhelmed her again as she heard Dino say,

'Fen darling, you were fantastic, a bloody miracle. I never figured I'd want another country to beat America, but you were just great, great, great.'

'Dino,' said Fen in a small voice. 'I've got something to tell you. I didn't mean to force your hand. But they goaded me about Rupert at the press conference and I told them I was going to marry you.'

'I know,' said Dino. 'Best programme I've ever seen.'

'You saw it?' said Fen in amazement.

'I taped it, so you can't change your mind. Means we won't have to put an announcement in the *New York Times*, either.'

Fen giggled. 'Oh, you are lovely. I didn't want to trap you.'

'Baby, how many times do I have to tell you? Look, are you coming home tomorrow? I've got the most god-awful withdrawal symptoms.'

'Oh, yes,' said Fen. 'I can't bear another minute away from you.'

'And when you get back, I'm going to frog-march you into the nearest Registrar's office and marry you. What the bloody hell's Billy doing out there?'

'Were you jealous?'

'Insanely – that's why I want you home. I don't trust either of those bastards.'

For a few minutes they talked nonsense.

'Have you said anything to Tory about us?'

'No, not really. I guess she knows. She's not in very good shape.'

Tory, who had been listening at the top of the stairs, desperate for some crumb of comfort, some tiny piece of news about Jake, slunk back to bed. Only when Dino had checked that she was asleep did she give way to tears.

63

Autumn came, bringing huge red suns and frosty mornings and clogging the mill stream with yellow leaves. Tory carried on as though there was a key in her back. There were no money problems. Fen came back from L.A. to a heroine's welcome. She and Dino carried on taking the horses to shows and trying to keep their delirious happiness within bounds, at least when they were with Tory. The children, particularly Isa, were at first bewildered, even distraught, by Jake's disappearance, but soon got involved in a new term, where they were both the object of increased sympathy and interest. Dino, whom they both adored, was back, and Fen and he infected the children with their happiness and took them out a lot, to give Tory a break. To Tory they seemed like four children, or very young parents with two kids. She was glad Dino and Fen had finally got it together, but it didn't ease her own despair.

Tory normally loved autumn best of all, chopping logs for huge fires, making chutney, jam and elderberry wine, loading up the deep freeze with vegetables and apple pies. But this year there seemed to be a glut of everything. Too many green tomatoes, too many apples thudding from the trees. She tried to pick them and gave up. She was always cold, always shivering. She covered herself up with three or four jerseys, so that no one should realize how much weight she had lost, or that she wasn't eating. Alone in the house, she spent her time crying, then crept into bed at night to clutch an equally shivering Wolf, who missed Jake as much as she did. Malise came down to offer comfort, but was daunted by her grief. His own sadness that Helen had run off, he kept to himself.

To buck Tory up, Dino and Fen tried to persuade her to go to Wembley. But she couldn't face the prying eyes or the memories. Billy Lloyd-Foxe had a brilliant week and won the Victor Ludorum. Every night Ivor Braine, Fen and Rupert, with his arm in a sling, appeared at the end of the Personality Parade, and brought the house down as they displayed their gold medals. Otherwise, Rupert was off the circuit for two months. The doctor in L.A. had, in fact, trapped a nerve when he put Rupert's shoulder back. An operation was needed to sort it out. That Rupert had been brave enough to carry on jumping, despite such excruciating pain, only enhanced his almost magical prestige. The press reported his increased interest in politics. He was tipped to take over a safe seat in Gloucestershire.

The press were also wildly interested in Jake, keeping a watch on all the airports, and continually ringing the Mill House in case there was news of him. But there was none. He simply hadn't got in touch. Heaven only knew what he and Helen were living on.

Then, in the middle of October, the press caught Jake and Helen arriving at Heathrow, both wearing dark glasses. Neither would say a word to anyone, and somehow, as elusive as his gipsy forebears, Jake managed to shake off a pack of reporters and vanish. But not for long. The press's blood was up and within a few days they had hunted them down, staying near Gloucester with a horse-dealing friend of Jake's. Again, he and Helen refused to talk, despite the astronomical sums of money which were offered for their story. And two days later, blazoned across every paper, were pictures of Jake, again in dark glasses, applying for the dole at Gloucester Labour Exchange.

The fact that Jake was so near, yet still hadn't contacted Tory, was for Dino the final straw. He saw how Tory was being crucified. He was all for driving over to Gloucester and beating the hell out of Jake, but Fen managed to restrain him.

'You can't make him come back if he doesn't want to. Tory would hate that more than anything.'

Once back in England, when he wasn't dodging the press, Jake made heroic efforts to get work, but found every door shut. There was no point in ringing Garfield Boyson, as he hadn't kept his nose clean, but he rang all the other sponsors who'd been pursuing him before the games. They all gave him an earful or hung up. He buried his pride and applied for jobs running riding schools or working as a stud groom. A few people saw him out of curiosity before rejecting him. No one wanted a fallen idol.

Horse and Hound had announced that the inquiry into his defection at the Olympic Games would be held at the BSJA headquarters in November. Jake was expected to turn up and defend himself. If he didn't, the general consensus of opinion was that he'd be suspended for at least ten years, if not for life.

Jake could have handled all that if he and Helen had been happy. But, as the days passed, he began to realize the full extent of her neurosis and egoism. Even if he did get a job, her insecurity was such that she couldn't bear him out of her sight for an instant.

Before the Games, all they had really talked about was their love for one another and The Situation. Like a prisoner of war, Helen had dreamed of escape; now, having escaped, she now found she was living in some bleak grey Eastern European zone. By running off, she and Jake had deprived themselves of everything except each other. Claustrophobically thrown on their own resources, they found they had nothing in common.

Helen longed for her beautiful house and garden, her children, particularly Marcus, her cheque book and her status as Rupert's wife. Rupert blocked her application to see the children, so she would have to go to court and, as they had no money, that would mean applying for legal aid.

Horses had been Jake's life. Deprived of them, he was like a junkie without a fix. He missed the Mill House, the children, Wolf, but most of all he found he missed Tory. And yet some strange pride stopped him getting in touch. He was convinced they were all managing perfectly without him. It would look as though he was only slinking back because he'd run out of money and couldn't cope. He also realized the enormity of his crime towards her and towards his country and was too ashamed to show his face. Above all, he'd given Helen the handkerchief; he must stick by the rules.

He never blamed her once for forcing his hand, but he retreated inside himself. Knowing he was miserable, she became obsessively jealous of Tory, the good wife, who never made a fuss. Why the hell couldn't Jake bitch about her occasionally? But Jake realized now that Tory had loved him for himself. Helen only loved the new, infinitely desirable image of herself which his love had created, and which must be preserved at all costs.

Feeling that the horse dealer who'd put them up shouldn't be subjected to such a bombardment from the press, Helen and Jake moved into a bedsitter in Gloucester. But they were absolutely skint. The Social Security office came up with one reason after another why they shouldn't give Jake any money. He sold his cuff-links and some of Helen's jewellery. Soon, the only thing left would be his silver medal. And all the time Fleet Street was tempting him, offering more than a quarter of a million pounds for their story.

Jake was accustomed to being poor. Helen was not. She tried to economize, but she was used to going to the hairdressers at least twice a week, and never having a run in her tights, and paying £15 for a pot of face cream. If she paid any less, she was convinced Jake would go off her. Having run away in Los Angeles with only summer clothes, she was desperate to buy winter ones, and thought wistfully of her furs in the wardrobe at Penscombe.

The last Monday in October began badly for Tory. She got up and took the children to school, only realizing when

900

she got there and found the doors locked that it was half-term. Later, making her bed, she retrieved her hot water bottle from the bottom and, unscrewing it, found herself solemnly emptying it into her jersey drawer. In the middle of the morning Dino found her in floods of tears, turning out the contents of the vacuum cleaner in the sitting-room, because she'd hoovered up a moth by mistake.

'The poor little thing was alive,' she sobbed, scrabbling frantically through the dust. 'I can't find it anywhere.'

Dino cleared up the mess, then sat her down.

'Angel, you're very very tired. Fen and I have got to go up to London for this programme.' (They were doing Billy Lloyd-Foxe on *This is Your Life* that evening.) 'We're going to take the kids to get them out of your hair for twenty-four hours. They'll enjoy seeing the inside of a studio. Hannah will be here to keep an eye on you. Sarah'll be back first thing tomorrow morning, so you don't have to worry about the horses. Tomorrow, when we get back, I am taking you to the doctor.'

'I'm all right,' protested Tory.

But the children's wild delight at the prospect of a jaunt only depressed her more. They're bored by me, she thought miserably. I'm no fun anymore.

'You do promise to look after her, don't you?' said Fen to Hannah as they left.

After they'd gone, Tory tried to pull herself together and get down to making green tomato chutney. But as she was chopping the onions, she remembered it had been Jake's favourite, and how he used to eat it neat out of the jar with a spoon, which made her cry again.

She started as the doorbell rang. Why did she still harbour some inside hope that it might be Jake? But it was her mother, in a new burgundy suit, looking very chic despite a burgundy face from the car heater.

'I'm not crying,' lied Tory, wiping her hands on her skirt.

'No, I can smell you're not,' said Molly, backing off slightly. 'We're on our way to stay with some of Bernard's dreary relations. I left him in the car.' As though he was a smelly old labrador behind a grille, thought Tory.

'Doesn't he want to come in?'

'No, we won't be able to gossip.'

'Would you like a cup of coffee?'

Molly looked pointedly at her watch.

'I would have thought it was more like sherry time.'

As Tory poured her a glass, Molly said how pleased she was about Fen and Dino. Tory returned to chopping onions.

'Seems a nice chap,' Molly went on. 'Very good-looking and very rich. You should have married someone like that in the first place. Now I want to have a serious talk with you.'

Tory gritted her teeth.

'What are you going to do about your future?' said Molly. 'Fen and Dino won't want to stay here for ever with you and the children. They'll need a place of their own – perhaps they'll go back to America.'

Tory looked up in horror. 'D'you think so?'

'I know so. Of course, they're too nice to say anything, but you can't hold them back for ever.'

Tory said nothing, but chopped one piece of onion to pulp.

'And when are you going to divorce Jake? I mean, he's deserted you, so you shouldn't have any difficulty. His father did the same thing to his mother. Like father like son, I suppose.'

'Please, Mummy, don't.' Tory's voice broke. 'I can't bear it.'

'Can't think why you mind so much,' said Molly. 'You always knew he never loved you. Only married you for your money. What d'you expect?'

Tory looked down at the sink tidy. It was a disgusting mess of bacon rinds, spaghetti hoops, rusty Brillo pads and old tea bags. Like me, she thought, I'm as useless as an old tea bag.

'Let's be positive,' Molly was going on. 'I'm pleased to see you've lost a lot of weight. You may be looking quite

902

frightful, but at least you've got a waist, and even ankles now. But you really shouldn't have let yourself go like that. Can't blame Jake pushing off, really. You never tried to hold him.

'However, Bernard and I have a plan. We're going to send you to a health farm for a week. There's a special offer for one in *Harpers* this month. No, I won't take no for an answer. We've filled in the form and sent it off. You can have it as an early Christmas present.'

Tory was obviously not going to offer her another glass of sherry, so Molly helped herself. She wondered if the child was quite right in the head at the moment.

'Cheer up,' she said. 'You're only twenty-eight. If you smarten yourself up, you might easily get another man. One of your own class this time.'

After her mother had gone, Tory sat down and cried and cried. Wolf sat at her feet, raking her knee with his paw, licking her face, desperately trying to comfort her.

Eventually she responded to his sympathy. She had to go up to the village to buy brown sugar for the chutney, and afterwards she'd take him for a walk. She couldn't be bothered with lunch. As she got her coat and purse, the telephone rang. But it was for Hannah, who took it in the tackroom.

Going out into the yard Tory met Hannah, standing on one leg. Her boyfriend, she explained, had got tickets for the Rolling Stones concert that night. Of course she must go, said Tory. If Hannah gave the horses their final feed Tory would check them last thing to see everything was all right.

'Are you sure you'll be O.K.?' said Hannah.

'I'll be fine,' Tory reassured her. 'It'll be rather peaceful to have the house to myself.'

She didn't need a lead for Wolf any more. Since Jake had gone he never left her heels, waiting outside the village shop for her, with an anxious expression on his pointed brindle face. As she came out of the bakers, the low afternoon sun shone directly into her eyes. Suddenly she gave a gasp of excitement. Across the road a black-haired man was watching them. Then she felt a desperate thud of disappointment. It was very like him – but it was not Jake. Wolf, however, gave a bark of joyful recognition and shot across the road into the path of an oncoming lorry. The passers-by, watching in horror, couldn't be sure if it was the dog or the girl crouched over him who was screaming.

Everyone was very kind. They recognized poor Mrs Lovell. A man offered her a lift to the vet, but Wolf died on the way. He licked Tory's hand and gave a last thump of his shepherd's crook tail, as if to apologize for deserting her too, and his head fell back.

The vet drove Tory home, and dug a grave for Wolf beside Sailor and various of the children's guinea pigs and hamsters, and buried him in his blanket with his old shoe. He didn't like what he saw. Tory was shivering uncontrollably; there was no colour in her cheeks; her clothes hung off her. She insisted on making him a cup of tea, but forgot to put any tea in the pot and didn't even notice that she'd handed him just hot water and milk.

'It was Jake's dog,' she kept saying. 'I should have had him on a lead.'

'Now, you're not going to be by yourself?' asked the vet.

'No, no, the others'll be back soon.'

Hannah, going off at dusk, her thoughts full of her boyfriend and the Rolling Stones, wondered if she ought to ring Dino and Fen in London. Tory was just sitting at the kitchen table, twisting a drying-up cloth, gazing unseeingly at a mountain of chopped onions.

'Honestly, I'm perfectly O.K.,' she said. 'Sarah'll be back first thing and I've got an awful lot of chutney to make.'

At nine o'clock, Tory checked the horses. They were all dozing or lying down. She gave Macaulay an apple and a cuddle and then shut all the top doors. Then she took a torch and looked at Wolf's grave.

'You're lucky,' she said. 'You won't miss him anymore.'

Life without Jake, she reflected, wasn't worth a farthing. A far thing. Nothing could be further away now than he was. She was useless as a mother, no good as a human being. If she wasn't there, Jake could come home with Helen when Dino and Fen went to America and take over the yard.

The note took her hours to write, her mind was working so slowly. She screwed up several drafts and chucked them in the bin. In the top of Jake's chest of drawers in the bedroom, under the lining paper, she found the key to the poison cupboard. Back in the tackroom, she had to stand on a chair to open it. What a choice awaited her. Like Jake asking her what she wanted to drink the first time he'd taken her to a pub. There was henbane, used by Doctor Crippen, and hemlock water dropwort, which Jake often used as a poultice for horses with sore backs. Deadly poison it was, but it also paralysed you, leaving your mind clear to the end. She couldn't cope with that. Then there was deadly nightshade, or bella donna as it was called. A more appropriate name for Helen than herself. Jake had once told her that there was enough poison in that bottle to kill off a dozen Campbell-Blacks, with all their phenomenal strength. It should be enough for her. She took down the bottle.

Next morning Jake walked towards the Social Security office to have another crack at getting some dole. It was totally against his nature, hustling or wheedling for money – but things were getting desperate. A conker fell at his feet. Automatically he picked it up and was about to put it in his pocket for Isa. Then he realized there was no point and savagely hurled it across the car park.

'Hullo, Jake,' said a voice.

Wary of rejection, he turned, frowning. But it was Tanya, his old groom, now married and wheeling a baby in a pushchair. Jake knelt down to admire the child, picking up his little hands, tickling his ribs to make him laugh. He'd always been sweet with kids, thought Tanya. He must miss his own terribly, his swarthy face grey, his eyes deeply shadowed. The cotton jacket and jeans were far too thin for a bitter cold morning.

'He's beautiful,' he said, reluctantly getting to his feet.

'I'm sorry about Wolf,' she said.

'What about him?' said Jake, suddenly tense.

'Oh, God, perhaps I shouldn't have told you. Hannah rang me. He was run over yesterday afternoon.'

An hour later Jake got back to the bedsit to find Helen painting her nails and not in a good mood. She had just read in the *Daily Mail* that her husband had joined the Tory party and was expecting to be given a safe seat at any minute. Tory, Helen reflected bitterly, was not her favourite word at the moment. She thought so even less when she saw Jake's face.

'What's the matter?' she asked in alarm.

'I've got to go home.' She winced at the word. 'There's been an accident.'

'Oh, God, not one of the kids?'

'No, Wolf.'

'Wolf? Is that a horse?'

'No, the dog. He was run over yesterday.'

'A dog?' said Helen incredulously. 'A dog! You're going back just for that? I could appreciate it if it was a child.'

'Wolf was like a child to Tory.' And to me, he wanted to add.

Helen looked at him in bewilderment. It was all part of this hideous conspiracy between the English and their animals.

'I simply don't get it,' she said. 'You refuse to go back when Malise appeals to you over and over again to jump for your country, then you scuttle home because some goddam dog's been run over. I just don't understand you.'

There was a pause.

'How long will you be?' she asked. 'I suppose you'll want the car.'

Jake looked at his watch. 'I'll be back in time for you to go to the hairdressers. If I get delayed, take a taxi.'

'We can't afford it, and I've got to pay the hairdressers.'

Jake pulled a huge wad of tenners out of his pocket.

'Did you rob a bank?' asked Helen in amazement.

Jake shook his head. 'I flogged my silver.'

'Oh Jake,' she wailed. 'How could you? It was the one thing we had to cling on to, your one link with immortality. We've scrimped and saved so much so that you could keep it.'

He gave her eight hundred and fifty pounds – 'Now you can buy some winter clothes' – and kept a hundred and fifty for himself.

With it, he went to his friend Harry, who bred lurchers, and bought a puppy: a tiny replica of Wolf, with a brindle, fluffy coat, a nose like an ant-eater and huge, anxious eyes. By the time he drove over the bridge at Withrington the puppy had been sick five times. As he gently lifted the little creature out of the car, she was sick again all over Jake's coat. Jake hardly noticed. Unsure of his reception, his heart was thumping, his throat dry.

The yard seemed curiously deserted, except for the stable cat, who arched his back at the puppy, and the horses, particularly Macaulay, who nearly broke down their half-doors with delight at seeing their master again. The back door was open but there was no one in the house. As Jake washed the sick off, he was tempted to go upstairs and get a sweater. But Helen would do her nut if he came back wearing something different. His heart was still thumping when the telephone rang and he automatically picked it up. He had great difficulty in even saying 'Hullo'.

'Dino,' said a voice, 'this is Malise. I'm desperately sorry. Just wondered if there was any more news of Tory.'

'What about Tory?' snapped Jake.

'Who's that?'

'Jake.'

'What the hell are you doing there?'

'What about Tory?' said Jake, on a rising note of fear.

'She tried to commit suicide last night.'

'Must have been a mistake.'

'I'm afraid not,' said Malise, losing his temper. 'She took a massive overdose of one of your bloody poisons. She wasn't expecting anyone back till this morning. Dino and Fen got worried, came back and found her last night.'

'Oh, my God,' whispered Jake. 'Is she, is she . . .?'

Malise realized he'd been too harsh. 'I'm afraid she's dying, Jake.'

'Where is she?'

'The Great Warwickshire.'

Jake took Fen's car because it was faster. It had never been driven so fast in its life. The poor puppy rattled back and forth in the back like a shuttle. The hospital steps were swarming with press.

'Hullo Gyppo. Shown up at last, have you?' shouted the *Daily Mail*.

'About bloody time. You come to pay for the funeral?' asked *The Sun*.

'Fuck off,' snarled Jake.

Mrs Lovell was in Intensive Care on the second floor, said the receptionist, giving Jake a strange look. 'You can't bring that puppy in here.'

But Jake was off, limping across the polished floor, pulling the heavy gates of the lift with one hand, holding the puppy with the other. On the way up, it licked Jake's face. Oh, please God, he prayed frantically, don't let her die.

As he walked down the passage, a voice said, 'What the hell are you doing here?'

It was Dino towering over him, barring his way, like the Archangel Michael with the flaming sword. For a second Jake thought Dino was going to smash his face in, knocking him flying back into a trolley of instruments. Jake stood his ground.

'I want to see Tory.'

'Well, you bloody can't. She's in a coma and fading fast, and it's all your bloody fault, you bastard, you and your lousy poisons. My God, you wouldn't treat a horse, or even a dog, the way you treated her, leaving her without a fucking word, never getting in touch, letting her just pine away.'

For two minutes Dino carried on in the same vein, calling

908

Jake every name under the sun. His eloquence was fuelled by misery and guilt that he and Fen had left Tory on her own, not appreciating how desperate she was. Jake let him finish.

'Everything you say is true,' he said.

Hearing the din, a nurse came out of Tory's room.

'If you'd like to come in, Mr Ferranti.'

Jake stepped forward. 'I'm her husband, I've got to see her.'

But at that moment Fen came out, fighting back the tears, and went straight into Dino's arms.

'Look who's just turned up,' said Dino bitterly.

Fen spun around. 'Jake, where the hell have you been?' She gave a sob. 'You're too bloody late, that's all; she's dying. She was just conscious when we got to her, but she's got no will to live.'

Not waiting to hear any more, Jake pushed past them and into the room. At first he thought he was hallucinating. For there on the bed was Fen. Then he realized it was Tory – she'd lost so much weight since he'd seen her. Her face, still flushed from the bella donna, gave an illusion of health. Long lashes swept her hollowed cheeks. All Jake could think was how beautiful she looked. He sat down beside the bed, taking her hand. It felt so small and bony now, almost like Helen's. Oh, Christ, how could he have done this to her? It was he who'd killed her, not the poison.

The doctor came in, and decided to overlook the sleeping puppy curled up on Jake's knee. This was really no time to worry about hygiene.

'Can't you do anything?' asked Jake, in desperation.

The doctor shook his head. 'We've done all we can. She took a massive overdose, enough to kill four people. Luckily we caught it very early, but I'm surprised she's lasted this long. We washed out her stomach, of course, but she's got no resistance. There was nothing in her stomach. She can't have eaten for days. I'm afraid there's very little hope she'll ever regain consciousness. I'm so sorry.'

Jake was frantically wracking his brain. When he was

living with the gipsies one of the girls had taken an overdose of bella donna after her lover had walked out. The old gipsy grandmother had produced some antidote or emetic and saved her. What the hell had she used? But it was such a long time ago. He must concentrate and try to remember.

'Did she leave a note?' he asked Fen.

Fen got it out of her jeans pocket. 'It was addressed to you. She's left you everything. She knew horses were the only thing that mattered to you, that you and Helen could only come back if she was out of the way.'

But Jake was reading the note.

'She loved you,' said Fen bitterly. 'Isa, Darklis, me, the horses, Wolf, were only extensions of how much she loved you. She knew you didn't love her, but she felt you needed her. That she made life easier, that was enough.'

'Oh, Christ,' Jake groaned, putting his head in his hands. 'I only realized in L.A. how much I loved her. Then Helen spilled the beans to Rupert. I couldn't let her down. I was frightened at what Rupert would do to her. I'd got myself into such a stupid fucking corner.'

'You could have got in touch,' said Fen bleakly. 'Nothing, not a word to anyone since you walked out.'

'I didn't know what to say. I'd treated her so horrendously. I felt so guilty, and beside I'd given Helen the handkerchief.'

Fen lost her temper. 'What about the handkerchief you once gave Tory?' she hissed. 'You conveniently forgot about that when it suited you, didn't you? So much for your bloody gipsy integrity. Tory was clutching it when we found her.'

Jake was stunned. 'She always seemed so strong that she could cope with anything. I didn't realize I meant so much to her.' He looked down at Tory, touching her cheek. With a lurch of fear, he realised her breathing was even fainter. Both he and Fen jumped as Dino came in.

'You've been here long enough,' he said to Jake, making absolutely no attempt to conceal his contempt and loathing.

Suddenly Jake seemed roused out of his state of apathy.

'She's my wife,' he snarled, 'and I love her.'

'Funny way of showing it,' said Dino, holding the door open for him.

Tipping the puppy gently on to the floor, Jake stood up. 'Well, they won't cure her in here.'

'What the hell are you doing?'

'Taking her home.'

'She's dying, Godammit.'

'Then she might as well die at home, surrounded by people and the animals she loves.'

Pulling one of the thick grey blankets off the bed, Jake wrapped it around Tory and picked her up. She was so light now, he could carry her easily. The puppy, already recognizing Jake as her new master, wagged her tail and trotted after him out of the room. Deaf to the protestations of doctors and nurses, desperately trying to remember the name of that miracle cure of the old gipsy grandmother, Jake hardly seemed to recognize Malise coming out of the lift.

'Where d'you think you're going?' said Malise icily.

'Home.'

'What about Helen?'

'Helen?' Jake wrinkled his brow. It was as if Malise were asking him whether he'd turned off the tap in his cabin as the *Titanic* sank under the waves.

'Yes, Helen,' said Malise grimly, holding the lift door shut, blocking Jake's path.

Dragging his mind back, Jake gave Malise the address in Gloucester. 'She doesn't know what's happened. Could you go to her, explain to her, look after her, and say I'm sorry?'

Back at the Mill House, Jake tucked Tory up in the big double bed and lit a fire in the grate. Then he settled down in an armchair, as near her as possible, to pore over his ancient flower books and herbals, frantically searching for a clue to the missing ingredient that might cure her.

Late in the afternoon the children came home. Jake braced himself, longing to see them but prepared for sullen antagonism, even abuse. He nearly wept at their incredulous joy that he was home again, hurling themselves into his arms without a word of reproach.

Isa was clearly demented with worry about his mother. Darklis was young enough to be distracted. The puppy was a godsend and was soon taken over by both children. What frightened Jake was their touching faith that, now he was back, their mother would recover. Macaulay and Hardy had been close to death, numerous other horses, dogs and members of the family had been ill and Jake had cured them.

'Mummy definitely won't have to be put down now,' Jake heard Darklis telling Dino.

But Tory showed absolutely no sign of regaining consciousness, gradually growing weaker and weaker. Jake hardly left her side, not eating or sleeping. His anguish was so obvious, Fen, and even Dino, came to respect it, leaving him on his own with Tory. They fended off the press, keeping the children away if they became quarrelsome, even though most of the time Jake seemed to gain strength from their presence.

Two more days crawled by. Doctors and specialists, wheeled in by Dino, came and shook their heads. They no longer suggested Tory should go back into hospital; there was nothing anyone could do.

Jake refused to give up. If only it had been high summer, or even spring, some of the plants he suspected might cure her might have been flowering, or at least in leaf, and identifiable. Anyway, he was terrified to leave her too long in order to search, in case she died when he wasn't there. Hour after hour he turned the pages with his right hand, holding her hand with his left, hoping against hope that she might return the pressure, showing some sign of life.

And now it was midnight on the third day. Outside, the foxes were barking. The fire was dying in the grate. Tory's breathing had almost stopped. Her heartbeat was so faint he kept thinking he had lost her. She was deathly pale; the bella donna flush had long since gone. If only she could regain consciousness just for a second, so she could die knowing how much he loved her.

In one last desperate hope, he turned back to his most ancient flower book. He was so exhausted and he'd been reading small print for so long now that the words blurred before his eyes.

The only possibility had been the lesser spearwort, but it was such a strong emetic it would finish Tory off completely in her hopelessly weakened state. It was no good; he was powerless to save her.

Frantic, he took her in his arms, trying to warm some life into the frail body. He remembered how she had held Africa for him when he'd rushed off to be sick that first hot afternoon at the Bilborough Show, never letting on she was scared stiff of horses. He remembered how she'd got tight and bought Africa for him, and how she'd never complained at the long hours away, had always welcomed him home, delighting in every victory, yet boosting his morale, professing her faith in him whenever he lost. Believing she would always be there, he had taken her for granted. He knew she was going to be taken away from him. At the end he had failed her again, by not being able to remember that missing ingredient.

'Don't die,' he pleaded for the thousandth time. 'Please don't die.'

Laying her gently back on the pillow, he noticed the fire was nearly out and got up to put on another log. He hadn't even bothered to draw the curtains. Stiff from sitting so long, he went to the window. There were no stars. The sky was already in mourning. He couldn't bear it. Despairingly, he pressed his forehead against the cold window-pane. He had no idea how long he stood there.

'Jake,' came the faintest, faintest whisper.

He swung around in terror, drenched in sweat, his heart pounding. It must be her ghost, come back to mock him.

'Jake,' she whispered again.

913

He was beside her in an instant, seizing her hands, willing her to speak.

'Is it really you?' she murmured.

'Really me.'

'You came back.' The words were so faint he had to bend close to catch them. 'Or have I gone to Heaven?'

'Must be Hell,' he said unsteadily, 'if you found me there. Please don't die, I love you so much.'

'You need a shave,' she said, drifting back into unconsciousness.

Sick with terror, Jake had to wait, cradling her in his arms, frightened even to move. He'd only asked to be able to have time to tell her he loved her, but now it wasn't enough and didn't make him feel any better. He longed to call for Fen and Dino, but panic-stricken that she might die at any moment, he knew he could only face it alone.

After a couple of hours she gave a little sigh, shuddered, and opened her eyes again.

'I'm sorry I took all your bella donna. I couldn't go on without you.'

Jake kissed her forehead. 'I was the same. I just didn't know how to come back. Please get better. I'll never survive unless you do.'

'I'm sorry about Wolf. I should have had him on a lead, but he stuck so close since you, since you . . .' Her voice faltered.

'I know. I got you a puppy.' He picked the sleeping lurcher out of the basket, and laid her beside Tory on the bed, placing Tory's hand on the fluffy narrow head. The puppy gave a deep contented sigh, licked the inside of Tory's wrist and snuggled back to sleep again.

Tory smiled weakly. 'He's lovely. I didn't mean to blackmail you into coming back.'

'You didn't have to. I didn't even know you'd taken the bella donna until I turned up here with the puppy. Tanya told me about Wolf being run over. All I needed was an excuse to come back. I never stopped missing you the whole time I was away. Please don't talk. You must rest.'

'Can I see your silver?' she said drowsily.

'I flogged it to buy the puppy.'

As he drew the blankets up around her, the door opened softly. It was Fen. Jake put his finger to his lips. Shaking with sudden hope, Fen tiptoed towards the bed.

'You were speaking to her?'

'Twice.'

'Did she make sense?'

'Perfect.'

'Oh, my God. Is she going to be all right?'

'I don't know. It's too early to say.'

Together they gazed at the sleeping Tory. Then Fen put a hand on Jake's shoulder.

'You made her better,' she said softly.

For a second, he glanced up, his face soaked with tears.

'I failed her,' he mumbled. 'I tried and tried, but I couldn't remember the missing ingredient.'

'You blind, stupid idiot,' said Fen very gently. 'Only you could have cured her. Don't you understand? The missing ingredient was love.'

Epilogue

The following afternoon, Rupert Campbell-Black passed his first interview with the Birdlip and Chalford constituency committee with flying colours. There was only one sticky moment, when deaf old Lady Oakridge, who never read the papers, asked Rupert if he and his wife would be living in the constituency.

Everyone held their breath in embarrassment.

'My wife will certainly be living in the constituency,' said Rupert emphatically.

'Good, good, glad to hear it,' said Lady Oakridge.

'But not actually with me,' said Rupert.

Everyone, except Lady Oakridge, suppressed smiles.

'Better to have a wife,' she said.

'I absolutely agree,' said Rupert. 'Unfortunately mine's only just pushed off, so I haven't had time to get another one.'

'Fellow's certainly got charm,' said Lord Oakridge after the meeting.

'Views are sound too,' said the Brigadier. 'Think we should seriously consider him.'

'You did so well,' said Amanda, patting Rupert's thigh as she drove him back to London. 'It's a cinch.'

'Glad you think so.' Privately Rupert wondered how much he would enjoy listening to his constituents grumbling about one-way streets and their rows with their neighbours. Being off the circuit for two months had made him realize how desperately he missed show-jumping. With any luck he should be back for Olympia.

'Oh, damn,' said Amanda, as they drew up at her house

in Rutland Gate. 'Conceptione's left the drawing-room light on. She's getting awfully slack.'

'Hope it isn't Rollo.'

'Rollo's in Paris,' said Amanda, opening the front door. 'Anyway, he knows I'm driving you around. Georgina!' she cried in outraged tones as she went into the drawing-room. 'What on earth are you doing here?'

'The rest of the form's gone to the Old Vic. I couldn't face it. I thought it would be more fun to come and see you,' said Georgina. 'Hullo,' she turned to Rupert. 'Mummy's never allowed us to meet.'

'Oh, Christ,' thought Rupert helplessly.

For there, in school uniform, exuding lascivious innocence, was a replica of Amanda, just as beautiful, but twenty-five years younger. No, he told himself firmly, it simply wouldn't do. Now he was almost a prospective Tory candidate, he'd got to behave himself – although, heaven knows, they all seemed to be at it.

'What was the play?' he heard himself saying in an abnormally avuncular voice.

'All's Well that Ends Well,' said Georgina smiling dreamily. 'I hear you're going into politics.'

'Not sure I'll be very good,' said Rupert. 'The only babies I like kissing are female and over fifteen.'

'Oh, brill!' said Georgina. 'I was sixteen last week.'

Billy Lloyd-Foxe, just back from Amsterdam, watched his beautiful wife feeding his beautiful son with enormous pride and decided against pouring himself another glass of whisky. He was just getting over the glow of being on *This is Your Life*. So many people had emerged from his past and said such amazingly nice things.

'I heard the most riveting bit of gossip today,' said Janey.

'What was it?'

'Well, Tracey told me she heard it from Dizzy, who heard it from Sarah, who heard it from Bridie, who's just got this tremendously intellectual boyfriend, who actually takes her to the opera. Poor Bridie had to sit through *Parsifal* the

917

other night. Said she nearly died of boredom.'

'Oh, get on with it,' said Billy grinning.

Janey's eyes gleamed. 'I'll give you three guesses who she saw in the stalls together, looking radiant and not at all bored.'

'You know I can never guess anything.'

'Malise and Helen.'

'Good God,' said Billy astounded. 'Isn't Helen rather too old for him?'

'I would have thought so,' said Janey, 'and Monica Carlton will certainly call Malise out.'

Tory was getting better by the minute, but Jake, terrified that she might still elude him, hardly left her alone for a second.

'From the way he bullies her into resting and polices her every mouthful, you'd think she was Macaulay,' grumbled Fen, but she was so happy for them both.

As the doctor said, it was little short of a miracle.

A few days later, however, when Tory was definitely out of danger, Jake was persuaded downstairs to see Garfield Boyson.

'Well, lad,' said Boyson.

'Well,' said Jake.

'You've made a right cock-up of your career, haven't you?'

'I don't need anyone else to tell me.'

'I gather you've been to see every other sponsor, touting for business. Didn't come to me. Not much faith, have you? I said I'd keep my side of the bargain, if you kept yours, and you did. You got your medal. I'm still ready to back you.'

'The BSJA are going to suspend me.'

'Happen they won't. Under the circs, you may get off with a hefty fine.'

'I'm not interested,' said Jake. 'I'm not going back on the circuit. I'm going to train instead. I don't want to leave Tory or the children any more, and Dino and Fen are going back to the States.'

Looking out of the kitchen window, he saw Fen ride into the yard and collapse off Macaulay and into Dino's arms. He wouldn't have believed it was possible for anyone to go on kissing for so long. Boyson brought him back to earth.

'You'll be looking for riders, then. My lad can be your first jockey.'

Jake looked sceptical, so Boyston went on:

'I've just had a look at Africa's foal. Dino said she jumped six foot out of her field this morning.'

Jake laughed for the first time since the night he won his silver.

'I suppose you're trying to tell me that she and your boy'll be ready for the next Olympics,' he said.

THE END

RIVALS By Jilly Cooper

'A combination of drama, sex and good social comedy . . . unputdownable'
Sunday Times

'It is satisfyingly long, addictive, bitchy, endearing and full of sex and hilarious one-liners'
Books

Jilly Cooper's outrageous new novel is a riotous story of life behind the television screen. It marks the return of Rupert Campbell-Black, the unscrupulous hero of Riders, and explores the machinations and pleasures of the very rich, from the agonies of obsession to the passions and betrayals of men and women used to getting what they want.

'All the behind-the-scenes detail of tough wheeler-dealing in the media world is both fascinating and horrifyingly convincing'
Options

'I couldn't put it down'
Sunday Express

0 552 13264 0

JILLY COOPER TITLES AVAILABLE FROM CORGI

Fiction

EMILY: 'Emily opens windows onto a new romantic landscape.
. . . The young and young-at-heart will revel in it.'
Newsagent and Bookshop

BELLA: There is no doubt Bella Parkinson was a success: the
most promising actress in London, bright, sexy and hopelessly
scatterbrained – she was taking the town by storm. But Bella had
a secret in her past . . .

HARRIET: Shy, dreamy, and incurably romantic, Harriet Poole
was shattered when her brief affair with Simon ended abruptly,
But that was only the beginning of even more complications!

OCTAVIA: As soon as Octavia caught a glimpse of Jeremy, she
knew she just had to have him. It didn't matter that he'd just got
engaged to an old school friend of hers; he was looking at Octavia
in a way that suggested bed rather than breakfast, and she was
weak at the knees . . .

PRUDENCE: It was only when she noticed the way her boyfriend
Pendle looked at Jack's wife Maggie that it began to dawn on
Prudence that there was more to this weekend than met the eye.

IMOGEN: The path of a jet-set virgin on The Riviera was a hard
one. Imogen began to wonder if virtue really was its own reward.

LISA & CO: A collection of short love stories as only Jilly Cooper
can write them.

Non-Fiction

CLASS: A devastatingly funny expòsé of the English class system.
'Highly entertaining, acerbic and wickedly observant.'
The Economist

JILLY COOPER TITLES
AVAILABLE FROM CORGI

THE PRICES SHOWN BELOW WERE CORRECT AT THE TIME OF GOING TO PRESS. HOWEVER TRANSWORLD PUBLISHERS RESERVE THE RIGHT TO SHOW NEW RETAIL PRICES ON COVERS WHICH MAY DIFFER FROM THOSE PREVIOUSLY ADVERTISED IN THE TEXT OR ELSEWHERE.

☐	10427 2	**Bella**	£2.50
☐	10277 6	**Emily**	£2.50
☐	10576 7	**Harriet**	£2.50
☐	11149 X	**Imogen**	£2.50
☐	10241 3	**Lisa & Co.**	£2.50
☐	10717 4	**Octavia**	£2.50
☐	10878 2	**Prudence**	£2.50
☐	12486 9	**Riders**	£4.99
☐	11525 8	**Class**	£3.50
☐	13264 0	**Rivals**	£4.99

All Corgi/Bantam Books are available at your bookshop or newsagent, or can be ordered from the following address:
Corgi/Bantam Books,
Cash Sales Department,
P.O. Box 11, Falmouth, Cornwall TR10 9EN

Please send a cheque or postal order (no currency) and allow 60p for postage and packing for the first book plus 25p for the second book and 15p for each additional book ordered up to a maximum charge of £1.90 in UK.

B.F.P.O. customers please allow 60p for the first book, 25p for the second book plus 15p per copy for the next 7 books, thereafter 9p per book.

Overseas customers, including Eire, please allow £1.25 for postage and packing for the first book, 75p for the second book, and 28p for each subsequent title ordered.

NAME (Block Letters) ....

ADDRESS ....

....